THE
HEROES

JOE ABERCROMBIE

The right of Joe Abercrombie to be identified as the
author of this work has been asserted by him in accordance
with the Copyright, Designs and Patents Act 1988.

First published in Great Britain in 2011 by
Gollancz
An imprint of the Orion Publishing Group
Orion House, 5 Upper St Martin's Lane,
London WC2H 9EA
An Hachette UK Company

This edition published in Great Britain in 2012
by Gollancz

7 9 10 8 6

A CIP catalogue record for this book
is available from the British Library

ISBN 978 0 575 08385 1

Typeset at The Spartan Press Ltd,
Lymington, Hants

Printed and bound by CPI Group (UK) Ltd,
Croydon, CRO 4YY

The Orion Publishing Group's policy is to use papers that
are natural, renewable and recyclable products and made
from wood grown in sustainable forests. The logging and
manufacturing processes are expected to conform to the
environmental regulations of the country of origin.

www.joeabercrombie.com
www.orionbooks.co.uk

'Storms along at a breakneck pace. Each character has a history of betrayal and a wobbly moral compass, giving further realism and depth to Abercrombie's world. The violence is plentiful, the methods of exacting revenge are eye-wateringly inventive and the characters well fleshed out. A fan of Bernard Cornwell's historical escapades could easily fall for it. Believe the hype'

Waterstones Books Quarterly

'Abercrombie's narrative twists and turns, playing with but also against the reader's expectations. His characters do likewise. Their realistic unpredictability means that it is almost impossible to determine what will eventually happen. One of the great pleasures of Joe Abercrombie's fiction is that his characters are so lifelike'

Interzone

'All in all, we can't say enough good things about Mr Abercrombie's latest addition to the genre. It's intelligent, measured, thoughtful, well paced and considered, but retains a sense of fun. We can't recommend it enough'

Sci-Fi Now

THE
HEROES

Also by Joe Abercrombie from Gollancz:

THE FIRST LAW TRILOGY
The Blade Itself
Before They Are Hanged
Last Argument of Kings

Best Served Cold
The Heroes

For Eve
One day you will read this
And say, 'Dad, why all the swords?'

Order of Battle

THE UNION

High Command

Lord Marshal Kroy – commander-in-chief of his Majesty's armies in the North.

Colonel Felnigg – his chief of staff, a remarkably chinless man.

Colonel Bremer dan Gorst – royal observer of the Northern War and disgraced master swordsman, formerly the king's First Guard.

Rurgen and **Younger** – his faithful servants, one old, one . . . younger.

Bayaz, the First of the Magi – a bald wizard supposedly hundreds of years old and an influential representative of the Closed Council, the king's closest advisors.

Yoru Sulfur – his butler, bodyguard and chief bookkeeper.

Denka and **Saurizin** – two old Adepti of the University of Adua, academics conducting an experiment for Bayaz.

Jalenhorm's Division

General Jalenhorm – an old friend of the king, fantastically young for his position, described as brave yet prone to blunders.

Retter – his thirteen-year-old bugler.

Colonel Vallimir – ambitious commanding officer of the King's Own First Regiment.

First Sergeant Forest – chief non-commissioned officer with the staff of the First.

Corporal Tunny – long-serving profiteer, and standard-bearer of the First.
Troopers Yolk, Klige, Worth, and Lederlingen – clueless recruits attached to Tunny as messengers.

Colonel Wetterlant – punctilious commanding officer of the Sixth Regiment.
Major Culfer – his panicky second in command.
Sergeant Gaunt, Private Rose – soldiers with the Sixth.

Major Popol – commanding the first battalion of the Rostod Regiment.
Captain Lasmark – a poor captain with the Rostod Regiment.

Colonel Vinkler – courageous commanding officer of the Thirteenth Regiment.

Mitterick's Division

General Mitterick – a professional soldier with much chin and little loyalty, described as sharp but reckless.
Colonel Opker – his chief of staff.
Lieutenant Dimbik – an unconfident young officer on Mitterick's staff.

Meed's Division

Lord Governor Meed – an amateur soldier with a neck like a turtle, in peacetime the governor of Angland, described as hating Northmen like a pig hates butchers.
Colonel Harod dan Brock – an honest and hard-working member of Meed's staff, the son of a notorious traitor.
Finree dan Brock – Colonel Brock's venomously ambitious wife, the daughter of Lord Marshal Kroy.
Colonel Brint – senior on Meed's staff, an old friend of the king.
Aliz dan Brint – Colonel Brint's naive young wife.
Captain Hardrick – an officer on Meed's staff, affecting tight trousers.

The Dogman's Loyalists

The Dogman – Chief of those Northmen fighting with the Union. An old companion of the Bloody-Nine, once a close friend of Black Dow, now his bitter enemy.

Red-Hat – the Dogman's Second, who wears a red hood.

Hardbread – a Named Man of long experience, leading a dozen for the Dogman.

Redcrow – one of Hardbread's Carls.

THE NORTH

In and Around Skarling's Chair

Black Dow – the Protector of the North, or stealer of it, depending on who you ask.

Splitfoot – his Second, meaning chief bodyguard and arse-licker.

Ishri – his advisor, a sorceress from the desert South, and sworn enemy of Bayaz.

Caul Shivers – a scarred Named Man with a metal eye, who some call Black Dow's dog.

Curnden Craw – a Named Man thought of as a straight edge, once Second to Rudd Threetrees, then close to Bethod, now leading a dozen for Black Dow.

Wonderful – his long-suffering Second.

Whirrun of Bligh – a famous hero from the utmost North, who wields the Father of Swords. Also called Cracknut, on account of his nut being cracked.

Jolly Yon Cumber, Brack-i-Dayn, Scorry Tiptoe, Agrick, Athroc and Drofd – other members of Craw's dozen.

Scale's Men

Scale – Bethod's eldest son, now the least powerful of Dow's five War Chiefs, strong as a bull, brave as a bull, and with a bull's brain too.

Pale-as-Snow – once one of Bethod's War Chiefs, now Scale's Second.

White-Eye Hansul – a Named Man with a blind eye, once Bethod's herald.

'Prince' Calder – Bethod's younger son, an infamous coward and schemer, temporarily exiled for suggesting peace.

Seff – his pregnant wife, the daughter of Caul Reachey.

Deep and **Shallow** – a pair of killers, watching over Calder in the hope of riches.

Caul Reachey's Men

Caul Reachey – one of Dow's five War Chiefs, an elderly warrior, famously honourable, father to Seff, father-in-law to Calder.

Brydian Flood – a Named Man formerly a member of Craw's dozen.

Beck – a young farmer craving glory on the battlefield, the son of Shama Heartless.

Reft, Colving, Stodder and **Brait** – other young lads pressed into service with Beck.

Glama Golden's Men

Glama Golden – one of Dow's five War Chiefs, intolerably vain, locked in a feud with Cairm Ironhead.

Sutt Brittle – a famously greedy Named Man.

Lightsleep – a Carl in Golden's employ.

Cairm Ironhead's Men

Cairm Ironhead – one of Dow's five War Chiefs, notoriously stubborn, locked in a feud with Glama Golden.

Curly – a stout-hearted scout.

Irig – an ill-tempered axeman.

Temper – a foul-mouthed bowman.

Others

Brodd Tenways – the most loyal of Dow's five War Chiefs, ugly as incest.

Stranger-Come-Knocking – a giant savage obsessed with civilisation, Chief of all the lands east of the Crinna.

Back to the Mud (dead, thought dead, or long dead)

Bethod – the first King of the Northmen, father to Scale and Calder.

Skarling Hoodless – a legendary hero who once united the North against the Union.

The Bloody-Nine – once Bethod's champion, the most feared man in the North, and briefly King of the Northmen before being killed by Black Dow (supposedly).

Rudd Threetrees – a famously honourable Chief of Uffrith, who fought against Bethod and was beaten in a duel by the Bloody-Nine.

Forley the Weakest – a notoriously weak fighter, companion to Black Dow and the Dogman, ordered killed by Calder.

Shama Heartless – a famous champion killed by the Bloody-Nine. Beck's father.

BEFORE
THE BATTLE

'Unhappy the land that
is in need of heroes'

Bertolt Brecht

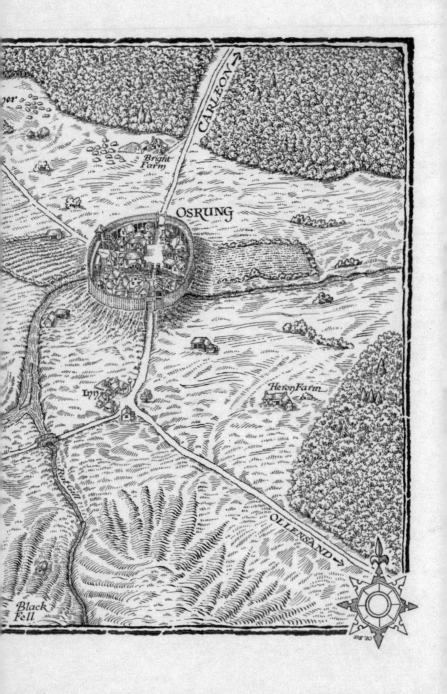

The Times

'Too old for this shit,' muttered Craw, wincing at the pain in his dodgy knee with every other step. High time he retired. Long past high time. Sat on the porch behind his house with a pipe, smiling at the water as the sun sank down, a day's honest work behind him. Not that he had a house. But when he got one, it'd be a good one.

He found his way through a gap in the tumble-down wall, heart banging like a joiner's mallet. From the long climb up the steep slope, and the wild grass clutching at his boots, and the bullying wind trying to bundle him over. But mostly, if he was honest, from the fear he'd end up getting killed at the top. He'd never laid claim to being a brave man and he'd only got more cowardly with age. Strange thing, that – the fewer years you have to lose the more you fear the losing of 'em. Maybe a man just gets a stock of courage when he's born, and wears it down with each scrape he gets into.

Craw had been through a lot of scrapes. And it looked like he was about to snag himself on another.

He snatched a breather as he finally got to level ground, bent over, rubbing the wind-stung tears from his eyes. Trying to muffle his coughing which only made it louder. The Heroes loomed from the dark ahead, great holes in the night sky where no stars shone, four times man-height or more. Forgotten giants, marooned on their hilltop in the scouring wind. Standing stubborn guard over nothing.

Craw found himself wondering how much each of those great slabs of rock weighed. Only the dead knew how they'd dragged the bastard things up here. Or who had. Or why. The dead weren't telling, though, and Craw had no plans on joining 'em just to find out.

He saw the faintest glow of firelight now, at the stones' rough edges. Heard the chatter of men's voices over the wind's low growl. That brought back the risk he was taking, and a fresh wave of fear washed up with it. But fear's a healthy thing, long as it makes you think. Rudd Threetrees told him that, long time ago. He'd thought it through, and this was the right thing to do. Or the least wrong thing, anyway. Sometimes that's the best you can hope for.

So he took a deep breath, trying to remember how he'd felt when he was young and had no dodgy joints and didn't care a shit for nothing, picked out a likely gap between two of those big old rocks and strolled through.

Maybe this had been a sacred place, once upon an ancient day, high magic in these stones, the worst of crimes to wander into the circle uninvited. But if any old Gods took offence they'd no way of showing it. The wind dropped away to a mournful sighing and that was all. Magic was in scarce supply and there wasn't much sacred either. Those were the times.

The light shifted on the inside faces of the Heroes, faint orange on pitted stone, splattered with moss, tangled with old bramble and nettle and seeding grass. One was broken off half way up, a couple more had toppled over the centuries, left gaps like missing teeth in a skull's grin.

Craw counted eight men, huddled around their wind-whipped campfire with patched cloaks and worn coats and tattered blankets wrapped tight. Firelight flickered on gaunt, scarred, stubbled and bearded faces. Glinted on the rims of their shields, the blades of their weapons. Lots of weapons. Fair bit younger, in the main, but they didn't look much different to Craw's own crew of a night. Probably they weren't much different. He even thought for a moment one man with his face side-on was Jutlan. Felt that jolt of recognition, the eager greeting ready on his lips. Then he remembered Jutlan was twelve years in the ground, and he'd said the words over his grave.

Maybe there are only so many faces in the world. You get old enough, you start seeing 'em used again.

Craw lifted his open hands high, palms forward, doing his best to stop 'em shaking any. 'Nice evening!'

The faces snapped around. Hands jerked to weapons. One

man snatched up a bow and Craw felt his guts drop, but before he got close to drawing the string the man beside him stuck out an arm and pushed it down.

'Whoa there, Redcrow.' The one who spoke was a big old lad, with a heavy tangle of grey beard and a drawn sword sitting bright and ready across his knees. Craw found a rare grin, 'cause he knew the face, and his chances were looking better.

Hardbread he was called, a Named Man from way back. Craw had been on the same side as him in a few battles down the years, and the other side from him in a few more. But he'd a solid reputation. A long-seasoned hand, likely to think things over, not kill then ask the questions, which was getting to be the more popular way of doing business. Looked like he was Chief of this lot too, 'cause the lad called Redcrow sulkily let his bow drop, much to Craw's relief. He didn't want anyone getting killed tonight, and wasn't ashamed to say that counted double for his self.

There were still a fair few hours of darkness to get through, though, and a lot of sharpened steel about.

'By the dead.' Hardbread sat still as the Heroes themselves, but his mind was no doubt doing a sprint. ''Less I'm much mistaken, Curnden Craw just wandered out o' the night.'

'You ain't.' Craw took a few slow paces forwards, hands still high, doing his best to look light-hearted with eight sets of unfriendly eyes weighing him down.

'You're looking a little greyer, Craw.'

'So are you, Hardbread.'

'Well, you know. There's a war on.' The old warrior patted his stomach. 'Plays havoc with my nerves.'

'All honesty, mine too.'

'Who'd be a soldier?'

'Hell of a job. But they say old horses can't jump new fences.'

'I try not to jump at all these days,' said Hardbread. 'Heard you was fighting for Black Dow. You and your dozen.'

'Trying to keep the fighting to a minimum, but as far as who I'm doing it for, you're right. Dow buys my porridge.'

'I love porridge.' Hardbread's eyes rolled down to the fire and he poked thoughtfully at it with a twig. 'The Union pays for mine now.' His lads were twitchy – tongues licking at lips, fingers tickling at weapons, eyes shining in the firelight. Like the audience at a duel, watching the opening moves, trying to suss who had the upper hand. Hardbread's eyes came up again. 'That seems to put us on opposite sides.'

'We going to let a little thing like sides spoil a polite conversation?' asked Craw.

As though the very word 'polite' was an insult, Redcrow had another rush of blood. 'Let's just kill this fucker!'

Hardbread turned slowly to him, face squeezed up with scorn. 'If the impossible happens and I feel the need for your contribution, I'll tell you what it is. 'Til then keep it shut, halfhead. Man o' Curnden Craw's experience don't just wander up here to get killed by the likes o' you.' His eyes flicked around the stones, then back to Craw. 'Why'd you come, all by your lone self? Don't want to fight for that bastard Black Dow no more, and you've come over to join the Dogman?'

'Can't say I have. Fighting for the Union ain't really my style, no disrespect to those that do. We all got our reasons.'

'I try not to damn a man on his choice o' friends alone.'

'There's always good men on both sides of a good question,' said Craw. 'Thing is, Black Dow asked me to stroll on down to the Heroes, stand a watch for a while, see if the Union are coming up this way. But maybe you can spare me the bother. Are the Union coming up this way?'

'Dunno.'

'You're here, though.'

'I wouldn't pay much mind to that.' Hardbread glanced at the lads around the fire without great joy. 'As you can see, they more or less sent me on my own. The Dogman asked me to stroll up to the Heroes, stand a watch, see if Black Dow or any of his lot showed up.' He raised his brows. 'You think they will?'

Craw grinned. 'Dunno.'

'You're here, though.'

'Wouldn't pay much mind to that. It's just me and my dozen. 'Cept for Brydian Flood, he broke his leg a few months ago, had to leave him behind to mend.'

Hardbread gave a rueful smile, prodded the fire with his twig and sent up a dusting of sparks. 'Yours always was a tight crew. I daresay they're scattered around the Heroes now, bows to hand.'

'Something like that.' Hardbread's lads all twitched to the side, mouths gaping. Shocked at the voice coming from nowhere, shocked on top that it was a woman's. Wonderful stood with her arms crossed, sword sheathed and bow over her shoulder, leaning up against one of the Heroes as careless as she might lean on a tavern wall. 'Hey, hey, Hardbread.'

The old warrior winced. 'Couldn't you even nock an arrow, make it look like you take us serious?'

She jerked her head into the darkness. 'There's some boys back there, ready to put a shaft through your face if one o' you looks at us wrong. That make you feel better?'

Hardbread winced even more. 'Yes and no,' he said, his lads staring into the gaps between the stones, the night suddenly heavy with threat. 'Still acting Second to this article, are you?'

Wonderful scratched at the long scar through her shaved-stubble hair. 'No better offers. We've got to be like an old married couple who haven't fucked for years, just argue.'

'Me and my wife were like that, 'til she died.' Hardbread's finger tapped at his drawn sword. 'Miss her now, though. Thought you'd have company from the first moment I saw you, Craw. But since you're still jawing and I'm still breathing, I reckon you're set on giving us a chance to talk this out.'

'Then you've reckoned the shit out o' me,' said Craw. 'That's exactly the plan.'

'My sentries alive?'

Wonderful turned her head and gave one of her whistles, and Scorry Tiptoe slid out from behind one of the stones. Had his arm around a man with a big pink birthmark on his cheek. Looked almost like two old mates, 'til you saw Scorry's hand had a blade in it, edge tickling at Birthmark's throat.

'Sorry, Chief,' said the prisoner to Hardbread. 'Caught me off guard.'

'It happens.'

A scrawny lad came stumbling into the firelight like he'd been shoved hard, tripped over his own feet and sprawled in the long grass with a squawk. Jolly Yon stalked from the darkness behind him, axe held loose in one fist, heavy blade gleaming down by his boot, heavy frown on his bearded face.

'Thank the dead for that.' Hardbread waved his twig at the

lad, just clambering up. 'My sister's son. Promised I'd keep an eye out. If you'd killed him I'd never have heard the end of it.'

'He was asleep,' growled Yon. 'Weren't looking out too careful, were you?'

Hardbread shrugged. 'Weren't expecting anyone. If there's two things we've got too much of in the North it's hills and rocks. Didn't reckon a hill with rocks on it would be a big draw.'

'It ain't to me,' said Craw, 'but Black Dow said come down here—'

'And when Black Dow says a thing . . .' Brack-i-Dayn half-sang the words, that way the hillmen tend to. He stepped into the wide circle of grass, tattooed side of his great big face turned towards the firelight, shadows gathered in the hollows of the other.

Redcrow made to jump up but Hardbread weighed him down with a pat on the shoulder. 'My, my. You lot just keep popping up.' His eyes slid from Jolly Yon's axe, to Wonderful's grin, to Brack's belly, to Scorry's knife still at his man's throat. Judging the odds, no doubt, just the way Craw would've done. 'You got Whirrun of Bligh with you?'

Craw slowly nodded. 'I don't know why, but he insists on following me around.'

Right on cue, Whirrun's strange valley accent floated from the dark. 'Shoglig said . . . I would be shown my destiny . . . by a man choking on a bone.' It echoed off the stones, seeming to come from everywhere at once. He'd quite the sense of theatre, Whirrun. Every real hero needs one. 'And Shoglig is old as these stones. Hell won't take her, some say. Blade won't cut her. Saw the world born, some say, and will see it die. That's a woman a man has to listen to, ain't it? Or so some say.'

Whirrun strolled through the gap one of the missing Heroes had left and into the firelight, tall and lean, face in shadow from his hood, patient as winter. He had the Father of Swords across his shoulders like a milkmaid's yoke, dull grey metal of the hilt all agleam, arms slung over the sheathed blade and his long hands dangling. 'Shoglig told me the time, and the place, and the manner of my death. She whispered it, and made me swear to keep it secret, for magic shared is no magic at all. So I cannot tell you where it will be, or when, but it is not here, and it is not now.' He stopped a few paces from the fire. 'You boys, on the other hand . . .' Whirrun's hooded head tipped to one side, only the end of his sharp nose, and the line of his sharp jaw, and his thin mouth showing. 'Shoglig didn't say when you'd be going.' He didn't move. He didn't have to. Wonderful looked at Craw, and rolled her eyes towards the starry sky.

But Hardbread's lads hadn't heard it all a hundred times before. 'That Whirrun?' one muttered to his neighbour. 'Cracknut Whirrun? That's him?'

His neighbour said nothing, just the lump on the front of his throat moving as he swallowed.

'Well, my old arse if I'm fighting my way out o' this,' said Hardbread, brightly. 'Any chance you'd let us clear out?'

'I've a mind to insist on it,' said Craw.

'We can take our gear?'

'I'm not looking to embarrass you. I just want your hill.'

'Or Black Dow does, at any rate.'

'Same difference.'

'Then you're welcome to it.' Hardbread slowly got to his feet, wincing as he straightened his legs, no doubt cursed with some sticky joints of his own. 'Windy as anything up here. Rather be down in Osrung, feet near a fire.' Craw had to admit he'd a point there. Made him wonder who'd got the better end of the deal. Hardbread sheathed his sword, thoughtful, while his lads gathered their gear. 'This is right decent o' you, Craw. You're a straight edge, just like they say. Nice that men on different sides can still talk things through, in the midst of all this. Decent behaviour . . . it's out o' fashion.'

'Those are the times.' Craw jerked his head at Scorry and he slipped his knife away from Birthmark's throat, gave this little bow and held his open hand out towards the fire. Birthmark backed off, rubbing at the new-shaved patch on his stubbly neck, and started rolling up a blanket. Craw hooked his thumbs in his sword-belt and kept his eyes on Hardbread's crew as they made ready to go, just in case anyone had a mind to play hero.

Redcrow looked most likely. He'd slung his bow over his shoulder and now he was standing there with a black look, an axe in one white-knuckled fist and a shield on his other arm, a red bird painted on it. If he'd been for killing Craw before, didn't

17

seem the last few minutes had changed his mind. 'A few old shits and some fucking woman,' he snarled. 'We're backing down to the likes o' these without a fight?'

'No, no.' Hardbread slung his own scarred shield onto his back. 'I'm backing down, and these fellows here. You're going to stay, and fight Whirrun of Bligh on your own.'

'I'm what?' Redcrow frowned at Whirrun, twitchy, and Whirrun looked back, what showed of his face still stony as the Heroes themselves.

'That's right,' said Hardbread, 'since you're itching for a brawl. Then I'm going to cart your hacked-up corpse back to your mummy and tell her not to worry 'cause this is the way you wanted it. You loved this fucking hill so much you just had to die here.'

Redcrow's hand worked nervously around his axe handle. 'Eh?'

'Or maybe you'd rather come down with the rest of us, blessing the name o' Curnden Craw for giving us a fair warning and letting us go without any arrows in our arses.'

'Right,' said Redcrow, and turned away, sullen.

Hardbread puffed his cheeks at Craw. 'Young ones these days, eh? Were we ever so stupid?'

Craw shrugged. 'More'n likely.'

'Can't say I felt the need for blood like they seem to, though.'

Craw shrugged again. 'Those are the times.'

'True, true, and three times true. We'll leave you the fire, eh? Come on, boys.' They made for the south side of the hill, still stowing the last of their gear, and one by one faded into the night between the stones.

Hardbread's nephew turned in the gap and gave Craw the fuck yourself finger. 'We'll be back here, you sneaking bastards!' His uncle cuffed him across the top of his scratty head. 'Ow! What?'

'Some respect.'

'Ain't we fighting a war?'

Hardbread cuffed him again and made him squeal. 'No reason to be rude, you little shit.'

Craw stood there as the lad's complaints faded into the wind beyond the stones, swallowed sour spit, and eased his thumbs out from his belt. His hands were trembling, had to rub 'em together to hide it, pretending he was cold. But it was done, and everyone involved still drawing breath, so he guessed it had worked out as well as anyone could've hoped.

Jolly Yon didn't agree. He stepped up beside Craw frowning like thunder and spat into the fire. 'Time might come we regret not killing those folks there.'

'Not killing don't tend to weigh as heavy on my conscience as the alternative.'

Brack tut-tutted from Craw's other side. 'A warrior shouldn't carry too much conscience.'

'A warrior shouldn't carry too much belly either.' Whirrun had shrugged the Father of Swords off his shoulders and stood it on end, the pommel coming up to his neck, watching how the light moved on the crosspiece as he turned it round and round. 'We all got our weights to heft.'

'I've got just the right amount, you stringy bastard.' And the hillman gave his great gut a proud pat like a father might give his son's head.

'Chief.' Agrick strode into the firelight, bow loose in his hand and an arrow dangling between two fingers.

'They away?' asked Craw.

'Watched 'em down past the Children. They're crossing the river now, heading towards Osrung. Athroc's keeping a watch on 'em, though. We'll know if they double back.'

'You reckon they will?' asked Wonderful. 'Hardbread's cut from the old cloth. He might smile, but he won't have liked this any. You trust that old bastard?'

Craw frowned into the night. ''Bout as much as I'd trust anyone these days.'

'Little as that? Best post guards.'

'Aye,' said Brack. 'And make sure ours stay awake.'

Craw thumped his arm. 'Nice o' you to volunteer for first shift.'

'Your belly can keep you company,' said Yon.

Craw thumped his arm next. 'Glad you're in favour, you can go second.'

'Shit!'

'Drofd!'

You could tell the curly lad was the newest of the crew 'cause he actually hurried up with some snap. 'Aye, Chief?'

'Take the saddle horse and head back up the Yaws Road. Not sure whose lads you'll meet first – Ironhead's most likely, or maybe Tenways'. Let 'em know we ran into one of the Dogman's dozens at the Heroes. More'n likely just scouting, but . . .'

'Just scouting.' Wonderful nibbled some scab off one knuckle and spat it from the tip of her tongue. 'The Union are miles away, split up and spread out, trying to make straight lines out of a country with none.'

'More'n likely. But hop on the horse and pass on the message anyway.'

'Now?' Drofd's face was all dismay. 'In the dark?'

'No, next summer'll be fine,' snapped Wonderful. 'Yes, now, fool, all you've got to do is follow a road.'

Drofd heaved a sigh. 'Hero's work.'

'All war work is hero's work, boy,' said Craw. He'd rather have sent someone else, but then they'd have been arguing 'til dawn over why the new lad wasn't going. There are right ways of doing things a man can't just step around.

'Right y'are, Chief. See you in a few days, I reckon. And with a sore arse, no doubt.'

'Why?' And Wonderful gave a few thrusts of her hips. 'Tenways a special friend o' yours is he?' That got some laughs. Brack's big rumble, Scorry's little chuckle, even Yon's frown got a touch softer which meant he had to be rightly tickled.

'Ha, bloody ha.' And Drofd stalked off into the night to find the horse and make a start.

'I hear chicken fat can ease the passage!' Wonderful called after him, Whirrun's cackle echoing around the Heroes and off into the empty dark.

With the excitement over Craw was starting to feel all burned out. He dropped down beside the fire, wincing as his knees bent low, the earth still warm from Hardbread's rump. Scorry had found a place on the far side, sharpening his knife, the scraping of metal marking the rhythm to his soft, high singing. A song of Skarling Hoodless, greatest hero of the North, who brought the clans together long ago to drive the Union out. Craw sat and listened, chewed at the painful skin around his fingernails and thought about how he really had to stop doing it.

Whirrun set the Father of Swords down, squatted on his haunches and pulled out the old bag he kept his runes in. 'Best do a reading, eh?'

'You have to?' muttered Yon.

'Why? Scared o' what the signs might tell you?'

'Scared you'll spout a stack of nonsense and I'll lie awake half the night trying to make sense of it.'

'Guess we'll see.' Whirrun emptied his runes into his cupped hand, spat on 'em then tossed 'em down by the fire.

Craw couldn't help craning over to see, though he couldn't read the damn things for any money. 'What do the runes say, Cracknut?'

'The runes say . . .' Whirrun squinted down like he was trying to pick out something a long way off. 'There's going to be blood.'

Wonderful snorted. 'They always say that.'

'Aye.' Whirrun wrapped himself in his coat, nuzzled up against the hilt of his sword like a lover, eyes already shut. 'But lately they're right more often than not.'

Craw frowned around at the Heroes, forgotten giants, standing stubborn guard over nothing. 'Those are the times,' he muttered.

The Peacemaker

He stood by the window, one hand up on the stone, fingertips drumming, drumming, drumming. Frowning off across Carleon. Across the maze of cobbled streets, the tangle of steep slate roofs, the looming city walls his father built, all turned shiny black by the drizzle. Into the hazy fields beyond, past the fork of the grey river and towards the streaky rumour of hills at the head of the valley. As if, by sulking hard enough, he could see further. Over two score miles of broken country to Black Dow's scattered army. Where the fate of the North was being decided.

Without him.

'All I want is just for everyone to do what I tell them. Is that too much to ask?'

Seff slid up behind him, belly pressing into his back. 'I'd say it's no more than good sense on their part.'

'I know what's best anyway, don't I?'

'I do, and I tell you what it is, so . . . yes.'

'It seems there are a few pig-headed bastards in the North who don't realise we have all the answers.'

Her hand slipped up his arm and trapped his restless fingers against the stone. 'Men don't like to come out for peace, but they will. You'll see.'

'And until then, like all visionaries, I find myself spurned. Scorned. Exiled.'

'Until then, you find yourself locked in a room with your wife. Is that so bad?'

'There's nowhere I'd rather be,' he lied.

'Liar,' she whispered, lips tickling his ear. 'You're almost as much of a liar as they say you are. You'd rather be out there, beside your brother, with your armour on.' Her hands slid under his armpits and across his chest, giving him a ticklish shiver. 'Hacking the heads from cartloads of Southerners.'

'Murder is my favourite hobby, as you know.'

'You've killed more men than Skarling.'

'And I'd wear my armour to bed if I could.'

'It's only concern for my soft, soft skin that stops you.'

'But severed heads are prone to squirt.' He wriggled around to face her and pushed one lazy fingertip into her breastbone. 'I prefer a quick thrust through the heart.'

'Just like you've skewered mine. Aren't you the swordsman.'

He squeaked as he felt her hand between his legs and slid away sniggering across the wall, arms up to fend her off. 'All right, I admit it! I'm more lover than fighter!'

'At last the truth. Only look what you've done to me.' Putting one hand on her stomach and giving him a disapproving frown. It turned into a smile as he came close, slid his hand over hers, fingertips between hers, stroking her swollen belly.

'It's a boy,' she whispered. 'I feel it. An heir to the North. You'll be king, and then—'

'Shhhhh.' And he stopped her mouth with a kiss. There was no way of knowing when someone might be listening, and anyway, 'I've got an older brother, remember?'

'A pinhead of an older brother.'

Calder winced, but didn't deny it. He sighed as he looked down at that strange, wonderful, frightening belly of hers. 'My father always said there's nothing more important than family.' Except power. 'Besides, there's no point arguing over what we don't have. Black Dow's the one who wears my father's chain. Black Dow's the one we need to worry on.'

'Black Dow's nothing but a one-eared thug.'

'A thug with all the North under his boot and its mightiest War Chiefs taking his say-so.'

'Mighty War Chiefs.' She snorted in his face. 'Dwarves with big men's names.'

'Brodd Tenways.'

'That rotten old maggot? Even the thought of him makes me sick.'

'Cairm Ironhead.'

'I hear he has a tiny little prick. That's why he frowns all the time.'

'Glama Golden.'

'Even tinier. Like a baby's finger. And you have allies.'

'I do?'

'You know you do. My father likes you.'

Calder screwed up his face. 'Your father doesn't hate me, but I doubt he'll be leaping up to cut the rope if they hang me.'

'He's an honourable man.'

'Of course he is. Caul Reachey's a real straight edge, everyone knows it.' For what that was worth. 'But you and I were promised when I was the son of the King of the Northmen and the world was all different. He was getting a prince for a son-in-law, not just a well-known coward.'

She patted his cheek, hard enough to make a gentle slapping sound. 'A beautiful coward.'

'Beautiful men are even less well liked in the North than cowardly ones. I'm not sure your father's happy with the way my luck's turned.'

'Shit on your luck.' She took a fistful of his shirt and dragged him closer, much stronger than she looked. 'I wouldn't change a thing.'

'Neither would I. I'm just saying your father might.'

'And I'm saying you're wrong.' She caught his hand in hers and pressed it against her bulging stomach again. 'You're family.'

'Family.' He didn't bother saying that family could be as much a weakness as a strength. 'So we have your honourable father and my pinhead brother. The North is ours.'

'It will be. I know it.' She was swaying backwards slowly, leading him away from the window and towards the bed. 'Dow may be the man for war, but wars don't last forever. You're better than him.'

'Few would agree.' But it was nice to hear it, especially whispered in his ear in that soft, low, urgent voice.

'You're cleverer than him.' Her cheek brushing his jaw. 'Far cleverer.' Her nose nuzzling his chin. 'The cleverest man in the North.' By the dead, how he loved flattery.

'Go on.'

'You're certainly better looking than him.' Squeezing his hand

and sliding it down her belly. 'The most handsome man in the North . . .'

He licked her lips with the tip of his tongue. 'If the most beautiful ruled you'd be Queen of the Northmen already . . .'

Her fingers were busy with his belt. 'You always know just what to say, don't you, Prince Calder . . .'

There was a thumping at the door and he froze, the blood suddenly pounding in his head and very much not in his cock. Nothing like the threat of sudden death for killing a romantic mood. The thumping came again, making the heavy door rattle. They broke apart, flushed and fussing with their clothes. More like a pair of child lovers caught by their parents than a man and woman five years married. So much for his dreams of being king. He didn't even command the lock on his own door.

'The damn bolt's on your side isn't it?' he snapped.

Metal scraped and the door creaked open. A man stood in the archway, shaggy head almost touching the keystone. The ruined side of his face was turned forwards, a mass of scar running from near the corner of his mouth, through his eyebrow and across his forehead, the dead metal ball in his blind socket glinting. If any trace of romance had been lingering in the corners, or in Calder's trousers, that eye and that scar were its grisly end. He felt Seff stiffen and, since she was a long stretch braver than he was, her fear did nothing for his own. Caul Shivers was about the worst omen a man could see. Folk called him Black Dow's dog, but never to his burned-out face. The man the Protector of the North sent to do his blackest work.

'Dow wants you.' If the sight of Shivers' face had only got some hero half way horrified, his voice would have done the rest of the job. A broken whisper that made every word sound like it hurt.

'Why?' asked Calder, keeping his own voice sunny as a summer morning in spite of his hammering heart. 'Can't he beat the Union without me?'

Shivers didn't laugh. He didn't frown. He stood there, in the doorway, a silent slab of menace.

Calder tried his best at a carefree shrug. 'Well, I suppose everyone serves someone. What about my wife?'

Shivers' good eye flicked across to Seff. If he'd looked with leering lust, or sneering disgust, Calder would've been happier. But Shivers looked at a pregnant woman like a butcher at a carcass, only a job to be done. 'Dow wants her to stay and stand hostage. Make sure everyone behaves. She'll be safe.'

'As long as everyone behaves.' Calder found he'd stepped in front of her, as if to shield her with his body. Not much of a shield against a man like Shivers.

'That's it.'

'And if Black Dow misbehaves? Where's my hostage?'

Shivers' eye slid back to Calder, and stuck. 'I'll be your hostage.'

'And if Dow breaks his word I can kill you, can I?'

'You can try.'

'Huh.' Caul Shivers had one of the hardest names in the North. Calder, it hardly needed to be said, didn't. 'Can you give us a moment to say our goodbyes?'

'Why not?' Shivers slid back until only the glint of his metal eye showed in the shadows. 'I'm no monster.'

'Back to the snake pit,' muttered Calder.

Seff caught his hand, eyes wide as she looked up at him, fearful and eager at once. Almost as fearful and eager as he was. 'Be patient, Calder. Tread carefully.'

'I'll tiptoe all the way there.' If he even made it. He reckoned there was about a one in four Shivers had been told to cut his throat on the way and toss his corpse in a bog.

She took his chin between her finger and thumb and shook it, hard. 'I mean it. Dow fears you. My father says he'll take any excuse to kill you.'

'Dow should fear me. Whatever else I am, I'm my father's son.'

She squeezed his chin even harder, looking him right in the eye. 'I love you.'

He looked down at the floor, feeling the sudden pressure of tears at the back of his throat. 'Why? Don't you realise what an evil shit I am?'

'You're better than you think.'

When she said it he could almost believe it. 'I love you too.' And he didn't even have to lie. How he'd raged when his father announced the match. Marry that pig-nosed, dagger-tongued little bitch? Now she looked more beautiful every time he saw her. He loved her nose, and her tongue even more. It was almost enough to make him swear off other women. He drew her close, blinking back the wet, and kissed her once more. 'Don't worry. No one's less keen to attend my hanging than I am. I'll be back in your bed before you know it.'

'With your armour on?'

'If you like,' as he backed away.

'And no lying while you're gone.'

'I never lie.'

'Liar,' she mouthed at him before the guards closed the door and slid the bolt, leaving Calder in the shadowy hallway with only the sappy-sad thought that he might never see his wife again. That gave him a rare touch of bravery and he hurried after Shivers, catching up with him as he trudged away and slapping a hand down on his shoulder. He was more than a little unnerved by the wood-like solidity of it, but plunged on regardless.

'If anything happens to her, I promise you—'

'I hear your promises ain't up to much.' Shivers' eye went to the offending hand and Calder carefully removed it. He might only rarely be brave, but he was never brave past the point of good sense.

'Who says so? Black Dow? If there's anyone in the North whose promises are worth less than mine it's that bastard's.' Shivers stayed silent, but Calder wasn't a man to be easily put off. Good treachery takes effort. 'Dow won't ever give you more than you can rip from him with both hands, you know. There'll be nothing for you, however loyal you are. In fact, the more loyal you are, the less there'll be. You'll see. Not enough meat and too many hungry dogs to feed.'

Shivers' one eye narrowed just the slightest fraction. 'I'm no dog.'

That chink of anger would have been enough to scare most men silent, but to Calder it was only a crack to chisel at. 'I see that,' he whispered, as low and urgent as Seff had whispered to him. 'Most men don't see past their fear of you, but I do. I see what you are. A fighter, of course, but a thinker too. An ambitious man. A proud man, and why not?' Calder brought them to a halt in a shadowy stretch of the hallway, leaned in to a conspiratorial distance, smothering his instinct to cringe away as that awful scar turned towards him. 'If I had a man like you working for me I'd make better use of him than Black Dow does, that much I promise.'

Shivers raised one beckoning hand, a big ruby on his little finger gleaming the colour of blood in the gloom. Giving Calder no choice but to come closer, closer, far too close for comfort. Close enough to feel Shivers' warm breath. Close enough almost to kiss. Close enough so all Calder could see was his own distorted, unconvincing grin reflected in that dead metal ball of an eye.

'Dow wants you.'

The Best of Us

Your August Majesty,

We are entirely recovered from the reverse at Quiet Ford and the campaign proceeds. For all Black Dow's cunning, Lord Marshal Kroy is driving him steadily north towards his capital at Carleon. We are no more than two weeks' march from the city, now. He cannot fall back for ever. We will have him, your Majesty can depend upon it.

General Jalenhorm's division won a small engagement on a chain of hills to the northeast yesterday. Lord Governor Meed leads his division south towards Ollensand in the hope of forcing the Northmen to split their forces and give battle at a disadvantage. I travel with General Mitterick's division, close to Marshal Kroy's headquarters. Yesterday, near a village called Barden, Northmen ambushed our supply column as it was stretched out along the bad roads. Through the alertness and bravery of our rearguard they were beaten back with heavy losses. I recommend to your Majesty one Lieutenant Kerns who showed particular valour and lost his life in the engagement, leaving, I understand, a wife and young child behind him.

The columns are well ordered. The weather is fair. The army moves freely and the men are in the highest spirits.

I remain your Majesty's most faithful and unworthy servant, Bremer dan Gorst, Royal Observer of the Northern War

The column was in chaos. The rain poured down. The army was mired in the filth and the men were in the most rotten spirits. *And mine the most rotten in the whole putrefying swarm.*

Bremer dan Gorst forced his way through a mud-spattered crush of soldiers, all wriggling like maggots, their armour running with wet, their shouldered pikes poking lethally in all directions. They were stopped as solid as milk turned rank in a bottle but men still squelched up from behind, adding their own burdens of ill temper to the jostling mass, choking the thread of muck that passed for a road and forcing men cursing into the trees. Gorst was already late and had to assert himself as the press tightened, brushing men aside. Sometimes they would turn to argue as they stumbled in the slop, but they soon shut their mouths when they saw who he was. They knew him.

The adversary that had so confounded his Majesty's army proved to be one of its own wagons, slid from the ankle-deep mud of the track and into the considerably deeper bog beside. Following the universal law that the most frustrating thing will always happen, no matter how unlikely, it had somehow ended up almost sideways, back wheels mired to their axles. A snarling driver whipped two horses into a pointless lather of terror while a half-dozen bedraggled soldiers floundered ineffectually about the back. On both sides of the road men slithered through the sodden undergrowth, cursing as gear was torn by brambles, pole-arms were tangled by branches, eyes were whipped at by twigs.

Three young officers stood nearby, the shoulders of their scarlet uniforms turned soggy maroon by the downpour. Two were arguing, stabbing at the wagon with pointed fingers while the other stood and watched, one hand carelessly resting on the gilded hilt of his sword, idle as a mannequin in a military tailor's.

The enemy could scarcely have arranged a more effective blockage with a thousand picked men.

'What is this?' Gorst demanded, fighting and, of course, failing, to sound authoritative.

'Sir, the supply train should be nowhere near this track!'

'That's nonsense, sir! The infantry should be held up while—'

Because the blame is what matters, of course, not the solution. Gorst shouldered the officers aside and squelched into the quagmire, wedging himself between the muddy soldiers, delving into the muck for the wagon's back axle, boots twisting through the slime to find a solid footing. He took a few short breaths and braced himself.

'Go!' he squeaked at the driver, for once forgetting even to try to lower his voice.

Whip snapped. Men groaned. Horses snorted. Mud sucked. Gorst strained from his toes to his scalp, every muscle locked and vibrating with effort. The world faded and he was left alone with his task. He grunted, then growled, then hissed, the rage boiling up in him as if he had a bottomless tank of it instead of a heart and he only had to turn the tap to rip this wagon apart.

The wheels gave with a protesting shriek, lurched from the bog and forward. Suddenly straining at nothing Gorst stumbled despairingly then flopped face down in the mire, one of the soldiers falling beside him. He struggled up as the wagon rattled away, the driver fighting to bring his plunging horses under control.

'Thanks for the help, sir.' The mud-caked soldier reached out with a clumsy paw and managed to smear the muck that now befouled Gorst's uniform even more widely. 'Sorry, sir. Very sorry.'

Keep your axles oiled you retarded scum. Keep your cart on the road you gawping halfwits. Do your damn jobs you lazy vermin. Is that too much to ask? 'Good,' muttered Gorst, brushing the man's hand away and making a futile attempt to straighten his jacket. 'Thank you.' He stalked off into the drizzle after the wagon, and could almost hear the mocking laughter of the men and their officers prickling at his back.

Lord Marshal Kroy, commander-in-chief of his Majesty's armies in the North, had requisitioned for his temporary headquarters the grandest building within a dozen miles, namely a squat cottage so riddled with moss it looked more like an abandoned dunghill. A toothless old woman and her even more ancient husband, presumably the dispossessed owners, sat in the doorway of the accompanying barn under a threadbare shawl, and watched Gorst squelch up towards their erstwhile front door. They did not look impressed. Neither did the four guards loitering about the porch in wet oilskins. Nor the collection of damp officers infesting the low living room, who all looked around expectantly when Gorst ducked through the door, and all looked equally crestfallen when they realised who it was.

'It's Gorst,' sneered one, as if he had been expecting a king and got a pot-boy.

It was quite the concentration of martial splendour. Marshal Kroy was the centrepiece, sitting with unflinching discipline at the head of the table, impeccable as always in a freshly pressed black uniform, stiff collar encrusted with silver leaves, every iron-grey hair on his skull positioned at rigid attention. His chief of staff Colonel Felnigg sat bolt upright beside him, small, nimble, with sparkling eyes that missed no detail, his chin lifted uncomfortably high. Or rather, since he was a remarkably chinless man, his neck formed an almost straight line from his collar to the nostrils of his beaked nose. *Like an over-haughty vulture waiting for a corpse to feast upon.*

General Mitterick would have made a considerable meal. He was a big man with a big face, oversized features positively stuffed into the available room on the front of his head. Where Felnigg had too little chin Mitterick had far too much, and with a big, reckless cleft down the middle. *As if he had an arse suspended from his magnificent moustache.* He had affected buff leather gauntlets reaching almost to the elbow, probably intended to give the impression of a man of action, but which put Gorst in mind of the gloves a farmer might wear to wind a troubled cow.

Mitterick cocked an eyebrow at Gorst's mud-crusted uniform. 'More heroics, Colonel Gorst?' he asked, accompanied by some light sniggering.

Ram it up your chin-arse, you cow-winding bladder of vanity. The words tickled Gorst's lips. But in his falsetto, whatever he said the joke would be on him. He would rather have faced a thousand Northmen than this ordeal by conversation. So he turned the first sound into a queasy grin, and smiled along with his humiliation as he always did. He found the gloomiest corner, crossed his arms over his filthy jacket and dampened his fury by imagining the smirking heads of Mitterick's staff impaled on the pikes of Black Dow's army. Not the most patriotic pastime, perhaps, but among his most satisfying.

It's an upside-down sham of a world in which men like these, if they can be called men at all, can look down on a man like me. I am worth twice the lot of you. And this is the best the Union has to offer? We deserve to lose.

'Can't win a war without getting your hands dirty.'

'What?' Gorst frowned sideways. The Dogman was leaning

beside him in his battered coat, a look of world-weary resignation on his no less battered face.

The Northman let his head tip back until it bumped gently against the peeling wall. 'Some folk would rather keep clean, though, eh? And lose.'

Gorst could ill afford to strike up an alliance with the one man even more of an outsider than himself. He slipped into his accustomed silence like a well-worn suit of armour, and turned his attention to the nervous chatter of the officers.

'When are they getting here?'

'Soon.'

'How many of them?'

'I heard three.'

'Only one. It only takes one member of the Closed Council.'

'The Closed Council?' squeaked Gorst, voice driven up almost beyond the range of human hearing by a surge of nerves. A nauseating after-taste of the horror he had felt the day those horrible old men had stripped him of his position. *Squashing my dreams as carelessly as a boy might squash a beetle.* 'And next . . .' as he was ushered into the hallway and the black doors were shut on him like coffin lids. *No longer commander of the king's guards. No longer a Knight of the Body. No longer anything but a squealing joke, my name made a byword for failure and disgrace.* He could see that panel of creased and sagging sneers still. And at the head of the table the king's pale face, jaw clenched, refusing to meet Gorst's eye. *As though the ruin of his most loyal servant was no more than an unpleasant chore . . .*

'Which of them will it be?' Felnigg was asking. 'Do we know?'

'It hardly matters.' Kroy looked towards the window. Beyond the half-open shutters the rain was getting heavier. 'We already know what they will say. The king demands a great victory, at twice the speed and half the cost.'

'As always!' Mitterick crowed with the regularity of an over-eager cockerel. 'Damn politicians, sticking their noses into our business! I swear those swindlers on the Closed Council cost us more lives than the bloody enemy ever—'

The doorknob turned with a loud rattle and a heavy-set old man entered the room, entirely bald with a short grey beard. He gave no immediate impression of supreme power. His clothes were only slightly less rain-soaked and mud-spattered than Gorst's own. His staff was of plain wood shod with steel, more walking stick than rod of office. But still, though he and the single, unassuming servant who scraped in after him were outnumbered ten to one by some of the finest peacocks in the army, it was the officers who held their breath. The old man carried about him an air of untouchable confidence, disdainful ownership, masterful control. *The air of a slaughterman casting an eye over that morning's hogs.*

'Lord Bayaz.' Kroy's face had paled, slightly. It might have been the very first time Gorst had seen the marshal surprised, and he was not alone. The crowded room could not have been more dumbstruck if the corpse of Harod the Great had been trundled in on a trolley to address them.

'Gentlemen.' Bayaz tossed his staff carelessly to his curly-headed servant, wiped the beads of moisture from his bald pate with a faint hissing and flicked them from the edge of his hand. For a legendary figure, there was no ceremony to him. 'Some weather we're having, eh? Sometimes I love the North and sometimes . . . less so.'

'We were not expecting—'

'Why would you be?' Bayaz chuckled with a show of good humour that somehow managed to seem a threat. 'I am retired! I had left my seat on the Closed Council empty once again and was seeing out my dotage at my library, far removed from the grind of politics. But since this war is taking place on my very doorstep, I thought it would be neglectful of me not to stop by. I have brought money with me – I understand pay is standing somewhat in arrears.'

'A little,' conceded Kroy.

'A little more and the soldier's veneer of honour and obedience might swiftly rub away, eh, gentlemen? Without its golden lubricant the great machine of his Majesty's army would soon stutter to a halt, would it not, as with so much in life?'

'Concern for the welfare of our men is always uppermost in our minds,' said the marshal, uncertainly.

'And mine!' answered Bayaz. 'I am here only to help. To keep the wheels oiled, if you will. To observe and perhaps, should the occasion call, offer some trifling guidance. Yours is the command, Lord Marshal, of course.'

'Of course,' echoed Kroy, but no one was convinced. This, after all, was the First of the Magi. A man supposedly hundreds of years old, supposedly possessed of magical powers, who had supposedly forged the Union, brought the king to his throne, driven out the Gurkish and laid a good section of Adua to waste doing it. Supposedly. *Hardly a man noted for a reluctance to interfere.* 'Er . . . might I introduce General Mitterick, commander of his Majesty's second division?'

'General Mitterick, even sealed away with my books I have heard tales of your valour. An honour.'

The general fluffed up with happiness. 'No, no! The honour is mine!'

'Yes,' said Bayaz, with casual brutality.

Kroy charged boldly into the ensuing silence. 'This is my chief of staff, Colonel Felnigg, and this the leader of those Northmen who oppose Black Dow and fight alongside us, the Dogman.'

'Ah, yes!' Bayaz raised his brows. 'I believe we had a mutual friend in Logen Ninefingers.'

The Dogman stared evenly back, the one man in the room who showed no sign of being overawed. 'I'm a long way from sure he's dead.'

'If anyone can cheat the Great Leveller it was – or is – he. Either way, he is a loss to the North. To the world. A great man, and much missed.'

Dogman shrugged. 'A man, anyway. Some good and some bad in him, like most. As for much missed, depends on who you ask, don't it?'

'True.' Bayaz gave a rueful smile, and spoke a few words in fluent Northern: 'You have to be realistic about these things.'

'You do,' replied the Dogman. Gorst doubted whether anyone else in the room had understood their little exchange. He was not entirely sure he had, for all he knew the language.

Kroy tried to usher things on. 'And this is—'

'Bremer dan Gorst, of course!' Bayaz shocked Gorst to his boots by warmly shaking his hand. For a man of his years, he had quite the grip. 'I saw you fence against the king, how long ago, now? Five years? Six?'

Gorst could have counted the hours since. *And it says a great deal for my shadow of a life that my proudest moment is still being humiliated in a fencing match.* 'Nine.'

'Nine, imagine that! The decades flit past me like leaves on the wind, I swear. No man ever deserved the title more.'

'I was fairly beaten.'

Bayaz leaned close. 'You were beaten, anyway, which is all that really counts, eh?' And he slapped Gorst on the arm as if they had shared a private joke, though if they had it was private to Bayaz alone. 'I thought you were with the Knights of the Body? Were you not guarding the king at the Battle of Adua?'

Gorst felt himself colouring. *I was, as everyone here well knows, but now I am nothing but a wretched scapegoat, used and discarded like some stuttering serving girl by his lordship's caddish youngest son. Now I am—*

'Colonel Gorst is here as the king's observer,' ventured Kroy, seeing his discomfort.

'Of course!' Bayaz snapped his fingers. 'After that business in Sipani.'

Gorst's face burned as though the city's very name was a slap. *Sipani.* And as simply as that the best part of him was where he spent so much of his time: four years ago, back in the madness of Cardotti's House of Leisure. Stumbling through the smoke, searching desperately for the king, reaching the staircase, seeing that masked face – and then the long, bouncing trip down the stairs, into unjust disgrace. He saw smirks among the over-bright smear of faces the room had suddenly become. He opened his dry mouth but, as usual, nothing of any use emerged.

'Ah, well.' The Magus gave Gorst's shoulder the kind of consoling pat one might give to a guard dog long ago gone blind, and occasionally tossed a bone for sentimental reasons. 'Perhaps you can work your way back into the king's good graces.'

Depend upon it, you arcane fuck-hole, if I must spill every drop of blood in the North. 'Perhaps,' Gorst managed to whisper.

But Bayaz had already drawn out a chair and was steepling his fingers before him. 'So! The situation, Lord Marshal?'

Kroy jerked the front of his jacket smooth as he advanced on the great map, so large it had been folded at the edges to fit on the biggest wall of the mean little building. 'General Jalenhorm's division is here, to our west.' Paper crackled as Kroy's stick hissed over it. 'He is pushing northwards, firing crops and villages in the hope of drawing the Northmen into battle.'

Bayaz looked bored. 'Mmmm.'

'Meanwhile Lord Governor Meed's division, accompanied by the majority of the Dogman's loyalists, have marched southeast to take Ollensand under siege. General Mitterick's division remains between the two.' Tap, tap, stick on paper, ruthlessly precise. 'Ready to lend support to either one. The route of supply runs south towards Uffrith over poor roads, no more than tracks, really, but we are—'

'Of course.' Bayaz rendered it all irrelevant with a wave of one meaty hand. 'I have not come to interfere in the details.'

Kroy's stick hovered uselessly. 'Then—'

'Imagine yourself a master mason, Lord Marshal, working upon one turret of a grand palace. A craftsman whose dedication, skill and attention to detail are disputed by no one.'

'Mason?' Mitterick looked baffled.

'Then imagine the Closed Council as the architects. Our responsibility is not the fitting of one stone to another, it is the design of the building overall. The politics, rather than the tactics. An army is an instrument of government. It must be used in such a way that it furthers the interests of government. Otherwise what use is it? Only an extremely costly machine for . . . minting medals.' The room shifted uncomfortably. *Hardly the sort of talk the toy soldiers appreciate.*

'The policies of government are subject to sudden change,' grumbled Felnigg.

Bayaz looked upon him like a schoolmaster at the dunce ruining the standard of his class. 'The world is fluid. We must be fluid also. And since these latest hostilities began, circumstances have not flowed for the better. At home the peasants are restless again. War taxes, and so on. Restless, restless, always restless.' He drummed his thick fingers restlessly on the table-top. 'And the new Lords' Round is finally completed, so the Open Council is in session and the nobles have somewhere to complain. They are doing so. At tremendous length. They are impatient with the lack of progress, apparently.'

'Damn windbags,' grunted Mitterick. *Lending considerable support to the maxim that men always hate in others what is most hateful in themselves.*

Bayaz sighed. 'Sometimes I feel I am building sandcastles against the tide. The Gurkish are never idle, there is no end to their intrigues. But once they were the only real challenge to us abroad. Now there is the Snake of Talins, too. Murcatto.' He frowned as if the name tasted foul, hard lines deepening across his face. 'While our armies are entangled here that cursed woman continues to tighten her grip on Styria, emboldened by the knowledge that the Union can do little to oppose her.' Some patriotic tutting stirred the assembly. 'Put simply, gentlemen, the costs of this war, in treasure, in prestige, in lost opportunities, are becoming too high. The Closed Council require a swift conclusion. Naturally, as soldiers, you all are prone to be sentimental about warfare. But fighting is only any use when it's cheaper than the alternatives.' He calmly picked a piece of fluff from his sleeve, frowned at it, and flicked it away. 'This is the North, after all. I mean to say . . . what's it worth?'

There was a silence. Then Marshal Kroy cleared his throat. 'The Closed Council require a swift conclusion . . . do they mean by the end of the campaigning season?'

'The end of the season? No, no.' The officers blew out their cheeks with evident relief. It was short-lived. 'Considerably sooner than that.'

The noise slowly built. Shocked gasps, then horrified splutters, then whispered swear-words and grumbles of disbelief, the officers' professional affront scoring a rare victory over their usually unconquerable servility.

'But we cannot possibly—!' Mitterick burst out, striking the table with one gauntleted fist then hastily remembering himself. 'I mean to say, I apologise, but we cannot—'

'Gentlemen, gentlemen.' Kroy ushered down his unruly brood, and appealed to reason. *The lord marshal is nothing if not a reasonable man.* 'Lord Bayaz . . . Black Dow continues to evade us. To manoeuvre and fall back.' He gestured at the map as though it was covered in realities that simply could not be argued with. 'He has staunch war leaders at his side. His men know the land, are sustained by its people. He is a master at swift movement and retreat, at swift concentration and surprise. He has already wrong-footed us once. If we rush to battle, there is every chance that—'

But he might as well have reasoned with the tide. The First of the Magi was not interested. 'You stray onto the details again, Lord Marshal. Masons and architects and so forth, did I speak about that? The king sent you here to fight, not march around. I have no doubt you will find a way to bring the Northmen to a decisive battle, and if not, well . . . every war is only a prelude to talk, isn't it?' Bayaz stood, and the officers belatedly struggled up after him, chairs screeching and swords clattering in an ill-coordinated shambles.

'We are . . . delighted you could join us,' Kroy managed, though the army's feelings were very clearly the precise opposite.

Bayaz appeared impervious to irony, however. 'Good, because I will be staying to observe. Some gentlemen from the University of Adua accompanied me. They have an invention that I am curious to see tested.'

'Anything we can do to assist.'

'Excellent.' Bayaz smiled broadly. *The only smile in the room.* 'I will leave the shaping of the stones in your . . .' He raised an eyebrow at Mitterick's absurd gauntlets. 'Capable hands. Gentlemen.'

The officers kept their nervous silence, as the First of the Magi's worn boots and those of his single servant receded down the hallway, like children sent early to bed, preparing to throw back the covers as soon as their parents reached a safe distance.

Angry babbling broke out the moment they heard the front door close. 'What the hell—'

'How dare he?'

'Before the end of the season?' frothed Mitterick. 'He is quite mad!'

'Ridiculous!' snapped Felnigg. 'Ridiculous!'

'Bloody politicians!'

But Gorst had a smile, and not just at the dismay of Mitterick and the rest. Now they would have to seek battle. *And whatever they came for, I came to fight.*

Kroy brought his fractious officers to order by banging at the table with his stick. 'Gentlemen, please! The Closed Council have

39

spoken, and so the king has spoken, and we can only strive to obey. We are but the masons, after all.' He turned towards the map as the room quieted, eyes running over the roads, the hills, the rivers of the North. 'I fear we must abandon caution and concentrate the army for a concerted push northwards. Dogman?'

The Northman stepped up to the table and snapped out a vibrating salute. 'Marshal Kroy, sir!' A joke, of course, since he was an ally rather than an underling.

'If we march for Carleon in force, is it likely that Black Dow will finally offer battle?'

The Dogman rubbed a hand over his stubbled jaw. 'Maybe. He ain't the most patient. Looks bad for him, letting you tramp all over his back yard these past few months. But he's always been an unpredictable bastard, Black Dow.' He had a bitter look on his face for a moment, as if remembering something painful. 'One thing I can tell you, if he decides on battle he won't offer nothing. He'll ram it right up your arse. Still, it's worth a try.' Dogman grinned around the officers. ''Specially if you like it up your arse.'

'Not my first choice, but they say a general should be prepared for anything.' Kroy traced a road to its junction, then tapped at the paper. 'What is this town?'

The Dogman leaned over the table to squint at the map, considerably inconveniencing a pair of unhappy staff officers and giving the impression of not caring in the least. 'That's Osrung. Old town, set in fields, with a bridge and a mill, might have, what . . . three or four hundred people in peacetime? Some stone buildings, more wood. High fence around the outside. Used to have a damn fine tavern but, you know, nothing's how it used to be.'

'And this hill? Near where the roads from Ollensand and Uffrith meet?'

'The Heroes.'

'Odd name for a hill,' grunted Mitterick.

'Named after a ring of old stones on top. Some warriors of ancient days are buried beneath 'em, or that's one rumour, anyway. You get quite a view from up there. I sent a dozen to have a look-see the other day, in fact, check if any of Dow's boys have shown their faces.'

'And?'

'Nothing yet, but no reason there should be. There's help nearby, if they get pressed.'

'That's the spot, then.' Kroy craned closer to the map, pressing the point of his stick into that hill as though he could will the army there. 'The Heroes. Felnigg?'

'Sir?'

'Send word to Lord Governor Meed to abandon the siege of Ollensand and march with all haste to meet us near Osrung.'

That got a few sharp in-breaths. 'Meed will be furious,' said Mitterick.

'He often is. That cannot be helped.'

'I'll be heading back that way,' said Dogman. 'Meet up with the rest o' my boys and get 'em moving north. I can take the message.'

'It might be better if Colonel Felnigg carries it personally. Lord Governor Meed is . . . not the greatest admirer of Northmen.'

'Unlike the rest of you, eh?' The Dogman showed the Union's finest a mouthful of sharp yellow teeth. 'I'll make a move, then. With any luck I'll see you up the Heroes in what . . . three days? Four?'

'Five, if this weather gets no better.'

'This is the North. Let's call it five.' And he followed Bayaz out of the low sitting room.

'Well, it might not be the way we wanted it.' Mitterick smashed a meaty fist into a meaty palm. 'But we can show them something, now, eh? Get those skulking bastards out in the open and *show* them something!' The legs of his chair shrieked as he stood. 'I will hurry my division along. We should make a night march, Lord Marshal! Get at the enemy!'

'No.' Kroy was already sitting at his desk and dipping pen in ink to write orders. 'Halt them for the night. On these roads, in this weather, haste will do more harm than good.'

'But, Lord Marshal, if we—'

'I intend to rush, General, but not headlong into a defeat. We must not push the men too hard. They need to be ready.'

Mitterick jerked up his gloves. 'Damn these damn roads!' Gorst stood aside to let him and his staff file from the room, silently wishing he was ushering them through into a bottomless pit.

Kroy raised his brows as he wrote. 'Sensible men . . . run away . . . from battles.' His pen scratched neatly across the paper. 'Someone will need to take this order to General Jalenhorm. To move with all haste to the Heroes and secure the hill, the town of Osrung, and any other crossings of the river that—'

Gorst stepped forwards. 'I will take it.' If there was to be action, Jalenhorm's division would be first into it. *And I will be at the front of the front rank. I will not bury the ghosts of Sipani in a headquarters.*

'There is no one I would rather entrust it to.' Gorst grasped the order but the marshal did not release it at once. He remained looking calmly up, the folded paper a bridge between them. 'Remember, though, that you are the king's observer, not the king's champion.'

I am neither. I am a glorified errand boy, here because nowhere else will have me. I am a secretary in a uniform. A filthy uniform, as it happens. I am a dead man still twitching. Ha ha! Look at the big idiot with the silly voice! Make him dance! 'Yes, sir.'

'Observe, then, by all means. But no more heroics, if you please. Not like the other day at Barden. A war is no place for heroics. Especially not this one.'

'Yes, sir.'

Kroy let go of the order and turned back to peer at his map, measuring distances between stretched-out thumb and forefinger. 'The king would never forgive me if we were to lose you.'

The king has abandoned me here, and no one will care a stray speck of piss if I am hacked apart and my brains splattered across the North. Least of all me. 'Yes, sir.' And Gorst strode out, through the front door and back into the rain, where he was struck by lightning.

There she was, picking her way across the boggy front yard towards him. In the midst of all that sullen mud her smiling face burned like the sun, incandescent. Delight crushed him, made his skin sing and his breath catch. The months he had spent away from her had done not the slightest good. He was as desperately, hopelessly, helplessly in love as ever.

'Finree,' he whispered, voice full of awe, as in some silly story a wizard might pronounce a word of power. 'Why are you here?' Half-expecting she would fade into nothing, a figment of his overwrought imagination.

'To see my father. Is he in there?'

'Writing orders.'

'As always.' She looked down at Gorst's uniform and raised one eyebrow, darkened from brown to almost black and spiked to soft points by the rain. 'Still playing in the mud, I see.'

He could not even bring himself to be embarrassed. He was lost in her eyes. Some strands of hair were stuck across her wet face. He wished he was. *I thought nothing could be more beautiful than you used to be, but now you are more beautiful than ever.* He dared not look at her and he dared not look away. *You are the most beautiful woman in the world – no – in all of history – no – the most beautiful thing in all of history. Kill me, now, so that your face can be the last thing I see.* 'You look well,' he murmured.

She looked down at her sodden travelling coat, mud-spotted to the waist. 'I suspect you're not being entirely honest with me.'

'I never dissemble.' *I love you I love you I love you I love you I love you I love you I love you . . .*

'And are you well, Bremer? I may call you Bremer, may I?'

You may crush my eyes out with your heels. Only say my name again. 'Of course. I am . . .' *Ill in mind and body, ruined in fortune and reputation, hating of the world and everything in it, but none of that matters, as long as you are with me.* 'Well.'

She held out her hand and he bent to kiss it like a village priest who had been permitted to touch the hem of the Prophet's robe—

There was a golden ring on her finger with a small, sparkling blue stone.

Gorst's guts twisted so hard he nearly lost control of them entirely. It was only by a supreme effort that he stayed standing. He could scarcely whisper the words. 'Is that . . .'

'A marriage band, yes!' Could she know he would rather she had dangled a butchered head in his face?

He gripped to his smile like a drowning man to the last stick of wood. He felt his mouth move, and heard his own squeak. His repugnant, womanly, pathetic little squeak. 'Who is the gentleman?'

'Colonel Harod dan Brock.' A hint of pride in her voice. Of love. *What would I give to hear her say my name like that? All I have. Which is nothing but other men's scorn.*

'Harod dan Brock,' he whispered, and the name was sand in his mouth. He knew the man, of course. They were distantly related, fourth cousins or some such. They had sometimes spoken years ago, when Gorst had served with the guard of his father, Lord Brock. Then Lord Brock had made his bid for the crown, and failed, and been exiled for the worst of treasons. His eldest son had been granted the king's mercy, though. Stripped of his many lands, and his lofty titles, but left with his life. How Gorst wished the king was less merciful now.

'He is serving on Lord Governor Meed's staff.'

'Yes.' Brock was nauseatingly handsome, with an easy smile and a winning manner. *The bastard.* Well spoken of and well liked, in spite of his father's disgrace. *The snake.* Had earned his place by bravery and bonhomie. *The fucker.* He was everything Gorst was not.

He clenched his right fist trembling hard, and imagined it ripping the easy-smiling jaw out of Harod dan Brock's handsome head. 'Yes.'

'We are very happy,' said Finree.

Good for you. I want to kill myself. She could not have given him sharper pain if she had crushed his cock in a vice. Could she be such a fool as to not see through him? Some part of her must have known, must have delighted in his humiliation. *Oh, how I love you. Oh, how I hate you. Oh, how I want you.*

'My congratulations to you both,' he murmured.

'I will tell my husband.'

'Yes.' *Yes, yes, tell him to die, tell him to burn, and soon.* Gorst kept the rictus smile clinging to his face while vomit tickled at his throat. 'Yes.'

'I must go to my father. Perhaps we will see each other again, soon?'

Oh, yes. Very soon. Tonight, in fact, while I lie awake with my cock in my hand, pretending it's your mouth . . . 'I hope so.'

She was already walking past. *For her, a forgettable encounter with an old acquaintance.* For him, as she turned away it was as if night fell. *The soil is heaped upon me, the grit of burial in my mouth.* He watched the door rattle shut behind her, and stood there for a long moment, in the rain. He wanted to weep, and weep, and weep for all his ruined hopes. He wanted to kneel in the mud and tear out the hair he still had. He wanted to murder someone, and hardly cared who. *Myself, perhaps?*

Instead he took a sharp breath, squeaking slightly in one nostril, and squelched away through the mud, into the gathering dusk.

He had a message to carry, after all. With no heroics.

Black Dow

The stable doors shut with a bang like a headsman's axe, and it took all of Calder's famous arrogance not to jump clean in the air. War meetings had never been his favourite style of gathering, especially ones full of his enemies. Three of Dow's five War Chiefs were in attendance and, as Calder's ever-worsening luck would have it, they were the three that liked him least.

Glama Golden looked the hero from his scalp to his toes, big-knuckle brawny and heavy-jaw handsome, his long hair, his bristling moustache, his eyelashes to their tips all the colour of pale gold. He wore more yellow metal than a princess on her wedding day – golden torc around his thick neck, bracelets at his thick wrists and fistfuls of rings on his thick fingers, every part of him buffed to a pretty shine with bluster and self-love.

Cairm Ironhead was a very different prospect. His scar-crossed face was a fortress of frown you could've blunted an axe on, eyes like nails under a brow like an anvil, cropped hair and beard an uncompromising black. He was shorter than Golden but wider still, a slab of a man, chain mail glinting under a cloak of black bear-fur. The rumour was he'd strangled that bear. Possibly for looking at him wrong. Neither Ironhead nor Golden had much beyond contempt for Calder, but luckily they'd always despised each other like night hates day and their feud left no hatred in the quiver for anyone else.

When it came to hatred, Brodd Tenways had a bottomless supply. He was one of those bastards who can't even breathe quietly, ugly as incest and always delighted to push it in your face, leering from the shadows like the village pervert at a passing milkmaid. Foul-mouthed, foul-toothed, foul-smelling, and with some kind of hideous rash patching his twisted face he gave every sign of taking great pride in. He'd made a bitter enemy of Calder's father, lost to him in battle twice, and been forced to kneel and give up everything he had. Getting it back only seemed to have worsened his mood, and he'd easily shifted all his years of bile from Bethod to his sons, and Calder in particular.

Then there was the head of this mismatched family of villains, the self-styled Protector of the North, Black Dow himself. He sat easy in Skarling's Chair, one leg folded under him while the other boot tapped gently at the ground. He had something like a smile on his deep-lined, hard-scarred face but his eyes were narrowed, sly as a hungry tomcat that just now spied a pigeon. He'd taken to wearing fine clothes, the sparkling chain that Calder's father used to wear around his shoulders. But he couldn't hide what he was, and didn't want to either. A killer to the tips of his ears. Or ear, since the left one was no more than a flap of gristle.

As if Black Dow's name and his grin weren't threats enough, he'd made sure they were shored up with plenty of steel. A long, grey sword leaned against Skarling's Chair on one side, an axe on the other, notched with long use, in easy reach of his dangling fingers. Killer's fingers – scuffed, and swollen, and scarred at the knuckles from a lifetime of the dead knew what dark work.

Splitfoot stood in the gloom at Dow's shoulder. His Second, meaning his closest bodyguard and chief arse-licker, stuck to his master tight as his shadow with thumbs hooked in his silver-buckled sword-belt. Two of his Carls lurked behind, armour, and shield-rims, and drawn swords all agleam, others dotted about the walls, flanking the door. There was a smell of old hay and old horses, but far stronger was the reek of ready violence, thick as the stink in a marsh.

And as if all that wasn't enough to make Calder shit his well-tailored trousers, Shivers still loomed at his shoulder, adding his own chill threat to the recipe.

'Well, if it ain't brave Prince Calder.' Dow looked him up and down like the tomcat at the shrub it was about to piss on. 'Welcome back to the good fight, lad. You going to do as you're fucking told this time around?'

Calder swept out a bow. 'Your most obedient servant.' He smirked as if the very words didn't burn his tongue. 'Golden. Ironhead.' He gave each a respectful nod. 'My father always said there weren't two stouter hearts in all the North.' His father always said there weren't two thicker heads in all the North, but his lies were no more use than money down a well in any case. Ironhead and Golden did nothing but glower at each other. Calder felt a burning need for someone who liked him. Or at least didn't want him dead. 'Where's Scale?'

'Your brother's out west,' said Dow. 'Doing some fighting.'

'You know what that is, do you, boy?' Tenways turned his head and spat through the gap in his brown front teeth.

'Is it . . . the thing with all the swords?' Calder took a hopeful look around the stable but no allies had crept in, and he ended up glancing at Shivers' ruined frown, which was even worse than Dow's smile. However often he saw that scar, it was always more hideous than he remembered. 'How about Reachey?'

'Your wife's daddy's a day or so east,' said Dow. 'Putting on a weapontake.'

Golden snorted. 'I'd be surprised if there's a boy can grip a blade isn't pressed already.'

'Well, he's scraping up what there is. Reckon we'll need every ready hand when it comes to a battle. Yours too, maybe.'

'Oh, you'll have to hold me back!' Calder slapped the hilt of his sword. 'Can't wait to get started!'

'You ever even drawn the fucking thing?' sneered Tenways, stretching his neck out to spit again.

'Just the once. I had to trim your daughter's hairy cunt before I could get at it.'

Dow burst out laughing. Golden chuckled. Ironhead gave the faintest of grins. Tenways choked on his spit and left a string of glistening drool down his chin, but Calder didn't much care. He was better off scoring points with those who weren't quite a lost cause yet. Somehow he needed to win at least one of these unpromising bastards over to his side.

'Never thought I'd say this,' Dow sighed and wiped one eye with a finger, 'but I've missed you, Calder.'

'Likewise. I'd much rather be trading horseshit in a stable than back at Carleon kissing my wife. What's to do?'

'You know.' Dow took the pommel of his sword between finger and thumb, turning it this way and that so the silver mark near the hilt glinted. 'War. Skirmish here, raid there. We cut off some stragglers, they burn out some villages. War. Your brother's been hitting fast, giving the Southerners something to think about. Useful man your brother, got some sting in him.'

'Shame your father didn't have more'n one son,' growled Tenways.

'Keep talking, old man,' said Calder, 'I can make you look a prick all day.'

Tenways bristled but Dow waved him down. 'Enough cock-measuring. We've a war to fight.'

'And how many victories, so far?'

A brief, unhappy pause. 'No battle,' grunted Ironhead.

'This Kroy,' sneered Golden back across the stable, 'the one in charge o' the Union.'

'Marshal, they call him.'

'Whatever they call him, he's a cautious bastard.'

'Baby-stepping coward fuck,' growled Tenways.

Dow shrugged. 'Naught cowardly about stepping careful. Wouldn't be my style with his numbers, but . . .' And he turned his grin on Calder. 'Your father always used to say, "In war it's the winning counts. The rest is for fools to sing about." So Kroy's going slow, hoping to wear out our patience. We Northmen ain't known for it, after all. He's split his army in three parts.'

'Three big bloody parts,' said Ironhead.

Golden agreed, for once. 'Might be ten thousand fighting men each, not even counting all the fetchers and carriers.'

Dow leaned forwards like a grandfather teaching a child about fish. 'Jalenhorm to the west. Brave but sluggish and apt to blunder. Mitterick in the centre. Sharpest of the three by all accounts, but reckless. Loves his horses, I hear. Meed to the east. Not a soldier, and he hates Northmen like a pig hates butchers. Could make him short-sighted. Then Kroy's got some North-men of his own, spread out scouting mostly, but a fair few fighters too, and some good ones among 'em.'

'The Dogman's men,' said Calder.

'Fucking traitor that he is,' hissed Tenways, making ready to spit.

'Traitor?' Dow jerked forwards in Skarling's Chair, knuckles white on its arms. 'You dumb old rashy *fuck*! He's the one man in the North who's always stuck to the same side!' Tenways looked up, slowly swallowed whatever scum he'd been about to spit and leaned back into the shadows. Dow slid down limp again. 'Shame it's the wrong side, is all.'

'Well, we're going to have to move soon,' said Golden. 'Meed may be no soldier, but he's put Ollensand under siege. Town's got good walls but I ain't sure how long they can—'

'Meed broke off the siege yesterday morning,' said Dow. 'He's heading back north and most o' the Dogman's lot are with him.'

'Yesterday?' Golden frowned. 'How d'you know—'

'I've got my ways.'

'I didn't hear anything.'

'That's why I give the orders and you listen to 'em.' Ironhead smiled to see his rival cut down a peg. 'Meed's turned back north, and in quite the hurry. My guess is he'll be joining up with Mitterick.'

'Why?' asked Calder. 'Slow and steady all these months, then they just decide to take a rush?'

'Maybe they got tired o' cautious. Or maybe someone who has the say-so did. Either way, they're coming.'

'Might give us a chance to catch 'em off guard.' Ironhead's eyes were sparkling like a starving man just saw the roast brought in.

'If they're set on looking for a fight,' said Dow, 'I'd hate not to give 'em one. We got someone down at the Heroes?'

'Curnden Craw's there with his dozen,' said Splitfoot.

'Safe hands,' muttered Calder. He almost wished he was down at the Heroes with Curnden Craw, rather than here with these bastards. No power, maybe, but a lot more laughs.

'Had word from him an hour or two back, as it goes,' said Ironhead. 'He ran into some o' the Dogman's scouts up there and seen 'em off.'

Dow looked down at the ground for a moment, rubbing at his lips with one fingertip. 'Shivers?'

'Chief?' Whispered so soft it was hardly more than a breath.

'Ride down to the Heroes and tell Craw I want that hill held on to. Just might be one or other o' these Union bastards try to come through that way. Cross the river at Osrung, maybe.'

'Good ground for a fight,' said Tenways.

Shivers paused a moment. Long enough for Calder to see he

wasn't happy playing messenger boy. Calder gave him the barest look, just a reminder of what was said in the hallway at Carleon. Just to give whatever seeds were planted a little water.

'Right y'are, Chief.' And Shivers slid out through the doorway.

Golden gave a shiver of his own. 'That one gives me the worries.'

Dow only grinned the wider. 'That's the point of him. Ironhead?'

'Chief.'

'You're leading off down the Yaws Road. Point o' the spear.'

'We'll be in Yaws evening tomorrow.'

'Make it sooner.' That got a deeper frown from Ironhead and a matching grin from Golden. It was as if the two sat on a pair of scales. You couldn't nudge one down without hoisting the other up. 'Golden, you take the Brottun Road and join up with Reachey. Get him on the way soon as his weapontake's done, that old boy sometimes needs the spur.'

'Aye, Chief.'

'Tenways, bring your foragers in and get your lot ready to move, you'll be bringing up the back with me.'

'Done.'

'And all of you march your lads hard, but keep your eyes open. Be nice to give the Southerners a shock and not the other way around.' Dow showed even more of his teeth. 'If your blades ain't sharpened already, I reckon now's the time.'

'Aye,' the three of them chimed in, competing to sound the most bloodthirsty.

'Oh, aye,' said Calder on the end, and giving his best smirk to go with it. He might not be much with a sword, but there were few men in the North who could handle a smirk better. It was wasted this time, though. Splitfoot was leaning down to mutter something in Dow's ear.

The Protector of the North sat back frowning. 'Send him in, then!'

The doors were hauled open, wind sighing through and whisking loose straw across the stable floor. Calder squinted into the evening outside. Had to be some trick of the fading light, because the figure in the doorway seemed to fill it almost to the beam above. Then he took the step up. Then he straightened. It was quite the entrance, the room silent as he strode slowly to its centre except for the floor groaning under his every step. But then it's easy to make the big entrance when you're the size of a cliff. You just walk in and stand there.

'I am Stranger-Come-Knocking.'

Calder knew the name. Stranger-Come-Knocking called himself Chief of a Hundred Tribes, called everything east of the Crinna his land and all the people who lived on it his property. Calder had heard he was a giant but hadn't taken it too seriously. The North was full of swollen men with swollen opinions of themselves and even more swollen reputations. More often than not you found the man a good deal smaller than the name. So this came as a bit of a shock.

When you said the word 'giant', Stranger-Come-Knocking was pretty much what you thought of, stepped straight out from the age of heroes and into this petty latter time. He towered over Dow and his mighty War Chiefs, head among the rafters, black hair streaked with grey hanging around his craggy, bearded face. Glama Golden looked a gaudy dwarf beside him, and Splitfoot and his Carls a set of toy soldiers.

'By the dead,' Calder whispered under his breath. 'That is a big one.'

But Black Dow showed no awe. He sprawled in Skarling's Chair easily as ever, one boot still tapping the straw, killer's hands still dangling, wolf grin still curled around his face. 'Wondered when you'd . . . come knocking. Didn't think you'd come all this way your own self, though.'

'An alliance should be sealed face to face, man to man, iron to iron and blood to blood.' Calder had been expecting the giant to roar every word like the monsters in children's stories, but he had a soft sort of voice. Slow, as if he was puzzling out every word.

'The personal touch,' said Dow. 'I'm all for it. We've a deal, then?'

'We have.' Stranger-Come-Knocking spread one massive hand, put the web between thumb and forefinger in his mouth and bit into it, held it up, blood starting to seep from the marks.

Dow slid his palm down his sword, leaving the edge gleaming red. Then he was out of Skarling's Chair in a flash and caught the giant's hand with his own. The two men stood there as blood streaked their forearms and started to drip from their elbows. Calder felt a little fear and a lot of contempt at the level of manliness on display.

'Right y'are.' Dow let go of the giant's hand and slowly sat back in Skarling's Chair, leaving a bloody palm-print on one arm. 'Reckon you can bring your men over the Crinna.'

'I already did.'

Golden and Ironhead exchanged a glance, not much caring for the idea of a lot of savages crossing the Crinna and, presumably, their land. Dow narrowed his eyes. 'Did you, indeed?'

'On this side of the water they can fight the Southerners.' Stranger-Come-Knocking looked slowly about the stable, fixing each man with his black eyes. 'I came to *fight*!' He roared the last word, echoes ringing from the roof. A ripple of fury passed through him from his feet to his head, making his fists clench, and his chest swell, and his monstrous shoulders rise, seeming in that moment more outsize than ever.

Calder found himself wondering what fighting this bastard would feel like. How the hell would you stop him, once he was moving? Just the sheer weight of meat. What weapon would put him down? He reckoned everyone else in the room was thinking the same thing, and not much enjoying the experience.

Except Black Dow. 'Good! That's what I want you for.'

'I want to fight the Union.'

'There's plenty to go round.'

'I want to fight Whirrun of Bligh.'

'Can't promise you that, he's on our side and has some odd notions. But I can ask if he'll give you a bout.'

'I want to fight the Bloody-Nine.'

The hairs on the back of Calder's neck prickled. Strange, how that name still weighed heavy, even in company like this, even if the man was eight years dead. Dow wasn't grinning any more.

'You missed your chance. Ninefingers is back in the mud.'

'I hear he is alive, and standing with the Union.'

'You hear wrong.'

'I hear he is alive, and I will kill him.'

'Will you now?'

'I am the greatest warrior in the Circle of the World.' Stranger-Come-Knocking didn't boast it, puffed up and pouting as Glama

Golden might have. He didn't threaten it, fists clenched and glowering as Cairm Ironhead might have. He stated the fact.

Dow scratched absently at the scar where his ear used to be. 'This is the North. Lot of hard men about. Couple of 'em in this room. So that's quite a claim you're making.'

Stranger-Come-Knocking unhooked his great fur cloak and shrugged it off, stood there stripped to the waist like a man ready to wrestle. Scars had always been almost as popular in the North as blades. Every man who reckoned himself a man had to have a couple of both. But Stranger-Come-Knocking's great expanse of body, sinew-knotted like an ancient tree, was almost more scar than skin. He was ripped, pocked, gouged with wounds, enough to make a score of champions proud.

'At Yeweald I fought the Dog Tribe and was pierced with seven arrows.' He pointed out some pink blobs scattered across his ribs with his club of a forefinger. 'But I fought on, and made a hill of their dead, and made their land my land, and their women and children my people.'

Dow sighed, as if he had a half-naked giant at most of his war meetings and was getting tired of it. 'Maybe it's time to think about a shield.'

'They are for cowards to hide behind. My wounds tell the story of my strength.' The giant jerked his thumb at a star-shaped mass that covered one shoulder, and his back, and half his left arm with flesh lumped and mottled as oak-bark. 'The dreaded witch Vanian sprayed me with a liquid fire, and I carried her into the lake and drowned her while I burned.'

Dow picked a fingernail. 'Reckon I'd have tried to put it out first.'

The giant shrugged, the pink burn across his shoulder creasing like a ploughed field. 'It went out when she died.' He pointed to a ragged pink mark that left a bald streak through the pelt of black hair on his chest and appeared to have taken a nipple off. 'The brothers Smirtu and Weorc challenged me to single combat. They said because they grew together in one womb they counted as one man.'

Dow snorted. 'You fell for that?'

'I do not look for reasons *not* to fight. I split Smirtu in half with an axe, then crushed his brother's skull in my hand.' The

54

giant slowly closed one massive fist and squeezed the fingers white, muscle squirming in his arm like a giant sausage being stuffed.

'Messy,' said Dow.

'In my country, men are impressed by messy deaths.'

'Honestly, they're much the same here. Tell you what – anyone I call my enemy you can kill when you please. Anyone I call my friend . . . let me know before you give 'em a messy death. I'd hate for you to slaughter Prince Calder by accident.'

Stranger-Come-Knocking looked around. 'You are Calder?'

That awkward moment wondering whether to deny it. 'I am.'

'Bethod's second son?'

'The same.'

He slowly nodded his monstrous head, long hair swaying. 'Bethod was a great man.'

'A great man for getting other men to fight for him.' Tenways sucked his rotten teeth and spat one more time. 'Not much of a fighter himself.'

The giant's voice had suddenly softened again. 'Why is everyone so bloodthirsty this side of the Crinna? There is more to life than fighting.' He leaned down and dragged up his cloak between two fingers. 'I will be at the place agreed upon, Black Dow. Unless . . . any of the little men wish to wrestle?' Golden, and Ironhead, and Tenways all took their turns to peer off into the furthest corners of the stable.

Calder was used to being scared out of his wits, though, and met the giant's eye with a smile. 'I would, but I make a point of never stripping unless there are women present. Which is a shame, actually, because I have an almighty spot on my back that I think would quite impress everyone.'

'Oh, I cannot wrestle with you, son of Bethod.' The giant might even have had a knowing smirk of his own as he turned away. 'You are made for other things.' And he threw his cloak over his scarred shoulder and stooped under the high lintel, the Carls swinging the doors shut on the gust of wind that blew in behind him.

'He seems a good sort,' said Calder, brightly. 'Nice of him not to show off the scars on his cock.'

'Fucking savages!' cursed Tenways, which was rich coming from him.

'Greatest warrior in the world,' scoffed Golden, though he hadn't done much scoffing while the giant was in the room.

Dow rubbed his jaw thoughtfully. 'The dead know I'm no fucking diplomat, but I'll take the allies I can get. And a man that size'll stop a lot of arrows.' Tenways and Golden had themselves an arse-licking chuckle, but Calder saw beyond the joke. If the Bloody-Nine was still alive, maybe a man that size might stop him too. 'You all know your tasks, eh? Let's get to 'em.'

Ironhead and Golden gave each other a deadly glare on the way out. Tenways spat at Calder's feet but he only grinned back, promising himself he'd get the last laugh as the ugly old bastard shambled into the evening.

Dow stood, blood still dotting the ground from the tip of his middle finger, watching the doors as they were closed. Then he gave a sigh. 'Feuding, feuding, always bloody feuding. Why can no one just get on, eh, Calder?'

'My father used to say, "Point three Northmen the same way, they'll be killing each other before you can order the charge."'

'Hah! He was a clever bastard, Bethod, whatever else he was. Couldn't stop the warring, though, once he'd started.' Dow frowned at his blood-daubed palm, working the fingers. 'Once your hands get bloody it ain't so easy to get 'em clean. The Dogman told me that. My hands been bloody all my life.' Calder flinched as Splitfoot tossed something into the air, but it was only a cloth. Dow snatched it out of the darkness and started winding it around his cut hand. 'Guess it's a bit late to clean 'em now, eh?'

'It'll just have to be more blood,' said Splitfoot.

'I reckon.' Dow wandered into one of the empty stalls, tipped his head back, rolled his eyes to the ceiling and winced. A moment later Calder heard the sound of his piss spattering the straw. 'There . . . we . . . go.'

If the aim was to make him feel even more insignificant, it worked. He'd been half-expecting them to murder him. Now it seemed they couldn't be bothered, and that pricked at Calder's pride. 'Got any orders for me?' he snapped.

Dow glanced over his shoulder. 'Why? You'd only fuck 'em up or ignore 'em.'

Probably true. 'Why send for me, then?'

'The way your brother tells it, you've got the sharpest mind in the whole North. I got sick of him telling me he couldn't do without you.'

'I thought Scale was up near Ustred?'

'Two days' ride away, and soon as I learned the Union were moving I sent to him to join up with us.'

'Not much point me going, then.'

'Wouldn't say so . . .' The sound of pissing stopped. 'There it is!' And started up again.

Calder ground his teeth. 'Maybe I'll go see Reachey. Watch this weapontake of his.' Or talk him into helping Calder live out the month, even better.

'You're a free man, ain't you?' They both knew the answer to that one. Free as a pigeon already plucked and in the pot. 'Things are just like they were in your father's day, really. Any man can do what he likes. Right, Splitfoot?'

'Right, Chief.'

'Just as long as it's exactly what I fucking tell 'em to do.' And Dow's Carls all chuckled away like they never heard finer wit. 'Give Reachey my regards.'

'I will.' Calder turned for the door.

'And Calder!' Dow was just tapping off the drips. 'You ain't going to make more trouble for me, are you?'

'Trouble? Wouldn't know how, Chief.'

''Cause what with all those Southerners to fight . . . and unknowable fucks like Whirrun of Bligh and this Crinna-Come-Boasting weirdness . . . and my own people treading all over each other . . . I've got about as much arse-ache as I need. Can't stand for anyone playing their own games. Someone tries to dig my roots from under me at a time like this, well, I've got to tell you, things'll get *fucking ugly*!' He screamed the last two words, eyes suddenly bulging from his face, veins popping from his neck, fury boiling out of him with no warning and making every man in the room flinch. Then he was calm as a kitten again. 'Get me?'

Calder swallowed, trying not to let his fear show even though his skin was all prickling. 'I think I have the gist.'

'Good lad.' Dow worked his hips about as he finished lacing

up, then grinned around like a fox grins at a chicken coop left open. 'I'd hate to hurt your wife, she's a pretty little thing. Not so pretty as you, o' course.'

Calder hid his fury under another smirk. 'Who is?'

He strode between the grinning Carls and out into the evening, all the while thinking about how he was going to kill Black Dow, and take back what was stolen from his father.

What War?

'**B**eautiful, ain't it?' said Agrick, big grin across his freckled face.

'Is it?' muttered Craw. He'd been thinking about the ground, and how he might use it, and how an enemy might do the same. An old habit. It had been the better half of Bethod's talk, when they were on campaign. The ground, and how to make a weapon of it.

The hill the Heroes stood on was ground an idiot could've seen the value of. It sprouted alone from the flat valley, so much alone and so oddly smooth a shape it seemed almost a thing man-made. Two spurs swelled from it – one pushing west with a single needle of rock raised up on end which folk had named Skarling's Finger, one to the southeast, a ring of smaller stones on top they called the Children.

The river wound through the valley's shallow bottom, skirting golden barley fields to the west, losing itself in a bog riddled with mirror-pools, then under the crumbling bridge Scorry Tiptoe was watching, which was called, with a stubborn lack of imagination, the Old Bridge. The water flowed on fast around the foot of the hill, flaring out in sparkling shallows streaked with shingle. Somewhere down there among the scraggy brush and driftwood Brack was fishing. Or, more likely, sleeping.

On the far side of the river, off to the south, Black Fell rose up. A rough-heaped mass of yellow grass and brown bracken, stained with scree and creased with white-watered gills. To the east Osrung straddled the river, a cluster of houses around a bridge and a big mill, huddled inside a high fence. Smoke drifted from chimneys, into the bright blue and off to nowhere. All normal, and nothing to remark upon, and no sign whatever of the Union, or Hardbread, or any of the Dogman's boys.

Hard to believe there was any war at all.

But then in Craw's experience, and he'd plenty, wars were made from ninety-nine parts boredom, usually in the cold and damp, hungry and ill, often hauling a great weight of metal uphill, to one part arse-opening terror. Made him wonder yet again why the hell he ever got into the black business, and why the hell he still hadn't got out. Talent for it, or a lack of talent for aught else. Or maybe he'd just gone with the wind and the wind had blown him here. He peered up, shreds of cloud shifting across the deep sky, now one memory, now another.

'Beautiful,' said Agrick again.

'Everything looks prettier in the sun,' said Craw. 'If it was raining you'd be calling it the ugliest valley in the world.'

'Maybe.' Agrick closed his eyes and tipped his face back. 'But it ain't raining.'

That was a fact, and not necessarily a happy one. Craw had a long-established tendency to sunburn, and had spent most of yesterday edging around the tallest of the Heroes along with the shade. Only thing he liked less than the heat was the cold.

'Oh, for a roof,' he muttered. 'Damn fine invention for keeping the weather off.'

'Bit o' rain don't bother me none,' grunted Agrick.

'You're young. Wait 'til you're out in all weathers at my age.'

Agrick shrugged. 'By then I hope to have a roof, Chief.'

'Good idea,' said Craw. 'You cheeky little bastard.' He opened his battered eyeglass, the one he'd taken from a dead Union officer they found frozen in the winter, and peered towards the Old Bridge again. Nothing. Checked the shallows. Nothing. Eyed the Ollensand Road, jerked up at a moving spot there, then realised it was some tiny fly on the end of the glass and sank back. 'Guess a man can see further in fine weather, at least.'

'It's the Union we're watching for, ain't it? Those bastards couldn't creep up on a corpse. You worry too much, Chief.'

'Someone has to.' But Agrick had a point. Worrying too much or not enough is ever a fine balance, and Craw always found himself falling heavily on the worried side of it. Every hint of movement had him starting, ripe to call for weapons. Birds flapping lazily into the sky. Sheep grazing on the slopes of the fells. Farmers' wagons creeping along the roads. A little while ago

Jolly Yon had started up axe practice with Athroc, and the sudden scrape of metal had damn near made him soak his trousers. Craw worried too much, all right. Shame is, a man can't just choose not to worry.

'Why are we here, Agrick?'

'Here? Well, you know. Sit on the Heroes, watch to see if the Union come, tell Black Dow if they do. Scouting, like always.'

'I know that. It was me told it to you. I mean, *why* are we here?'

'What, like, meaning of life and that?'

'No, no.' Craw grabbed at the air as though what he meant was something he couldn't quite get a hold of. 'Why are we *here*?'

Agrick's face puckered up as he thought on it. 'Well . . . The Bloody-Nine killed Bethod, and took his chain, and made himself King o' the Northmen.'

'True.' Craw remembered the day well enough, Bethod's corpse sprawled out bloody in the circle, the crowd roaring Ninefingers' name, and he shivered in spite of the sun. 'And?'

'Black Dow turned on the Bloody-Nine and took the chain for his self.' Agrick realised he might have used some risky phrasing there, started covering his tracks. 'I mean, he had to do it. Who'd want a mad bastard like the Bloody-Nine for king? But the Dogman called Dow traitor, and oath-breaker, and most of the clans from down near Uffrith, they tended to his way of seeing things. The King of the Union, too, having been on some mad journey with Ninefingers and made a friend of him. So the Dogman and the Union decided to make war on Black Dow, and here we all are.' Agrick slumped back on his elbows, closing his eyes and looking quite heavily pleased with himself.

'That's a fine understanding of the politics of the current conflict.'

'Thanks, Chief.'

'Why Black Dow and the Dogman got a feud. Why the Union's taken the Dogman's side in it, though I daresay that's got more to do with who owns what than who made a friend of who.'

'All right. There you are then.'

'But why are *we* here?'

Agrick sat up again, frowning. Behind them, metal clonked on wood as his brother took a swipe at Yon's shield and got knocked over for his pains.

'Sideways, I said, y'idiot!' came Yon's un-jolly growl.

'Well . . .' tried Agrick, 'I guess we stand with Dow because Dow stands for the North, rough bastard or not.'

'The North? What?' Craw patted the grass beside him. 'The hills and the forests and the rivers and that, he stands for them, does he? Why would they want armies tramping all over 'em?'

'Well, not the land of it. The people in it, I mean. You know. The North.'

'But there's all kinds of people in the North, ain't there? Lot of 'em don't care much for Black Dow, and he certainly don't care much for them. Most just want to keep their heads down low and scratch out a living.'

'Aye, I suppose.'

'So how can Black Dow be for everyone?'

'Well . . .' Agrick squirmed about a bit. 'I don't know. I guess, just . . .' He squinted down into the valley as Wonderful walked up behind them. 'Why are we here, then?'

She clipped him across the back of the head and made him grunt. 'Sit on the Heroes, watch for the Union. Scouting, like always, idiot. Damn fool bloody question.'

Agrick shook his head at the injustice of it all. 'That's it. I'm never talking again.'

'You promise?' asked Wonderful.

'Why are we bloody here . . .' Agrick muttered to himself as he walked off to watch Yon and Athroc training, rubbing the back of his head.

'I know why I'm here.' Whirrun had slowly raised one long forefinger, stalk of grass between his teeth thrashing around as he spoke. Craw had thought he was asleep, sprawled out on his back with the hilt of his sword for a pillow. But then Whirrun always looked asleep, and he never was. 'Because Shoglig told me a man with a bone caught in his throat would—'

'Lead you to your destiny.' Wonderful planted her hands on her hips. 'Aye, we've heard it before.'

Craw puffed out his cheeks. 'Like the care of eight lives weren't a heavy enough burden, I need a madman's destiny to weigh me down.'

Whirrun sat up and pushed his hood back. 'I object to that, I'm not mad in the least. I just . . . got my own way of seeing things.'

'A mad way,' muttered Wonderful under her breath as Whirrun stood, slapped the arse of his stained trousers and dragged his sheathed sword up and over his shoulder.

He frowned, shifted from one leg to the other, then rubbed at his fruits. 'I'm needing a wee, though. Would you go in the river, or up against one o' these stones, do you reckon?'

Craw thought about it. 'River. Up against the stones would seem . . . disrespectful.'

'You think there are Gods watching?'

'How do you tell?'

'True.' Whirrun chewed his grass stalk across to the other side of his mouth and started off down the hill. 'River it is, then. Maybe I'll give Brack a hand with the fishing. Shoglig used to be able to just talk the fish out of the water and I've never quite been able to get the trick of it.'

'You could hack 'em out with that tree-cutter of yours!' Wonderful shouted after him.

'Maybe I will!' He lifted the Father of Swords high over his head, not much shorter'n a man from pommel to point. 'High time I killed something!'

Craw wouldn't have complained if he held off for a spell. Leaving the valley with nothing dead was the sum of his hopes, right then. Which was an odd ambition for a soldier, when you thought about it. Him and Wonderful stood there silent for a while, side by side. Behind them steel squealed as Yon brushed Athroc away and sent him stumbling. 'Put some effort in, you limp-wristed fuck!'

Craw found himself coming over nostalgic, like he did more and more these days. 'Colwen loved the sunshine.'

'That so?' asked Wonderful, lifting one brow at him.

'Always mocked at me about sticking to the shade.'

'That so?'

'I should've married her,' he muttered.

'Aye, you should've. Why didn't you?'

'You told me not to, apart from aught else.'

63

'True. She had a sharp old tongue on her. But you don't usually have trouble ignoring me.'

'Fair point. Guess I was just too coward to ask.' And he couldn't wait to leave. Win a big name with high deeds. He hardly even knew the man who'd thought that way. 'Didn't really know what I wanted back then, just thought I didn't have it, and I could get it with a sword.'

'Think about her, at all?' asked Wonderful.

'Not often.'

'Liar.'

Craw grinned. She knew him too bloody well. 'Call it half a lie. I don't think about her, really. Can't hardly remember her face half the time. But I think about what my life might've been, if I'd taken that path 'stead o' this.' Sitting with his pipe, under his porch, smiling at the sunset on the water. He gave a sigh. 'But, you know, choices made, eh? What about your husband?'

Wonderful took a long breath. 'Probably he's getting ready to bring the harvest in about now. The children too.'

'Wish you were with 'em?'

'Sometimes.'

'Liar. How often you been back this year? Twice, is it?'

Wonderful frowned down into the still valley. 'I go when I can. They know that. They know what I am.'

'And they still put up with you?'

She was silent a moment, then shrugged. 'Choices made, eh?'

'Chief!' Agrick was hurrying over from the other side of the Heroes. 'Drofd's back! And he ain't alone.'

'No?' Craw winced as he worked some movement into his dodgy knee. 'Who's he got with him?'

Agrick had a face like a man sat on a thistle. 'Looked like Caul Shivers.'

'Shivers?' growled Yon, head snapping sideways. Athroc seized his moment, stepped around Yon's drooping shield and kneed him in the fruits. 'Awwww, you little bastard . . .' And Yon went down, eyes bulging.

Craw might've laughed half his teeth out any other time, but Shivers' name had chased the fun right out of him. He strode across the circle of grass, hoping all the way Agrick might've got it wrong but knowing it wasn't likely. Craw's hopes had a habit of coming out bloodstained, and Caul Shivers was a difficult man to mistake.

Up he came towards the Heroes now, riding up that steep track on the north side of the hill. Craw watched him all the way, feeling like a shepherd watching a storm-cloud blow in.

'Shit,' muttered Wonderful.

'Aye,' said Craw. 'Shit.'

Shivers left Drofd to hobble their horses down at the drystone wall and came the rest of the way on foot. He looked at Craw, and Wonderful, and Jolly Yon too, half-ruined face slack as a hanged man's, the left side not much more'n a great line of burn through that metal eye. A spookier-looking bastard you never did see.

'Craw.' Said in his whispery croak.

'Shivers. What brings you down here?'

'Dow sent me.'

'That much I guessed. It's the why I'm after.'

'He says you're to keep hold o' this hill and watch for the Union.'

'He told me that already.' Bit more snappish than Craw had meant. There was a pause. 'So why send you here?'

Shivers shrugged. 'To make sure you do it.'

'Many thanks for the support.'

'Thank Dow.'

'I will.'

'He'll like that. Have you seen the Union?'

'Not since Hardbread was up here, four nights ago.'

'I know Hardbread. Stubborn old prick. He might come back.'

'If he does there's only three ways across the river, far as I know.' Craw pointed 'em out. 'The Old Bridge over west near the bogs, the new bridge in Osrung and the shallows at the bottom of the hill there. We got eyes on all of 'em, and the valley's open. We could see a sheep cross the river from here.'

'Don't reckon we need to tell Black Dow about a sheep.' Shivers brought the ruined side of his face close. 'But we better if the Union come. Maybe we can sing some songs, while we wait?'

'Can you carry a tune?' asked Wonderful.

'Shit, no. Don't stop me trying, though.' And he strolled off across the circle of grass, Athroc and Agrick backing away to give him room. Craw couldn't blame 'em. Shivers was one of those men seemed to have a space around him where you'd better not be.

Craw turned slowly to Drofd. 'Great.'

The lad held his hands up. 'What was I supposed to do? Tell him I didn't want the company? Least you didn't have to spend two days riding with him, and two nights sleeping next to him at the fire. He never closes that eye, you know. It's like he's looking at you all night long. I swear I haven't slept a wink since we set out.'

'He can't see out of it, fool,' said Yon, 'any more'n I can see out your belt buckle.'

'I know that, but still.' Drofd looked around at them all, voice dropping. 'Do you really reckon the Union are coming this way?'

'No,' said Wonderful. 'I don't.' She gave Drofd one of her looks, and his shoulders slumped, and he walked away muttering to himself on the theme of what else he could've done. Then she came up beside Craw, and leaned close. 'Do you really reckon the Union are coming this way?'

'Doubt it. But I've got a bad feeling.' He frowned across at Shivers' black outline, leaning against one of the Heroes, the valley drenched in sunlight beyond, and he put one hand on his stomach. 'And I've learned to listen to my gut.'

Wonderful snorted. 'Hard to ignore something so bloody big, I guess.'

Old Hands

'Tunny.'

'Uh?' He opened one eye and the sun stabbed him directly in the brains. 'Uh!' He snapped it shut again, wormed his tongue around his sore mouth. It tasted like slow death and old rot. 'Uh.' He tried his other eye, just a crack, trained it on the dark shape hovering above him. It loomed closer, sun making glittering daggers down its edges.

'Tunny!'

'I hear you, damn it!' He tried to sit and the world tossed like a ship in a storm. 'Gah!' He became aware he was in a hammock. He tried to rip his feet clear, got them tangled in the netting, almost tipped himself over in his efforts to get free, somehow ended up somewhere near sitting, swallowing the overwhelming urge to vomit. 'First Sergeant Forest. What a delight. What time is it?'

'Past time you were working. Where did you get those boots?'

Tunny peered down, puzzled. He was wearing a pair of superbly polished black cavalry boots with gilded accoutrements. The reflection of the sun in the toes was so bright it was painful to look at. 'Ah.' He grinned through the agony, some of the details of last night starting to leak from the shadowy crannies of his mind. 'Won 'em . . . from an officer . . . called . . .' He squinted up into the branches of the tree his hammock was tied to. 'No. It's gone.'

Forest shook his head in amazement. 'There's still someone in the division stupid enough to play cards with you?'

'Well, this is one of the many fine things about wartime, Sergeant. Lots of folks leaving the division.' Their regiment had left two score in sick tents over the last couple of weeks alone. 'That means lots of new card-players arriving, don't it?'

'Yes it does, Tunny, yes it does.' Forest had that mocking little grin on his scarred face.

'Oh no,' said Tunny.

'Oh yes.'

'No, no, no!'

'Yes. Up you come, lads!'

And up they came indeed. Four of them. New recruits, fresh off the boat from Midderland by their looks. Seen off at the docks with kisses from Mummy or sweetheart or both. New uniforms pressed, straps polished, buckles gleaming and ready for the noble soldiering life, indeed. Forest gestured towards Tunny like a showman towards his freak, and trotted out that same little address he always gave.

'Boys, this here is the famous Corporal Tunny, one of the longest serving non-commissioned officers in General Jalenhorm's division. A veteran of the Starikland Rebellion, the Gurkish War, the last Northern War, the Siege of Adua, this current unpleasantness and a quantity of peacetime soldiering that would have bored a keener mind to death. He has survived the runs, the rot, the grip, the autumn shudders, the caresses of Northern winds, the buffets of Southern women, thousands of miles of marching, many years of his Majesty's rations and even a tiny bit of actual fighting to stand – or sit – before you now. He has four times been Sergeant Tunny, once even Colour Sergeant Tunny, but always, like a homing pigeon to its humble cage, returned to his current station. He now holds the exalted post of standard-bearer of his August Majesty's indomitable First Regiment of cavalry. That gives him responsibility—' Tunny groaned at the mere mention of the word '—for the regimental riders, tasked with carrying messages to and from our much admired commanding officer, Colonel Vallimir. Which is where you boys come in.'

'Oh, bloody hell, Forest.'

'Oh, bloody hell, Tunny. Why don't you introduce yourselves to the corporal?'

'Klige.' Chubby-faced, with a big sty that had closed one eye and his strapping on the wrong way round.

'Previous profession, Klige?' asked Forest.

'Was going to be a weaver, sir. But I hadn't been 'prenticed

68

more than a month before my master sold me out to the recruiter.'

Tunny gave a further grimace. The replacements they were getting lately were an insult to the bottom of the barrel.

'Worth.' The next was gaunt and bony with an ill-looking grey sheen to his skin. 'I was in the militia and they disbanded the company, so we all got drafted.'

'Lederlingen.' A tall, rangy specimen with big hands and a worried look. 'I was a cobbler.' He offered no further detail on the mechanics of his entry into the King's Own and Tunny's head was hurting too much for him to pry. The man was here now, unfortunately for everyone involved.

'Yolk.' A short lad with a lot of freckles, dwarfed by his pack. He glanced guiltily about. 'They called me a thief but I never done it. Judge said it was this or five year in prison.'

'I rather think we may all come to regret that choice,' grunted Tunny, though probably as a thief he was the only one with transferrable skills. 'Why's your name Yolk?'

'Er . . . don't know. Was my father's name . . . I guess.'

'Think you're the best part of the egg, do you, Yolk?'

'Well . . .' He looked doubtfully at his neighbours. 'Not really.'

Tunny squinted up at him. 'I'll be watching you, boy.' Yolk's bottom lip almost trembled at the injustice.

'You lads stick close to Corporal Tunny here. He'll keep you out of danger.' Forest had a smile that was tough to define. 'If there was ever a soldier for staying clear of danger, it's Corporal Tunny. Just don't play cards with him!' he shouted over his shoulder as he made off through the shambles of ill-kempt canvas that was their camp.

Tunny took a deep breath, and stood. The recruits snapped to ill-coordinated attention. Or three of them did. Yolk followed up a moment later. Tunny waved them down. 'For pity's sake don't salute. I might be sick on you.'

'Sorry, sir.'

'I'm not sir, I'm Corporal Tunny.'

'Sorry, Corporal Tunny.'

'Now look. I don't want you here and you don't want to be here—'

'I want to be here,' said Lederlingen.

'You do?'

'Volunteered.' A trace of pride in his voice.

'Vol . . . un . . . teered?' Tunny wrestled with the word as if it belonged to a foreign language. 'So they do exist. Just make damn sure you don't volunteer me for anything while you're here. Anyway . . .' He drew the lads into a conspiratorial huddle with a crooked finger. 'You boys have landed right on your feet. I've done all kind of jobs in his Majesty's army and this right here,' and he pointed an affectionate finger at the standard of the First, rolled up safe under his hammock in its canvas cover, 'this is a sweet detail. Now I may be in charge, that's true. But I want you lads to think of me as, let's say . . . your kindly uncle. Anything you need. Anything *extra*. Anything to make this army life of ours worth living.' He leaned in closer' and gave the suggestive eyebrows. '*Anything*. You can come to me.'

Lederlingen held up a hesitant finger. 'Yes?'

'We're cavalrymen, aren't we?'

'Yes, trooper, we are.'

'Shouldn't we have horses?'

'That's an excellent question and a keen grasp of tactics. Due to an administrative error, our horses are currently with the Fifth, attached to Mitterick's division, which, as a regiment of infantry, is not in a position to make best use of them. I'm told they'll be catching up with us any day, though they've been telling me that a while. For the time being we are a regiment of . . . horseless horse.'

'Foot?' offered Yolk.

'You might say that, except we still . . .' and Tunny tapped his skull, 'think like cavalry. Other than horses, which is a deficiency common to every man in the unit, is there anything else you need?'

Klige was next to lift his arm. 'Well, sir, Corporal Tunny, that is . . . I'd really like something to eat.'

Tunny grinned. 'Well, that's definitely extra.'

'Don't we get food?' asked Yolk, horrified.

'Of course his Majesty provides his loyal soldiers with rations, Yolk, of course he does. But nothing anyone would actually *want* to eat. You get sick of eating things you don't want to eat, well, you come to me.'

'At a price, I suppose.' Lederlingen, sour of face.

'A *reasonable* price. Union coin, Northern coin, Styrian coin, Gurkish coin. Any kind of coin, in fact. But if you're short of currency I'm prepared to consider all manner of things in trade. Arms salvaged from dead Northmen, for example, are popular at present. Or perhaps we can work on the basis of favours. Everyone has something to trade, and we can always come to some—'

'Corporal?' An odd, high, strained voice, almost like a woman's, but it wasn't a woman who stood behind Tunny when he turned, to his great disappointment if not surprise. It was a very large man, black uniform mud-spotted from hard riding, colonel's markings at the sleeves, long and short steels of a businesslike design at his belt. His hair was shaved to stubble, dusted with grey at the ears and close to bald on top. Heavy-browed, broadnosed and slab-jawed like a prizefighter, dark eyes fixed on Tunny. Perhaps it was his notable lack of neck, or the way the big knuckles stuck white from his clenched fists, or that his uniform looked as if it was stretched tight over rock, but even standing still he gave the impression of fearsome strength.

Tunny could salute with the very best when it seemed a wise idea, and now he snapped to vibrating attention. 'Sir! Corporal Tunny, sir, standard-bearer of his Majesty's First Regiment!'

'General Jalenhorm's headquarters?' The newcomer's eyes flicked over the recruits, as if daring them to laugh at his piping voice.

Tunny knew when to laugh, and now was not the moment. He pointed across the rubbish and tent-strewn meadow towards the farmhouse, smudges of smoke rising from the chimney and staining the bright sky. 'You'll find the general just there, sir! In the house, sir! Probably still in bed, sir!'

The officer nodded once then strode off, head down, in a way that suggested he'd simply walk through anything and anyone in his way.

'Who was that?' muttered one of the lads.

'I believe that . . .' Tunny let it hang in the air for a moment, 'was Bremer dan Gorst.'

'The one who fenced with the king?'

'That's right, and was his bodyguard until that mess in Sipani. Still has the king's ear, some say.' Not a good thing, that such a notable personage should be here. Never stand near anyone notable.

'What's he doing here?'

'Couldn't say for sure. But I hear he's a hell of a *fighter*.' And Tunny gave his front teeth a worried sucking.

'Ain't that a good thing in a soldier?' asked Yolk.

'Bloody hell, no! Take it from me, who's lived through more than one melee, wars are hard enough work without people *fighting* in the middle of 'em.' Gorst stalked into the front yard of the house, pulling something from his jacket. A folded paper. An order, by the look of it. He saluted the guards and went in. Tunny rubbed at his rebelling stomach. Something didn't feel right, and not just last night's wine.

'Sir?'

'Corporal Tunny.'

'I . . . I . . .' It was the one called Worth, and he was in a fix. Tunny knew the signs, of course. The shifting from one leg to another, the pale features, the slightly dewy eyes. No time to spare.

He jerked his thumb towards the latrine pits. 'Go!' The lad took off like a scared rabbit, hopping bow-legged through the mud. 'But make sure you crap in the proper place!' Tunny turned to wag one lecturing finger at the rest of the litter. '*Always* crap in the proper place. This is a principle of soldiering of far greater importance than any rubbish about marching, or weapons, or ground.' Even at this distance Worth's long groan could be heard, followed by some explosive farting. 'Trooper Worth is fighting his first engagement with our real enemy out here. An implacable, merciless, liquid foe.' He slapped a hand down on the shoulder of the nearest trooper. Yolk, as it happened, who nearly collapsed under the added weight. 'Sooner or later, I've no doubt, you will all be called upon to fight your own battle of the latrines. Courage, boys, courage. Now, while we wait for Worth to force out the enemy or die bravely in the attempt, would any of you boys care for a friendly game of cards?' He produced the deck from nowhere, fanning it out under the recruits' surprised eyes, or eye in Klige's case, the mesmerising effect only mildly damaged by Trooper Worth's ongoing arse music. 'We'll just play for honour. To begin with. Nothing you can't afford to lose, eh? Nothing you can't . . . Uh-oh.'

General Jalenhorm had emerged from his headquarters, jacket wide open, hair in disarray, face flushed beetroot red, and shouting. He was always shouting, but this time he appeared, for once, to have a purpose. Gorst came after him, hunched and silent.

'Uh-oh.' Jalenhorm stomped one way, seemed to think better of it, swivelled, roared at nobody, struggled with a button, slapped an assisting hand angrily away. Staff officers began to scatter from the house in all directions like birds whacked from the brush, chaos spreading rapidly from the general and infecting the entire camp.

'Damn it,' muttered Tunny, shouldering his way into his bracers. 'We'd best get ready to move.'

'We just got here, Corporal,' grumbled Yolk, pack half way off.

Tunny took hold of the strap and tugged it back over Yolk's shoulder, turned him by it to face towards the general. Jalenhorm was trying to shake his fist at a well-presented officer and button his own jacket at the same time, and failing. 'You have before you a perfect demonstration of the workings of the army – the chain of command, trooper, each man shitting on the head of the man below. The much-loved leader of our regiment, Colonel Vallimir, is just getting shat on by General Jalenhorm. Colonel Vallimir will shit on his own officers, and it won't take long to roll downhill, believe me. Within a minute or two, First Sergeant Forest will arrive to position his bared buttocks above my undeserving head. Guess what that means for you lot?' The lads stayed silent for a moment, then Klige raised a tentative hand. 'The question was meant to be rhetorical, numbskull.' He carefully lowered it again. 'For that you get to carry my pack.'

Klige's shoulders slumped.

'You. Ladderlugger.'

'Lederlingen, Corporal Tunny.'

73

'Whatever. Since you love volunteering so much, you just volunteered to take my other pack. Yolk?'

'Sir?' Plain to see he could hardly stand under the weight of his own gear.

Tunny sighed. 'You carry the hammock.'

New Hands

Beck raised the axe high and snarled as he brought it down, split that log in two and pretended all the while it was some Union soldier's head. Pretended there was blood spraying from it rather'n splinters. Pretended the babbling of the brook was the sound of men cheering for him and the leaves across the grass were women swooning at his feet. Pretended he was a great hero, like his father had been, won himself a high name on the battlefield and a high place at the fire and in the songs. He was the hardest bastard in the whole damn North, no doubt. Far as pretending went.

He tossed the split wood onto the pile, stooped down to drag up another log. Wiped his forehead on his sleeve and frowned across the valley, humming to himself from the Lay of Ripnir. Somewhere out there beyond the hills, Black Dow's army was fighting. Out there beyond the hills high deeds were being done and tomorrow's songs written. He spat into his palms, rough from wood-axe, and plough, and scythe, and shovel, and wash-board even. He hated this valley and the people in it. Hated this farm and the work he did on it.

He was made to fight, not chop logs.

He heard footsteps slapping, saw his brother struggling up the steep path from the house, bent over. Back from the village already, and it looked like he'd run the whole way. Beck's axe went up into the bright sky and came down, and one more Southerner's skull was laid to waste. Festen made it to the top of the path and stood there, bent over, shaking hands on his wobbly knees, round cheeks blotchy pink, struggling for breath.

'What's the hurry?' asked Beck, bending for more wood.

'There's . . . there's . . .' Festen fought to talk and breathe and stand up all at once. 'There's men in the village!' he got out in a rush.

'What sort o' men?'

'Carls! Reachey's Carls!'

'What?' The axe hovered over Beck's head, forgotten.

'Aye. And they got a weapontake on!'

Beck stood there for a moment longer, then tossed the axe down on the pile of split logs and strode for the house. Strode fast and hard, his skin all singing. So fast Festen had to trot along to keep up, asking, 'What you going to do?' over and over and getting no reply.

Past the pen and the staring goats and the five big tree stumps all hacked and scarred from years of Beck's blade practice every morning. Into the smoke-smelling darkness of the house, slashes of sunlight through the ill-fitting shutters, across bare boards and bald old furs. Wood creaked under his boots as he strode to his chest, knelt, pushed back the lid, tore his clothes out of the way with small patience. Lifted it with fingers tender as a lover's. The only thing he cared for.

Gold glimmered in the gloom and he wrapped his fingers around the hilt, feeling the perfect balance of it, slid a foot-length of steel from the scabbard. Smiled at that sound, that scraping, singing sound that set his already jangling nerves to thrill. How often had he smiled down like this, polishing, sharpening, polishing, dreaming of this day, and now it was come. He slapped the sword back in its sheath, turned . . . and froze.

His mother stood in the doorway, watching. A black shadow with the white sky behind.

'I'm taking my father's sword,' he snapped, shaking the hilt at her.

'He was killed with that sword.'

'It's mine to take!'

'It is.'

'You can't make me stay here no more.' He stuffed a few things in the pack he kept ready. 'You said this summer!'

'I did.'

'You can't stop me going!'

'Do you see me trying?'

'By my age Shubal the Wheel had been seven years on campaign!'

'Lucky him.'

'It's time. It's past time!'

'I know.' She watched as he took his bow down, unstrung and wrapped up with a few shafts. 'It'll be cold nights, next month or two. Best take my good cloak with you.'

That caught him off guard. 'I . . . no, you should keep it.'

'I'd be happier knowing you had it.'

He didn't want to argue in case he lost his nerve. Off all big and bold to face down a thousand thousand Southerners but scared of the one woman who'd birthed him. So he snatched her good green-dyed cloak down from the peg and over his shoulder as he stalked for the door. Treated it like nothing even though he knew it was the best thing she had.

Festen was standing outside, nervous, not really understanding what was happening. Beck ruffled his red hair for him. 'You're the man here, now. Get them logs chopped and I'll bring you something back from the wars.'

'They've got nothing there we need,' said his mother, eyeing him from the shadows. Not angry, like she used to be. Just sad. He'd hardly realised 'til that moment how much bigger'n her he was now. The top of her head hardly came up to his neck, even.

'We'll see.' He took the two steps down to the ground outside, under the mossy eaves of the house, couldn't help turning back. 'Well, then.'

'One last thing, Beck.' She leaned down, and kissed him on his forehead. The softest of kisses, gentle as the rain. She touched his cheek, and she smiled. 'My son.'

He felt the tightness of tears in his throat, and he was guilty for what he'd said, and joyful to get his way at last, and angry for all the months he hadn't, and sad to go, and afraid, and excited all at once. He could hardly make his face show one thing or another for all the different ways it was pulled. He touched the back of her hand quickly, and he turned before he started weeping and strode away down the path, and off to war.

Strode the way he thought his father might've.

*

The weapontake weren't quite what Beck had hoped for.

Rain flitted down, not enough to make anyone wet, really, but enough to make everyone squint and hunch, to damp down the feel of the whole business. And the feel was pretty damn soggy already. Folk who'd come to join up, or been made to come, more likely, stood in things that might've started off as rows but had melted into squelching, jostling, grumbling tangles. Most of 'em were young lads, too young for this by Beck's reckoning. Lads who might never have seen the next valley let alone a battle. Most of the rest were grey with age. A few cripples of one kind or another rounded out the numbers. At the edge of the crowd some of Reachey's Carls stood leaning on spears or sat mounted, looking every bit as unimpressed by the new recruits as Beck was. All in all, it was a long, low way from the noble band of brothers he'd been hoping to play a hero's part in.

He shook his head, one fist holding his mother's cloak tight at his neck, the other underneath it, gripping the warm hilt of his father's sword. He didn't belong with this lot. Maybe Skarling Hoodless had started out with an unpromising crowd, and made an army of 'em that beat the Union, but Beck couldn't see anyone telling high tales about this gathering of the hopeless. At one point he'd seen a new-made crew shambling by and two little lads at the front only had one spear between 'em. A weapontake without enough weapons to go round, you don't hear much about that in the songs.

For some reason, most likely on account of daydreaming it so often, he'd been half-expecting old Caul Reachey himself to be looking on, a man who'd fought in every battle since whenever, a man who did everything the old way. Maybe catching Beck's eye or giving him a slap on the back. Here's the kind o' lad we need! Everyone look at this lad! Let's find us some more like him! But there was no sign of Reachey. Or anyone else who knew what they were doing. For a moment he looked at the muddy way he'd come, and gave some hard thought to heading back to the farm. He could be home before dawn—

'Come to join up?' A short man but heavy in the shoulder, hair and stubble full of grey, a mace at his belt looked like it had seen some action. He stood with his weight all on one leg, like the other might not take it.

Beck weren't about to look the fool. He packed away any thoughts of quitting. 'I've come to fight.'

'Good for you. My name's Flood, and I'll be taking charge o' this little crew when it's mustered.' He pointed out an unpromising row of boys, some with worn bows or hatchets, most with nothing but the clothes they stood in and those in a sorry state. 'You want to do more'n talk about fighting, get in line.'

'Reckon I will.' Flood looked like he might know a sword from a sow at least, and one line looked pretty much as bad as another. So Beck swaggered up, chest out, and pushed his way in among the lads at the back. He fair towered over 'em, young as they were. 'I'm Beck,' he said.

'Colving,' muttered one. Couldn't have been more'n thirteen and tubby with it, staring about wide-eyed, looking scared of everything.

'Stodder,' mumbled around a mouthful of some rotten-looking meat by a hangdog lad with a fat lower lip, wet and dangling like he was touched in the head.

'I'm Brait,' piped a boy even smaller'n Colving, ragged as a beggar, dirty toes showing through the end of one split boot. Beck was getting ready to feel sorry for him until he realised how bad he smelled. Brait offered his skinny hand but Beck didn't take it. He was busy sizing up the last of the group, older'n the others with a bow over his shoulder and a scar through one dark eyebrow. Probably just fell off a wall, but it made him look more dangerous than he'd any right to. Beck wished he had a scar.

'What about you?'

'Reft.' He'd this knowing little grin on his face Beck didn't much like the look of. Felt right away like he was being laughed at.

'Something funny?'

Reft waved a hand at the muddle all around 'em. 'Something not funny?'

'You laughing at me?'

'Not everything's about you, friend.'

Beck weren't sure if this lad was making him look a fool, or if he was doing it to himself, or if he was just hacked off 'cause none of this matched his hopes, but he was getting angry, and fast. 'You might want to watch your fucking—'

But Reft weren't listening. He was looking over Beck's shoulder, and so were the rest of the lads. Beck turned to see what at, got a shock to find a rider looming over him on a high horse. A good horse with an even better saddle, metal on the harness polished to a neat twinkle. A man of maybe thirty years, by Beck's guess, clear-skinned and sharp-eyed. He wore a fine cloak with a stitched edge and a rich fur collar, might've made Beck shamed of the one his mother had given him if most of the others in the row hadn't been wearing little better'n rags.

'Evening.' The rider's voice was soft and smooth, the word hardly even sounding like Northern.

'Evening,' said Reft.

'Evening,' said Beck, no chance he was going to let Reft play at being leader.

The rider smiled down from his fancy saddle, just like they were all old mates together. 'I don't suppose you lads could point me to Reachey's fire?'

Reft stuck a finger into the gathering gloom. 'Over yonder, I reckon, on that rise there, lee o' them trees.' Black outlines against the evening sky, branches lit underneath by firelight.

'Much obliged to you.' The man nodded to each of them, even Brait and Colving, then clicked his tongue and nudged his horse through the press, smirk still at the corner of his mouth. Like he'd said something funny. Beck didn't see what.

'Who was that bastard?' he snapped, once the rider was well out of earshot.

'Don't know,' whispered Colving.

Beck curled his lip at the lad. ''Course you don't. Weren't asking you, was I?'

'Sorry.' He flinched like he was expecting a slap. 'Just saying . . .'

'Reckon that was the great Prince Calder,' said Reft.

Beck's lip curled further. 'What, Bethod's son? Ain't a prince no more, then, is he?'

'Reckon he thinks he is.'

'Married to Reachey's daughter, ain't he?' said Brait in his high little voice. 'Come to pay respects to his wife's father, maybe.'

'Come to try and lie his way back into his father's chair, judging on his reputation,' said Reft.

Beck snorted. 'Don't reckon he'll get much change out o' Black Dow.'

'Get the bloody cross cut in him for the effort, more'n likely,' grunted Stodder, licking his fingers as he finished eating.

'Get hung and burned, I reckon,' piped up Colving. 'That's what he does, Black Dow, wi' cowards and schemers.'

'Aye,' said Brait, as though he was the great expert. 'Puts the flame to 'em himself and watches 'em dance.'

'Can't say I'll weep any.' Beck threw a dark glance after Calder, still easing through the press, high above everyone else in his saddle. If there was an opposite of a straight edge it was that bastard. 'He don't look much of a fighter.'

'So?' Reft's grin dropped down to the hem of Beck's cloak where the blunt end of the sword's sheath showed. 'You do look a fighter. Don't necessarily make it so.'

Beck weren't having that. He twitched his mother's cloak back over his shoulder to give him room, fists clenched. 'You calling me a fucking coward?' Stodder slid carefully out of his way. Colving turned his scared eyes to the ground. Brait just had this helpless little smile.

Reft shrugged, not quite rising to it, but not quite backing down either. 'Don't know you well enough to say what y'are. Stood in the line, have you, in battle?'

'Not in the line,' snapped Beck, hoping they might think he'd fought a few skirmishes when in fact aside from some bare-handed tussles with boys in the village he'd only fought trees.

'Then you don't know yourself, do you? Never can tell what a man'll do once the blades are drawn, shoulder to shoulder, waiting for the charge to come. Maybe you'll stand and fight like Skarling his self. Or maybe you'll run. Maybe you only talk a good fight.'

'I'll show you a fight, you fucker!' Beck stepped forwards, one fist going up. Colving gave a whimper, covered his face like he was the one might get hit. Reft took a pace back, pulling his coat open with one hand. Beck saw the handle of a long knife there, and he realised when he pushed the cloak back he'd showed the hilt of his father's sword, and it was right by his hand, and it came to him of a sudden how high the stakes had climbed all out of nothing. It came to him in a flash this might not end up a tussle between boys in the village, and he saw the fear in Reft's eyes, and the willingness, and the guts dropped out of him, and he faltered for a moment, not knowing how he got here or what he should do—

'Oy!' Flood lurched out of the crowd, dragging his bad leg behind him. 'Enough o' that!' Beck slowly let his fist drop, mightily glad of the interruption if he was honest. 'Good to see you've some fire in you, but there'll be plenty of fight to go round with the Southerners, don't you worry about that. We got marching to do on the morrow, and you'll march better without smashed mouths.' Flood held his big fist up between Beck and Reft, grey hairs on the back, knuckles scuffed from a hundred old scrapes. 'And that's what you'll be getting 'less you behave yourselves, understand?'

'Aye, Chief,' growled Beck, giving Reft the eye though his heart was going so hard in his ears he thought it might pop 'em right off.

'Aye, 'course,' said Reft, letting his coat fall closed.

'First thing a fighter has to learn is when not to fight. Now get up there, the pair o' you.'

Beck realised the row of lads had melted away in front of him and there was just a stretch of trampled mud between him and a table, an awning of dripping canvas over it to keep the rain off. An old greybeard sat there waiting for him, and looking somewhat sour about it. He'd lost an arm, coat-sleeve folded up and stitched across his chest. In the other hand he'd got a pen. Seemed they were taking each man's name and marking it down in a big book. New ways of doing things, with writing and what have you. Beck didn't reckon his father would've cared much for that, and neither did he. What was the purpose to fighting the Southerners if you took their ways yourselves? He trudged up through the slop, frowning.

'Name?'

'My name?'

'Who the bloody hell else's?'

'Beck.'

The greybeard scratched it on his paper. 'From?'

'A farm just up the valley there.'

'Age?'

'Seventeen year.'

The man frowned up at him. 'And a big one too. You're a few summers late, lad. Where you been at?'

'Helping my mother on the farm.' Someone behind snorted and Beck whipped around to give him a proper glare. Brait's sorry little grin wilted, and he looked down at his knackered shoes. 'She's two little 'uns to care for, so I stayed to help her. That's man's work too.'

'Guess you're here now, anyway.'

'That's right.'

'Your father's name?'

'Shama Heartless.'

His head jerked right back up at that. 'Don't poke me, lad!'

'I won't, old man. Shama Heartless was my father. This here is his sword.' And Beck drew it, metal hissing, the weight in his hand putting heart right back in him, and stood it point-down on the table.

The one-armed old man looked it up and down for a moment, gold glinting with the sunset, mirror-brightness of good steel. 'Well, there's a turn-up. Let's hope you're forged from the same iron as your father.'

'I am.'

'Reckon we'll see. Here's your first staple, lad.' And he pressed a tiny silver coin into Beck's palm and took up his pen again. 'Next man.'

And there you go, farmer no more. Joined up with Caul Reachey and ready to fight for Black Dow against the Union. Beck sheathed his sword and stood frowning in the thickening rain, in the gathering darkness. A girl with red hair turned brown by the damp was pouring out grog for those who'd given their names and Beck took his own measure and threw it burning down his gullet. He tossed the cup aside, watching Reft, and Colving, and Stodder give their answers, thinking how it didn't matter a shit what these fools thought. He'd win his name. He'd show 'em who was the coward.

And who was the hero.

Reachey

'If it ain't my daughter's husband!' called out Reachey, fire-light shining on a gap-toothed grin. 'No need to tiptoe, lad.'

'Muddy going,' said Calder.

'And you always did like to keep your boots clean.'

'Styrian leather, shipped in from Talins.' And he planted one on a stone by the fire so Reachey's old Named Men could get a better look.

'Shipping in boots,' grumbled Reachey, as if bemoaning the loss of all that was good in the world. 'By the dead. How did a clever girl like my daughter fall for a tailor's dummy like you?'

'How did a butcher's block like you father such a beauty as my wife?'

Reachey grinned, so his men did too, the rustling flames picking out every crease and crinkle on their leathery faces. 'I've always wondered at it myself. Less'n you, though. I knew her mother.' A couple of the older lads grunted, faraway looks in their eyes. 'And I was quite the beauty myself before life's buffets wore down my looks.' The self-same older lads chuckled. Old men's jokes, all about how fine things used to be.

'Buffets,' said one, shaking his head.

'Could I have a word?' asked Calder.

'Anything for my son. Lads.' Reachey's closest stood, some with evident effort, and made their way grunting off into the dark. Calder picked a spot by the fire and squatted down, hands out to the flames.

'You want the pipe?' Reachey offered it, smoke curling from the bowl.

'No, thanks.' Calder had to keep a straight head, even among supposed friends. It was a damn narrow path he was always treading these days, and he couldn't afford to weave about. There

84

was a long drop on both sides of it and nothing soft at the bottom.

Reachey took a suck himself, sent up a couple of little brown smoke rings and watched them drift apart. 'How's my daughter?'

'She's the best woman in the world.' And he didn't even have to lie.

'You always know what to say, don't you, Calder? I won't disagree. And my grandson?'

'Still a little small to help out against the Union this time around, but he's swelling. You can feel him kick.'

'Can't believe it.' Reachey looked into the flames and slowly shook his head, scrubbing at his white stubble with his fingernails. 'Me, a grandfather. Hah! Seems like just yesterday I was a child myself. Just this morning I was watching Seff kick at her mother's belly. It all slips by so fast. Slips by and you hardly notice, like leaves on the water. Savour the little moments, son, that's my advice. They're what life is. All the things that happen while you're waiting for something else. I've heard Black Dow wants you dead.'

Calder tried not to show he'd been thrown by the shift of subject and failed. 'Who says?'

'Black Dow.'

No great surprise, but hearing it laid out stark as that didn't help Calder's shredded spirits. 'I reckon he'd know.'

'I think he's brought you back out here so he can find an easy way to kill you, or so someone else can in hopes of earning favours from him. I think he thinks you'll start scheming, and turning men against him, and trying to steal his chair. Then he'll find out about it, and be able to hang you fair, and no one can complain over much.'

'He thinks if he hands me the knife I'll stab myself.'

'Something like that.'

'Maybe I'm quicker fingered than he reckons.'

'I hope y'are. All I'm saying is, if you're planning on hatching a scheme or two, be aware he's aware, and he's waiting for you to miss a step. Providing he don't tire of tiptoeing around the issue and tell Caul Shivers to sharpen his axe on your brains.'

'There'd be a few folk unhappy about that.'

'True, and half the North's unhappy as it is. Too much war.

Too much tax. War's got a fine tradition round these parts, o' course, but tax has never been popular. Dow needs to tread careful on folks' feelings these days, and he knows it. But it'd be a fool presumed too far on Black Dow's patience. He ain't a man made for treading carefully.'

'But I suppose I am?'

'There's no shame in a soft footfall, lad. We like big, stupid men in the North, men who wade about in blood and so on. We sing songs about 'em. But those men get nothing done alone, and that's a fact. We need the other kind. Thinkers. Like you. Like your father. And we don't make half way enough of 'em. You want my advice?'

Reachey could stick his advice up his arse as far as Calder was concerned. He'd come for men, and swords, and cold hearts ready to do treachery. But he'd long ago learned that most men love nothing better than to be listened to. Especially powerful men. And Reachey was one of Dow's five War Chiefs, about as powerful as it got these days. So Calder did what he was best at, and lied. 'It's your advice I came for.'

'Then leave things be. 'Stead o' swimming out against a fierce current, risking it all in the cold deep, sit on the beach awhile, take your ease. Who knows? Maybe in good time the sea'll just wash up what you want.'

'You reckon?' As far as Calder could tell, the sea had been washing up nothing but shit ever since his father died.

Reachey shuffled a little closer, speaking low. 'Black Dow ain't sat too firmly in Skarling's Chair, for all he carts it around with him. He's the best bet for most, still, but outside o' that rotten old fuck Tenways he ain't got much loyalty. Lot less than your father had, and men these days, the likes of Ironhead and Golden? Pah!' And he snorted his contempt into the fire. 'They're fickle as the wind. Folk fear Black Dow, but that only works long as you're fearsome, and if things keep dragging on, and he don't fight . . . folk got better things to do than sit around here going hungry and shitting in holes. I've lost as many men wandering off home to the harvest the last month as I'll pick up at this weapontake here. Dow has to fight, and soon, and if he don't, or if he loses, well, everything could spin around in an instant.' And Reachey took a long, self-satisfied suck at his pipe.

'And what if he fights the Union and wins?'

'Well . . .' The old man squinted up at the stars as he finished blowing out his latest plume. 'That is a point you've got there. If he wins he'll be everyone's hero.'

'Not mine, I daresay.' It was Calder's turn to lean close and whisper. 'And in the meantime, we're not on the beach. What if Dow tries to murder me, or gives me some task I can't but fail at, or puts me in the line somewhere I'm good as dead? Will I have any friends at my back?'

'You're my daughter's husband, better or worse. Me and your father agreed to it when you and Seff weren't much more'n babies. I was proud to take you when you had the world at your feet. What kind of a man would I be if I turned my back now you've got the world on your shoulders? No. You're family.' And he showed that missing tooth again, slapping his heavy hand down on Calder's shoulder. 'I do things the old way.'

'Straight edge, eh?'

'That's right.'

'So you'd draw your sword for me?'

'Shit, no.' And he gave Calder's shoulder a parting squeeze and took his hand away. 'I'm just saying I won't draw it against you. If I have to burn, I'll burn, but I ain't setting myself on fire.' About what Calder had expected, but still a disappointment. However many life gives you, each new one still stings. 'Where you going, lad?'

'I think I'll meet up with Scale, help him with what's left of my father's men.'

'Good idea. Strong as a bull, your brother, and brave as one with it but, well, might be he's got a bull's brain, too.'

'Might be.'

'Word's come from Dow, he's calling the army together. We're all marching for Osrung tomorrow morning. Heading for the Heroes.'

'Guess I'll catch up with Scale there, then.'

'And a warming reunion, I don't doubt.' Reachey waved a gnarled paw at him. 'Watch your back, Calder.'

'That I will,' he muttered under his breath.

'And Calder?'

Everyone always had just one more thing to say, and it never seemed to be something nice. 'Aye?'

'You get yourself killed, that's one thing. But my daughter's stood hostage for you. Done it willingly. I don't want you doing anything that's going to bring harm to her or to her child. I won't stand for that. I've told Black Dow and I'm telling you. I won't stand for it.'

'You think I will?' Calder snapped back, with a heat he hadn't expected. 'I'm not quite the bastard they say I am.'

'I know you're not.' And Reachey gave him a pointed look from under his craggy brows. 'Not quite.'

Calder left the fire with worry weighing on his shoulders like a coat of double mail. When the best you can get from your wife's father is that he won't help to kill you, it doesn't take a clever man to see you're in shit to your chin.

Music was coming from somewhere, old songs badly sung about men long dead and the men they'd killed. Drunken laughter too, figures around the fire-pits, drinking to nothing. A hammer rang from the darkness and Calder caught the shape of the smith, frozen against the sparks of his forge. They'd be working all night arming up Reachey's new recruits. Blades, axes, arrowheads. The business of destruction. He winced at the shriek of a whetstone. Something about that sound had always set his teeth on edge. He'd never understood what men saw in weapons. Probably a weapontake wasn't the best place for him, when you thought about it. He stopped, peering into the darkness. Somewhere around here he'd tied his horse—

A boot squelched and he frowned over his shoulder. The shapes of two men, shaggy in the dark, a hint of a stubbly face. Somehow, right away he knew. And right away he took off running.

'Shit!'

'Stop him!'

He pounded to nowhere, not thinking about anything, which was a strange relief for a moment, and then, as the first flush of action faded and he realised they were going to kill him . . . not.

'Help!' he screamed at no one. 'Help me!'

Three men about a fire looked over, part-curious, part-annoyed at being disturbed. None of them so much as reached for weapons. They didn't care a shit. People don't, on the whole. They didn't know who he was, and even if they had he was widely hated, and even if he'd been widely loved, still, on the whole, no one cares a shit.

He left them behind, scared breath starting to burn, slithered down a bank and up another, crashed through a patch of bushes, twigs snatching at him, not caring much about the state of his Styrian boots now as the fear clawed up his throat. He saw a shape looming out of the murk, a pale face, startled.

'Help!' he screeched. 'Help!'

Someone squatting, pinching off a turd. 'What?'

And Calder was past, thumping through the mud, leaving the fires of Reachey's camp behind. He snatched a glance over his shoulder, couldn't see a thing beyond the wobbling black outline of the land. But he could hear them still, too close behind. Far too close. He caught water glimmering at the bottom of a slope, then his lovely Styrian boot toe caught something and he was in the air.

He came down mouth first, crumpled, tumbled, head filled with his own despairing whimpers as the earth battered at him. Slid to what might've been a stop though it felt like he was still going. Struggled up, arms clutching at him.

'Off me, bastards!' It was his own cloak, heavy with mud. He floundered a half-step, realised he was going up the bank as the killers came down it. He tried to turn and flopped over in the stream, gasping for air, cold water gripping him.

'Some runner, ain't he?' The voice boomed through the surging blood in Calder's head, a nasty kind of chuckle on the end. Why do they always have to laugh?

'Oh, aye. Come here.' That scraping sound as one drew a blade. Calder remembered he had a sword himself, fished numbly for it, trying to struggle up out of the freezing water. He only got as far as his knees. The nearest killer came at him, then fell over sideways.

'What you doing?' said the other. Calder wondered if he'd drawn and stabbed him, then realised his sword was still all tangled up with his cloak. He couldn't have got it free even if he had the strength to move his arm – which, at that moment, he didn't.

'What?' His tongue felt twice its normal size.

A shape flashed from nowhere. Calder gave a kind of squeal, arms jerking pointlessly to cover his face. He felt the wind of something passing, it crashed into the second killer and he went down on his back. The first was trying to crawl away up the bank, making a wet groan. The outline of a man walked down to him, slinging a bow over his shoulder and drawing a sword, and stabbed him through the back without breaking stride. He strolled up close and stood there, a blacker shape in the darkness. Calder stared at him through the spread-out fingers over his face, cold water bubbling at his knees. Thinking of Seff. Waiting for his death.

'If it ain't Prince Calder. Wouldn't expect to chance on you in such surroundings.'

Calder slowly prised his trembling hands away from his face. He knew that voice. 'Foss Deep?'

'Yes.'

Relief spouted up in Calder like a fountain, so much he almost wanted to laugh. Laugh or be sick. 'My brother sent you?'

'No.'

'Scale's busy . . . busy . . . busy these days,' grunted Shallow, still stabbing the second killer, blade squelching in and out.

'Very busy.' Deep watched his brother as if he was watching a man dig a ditch. 'Fighting and so forth. War. The old swords-and-marching game. Loves him some war, Scale, can't get enough. If that's not dead yet, by the way, ain't never going to be.'

'True.' Shallow stabbed his man once more then rocked back on his haunches, his blade, and his hand, and his arm to the elbow all sticky black with blood in the moonlight.

Calder made himself not look at it, trying to keep his mind off his rising gorge. 'Where the hell did you come from?'

Deep offered a hand and Calder took it. 'We heard you were returned from exile and – aware what a popular boy you are – thought we'd come and stand lookout. Case someone tried something. And whatever do you know . . .'

Calder held Deep's forearm a moment longer as the dark world started to steady. 'Good thing you came when you did. Moment longer I'd have had to kill those bastards myself.' He stood, the blood rushed to his head, and he doubled up and puked all over his Styrian boots.

'Things were about to get ugly, all right,' said Deep solemnly.

'If you could just've got your sword free from your fancy-arsed cloak you'd have cut those bastards up every which way.' Shallow was coming down the slope and dragging something after him. 'We caught this one. He was holding their horses.' And he shoved a shape down in the mud in front of Calder. A young lad, pale face dirt-speckled in the half-light.

'That's some good work.' Calder wiped his sour mouth on the back of his sleeve. 'My father always said you were two of the best men he knew.'

'Funny.' He could see Shallow's teeth as he grinned. 'He used to tell us we were the worst.'

'Either way, don't know how I'll thank you.'

'Gold,' said Shallow.

'Aye,' said Deep. 'Gold will go most of the way.'

'You'll have it.'

'I know we will. That's why we love you, Calder.'

'Well, that and the winning sense of humour,' said Shallow.

'And that beautiful face, and those beautiful clothes, and the smirk that makes you want to punch it.'

'And the bottomless respect we had for your father.' Shallow gave a little bow. 'But, yes, mostly it's the old goldy-woldy.'

'What rites for the dead?' asked Deep, poking one of the corpses with the toe of his boot.

Now that Calder's head was settling, the surging of blood in his ears was quieting, the pounding in his face was dulling to a throb, he was starting to think. To wonder what could be gained. He could show these boys to Reachey, try and get him riled up. Murdering his daughter's husband in his own camp, it was an insult. Especially to an honourable man. Or he could have them dragged before Black Dow, fling them at his feet and demand justice. But both options held risks, especially when he didn't know for a fact who was behind it. When you're planning what to do, always think of doing nothing first, see where that gets you. It was better to let these bastards wash away, pretend it never happened, and keep his enemies guessing.

'In the river,' he said.

'And this one?' Shallow waved his knife at the lad.

Calder stood over him, lips pursed. 'Who sent you?'

'I just mind the horses,' whispered the boy.

'Come on, now,' said Deep, 'we don't want to cut you up.'

'I don't mind,' said Shallow.

'No?'

'Not bothered.' He grabbed the boy around the throat and stuck his knife up his nose.

'No! No!' he squeaked. 'Tenways, they said! They said Brodd Tenways!' Shallow let him drop back in the mud, and Calder gave a sigh.

'That flaking old fuck.' How toweringly unsurprising. Maybe Dow had asked him to get it done, or maybe he'd taken his own initiative. Either way, this lad wouldn't know enough to help.

Shallow spun his knife around, blade flashing moonlight as it turned. 'And for young master I-just-mind-the-horsey-boy?'

Calder's instinct was just to say, 'Kill him,' and be done. Quicker, simpler, safer. But these days, he tried always to think about mercy. A long time ago when he'd been a young idiot, or perhaps a younger idiot, he'd ordered a man killed on a whim. Because he'd thought it would make him look strong. Because he'd thought it might make his father proud. It hadn't. 'Before you make a man into mud,' his father had told him afterwards in his disappointed voice, 'make sure he's no use to you alive. Some men will smash a thing just because they can. They're too stupid to see that nothing shows more power than mercy.'

The lad swallowed as he looked up, eyes big and hopeless, gleaming in the darkness with maybe a sorry tear or two. Power was what Calder wanted most, and so he thought about mercy. Thought all about it. Then he pressed his tongue into his split lip, and it really hurt a lot.

'Kill him,' he said, and turned away, heard the lad make a surprised yelp, quickly cut off. It always catches people by surprise, the moment of their death, even when they should see it coming. They always think they're special, somehow expect a reprieve. But no one's special. He heard the splash as Shallow rolled the lad's body into the water, and that was that. He struggled back up the slope, cursing at his soaked-through, clinging cloak, and his mud-caked boots, and his battered mouth. Calder wondered if he'd be surprised, when his moment came. Probably.

The Right Thing

'Is it true?' asked Drofd.

'Eh?'

'Is it true?' The lad nodded towards Skarling's Finger, standing proud on its own tump of hill, casting no more'n a stub of shadow since it was close to midday. 'That Skarling Hoodless is buried under there?'

'Doubt it,' said Craw. 'Why would he be?'

'Ain't that why they call it Skarling's Finger, though?'

'What else would they call it?' asked Wonderful. 'Skarling's Cock?'

Brack raised his thick brows. 'Now you mention it, it does look a bit like a—'

Drofd cut him off. 'No, I mean, why call it that if he ain't buried there?'

Wonderful looked at him like he was the biggest idiot in the North. He might've been in the running. 'There's a stream near my husband's farm – my farm – they call Skarling's Beck. There's probably fifty others in the North. Most likely there's a legend he wet his manly thirst in their clear waters before some speech or charge or noble stand from the songs. Daresay he did no more'n piss in most of 'em if he ever even came within a day's ride. That's what it is to be a hero. Everyone wants a little bit of you.' She nodded at Whirrun, kneeling before the Father of Swords with hands clasped and eyes closed. 'In fifty years there'll more'n likely be a dozen Whirrun's Becks scattered across farms he never went to, and numbskulls will point at 'em, all dewy-eyed, and ask – "Is it true Whirrun of Bligh's buried under that stream?"' She walked off, shaking her cropped head.

Drofd's shoulders slumped. 'I only bloody asked, didn't I? I thought that was why they called 'em the Heroes, 'cause there are heroes buried under 'em.'

'Who cares who's buried where?' muttered Craw, thinking about all the men he'd seen buried. 'Once a man's in the ground he's just mud. Mud and stories. And the stories and the men don't often have much in common.'

Brack nodded. 'Less with every time the story's told.'

'Eh?'

'Bethod, let's say,' said Craw. 'You'd think to hear the tales he was the most evil bastard ever set foot in the North.'

'Weren't he?'

'All depends on who you ask. His enemies weren't keen on him, and the dead know he made a lot o' the bastards. But look at all he did. More'n Skarling Hoodless ever managed. Bound the North together. Built the roads we march on, half the towns. Put an end to the warring between the clans.'

'By starting wars with the Southerners.'

'Well, true. There's two sides to every coin, but there's my very point. People like simple stories.' Craw frowned at the pink marks down the edges of his nails. 'But people ain't simple.'

Brack slapped Drofd on the back and near made him fall. 'Except for you, eh, boy?'

'Craw!' Wonderful's voice had that note in it made everyone turn. Craw sprang up, or as close as he got to springing these days, and hurried over to her, wincing as his knee crunched like breaking twigs, sending stings right up into his back.

'What am I looking at?' He squinted at the Old Bridge, at the fields and pastures and hedgerows, at the river and the fells beyond, struggling to shield his watery eyes from the wind and make the blurry valley come sharp.

'Down there, at the ford.'

Now he saw them and his guts hollowed out. Little more'n dots to his eyes, but men for sure. Wading through the shallows, picking their way over the shingle, dragging themselves up onto the bank. The north bank. Craw's bank.

'Shit,' he said. Not enough of 'em to be Union men, but coming from the south, which meant they were the Dogman's boys. Which meant more'n likely—

'Hardbread's back.' Shivers' whisper was the last thing Craw needed behind him. 'And he's found himself some friends.'

'Weapons!' shouted Wonderful.

'Eh?' Agrick stood staring with a cookpot in his hands.

'Weapons, idiot!'

'Shit!' Agrick and his brother started running around, shouting at each other, dragging their packs open and spilling gear about the trampled grass.

'How many do you count?' Craw patted his pocket but his eyeglass was missing. 'Where the bloody hell—'

Brack had it pressed to his face. 'Twenty-two,' he grunted.

'You sure?'

'I'm sure.'

Wonderful rubbed at the long scar down her scalp. 'Twenty-two. *Twenty*-two. Twenty . . . *two*.'

The more she said it the worse it sounded. A particularly shitty number. Too many to beat without taking a terrible chance, but few enough that – with the ground on their side and a happy fall of the runes – it might be done. Too few to just run away from, without having to tell Black Dow why. And fighting out-numbered might be the lighter risk than telling Black Dow why.

'Shit.' Craw glanced across at Shivers and caught his good eye looking back. Knew he'd juggled the same sum and come up with the same answer, but that he didn't care how much blood got spilled along the way, how many of Craw's dozen went back to the mud for this hill. Craw did care. Maybe too much, these days. Hardbread and his boys were out of the river now, last of 'em disappearing into the browning apple trees between the shallows and the foot of the hill, heading for the Children.

Yon appeared between two of the Heroes, bundle of sticks in his arms, puffing away from the climb. 'Took a while, but I found some— What?'

'Weapons!' bellowed Brack at him.

'Hardbread's back!' added Athroc.

'Shit!' Yon let his sticks fall in a tangle, near tripped over them as he ran for his gear.

It was a bastard of a call and Craw couldn't dither on it. But that's what it is to be Chief. If he'd wanted easy choices he could've stayed a carpenter, where you might on occasion have to toss out a botched joint but rarely risk a friend's life.

He'd stuck all his days to the notion there's a right way to do things, even as it seemed to be going out of fashion. You pick your Chief, you pick your side, you pick your crew and then you stand by 'em, whatever the wind blows up. He'd stood by Threetrees 'til he lost to the Bloody-Nine. Stood by Bethod 'til the end. Now he stood with Black Dow and, whatever the rights and wrongs of it, Black Dow said hold this hill. They were fighters by trade. Time comes a fighter has to toss the runes and fight. It was the right thing to do.

'The right thing,' he hissed to himself. Or maybe it was just that, deep under his worries and his grumbles and his blather about sunsets, there was still a jagged little splinter left in him of that man he'd been years ago. That dagger-eyed fucker who would've bled all the blood in the North before he backed down a stride. The one who stuck himself in everyone's craw.

'Weapons,' he growled. 'Full gear! Battle gear!' Hardly needed saying, really, but a good Chief should shout a lot. Yon was delving into the packhorse's bags for the mail, dragging Brack's big coat rattling free. Scorry pulling his spear from the other side, jerking the oilskin from the bright blade, humming to himself while he did it. Wonderful stringing her bow with quick hands, making it sing its own note as she tested it. All the while Whirrun knelt still, eyes closed, hands clasped before the Father of Swords.

'Chief.' Scorry tossed Craw's blade over, stained belt wrapped around it.

'Thanks.' Though he didn't feel too thankful as he snatched it out of the air. Started to buckle it on, memories of other bright, fierce times he'd done it flashing by. Memories of other company, long gone back to the mud. By the dead, but he was getting old.

Drofd stared around for a moment, hands opening and closing. Wonderful gave him a slap on the side of the head as she passed and he came round, started loosening the shafts in his quiver with twitchy fingers.

'Chief.' She handed Craw his shield and he slid it onto his arm, strap fitting into his clenched fist snug as a foot into an old boot.

'Thanks.' Craw looked over at Shivers, standing still with his arms folded, watching the dozen make ready. 'How about you, lad? Front rank?'

Shivers tipped his face back, little grin on the side that wasn't stiff with scar. 'Front and middle,' he croaked. Then he ambled off towards the ashes of the fire.

'We could kill him,' Wonderful muttered in Craw's ear. 'Don't care how hard he is, arrow in the neck, job done.'

'He's just passing the message.'

'Shooting the messenger ain't always a bad idea.' Joking, but only half. 'Stops him taking messages back.'

'Whether or not he's here we've the same job. Keep hold o' the Heroes. We're meant to be fighters. A little fight shouldn't get us shitting ourselves.' He almost choked on the words, since he was mostly shitting himself from morning to night, and especially in fights.

'A little fight?' she muttered, loosening her sword in its sheath. 'Near three to one? Do we really need this hill?'

'Closer to two to one.' As if that made it good odds. 'If the Union do come, this hill's the key to the whole valley.' Giving himself reasons as much as her. 'Better to fight for it now while we're up here than give it away so we can fight our way up it later. That and it's the right thing to do.' She opened her mouth like she was going to argue. 'The right thing!' snapped Craw, and held his hand out, not wanting to give her the chance to talk him round.

She took a breath. 'All right.' She gave his hand a squeeze, almost painful. 'We fight.' And she walked away, pulling her archery guard on with her teeth. 'Arm up, you bastards! We fight!'

Athroc and Agrick were ready, helmets on, bashing their shields together and grunting in each other's faces, working themselves up to it. Scorry was holding his spear just under the blade, using it to shave bits of Shudder Root off a lump and into his mouth. Whirrun had finally stood up and now he was smiling into the blue sky with his eyes closed, sun on his face. His preparations didn't go much beyond taking his coat off.

'No armour.' Yon was helping Brack into his mail, shaking his head as he frowned over at Whirrun. 'What kind of a bloody hero don't wear bloody armour?'

'Armour . . .' mused Whirrun, licking a finger and scrubbing some speck of dirt from the pommel of his sword, 'is part of a state of mind . . . in which you admit the possibility . . . of being hit.'

'What the *fuck*?' Yon tugged hard at the straps and made Brack grunt. 'What does that even mean?'

Wonderful clapped her hand down on Whirrun's shoulder and leaned against him, one foot propped on its boot-toe. 'How many years and you're still expecting sense out o' this article? He's mad.'

'We're all fucking mad, woman!' Brack was red in the face from holding his breath out while Yon struggled to get the buckles closed at his back. 'Why else would we be fighting for a hill and some old rocks?'

'War and madness have a lot in common.' Scorry, not very helpfully, talking around his cheekful of mush.

Yon finally got the last buckle shut and held his arms out so Brack could start getting him into his mail. 'Being mad don't stop you wearing bloody armour, though, does it?'

Hardbread's crew had made it through the orchards, and two sets of three split from the rest – one heading west around the base of the hill, the other north. Getting around their flanks. Drofd's eyes were wide as he watched 'em moving, then the others getting their gear ready. 'How can they make jokes? How can they make bloody jokes?'

'Because every man finds courage his own way.' Craw didn't admit that giving advice was his. There's nothing better for a dose of terror than standing by someone even more terrified than yourself. He clasped Drofd's hand and gave it a squeeze. 'Just breathe, lad.'

Drofd took a shuddering breath in and forced it out. 'Right y'are, Chief. Breathe.'

Craw turned to face the rest of the crew. 'Right, then! They've two parties of three trying to get on our flanks, then a few less than a score coming up front.' He rushed through the numbers, maybe hoping no one would notice the odds. Maybe hoping he wouldn't. 'Athroc, Agrick, Wonderful to skirmish, Drofd too, give 'em arrows while they climb, spread 'em out on the slope. When they get in close to the stones . . . we charge.' He saw Drofd swallow, not much taken with the idea of charging. The dead knew Craw could think of other ways to spend an afternoon himself. 'There aren't enough of 'em to get all around us, and we've got the ground. We can pick where we hit 'em, and hit 'em hard. Any luck we'll break 'em before they get set, then if the other six have a mind to fight we can mop up.'

'Hit 'em hard!' growled Yon, clasping hands with the others one after another.

'Just wait for my word, and move together.'

'Together.' Wonderful slapped her right hand into Scorry's and punched him on the arm with her left.

'Me, Shivers, Brack, Yon, we're front and centre.'

'Aye, Chief,' said Brack, still struggling with Yon's mail.

'Fucking aye!' Yon took a practice swipe with his axe and jerked the buckles out of Brack's hands.

Shivers grinned and stuck his tongue out, not especially reassuring.

'Athroc and Agrick fall back to the wings.'

'Aye,' they chimed in together.

'Scorry, anyone tries to get around the side early on, give 'em a poke. Once we close up, you're the back rank.'

Scorry just hummed to himself, but he'd heard.

'Whirrun. You're the nut in the shell.'

'No.' Whirrun took the Father of Swords from its place against the stone and lifted it high, pommel glinting with the sunlight. 'This is. Which makes me . . . I guess . . . that kind of . . . flaky bit between the nut and the shell.'

'You're flaky all right,' muttered Wonderful, under her breath.

'You can be whatever bit of the nut you like,' said Craw, 'long as you're there when it cracks.'

'Oh, I'm going nowhere until you show me my destiny.' Whirrun pushed back his hood and scrubbed a hand through his flattened hair. 'Just like Shoglig promised me you would.'

Craw sighed. 'Can't wait. Questions?' No sound except the wind fumbling across the grass, the clapping of palms as they all finished shaking hands, the grunt and jingle as Brack finally got Yon's armour buckled. 'All right. 'Case I don't have the chance to say it again, been an honour fighting with you all. Or an honour slogging across the North in all weathers, anyway. Just keep in mind what Rudd Threetrees once told me. Let's us get them killed, and not the other way round.'

Wonderful grinned. 'Best damn advice about war I ever heard.'

The rest of Hardbread's lads were coming now. The big group. Coming slowly, taking time, up the long slope towards the Children. More than dots now. A lot more'n dots. Men, with a purpose, the odd glint of sunlight on sharp metal. A heavy hand thumped down on his shoulder and Craw jumped, but it was only Yon behind him.

'A word, Chief?'

'What's to do?' Though he knew already.

'The usual. If I'm killed—'

Craw nodded, keen to cut it short. 'I'll find your sons, and give 'em your share.'

'And?'

'I'll tell 'em what you were.'

'All of it.'

'All of it.'

'Good. And don't dress it up any, you old bastard.'

Craw waved a hand at his stained coat. 'When did you last see me dress anything up?'

Yon might've had a trace of a smile as they clasped hands. 'Not lately, Chief, that's sure.' Left Craw wondering who'd need telling when he went back to the mud. His family were all here.

'Talking time,' said Wonderful.

Hardbread had left his men behind at the Children and was climbing the grassy slope with empty hands and open grin turned up towards the Heroes. Craw drew his sword, felt the frightening, reassuring weight of it in his hand. Knew the sharpness of it, worked at with whetstone every day for a dozen years. Life and death in a length of metal.

'Makes you feel big, don't it?' Shivers spun his own axe around in one fist. A brutal-looking article, studs through the heavy wooden shaft, bearded head notched and gleaming. 'A man should always be armed. If only for the feel of it.'

'An unarmed man is like an unroofed house,' muttered Yon.

'They'll both end up leaking,' Brack finished for him.

Hardbread stopped well within bowshot, long grass brushing at his calves. 'Hey, hey, Craw! Still up there, then?'

'Sadly, yes.'

'Sleeping well?'

'I'd rather have a feather pillow. You brought me one?'

'Wish I had one spare. That Caul Shivers up there with you?'

'Aye. And he brought two dozen Carls with him.' It was worth a stab, but Hardbread only grinned.

'Good try. No, he didn't. Haven't seen you in a while, Caul. How are things?'

Shivers gave the smallest shrug. Nothing more.

Hardbread raised his brows. 'Like that, is it?'

Another shrug. Like the sky could fall in and it'd make no difference to him.

'Have it your way. How about it, then, Craw? Can I have my hill back?'

Craw worked his hand around the grip of his sword, raw skin at the corners of his chewed fingernails burning. 'I've a mind to sit here a few days more.'

Hardbread frowned. Not the answer he'd been hoping for. 'Look, Craw, you gave me a chance the other night, so I'm giving you one. There's a right way o' doing things, and fair's fair. But you might've noticed I had some friends come up this morning.' And he jerked his thumb over his shoulder towards the Children. 'So I'll ask one more time. Can I have my hill back?'

Last chance. Craw gave a long sigh, and shouted it into the wind. ''Fraid not, Hardbread! 'Fraid you'll have to come up here and take it off me!'

'How many you got up there? Nine? Against my two dozen?'

'We've faced down worse odds!' Though he couldn't remember ever picking 'em willingly.

'Good for fucking you, I wouldn't fancy it!' Hardbread brought his voice back down from angry to reasonable. 'Look, there ain't no need for this to get out of hand—'

''Cept we're in a *war*!' And Craw found he'd roared the last word with a sight more venom than he'd planned on.

Far as he could tell over the distance, Hardbread had lost his grin. 'Right y'are. Thought I'd give you the chance you gave me is all.'

'That's good o' you. Appreciate it. Just can't move.'

'That's a shame all round.'

'Aye. But there 'tis.'

Hardbread took a breath, like he was about to speak, but he didn't. He just stood still. So did Craw. So did all his crew behind him, looking down. So did all Hardbread's too, looking up. Silent on the Heroes, except for the wind sighing, a bird or two warbling somewhere, a few bees buzzing in the warm, tending to the flowers. A peaceful moment. Considering they had a war to be about.

Then Hardbread snapped his mouth shut, turned around and walked back down the steep slope towards the Children.

'I could shoot him,' muttered Wonderful.

'I know you could,' said Craw. 'And you know you can't.'

'I know. Just saying.'

'Maybe he'll think it over, and decide against.' But Brack didn't sound all that hopeful.

'No. He don't like this any more'n us, but he backed down once already. His odds are too good to do it again.' Craw almost whispered the last words. 'Wouldn't be right.' Hardbread reached the Children and vanished among the stones. 'Everyone without a bow, back inside the Heroes and wait for the moment.'

The quiet stretched out. Niggling pain in Craw's knee as he shifted his weight. Raised voices behind, Yon and Brack arguing about nothing as they got their stub of a line ready. More quiet. War's ninety-nine parts boredom and, now and then, one part arse-opening terror. Craw had a powerful sense one of those was about to drop on him from a height.

Agrick had planted a few arrows in the earth, flights fluttering like the seed heads on the long grass. Now he rocked back on his heels, rubbing at his jaw. 'Might be he'll wait for dark.'

'No. If he's been sent more men, it's 'cause the Dogman wants this hill. The Union wants this hill. He won't risk us getting help by tonight.'

'Then . . .' muttered Drofd.

'Aye. I reckon they'll be coming now.'

By some unhappy chance, as Craw said the word 'now', men

started to ease out from the shadows of the Children. They formed up in an orderly row, at a steady pace. A shield wall perhaps a dozen men wide, spear-points of a second row glittering behind, archers on the flanks, staying in the cover of the shields.

'Old style,' said Wonderful, nocking an arrow.

'Wouldn't expect nothing else from Hardbread. He's old style himself.' A bit like Craw. Two old leftover fools lasted longer than they'd any right to, setting to knock chunks out of each other. The right way, at least. They'd do it the right bloody way. He looked to the sides, straining for some sign of the two little groups who'd broken off. Couldn't see no one. Crawling in the long grass, maybe, or just biding their time.

Agrick drew his bowstring back to his frown. 'When d'you want me to shoot?'

'Soon as you can hit something.'

'Anyone in particular?'

Craw scraped his tongue over his front teeth. 'Anyone you can put down.' Say it straight, why not, he ought to have the bones to say it, at least. 'Anyone you can kill.'

'I'll do my best.'

'Do your worst and I'll be happier.'

'Right y'are.' Agrick let fly, just a ranging shot, flitting over the heads of Hardbread's lot and making 'em duck. Wonderful's first arrow stuck humming into a shield and the man behind it dropped back, dragging the shield wall apart. It was starting to break up anyway, for all Hardbread's shouting. Some men moving quicker, some tiring faster on that bastard of a slope.

Drofd shot too, his arrow going way high, lost somewhere short of the Children. 'Shit!' he cursed, snatching at another arrow with a trembling hand.

'Easy, Drofd, easy. Breathe.' But Craw was finding easy breathing a bit of a challenge himself. He'd never cared for arrows. 'Specially, it hardly needed saying, when they were falling out of the sky at him. They didn't look much but they could have your death on the end, all right. He remembered seeing the shower of 'em dropping down towards their line at Ineward, like a flock of angry birds. Nowhere to run to. Just had to hope.

One sailed up now and he stepped sideways, behind the

nearest Hero, crouching in the cover of his shield. Not much fun watching that shaft spin down, wondering whether the wind would snatch it at the last moment and put it right through him. It glanced off the stone and spun harmlessly away. Not a lot of air between your death and an arrow in the grass.

The man who'd shot it paused on one knee, fiddling with his quiver as the safety of the shields crept up the slope away from him. Athroc's shaft took him in the stomach. Craw saw his mouth open wide, his own arrow flying from his hand, his scream coming a moment later, sputtering out into a long-drawn wail. Maybe it was the sound of their odds getting that little bit better, but Craw still didn't much like hearing it. Didn't like the notion that he might be making a sound like that himself before the hour was out.

The end of the shield wall got ragged as men looked over at the howling archer, wondering whether to help or press on, or just wondering whether they'd be next. Hardbread barked orders, straightened up his line, but Wonderful's next arrow flitted close over their heads and bent 'em out of shape again. Craw's people had the height as an ally, could shoot fast and flat. Hardbread's had to shoot high, where the wind was sure to drag their shafts around. Still, there was no call to take chances. They wouldn't be settling this with arrows.

Craw let Drofd loose one more, then grabbed his arm. 'Back to the others.'

The lad jerked around, looking like he was about to scream. Battle lust on him, maybe. You never could tell who'd get it. Mad fear and mad courage are two leaves on one nettle all right, and you wouldn't want to grab a hold of either one. Craw dug his fingers into the lad's shoulder and dragged him close. 'Back to the others, I said!'

Drofd swallowed, Craw's hand squeezing the sense back into him. 'Chief.' And he stumbled back between the stones, bent double.

'Fall back when you have to!' Craw shouted at Wonderful. 'Take no chances!'

'Too fucking right!' she hissed over her shoulder, nocking another shaft.

Craw crept backwards, keeping an eye out for arrows until he was past the stones, then hurrying across the circle of grass, stupidly happy to get another couple of moments safe and feeling a coward because of it. 'They're on the— Gah!'

Something caught his foot and he twisted his ankle, pain stabbing up his leg. Limped the rest of the way, teeth bared, and fell into line in the centre.

'Evil, those rabbit holes,' whispered Shivers.

Before Craw could gather the wits to answer, Wonderful came running between two of the Heroes, waving her bow. 'They're past the wall! Got one more o' the bastards!'

Agrick was at her heels, swinging his shield off his back, an arrow looping over from behind and sticking into the turf by his boots as he ran. 'The rest are coming!'

Craw could hear their shouting from down below, still the faint scream of the stuck archer, all turned strange by the wind. 'Get back 'ere!' he heard Hardbread bellow, short on breath. Sounded like they were still losing shape on the run up, some eager, some the opposite, not used to fighting together. That favoured Craw's crew, most of 'em been together for what felt like centuries.

He stole a glance over his shoulder and Scorry winked back, chewing away. Old friends, old brothers. Whirrun had his sword out of its sheath, great length of dull grey metal with hardly a gleam to its edge even in the sun. Like the runes had said, there was going to be blood. The only question was whose. It passed between 'em as their eyes met, no words spoken and none needed.

Wonderful knelt at the end of their little line in the shadow of Athroc's shield, nocked an arrow, and Craw's dozen were ready as they'd ever get.

Someone crept around one of the stones. His shield might've had something painted on it once but so scuffed by war and weather there was no telling what. Sword bright in his hand, helmet on, but he hardly looked like anyone's enemy. He looked knackered, mouth hanging open, panting from the long climb.

He stood staring at 'em, and they stared back. Craw felt Yon straining next to him, bursting to go, heard Shivers' breath crackling through gritted teeth, heard Brack growling deep in his throat, everyone's jangling nerves setting everyone else's jangling even worse.

'Steady,' Craw hissed, 'steady.' Knew the hardest thing at a time like that was just to stand. Men ain't made for it. You need to charge or you need to flee, but either way you're desperate to move, to run, to scream. Had to wait, though. Finding the right moment was everything.

Another of Hardbread's crew showed themselves, knees bent low, peering over his shield. It had a fish painted on it, and badly. Craw wondered if his name was Fishy, felt a stupid urge to laugh, quickly gone.

They had to go soon. Use the ground. Catch 'em on the slope. Break 'em fast. It was up to him to feel the moment. Like he knew. Time was stretched out, full of details. Breath in his sore throat. Breeze tickling the back of his hand. Blades of grass shifting with the wind. His mouth so dry he wasn't sure he'd be able to say the word even if he thought the time was right.

Drofd loosed an arrow and the two men ducked down. But the sound of the string loosed something in Craw and, before he'd even thought whether it was the right moment or not, he'd given a great roar. Hardly even a word but his crew got the gist, and like a pack of dogs suddenly slipped the leash, they were away. Too late now. Maybe one moment's good as another anyway.

Feet pounding the ground, jolting his teeth, jolting his sore knee. Wondering if he'd hit another rabbit hole, go sprawling. Wondering where the six men were who'd gone around 'em. Wondering whether they should've backed off. What those two idiots, three now, they were charging at were thinking. What lies he'd tell Yon's sons.

The others matched him step for step, rims of their shields scraping against his, jostling at his shoulders. Jolly Yon on one side and Caul Shivers on the other. Men who knew how to hold a line. It occurred to Craw he was probably the weak link in here. Then that he thought too much.

Hardbread's boys skipped and wobbled with each footfall, more of 'em up now, trying to get some shape between the stones. Yon let go his war cry, high and shrill, then Athroc and his brother too, then they were all giving it the screech and wail, boots hammering the old sod of the Heroes. Ground where men prayed once, maybe, long ago. Prayed for better times.

Craw felt the terror and joy of battle burning in his chest, burning up his throat, Hardbread's men a buckled line of shields, blurred weapons between, blades swaying, twinkling.

They were between the stones, they were on 'em.

'Break!' roared Craw.

Him and Yon went left, Shivers and Brack went right, and Whirrun came out of the gap they left, howling his devil shriek. Craw caught a glimpse of the nearest face, jaw dropping, eyes wide. Men ain't just brave or not. It all depends on how things stand. Who stands beside 'em. Whether they've just had to run up a great big fucking hill with arrows falling on 'em. He seemed to shrink, this lad, trying to get his whole body behind his shield as the Father of Swords fell on him like a mountain. A mountain sharpened to a razor-edge.

Metal screamed, wood and flesh burst apart. Blood roaring and men roaring in Craw's ears. He twisted himself sideways, missed a spear-thrust, crashed on, blade rattling off wood, turning him, went into someone shield-first with a bone-jarring crunch and sent him over backwards, sliding down the hillside.

He saw Hardbread, long grey hair tangled around his face. His sword went up quick but Whirrun was quicker, arm snaking out and ramming the pommel of the Father of Swords into Hardbread's mouth, snapping his head back and sending him toppling. Craw had other worries. Crushed against a snarling cave of a face, sour breath blasting him. Dragging at his snagged sword, trying to get space to swing. He shoved with his shield, had the slope on his side, drove his man back enough to make room.

Athroc whacked a shield with his axe, got his whacked in reply. Craw chopped, his elbow caught on the shaft of a spear, tangled with it, his sword just tapped someone with the flat. A friendly pat on the shoulder.

Whirrun was in the midst of 'em, Father of Swords making blurred circles, scattering men squealing. Someone got in the way. Hardbread's nephew. 'Oh—' And he fell in half. His arm flew in the air, body turning over and around, legs toppling. The long blade pinged like ice shifting as the weather warms, spots of blood showering off it. Craw gasped as they pit-pattered on his face, hacked away at a shield, teeth squeezed together so hard seemed they'd crack. Still snarling something through 'em, didn't know what, splinters in his face. Movement at the corner of his eye, shield up on an instinct and something thudded into it, cracking the rim into his jaw, making him stumble sideways, arm numbed.

He saw a weapon black against bright sky, caught it on his own as it came down. Blades clashing, scraping, grunting in someone's face, looked like Jutlan but Jutlan was years in the ground. Staggering around, off-balance on the slope, fingers clutching. His knee burned, his lungs burned. Gleam of Shivers' eye, battle smile creasing his ruined face. His axe split Jutlan's head open wide, dark pulp smeared down Craw's shield. Shoved him off, corpse tumbling through the grass. Father of Swords ripped armour beside him, bent mail rings flying, stinging the back of Craw's hand.

Clash and clatter, scrape and rattle, scream and hiss, thump, crack, men swearing and bellowing like animals at the slaughterhouse. Was Scorry singing? Something across Craw's cheek, in his eye, snatched his head away. Blood, blade, dirt, no way of knowing, lurched sideways as something came at him and he slid onto his elbow. Spear, snarling face with a birth-mark behind, spear jabbing, flapped it away clumsily with his shield, trying to scramble up. Scorry stuck the man in the shoulder and he fumbled his spear, wound welling.

Wonderful with blood all over her face. Hers or someone else's or both. Shivers laughing, smashing the metal rim of his shield into someone's mouth as they lay. Crunch, crunch, die, die. Yon shouting, axe going up and clattering down. Drofd stumbling, holding his bloody arm, broken wreck of his bow all tangled around his back.

Someone jumped after him with a spear and Craw stepped in his way, head buzzing with his own hoarse roar, sword lashing across. Grip jolted in his fist, cloth and leather flapped, split, bloody. Man's spear dropping, mouth open, long shriek drooling out of it. Craw hacked him down on the backswing, body spinning as it fell, severed arm flopping in his sleeve, black blood frozen in white cloud.

Someone was running away down the hill. Arrow flitted past,

missed. Craw leaped at him, missed. Tangled with Agrick's elbow. Slid and fell hard, dug himself with his sword hilt, left himself open. But the runner didn't care, bounding off, flinging his shield away bouncing on its edge.

Craw tore his sword up along with a handful of grass. Nearly swung at someone, stopped himself. Scorry, gripping to his spear. All of Hardbread's lot were running. The ones that were alive. When men break they break all at once, like a wall falling, like a cliff splitting off into the sea. Broken. Thought he saw Hardbread stumbling after, bloody-mouthed. Half wanted the old bastard to get away, half wanted to charge on and kill him.

'Behind! Behind!' He tottered around, fear dragging at his guts, saw men among the stones. There was no shape left to any of it. Sun twinkling bright, blinding. He heard screams, clashing metal. He was running back, back between the stones, shield clattering against rock, arm numb. Breath wheezing now, aching. Coughing and running on.

The packhorse was dead beside the fire, arrow poking from its ribs. Shield with a red bird on it, blade rising and falling. Wonderful loosed a shaft, missed. Redcrow turned and ran, a bowman behind shooting an arrow and it looped over towards Wonderful. Craw stepped in front of it, eyes rooted to it, caught it on his shield and it glanced away into the tall grass.

And they were gone.

Agrick was looking down at something, not far from the fire. Staring down, axe in one hand, helmet in the other. Craw didn't want to know what he was looking at, but he already knew.

One of Hardbread's lot was crawling away, making the grass thrash as he dragged bloody legs behind him. Shivers walked up and split his head with the back of his axe. Not that hard, but hard enough. Neat. Like a practised miner testing the ground. Someone was still screaming, somewhere. Or maybe it was just in Craw's head. Maybe just the sighing breath in his throat. He blinked around. Why the hell had they stayed? He shook his head like it might shake the answer out. Just made his jaw ache worse.

'The leg move?' Scorry was asking, squatting down over Brack, sitting on the ground gripping a bloody hand to one big thigh.

'Aye, it fucking moves! It just fucking hurts to fucking move it!'

Craw was sticky with sweat, scratchy, burning hot. His jaw was throbbing where his shield had cracked it, arm throbbing too. Dodgy knee and ankle doing their usual whining, but he didn't seem hurt. Not really. Not sure how he'd come out of that not hurt. The hot glow of battle was fading fast, his aching legs shaky as a new-born calf's, his sight swimming. Like he'd borrowed all the strength he'd used and had to pay it back with interest. He took a few steps towards the burned-out fire and the dead packhorse. No sign of the saddle horses. Run off or dead. He dropped down on his arse in the middle of the Heroes.

'You all right?' Whirrun was leaning over him, great long sword held below the crosspiece in one fist, blade all spattered and dashed. Blooded, the way it had to be. Once the Father of Swords is drawn, it has to be blooded. 'You all right?'

'I reckon.' Craw's fingers were so tight around the strap of his shield he could hardly remember how to make them unclench. Finally forced 'em open, let the shield drop into the grass, its face showing a few fresh gouges to go with a hundred old wounds, a new dent in the dull boss.

Wonderful's stubbly hair was matted with blood. 'What happened?' Rubbing her eyes on the back of her arm. 'Am I cut?'

'Scratch,' Scorry said, prodding at her scalp with his thumbs.

Drofd was kneeling beside her, rocking back and forward, gripping tight to his arm, blood streaked to his fingertips.

The sun flashed in Craw's eyes, made his lids flicker. He could hear Yon screaming, over by the stones, roaring after Hardbread and his lads. 'Come back 'ere, you fuckers! Come on, you bastard cowards!' Couldn't make no difference. Every man's a coward. A coward and a hero, depending how things stand. They weren't coming back. Looked like they'd left eight corpses behind. They weren't coming back. Craw prayed to the old dead Gods of this place they weren't coming back.

Scorry was singing, soft and low and sad as he took needle and thread from his pouch to start the stitching. You get no happy songs after a battle. The jaunty tunes come beforehand and they usually do some injury to the truth.

Craw caught himself thinking they'd come out of it well. Very well. Just the one dead. Then he looked at Athroc's silly-slack face, eyes all crossed, jerkin all ripped up by Redcrow's axe and turned sloppy red with his insides, and was sick with himself for thinking it. He knew this would stay with him, along with all the others. We all got our weights to heft.

He lay back in the grass and watched the clouds move, shift. Now one memory, now another. A good leader can't dwell on the choices he's made, Threetrees used to tell him, and a good leader can't help dwelling on 'em.

He'd done the right thing. Maybe. Or maybe there's no such thing.

DAY ONE

'A rational army would run away'

Montesquieu

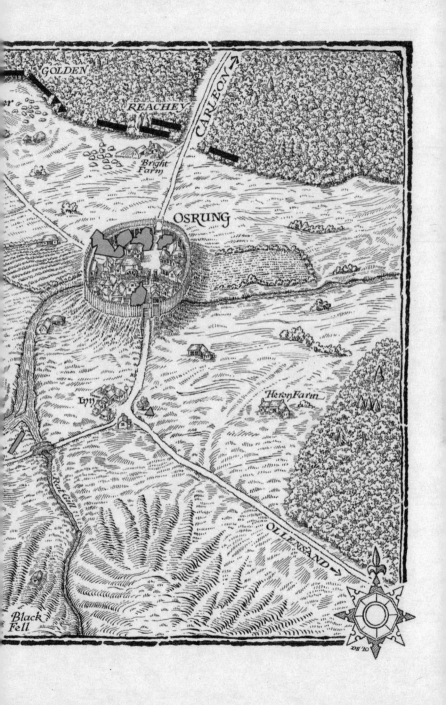

Silence

Your August Majesty,

Lord Bayaz, the First of the Magi, has conveyed to Marshal Kroy your urgent desire that the campaign be brought to a swift conclusion. The marshal has therefore devised a plan to bring Black Dow to a decisive battle with all despatch, and the entire army hums with gainful activity.

General Jalenhorm's division leads the way, marching from first light to last and with the vanguard of General Mitterick's but a few hours behind. One could almost say there is a friendly rivalry between the two to be first to grapple with the enemy. Lord Governor Meed, meanwhile, has been recalled from Ollensand. The three divisions will converge near a town called Osrung, then, united, drive north towards Carleon itself, and victory.

I accompany General Jalenhorm's staff, at the very spear-point of the army. We are somewhat hampered by the poor roads and changeable weather, which switches with little warning from sunshine to sharp downpours. The general is not a man to be stopped, however, either by the actions of the skies or the enemy. If we do come into contact with the Northmen I will, of course, observe, and immediately inform your Majesty of the outcome.

I remain your Majesty's most faithful and unworthy servant, Bremer dan Gorst, Royal Observer of the Northern War

You could barely have called it dawn. That funeral-grey light before the sun crawls up that has no colour in it. Few faces abroad, and those that were made ghosts. The empty country turned into the land of the dead. Gorst's favourite time of the day. *One could almost pretend no one will ever talk again.*

He had already been running for the best part of an hour, feet battering the rutted mud. Long slits of cartwheel puddle reflected the black tree branches and the washed-out sky. Happy mirror-worlds in which he had all he deserved, smashed apart as his heavy boots came down, spraying his steel-cased calves with dirty water.

It would have been madness to run in full armour, so Gorst wore only the essentials. Breast and back-plates with fauld to the hip and greaves at the shin. On the right arm, vambrace and fencing glove only to allow free movement of the sword. On the left, full-jointed steel of the thickest gauge, encasing the parrying arm from fingertips to weighty shoulder-plate. A padded jacket beneath, and thick leather trousers reinforced with metal strips, his wobbling window on the world the narrow slot in the visor of his sallet.

A piebald dog yapped wheezily at his heels for a while, its belly grotesquely bloated, but abandoned him to root through a great heap of refuse beside the track. *Is our rubbish the only lasting mark we will leave upon this country? Our rubbish and our graves?* He pounded through the camp of Jalenhorm's division, a sprawling maze of canvas all in blissful, sleeping silence. Fog clung to the flattened grass, wreathed the closest tents, turned distant ones to phantoms. A row of horses watched him glumly over their nosebags. A lone sentry stood with pale hands stretched out to a brazier, a bloom of crimson colour in the gloom, orange sparks drifting about him. He stared open-mouthed at Gorst as he laboured past, and away.

His servants were waiting for him in the clearing outside his tent. Rurgen brought a bucket and he drank deep, cold water running down his burning neck. Younger brought the case, straining under the weight, and Gorst slid his practice blades from inside. Great, blunt lengths of battered metal, their pommels big as half-bricks to lend some semblance of balance, three times the weight of his battle steels which were already of a particularly heavy design.

In wonderful silence they came for him, Rurgen with shield and stick, Younger jabbing away with the pole, Gorst struggling to parry with his unwieldy iron. They gave him no time and no chances, no mercy and no respect. He wanted none. He had been given chances before Sipani, and allowed himself to grow soft. To grow blunt. When the moment came he was found wanting. Never again. If another moment came, it would find him forged from steel, sharpened to a merciless, murderous razor's edge. And so, every morning for the last four years, every morning since Sipani, every morning without fail, in rain or heat or snow – this.

The clonk and scrape of wood on metal. The occasional thud and grunt as sticks bounced off armour or found their marks between. The rhythm of his ripping breath, his pounding heart, his savage effort. The sweat soaking his jacket, tickling his scalp, flying in drops from his visor. The burning in every muscle, worse and worse, better and better, as if he could burn away his disgrace and live again.

He stood there, mouth gaping, eyes closed, while they unbuckled his armour. When they lifted the breastplate off it felt as if he was floating away. Off into the sky never to come down. *What is that up there, above the army? Why, none other than famous scapegoat Bremer dan Gorst, freed from the clutching earth at last!*

He peeled off his clothes, soaked through and reeking, arms so swollen he could hardly bend them. He stood naked in the chill morning, blotched all over with chafe-marks, steaming like a pudding from the oven. He gasped with shock when they doused him with icy water, fresh from the stream. Younger tossed him a cloth and he rubbed himself dry, Rurgen brought fresh clothes and he dressed while they scrubbed his armour to its usual workmanlike dull sheen.

The sun was creeping over the ragged horizon, and through the gap in the trees Gorst could see the troopers of the King's Own First Regiment wriggling from their tents, breath smoking in the chilly dawn. Buckling on their own armour, poking hopefully at the embers of dead fires, preparing for the morning's march. One group had been drawn yawning up to see one of their fellows whipped for some infringement, the lash leaving faint red lines across his stripped back, its sharp crack reaching Gorst's ear a moment later followed by the soldier's whimper. *He does not realise his luck. If only my punishment had been so short, so sharp, and so deserved.*

Gorst's battle steels had been made by Calvez, greatest sword-smith of Styria. Gifts from the king, for saving his life at the Battle of Adua. Rurgen drew the long steel from the scabbard and displayed both sides, immaculately polished metal flashing with the dawn. Gorst nodded. His servant showed him the short steel next, edges coldly glittering. Gorst nodded, took the harness and buckled it on. Then he rested one hand on Younger's shoulder, one on Rurgen's, gave them a gentle squeeze and smiled.

Rurgen spoke softly, respecting the silence. 'General Jalenhorm asked that you join him at the head of the column, sir, as soon as the division begins to march.'

Younger squinted up into the brightening sky. 'Only six miles from Osrung, sir. Do you think there'll be a battle today?'

'I hope not.' *But by the Fates, I hope there is. Oh please, oh please, oh please, I beg you only for this one thing. Send me a battle.*

Ambition

'Fin?'

'Mmmm?'

He propped himself up on his elbow, grinning down at her. 'I love you.'

'Mmmm.'

A pause. She had long ago stopped expecting love to fall upon her like a bolt of lightning. Some people are prone to love of that kind. Others are harder-headed.

'Fin?'

'Mmmm?'

'Really. I love you.'

She did love him, even if she somehow found it hard to say the words. Something very close to love. He looked magnificent in a uniform and even better without one, sometimes surprised her by making her laugh, and there was definite fire when they kissed. He was honourable, generous, diligent, respectful, good-smelling . . . no towering intellect, true, but probably that was just as well. There is rarely room for two of those in one marriage.

'Good boy,' she murmured, patting him on his cheek. She had great affection for him, and only occasionally a little contempt, which was better than she could say for most men. They were well matched. Optimist and pessimist, idealist and pragmatist, dreamer and cynic. Not to mention his noble blood and her burning ambition.

He gave a disappointed sigh. 'I swear every man in the whole damn army loves you.'

'Your commanding officer, Lord Governor Meed?'

'Well . . . no, probably not him, but I expect even he'd warm to you if you stopped making such a bloody fool of him.'

'If I stopped he'd only do it to himself.'

'Probably, but men have a higher tolerance for that.'

'There's only one officer whose opinion I give a damn about, anyway.'

He smiled as he traced her ribs with a fingertip. 'Really?'

'Captain Hardrick.' She clicked her tongue. 'I think it's those very, very tight cavalry trousers of his. I like to drop things so he'll pick them up for me. Ooops.' She touched her finger to her lip, fluttering her lashes. 'Curse my clumsiness, I've let fall my fan again! You couldn't just reach for it, could you, Captain? You've almost got it. Only bend a little lower, Captain. Only bend . . . a little . . . *lower*.'

'Shameless. I don't think Hardrick would suit you at all, though. The man's dull as a plank. You'd be bored in minutes.'

Finree puffed out her cheeks. 'You're probably right. A good arse only goes so far. Something most men never realise. Maybe . . .' She thought through her acquaintance for the most ridiculous lover, smiled as she lighted on the perfect candidate. 'Bremer dan Gorst, then? Can't really say he's got the looks . . . or the wit . . . or the standing, but I've a feeling there's a deep well of emotion beneath that lumpen exterior. The voice would take some getting used to, of course, if one could coax out more than two words together, but if you like the strong and silent type, I'd say he scores stupendously high on both counts— What?' Hal wasn't smiling any more. 'I'm joking. I've known him for years. He's harmless.'

'Harmless? Have you ever seen him fight?'

'I've seen him fence.'

'Not quite the same.'

There was something in the way he was holding back that made her want to know more. 'Have you seen him fight?'

'Yes.'

'And?'

'And . . . I'm glad he's on our side.'

She brushed the tip of his nose with a finger. 'Oh, my poor baby. Are you scared of him?'

He rolled away from her, onto his back. 'A little. Everyone should be at least a little scared of Bremer dan Gorst.' That surprised her. She hadn't thought Hal was afraid of anything.

They lay there, for a moment, the canvas above them flapping gently with the wind outside.

Now she felt guilty. She did love Hal. She had marked down all the points the day he proposed. Considered all the pros and cons and categorically proved it to herself. He was a good man. One of the best. Excellent teeth. Honest, brave, loyal to a fault. But those things are not always enough. That was why he needed someone more practical to steer him through the rapids. That was why he needed her.

'Hal.'

'Yes?'

She rolled towards him, pressing herself against his warm side, and whispered in his ear. 'I love you.'

She had to admit to enjoying the power she had over him. That was all it took to make him beam with happiness. 'Good girl,' he whispered, and he kissed her, and she kissed him back, tangling her fingers in his hair. What is love anyway, but finding someone who suits you? Someone who makes up for your shortcomings?

Someone you can work with. Work on.

Aliz dan Brint was pretty enough, clever enough and well-born enough not to constitute an embarrassment, but neither pretty enough, clever enough nor well-born enough to pose any threat. A comparatively narrow band in which Finree felt it was safe to cultivate a friend without danger of being overshadowed. She had never liked being overshadowed.

'I find it something of a difficult adjustment,' murmured Aliz, glancing at the column of marching soldiers beside them from beneath her blonde lashes. 'Being surrounded by men takes some getting used to—'

'I wouldn't know. The army has always been my home. My mother died when I was very young, and my father raised me.'

'I'm . . . I'm sorry.'

'Why? My father misses her, I think, but how can I? I never knew her.'

An awkward silence, hardly surprising since, Finree realised, that had been the conversational equivalent of a mace to the head. 'Your parents?'

'Both dead.'

'Oh.' That made Finree feel worse. She seemed to spend most conversations see-sawing between impatience and guilt. She resolved to be more tolerant, though she did that often and it never worked. Perhaps she should have resolved simply to keep her mouth shut, but she did that often too, with even more negligible results. Hooves clapped at the track, tramping boots rumbled in unison, punctuated by the occasional calls of officers annoyed by some break in the rhythm.

'We are heading . . . north?' asked Aliz.

'Yes, towards the town of Osrung to rendezvous with the other two divisions, under Generals Jalenhorm and Mitterick. They might be as little as ten miles from us now, on the other side of those hills,' and she gestured towards the lowering fells on their left with her riding crop.

'What sort of men are they?'

'General Jalenhorm is . . .' Tact, tact. 'A brave and honest man, an old friend of the king.' And promoted far beyond his limited ability as a result. 'Mitterick is a competent and experienced soldier.' As well as a disobedient blowhard with his eyes firmly on her father's position.

'And each commanding as many men as our own Lord Governor Meed?'

'Seven regiments apiece, two of cavalry and five of foot.' Finree could have reeled off their numbers, titles and senior officers, but Aliz looked as though she was reaching the limits of comprehension as it was. The limits of her comprehension never seemed to be far off, but Finree was determined to make a friend of her even so. Her husband, Colonel Brint, was said to be close to the king himself, which made him a very useful man to know. That was why she always made a point of laughing at his tiresome jokes.

'So many people,' said Aliz. 'Your father certainly carries a great responsibility.'

'He does.' The last time Finree had seen her father she had been shocked by how worn down he seemed. She had always thought of him as cast in iron, and the realisation that he might be soft in the middle was most disconcerting. Perhaps that was the moment you grew up, when you learned your parents were just as fallible as everyone else.

'How many soldiers on the other side?'

'The line between soldier and citizen is not sharply drawn in the North. They have a few thousand Carls, perhaps – professional fighters with their own mail and weapons, bred to a life of warfare, who form the spear-point of the charge and the front rank in the shield wall. But for each Carl there will be several Thralls – farmers or tradesmen pressed or paid to fight and labour, usually lightly armed with spear or bow but often hardened warriors even so. Then there are Named Men, veterans who have won a celebrated place through deeds on the battlefield and serve as officers, bodyguards or scouts in small groups called dozens. Like them.' She pointed out a shabby set of the Dogman's men, shadowing the column on the ridge-line to their right. 'I'm not sure anyone knows how many Black Dow has, altogether. Probably not even Black Dow does.'

Aliz blinked. 'You're so knowledgeable . . .'

Finree very much wanted to say, 'Yes, I am' but settled for a careless shrug. There was no magic to it. She simply listened, observed, and made sure she never spoke until she knew what she was speaking of. Knowledge is the root of power, after all.

Aliz sighed. 'War is terrible, isn't it?'

'It blights the landscape, throttles commerce and industry, kills the innocent and rewards the guilty, thrusts honest men into poverty and lines the pockets of profiteers, and in the end produces nothing but corpses, monuments and tall tales.' Finree neglected to mention that it also offered enormous opportunities, however.

'So many men injured,' said Aliz. 'So many dead.'

'An awful thing.' Though dead men leave spaces into which the nimble-footed can swiftly step. Or into which nimble wives can swiftly manoeuvre their husbands . . .

'And all these people. Losing their homes. Losing everything.' Aliz was gazing moist-eyed at a miserable procession coming the other way, forced from the track by the soldiers and obliged to toil through their choking dust.

They were mostly women, though it was not easy to tell, they were so ragged. Some old men, and some children along with them. Northern, certainly. Poor, undoubtedly. Beyond poor, for they had virtually nothing, their faces pinched with hunger, jaws dangling with exhaustion, clutching at heartbreakingly meagre possessions. They did not look at the Union soldiers tramping the other way with hatred, or even with fear. They looked too desperate to register emotion of any kind.

Finree did not know who they were running from exactly, or where they were going. What horror had set them in motion or what others they might still face. Shaken from their homes by the blind tremors of war. Looking at them, Finree felt shamefully secure, revoltingly lucky. It is easy to forget how much you have, when your eyes are always fixed on what you have not.

'Something should be done,' murmured Aliz, wistfully.

Finree clenched her teeth. 'You're right.' She gave her horse the spurs, possibly flicking a few specks of mud over Aliz' white dress, covered the ground in no time and slid her mount into the knot of officers that was the frequently misfiring brain of the division.

They spoke the language of war up here. Timing and supply. Weather and morale. Rates of march and orders of battle. It was no foreign tongue to Finree, and even as she slipped her horse between them she noticed mistakes, oversights, inefficiencies. She had been brought up in barracks, and mess halls, and head-quarters, had spent longer in the army than most of the officers here and knew as much about strategy, tactics and logistics as any of them. Certainly a great deal more than Lord Governor Meed, who until last year had never presided over anything more dangerous than a formal banquet.

He rode at the very centre of the press, under a standard bearing the crossed hammers of Angland, and wearing a magnificent azure uniform rigged with gold braid, better suited to an actor in a tawdry production than a general on campaign. Despite all that money wasted on tailoring, his splendid collars never seemed quite to fit and his sinewy neck always stuck from them like a turtle's from its shell.

He had lost his three nephews years ago at the Battle of Black Well and his brother, the previous lord governor, not long after. He had nursed an insurmountable hatred for Northmen ever since and been such a keen advocate of war he had outfitted half his division at his own expense. Hatred of the enemy was no qualification for command, however. Quite the reverse.

'Lady Brock, how wonderful that you could join us,' he said, with mild disdain.

'I was simply taking part in the advance and you all got in my way.' The officers chuckled with, in Hal's case, a slightly desperate note. He gave her a pointed look sideways, and she gave him one back. 'I and some of the other ladies noticed the refugees on our left. We were hoping you could be prevailed upon to spare them some food?'

Meed turned his watery eyes on the miserable file with the scorn one might have for a trail of ants. 'I am afraid the welfare of my soldiers must come first.'

'Surely these strapping fellows could afford to miss a meal in a good cause?' She thumped Colonel Brint's breastplate and made him give a nervous laugh.

'I have assured Marshal Kroy that we will be in position outside Osrung by midnight. We cannot stop.'

'It could be done in—'

Meed turned rudely away from her. 'Ladies and their charitable projects, mmm?' he tossed to his officers, provoking a round of sycophantic laughter.

Finree cut through it with a shrill titter of her own. 'Men and their playing at war, mmm?' She slapped Captain Hardrick on the shoulder with her gloves, hard enough to make him wince. 'What *silly, womanly nonsense,* to try to save a life or two. Now I see it! We should be letting them drop like flies by the roadside, spreading fire and pestilence wherever possible and leaving their country a blasted wasteland. That will teach them the proper respect for the Union and its ways, I am sure! *There's* soldiering!' She looked around at the officers, eyebrows raised. At least they had stopped laughing. Meed, in particular, had never looked more humourless, which took some doing.

'Colonel Brock,' he forced through tight lips. 'I think your wife might be more comfortable riding with the other ladies.'

'I was about to suggest it,' said Hal, pulling his horse in front of hers and bringing them both to a sharp halt while Meed's party carried on up the track. 'What the *hell* are you doing?' he hissed under his breath.

'The man's a callous idiot! A farmer playing at soldiers!'

'We have to work with what we have, Fin! Please, don't bait him. For me! My bloody nerves won't stand it!'

'I'm sorry.' Impatience back to guilt, yet again. Not for Meed, of course, but for Hal, who had to be twice as good, twice as brave and twice as hard-working as anyone else simply to stay free of his father's suffocating shadow. 'But I hate to see things done badly on account of some old fool's pride when they could just as easily be done well.'

'Did you consider that it's bad enough having an amateur general without having one who's a bloody laughing stock besides? Maybe with some support he'd do better.'

'Maybe,' she muttered, unconvinced.

'Can't you stay with the other wives?' he wheedled. 'Please, just for now?'

'That prattling coven?' She screwed up her face. 'All they talk about is who's barren, who's unfaithful, and what the queen's wearing. They're idiots.'

'Have you ever noticed that everyone's an idiot but you?'

She opened her eyes wide. 'You see it too?'

Hal took a hard breath. 'I love you. You know I do. But think about who you're actually helping. You could have fed those people if you'd trodden softly.' He rubbed at the bridge of his nose. 'I'll talk to the quartermaster, try to arrange something.'

'Aren't you a hero.'

'I try, but bloody hell, you don't make it easy. Next time, for me, please, think about saying something bland. Talk about the weather, maybe!' As he rode off back towards the head of the column.

'Shit on the weather,' she muttered at his back, 'and Meed too.' She had to admit Hal had a point, though. She wasn't doing herself, or her husband, or the Union cause, or even the refugees any good by irritating Lord Governor Meed.

She had to destroy him.

Give and Take

'**U**p you get, old man.'

Craw was half in a dream still. At home, wherever that was. A young man, or retired. Was it Colwen smiling at him from the corner? Turning wood on the lathe, curled shavings scattering, crunching under his feet. He grunted, rolled over, pain flaring up his side, stinging him with panic. He tried to rip back his blanket.

'What's the—'

'It's all right.' Wonderful had a hand on his shoulder. 'Thought I'd let you sleep in.' She had a long scab down the other side of her head now, stubble hair clumped with dried blood. 'Thought you could use it.'

'I could use a few hours yet.' Craw gritted his teeth against ten different aches as he tried to sit up, first fast then very, very slow. 'Bloody hell, but war's a young man's business.'

'What's to do?'

'Not much.' She handed him a flask and he sluiced water around his foul mouth and spat. 'No sign of Hardbread. We buried Athroc.' He paused, flask half way to his mouth, slowly let it drop. There was a heap of fresh dirt at the foot of one of the stones on the far side of the Heroes. Brack and Scorry stood in front of it, shovels in their hands. Agrick was between the two, looking down.

'You say the words yet?' asked Craw, knowing they wouldn't have but still hoping.

'Waiting for you.'

'Good,' he lied, and clambered up, gripping to her forearm. It was a grey morning with a nip in the wind, low clouds pawing at the craggy summits of the fells, mist still clinging to the creases in their sides, shrouding the bogs down in the valley's bottom.

Craw limped to the grave, shifting his hips, trying to wriggle away from the pain in his joints. He'd rather have gone anywhere else, but there are some things you can't wriggle away from. They were all drifting over there, gathering in a half-circle. All sad and quiet. Drofd trying to cram down a whole crust of bread at once, wiping his hands on his shirt. Whirrun with hood drawn up, cuddling the Father of Swords like a man might cuddle his sick child. Yon with a face even grimmer'n usual, which took some doing. Craw found his place at the foot of the grave, between Agrick and Brack. The hillman's face had lost its usual ruddy glow, the bandage on his leg showing a big fresh stain.

'That leg all right?' he asked.

'Scratch,' said Brack.

'Bleeding a lot for a scratch, ain't it?'

Brack smiled at him, tattoos on his face shifting. 'Call that a lot?'

'Guess not.' Not compared to Hardbread's nephew when Whirrun cut him in half, anyway. Craw glanced over his shoulder, towards where they'd piled the corpses in the lee of the crumbling wall. Out of sight, maybe, but not forgotten. The dead. Always the dead. Craw looked at the black earth, wondering what to say. Looked at the black earth like it had answers in it. But there's nothing in the earth but darkness.

'Strange thing.' His voice came out a croak, he had to cough to clear it. 'The other day Drofd was asking me whether they call these stones the Heroes 'cause there are Heroes buried here. I said not. But maybe there's one buried here now.' Craw winced saying it, not out of sadness but 'cause he knew he was talking shit. Stupid shit wouldn't have fooled a child. But the dozen all nodded, Agrick with a tear-track down his cheek.

'Aye,' said Yon.

You can say things at a grave would get you laughed out of a tavern, and be treated like you're brimming over with wisdom. Craw felt every word was a knife he had to stick in himself, but there was no stopping.

'Hadn't been with us long, Athroc, but he made his mark. Won't be forgot.' Craw thought on all the other lads he'd buried, faces and names worn away by the years, and couldn't even guess the number of 'em. 'He stood with his crew. Fought well.' Died badly, hacked with an axe, on ground that meant nothing. 'Did the right thing. All you can ask of a man, I reckon. If there's any—'

'Craw!' Shivers was standing maybe thirty strides away on the south side of the circle.

'Not now!' he hissed back.

'Aye,' said Shivers. 'Now.'

Craw hurried over, the grey valley opening up between two of the stones. 'What am I looking— Uh.' Beyond the river, at the foot of Black Fell, there were horsemen on the brown strip of the Uffrith Road. Riding fast towards Osrung, smudges of dust rising behind. Could've been forty. Could've been more.

'And there.'

'Shit.' Another couple of score coming the other way, towards the Old Bridge. Taking the crossings. Getting around both sides of the Heroes. The surge of worry was almost a pain in Craw's chest. 'Where's Scorry at?' Staring about like he'd put something down and couldn't remember where. Scorry was right behind him, holding up one finger. Craw breathed out slow, patting him on the shoulder. 'There you are. There you are.'

'Chief,' muttered Drofd.

Craw followed his pointing finger. The road south from Adwein, sloping down into the valley from the fold between two fells, was busy with movement. He snapped his eyeglass open and peered towards it. 'It's the Union.'

'How many, d'you reckon?'

The wind swept some mist away and, for just a moment, Craw could see the column stretching back between the hills, men and metal, spears prickling and flags waving above. Stretching back far as he could see.

'Looks like all of 'em,' breathed Wonderful.

Brack leaned over. 'Tell me we ain't fighting this time.'

Craw lowered his eyeglass. 'Sometimes the right thing to do is run like fuck. Pack up!' he bellowed. 'Right now! We're moving out!'

His crew always kept most of their gear stowed and they were busy packing the rest quick sharp, Scorry with a jaunty marching tune on the go. Jolly Yon was stomping the little fire out with one boot while Whirrun watched, already packed since all he owned was the Father of Swords and he had it in one hand.

'Why put it out?' asked Whirrun.

'I ain't leaving those bastards my fire,' grunted Yon.

'Don't reckon they'll all be able to fit around it, do you?'

'Even so.'

'We can't even all fit around it.'

'Still.'

'Who knows? You leave it, maybe one of those Union fellows burns himself and they all get scared and go home.'

Yon looked up for a moment, then ground the last embers out under his boot. 'I ain't leaving those bastards my fire.'

'That's it then?' asked Agrick. Craw found it hard to look in his eye. There was something desperate in it. 'That's all the words he gets?'

'We can say more later, maybe, but for now there's the living to think on.'

'We're giving it up.' Agrick glared at Shivers, fists clenched, like he was the one killed his brother. 'He died for nothing. For a fucking hill we ain't even holding on to! If we hadn't fought he'd still be alive! You hear that!' He took a step, might've gone for Shivers if Brack hadn't grabbed him from behind, Craw from in front, holding him tight.

'I hear it.' Shivers shrugged, bored. 'And it ain't the first time. If I hadn't gone to Styria I'd still have both my eyes. I went. One eye. We fought. He died. Life only rolls one way and it ain't always the way we'd like. There it is.' He turned and strolled off towards the north, axe over his shoulder.

'Forget about him,' muttered Craw in Agrick's ear. He knew what it was to lose a brother. He'd buried all three of his in one morning. 'You need a man to blame, blame me. I chose to fight.'

'There was no choice,' said Brack. 'It was the right thing to do.'

'Where'd Drofd get to?' asked Wonderful, slinging her bow over her shoulder as she walked past. 'Drofd?'

'Over here! Just packing up!' He was down near the wall, where they'd left the bodies of Hardbread's lot. When Craw got there he was kneeling by one of 'em, going through his pockets. He grinned around, holding out a few coins. 'Chief, this one had some . . .' He trailed off when he saw Craw's frown. 'I was going to share it out—'

'Put it back.'

Drofd blinked at him. 'But it's no good to him now—'

'Ain't yours is it? Leave it there with Hardbread's lad and when Hardbread comes back he'll decide who gets it.'

'More'n likely it'll be Hardbread gets it,' muttered Yon, coming up behind with his mail draped over his shoulder.

'Maybe it will be. But it won't be any of us. There's a right way of doing things.'

That got a couple of sharp breaths and something close to a groan. 'No one thinks that way these days, Chief,' said Scorry, leaning on his spear.

'Look how rich some no-mark like Sutt Brittle's made himself,' said Brack.

'While we scrape by on a piss-pot staple and the odd gild,' growled Yon.

'That's what you're due, and I'll see you get a gild for yesterday's work. But you'll leave the bodies be. You want to be Sutt Brittle you can beg a place with Glama Golden's lot and rob folk all day long.' Craw wasn't sure what was making him so prickly. He'd let it pass before. Helped himself more'n once when he was younger. Even Threetrees used to overlook his boys picking a corpse or two. But prickly he was, and now he'd chosen to stand on it he couldn't back down. 'What're we?' he snapped, 'Named Men or pickers and thieves?'

'Poor is what we are, Chief,' said Yon, 'and starting to—'

'What the *fuck*?' Wonderful slapped the coins from Drofd's hand and sent 'em scattering into the grass. 'When you're Chief, Jolly Yon Cumber, you can do it your way. 'Til then, we'll do it Craw's. We're Named Men. Or I am, at least – I ain't convinced about the rest of you. Now move your fat arses before you end up bitching to the Union about your poverty.'

'We ain't in this for the coin,' said Whirrun, ambling past with the Father of Swords over his shoulder.

Yon gave him a dark look. 'You might not be, Cracknut. Some of us wouldn't mind a little from time to time.' But he walked off shaking his head, mail jingling, and Brack and Scorry shrugged at each other, then followed.

Wonderful leaned close to Craw. 'Sometimes I think the more other folk don't care a shit the more you think you've got to.'

'Your point?'

'Can't make the world a certain way all on your own.'

'There's a right way of doing things,' he snapped.

'You sure the right way isn't just trying to keep everyone happy and alive?'

The worst thing was that she had a point. 'Is that where we've come to now?'

'I thought that's about where we've always been.'

Craw raised a brow at her. 'You know what? That husband o' yours really should teach you some respect.'

'That bitch? He's almost as scared o' me as you lot. Let's go!' She pulled Drofd up by his elbow, and the dozen made their way through the gap in the wall, moving fast. Or as fast as Craw's knees would go. They headed north down the ragged track the way they'd come and left the Heroes to the Union.

Craw worked his way through the trees, chewing at the fingernails of his sword hand. He'd already gnawed his shield hand down to his knuckles, more or less. Damn things never grew back fast enough. He'd felt less scared on the way up the Heroes at night than he did going to tell Black Dow he'd lost a hill. Can't be right when you're less scared of the enemy than your own Chief, can it? He wished he had some friendly company, but if there was going to be blame he wanted to shoulder it alone. He'd made the choices.

The woods were crawling with men thick as ants in the grass. Black Dow's own Carls – veterans, cold-headed and cold-hearted and with lots of cold steel to share out. Some had plate armour like the Union wore, others strange weapons, beaked, picked and hooked for punching through steel, all manner of savage inventions new to the world that the world was more'n likely better off without. He doubted any of these would be thinking twice before robbing a few coins off the dead, or the living either.

Craw had been most of his life a fighting man, but crowds of 'em still somehow made him nervous, and the older he got the less he felt he fit. Any day now they'd spot him for a fraud. Realise that keeping his threadbare courage stitched together was harder work every morning. He winced as his teeth bit into the quick and jerked his nails away.

'Can't be right,' he muttered to himself, 'for a Named Man to be scared all the time.'

'What?' Craw had almost forgotten Shivers was there, he moved so silent.

'You get scared, Shivers?'

A pause, that eye of his glinting as the sun peeped through the branches. 'Used to. All the time.'

'What changed?'

'Got my eye burned out o' my head.'

So much for calming small talk. 'Reckon that could change your outlook.'

'Halves it.'

Some sheep were bleating away beside the track, pressed tight into a pen much too small. Foraged, no doubt, meaning stolen, some unlucky shepherd's livelihood vanished down the gullets and out the arses of Black Dow's army. Behind a screen of hides, not two strides from the flock, a woman was slaughtering 'em and three more doing the skinning and gutting and hanging the carcasses, all soaked to the armpits in blood and not caring much about it either.

Two lads, probably just reached fighting age, were watching. Laughing at how stupid the sheep were, not to guess what was happening behind those hides. They didn't see that they were in the pen, and behind a screen of songs and stories and young men's dreams, war was waiting, soaked to the armpits and not caring. Craw saw it all well enough. So why was he still sitting meek in his pen? Might be old sheep can't jump new fences either.

The black standard of the Protector of the North was dug into the earth outside some ivy-wrapped ruin, long ago conquered by the forest. More men busy in the clearing before it, and stirring horses tethered in long rows. A grindstone being pedalled, metal shrieking, sparks spraying. A woman hammering at a cartwheel. A smith working at a hauberk with pincers and a mouthful of mail rings. Children hurrying about with armfuls of shafts, slopping buckets on yokes, sacks of the dead knew what. A complicated business, violence, once the scale gets big enough.

A man sprawled on a stone slab, oddly at ease in the midst of all this work that made nothing, on his elbows, head tipped back, eyes closed. Body all in shadow but a chink of sun from between the branches coming down across his smirk so it was bathed in double brightness.

'By the dead.' Craw walked to him and stood looking down. 'If it ain't the prince o' nothing much. Those women's boots you're wearing?'

'Styrian leather.' Calder's lids drifted open a slit, that curl to his lip he'd had since a boy. 'Curnden Craw. You still alive, you old shit?'

'Bit of a cough, as it goes.' He hawked up and spat phlegm onto the old stone between Calder's fancy foot-leather. 'Reckon I'll survive, though. Who made the mistake o' letting you crawl back from exile?'

Calder swung his legs off the slab. 'None other than the great Protector himself. Guess he couldn't beat the Union without my mighty sword-arm.'

'What's his plan? Cut it off and throw it at 'em?'

Calder spread his arms out wide. 'How would I hold you then?' And they folded each other tight. 'Good to see you, you stupid old fool.'

'Likewise, you lying little fuck.'

Shivers frowned from the shadows all the while. 'You two seem tight,' he muttered.

'Why, I practically raised this little bastard!' Craw scrubbed Calder's hair with his knuckles. 'Fed him milk from a squeezed cloth, I did.'

'Closest thing I ever had to a mother,' said Calder.

Shivers nodded slowly. 'Explains a lot.'

'We should talk.' Calder gave Craw's arm a squeeze. 'I miss our talks.'

'And me.' Craw took a careful step back as a horse reared nearby, knocked its cart sideways and sent a tangle of spears clattering to the ground. 'Almost as much as I miss a decent bed. Today might not be the day, though.'

'Maybe not. I hear there's some sort of battle about to happen?' Calder backed off, throwing up his hands. 'It's going to kill my whole afternoon!'

He passed a cage as he went, a couple of filthy Northmen squatting naked inside, one sticking an arm out through the bars in hopes of water, or mercy, or just so some part of him could be free. Deserters would've been hanged already which made these thieves or murderers. Waiting on Black Dow's pleasure, which was more'n likely going to be to hang 'em anyway, and probably burn 'em into the bargain. Strange, to lock men up for thieving when the whole army lived on robbery. To dangle men for murder when they were all at the business of killing. What makes a crime in a time when men take what they please from who they please?

'Dow wants you.' Splitfoot stood frowning in the ruin's archway. He'd always been a dour bastard but he looked 'specially put upon today. 'In there.'

'You want my sword?' Craw was already sliding it out.

'No need.'

'No? When did Black Dow start trusting people?'

'Not people. Just you.'

Craw wasn't sure if that was a good sign. 'All right, then.'

Shivers made to follow but Splitfoot held him back with one hand. 'Dow didn't ask for you.'

Craw caught Shivers' narrowed eye for a moment, and shrugged, and ducked through the ivy-choked archway, feeling like he was sticking his head in a wolf's mouth and wondering when he'd hear the teeth snap. Down a passage hung with cobweb, echoing with dripping water. Into a wide stretch of brambly dirt, broken pillars scattered around its edge, some still holding up a crumbling vault, but the roof long gone and the clouds above starting to show some bright blue between. Dow sat in Skarling's Chair at the far end of the ruined hall, toying with the pommel of his sword. Caul Reachey sat near him, scratching at his white stubble.

'When I give the word,' Dow was saying, 'you'll lead off alone. Move on Osrung with everything you've got. They're weak there.'

'How d'you know that?'

Dow winked. 'I've got my ways. They've too many men and not enough road, and they rushed to get here so they're stretched out thin. Just some horsemen in the town, and a few o' the

Dogman's lads. Might've got some foot up there by the time we go, but not enough to stop you if you take a proper swing at it.'

'Oh, I'll swing at it,' said Reachey. 'Don't worry on that score.'

'I'm not. That's why you're leading off. I want your lads to carry my standard, nice and clear up at the front. And Golden's, and Ironhead's, and yours. Where everyone can see.'

'Make 'em think it's our big effort.'

'Any luck they'll pull some men off from the Heroes, leave the stones weaker held. Once they're in the open fields between hill and town, I'll let slip Golden's boys and he'll tear their arses out. Meantime me, and Ironhead, and Tenways'll make the proper effort on the Heroes.'

'How d'you plan to work it?'

Dow flashed that hungry grin of his. 'Run up that hill and kill everything living.'

'They'll have had time to get set, and that's some tough ground to charge. It's where they'll be strongest. We could go around—'

'Strongest here.' Dow dug his sword into the ground in front of Skarling's Chair. 'Weakest here.' And he tapped at his chest with a finger. 'We've been going around the sides for months, they won't be expecting us front on. We break 'em at the Heroes, we break 'em here,' and he thumped his chest again, 'and the rest all crumbles. Then Golden can follow up, chase 'em right across the fords if need be. All the way to Adwein. Scale should be ready on the right by then, can take the Old Bridge. With you in Osrung in weight, when the rest o' the Union turn up tomorrow all the best ground'll be ours.'

Reachey slowly stood. 'Right y'are, Chief. We'll make it a red day. A day for the songs.'

'Shit on the songs,' said Dow, standing himself. 'I'll take just victory.'

They clasped hands a moment, then Reachey moved for the entrance, saw Craw and gave a big gap-toothed smile.

'Old Caul Reachey.' And Craw held out his hand.

'Curnden Craw, as I live and breathe.' Reachey folded it in one of his then slapped the other down on top. 'Ain't enough of us good men left.'

'Those are the times.'

'How's the knee?'

'You know. It is how it is.'

'Mine too. Yon Cumber?'

'Always with a joke ready. How's Flood getting on?'

Reachey grinned. 'Got him looking after some new recruits. Right shower o' piss-water, in the main.'

'Maybe they'll shape up.'

'They better had, and fast. I hear we got a battle coming.' Reachey clapped him on the arm as he passed. 'Be waiting for your order, Chief!' And he left Craw and Black Dow watching each other over a few strides of rubble-strewn, weed-sprouting, nettle-waving old mud. Birds twittered, leaves rustled, the hint of distant metal serving notice there was bloody business due.

'Chief.' Craw licked his lips, no idea how this was going to go.

Dow took a long breath in and screamed at the top of his voice. 'Didn't I tell you to hold on to that *fucking* hill!'

Craw went cold as the echoes rang from the crumbling walls. Looked like it might not go well at all. He wondered if he might find himself stripped in a cage before sundown. 'Well, I was holding on to it all right . . . until the Union showed up . . .'

Dow came closer, sheathed sword still in one fist, and Craw had to make himself not back off. Dow leaned forwards and Craw had to make himself not flinch. Dow raised one hand and put it gently down on Craw's sore shoulder, and he had to make himself not shudder. 'Sorry 'bout this,' said Dow quietly, 'but I've a reputation to look to.'

A wave of giddy relief. ''Course, Chief. Let rip.' He narrowed his eyes as Dow took another breath.

'You *useless* old limping *fuck*!' Spraying Craw with spit, then patting the bruised side of his face, none too gently. 'You made a fight of it, then?'

'Aye. With Hardbread and a few of his lads.'

'I remember that old bastard. How many did he have?'

'Twenty-two.'

Dow bared his teeth somewhere between smile and scowl. 'And you, what, ten?'

'Aye, with Shivers.'

'And you saw 'em off?'

'Well—'

'Wish I'd fucking been there!' Dow twitched with violence, eyes fixed on nothing like he could see Hardbread and his boys coming up that slope and they couldn't come fast enough for him. '*Wish* I'd been there!' And he lashed out with the pommel of his sheathed sword and struck splinters from the nearest pillar, making Craw take a careful step back. ''Stead of sitting back here fucking *talking*. Talking, talking, fucking talking!' Dow spat, and took a breath, then seemed to remember Craw was there, eyes sliding back towards him. 'You saw the Union come up?'

'At least a thousand on the road to Adwein and I got the feeling there were more behind.'

'Jalenhorm's division,' said Dow.

'How d'you know that?'

'He has his ways.'

'By the—' Craw took a startled pace, got his feet caught in a bramble and nearly fell. There was a woman lying on one of the highest walls. Draped over it like a wet cloth, one arm and one leg dangling, head hanging over the side like she was resting on some garden bench 'stead of a tottering heap of masonry six strides above the dirt.

'Friend o' mine.' Dow didn't even look up. 'Well – when I say friend—'

'Enemy's enemy.' She rolled off the back of the wall. Craw stared, waiting for the sound of her hitting the ground. 'I am Ishri.' The voice whispered in his ear.

This time he went right on his arse in the dirt. She stood over him, skin black, and smooth, and perfect, like the glazing on a good pot. She wore a long coat, tails dragging on the dirt, hanging open, body all bound in white bandages underneath. If anyone ever looked like a witch, she was it. Not that there was much more evidence of witchery needed past vanishing from one place and stepping out of another.

Dow barked with laughter. 'You never can tell where she'll spring from. I'm always worried she'll pop out o' nowhere while I'm . . . you know.' And he mimed a wanking action with one fist.

'You wish,' said Ishri, looking down at Craw with eyes blacker than black, unblinking, like a jackdaw staring at a maggot.

'Where did you come from?' muttered Craw as he scrambled up, hopping a little on account of his stiff knee.

'South,' she said, though that much was clear enough from her skin. 'Or do you mean, why did I come?'

'I'll take why.'

'To do the right thing.' There was a faint smile on her face, at that. 'To fight against evil. To strike mighty blows for right-eousness. Or . . . do you mean who sent me?'

'All right, who sent you?'

'God.' Her eyes rolled to the sky, framed by jutting weeds and saplings. 'And how could it be otherwise? God puts us all where he wants us.'

Craw rubbed at his knee. 'Got a shitty sense o' humour, don't he?'

'You do not know the half of it. I came to fight against the Union, is that enough?'

'It's enough for me,' said Dow.

Ishri's black eyes flicked away to him, and Craw felt greatly relieved. 'They are moving onto the hill in numbers.'

'Jalenhorm's lot?'

'I believe so.' She stretched up tall, wriggling all over the place like she had no bones in her. Reminded Craw of the eels they used to catch from the lake near his workshop, spilling from the net, squirming in the children's hands and making them squeal. 'You fat pink men all look the same to me.'

'What about Mitterick?' asked Dow.

Her bony shoulders drifted up and down. 'Some way behind, chomping at the bit, furious that Jalenhorm is in his way.'

'Meed?'

'Where is the fun in knowing everything?' She pranced past Craw, up on her toes, almost brushing against him so he had to nervously step back and nearly trip again. 'God must be so *bored*.' She wedged one foot into a crack in the wall too narrow for a cat to squeeze through, twisting her leg, somehow working it in up to the hip. 'To it, then, my heroes!' She writhed like a worm cut in half, wriggling into the ruined masonry, her coat dragging up the mossy stonework behind her. 'Do you not have a battle to fight?' Her skull somehow slid into the gap, then her arms, she clapped her bandaged hands once and just a finger was left sticking from the crack. Dow walked over to it, reached out, and snapped it off. It wasn't a finger at all, just a dead bit of twig.

'Magic,' muttered Craw. 'Can't say I care for the stuff.' In his experience it did more harm than good. 'I daresay a sorcerer's got their uses and all but, I mean, do they always have to act so bloody *strange*?'

Dow flicked the twig away with a wrinkled lip. 'It's a war. I care for whatever gets the job done. Best not mention my black-skinned friend to anyone else though, eh? Folks might get the wrong idea.'

'What's the right idea?'

'Whatever I fucking say it is!' snarled Dow, and he didn't look like he was faking the anger this time.

Craw held up his open hands. 'You're the Chief.'

'Damn right!' Dow frowned at that crack. 'I'm the Chief.' Almost like it was himself he was trying to convince. Just for a moment Craw wondered whether Black Dow ever felt like a fraud. Whether Black Dow's courage needed stitching together every morning.

He didn't like that thought much. 'We're fighting, then?'

Dow's eyes swivelled sideways and his killing smile broke out fresh, no trace of doubt in it, or fear neither. 'High fucking time, no? You hear what I was telling Reachey?'

'Most of it. He'll try and draw 'em off towards Osrung, then you'll go straight at the Heroes.'

'Straight at 'em!' barked Dow, like he could make it work by shouting it. 'The way Threetrees would've done it, eh?'

'Would he?'

Dow opened his mouth, then paused. 'What does it matter? Threetrees is seven winters in the mud.'

'True. Where do you want me and my dozen?'

'Right beside me when I charge up to the Heroes, o' course. Expect there's nothing in the world you'd like more'n to take that hill back from those Union bastards.'

Craw gave a long sigh, wondering what his dozen would have to say about that. 'Oh, aye. It's top o' my list.'

The Very Model

'An officer should command from horseback, eh, Gorst? The proper place for a headquarters is the saddle!' General Jalenhorm affectionately patted the neck of his magnificent grey, then leaned over without waiting for an answer to roar at a spotty-faced courier. 'Tell the captain that he must simply clear the road by whatever means necessary! Clear the road and move them up! Haste, all haste, lad, Marshal Kroy wants the division moving north!' He swivelled to bellow over the other shoulder. 'Speed, gentlemen, speed! Towards Carleon, and victory!'

Jalenhorm certainly looked a conquering hero. Fantastically young to command a division and with a smile that said he was prepared for anything, dressed with an admirable lack of pretension in a dusty trooper's uniform and as comfortable in the saddle as a favourite armchair. If he had been half as fine a tactician as he was a horseman, they would long ago have had Black Dow in chains and on public display in Adua. *But he is not, and we do not.*

A constantly shifting body of staff officers, adjutants, liaisons and even a scarcely pubescent bugler trailed eagerly along in the general's wake like wasps after a rotten apple, fighting to attract his fickle attention by snapping, jostling and shouting over one another with small dignity. Meanwhile Jalenhorm himself barked out a volley of confusing and contradictory replies, questions, orders and occasional musings on life.

'On the right, on the right, of course!' to one officer. 'Tell him not to worry, worrying solves nothing!' to another. 'Move them up, Marshal Kroy wants them all up by lunch!' A large body of infantry were obliged to shuffle exhausted from the road, watch the officers pass, then chew on their dust. 'Beef, then,' bellowed

Jalenhorm with a regal wave, 'or mutton, whichever, we have more important business! Will you come up the hill with me, Colonel Gorst? Apparently one gets quite the view from the Heroes. You are his Majesty's observer, are you not?'

I am his Majesty's fool. Almost as much his Majesty's fool as you are. 'Yes, General.'

Jalenhorm had already whisked his mount from the road and down the shingle towards the shallows, pebbles scattering. His hangers-on strained to follow, splashing out into the water and heedlessly showering a company of heavily loaded foot who were struggling across, up to their waists in the river. The hill rose out of the fields on the far side, a great green cone so regular as to seem artificial. The circle of standing stones that the Northmen called the Heroes jutted from its flat top, a much smaller circle on a spur to the right, a single tall needle of rock on another to the left.

Orchards grew on the far bank, the twisted trees heavy with reddening apples, thin grass underneath patched with shade and covered in half-rotten windfalls. Jalenhorm leaned out to pluck one from a low-hanging branch and happily bit into it. 'Yuck.' He shuddered and spat it out. 'Cookers, I suppose.'

'General Jalenhorm, sir!' A breathless messenger whipping his horse down one row of trees towards them.

'Speak, man!' Without slowing from a trot.

'Major Kalf is at the Old Bridge, sir, with two companies of the Fourteenth. He wonders whether he should push forward to a nearby farm and establish a perimeter—'

'Absolutely! Forward. We need to make room! Where are the rest of his companies?' The messenger had already saluted and galloped off westwards. Jalenhorm frowned around at his staff. 'Major Kalf's other companies? Where's the rest of the Fourteenth?'

Dappled sunlight slid over baffled faces. An officer opened his mouth but said nothing. Another shrugged. 'Perhaps held up in Adwein, sir, there is considerable confusion on the narrow roads—'

He was interrupted by another messenger, bringing a well-lathered horse from the opposite direction. 'Sir! Colonel Vinkler wishes to know whether he should turn the residents of Osrung out of their houses and garrison—'

'No, no, turn them out? No!'

'Sir!' The young man pulled his horse about.

'Wait! Yes, turn them out. Garrison the houses. Wait! No. No. Hearts and minds, eh, Colonel Gorst? Hearts and mind, don't you think? What do you think?'

I think your close friendship with the king has caused you to be promoted far beyond the rank at which you were most effective. I think you would have made an excellent lieutenant, a passable captain, a mediocre major and a dismal colonel, but as a general you are a liability. I think you know this, and have no confidence, which makes you behave, paradoxically, as if you have far too much. I think you make decisions with little thought, abandon some with none and stick furiously to others against all argument, thinking that to change your mind would be to show weakness. I think you fuss with details better left to subordinates, fearing to tackle the larger issues, and that makes your subordinates smother you with decisions on every trifle, which you then bungle. I think you are a decent, honest, courageous man. And I think you are a fool. 'Hearts and minds,' said Gorst.

Jalenhorm beamed. The messenger tore off, presumably to win the people of Osrung to the Union cause by allowing them keep their own houses. The rest of the officers emerged from the shade of the apple trees and into the sun, the grassy slope stretching away above them.

'With me, boys, with me!' Jalenhorm urged his charger uphill, maintaining an effortless balance in the saddle while his retainers struggled to keep up, one balding captain almost torn from his seat as a low branch clubbed him in the head.

An old drystone wall ringed the hill not far from the top, sprouting with seeding weeds, no higher than a stride or two even on its outside face. One of the more impetuous young ensigns tried to show off by jumping it, but his horse shied and nearly dumped him. *A fitting metaphor for the Union involvement in the North so far – a lot of vainglory but it all ends in embarrassment.*

Jalenhorm and his officers passed in file through a narrow gap, the ancient stones on the summit looming larger with every hoofbeat, then rearing over Gorst and the rest as they crested the hill's flat top.

It was close to midday, the sun was high and hot, the morning mists were all burned off and, aside from some towers of white cloud casting ponderous shadows over the forests to the north, the valley was bathed in golden sunlight. The wind made waves through the crops, the shallows glittered, a Union flag snapped proudly over the tallest tower in the town of Osrung. To the south of the river the roads were obscured by the dust of thousands of marching men, the occasional twinkle of metal showing where bodies of soldiers moved: infantry, cavalry, supplies, rolling sluggishly from the south. Jalenhorm had drawn his horse up to take in the view, and with some displeasure.

'We aren't moving fast enough, damn it. Major!'

'Sir?'

'I want you to ride down to Adwein and see if you can hurry them along there! We need to get more men on this hill. More men into Osrung. We need to move them up!'

'Sir!'

'And Major?'

'Sir?'

Jalenhorm sat, open-mouthed, for a moment. 'Never mind. Go!'

The man set off in the wrong direction, realised his error and was gone down the hill the way they had come.

Confusion reigned in the wide circle of grass within the Heroes. Horses had been tethered to two of the stones but one had got loose and was making a deafening racket, scaring the others and kicking out alarmingly while several terrified grooms tried desperately to snatch its bridle. The standard of the King's Own Sixth Regiment hung limp in the centre of the circle beside a burned-out fire where, utterly dwarfed by the sullen slabs of rock that surrounded it on every side, it did little for morale. *Although, let us face the facts, my morale is beyond help.*

Two small wagons that had somehow been dragged up the hill had been turned over onto their sides and their eclectic contents – from tents to pans to smithing instruments to a shining new washboard – scattered across the grass while soldiers rooted through the remainder like plunderers after a rout.

'What the hell are you about, Sergeant?' demanded Jalenhorm, spurring his horse over.

The man looked up guiltily to see the attention of a general and two dozen staff officers all suddenly focused upon him, and swallowed. 'Well, sir, we're a little short of flatbow bolts, General, sir.'

'And?'

'It seems ammunition was considered very important by those that packed the supplies.'

'Naturally.'

'So it was packed first.'

'First.'

'Yes, sir. Meaning, on the bottom, sir.'

'The bottom?'

'Sir!' A man with a pristine uniform hastened over, chin high, giving Jalenhorm a salute so sharp that the snapping of his well-polished heels was almost painful to the ear.

The general swung from his saddle and shook him by the hand. 'Colonel Wetterlant, good to see you! How do things stand?'

'Well enough, sir, most of the Sixth is up here now, though lacking a good deal of our equipment.' Wetterlant led them across the grass, soldiers doing the best they could to make room amid the chaos. 'One battalion of the Rostod Regiment too, though what happened to their commanding officer is anyone's guess.'

'Laid up with the gout, I believe—' someone muttered.

'Is that a grave?' asked Jalenhorm, pointing out a patch of fresh-turned earth in the shadow of one of the stones, trampled with boot-prints.

The colonel frowned at it. 'Well, I suppose—'

'Any sign of the Northmen?'

'A few of my men have seen movement in the woods to the north but nothing we could say for certain was the enemy. More likely than not it's sheep.' Wetterlant led them between two of the towering stones. 'Other than that, not a sniff of the buggers. Apart from what they left behind, that is.'

'Ugh,' said one of the staff officers, looking sharply away. Several bloodstained bodies were laid out in a row. One of them had been sliced in half and had lost his lower arm besides, flies busy on his exposed innards.

'Was there combat?' asked Jalenhorm, frowning at the corpses.

'No, those are yesterday's. And they were ours. Some of the Dogman's scouts, apparently.' The colonel pointed out a small group of Northmen, a tall one with a red bird on his shield and a heavy set old man conspicuous among them, busy digging graves.

'What about the horse?' It lay on its side, an arrow poking from its bloated belly.

'I really couldn't say.'

Gorst took in the defences, which were already considerable. Spearmen were manning the drystone wall on this side of the hill, packed shoulder to shoulder at a gap where a patchy track passed down the hillside. Behind them, higher up the slope, a wide double curve of archers fussed with bolts and flatbows or simply lazed about, chewing disconsolately at dried rations, a couple apparently arguing over winnings at dice.

'Good,' said Jalenhorm, 'good,' without specifying exactly what met his approval. He frowned out across the patchwork of field and pasture, over the few farms and towards the woods that blanketed the north side of the valley. Thick forest, of the kind that covered so much of the country, the monotony of trees only relieved by the vague stripes of two roads leading north between the fells. One of them, presumably, to Carleon. *And victory.*

'There could be ten Northmen out there or ten thousand,' muttered Jalenhorm. 'We must be careful. Mustn't under-estimate Black Dow. I was at the Cumnur, you know, Gorst, where Prince Ladisla was killed. Well, the day before the battle, in fact, but I was there. A dark day for Union arms. Can't be having another of those, eh?'

I strongly suggest that you resign your commission, then, and allow someone with better credentials to take command. 'No, sir.'

Jalenhorm had already turned away to speak to Wetterlant. Gorst could hardly blame him. *When did I last say anything worth hearing? Bland agreements and non-committal splutterings. The bleating of a goat would serve the same purpose.* He turned his back on the knot of staff officers and wandered over to where the Northmen were digging graves. The grey-haired one watched him come, leaning on his spade.

'My name is Gorst.'

The older man raised his brows. *Surprise that a Union man should speak Northern, or surprise that a big man should speak like a little girl?* 'Hardbread's mine. I fight for the Dogman.' His words slightly mangled in a badly battered mouth.

Gorst nodded to the corpses. 'These are your men?'

'Aye.'

'You fought up here?'

'Against a dozen led by a man called Curnden Craw.' He rubbed at his bruised jaw. 'We had the numbers but we lost.'

Gorst frowned around the circle of stones. 'They had the ground.'

'That and Whirrun of Bligh.'

'Who?'

'Some fucking hero,' scoffed the one with a red bird on his shield.

'From way up north in the valleys,' said Hardbread, 'where it snows every bloody day.'

'Mad bastard,' grunted one of Hardbread's men, nursing a bandaged arm. 'They say he drinks his own piss.'

'I heard he eats children.'

'He has this sword they say fell out of the sky.' Hardbread wiped his forehead on the back of one thick forearm. 'They worship it, up there in the snows.'

'They worship a sword?' asked Gorst.

'They think God dropped it or something. Who knows what they think up there? Either way, Cracknut Whirrun is one dangerous bastard.' Hardbread licked at a gap in his teeth, and from his grimace it was a new one. 'I can tell you that from my own experience.'

Gorst frowned towards the forest, trees shining dark green in the sun. 'Do you think Black Dow's men are near?'

'I reckon they are.'

'Why?'

'Because Craw fought against the odds, and he ain't a man to fight over nothing. Black Dow wanted this hill.' Hardbread shrugged as he bent back to his task. 'We're burying these poor bastards then we're going down. I'll be leaving a tooth back there on the slope and a nephew in the mud and I don't plan on leaving aught else in this bloody place.'

'Thank you.' Gorst turned back towards Jalenhorm and his staff, now engaged in a heated debate about whether the latest company to arrive should be placed behind or in front of the ruined wall. 'General!' he called. 'The scouts think Black Dow might be nearby!'

'I hope he is!' shot back Jalenhorm, though it was obvious he was scarcely listening. 'The crossings are in our hands! Take control of all three crossings, that's our first objective!'

'I thought there were four crossings.' It was said quietly, one man murmuring to another, but the hubbub dropped away at that moment. Everyone turned to see a pale young lieutenant, somewhat surprised to have become the centre of attention.

'Four?' Jalenhorm rounded on the man. 'There is the Old Bridge, to the west.' He flung out one arm, almost knocking down a portly major. 'The bridge in Osrung, to the east. And the shallows where we made the passage. Three crossings.' The general waved three big fingers in the lieutenant's face. 'All in our hands!'

The young man flushed. 'One of the scouts told me there is a path through the bogs, sir, further west of the Old Bridge.'

'A path through the bogs?' Jalenhorm squinted off to the west. 'A secret way? I mean to say, Northmen could use that path and get right around us! Damn good work, boy!'

'Well, thank you, sir—'

The general spun one way, then back the other, heel twisting up the sod, casting around as though the right strategy was always just behind him. 'Who hasn't crossed the river yet?'

His officers milled about in their efforts to stay in his line of sight.

'Are the Eighth up?'

'I thought the rest of the Thirteenth—'

'Colonel Vallimir's first cavalry are still deploying there!'

'I believe they have one battalion in order, just reunited with their horses—'

'Excellent! Send to Colonel Vallimir and ask him to take that battalion through the bogs.'

A couple of officers grumbled their approval. Others glanced somewhat nervously at each other. 'A whole battalion?' one muttered. 'Is this path suitable for—'

Jalenhorm swatted them away. 'Colonel Gorst! Would you ride back across the river and convey my wishes to Colonel Vallimir, make sure the enemy can't give us an unpleasant surprise.'

Gorst paused for a moment. 'General, I would prefer to remain where I can—'

'I understand entirely. You wish to be close to the action. But the king asked specifically in his last letter that I do everything possible to keep you out of danger. Don't worry, the front line will hold perfectly well without you. We friends of the king must stick together, mustn't we?'

All the king's fools, capering along in military motley to the same mad bugle music! Make the one with the silly voice turn another cartwheel, my sides are splitting! 'Of course, sir.' And Gorst trudged back towards his horse.

Scale

Calder nudged his horse down a path so vague he wasn't even sure it was one, smirk clamped tight to his face. If Deep and Shallow were keeping an eye on him – and since he was their best source of money it was a certainty – he couldn't tell. Admittedly, there wasn't much point to men like Deep and Shallow if a man like Calder could tell where they were, but by the dead he would've liked some company. Like a starving man tossed a crust, seeing Curnden Craw had only whetted Calder's appetite for friendly faces.

He'd ridden through Ironhead's men, soaking up their scorn, and Tenways', soaking up their hostility, and now he was getting into the woods at the west end of the valley, where Scale's men were gathered. His brother's men. His men, he supposed, though they didn't feel much like his. Tough-looking bastards, ragged from hard marching, bandaged from hard fighting. Worn down from being far from Black Dow's favour where they did the toughest jobs for the leanest rewards. They didn't look in a mood to celebrate anything, and for damn sure not the arrival of their Chief's coward brother.

It didn't help that he'd struggled into his chain mail shirt, hoping to at least look like a warrior prince for the occasion. It had been a gift from his father, years ago, made from Styrian steel, lighter than most Northern mixtures but still heavy as an anvil and hot as a sheepskin. Calder had no notion how men could wear these damn things for days at a time. Run in them. Sleep in them. Fight in them. Mad business, fighting in this. Mad business, fighting. He'd never understood what men saw in it.

And few men saw more in it than his own brother, Scale.

He was squatting in a clearing with a map spread out in front of him. Pale-as-Snow was at his left elbow and White-Eye Hansul at his right, old comrades of Calder's father from the time when he ruled the best part of the North. Men who'd fallen a long way when the Bloody-Nine threw Calder's father from his battlements. Almost as far as Calder had fallen himself.

Him and Scale were born to different mothers, and the joke always was that Scale's must've been a bull. He looked like a bull, and a particularly mean and muscular one at that. He was Calder's opposite in almost every way – blond where Calder was dark, blunt-featured where Calder was sharp, quick to anger and slow to think. Nothing like their father. Calder was the one who'd taken after Bethod, and everyone knew it. One reason why they hated him. That and he'd spent so much of his life acting like a prick.

Scale looked up when he heard the hooves of Calder's horse, gave a great smile as he strode over, still carrying that trace of a limp the Bloody-Nine had given him. He wore his chain mail lightly as a maiden wears a shift even so, a heavy black-forged double coat of it, plates of black steel strapped on top, all scratched and dented. 'Always be armed,' their father had told them, and Scale had taken it literally. He was criss-crossed with belting and bristling with weapons, two swords and a great mace at his belt, three knives in plain sight and probably others out of it. He had a bandage around his head stained brown on one side, and a new nick through his eyebrow to add to a rapidly growing collection of scars. It looked as if Calder's frequent attempts to persuade Scale to stay out of battle had been as wasted as Scale's frequent attempts to persuade Calder to charge into it.

Calder swung from his saddle, finding it a straining effort in his mail and trying to make it look like he was only stiff from a hard ride. 'Scale, you thick bastard, how've you—'

Scale caught him in a crushing hug, lifted his feet clear of the ground and gave him a slobbery kiss on the forehead. Calder hugged him back the best he could with all the breath squeezed out of his body and a sword hilt poking him in the gut, so suddenly, pathetically happy to have someone on his side he wanted to cry.

'Get off!' he wheezed, hammering at Scale's back with the heel of his hand like a wrestler submitting. 'Off!'

'Just good to see you back!' And Scale spun him helplessly around like a husband with his new bride, gave him a fleeting view of Pale-as-Snow and White-Eye Hansul. Neither of them looked like hugging Calder any time soon. The eyes on him from the Named Men scattered about the clearing were no more enthusiastic. Men he recognised from way back, kneeling to his father or sitting at the long table or cheering victory in the good old days. No doubt they were wondering whether they'd have to take Calder's orders now, and not much caring for the idea. Why would they? Scale was all those things warriors admire – loyal, strong and brave beyond the point of stupidity. Calder was none of them, and everyone knew it.

'What happened to your head?' he asked, once Scale had let his feet touch earth again.

'This? Bah. Nothing.' Scale tore the bandage off and tossed it away. It didn't look like nothing, his yellow hair matted brown with dry blood on one side. 'Seems you've a wound of your own though.' Patting Calder's bruised lip none too gently. 'Some woman bite you?'

'If only. Brodd Tenways tried to have me killed.'

'What?'

'Really. He sent three men after me to Caul Reachey's camp. Luckily Deep and Shallow were looking out and . . . you know . . .'

Scale was moving fast from bafflement to fury, his two favourite emotions and never much of a gap between the two, little eyes opening wider and wider until the whites showed all the way around. 'I'll kill the rotten old bastard!' He started to draw a sword, as if he was going to charge off through the woods to the ruin where Black Dow had their father's chair and slaughter Brodd Tenways on the spot.

'No, no, no!' Calder grabbed his wrist with both hands, managed to stop him getting his sword from the sheath and was nearly dragged off his feet doing it.

'Fuck him!' Scale shrugged Calder off, punched the nearest tree trunk with one gauntleted fist and tore a chunk of bark off it. 'Fuck the shit out of him! Let's kill him! Let's just *kill* him!' He punched it again and brought a shower of seeds fluttering down. White-Eye Hansul looked on warily, Pale-as-Snow looked on wearily, both giving the strong impression this wasn't the first rage they'd had to deal with.

'We can't run around killing important people,' coaxed Calder, palms up.

'He tried to kill you, didn't he?'

'I'm a special case. Half the North wants me dead.' That was a lie, it was closer to three-quarters. 'And we've no proof.' Calder put his hand on Scale's shoulder and spoke softly, the way their father used to. 'It's politics, brother. Remember? It's a delicate balance.'

'Fuck politics and shit on the balance!' But the rage had flickered down now. Far enough that there was no danger of Scale's eyes popping out of his head. He rammed his sword back, hilt snapping against the scabbard. 'Can't we just fight?'

Calder took a long breath. How could this unreasoning thug be his father's son? And his father's heir, besides? 'There'll be a time to fight, but for now we need to tread carefully. We're short on allies, Scale. I spoke to Reachey, and he won't move against me but he won't move for.'

'Creeping bloody coward!' Scale raised his fist to punch the tree again and Calder pushed it gently down with one finger.

'Just worried for his daughter.' And he wasn't the only one. 'Then there's Ironhead and Golden, neither too well disposed to us. If it weren't for their feud with each other I daresay they'd have been begging Dow for the chance to kill me.'

Scale frowned. 'You think Dow was behind it?'

'How could he not be?' Calder had to squeeze down his frustration and his voice with it. He'd forgotten how much talking to his brother could be like talking to a tree stump. 'And anyway, Reachey had it from Dow's own mouth that he wants me dead.'

Scale shook his head, worried. 'I hadn't heard that.'

'He's not likely to tell you, is he?'

'But he had you hostage.' Scale's brow was wrinkled with the effort of thinking it out. 'Why let you come back?'

'Because he's hoping I'll start plotting, and then he'll be able to bring it all out and hang me nice and fair.'

'Don't plot, then, you should be right enough with everyone.'

'Don't be an *idiot*.' A couple of Carls looked up from their water cups, and he pushed his voice back down. Scale could afford to lose his temper, Calder couldn't. 'We need to protect ourselves. We have enemies everywhere.'

'True, and there's one you haven't talked about at all. Most dangerous of the lot, far as I can tell.' Calder froze for a moment, wondering who he might have left out of his calculations. 'The fucking Union!' Scale pointed through the trees towards the south with one thick finger. 'Kroy, and the Dogman, and their forty thousand soldiers! The ones we've been fighting a war against! I've been, anyway.'

'That's Black Dow's war, not mine.'

Scale slowly shook his head. 'Did you ever think it might be the easier, cheaper, safer path just to do what you're told?'

'Thought about it, decided against. What we need—'

'Listen to me.' Scale came close, looking him right in the eye. 'There's a battle coming, and we have to fight. Do you understand? This is the North. We have to fight.'

'Scale—'

'You're the clever one. Far cleverer than me, everyone knows it. The dead know I know it.' He leaned closer still. 'But the men won't follow cleverness. Not without strength. You have to earn their respect.'

'Huh.' Calder glanced around at the hard eyes in the trees. 'Can't I just borrow it from you?'

'One day I might not be here, and you'll need some respect of your own. You don't have to wade in blood. You just have to share the hardships and share the danger.'

Calder gave a watery smile. 'It's the danger that scares me.' He wasn't over keen on the hardships either, if the truth be known.

'Fear is good.' Easy for him to say whose skull was so thick fear couldn't get in. 'Our father was scared every day of his life. Kept him sharp.' Scale took Calder's shoulder in a grip that wasn't to be resisted and turned him to face south. Between the trunks of the trees at the edge of the woods he could see a long expanse of fields, gold, and green, and fallow brown. The western spur of the Heroes loomed up on the left, Skarling's Finger sticking from the top, the grey streak of a road through the crops at its foot. 'That track leads to the Old Bridge. Dow wants us to take it.'

'Wants *you* to take it.'

'Us. It's barely defended. Do you have a shield?'

'No.' Nor the slightest wish to go where he might need one.

'Pale-as-Snow, lend me your shield there.'

The waxy-faced old warrior handed it over to Calder. Painted white, appropriately enough. It had been a long time since he'd handled one, battered about a courtyard at sword practice, and he'd forgotten how much the damn things weighed. The feel of it on his arm brought back ugly memories of old humiliations, most of them at his brother's hands. But they'd probably be eclipsed by new ones before the day was out. If he lived through it.

Scale patted Calder on his sore cheek again. Unpleasantly firm, again. 'Stay close to me and keep your shield up, you'll get through all right.' He jerked his head towards the men scattered in the trees. 'And they'll think more of you just for seeing you up front.'

'Right.' Calder hefted the shield with scant enthusiasm.

'Who knows?' His brother slapped him on the back and nearly knocked him over. 'Maybe you will too.'

Ours Not to Reason Why

'**Y**ou just love that bloody horse, don't you, Tunny?'

'She makes better conversation than you, Forest, that's for sure, and she's a damn sight better than walking. Aren't you, my darling?' He nuzzled at her long face and fed her an extra handful of grain. 'My favourite animal in the whole bloody army.'

He felt a tap on his arm. 'Corporal?' It was Yolk, looking off towards the hill.

'No, Yolk, I'm afraid to say you're nowhere near. In fact you need to work hard at not being my least favourite animal—'

'No, Corporal. Ain't that that Gurts?'

Tunny frowned. 'Gorst.' The neckless swordsman was riding across the river from the direction of the orchards on the far bank, horse's hooves dashing up spray, armour glinting dully in what had turned out to be bright sunlight. He spurred up the bank and into the midst of the regiment's officers, almost knocking one young lieutenant down. Tunny might have been amused, except there was something about Gorst that drained all the laughs from the world. He swung from the saddle, nimbly for all his bulk, lumbered straight up to Colonel Vallimir and gave a stiff salute.

Tunny tossed his brush down and took a few steps towards them, watching closely. Long years in the military had given him a razor-keen sense of when he was about to get fucked, and he was having a painful premonition right now. Gorst spoke for a few moments, face a blank slab. Vallimir shook an arm at the hill, then off to the west. Gorst spoke again. Tunny edged closer, trying to catch the details. Vallimir flung up his hands in frustration, then stalked over, shouting.

'First Sergeant Forest!'

'Sir.'

'Apparently there's a path through those bogs to our west.'

'Sir?'

'General Jalenhorm wants us to send the First Battalion through it. Make sure the Northmen can't use it against us.'

'The bog beyond the Old Bridge?'

'Yes.'

'We won't be able to get horses through that—'

'I know.'

'We only just got them back, sir.'

'I know.'

'But . . . what will we do with them in the meantime?'

'You'll just have to bloody well leave them here!' snapped Vallimir. 'Do you think I like sending half my regiment across a bloody bog without their horses? Do you?'

Forest worked his jaw, scar down his cheek shifting. 'No, sir.'

Vallimir strode away, beckoning over some of the officers. Forest stood a moment, rubbing fiercely at the back of his head.

'Corporal?' whispered Yolk, in a small voice.

'Yes?'

'Is this another example of everyone shitting on the head of the man below?'

'Very good, Yolk. We may make a soldier of you yet.'

Forest stopped in front of them, hands on hips, frowning off upriver. 'Seems the First Battalion have a mission.'

'Marvellous,' said Tunny.

'We'll be leaving our horses here and heading west to cross that bog.' A chorus of groans greeted him. 'You think I like it? Get packed and get moving!' And Forest stomped off to break the happy news elsewhere.

'How many men in the battalion?' muttered Lederlingen.

Tunny took a long breath. 'About five hundred when we left Adua. Currently four hundred, give or take a recruit or two.'

'Four hundred men?' said Klige. 'Across a bog?'

'What sort of a bog is it?' muttered Worth.

'A bog!' Yolk squealed, like a tiny, angry dog yapping at a bigger one. 'A bloody bog! A massive load of mud! What other sort of bog would it be?'

'But . . .' Lederlingen stared after Forest, and then at his horse, onto which he'd just loaded most of his gear and some of Tunny's. 'This is stupid.'

Tunny rubbed at his tired eyes with finger and thumb. How often had he had to explain this to a set of recruits? 'Look. You think how stupid people are most of the time. Old men drunk. Women at a village fair. Boys throwing stones at birds. Life. The foolishness and the vanity, the selfishness and the waste. The *pettiness,* the *silliness.* You think in a war it must be different. Must be better. With death around the corner, men united against hardship, the cunning of the enemy, people must think harder, faster, be . . . better. Be *heroic.*'

He started to heave his packages down from his horse's saddle. 'Only it's just the same. In fact, do you know, because of all that pressure, and worry, and fear, it's worse. There aren't many men who think clearest when the stakes are highest. So people are even stupider in a war than the rest of the time. Thinking about how they'll dodge the blame, or grab the glory, or save their skins, rather than about what will actually *work.* There's no job that forgives stupidity more than soldiering. No job that encourages it more.'

He looked at his recruits and found they were all staring back, horrified. Except for an oblivious Yolk, straining on tiptoe to get his spear down from his horse, perhaps the largest in the regiment. 'Never mind,' he snapped. 'This bog won't cross itself.' He turned his back on them, patted his horse gently on the neck and sighed. 'Oh well, old girl. Guess you'll have to manage a little longer without me.'

Cry Havoc and . . .

Scorry was cutting hair when Craw got back to his dozen, or the seven who were left, leastways. Eight including him. He wondered if there'd ever been a dozen that actually had the full twelve. Sure as hell his never had. Agrick sat on a fallen tree trunk all coated with ivy, frowning into nowhere as the shears snip-snipped around his face.

Whirrun was leaning against a tree, the Father of Swords stood up on its point and the hilt cradled in his folded arms. He'd stripped his shirt off for some reason and stood there in a leather vest, a big grey stain of old sweat down the front and his long, sinewy arms sticking out. Seemed as if the more dangerous things got the more clothes he liked to lose. Probably have his arse out by the time they were finished with this valley.

'Craw!' he shouted, lifting his sword and shaking it around.

'Hey, Chief.' Drofd sitting on a branch above with back against trunk. Whittling a stick for an arrow shaft, shavings fluttering down.

'Black Dow didn't kill you, then?' asked Wonderful.

'Not right on the spot, anyway.'

'Did he tell you what's to do?' Yon nodded towards the men crowding the woods all around. He had a lot less hair than when Craw left and it made him look older somehow, creases around his eyes and grey in his brows Craw never noticed before. 'I get the feeling Dow's planning to go.'

'That he is.' Craw winced as he squatted down in the brush, peering south. Seemed a different world out there beyond the treeline. All dark and comforting under the leaves. Quiet, like being sunk in cool water. All bathed in harsh sunlight outside. Yellow-brown barley under the blue sky, the Heroes bulging up vivid green from the valley, the old stones on top, still standing their pointless watch.

Craw pointed over to their left, towards Osrung, the town no more'n a hint of a high fence and a couple of grey towers over the crops. 'Reachey's going to move first, make a charge on Osrung.' He found he was whispering, even though the Union were a good few hundred strides away on top of a hill and could hardly have heard him if he screamed. 'He'll be carrying all the standards, make it look like that's the big push. Hope to draw some men down off the Heroes.'

'Reckon they'll fall for that?' asked Yon. 'Pretty thin, ain't it?'

Craw shrugged. 'Any trick looks thin to them who know it's coming.'

'Don't make too much difference whether they go or not, though.' Whirrun was stretching now, hanging from a tree branch, sword slung over his back. 'We still got the same hill to climb.'

'Might help if there's half as many Union at the top when we get there,' Drofd tossed down from his own perch.

'Let's hope they fall for it then, eh?' Craw moved his hand to the right, towards the field and pasture between Osrung and the Heroes. 'If they do send men down from the hill, that's when Golden's going with his horse. Catch those boys trousers down in the open and spill 'em all the way back to the river.'

'Drown those fuckers,' grunted Agrick, with rare bloodthirstiness.

'Meantime Dow's going to make the main effort. Straight at the Heroes, Ironhead and Tenways alongside with all their lads.'

'How's he going to work it?' asked Wonderful, rubbing at her new scar.

Craw gave her a look. 'Black Dow, ain't it? He's going to run up there head on and make mud of everything ain't mud already.'

'And us?'

Craw swallowed. 'Aye. We'll be along.'

'Front and centre, eh?'

'Up that bloody hill again?' growled Yon.

'Almost makes you wish we'd fought the Union for it last time,' said Whirrun, swinging from one branch to another.

Craw pointed to their right. 'Scale's over there in the woods under Salt Fell. Once Dow's made his move, he's going to charge his horsemen down the Ustred Road and snatch the Old Bridge. Him and Calder.'

Amazing how much Yon could disapprove with just a shake of his head. 'Your old mate Calder, eh?'

'That's right.' Craw looked straight at him. 'My old mate Calder.'

'Then this lovely valley and all its nothing much shall be ours!' sang Whirrun. 'Again.'

'Dow's, at any rate,' said Wonderful.

Drofd was counting the names off on his fingers. 'Reachey, Golden, Ironhead, Tenways, Scale and Dow himself . . . that's a lot o' men.'

Craw nodded. 'Might be the most ever fought for the North in one spot.'

'There's going to be quite a battle here,' said Yon. 'Quite the hell of a battle.'

'One for the songs!' Whirrun had hooked his legs over the branch and was hanging upside down now, for some reason best known to his self.

'We're going to make a right mess o' those Southerners.' Drofd didn't sound entirely convinced, though.

'By the dead, I hope so,' mouthed Craw.

Yon edged forwards. 'Did you get our gild, Chief?'

Craw winced. 'Dow weren't in the mood to bring it up.' There was a round of groans at that, just like he'd known there would be. 'I'll get it later, don't worry. It's owed and you'll get it. I'll talk to Splitfoot.'

Wonderful sucked her teeth. 'You'd be better trying to get sense from Whirrun than coin out o' Splitfoot.'

'I heard that!' called Whirrun.

'Think on this,' said Craw, slapping Yon's chest with the back of his hand. 'You get up that hill you'll be owed another gild. Two at once. Ain't going to be time to spend it now anyway, is there? We got a battle to fight.'

That much no one could argue with. Men were moving through the woods now, all geared-up and ready. Rustling and rattling, whispering and clattering, forming a kneeling line stretching off both ways between the tree trunks. Sunlight came ragged through the branches, patching on frowning faces, glinting on helmet and drawn sword.

'When were we last in a proper battle, anyway?' muttered Wonderful.

'There was that skirmish down near Ollensand,' said Craw.

Yon spat. 'Don't hardly call that proper.'

'Up in the High Places,' said Scorry, finishing the cutting and brushing the hair from Agrick's shoulders. 'Trying to prise Ninefingers out of that bloody crack of a valley.'

'Seven years ago, was it? Eight?' Craw shuddered at the memory of that nightmare, scores of fighters crowded into a gap in the rock so tight no one could hardly breathe, so tight no one could swing, just prick at each other, knee at each other, bite at each other. Never thought he'd come through that little slice of horror alive. Why the hell would a man choose to risk it again?

He looked at that shallow bowl of crop-filled country between the woods and the Heroes. Looked a bloody long way for an old man with more'n one dodgy leg to run. Glorious charges came up a lot in the songs, but there was one advantage to the defensive no one could deny – the enemy come to you. He shifted from one leg to the other, trying to find the best spot for his knee, and his ankle, and his hip, but a variety of agony was the best he could manage. He snorted to himself. True of life in general, that was.

He looked around to check his dozen were all ready. Got quite the shock to see Black Dow himself down on one knee in the ferns not ten strides distant, axe in one hand, sword in the other, Splitfoot and Shivers and his closest Carls at his back. He'd put aside his furs and finery and looked about like any other man in the line. Except for his fierce grin, like he was looking forward to this as much as Craw was wondering if there was a way free of it.

'Nobody get killed, aye?' He looked around 'em all as he pressed Scorry's hand. They all shook their heads, gave frowns or nervous grins, said 'no', or 'aye', or 'not me'. All except Brack, sat staring out towards the trees like he was on his own, sweat beading his big, pale face.

'Don't get killed, eh, Brack?'

The hillman looked at Craw as if he'd only just realised he was there. 'What?'

'You all right?'

'Aye.' Taking Craw's hand and giving it a clammy press. ''Course.'

'That leg good to run on?'

'I've had more pain taking a shit.'

Craw raised his brows. 'Well, a good shit can be quite punishing, can't it?'

'Chief.' Drofd nodded over towards the light beyond the trees and Craw hunched a little lower. There were men moving out there. Mounted men, though only their heads and shoulders showed from where Craw was crouching.

'Union scouts,' whispered Wonderful in his ear. Dogman's lads, maybe, worked their way through the fields and the farmhouses and were casting out towards the treeline. The forest the whole length of the valley was crawling with armed and armoured Northmen. It was a wonder they weren't seen yet.

Dow knew it, 'course. He coolly waved his axe over to the east, like he was asking for some beer to be brought over. 'Best tell Reachey to go, 'fore they spoil our surprise.' The word went out, that same gesture of Dow's arm copied down the line in a wave.

'Here we bloody go again, then,' grunted Craw between chewing on his nails.

'Here we go,' Wonderful forced through tight lips, sword drawn in her hand.

'I'm too old for this shit.'

'Yep.'

'Should've married Colwen.'

'Aye.'

'High time I retired.'

'True.'

'Could you stop fucking agreeing with me?'

'Ain't that the point of a Second? Support the Chief, no matter what! So I agree. You're too old and you should've married Colwen and retired.'

Craw sighed as he offered his hand. 'My thanks for your support.'

She gave it a squeeze. 'Always.'

The deep, low blast of Reachey's horn throbbed out from the east. Seemed to make the earth buzz, tickle at the roots of Craw's hair. More horns, then came the feet, like distant thunder mixed with metal. He strained forwards, peering between the black tree trunks, trying to get a glimpse of Reachey's men. Could hardly see more than a few of Osrung's roofs across the sun-drenched fields. Then the war cries started, floating out over the valley, echoing through the trees like ghosts. Craw felt his skin tingling, part fear at what was coming and part wanting to spring up and add his own voice to the clamour.

'Soon enough,' he whispered, licking his lips as he stood, hardly noticing the pain in his leg no more.

'I'd say so.' Whirrun came up beside him, Father of Swords drawn and held under the crosspiece, his other hand pointing towards the Heroes. 'Do you see that, Craw?' Looked like there might be men moving at the top of the green slopes. Gathering around a standard, maybe. 'They're coming down. Going to be a happy meeting with Golden's lads out in those fields, ain't it?' He gave his soft, high chuckle. 'A happy meeting.'

Craw slowly shook his head. 'Ain't you worried at all?'

'Why? Didn't I say? Shoglig told me the time and place of my death, and—'

'It's not here and it's not now, aye, only about ten thousand bloody times.' Craw leaned in to whisper. 'Did she tell you whether you'd get both your legs cut off here, though?'

'No, that she didn't,' Whirrun had to admit. 'But what difference would that make to my life, will you tell me? You can still sit around a fire and talk shit with no legs.'

'Maybe they'll cut your arms off too.'

'True. If that happens . . . I'll have to at least consider retirement. You're a good man, Curnden Craw.' And Whirrun poked him in the ribs. 'Maybe I'll pass the Father of Swords on to you, if you're still breathing when I cross to the distant shore.'

Craw snorted. 'I ain't carrying that bastard thing around.'

'You think I *chose* to carry it? Daguf Col picked me out for the task, on his death-pyre after the Shanka tore out his innards. Purplish.'

'What?'

'His innards. It has to go to someone, Craw. Ain't you the one always saying there's a right way to do things? Has to go to someone.'

They stood in silence for a moment longer, peering into the brightness beyond the trees, the wind stirring the leaves and making them rustle, shaking a few dry bits of green down onto the spears, and helmets, and shoulders of all those men kneeling in the brush. Birds chirping in the branches, tweet bloody tweet, and even quieter the distant screaming of Reachey's charge.

Men were moving on the eastern flank of the Heroes. Union men, coming down. Craw rubbed his sweaty palms together, and drew his sword. 'Whirrun.'

'Aye?'

'You ever wonder if Shoglig might've been wrong?'

'Every bloody fight I get into.'

Devoutly to be Wished

Y*our August Majesty,*
    General Jalenhorm's division has reached the town of Osrung, seized the crossings of the river with the usual focused competence, and the Sixth and Rostod Regiments have taken up a strong position on a hill the Northmen call the Heroes. From its summit one receives a commanding view of the country for miles around, including the all-important road north to Carleon, but, aside from a dead fire, we have seen no sign of the enemy.

The roads continue to be our most stubborn antagonists. The leading elements of General Mitterick's division have reached the valley, but become thoroughly entangled with the rearmost units of Jalenhorm's, making—

Gorst looked up sharply. He had caught the faintest hint of voices on the wind, and though he could not make out the words there was no mistaking a note of frantic excitement.

Probably deluding myself. I have a talent for it. There was no sign of excitement here behind the river. Men were scattered about the south bank, lazing in the sun while their horses grazed contentedly around them. One coughed on a chagga pipe. Another group were singing quietly as they passed around a flask. Not far away their commander, Colonel Vallimir, was arguing with a messenger over the precise meaning of General Jalenhorm's latest order.

'I see that, but the general asks you to hold your current position.'

'Hold, by all means, but on the road? Did he not mean for us to cross the river? Or at least arrange ourselves on the bank? I have lost one battalion across a bog and now the other is in everyone's way!' Vallimir pointed out a dust-covered captain whose company was stalled in grumbling column further down the road. Possibly one of the companies the regiments on the hill were missing. *Or not.* The captain was not offering the information and no one was seeking it out. 'The general cannot have meant for us to sit *here*, surely you see that!'

'I do see that,' droned the messenger, 'but the general asks you to hold your current position.'

Only the usual random incompetence. A team of bearded diggers tramped past in perfect unison, shovels shouldered and faces stern. *The most organised body of men I've seen today, and probably his Majesty's most valuable soldiers too.* The army's appetite for holes was insatiable. Fire-pits, grave-pits, latrine-pits, dugouts and dig-ins, ramparts and revetments, ditches and trenches of every shape, depth and purpose imaginable and some that would never come to you in a month of thinking. *Truly the spade is mightier than the sword. Perhaps, instead of blades, generals should wear gilded trowels as the badge of their vocation. So much for excitement.*

Gorst turned his attention back to his letter, wrinkled his lip as he realised he had made an unsightly inkblot and crumpled it angrily in his fist.

Then the wind wafted up again and carried more shouts to his ear. *Do I truly hear it? Or do I only want to so badly that I am imagining it?* But a few of the troopers around him were frowning up towards the hill as well. Gorst's heart was suddenly thumping, his mouth dry. He stood and walked towards the water like a man under a spell, eyes fixed on the Heroes. He thought he could see men moving there now, tiny figures on the hill's grassy flank.

He crunched down the shingle to where Vallimir was standing, still arguing pointlessly over which side of the river his men should be doing nothing on. *I suspect that might soon be irrelevant.* He prayed it would be.

'. . . But surely the general does not—'

'Colonel Vallimir.'

'What?'

'You should ready your men.'

'I should?'

Gorst did not for a moment take his eyes from the Heroes.

From the silhouettes of soldiers on the eastern slope. A considerable body of them. No messengers had crossed the shallows from Marshal Kroy. Which meant the only reason he could see for so many men to be leaving the hill was . . . *an attack by the Northmen elsewhere. An attack, an attack, an attack . . .*

He realised he was still gripping his half-finished letter white-knuckle hard. He let the crumpled paper flutter down into the river, to be carried spinning away by the current. More voices came, even more shrill than before, no question now that they were real.

'That sounds like shouting,' said Vallimir.

A fierce joy had begun to creep up Gorst's throat and made his voice rise higher than ever. He did not care. 'Get them ready now.'

'To do what?'

Gorst was already striding towards his horse. 'Fight.'

Casualties

Captain Lasmark thrashed through the barley at something between a brisk walk and a jog, the Ninth Company of the Rostod Regiment toiling after him as best they could, despatched towards Osrung with the ill-defined order to 'get at the enemy!' still ringing in their ears.

The enemy were before them now, all right. Lasmark could see scaling ladders against the mossy logs of the town's fence. He could see missiles flitting up and down. He could see standards flapping in the breeze, a ragged black one over all the rest, the standard of Black Dow himself, the Northern scouts had said. That was when General Jalenhorm had given the order to advance, and made it abundantly clear nothing would change his mind.

Lasmark turned, hoping he wouldn't trip and catch a mouthful of barley, and urged his men forward with what was intended to be a soldierly jerk of the hand.

'On! On! To the town!'

It was no secret General Jalenhorm was prone to poorly considered orders, but saying so would have been terrible form. Usually officers quietly ignored him where possible and creatively interpreted him where not. But there was no room for interpretation in a direct order to attack.

'Steady, men, keep even!'

They kept even to no noticeable degree, indeed in the main they appeared rather ragged and reluctant, and Lasmark could hardly blame them. He didn't much care for charging unsupported into an empty mass of barley himself, especially since a good part of the regiment was still clogged up in the shambles of men and equipment on the bad roads south of the river. But an officer has his duty. He had made representations to Major

Popol, and the major had made representations to Colonel Wetterlant of the Sixth, who was ranking officer on the hill. The colonel had appeared too busy to take much notice. The battlefield was no place for independent thought, Lasmark supposed, and perhaps his superiors simply knew better than he did.

Alas, experience did not support that conclusion.

'Careful! Watch the treeline!'

The treeline was some distance away to the north and seemed to Lasmark particularly gloomy and threatening. He did not care to imagine how many men could be concealed in its shadows. But then he thought that whenever he saw woods, and the North was bloody full of them. It was unclear what good watching them would do. Besides, there was no turning back now. On their right, Captain Vorna was urging his company ahead of the rest of the regiment, desperate to get into the action, as ever, so he could go home with a chestful of medals and spend the balance of his life boasting.

'That fool Vorna's going to pull us all out of formation,' growled Sergeant Lock.

'The captain is simply obeying orders!' snapped Lasmark and then, under his breath, 'The arsehole. Forward, men, at the double!' If the Northmen did come, the worst thing of all would be to leave gaps in the line.

They upped the pace, all tiring, men occasionally catching a boot and sprawling in the crops, their order fraying with every stride. They might have been half way between the hill and the town now, Major Popol in the lead on horseback, waving his sabre and bellowing inaudible encouragements.

'Sir!' roared Lock. 'Sir!'

'I bloody know,' gasped Lasmark, no breath to spare for moaning now, 'I can't hear a word he's . . . oh.'

He saw what Lock was desperately stabbing towards with his drawn sword and felt a horrible wave of cold surprise. There is a gulf of difference, after all, between expecting the worst and seeing it happen. Northmen had broken from the woods and were rushing across the pastures towards them. It was hard to tell how many from this angle – the dipping ground was cut up by ditches and patchy hedgerows – but Lasmark felt himself go colder yet as his eyes registered the width of their front, the glimmer of metal, the dots of colour that were their painted shields.

The Rostod Regiment was outnumbered. Several companies were still following Popol blithely off towards Osrung where even more Northmen waited. Others had stopped, aware of the approaching threat on their left and seeking desperately to form lines. The Rostod Regiment was heavily outnumbered, and out of formation, and caught unsupported in the open.

'Halt!' he screamed, rushing into the barley ahead of his company, spinning about and throwing his arms up at his men. 'Form line! Facing north!' That was the best thing to do, wasn't it? What else could they do? His soldiers began to perform a shambolic mockery of a wheel, some faces purposeful, others panicked as they scrambled into position.

Lasmark drew his sword. He'd picked it up cheap, an antique, really, the hilt was prone to rattle. He'd paid less for it than he had for his dress hat. That seemed a foolish decision now. But then one sword looked much like another and Major Popol had been very particular about the appearance of his officers on parade. They were not on parade now, more the pity. Lasmark glanced over his shoulder, found he was chewing so hard at his lip he could taste blood. The Northmen were closing swiftly. 'Archers, ready your bows, spearmen to the—'

The words froze in his throat. Cavalry had emerged from behind a village even further to their left. A considerable body of cavalry, bearing down on their flank, hooves threshing up a pall of dust. He heard the gasps of alarm, felt the mood shift from worried resolve to horror.

'Steady!' he shouted, but his own voice quavered. When he turned, many of his men were already running. Even though there was nowhere to run to. Even though their chances running were even worse than they were fighting. A calm assessment of the odds was evidently not foremost in their minds. He saw the other companies falling apart, scattering. He caught a glimpse of Major Popol bouncing in his saddle as he rode full tilt for the river, no longer interested in presentation. Perhaps if captains had horses Lasmark would have been right beside him. But captains didn't get horses. Not in the Rostod Regiment. He really should have joined a regiment where the captains got horses, but then he could never have afforded one. He'd had to borrow the money to purchase his captaincy at an outrageous interest and had nothing to spare . . .

The Northmen were already horrifyingly close, breaking through the nearest hedgerow. He could pick out faces across their line. Snarling, screaming, grinning faces. Like animals, weapons raised high as they bounded on through the barley. Lasmark took a few steps backwards without thinking. Sergeant Lock stood beside him, his jaw muscles clenched.

'Shit, sir,' he said.

Lasmark could only swallow and ready himself as his men flung down their weapons around him. As they turned and ran for the river or the hill, too far, far too far away. As the makeshift line of his company and the company beside them dissolved leaving only a few knots of the most stunned and hard-bitten to face the Northmen. He could see how many there were, now. Hundreds of them. Hundreds upon hundreds. A flung spear impaled a man beside him with a thud, and he fell screaming. Lasmark stared at him for a moment. Stelt. He'd been a baker.

He looked up at the tide of howling men, open-mouthed. You hear about this kind of thing, of course, but you assume it won't happen to you. You assume you're more important than that. He'd done none of the things he'd promised himself he'd do by the time he was thirty. He wanted to drop his sword and sit down. Caught sight of his ring and lifted his hand to look at it. Emlin's face carved into the stone. Didn't look likely he'd be coming back for her now. Probably she'd marry that cousin of hers after all. Marrying cousins, a deplorable business.

Sergeant Lock charged forward, wasted bravery, hacked a lump from the edge of a shield. The shield had a bridge painted on it. He chopped at it again, just as another Northman ran up and hit him with an axe. He was knocked sideways, then back the other way by a sword that left a long scratch across his helmet and a deep cut across his face. He spun, arms up like a dancer, then was barged over in the rush and lost in the barley.

Lasmark sprang at the shield with the bridge, for some reason barely taking note of the man behind it. Perhaps he wanted to pretend there was no man behind it. His sword instructor would have been livid with him. Before he got there a spear caught his breastplate, sent him stumbling. The point scraped past and he swung at the man who thrust it, an ugly-looking fellow with a badly broken nose. The sword split his skull open and brains flew out. It was surprisingly easy to do. Swords are heavy and sharp, he supposed, even cheap ones.

There was a clicking sound and everything turned over, mud thumped and barley tangled him. One of his eyes was dark. There was a ringing, stupidly loud, as if his head was the clapper in a great bell. He tried to get up but the world was spinning. None of the things he'd promised to do by the time he was thirty. Oh. Except join the army.

The Southerner tried to push himself up and Lightsleep knocked him on the back of the head with his mace and bonked his helmet in. One boot kicked a little and he was done.

'Lovely.' The rest of the Union men were all surrounded and going down fast or scattering like a flock o' starlings, just like Golden said they would. Lightsleep knelt, tucked his mace under his arm and started trying to twist a nice-looking ring off the dead Southerner's finger. Couple of other lads were claiming their prizes, one was screaming with blood running down his face, but, you know, it's a battle, ain't it? If everyone came out smiling there'd be no point. Away south Golden's riders were mopping up, driving the fleeing Southerners to the river.

'Turn for the hill!' Scabna was bellowing, pointing at it with his axe, the smug arse. 'To the hill, you bastards!'

'You turn for the hill,' grunted Lightsleep, legs still sore from all that running, throat sore from all that screaming besides. 'Hah!' Finally got the Union lad's ring off. Held it up to the light and frowned. Just some polished rock with a face cut into it, but he guessed it might fetch a couple of silvers. Tucked it into his jerkin. Took the lad's sword for good measure and stuck it through his belt, though it was a light little toothpick of a thing and the hilt rattled.

'Get on!' Scabna dragged one scavenger up and booted him in the arse to set him going. 'Bloody get on!'

'All right, all right!' Lightsleep jogged on after the others, towards the hill. Upset at not getting the chance to go through the Southerner's pockets, maybe get his boots off. It'd all be swept by the pickers and the women following after now. Beggar bastards too cowardly to fight, turning a profit out of other men's work. A disgrace, but he guessed there was no stopping it. Facts of life, like flies and bad weather.

There were Union men up on the Heroes, he could see metal glinting round the drystone wall near the top, spears pricking the sky. He kept his shield up, peering over the rim. Didn't want to get stuck with one of those evil little arrows they used. Get stuck with one o' those, you won't never get yourself unstuck.

'Will you look at that,' Scabna grunted.

Now they'd climbed a little higher they could see all the way to the woods up north, and the land between was full of men. Black Dow's Carls, and Tenways', and Ironhead's too. Thralls surging after. Thousands of 'em, all streaming across towards the Heroes. Lightsleep had never seen so many fighters in one place, not even when he fought with Bethod's army. Not at the Cumnur, or Dunbrec, or in the High Places. He'd half a mind to let 'em take the Heroes while he hung back, maybe pleading a twisted ankle, but he weren't going to raise a sharp dowry for his daughters on a cheap ring and a little sword, now, was he?

They hopped over a ditch patched with brown puddles and were out of the trampled crops at the foot of the slope. 'Up the hill, you bastards!' screeched Scabna, waving his axe.

Lightsleep had swallowed about enough of that fool's carping, only Chief 'cause he was some friend to one of Golden's sons. He twisted sideways, snarling, 'You get up the fucking hill, you—'

There was a thud and an arrowhead stuck out of his jerkin. He spent a silent moment just staring at it, then he took a great whooping breath in and screamed. 'Ah, *fuck*!' He whimpered, shuddered, pain stabbing into his armpit as he tried to breathe again, coughed blood down his front, dropped on his knees.

Scabna stared at him, shield up to cover them both. 'Lightsleep, what the hell?'

'Bloody . . . I'm stuck right . . . through.' He had to spit blood out, gurgling with every word. He couldn't kneel any more, it was hurting him too much. He slumped over on his side. Seemed a shitty way to go back to the mud, but maybe they all are. Boots hammered around him as men started thumping up that hill, spraying spots of dirt in his face.

Scabna knelt, started to unbutton Lightsleep's jerkin. 'Let's have a look here.'

Lightsleep couldn't move hardly. Everything was going blurry. 'By the . . . dead, it . . . hurts.'

'Bet it does. Where did you put that ring?'

Gaunt lowered his bow, watched a few Northmen in the crowd topple over as the rest of the volley flickered down into them. From this height, the bolts from a heavy flatbow could split their shields and punch through chain mail easily as a lady's gown. One of them threw his weapons down and ran off hooting, clutching his stomach, left a gently curving trail through the crops. Gaunt had no way of knowing if his own bolt had found a mark or not, but it hardly mattered. It was all about quantity. Crank, load, level, shoot, crank, load . . .

'Come on, lads!' he shouted at the men around him. 'Shoot! Shoot!'

'By the Fates,' he heard Rose whisper, voice all choked off, pointing a wavering forefinger towards the north. The enemy were still pouring from the trees in fearsome numbers. The fields were crawling with them already, surging south towards the hill in a dully twinkling tide. But it took more than a pack of angry apes to make Sergeant Gaunt nervy. He'd watched the number-less Gurkish charge their little hill at Bishak and he'd cranked his flatbow just as hard as he could for the best part of an hour and in the end he'd watched them all run back again. Apart from those they left peppered in heaps. He grabbed Rose by the shoulder and steered him back to the wall.

'Never mind about that. The next bolt is all that matters.'

'Sergeant.' And Rose bent over his bow again, pale but set to his task.

'Crank, lads, crank!' Gaunt turned his own at a nice, measured pace, all oiled and clean and working smoothly. Not too fast, not too slow, making sure he did the job right. He fished out another bolt, frowning to himself. No more than ten left in his quiver. 'What happened to that ammunition?' he roared over his shoulder, and then at his own people, 'Pick your targets, nice and careful!' And he stood, levelled his bow, stock pressing into his shoulder.

The sight below gave a moment's pause, even to a man of his experience. The foremost Northmen had reached the hill and were charging up, slowing on the grassy slope but showing no sign of stopping. Their war cry got worryingly louder as he came up from behind the wall, the vague keening becoming a shrill howl.

He gritted his teeth, aiming low. Squeezed the trigger, felt the jolt, string humming. He saw where this one went, thudding straight into a shield and knocking the man who held it over backwards. Rattle and pop as a dozen or more bows went on his left, two or three Northmen dropping, one shot in the face, going over backwards and his axe spinning into the blue sky.

'That's the recipe, lads, keep shooting! Just load and—' There was a loud click beside him. Gaunt felt a searing pain in his neck, and all the strength went out of his legs.

It was an accident. Rose had been tinkering with the trigger of his flatbow for a week or longer, trying to stop it wobbling, worried it might go off at the wrong moment, but he'd never been any good with machines. Why they'd made him a bowman he'd no clue. Would have been better off with a spear. Sergeant Gaunt would have been a lot better off if they'd given Rose a spear, that was a fact most definite. It just went off as he was lifting it, the point of the metal lath leaving a long scratch down his arm. As he was cursing at that, he looked sideways, and Gaunt had the bolt through his neck.

They stared at each other for a moment, then Gaunt's eyes rolled down, crossed, towards the flights, and he dropped his own bow and reached up to his neck. His quivering fingers came away bloody. 'Gurgh,' he said. 'Bwuthers.' And his lids flickered, and he dropped all of a sudden, his skull smacking against the wall and knocking his helmet skewed across his face.

'Gaunt? Sergeant Gaunt?' Rose slapped his cheek as though trying to wake him from an unauthorised nap, smeared blood across his face. There was more and more blood welling out of him all the time. Out of his nose, out of the neat slit where the bolt entered his neck. Oily dark, almost black, and his skin so white.

'He's dead!' Rose felt himself dragged towards the wall.

Someone shoved his empty flatbow back into his bloody hands. 'Shoot, damn you! Shoot!' A young officer, one of the new ones, Rose couldn't remember his name. Could hardly remember his own name.

'What?'

'Shoot!'

Rose started cranking, aware of other men around him doing the same. Sweating, struggling, cursing, leaning over the wall to shoot. He could hear wounded men screaming, and above that a strange howl. He fumbled a bolt from his quiver, slotted it into the groove, cursing to himself at his trembling fingers, all smeared pink from Gaunt's blood.

He was crying. There were tears streaming down his face. His hands felt very cold, though it wasn't cold. His teeth were chattering. The man beside him threw down his bow and ran towards the top of the hill. There were a lot of men running, ignoring the desperate bellows of their officers.

Arrows flitted down. One went spinning from a steel cap just beside him. Others stuck into the hillside behind the wall. Silent, still, as if they'd suddenly sprung from the ground by magic rather than dropped from the sky. Someone else turned to run, but before he got a step the officer cut him down with his sword.

'For the king!' he squealed, his eyes gone all mad. 'For the king!'

Rose had never seen the king. A Northman jumped up on the wall just to his left. He was stabbed with two spears right away, screamed and fell back. The man beside Rose stood, cursing as he raised his flatbow. The top of his head came off and he stumbled, shot his bolt high into the sky. A Northman sprang over the wall into the gap he left, young-looking, face all twisted up with rage. A devil, screaming like a devil. A Union man came at him with a spear but he turned it away with his shield, swung as he dropped from the wall, axe blade thudding into the man's shoulder and sending blood flying in dark streaks. Northmen were coming over the wall all around. The gap to their left was choked with straining bodies, a tangle of spears, slipping boots ripping at the muddy grass.

Rose's head was full of mad noise, clash and clatter of weapons and armour, war cries and garbled orders and howls of pain all mingled with his own terrified, whimpering breath. He was just staring, bow forgotten. The young Northerner blocked the officer's sword and hit him in the side, twisted him up, chopped into his arm on the next blow, hand flying up bonelessly in its embroidered sleeve. The Northman kicked the officer's legs away and hacked at him on the ground, grin speckled with blood. Another was clambering over the wall beside him, a big face with a black and grey beard, shouting something in a gravelly voice.

A great tall one with long bare arms leaped clean over the jumble of stones, boots flicking at the grass that sprouted from the top, the biggest sword Rose had ever seen raised high. He didn't see how a man could swing a sword so big. The dull blade took an archer in the side, folded him up and sent him tumbling across the hillside in a mist of blood. It was as if Rose's limbs came suddenly unstuck and he turned and ran, was jostled by someone else doing the same, slipped, ankle twisting. He scrambled up, took one lurching stride, and was hit so hard on the back of his head he bit his tongue off.

Agrick hacked the archer between the shoulder-blades to make sure, haft jolting in his raw hand, sticky with blood. He saw Whirrun struggling with a big Union man, hit him in the back of the leg with his axe, made a mess of it and only caught him with the flat, still hard enough to bring him down where Scorry could spear him as he slipped over the wall.

Agrick never saw Union men in numbers before, and they all looked the same, like copies o' one man with the same armour, the same jackets, the same weapons. It was like killing one man over and over. Hardly like killing real people at all. They were running, now, up the slope, scattering from the wall, and he ran after like a wolf after sheep.

'Slow down, Agrick, you mad bastard!' Jolly Yon, wheezing at his back, but Agrick couldn't stop. The charge was a great wave and all he could do was be carried along by it, forwards, upwards, get at them who'd killed his brother. On up the hill, Whirrun at the wall behind, the Father of Swords cutting into a knot of Southerners still standing, hacking 'em apart, armour or not. Brack near him, roaring as he swung his hammer.

'On! Fucking on!' Black Dow himself, lips curled from bloody teeth, shaking his axe at the summit, blade flashing red and steel in the sun. Lit a fire in Agrick knowing his leader was there, fighting beside him in the front rank. He came up level with a stumbling Union man, clawing at the slope, hit him in the face with his axe and knocked him shrieking back.

He burst between two of the great stones, head spinning like he was drunk. Blood-drunk, and needing more. Lots of corpses in the circle of grass inside the Heroes. Union men hacked in the back, Northmen stuck with arrows.

Someone shouted, and flatbows clattered, and a few dropped around him but Agrick ran right on, towards a flag in the middle of the Union line, voice hoarse from screaming. He chopped an archer down, broken bow tumbling. Swung at the big Southerner carrying the standard. He caught Agrick's first blow with the flagstaff, got it tangled with the blade. Agrick let go, pulled out his knife and stabbed the standard-bearer overhand though the open face of his helmet. He dropped like a hammered cow, mouth yawning all twisted and silent. Agrick tried to drag the standard from his dead-gripping fists, one hand on the pole, the other on the flag itself.

He heard himself make a weird whoop, sounded like someone else's voice. A half-bald man with grey hair round his ears pulled his arm back and his sword slid out of Agrick's side, scraping the bottom rim of his shield. It had been in him right to the hilt, the blade came out all bloody. Agrick tried to swing his axe but he'd dropped it just before and his knife was stuck in the standard-bearer's face, he just flapped his empty hand around. Something hit him in the shoulder and the world reeled.

He was lying in some dirt. A pile of trampled dirt, in the shadow of one of the stones. He had the torn flag in one hand.

He wriggled, but he couldn't get comfortable.

All numb.

Colonel Wetterlant was still having trouble believing it, but it appeared the King's Own Sixth Regiment was in a great deal of difficulty. The wall, he thought, was lost. Knots of resistance but basically overrun, and Northmen were flooding into the circle of stones from the north. Where else would Northmen come from? It had all happened so damnably fast.

'We have to withdraw!' screamed Major Culfer over the din of combat. 'There are too many of them!'

'No! General Jalenhorm will bring reinforcements! He promised us—'

'Then where the hell is he?' Culfer's eyes were bulging. Wetterlant would never have had him down as the panicky type. 'He's left us here to die, he's—'

Wetterlant simply turned away. 'We stand! We stand and fight!' He was a proud man of a proud family, and he would stand. He would stand until the bitter end, if necessary, and die fighting with sword in hand, as his grandfather was said to have done. He would die under the regimental colours. Well, he wouldn't, in fact, because that boy he ran through had torn them from the pole when he fell. But Wetterlant would stand, there was no question. He had often told himself so. Usually while admiring his reflection in the mirror after dressing for one official function or another. Straightening his sash.

These were very different circumstances, however, it had to be admitted. No one was wearing a sash, not even him. And there was the blood, the corpses, the spreading panic. The unearthly wailing of the Northmen, who were flooding through the gaps between the stones and into the trampled circle of grass at their centre. Virtually a constant press of them now, as far as Wetterlant could see. The difficulty with a ring of standing stones as a defensive position is undoubtedly the gaps between them. The Union line, if you could use the phrase about an improvised clump of soldiers and officers fighting desperately wherever they stood, was bulging back under the pressure, in imminent danger of dissolving all together, and with nowhere defensible to dissolve back to.

Orders. He was in command, and had to give orders. 'Er!' he shouted, brandishing his sword. 'Er . . .' It had all happened so very, very fast. What orders would Lord Marshal Varuz have given at a time like this? He had always admired Varuz. Unflappable.

Culfer gave a thin scream. A narrow split had appeared in his shoulder, right down to his chest, splinters of white bone showing through it. Wetterlant wanted to tell him not to scream in a manner so unbefitting of an officer in the King's Own. A scream like that might be good enough for one of the levy regiments, but in the Sixth he expected a manly roar. Culfer almost gracefully subsided to the ground, blood bubbling from the wound, and a large Northman stepped up with an axe in his fist and began to cleave him into pieces.

Wetterlant was vaguely conscious that he should have jumped to the aid of his second-in-command. But he found himself unable to move, fascinated by the Northman's expression of businesslike calm. As if he was a bricklayer getting a difficult stretch of wall to meet his high standards. Eventually satisfied by the number of pieces he had made of Culfer – who still, impossibly, seemed to be making a quiet squealing sound – the Northman turned to look at Wetterlant.

The far side of his face was crossed by a giant scar, a bright ball of dead metal in his eye socket.

Wetterlant ran. There was not the slightest thought involved. His mind was turned off like a candle snuffed out. He ran faster than he had in thirty years or more, faster than he thought a man of his years possibly could. He sprang between two of the ancient stones and jolted down the hillside, boots thrashing at the grass, vaguely conscious of other men running all around him, of screams and hisses and threats, of arrows whipping through the air about his head, shoulders itching with the inevitability of death at his back.

He passed the Children, then a column of dumbstruck soldiers who had been on their way up the hill and were just now scattering back down it. His foot found a small depression and the shock made his knee buckle. He bit his tongue, flew headlong, hit the ground and tumbled over and over, no way of stopping himself. He slid into shadow, finally coming to an ungainly stop in a shower of leaves, twigs, dirt.

He rolled stiffly over, groaning. His sword was gone, his right hand red raw. Twisted from his grip as he fell. The blade his father had given him the day he received his commission in the King's Own. So proud. He wondered if his father would have been proud now. He was in among trees. The orchard? He had abandoned his regiment. Or had they abandoned him? The rules of military behaviour, so unshakeable a foundation until a few moments ago, had vanished like smoke in a breeze. It had happened so fast.

His wonderful Sixth Regiment, his life's work, built out of copious polish, and rigorous drill, and unflinching discipline, utterly shattered in a few insane moments. If any survived it would be those who had chosen to run first. The rawest recruits and most craven cowards. And he was one of them. His first instinct was to ask Major Culfer for his opinion. He almost opened his mouth to do it, then realised the man had been butchered by a lunatic with a metal eye.

He heard voices, the sounds of men crashing through the trees, shrank against the nearest trunk, peering around it like a scared child over their bedclothes. Union soldiers. He shuddered with relief, stumbled from his hiding place, waving one arm.

'You! Men!'

They snapped around, but not at attention. In fact they stared at him as if he was a ghost risen from a grave. He thought he knew their faces, but it seemed they had turned suddenly from the most disciplined of soldiers into trembling, mud-smeared animals. Wetterlant had never been afraid of his own men before, had taken their obedience entirely for granted, but he had no choice but to blather on, his voice shrill with fear and exhaustion.

'Men of the Sixth! We must hold here! We must—'

'Hold?' one of them screeched, and hit Wetterlant with his sword. Not a full-blooded blow, only a jarring knock in the arm that sent him sliding onto his side, gasping more from shock than pain. He cringed as the soldier half-raised the sword again. Then one of the others squealed and scrambled away, and soon they were all running. Wetterlant looked over his shoulder, saw shapes moving through the trees. Heard shouting. A deep voice, and the words were in Northern.

Fear clutched him again and he whimpered, floundered through the slick of twigs and fallen leaves, the slime of rotten fruit smeared up his trouser leg, his own terrified breath echoing in his ears. He paused at the edge of the trees, the back of one sleeve pressed to his mouth. There was blood on his dangling hand. Seeing the torn cloth on his arm made him want to be sick. Was it torn cloth, or torn flesh?

He could not stay here. He would never make it to the river.

But he could not stay here. It had to be now. He broke from the undergrowth, running for the shallows. There were other runners everywhere, most of them without weapons. Mad, desperate faces, eyes rolling. Wetterlant saw the cause of their terror. Horsemen. Spread out across the fields, converging on the shallows, herding the fleeing Union soldiers southwards. Cutting them down, trampling them, their howls echoing across the valley. He ran on, ran on, stumbling forwards, snatched another look. A rider was bearing down on him, he could see the curve of his teeth in a tangled beard.

Wetterlant tried to run faster but he was so tired. Lungs burning, heart burning, breath whooping, the land jerking and see-sawing wildly with every step, the glittering hint of the shallows getting gradually closer, the thunder of hooves behind him—

And he was suddenly on his side, in the mud, an unspeakable agony burning out from his back. A crushing pressure on his chest as if there were rocks piled on it. He managed to move his head to look down. There was something glinting there. Something shining on his jacket in the midst of the dirt. Like a medal. But he hardly deserved a medal for running away.

'How silly,' he wheezed, and the words tasted like blood. He found to his surprise, and then to his mounting horror, that he could not breathe. It had all happened so very, very fast.

Sutt Brittle tossed the splintered shaft of his spear away. The rest was stuck in the back of that running fool. He'd run fast, for an old man, but not near as fast as Sutt's horse, which was no surprise. He hauled the old sword out, keeping the reins in his shield hand, and dug in his heels. Golden had promised a hundred gold coins to the first of his Named Men across the river, and Brittle wanted that money. Golden had showed it, in an iron box. Let 'em feel it, even, everyone's eyes on fire with looking at it. Strange coins, a head stamped on each side. Came from the desert, far away, someone had said. Sutt didn't know how Glama Golden came by desert coins, but he couldn't say he much cared either.

Gold was gold.

And this was almost too easy. The Union ran – knackered,

stumbling, crying, and Sutt just leaned from the saddle and chopped 'em down, one side then t'other, whack, whack, whack. It was this Sutt got into the business for, not the skulking around and scouting they'd been doing, the pulling back over and over, trying to find the right spot and never getting there. He hadn't joined the grumblers, though, not him. He'd said Black Dow would bring 'em a red day afore too long, and here it was.

All the killing was slowing him down, though. Frowning over into the wind on his left he saw he weren't quite at the front of the pack no more. Feathers had pulled ahead, bent low over his saddle, not bothering about the work and just riding straight through the rabbiting Southerners and down the bank into the shallows.

Sutt was damned if he was going to let a liar like Hengul Feathers steal his hundred coins. He dug his heels harder, wind and mane whipping at his eyes, tongue wedged into the big gap in his teeth. He plunged down into the river, water showering, Union men flailing up to their hips around him. He urged his horse on, eyes for nothing but Feathers' back as he trotted up onto the shingle and—

Went flying out of his saddle, war whoop cut off in a spray of blood.

Brittle weren't sure whether to be pleased or not as Feathers' corpse flopped over and over into the water. On the sunny side it looked like he was at the front of Golden's whole crew now. On the shady, there was a strange-looking bastard bearing down on him, well armoured and well horsed, short sword and the reins in one hand, long sword ready in the other, catching the sun and glistening with Feathers' blood. He had a plain round helmet with a slot in the front to see through and nothing but a big mouthful of gritted teeth showing below it. Riding at Golden's cavalry all on his own while the rest of the Union fled the other way.

In the midst of all Sutt's greed and bloodlust he felt this niggling moment of doubt made him check his horse to the right, get his shield between him and this steel-headed bastard. Just as well, 'cause a twinkling later his sword crashed into Sutt's shield and nearly ripped it off his arm. The shorter one came stabbing at him before the noise had faded, would've stuck him right in the chest if his own sword hadn't got in the way by blind chance.

By the dead he was fast, this bastard. Sutt couldn't believe how fast he was in all that armour. The swords came flickering out of nowhere. Sutt managed to block the short blade, the force of it near dumping him from the saddle. Tried to swing himself as he rocked back, screaming at the top of his lungs. 'Die, you fuck-ing— Uh?' His right hand wasn't there. He stared at the stump, blood squirting out of it. How had that happened? He saw something at the corner of his eye, felt a great crunching in his chest, and his howl of pain was cut off in a squawk of his own.

He was flung straight out of his saddle, no breath in him, and splashed down in the cold water where there was nothing but bubbles gurgling around his face.

Even before the gap-toothed Northman had toppled from his horse, Gorst had twisted in his saddle and brought his long steel blurring down on the other side. The next one had a patchy fur across his shoulders, managed to raise his axe to parry, but it was wasted effort. Gorst's blow splintered the haft and drove the pick on the back deep into him below the collarbone, the point of Gorst's long steel opening a gaping red wound in his neck. *A touch to me.*

The man was just opening his mouth, presumably to scream, when Gorst stabbed him through the side of the head with his short steel so the point came out of his cheek. *And another.* Gorst wrenched it free in time to deflect a sword with his buckler, shrug the blade harmlessly off his armoured shoulder. Someone clutched at him. Gorst smashed his nose apart with the pommel of his long steel. Smashed it again and drove it deep into his head.

They were all around him. The world was a strip of brightness through the slot in his helmet filled with plunging horses, and flailing men, and flashing weapons, his own swords darting by instinct to block, chop, stab, jerking the reins at the same time and dragging his panicked mount about in mindless circles. He swatted another man from his saddle, twisted chain-mail rings flying like dust from a beaten carpet. He parried a sword and the tip glanced from his helmet and made his ears ring. Before its owner could swing again he was cut across the back and fell shrieking forward. Gorst caught him in a hug and bundled him down among the thrashing hooves.

Union cavalry were splashing through the shallows around him, meeting the Northmen as they charged in from the north bank and mingling in a clattering, shattering melee. Vallimir's men. *How nice that you could join us!* The river became a mass of stomping hooves and spray, flying metal and blood, and Gorst hacked his way through it, teeth ground together in a frozen smile. *I am home.*

He lost his short steel in the madness, stuck in someone's back and wrenched from his hand. It might have been a Union man. He was a long way from caring. He could scarcely hear a thing apart from his own breath, his own grunts, his own girlish squeaks as he swung, and swung, and swung, denting armour, smashing bone, splitting flesh, every jolting impact up his arm a burning thrill. Every blow like a swallow to a drunkard, better, and better, but never enough.

He chopped a horse's head half-off. The Northman riding it had a look of comical surprise, a clown in a cheap stage show, still pulling at the reins as his flopping mount collapsed under him. A rider squealed, hands full of his own guts. Gorst backhanded him across the head with his buckler and it tore from his fist with a crash of steel and flew into the air in a fountain of blood and bits of teeth, spinning like a flipped coin. *Heads or tails? Anyone?*

A big Northman sat on a black horse in the midst of the river, chopping around him with an axe. His horned helmet, his armour, his shield, all chased with whorls of gold. Gorst spurred straight through the combat at him, hacking a Northman across the back as he went and dumping another from the saddle by chopping into his horse's hind leg. His long steel was bright red with blood. Slathered with it, like an axle with grease.

It caught the golden shield with a shattering impact, left a deep dent through all that pretty craftsmanship. Gorst chopped at it again and crossed the one scar with another, sent the golden man lurching in his saddle. Gorst lifted his long steel for a finishing blow then felt it suddenly twisted from his hand.

A Northman with a shaggy red beard had knocked it away with a mace and now swung it at Gorst's head. *Bloody rude.* Gorst caught the shaft in one hand, pulled out his dagger in the other and rammed it up under the Northman's jaw to the crosspiece, left it stuck there as he toppled backwards. *Manners, manners.* The golden man had his balance back, standing in the stirrups with his axe raised high.

Gorst clutched hold of him, dragged him into an ungainly embrace between their two jostling horses. The axe came down but the shaft caught Gorst's shoulder and the blade only scraped harmlessly against his back-plate. Gorst caught one of the absurd horns on the man's gilded helmet and twisted it, twisted it, twisting his head with it until it was pressed against Gorst's breastplate. The golden man snarled and spluttered, most of the way out of his saddle, one leg caught in his stirrup. He tried to drop his axe and wrestle but it was on a loop around his wrist, snagged on Gorst's armour, his other arm trapped by his battered shield.

Gorst bared his teeth, raised his fist and started punching the man in the face, his gauntlet crunching against one side of the golden helmet. Up and down, up and down, his fist was a hammer and gradually it marked, then dented, then twisted the helmet out of shape until one side of it dug into the man's face. *Even better than the sword.* Crunch, crunch, and it bent further, cutting into his cheek. *More personal.* No need for discussion or justification, for introductions or etiquette, for guilt or excuses. Only the incredible release of violence. So powerful that he felt this golden-armoured man must be his best friend in all the world. *I love you. I love you, and that is why I must smash your head apart.* He was laughing as he pounded his gauntleted knuckles into the man's bloody-blond moustache again. Laughing and crying at once.

Then something hit him in the backplate with a dull clang, his head snapped back and he was out of the saddle, jostled upside down between their two horses, gripped by cold and his helmet full of bubbling river. He came up coughing, water sprayed in his face by thrashing hooves.

The man in the golden armour had floundered to a riderless horse and was dragging himself drunkenly into the saddle. There were corpses everywhere: horses and men, Union and Northman, sprawled on the shingle, bobbing in the ford, carried gently by the soft current. He hardly saw any Union cavalry left. Only Northmen, weapons raised, nudging their horses cautiously towards him.

Gorst fumbled with the buckle on his helmet and dragged it off, the wind shockingly cold on his face. He clambered to his feet, armour leaden with river water. He held his arms out, as if to embrace a dear friend, and smiled as the nearest Northman raised his sword.

'I am ready,' he whispered.

'Shoot!' There was a volley of clicks and rattles behind him. The Northman toppled from his saddle, stuck through with flatbow bolts. Another shrieked, axe tumbling as he clapped his hand to a bolt in his cheek. Gorst turned, stupidly, to look over his shoulder. The south bank of the shallows was one long row of kneeling flatbowmen. Another rank stepped between them as they started to reload, knelt and levelled their bows with mechanical precision.

A big man sat on a large grey at the far end of the line. General Jalenhorm. 'Second rank!' he roared, slashing his hand down. 'Shoot!' Gorst ducked on an instinct, head whipping around as he followed the bolts flickering overhead and into the Northmen, already turning their horses to flee, men and beasts screaming and snorting as they dropped in the shallows.

'Third rank! Shoot!' The hiss and twitter of another volley. A few more fell peppered, one horse rearing and going over backwards, crushing its rider. But most of the rest had made it up the bank and were away into the barley on the other side, tearing off to the north as quickly as they had arrived.

Gorst slowly let his arms drop as the sound of hooves faded and left, aside from the chattering of the water and the moaning of the wounded, an uncanny silence.

Apparently the engagement was over, and he was still alive.

How strangely disappointing.

The Better Part of Valour

By the time Calder pulled up his horse some fifty paces from the Old Bridge, the fighting was over. Not that he was shedding too many tears for having missed his part in it. That had been the point of hanging back.

The sun was starting to sink in the west and the shadows were stretching out towards the Heroes, insects floating lazily above the crops. Calder could almost have convinced himself he was out for an easy ride in the old days, son of the King of the Northmen and master of all he saw. Except for the few corpses of men and horses scattered on the track, one Union soldier spreadeagled on his face with a spear sticking straight up from his back, the dust underneath him stained dark.

It looked like the Old Bridge – a moss-crusted double span of ancient stone that looked as if it was about to collapse under its own weight – had been only lightly held, and when the Union men saw their fellows fleeing from the Heroes they'd pulled back to the other bank just as quickly as ever they could. Calder couldn't say he blamed them.

Pale-as-Snow had found a big rock to sit on, spear dug point first into the ground beside him, his grey horse nibbling at the grass and the grey fur around his shoulders blowing in the breeze. Whatever the weather, he never seemed warm. It took Calder a moment to find the end of his scabbard with the point of his sword – not usually a problem of his – before he sheathed it and sat down beside the old warrior.

'You took your time getting here,' said Pale-as-Snow, without looking up.

'I think my horse might be lame.'

'Something's lame, all right. You know your brother was right about one thing.' He nodded towards Scale, striding about in the open ground at the north end of the bridge, shouting and waving his mace around. He still had his shield in the other fist, a flatbow bolt lodged near the rim. 'Northmen won't follow a man reckoned a coward.'

'What's that to me?'

'Oh, nothing.' Pale-as-Snow's grey eyes showed no sign he was joking. 'You're everyone's hero.'

White-Eye Hansul was trying to argue with Scale, open hands up for calm. Scale shoved him over onto his back with an ill-tempered flick of his arm and started bellowing again. It looked as though there hadn't been enough fighting for his taste, and he was for pushing on across the river right away to find some more. It looked as though no one else thought that was a very good idea.

Pale-as-Snow gave a resigned sort of sigh, as if this had been happening a lot. 'By the dead, but once your brother gets the fire under him it can be hard work putting it out. Maybe you can play at the voice of reason?'

Calder shrugged. 'I've played at worse. Here's your shield back.' And he tossed it at Pale-as-Snow's stomach so he almost fell off his rock catching it. 'Oy! Pinhead!' Calder swaggered towards Scale with hands on his hips. 'Pinhead Scale! Brave as a bull, strong as a bull, thick as a bull's arse.' Scale's eyes bulged right out of his livid face as they followed him. So did everyone else's, but Calder didn't mind that. He liked nothing better than an audience.

'Good old stupid Scale! Great fighter but, you know . . . nothing but shit in his head.' Calder tapped at his skull as he said it, then slowly stretched out his arm to point up towards the Heroes. 'That's what they say about you.' Scale's expression grew a touch less furious and a touch more thoughtful, but only a touch. 'Up there, at Dow's little wank-parties. Tenways, and Golden, and Ironhead, and the rest. They think you're a fucking idiot.' Calder didn't entirely disagree, if it came to that. He leaned in close to Scale, well within punching range, he was painfully aware. 'Why don't you ride on over that bridge, and prove them all right?'

'Fuck them!' barked Scale. 'We could get over that bridge and into Adwein. Get astride the Uffrith Road! Cut those Union bastards off at the roots. Get in behind 'em!' He was punching at the air with his shield, trying to stoke his rage up again, but the moment he'd started talking instead of doing he'd lost and Calder had won. Calder knew it, and had to smother his contempt. That was no challenge, though. He'd been hiding contempt around his brother for years.

'Astride the Uffrith Road? Might be half the Union army coming up that road before sunset.' Calder looked at Scale's horsemen, no more than ten score and most of their horses ridden out, the foot still hurrying through the fields far behind or stopped at a long wall that reached almost all the way to Skarling's Finger. 'No offence to the valour of our father's proud Named Men here, but are you really going to take on countless thousands with this lot?'

Scale gave them a look himself, jaw muscles squirming in the side of his head as he ground his teeth. White-Eye Hansul, who'd picked himself up and was dusting his dented armour down, shrugged his shoulders. Scale flung his mace on the ground. 'Shit!'

Calder risked a calming hand on his shoulder. 'We were told to take the bridge. We took the bridge. If the Union want it back, they can cross over and fight us for it. On our ground. And we'll be waiting for them. Ready and rested, dug in and close to supplies. Honestly, brother, if Black Dow doesn't kill the pair of us through pure meanness you'll more than likely do it through pure rashness.'

Scale took a long breath, and blew it out. He didn't look at all happy. But he didn't look like he was about to tear anyone's head off. 'All right, damn it!' He frowned across the river, then back at Calder, then shook off his hand. 'I swear, sometimes talking to you is like talking to our father.'

'Thanks,' said Calder. He wasn't sure it was meant as a compliment, but he took it as one anyway. One of their father's sons had to keep his temper.

Paths of Glory

Corporal Tunny tried to hop from one patch of yellow weed to another, the regimental standard held high above the filth in his left hand, his right already spattered to the shoulder from slips into the scum. The bog was pretty much what Tunny had been expecting. And that wasn't a good thing.

The place was a maze of sluggish channels of brown water, streaked on the surface with multicoloured oil, with rotten leaves, with smelly froth, ill-looking rushes scattered at random. If you put down your foot and it only squelched in to the ankle, you counted yourself lucky. Here and there some species of hell-tree had wormed its leathery roots deep enough to stay upright and hang out a few lank leaves, festooned with beards of brown creeper and sprouting with outsize mushrooms. There was a persistent croaking that seemed to come from everywhere and nowhere. Some cursed variety of bird, or frog, or insect, but Tunny couldn't see any of the three. Maybe it was just the bog itself, laughing at them.

'Forest of the fucking damned,' he whispered. Getting a battalion across this was like driving a herd of sheep through a sewer. And, as usual, for reasons he could never understand, him and the four rawest recruits in the Union army were playing vanguard.

'Which way, Corporal Tunny?' asked Worth, doubled up around his guts.

'Stick to the grassy bits, the guide said!' Though there wasn't much around that an honest man could've called grass. Not that there were many honest men around either. 'Have you got a rope, boy?' he asked Yolk, struggling through the mulch beside him, a long smear of mud down his freckled cheek.

'Left 'em with the horses, Corporal.'

'Of course. Of course we bloody did.' By the Fates, how Tunny wished he'd been left with the horses. He took one step and cold water rushed over the top of his boot like a clammy hand clamping around his foot. He was just setting up to have a proper curse at that when a shrill cry came from behind.

'Ah! My boot!'

Tunny spun round. 'Keep quiet, idiot!' Totally failing to keep quiet himself. 'The Northmen'll hear us in bloody Carleon!'

But Klige wasn't listening. He'd strayed well away from the rushes and left one of his boots behind, sucked off by the bog. He was wading out to get it, sliding in up to his thighs. Yolk snickered at him as he started delving into the slime.

'Leave it, Klige, you fool!' snapped Tunny, floundering back towards him.

'Got it!' The bog made a squelching suck as Klige dragged his boot free, looking like it was caked in black porridge. 'Whoa!' He lurched one way, then the other. 'Whoa!' And he was in up to his waist, face flipped from triumph to panic in an instant. Yolk snickered again, then suddenly realised what was happening.

'Who's got a rope?' shouted Lederlingen. 'Someone get a rope!' He floundered out towards Klige, grabbing hold of the nearest piece of tree, a leafless twig thrust out over the mire. 'Take my hand! Take my hand!'

But Klige was panicking, thrashing around and only working himself deeper. He went down with shocking speed, face tipped back, only just above the level of the filth, a big black leaf stuck across one cheek.

'Help me!' he squealed, stretching fingers still a good stride short of Lederlingen's. Tunny slopped up, shoving the flagstaff out towards Klige. 'Help murghhh—' His bulging eyes rolled towards Tunny, then they were lost, his floating hair vanished, a few bubbles broke on the foetid surface, and that was it. Tunny poked at the mush uselessly, but Klige was gone. Aside from his rescued boot, floating slowly away, no trace he'd ever existed.

They struggled the rest of the way in silence, the other recruits looking stunned, Tunny with his jaw furiously clenched, all sticking to the tumps of yellow weed as close as new foals to their mothers. Soon enough the ground started to rise, the trees turned from twisted swamp monsters to firs and oaks. Tunny leaned the filthy standard against a trunk and stood, hands on hips. His magnificent boots were ruined.

'Shit!' he snarled. 'Fucking *shit*!'

Yolk sank down in the muck, staring into nowhere, white hands trembling. Lederlingen licked his pale lips, breathing hard and saying nothing. Worth was nowhere to be seen, though Tunny thought he could hear someone groaning in the undergrowth. Even the drowning of a comrade couldn't delay the working of that lad's troublesome bowels. If anything it had made them accelerate. Forest walked up, caked to the knees in black mud. They all were caked, daubed, spattered with it, and Tunny in particular.

'I hear we lost one of our recruits.' Forest had said it often enough that he could say it deadpan. That he had to.

'Klige,' Tunny squeezed between gritted teeth. 'Was going to be a weaver. We lost a man in a fucking *bog*. Why are we here, even?' The bottom half of his coat was heavy with oily filth and he peeled it off and flung it down.

'You did the best you could.'

'I know,' snapped Tunny.

'Nothing more you—'

'He had some of my bloody gear in his pack! Eight good bottles of brandy! You know how much that could've made me?'

There was a pause.

'Eight bottles.' Forest slowly nodded. 'Well, you're a piece of work, Corporal Tunny, you know that? Twenty-six years in his Majesty's army but you can always find a way to surprise me. I tell you what, you can get up that rise and find out where in the pit of hell we are while I try and get the rest of the battalion across without sinking any more bottles. Maybe that'll take your mind off the depth of your loss.' And he stalked away, hissing to some men who were trying to heave a trembling mule out of the knee-deep muck.

Tunny stood fuming a moment longer, but fuming was going to do no good. 'Yolk, Latherlister, Worth, get over here!'

Yolk stood up, wide-eyed. 'Worth . . . Worth—'

'Still squirting,' said Lederlingen, busy rooting through his pack and hanging various sodden items up on branches to dry.

''Course he is. What else would he be doing? You wait for him, then. Yolk, follow me and try not to bloody die.' He stalked off up the slope, sodden trousers chafing horribly, kicking bits of fallen wood out of his way.

'Shouldn't we be keeping quiet?' whispered Yolk. 'What if we run into the enemy?'

'Enemy!' snorted Tunny. 'Probably we'll run into the other bloody battalion, just trotted over the Old Bridge and up a path and got there ahead of us all nice and dry. That'll make a fine bloody picture, won't it?'

'Couldn't say, sir,' muttered Yolk, dragging himself up the muddy slope almost on all fours.

'Corporal Tunny! And I wasn't soliciting an opinion. Some big bloody grins they'll have when they see the state of us. Some laugh they'll all have!' They were coming to the edge of the trees. Beyond the branches he could see the faint outline of the distant hill, the stones sticking from the top. 'At least we're in the right bloody place,' and then, under his breath, 'to get wet, sore, hungry and poor, that is. General fucking Jalenhorm, I swear, a soldier expects to get shat on, but this . . .'

Beyond the trees the ground sloped down, studded with old stumps and new saplings where some woodcutters had once been busy, their slumping sheds abandoned and already rotting back to the earth. Beyond them a gentle river babbled, hardly more than a stream, really, flowing south to empty into the nightmare of swamp they'd just crossed. There was an earthy overhang on the far bank, then a grassy upslope on which some boundary-conscious farmer seemed to have built an irregular drystone wall. Above the wall Tunny saw movement. Spears, their tips glinting in the fading light. So he'd been right. The other battalion were there ahead of them. He just couldn't work out why they were on the north side of the wall . . .

'What is it, Corporal—'

'Didn't I tell you to stay bloody quiet?' Tunny dragged Yolk down into the bushes and pulled out his eyeglass, a good three-part brass one he won in a game of squares with an officer from the Sixth. He edged forwards, finding a gap in the undergrowth. The ground rose sharply on the other side of the stream then dipped away, but there were spears behind the whole length of wall that he could see. He glimpsed helmets too. Some smoke, perhaps from a cook-fire. Then he saw a man wading out into the stream, waving a fishing rod made from a spear and some twine, wild-haired and stripped to the waist, and very definitely not a Union soldier. Perhaps only two hundred strides from where they were squatting in the brush.

'Uh-oh,' he breathed.

'Are those Northmen?' whispered Yolk.

'Those are a lot of bloody Northmen. And we're right on their flank.' Tunny handed his eyeglass over, half-expecting the lad to look through the wrong end.

'Where did they come from?'

'I'd guess the North, wouldn't you?' He snatched back his eyeglass. 'Someone's going to have to go back. Let someone higher up the dunghill know the bother we're in here.'

'They must know already, though. They'll have run into the Northmen themselves, won't they?' Yolk's voice, never particularly calm, had taken on a slightly hysterical note. 'I mean, they must've! They must know!'

'Who knows what who knows, Yolk? It's a battle.' As he said the words, Tunny realised with mounting worry they were true. If there were Northmen behind that wall, there must have been fighting. It was a battle, all right. Maybe the start of a big one. The Northman in the river had landed something, a flashing sliver of a fish flapping on the end of his line. Some of his mates stood up on the wall, shouting and waving. All bloody smiles. If there had been fighting, it looked pretty damn clear they won.

'Tunny!' Forest was creeping up through the brush behind them, bent double. 'There are Northmen on the other side of that stream!'

'And fishing, would you believe. That wall's crawling with the bastards.'

'One of the lads shinned up a tree. Said he could see horsemen at the Old Bridge.'

'They took the bridge?' Tunny was starting to think that if he left this valley with no greater losses than eight bottles of brandy he might count himself lucky. 'They cross it, we'll be cut off!'

'I'm aware of that, Tunny. I'm very bloody well aware of that. We need to take a message back to General Jalenhorm. Pick someone out. And stay out of bloody sight!' And he crawled away through the undergrowth.

'Someone's got to go back through the bog?' whispered Yolk.

'Unless you can fly there.'

'Me?' The lad's face was grey. 'I can't do it, Corporal Tunny, not after Klige . . . I just can't do it!'

Tunny shrugged. 'Someone has to go. You made it across, you can make it back. Just stick to the grassy bits.'

'Corporal!' Yolk had grabbed Tunny's dirty sleeve and come close, freckled face uncomfortably near. He let his voice drop down quiet. That intimate, urgent little tone that Tunny always liked to hear. The tone in which deals were made. 'You told me, if I ever needed anything . . .' His wet eyes darted left and right, checking they were unobserved. He reached into his jacket and slid out a pewter flask, pressed it into Tunny's hand. Tunny raised a brow, unscrewed the cap, took a sniff, replaced the cap and slipped it into his own jacket. Then he nodded. Hardly made a dent in what he'd lost in the bog, but it was something.

'Leatherlicker!' he hissed as he crept back through the brush. 'I need a volunteer!'

The Day's Work

'**B**y the dead,' grunted Craw, and there were enough of 'em. They were scattered up the north slope of the hill as he limped past, a fair few wounded too, howling and whimpering as the wounded do, a sound that set Craw's teeth on edge more with every passing year. Made him want to scream at the poor bastards to shut up, then made him guilty that he wanted to, knowing he'd done plenty of his own squealing one time or another, and probably wasn't done with it yet.

Lots more dead around the drystone wall. Enough almost to climb the bloody hill without once stepping on the mangled grass. Ended men from both sides, all on the same side now – the pale and gaping, cold far side of the great divide. One young Union lad seemed to have died on his face, arse in the air, staring sideways at Craw with a look of baffled upset, like he was about to ask if someone could lay him out in a fashion more dignified.

Craw didn't bother. Dignity ain't much use to the living, it's none to the dead.

The slopes were just a build-up to the carnage inside the Heroes, though. The Great Leveller was a joker today, wending his long way up to the punchline. Craw wasn't sure he ever saw so many dead men all squeezed into one space. Heaps of 'em, all tangled up in the old grave-pit embrace. Hungry birds danced over the stones, waiting their chance. Flies already busy at the open mouths, open eyes, open wounds. Where do all the flies come from, on a sudden? The place had that hero's smell already. All those bodies bloating in the evening sun, emptying out their innards.

Should've been a sight to get anyone pondering his own mortality, but the dozens of Thralls picking over the wreckage seemed no more concerned than if they'd been picking daisies.

Stripping off clothes and armour, stacking up weapons and shields good enough to be used. If they were upset it was 'cause the Carls who'd led the charge had snaffled the best booty.

'Too old for this shit,' muttered Craw, leaning down to grip at his sore knee, a cold cord of pain running through it from ankle to hip.

'If it ain't Curnden Craw, at last!' Whirrun had been sitting against one of the Heroes and now he stood, brushing dirt from his arse. 'I'd almost given up on waiting.' He swung the Father of Swords up onto one shoulder, sheathed again, and pointed into the valley with it, the way they'd come. 'Thought maybe you'd decided to settle down in one of those farms on the way over here.'

'I wish I had.'

'Aw, but then who'd show me my destiny?'

'Did you fight?'

'I did, yes, as it happens. Stuck into the midst of it. I'm quite a one for fighting, according to the songs. Lots of fighting here.' Not that he had a scratch on him. Craw had never seen Whirrun come out of a fight with a single mark. He frowned around the circle of butchery, scrubbing at his hair, and the wind chose that moment to freshen, stirring the tattered clothes of the corpses. 'Lot of dead men, ain't there.'

'Aye,' said Craw.

'Heaps and heaps.'

'Aye.'

'Union mostly, though.'

'Aye.'

Whirrun shrugged his sword off his shoulder and stood it on its tip, hilt in both hands, leaning forward so his chin rested on the pommel. 'Still, even when it's enemies, a sight like this, well . . . makes you wonder whether war's really such a good thing after all.'

'You joking?'

Whirrun paused, turning the hilt round and round so the end of the stained scabbard twisted into the stained grass. 'I don't really know any more. Agrick's dead.' Craw looked up, mouth open. 'He charged off right at the head. Got killed in the circle.

Stabbed, I think, with a sword, just about here,' and he poked at his side, 'under the ribs and went right through, probably—'

'Don't matter exactly how, does it?' snapped Craw.

'I guess not. Mud is mud. He had the shadow over him since his brother died, though. You could see it on him. I could, anyway. The boy wasn't going to last.'

Some consolation, that. 'The rest?'

'Jolly Yon got a nick or two. Brack's leg's still bothering him, though he won't say so. Other than that, they're all good. Good as before, leastways. Wonderful thought we could try and bury Agrick next to his brother.'

'Aye.'

'Let's get a hole dug, then, shall we, 'fore someone else digs there?'

Craw took a long breath as he looked around them. 'If you can find a spare shovel. I'll come say the words.' A fitting end to the day that'd be. Before he got more'n a couple of steps, though, he found Caul Shivers in his way.

'Dow wants you,' he said, and with his whisper, and his scar, and his careless frown, he might've been the Great Leveller his self.

'Right.' Craw fought the urge to start chewing his nails again. 'Tell 'em I'll be back soon. I'll be back soon, will I?'

Shivers shrugged.

Craw might not much have cared for what they'd done with the place, but Black Dow looked happy enough with the day's work, leaning against one of the stones with a mostly eaten apple in one hand. 'Craw, you old bastard!' As he turned, Craw saw one side of his grinning face was all dashed and speckled with blood. 'Where the hell did you get to?'

'All honesty, limping along at the back.' Splitfoot and a few of his Carls were scattered about, swords drawn and eyes peeled. A lot of bare steel, considering they'd won a victory.

'Thought maybe you got yourself killed,' said Dow.

Craw winced as he worked his burning foot around, thinking there was still time. 'I wish I could run fast enough to get myself killed. I'll stand wherever you tell me, but this charging business is a young man's game.'

'I managed to keep up.'

'Don't all have your taste for blood, Chief.'

'It's been the making of me. Don't reckon I've done a better day's work than this, though.' Dow put a hand on Craw's shoulder and drew him out between the stones, out to the edge of the hill where they could get a look south across the valley. The very spot Craw had stood when they first saw the Union come. Things had changed a lot in a few hours.

The tumbledown wall bristled with weapons, shining dully in the fading light. Men on the slope below as well, digging pits, whittling stakes, making the Heroes a fortress. Below them the south side of the hill was littered with bodies, all the way down to the orchards. Scavengers flitted from one to another, first men then crows, feathered undertakers croaking a happy chorus. Thralls were starting to drag the stripped shapes into heaps for burying. Strange constructions in which one corpse couldn't be told from another. When a man dies in peacetime it's all tears and processions, friends and neighbours offering each other comfort. A man dies in war and he's lucky to get enough mud on top to stop him stinking.

Dow crooked a finger. 'Shivers.'

'Chief.'

'I hear tell they got a choice prisoner down in Osrung. A Union officer or some such. Why don't you bring him up here, see if we can prick anything out of him worth hearing?'

Shivers' eye twinkled orange with the setting sun each time he nodded. 'Right.' And he strode off, stepping over corpses as careless as autumn leaves.

Dow frowned after him. 'Some men you have to keep busy, eh, Craw?'

'I guess.' Wondering what the hell Dow planned to keep him busy with.

'Quite the day's work.' He tossed his apple core away and patted his stomach like a man who'd had the best meal of his life and a few hundred dead men were the leftovers.

'Aye,' muttered Craw. Probably he should've been celebrating himself. Doing a little jig. A one-legged one, anyway. Singing and clashing ale cups and all the rest. But he just felt sore. Sore and he wanted to go to sleep, and wake up in that house of his by the water, and never see another battlefield. Then he wouldn't have to say the lies over Agrick's mud.

'Pushed 'em back to the river. All across the line.' Dow waved at the valley, blood dried black into the skin around his finger-nails. 'Reachey got over the fence and kicked the Union out of Osrung. Scale got a hold o' the Old Bridge. Golden drove this lot clean across the shallows. He got stopped there but . . . I'd worry if I started getting everything my way.' Black Dow winked at him, and Craw wondered if he was about to get stabbed in the back. 'Guess folk won't be carping that I ain't the fighter they thought I was, eh?'

'Guess not.' As if that was all that mattered. 'Shivers said you needed me for something.'

'Can't a pair of old fighters have a chat after a battle?'

That gave Craw a much bigger surprise than the blade in the back might've. 'I reckon they can. Just didn't reckon you'd be one of 'em.'

Dow seemed to think about that for a moment. 'Neither did I. Guess we're both surprised.'

'Aye,' said Craw, no idea what else to say.

'We can let the Union come to us tomorrow,' said Dow. 'Spare your old legs.'

'You reckon they'll come on? After this?'

Dow's grin was wider'n ever. 'We gave Jalenhorm a hell of a beating, but half his men never even got across the river. And that's only one division out of three.' He pointed over towards Adwein, lights starting to twinkle in the dusk, bright dots mark-ing the path of the road as marching men got torches lit. 'And Mitterick's just bringing his men up over there. Fresh and ready. Meed on the other side, I hear.' And his finger moved over to the left, towards the Ollensand Road. Craw picked out lights there too, further back, his heart sinking all the time. 'There's still heaps more work here, don't worry about that.' Dow leaned close, fingers squeezing at Craw's shoulder. 'We're just getting started.'

The Defeated

Your August Majesty,
    I regret to inform you that today your army and interests in the North suffered a most serious reverse. The foremost elements of General Jalenhorm's division reached the town of Osrung this morning and took up a powerful position on a hill surmounted by a ring of ancient stones called the Heroes. Reinforcements were held up on the bad roads, however, and before they could move across the river the Northmen attacked in great numbers. Although they fought with the greatest courage, the Sixth and Rostod Regiments were overwhelmed. The standard of the Sixth was lost. Casualties may well be close to a thousand dead, perhaps the same number of wounded, and many more in the hands of the enemy.

    It was only by a valiant action of your Majesty's First Cavalry that further disaster was averted. The Northmen are now well entrenched around the Heroes. One can see the lights of their campfires on the slopes. One can almost hear their singing when the wind shifts northerly. But we yet hold the ground south of the river, and the divisions of General Mitterick on the western flank, and Lord Governor Meed on the eastern, have begun to arrive and are preparing to attack at first light.

    Tomorrow, the Northmen will not be singing.

    I remain your Majesty's most faithful and unworthy servant,
    Bremer dan Gorst, Royal Observer of the Northern War

The gathering darkness was full of shouts, clanks and squeals, sharp with the tang of woodsmoke, the even sharper sting of defeat. Fires rustled in the wind and torches sputtered in pale hands, illuminating faces haggard from a day of marching, waiting, worrying. *And perhaps, in a few cases, even fighting.*

The road up from Uffrith was an endless parade of overloaded wagons, mounted officers, marching men. Mitterick's division grinding through, seeing the wounded and the beaten, catching the contagion of fear before they even caught a whiff of the enemy. Things that might have been just objects before the rout on the Heroes had assumed a crushing significance. A dead mule, lamplight shining in its goggling eyes. A cart with a broken axle tipped off the road and stripped down for firewood. An abandoned tent, blown from its moorings, the yellow sun of the Union stitched into the trampled canvas. *All become emblems of doom.*

Fear had been a rarity over the past few months, as Gorst took his morning runs through the camps of one regiment or another. Boredom, exhaustion, hunger, illness, hopelessness and homesickness, all commonplace. *But not fear of the enemy.* Now it was everywhere, and the stink of it only grew stronger as the clouds rolled steadily in and the sun sank below the fells.

If victory makes men brave, defeat renders them cowards.

Progress through the village of Adwein had been entirely stalled by several enormous wagons, each drawn by a team of eight horses. An officer was bellowing red-faced at an old man huddled on the seat of the foremost one.

'I am Saurizin, Adeptus Chemical of the University of Adua!' he shouted back, waving a document smudged by the first spots of rain. 'This equipment must be allowed through, by order of Lord Bayaz!'

Gorst left them arguing, strode past a quartermaster hammering on doors, searching for billets. A Northern woman stood in the street with three children pressed against her legs, staring at a handful of coins as the drizzle grew heavier. *Kicked out of their shack to make way for some sneering lieutenant, who'll be elbowed off to make way for some preening captain, who'll be shuffled on to make way for some bloated major. Where will this woman and her children be by then? Will they slumber peacefully in my tent while I doss heroically on the damp sod outside? I need only reach out my hand* . . . Instead he put his head down and trudged by them in silence.

Most of the village's mean buildings were already crowded with wounded, the less serious cases spilling out onto the doorsteps. They looked up at him, pain-twisted, dirt-smeared or bandaged faces slack, and Gorst looked back in silence. *My skills are for making casualties, not comforting them.* But he pulled the stopper from his canteen and offered it out, and each in turn they took a mouthful until it was empty. Apart from one who gripped his hand for a moment they did not thank him and he did not care.

A surgeon in a smeared apron appeared at a doorway, blowing out a long sigh. 'General Jalenhorm?' Gorst asked. He was pointed down a rutted side-track and after a few strides heard the voice. That same voice he'd heard blathering orders for the last few days. Its tone was different now.

'Lay them down here, lay them here! Clear a space! You, bring bandages!' Jalenhorm was kneeling in the mud, clasping the hand of a man on a stretcher. He seemed to have shaken off his huge staff, finally, if he had not left them dead on the hill. 'Don't worry, you'll have the best of care. You're a hero. You're all heroes!' His knees squelched into the muck beside the next man. 'You did everything that could have been asked. Mine was the fault, my friends, mine were the mistakes.' He squeezed the casualty's shoulder then stood, slowly, staring down. 'Mine is the guilt.'

Defeat, it seems, brings out the best in some men.

'General Jalenhorm.'

He looked up, face tipping into the torchlight, looking suddenly very old for a man so young. 'Colonel Gorst, how are you—'

'Marshal Kroy is here.' The general visibly deflated, like a pillow with half the stuffing pulled out.

'Of course he is.' He straightened his dirt-smudged jacket, twisted his sword-belt into the correct position. 'How do I look?' Gorst opened his mouth to speak, but Jalenhorm cut him off. 'Don't bother to humour me. I look defeated.' *True.* 'Please don't deny it.' *I didn't.* 'That's what I am.' *It is.*

Gorst led the way back down the crowded alleys, through the steam of the army's kitchens and the glow from the stalls of enterprising pedlars, hoping for silence. He was disappointed. *As so very often.*

'Colonel Gorst, I need to thank you. That charge of yours saved my division.'

Perhaps it will also have saved my career. Your division can all drown if I can be the king's First Guard again. 'My motives were not selfless.'

'Whose are? It's the results that go down in history. Our reasons are written in smoke. And the fact is I nearly destroyed my division. *My* division.' Jalenhorm snorted bitterly. 'The one the king had most foolishly lent me. I tried to turn it down, you know.' *It seems you did not try hard enough.* 'But you know the king.' *All too well.* 'He has romantic notions about his old friends.' *He has romantic notions about everything.* 'No doubt I will be laughed at when I return home. Humiliated. Shunned.' *Welcome to my life.* 'Probably I deserve it.' *Probably you do. I don't.*

And yet, as Gorst frowned sideways at Jalenhorm's hanging head, hair plastered to his skull, a drop of rain clinging to the point of his nose, as thorough a picture of dejection as he could find without a mirror, he was swept up by a surprising wave of sympathy.

He found he had put his hand on the general's shoulder. 'You did what you could,' he said. 'You should not blame yourself.' *If my experience is anything to go by, there will soon be legions of self-righteous scum queuing up to do it for you.* 'You must not blame yourself.'

'Who should I blame, then?' Jalenhorm whispered into the rain. 'Who?'

If Lord Marshal Kroy was infected by fear he showed no symptoms, and nor did anyone else in range of his iron frown. Within his sight soldiers marched in perfect step, officers spoke clearly but did not shout, and the wounded bit down on their howls and remained stoically silent. Within a circle perhaps fifty strides across, with Kroy bolt upright in his saddle at its centre, there was no lag in morale, there was no lapse in discipline, and there had certainly been no defeat.

Jalenhorm's bearing noticeably stiffened as he strode up and gave a rigid salute. 'Lord Marshal Kroy.'

'General Jalenhorm.' The marshal glared down from on high. 'I understand there was an engagement.'

'There was. The Northmen came in very great numbers. Very great, and very quickly. A well-coordinated assault. They made a feint for Osrung and I sent a regiment to reinforce the town. I went to find more but, by that time . . . it was too late to do anything but try to keep them on the far side of the river. Too late to—'

'The condition of your division, General.'

Jalenhorm paused. In one sense the condition of his division was painfully obvious. 'Two of my five regiments of foot were held up on the bad roads and have yet to see action. The Thirteenth were holding Osrung and withdrew in good order when the Northmen breached the gate. Some casualties.' Jalenhorm recited the butcher's bill in a dull monotone. 'The majority of the Rostod Regiment, some nine companies, I believe, were caught in the open and routed. The Sixth were holding the hill when the Northmen attacked. They were comprehensively broken. Ridden down in the fields. The Sixth has . . .' Jalenhorm's mouth twitched silently. 'Ceased to exist.'

'Colonel Wetterlant?'

'Presumed among the dead on the far side of the river. There are very many dead there. Many wounded we cannot reach. You can hear them crying for water. They always want water, for some reason.' Jalenhorm gave a horrifically inappropriate snort of nervous laughter. 'I'd have thought they might want . . . spirits, or something.'

Kroy kept his silence. Gorst was unlikely to break it.

Jalenhorm droned on, as if he could not bear the quiet. 'One regiment of cavalry took losses near the Old Bridge and withdrew, but held the south bank. The First is split in two. One battalion made their way through the marshes to a position in the woods on our left flank.'

'That could be useful. The other?'

'Fought valiantly alongside Colonel Gorst in the shallows, and turned back the enemy at great cost on both sides. Our one truly successful action of the day.'

Kroy turned his frown on Gorst. 'More heroics, eh, Colonel?'

Only the bare minimum of action necessary to prevent disaster turning into catastrophe. 'Some action, sir. No heroics.'

'I was mindful, Lord Marshal,' cut in Jalenhorm, 'of the urgency. You wrote to me of some urgency.'

'I did.'

'I was mindful that the king wished for quick results. And so I seized the chance to get at the enemy. Seized it . . . much too ardently. I made a terrible mistake. A most terrible mistake, and I alone bear the full responsibility.'

'No.' Kroy gave a heavy sigh. 'You share it with me. And with others. The roads. The nature of the battlefield. The undue haste.'

'Nonetheless, I have failed.' Jalenhorm drew his sword and offered it up. 'I humbly request that I be removed from command.'

'The king would not hear of it. Neither will I.'

Jalenhorm's sword drooped, the point scraping against the mud. 'Of course, Lord Marshal. I should have scouted the trees more thoroughly—'

'You should have. But your orders were to push north and find the enemy.' Kroy looked slowly around the torchlit chaos of the village. 'You found the enemy. This is a war. Mistakes happen, and when they do . . . the stakes are high. But we are not finished. We have barely even begun. You will spend tonight and tomorrow behind the shallows where Colonel Gorst fought his unheroic action this afternoon. Regrouping in the centre, re-equipping your division, looking to the welfare of the wounded, restoring morale and,' glowering balefully around at the decidedly unmilitary state of the place, 'imposing *discipline*.'

'Yes, Lord Marshal.'

'I will be making my headquarters on the slopes of Black Fell, where there should be a good view of the battlefield tomorrow. Defeat is always painful, but I have a feeling you will get another chance to be involved in this particular battle.'

Jalenhorm drew himself up, something of his old snap returning at being given a straightforward goal. 'My division will be ready for action the day after tomorrow, you may depend upon it, Lord Marshal!'

'Good.' And Kroy rode off, his indomitable aura fading into the night along with his staff. Jalenhorm stood frozen in a parting salute as the marshal clattered away, but Gorst looked back, when he had made it a few steps further down the road.

The general still stood beside the track, alone, hunched over as the rain grew heavier, white streaks through the fizzing torchlight.

Fair Treatment

At a pace no faster'n Flood's limping, which wasn't that fast at all, they made their way down the road towards Osrung, in the flitting rain. They'd only the light of Reft's one guttering torch to see by, which showed just a few strides of rutted mud ahead, some flattened crops on either side, the scared little-boy faces of Brait and Colving and the clueless gawp of Stodder. All staring off towards the town, a cluster of lights up ahead in the black country, touching the weighty clouds above with the faintest glow. All holding tight to what passed for weapons in their little crew of beggars. As if they were going to be fighting now. Today's fighting was all long done with, and they'd missed it.

'Why the hell were we left at the back?' grumbled Beck.

'Because of my dodgy leg and your lack o' practice, fool,' snapped Flood over his shoulder.

'How we going to get practice left at the back?'

'You'll get practice at not getting killed, which is a damn fine thing to have plenty o' practice at, if you're asking me.'

Beck hadn't been asking. His respect for Flood was waning with every mile they marched together. All the old prick seemed to care about was keeping the lads he led out of the fight and set to idiot's tasks like digging, and carrying, and lighting fires. That and keeping his leg warm. If Beck had wanted to do women's work he could've stayed on the farm and spared his self a few nights out in the wind. He'd come to fight, and win a name, and do business fit for the singing of. He was about to say so too, when Brait tugged at his sleeve, pointing up ahead.

'There's someone there!' he squeaked. Beck saw shapes moving in the dark, felt a stab of nerves, hand fumbling for his sword. The torchlight fell across three somethings hanging from a tree by chains. All blackened up by fire, branch creaking gently as they turned.

'Deserters,' said Flood, hardly breaking his limping stride. 'Hanged and burned.'

Beck stared at 'em as he passed. Didn't hardly look like men at all, just charred wood. The one in the middle might've had a sign hanging round his neck, but it was all scorched off and Beck couldn't read anyway.

'Why burn 'em?' asked Stodder.

''Cause Black Dow got a taste for the smell o' men cooking long time ago and it hasn't worn off.'

'It's a warning,' Reft whispered.

'Warning what?'

'Don't desert,' said Flood.

'Y'idiot,' added Beck, though mostly 'cause looking at those strange man-shaped ashes was making him all kinds of jumpy. 'No better'n a coward deserves, if you're asking—' Another squeak, Colving this time, and Beck went for his sword again.

'Just townsfolk.' Reft lifted his torch higher and picked out a handful of worried faces.

'We ain't got nothing!' An old man at the front, waving bony hands. 'We ain't got nothing!'

'We don't want nothing.' Flood jerked his thumb over his shoulder. 'Go your ways.'

They trudged on past. Mostly old men, a few women too, a couple of children. Children even younger than Brait, which meant barely talking yet. They were all weighed down by packs and gear, one or two pushing creaking barrows of junk. Bald furs and old tools and cookpots. Just like the stuff might've come out of Beck's mother's house.

'Clearing out,' piped Colving.

'They know what's coming,' said Reft.

Osrung slunk out of the night, a fence of mossy logs whittled to points, a high stone tower looming up by the empty gateway with lights at slitted windows. Sullen men with spears kept watch, eyes narrowed against the rain. Some young lads were digging a big pit, working away in the light of a few guttering torches on poles, all streaked with mud in the drizzle.

'Shit,' whispered Colving.

'By the dead,' squeaked Brait.

'They's the dead all right.' Stodder, his fat lip dangling.

Beck found he'd nothing to say. What he'd taken without thinking for some pile of pale clay or something was actually a pile of corpses. He'd seen Gelda from up the valley laid out waiting to be buried after he drowned in the river and not thought much about it, counted himself hard-blooded, but this was different. They looked all strange, stripped naked and thrown together, face up and face down, slippery with the rain. Men, these, he had to tell himself, and the thought made him dizzy. He could see faces in the mess, or bits of faces. Hands, arms, feet, mixed up like they was all one monstrous creature. He didn't want to guess at how many were there. He saw a leg sticking out, a wound in the thigh yawning black like a big mouth. Didn't look real. One of the lads doing the digging stopped a moment, shovel clutched in white hands as they trudged past. His mouth was all twisted like he was about to cry.

'Come on,' snapped Flood, leading them in through the archway, broken doors leaning against the fence inside. A great tree trunk lay near, branches hacked off to easily held lengths, the heavy end filed to a point and capped with rough-forged black iron, covered with shiny scratches.

'You reckon that was the ram?' whispered Colving.

'I reckon,' said Reft.

The town felt strange. Edgy. Some houses were shut up tight, others had windows and doorways wide and full of darkness. A set of bearded men sat in front of one, mean-eyed, passing round a flask. Some children hid in an alley mouth, eyes gleaming in the shadows as the torch passed 'em by. Odd sounds came from everywhere. Crashing and tinkling. Thumping and shouting. Groups of men darted between the buildings, torches in hands, blades glinting, all moving at a hungry half-jog.

'What's going on?' asked Stodder, in that stodgy-stupid voice of his.

'They're at a bit of sacking.'

'But . . . ain't this our town?'

Flood shrugged. 'They fought for it. Some of 'em died for it. They ain't leaving empty-handed.'

A Carl with a long moustache sat under dripping eaves with a

214

bottle in his hand, sneering as he watched 'em walk past. Beside him a corpse lay in the doorway, half-in, half-out, the back of its head a glistening mass. Beck couldn't tell if it was someone who'd lived in the house or someone who'd been fighting in it. Whether it was a man or a woman, even.

'You're quiet all of a sudden,' said Reft.

Beck wanted to think of something sharp, but all he could manage was, 'Aye.'

'Wait here.' And Flood limped up to a man in a red cloak, pointing Carls off this way and that. Some figures sat slumped in an alleyway nearby, hands tied, shoulders hunched against the drizzle.

'Prisoners,' said Reft.

'They don't look much different than our lot,' said Colving.

'They ain't.' Reft frowned at 'em. 'Some o' the Dogman's boys, I guess.'

'Apart from him,' said Beck. 'That's a Union man.' He had a bandage round his head and a funny Union jacket, one red sleeve ripped and the skin underneath covered in grazes, the other with some kind of fancy gold thread all around the cuff.

'Right,' said Flood as he walked back over. 'You're going to look to these prisoners while I find out what the work'll be tomorrow. Just make sure none o' them, and none o' you, end up dead!' he shouted as he made off up the street.

'Looking to prisoners,' grumbled Beck, some of his bitterness bubbling back as he looked down at their hangdog faces.

'Reckon you deserve better work, do you?' The one who spoke had a crazy look to him, a big bandage around his belly, stained through brown with some fresh red in the middle, ankles tied as well as wrists. 'Bunch o' fucking boys, don't even have their Names yet!'

'Shut up, Crossfeet,' grunted one of the other prisoners, not hardly looking up.

'*You* shut up, y'arsehole!' Crossfeet gave him a look like he might tear him with his teeth. 'Whatever happens tonight, the Union'll be here tomorrow. More o' those bastards than ants in a hill. The Dogman too, and you know who the Dogman's got with him?' He grinned, eyes going huge as he whispered the name. 'The Bloody-Nine.' Beck felt his face go hot. The

Bloody-Nine had killed his father. Killed him in a duel with his own sword. The one he had sheathed beside him now.

'That's a lie,' squeaked Brait, looking scared to his bones even though they had weapons and the prisoners were trussed up tight. 'Black Dow killed Ninefingers, years ago!'

Crossfeet kept giving him that crazy grin. 'We'll see. To-morrow, you little bastard. We'll—'

'Let him alone,' said Beck.

'Oh aye? And what's your name?'

Beck stepped up and booted Crossfeet in the fruits. 'That's my name!' He kept on kicking him as he folded up, all his anger boiling out. 'That's my name! That's my fucking name, you heard it enough?'

'Hate to interrupt.'

'What?' snarled Beck, spinning round with his fists clenched.

A big man stood behind him, a half-head taller'n Beck, maybe, fur on his shoulders glistening with the rain. All across one side of his face, the biggest and most hideous scar Beck had ever seen, the eye on that side not an eye at all but a ball of dead metal.

'Name's Caul Shivers,' voice a ground-down whisper.

'Aye,' croaked Beck. He'd heard stories. Everyone had. They said Shivers did tasks for Black Dow too black for his own hands. They said he'd fought at Black Well, and the Cumnur, and Dunbrec, and the High Places, fought beside old Rudd Three-trees, and the Dogman. The Bloody-Nine too. They said he'd gone south across the sea and learned sorcery. That he'd traded his eye willingly for that silver one, and that a witch had made it, and through it he could see what a man was thinking.

'Black Dow sent me.'

'Aye,' whispered Beck, all his hairs standing up on end.

'To get one o' these. A Union officer.'

'Reckon that's this one.' Colving used his toe to poke at the man with the tattered sleeve and made him grunt.

'If it ain't Black Dow's bitch!' Crossfeet was smiling up, teeth shining red, bandages round him reddened too. 'Why don't you bark, eh, Shivers? Bark, you bastard!' Beck could hardly believe it. None of 'em could. Maybe he knew that wound in his gut was death, and it'd sent him mad.

'Huh.' Shivers jerked his trousers up so it was easy for him to squat down, boots grinding the dirt as he did it. When he got there he had a knife in his hand. Just a little one, blade no longer'n a man's finger, glinting red and orange and yellow. 'You know who I am, then?'

'Caul Shivers, and I ain't fucking scared of a dog!'

Shivers raised one brow, the one above his good eye. The one above his metal eye didn't shift much. 'Well, ain't you the hero?' And he poked Crossfeet in the calf with the blade. Not much weight behind it. Like Beck might've poked his brother with a finger to wake him up of a frosty morning. The knife stuck into his leg, silent, and back out, and Crossfeet snarled and wriggled.

'Black Dow's bitch, am I?' Shivers poked him in the other leg, knife going deeper into his thigh. 'It's true I get some shitty jobs.' Poked him again, somewhere around his hip. 'Dog can't hold a knife, though, can it?' He didn't sound angry. Didn't look angry. Bored, almost. 'I can.' Poke, poke.

'Gah!' Crossfeet twisted and spat. 'If I had a blade—'

'If?' Shivers poked him in the side, where his bandages were. 'You don't, so there's the end o' that.' Crossfeet had twisted over, so Shivers poked him in the back. 'I've got one, though. Look.' Poke, poke, poke. 'Look at that, hero.' Poked him in the backs of his legs, poked him in the arse, poked him all over, blood spreading out into his trousers in dark rings.

Crossfeet moaned and shuddered, and Shivers puffed out his cheeks, and wiped his knife on the Union man's sleeve, making the gold thread glint red. 'Right, then.' He made the Union man grunt as he jerked him to his feet, carefully sheathed his little knife somewhere at his belt. 'I'll take this one off.'

'What should we do with him?' Beck found he'd asked in a reedy little voice, pointing at Crossfeet, moaning softly in the mud, torn clothes all glistening sticky black.

Shivers looked straight at Beck, and it felt like he was looking into him. Right into his thoughts, like they said he could. 'Do nothing. You can manage that, no?' He shrugged as he turned to go. 'Let him bleed.'

Tactics

The valley was spread out below them, a galaxy of twinkling points of orange light. The torches and campfires of both sides, occasionally smudged as a new curtain of drizzle swept across the hillside. One cluster must have been the village of Adwein, another the hill they called the Heroes, a third the town of Osrung.

Meed had made his headquarters at an abandoned inn south of the town and left his leading regiment digging in just out of bowshot of its fence, Hal with them, nobly wrestling to stamp some order on the darkness. More than half the division was still slogging up, ill-tempered and ill-disciplined, along a road that had begun the day as an uneven strip of dust and ended it churned to a river of mud. The rearmost elements would probably still not have arrived at first light tomorrow.

'I wanted to thank you,' said Colonel Brint, rain dripping from the peak of his hat.

'Me?' asked Finree, all innocence. 'Whatever for?'

'For looking after Aliz these past few days. I know she's not terribly worldly—'

'It's been my pleasure,' she lied. 'You've been such a good friend to Hal, after all.' Just a gentle reminder that she damn well expected him to carry on being one.

'Hal's an easy man to like.'

'Isn't he, though?'

They rode past a picket, four Union soldiers swaddled in sodden cloaks, spear-points glistening in the light of the lanterns of Meed's officers. There were more men beyond, unloading rain-spoiled gear from packhorses, struggling to pitch tents, wet canvas flapping in their faces. An unhappy queue of them were hunched beside a dripping awning clutching an assortment of tins, cups and boxes while rations were weighed out.

'There's no bread?' one was asking.

'Regulations say flour's an acceptable substitute,' replied the quartermaster, measuring out a tiny quantity on his scales with frowning precision.

'Acceptable to who? What are we going to bake it on?'

'You can bake it on your fat arse far as I'm— Oh, begging your pardon, my lady,' tugging his forelock as Finree rode past. As though seeing men go hungry for no good reason could cause no offence but the word 'arse' might overcome her delicate sensibilities.

What looked at first to be a hump in the steep hillside turned out to be an ancient building, covered with wind-lashed creeper, somewhere between a cottage and a barn and probably serving as both. Meed dismounted with all the pomp of a queen at her coronation and led his staff in file through the narrow doorway, leaving Colonel Brint to hold back the queue so Finree could slip through near the front.

The bare-raftered room beyond smelled of damp and wool, wet-haired officers squeezed in tight. The briefing had the charged air of a royal funeral, every man vying to look the most solemn while they wondered eagerly whether there might be anything for them in the will. General Mitterick stood against one rough stone wall, frowning mightily into his moustache with one hand thrust between two buttons of his uniform, thumb sticking up, as if he was posing for a portrait, and an insufferably pretentious one at that. Not far from him Finree picked out Bremer dan Gorst's impassive slab of a face in the shadows, and smiled in acknowledgement. He scarcely tipped his head in return.

Finree's father stood before a great map, pointing out positions with expressive movements of one hand. She felt the warm glow of pride she always did when she saw her father at work. He was the very definition of a commander. When he saw them enter, he came over to shake Meed's hand, catching Finree's eye and giving her the slightest smile.

'Lord Governor Meed, I must thank you for moving north with such speed.' Though if it had been left to his Grace to

219

navigate they would still have been wondering which way was north.

'Lord Marshal Kroy,' grated the governor, with little enthusiasm. Their relationship was a prickly one. In his own province of Angland, Meed was pre-eminent, but as a lord marshal carrying the king's commission, in time of war Finree's father outranked him.

'I realise it must have been a wrench to abandon Ollensand, but we need you here.'

'So I see,' said Meed, with characteristic bad grace. 'I understand there was a serious—'

'Gentlemen!' The press of officers near the door parted to let someone through. 'I must apologise for my late arrival, the roads are quite clogged.' A stocky bald man emerged from the crowd, flapping the lapels of a travel-stained coat and heedlessly spraying water over everyone around him. He was attended by only one servant, a curly-haired fellow with a basket in one hand, but Finree had made it her business to know every person in his Majesty's government, every member of the Open Council and the Closed and the exact degrees of their influence, and the lack of pomp did not fool her for a moment. Put simply, whether he was said to be retired or not, Bayaz, the First of the Magi, outranked everyone.

'Lord Bayaz.' Finree's father made the introductions. 'This is Lord Governor Meed, of Angland, commanding his Majesty's third division.'

The First of the Magi somehow managed to press his hand and ignore him simultaneously. 'I knew your brother. A good man, much missed.' Meed attempted to speak but Bayaz was distracted by his servant, who at that moment produced a cup from his basket. 'Ah! Tea! Nothing seems quite so terrible once there is a cup of tea in your hand, eh? Would anyone else care for some?' There were no takers. Tea was generally considered an unpatriotic Gurkish fashion, synonymous with moustache-twiddling treachery. 'Nobody?'

'I would love a cup.' Finree slipped smoothly in front of the lord governor, obliging him to take a spluttering step back. 'The perfect thing in this weather.' She despised tea, but would happily have drunk an ocean of it for the chance to exchange words with one of the most powerful men in the Union.

Bayaz' eyes flickered briefly over her face like a pawnshop owner's asked for an estimate on some gaudy heirloom. Finree's father cleared his throat, somewhat reluctantly. 'This is my daughter—'

'Finree dan Brock, of course. My congratulations on your marriage.'

She smothered her surprise. 'You are very well informed, Lord Bayaz. I would have thought myself beneath notice.' She ignored a cough of agreement from Meed's direction.

'Nothing can be beneath the notice of a careful man,' said the Magus. 'Knowledge is the root of power, after all. Your husband must be a fine fellow indeed to outshine the shadow of his family's treason.'

'He is,' she said, unabashed. 'He in no way takes after his father.'

'Good.' Bayaz still smiled, but his eyes were hard as flints. 'I would hate to bring you pain by seeing him hanged.'

An awkward silence. She glanced at Colonel Brint, then at Lord Governor Meed, wondering if either of them might offer some support for Hal in reward for his unstinting loyalty. Brint at least had the decency to look guilty. Meed looked positively delighted. 'You will find no more loyal man in his Majesty's whole army,' she managed to grate out.

'I am all delight. Loyalty is a fine thing in an army. Victory is another.' Bayaz frowned about at the assembled officers. 'Not the best of days, gentlemen. A long way from the best of days.'

'General Jalenhorm overreached himself,' said Mitterick, out of turn and with little empathy, behaviour entirely characteristic of the man. 'He should never have been so damn spread out—'

'General Jalenhorm acted under my orders,' snapped Marshal Kroy, leaving Mitterick to subside into a grumpy silence. 'We overreached, yes, and the Northmen surprised us . . .'

'Your tea.' A cup was insinuated into Finree's hand and the eyes of Bayaz' servant met hers. Odd-coloured eyes, one blue, one green. 'I am sure your husband is as loyal, honest and hard-working as ever a man could be,' he murmured, a most unservile curl to the corner of his mouth, as if they shared some private joke. She did not see what, but the man had already oozed back, pot in hand, to charge Bayaz' cup. Finree wrinkled her lip, checked she was unobserved and furtively tossed the contents of hers down the wall.

'. . . our choices were most limited,' her father was saying, 'given the great need for haste impressed upon us by the Closed Council—'

Bayaz cut him off. 'The need for haste is a fact of our situation, Marshal Kroy, a fact no less compelling for being a political imperative rather than a physical.' He slurped tea through pursed lips, but the room was held so silent for the duration one could have heard a flea jump. Finree wished she understood the trick, and could rely on her every facile utterance being given rapt attention, rather than endlessly chewing on her usual diet of sidelinings, humourings and brushings-off. 'If a mason builds a wall upon a slope and it collapses, he can hardly complain that it would have stood a thousand years if only he had been given level ground to work with.' Bayaz slurped again, again in utter silence. 'In war, the ground is never level.'

Finree felt an almost physical pressure to jump to her father's defence, as if there was a wasp down her back that had to be smashed, but she bit her tongue. Taunting Meed was one thing. Taunting the First of the Magi quite another.

'It was not my intention to offer excuses,' said her father stiffly. 'For the failure I take all the responsibility, for the losses I take all the blame.'

'Your willingness to shoulder the blame does you much credit but us little good.' Bayaz sighed as if reproving a naughty grandson. 'But let us learn the lessons, gentlemen. Let us put yesterday's defeats behind us, and look to tomorrow's victories.' Everyone nodded as though they had never heard anything so profound, even Finree's father. Here was power.

She could not remember ever coming to dislike anyone so much, or admire anyone so much, in so short a time.

Dow's meet was held around a big fire-pit in the centre of the Heroes, shimmering with heat, hissing and fizzing with the drizzle. There was an edgy feel about the gathering, somewhere between a wedding and a hanging. Firelight and shadow make men look like devils, and Craw had seen 'em make men act like devils more'n once. They all were there – Reachey, Tenways, Scale and Calder, Ironhead, Splitfoot and a couple score Named Men besides. The biggest names and the hardest faces in the North, less a few up in the hills and a few more with the other side.

Looked like Glama Golden had got in the fight. Looked like someone had used his face for an anvil. His left cheek was one big welt, mouth split and bloated, blooms of bruise already spreading. Ironhead smirked across the ring of leering faces like he'd never seen a thing so pretty as Golden's broken nose. They had bad blood between 'em, those two, so bad it poisoned everything around.

'What the hell are you doing here, old man?' murmured Calder as Craw jostled into place beside him.

'Damned if I know. My eyes ain't all they used to be.' Craw took a hold on his belt buckle and squinted around. 'Ain't this where we go to shit?'

Calder snorted. 'It's where we go to talk it. Though if you want to drop your trousers and give Brodd Tenways some polish for his boots I won't complain.'

Now Black Dow strolled out of the shadows, around the side of Skarling's Chair, chewing at a bone. The chatter quieted then died altogether, leaving only the crackle and crunch of sagging embers, faint snatches of song floating from outside the circle. Dow stripped his bone to nothing and tossed it into the fire, licking his fingers one by one while he took in every shadow-pitted face. Drew out the silence. Made 'em all wait. Left no doubts who was the biggest bastard on the hill.

'So,' he said in the end. 'Good day's work, no?' And a great clatter went up, men shaking their sword hilts, thumping shields with gauntlets, beating their armour with their fists. Scale joined in, banging his helmet on one scratched thigh-plate. Craw rattled his sword in its sheath, somewhat guiltily, since he hadn't run fast enough to draw it. Calder stayed quiet, he noticed, just sourly sucked his teeth as the clamour of victory faded.

'A good day!' Tenways leered around the fire.

'Aye, a good day,' said Reachey.

'Might've been better yet,' said Ironhead, curling his lip at Golden, 'if we'd only made it across the shallows.'

Golden's eyes burned in their bruised sockets, jaw muscles squirming on the side of his head, but he kept his peace. Probably 'cause talking hurt too much.

'Men are always telling me the world ain't what it was.' Dow held up his sword, grinning so the sharp point of his tongue stuck out between his teeth. 'Some things don't change, eh?' Another clattering chorus of approval, so much steel thrust up it was a wonder no one got stabbed by accident. 'For them who said the clans o' the North can't fight as one . . .' Dow curled his tongue and blew spit hissing into the fire. 'For them who said the Union are too many to beat . . .' He sent another gob sailing neatly into the flames. Then he looked up, eyes shining orange. 'And for them who say I'm not the man to do it . . .' And he rammed his sword point-first into the fire with a snarl, sparks whirling up around the hilt.

A hammering of approval loud as a busy smithy, loud enough to make Craw wince. 'Dow!' shrieked Tenways, smashing the pommel of his sword with one scabby hand. 'Black Dow!'

Others joined in, and found a rhythm with his name and with their fists on metal. 'Black! Dow! Black! Dow!' Ironhead with it, and Golden mumbling through his battered mouth, and Reachey too. Craw kept his silence. Take victory quiet and careful, Rudd Threetrees used to say, 'cause you might soon be called on to take defeat the same way. Across the fire, Craw caught the glint of Shivers' eye in the shadows. He wasn't chanting neither.

Dow settled back in Skarling's Chair just the way Bethod used to, basking in the love like a lizard in the sun then halting it with a kingly wave. 'All right. We've got all the best ground in the valley. They've got to back off or come at us, and there ain't many places they can do it. So there's no need for anything clever. Clever'd be wasted on the likes o' you lot, anyway.' A range of chuckles. 'So I'll take blood, and bones, and steel, like today.' More cheering. 'Reachey?'

'Aye, Chief.' The old warrior stepped into the firelight, mouth pressed into a hard line.

'I want your boys to hold Osrung. They'll come at you hard tomorrow, I reckon.'

Reachey shrugged. 'Only fair. We came at 'em pretty damn hard today.'

'Don't let 'em get across that bridge, Reachey. Ironhead?'

'Aye, Chief.'

'I'm giving you the shallows to mind. I want men in the orchard, I want men holding the Children, I want men ready to die but happier to kill. It's the one place they could come across in numbers, so if they try it we got to step on 'em hard.'

'That's what I do.' Ironhead sent a mocking look across the fire. 'Won't nobody be turning me back.'

'Whassat mean?' snarled Golden.

'You'll all get a stab at glory,' said Dow, bringing the pair of 'em to heel. 'Golden, you fought hard today so you'll be hanging back. Cover the ground between Ironhead and Reachey, ready to lend help to either one if they get pressed more'n they're comfortable with.'

'Aye.' Licking at his bloated lip with the point of his bloated tongue.

'Scale?'

'Chief.'

'You took the Old Bridge. Hold the Old Bridge.'

'Done.'

'If you have to fall back—'

'I won't,' said Scale, with all the confidence of youth and limited brains.

'—it'd be worth having a second line at that old wall. What do they call it?'

'Clail's Wall,' said Splitfoot. 'Some mad farmer built it.'

'Might be a good thing for us he did,' said Dow. 'You won't be able to use all you've got in the space behind that bridge anyway, so plant some further back.'

'I will,' said Scale.

'Tenways?'

'Made for glory, Chief!'

'You've got the slope o' the Heroes and Skarling's Finger to look to, which means you shouldn't get into any scrapes right off. Scale or Ironhead need your help, maybe you can find 'em some.'

Tenways sneered across the fire at Scale and Calder and,

hopefully just 'cause he was standing with 'em, Craw. 'I'll see what I can root out.'

Dow leaned forward. 'Splitfoot and me will be up here at the top, behind the drystone wall. Reckon I'll lead from the back tomorrow, like our friends in the Union do.' Another round of harsh laughter. 'So there it is. Anyone got any better ideas?' Dow slowly worked the gathering over with his grin. Craw had never felt less like speaking in his life, and it didn't seem likely anyone else would want to make a spectacle of themselves—

'I have.' Calder held up a finger, always wanting to make a spectacle of himself.

Dow's eyes narrowed. 'What a surprise. And what's your strategy, Prince Calder?'

'Put our backs to the Union and run?' asked Ironhead, a wave of chuckling following after.

'Put our backs to the Union and bend over?' asked Tenways, followed by another. Calder only smiled through it, and waited for the laughter to fade, and leave things silent.

'Peace,' he said.

Craw winced. It was like getting up on a table and calling for chastity in a brothel. He felt a strong urge to step away, like you might from a man doused in oil when there are a lot of naked flames about. But what kind of man steps away from a friend just 'cause he isn't popular? Even if he is in danger of becoming a fireball. So Craw stayed shoulder to shoulder with him, wondering what the hell his game was, since sure as sure Calder always had some game in mind. The disbelieving silence stretched out long enough for a sudden gust to whip up, make cloaks flap and torch flames dance, throwing wild light across that circle of frowns.

'Why, you bastard fucking *coward*!' Brodd Tenways' rashy face was so twisted up with scorn it looked like it might split.

'Call my brother a coward?' snarled Scale, eyes bulging. 'I'll twist your flaky fucking neck!'

'Now, now,' said Dow. 'If any necks need twisting I'll do the picking out. Prince Calder's known to have a way with words. I brought him out here to hear what he has to say, didn't I? So let's hear it, Calder. Why peace?'

'Careful, Calder,' muttered Craw, trying not to move his lips. 'Careful.'

If Calder heard the warning, he chose to piss all over it. 'Because war's a waste of men's time, and money, and lives.'

'Fucking *coward*!' barked Tenways again, and this time even Scale didn't disagree, just stood staring at his brother. There was a chorus of disgust, and cursing, and spitting, almost as loud as the chorus of approval for Dow. But the louder it got the more Calder smiled. Like he thrived on their hatred like a flower on shit.

'War's a way of getting things,' he said. 'If it gets you nothing, what's the point? How long have we been marching around out here?'

'You've had a trip back home, bastard,' someone called.

'Aye, and it was talk o' peace landed you there,' said Ironhead.

'All right, how long have *you* been out here, then?' Pointing right in Ironhead's face. 'Or you?' At Golden. 'Or him?' Jerking a thumb sideways at Craw. Craw frowned, wishing he'd been left out of it. 'Months? Years? Marching, and riding, and fearing, and lying out under the stars with your sickness and your wounds. In the wind, in the cold, while your fields, and your herds, and your workshops, and your wives go untended. For what? Eh? What plunder? What glory? If there are ten-score men in all this host who are richer because o' this I'll eat my own cock.'

'Coward's fucking talk!' snarled Tenways, turning away. 'I won't hear it!'

'Cowards run away from things. Scared of words, are you, Tenways? What a hero.' Calder even got a ragged scatter of laughter for that. Made Tenways stop and turn back, bristling. 'We won a victory here today! Legends, every man!' And Calder slapped at his sword hilt. 'But it was just a little one.' He jerked his head towards the south, where everyone knew the campfires of the enemy were lighting up the whole valley. 'There's plenty more Union. There'll be harder fighting on the morrow, and heavier losses. Far heavier. And if we win it's to end up in the same spot, just with more dead men for company. No?' Some were still shaking their heads, but more were listening, thinking it over. 'As for those who said the clans of the North can't fight as one, or the Union are too many to beat, well, I don't reckon those questions are quite settled yet.' Calder curled his tongue, and sent a bit of his own spittle spinning into Dow's fire. 'And any man can spit.'

'Peace,' snorted Tenways, who'd stuck around to listen after all. 'We all know what a lover o' peace your father was! Didn't he take us to war with the Union in the first place?'

Didn't slow Calder down a step. 'He did, and it was the end of him. Might be I learned from his mistake. Have you, is my question?' Looking every man in the eye. ''Cause if you ask me, it'd be a damn fool who risked his life for what he could get just by the asking.' There was silence for a while. A grudging, guilty silence. The wind flapped clothes some more, whipped sparks from the fire-pit in showers. Dow leaned forward, propping himself up on his sword.

'Well, you've done quite the job o' pissing on my cookfire, ain't you, Prince Calder?' Harsh chuckles all round, and the thoughtful moment was gone. 'How about you, Scale? You want peace?'

The brothers eyed each other for a moment, while Craw tried to ease back gently from between the two. 'No,' said Scale. 'I'm for fighting.'

Dow clicked his tongue. 'There we go. Seems you didn't even convince your own brother.' More chuckling, and Calder laughed with the rest, if somewhat sickly. 'Still, you've got quite the way with words, all right, Calder. Maybe the time'll come we need to talk peace with the Union. Then I'll be sure to give you the call.' He showed his teeth. 'Won't be tonight, though.'

Calder swept out a fancy bow. 'As you command, Protector of the North. You're the Chief.'

'That's right,' growled Dow, and most nodded along with him. 'That's right.' But Craw noticed a few had more thoughtful looks on their faces as they started to drift away into the night. Pondering their untilled fields, maybe, or their untilled wives. Could be Calder weren't so mad as he seemed. Northmen love battle, sure, but they love beer too. And like beer, there's only so much battle most can stomach.

'We suffered a reverse today. But tomorrow will be different.' Marshal Kroy's manner did not allow for the possibility of disagreement. It was stated as fact. 'Tomorrow we will take the fight to our enemy, and we will be victorious.' The room rustled, starched collars shifting as men nodded in unison.

'Victory,' someone murmured.

'By tomorrow morning all three divisions will be in position.' *Though one is ruined and the others will have marched all night.* 'We have the weight of numbers.' *We will crush them under our corpses!* 'We have right on our side.' *Good for you. I have a huge bruise on mine.* But the rest of the officers seemed cheered by the platitudes. *As idiots often are.*

Kroy turned to the map, pointing out the south bank of the shallows. The spot where Gorst had fought that very morning. 'General Jalenhorm's division needs time to regroup, so they will stay out of action in the centre, demonstrating towards the shallows but not crossing them. We will attack instead on both flanks.' He strode purposefully to the right side of the map, pushing his hand up the Ollensand Road towards Osrung. 'Lord Governor Meed, you are our right fist. Your division will attack Osrung at first light, carry the palisade, occupy the southern half of the town, then aim to take the bridge. The northern half is the more built up, and the Northmen have had time to strengthen their positions there.'

Meed's gaunt face was blotchy with intensity, eyes bright at the prospect of grappling with his hated enemy at last. 'We will flush them out and put every one of them to the sword.'

'Good. Be cautious, though, the woods to the east have not been thoroughly scouted. General Mitterick, you are the left hook. Your objective is to force your way across the Old Bridge and establish a presence on the far side.'

'Oh, my men will take the bridge, don't concern yourself about that, Lord Marshal. We'll take the bridge and drive them all the way to bloody Carleon—'

'Taking the bridge will be adequate, for today.'

'A battalion of the First Cavalry are being attached to your command.' Felnigg glared down his beak of a nose as if he thought attaching anything to Mitterick deeply ill-advised. 'They found a route through the marshes and a position in the woods beyond the enemy's right flank.'

Mitterick did not deign even to look at Kroy's chief of staff.

'I've asked for volunteers to lead the assault on the bridge, and my men have already built a number of sturdy rafts.'

Felnigg's glare intensified. 'I understand the current is strong.'

'It's worth a try, isn't it?' snapped Mitterick. 'They could hold us up all morning on that bridge!'

'Very well, but remember we are seeking victory, not glory.' Kroy looked sternly around the room. 'I will be sending written orders to each one of you. Are there any questions?'

'I have one, sir.' Colonel Brint held up a finger. 'Is it possible for Colonel Gorst to refrain from his heroics long enough for the rest of us to contribute?' There was a scattering of chuckles, utterly disproportionate to the humour displayed, the soldiers seizing on a rare chance to laugh. Gorst had been entirely occupied staring across the room at Finree and pretending not to. Now he found to his extreme discomfort that everyone was grinning at him. Someone started to clap. Soon there was a modest round of applause. He would have vastly preferred it if they had jeered at him. *That at least I could have joined in with.*

'I will observe,' he grunted.

'As will I,' said Bayaz, 'and perhaps conduct my little experiment on the south bank.'

The marshal bowed. 'We stand entirely at your disposal, Lord Bayaz.'

The First of the Magi slapped his thighs as he rose, his servant leaning forward to whisper something in his ear and, as though that was a call for the advance, the room began quickly to empty, officers hurrying back to their units to make preparations for the morning's attacks. *Make sure to pack plenty of coffins, you—*

'I hear you saved the army today.'

He spun about with all the dignity of a startled baboon and found himself staring into Finree's face at paralysingly close quarters. News of her marriage should have allowed him to finally bury his feelings for her as he had buried all the others worth having. But it seemed they were stronger than ever. A vice in his guts clamped down whenever he saw her, screwed tighter the longer they spoke. If you could call it speaking.

'Er,' he muttered. *I floundered around in a stream and killed seven men that I am sure of, but without doubt maimed several more. I hacked them apart in the hope that our fickle monarch* would hear of it, and commute my undeserved sentence of undeath. I made myself guilty of mass murder so I could be proclaimed innocent of incompetence. Sometimes they hang men for this type of thing, and sometimes they applaud. 'I am . . . lucky to be alive.'

She came closer and he felt a dizzy rush of blood, a lightness in his head not unlike serious illness. 'I have a feeling we are all lucky you are alive.'

I have a feeling in my trousers. If I was truly lucky you would put your hand down them. Is that too much to ask? After saving the army, and so on? 'I . . .' *I'm so sorry. I love you. Why am I sorry? I didn't say anything. Does a man need to feel sorry for what he thinks? Probably.*

She had already walked off to speak to her father, and he could hardly blame her. *If I was her, I wouldn't even look at me, let alone listen to me squeak my halting way through half a line of insipid drivel. And yet it hurts. It hurts so much when she goes.* He trudged for the door.

Fuck, I'm pathetic.

Calder slipped out of Dow's meet before he had to explain himself to his brother and hurried away between the fires, ignoring grumbled curses from the men gathered around them. He found a path between two of the torchlit Heroes, saw gold glinting on the slope and caught up with its owner as he strode angrily downhill.

'Golden! Golden, I need to talk to you!'

Glama Golden frowned over his shoulder. Perhaps the intention was fearsome fury, but the swellings on his cheek made him look like he was worried at the taste of something he was eating. Calder had to bite back a giggle. That smashed-up face was an opportunity for him, one he could ill afford to miss.

'What would I have to thay to you, Calder?' he snarled, three of his Named Men bristling behind him, hands tickling their many weapons.

'Quietly, we're watched!' Calder came close, huddling as though he had secrets to share. An attitude he'd noticed tended to make men do the same, however little they were inclined to. 'I thought we could help each other, since we find ourselves in the same position—'

'The thame?' Golden's bloated, blotched and bloodied face loomed close. Calder shrank back, all fear and surprise, while on the inside he was a fisherman who feels the tug on his line. Talk was his battlefield, and most of these fools were as useless on it as he was on a real one. 'How are we the thame, *peathemaker*?'

'Black Dow has his favourites, doesn't he? And the rest of us have to struggle over the scraps.'

'Favourith?' Golden's battered mouth was giving him a trace of a lisp and every time he slurred a word he looked even more enraged.

'You led the charge today, while *others* lagged at the back. You put your life in the balance, were wounded fighting Dow's battle. And now *others* are getting the place of honour, in the front line, while you sit at the rear? Wait, in case you're needed?' He leaned even closer. 'My father always admired you. Always told me you were a clever man, a righteous man, the kind who could be relied on.' It's amazing how well the most pathetic flattery can work. On enormously vain people especially. Calder knew that well enough. He used to be one.

'He never told me,' muttered Golden, though it was plain he wanted to believe it.

'How could he?' wheedled Calder. 'He was King of the Northmen. He didn't have the luxury of telling men what he really thought.' Which was just as well, because he'd thought Golden was a puffed-up halfhead, just as Calder did. 'But I can.' He just chose not to. 'There's no reason you and I need to stand on different sides. That's what Dow wants, to divide us. So he can share all the power, and the gold, and the glory with the likes of Splitfoot, and Tenways . . . and Ironhead.' Golden twitched at the name as if it was a hook tugging at his battered face. Their feud was so big he couldn't see around it, the idiot. 'We don't need to let that happen.' Almost a lover's whisper, and Calder risked slipping his hand gently onto Golden's shoulder. 'Together, you and I could do great things—'

'Enough!' mumbled Golden through his split lips, slapping away Calder's hand. 'Peddle your lieth elthewhere!' But Calder could smell the doubt as Golden turned away, and a little doubt was all he was after. If you can't make your enemies trust you, you can at least make them mistrust each other. Patience, his father would have told him, patience. He allowed himself a smirk as Golden and his men stomped off into the night. He was just sowing seeds. Time would bring the harvest. If he lived long enough to swing the scythe.

Lord Governor Meed gave Finree one last disapproving frown before leaving her alone with her father. He clearly could not stand anyone being in a position of power over him, especially a woman. But if he supposed she would give him a lacklustre report behind his back, he had profoundly underestimated her.

'Meed is a primping dunce,' she shot over her shoulder. 'He'll be as much use on a battlefield as a two-copper whore.' She thought about it a moment. 'Actually, I'm not being fair. The whore at least might improve morale. Meed is about as inspiring as a mouldy flannel. Just as well for him you called off the siege of Ollensand before it turned into a complete fiasco.'

She was surprised to see her father had dropped into a chair behind a travelling desk, head in his hands. He looked suddenly like a different man. Shrunken, and tired, and old. 'I lost a thousand men today, Fin. And a thousand more wounded.'

'Jalenhorm lost them.'

'Every man in this army is my responsibility. I lost them. A *thousand* of them. A number, easily said. Now rank them up. Ten, by ten, by ten. See how many there are?' He grimaced into the corner as though it was stacked high with bodies. 'Every one a father, a husband, a brother, a son. Every life lost a hole I can never fill, a debt I can never repay.' He stared through his spread fingers at her with red-rimmed eyes. 'Finree, I lost a thousand men.'

She took a step or two closer to him. 'Jalenhorm lost them.'

'Jalenhorm is a good man.'

'That's not enough.'

'It's something.'

'You should replace him.'

'You have to put some trust in your officers, or they'll never be worthy of it.'

'Is it possible for that advice to be as lame as it sounds?'

They frowned at each other for a moment, then her father waved it away. 'Jalenhorm is an old friend of the king, and the king is most particular about his old friends. Only the Closed Council can replace him.'

She was by no means out of suggestions. 'Replace Meed, then. The man's a danger to everyone in the army and a good few who aren't. Leave him in charge for long and today's disaster will soon be forgotten. Buried under one much worse.'

Her father sighed. 'And who would I put in his place?'

'I have the perfect man in mind. A very fine young officer.'

'Good teeth?'

'As it happens, and high born to a fault, and vigorous, brave, loyal and diligent.'

'Such men often come with fearsomely ambitious wives.'

'Especially this one.'

He rubbed his eyes. 'Finree, Finree, I've already done everything possible in getting him the position he has. In case you've forgotten, his father—'

'Hal is not his father. Some of us surpass our parents.'

He let that go, though it looked as if it took some effort. 'Be realistic, Fin. The Closed Council don't trust the nobility, and his family was the first among them, a heartbeat from the crown. Be patient.'

'Huh,' she snorted, at realism and patience both.

'If you want a higher place for your husband—' she opened her mouth but he raised his voice and talked over her. '—you'll need a more powerful patron than me. But if you want my advice – I know you don't, but still – you'll do without. I've sat on the Closed Council, at the very heart of government, and I can tell you power is a bloody mirage. The closer you seem to get the further away it is. So many demands to balance. So many pressures to endure. All the consequences of every decision weighing on you . . . small wonder the king never makes any. I never thought I would look forward to retirement, but perhaps without any power I can actually get something done.'

She was not ready to retire. 'Do we really have to wait for Meed to cause some catastrophe?'

He frowned up at her. 'Yes. Really. And then for the Closed Council to write to me demanding his replacement and telling me who it will be. Providing they don't replace me first, of course.'

'Who would they find to replace you?'

'I imagine General Mitterick would not turn down the appointment.'

'Mitterick is a vainglorious backbiter with the loyalty of a cuckoo.'

'He should suit the Closed Council perfectly, then.'

'I don't know how you can stand him.'

'I used to think I had all the answers myself, in my younger days. I maintain a guilty sympathy with those who still labour under the illusion.' He gave her a significant look. 'They are not few in number.'

'And I suppose it's a woman's place to simper on the sidelines and cheer as idiots rack up the casualties?'

'We all find ourselves cheering for idiots from time to time, that's a fact of life. There really is no point heaping scorn on my subordinates. If a person is worthy of contempt, they'll bury themselves soon enough without help.'

'Very well.' She did not plan to wait that long, but it was plain she would do no more good here. Her father had enough to worry about, and she was supposed to be lifting his spirits rather than weighing them down. Her eye fell on the squares board, still set out in the midst of their last game.

'You still have the board set?'

'Of course.'

'Then . . .' She had been planning her move ever since she last saw him, but made it as if it had only just occurred to her, brushing the piece forward with a shrug.

Her father looked up in that indulgent way he used to when she was a girl. 'Are you entirely sure about that?'

She sighed. 'It's as good as another.'

He reached for a piece, and paused. His eyes darted around the board, hand hovering. His smile faded. He slowly withdrew the hand, touched one finger to his bottom lip. Then he started to smile. 'Why, you—'

'Something to take your mind off the casualties.'

'I have Black Dow for that. Not to mention the First of the Magi and his colleagues.' He sourly shook his head. 'Are you staying here tonight? I could find you a—'

'I should be with Hal.'

'Of course. Of course you should.' She bent and kissed him on the forehead, and he closed his eyes, held her shoulder for a moment. 'Be careful tomorrow. I'd sooner lose ten thousand than lose you.'

'You won't shake me off that easily.' She headed for the door. 'I mean to live to see you get out of that move!'

The rain had stopped for the time being and the officers had drifted back to their units. All except one.

It looked as if Bremer dan Gorst had been caught between leaning nonchalantly against the rail their horses were tied to or standing proudly straight, and had ended up posed awkwardly in no-man's-land between the two.

Even so, Finree could not think of him as quite the harmless figure she once had, when they used to share brief and laughably formal conversations in the sunny gardens of the Agriont. Only a graze down the side of his face gave any indication that he had been in action at all that day, and yet she had it from Captain Hardrick that he had charged alone into a legion of Northmen and killed six. When she heard the story from Colonel Brint it had become ten. Who knew what story the enlisted men were telling by now? The pommel of his steel glinted faintly as he straightened, and she realised with an odd cold thrill that he had killed men with that sword, only a few hours before. Several men, whichever story you believed. It should not have raised him in her estimation in the least, and yet it did, very considerably. He had acquired the glamour of violence.

'Bremer. Are you waiting for my father?'

'I thought . . .' in that strangely incongruous, piping voice of his, and then, slightly lower, 'you might need an escort.'

She smiled. 'So there are still some heroes left in the world? Lead the way.'

Calder sat in the damp darkness, a long spit from the shit-pits, listening to other men celebrate Black Dow's victory. He didn't like admitting it, but he missed Seff. He missed the warmth and safety of her bed. He certainly missed the scent of her as the breeze picked up and wafted the smell of dung under his nose. But in all this chaos of campfires, drunken singing, drunken boasting, drunken wrestling, there was only one place he could think of where you could be sure of catching a man alone. And treachery needs privacy.

He heard heavy footsteps thumping towards the pit. Their maker was no more than a black outline with orange firelight down the edges, the very faintest grey planes of a face, but even so Calder recognised him. There were few men, even in this company, who were quite so wide. Calder stood, stretching out his stiff legs, and walked up to the edge of the pit beside the newcomer, wrinkling his nose. Pits full of shit, and pits full of corpses. That's all war left behind, as far as he could see.

'Cairm Ironhead,' he said quietly. 'What are the chances?'

'My, my.' The sound of spittle sucked from the back of a mouth, then sent spinning into the hole. 'Prince Calder, this is an honour. Thought you were camped over to the west with your brother.'

'I am.'

'My pits smell sweeter than his, do they?'

'Not much.'

'Come to measure cocks with me, then? It ain't how much you've got, you know, but what you do with it.'

'You could say the same about strength.'

'Or guile.' Nothing else but silence. Calder didn't like a silent man. A boastful man like Golden, an angry man like Tenways, even a savage man like Black Dow, they give you something to work with. A quiet man like Ironhead gives nothing. Especially in the dark, where Calder couldn't even guess at his thoughts.

'I need your help,' he tried.

'Think of running water.'

'Not with that.'

'With what, then?'

'I've heard it said Black Dow wants me dead.'

'More'n I know. But if it's true, what's my interest? We don't all love you as much as you love yourself, Calder.'

'You'll have need of allies of your own before too long, and you well know it.'

'Do I?'

Calder snorted. 'No fool gets where you are, Ironhead. Black Dow scarcely has more liking for you than me, I think.'

237

'No liking? Has he not put me in the place of honour? Front and middle, boy!'

Calder got the unpleasant feeling there was a trace of mocking laughter in Ironhead's voice. But it was some kind of opening and he had no choice but to charge in with his most scornful chuckle. 'The place of *honour*? Black Dow? He turned on the man who spared his life, and stole my father's chain for himself. The place of *honour*? He's done what I'd do to the man I fear most. Put you where you'll take the brunt of the enemy's fury. My father always said you were the toughest fighter in the North, and Black Dow knows it. Knows you'll never back down. He's put you where your own strength will work against you. And who's to benefit? Who's been left out of the fight? Tenways and Golden.' He'd been hoping for that name to work some magic, but Ironhead didn't move so much as a hair. 'They hang back while you, and my brother, and my wife's father do the fighting. I hope your honour can stop a knife in the back, when it comes.'

There was a grunt. 'Finally.'

'Finally what?'

The sound of piss spattering below them. 'That. You know, Calder, you said it yourself.'

'Said what?'

'No fool gets where I am. I'm a long way from convinced Black Dow's set on my doom or even on yours. But if he is, what help can you offer me? Your father's praise? That lost most of its worth when he got bested in the High Places, and all the rest when the Bloody-Nine smashed his skull to porridge. Oops.' Calder felt piss spattering over his boots. 'Sorry 'bout that. Guess we're not all as nimble with our cocks as you are. Reckon I'll stick with Dow, touched though I am by your offer of alliance.'

'Black Dow's got nothing to offer but war and the fear men have of him. If he dies there's nothing left.' Silence, while Calder wondered if he'd gone a step too far.

'Huh.' There was a jingling as Ironhead fastened his belt. 'Kill him, then. But until you do, find other ears for your lies. Find another piss-pit too, you wouldn't want to drown in this one.' Calder was slapped on the back, hard enough to leave him teetering at the brink, waving his arms for balance. When he found it, Ironhead was gone.

238

Calder stood there for a moment. If talk sows seeds, he wasn't sure at all what harvest he could expect from this. But that didn't have to be a bad thing. He'd learned Cairm Ironhead was a subtler man than he appeared. That alone was worth some piss on his boots.

'One day I'll sit in Skarling's Chair,' Calder whispered into the darkness. 'And I'll make you eat my shit, and you'll tell me nothing ever tasted so sweet.' That made him feel a little better.

He shook the wet from his boots as best he could, and strutted off into the night.

Rest and Recreation

Finree did not make much noise. Neither did Gorst. But that suited him well enough. Knobs of backbone showed through pale skin, thin muscles in her hunched shoulders tensing and relaxing, an unsightly ripple going through her arse with every thrust of his hips. He closed his eyes. In his head it was prettier.

They were in her husband's tent. *Or no.* That wasn't working. *My quarters in the palace.* The ones he used to have when he was the king's First Guard. *Yes.* That was better. Nice feel, they'd had. *Airy.* Or maybe her father's headquarters? *On his desk? In front of the other officers at a briefing?* Hell, no. *Urgh.* His quarters in the palace were easiest, familiar from a thousand well-worn fantasies in which the Closed Council had never stripped him of his position.

I love you, I love you, I love you. It hardly felt like love, though. It hardly felt like much of anything. Certainly nothing beautiful. A mechanical action. *Like winding a clock or peeling a carrot or milking a cow.* How long had he been at it now? His hips were aching, his stomach was aching, his back and his shoulder were bruised as a trampled apple from the fight in the shallows. Slap, slap, slap, skin on skin. He bared his teeth, gripping hard at her hips, forcing himself back to his airy quarters at the palace . . .

Getting there, getting there, getting there—

'Are you nearly done?'

Gorst stopped dead, snatched to reality with an icy shock. Nothing like Finree's voice. The side of her face turned towards him, gleaming damply in the light of the one candle, the dimple of an old acne scar inadequately covered by thick powder. Nothing like Finree's face. All his thrusting seemed to have made little impression. She might have been a baker asking his apprentice if the pies were done.

His rasping breath echoed back from the canvas. 'I thought I told you not to talk.'

'I've a queue.'

So much for nearly there. His cock was already wilting. He struggled to his feet, sore head brushing against the ceiling of the tent. She was one of the cleaner ones, but still the air had a cloying feel. Too much sweat and breath, and other things, inadequately smothered by cheap flower-water. He wondered how many other men had already been through here tonight, how many more would come through. He wondered if they pretended they were somewhere else, she was someone else. *Does she pretend that we are someone else? Does she care? Does she hate us? Or are we a procession of clocks to be wound, carrots to be peeled, cows to be milked?*

She had her back to him, shrugging her dress on so she could shrug it off again. He felt as if he was suffocating. He dragged his trousers up and fumbled his belt shut. He tossed coins on a wooden box without counting, tore his way out through the flap into the night and stood there, eyes closed, breathing the damp air and swearing never to do this again. *Again.*

One of the pimps stood outside, apparently unbothered by the water gently dripping from the brim of his hat, with that knowing and slightly threatening smile they have to wear like uniforms. 'Everything to your liking?'

My liking? I seem unable even to come in the allotted time. Most men are capable of that level of social interaction, at least, if no other, are they not? What am I, that I must debase and ruin even the one decent emotion I have? If one can call an entirely unhealthy obsession with another man's wife decent. I don't suppose one can. Well, probably he could.

Gorst looked at the man. Really looked, right in his eyes. Through that empty smile to the greed, and ruthlessness, and limitless boredom behind.

My liking? Shall I guffaw, and hug you like a brother? Hug you and hug you and twist your head all the way around, and your stupid fucking hat with it? If I beat your face until it has no bones in it, if I crush your scrawny throat with my hands, will that be a loss to the world, do you think? Will anyone even notice? Would I even notice? Would it be an evil deed, or a good? One less worm to get fat burrowing through the shit of the king's glorious army?

Gorst's mask must have slipped for a moment, or perhaps the man was more attuned by years of practice to hints of violence in a face than the cultured members of Jalenhorm's staff and Kroy's headquarters. His eyes narrowed and he took a cautious step back, one hand straying towards his belt.

Gorst found himself hoping the man would pull out a blade, excitement flaring briefly at the thought of seeing steel. *Is that all that excites me now? Death? Facing it and causing it?* Did he even feel the slightest renewed stirring in his sore groin at the possibility of violence? But the pimp only stood there, watching.

'Everything is fine.' And Gorst trudged past, boots squelching in the muck, away between the tents and into the mad carnival that sprang up behind the lines, as if by magic, whenever the army stopped for more than a couple of hours together. As full of bustle and variety as any market of the Thousand Isles, as full of blinding colour and choking fragrance as any Dagoskan bazaar, every need, taste or whim catered for a dozen times over.

Fawning merchants held swatches of bright cloth against officers too drunk to stand. Armourers battered out a shattering anvil music while salesmen demonstrated the strength, sharpness or beauty of wares nimbly replaced with trash when the money was handed over. A major with a bristling moustache sat frozen in double-chinned belligerence while a painter dashed off a shoddy representation by candlelight. Joyless laughter and meaningless babble hammered at Gorst's aching head. Everything the best, the finest, the bespoke and renowned.

'The new self-sharpening sheath!' someone roared. 'Self-sharpening!'

'Advances to officers! Loans at first-rate rates!'

'Suljuk girls here! Best fuckery you'll ever get!'

'Flowers!' in a voice somewhere between song and scream. 'For your wife! For your daughter! For your lover! For your whore!'

'For pet or pot!' a woman shrieked, thrusting up a bemused puppy. 'For pet or pot!'

Children old long before their time darted through the crowd offering polishing or prophecy, sharpening or shaving, grooming or gravedigging. Offering anything and everything that could be bought or paid for. A girl whose age could not be reckoned slipped all around Gorst in a capering dance, bare feet mud-caked to the knee. Suljuk, Gurkish, Styrian, who knew of what mongrel derivation. 'Like this?' she cooed, gesturing at a stick upon which samples of gold braid were stapled.

Gorst felt a sudden choking need to weep, and gave her a sad smile, and shook his head. She spat at his feet, and was gone. A pair of elderly ladies stood at the flap of a dripping tent, handing out printed papers extolling the virtues of temperance and sobriety to illiterate soldiers who had already left them trampled in the mud for a half-mile in every direction, worthy lessons gently erased by the rain.

A few more steps, each an unimaginable effort, and Gorst stopped in the track, alone in the midst of all that crowd. Cursing soldiers slopped through the mud around him, all stranded like him with their petty despairs, all shopping like him for what cannot be bought. He looked up, open-mouthed, rain tickling his tongue. Hoping for guidance, perhaps, but the stars were shrouded in cloud. *They light the happy way for better men. Harod dan Brock, and his like.* Shoulders and elbows knocked and jostled him. *Someone help me, please.*

But who?

DAY TWO

'You can't say that civilisation don't
advance, however, for in every war they
kill you in a new way'

Will Rogers

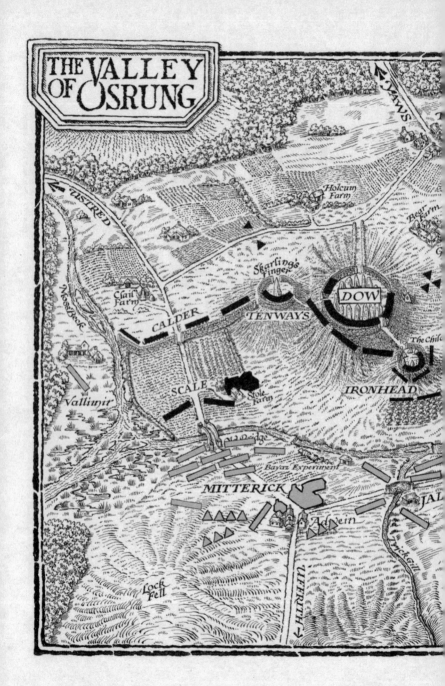

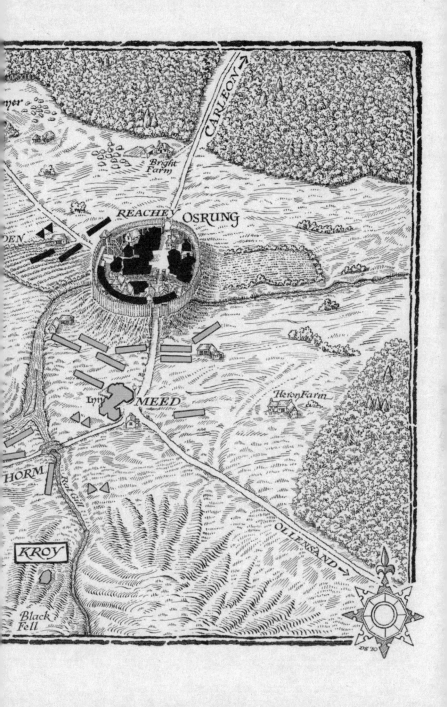

Dawn

When Craw dragged himself from his bed, cold and clammy as a drowned man's grave, the sun was no more'n a smear of mud-brown in the blackness of the eastern sky. He fumbled his sword through the clasp at his belt then stretched, creaked and grunted through his morning routine of working out exactly how much everything hurt. His aching jaw he could blame on Hardbread and his lads, his aching legs on a lengthy jog across some fields and up a hill followed by a night huddled in the wind, but the bastard of a headache he'd have to take the blame for himself. He'd had a drink or two or even a few more last night, softening the loss of the fallen, toasting the luck of the living.

Most of the dozen were already gathered about the pile of damp wood that on a happier day would've been a fire. Drofd was bent over it, cursing softly while he failed to get it lit. Cold breakfast, then.

'Oh, for a roof,' whispered Craw as he limped over.

'I slice the bread thin, d'you see?' Whirrun had the Father of Swords gripped between his knees with a hand's length drawn, and now he was rubbing loaf against blade with ludicrous care, like a carpenter chiselling at a vital joint.

'Sliced bread?' Wonderful turned away from the black valley to watch him. 'Can't see it catching on, can you?'

Yon spat over his shoulder. 'Either way, could you bloody get on with it? I'm hungry.'

Whirrun ignored 'em. 'Then, when I've got two cut,' and he dropped a pale slab of cheese on one slice then slapped the other on top like he was catching a fly, 'I trap the cheese between them, and there you have it!'

'Bread and cheese.' Yon weighed the half-loaf in one hand and the cheese in the other. 'Just the same as I've got.' And he bit a lump off the cheese and tossed it to Scorry.

Whirrun sighed. 'Have none of you no *vision*?' He held up his masterpiece to such light as there was, which was almost none. 'This is no more bread and cheese than a fine axe is wood and iron, or a live person is meat and hair.'

'What is it, then?' asked Drofd, rocking back from his wet wood and tossing the flint aside in disgust.

'A whole new thing. A forging of the humble parts of bread and cheese into a greater whole. I call it . . . a cheese-trap.' Whirrun took a dainty nibble from one corner. 'Oh, yes, my friends. This tastes like . . . progress. Works with ham, too. Works with anything.'

'You should try it with a turd,' said Wonderful.

Drofd laughed up snot but Whirrun hardly seemed to notice. 'This is the thing about war. Forces men to do new things with what they have. Forces them to think new ways. No war, no progress.' He leaned back on one elbow. 'War, d'you see, is like the plough that keeps the earth rich, like the fire that clears the fields, like—'

'The shit that makes the flowers grow?' asked Wonderful.

'Exactly!' Whirrun pointed at her sharply with his whole new thing and the cheese fell out into the unlit fire. Wonderful near fell over from laughing. Yon snorted so hard he blew bread out of his nose. Even Scorry stopped his singing to have a high chuckle. Craw laughed along, and it felt good. Felt like too long since the last time. Whirrun frowned at his two flapping slices of bread. 'Don't think I trapped it tight enough.' And he shoved 'em in his mouth all at once and started rooting through the damp twigs for the cheese.

'Union showed any sign of moving?' asked Craw.

'None that we've seen.' Yon squinted up at the stains of brightness in the east. 'Dawn's on the march, though. Reckon we'll see more soon.'

'Best get Brack up,' said Craw. 'He'll be pissy all day if he misses breakfast.'

'Aye, Chief.' And Drofd trotted off to where the hillman was sleeping.

Craw pointed down at the Father of Swords, short stretch of grey blade drawn. 'Don't it have to be blooded now?'

'Maybe crumbs count,' said Wonderful.

'Alas, they don't.' Whirrun brushed the heel of his hand against its edge, then wiped it with his last bit of crust and slid the sword gently back into its scabbard. 'Progress can be painful,' he muttered, sucking the cut.

'Chief?' Far as Craw could tell in the gloom, and with Drofd's hair blown across his face by the wind, the lad looked worried. 'Don't reckon Brack wants to get up.'

'We'll see.' Craw strode over to him, a big shape swaddled up on his side, shadow pooling in the folds of his blanket. 'Brack.' He poked him with the toe of his boot. 'Brack?' The tattooed side of Brack's face was all beaded with dew. Craw put his hand on it. Cold. Didn't feel like a person at all. Meat and hair, like Whirrun said.

'Up you get, Brack, you fat hog,' snapped Wonderful. 'Before Yon eats all your—'

'Brack's dead,' said Craw.

Finree could not have said how long she had been awake, sitting on her travelling chest at the window with her arms resting on the cold sill and her chin resting on her wrists. Long enough to watch the ragged line of the fells to the north become distinct from the sky, for the quick-flowing river to emerge glittering from the mist, for the forests to the east to take on the faintest texture. Now, if she squinted, she could pick out the jagged top of the fence around Osrung, a light twinkling at the window of a single tower. In the few hundred strides of black farmland between her and the town a ragged curve of flickering torches marked out the Union positions.

A little more light in the sky, a little more detail in the world, and Lord Governor Meed's men would be rushing from those trenches and towards the town. The strong right fist of her father's army. She bit down on the tip of her tongue, so hard it was painful. Excited and afraid at once.

She stretched, looking over her shoulder into the cobwebby little room. She had made a desultory effort at cleaning but had to admit she was pathetic as a homemaker. She wondered what had become of the owners of the inn. Wondered what its name was, even. She thought she had seen a pole over the gate, but the sign was gone. That's what war does. Strips people and places of their identities and turns them into enemies in a line, positions to be taken, resources to be foraged. Anonymous things that can be carelessly crushed, and stolen, and burned without guilt. War is hell, and all that. But full of opportunities.

She crossed to the bed, or the straw-filled mattress they were sharing, and leaned down over Hal, studying his face. He looked young, eyes closed and mouth open, cheek squashed against the sheet, breath whistling in his nose. Young, and innocent, and ever so slightly stupid.

'Hal,' she whispered, and sucked gently at his top lip. His eyelids fluttered open and he stretched back, arms above his head, craned up to kiss her, then saw the window and the glimmer of light in the sky.

'Damn it!' He threw the blankets back and scrambled out of bed. 'You should've woken me sooner.' He splashed water from the cracked bowl onto his face and rubbed it with a cloth, started pulling yesterday's trousers on.

'You'll still be early,' she said, leaning back on her elbows and watching him dress.

'I have to be twice as early. You know I do.'

'You looked so peaceful. I didn't have the heart to wake you.'

'I'm supposed to be helping coordinate the attack.'

'I suppose someone has to.'

He froze for a moment with his shirt over his head, then pulled it down. 'Perhaps . . . you should stay at your father's head-quarters today, up on the fell. Most of the other wives have already headed back to Uffrith.'

'If we could only pack Meed off along with the rest of the clothes-obsessed old women, perhaps we'd have a chance of victory.'

Hal soldiered on. 'There's only you and Aliz dan Brint, now, and I worry about you—'

He was painfully transparent. 'You worry that I'll make a scene with your incompetent commanding officer, you mean.'

'That too. Where's my—'

She kicked his sword rattling across the boards and he had to stoop to retrieve it. 'It's a shame, that a man like you should have to take orders from a man like Meed.'

'The world is full of shameful things. That's a long way from the worst.'

'Something really should be done about him.'

Hal was still busy fumbling with his sword-belt. 'There's nothing to be done but to make the best of it.'

'Well . . . someone could mention the mess he's making to the king.'

'You may not be aware of this, but my father and the king had a minor falling-out. I don't stand very high in his Majesty's favour.'

'Your good friend Colonel Brint does.'

Hal looked up sharply. 'Fin. That's low.'

'Who cares how high it is if it helps you get what you deserve?'

'*I* care,' he snapped, dragging the buckle closed. 'You get on by doing the right thing. By hard work, and loyalty, and doing as you're told. You don't get on by . . . by . . .'

'By what?'

'Whatever it is you're doing.'

She felt a sudden, powerful urge to hurt him. She wanted to say she could easily have married a man with a father who wasn't the most infamous traitor of his generation. She wanted to point out he only had the place he had now through her father's patronage and her constant wheedling, and that left to his own devices he'd have been demonstrating hard work and loyalty as a poor lieutenant in a provincial regiment. She wanted to tell him he was a good man, but the world was not the way good people thought it was. Fortunately, he got in first.

'Fin, I'm sorry. I know you want what's best for us. I know you've done a lot for me already. I don't deserve you. Just . . . let me do things my way. Please. Just promise me you won't do anything . . . rash.'

'I promise.' She'd make sure whatever she did was well thought out. That or she'd just break her promise. She didn't take them terribly seriously.

He smiled, somewhat relieved, and bent to kiss her. She returned it half-heartedly, but then, when she felt his shoulders slump, remembered he'd be in danger today, and she pinched his cheek and shook it about. 'I love you.' That was why she had come up here, no? Why she was slogging through the mud along with the soldiers? To be with him. To support him. To steer him in the right direction. The Fates knew, he needed it.

'I love you more,' he said.

'It's not a competition.'

'No?' And he went out, pulling on his jacket. She loved Hal. Really she did. But if she waited for him to get what they deserved through honesty and good nature she'd be waiting until the sky fell in.

And she did not plan to live out her days as some colonel's wife.

Corporal Tunny had long ago acquired a reputation as the fiercest sleeper in his Majesty's army. He could sleep on anything, in any situation, and wake in an instant ready for action or, better still, to avoid it. He'd slept through the whole assault at Ulrioch in the lead trench fifty strides from the breach, then woken just in time to hop between the corpses as the fighting petered out and snatch as fine a share of the booty as anyone who actually drew steel that day.

So a patch of waterlogged forest in the midst of a spotty drizzle with nothing but a smelly oilskin over his head was good as a feather bed to him. His recruits weren't anywhere near so tough in the eyelids, though. Tunny snapped awake in the chill gloom around dawn, back against a tree and the regimental standard in one fist, and nudged his oilskin up with one finger to see the two men he had left hunched over the damp ground.

'Like this?' Yolk was squeaking.

'No,' whispered Worth. 'Tinder under there, then strike it like—'

Tunny was up in a flash, stomped down hard on their pile of slimy sticks and crushed it flat. 'No fires, idiots, if the enemy miss the flames they'll see the smoke for sure!' Not that Yolk would've got that pitiable collection of soaked rot lit in ten years of trying. He wasn't even holding the flint properly.

'How we going to cook our bacon, though, Corporal?' Worth held up his skillet, a pale and unappetising slice lying limp inside.

'You're not.'

'We'll eat it raw?'

'Can't advise it,' said Tunny, 'especially not to you, Worth, given the sensitivity of your intestines.'

'My what?'

'Your dodgy guts.'

His shoulders slumped. 'What do we eat, then?'

'What have you got?'

'Nothing.'

'That's what you're eating, then. Unless you can find something better.' Even considering he'd been woken before dawn, Tunny was unusually grumpy. He had a lurking sense he had something to be very annoyed about, but wasn't sure what. Until he remembered the dirty water closing over Klige's face, and kicked Yolk's embarrassment of a fire away into the dripping brush.

'Colonel Vallimir came up a while ago,' murmured Yolk, as though that was the very thing Tunny needed to lift his spirits.

'Wonderful,' he hissed. 'Maybe we can eat him.'

'Might be some food came up with him.'

Tunny snorted. 'All officers ever bring up is trouble, and our boy Vallimir's the worst kind.'

'Stupid?' muttered Worth.

'Clever,' said Tunny. 'And ambitious. The kind of officer climbs to a promotion over the bodies of the common man.'

'Are we the common man?' asked Yolk.

Tunny stared at him. 'You are the fucking definition.' Yolk even looked pleased about it. 'No sign of Latherliver yet?'

'Lederlingen, Corporal Tunny.'

'I know his name, Worth. I choose to mispronounce it because it amuses me.' He puffed out his cheeks. His standard for amusement really had plummeted since this campaign got underway.

'Haven't seen him,' said Yolk, gazing sadly at that forlorn slice of bacon.

'That's something, at least.' Then, when the two lads looked blankly at him. 'Leperlover went to tell the tin-soldier pushers where we are. Chances are he'll be the one bringing the orders back.'

'What orders?' asked Yolk.

'How the hell should I know what orders? But any orders is a bad thing.' Tunny frowned off towards the treeline. He couldn't see much through the thicket of trunk, branch, shadow and mist, but he could just hear the sound of the distant stream, swollen with half the drizzle that had fallen last night. The other half felt like it was in his underwear. 'Might even be an order to attack. Cross that stream and hit the Northmen in the flank.'

Worth carefully set his pan down, pressing at his stomach. 'Corporal, I think—'

'Well, I don't want you doing it here, do I?'

Worth dashed off into the shadowy brush, already fumbling with his belt. Tunny sat back against his trunk, slipped out Yolk's flask and took the smallest nip.

Yolk licked his pale lips. 'Could I—'

'No.' Tunny regarded the recruit through narrowed eyes as he took another. 'Unless you've something to pay with.' Silence. 'There you go, then.'

'A tent would be something,' whispered Yolk in a voice almost too soft to hear.

'It would, but they're with the horses, and the king has seen fit to supply his loyal soldiers with a new and spectacularly inefficient type which leaks at every seam.' Leading, as it happened, to a profitable market in the old type in which Tunny had already twice turned a handsome profit. 'How would you pitch one here anyway?' And he wriggled back against his tree so the bark scratched his itchy shoulder blades.

'What should we do?' asked Yolk.

'Nothing whatsoever, trooper. Unless specifically and precisely instructed otherwise, a good soldier always does nothing.' In a narrow triangle between black branches, the sky was starting to show the faintest sickly tinge of light. Tunny winced, and closed his eyes. 'The thing folks at home never realise about war is just how bloody boring it is.'

And like that he was asleep again.

Calder's dream was the same one as always.

Skarling's Hall in Carleon, dim with shadows, sound of the river outside the tall windows. Years ago, when his father was King of the Northmen. He was watching his younger self, sitting in Skarling's Chair and smirking. Smirking down at Forley the Weakest, all bound up, Bad-Enough standing over him with his axe out.

Calder knew it for a dream, but he felt the same freezing dread as ever. He was trying to shout, but his mouth was all stopped up. He was trying to move, but he was bound as tight as Forley. Bound by what he'd done, and what he hadn't.

'What shall we do?' asked Bad-Enough.

And Calder said, 'Kill him.'

He woke with a jolt as the axe came down, floundering with his blankets. The room was fizzing black. There was none of that warm wash of relief you get when you wake from a nightmare. It had happened. Calder swung from his bed, rubbing at his sweaty temples. He'd given up on being a good man long ago, hadn't he?

Then why did he still dream like one?

'Peace?' Calder looked up with a start, heart jumping at his ribs. There was a great shape in the chair in the corner. A blacker shape than the darkness. 'It was talk of peace got you banished in the first place.'

Calder breathed out. 'And a good morning to you, brother.' Scale was wearing his armour, but that was no surprise. Calder was starting to think he slept in it.

'I thought you were the clever one? At this rate you'll clever yourself right back into the mud, and me along with you, and so much for our father's legacy then. Peace? On a day of victory?'

'Did you see their faces, though? Plenty even at that meet are ready to stop fighting, day of victory or not. There'll be harder days coming, and when they come more and more will see it our way—'

'*Your* way,' snapped Scale. 'I've a battle to fight. A man doesn't get to be reckoned a hero by talking.'

Calder could hardly keep the contempt out of his voice. 'Maybe what the North needs is fewer heroes and more thinkers. More builders. Maybe our father's remembered for his battles, but his legacy is the roads he laid, the fields he cleared, the towns, and the forges, and the docks, and the—'

'He built the roads to march his armies on. He cleared the

fields to feed them. The towns bred soldiers, the forges made swords, the docks brought in weapons.'

'Our father fought because he had to, not because he—'

'This is the North!' bellowed Scale, voice making the little room ring. 'Everyone has to fight!' Calder swallowed, suddenly unsure of himself and ever so slightly scared. 'Whether they want to or not. Sooner or later, everyone has to fight.'

Calder licked his lips, not ready to admit defeat. 'Our father preferred to get what he wanted with words. Men listened to—'

'Men listened because they knew he had *iron in him*!' Scale smashed the arm of his chair with his fist, wood cracking, struck it again and broke it off, sent it clattering across the boards. 'Do you know what I remember him telling me? "Get what you can with words, because words are free, but the words of an armed man ring that much sweeter. So when you talk, bring your sword."' He stood, and tossed something across the room. Calder squeaked, half-caught it, half-hit painfully in the chest by it. Heavy and hard, metal gleaming faintly. His sheathed sword. 'Come outside.' Scale loomed over him. 'And bring your sword.'

It was hardly any lighter outside the ramshackle farmhouse. Just the first smear of dawn in the heavy eastern sky, picking out the Heroes on their hilltop in solemn black. The wind was coming up keen, whipping drizzle in Calder's eyes, sweeping waves through the barley and making him hug himself tight. A scarecrow danced a mad jig on a pole near the house, torn gloves endlessly beckoning for a partner. Clail's Wall was a chest-high heap of moss running through the fields from beyond a rise on their right to a good way up the steep flank of the Heroes. Scale's men were huddled in its lee, most still swaddled in blankets, exactly where Calder wished he was. He couldn't remember the last time he'd seen the world this early and it was an even uglier place than usual.

Scale pointed south, through a gap in the wall and down a rough track scarred with puddles. 'Half the men are hidden in sight of the Old Bridge. When the Union try to cross, we'll stop the bastards.'

Calder didn't want to deny it, of course, but he had to ask. 'How many Union on the other side of the river now?'

'A lot.' Scale looked at him as if daring him to say something.

Calder only scratched his head. 'You're staying back here, with Pale-as-Snow and the rest of the men, behind Clail's Wall.' Calder nodded. Staying behind a wall sounded like his kind of job. 'Sooner or later, though, chances are I'll need your help. When I send for it, come forward. We'll fight together.' Calder winced into the wind. That sounded less like his kind of job. 'I can trust you to do that, right?'

Calder frowned sideways. 'Of course.' Prince Calder, a byword for trustiness. 'I won't let you down.' Brave, bold, good Prince Calder.

'Whatever we've lost, we've got each other still.' Scale put his big hand on Calder's shoulder. 'It's not easy, is it? Being a great man's son. You'd have thought it would come with all kinds of advantages – with borrowed admiration, and respect. But it's only as easy as it is for the seeds of a great tree, trying to grow in its choking shadow. Not many make it to the sunlight for themselves.'

'Aye.' Calder didn't mention that being a great man's younger son was twice the trial. Then you've two trees to take the axe to before you can spread your leaves in the sunshine.

Scale nodded up towards Skarling's Finger. A few fires still twinkled on the flanks of the hill where Tenways' men had their camps. 'If we can't hold up, Brodd Tenways is meant to be helping.'

Calder raised his brows. 'I'll expect Skarling himself to ride to my aid before I count on that old bastard.'

'Then it's you and me. We might not always agree, but we're family.' Scale held out his hand, and Calder took it.

'Family.' Half-family, anyway.

'Good luck, brother.'

'And to you.' Half-brother. Calder watched Scale swing up onto his horse and spur off sharply down that track towards the Old Bridge.

'Got a feeling you'll need more'n luck today, your Highness.' Foss Deep was under the dripping ruins of a porch beside the house, his weathered clothes and his weathered face fading into the weathered wall behind.

'I don't know.' Shallow sat wrapped in a grey blanket so only his grinning head showed, disembodied. 'The biggest mountain of best luck ever might do it.'

Calder turned away from them in sulky silence, frowning across the fields to the south. He'd a feeling they might have the truth of it.

Theirs wasn't the only bit of earth being turned over. Few other wounded men must've died in the night. You could see the little groups, hunched in the drizzle with sorrow, or more likely self-pity, which looks about the same and serves just as well at a funeral. You could hear the Chiefs trotting out their empty babble, all aiming at that same sorry tone. Splitfoot was one, standing over the grave of one of Dow's Named Men not twenty paces distant, giving it the moist eye. No sign of Dow himself, mind you. Moist eyes weren't really his style.

Meanwhile the ordinary business of the day got started like the burial parties were ghosts themselves, invisible. Men grumbling as they crawled from wet beds, cursing at damp clothes, rubbing down damp weapons and armour, searching out food, pissing, scratching, sucking the last drops from last night's bottles, comparing trophies stolen from the Union, chuckling over one joke or another. Chuckling too loud because they all knew there'd be more dark work today and chuckles had to be grabbed where they could be.

Craw looked at the others, all with heads bowed. All except Whirrun, who was arching back, hugging the Father of Swords in his folded arms, letting the rain patter on his tongue. Craw was a little annoyed by that, and a little jealous of it. He wished he was known as a madman and didn't have to go through the empty routines. But there's a right way of doing things, and for him there was no dodging it.

'What makes a man a hero?' he asked the wet air. 'Big deeds? Big name? Tall glory and tall songs? No. Standing by your crew, I reckon.' Whirrun grunted his agreement, then stuck his tongue out again. 'Brack-i-Dayn, come down from the hills fifteen years ago, fought beside me fourteen of 'em, and always thought of his crew 'fore himself. Lost count on the number o' times that big bastard saved my life. Always had a kind word, or a funny one. Think he even made Yon laugh one time.'

'Twice,' said Yon, face harder'n ever. Got any harder he'd be knocking lumps from the Heroes with it.

'He made no complaints. Except not enough to eat.' Craw's voice went for a moment and he gave a kind of squeaky croak. Stupid bloody noise for a Chief to make, 'specially at a time like this. He cleared his throat and hammered on. 'Never enough for Brack to eat. He died . . . peaceful. Reckon he'd have liked that, even if he loved a good fight. Dying in your sleep is a long stretch better'n dying with steel in your guts, whatever the songs say.'

'Fuck the songs,' said Wonderful.

'Aye. Fuck 'em. Don't know who's buried under here, really. But if it's Skarling his self he should be proud to share some earth with Brack-i-Dayn.' Craw curled his lips back. 'And if not, fuck him too. Back to the mud, Brack.' He knelt, not having to try too hard to look in pain since his kneecap felt like it was going to pop off, clawed up a fistful of damp black soil and shook it out again over the rest.

'Back to the mud,' muttered Yon.

'Back to the mud,' came Wonderful's echo.

'Looking on the sunny side,' said Whirrun, 'it's where we're all headed, one way or another. No?' He looked about as though expecting that to lift spirits, and when it didn't, shrugged and turned away.

'Old Brack's all done.' Scorry squatted by the grave, one hand on the wet ground, brow furrowed like at a puzzle he couldn't work out. 'Can't believe it. Good words, though, Chief.'

'You reckon?' Craw winced as he stood, slapping the dirt from his hands. 'I'm not sure how many more o' these I can stand.'

'Aye,' murmured Scorry. 'I guess those are the times.'

Opening Remarks

'**G**et up.'

Beck shoved the foot away, scowling. He didn't care for a boot in the ribs at any time, but 'specially not from Reft, and 'specially not when it felt like he only just got off to sleep. He'd lain awake in the darkness a long time, thinking on Caul Shivers stabbing that man, turning it over and over as he twisted about under his blanket. Not able to get comfortable. Not with his blanket or with the thought of that little knife poking away. 'What?'

'The Union are coming, that's what.'

Beck tore his blanket back and strode across the garret room, ducking under the low beam, sleep and anger forgotten both at once. He kicked the creaking door of the big cupboard closed, shouldered Brait and Stodder out of the way and stared through one of the narrow windows.

He'd half-expected to see men slaughtering each other outside in the lanes of Osrung, blood flying and flags waving and songs being sung right under his window. But the town was quiet at a first glance. Weren't much beyond dawn and the rain was flitting down, drawing a greasy haze over the huddled buildings.

Maybe forty strides away across a cobbled square the brown river was churning past, swollen with rain off the fells. The bridge didn't look much for all the fuss being made of it – a worn stone span barely wide enough for two riders to pass each other. A mill house stood on its right, a row of low houses on its left, shutters open with a few nervy faces at the windows, most looking off to the south, just like Beck. Beyond the bridge a rutted lane led between wattle shacks and up to the fence on the south side of town. He thought he could see men moving there on the walkways, dim through the drizzle. Maybe a couple with flatbows already shooting.

While he was looking, men started hurrying from an alley and into the square below, forming up a shield wall at the north end of the bridge while a man in a fine cloak bellowed at 'em. Carls to the front, ready to lock their painted shields together. Thralls behind, spears ready to bring down.

There was a battle on the way, all right.

'You should've told me sooner,' he snapped, hurrying back to his blanket and dragging on his boots.

'Didn't know sooner,' said Reft.

'Here.' Colving offered Beck a hunk of black bread, his eyes scared circles in his chubby face.

Even the thought of eating made Beck feel sick. He snatched up his sword, then realised he'd nowhere to take it to. Weren't like he had a place at the fence, or in the shield wall, or anywhere else in particular. He looked towards the stairs, then towards the window, free hand opening and closing. 'What do we do?'

'We wait.' Flood dragged his stiff leg up the steps and into the attic. He'd got his mail on, glistening with drizzle across the shoulders. 'Reachey's given us two houses to hold, this and one just across the street. I'll be in there.'

'You will?' Beck realised he'd made himself sound scared, like a child asking his mummy if she was really going to leave him in the dark. 'You know, some o' these boys could do with a man to look to—'

'That'll have to be you and Reft. You might not believe it, but the lads in the other house are even greener'n you lot.'

'Right. 'Course.' Beck had spent the past week chafing at Flood being always around, keeping him back. Now the thought of the old boy going only made him feel more jittery.

'There'll be you five and five more in this house. Some other lads from the weapontake. For the time being just sit tight. Block up the windows downstairs best you can. Who's got a bow?'

'I have,' said Beck.

'And me.' Reft held his up.

'I've got my sling,' said Colving, hopefully.

'You any good with it?' asked Reft.

The boy shook his head sadly. 'Couldn't use it at a window, anyway.'

'Why bring it up, then?' snapped Beck, fingering his own bow. His palm was all sweaty.

Flood walked to the two narrow windows and pointed towards the river. 'Maybe we'll hold 'em at the fence, but if not we're forming up a shield wall at the bridge. If we don't hold 'em there, well, anyone with a bow start shooting. Careful, though, don't go hitting any of our boys in the back, eh? Better not to shoot at all than risk killing our own, and when the blood's up it can get hard to make out the difference. The rest of you downstairs, ready to keep 'em out of the house if they make it across.' Stodder chewed at his big bottom lip. 'Don't worry. They won't make it across, and even if they do they'll be in a right mess. Reachey'll be getting ready to hit back by then, you can bet on that. So if they try to get in, just keep 'em out 'til help gets here.'

'Keep 'em out,' piped Brait, jabbing happily at nothing with his twig of a spear. He didn't look like he could've kept a cat out of a chicken coop with that.

'Any questions?' Beck didn't feel he had a clue what to do, but it hardly seemed one question would plug the gap, so he kept quiet. 'Right, then. I'll check back if I can.' Flood limped to the stairway and was gone. They were on their own. Beck strode to a window again, thinking it was better'n doing nothing, but naught had changed that he could see.

'They over the fence yet?' Brait was up on tiptoe, trying to look over Beck's shoulder. He sounded all excited, eyes bright like a boy on his birthday, waiting to see what his present might be. He sounded a little bit like Beck always thought he'd feel facing battle. But he didn't feel that way. He felt sick and hot in spite of the damp breeze on his face.

'No. And ain't you supposed to be downstairs?'

'Not 'til they come, I'm not. Don't get to see this every day, do you?'

Beck brushed him off with an elbow. 'Just get out of it! Your stink's making me sick!'

'All right, all right.' Brait shambled away, looking hurt, but Beck couldn't bring up much sympathy. It was the best he could do not to bring up the breakfast he hadn't had.

Reft was stood at the other window, bow over his shoulder. 'Thought you'd be happy. Looks like you'll get your chance to be a hero.'

'I am happy,' snapped Beck. And not shitting himself at all.

Meed had established his headquarters in the inn's common hall, which by the standards of the North was a palatial space, double height and with a gallery at first-floor level. Overnight it had been decorated like a palace too with gaudy hangings, inlaid cupboards, gilded candlesticks and all the pompous trappings one would expect in a lord governor's own residence, presumably carted half way across the North at monstrous expense. A pair of violinists had set up in the corner and were grinning smugly at each other as they sawed out jaunty chamber music. Three huge oil paintings had even been hoisted into position by Meed's industrious servants: two renderings of great battles from the Union's history and, incredibly, a portrait of Meed himself, glowering from on high in antique armour. Finree gaped at it for a moment, hardly knowing whether to laugh or cry.

Large windows faced south into the inn's weed-colonised courtyard, east across fields dotted with trees towards brooding woods, and north towards the town of Osrung. With all the shutters wide open a chilly breeze drifted through the room, ruffling hair and snatching at papers. Officers clustered about the northern windows, eager to catch a glimpse of the assault, Meed in their midst in a uniform of eye-searing crimson. He glanced sideways as Finree slipped up beside him and gave the slightest sneer of distaste, like a fastidious eater who has spied an insect in his salad. She returned it with a beaming smile.

'Might I borrow your eyeglass, your Grace?'

He worked his mouth sourly for a moment but was held prisoner by etiquette, and handed it stiffly over. 'Of course.'

The road curved off to the north, a muddy stripe through muddy fields overflowing with the sprawling camp, tents haphazardly scattered like monstrous fungi sprouted in the night. Beyond them were the earthworks Meed's men had thrown up in the darkness. Beyond them, through the haze of mist and drizzle, she could just make out the fence around Osrung, perhaps even the suggestion of scaling ladders against it.

Her imagination filled in the blanks. Ranks of marching men ordered forward to the palisade, grim-faced and determined as arrows showered down. The wounded dragged for the rear or left screaming where they lay. Rocks tumbling, ladders shoved from the fence, men butchered as they tried to climb over onto the walkways, thrust screaming back to be dashed on the ground below.

She wondered whether Hal was in the midst of that, playing the hero. For the first time she felt a stab of worry for him, a cold shiver through her shoulders. This was no game. She lowered Meed's eyeglass, chewing at her lip.

'Where the hell is the Dogman and his rabble?' the lord governor was demanding of Captain Hardrick.

'I believe they were behind us on the road, your Grace. His scouts came upon a burned-out village and the lord marshal gave him leave to investigate. They should be here within an hour or two—'

'Typical. You can rely on him for a knowing shrug but when the battle begins he is nowhere to be seen.'

'Northmen are treacherous by nature,' someone tossed out.

'Cowardly.'

'Their presence would only slow us down, your Grace.'

'That much is true,' snorted Meed. 'Order every unit into the attack. I want them overwhelmed. I want that town crushed into the dust and every Northman in it dead or running.'

Finree could not help herself. 'Surely it would be wise to leave at least one regiment behind? As I understand it, the woods to the east have not been thoroughly—'

'Do you seriously suppose you will hit upon some scheme by which you will replace me with your husband?'

There was a pause that seemed impossibly long, while Finree wondered if she might be dreaming. 'I beg your—'

'He is a pleasant enough man, of course. Brave and honest and all those things housewives like to coo about. But he is a fool and, what is worse, the son of a notorious traitor and the husband of a shrew to boot. His only significant friend is your father, and your father's days in the sun are numbered in small digits.' Meed spoke softly, but not so softly that he could not easily be overheard. One young captain's mouth fell open with surprise.

It seemed Meed was not held quite so tightly by the bonds of etiquette as she had supposed.

'I frustrated an attempt by the Closed Council to prevent me taking my brother's place as lord governor, did you know that? The Closed Council. Do you really suppose some soldier's daughter might succeed where they failed? Address me only once again without the proper respect and I will crush you and your husband like the pretty, ambitious, irrelevant lice you are.' He calmly plucked his eyeglass from her limp hand and looked through it towards Osrung, precisely as if he had never spoken and she did not exist.

Finree should have whipped out some acid rejoinder, but the only thing in her mind was an overpowering urge to smash the front of Meed's eyeglass with her fist and drive the other end into his skull. The room seemed uncomfortably bright. The violins ripped at her ears. Her face burned as if she had been slapped. All she could do was blink, and meekly retreat. It was as if she floated to the other side of the room without moving her feet. A couple of the officers watched her get there, muttering among themselves, evidently party to her one-sided humiliation and no doubt relishing it too.

'Are you all right?' asked Aliz. 'You look pale.'

'I am perfectly well.' Or, in fact, seething with fury. Insulting her was one thing, no doubt she deserved it. Insulting her husband and her father were other things entirely. That she would make the old bastard pay for, she swore it.

Aliz leaned close. 'What do we do now?'

'Now? We sit here like good little girls and applaud while idiots stack up the coffins.'

'Oh.'

'Don't worry. Later on they might let you weep over a wound or two and, if the mood takes you, you can flutter your eyelashes at the awful futility of it all.'

Aliz swallowed, and looked away. 'Oh.'

'That's right. Oh.'

So this was battle. Beck and Reft had never had too much to say to each other, but since the Union first started fighting their way over the fence they hadn't said a word. Just stood silent at the windows. Beck wished he'd got friends beside him. Or wished he'd tried harder to make friends of the lads he'd found beside him. But it was too late now.

His bow was in his hand, an arrow nocked and the string ready to draw. He'd had it ready the best part of an hour, but there was no one he could shoot at. Nothing he could do but watch, and sweat, and lick his lips, and watch. He'd started off wishing he could see more, but now the rain had slacked off, and the sun was getting up, and Beck found he was seeing far more than he wanted to.

The Union were over the fence in three or four places, into the town in numbers. There was fighting all over, everything broken up into separate little scraps facing every which way. No lines, just a mass of confusion and mad noise. Shouts and howls mashed together, din of clashing metal and breaking wood.

Beck was no expert. He didn't know how anyone could be at this. But he could feel the balance shifting over there on the south side of the river. More and more Northmen were scurrying back across the bridge, some limping or holding wounds, some shouting and pointing off south, threading their way through the shield wall at the north end of the span and into the square under Beck's window. Safety. He hoped. Felt a long bloody way from safe, though. Felt about as far from safe as Beck had in his whole life.

'I want to see!' Brait was dragging at Beck's shirt, trying to get a peek through the window. 'What's going on?'

Beck didn't know what to say. Didn't know if he could find his voice, even. Right under them some wounded man was screaming. Gurgling, retching screams. Beck wished he'd stop. He felt dizzy with it.

The fence was mostly lost. He could see one tall Union man on the walkway, pointing towards the bridge with a sword, clapping men on their backs as they flooded off the ladders to either side of him. There were still a few dozen Carls at the gate, clustered around a tattered standard, painted shields facing out in a half-circle but they were surrounded and well outnumbered, shafts hissing down into 'em from the walkways.

Some of the bigger buildings were still in Northern hands. Beck could see men at the windows, shooting arrows out, ducking back in. Doors nailed shut and barricaded, but Union men swarming around 'em like bees around a hive. They'd managed to set fires for a couple of the most stubborn holdouts, in spite of the damp. Now brown smoke billowed out and was carried off east by the wind, lit by the dull orange of flames flickering.

A Northman came charging from a burning building, swinging an axe around his head in both hands. Beck couldn't hear him shouting, could see he was, though. In the songs he'd have taken a load down with him and joined the dead proud. Couple of Union men scattered away before some others herded him back against the wall with spears. One stuck him in the arm and he dropped his axe, held his other hand up, shouting more. Giving up, maybe, or insults, didn't make much difference. They stuck him in the chest and he slumped down. Stuck him on the ground, spear shafts going up and down like a couple of men digging in the fields.

Beck's wide-open, watery eyes kept on darting across the buildings, murder in plain view all along the riverbank not a hundred strides from where he stood. They dragged someone struggling out from a hovel and bent him over. There was the twinkle of a knife, then they shoved him into the water and he floated away on his face while they wandered back inside the house. Cut his throat, Beck reckoned. Cut his throat, just like that.

'They've got the gate.' Reft's voice sounded strangled. Like he'd never spoken before. Beck saw he was right, though. They'd cut down the last defenders, and were dragging the bars clear, and pulling the gates open, and daylight showed through the square archway.

'By the dead,' whispered Beck, but it came out just a breath. Hundreds of the bastards started flowing into Osrung, pouring out into the smoke and the scattered buildings, flooding down the lane towards the bridge. The triple row of Northmen at its north end looked a pitiful barrier all of a sudden. A sand wall to hold back the ocean. Beck could see them stirring. Wilting, almost. Could feel their deep desire to join the men who were scattering back across the bridge and through their ranks, trying to escape the slaughter on the far bank.

Beck felt it too, that tickling need to run. To do something, and run was all he could think of. His eyes flickered over the burning buildings on the south side of the river, flames reaching higher now, smoke spreading over the town.

Beck wondered what it was like inside those houses. No way out. Thousands of Union bastards beating at the doors, at the walls, shooting arrows in. Low rooms filling up with smoke. Wounded men with small hopes of mercy. Counting their last shafts. Counting their dead friends. No way out. Time was Beck's blood would've run hot at thoughts like that. It was on the chilly side now, though. Those weren't no fortresses built for defending on the other side of the river, they were little wooden shacks.

Just like the one he was in.

The Infernal Contraptions

Your August Majesty,

    *Morning on the second day of battle, and the North-
men occupy strong positions on the north side of the river.
They hold the Old Bridge, they hold Osrung, and they hold the
Heroes. They hold the crossings and invite us to take them. The
ground is theirs, but they have handed the initiative to Lord
Marshal Kroy and, now that all our forces have reached the
battlefield, he will not be slow to seize it.*

    *On the eastern wing, Lord Governor Meed has already begun
an attack in overwhelming force upon the town of Osrung. I find
myself upon the western, observing General Mitterick's assault
upon the Old Bridge.*

    *The general delivered a rousing speech this morning as the first
light touched the sky. When he asked for volunteers to lead the
attack every man put up his hand without hesitation. Your
Majesty would be most proud of the bravery, the honour, and the
dedication of your soldiers. Truly, every man of them is a hero.*

    *I remain your Majesty's most faithful and unworthy servant,
Bremer dan Gorst, Royal Observer of the Northern War*

Gorst blotted the letter, folded it and passed it to Younger, who
sealed it with a blob of red wax and slid it into a courier's satchel
with the golden sun of the Union worked into the leather in
elaborate gilt.

'It will be on its way south within the hour,' said the servant,
turning to go.

'Excellent,' said Gorst.

*But is it? Does it truly matter whether it goes sooner, or later, or if
Younger tosses it into the latrine pits along with the rest of the camp's
ordure? Does it matter whether the king ever reads my pompous*

platitudes about General Mitterick's pompous platitudes as the first light touched up the sky? When did I last get a letter back? A month ago? Two? Is just a note too much to ask? Thanks for the patriotic garbage, hope you're keeping well in ignominious exile?

He picked absently at the scabs on the back of his right hand, wanting to see if he could make them hurt. He winced as he made them hurt more than he had intended to. *Ever a fine line.* He was covered with grazes, cuts and bruises he could not even recall the causes of, but the worst pain came from the loss of his Calvez-made short steel, drowned somewhere in the shallows. One of the few relics remaining of a time when he was the king's exalted First Guard rather than an author of contemptible fantasies. *I am like a jilted lover too cowardly to move on, clinging tremble-lipped to the last feeble mementoes of the cad who abandoned her. Except sadder, and uglier, and with a higher voice. And I kill people for a hobby.*

He stepped from under the dripping awning outside his tent. The rain had slackened to a few flitting specks, and there was even some blue sky torn from the pall of cloud that smothered the valley. He surely should have felt some flicker of optimism at the simple pleasure of the sun on his face. But there was only the unbearable weight of his disgrace. The fool's tasks lined up in crushingly tedious procession. *Run. Practice. Shit a turd. Write a letter. Eat. Watch. Write a turd. Shit a letter. Eat. Bed. Pretend to sleep but actually lie awake all night trying to wank. Up. Run. Letter . . .*

Mitterick had already presided over one failed attempt on the bridge: a bold, rash effort by the Tenth Foot which had crossed unresisted to a lot of victorious whooping. The Northmen had met them with a hail of arrows as they attempted to find their order on the far side, then sprang from hidden trenches in the barley and charged with a blood-freezing wail. Whoever was in command of them knew his business. The Union soldiers fought hard but were surrounded on three sides and quickly cut down, forced back into the river to flounder helplessly in the water, or crushed into a hellish confusion on the bridge itself, mingled with those still striving mindlessly to cross from behind.

A great line of Mitterick's flatbowmen had then appeared from behind a hedgerow on the south bank and raked the Northmen with a savage volley, forcing them into a disorganised retreat back to their trenches, leaving the dead scattered in the trampled crops on their side of the bridge. The Tenth had been too mauled to take advantage of the opening, though, and now archers on both sides were busy with a desultory exchange of ammunition across the water while Mitterick and his officers marshalled their next wave. *And, one imagines, their next batch of coffins too.*

Gorst watched the whirling clouds of gnats that haunted the bank, and the corpses that floated past beneath them. *The bravery.* Turning with the current. *The honour.* Face up and face down. *The dedication of the soldiers.* One sodden Union hero wallowed to a halt in some rushes, bobbing for a moment on his side. A Northman drifted up, bumped gently into him and carried him from the bank and through a patch of frothy yellow scum in an awkward embrace. *Ah, young love. Perhaps someone will hug me after my death. I certainly haven't had many before.* Gorst had to stop himself snorting with spectacularly inappropriate laughter.

'Why, Colonel Gorst!' The First of the Magi strolled up with staff in one hand and teacup in the other. He took in the river and its floating cargo, heaved a long breath through his nose and exhaled satisfaction. 'Well, you couldn't say they aren't giving it a good try, anyway. Successes are all very well, but there's something grand about a glorious failure, isn't there?'

I can't see what, and I should know.

'Lord Bayaz.' The Magus' curly-headed servant snapped open a folding chair, brushed an imaginary speck of dust from its canvas seat and bowed low.

Bayaz tossed his staff on the wet grass without ceremony and sat, eyes closed, tipping his smiling face towards the strengthening sun. 'Wonderful thing, a war. Done in the right way, of course, for the right reasons. Separates the fruit from the chaff. Cleans things up.' He snapped his fingers with an almost impossibly loud crack. 'Without them societies are apt to become soft. Flabby. Like a man who eats only cake.' He reached up and punched Gorst playfully on the arm, then shook out his limp fingers in fake pain. 'Ouch! I bet you don't eat only cake, do you?'

'No.'

Like virtually everyone Gorst ever spoke to, Bayaz was hardly listening. 'Things don't change just by the asking. You have to give them a damn good shake. Whoever said war never changes anything, well . . . they just haven't fought enough wars, have they? Glad to see this rain's clearing up, though. It's been playing hell with my experiment.'

The experiment consisted of three giant tubes of dull, grey-black metal, seated upon huge wooden cradles, each closed at one end with the other pointed across the river in the vague direction of the Heroes. They had been set up with immense care and effort on a hump of ground a hundred strides from Gorst's tent. The ceaseless din of men, horses and tackle would have kept him awake all night had he not been half-awake anyway, as he always was. Lost in the smoke of Cardotti's House of Leisure, searching desperately for the king. Seeing a masked face in the gloom, at the stairway. Before the Closed Council as they stripped him of his position, the bottom dropping out of the world all over again. Twisted up with Finree, holding her. Holding smoke. Coughing smoke, as he stumbled through the twisted corridors of Cardotti's House of—

'Pitiful, isn't it?' asked Bayaz.

For a moment, Gorst wondered if the Magus had read his thoughts. *And yes, it certainly fucking is.* 'Pardon?'

Bayaz spread his arms to encompass the scene of crawling activity. 'All the doings of men, still at the mercy of the fickle skies. And war most of all.' He sipped from his cup again, grimaced and flung the dregs out across the grass. 'Once we can kill people at any time of day, in any season, in any weather, why, *then* we'll be civilised, eh?' And he chuckled away to himself.

The two old Adepti from the University of Adua scraped up like a pair of priests given a personal audience with God. The one called Denka was ghoul-pale and trembling. The one called Saurizin had a sheen of sweat across his wrinkled forehead which sprang back as fast as he could wipe it off.

'Lord Bayaz.' He tried to bow and grin at once and couldn't manage either with any conviction. 'I believe the weather has improved to the point where the devices can be tested.'

'At last,' snapped the Magus. 'Then what are you waiting for, the Midwinter Festival?'

The two old men fled, Saurizin snarling fiercely at his colleague. They had an ill-tempered discussion with the dozen aproned engineers about the nearest tube, including a deal of arm-waving, pointing at the skies and reference to some brass instruments. Finally one produced a long torch, flames licking at the tarred end. The Adepti and their minions hurried away, squatting behind boxes and barrels, covering their ears. The torch-bearer advanced with all the enthusiasm of a condemned man to the scaffold, touched the brand at arm's length to the top of the tube. A few sparks flew, a lick of smoke curled up, a faint pop and fizzle were heard.

Gorst frowned. 'What is—'

There was a colossal explosion and he shrank to the ground, hands clasped over his head. He had heard nothing like it since the Siege of Adua, when the Gurkish put fire to a mine and blew a hundred strides of the walls to gravel. Guardsmen peeped terrified from behind their shields. Exhausted labourers scrambled gaping from their fires. Others struggled to control terrified horses, two of which had torn a rail free and were galloping away with it clattering behind them.

Gorst slowly, suspiciously, stood. Smoke was issuing gently from the end of one of the pipes, engineers swarming around it. Denka and Saurizin were arguing furiously with each other. What had been the effect of the device beyond the noise, Gorst had not the slightest idea.

'Well.' Bayaz stuck a finger in one ear and waggled it around. 'They're certainly loud enough.'

A faint rumble echoed over the valley. Something like thunder, though it seemed to Craw the weather was just clearing up.

'You hear that?' asked Splitfoot.

Craw could only shrug up at the sky. Plenty of cloud still, even if there were a few blue patches showing. 'More rain, maybe.'

Dow had other things on his mind. 'How are we doing at the Old Bridge?'

'They came just after first light but Scale held 'em,' said Splitfoot. 'Drove 'em back across.'

'They'll be coming again, 'fore too long.'

'Doubtless. Reckon he'll hold?'

'If he don't we got a problem.'

'Half his men are across the valley with Calder.'

Dow snorted. 'Just the man I'd want at my back if I was fighting for my life.'

Splitfoot and a couple of the others chuckled.

There was a right way of doing things, far as Craw was concerned, and it didn't include letting men laugh at your friends behind their backs, however laughable they may be. 'That lad might surprise you,' he said.

Splitfoot smirked wider. 'Forgot you and him were tight.'

'Practically raised the boy,' said Craw, squaring up and giving him the eye.

'Explains a lot.'

'Of what?'

Dow spoke over 'em, an edge to his voice. 'The pair o' you can wank Calder off once the light's gone. In case you hadn't noticed we've got bigger business. What about Osrung?'

Splitfoot gave Craw a parting look, then turned back to his Chief. 'Union are over the fence, fighting on the south side of town. Reachey'll hold 'em, though.'

'He better,' grunted Dow. 'And the middle? Any sign of 'em crossing the shallows?'

'They keep marching around down there, but no—'

Splitfoot's head vanished and something went in Craw's eye.

There was a cracking sound then all he could hear was a long, shrill whine.

He got knocked in the back hard and he fell, rolled, scrambled up, bent over like a drunken man, the ground weaving.

Dow had his axe out, waving it at something, shouting, but Craw couldn't hear him. Just that mad ringing. There was dust everywhere. Choking clouds, like fog.

He nearly tripped over Splitfoot's headless corpse, blood welling out of it. Knew it was his from the collar of his mail coat. He was missing an arm as well. Splitfoot was. Not Craw. He had both his. He checked. Blood on his hands, though, not sure whose.

Probably he should've drawn his sword. He waved at the hilt but couldn't work out how far away it was. People ran about, shapes in the murk.

Craw rubbed at his ears. Still nothing but that whine.

A Carl was sitting on the ground, screaming silently, tearing at his bloody chain mail. Something was sticking out of it. Too fat to be an arrow. A splinter of stone.

Were they attacked? Where from? The dust was settling. People shambling about, knocking into each other, kneeling over wounded men, pointing every which way, cowering on their faces.

The top half of one of the Heroes was missing, the old stone sheared off jagged in a fresh, shiny edge. Dead men were scattered around its base. More'n dead. Smashed apart. Folded and twisted. Split open and gutted. Ruined like Craw had never seen before. Even after the Bloody-Nine did his black work up in the High Places.

A boy sat alive in the midst of the bodies and the chunks of rock, blood-sprayed, blinking at a drawn sword on his knees, a whetstone held frozen in one hand. No sign how he'd been saved, if he had been.

Whirrun's face loomed up. His mouth moved like he was talking but Craw could only hear a crackle.

'What? What?' Even his own words made no sound. Thumbs poked at his cheek. It hurt. A lot. Craw touched his face and his fingers were bloody. But his hands were bloody anyway. Everything was.

He tried to push Whirrun away, tripped over something and sat down heavily on the grass.

Probably best all round if he stayed there a bit.

'A hit!' cackled Saurizin, shaking a mystifying arrangement of brass screws, rods and lenses at the sky like a geriatric warrior brandishing a sword in victory.

'A palpable hit with the second discharge, Lord Bayaz!' Denka could barely contain his delight. 'One of the stones on the hill was struck directly and destroyed!'

The First of the Magi raised an eyebrow. 'You talk as if destroying stones was the point of the exercise.'

'I am sure considerable injury and confusion were inflicted upon the Northmen at the summit as well!'

'Considerable injury and confusion!' echoed Saurizin.

'Fine things to visit upon an enemy,' said Bayaz. 'Continue.'

The mood of the two old Adepti sagged. Denka licked his lips. 'It would be prudent to check the devices for evidence of damage. No one knows what the consequences of discharging them frequently might be—'

'Then let us find out,' said Bayaz. 'Continue.'

The two old men clearly feared carrying on. *But a great deal less than they fear the First of the Magi.* They scraped their way back towards the tubes, where they began to bully their helpless engineers as they themselves had been bullied. *And the engineers no doubt will harangue the labourers, and the labourers will whip the mules, and the mules will kick at the dogs, and the dogs will snap at the wasps, and with any luck one of the wasps will sting Bayaz on his fat arse, and thus the righteous wheel of life will be ready to turn once again . . .*

Away to the west a second attempt on the Old Bridge was just petering out, having achieved no more than the first. This time an ill-advised effort had been made to cross the river on rafts. A couple had broken up not long after pushing off, leaving their passengers floundering in the shallows or dragged under by their armour in deeper water. Others were swept off merrily downstream while the men on board flailed pointlessly with their paddles or their hands, arrows plopping around them.

'Rafts,' murmured Bayaz, sticking out his chin and scratching absently at his short beard.

'Rafts,' murmured Gorst, watching an officer on one furiously brandish his sword at the far bank, about as likely ever to reach it as he was the moon.

There was another thunderous explosion, followed almost immediately by a chorus of gasps, sighs and cheers of wonder from the swelling audience, gathered at the top of the rise in a curious crescent. This time Gorst scarcely flinched. *Amazing how quickly the unbearable becomes banal.* More smoke issued from the nearest tube, wandering gently up to join the acrid pall already hanging over the experiment.

That weird rumble rolled out again, smoke rising from somewhere across the river to the south. 'What the hell are they up to?'

muttered Calder. Even standing on the wall, he couldn't see a thing.

He'd been there all morning, waiting. Pacing up and down, in the drizzle, then the dry. Waiting, every minute an age, with his thoughts darting round and round like a lizard in a jar. Peering to the south and not being able to see a thing, the sounds of combat drifting across the fields in waves, sometimes sounding distant, sometimes worryingly near. But no call for help. Nothing but a few wounded carried past, scant reinforcement for Calder's wavering nerve.

'Here's news,' said Pale-as-Snow.

Calder stretched up, shading his eyes. It was White-Eye Hansul, riding up hard from the Old Bridge. He had a smile on his wrinkled face as he reined in, though, which gave Calder a trace of hope. Right then putting off the fighting seemed almost as good as not doing it at all.

He wedged a boot up on the gate in what he hoped was a manly style, trying to sound cool as snow while his heart was burning. 'Scale got himself in a pickle, has he?'

'It's the Southerners pickled so far, the stupid bastards.' White-Eye pulled his helmet off and wiped his forehead on the back of his sleeve. 'Twice Scale's driven them back. First time they came strolling across like they thought we'd just give the bridge over. Your brother soon cured them of that notion.' He chuckled to himself and Pale-as-Snow joined him. Calder offered up his own, though it tasted somewhat sour. Everything did today.

'Second time they tried rafts as well.' White-Eye turned his head and spat into the barley. 'Could've told them the current's way too strong for that.'

'Good thing they never asked you,' said Pale-as-Snow.

'That it is. I reckon you lot can sit back here and take your boots off. We'll hold 'em all day at this rate.'

'There's a lot of day still,' Calder muttered. Something flashed by. His first thought was that it was a bird skimming the barley, but it was too fast and too big. It bounced once in the fields, sending up a puff of stalk and dust and leaving a long scar through the crop. A couple of hundred strides to the east, down at the grassy foot of the Heroes, it hit Clail's Wall.

Broken stones went spinning high, high into the air, showering out in a great cloud of dust and bits. Bits of tents. Bits of gear. Bits of men, Calder realised, because there were men camped behind the whole length of the wall.

'By—' said Hansul, gaping at the flying wreckage.

There was a sound like a whip cracking but a thousand times louder. White-Eye's horse reared up and he went sliding off the back, tumbling down into the barley, arms flailing. All around men gawped and shouted, drew weapons or flung themselves on the ground.

That last looked a good idea.

'Shit!' hissed Calder, scrambling from the gate and throwing himself in a ditch, his desire to look manly greatly outweighed by his desire to stay alive. Earth and stones rattled down around them like unseasonal hail, pinging from armour, bouncing in the track.

'Sticking to the sunny side,' said Pale-as-Snow, utterly unmoved, 'that's Tenways' stretch of wall.'

Bayaz' servant lowered an eyeglass with a curl of mild disappointment to his mouth. 'Wayward,' he said.

A towering understatement. The devices had been discharged perhaps two dozen times and their ammunition, which appeared to be large balls of metal or stone, scattered variously across the slope of the hill ahead, the fields to each side, the orchard at the foot, the sky above and on one occasion straight into the river sending up an immense fountain of spray.

How much the cost of this little aside, so we could dig a few holes in the Northern landscape? How many hospitals could have been built with the money? How many alms-houses? Anything worthier? Burials for dead pauper children? Gorst struggled to care, but could not quite get there. *We probably could have paid the Northmen to kill Black Dow themselves and go home. But then what would I find to fill the blasted desert between getting out of bed and—*

There was an orange flash, and the vague perception of things flying. He thought he saw Bayaz' servant punch at nothing beside his master, his arm an impossible blur. A moment later Gorst's skull was set ringing by an explosion even more colossal than usual, accompanied by a note something like the tolling of a great bell. He felt the blast ripping at his hair, stumbled to keep his balance. The servant had a ragged chunk of curved metal the size of a dinner plate in his hand. He tossed it onto the ground, where it smoked gently in the grass.

Bayaz raised his brows at it. 'A malfunction.'

The servant rubbed black dirt from his fingers. 'The path of progress is ever a crooked one.'

Pieces of metal had been flung in all directions. A particularly large one had bounced straight through a group of labourers leaving several dead and the rest spotted with blood. Other fragments had knocked little gaps in the stunned audience, or flicked over guardsmen like skittles. A great cloud of smoke was billowing from where one of the tubes had been. A blood and dirt-streaked engineer wandered out of it, his hair on fire, walking unsteadily at a diagonal. He didn't have any arms, and soon toppled over.

'Ever,' as Bayaz sank unhappily into his folding chair, 'a crooked one.'

Some people sat blinking. Others screamed. Yet more rushed about, trying to help the many wounded. Gorst wondered whether he should do the same. *But what good could I do? Boost morale with jokes? Have you heard the one about the big idiot with the stupid voice whose life was ruined in Sipani?*

Denka and Saurizin were sidling towards them, black robes smudged with soot. 'And here, the penitents,' murmured Bayaz' servant. 'With your leave, I should attend to some of our business on the other side of the river. I have a feeling the Prophet's little disciples are not idle over there.'

'Then we cannot be idle either.' The Magus waved his servant away with a careless hand. 'There are more important things than pouring my tea.'

'A very few.' The servant gave Gorst a faint smile as he slipped away. 'Truly, as the Kantic scriptures say, the righteous can afford no rest . . .'

'Lord Bayaz, er . . .' Denka looked across at Saurizin, who made a frantic get-on-with-it motion. 'I regret to inform you that . . . one of the devices has exploded.'

The Magus let them stand for a moment while, out of sight, a woman shrieked like a boiling kettle. 'Do you suppose I missed that?'

'Another jumped from its carriage upon the last discharge, and I fear will take some considerable time to realign.'

'The third,' wheedled Denka, 'is displaying a tiny crack which requires some attention. I am . . .' his face crumpling up as though he feared someone was going to stick a sword in it, 'reluctant to risk charging it again.'

'Reluctant?' Bayaz' displeasure was as a mighty weight. Even standing beside him Gorst felt a powerful urge to kneel.

'A defect in the casting of the metal,' Saurizin managed to gasp, sending a poisonous glance at his colleague.

'My alloys are perfect,' whined Denka. 'It was an inconsistency in the explosive powders that was to—'

'Blame?' The voice of the Magus was almost as fearsome as the explosion had been. 'Believe me, gentlemen, there is always plenty of that left over after a battle. Even on the winning side.' The two old men positively grovelled. Then Bayaz waved a hand and the menace was gone. 'But these things happen. Overall it has been . . . a most interesting demonstration.'

'Why, Lord Bayaz, you are far too kind . . .'

Their servile mutterings faded as Gorst picked his way to where a guard had been standing a few moments before. He was lying in the long grass, arms out wide, a ragged chunk of curved metal embedded in his helmet. One eye could still be seen through the twisted visor, staring at the sky in a last moment of profound surprise. *Truly, every man of them is a hero.*

The guard's shield lay nearby, the golden sun on the face gleaming as its counterpart showed through the clouds. Gorst picked it up, slid his left hand into the straps and trudged off, upstream, towards the Old Bridge. As he passed, Bayaz was sitting back in his folding chair with one boot crossed over the other, his staff forgotten in the wet grass beside him.

'What should they be called? They are engines that produce fire, so . . . fire engines? No, silly. Death tubes? Names are so important, and I've never had the trick of them. Have you two any ideas?'

'I liked death tubes . . .' muttered Denka.

Bayaz was not listening. 'I daresay someone will think up something suitable in due course. Something simple. I've a feeling we'll be seeing a great deal more of these devices . . .'

Reasoned Debate

Far as Beck could tell, things were coming apart.

The Union had a double row of archers on the south bank of the river. Squatting down behind a fence to load their evil little bows. Popping up every now and then to loose a clattering hail of bolts at the north end of the bridge. The Carls there were hunched behind their arrow-prickled shield wall, the Thralls huddling tight behind them, spears in a thoughtless tangle. A couple of men had ended up arrow-prickled too, been dragged squealing back through the ranks, doing nothing for the courage of the rest. Or for Beck's courage either. What there was of it left.

He was almost saying the words with every breath. Let's run. Plenty of others had. Grown men with names and everything, running for their lives from the fight across the river. Why the hell were Beck and the rest staying? Why should they care a shit whether Caul Reachey got to hold some town, or Black Dow got to keep wearing Bethod's old chain?

South of the river the fighting was done. The Union had broken into the last houses and slaughtered the defenders or burned 'em out with about the same results, the smoke of it still drifting across the water. Now they were getting ready to try the bridge, a wedge of soldiers coming together on the far side. Beck had never seen men so heavy armoured, cased head to toe in metal so they looked more like something forged than born. He thought of the lame weapons his half-arsed crew had. Dull knives and bent spears. It'd be like trying to bring down a bull with a pin.

Another hail of little arrows came hissing across the water and a great big Thrall leaped up, making a mad shriek, shoving men out of his way then toppling off the bridge and into the water.

The shield wall loosened where he'd passed, the back rank drifting apart, going ragged. None of 'em wanted to just squat there and get peppered, and they wanted to face those armoured bastards close up even less. Maybe Black Dow liked the smell of burning cowards, but Black Dow was far away. The Union were awful near and fixing to get nearer. Beck could almost see the bones going out of 'em, all edging back together, shields coming unlocked, spears wobbling.

The Named Man who led the shield wall turned to shout, waving his axe, then fell on his knees, trying to reach over his back at something. He keeled over on his face, a bolt poking out of his fine cloak. Then someone gave a long shout on the other side of the bridge and the Union came on. All that polished metal tramping up together like some single angry beast. Not the wild charge of a crowd of Carls but a steady jog, full of purpose. Like that, without even a blow given, the shield wall broke apart and men ran. The next hail of arrows dropped a dozen or more as they showed their backs and scattered the rest across the square like Beck used to scatter starlings with a clap.

Beck watched a man drag himself over the cobbles with three bolts in him. Watched him wide-eyed, breath slithering in his throat. What did it feel like when the arrow went in you? Deep into your flesh? In your neck. In your chest. In your fruits. Or a blade? All that sharp metal, and a body so soft. What did it feel like to have a leg cut off? How much could something hurt? All the time he'd spent dreaming of battle, but somehow he'd never thought of it before.

Let's run. He turned to Reft to say it but he was letting an arrow fly, cursing and reaching for another. Beck should've been doing the same, like Flood told him, but his bow seemed to weigh a ton, his hand so weak he could hardly grip it. By the dead he was sick. They had to run, but he was too coward even to say it. Too coward to show his shitting, screaming, trembling fear to the lads downstairs. All he could do was stand there, with his bow out the window but the string not even drawn like a lad who's got his prick out to piss but found he couldn't manage it with someone watching.

He heard Reft's bow string go again. Heard him shout, 'I'm going down!' Pulling out his long knife in one hand, his hatchet in the other and heading for the stairs. Beck watched him with his mouth half open but nothing to say. Trapped between his fear of staying here alone and his fear of going downstairs.

He had to force himself to look out of the window. Union men flooding across the square, the heavy armoured ones and more behind. Dozens. Hundreds. Arrows flitting from the buildings and down into them. Corpses all over. A rock came from the roof of the mill and stove in a Union helmet, sent the man toppling. But they were everywhere, charging through the streets, beating at the doors, hacking down the wounded as they tried to limp away. A Union officer stood near the bridge, waving his sword towards the buildings, dressed in a fancy jacket with gold thread like the prisoner Shivers had taken. Beck raised his bow, found his mark, finally drew the string back.

Couldn't do it. His ears were full of mad din, he couldn't think. He started trembling so bad he could hardly see, and in the end he squeezed his eyes shut and shot the arrow off at nothing. The only one he'd shot. Too late to run. They were all around the house. Trapped. He'd had his chance and now the Union was everywhere. Splinters flew in his face and he tumbled back inside the attic, slipped and fell on his arse, heels scraping at the boards. A flatbow bolt was buried in the window frame, splitting the timber, its gleaming point coming through into the room. He lay, propped on his elbows, staring at it.

He wanted his mother. By the dead, he wanted his mother. What kind of a thing was that for a man to want?

Beck scrambled up, could hear crashes and bangs everywhere, wails and roars sounding hardly human, downstairs, outside, inside, his head snapping round at every hint of a noise. Were they in the house already? Were they coming for him? All he could do was stand there and sweat. His legs were wet with it. Too wet. He'd pissed himself. Pissed himself like a child and hardly even known 'til it started going cold.

He drew his father's sword. Felt the weight of it. Should've made him feel strong, the way it always had before. But instead it made him feel homesick. Sick for the smelly little room he'd always drawn it in, the brave dreams that had hissed out of the sheath along with it. He could hardly believe he'd wished for this. He edged to the stairs, head turned away, looking out of the corner of one narrowed eye as if not seeing clearly might somehow keep him safe.

The room at the bottom was full of mad movement, shadows and darker shadows and splashes of light through broken shutters, furniture scattered, blades glinting. A regular splintering of wood, someone trying to break their way in. Voices, mangled up and saying nothing, Union words or no words at all. Screams and whimpers.

Two of Flood's Northern lads were lying on the floor. One was leaking blood everywhere. The other was saying, 'No, no, no,' over and over. Colving had this wild, mad look on his chubby face, jabbing at a Union man who'd squeezed in through the door. Reft came out of the shadows and hit him in the back of the helmet with his hatchet, knocked him sprawling on top of Colving, hacked away at his back-plate as he tried to get up, finally found the gap between plate and helmet and put him down with his head hanging off.

'Keep 'em out!' Reft screamed, jumping back to the door and heaving it shut with his shoulder.

A Union man burst through the shutters not far from the bottom of the steps. Beck could've stabbed him in the back. Probably without even being seen. But he couldn't help thinking about what would happen if it went wrong. What would happen after he did it. So he didn't do anything. Brait squealed, spun around to poke at the Union man with his spear, but before he could do it the soldier's sword thudded into Brait's shoulder and split him open to his chest. He gave this breathy shriek, waving his spear about while the Union man struggled to rip his sword out of him, blood squirting out black over the pair of 'em.

'Help!' roared Stodder at no one, pressed against the wall with a cleaver dangling from one hand. 'Help!'

Beck didn't turn and run. He just backed softly up the stairs the way he came, and he hurried to the open cupboard, ripped its single shelf out then ducked into the cobwebby shadows inside. He worked his fingertips into a gap between two planks of the door and he dragged it shut, bent over with his back against the rafters. Pressed into the darkness, in a child's bad hiding place. Alone with his father's sword, and his own whimpering breath, and the sounds of his crew being slaughtered downstairs.

*

Lord Governor Meed gazed imperiously out of the northern window of the common hall with hands clasped behind his back, nodding knowingly at scraps of information as if he understood them, his officers crowding about him and gabbling away like eager goslings around their mother. An apt metaphor, as the man had all the military expertise of a mother goose. Finree lurked at the back of the room, an ugly secret, desperately wanting to know what was going on but desperately not wanting to give anyone the satisfaction of asking, chewing at her nails, silently stewing and turning over various unlikely scenarios for her revenge.

Mostly, though, she was forced to admit, she was annoyed at herself. She saw now it would have been much better if she had pretended to be patient, and charming, and humble just as Hal had wanted, clapped her hands at Meed's pitiful soldiering and slid into his confidence like a cuckoo into an old pigeon's nest.

Still, the man was vain enough to haul an overblown portrait of himself around on campaign. It might not be too late to play the wayward lamb, and worm her way into his good graces through simpering contrition. Then, when the opportunity presented, she could stab him in the back from a nice, short distance. She'd stab him one way or another, that was a promise. She could hardly wait to see the look on Meed's papery old face when she finally—

Aliz let go a snort of laughter. 'Why, who's that?'

'Who's what?' Finree glanced out of the eastern window, entirely ignored since the battle was happening to the north. A ragged man had emerged from the woods and was standing on a small outcropping of rock, staring towards the inn, long black hair twitched by the wind. Clearly, he was by no stretch of the imagination a Union soldier.

Finree frowned. Most of the Dogman's men were supposed to be well behind them, and in any case there was something about this lonely figure that just looked . . . *wrong*.

'Captain Hardrick!' she called. 'Is he one of the Dogman's men?'

'Who?' Hardrick strolled up beside them. 'All honesty I couldn't say . . .'

The man on the rock lifted something to his mouth and bent

288

his head back. A moment later a long, mournful note echoed out over the empty fields.

Aliz laughed. 'A horn!'

Finree felt that note right in her stomach, and straight away she knew. She grabbed Hardrick's arm. 'Captain, you need to ride to General Jalenhorm and tell him we are under attack.'

'What? But there's . . .' His gormless grin slowly faded as he looked towards the east.

'Oh,' said Aliz. The whole treeline was suddenly alive with men. Wild, they looked, even at this distance. Long-haired, rag-clothed, many half-naked. Now that he stood in the midst of hundreds of others and there was some sense of scale, Finree realised what had puzzled her about the man with the horn. He was a giant, in the truest sense of the word.

Hardrick stared, his mouth hanging open, and Finree dug her fingers into his arm and dragged him towards the door. 'Now! Find General Jalenhorm. Find my father. Now!'

'I should have orders—' His eyes flickered over to Meed, still blithely observing his attack on Osrung, along with all the other officers except for a couple who had drifted over without much urgency to investigate the sound of the horn.

'Who are they?' one asked.

Finree had no time to argue her case. She gave vent to the shrillest, longest, most blood-curdling girlish scream she could manage. One of the musicians issued a screeching wrong note, the other played on for a moment before leaving the room in silence, every head snapping towards Finree, except Hardrick's. She was relieved to see she had shocked him into running for the door.

'What the hell—' Meed began.

'Northmen!' somebody wailed. 'To the east!'

'What Northmen? Whatever are you—'

Then everyone was shouting. 'There! There!'

'Bloody hell!'

'Man the walls!'

'Do we have walls?'

Men out in the fields – drivers, servants, smiths and cooks – were scattering wildly from tents and wagons, back towards the inn. There were already horsemen among them, mounted on shaggy ponies, without stirrups, even, but moving quickly nonetheless. She thought they might have bows, and a moment later arrows clattered against the north wall of the inn. One looped through a window and skittered across the floor. A black, jagged, ill-formed thing, but no less dangerous for that. Someone drew their sword with a faint ring of metal, and soon there were blades flashing out all around the hall.

'Get some archers on the roof!'

'Do we have archers?'

'Get the shutters!'

'Where is Colonel Brint?'

A folding table squealed in protest as it was dragged in front of one of the windows, papers sliding across the floor.

Finree snatched a look out as two officers struggled to get the rotten shutters closed. A great line of men was surging through the fields towards them, already half way between the trees and the inn and closing rapidly, spreading out as they charged. Torn standards flapped behind them, adorned with bones. At her first rough estimate there were at least two thousand, and no more than a hundred in the inn, most lightly armed. She swallowed at the simple horror of the arithmetic.

'Are the gates closed?'

'Prop them!'

'Recall the Fifteenth!'

'Is it too late to take—'

'By the Fates.' Aliz' eyes had gone wide, white showing all the way around, darting about as if looking for some means of escape. There was none. 'We're trapped!'

'Help will be coming,' said Finree, trying to sound as calm as she could with her heart threatening to burst her ribs.

'From who?'

'From the Dogman,' who had very reasonably made every effort to put as much ground between himself and Meed as possible, 'or General Jalenhorm,' whose men were in such a disorganised shambles after yesterday's disaster they were no help to themselves let alone anyone else, 'or from our husbands,' who were both thoroughly entangled with the attack on Osrung and probably had not the slightest idea that a new threat had emerged right behind them. 'Help will be coming.' It sounded pathetically unconvincing even to her.

Officers dashed to nowhere, pointed everywhere, screeched contradictory orders at each other, the room growing steadily darker and more confused as the windows were barricaded with whatever gaudy junk was to hand. Meed stood in the midst, suddenly ignored and alone, staring uncertainly about with his gilded sword in one hand and the other opening and closing powerlessly. Like a nervous father at a great wedding so carefully planned that he found himself entirely unwanted on the big day. Above him, his masterful portrait frowned scornfully down.

'What should we do?' he asked of no one in particular. His desperately wandering eyes lighted on Finree. 'What should we do?'

It wasn't until she opened her mouth that she realised she had no answer.

Chains of Command

After a brief spell of fair weather the clouds had rolled back in and rain had begun to fall again, gently administering Marshal Kroy and his staff another dose of clammy misery and entirely obscuring both flanks of the battlefield.

'Damn this drizzle!' he snapped. 'I might as well have a bucket on my head.'

People often supposed that a lord marshal wielded supreme power on the battlefield, even beyond an emperor in his throne room. They did not appreciate the infinite constraints on his authority. The weather, in particular, was prone to ignore orders. Then there was the balance of politics to consider: the whims of the monarch, the mood of the public. There were a galaxy of logistical concerns: difficulties of supply and transport and signalling and discipline, and the larger the army the more staggeringly cumbersome it became. If one managed, by some miracle, to prod this unwieldy mass into a position to actually fight, a headquarters had to be well behind the lines and even with the opportunity to choose a good vantage point a commander could never see everything, if anything. Orders might take half an hour or longer to reach their intended recipients and so were often useless or positively dangerous by the time they got there, if they ever got there.

The higher you climbed up the chain of command, the more links between you and the naked steel, the more imperfect the communication became. The more men's cowardice, rashness, incompetence or, worst of all, good intentions might twist your purposes. The more chance could play a hand, and chance rarely played well. With every promotion, Marshal Kroy had looked forward to finally slipping the shackles and standing all powerful.

And with every promotion he had found himself more helpless than before.

'I'm like a blind old idiot who's got himself into a duel,' he murmured. Except there were thousands of lives hanging on his clueless flailing, rather than just his own.

'Would you care for your brandy and water, Lord—'

'No, I would not bloody care for it!' he snapped at his orderly, then winced as the man backed nervously away with the bottle. How could he explain that he had been drinking it yesterday when he heard that he was responsible for the deaths of hundreds of his men, and now the very idea of brandy and water utterly sickened him?

It was no help that his daughter had placed herself so close to the front lines. He kept finding his eyeglass drawn towards the eastern side of the battle, trying to pick out the inn Meed was using as his headquarters through the drizzle. He scratched unhappily at his cheek. He had been interrupted while shaving by a worrying report sent from the Dogman, signs of savages from beyond the Crinna loose in the countryside to their east. Men the Dogman reckoned savage were savage indeed. Now Kroy was deeply distracted and, what was more, one side of his face was smooth and the other stubbly. Those sorts of details had always upset him. An army is made of details the way a house is made of bricks. One brick carelessly laid and the whole is compromised. But attend to the perfect mortaring of every—

'Huh,' he muttered to himself. 'I am a bloody mason.'

'Latest report from Meed says things are going well on the right,' said Felnigg, no doubt trying to allay his fears. His chief of staff knew him too well. 'They've got most of southern Osrung occupied and are making an effort on the bridge.'

'So things were going well half an hour ago?'

'Best one could say for them, sir.'

'True.' He looked for a moment longer, but could scarcely make out the inn, let alone Osrung itself. There was nothing to be gained by worrying. If his entire army had been as brave and resourceful as his daughter they would already have won and been on their way home. He almost pitied the Northman who ran across her in a bad mood. He turned to the west, following the line of the river with his eyeglass until he came to the Old Bridge.

Or thought he did. A faint, straight, light line across the faint, curved, dark line which he assumed was the water, all of it drifting in and out of existence as the rain thickened or slackened in the mile or two between him and the object. In truth he could have been looking at anything.

'Damn this drizzle! What about the left?'

'Last word from Mitterick was that his second assault had, how did he put it? Been blunted.'

'By now it will have failed, then. Still, tough work, carrying a bridge against determined resistance.'

'Huh,' grunted Felnigg.

'Mitterick may lack many things—'

'Huh,' grunted Felnigg.

'—but persistence is not one of them.'

'No, sir, he is persistently an arse.'

'Now, now, let us be generous.' And then, under his breath, 'Every man needs an arse, if only to sit on.' If Mitterick's second assault had recently failed he would be preparing another. The Northmen facing him would be off balance. Kroy snapped his eyeglass closed and tapped it against his palm.

The general who waited to make a decision until he knew everything he needed to would never make one, and if he did it would be far too late. He had to feel out the moment. Anticipate the ebb and flow of battle. The shifting of morale, of pressure, of advantage. One had to trust one's instincts. And Marshal Kroy's instincts told him the crucial moment on the left wing was soon coming.

He strode through the door of his barn-cum-headquarters, making sure he ducked this time, as he had no need of another painful bruise on the crown of his head, and went straight to his desk. He dipped pen in ink without even sitting and wrote upon the nearest of several dozen slips of paper prepared for the purpose:

Colonel Vallimir
  General Mitterick's troops are heavily engaged at the Old Bridge. Soon he will force the enemy to commit all his reserves. I

wish you to begin your attack immediately, therefore, as discussed, and with every man at your disposal. Good luck.

    Kroy

He signed it with a flourish. 'Felnigg, I want you to take this to General Mitterick.'

'He might take it better from a messenger.'

'He can take it however he damn well pleases, but I don't want him to have any excuse to ignore it.'

Felnigg was an officer of the old school and rarely betrayed his feelings; it was one of the things Kroy had always admired about the man. But his distaste for Mitterick was evidently more than he could suppress. 'If I must, Lord Marshal.' And he plucked the order sourly from Kroy's hand.

Colonel Felnigg stalked from the headquarters, nearly clubbing himself on the low lintel and only just managing to disguise his upset. He thrust the order inside his jacket pocket, checked that no one was looking and took a quick nip from his flask, then checked again and took another, pulled himself into the saddle and whipped his horse away down the narrow path, sending servants, guardsmen and junior officers scattering.

If it had been Felnigg put in command of the Siege of Ulrioch all those years ago and Kroy sent off on a fruitless ride to dusty nowhere, Felnigg who had reaped the glory and Kroy who had ridden thirsty back with his twenty captured wagons to find himself a forgotten man, things could so easily have been different. Felnigg might have been the lord marshal now, and Kroy his glorified messenger boy.

He clattered down from the hillside, spurring west towards Adwein along the puddle-pocked track. The ground sloping down to the river crawled with Jalenhorm's men, still struggling to find some semblance of organisation. Seeing things done in so slovenly a manner caused Felnigg something close to physical pain. It was the very most he could do not to pull up his horse, start screaming orders at all and sundry and put some damn purpose into them. *Purpose* – was that too much to ask in an army?

'Bloody Jalenhorm,' Felnigg hissed. The man was a joke, and

not even a funny one. He had neither the wit nor experience for a sergeant's place, let alone a general's, but apparently having been the king's old drinking partner was better qualification than years of competent and dedicated service. It would have been enough to make a lesser man quite bitter, but Felnigg it only drove to greater heights of excellence. He slowed for a moment to take another nip from his flask.

On the grassy slope to his right there had been some manner of accident. Aproned engineers fussed around two huge tubes of dark metal and a large patch of blackened grass. Bodies were laid out by the road, bloody sheets for shrouds. No doubt the First of the Magi's damn fool experiment blown up in everyone's faces. Whenever the Closed Council became directly involved in warfare there was sure to be some heavy loss of life and, in Felnigg's experience, rarely on the enemy's side.

'Out of the way!' he roared, forcing a path through a herd of foraged cattle that should never have been allowed on the road and making one of its handlers dive for the verge. He cantered through Adwein, as miserable a village as he had ever seen and packed today with miserable faces, injured men and filthy remnants of who-knew-what units. The useless, self-pitying flotsam of Mitterick's failed assaults, swept out the back of his division like dung from a stables.

At least Jalenhorm, fool that he was, could obey an order. Mitterick was forever squirming out from under his to do things his own way. Incompetence was unforgivable, but disobedience was . . . still less forgivable, damn it. If everyone simply did as they pleased, there would be no coordination, no command, no purpose. No army at all, just a great crowd of men indulging their own petty vanities. The very idea made him—

A servant carrying a bucket stepped suddenly from a doorway and right into Felnigg's path. His horse skittered to a stop, rearing up and nearly throwing him from the saddle.

'Out of the way!' Without thinking, Felnigg struck the man across the face with his riding crop. The servant cried out and went sprawling in the gutter, his bucket spraying water across the wall. Felnigg gave his horse the spurs and rode on, the heat of spirits in his stomach turned suddenly cold. He should not have done that. He had let anger get the better of him and the realisation only made him angrier than ever.

Mitterick's headquarters was the most unruly place in his unruly division. Officers dashed about, spraying mud and shouting over one another, the loudest voice obeyed and the finest ideas ignored. A commander set the tone for his entire command. A captain for his company, a major for his battalion, a colonel for his regiment and Mitterick for his entire division. Sloppy officers meant sloppy men, and sloppy soldiering meant defeat. Rules saved lives at times like these. What kind of officer allowed things to degenerate into chaos in his own headquarters? Felnigg reined his horse up and made a direct line for the flap of Mitterick's great tent, clearing excitable young adjutants from his path by sheer force of disapproval.

Inside the confusion was redoubled. Mitterick was leaning over a table in the midst of a clamouring press of crimson uniforms, an improvised map of the valley spread out upon it, holding forth at tremendous volume. Felnigg felt his revulsion for the man almost like a headwind. He was the worst kind of soldier, the kind that dresses his incompetence up as flair and, to make matters worse, he fooled people more often than not. But he did not fool Felnigg.

Felnigg stepped up and gave an impeccable salute. Mitterick gave the most peremptory movement of his hand, barely looking up from his map.

'I have an order for the King's Own First Regiment from Lord Marshal Kroy. I would be gratified if you could despatch it *at once*.' He could not entirely keep the contempt out of his voice, and Mitterick evidently noticed.

'We're a little busy *soldiering* here, perhaps you could leave it—'

'I am afraid that will not be good enough, General.' Felnigg only just prevented himself from slapping Mitterick across the face with his gloves. 'The lord marshal was most specific, and I must insist on haste.'

Mitterick straightened, the jaw muscles working on the side of his outsized head. 'Must you?'

'Yes. I absolutely must.' And Felnigg thrust the order at him as if he would throw it in his face, only by a last shred of restraint keeping it in his fingertips.

Mitterick snatched the paper from Felnigg's hand, only just preventing himself from punching him in the face with his other fist, and tore it open.

Felnigg. What an arse. What an arrogant, pedantic fool. A prickly stickler with no imagination, no initiative, none of what the Northmen called, with their gift for simplicity, 'bones'. He was lucky he had Marshal Kroy for a friend, lucky Kroy had dragged him up through the ranks behind him or he would most likely have remained all his career a tight-buttoned captain.

Felnigg. What an *arse*. Mitterick remembered him bringing in those six wretched wagons after Kroy won his great victory at Ulrioch. Remembered him demanding to have his contribution noted. His battalion ground down to a dusty stub for the sake of six bloody wagons. His contribution had been noted, all right. Mitterick had thought then, *what an arse*, and his opinion had not changed in all the years between.

Felnigg. What a suppurating arse. Look at him. Arse. Probably he thought he was better than everyone else, still, even though Mitterick knew for a fact he could barely get up without a drink. Probably he thought he could have done Mitterick's job better. Probably he thought he should have had Kroy's. Bloody arse. He was the worst kind of soldier, the kind that dresses his stupidity up as discipline, and to make matters worse he fooled people more often than not. But he did not fool Mitterick.

Already two of his assaults on the bridge had failed, he had a third to prepare and no time to waste on this pompous streak of bureaucracy. He turned to Opker, his own chief of staff, stabbing at the map with the crumpled order. 'Tell them to get the Seventh ready, and I want the Second in place right behind. I want cavalry across that bridge as soon as we get a foothold, damn it, these fields are made for a charge! Get the Keln Regiment out of the way, clear out the wounded. Dump 'em in the river if we have to, we're giving the bloody Northmen time to get set. Time to have a bloody bath if they bloody want one! Tell them to get it done now or I'll go down there myself and lead the charge, whether I can fit my fat arse into my armour or not. Tell them to—'

A finger jabbed at his shoulder. 'This order must be attended to at once, General Mitterick. *At once!*' Felnigg nearly shrieked the last words, blasting Mitterick with spit. He could hardly believe the man's obsession with proper form. Rules cost lives at times like these. What kind of an officer insisted on them in a headquarters while outside men were fighting? Dying? He ran a furious eye over the order:

> *Colonel Vallimir*
> *General Mitterick's troops are heavily engaged at the Old Bridge. Soon he will force the enemy to commit all his reserves. I wish you to begin your attack immediately, therefore, as discussed, and with every man at your disposal. Good luck.*
> *Kroy*

The First had been attached to Mitterick's division and so, as their commander, it was his responsibility to clarify their instructions. Kroy's order was lean and efficient as the marshal himself, as always, and the timing was apt. But Mitterick was damned if he was going to miss an opportunity to frustrate the marshal's chinless stick-insect of a right-hand man. If he wanted it by the book, he could have it by the book and bloody choke on it. So he spread the paper out on top of his map, snapped his fingers until someone thrust a pen into them, and added a scratchy line of his own at the bottom almost without considering the content.

> *Ensure that the enemy are fully engaged before crossing the stream, and in the meantime take care not to give away your position on their flank. My men and I are giving our all. I will not have them let down.*
> *General Mitterick, Second Division*

He took a route to his tent flap that enabled him to shoulder Felnigg rudely out of the way. 'Where the hell is that boy from Vallimir's regiment?' he bellowed into the thinning drizzle. 'What was his name? Leperlisper?'

'Lederlingen, sir!' A tall, pale, nervous-looking young man

stepped forward, gave an uncertain salute and finished it off with an even more uncertain, 'General Mitterick, sir.' Mitterick would not have trusted him to convey his chamber pot safely to the stream, let alone to carry a vital order, but he supposed, as Bialoveld once said, 'In battle one must often make the best of contrary conditions.'

'Take this order to Colonel Vallimir at once. It's from the lord marshal, d'you understand? Highest importance.' And Mitterick pressed the folded, creased and now slightly ink-blotted paper into his limp hand.

Lederlingen stood there for a moment, staring at the order.

'Well?' snapped the general.

'Er . . .' He saluted again. 'Sir, yes—'

'Move!' roared Mitterick in his face. 'Move!'

Lederlingen backed away, still at absurd attention, then hurried through the boot-mashed mud and over to his horse.

By the time he'd struggled into his wet saddle, a thin, chinless officer in a heavily starched uniform had emerged from Mitterick's tent and was hissing something incomprehensible at the general while a collection of guards and officers looked on, among them a large, sad-eyed man with virtually no neck who seemed vaguely familiar.

Lederlingen had no time to waste trying to place him. Finally, he had a job worth the doing. He turned his back on the unedifying spectacle of two of his Majesty's most senior officers bitterly arguing with one another and spurred off to the west. He couldn't honestly say he was sorry to be going. A headquarters appeared to be an even more frightening and disorientating place than the front line.

He rode through the tight-packed men before the tent, shouting for them to give him room, then through the looser mass making ready for another attack on the bridge, all the time with one hand on the reins and the order clutched in the other. He should have put it in his pocket, it was only making it harder for him to ride, but he was terrified of losing it. An order from Lord Marshal Kroy himself. This was exactly the kind of thing he'd been hoping for when he first signed up, bright-eyed, was it really only three months ago?

He'd cleared the main body of Mitterick's division now, their clamour fading behind him. He upped the pace, bending low over his horse's back, thumping down a patchy track away from the Old Bridge and towards the marshes. He'd have to leave his horse with the picket at the south bank, unfortunately, and cross the bogs on foot to take the order to Vallimir. If he didn't put a foot wrong and end up taking the order down to Klige instead.

That thought gave him a shudder. His cousin had warned him not to enlist. Had told him wars were upside-down places where good men did worse than bad. Had told him wars were all about rich men's ambitions and poor men's graves, and there hadn't been two honest fellows to strike a spark of decency in the whole company he served with. That officers were all arrogance, ignorance and incompetence. That soldiers were all cowards, braggarts, bullies or thieves. Lederlingen had supposed his cousin to be exaggerating for effect, but now had to admit that he seemed rather to have understated the case. Corporal Tunny, in particular, gave the strong impression of being coward, braggart, bully and thief all at once, as thorough a villain as Lederlingen had laid eyes upon in his life, but by some magic almost celebrated by the other men as a hero. All hail good old Corporal Tunny, the shabbiest cheat and shirker in the whole division!

The track had become a stony path, threading through a gully alongside a stream, or at any rate a wide ditch full of wet mud, trees heavy with red berries growing out over it. The place smelled of rot. It was impossible to ride at anything faster than a bumpy trot. Truly, the soldier's life took a man to some beautiful and exotic locations.

Lederlingen heaved out a sigh. War was an upside-down place, all right, and he was rapidly coming around to his cousin's opinion that it was no place for him at all. He would just have to keep his head low, stay out of trouble and follow Tunny's advice never to volunteer for anything—

'Ah!' A wasp had stung his leg. Or that was what he thought at first, though the pain was considerably worse. When he looked down, there was an arrow in his thigh. He stared at it. A long, straight stick with grey and white flights. An arrow. He wondered if someone was playing a joke on him for a moment. A fake arrow. It hurt so much less than he'd ever thought it might. But there was blood soaking into his trousers. It was a real arrow.

Someone was shooting at him!

He dug his heels into his horse's flanks and screamed. Now the arrow hurt. It hurt like a flaming brand rammed through his leg. His mount jerked forwards on the rocky path and he lost his grip on the reins, bounced once in the saddle, the hand clutching the order flailing at the air. Then he hit the ground, teeth rattling, head spinning, tumbling over and over.

He staggered up, sobbing at the pain in his leg, half-hopped about, trying to get his bearings. He managed to draw his sword. There were two men on the path behind. Northmen. One was walking towards him, purposeful, a knife in his hand. The other had a bow raised.

'Help!' shouted Lederlingen, but it was breathy, weak. He wasn't sure when he last passed a Union soldier. Before he came into the gully, maybe, he'd seen some scouts, but that had been a while back. 'Help—'

The arrow stuck right through his jacket sleeve. Right through his arm inside it. This time it hurt from the start. He dropped his sword with a shriek. His weight went onto his right leg and it gave under him. He tumbled down the bank, jolts of agony shooting through his limbs whenever the ground caught at the broken shafts.

He was in the mud. Had the order in his fist still. He tried to get up. Heard the squelch of a boot beside him. Something hit him in the side of the neck and made his head jolt.

Foss Deep plucked the bit of paper out of the Southerner's hand, wiped his knife on the back of his jacket, then planted a boot on his head and pushed his face down into the bloody mud. Didn't want him screaming any. In part on account of stealth, but in part just because he found these days he didn't care for the sounds of persons dying. If it had to be done, so, so, but he didn't need to hear about it, thank you very much all the same.

Shallow was leading the Southerner's horse down the bank into the soggy stream bed. 'She's a good one, no?' he asked, grinning up at it.

'Don't call her she. It's a horse, not your wife.'

Shallow patted the horse on the side of its face. 'She's better looking than your wife was.'

'That's rude and uncalled for.'

'Sorry. What shall we do with . . . it, then? It's a good one. Be worth a pretty—'

'How you going to get it back over the river? I ain't dragging that thing through a bog, and there's a fucking battle on the bridge, in case you forgot.'

'I didn't forget.'

'Kill it.'

'Just a shame is all—'

'Just bloody kill it and let's get on.' He pointed down at the Southerner under his boot. 'I'm killing him, aren't I?'

'Well, he isn't bloody worth anything—'

'Just kill it!' Then, realising he shouldn't be raising his voice, since they was on the wrong side of the river and there might be Southerners anywhere, whispered, 'Just kill it and hide the bloody thing!'

Shallow gave him a sour look, but he dragged on the horse's bridle, put his weight across its neck and got it down, then gave it a quick stab in the neck, leaning on it while it poured blood into the muck.

'Shit on a shitty shit.' Shallow shook his head. 'There's no money in killing horses. We're taking risksies enoughsies coming over here in the first—'

'Stop it.'

'Stop what?' As he dragged a fallen tree branch over the horse's corpse.

Deep looked up at him. 'Talking like a child, what do you think? It's odd, is what it is. It's like your head's trapped at four years old.'

'My parts of speech upset you?' Chopping another branch free with his hatchet.

'They do, as it goes, yes.'

Shallow got the horse hidden to his satisfaction. 'Guess I'll have to stopsy wopsy, then.'

Deep gave a long sigh through gritted teeth. One day he'd kill Shallow, or the other way around, he'd known it ever since he was ten years old. He unfolded the paper and held it up to the light.

'What's the matter of it?' asked Shallow, peering over his shoulder.

Deep turned slowly to look at him. He wouldn't have been surprised if today turned out to be the day. 'What? Did I learn to read Southerner in my sleep and not realise? How in the land of the dead should I know what the bloody matter of it is?'

Shallow shrugged. 'Fair point. It has the look of import, though.'

'It do indeed have every appearance of significance.'

'So?'

'I guess it becomes a question of who we know might find 'emselves tempted to fork out for it.'

They looked at each other and said it together. 'Calder.'

This time White-Eye Hansul rode up fast, and with no hint of a smile. His shield had a broken arrow shaft in it and there was a cut across his forehead. He looked like a man who'd been in action. Calder felt sick just seeing him.

'Scale wants you to bring your men up.' There was no laughter in his voice now. 'The Southerners are coming across the bridge again and this time they've come hard. He can't hold out much longer.'

'All right.' Calder had known the moment would come, but that didn't make it any sweeter. 'Get them ready.'

'Aye.' And Pale-as-Snow strode off barking orders.

Calder reached for his sword hilt and made a show of loosening it as he watched his brother's men – his men – stand up from behind Clail's Wall and prepare to join the battle. Time to write the first verse in the song of bold Prince Calder. And hope it wasn't the last.

'Your prince-li-ness!'

Calder looked round. 'Foss Deep. You always come upon me at my brightest moments.'

'I can smell desperation.' Deep was dirty, and not just from a moral standpoint. Even dirtier than usual, as if he'd dived into a bog, which Calder didn't doubt he would have if he'd thought there was a coin at the bottom.

'What is it? I've a battle to die gloriously in.'

'Oh, I wouldn't want to stop 'em strumming ballads in your honour.'

'They already sing songs about him,' said Shallow.

Deep grinned. 'Not in his honour, though. We found something might be of interest.'

'Look!' Shallow pointed off to the south, white teeth smiling in his mud-spattered face. 'There's a rainbow!'

There was, in fact, a faint one, curving down towards the distant barley as the rain slackened and the sun showed itself again, but Calder was in no mood to appreciate it. 'Did you just want to draw my attention to the endless beauty all around us, or is there something more to the point?'

Deep held out a piece of folded paper, creased and dirty. Calder reached for it and he whipped it theatrically away. 'For a price.'

'The price for paper isn't high.'

''Course not,' said Deep. 'It's what's written on that paper gives it value.'

'And what's written on it?'

The brothers looked at each other. 'Something. We found it on some Union lad.'

'I've no time for this. Chances are high it's just some letter from Mother.'

'Letter?' asked Shallow.

Calder snapped his fingers. 'Give it me and I'll pay you what it's worth. Or you can peddle your rainbows elsewhere.'

The brothers exchanged glances again. Shallow shrugged. Deep slapped the paper into Calder's hand. It didn't appear to be worth much at a glance, spotted with mud and what looked suspiciously like blood. Knowing these two, definitely blood. There was neat writing inside.

Colonel Vallimir,

General Mitterick's troops are heavily engaged at the Old Bridge. Soon he will force the enemy to commit all his reserves. I wish you to begin your attack immediately, therefore, as discussed, and with every man at your disposal. Good luck.

Then what might have been a name but it was right in the crease, the paper was all scuffed and Calder couldn't make sense of it. It looked like an order, but he'd never heard of any Vallimir. An attack on the Old Bridge. That was hardly news. He was about to throw it away when he caught the second block of writing in a wilder, slanting hand.

Ensure that the enemy are fully engaged before crossing the stream, and in the meantime take care not to give away your position on their flank. My men and I are giving our all. I will not have them let down.
    General Mitterick, Second Division

Mitterick. Dow had mentioned that name. One of the Union's generals. Something about him being sharp and reckless. My men and I are giving our all? He sounded a pompous idiot. Ordering an attack across a stream, though. On the flank. Calder frowned. Not the river. And not the bridge. He blinked around at the terrain, thinking about it. Wondering where soldiers could be for that order to make sense.

'By the dead,' he whispered. There were Union men in the woods over to the west, ready to cross the beck and take them in their flank at any moment. There had to be!

'Worth something, then?' asked Shallow, smirking.

Calder hardly heard him. He pushed past the two killers and hurried up the rise to the west, shoving between the grim-faced men leaning against Clail's Wall so he could get a view across the stream.

'What is it?' asked White-Eye, bringing his horse up on the other side of the drystone.

Calder snapped open the battered eyeglass his father used to use and peered westwards, up that slope covered with old stumps, past the woodcutters' sheds and towards the shadowy trees beyond. Were they crawling with Union soldiers, ready to charge across the shallow water as soon as they saw him move? There was no sign of men there. Not even a glint of steel among the trees. Could it be a trick?

Should he keep his promise, charge to his brother's aid and risk offering the whole army's bare arse to the enemy? Or stay behind the wall and leave Scale the one with his backside in the breeze? That was the safe thing, wasn't it? Hold the line. Prevent disaster. Or was he only telling himself what he wanted to hear? Was he relieved to have found a way to avoid fighting? A way to get rid of his idiot older brother? Liar, liar, he didn't even know when he was telling himself the truth any more.

He desperately wanted someone to tell him what to do. He wished Seff was with him, she always had bold ideas. She was brave. Calder wasn't made for riding to the rescue. Hanging back was more his style. Saving his own skin. Killing prisoners. Not doing it himself, of course, but ordering it done. Poking other men's wives while they were doing the fighting, maybe, if he was really feeling adventurous. But this was a long way outside his expertise. What the hell should he do?

'What's going on?' asked Pale-as-Snow. 'The men are—'

'The Union are in the woods on the other side of that stream!'

There was a silence, in which Calder realised he'd spoken far louder than he needed to.

'The Union's over there? You sure?'

'Why haven't they come already?' White-Eye wanted to know.

Calder held up the paper. 'Because I've got their orders. But they'll get more.'

He could hear the Carls around him muttering. Knew they were passing the news from man to man. Probably that was no bad thing. Probably that was why he'd shouted it.

'What do we do, then?' hissed White-Eye. 'Scale's waiting for help.'

'I know that, don't I? No one knows that better than me!' Calder stood frowning towards the trees, his free hand opening and closing. 'Tenways.' By the dead, he was clutching at dust now, running for help to a man who'd tried to have him murdered a few days before. 'Hansul, get up to Skarling's Finger and tell Brodd Tenways we've got the Union out there in the woods to the west. Tell him Scale needs him. Needs him now, or we'll lose the Old Bridge.'

Hansul raised an eyebrow. 'Tenways?'

'Dow said he should help, if we needed it! We need it.'

'But—'

'Get up there!'

Pale-as-Snow and Hansul traded a glance. Then White-Eye clambered back up onto his horse and cantered off towards Skarling's Finger. Calder realised everyone was watching him. Wondering why he hadn't done the right thing already, and charged to his brother's rescue. Wondering whether they should stay loyal to this clueless idiot with the good hair.

'Tenways has to help,' he muttered, though he wasn't sure who he was trying to convince. 'We lose that bridge and we're all in the shit. This is about the whole North.' As if he'd ever cared a damn about the whole North, or even anyone much further away than the end of his own foot.

His patriotic bluster carried no more weight with Pale-as-Snow than it did with him. 'If the world worked that way,' said the old warrior, 'we'd have no need for swords in the first place. No offence, Calder, but Tenways hates you like the plague hates the living, and he doesn't feel a whole stretch warmer towards your brother. He won't put himself or his men on the line for your sakes, whatever Dow says. If you want your brother helped, I reckon you'll have to do it yourself. And soon.' He raised his white brows. 'So what do we do?'

Calder wanted very much to hit him, but he was right. He wanted to hit him because he was right. What should he do? He lifted his eyeglass again and scanned the treeline, slowly one way, then the other, then stopped dead.

Did he catch, just for a moment, the glint of another eyeglass trained on him?

Corporal Tunny peered through his eyeglass towards the dry-stone wall. He wondered if, just for an instant, he caught the glint of another trained on him? But probably he'd just imagined it. There certainly wasn't much sign of anything else going on.

'Movement?' squeaked Yolk.

'Nah.' Tunny slapped the glass closed then scratched at his increasingly stubbly, greasy, itchy neck. He'd a strong feeling something other than him had taken up residence in his collar. A decision hard to understand, since he'd rather have been pretty much anywhere else himself. 'They're just sitting there, far as I can tell.'

'Like us.'

'Welcome to the glory-fields, Trooper Yolk.'

'Still no damn orders? Where the hell has bloody Lederlingen got to?'

'No way of knowing.' Tunny had long ago given up feeling any surprise when the army didn't function quite as advertised. He glanced over his shoulder. Behind them, Colonel Vallimir was having another one of his rages, this time directed at Sergeant Forest.

Yolk leaned in to whisper, 'Every man shitting on the man below, Corporal?'

'Oh, you're developing a keen sense of the mechanisms of his Majesty's forces. I do believe you'll make a fine general one day, Yolk.'

'My ambition don't go past corporal, Corporal.'

'I think that's very wise. As you can tell.'

'Still no orders, sir,' Forest was saying, face screwed up like a man looking into a stiff wind.

'Bloody hell!' snapped Vallimir. 'It's the right time to go! Any fool can see that.'

'But . . . we can't go without orders, sir.'

'Of course we bloody can't! Dereliction of duty, that'd be! But now's the right time, so of course General bloody Mitterick will be demanding to know why I didn't act on my own initiative!'

'Very likely, sir.'

'Initiative, eh, Forest? *Initiative*. What the bloody hell is that except an excuse to demote a man? It's like a card game they won't tell you the rules to, only the stakes!' And on, and on, and on he went, just like always.

Tunny gave a sigh, and handed his eyeglass to Yolk.

'Where you going, Corporal?'

'Nowhere, I reckon. Absolutely nowhere.' He wedged himself back against his tree trunk and dragged his coat closed over him. 'Wake me if that changes, eh?' He scratched his neck, then pulled his cap down over his eyes. 'By some miracle.'

Closing Arguments

It was the noise that was the most unexpected thing about battle. It was probably the loudest thing Finree had ever heard. Several dozen men roaring and shrieking at the very highest extent of their broken voices, crashing wood, stamping boots, clanging metal, all amplified and rendered meaningless by the enclosed space, the walls of the room ringing with mindless echoes of pain, and fury, and violence. If hell had a noise, it sounded like this. No one could have heard orders, but it hardly mattered.

Orders could have made no difference now.

The shutters of another window were bludgeoned open, a gilded cupboard that had been blocking them flattening an unfortunate lieutenant and spewing an avalanche of shattering dress crockery across the floor. Men swarmed through the square of brightness, ragged black outlines at first, gaining awful detail as they burst into the inn. Snarling faces smeared with paint, and dirt, and fury. Wild hair tangled with bones, with rough-carved wooden rings and rough-cast metal. They brandished jagged axes and clubs toothed with dull iron. They wept and gurgled a mad clamour, eyes bulging with battle-madness.

Aliz screamed again, but Finree felt oddly cold-headed. Perhaps it was some kind of beginner's luck at bravery. Or perhaps it had yet to really dawn on her how bad things were. They were very, very bad. Her eyes darted around as she struggled to take it all in, not daring to blink in case she missed something.

In the middle of the room an old sergeant was wrestling with a grey-haired primitive, each holding the other's wrist with weapons waggling at the ceiling, dragging each other this way and that as though through the steps of some drunken dance, unable to agree on who should be leading. Nearby one of the violinists was beating at someone with his shattered instrument, reduced now to a tangle of strings and splinters. Outside in the courtyard the gates were shuddering, splinters flying from their inside faces while guardsmen tried desperately to prop them shut with their halberds.

She found herself rather wishing that Bremer dan Gorst was beside her. Probably she should have wished for Hal instead, but she had a feeling courage, and duty, and honour would do no good here. Brute strength and rage were what was needed.

She saw a plump captain with a scratch down his face, who was rumoured to be the bastard son of someone-or-other important, stabbing at a man wearing a necklace of bones, both of them slick with red. She saw a pleasant major who used to tell her bad jokes when she was a girl clubbed on the back of the head. He tottered sideways, knees buckling like a clown's, one hand fishing at his empty scabbard. He was caught with a sword and flung to the floor in a shower of blood. Another officer's backswing, she realised.

'Above us!' someone screamed.

The savages had somehow got up onto the gallery, were shooting arrows down. An officer just next to Finree slumped over a table with a shaft in his back, dragging one of the hangings down on top of him, his long steel clattering from his dangling hand. She reached out nervously and slid his short steel from the sheath, backed away again towards the wall with it hidden beside her skirts. As though anyone would complain at a theft in the midst of this.

The door burst open and savages spilled into the common hall from the rest of the inn. They must have taken the courtyard, killed the guards. Men desperately trying to keep the attackers out from the windows spun about, their frozen faces pictures of horror.

'The lord governor!' someone screamed. 'Protect his—' Cut off in a snivelling wail.

The melee had lost all shape. The officers were fighting hard for every inch of ground but they were losing, forced grimly back into a corner, cut down one by one. Finree was shoved against the wall, perhaps by some pointless act of chivalry, more likely by the random movement of the fight. Aliz was next to her, pale and blubbing, Lord Governor Meed on the other side, in a state little better. All three of them jostled by men's backs as they fought hopelessly for survival.

Finree could hardly see over the armoured shoulder of a guard, then he fell and a savage darted into the gap, a jagged iron sword in his fist. She got one quick, sharp look at his face. Lean, yellow-haired, splinters of bone pushed through the rim of one ear.

Meed held up a hand, breath whooshing in to speak, or scream, or beg. The jagged sword chopped into him between neck and collarbone. He took a wobbling step, eyes rolled up to the ceiling so the whites showed huge, tongue sticking out and his fingers plucking at the ragged wound while blood welled up from between them and down the torn braid on the front of his uniform. Then he crashed over on his face, catching a table on the way and knocking it half in the air, a sheaf of papers spilling across his back.

Aliz let go another piercing shriek.

The thought flashed through Finree's mind as she stared at Meed's corpse that this might all have been her fault. That the Fates had despatched this as the method of her vengeance. It seemed disproportionate, to say the least. She would have been happy with something considerably less—

'Ah!' Someone grabbed her left arm, twisted it painfully around, and she was staring into a leering face, a mouthful of teeth filed to points, one pitted cheek marked with a blue handprint and speckled red.

She shoved him away, he gave a whooping squeal and she realised she had the short steel in her hand, had rammed it into his ribs. He pressed her against the wall, wrenching her head up. She managed to drag the steel free, slippery now, work it between them, grunting as she pushed the point up into his jaw, blade sliding into his head. She could see the skin on his blue cheek bulge from the metal behind it.

He tottered back, one hand fishing at the bloody hilt under his jaw, left her gasping against the wall, hardly able to stand her knees were shaking so badly. She felt her head suddenly yanked sideways, a stab of pain in her scalp, in her neck. She yelped, cut off as her skull smacked—

Everything was bright for a moment.

The floor thumped her in the side. Boots shuffled and crunched.

Fingers around her neck.

She couldn't breathe, plucked at the hand with her nails, ears throbbing with her own heartbeat.

A knee pressed into her stomach, crushing her against a table. Hot, foul breath blasted at her cheek. It felt as if her head was going to burst. She could hardly see, everything was so bright.

Then there was silence. The hand at her throat released a fraction, enough for her to draw in a shuddering breath. Cough, gag, cough again. She thought she was deaf, then realised the room had gone deathly quiet. Corpses of both sides were tangled up with broken furniture, scattered cutlery, torn papers, piles of fallen plaster. A few weak groans came from dying men. Only three officers appeared to have survived, one holding his bloody arm, the other two sitting with hands up. One was crying softly. The savages stood over them, still as statues. Nervous, almost, as if waiting for something.

Finree heard a creaking footstep in the corridor outside. And then another. As though some great weight was pressing on the boards. Another groaning footstep. Her eyes rolled towards the doorway, straining to see.

A man came through. The shape of a man, at least, if not the size. He had to duck under the lintel and then stayed suspiciously stooped, as if he was below decks in a small ship, scared of catching his head on low beams. Black hair streaked with grey stuck to his knobbly face with wet, black beard jutting, tangled black fur across his great shoulders. He surveyed the scene of wreckage with an expression strangely disappointed. Hurt even. As if he had been invited to attend a tea party and found instead a slaughter-yard at the venue.

'Why is everything broken?' he said in a voice oddly soft. He stooped to pick up one of the fallen plates, no more than a saucer in his immense hand, licked a fingertip and rubbed a few specks of blood from the maker's mark on the back, frowning at it like a cautious shopper. His eyes lighted on Meed's corpse, and his frown grew deeper. 'Did I not ask for trophies? Who killed this old man?'

The savages stared at each other, eyes bulging in their painted faces. They were terrified, Finree realised. One raised a trembling arm to point at the man who was holding her down. 'Saluc did it!'

The giant's eyes slid across to Finree, then the man with his knee in her stomach, then narrowed. He put the plate on a gouged table, so gently it made no sound. 'What are you doing with my woman, Saluc?'

'Nothing!' The hand around Finree's neck released and she dragged herself back across the table, struggling to get a proper breath. 'She killed Bregga, I was just—'

'You were robbing me.' The giant took a step forwards, his head on one side.

Saluc stared desperately around but his friends were all scrambling away from him as if he was infected with the plague. 'But . . . I only wanted to—'

'I know.' The giant nodded sadly. 'But rules are rules.' He was across the space between them in an instant. With one great hand he caught the man's wrist while the other closed around his neck, fingers almost meeting thumb behind his head, lifting him squirming off his feet, smashing his skull crunching into the wall, once, twice, three times, blood spattering across the cracked plaster. It was over so quickly Finree did not have time to cower.

'You try to show them a better way . . .' The giant carefully set the dead man down in a sitting position against the wall, arranging his hands in his lap, resting his flattened head in a comfortable position, like a mother putting a child to sleep. 'But some men will never be civilised. Take my women away. And do not tamper with them. Alive they are worth something. Dead they are . . .' He rolled Meed's corpse over with one huge boot. The lord governor flopped onto his back, eyes goggling at the ceiling. 'Dirt.'

Aliz screamed yet again. Finree wondered how she could still produce so high and true a note after all that screaming. She did not make a sound herself as they dragged her out. Partly that blow to her head seemed to have knocked all the voice out of her. Partly she was still having trouble getting a good breath after being throttled. But mostly she was occupied trying desperately to think of a way to live through this nightmare.

*

The battle was still going outside, Beck could hear it. But it was quiet downstairs. Maybe the Union men reckoned they'd got everyone killed. Maybe they'd missed the little stairway somehow. By the dead, he hoped they'd missed the—

One of the steps creaked and the breath stopped in Beck's throat. Maybe one creak sounds like another, but somehow he knew this was made by the foot of a man aiming to keep quiet. Sweat sprang out of his skin. Trickling, tickling down his neck. Didn't dare move to scratch it. He strained with every muscle to make no sound, wincing at every smallest wheeze in his throat, not daring even to swallow. His fruits, and his arse, and his guts all felt like they were a huge, cold weight he could hardly stop from dropping out of him.

Another stealthy, creaking step. Beck thought he could hear the bastard hissing something. Taunting him. Knew he was there, then. Couldn't make out the words, his heart was thumping so loud in his ears, so hard it felt like it might pop his eyes right out. Beck tried to shrink back into the cupboard, one eye fixed on the ragged slit between two planks of the door, the slice of attic beyond. The point of the man's sword slid into view, glinting murder, then the blade, dotted with red. Colving's blood, or Brait's, or Reft's. And Beck's too, soon enough. A Union sword, he could tell from the twisted metal around the hilt.

Another creaking step, and Beck spread his fingertips out against the rough wood, hardly touching it in case the rusted hinges gave him away. He gripped the hot hilt of his own sword, a narrow strip of light across the bright blade, the rest gleaming in the darkness. He had to fight. Had to, if he wanted to see his mother, and his brothers, and their farm again. And that was all he wanted, now.

One more creaking step. He took a long, cutting breath, chest swelling with it, frozen, frozen, time stretching. How long could a man need to take a pace?

One more footstep.

Beck burst out, screaming, flinging back the door. The loose corner caught on the boards and he stumbled over it, plunging off balance, no choice but to charge.

The Union man stood in the shadows, head turning. Beck thrust wild, felt the point bite, crosspiece digging at his knuckles as the blade slid through the Union man's chest. They spun in a growling hug and something whacked Beck hard on the head. The low beam. He came down on his back with the weight of the Union man full across him, breath driven out in a whoosh, hand squashed around the grip of his sword. Took a moment for Beck's eyes to adjust, but when they did he was staring straight up into a twisted, bulge-eyed face.

Only it weren't a Union man at all. It was Reft.

He took a long, slow, wheezing breath in, cheeks trembling. Then he coughed blood into Beck's face.

Beck whimpered, kicked, squirmed free, rolled Reft off and scrambled clear of him. Knelt there, staring.

Reft lay on his side. One hand scratched at the floor, one eye rolled up towards Beck. He was trying to say something but the words were gurgles. Blood bubbling out from mouth and nose. Blood creeping from underneath him and down the grain of the boards. Black in the shadows. Dark red where it crossed a patch of light.

Beck put one hand on his shoulder. Almost whispered his name, knew there was no point. His other hand closed around the grip of his sword, slick with blood. It was a lot harder to get it out than it had been to put it in. Made a faint sucking sound as it came clear. Almost said Reft's name again. Found he couldn't speak. Reft's fingers had stopped moving, his eyes wide open, red on his lips, on his neck. Beck put the back of one hand against his mouth. Realised it was all bloody. Realised he was bloody all over. Soaked with it. Red with it. Stood, stomach suddenly rolling. Reft's eyes were still on him. He tottered over to the stairs and down 'em, sword scraping a pink groove in the plaster. His father's sword.

No one moved downstairs. He could hear fighting out in the street, maybe. Mad shouting. There was a faint haze of smoke, tang of it tickling his throat. His mouth tasted of blood. Blood and metal and raw meat. All the lads were dead. Stodder was on his face near the steps, one hand reaching for 'em. The back of his head was neatly split, hair matted to dark curls. Colving was against the wall, head back, hands clamped to his chubby gut, shirt soaked with blood. Brait just looked like a pile of rags in the corner. Never had looked like much more'n a pile a rags, the poor bastard.

There were four Union men dead too, all near each other, like they'd decided to stick together. Beck stood in the midst of 'em. The enemy. Such good gear they all had. Breastplates, and greaves, and polished helmets, all the same. And boys like Brait had died with not much more'n a split stick and a knife blade stuck in it. Weren't fair, really. None of it was fair.

One of 'em was on his side and Beck rolled him over with his boot, head flopping. He was left squinting up at the ceiling, eyes looking off different ways. Apart from his gear, there didn't look to be much special about him. He was younger'n Beck had thought, a downy effort at a beard on his cheeks. The enemy.

There was a crash. The shattered door was kicked out of the way and someone took a lurching step into the room, shield in front of him and a mace up in the other hand. Beck just stood staring. Didn't even raise his sword. The man limped forward, and gave a long whistle.

'What happened, lad?' asked Flood.

'Don't know.' He didn't know, really. Or at least, he knew what, but not how. Not why. 'I killed . . .' He tried to point upstairs, but he couldn't raise his arm. Ended up pointing at the dead Union boys at his feet. 'I killed . . .'

'You hurt?' Flood was pressing at his blood-soaked shirt, looking him over for a wound.

'Ain't mine.'

'Got four o' the bastards, eh? Where's Reft?'

'Dead.'

'Right. Well. You can't think about that. Least you made it.' Flood slid one arm around his shoulders and led him out into the bright street.

The wind outside felt cold through Beck's blood-soaked shirt and his piss-soaked trousers, made him shiver. Cobbles coated with dust and blowing ash, with splintered wood, fallen weapons. Dead of both sides tossed around and wounded too. Saw a Union man on the ground, holding up a helpless arm while two Thralls hacked at him with axes. Smoke still shifting across the square, but Beck could see there was a new struggle on the bridge, shadows of men and weapons in the murk, the odd flitting arrow.

A big old-timer in dark mail and a battered helmet sat on horseback at the front of a wedge of others, pointing across the square with a broken length of wood, roaring at the top of his lungs in a voice husky from smoke. 'Push 'em back over the bridge! Drive the bastards!' One of the men behind had a standard on a pole – white horse on green. Reachey's sign. Which he guessed made the old man Reachey his self.

Beck was only just starting to make sense of it. The Northmen had laid on an attack of their own, just the way Flood had said, and caught the Union as they got bogged down in the houses and the twisting lanes. Driven 'em back across the river. Looked like he might even not die today, and the thought made him want to cry. Maybe he would've, if his eyes hadn't been watering already from the smoke.

'Reachey!'

The old warrior looked over. 'Flood! Still alive, y'old bastard?'

'Half way to it, Chief. Hard fighting hereabouts.'

'I'll say. I broke my bloody axe! Union men got good helmets, eh? Not good enough, though.' Reachey tossed the splintered haft clattering across the ruined square. 'You did some decent work here.'

'Lost about all my boys, though,' said Flood. 'Just this one left.' And he clapped Beck on the shoulder. 'Got four o' the bastards on his own, he did.'

'Four? What's your name, lad?'

Beck gawped up at Reachey and his Named Men. All watching him. He should've put 'em all right. Told the truth. But even if he'd had the bones, and he didn't, he didn't have the breath in him to say that many words. So he just said, 'Beck.'

'Just Beck?'

'Aye.'

Reachey grinned. 'Man like you needs a bit more name than that, I reckon. We'll call you . . .' He looked Beck up and down for a moment, then nodded to himself like he had the answer. 'Red Beck.' He turned in his saddle and shouted to his Named Men. 'How d'you like that, lads? Red Beck!' And they started banging their shields with their sword hilts, and their chests with their gauntlets, and sending up a right clatter.

'You see this?' shouted Reachey. 'Here's the kind o' lad we

need! Everyone look at this lad! Let's find us some more like him! Some more bloody little bastards!' Laughter, and cheering, and nods of approval all round. Mostly for the Union being driven back past the bridge, but partly for him, and his bloody day. He'd always wanted respect, and the company of fighting men, and above all a fearsome name. Now he had the lot, and all he'd had to do was hide in a cupboard and kill someone on his own side, then take the credit for his work.

'Red Beck.' Flood grinned proudly like a father at his baby's first steps. 'What d'you reckon to that, boy?'

Beck stared down at the ground. 'Don't know.'

Straight Edge

'Ah!' Craw jerked away from the needle on an instinct and only made the thread tug at his cheek and hurt him worse. 'Ah!'

'Oftentimes,' murmured Whirrun, 'a man's better served embracing his pain than trying to escape it. Things are smaller when you face 'em.'

'Easily said when you're the one with the needle.' Craw sucked air through his teeth as the point nipped at his cheek again. Hardly the first stitches he ever had, but it's strange how quick you forget what a given kind of pain feels like. It was coming back to him now, and no mistake. 'Best thing might be to get it over with quick, eh?'

'I'm right there with you on that, but the sorry fact is I'm a much better killer than I am a healer. Tragedy of my life. I can stitch all right and I know Crow's Foot from the Alomanter and how to rub each one on a bandage and I can hum a charm or two—'

'They any use?'

'The way I sing 'em? Only for scaring off cats.'

'Ah!' grunted Craw as Whirrun pressed his cut closed between finger and thumb and pushed the needle through again. He really had to stop squawking, there were plenty about with far worse'n a scratch across the cheek.

'Sorry,' grunted Whirrun. 'You know, I've thought on it before, now and then, in the slow moments—'

'You get a lot o' those, don't you?'

'Well, you're taking your time about showing me this destiny of mine. Anyway, it seems to me a man can do an awful lot of evil in no time at all. Swing of a blade is all it takes. Doing good

320

needs time. And all manner of complicated efforts. Most men don't have the patience for it. 'Specially not these days.'

'Those are the times.' Craw paused, chewing at a flap of loose skin on his bottom lip. 'Do I say that too much? Am I turning into my father? Am I turning into a boring old fool?'

'All heroes do.'

Craw snorted. 'Those that live to hear their own songs.'

'Terrible strain on a man, hearing his self sung about. Enough to make anyone a shit.'

'Even if they weren't one in the first place.'

'Which isn't likely. I guess hearing songs about warriors makes men feel brave their own selves, but a great warrior has to be at least half way mad.'

'Oh, I've known a few great warriors weren't mad at all. Just heartless, careless, selfish bastards.'

Whirrun bit off the thread with his teeth. 'That is the other common option.'

'Which are you, then, Whirrun? Mad or a heartless prick?'

'I try to bridge the gap between the two.'

Craw chuckled in spite of the throbbing in his face. 'That right there. That right there is a bloody hero's effort.'

Whirrun settled back on his heels. 'You're done. And not a bad job either, though I'm singing my own praises. Maybe I'll give up the killing and turn to healing after all.'

A growling voice cut through the faint ringing still going in Craw's ears. 'After the battle, though, eh?'

Whirrun blinked up. 'Why, if it ain't the Protector of the North. I feel all . . . protected. Swaddled up, like in a good coat.'

'Had that effect all my life.' Dow looked down at Craw with his hands on his hips, the sun bright behind him.

'You going to bring me some fighting, Black Dow?' Whirrun slowly stood, pulling his sword up after him. 'I came here to fill graves, and the Father of Swords is getting thirsty.'

'I daresay I can scare you up something to kill before too long. In the meantime I need a private word with Curnden Craw, here.'

Whirrun clapped a hand to his chest. 'Wouldn't dream of putting myself in between two lovers.' And he swanned off up the hill, sword over one shoulder.

'Strange bastard, that,' said Dow as he watched Whirrun go.

Craw grunted as he unfolded his legs and slowly stood, shaking his aching joints out. 'He plays up to it. You know how it is, having a reputation.'

'Fame's a prison, no doubt. How's your face?'

'Lucky I've always been an ugly bastard. I'll look no worse'n before. Do we know what it was did the damage?'

Dow shook his head. 'Who knows with the Southerners? Some new weapon. Some style o' sorcery.'

'It's an evil one. That can just reach out and pluck men away like that.'

'Is it? The Great Leveller's waiting for all of us, ain't he? There'll always be someone stronger, quicker, luckier'n you, and the more fighting you do the quicker he's going to find you. That's what life is for men like us. The time spent plummeting towards that moment.'

Craw wasn't sure he cared for that notion. 'At least in the line, or the charge, or the circle a man can fight. Pretend to have a hand in the outcome.' He winced as he touched the fresh stitching with his fingertips. 'How do you make a song about someone whose head got splattered while he was half way through saying nothing much?'

'Like Splitfoot.'

'Aye.' Craw wasn't sure he'd ever seen anyone look deader than that bastard.

'I want you to take his place.'

'Eh?' said Craw. 'My ears are still whining. Not sure I heard you right.'

Dow leaned closer. 'I want you to be my Second. Lead my Carls. Watch my back.'

Craw stared. 'Me?'

'Aye, you, what did I fucking say?'

'But . . . why the hell *me*?'

'You got the experience, and the respect . . .' Dow looked at him for a moment, his jaw clenched tight. Then he waved a hand like he was swatting a fly. 'You remind me o' Threetrees.'

Craw blinked. It might've been one of the best things anyone had ever said to him, and not from a source prone to lazy compliments. Or any compliments at all, in fact. 'Well . . . I don't know what to say. Thank you, Chief. That means a lot. A hell of a bloody lot. If I ever get to be a tenth of the man he was then I'll be more'n satisfied—'

'Shit on that. Just tell me you'll do it. I need someone I can count on, Craw, and you do things the old way. You're a straight edge, and there ain't many left. Just tell me you'll do it.' He had a strange look to him, suddenly. An odd, weak twist to his mouth. If Craw hadn't known better, he'd have called it fear, and suddenly he saw it.

Dow had no one he could turn his back to. No friends but those he'd scared into serving him and a mountain of enemies. No choice but to trust to a man he hardly knew 'cause he reminded him of an old comrade long gone back to the mud. The cost of a great big name. The harvest of a lifetime in the black business.

''Course I'll do it.' And like that it was said. Maybe he felt for Dow in that moment, however mad it sounded. Maybe he understood the loneliness of being Chief. Or maybe the embers of his own ambitions, that he'd thought burned out beside his brothers' graves long ago, flared up one last time when Dow raked 'em over. Either way it was said, and there was no unsaying it. Without wondering if it was the right thing to do. For him, or for his dozen, or for anyone, and straight away Craw had a terrible feeling like he'd made a bastard of a mistake. 'Just while the battle's on, though,' he added, rowing back from the waterfall fast as he could. 'I'll hold the gap 'til you find someone better.'

'Good man.' Dow held out his hand, and they shook, and when Craw looked up again it was into that wolf grin, not a trace of weakness or fear or anything even close. 'You done the right thing, Craw.'

Craw watched Dow walk back up the hillside towards the stones, wondering whether he'd really let his hard mask slip or if he'd just slipped a soft one on. The right thing? Had Craw just signed up as right hand to one of the most hated men in the world? A man with more enemies than any other in a land where everyone had too many? A man he didn't even particularly like, promised to guard with his life? He gave a groan.

What would his dozen have to say about this? Yon shaking his head with a face like thunder. Drofd looking all hurt and confused. Brack rubbing at his temples with his— Brack was back to the mud, he realised with a jolt. Wonderful? By the dead, what would she have to—

'Craw.' And there she was, right at his elbow.

'Ah!' he said, taking a step away.

'How's the face?'

'Er . . . all right . . . I guess. Everyone else all right?'

'Yon got a splinter in his hand and it's made him pissier'n ever, but he'll live.'

'Good. That's . . . good. That everyone's all right, that is, not . . . not the splinter.'

Her brows drew in, guessing something was wrong, which wasn't too difficult since he was making a pitiful effort at hiding it. 'What did our noble Protector want?'

'He wanted . . .' Craw worked his lips for a moment, wondering how to frame it, but a turd's a turd however it's framed. 'He wanted to offer me Splitfoot's place.'

He'd been expecting her to laugh her arse off, but she just narrowed her eyes. 'You? Why?'

Good question, he was starting to wonder about it now. 'He said I'm a straight edge.'

'I see.'

'He said . . . I remind him of Threetrees.' Realising what a pompous cock he sounded even as the words came out.

He'd definitely been expecting her to laugh at that, but she just narrowed her eyes more. 'You're a man can be trusted. Everyone knows that. But I can see better reasons.'

'Like what?'

'You were tight with Bethod and his crowd, and with Three-trees before him, and maybe Dow thinks you'll bring him a few friends he hasn't already got. Or at any rate a few less enemies.' Craw frowned. Those were better reasons. 'That and he knows Whirrun'll go wherever you go, and Whirrun's a damn good man to have standing behind you if things get ugly.' Shit. She was double right. She'd sussed it all straight off. 'And knowing Black Dow, things are sure to get ugly . . . What did you tell him?'

Craw winced. 'I said yes,' and hurried after with, 'just while the battle's on.'

'I see.' Still no anger, and no surprise either. She just watched him. That was making him more nervy than if she'd punched him in the face. 'And what about the dozen?'

'Well . . .' Ashamed to say he hadn't really considered it. 'Guess you'll be coming along with me, if you'll have it. Unless you want to go back to your farm and your family and—'

'Retire?'

'Aye.'

She snorted. 'The pipe and the porch and the sunset on the water? That's you, not me.'

'Then . . . I reckon it's your dozen for the time being.'

'All right.'

'You ain't going to give me a tongue-lashing?'

'About what?'

'Not taking my own advice, for a start. About how I should keep my head down, not stick my neck out, get everyone in the crew through alive, how old horses can't jump new fences and blah, blah, blah—'

'That's what you'd say. I'm not you, Craw.'

He blinked. 'Guess not. Then you think this is the right thing to do?'

'The right thing?' She turned away with a hint of a grin. 'That's you an' all.' And she strolled back up towards the Heroes, one hand resting slack on her sword hilt, and left him stood there in the wind.

'By the bloody dead.' He looked off across the hillside, desperately searching for a finger that still had some nail left to chew at.

Shivers was standing not far off. Saying nothing. Just staring. Looking, in fact, like a man who felt himself stepped in front of. Craw's wince became a full grimace. Seemed that was getting to be the normal shape to his face, one way and another. 'A man's worst enemies are his own ambitions,' Bethod used to tell him. 'Mine have got me in all the shit I'm in today.'

'Welcome to the shit,' he muttered to himself through gritted teeth. That's the problem with mistakes. You can make 'em in an instant. Years upon years spent tiptoeing about like a fool, then you take your eye away for a moment and . . .

Bang.

Escape

Finree thought they were in some kind of shack. The floor was damp dirt, a chill draught across it making her shiver. The place smelled of fust and animals.

They had blindfolded her, and marched her lurching across the wet fields into the trees, crops tangling her feet, bushes clutching at her dress. It was a good thing she had been wearing her riding boots or she would probably have ended up barefoot. She had heard fighting behind them, she thought. Aliz had kept screaming for a while, her voice getting more and more hoarse, but eventually stopped. It changed nothing. They had crossed water on a creaking boat. Maybe over to the north side of the river. They had been shoved in here, heard a door wobble shut and the clattering of a bar on the outside.

And here they had been left, in the darkness. To wait for who knew what.

As Finree slowly got her breath back the pain began to creep up on her. Her scalp burned, her head thumped, her neck sent vicious stings down between her shoulders whenever she tried to turn her head. But no doubt she was a great deal better off than most who had been trapped in that inn.

She wondered if Hardrick had made it to safety, or if they had ridden him down in the fields, his useless message never delivered. She kept seeing that major's face as he stumbled sideways with blood running from his broken head, so very surprised. Meed, fumbling at the bubbling wound in his neck. All dead. All of them.

She took a shuddering breath and forced the thought away. She could not think of it any more than a tightrope walker could think about the ground. 'You have to look forward,' she remembered her father telling her, as he plucked another of her pieces from the squares board. 'Concentrate on what you can change.'

Aliz had been sobbing ever since the door shut. Finree wanted quite badly to slap her, but her hands were tied. She was reasonably sure they would not get out of this by sobbing. Not that she had any better ideas.

'Quiet,' Finree hissed. 'Quiet, please, I need to think. Please. Please.'

The sobbing stuttered back to ragged whimpering. That was worse, if anything.

'Will they kill us?' squeaked Aliz' voice, along with a slobbering snort. 'Will they murder us?'

'No. They would have done it already.'

'Then what will they do with us?'

The question sat between them like a bottomless abyss, with nothing but their echoing breath to fill it. Finree managed to twist herself up to sitting, gritting her teeth at the pain in her neck. 'We have to think, do you understand? We have to look forward. We have to try and escape.'

'How?' Aliz whimpered.

'Any way we can!' Silence. 'We have to try. Are your hands free?'

'No.'

Finree managed to worm her way across the floor, dress sliding over the dirt until her back hit the wall, grunting with the effort. She shifted herself along, fingertips brushing crumbling plaster, damp stone.

'Are you there?' squeaked Aliz.

'Where else would I be?'

'What are you doing?'

'Trying to get my hands free.' Something tugged at Finree's waist, cloth ripped. She wormed her shoulder blades up the wall, following the caught material with her fingers. A rusted bracket. She rubbed away the flakes between finger and thumb, felt a jagged point underneath, a sudden surge of hope. She pulled her wrists apart, struggling to find the metal with the cords that held them.

'If you get your hands free, what then?' came Aliz' shrill voice.

'Get yours free,' grunted Finree through gritted teeth. 'Then feet.'

'Then what? What about the door? There'll be guards, won't there? Where are we? What do we do if—'

'I don't know!' She forced her voice down. 'I don't know. One battle at a time.' Sawing away at the bracket. 'One battle at a—' Her hand slipped and she lurched back, felt the metal leave a burning cut down her arm. 'Ah!'

'What?'

'Cut myself. Nothing. Don't worry.'

'Don't worry? We've been captured by the Northmen! Savages! Did you see—'

'Don't worry about the cut, I meant! And yes, I saw it all.' And she had to concentrate on what she could change. Whether her hands were free or not was challenge enough. Her legs were burning from holding her up against the wall, she could feel the greasy wetness of blood on her fingers, of sweat on her face. Her head was pounding, agony in her neck with every movement of her shoulders. She wriggled the cord against that piece of rusted metal, back and forward, back and forward, grunting with frustration. 'Damn, bloody— Ah!'

Like that it came free. She dragged her blindfold off and tossed it away. She could hardly see more without it. Chinks of light around the door, between the planks. Cracked walls glistening with damp, floor scattered with muddy straw. Aliz was kneeling a stride or two away, dress covered in dirt, bound hands limp in her lap.

Finree jumped over to her, since her ankles were still tied, and knelt down. She tugged off Aliz' blindfold, took both of her hands and pressed them in hers. Spoke slowly, looking her right in her pink-rimmed eyes. 'We will escape. We must. We will.' Aliz nodded, mouth twisting into a desperately hopeful smile for a moment. Finree peered down at her wrists, numb fingertips tugging at the knots, tongue pressed between her teeth as she prised at them with her broken nails—

'How does he know I have them?' Finree went cold. Or even colder. A voice, speaking Northern, and heavy footsteps, coming closer. She felt Aliz frozen in the dark, not even breathing.

'He has his ways, apparently.'

328

'His ways can sink in the dark places of the world for all I care.' It was the voice of the giant. That soft, slow voice, but it had anger in it now. 'The women are mine.'

'He only wants one.' The other sounded like his throat was full of grit, his voice a grinding whisper.

'Which one?'

'The brown-haired one.'

An angry snort. 'No. I had in mind she would give me children.' Finree's eyes went wide. Her breath crawled in her throat. They were talking about her. She went at the knot on Aliz' wrists with twice the urgency, biting at her lip.

'How many children do you need?' came the whispering voice.

'Civilised children. After the Union fashion.'

'What?'

'You heard me. Civilised children.'

'Who eat with a fork and that? I been to Styria. I been to the Union. Civilisation ain't all it's made out to be, believe me.'

A pause. 'Is it true they have holes there in which a man can shit, and the turds are carried away?'

'So what? Shit is still shit. It all ends up somewhere.'

'I want civilisation. I want civilised children.'

'Use the yellow-haired one.'

'She pleases my eye less. And she is a coward. She does nothing but cry. The brown-haired one killed one of my men. She has bones. Children get their courage from the mother. I will not have cowardly children.'

The whispering voice dropped lower, too quiet for Finree to hear. She tugged desperately at the knots with her nails, mouthing curses.

'What are they saying?' came Aliz' whisper, croaky with terror.

'Nothing,' Finree hissed back. 'Nothing.'

'Black Dow takes a high hand with me in this,' came the giant's voice again.

'He takes a high hand with me and all. There it is. He's the one with the chain.'

'I shit on his chain. Stranger-Come-Knocking has no masters but the sky and the earth. Black Dow does not command—'

'He ain't commanding nothing. He's asking nicely. You can tell me no. Then I'll tell him no. Then we can see.'

There was a pause. Finree pressed her tongue into her teeth, the knot starting to give, starting to give—

The door swung open and they were left blinking into the light. A man stood in the doorway. One of his eyes was strangely bright. Too bright. He stepped under the lintel, and Finree realised that his eye was made of metal, and set in the midst of an enormous, mottled scar. She had never seen a more monstrous-looking man. Aliz gave a kind of stuttering wheeze. Too scared even to scream, for once.

'She got her hands free,' he whispered over his shoulder.

'I said she had bones,' came the giant's voice from outside. 'Tell Black Dow there will be a price for this. A price for the woman and a price for the insult.'

'I'll tell him.' The metal-eyed man came forward, pulling something from his belt. A knife, she saw the flash of metal in the gloom. Aliz saw it too, whimpered, gripped hard at Finree's fingers and she gripped back. She was not sure what else she could do. He squatted down in front of them, forearms on his knees and his hands dangling, the knife loose in one. Finree's eyes flickered from the gleam of the blade to the gleam of his metal eye, not sure which was more awful. 'There's a price for everything, ain't there?' he whispered to her.

The knife darted out and slit the cord between her ankles in one motion. He reached behind his back and pulled a canvas bag over her head with another, plunging her suddenly into fusty, onion-smelling darkness. She was dragged up by her armpit, hands slipping from Aliz' limp grip.

'Wait!' she heard Aliz shouting behind her. 'What about me? What about—'

The door clattered shut.

The Bridge

Your August Majesty,
*   If this letter reaches you I have fallen in battle, fighting*
for your cause with my final breath. I write it only in the
hope of letting you know what I could not in person: that the days
I spent serving with the Knights of the Body, and as your Majesty's
First Guard in particular, were the happiest of my life, and that
the day when I lost that position was the saddest. If I failed you I
hope you can forgive me, and think of me as I was before Sipani:
dutiful, diligent, and always utterly loyal to your Majesty.
*   I bid you a fond farewell,*
*   Bremer dan Gorst*

He thought better of 'a fond' and crossed it out, realised he
should probably rewrite the whole thing without it, then decided
he did not have the time. He tossed the pen away, folded the
paper without bothering to blot it and tucked it down inside his
breastplate.

Perhaps they will find it there, later, on my crap-stained corpse.
Dramatically bloodied at the corner, maybe? A final letter! Why, to
whom? Family? Sweetheart? Friends? No, the sad fool had none of
those, it is addressed to the king! And borne upon a velvet pillow into
his Majesty's throne room, there perhaps to wring out some wretched
drip of guilt. A single sparkling tear spatters upon the marble tiles.
Oh! Poor Gorst, how unfairly he was used! How unjustly stripped of
his position! Alas, his blood has watered foreign fields, far from the
warmth of my favour! Now what's for breakfast?

Down on the Old Bridge the third assault had reached its
critical moment. The narrow double span was one heaving mass,
rows of nervous soldiers waiting unenthusiastically to take their
turn while the wounded, exhausted and otherwise spent staggered

away in the opposite direction. The resolve of Mitterick's men was flickering, Gorst could see it in the pale faces of the officers, hear it in their nervous voices, in the sobs of the injured. Success or failure was balanced on a knife-edge.

'Where the hell is bloody Vallimir?' Mitterick was roaring at everyone and no one. 'Bloody coward, I'll have him cashiered in disgrace! I'll go down there my bloody self! Where did Felnigg get to? Where . . . what . . . who . . .' His words were buried in the hubbub as Gorst walked down towards the river, his mood lifting with every jaunty step as if a great weight was floating from his shoulders piece by leaden piece.

A wounded man stumbled by, one arm around a fellow, clutching a bloody cloth to his eye. *Someone will be missing from next year's archery contest!* Another was hauled past on a stretcher, crying out piteously as he bounced, the stump of his leg bound tightly with red-soaked bandages. *No more walks in the park for you!* He grinned at the injured men laid groaning at the verges of the muddy track, gave them merry salutes. *Unlucky, my comrades! Life is not fair, is it?*

He strode through a scattered crowd, then threaded through a tighter mass, then shouldered through a breathless press, the fear building around him as the bodies squeezed tighter, and with it his excitement. Feelings ran high. Men shoved at each other, thrashed with their elbows, screamed pointless insults. Weapons waved dangerously. Stray arrows would occasionally putter down, no longer in volleys but in apologetic ones and twos. *Little gifts from our friends on the other side. No, really, you shouldn't have!*

The mud beneath Gorst's feet levelled off, then began to rise, then gave way to old stone slabs. Between twisted faces he caught glimpses of the river, the bridge's mossy parapet. He began to make out from the general din the metallic note of combat and the sound tugged at his heart like a lover's voice across a crowded room. *Like the whiff of the husk pipe to the addict. We all have our little vices. Our little obsessions. Drink, women, cards. And here is mine.*

Tactics and technique were useless here, it was a question of brute strength and fury, and very few men were Gorst's match in either. He put his head down and strained at the press as he had strained at the mired wagon a few days before. He began to grunt, then growl, then hiss, and he rammed his way through the soldiers like a ploughshare through soil, shoving heedlessly with shield and shoulder, tramping over the dead and wounded. *No small talk. No apologies. No petty embarrassments here.*

'Out of my fucking *way*!' he screeched, sending a soldier sprawling on his face and using him for a carpet. He caught a flash of metal and a spear-point raked his shield. For a moment he thought a Union man had taken objection, then he realised the spear had a Northman on the other end. *Greetings, my friend!* Gorst was trying to twist his sword free of the press and into a useful attitude when he was given an almighty shove from behind and found himself suddenly squashed up against the owner of the spear, their noses almost touching. A bearded face, with a scar on the top lip.

Gorst smashed his forehead into it, and again, and again, shoved him down and stomped on his head until it gave under his heel. He realised he was shouting at the falsetto top of his voice. He wasn't even sure of the words, if they were words. All around him men were doing the same, spitting curses in each other's faces that no one on the other side could possibly understand.

A glimpse of sky through a thicket of pole-arms and Gorst thrust his sword into it, another Northman bent sideways, breath wheezing silently through a mouth frozen in a drooling ring of surprise. Too tangled to swing, Gorst gritted his teeth and jabbed away, jabbed, jabbed, jabbed, point grating against armour, pricking at flesh, opening an arm up in a long red slit.

A growling face showed for a moment over the rim of Gorst's shield and he set his boots and drove the man back, battering at his chest, jaw, legs. Back he went, and back, and squealing over the parapet, his spear splashing into the fast-flowing water below. Somehow he managed to cling on with the other hand, desperate fingers white on stone, blood leaking from his bloated nose, looking up imploringly. *Mercy? Help? Forbearance, at least? Are we not all just men? Brothers eternal, on this crooked road of life? Could we be bosom friends, had we met in other circumstances?*

Gorst smashed his shield down on the hand, bones crunching under the metal edge, watched the man fall cartwheeling into the river. 'The Union!' someone shrieked. 'The Union!' Was it him? He felt soldiers pushing forward, their blood rising, surging across the bridge with an irresistible momentum, carrying him northwards, a stick on the crest of a wave. He cut someone down with his long steel, laid someone's else's head open with the corner of his shield, strap twisting in his hand, his face aching he was smiling so hard, every breath burning with joy. *This is living! This is living! Well, not for them, but—*

He tottered suddenly into empty space. Fields opened wide before him, crops shifting in the breeze, golden in the evening sun like the paradise the Prophet promises to the Gurkish righteous. Northmen ran. Some running away, and more running towards. A counter-attack, and leading it a huge warrior, clad in plates of black metal strapped over black chain mail, a long sword in one gauntleted fist, a heavy mace in the other, steel glinting warm and welcoming in the mellow afternoon. Carls followed in a mailed wedge, painted shields up and offering their bright-daubed devices, screaming a chant – 'Scale! Scale!' in a thunder of voices.

The Union drive faltered, the vanguard still shuffling reluctantly forward from the weight of those behind. Gorst stood at their front and watched, smiling into the dropping sun, not daring to move a muscle in case the feeling ended. It was sublime. Like a scene from the tales he had read as a boy. Like that ridiculous painting in his father's library of Harod the Great facing Ardlic of Keln. *A meeting of champions! All gritted teeth and clenched buttocks! All glorious lives, glorious deaths and glorious . . . glory?*

The man in black hammered up onto the bridge, big boots thumping the stones. His blade came whistling at shoulder height and Gorst set himself to parry, the breathtaking shock humming up his arm. The mace came a moment later and he caught it on his shield, the heavy head leaving a dent just short of his nose.

Gorst gave two savage cuts in return, high and low, and the man in black ducked the first and blocked the second with the shaft of his mace, lashed at Gorst with his sword and made him spin away, using a Union soldier's shield as a backrest.

He was strong, this champion of the North, and brave, but strength and bravery are not always enough. He had not studied every significant text on swordsmanship ever committed to paper. Had not trained three hours a day every day since he was fourteen. Had run no ten thousand miles in his armour. Had endured no bitter, enraging years of humiliation. *And, worst of all, he cares whether he loses.*

Their blades met in the air with a deafening crash but Gorst's timing was perfect and it was the Northman who staggered off balance, favouring perhaps a weak left knee. Gorst was on him in a flash but someone else's stray weapon struck him on the shoulder-plate before he could swing, sent him stumbling into the man in black's arms.

They lumbered in an awkward embrace. The Northman tried to beat at him with the haft of his mace, trip him, shake him off. Gorst held tight. He was vaguely aware of fighting around them, of men locked in their own desperate struggles, of the screams of tortured flesh and tortured metal, but he was lost in the moment, eyes closed.

When was the last time I truly held someone? When I won the semi-final in the contest, did my father hug me? No. A firm shake of the hand. An awkward clap on the shoulder. Perhaps he would have hugged me if I'd won, but I failed, just as he said I would. When, then? Women paid to do it? Men I scarcely know in meaningless drunken camaraderie? But not like this. By an equal, who truly understands me. If only it could last . . .

He leaped back, jerking his head away from the whistling mace and letting the man in black stumble past. Gorst's steel flashed towards his head as he righted himself and he only just managed to deflect the blow, sword wrenched from his hand and sent skittering away among the pounding boots. The man in black bellowed, twisting to swing his mace at a vicious diagonal.

Too much brawn, not enough precision. Gorst saw it coming, let it glance harmlessly from his shield and slid around it into space, aimed a carefully gauged chop, little more than a fencer's flick, at that weak left knee. The blade of his steel caught the thigh-plate, found the chain mail on the joint and bit through. The man in black lurched sideways, only staying upright by clawing at the parapet, his mace scraping the mossy stone.

Gorst blew air from his nose as he brought the steel scything up and over, no fencer's movement this. It chopped cleanly through the man's thick forearm, armour, flesh and bone, and clanged against the old rock underneath, streaks of blood, rings of mail, splinters of stone flying.

The man in black gave an outraged snort as he struggled up, roared as he swung his mace at Gorst's head with a killing blow. Or would have, had his hand still been attached. Somewhat to the disappointment of them both, Gorst suspected, his gauntlet and half his forearm were hanging by a last shred of chain mail, the mace dangling puppet-like from the wrist by a leather thong. As far as Gorst could tell without seeing his face, the man was greatly confused.

Gorst smashed him in the head with his shield and snapped his helmet back, blood squirting from his severed arm in thick black drops. He was pawing clumsily for a dagger at his belt when Gorst's long steel clanged into his black faceplate and left a bright dent down the middle. He tottered, arms out wide, then toppled backwards like a great tree felled.

Gorst held up his shield and bloody sword, shaking them at the last few dismayed Northmen like a savage, and gave a great shrill scream. *I win, fuckers! I win! I win!*

As if that were an order, the lot of them turned and fled northwards, thrashing through the crops in their desperate haste to get away, weighed down by their flapping mail and their fatigue and their panic, and Gorst was among them, a lion among the goats.

Compared to his morning routine this was like dancing on air. A Northman slipped beside him, yelping in terror. Gorst charted the downward movement of his body, timed the downward movement of his arm to match and neatly cut the man's head off, felt it bounce from his knee as he plunged on up the track. A young lad tossed away a spear, face contorted with fear as he looked over his shoulder. Gorst chopped deep into his backside and he went down howling in the crops.

It was so easy it was faintly ridiculous. Gorst hacked the legs out from one man, gained on another and dropped him with a cut across the back, struck an arm from a third and let him stumble on for a few wobbling steps before he smashed him over backwards with his shield.

Is this still battle? Is this still the glorious matching of man against man? Or is this just murder? He did not care. *I cannot tell jokes, or make pretty conversation, but this I can do. This I am made for. Bremer dan Gorst, king of the world!*

He chopped them down on both sides, left their blubbing, leaking bodies wrecked in his wake. A couple turned stumbling to face him and he chopped them down as well. Made meat of them all, regardless. On he went, and on, hacking away like a mad butcher, the air whooping triumphantly in his throat. He passed a farm on his right, half way or more to a long wall up ahead. No Northmen within easy reach, he stole a glance over his shoulder, and slowed.

None of Mitterick's men were following. They had stopped near the bridge, a hundred strides behind him. He was entirely alone in the fields, a one-man assault on the Northmen's positions. He stopped, uncertainly, marooned in a sea of barley.

A lad he must have overtaken earlier jogged up. Shaggy-haired, wearing a leather jerkin with a bloody sleeve. No weapon. He spared Gorst a quick glance, then laboured on. He passed close enough that Gorst could have stabbed him without moving his feet, but suddenly he could not see the point.

The elation of combat was leaking out of him, the familiar weight gathering on his shoulders again. *So quickly I am sucked back into the bog of despond. The foetid waters close over my face. Only count three, and I am once again the very same sad bastard who all know and scorn.* He looked back towards his own lines. The trail of broken bodies no longer felt like anything to take pride in.

He stood, skin prickling with sweat, sucking air through gritted teeth. Frowning towards the wall through the crops to the north, and the spears bristling up behind it, and the beaten men still struggling back towards it. *Perhaps I should charge on, all alone. Glorious Gorst, there he goes! Falling upon the enemy like a shooting star! His body dies but his name shall live for ever!* He snorted. *Idiot Gorst, throwing his life away, the stupid, squeaking arse. Dropping into his pointless grave like a turd into a sewer, and just as quickly forgotten.*

He shook the ruined shield from his arm and let it drop to the track, pulled the folded letter from his breastplate between two fingers, crumpled it tightly in his fist, then tossed it into the barley. *It was a pathetic letter anyway. I should be ashamed of myself.*

Then he turned, head hanging, and trudged back towards the bridge.

One Union soldier, for some reason, had chased far down the track after Scale's fleeing troops. A big man wearing heavy armour and with a sword in his hand. He didn't look particularly triumphant as he stared up the road, standing oddly alone in that open field. He looked almost as defeated as Calder felt. After a while he turned and plodded back towards the bridge. Back towards the trenches Scale's men had dug the previous night, and where the Union were now taking up positions.

Not all dramas on the battlefield spring from glorious action. Some slink from everyone just sitting there, doing nothing. Tenways had sent no help. Calder hadn't moved. He hadn't even got as far as making his mind up not to move. He'd just stood, staring at nothing through his eyeglass, in a frozen agony of indecision, and then suddenly all of Scale's men who still could were running, and the Union had carried the bridge.

Thankfully, it looked as if they were satisfied for now. Probably they didn't want to risk pushing further with the light fading. They could push further tomorrow, after all, and everyone knew it. They had a good foothold on the north bank of the river, and no shortage of men in spite of the price Scale had made them pay. It looked as if the price Scale had paid had been heavier yet.

The last of his defeated Carls were still hobbling back, clambering over the wall to lie scattered in the crops behind, dirt and blood-smeared, broken and exhausted. Calder stopped a man with a hand on his shoulder.

'Where's Scale?'

'Dead!' he screamed, shaking him off. 'Dead! Why didn't you come, you bastards? Why didn't you help us?'

'Union men over the stream there,' Pale-as-Snow was explaining as he led him away, but Calder hardly heard. He stood at the gate, staring across the darkening fields towards the bridge.

He'd loved his brother. For being on his side when everyone

else was against him. Because nothing's more important than family.

He'd hated his brother. For being too stupid. For being too strong. For being in his way. Because nothing's more important than power.

And now his brother was dead. Calder had let him die. Just by doing nothing. Was that the same as killing a man?

All he could think about was how it might make his life more difficult. All the extra tasks he'd have to do, the responsibilities he didn't feel ready for. He was the heir, now, to all his father's priceless legacy of feuds, hatred and bad blood. He felt annoyance rather than grief, and puzzled he didn't feel more. Everyone was looking at him. Watching him, to see what he'd do. To judge what kind of man he was. He was embarrassed, almost, that this was all his brother's death made him feel. Not guilty, not sad, just cold. And then angry.

And then very angry.

Strange Bedfellows

The hood was pulled from her head and Finree squinted into the light. Such as it was. The room was dim and dusty with two mean windows and a low ceiling, bowing in the middle, cobwebs drifting from the rafters.

A Northman stood a couple of paces in front of her, feet planted wide and hands on hips, head tipped slightly back in the stance of a man used to being obeyed, and quickly. His short hair was peppered with grey and his face was sharp as a chisel, notched with old scars, an appraising twist to his mouth. A chain of heavy golden links gleamed faintly around his shoulders. An important man. Or one who thought himself important, at least.

An older man stood behind him, thumbs in his belt near a battered sword hilt. He had a shaggy grey growth on his jaw somewhere between beard and stubble and a fresh cut on his cheek, dark red and rimmed with pink, closed with ugly stitches. He wore an expression somewhat sad, somewhat determined, as if he did not like what was coming but could see no way to avoid it, and now was fixed on seeing it through, whatever it cost him. A lieutenant of the first man.

As Finree's eyes adjusted she saw a third figure in the shadows against the wall. A woman, she was surprised to see, and with black skin. Tall and thin, a long coat hanging open to show a body wrapped in bandages. Where she stood in this, Finree could not tell.

She did not turn her head to look, in spite of the temptation, but she knew there was another man behind her, his gravelly breath at the edge of her hearing. The one with the metal eye. She wondered if he had that little knife in his hand, and how close the point was to her back. Her skin prickled inside her dirty dress at the thought.

'This is her?' sneered the man with the chain at the black-skinned woman, and when he turned his head Finree saw there was only a fold of old scar where his ear should have been.

'Yes.'

'She don't look much like the answer to all my problems.'

The woman stared at Finree, unblinking. 'Probably she has looked better.' Her eyes were like a lizard's, black and empty.

The man with the chain took a step forwards and Finree had to stop herself cringing. There was something in the set of him that made her feel he was teetering on the edge of violence. That his every smallest movement was the prelude to a punch, or a headbutt, or worse. That his natural instinct was to throttle her and it took a constant effort to stop himself doing it, and talk instead. 'Do you know who I am?'

She lifted her chin, trying to look undaunted and almost certainly failing. Her heart was thumping so hard she was sure they must be able to hear it against her ribs. 'No,' she said in Northern.

'You understand me, then.'

'Yes.'

'I'm Black Dow.'

'Oh.' She hardly knew what to say. 'I thought you'd be taller.'

Dow raised one scar-nicked brow at the older man. The older man shrugged. 'What can I say? You're shorter'n your repu-tation.'

'Most of us are.' Dow looked back at Finree, eyes narrowed, judging her response. 'How 'bout your father? Taller'n me?'

They knew who she was. Who her father was. She had no idea how, but they knew. That was either a good thing or a very bad one. She looked at the older man and he gave her the faintest, apologetic smile, then winced since he must have stretched his stitches doing it. She felt the man with the metal eye shift his weight behind her, a floorboard creaking. This did not seem like a group from which she could expect good things.

'My father is about your height,' she said, her voice whispery.

Dow grinned, but there was no humour in it. 'Well, that's a damn good height to be.'

'If you mean to gain some advantage over him through me, you will be disappointed.'

'Will I?'

'Nothing will sway him from his duty.'

'Won't be sorry to lose you, eh?'

'He'll be sorry. But he'll only fight you harder.'

'Oh, I'm getting a fine sense for the man! Loyal, and strong, and bulging with righteousness. Like iron on the outside, but . . .' And he thumped at his chest with one fist and pushed out his bottom lip. 'He feels it. *Feels* it all, right here. And weeps at the quiet times.'

Finree looked right back. 'You have him close enough.'

Dow whipped out his grin like a killer might a knife. 'Sounds like my fucking twin.' The older man gave a snort of laughter. The woman smiled, showing a mouthful of impossibly perfect white teeth. The man with the metal eye made no sound. 'Good thing you won't be relying on your father's tender mercies, then. I got no plans to bargain with you, or ransom you, or even send your head over the river in a box. Though we'll see how the conversation goes, you might yet change my mind on that score.'

There was a long pause, while Dow watched her and she watched him. Like the accused waiting for the judge to pass sentence.

'I've a mind to let you go,' he said. 'I want you to take a message back to your father. Let him know I don't see the purpose shedding any more blood over this worthless fucking valley. Let him know I'm willing to talk.' Dow gave a loud sniff, worked his mouth as if it tasted bad. 'Talk about . . . *peace*.'

Finree blinked. 'Talk.'

'That's right.'

'About peace.'

'That's right.'

She felt dizzy. Drunk on the sudden prospect of living to see her husband and her father again. But she had to put that to one side, think past it. She took a long breath through her nose and steadied herself. 'That will not be good enough.'

She was pleased to see Black Dow look quite surprised. 'Won't it, now?'

'No.' It was difficult to appear authoritative while bruised, beaten, dirt-spattered and surrounded by the most daunting enemies, but Finree did her very best. She would not get through this with meekness. Black Dow wished to deal with someone powerful. That would make him feel powerful. The more powerful she made herself, the safer she was. So she raised her chin and looked him full in the eye. 'You need to make a gesture of goodwill. Something to let my father know you are serious. That you are willing to negotiate. Proof you are a reasonable man.'

Black Dow snorted. 'You hear that, Craw? Goodwill. Me.'

The older man shrugged. 'Proof you're reasonable.'

'More proof than sending back his daughter without a hole in her head?' grated Dow, looking her up and down. 'Or her head in her hole, for that matter.'

She floated over it. 'After the battle yesterday, you must have prisoners.' Unless they had all been murdered. Looking into Black Dow's eyes, it did not seem unlikely.

''Course we've got prisoners.' Dow cocked his head on one side, drifting closer. 'You think I'm some kind of an animal?'

Finree did, in fact. 'I want them released.'

'Do you, now? All of 'em?'

'Yes.'

'For nothing?'

'A gesture of—'

He jerked forwards, nose almost touching hers, thick veins bulging from the side of his thick neck. 'You're in no place to negotiate, you fucking little—'

'You aren't negotiating with me!' Finree barked back at him, showing her teeth. 'You're negotiating with my father, and he is in every position! Otherwise you wouldn't be *fucking* asking!'

A ripple of twitches went through Dow's cheek, and for an instant she was sure he was going to beat her to a pulp. Or give the smallest signal to his metal-eyed henchman and she would be slit from her arse to the back of her head. Dow's arm jerked up, and for an instant she was sure her death was a breath away. But all he did was grin, and gently wag his finger in her face. 'Oh, you're a sharp one. You didn't tell me she was so sharp.'

'I am shocked to my very roots,' intoned the black-skinned woman, looking about as shocked as the wall behind her.

'All right.' Dow puffed out his scarred cheeks. 'I'll let some of the wounded ones go. Don't need their sobbing keeping me awake tonight anyway. Let's say five dozen men.'

'You have more?'

'A lot more, but my goodwill's a brittle little thing. Five dozen is all it'll stretch around.'

An hour ago she had not seen any way to save herself. Her knees were almost buckling at the thought of coming out of this alive and saving sixty men besides. But she had to try one more thing. 'There was another woman taken with me—'

'Can't do it.'

'You don't know what I'm going to ask—'

'Yes, I do, and I can't do it. Stranger-Come-Knocking, that big bastard who took you prisoner? Man's mad as a grass helmet. He don't answer to me. Don't answer to nothing. You've no idea what it's cost me getting you. I can't afford to buy anyone else.'

'Then I won't help you.'

Dow clicked his tongue. 'Sharp is good, but you don't want to get so sharp you cut your own throat. You won't help me, you're no use to me at all. Might as well send you back to Stranger-Come-Fucking, eh? The way I see it, you got two choices. Back to your father and share in the peace, or back to your friend and share in . . . whatever she's got coming. Which appeals?'

Finree thought of Aliz' scared breath, in the darkness. Her whimper as Finree's hand slipped out of hers. She thought of that scarred giant, smashing his own man's head apart against the wall. She wished she was brave enough to have tried to call the bluff, at least. But who would be?

'My father,' she whispered, and it was the most she could do to stop herself crying with relief.

'Don't feel bad about it.' Black Dow drew his murderer's grin one more time. 'That's the choice I'd have made. Happy fucking journey.'

The bag came down over her head.

Craw waited until Shivers had bundled the hooded girl through the door before leaning forward, one finger up, and gently asking his question. 'Er . . . what's going on, Chief?'

Dow frowned at him. 'You're supposed to be my Second, old man. You should be the last one questioning me.'

Craw held up his palms. 'And I will be. I'm all for peace, believe me, just might help if I understood why you want it of a sudden.'

'Want?' barked Dow, jerking towards him like a hound got the scent. '*Want?*' Closer still, making Craw back up against the wall. 'I got what I want I'd hang the whole fucking Union and choke this valley with the smoke o' their cooking meat and sink Angland, Midderland and all their bloody other land in the bottom o' the Circle Sea, how's that for peace?'

'Right.' Craw cleared his throat, rightly wishing he hadn't asked the question. 'Right y'are.'

'But that's being Chief, ain't it?' snarled Dow in his face. 'A dancing fucking procession o' things you don't want to do! If I'd known what it meant when I took the chain I'd have tossed it in the river along with the Bloody-Nine. Threetrees warned me, but I didn't listen. There's no curse like getting what you want.'

Craw winced. 'So . . . why, then?'

'Because the dead know I'm no peacemaker but I'm no idiot either. Your little friend Calder may be a pissing coward but he's got a point. It's a damn fool risks his life for what he can get just by the asking. Not everyone's got my appetite for the fight. Men are getting tired, the Union are too many to beat and in case you hadn't noticed we're trousers down in a pit full of bloody snakes. Ironhead? Golden? Stranger-Come-Bragging? I don't trust those bastards further'n I can piss with no hands. Better finish this up now while we can call it a win.'

'Fair point,' croaked Craw.

'Got what I want there'd be no bloody talk at all.' Dow's face twitched, and he looked over at Ishri, leaning in the shadows against the wall, face a blank, black mask. He ran his tongue around the inside of his sneering mouth and spat. 'But calmer heads have prevailed. We'll try peace on, see whether it chafes. Now get that bitch back to her father 'fore I change my mind and cut the bloody cross in her for the fucking exercise.'

Craw edged for the door sideways, like a crab. 'On my way, Chief.'

Hearts and Minds

'How long should we spend out here, Corporal?'

'As short a time as is possible without disgrace, Yolk.'

'How long's that?'

'Until it's too dark for me to see your gurning visage would be a start.'

'And we patrol, do we?'

'No, Yolk, we'll just walk a few dozen strides and sit down for a while.'

'Where will we find to sit that isn't wet as an otter's—'

'Shh,' hissed Tunny, waving at Yolk to get down. There were men in the trees on the other side of the rise. Three men, and two of them in Union uniforms. 'Huh.' One was Lance Corporal Hedges. A squinty, mean-spirited rat of a man who'd been with the First for about three years and thought himself quite the rogue but was no better than a nasty idiot. The kind of bad soldier who gives proper bad soldiers a bad name. His gangly sidekick was unfamiliar, probably a new recruit. Hedges' version of Yolk, which was truly a concept too horrifying to entertain.

They both had swords drawn and pointed at a Northman, but Tunny could tell right off he was no fighter. Dressed in a dirty coat with a belt around it, a bow over one shoulder and some arrows in a quiver, no other weapon visible. A hunter, maybe, or a trapper, he looked somewhat baffled and somewhat scared. Hedges had a black fur in one hand. Didn't take a great mind to work it all out.

'Why, Lance Corporal Hedges!' Tunny grinned wide as he stood and strolled down the bank, his hand loose on the hilt of his sword, just to make sure everyone realised he had one.

Hedges squinted guiltily over at him. 'Keep out o' this, Tunny. We found him, he's ours.'

'Yours? Where in the rule book does it say prisoners are yours to abuse because you found them?'

'What do you care about the rules? What're you doing here, I'd like to know.'

'As it happens, First Sergeant Forest sent me and Trooper Yolk on patrol to make sure none of our men were out beyond the picket causing mischief. And what should I find but you, out beyond the picket and in the process of robbing this civilian. I call that mischievous. Do you call that mischievous, Yolk?'

'Well, er . . .'

Tunny didn't wait for an answer. 'You know what General Jalenhorm said. We're out to win hearts and minds as much as anything else. Can't have you robbing the locals, Hedges. Just can't have it. Contrary to our whole approach up here.'

'General fucking Jalenhorm?' Hedges snorted. 'Hearts and minds? You? Don't make me laugh!'

'Make you laugh?' Tunny frowned. 'Make you *laugh*? Trooper Yolk, I want you to raise your loaded flatbow and point it at Lance Corporal Hedges.'

Yolk stared. 'What?'

'What?' grunted Hedges.

Tunny threw up an arm. 'You heard me, point your bow!'

Yolk raised the bow so that the bolt was aimed uncertainly at Hedges' stomach. 'Like this?'

'How else exactly? Lance Corporal Hedges, how's this for a laugh? I will count to three. If you haven't handed that Northman back his fur by the time I get there I will order Trooper Yolk to shoot. You never know, you're only five strides away, he might even hit you.'

'Now, look—'

'One.'

'Look!'

'Two.'

'All right! All right.' Hedges tossed the fur in the Northman's face then stomped angrily away through the trees. 'But you'll fucking pay for this, Tunny, I can tell you that!'

Tunny turned, grinning, and strolled after him. Hedges was

347

opening his mouth for another prize retort when Tunny coshed him across the side of the head with his canteen, which represented a considerable weight when full. It happened so fast Hedges didn't even try to duck, just went down hard in the mud.

'You'll fucking pay for this, *Corporal* Tunny,' he hissed, and booted Hedges in the groin to underscore the point. Then he took Hedges' new canteen, and tucked his own badly dented one into his belt where it had been. 'Something to keep me in your thoughts.' He looked up at Hedges' lanky sidekick, fully occupied gawping. 'Anything to add, pikestaff?'

'I . . . I—'

'I? What do you think that adds? Shoot him, Yolk.'

'What?' squeaked Yolk.

'What?' squeaked the tall trooper.

'I'm joking, idiots! Bloody hell, does no one think at all but me? Drag your prick of a lance corporal back behind the lines, and if I see either one of you out here again I'll bloody shoot you myself.' The lanky one helped Hedges up, whimpering, bow-legged and bloody-haired, and the two of them shuffled off into the trees. Tunny waited until they'd disappeared from sight. Then he turned to the Northman and held out his hand. 'Fur, please.'

To be fair to the man, in spite of any troubles with the language, he fully understood. His face sagged, and he slapped the fur down into Tunny's hand. It wasn't that good a one, even, now he got a close look at it, rough-cured and sour-smelling. 'What else you got there?' Tunny came closer, one hand on the hilt of his sword, just in case, and started patting the man down.

'We're robbing him?' Yolk had his bow on the Northman now, which meant it was a good deal closer to Tunny than he'd have liked.

'That a problem? Didn't you tell me you were a convicted thief?'

'I told you I didn't do it.'

'Exactly what a thief would say! This isn't robbery, Yolk, it's war.' The Northman had some strips of dried meat, Tunny pocketed them. He had a flint and tinder, Tunny tossed them. No money, but that was far from surprising. Coinage hadn't fully caught on up here.

348

'He's got a blade!' squeaked Yolk, waving his bow about.

'A skinning knife, idiot!' Tunny took it and put it in his own belt. 'We'll stick some rabbit blood on it, say it came off a Named Man dead in battle, and you can bet some fool will pay for it back in Adua.' He took the Northman's bow and arrows too. Didn't want him trying a shot at them out of spite. He looked a bit on the spiteful side, but then Tunny probably would've looked spiteful himself if he'd just been robbed. Twice. He wondered about taking the trapper's coat, but it wasn't much more than rags, and he thought it might have been a Union one in the first place anyway. Tunny had stolen a score of new Union coats out of the quartermaster's stores back in Ostenhorm, and hadn't been able to shift them all yet.

'That's all,' he grunted, stepping back. 'Hardly worth the trouble.'

'What do we do, then?' Yolk's big flatbow was wobbling all over the place. 'You want me to shoot him?'

'You bloodthirsty little bastard! Why would you do that?'

'Well . . . won't he tell his friends across the stream we're over here?'

'We've had, what, four hundred men sitting around in a bog for over a day. Do you really think Hedges has been the only one wandering about? They know we're here by now, Yolk, you can bet on that.'

'So . . . we just let him go?'

'You want to take him back to camp and keep him as a pet?'

'No.'

'You want to shoot him?'

'No.'

'Well, then?'

The three of them stood there for a moment in the fading light. Then Yolk lowered his bow, and waved with the other hand. 'Piss off.'

Tunny jerked his head into the trees. 'Off you piss.'

The Northman blinked for a moment. He scowled at Tunny, then at Yolk, then stalked off into the woods, muttering angrily.

'Hearts and minds,' murmured Yolk.

Tunny tucked the Northman's knife inside his coat. 'Exactly.'

Good Deeds

The buildings of Osrung crowded in on Craw, all looking like they'd bloody stories to tell, each corner turned opening up a new stretch of disaster. A good few were all burned out, charred rafters still smouldering, air sharp with the tang of destruction. Windows gaped empty, shutters bristled with broken shafts, axe-scarred doors hung from hinges. The stained cobbles were scattered with rubbish and twisting shadows and corpses too, cold flesh that once was men, dragged by bare heels to their places in the earth.

Grim-faced Carls frowned at their strange procession. A full sixty wounded Union soldiers shambling along with Caul Shivers at the back like a wolf trailing a flock and Craw up front with his sore knees and the girl.

He found he kept glancing sideways at her. Didn't get a lot of chances to look at women. Wonderful, he guessed, but that wasn't the same, though she probably would've kicked him in the fruits for saying so. Which was just the point. This girl was a girl, and a pretty one too. Though probably she'd been prettier that morning, just like Osrung had. War makes nothing more beautiful. Looked as if she'd had a clump of hair torn from her head, the rest matted with clot on one side. A big bruise at the corner of her mouth. One sleeve of her dirty dress ripped and brown with dry blood. She shed no tears, though, not her.

'You all right?' asked Craw.

She glanced over her shoulder at the shambling column, and its crutches, and stretchers, and pain-screwed faces. 'I could be worse.'

'Guess so.'

'Are you all right?'

'Eh?'

She pointed at his face and he touched the stitched cut on his cheek. He'd forgotten all about it until then. 'What do you know, I could be worse myself.'

'Just out of interest – if I wasn't all right, what could you do about it?'

Craw opened his mouth, then realised he didn't have much of an answer. 'Don't know. A kind word, maybe?'

The girl looked around at the ruined square they were crossing, the wounded men propped against the wall of a house on the north side, the wounded men following them. 'Kind words wouldn't seem to be worth much in the midst of this.'

Craw slowly nodded. 'What else have we got, though?'

He stopped maybe a dozen paces from the north end of the bridge, Shivers walking up beside him. That narrow path of stone flags stretched off ahead, a pair of torches burning at the far end. No sign of men, but Craw was sure as sure the black buildings beyond the far bank were crammed full of the bastards, all with flatbows and tickly trigger-hands. Wasn't that big a bridge, but it looked a hell of a march across right then. An awful lot of steps, and at every footfall he might get an arrow in his fruits. Still, waiting about wasn't going to make that any less likely. More, in fact, since it was getting darker every moment.

So he hawked up some snot, made ready to spit it, realised the girl was watching him and swallowed it instead. Then he shrugged his shield off his shoulder and set it down by the wall, dragged his sword out from his belt and handed it to Shivers. 'You wait here with the rest, I'll go across and see if there's someone around with an ear for reason.'

'All right.'

'And if I get shot . . . weep for me.'

Shivers gave a solemn nod. 'A river.'

Craw held his hands up high and started walking. Didn't seem that long ago he was doing more or less the same thing up the side of the Heroes. Walking into the wolf's den, armed with nothing but a nervy smile and an overwhelming need to shit.

'Doing the right thing,' he muttered under his breath. Playing peacemaker. Threetrees would've been proud. Which was a great comfort, because when he got shot in the neck he could use a dead man's pride to pull the arrow out, couldn't he? 'Too bloody old for this.' By the dead, he should be retired. Smiling at the water with his pipe and his day's work behind him. 'The right thing,' he whispered again. Would've been nice if, just one time, the right thing could've been the safe thing too. But Craw guessed life wasn't really set up that way.

'That's far enough!' came a voice in Northern.

Craw stopped, all kinds of lonely out there in the gloom, water chattering away underneath him. 'Couldn't agree more, friend! Just need to talk!'

'Last time we talked it didn't come out too well for anyone concerned.' Someone was walking up from the other end of the bridge, a torch in his hand, orange light on a craggy cheek, a ragged beard, a hard-set mouth with a pair of split lips.

Craw found he was grinning as the man stopped an arm's length away. He reckoned his chances at living through the night just took a leap for the better. 'Hardbread, 'less I'm mistook all over the place.' In spite of the fact they'd been struggling to kill each other not a week before, it felt more like greeting an old friend than an old enemy. 'What the hell are you doing over here?'

'Lot o' the Dogman's boys hereabouts. Stranger-Come-Knocking and his Crinna bastards showed up without an invite, and we been guiding 'em politely to the door. Some messed-up allies your Chief makes, don't he.'

Craw looked over towards some Union soldiers who'd gathered in the torchlight at the south end of the bridge. 'I could say the same o' yours.'

'Aye, well. Those are the times. What can I do for you, Craw?'

'I got some prisoners Black Dow wants handed back.'

Hardbread looked profoundly doubtful. 'When did Dow start handing anything back?'

'He's starting now.'

'Guess it ain't never too late to change, eh?' Hardbread called something in Union, over his shoulder.

'Guess not,' muttered Craw, under his breath, though he was far from sure Dow had made that big a shift.

A man came warily up from the south side of the bridge. He wore a Union uniform, high up by the markings but young, and fine-looking too. He nodded to Craw and Craw nodded back, then he traded a few words with Hardbread, then he looked over at the wounded starting to come across the bridge and his jaw dropped.

Craw heard quick footsteps at his back, saw movement as he turned. 'What the—' He made a tardy grab for his sword, realised it wasn't there, by which point someone had already flashed past. The girl, and straight into the young man's arms. He caught her, and they held each other tight, and they kissed, and Craw watched with his hand still fishing at the air where his hilt usually was and his eyebrows up high.

'That was unexpected,' he said.

Hardbread's were no lower. 'Maybe men and women always greet each other that way down in the Union.'

'Reckon I'll have to move down there myself.'

Craw leaned back against the pitted parapet of the bridge. Leaned back next to Hardbread and watched those two hold each other, eyes closed, swaying gently in the light of the torch like dancers to a slow music none could hear. He was whispering something in her ear. Comfort, or relief, or love. Words foreign to Craw, no doubt, and not just on account of the language. He watched the wounded shuffling across around the couple, a spark of hope lit in their worn-out faces. Going back to their own people. Hurt, maybe, but alive. Craw had to admit, the night might've been coming on cold but he'd a warmth inside. Not like that rush of winning a fight, maybe, not so strong nor so fierce as the thrill of victory.

But he reckoned it might last longer.

'Feels good.' As he watched the soldier and the girl make their way across the bridge to the south bank, his arm around her. 'Making a few folk happier, in the midst o' this. Feels damn good.'

'It does.'

'Makes you wonder why a man chooses to do what we do.'

Hardbread took in a heavy breath. 'Too coward to do aught else, maybe.'

'You might be right.' The woman and the officer faded into darkness, the last few wounded shambling after. Craw pushed himself away from the parapet and slapped the damp from his hands. 'Right, then. Back to it, eh?'

'Back to it.'

'Good to see you, Hardbread.'

'Likewise.' The old warrior turned away and followed the others back towards the south side of the town. 'Don't get killed, eh?' he tossed over his shoulder.

'I'll try to avoid it.'

Shivers was waiting at the north end of the bridge, offering out Craw's sword. The sight of his eye gleaming in his lopsided smile was enough to chase any soft feelings away sharp as a rabbit from a hunter.

'You ever thought about a patch?' asked Craw, as he took his sword and slid it through his belt.

'Tried one for a bit.' Shivers waved a finger at the mass of scar around his eye. 'Itched like a bastard. I thought, why wear it just to make other fuckers more comfortable? If I can live with having this face, they can live with looking at it. That or they can get fucked.'

'You've a point.' They walked on through the gathering gloom in silence for a moment. 'Sorry to take the job.'

Shivers said nothing.

'Leading Dow's Carls. More'n likely you should've had it.'

Shivers shrugged. 'I ain't greedy. I've seen greedy, and it's a sure way back to the mud. I just want what's owed. No more and no less. A little *respect.*'

'Don't seem too much to ask. Anyway, I'll only be doing it while the battle's on, then I'm done. I daresay Dow'll want you for his Second then.'

'Maybe.' Another stretch of silence, then Shivers turned to look at him. 'You're a decent man, aren't you, Craw? Folk say so. Say you're a straight edge. How d'you stick at it?'

Craw didn't feel like he'd stuck at it too well at all. 'Just try to do the right thing, I reckon. That's all.'

'Why? I tried it. Couldn't make it root. Couldn't see the profit in it.'

'There's your problem. Anything good I done, and the dead know there ain't much, I done for its own sake. Got to do it because you want to.'

'It ain't no kind o' sacrifice if you want to do it, though, is it?

How does doing what you want make you a fucking hero? That's just what I do.'

Craw could only shrug. 'I haven't got the answers. Wish I did.'

Shivers turned the ring on his little finger thoughtfully round and round, red stone glistening. 'Guess it's just about getting through each day.'

'Those are the times.'

'You think other times'll be any different?'

'We can hope.'

'Craw!' His own name echoed at him and Craw whipped around, frowning into the darkness, wondering who he'd upset recently. Pretty much everyone, was the answer. He'd made a shitpile of enemies the moment he said yes to Black Dow. His hand strayed to his sword again, which at least was in the sheath this time around. Then he smiled. 'Flood! I seem to run into men I know all over the damn place.'

'That's what it is to be an old bastard.' Flood stepped over with a grin of his own, and a limp of his own too.

'Knew there had to be an upside to it. You know Caul Shivers, do you?'

'By reputation.'

Shivers showed his teeth. 'It's a fucking beauty, ain't it?'

'How's the day been over here with Reachey?' asked Craw.

'It's been bloody,' was Flood's answer. 'Had a few young lads calling me Chief. Too young. All but one back to the mud.'

'Sorry to hear that.'

'Me too. But it's a war. Thought I might come back over to your dozen, if you'll have me, and I thought I might bring this one with me.' Flood jerked his thumb at someone else. A big lad, hanging back in the shadows, wrapped up in a stained green cloak. He was looking at the ground, dark hair across his forehead so Craw couldn't see much more'n the gleam of one eye in the dark. He'd a good sword at his belt, though, gold on the hilt. Craw saw the gleam of that quick enough. 'He's a good hand. Earned his name today.'

'Congratulations,' said Craw.

The lad didn't speak. Not full of bragging and vinegar like some might be who'd won a name that day. Like Craw had been the day he won his, for that matter. Craw liked to see it. He didn't need any fiery tempers landing everyone in the shit. Like his had landed him in the shit, years ago.

'What about it then?' Flood asked. 'You got room for us?'

'Room? I can't remember ever having more'n ten in the dozen, and there's not but six now.'

'Six? What happened to 'em all?'

Craw winced. 'About the same as happened to your lot. About what usually happens. Athroc got killed up at the Heroes day before yesterday. Agrick a day later. Brack died this morning.'

There was a bit of a silence. 'Brack died?'

'In his sleep,' said Craw. 'From a bad leg.'

'Brack's back to the mud.' Flood shook his head. 'That's a tester. Didn't think he'd ever die.'

'Nor me. The Great Leveller's lying in wait for all of us, no doubt, and he takes no excuses and makes no exceptions.'

'None,' whispered Shivers.

''Til then, we could certainly use the pair o' you, if Reachey'll let you go.'

Flood nodded. 'He said he would.'

'All right then. You ought to know Wonderful's running the dozen for now, though.'

'She is?'

'Aye. Dow offered me charge of his Carls.'

'You're Black Dow's Second?'

'Just 'til the battle's done.'

Flood puffed out his cheeks. 'What happened to never sticking your neck out?'

'Didn't take my own advice. Still want in?'

'Why not?'

'Happy to have you back, then. And your lad too, if you say he's up to it.'

'Oh, he's up to it, ain't you, boy?'

The boy didn't say a thing.

'What's your name?' asked Craw.

'Beck.'

Flood thumped him on the arm. '*Red* Beck. Best get used to using the whole thing, eh?'

The lad looked a bit sick, Craw thought. Small wonder, given the state of the town. Must've been quite a scrap he'd been through. Quite an introduction to the bloody business. 'Not much of a talker, eh? Just as well. We got more'n enough talk with Wonderful and Whirrun.'

'Whirrun of Bligh?' asked the lad.

'That's right. He's one of the dozen. Or the half-dozen, leastways. Do you reckon I need to give him the big speech?' Craw asked Flood. 'You know, the one I gave you when you joined up, 'bout looking out for your crew and your Chief, and not getting killed, and doing the right thing, and all that?'

Flood looked at the lad, and shook his head. 'You know what, I think he learned today the hard way.'

'Aye,' said Craw. 'Reckon we all did. Welcome to the dozen, then, Red Beck.'

The lad just blinked.

One Day More

It was the same path she had ridden up the night before. The same winding route up the windswept hillside to the barn where her father had made his headquarters. The same view out over the darkened valley, filled with the pinprick lights of thousands of fires, lamps, torches, all glittering in the wet at the corners of her sore eyes. But everything felt different. Even though Hal was riding beside her, close enough to touch, jawing away to fill the silence, she felt alone.

'. . . good thing the Dogman turned up when he did, or the whole division might've come apart. As it is we lost the northern half of Osrung, but we managed to push the savages back into the woods. Colonel Brint was a rock. Couldn't have done it without him. He'll want to ask you . . . want to ask you about—'

'Later.' There was no way she could face that. 'I have to talk to my father.'

'Should you wash first? Change your clothes? At least catch your breath for a—'

'My clothes can wait,' she snapped at him. 'I've a message from Black Dow, do you understand?'

'Of course. Stupid of me. I'm sorry.' He kept flipping from fatherly stern to soppy soft, and she could not decide which was annoying her more. She felt as if he was angry, but lacked the courage to say so. At her for coming to the North when he had wanted her to stay behind. At himself for not being there to help her when the Northmen came. At both of them for not knowing how to help her now. Probably he was angry that he was angry, instead of revelling in her safe return.

They reined in their horses and he insisted on helping her down. They stood in awkward silence, with an awkward distance between them, he with an awkward hand on her shoulder that offered less than no comfort. She badly wanted him to find some words that might help her see some sense in what had happened that day. But there was no sense in it, and any words would fall pathetically short.

'I love you,' he said lamely, in the end, and it seemed few words could have fallen as pathetically short as those did.

'I love you too.' But all she felt was a creeping dread. A sense that there was an awful weight at the back of her mind she was forcing herself not to look at, but that at any moment it might fall and crush her utterly. 'You should go back down.'

'No! Of course not. I should stay with—'

She put a firm hand on his chest. She was surprised how firm it was. 'I'm safe now.' She nodded towards the valley, its fires prickling at the night. 'They need you more than I do.'

She could almost feel the relief coming off him. To no longer be taunted by his inability to make everything better. 'Well, if you're sure—'

'I'm sure.'

She watched him mount up, and he gave her a quick, uncertain, worried smile, and rode away into the gathering darkness. Part of her wished he had fought harder to stay. Part of her was glad to see the back of him.

She walked to the barn, pulling Hal's coat tight around her, past a staring guard and into the low-raftered room. It was a much more intimate gathering than last night's. Generals Mitterick and Jalenhorm, Colonel Felnigg, and her father. For a moment she felt an exhausting sense of relief to see him. Then she noticed Bayaz, sitting slightly removed from the others, his servant occupying the shadows behind him with the faintest of smiles, and any relief died a quick death.

Mitterick was holding forth, as ever, and, as ever, Felnigg listening with the expression of a man forced to fish something from a latrine. 'The bridge is in our hands and my men are crossing the river even as we speak. I'll have fresh regiments on the north bank well before dawn, including plenty of cavalry and the terrain to make use of it. The standards of the Second and Third are flying in the Northmen's trenches. And tomorrow I'll get Vallimir off his arse and into action if I have to kick him across that stream myself. I'll have those Northern bastards on the run by . . .'

His eyes drifted over to Finree, and he awkwardly cleared his throat and fell silent. One by one the other officers followed his gaze, and she saw in their faces what a state she must look. They could hardly have appeared more shocked if they had witnessed a corpse clamber from its grave. All except for Bayaz, whose stare was as calculating as ever.

'Finree.' Her father started up, gathered her in his arms and held her tight. Probably she should have dissolved into grateful tears, but he was the one who ended up dashing something from his eye on one sleeve. 'I thought maybe . . .' He winced as he touched her bloody hair, as though to finish the thought was more than he could bear. 'Thank the Fates you're alive.'

'Thank Black Dow. He's the one who sent me back.'

'Black Dow?'

'Yes. I met him. I spoke to him. He wants to talk. He wants to talk about peace.' There was a disbelieving silence. 'I persuaded him to let some wounded men go, as a gesture of good faith. Sixty. It was the best I could do.'

'You persuaded Black Dow to release prisoners?' Jalenhorm puffed out his cheeks. 'That's quite a thing. Burning them is more his style.'

'That's my girl,' said her father, and the pride in his voice made her feel sick.

Bayaz sat forward. 'Describe him.'

'Tallish. Strong-built. Fierce-looking. He was missing his left ear.'

'Who else was with him?'

'An older man called Craw, who led me back across the river. A big man with a scarred face and . . . a metal eye. And . . .' It seemed so strange now she was starting to wonder whether she had imagined the whole thing. 'A black-skinned woman.'

Bayaz' eyes narrowed, his mouth tightened, and Finree felt the hairs prickling on the back of her neck. 'A thin, black-skinned woman, wrapped in bandages?'

She swallowed. 'Yes.'

The First of the Magi sat slowly back, and he and his servant exchanged a long glance. 'They *are* here.'

'I did say.'

'Can nothing ever be straightforward?' snapped Bayaz.

'Rarely, sir,' replied the servant, his different-coloured eyes shifting lazily from Finree, to her father, and back to his master.

'Who are here?' asked a baffled Mitterick.

Bayaz did not bother to answer. He was busy watching Finree's father, who had crossed to his desk and was starting to write. 'What are you about, Lord Marshal?'

'It seems best that I should write to Black Dow and arrange a meeting so we can discuss the terms of an armistice—'

'No,' said Bayaz.

'No?' There was a pregnant silence. 'But . . . it sounds as if he is willing to be reasonable. Should we not at least—'

'Black Dow is not a reasonable man. His allies are . . .' Bayaz' lip curled and Finree drew Hal's coat tight around her shoulders. 'Even less so. Besides, you have done so well today, Lord Marshal. Such fine work from you, and General Mitterick, and Colonel Brock, and the Dogman. Ground taken and sacrifices made and so on. I feel your men deserve another crack at it tomorrow. Just one more day, I think. What's one day?'

Finree found she was feeling awfully weak. Dizzy. Whatever force had been holding her up for the past few hours was ebbing fast.

'Lord Bayaz . . .' Her father looked trapped in no-man's-land between pain and bafflement. 'A day is just a day. We will strive, of course, with every sinew if that is the king's pleasure, but there is a very good chance that we will not be able to secure a decisive victory in one day—'

'That would be a question for tomorrow. Every war is only a prelude to talk, Lord Marshal, but it's all about,' and the Magus looked up at the ceiling, rubbing one thick thumb against one fingertip, 'who you talk to. It would be best if we kept news of this among ourselves. Such things can be bad for morale. One more day, if you please.'

Finree's father obediently bowed his head, but when he crumpled up his half-written letter in one fist his knuckles were white with force. 'I serve at his Majesty's pleasure.'

'So do we all,' said Jalenhorm. 'And my men are ready to do their duty! I humbly entreat the right to lead an assault upon the

Heroes, and redeem myself on the battlefield.' As though anyone was redeemed on the battlefield. They were only killed there, as far as Finree could see. Her legs seemed to weigh a ton a piece as she made for the door at the back of the room.

Mitterick was busy gushing his own military platitudes behind her. 'My division is champing at the bloody bit, don't worry on that score, Marshal Kroy! Don't worry about that, Lord Bayaz!'

'I am not.'

'We have a bridgehead. Tomorrow we'll drive the bastards, you'll see. Just one day more . . .'

Finree shut the door on their posturing, her back against the wood. Maybe whatever herder had built this barn had lived in this room. Now her father was sleeping there, his bed against one unplastered wall, travelling chests neatly organised against the others like soldiers around a parade ground.

Everything was painful, suddenly. She pulled the sleeve of Hal's coat back, grimacing at the long cut down her forearm, flesh angry pink along both sides. Probably it would need stitching, but she could not go back out there. Could not face their pitying expressions and their patriotic drivel. It felt as if her neck had ten strings of agony through it and however she moved her head it tugged at one or another. She touched her fingertips to her burning scalp. There was a mass of scab under her greasy hair. She could not stop her hand trembling as she took it away. She almost laughed it was shaking so badly, but it came out as an ugly snort. Would her hair grow back? She snorted again. What did it matter, compared to what she had seen? She found she could not stop snorting. Her breath came ragged, and shuddering, and in a moment her aching ribs were heaving with sobs, the quick breath whooping in her throat, her face crushed up and her mouth twisted, tugging at her split lip. She felt a fool, but her body would not let her stop. She slid down the door until her backside hit stone, and bit on her knuckle to smother her blubbering.

She felt absurd. Worse still, ungrateful. Treacherous. She should have been weeping with joy. She, after all, was the lucky one.

Bones

'**W**here's that scab-faced old cunt hiding?'

The man's eyes flickered about uncertainly, caught off balance with his cup frozen half way to the water butt. 'Tenways is up on the Heroes with Dow and the rest, but if you're—'

'Get to *fuck*!' Calder shoved past him, striding on through Tenways' puzzled Carls, away from Skarling's Finger and towards the stones, picked out on their hilltop by the light of campfires behind.

'We won't be coming along up there,' came Deep's voice in his ear. 'Can't watch your arse if you're minded on sticking it in the wolf's mouth.'

'No money's worth going back to the mud for,' said Shallow. 'Nothing is, in my humble opinion.'

'That's an interesting point o' philosophy you've stumbled upon,' said Deep, 'what's worth dying for and what ain't. Not one we're likely to—'

'Stay and talk shit, then.' Calder kept walking, uphill, the cold air nipping at his lungs and a few too many nips from Shallow's flask burning at his belly. The scabbard of his sword slapped against his calf, as if with every step it was gently reminding him it was there, and that it was far from the only blade about either.

'What're you going to do?' asked Pale-as-Snow, breathing hard from keeping up.

Calder didn't say anything. Partly because he was too angry to say anything worth hearing. Partly because he thought it made him look big. And partly because he hadn't a clue what he was going to do, and if he started thinking about it there was every chance his courage would wilt, and quick. He'd done enough nothing that day. He strode through the gap in the drystone wall

363

that ringed the hill, a pair of Black Dow's Carls frowning as they watched him pass.

'Just keep calm!' Hansul shouted from further back. 'Your father always kept calm!'

'Shit on what my father did,' Calder snapped over his shoulder. He was enjoying not having to think and just letting the fury carry him. Sweep him up onto the hill's flat top and between two of the great stones. Fires burned inside the circle, flames tugged and snapped by the wind, sending up whirls of sparks into the black night. They lit up the inside faces of the Heroes in flickering orange, lit up the faces of the men clustered around them, catching the metal of their mail coats, the blades of their weapons. They clucked and grumbled as Calder strode heedless through them towards the centre of the circle, Pale-as-Snow and Hansul following in his wake.

'Calder. What are you about?' Curnden Craw, some staring lad Calder didn't know beside him. Jolly Yon Cumber and Wonderful were there too. Calder ignored the lot of them, brushed past Cairm Ironhead as he stood watching the flames with his thumbs in his belt.

Tenways was sitting on a log on the other side of the fire, and his flaking horror of a face broke out in a shining grin as he saw Calder coming. 'If it ain't pretty little Calder! Help your brother out today, did you, you—' His eyes went wide for a moment and he tensed, shifting his weight to get up.

Then Calder's fist crunched into his nose. He squawked as he went over backwards, boots kicking, and Calder was on top of him, flailing away with both fists, bellowing he didn't even know what. Punching mindlessly at Tenways' head, and his arms, and his flapping hands. He got another good one on that scabby nose before someone grabbed his elbow and dragged him off.

'Whoa, Calder, whoa!' Craw's voice, he thought, and he let himself be pulled back, thrashing about and shouting like you're supposed to. As if all he wanted to do was keep fighting when in fact he was all relief to let it be stopped, as he'd run right out of ideas and his left hand was really hurting.

Tenways stumbled up, blood bubbling out of his nostrils as he snarled curses, slapping away a helping hand from one of his men. He drew his sword with that soft metal whisper that somehow sounds so loud, steel gleaming in the firelight. There was a silence, the crowd of curious men around them all heaving a nervous breath together. Ironhead raised his brows, and folded his arms, and took a pace out of the way.

'You little fucker!' growled Tenways, and he stepped over the log he'd been sitting on.

Craw dragged Calder behind him and suddenly his sword was out too. Not a moment later a pair of Tenways' Named Men were beside their Chief, a big bearded bastard and a lean one with a lazy eye, weapons ready, though they looked like men who never had to reach too far for them. Calder felt Pale-as-Snow slide up beside him, blade held low. White-Eye Hansul on his other side, red-faced and puffing from his trek up the hillside but his sword steady. More of Tenways' boys sprang up, and Jolly Yon Cumber was there with his axe and his shield and his slab of frown.

It was then Calder realised things had gone a bit further than he'd planned on. Not that he'd planned at all. He thought it was probably bad form to leave his sword sheathed, what with everyone else drawing and him having stirred the pot in the first place. So he drew himself, smirking in Tenways' bloody face.

He'd felt grand when he'd seen his father put on the chain and sit in Skarling's Chair, three hundred Named Men on their knee to the first King of the Northmen. He'd felt grand when he put his hand on his wife's belly and felt his child kick for the first time. But he wasn't sure he'd ever felt such fierce pride as he did in the moment Brodd Tenways' nose-bone broke under his knuckles.

No way he would've said no to more of that feeling.

'Ah, shit!' Drofd scrambled up, kicking embers over Beck's cloak and making him gasp and slap 'em off.

A right commotion had flared up, folk stomping, metal hissing, grunts and curses in the darkness. There was some sort of a fight, and Beck had no idea who'd started it or why or what side he was supposed to be on. But Craw's dozen were all piling in so he just went with the current, drew his father's sword and stood shoulder to shoulder with the rest, Wonderful on his left with her curved blade steady, Drofd on his right with a hatchet in his fist and his tongue stuck out between his teeth. Wasn't so difficult to do, what with everyone else doing it. Would've been damn near impossible not to, in fact.

Brodd Tenways and some of his boys were facing 'em across a wind-blown fire, and he had a lot of blood on his rashy face and maybe a broken nose too. Might be that Calder had been the one to do it, given how he'd come stomping past like that and now was standing next to Craw with sword in hand and smirk on face. Still, the whys didn't seem too important right then. It was the what nexts that were looming large on everyone's minds.

'Put 'em away.' Craw spoke slow but there was a kind of iron to his voice said he'd be backing down from nothing. It put iron in Beck's bones, made him feel like he'd be backing down from nothing neither.

Tenways didn't look like taking any backward steps himself, though. 'You fucking put 'em away.' And he spat blood into the fire.

Beck found his eyes had caught a lad's on the other side, maybe a year or two older'n him. Yellow-haired lad with a scar on one cheek. They turned a little to face each other. As if on an instinct they were all pairing off with the partner who suited 'em best, like folk at a harvest dance. Except this dance seemed likely to shed a lot of blood.

'Put 'em up,' growled Craw, and his voice had more iron now. A warning, and the dozen all seemed to shift forwards around him at it, steel rattling.

Tenways showed his rotten teeth. 'Fucking make me.'

'I'll give it a try.'

A man came strolling out of the dark, just his sharp jaw showing in the shadows of his hood, boots crunching heedless through the corner of the fire and sending a flurry of sparks up around his legs. Very tall, very lean and he looked like he was carved out of wood. He was chewing meat from a chicken bone in one greasy hand and in the other, held loose under the cross-piece, he had the biggest sword Beck had ever seen, shoulder-high maybe from point to pommel, its sheath scuffed as a beggar's boot but the wire on its hilt glinting with the colours of the fire-pit.

He sucked the last shred of meat off his bone with a noisy

slurp, and he poked at all the drawn steel with the pommel of his sword, long grip clattering against all those blades. 'Tell me you lot weren't working up to a fight without me. You know how much I love killing folk. I shouldn't, but a man has to stick to what he's good at. So how's this for a recipe . . .' He worked the bone around between finger and thumb, then flicked it at Tenways so it bounced off his chain mail coat. 'You go back to fucking sheep and I'll fill the graves.'

Tenways licked his bloody top lip. 'My fight ain't with you, Whirrun.'

And it all came together. Beck had heard songs enough about Whirrun of Bligh, and even hummed a few himself as he fought his way through the logpile. Cracknut Whirrun. How he'd been given the Father of Swords. How he'd killed his five brothers. How he'd hunted the Shimbul Wolf in the endless winter of the utmost North, held a pass against the countless Shanka with only two boys and a woman for company, bested the sorcerer Daroum-ap-Yaught in a battle of wits and bound him to a rock for the eagles. How he'd done all the tasks worthy of a hero in the valleys, and so come south to seek his destiny on the battlefield. Songs to make the blood run hot, and cold too. Might be his was the hardest name in the whole North these days, and standing right there in front of Beck, close enough to lay a hand on. Though that probably weren't a good idea.

'Your fight ain't with me?' Whirrun glanced about like he was looking for who it might be with. 'You sure? Fights are twisty little bastards, you draw steel it's always hard to say where they'll lead you. You drew on Calder, but when you drew on Calder you drew on Curnden Craw, and when you drew on Craw you drew on me, and Jolly Yon Cumber, and Wonderful there, and Flood – though he's gone for a wee, I think, and also this lad here whose name I've forgotten.' Sticking his thumb over his shoulder at Beck. 'You should've seen it coming. No excuse for it, a proper War Chief fumbling about in the dark like you've nothing in your head but shit. So my fight ain't with you either, Brodd Tenways, but I'll still kill you if it's called for, and add your name to my songs, and I'll still laugh afterwards. So?'

'So what?'

'So shall I draw? And you'd best keep always before you that if

367

the Father of Swords is drawn it must be blooded. That's the way it's been since before the Old Time, and the way it must be still, and must always be.'

They stood there for a moment longer, the lot of 'em, all still, all waiting, then Tenways' brows drew in, and his lips curled back, and Beck felt the guts dropping out of him, because he could feel what was coming, and—

'What the *fuck*?' Another man stalked up into the firelight, eyes slits and teeth bared, head forwards and shoulders up like a fighting dog, no want in it but killing. His scowl was crossed with old scars, one ear missing, and he wore a golden chain, a big jewel alive with orange sparks in the middle.

Beck swallowed. Black Dow, no question. Who beat Bethod's men six times in the long winter then burned Kyning to the ground with its people in the houses. Who fought the Bloody-Nine in the circle and nearly won, was left with his life and bound to serve. Fought alongside him then, and with Rudd Threetrees, and Tul Duru Thunderhead, and Harding Grim, as tough a crew as ever walked the North since the Age of Heroes and of which, aside from the Dogman, he was the last drawing breath. Then he betrayed the Bloody-Nine, and killed him who men said couldn't die, and took Skarling's Chair for himself. Black Dow, right before him now. Protector of the North, or stealer of it, depending on who you asked. He'd never dreamed of coming so close to the man.

Black Dow looked over at Craw, and he looked an awful long way from happy. Beck weren't sure how that pickaxe of a face ever could. 'Ain't you supposed to be keeping the peace, old man?'

'That's what I'm doing.' Craw's sword was still out but the point had dropped towards the ground now. Most of 'em had.

'Oh, aye. Here's a peaceful fucking picture.' Dow swept the lot of 'em with his scowl. 'No one draws steel up here without my say so. Now put 'em away, the lot o' you, you're embarrassing yourselves.'

'Boneless little fucker broke my nose!' snarled Tenways.

'Spoil your looks, did he?' snapped Dow. 'Want me to kiss it better? Let me frame this in terms you fucking halfheads can understand. Anyone still holding a blade by the time I get to five is stepping into the circle with me, and I'll do things like I used to 'fore old age softened me up. One.'

He didn't even need to get to two. Craw put up right away, and Tenways just after, and all the rest of that steel was good and hidden almost as swift as it had come to light, leaving the two lines of men frowning somewhat sheepishly across the fire at each other.

Wonderful whispered in Beck's ear. 'Might want to put that away.'

He realised he still had his steel out, shoved it back so fast he damn near cut his leg. Only Whirrun was left there, between the two sides, one hand on the hilt of his sword and the other on the scabbard, still ready to draw, and looking at it with the smallest curl of a smile to his mouth. 'You know, I'm just a little tempted.'

'Another time,' growled Dow, then threw one arm up. 'Brave Prince Calder! I'm honoured all the way to fuck! I was about to send over an invitation but you've got in first. Come to tell me what happened at the Old Bridge today?'

Calder still had the fine cloak he'd been wearing when Beck first saw him up at Reachey's camp, but he had mail underneath it now, and a scowl instead of a grin. 'Scale got killed.'

'I heard. Can't you tell? I'm weeping a sea o' tears. What happened at my bridge is what I'm asking.'

'He fought as hard as he could. Hard as anyone could.'

'Went down fighting. Good for Scale. What about you? Don't look like you fought that hard.'

'I was ready to.' Calder slid a piece of paper out from his collar and held it up between two fingers. 'Then I got this. An order from Mitterick, the Union general.' Dow snatched it from his hand and pulled it open, frowning down at it. 'There are Union men in the woods to our west, ready to come across. It's lucky I found out, because if I'd gone to help Scale they'd have taken us in the flank and there's a good chance the lot of you would be dead now, rather than arguing the toss over whether I've got no bones.'

'I don't think anyone's arguing you've got bones, Calder,' said Dow. 'Just sat there behind the wall, did you?'

'That, and sent to Tenways for help.'

369

Dow's eyes slid sideways, glittering with the flames. 'Well?'

Tenways rubbed blood from under his broken nose. 'Well what?'

'Did he send for help?'

'Spoke to Tenways myself,' piped up one of Calder's men. An old boy with a scar down his face and the eye on that side milky white. 'Told him Scale needed help, but Calder couldn't go on account of the Southerners across the stream. Told him the whole thing.'

'And?'

The half-blind old man shrugged. 'Said he was busy.'

'Busy?' whispered Dow, face getting harder'n ever if that was possible. 'So you just sat there and all, did you?'

'I can't just move soon as that bastard tells me to—'

'You sat on the hill with Skarling's Finger up your arse and fucking *watched*?' Dow roared. 'Sat and watched the Southerners have *my bridge*?' Stabbing at his chest with his thumb.

Tenways flinched back, one eye twitching. 'There weren't no Southerners over the river, that's all lies! Lies like he always tells.' He pointed across the fire with a shaking finger. 'Always some fucking excuse, eh, Calder? Always some trick to keep your hands clean! Talk of peace, or talk of treachery, or some kind of bloody talk—'

'Enough.' Black Dow's voice was quiet, but it cut Tenways off dead. 'I don't care a runny shit whether there are Union men out west or if there aren't.' He crumpled the paper up in his trembling fist and flung it at Calder. 'I care whether you do as you're told.' He took a step towards Tenways, and leaned in close.

'You won't be sitting watching tomorrow, no, no, no.' And he sneered over at Calder. 'And nor will you, prince of nothing fucking much. Your sitting days are over, the pair o' you. You two lovers'll be down there on that wall together. That's right. Side by side. Arm in arm from dawn to dusk. Making sure this shitcake you've cooked up between you don't start stinking any worse. Doing what I brought you idiots here for – which, in case anyone's started wondering, is *fighting the fucking Union*!'

'What if they are across that stream?' asked Calder. Dow turned towards him, brow furrowed like he couldn't believe what he was hearing. 'We're stretched thin as it is, lost a lot of men today and we're well outnumbered—'

'It's a fucking *war*!' roared Dow, leaping over to him and making everyone shuffle back. 'Fight the bastards!' He tore at the air as if he was only just stopping himself from tearing Calder's face apart with his hands. 'Or you're the planner, ain't you? The great trickster? Trick 'em! You wanted your brother's place? Then deal with it, you little arsehole, or I'll find a man who will! And if anyone don't do his bit tomorrow, anyone with a taste for *sitting out* . . .' Black Dow closed his eyes and tipped his face back towards the sky. 'By the dead, I'll cut the bloody cross in you. And I'll hang you. And I'll burn you. And I'll make such an end of you the very song of it will turn the bards white. Am I leaving room for doubts?'

'No,' said Calder, sullen as a whipped mule.

'No,' said Tenways, no happier.

Beck didn't get the feeling the bad blood between 'em was anywhere near settled, though.

'Then this is the fucking end o' this!' Dow turned, saw one of Tenways' lads was in his way, grabbed hold of his shirt and flung him cringing onto the ground, then stalked back into the night the way he came.

'With me,' Craw hissed in Calder's ear, then took him under the armpit and marched him off.

Tenways and his boys found their way back to their seats, grumbling, the yellow-haired lad giving Beck a hard look as he went. Time was Beck would've given him one back, maybe even a hard word or two to go with it. After the day he'd had he just looked away quick as he could, heart thumping in his ears.

'Shame. I was enjoying that.' Whirrun of Bligh pulled his hood back and scrubbed at his flattened hair with his fingernails. 'What is your name, anyway?'

'Beck.' He thought he'd best leave it at just that. 'Is every day with you lot like this?'

'No, no, no, lad. Not every day.' And Whirrun's pointed face broke into a mad grin. 'Only a precious few.'

Craw had always had rooted suspicions that one day Calder would land him in some right shit, and it seemed this was the day. He marched him down the hillside away from the Heroes, through the cutting wind, gripping him tight by the elbow. He'd spent a good twenty years trying to keep his enemies to a strict few. One afternoon as Dow's Second and they were sprouting up like saplings in a wet spring, and Brodd Tenways was one he could have very well done without. That man was as ugly inside as out and had a bastard of a memory for slights.

'What the hell was that?' He dragged Calder to a halt a good way from fires or prying ears. 'You could've got us all killed!'

'Scale's dead. That's what that was. Because that rotting fucker did nothing, Scale's dead.'

'Aye.' Craw felt himself softening. Stood there for a moment while the wind lashed the long grass against his calves. 'I'm sorry for that. But adding more corpses ain't going to help matters. 'Specially not mine.' He stuck a hand on his ribs, heart thumping away behind 'em. 'By the dead, I think I might die just o' the excitement.'

'I'm going to kill him.' Calder scowled up towards the fire, and he did seem to have a purpose in him Craw hadn't seen before. Something that made him put a warning hand on Calder's chest and gently steer him back.

'Keep it for tomorrow. Save it for the Union.'

'Why? My enemies are here. Tenways sat there while Scale died. Sat there and laughed.'

'And you're angry because he sat there, or because you did?' He put his other hand down on Calder's shoulder. 'I loved your father, in the end. I love you, like the son I never had. But why the hell is it the pair o' you always had to take on every fight you were offered? There'll always be more. I'll stand by you if I can, you know I will, but there's other things to think about than just—'

'Yes, yes.' Calder slapped Craw's hands away. 'Keeping your crew alive, and not sticking your neck out, and doing the right thing, even when it's the wrong thing—'

Craw grabbed hold of his shoulders again and gave him a shake. 'I have to keep the peace! I'm in charge o' Dow's Carls now, his Second, and I can't—'

'You're what? You're guarding him?' Calder's fingers dug into

Craw's arms, his eyes suddenly wide and bright. Not anger. A kind of eagerness. 'You're at his back, with your sword drawn? That's your job?' And Craw suddenly saw the pit he'd dug for himself opening under his feet.

'No, Calder!' snarled Craw, trying to wriggle free. 'Shut your—'

Calder kept his grip, dragging him into an awkward hug, and Craw could smell the drink on his breath as he hissed in his ear. 'You could do it! Put an end to this!'

'No!'

'Kill him!'

'No!' Craw tore free and shoved him off, hand tight around the grip of his sword. 'No, you bloody fool!'

Calder looked like he couldn't understand what Craw was saying. 'How many men have you killed? That's what you do for a living. You're a killer.'

'I'm a Named Man.'

'So you're better at it than most. What's killing one more? And this time for a purpose! You could stop all this. You don't even like the bastard!'

'Don't matter what I like, Calder! He's Chief.'

'He's Chief now, but stick an axe in his head he's just mud. No one'll care a shit then.'

'I will.' They watched each other for what felt like a long while, still in the darkness, not much more to see but the gleam of Calder's eyes in his pale face. They slid down to Craw's hand, still on the hilt of his sword.

'Going to kill me?'

''Course I'm not.' Craw straightened, letting his hand drop. 'But I'll have to tell Black Dow.'

More silence. Then, 'Tell him what, exactly?'

'That you asked me to kill him.'

And another. 'I don't think he'll like that very much.'

'Nor do I.'

'I think cutting the bloody cross in me, then hanging me, then burning me, is the least of what he'll do.'

'Reckon so. Which is why you'd better run.'

'Run where?'

'Wherever you like. I'll give you a start. I'll tell him tomorrow.

I have to tell him. That's what Threetrees would've done.' Though Calder hadn't asked for a reason, and that sounded a particularly lame one right then.

'Threetrees got killed, you know. For nothing, out in the middle of nowhere.'

'Don't matter.'

'Ever think you should be looking for another man to imitate?'

'I gave my word.'

'Killer's honour, eh? Swear it, did you, on Skarling's cock, or whatever?'

'Didn't have to. I gave my word.'

'To Black Dow? He tried to have me killed a few nights back, and I'm supposed to sit on my hands waiting for him to do it again? The man's more treacherous than winter!'

'Don't matter. I said yes.' And by the dead how he wished he hadn't now.

Calder nodded, little smile at the corner of his mouth. 'Oh, aye. Gave your word. And good old Craw's a straight edge, right? No matter who gets cut.'

'I have to tell him.'

'But tomorrow.' Calder backed away, still with that smirk on his face. 'You'll give me a start.' One foot after another, down the hillside. 'You won't tell him. I know you, Craw. Raised me from a babe, didn't you? You've got more bones than that. You're not Black Dow's dog. Not you.'

'It ain't a question of bones, nor dogs neither. I gave my word, and I'll tell him tomorrow.'

'No, you won't.'

'Yes, I will.'

'No.' And Calder's smirk was gone into the darkness. 'You won't.'

Craw stood there for a moment, in the wind, frowning at nothing. Then he gritted his teeth, and pushed his fingers into his hair, bent over and gave a strangled roar of frustration. He hadn't felt this hollow since Wast Never sold him out and tried to kill him after eight years a friend. Would've done it too if it hadn't been for Whirrun. Wasn't clear who'd get him out of this particular scrape. Wasn't clear how anyone could. This time it was him doing the betraying. He'd be doing it to someone whatever he did.

Always do the right thing sounds an easy rule to stick to. But when's the right thing the wrong thing? That's the question.

The King's Last Hero

Your August Majesty,
            *Darkness has finally covered the battlefield. Great
            gains were made today. Great gains at great cost. I deeply
regret to inform you that Lord Governor Meed was killed, fighting
with the highest personal courage for your Majesty's cause alongside many of his staff.*

*There was bitter combat from dawn to dusk in the town of
Osrung. The fence was carried in the morning and the Northmen
driven across the river, but they launched a savage counterattack
and retook the northern half of the town. Now the water separates
the two sides once again.*

*On the western wing, General Mitterick had better fortune.
Twice the Northmen resisted his assaults on the Old Bridge, but
on the third attempt they were finally broken and fled to a low
wall some distance away over open fields. Mitterick is moving his
cavalry across the river, ready for an attack at first light tomorrow.
From my tent I can see the standards of your Majesty's Second and
Third Regiments, defiantly displayed on ground held by the
Northmen only a few hours ago.*

*General Jalenhorm, meanwhile, has reorganised his division,
augmented by reserves from the levy regiments, and is prepared for
an attack upon the Heroes in overwhelming force. I mean to stay
close to him tomorrow, witness his success at first hand, and
inform your Majesty of Black Dow's defeat as soon as the stones are
recaptured.*

I remain your Majesty's most faithful and unworthy servant,
Bremer dan Gorst, Royal Observer of the Northern War

Gorst held the letter out to Rurgen, clenching his teeth as pain
flashed through his shoulder. Everything was hurting. His ribs

were even worse than yesterday. His armpit was one great itching graze where the edge of his breastplate had been ground into it. For some reason there was a cut between his shoulder blades just where it was hardest to reach. *Though no doubt I deserve far worse, and probably will get it before we're done with this worthless valley.*

'Can Younger take this?' he grunted.

'Younger!' called Rurgen.

'What?' from outside.

'Letter!'

The younger man ducked his head through the tent flap, stretching for it. He winced, had to come a step closer, and Gorst saw that the right side of his face was covered by a large bandage, soaked through with a long brown mark of dried blood.

Gorst stared at him. 'What happened?'

'Nothing.'

'Huh,' grunted Rurgen. 'Tell him.'

Younger frowned at his colleague. 'It doesn't matter.'

'Felnigg happened,' said Rurgen. 'Since you ask.'

Gorst was out of his seat, pains forgotten. 'Colonel Felnigg? Kroy's chief of staff?'

'I got in his way. That's all. That's the end of it.'

'Whipped him,' said Rurgen.

'Whipped . . . you?' whispered Gorst. He stood staring for a moment. Then he snatched up his long steel, cleaned, sharpened and sheathed just beside him on the table.

Younger blocked his way, hands up. 'Don't do anything stupid.' Gorst brushed him aside and was out through the tent flap, into the chilly night, striding across the trampled grass. 'Don't do anything stupid!'

Gorst kept walking.

Felnigg's tent was pitched on the hillside not far from the decaying barn Marshal Kroy had taken for his headquarters. Lamplight leaked from the flap and into the night, illuminating a slit of muddy grass, a tuft of dishevelled sedge and the face of a guard, epically bored.

'Can I help you, sir?'

Help me, you bastard? Rather than giving him the opportunity to consider his position, the long walk up from the valley had only stoked Gorst's fury. He grabbed the guard's breastplate by one armhole and flung him tumbling down the hillside, ripping the tent flap wide. 'Felnigg—!'

He came up short. The tent was crammed with officers. Senior members of Kroy's staff, some of them clutching cards, others drinks, most with uniforms unbuttoned to some degree, clustered around an inlaid table that looked as if it had been salvaged from a palace. One was smoking a chagga pipe. Another was sloshing wine from a green bottle. A third hunched over a heavy book, making interminable entries by candlelight in an utterly unreadable script.

'—that bloody captain wanted to charge fifteen for each cabin!' Kroy's chief quartermaster was braying as he clumsily sorted his hand. 'Fifteen! I told him to be damned.'

'What happened?'

'We settled on twelve, the bloody sea-leech . . .' He trailed off as, one by one, the officers turned to look at Gorst, the bookkeeper peering over thick spectacles that made his eyes appear grotesquely magnified.

Gorst was not good with crowds. Even worse than with individuals, which was saying something. *But witnesses will only add to Felnigg's humiliation. I will make him beg. I will make all of you bastards beg.* Yet Gorst had stopped dead, his cheeks prickling with heat.

Felnigg sprang up, looking slightly drunk. They all looked drunk. Gorst was not good with drunk. Even worse than with sober, which was saying something. 'Colonel Gorst!' He lurched forwards, beaming. Gorst raised his open hand to slap the man across the face, but there was a strange delay in which Felnigg managed to grasp it with his own and give it a hearty shake. 'I'm delighted to see you! Delighted!'

'I . . . What?'

'I was at the bridge today! Saw the whole thing!' Still pumping away at Gorst's hand like a demented washerwoman at a mangle. 'Crashing through the crops after them, cutting them down!' And he slashed at the air with his glass, slopping wine about. 'Like something out of a storybook!'

'Colonel Felnigg!' The guard from outside, shoving through the flap with mud smeared all down his side. 'This man—'

'I know! Colonel Bremer dan Gorst! Never saw such personal courage! Such skill at arms! The man's worth a regiment to his Majesty's cause! Worth a division, I swear! How many of the bastards did you get, do you think? Must've been two dozen! Three dozen, if it was a single one!'

The guard scowled but, seeing that things were not running his way, was forced to retreat into the night. 'No more than fifteen,' Gorst found he had said. *And only a couple on our side! A heroic ratio if ever there was one!* 'But thank you.' He tried unsuccessfully to lower his voice to somewhere around a tenor. 'Thank you.'

'It's us who should be thanking you! That bloody idiot Mitterick certainly should be. His fiasco of an attack would have sunk in the river without you. No more than fifteen, did you hear that?' And he slapped one of his fellows on the arm and made him spill his wine. 'I've already written to my friend Halleck on the Closed Council, told him what a bloody hero you are! Didn't think there was room for 'em in the modern age, but here you are, large as life.' He clapped Gorst jauntily on the shoulder. 'Larger! I've been telling everyone I could find all about it!'

'I'll say he has,' grunted one of the officers, peering down at his cards.

'That is . . . most kind.' *Most kind? Kill him! Hack his head off like you hacked the head from that Northman today. Throttle him. Murder him. Punch all his teeth out, at least. Hurt him. Hurt him now!* 'Most . . . kind.'

'I'd be bloody honoured if you'd consent to have a drink with me. We all would!' Felnigg spun about and snatched up the bottle. 'What brings you up here onto the fell, anyway?'

Gorst took a heavy breath. *Now. Now is the time for courage. Now do it.* But he found each word was an immense effort, excruciatingly aware of how foolish his voice sounded. How singularly lacking in threat or authority, the nerve leaking out of him with every slobbering movement of his lips. 'I am here . . . because I heard that earlier today . . . you whipped . . .' *My friend. One of my only friends. You whipped my friend, now prepare for your last moments.* 'My servant.'

Felnigg spun about, his jaw falling open. 'That was your servant? By the . . . you must accept my apologies!'

'You whipped someone?' asked one of the officers.

'And not even at cards?' muttered another, to scattered chuckles.

Felnigg blathered on. 'So very sorry. No excuse for it. I was in a terrible rush with an order from the lord marshal. No excuse, of course.' He grabbed Gorst by the arm, leaning close enough to blast him with a strong odour of spirits. 'You must understand, I would never have . . . never, had I known he was *your* servant . . . of course I would never have done any such thing!'

But you did, you chinless satchel of shit, and now you will pay. There must be a reckoning, and it will be now. Must be now. Definitely, positively, absolutely bloody now. 'I must ask—'

'Please say you'll drink with me!' And Felnigg thrust the overfull glass into Gorst's hand, wine slopping onto his fingers. 'A cheer for Colonel Gorst! The last hero in his Majesty's army!' The other officers hurried to raise their own glasses, all grinning, one thumping at the table with his free hand and making the silverware jingle.

Gorst found he was sipping at the glass. And he was smiling. Worse yet, he was not even having to force himself. He was enjoying their adulation.

I slaughtered men today who had done me not the slightest grain of harm. No more than fifteen of them. And here I stand with a man who whipped one of my only friends. What horrors should I visit upon him? Why, to smile, and slurp up his cheap wine, and the congratulations of pandering strangers too, what else? What will I tell Younger? That he need not worry about his pain and humiliation because his tormentor warmly approved of my murderous rampage? The king's last hero? I want to be fucking sick. He became acutely aware that he was still clutching his sheathed long steel in one white knuckled fist. He attempted, unsuccessfully, to hide it behind his leg. *I want to vomit up my own liver.*

'It's certainly a hell of a story the way Felnigg tells it,' one of the officers was droning while he rearranged his cards. 'I daresay it's the second bravest thing I've heard about today.'

'Risking his Majesty's rations hardly counts,' someone frothed, to more drunken laughter.

'I was speaking of the lord marshal's daughter, in fact. I

do prefer a heroine to a hero, they look much better in the paintings.'

Gorst frowned. 'Finree dan Kroy? I thought she was at her father's headquarters?'

'You didn't hear?' asked Felnigg, giving him another dose of foul breath. 'The damnedest thing! She was with Meed at the inn when the Northmen butchered him and his whole staff. Right there, in the room! She was taken prisoner, but she talked her way free, and negotiated the release of sixty wounded men besides! What do you make of that! More wine?'

Gorst did not know what to make of it, except that he felt suddenly hot and dizzy. He ignored the proffered bottle, turned without another word and pushed through the tent flap into the chill night air. The guard he had thrown was outside, making a futile effort to brush himself clean. He gave an accusing look and Gorst glanced guiltily away, unable to summon the courage even to apologise—

And there she was. Standing by a low stone wall before Marshal Kroy's headquarters and frowning down into the valley, a military coat wrapped tight around her, one pale hand holding it closed at her neck.

Gorst went to her. He had no choice. It was as if he was pulled by a rope. *A rope around my cock. Dragged by my infantile, self-destructive passions from one cringingly embarrassing episode to another.*

She looked up at him, and the sight of her red-rimmed eyes froze the breath in his throat. 'Bremer dan Gorst.' Her voice was flat. 'What brings you up here?'

Oh, I came to murder your father's chief of staff but he offered me drunken praise so instead I drank a toast with him to my heroism. There is a joke there somewhere . . .

He found he was staring at the side of her darkened face. Staring and staring. A lantern beyond her picked out her profile in gold, made the downy hairs on her top lip glow. He was terrified that she would glance across, and catch him looking at her mouth. *No innocent reason, is there, to stare at a woman's mouth like this? A married woman? A beautiful, beautiful, married woman?* He wanted her to look. Wanted her to catch him looking. But of course she did not. *What possible reason would a woman have to look at me? I love you. I love you so much it hurts me. More than all the blows I took today. More even than all the blows I gave. I love you so much I want to shit. Say it. Well, not the part about shit, but the other part. What is there to lose? Say it and be damned!*

'I heard that—' he almost whispered.

'Yes,' she said.

An exquisitely uncomfortable pause. 'Are you—'

'Yes. Go on, you can tell me. Tell me I shouldn't have been down there in the first place. Go on.'

Another pause, more uncomfortable yet. For him there was a chasm between mind and mouth he could not see how to bridge. Did not dare to bridge. She did it so easily it quite took his breath away. 'You brought men back,' he managed to murmur in the end. 'You saved lives. You should be proud of—'

'Oh, yes, I'm a real hero. Everyone's terribly proud. Do you know Aliz dan Brint?'

'No.'

'Neither did I, really. Thought she was a fool, if I'm honest. She was with me. Down there.' She jerked her head towards the dark valley. 'She's still down there. What's happening to her now, do you think, while we stand here, talking?'

'Nothing good,' said Gorst, before he had considered it.

She frowned sideways at him. 'Well. At least you say what you really think.' And she turned her back and walked away up the slope towards her father's headquarters, leaving him standing there as she always did, mouth half-open to say words he never could.

Oh yes, I always say what I really think. Would you like to suck my cock, by the way? Please? Or a tongue in the mouth? A hug would be something. She disappeared inside the low barn, and the door was closed, and the light shut in. *Hold hands? No? Anyone?*

The rain had started to come down again.

Anyone?

My Land

Calder took his time strolling up out of the night, towards the fires behind Clail's Wall, spitting and hissing in the drizzle. He'd been in danger for a long time, and never deeper than now, but the strange thing was he still had his smirk.

His father was dead. His brother was dead. He'd even managed to turn his old friend Craw against him. His scheming had got him nowhere. All his careful seeds had yielded not the slightest bitter little fruit. With the help of an impatient mood and a bit too much of Shallow's cheap booze he'd made a big, big mistake tonight, and there was a good chance it was going to kill him. Soon. Horribly.

And he felt strong. Free. No more the younger son, the younger brother. No more the cowardly one, the treacherous one, the lying one. He was even enjoying the throbbing pain in his left hand where he'd skinned his knuckles on Tenways' mail. For the first time in his life he felt . . . brave.

'What happened up there?' Deep's voice came out of the darkness behind him without warning, but Calder was hardly surprised.

He gave a sigh. 'I made a mistake.'

'Whatever you do, don't make another, then,' came Shallow's whine from the other side.

Deep's voice again. 'You ain't thinking of fighting tomorrow, are you?'

'I am, in fact.'

A pair of sharp in-breaths. 'Fighting?' said Deep.

'You?' said Shallow.

'Get moving now, we could be ten miles away before sun up. No reason to—'

'No,' said Calder. There was nothing to think about. He

383

couldn't run. The Calder of ten years ago, who'd ordered Forley the Weakest killed without a second thought, would already have been galloping off on the fastest horse he could steal. But now he had Seff, and an unborn child. If Calder stayed to pay for his own stupidity, Dow would probably stop at ripping him apart in front of a laughing crowd but spare Seff so Reachey would be left owing him. If Calder ran, Dow would see her hanged, and he couldn't let that happen. It wasn't in him.

'Can't recommend this,' said Deep. 'Battles. Never a good idea.'

Shallow clicked his tongue. 'You want to kill a man, by the dead, you do it while he's facing the other way.'

'I heartily concur,' said Deep. 'I thought you did too.'

'I did.' Calder shrugged. 'Things change.'

Whatever else he might be, he was Bethod's last son. His father had been a great man, and he wasn't about to put a cowardly joke on the end of his memory. Scale might have been an idiot but at least he'd had the dignity to die in battle. Better to follow his example than be hunted down in some desolate corner of the North, begging for his worthless hide.

But more than that, Calder couldn't run because . . . fuck them. Fuck Tenways, and Golden, and Ironhead. Fuck Black Dow. Fuck Curnden Craw, too. He was sick of being laughed at. Sick of being called a coward. Sick of being one.

'We don't do battles,' said Shallow.

'Can't watch over you if you're fixed on fighting,' said Deep.

'Wasn't expecting you to.' And Calder left them in the darkness without a backward glance and strolled on down the track to Clail's Wall, past men darning shirts, and cleaning weapons, and discussing their chances on the morrow. Not too good, the general opinion. He put one foot up on a crumbled patch of drystone and grinned over at the scarecrow, hanging sadly limp. 'Cheer up,' he told it. 'I'm going nowhere. These are my men. This is my land.'

'If it ain't Bare-Knuckle Calder, the punching prince!' Pale-as-Snow came swaggering from the night. 'Our noble leader returns! Thought maybe we'd lost you.' He didn't sound too upset at the possibility.

'I was giving some thought to running for the hills, in fact.'

Calder worked his toes inside his boot, enjoying the feel of it. He was enjoying little things a lot, tonight. Maybe that's what happened when you saw your death coming at you fast. 'But the hills are probably turning cold this time of year.'

'The weather's on our side, then.'

'We'll see. Thanks for drawing your sword for me. I always had you down as a man to back the favourite.'

'So did I. But for a moment up there you reminded me of your father.' Pale-as-Snow planted his own boot on the wall beside Calder's. 'I remembered how it felt to follow a man I admire.'

Calder snorted. 'I wouldn't get used to that feeling.'

'Don't worry, it's gone already.'

'Then I'll spend every moment I've got left struggling to bring it back for you.' Calder hopped up onto the wall, waving his arms for balance as a loose stone rocked under his feet, then stood, peering off across the black fields towards the Old Bridge. The torches of the Union pickets formed a dotted line, others moving about as soldiers poured across the river. Making ready to come flooding across the fields tomorrow morning, and over their tumbledown little wall, and murder the lot of them, and leave Bethod's memory a joke regardless.

Calder squinted, shading his eyes from the light of his own fires. It looked as if they'd stuck two tall flags right up at the front. He could see them shifting in the wind, gold thread faintly glinting. It seemed strange that they were so easy to see, until he realised they were lit up on purpose. Some sort of display. Some show of strength, maybe.

'By the dead,' he muttered, and snorted with laughter. His father used to tell him it's easy to see the enemy one of two ways. As some implacable, terrifying, unstoppable force that can only be feared and never understood. Or some block of wood that doesn't think, doesn't move, a dumb target to shoot your plans at. But the enemy is neither one. Imagine he's you, that he's no more and no less of a fool, or a coward, or a hero than you are. If you can imagine that, you won't go too far wrong. The enemy is just a set of men. That's the realisation that makes war easy. And the one that makes it hard.

The chances were high that General Mitterick and the rest were just as big a set of idiots as Calder was himself. Which meant they were big ones. 'Have you seen those bloody flags?' he called down.

Pale-as-Snow shrugged. 'It's the Union.'

'Where's White-Eye?'

'Touring the fires, trying to keep mens' spirits up.'

'Not buoyed by having me in charge, then?'

Pale-as-Snow shrugged again. 'They don't all know you like I do. Probably Hansul's busy singing the song of how you punched Brodd Tenways in the face. That'll do their love for you no harm.'

Maybe not, but punching men on his own side wasn't going to be enough. Calder's men were beaten and demoralised. They'd lost a leader they loved and gained one nobody did. If he did any more nothing, the chances were high they'd fall apart in battle tomorrow morning, if they were even there when the sun rose.

Scale had said it. This is the North. Sometimes you have to fight.

He pressed his tongue into his teeth, the glimmers of an idea starting to take shape from the darkness. 'Mitterick, is it, across the way?'

'The Union Chief? Aye, Mitterick, I think.'

'Sharp, Dow told me, but reckless.'

'He was reckless enough today.'

'Worked for him, in the end. Men tend to stick to what works. He loves horses, I heard.'

'What? Loves 'em?' Pale-as-Snow mimed a grabbing action and gave a couple of thrusts of his hips.

'Maybe that too. But I think fighting on them was more the point.'

'That's good ground for horses.' Pale-as-Snow nodded at the sweep of dark crops to the south. 'Nice and flat. Maybe he thinks he'll ride all over us tomorrow.'

'Maybe he will.' Calder pursed his lips, thinking about it. Thinking about the order crumpled in his shirt pocket. *My men and I are giving our all.* 'Reckless. Arrogant. Vain.' Roughly what men said about Calder, as it went. Which maybe gave him a little insight into his opponent. His eyes shifted back to those idiot flags, thrust out front, lit up like a dance on midsummer eve. His mouth found that familiar smirk, and stayed there. 'I want you to get your best men together. No more than a few score. Enough to keep together and work quickly at night.'

'What for?'

'We're not going to beat the Union moping back here.' He kicked the bit of loose stone from the top of the wall. 'And I don't think some farmer's boundary mark is going to keep them out either, do you?'

Pale-as-Snow showed his teeth. 'Now you're reminding me of your father again. What about the rest of the lads?'

Calder hopped down from the wall. 'Get White-Eye to round them up. They've got some digging to do.'

DAY THREE

'I'm not sure how much violence and
butchery the readers will stand'

Robert E. Howard

THE VALLEY OF OSRUNG

JAWS

USTRED

Holcum Farm

Bear Farm

Clail Farm

Skarling's Finger

DOW

TENWAYS

Wall

Clail

CALDER

The Child

Vallimir

Stile Farm

IRONHEAD

MITTERICK

Old Bridge

JAL

Adwein

UFRITH

Lock Fell

The Standard Issue

The light came and went as the clouds tore across the sky, showing a glimpse of the big full moon then hiding it away, like a clever whore might show a glimpse of tit once in a while, just to keep the punters eager. By the dead, Calder wished he was with a clever whore now, rather than crouching in the middle of a damp barley-field, peering through the thrashing stalks in the vain hope of seeing a whole pile of night-dark nothing. It was a sad fact, or perhaps a happy one, that he was a man better suited to brothels than battlefields.

Pale-as-Snow was rather the reverse. The only part of him that had moved in an hour or more was his jaw, slowly shifting as he ground a lump of chagga down to mush. His flinty calm only made Calder more jumpy. Everything did. The scraping of shovels dug at his nerves behind them, sounding just a few strides distant one moment then swallowed up by the wind the next. The same wind that was whipping Calder's hair in his face, blasting his eyes with grit and cutting through his clothes to the bone.

'Shit on this wind,' he muttered.

'Wind's a good thing,' grunted Pale-as-Snow. 'Masks the sound. And if you're chill, brought up to the North, think how they feel over there, used to sunnier climes. All in our favour.' Good points, maybe, and Calder was annoyed he hadn't thought of them, but they didn't make him feel any warmer. He clutched his cloak tight at his chest, other hand wedged into his armpit, and pressed one eye shut.

'I expected war to be terrifying but I never thought it'd be so bloody boring.'

'Patience.' Pale-as-Snow turned his head, softly spat and licked the juice from his bottom lip. 'Patience is as fearsome a weapon as rage. More so, in fact, 'cause fewer men have it.'

'Chief.' Calder spun about, fumbling for his sword hilt. A man had slithered from the barley beside them, mud smeared on his face, eyes standing out strangely white in the midst of it. One of theirs. Calder wondered if he should've smeared some mud on his face too. It made a man look like he knew his business. He waited for Pale-as-Snow to answer for a while. Then he realised he was the Chief.

'Oh, right.' Letting go of his sword and pretending he hadn't been surprised at all. 'What?'

'We're in the trenches,' whispered the newcomer. 'Sent a few Union boys back to the mud.'

'They seem ready?' asked Pale-as-Snow, who hadn't so much as looked round.

'Shit, no.' The man's grin was a pale curve in his blacked-out face. 'Most of 'em were sleeping.'

'Best time to kill a man.' Though Calder had to wonder whether the dead would agree. The old warrior held out one hand. 'Shall we?'

'We shall.' Calder winced as he set off crawling through the barley. It was far sharper, rougher, more painful stuff to sneak through than you could ever have expected. It didn't take long for his hands to chafe raw, and it hardly helped that he knew he was heading towards the enemy. He was a man better suited to the opposite direction. 'Bloody barley.' When he took his father's chain back he'd make a law against growing the bastard stuff. Only soft crops allowed, on pain of— He ripped two more bristly wedges out of his way and froze.

The standards were right ahead, no more than twenty strides off, flapping hard on their staves. Each was embroidered with a golden sun, glittering in the light of a dozen lanterns. Beyond them the stretch of bald, soggy ground Scale had died defending sloped down towards the river, crawling with Union horses. Hundreds of tons of big, glossy, dangerous-looking horseflesh and, as far as he could tell by the patchy torchlight, they were still coming across, hooves clattering on the flags of the bridge, panicked whinnies echoing out as they jostled each other in the darkness. There was no shortage of men either, shouting as they struggled to get their mounts into position, bellowed orders fading on the wind. All making good and ready to trample Calder and his boys into the mud in a few short hours. Not a particularly comforting thought, it had to be said. Calder didn't mind the odd trampling but he much preferred being in the saddle to being under the hooves.

A pair of guards flanked the standards, one with his arms wrapped around him and a halberd hugged tight in the crook of his elbow, the other stamping his feet, sword sheathed and using his shield as a windbreak.

'Do we go?' whispered Pale-as-Snow.

Calder looked at those guards, and he thought about mercy. Neither one seemed the slightest bit ready for what was coming. They looked even more unhappy about being here than he was, which was quite the achievement. He wondered whether they had wives waiting for them too. Wives with children in their soft bellies, maybe, curled up asleep under the furs with a warm space beside them. He sighed. Damn shame they weren't all with their wives, but mercy wasn't going to drive the Union out of the North, or Black Dow out of his father's chair either.

'We go,' he said.

Pale-as-Snow held up a hand and made a couple of gestures. Then he did the same on the other side and settled back onto his haunches. Calder wasn't sure who he was even waving at, let alone what the meaning was, but it worked like magic.

The guard with the shield suddenly went over backwards. The other turned his head to look then did the same. Calder realised they'd both had their throats cut. Two black shapes lowered them gently to the ground. A third had caught the halberd as it dropped and now he turned, hugging it in the crook of his own elbow, giving them a gap-toothed grin as he imitated the Union guard.

More Northmen had broken from the crops and were scurrying forwards, bent double, weapons gleaming faintly as the moon slipped from the clouds again. Not twenty strides away from them three Union soldiers were struggling with a wind-torn tent. Calder chewed at his lip, hardly able to believe they weren't seen as they crept across the open ground and into the lamplight, one of them taking a hold of the right-hand flag, starting to twist it free of the earth.

'You!' A Union soldier, a flatbow part-raised, a look of mild puzzlement on his face. There was a moment of awkward silence, everyone holding their breath.

'Ah,' said Calder.

'Shit,' said Pale-as-Snow.

The soldier frowned. 'Who are—' Then he had an arrow in his chest. Calder didn't hear the bowstring but he could see the black line of the shaft. The soldier shot his flatbow into the ground, gave a high shriek and fell to his knees. Not far away some horses startled, one dragging its surprised handler over onto his face and bumping across the mud. The three soldiers with the tent all snapped around at the same moment, two of them letting go of the canvas so that it was blown straight into the face of the third. Calder felt a sucking feeling in his stomach.

More Union men spilled into the light with frightening suddenness, a dozen or more, a couple with torches, flames whipped out sideways by a new gust. High wails echoed on Calder's right and men darted from nowhere, steel glinting as swords were swung. Shadows flickered in the darkness, a weapon, or an arm, or the outline of a face caught for an instant against the orange glow of fire. Calder could hardly tell what was happening, then one of the torches guttered out and he couldn't tell at all. It sounded as if there was fighting over on the left now too, his head yanked about by every sound.

He nearly jumped into the sky when he felt Pale-as-Snow's hand on his shoulder. 'Best be moving.'

Calder needed no further encouragement, he was off through the barley like a rabbit. He could hear other men, whooping, laughing, cursing, no clue whether they were his or the enemy. Something hissed into the crops next to him. An arrow, or just the wind blowing stalks about. Crops tangled his ankles, thrashed at his calves. He tripped and fell on his face, tore his way back up with Pale-as-Snow's hand under his arm.

'Wait! Wait.'

He stood frozen in the dark, bent over with his hands on his knees, ribcage going like a bellows. Voices were gabbling over each other. Northern voices, he was greatly relieved to hear.

'They following?'

'Where's Hayl?'

'Did we get the bloody flags?'

'Those bastards wouldn't even know which way to go.'

'Dead. Caught an arrow.'

'We got 'em!'

'They were just dragging their bloody horses around!'

'Thought we'd have nothing to say about it.'

'But Prince Calder had something to say.' Calder looked up at his name and found Pale-as-Snow smiling at him, one of the standards in his fist. Something like the smile a smith might have when his favourite apprentice finally hammers out something worth selling on the anvil.

Calder felt a poke in his side, started, then realised it was the other standard, the flag rolled up tight. One of the men was offering it out to him, grin shining in the moonlight in the midst of his muddy face. There was a whole set of grins pointed at him. As if he'd said something funny. As if he'd done something great. It didn't feel that way to Calder. He'd just had the idea, which had been no effort at all, and set other men to work out how, and others still to take the risks. Hardly seemed possible that Calder's father had earned his great reputation like this. But maybe that's how the world works. Some men are made for doing violence. Some are meant for planning it. Then there are a special few whose talent is for taking the credit.

'Prince Calder?' And the grinning man offered him the flag again.

Well. If they wanted someone to admire, Calder wasn't about to disappoint them. 'I'm no prince.' He snatched the standard, swung one leg over the flagstaff and held it there, sticking up at an angle. He drew his sword, for the first time that night, and thrust it straight up into the dark sky. 'I'm the king of the fucking Union!'

It wasn't much of a joke, but after the night they'd had, and the day they'd had yesterday, they were ready to celebrate. A gale of laughter went up, Calder's men chuckling away, slapping each other on the backs.

'All hail his fucking Majesty!' shouted Pale-as-Snow, holding up the other flag, gold thread sparkling as it snapped in the wind. 'King bloody Calder!'

Calder just kept on grinning. He liked the sound of that.

Shadows

Your August Fuck-Hole,
    The truth? Under the wilful mismanagement of the old villains on your Closed Council, your army is rotting. Frittered away with cavalier carelessness, as a rake might fritter away his father's fortune. If they were the enemy's councillors they could scarcely do more to frustrate your Fuck-Hole's interests in the North. You could do better yourself, which is truly the most damning indictment of which I am capable. It would have been more honourable to load the men aboard in Adua, wave them off with a tear in the eye, then simply set fire to the ships and send them all to the bottom of the bay.

The truth? Marshal Kroy is competent, and cares for his soldiers, and I ardently desire to fuck his daughter, but there is only so much one man can do. His underlings, Jalenhorm, Mitterick and Meed, have been struggling manfully with each other for the place of worst general in history. I hardly know which deserves the higher contempt – the pleasant but incompetent dullard, the treacherous, reckless careerist, or the indecisive, warmongering pedant. At least the last has already paid for his folly with his life. With any luck the rest of us will follow.

The truth? Why would you care? Old friends like us need have no pretences. I know better than most you are a cringing cipher, a spineless figurehead, a self-pitying, self-loving, self-hating childman, king of nothing but your own vanity. Bayaz rules here, and he is bereft of conscience, scruple or mercy. The man is a monster. The worst I have seen, in fact, since I last looked in the mirror.

The truth? I am rotting too. I am buried alive, and already rotting. If I was not such a coward I would kill myself, but I am, and so I must content myself with killing others in the hope that one day, if I can only wade deep enough in blood, I will come out clean. While I wait breathlessly for rehabilitation that will never come, I will of course be delighted to consume any shit you might deign to squeeze into my face from the royal buttocks.

I remain your Fuck-Hole's most betrayed and vilified scapegoat, Bremer dan Gorst, Royal Observer of the Northern Fiasco

Gorst put down his pen, frowning at a tiny cut he had somehow acquired on the very tip of his forefinger where it rendered every slightest task painful. He blew gently over the letter until every gleam of wet ink had turned dry black, then folded it, running his one unbroken nail slowly along it to make the sharpest of creases. He took up the stick of wax, tongue pressed into the roof of his mouth. His eyes found the candle flame, twinkling invitingly in the shadows. He looked at that spark of brightness as a man scared of heights looks at the parapet of a great tower. It called to him. Drew him. Made him dizzy with the delightful prospect of self-annihilation. *Like that, and this shameful unpleasantness that I laughingly call a life could all be over.* Only seal it, and send it, and wait for the storm to break.

Then he sighed, and slid the letter into the flame, watched it slowly blacken, crinkle, dropped the last smouldering corner on the floor of his tent and ground it under his boot. He wrote at least one of these a night, savage punctuation points between rambling sentences of trying to force himself to sleep. Sometimes he even felt better afterwards. *For a very short while.*

He frowned up at a clatter outside, then started at a louder crash, the gabble of raised voices, something in their tone making him reach for his boots. Many voices, then the sounds of horses too. He snatched up his sword and ripped aside his tent flap.

Younger had been sitting outside, tapping the day's dents out of Gorst's armour by lamplight. He was standing up now, craning to see, a greave in one hand and the little hammer in the other.

'What is it?' Gorst squeaked at him.

'I've no— Woah!' He shrank back as a horse thundered past, flicking mud all over both of them.

'Stay here.' Gorst put a gentle hand on his shoulder. 'Stay out of danger.' He strode from his tent and towards the Old Bridge, tucking his shirt in with one hand, sheathed long steel gripped firmly in the other. Shouts echoed from the darkness ahead, lantern beams twinkling, glimpses of figures and faces mixed up with the after-image of the candle flame still fizzing across Gorst's vision.

A messenger jogged from the night, breathing hard, one cheek and the side of his uniform caked with mud. 'What's happening?' Gorst snapped at him.

'The Northmen have attacked in numbers!' he wheezed as he laboured past. 'We're overrun! They're coming!' His terror was Gorst's joy, excitement flaring up his throat so hot it was almost painful, the petty inconveniences of his bruises and aching muscles all burned away as he strode on towards the river. *Will I have to fight my way across that bridge for the second time in twelve hours?* He was almost giggling at the stupidity of it. *I cannot wait.*

Some officers pleaded for calm while others ran for their lives. Some men searched feverishly for weapons while others threw them away. Every shadow was the first of a horde of marauding Northmen, Gorst's palm itching with the need to draw his sword, until the tricking shapes resolved themselves into baffled soldiers, half-dressed servants, squinting grooms.

'Colonel Gorst? Is that you, sir?'

He stalked on, thoughts elsewhere. Back in Sipani. Back in the smoke and the madness at Cardotti's House of Leisure. Searching for the king in the choking gloom. *But this time I will not fail.*

A servant with a bloody knife was staring at a crumpled shape on the ground. *Mistaken identity.* A man came blundering from a tent, hair sticking wildly from his head, struggling to undo the clasp on a dress sword. *Pray excuse me.* Gorst swept him out of his way with the back of one arm and squawking over into the mud. A plump captain sat, surprised face streaked with blood, clasping a bandage to his head. 'What's happening? What's happening?' *Panic. Panic is happening. Amazing how quickly a steadfast army can dissolve. How quickly daylight heroes become night-time cowards. Become a herd, acting with the instincts of the animal.*

'This way!' someone shouted behind him. 'He knows!' Footsteps slapped after him in the mud. *A little herd of my own.* He did not even look around. *But you should know I'm going wherever the killing is.*

A horse plunged out of nowhere, eyes rolling. Someone had been trampled, was howling, pawing at the muck. Gorst stepped over them, following an inexplicable trail of fashionable lady's dresses, lace and colourful silk crushed into the filth. The press grew tighter, pale faces smeared across the dark, mad eyes shining with reflected fire, water glimmering with reflected torches. The Old Bridge was as packed and wild as it had been the previous day when they drove the Northmen across it. More so. Voices shouted over each other.

'Have you seen my—'

'Is that Gorst?'

'They're coming!'

'Out of my way! Out of my—'

'They're gone already!'

'It's him! He'll know what to do!'

'Everyone back! Back!'

'Colonel Gorst, could I—'

'Have to find some order! Order! I beseech you!'

Beseeching will not work here. The crowd swelled, surged, opening out then crushing tight, fear flashing up like lightning as a drawn sword or a lit torch wafted in someone's face. An elbow caught Gorst in the darkness and he lashed out with his fist, scuffed his knuckles on armour. Something grabbed at his leg and he kicked at it, tore himself free and shoved on. There was a shriek as someone was pushed over the parapet, Gorst caught a glimpse of his boots kicking as he vanished, heard the splash as he hit the fast-flowing water below.

He ripped his way clear on the far side of the bridge. His shirt was torn, the wind blowing chill through the rip. A ruddy-faced sergeant held a torch high and bellowed in a broken voice for calm. There was more shouting up ahead, horses plunging, weapons waving. But Gorst could not hear the sweet note of steel. He gripped his sword tight and stomped grimly on.

'No!' General Mitterick stood in the midst of a group of staff officers, perhaps the best example Gorst had ever seen of a man incandescent with rage. 'I want the Second and Third ready to charge at once!'

'But, sir,' wheedled one of his aides, 'it is still some time until dawn, the men are in disarray, we can't—'

Mitterick shook his sword in the young man's face. 'I'll give the orders here!' *Though it is obviously too dark to mount a horse safely, let alone ride several hundred at a gallop towards an invisible enemy.* 'Put guards on the bridge! I want any man who tries to cross hanged for desertion! *Hanged!*'

Colonel Opker, Mitterick's second-in-command, stood just outside the radius of blame, watching the pantomime with grim resignation.

Gorst clapped a hand down on his shoulder. 'Where are the Northmen?'

'Gone!' snapped Opker, shaking free. 'There were no more than a few score of them! They stole the standards of the Second and Third and were off into the night.'

'His Majesty will not countenance the loss of his standards, General!' someone was yelling. Felnigg. *Swooped down on Mitterick's embarrassment like a hawk on a rabbit.*

'I am well aware of what his Majesty will not countenance!' roared Mitterick back at him. 'I'll damn well get those standards back and kill every one of those thieving bastards, you can tell the lord marshal that! I *demand* you tell him that!'

'Oh, I'll be telling him all about it, never fear!'

But Mitterick had turned his back and was bellowing into the night. 'Where are the scouts? I told you to send scouts, didn't I? Dimbik? Where's Dimbik? The ground, man, the ground!'

'Me?' a white-faced young officer stammered out. 'Well, er, yes, but—'

'Are they back yet? I want to be sure the ground's good! Tell me it's good, damn it!'

The man's eyes darted desperately about, then it seemed he steeled himself, and snapped to attention. 'Yes, General, the scouts were sent, and have returned, in fact, very much returned, and the ground is . . . perfect. Like a card table, sir. A card table . . . with barley on it—'

'Excellent! I want no more bloody surprises!' Mitterick stomped off, loose shirt tails flapping. 'Where the bloody hell is Major Hockelman? I want these horsemen ready to charge as soon as we have light to piss by! Do you understand me? To *piss* by!'

His voice faded into the wind along with Felnigg's grating

complaints, and the lamps of his staff went with them, leaving Gorst frowning in the darkness, as choked with disappointment as a jilted groom.

A raid, then. An opportunistic little sally had caused all this, triggered by Mitterick's petty little display with his flags. *And there will be no glory and no redemption here. Only stupidity, cowardice and waste.* Gorst wondered idly how many had died in the chaos. *Ten times as many as the Northmen killed? Truly, the enemy are the least dangerous element of a war.*

How could we have been so ludicrously unready? Because we could not imagine they would have the gall to attack. If the Northmen had pushed harder they might have driven us back across the bridge, and captured two whole regiments of cavalry rather than just their standards. Five men and a dog could have done it. But they could not imagine we might be so ludicrously unready. A failure for everyone. Especially me.

He turned to find a small crowd of soldiers and servants with a mismatched assortment of equipment at his back. Those who had followed him down to the bridge, and beyond. A surprising number. *Sheep. Which makes me what? The sheep-dog? Woof, woof, you fools.*

'What should we do, sir?' asked the nearest of them.

Gorst could only shrug. Then he trudged slowly back towards the bridge, just as he had trudged back that afternoon, brushing through the deflated mob on the way. There was no sign of dawn yet, but it could not be far off.

Time to put on my armour.

Under the Wing

Craw picked his way down the hill, peering into the blackness for his footing, wincing at his sore knee with every other step. Wincing at his sore arm and his sore cheek and his sore jaw besides. Wincing most of all at the question he'd been asking himself most of a stiff, cold, wakeful night. A night full of worries and regrets, of the faint whimpering of the dying and the not-so-faint snoring of Whirrun of bloody Bligh.

Tell Black Dow what Calder had said, or not? Craw wondered whether Calder had already run. He'd known the lad since he was a child, and couldn't ever have accused him of courage, but there'd been something different about him when they talked last night. Something Craw hadn't recognised. Or rather something he had, but not from Calder, from his father. And Bethod hadn't been much of a runner. That was what had killed him. Well, that and the Bloody-Nine smashing his head apart. Which was probably better'n Calder could expect if Dow found out what had been said. Better'n Craw could expect himself, if Dow found out from someone else. He glanced over at Dow's frowning face, criss-cross scars picked out in black and orange by Shivers' torch.

Tell him or not?

'Fuck,' he whispered.

'Aye,' said Shivers. Craw almost took a tumble on the wet grass. 'Til he remembered there was an awful lot a man could be saying fuck about. That's the beauty of the word. It can mean just about anything, depending on how things stand. Horror, shock, pain, fear, worry. None were out of place. There was a battle on.

The little tumbledown house crept out of the dark, nettles sprouting from its crumbling walls, a piece of the roof fallen in and the rotten timbers sticking up like dead rib bones. Dow took Shivers' torch. 'You wait here.'

Shivers paused just a moment, then bowed his head and leaned back by the door, faintest gleam of moonlight settled on his metal eye.

Craw ducked through the low doorway, trying not to look worried. When he was alone with Black Dow, some part of him – and not a small one – always expected a knife in the back. Or maybe a sword in the front. But a blade, anyway. Then he was always the tiniest bit surprised when he lived out the meeting. He'd never felt that way with Threetrees, or even Bethod. Hardly seemed the mark of the right man to follow . . . He caught himself chewing at a fingernail, if you could even call it a fingernail there was that little left of the bastard thing, and made himself stop.

Dow took his torch over to the far side of the room, shadows creeping about the rough-sawn rafters as he moved. 'Ain't heard back from the girl, then, or her father neither.' Craw thought it best to stick to silence. Whenever he said a word these days it seemed to end up in some style of disaster. 'Looks like I put myself in debt to the bloody giant for naught.' Silence again. 'Women, eh?'

Craw shrugged. 'Don't reckon I'll be lending you any insights on that score.'

'You had one for a Second, didn't you? How did you make that work?'

'She made it work. Couldn't ask for a better Second than Wonderful. The dead know I made some shitty choices but that's one I've never regretted. Not ever. She's tough as a thistle, tough as any man I know. Got more bones than me and sharper wits too. Always the first to see to the bottom o' things. And she's a straight edge. I'd trust her with anything. No one I'd trust more.'

Dow raised his brows. 'Toll the fucking bells. Maybe I should've picked her for your job.'

'Probably,' muttered Craw.

'Got to have someone you can trust for a Second.' Dow crossed to the window, peering out into the windy night. 'Got to have trust.'

Craw snatched at another subject. 'We waiting for your black-skinned friend?'

'Not sure I'd call her a friend. But yes.'

'Who is she?'

'One o' those desert-dwellers. Don't the black give it away?'

'What's her interest in the North, is my question?'

'Couldn't tell you that for sure, but from what I've gathered she's got a war of her own to fight. An old war, and for now we've a battlefield in common.'

Craw frowned. 'A war between sorcerers? That something we want a part of?'

'We've a part of it already.'

'Where did you find her?'

'She found me.'

That was a long way from putting his fears to rest. 'Magic. I don't know—'

'You were up on the Heroes yesterday, no? You saw Splitfoot.'

Hardly a memory to lift the mood. 'I did.'

'The Union have magic, that's a fact, and they're happy to use it. We need to match fire with fire.'

'What if we all get burned?'

'I daresay we will.' Dow shrugged. 'That's war.'

'Can you trust her, though?'

'No.' Ishri was leaning against the wall by the door, one foot crossed over the other and a look like she knew what Craw was thinking and wasn't much impressed. He wondered if she knew he'd been thinking about Calder and tried not to, which only brought him more to mind.

Dow, meanwhile, didn't even turn around. Just slid his torch into a rusted bracket on the wall, watching the flames crackle.

'Seems our little gesture of peace fell on stony ground,' he tossed over his shoulder.

Ishri nodded.

Dow stuck his bottom lip out. 'Nobody wants to be my friend.'

Ishri made one thin eyebrow arch impossibly high.

'Well, who wants to shake hands with a man whose hands are bloody as mine?'

Ishri shrugged.

Dow looked down at his hand, made a fist of it and sighed. 'Reckon I'll just have to get 'em bloodier. Any idea where they're coming from today?'

'Everywhere.'

'Knew you'd say that.'

'Why ask, then?'

'Least I got you to speak.' There was a long silence, then Dow finally turned around, settling back with elbows on the narrow windowsill. 'Go on, go for some more.'

Ishri stepped away from the wall, letting her head drop back and roll in a slow circle. For some reason every movement of hers made Craw feel a little disgusted, like watching a snake slither. 'In the east, a man called Brock has taken charge, and prepares to attack the bridge in Osrung.'

'And what kind of man is he? Like Meed?'

'The opposite. He is young, pretty and brave.'

'I love those young brave pretty men!' Dow glanced over at Craw. 'It's why I picked one out for my Second.'

'None out of three ain't bad.' Craw realised he was chewing at his nail yet again, and whipped his hand away.

'In the centre,' said Ishri, 'Jalenhorm has a great number of foot ready to cross the shallows.'

Dow gave his hungry grin. 'Gives me something to look forward to today. I quite enjoy watching men try to climb hills I'm sat on top of.' Craw couldn't say he was looking forward to it, however much the ground might have taken their side.

'In the west Mitterick strains at the leash, keen to make use of his pretty horses. He has men across the little river too, in the woods on your western flank.'

Dow raised his brows. 'Huh. Calder was right.'

'Calder has been hard at work all night.'

'Damned if it ain't the first hard work that bastard's ever done.'

'He stole two standards from the Union in the darkness. Now he taunts them.'

Black Dow chuckled to himself. 'You'll not find a better hand at taunting. I've always liked that lad.'

Craw frowned over at him. 'You have?'

'Why else would I keep giving him chances? I got no shortage of men can kick a door down. I can use a couple who'll think to try the handle once in a while.'

'Fair enough.' Though Craw had to wonder what Dow would

408

say if he knew Calder was trying the handle on his murder. When he knew. It was a case of when. Wasn't it?

'This new weapon they've got.' Dow narrowed his eyes to lethal slits. 'What is it?'

'Bayaz.' Ishri did some fairly deadly eye-narrowing of her own. Craw wondered if there was a harder pair of eye-narrowers in the world than these two. 'The First of the Magi. He is with them. And he has something new.'

'That's the best you can do?'

She tipped her head back, looking down her nose. 'Bayaz is not the only one who can produce surprises. I have one for him, later today.'

'I knew there had to be a reason why I took you under my wing,' said Dow.

'Your wing shelters all the North, oh mighty Protector.' Ishri's eyes rolled slowly to the ceiling. 'The Prophet shelters under the wing of God. I shelter under the wing of the Prophet. That thing that keeps the rain from your head?' And she held her arm up, long fingers wriggling, boneless as a jar of bait. Her face broke out in a grin too white and too wide. 'Great or small, we all must find some shelter.' Dow's torch popped, its light flickered for a moment, and she wasn't there.

'Think on it,' came her voice, right in Craw's ear.

Names

Beck hunched his shoulders and stared at the fire. Not much more'n a tangle of blackened sticks, a few embers in the centre still with a glow to 'em and a little tongue of flame, whipped, and snatched, and torn about, helpless in the wind. Burned out. Almost as burned out as he was. He'd clutched at that dream of being a hero so long that now it was naught but ashes he didn't know what he wanted. He sat there under fading stars named for great men, great battles and great deeds, and didn't know who he was.

'Hard to sleep, eh?' Drofd shuffled up into the firelight cross-legged, blanket around his shoulders.

Beck gave the smallest grunt he could. Last thing he wanted to do was talk.

Drofd held out a piece of yesterday's meat to him, glistening with grease. 'Hungry?'

Beck shook his head. He weren't sure when he last ate. Just before he last slept, most likely, but the smell alone was making him sick.

'Might keep it for later, then.' Drofd stuck the meat into a pocket on the front of his jerkin, bone sticking out, rubbed his hands together and held 'em to the smear of fire, so dirty the lines on his palms were picked out black. He looked about of an age with Beck, but smaller and darker, some spare stubble on his jaw. Right then, in the darkness, he looked a little bit like Reft. Beck swallowed, and looked away. 'So you got yourself a name, then, eh?'

A little nod.

'Red Beck.' Drofd gave a chuckle. 'It's a good 'un. Fierce-sounding. You must be pleased.'

'Pleased?' Beck felt a stinging urge to say, 'I hid in a cupboard and killed one o' my own,' but instead he said, 'I reckon.'

'Wish I had a name. Guess it'll come in time.'

Beck kept staring into the fire, hoping to head off any more chatter. Seemed Drofd was the chattering sort, though.

'You got family?'

All the most ordinary, obvious, lame bloody talk a lad could've thought of. Dragging the words out felt like a painful effort to begin with. 'A mother. Two little brothers. One's 'prenticed to the smith in the valley.' Lame, maybe, but once he'd started talking, thoughts drifting homewards, he found he couldn't stop. 'More'n likely my mother's making ready to bring the harvest in. Was getting ripe when I left. She'll be sharpening the scythe and that. And Festen'll be gathering up after her . . .' And by the dead, how he wished he was with 'em. He wanted to smile and cry at once, didn't dare say more for fear of doing it.

'I got seven sisters,' said Drofd, 'and I'm the youngest. Like having eight mothers fussing over me, and putting me right all day long, and each with a tongue sharper'n the last. No man in the house, and no man's business ever talked of. Home was a special kind of hell, I can tell you that.'

A warm house with eight women and no swords didn't sound so awful right then. Beck had thought his home was a special kind of hell once. Now he had a different notion of what hell looked like.

Drofd blathered on.

'But I got a new family now. Craw, and Wonderful, and Jolly Yon and the rest. Good fighters. Good names. Stick together, you know, mind their own. Lost a couple o' people the last few days. Couple of good people, but . . .' Seemed he ran out of words himself for a moment. Didn't take him long to find more, though. 'Craw was Second to old Threetrees, you know, way back. Been in every battle since whenever. Does things the old way. Real straight edge. You fell on your feet to fall in with this lot, I reckon.'

'Aye.' Beck didn't feel like he'd fallen on his feet. He felt like he was still falling and, sooner or later but probably sooner, the ground would smash his brains out.

'Where did you get the sword?'

Beck blinked at the hilt, almost surprised to see it was still there beside him. 'It was my father's.'

'He was a fighter?'

'Named Man. Famous one, I guess.' And how he'd loved to boast about it once. Now the name was sour on his tongue. 'Shama Heartless.'

'What? The one who fought a duel against the Bloody-Nine? The one who . . .'

Lost. 'Aye. The Bloody-Nine brought an axe to the duel, and my father brought this blade, and they spun the shield, and the Bloody-Nine won, and he chose the sword.' Beck slid it out, stupidly worried he might stab someone without meaning to. He'd a respect of sharp metal he hadn't had the night before. 'They fought, and the Bloody-Nine split my father's belly wide open.' Seemed mad now that he'd rushed to follow the man's footsteps. A man he'd never known, whose footsteps led all the way to his own spilled guts.

'You mean . . . the Bloody-Nine held that sword?'

'Guess he must've.'

'Can I?'

Time was Beck would've told Drofd to fuck himself, but acting the loner hadn't worked out too well for anyone concerned. This time around maybe he'd try and coax out a friendship or two. So he handed the blade across, pommel first.

'By the dead, that's a damn good sword.' Drofd stared at the hilt with big eyes. 'There's still blood on it.'

'Aye,' Beck managed to croak.

'Well, well, well.' Wonderful strutted up, hands on hips, tip of her tongue showing between her teeth. 'Two young lads, handling each other's weapons by firelight? Don't worry, I see how it can happen. You think no one's watching, and there's a fight coming, and you might never get another chance to try it. Most natural thing in the world.'

Drofd cleared his throat and gave the sword back quick. 'Just talking about . . . you know. Names. How'd you come by yours?'

'Mine?' snapped Wonderful, narrowing her eyes at 'em. Beck didn't rightly know what to make of a woman fighting, let alone one who led a dozen. One who was his Chief, now, even. He had to admit she scared him a little, with that hard look and that knobbly head with an old scar down one side and a fresh one down the other. Being scared by a woman might've shamed him once, but it hardly seemed to matter now he was scared of everything. 'I got it giving a pair of curious young lads a wonderful kicking.'

'She got it off Threetrees.' Jolly Yon rolled over in his blankets and propped himself on an elbow, peering at the fire through one hardly open eye, scratching at his black and grey thatch of a beard. 'Her family had a farm just north of Uffrith. Stop me if I'm wrong.'

'I will,' she said, 'don't worry.'

'And when trouble started up with Bethod, some of his boys came down into that valley. So she shaved her hair.'

'Shaved it a couple of months before. Always got in my way when I was following the plough.'

'I stand corrected. You want to take over?'

'You're doing all right.'

'No need for the shears, then, but she took up a sword, and she got a few others in the valley to do the same, and she laid an ambush for 'em.'

Wonderful's eyes gleamed in the firelight. 'Did I ever.'

'And then Threetrees turned up, and me and Craw along with him, expecting to find the valley all burned out and the farmers scattered and instead he finds a dozen of Bethod's boys hanged and a dozen more prisoner and this bloody girl watching over 'em with quite the smile. What was it he said now?'

'Can't say I recall,' she grunted.

'Wonderful strange to have a woman in charge,' said Yon, putting on a gravelly bass. 'We called her Wonderful Strange for a week or two, then the strange dropped off, and there you have it.'

Wonderful nodded grimly at the fire. 'And a month later Bethod came in earnest and the valley got all burned out anyway.'

Yon shrugged. 'Still a good ambush, though.'

'And what about you, eh, Jolly Yon Cumber?'

Yon dragged his blankets off and sat up. 'Ain't much to it.'

'Don't be modest. Jolly was said straight in the old days, 'cause he used to be quite the joker, did Yon. Then his cock was tragically cut off in the battle at Ineward, a loss more mourned by the womenfolk of the North than all the husbands, sons and fathers killed there. Ever since then, not a single smile.'

'A cruel lie.' Yon pointed a thick finger across at Beck. 'I never had a sense o' humour. And it was just a little nick out of my thigh at Ineward. Lot of blood but no damage. Everything still working down below, don't you worry.'

Over his shoulder and out of his sight, Wonderful was pointing at her crotch. 'Cock and fruits,' she mouthed, miming a chopping action with one open hand. 'Cock . . . and . . .' Then when Yon looked around peered at her fingernails like she'd done nothing.

'Up already?' Flood came limping between the sleepers and the fires along with a man Beck didn't know, lean with a mop of grey-streaked hair.

'Our youngest woke us,' grunted Wonderful. 'Drofd was having a feel of Beck's weapon.'

'You can see how it can happen, though . . .' said Yon.

'You can check mine over if you like.' Flood grabbed the mace at his belt and stuck it up at an angle. 'It's got a big lump on the end!' Drofd gave a chuckle at that, but it seemed most of the rest weren't in a laughing mood. Beck surely weren't. 'No?' Flood looked around at 'em expectantly. 'It's 'cause I'm old, ain't it? You can say. It's 'cause I'm old.'

'Old or not, I'm glad you're here,' said Wonderful, one eyebrow up. 'The Union won't dare attack now we've got you two.'

'Never would have given 'em the chance but I had to go for a piss.'

'Third of the night?' asked Yon.

Flood peered up at the sky. 'Think it was the fourth.'

'Which is why they call him Flood,' murmured Wonderful under her breath. ''Case you were wondering.'

'I ran into Scorry Tiptoe on the way.' Flood jerked his thumb at the lean man beside him.

Tiptoe took a while weighing up the words, then spoke 'em soft. 'I was taking a look around.'

'Find anything out?' asked Wonderful.

He nodded, real slow, like he'd come upon the secret of life itself. 'There's a battle on.' He slid down next to Beck on crossed legs and held out a hand to him. 'Scorry Tiptoe.'

'On account of his gentle footfall,' said Drofd. 'Scouting, mostly. And back rank, with a spear, you know.'

Beck gave it a limp shake. 'Beck.'

'Red Beck,' threw in Drofd. 'That's his name. Got it yesterday. Off Reachey. Down in the fight in Osrung. Now he's joined up . . . with us . . . you know . . .' He trailed off, Beck and Scorry both frowning at him, and huddled down into his blanket.

'Craw give you the talk?' asked Scorry.

'The talk?'

'About the right thing.'

'He mentioned it.'

'Wouldn't take it too seriously.'

'No?'

Scorry shrugged. 'Right thing's a different thing for every man.' And he started pulling knives out and laying 'em on the ground in front of him, from a huge great thing with a bone handle only just this side of a short sword to a tiny little curved one without even a grip, just a pair of rings for two fingers to fit in.

'That for peeling apples?' asked Beck.

Wonderful drew a finger across her sinewy neck. 'Slitting throats.'

Beck thought she was probably having a laugh at him, then Scorry spat onto a whetstone and that little blade gleamed in the firelight and suddenly he weren't so sure. Scorry pressed it to the stone and gave it a lick both ways, snick, snick, and all of a sudden there was a thrashing of blankets.

'Steel!' Whirrun sprang up, reeling about, sword all tangled up with his bed. 'I hear steel!'

'Shut up!' someone called.

Whirrun tore his sword free, jerking his hood out of his eyes. 'I'm awake! Is it morning?' Seemed the stories about Whirrun of Bligh being always ready were a bit overdone. He let his sword drop, squinting up at the black sky, stars peeping between shreds of cloud. 'Why is it dark? Have no fear, children, Whirrun is among you and ready to fight!'

'Thank the dead,' grunted Wonderful. 'We're saved.'

'That you are, woman!' Whirrun pulled his hood back, scratched at his hair, plastered flat on one side and sticking out like a thistle on the other. He stared about the Heroes and, seeing nought but guttering fires, sleeping men and the same old stones as ever, crawled up close to the flames, yawning. 'Saved from dull conversation. Did I hear some talk of names?'

'Aye,' muttered Beck, not daring to say more. It was like having Skarling himself to talk to. He'd been raised on stories about Whirrun of Bligh's high deeds. Listened to old drunk Scavi tell 'em down in the village, and begged for more. Dreamed of standing beside him as an equal, claiming a place in his songs. Now here he was, sitting beside him as fraud, and coward, and friend-killer. He dragged his mother's cloak tight, felt something crusted under his fingers. Realised the cloth was still stiff with Reft's blood and had to stop a shiver. Red Beck. He'd blood on his hands, all right. But it didn't feel like he'd always dreamed it would.

'Names, is it?' Whirrun lifted his sword and stood it on end in the firelight, looking too long and too heavy ever to make much sense as a weapon. 'This is the Father of Swords, and men have a hundred names for it.' Yon closed his eyes and sank back, Wonderful rolled hers up towards the sky, but Whirrun droned on, deep and measured, like it was a speech he'd given often before. 'Dawn Razor. Grave-Maker. Blood Harvest. Highest and Lowest. Scac-ang-Gaioc in the valley tongue which means the Splitting of the World, the battle that was fought at the start of time and will be fought again at its end. This is my reward and my punishment both. My blessing and my curse. It was passed to me by Daguf Col as he lay dying, and he had it from Yorweel the Mountain who had it from Four-Faces who had it from Leef-reef-Ockang, and so on 'til the world was young. When Shoglig's words come to pass and I lie bleeding, face to face with the Great Leveller at last, I'll hand it on to whoever I think best deserves it, and will bring it fame, and the list of its names, and the list of the names of the great men who wielded it, and the great men who died by it, will grow, and lengthen, and stretch back into the dimness beyond memory. In the valleys where I was born they say it is God's sword, dropped from heaven.'

'Don't you?' asked Flood.

Whirrun rubbed some dirt from the crosspiece with his thumb. 'I used to.'

'Now?'

'God makes things, no? God is a farmer. A craftsman. A midwife. God gives things life.' He tipped his head back and looked up at the sky. 'What would God want with a sword?'

Wonderful pressed one hand to her chest. 'Oh, Whirrun, you're so fucking *deep*. I could sit here for hours trying to work out everything you meant.'

'Whirrun of Bligh don't seem so deep a name,' said Beck, and regretted it straight away when everyone looked at him, Whirrun in particular.

'No?'

'Well . . . you're from Bligh, I guess. Ain't you?'

'Never been there.'

'Then—'

'I couldn't honestly tell you how it came about. Maybe Bligh's the only place up there folk down here ever heard of.' Whirrun shrugged. 'Don't hardly matter. A name's got nothing in it by itself. It's what you make of it. Men don't brown their trousers when they hear the Bloody-Nine because of the name. They brown their trousers because of the man that had it.'

'And Cracknut Whirrun?' asked Drofd.

'Straightforward. An old man up near Ustred taught me the trick of cracking a walnut in my fist. What you do is—'

Wonderful snorted. 'That ain't why they call you Cracknut.'

'Eh?'

'No,' said Yon. 'It ain't.'

'They call you Cracknut for the same reason they gave Cracknut Leef the name,' and Wonderful tapped at the side of her shaved head. 'Because it's widely assumed your nut's cracked.'

'They do?' Whirrun frowned. 'Oh, that's less complimentary, the fuckers. I'll have to have words next time I hear that. You've completely bloody spoiled it for me!'

Wonderful spread her hands. 'It's a gift.'

'Morning, people.' Curnden Craw walked slowly up to the fire with his cheeks puffed out and his grey hair twitching in the wind. He looked tired. Dark bags under his eyes, nostrils rimmed pink.

'Everyone on their knees!' snapped Wonderful. 'It's Black Dow's right hand!'

Craw pretended to wave 'em down. 'No need to grovel.' Someone else came behind him. Caul Shivers, Beck realised with a sick lurch in his stomach.

'Y'all right, Chief?' asked Drofd, pulling the bit of meat out of his pocket and offering it over.

Craw winced as he bent his knees and squatted by the fire, put one finger on one nostril, then blew out through the other with a long wheeze like a dying duck. Then he took the meat and had a bite out of it. 'The definition of all right changes with the passing winters, I find. I'm about all right by the standards of the last few days. Twenty years ago I'd have considered this close to death.'

'We're on a battlefield, ain't we?' Whirrun was all grin. 'The Great Leveller's pressed up tight against us all.'

'Nice thought,' said Craw, wriggling his shoulders like there was someone breathing on his neck. 'Drofd.'

'Aye, Chief?'

'If the Union come later, and I reckon it's a set thing they will . . . might be best if you stay out of it.'

'Stay out?'

'It'll be a proper battle. I know you've got the bones but you don't have the gear. A hatchet and a bow? The Union got armour, and good steel and all the rest . . .' Craw shook his head. 'I can find you a place behind somewhere—'

'Chief, no, I want to fight!' Drofd looked across at Beck, like he wanted support. Beck had none to give. He wished he could be left behind. 'I want to win myself a name. Give me the chance!'

Craw winced. 'Name or not, you'll just be the same man. No better. Maybe worse.'

'Aye,' Beck found he'd said.

'Easy for those to say who have one,' snapped Drofd, staring surly at the fire.

'He wants to fight, let him fight,' said Wonderful.

Craw looked up, surprised. Like he'd realised he wasn't quite where he'd thought he was. Then he leaned back on one elbow, stretching one boot out towards the fire. 'Well. Guess it's your dozen now.'

'That's a fact,' said Wonderful, nudging that boot with hers. 'And they'll all be fighting.' Yon slapped Drofd on the shoulder, all flushed and grinning now at the thought of glory. Wonderful reached out and flicked the pommel of the Father of Swords with a fingernail. 'Besides, you don't need a great weapon to win yourself a name. Got yours with your teeth, didn't you, Craw?'

'Bite someone's throat out, did you?' asked Drofd.

'Not quite.' Craw had a faraway look for a moment, firelight picking out the lines at the corners of his eyes. 'First full battle I was in we had a real red day, and I was in the midst. I had a thirst, back then. Wanted to be a hero. Wanted myself a name. We was all sat around the fire-pit after, and I was expecting something fearsome.' He looked up from under his eyebrows. 'Like Red Beck. Then when Threetrees was considering it, I took a big bite from a piece of meat. Drunk, I guess. Got a bone stuck in my throat. Spent a minute hardly able to breathe, everyone thumping me on the back. In the end a big lad had to hold me upside down 'fore it came loose. Could barely talk for a couple of days. So Threetrees called me Craw, on account of what I'd got stuck in it.'

'Shoglig said . . .' sang Whirrun, arching back to look into the sky, 'I would be shown my destiny . . . by a man choking on a bone.'

'Lucky me,' grunted Craw. 'I was furious, when I got the name. Now I know the favour Threetrees was doing me. His way of trying to keep me level.'

'Seems like it worked,' croaked Shivers. 'You're the straight edge, ain't you?'

'Aye.' Craw licked unhappily at his teeth. 'A real straight edge.'

Scorry gave the straight edge of his latest knife one last flick with the whetstone and picked up the next. 'You met our latest recruit, Shivers?' Sticking his thumb sideways. 'Red Beck.'

'I have.' Shivers stared across the fire at him. 'Down in Osrung. Yesterday.'

Beck had that mad feeling Shivers could see right through him with that eye, and knew him for the liar he was. Made him wonder how none of the others could see it, writ across his face plain as a fresh tattoo. Cold prickled his back, and he pulled his blood-crusted cloak tight again.

'Quite a day yesterday,' he muttered.

'And I reckon today'll be another.' Whirrun stood and stretched up tall, lifting the Father of Swords high over his head. 'If we're lucky.'

Still Yesterday

The blue skin stretched as the steel slid underneath it, paint flaking like parched earth, stubbly hairs shifting, red threads of veins in the wide whites near the corners of his eyes. Her teeth ground together as she pushed it in, pushed it in, pushed it in, coloured patterns bursting on the blackness of her closed lids. She could not get that damned music out of her head. The music the violinists had been playing. Were playing still, faster and faster. The husk-pipe they had given her had blunted the pain just as they said it would, but they had lied about the sleep. She twisted the other way, huddling under the blankets. As though you can roll over and leave a day of murder on the other side of the bed.

Candlelight showed around the door, through the cracks between the slats. As the daylight had showed through the door of the cold room where they were kept prisoner. Kneeling in the darkness, plucking at the knots with her nails. Voices outside. Officers, coming and going, speaking with her father. Talking of strategy and logistics. Talking of civilisation. Talking of which one of them Black Dow wanted.

What had happened blurred with what might have, with what should have. The Dogman arrived an hour earlier with his Northmen, saw off the savages before they left the wood. She found out ahead of time, warned everyone, was given breathless thanks by Lord Governor Meed. Captain Hardrick brought help, instead of never being heard from again, and the Union cavalry arrived at the crucial moment like they did in the stories. Then she led the defence, standing atop a barricade with sword aloft and a blood-spattered breastplate, like a lurid painting of Monzcarro Murcatto at the battle of Sweet Pines she once saw on the wall of a tasteless merchant. All mad, and while she spun out the fantasies she knew they were mad, and she wondered if she was mad, but she did it all the same.

And then she would catch something at the edge of her sight, and she was there, as it had been, on her back with a knee crushing her in the stomach and a dirty hand around her neck, could not breathe, all the sick horror that she somehow had not felt at the time washing over her in a rotting tide, and she would rip back the blankets and spring up, and pace round and round the room, chewing at her lip, picking at the scabby bald patch on the side of her head, muttering to herself like a madwoman, doing the voices, doing all the voices.

If she'd argued harder with Black Dow. If she'd pushed, demanded, she could have brought Aliz with her, instead of . . . in the darkness, her blubbering wail as Finree's hand slipped out of hers, the door rattling shut. A blue cheek bulged as the steel slid underneath it, and she bared her teeth, and moaned, and clutched at her head, and squeezed her eyes shut.

'Fin.'

'Hal.' He was leaning over her, candlelight picking out the side of his head in gold. She sat up, rubbing her face. It felt numb. As if she was kneading dead dough.

'I brought you fresh clothes.'

'Thank you.' Laughably formal. The way one might address someone else's butler.

'Sorry to wake you.'

'I wasn't asleep.' Her mouth still had a strange taste, a swollen feeling from the husk. The darkness in the corners of the room fizzed with colours.

'I thought I should come . . . before dawn.' Another pause. Probably he was waiting for her to say she was glad, but she could not face the petty politeness. 'Your father has put me in charge of the assault on the bridge in Osrung.'

She did not know what to say. Congratulations. Please, no! Be careful. Don't go! Stay here. Please. Please. 'Will you be leading from the front?' Her voice sounded icy.

'Close enough to it, I suppose.'

'Don't indulge in any heroics.' Like Hardrick, charging out of the door for help that could never come in time.

'There'll be no heroics, I promise you that. It's just . . . the right thing to do.'

'It won't help you get on.'

'I don't do it to get on.'

'Why, then?'

'Because someone has to.' They were so little alike. The cynic and the idealist. Why had she married him? 'Brint seems . . . all right. Under the circumstances.' Finree found herself hoping that Aliz was all right, and made herself stop. That was a waste of hope, and she had none to spare.

'How should one feel when one's wife has been taken by the enemy?'

'Utterly desperate. I hope he will be all right.'

'All right' was such a useless, stilted expression. It was a useless, stilted conversation. Hal felt like a stranger. He knew nothing about who she really was. How can two people ever really know each other? Everyone went through life alone, fighting their own battle.

He took her hand. 'You seem—'

She could not bear his skin against hers, jerked her fingers away as though she was snatching them from a furnace. 'Go. You should go.'

His face twitched. 'I love you.'

Just words, really. They should have been easy to say. But she could not do it any more than she could fly to the moon. She turned away from him to face the wall, dragging the blanket over her hunched shoulder. She heard the door shut.

A moment later, or perhaps a while, she slid out of bed. She dressed. She splashed water on her face. She twitched her sleeves down over the scabbing chafe marks on her wrists, the ragged cut up her arm. She opened the door and went through. Her father was in the room on the other side, talking to the officer she saw crushed by a falling cupboard yesterday, plates spilling across the floor. No. A different man.

'You're awake.' Her father was smiling but there was a wariness to him, as if he was expecting her to burst into flames and he was ready to grab for a bucket. Maybe she would burst into flames. She would not have been surprised. Or particularly sorry, right then. 'How do you feel?'

'Well.' Hands closed around her throat and she plucked at them with her nails, ears throbbing with her own heartbeat. 'I killed a man yesterday.'

He stood, put his hand on her shoulder. 'It may feel that way, but—'

'It certainly does feel that way. I stabbed him, with a short steel I stole from an officer. I pushed the blade into his face. Into his face. So. I got one, I suppose.'

'Finree—'

'Am I going mad?' She snorted up a laugh, it sounded so stupid. 'Things could be so much worse. I should be glad. There was nothing I could do. What can anyone do? What should I have done?'

'After what you have been through, only a madman could feel normal. Try to act as though . . . it is just another day, like any other.'

She took a long breath. 'Of course.' She gave him a smile which she hoped projected reassurance rather than insanity. 'It is just another day.'

There was a wooden bowl, on a table, with fruit in it. She took an apple. Half-green, half-blood-coloured. She should eat while she could. Keep her strength up. It was just another day, after all.

Still dark outside. Guards stood by torchlight. They fell silent as she passed, watching while pretending not to watch. She wanted to spew all over them, but she tried to smile as if it was just another day, and they did not look exactly like the men who had strained desperately to hold the gates of the inn closed, splinters bursting around them as the savages hacked down the doors.

She stepped from the path and out across the hillside, pulling her coat tight around her. Wind-lashed grass sloped away into the darkness. Patches of sedge tangled at her boots. A bald man stood, coat-tails flapping, looking out across the darkened valley. He had one fist clenched behind him, thumb rubbing constantly, worriedly at forefinger. The other daintily held a cup. Above him, in the eastern sky, the first faint smudges of dawn were showing.

Perhaps it was the after-effects of the husk, or the sleeplessness, but after what she had seen yesterday the First of the Magi did not seem so terrible. 'Another day!' she called, feeling as if she might take off from the hillside and float into the dark sky. 'Another day's fighting. You must be pleased, Lord Bayaz!'

He gave her a curt bow. 'I—'

'Is it "Lord Bayaz" or is there a better term of address for the First of the Magi?' She pushed some hair out of her face but the wind soon whipped it back. 'Your Grace, or your Wizardship, or your Magicosity?'

'I try not to stand on ceremony.'

'How does one become First of the Magi, anyway?'

'I was the first apprentice of great Juvens.'

'And did he teach you magic?'

'He taught me High Art.'

'Why don't you do some then, instead of making men fight?'

'Because making men fight is easier. Magic is the art and science of forcing things to behave in ways that are not in their nature.' Bayaz took a slow sip from his cup, watching her over the rim. 'There is nothing more natural to men than to fight. You are recovered, I hope, from your ordeal yesterday?'

'Ordeal? I've almost forgotten about it already! My father suggested that I act as though this is just another day. Then, perhaps it will be one. Any other day I would spend feverishly trying to advance my husband's interests, and therefore my own.' She grinned sideways. 'I am venomously ambitious.'

Bayaz' green eyes narrowed. 'A characteristic I have always found most admirable.'

'Meed was killed.' His mouth opening and closing silently like a fish snatched from the river, plucking at the great rent in his crimson uniform, crashing over with papers sliding across his back. 'I daresay you are in need of a new lord governor of Angland.'

'His Majesty is.' The Magus heaved up a sigh. 'But making such a powerful appointment is a complicated business. No doubt some relative of Meed expects and demands the post, but we cannot allow it to become some family bauble. I daresay a score of other great magnates of the Open Council think it their due, but we cannot raise one man too close in power to the crown. The closer they come the less they can resist reaching for it, as your father-in-law could no doubt testify. We could elevate some bureaucrat but then the Open Council would rail about stoogery and they are troublesome enough as it is. So many balances to strike, so many rivalries, and jealousies, and dangers to navigate. It's enough to make one abandon politics altogether.'

'Why not my husband?'

Bayaz cocked his head on one side. 'You are very frank.'

'I seem to be, this morning.'

'Another characteristic I have always found most admirable.'

'By the Fates, I'm admirable!' she said, hearing the door clatter shut on Aliz' sobs.

'I am not sure how much support I could raise for your husband, however.' Bayaz wrinkled his lip as he tossed the dregs from his cup into the dewy grass. 'His father stands among the most infamous traitors in the history of the Union.'

'Too true. And the greatest of all the Union's noblemen, the first man on the Open Council, only a vote away from the crown.' She spoke without considering the consequences any more than a spinning stone considers the water it skims across. 'When his lands were seized, his power snuffed out as though it had never existed, I would have thought the nobles felt threatened. For all they delighted in his fall they saw in it the shadow of their own. I imagine restoring his son to some prudent fraction of his power might be made to play well with the Open Council. Asserting the rights of the ancient families, and so on.'

Bayaz' chin went up a little, his brows drew down. 'Perhaps. And?'

'And while the great Lord Brock had allies and enemies in abundance, his son has none. He has been scorned and ignored for eight years. He is part of no faction, has no agenda but faithfully to serve the crown. He has more than proved his honesty, bravery and unquestioning loyalty to his Majesty on the field of battle.' She fixed Bayaz with her gaze. 'It would be a fine story to tell. Instead of lowering himself to dabble in base politics, our monarch chooses to reward faithful service, merit and old-time heroism. The commoners would enjoy it, I think.'

'Faithful service, merit and heroism. Fine qualities in a soldier.' As though talking about fat on a pig. 'But a lord governor is first a politician. Flexibility, ruthlessness and an eye for expediency are more his talents. How is your husband there?'

'Weak, but perhaps someone close to him could supply those qualities.'

She fancied Bayaz had the ghost of a smile about his lips. 'I am beginning to suspect they could. You make an interesting suggestion.'

'You have not thought of everything, then?'

'Only the truly ignorant believe they have thought of everything. I might even mention it to my colleagues on the Closed Council when we next meet.'

'I would have thought it would be best to make a choice swiftly, rather than to allow the whole thing to become . . . an issue. I cannot be considered impartial but, even so, I truly believe my husband to be the best man in the Union.'

Bayaz gave a dry chuckle. 'Who says I want the best man? It may be that a fool and a weakling as lord governor of Angland would suit everyone better. A fool and a weakling with a stupid, cowardly wife.'

'That, I am afraid, I cannot offer you. Have an apple.' And she tossed it at him, made him juggle it with one hand before catching it in the other, his cup tumbling into the sedge, his brows up in surprise. Before he could speak she was already walking away. She could hardly even remember what their conversation had been about. Her mind was entirely taken up with the way that blue cheek bulged as steel slid underneath it, pushing it in, pushing it in.

For What We Are
About to Receive . . .

It's an awful fine line between being raised above folk like a leader and being raised above 'em like a hanged man on display. When Craw climbed up on an empty crate to give his little speech, he had to admit he felt closer to the latter. A sea of faces opened up in front of him, the Heroes packed with men from one side of the circle to the other and plenty more pressing in outside. Didn't help that Black Dow's own Carls were the grimmest, darkest, toughest-looking crowd you'd find anywhere in the North. And you'll find a lot of tough crowds in the North. Probably these were a long stretch more interested in doing plunder, rape and murder than anyone's idea of the right thing, and didn't care much who got on the pointy end of it either.

Craw was glad he had Jolly Yon, and Flood, and Wonderful stood frowning around the crate. He was even gladder he had Whirrun just beside. The Father of Swords was enough metal to add some weight to anyone's words. He remembered what Threetrees told him when he made him his Second. He was trying to be their leader, not their lover, and a leader's best feared first, and liked afterward.

'Men o' the North!' he bellowed into the wind. ''Case you didn't hear, Splitfoot's dead, and Black Dow's put me in his place.' He picked out the biggest, nastiest, most scornful-looking bastard in the whole crowd, a man looked like he shaved with an axe, and leaned towards him. 'Do what I fucking tell you!' he snarled. 'That's your job now.' He lingered on him for long enough to make the point he feared nothing, even if the opposite was closer to the truth. 'Keeping everyone alive, that's mine. There's a strong likelihood I ain't going to succeed in every case. That's war. Won't stop me trying, though. And by the dead it won't stop you lot trying either.'

They milled about a little, a long way from won over. Time to list the pedigree. Bragging weren't his strong suit these days but there'd be no prize for modesty. 'My name's Curnden Craw, and I'm thirty years a Named Man! I stood Second to Rudd Threetrees, back in the day.' That name got a nodding rustle of approval. 'The Rock of Uffrith himself. Held a shield for him when he fought his duel with the Bloody-Nine.' That name got a bigger one. 'Then I fought for Bethod, and now Black Dow. Every battle you pricks heard of I had a part in.' He curled his lip. 'So safe to say you needn't worry about whether I'm up to the task.' Even if Craw was worrying his bowels loose over it himself. But his voice rang out gruff and deep still. Thank the dead for his hero's voice, even if time had given him a coward's guts.

'I want each man here to do the right thing today!' he roared. 'And before you start sneering and I'm forced to stick my boot up your arse, I ain't talking about patting children on the head, or giving your last crust to a squirrel, or even being bolder'n Skarling once the blades are drawn. I ain't talking about acting the hero.' He jerked his head towards the stones around them. 'You can leave that to the rocks. They won't bleed for it. I'm talking about standing by your Chief! Standing with your crew! Standing with the man beside you! And above all I'm talking about not getting yourselves fucking killed!'

He picked Beck out with a pointed finger. 'Look at this lad here. Red Beck, his name.' Beck's eyes went wide as the whole front rank of killers turned to look at him. 'He did the right thing yesterday. Stuck in a house in Osrung with the Union breaking down the door. Listened to his Chief. Stood with his kind. Kept his head. Put four o' the bastards in the mud and came through alive.' Maybe Craw was flowering up the truth a little but that was the point of a speech, wasn't it? 'If a lad o' seventeen years can keep the Union out of a shack, I reckon men o' your experience should have no trouble keeping 'em off a hill like this one here. And since everyone knows how rich the Union is . . . no doubt they'll leave plenty behind 'em as they go running down that slope, eh?' That got a bit of a laugh at least. Nothing worked like tickling their greed.

'That's all!' he bellowed. 'Find your places!' And he hopped down, little wobble as his knee jarred but at least he kept standing. No applause, but he reckoned he'd won enough of 'em over not to get stabbed in his back before the battle was done. And in this company that was about as much as he could've hoped for.

'Nice speech,' said Wonderful.

'You reckon?'

'Not sure about the whole right thing bit, though. You have to say that?'

Craw shrugged. 'Someone should.'

'You may have heard some commotion this morning.' Colonel Vallimir gave the assembled officers and sergeants of his Majesty's First Regiment a stern glance. 'That was the sound of a raid by the Northmen.'

'That was the sound of someone fucking up,' muttered Tunny. He'd known that as soon as he heard the clamour floating across from the east. There's no better recipe for fuck-ups than night-time, armies and surprises.

'There was some confusion on the front line . . .'

'Further fuck-ups,' muttered Tunny.

'Panic spread in the darkness . . .'

'Several more,' muttered Tunny.

'And . . .' Vallimir grimaced. 'The Northmen made off with two standards.'

Tunny opened his mouth a crack, but he lacked the words for that. A disbelieving murmur went through the gathering, clear in spite of the wind shaking the branches. Vallimir shouted them down.

'The standards of the Second and Third were captured by the enemy! General Mitterick is . . .' The colonel gave the impression of choosing his words with great care. 'Not happy.'

Tunny snorted. Mitterick wasn't happy at the best of times. What effect having two of his Majesty's standards stolen from under his nose might have on the man was anyone's guess. Probably if you stuck a pin in him right now he'd explode and take half the valley with him. Tunny realised he was clutching the standard of the First with extra-special care, and made his fists relax.

'To make matters a great deal worse,' Vallimir went on,

'apparently we were sent orders to attack yesterday afternoon and they never reached us.' Forest gave Tunny a hard look sideways but he could only shrug. Of Lederlingen there was still no sign. Possibly he'd volunteered for desertion. 'By the time the next set came it was dark. So Mitterick wants us to make up for it today. As soon as there's light, the general will launch an assault on Clail's Wall in overwhelming force.'

'Huh.' Tunny had heard a lot about overwhelming force the last few days and the Northmen were still decidedly under-whelmed.

'The wall at this far western end he's going to leave to us, though. The enemy cannot possibly spare enough men to hold it once the attack is underway. As soon as we see them leave the wall, we cross the river and take them in the flank.' Vallimir slapped one hand with the other to illustrate the point. 'And that'll be the end of them. Simple. As soon as they leave the wall, we attack. Any questions?'

What if they don't leave the wall? was the one that im-mediately occurred, but Tunny knew a great deal better than to make himself conspicuous in front of a crowd of officers.

'Good.' Vallimir smiled as though silence meant the plan must be perfect, rather than just that his men were too thick, eager or cautious to point out its shortcomings. 'We're missing half our men and all our horses, but that won't stop his Majesty's First, eh? If everyone does his duty today, there's still time for all of us to be heroes.'

Tunny had to choke off his scornful laughter as the thick, eager, cautious officers broke up and began to drift into the trees to make their soldiers ready. 'You hear that, Forest? We can all be heroes.'

'I'll settle for living out the day. Tunny, I want you to get up to the treeline and keep a watch on the wall. Need some experienced eyes up there.'

'Oh, I've seen it all, Sergeant.'

'And then some more, I don't doubt. The very instant you see the Northmen start to clear out, you give the signal. And Tunny?' He turned back. 'You won't be the only one watching, so don't even think about pulling anything clever. I still remember what happened with that ambush outside Shricta. Or what didn't happen.'

'No evidence of wrongdoing, and I'm quoting the tribunal there.'

'Quoting the tribunal, you're a piece of work.'

'First Sergeant Forest, I am crushed that a colleague would hold so low an opinion of my character.'

'What character?' called Forest after him as he threaded his way uphill through the trees. Yolk was crouched in the bushes pretty much where they'd been crouching all night, peering across the stream through Tunny's eyeglass.

'Where's Worth?' Yolk opened his mouth. 'On second thought, I can guess. Any signs of movement?' Yolk opened his mouth again. 'Other than in Trooper Worth's bowels, that is?'

'None, Corporal Tunny.'

'Hope you don't mind if I check.' He snatched the eyeglass without waiting for an answer and scanned along the line of the wall, uphill from the stream, towards the east, where it disappeared over a hump in the land. 'Not that I doubt your expertise . . .' There was no one in front of the drystone but he could see spears behind it, a whole lot of them, just starting to show against the dark sky.

'No movement, right, Corporal?'

'No, Yolk.' Tunny lowered his eyeglass and gave his neck a scratch. 'No movement.'

General Jalenhorm's entire division, reinforced by two regiments from Mitterick's, was drawn up in parade-ground order on the gentle slope of grass and shingle that led down to the shallows. They faced north. Towards the Heroes. Towards the enemy. *So we got that much right, at least.*

Gorst had never seen so many arrayed for battle in one place and at one time, dwindling into darkness and distance on either side. Above their massed ranks a thicket of spears and barbed pole-arms jutted, the pennants of companies fluttered, and in one spot nearby the gilded standard of the King's Own Eighth Regiment snapped in the stiff breeze, proudly displaying several generations of battle honours. Lamps cast pools of light, picking out clutches of solemn faces, striking sparks from polished steel.

Here and there mounted officers waited to hear orders and give them, swords shouldered. A ragged handful of the Dogman's Northmen stood near the water's edge, gawping up towards this military multitude.

For the occasion General Jalenhorm had donned a thing more work of art than piece of armour: a breastplate of mirror-bright steel engraved front and back with golden suns whose countless rays became swords, lances, arrows, entwined with wreaths of oak and laurel in the most exquisite craftsmanship.

'Wish me luck,' he murmured, then gave his horse his heels and nudged it up the shingle towards the front rank.

'Good luck,' whispered Gorst.

The men were quiet enough that one could hear the faint ringing as Jalenhorm drew his sword. 'Men of the Union!' he thundered, holding it high. 'Two days ago many of you were among those who suffered a defeat at the hands of the Northmen! Who were driven from the hill you see ahead of us. The fault that day was entirely mine!' Gorst could hear other voices echoing the general's words. Officers repeating the speech to those too far away to hear the original. 'I hope, and I trust, that you will help me gain redemption today. Certainly I feel a great pride to be given the honour of leading men such as you. Brave men of Midderland, of Starikland, of Angland. Brave men of the Union!'

Staunch discipline prevented anyone from shouting out but a kind of murmur still went up from the ranks. Even Gorst felt a patriotic lifting of his chin. *A jingoistic misting of the eye. Even I, who should know so much better.*

'War is terrible!' Jalenhorm's horse pawed at the shingle and he brought it under control with a tug of the reins. 'But war is wonderful! In war, a man can find out all he truly is. All he can be. War shows us the worst of men – their greed, their cowardice, their savagery! But it also shows us the best – our courage, our strength, our mercy! Show me your best today! And more than that, show it to the enemy!'

There was a brief pause as the distant voices relayed the last sentence, and as members of Jalenhorm's staff let it be known that the address was at an end, then the men lifted their arms as one and gave a thunderous cheer. Gorst realised after a moment that he was making his own piping contribution, and stopped.

433

The general sat with his sword raised in acknowledgement, then turned his back on the men and rode towards Gorst, his smile fading.

'Good speech. Far as these things go.' The Dogman was slouched in the battered saddle of a shaggy horse, blowing into his cupped palms.

'Thank you,' answered the general as he reined in. 'I tried simply to tell the truth.'

'The truth is like salt. Men want to taste a little, but too much makes everyone sick.' The Dogman grinned at them both. Neither replied. 'Quite some piece of armour, too.'

Jalenhorm looked down, somewhat uncomfortably, at his magnificent breastplate. 'A gift from the king. It never seemed like quite the right occasion before . . .' *But if one shouldn't make an effort when charging to one's doom, then, really, when should one?*

'So what's the plan?' asked the Dogman.

Jalenhorm swept his arm towards his waiting division. 'The Eighth and Thirteenth Foot and the Stariksa Regiment will lead off.' *He makes it sound like a wedding dance. I suspect the casualties will be higher.* 'The Twelfth and the Aduan Volunteers will form our second wave.' *Waves break on a beach, and melt away into the sand, and are forgotten.* 'The remnants of the Rostod Regiment and the Sixth will follow in reserve.' *Remnants, remnants. We all will be remnants, in due course.*

The Dogman puffed his cheeks out as he looked at the massed ranks. 'Well, you've no shortage of bodies, anyway.' *Oh no, and no shortage of mud to bury them in either.*

'First we cross the shallows.' Jalenhorm pointed towards the twisting channels and sandbars with his sword. 'I expect they will have skirmishers hidden about the far bank.'

'No doubt,' said the Dogman.

The sword drifted up towards the rows of fruit trees, just becoming visible on the sloping ground between the glimmering water and the base of the hill. 'We expect some resistance as we pass through the orchards.' *More than some, I imagine.*

'We might be able to flush 'em out of the trees.'

'But you have no more than a few score men over here.'

The Dogman winked. 'There's more to war than numbers.

Few o' my boys are already across the river, lying low. Once you're over, just give us a chance. If we're able to shift 'em, fine, if not, you've lost nothing.'

'Very well,' said Jalenhorm. 'I am willing to take any course that might save lives.' *Ignoring the fact that the entire business is an exercise in slaughter.* 'Once the orchards are in our hands . . .' His sword drifted implacably up the bare hillside, pointing out the smaller stones on the southern spur, then the larger ones on the summit, glowing faintly orange in the light of guttering fires. He shrugged, letting his sword drop. 'We climb the hill.'

'You climb that hill?' asked the Dogman, eyebrows high.

'Indeed.'

'Fuck.' Gorst could only silently concur. 'They've been up there two days now. Black Dow's all kinds of things but he's no fool, he'll be ready. Stakes planted, and ditches dug, and men at the drystone walls, and arrows showering down, and—'

'Our purpose is not necessarily to drive them off,' Jalenhorm interrupted, grimacing as though there were arrows showering on him already. 'It is to fix them in place while General Mitterick on the left, and Colonel Brock on the right, force openings on the flanks.'

'Aye,' said the Dogman, somewhat uncertainly.

'But we hope we may achieve much more than that.'

'Aye, but, I mean . . .' The Dogman took a deep breath as he frowned up towards the hill. 'Fuck.' *I'm not sure I could have said it better.* 'You sure about this?'

'My opinion does not enter into the case. The plan is Marshal Kroy's, on the orders of the Closed Council and the wishes of the king. My responsibility is the timing.'

'Well, if you're going to go, I wouldn't leave it too long.' The Dogman nodded to them, then turned his shaggy horse away. 'Reckon we'll have rain later. And lots of it!'

Jalenhorm peered up at the sullen sky, bright enough now to see the clouds flowing quickly across it, and sighed. 'The timing is in my hands. Across the river, through the orchards, and straight up the hill. Just go north, basically. That should be within my capabilities, I would have thought.' They sat in silence for a moment. 'I wanted very much to do the right thing, but I have proved myself to be . . . not the greatest tactical mind in his

Majesty's army.' He sighed again. 'At least I can still lead from the front.'

'With the greatest respect, might I suggest you remain behind the lines?'

Jalenhorm's head jerked around, astonished. *At the words themselves or at hearing me speak more than three together? People talk to me as though they were talking to a wall, and they expect the same return.* 'Your concern for my safety is touching, Colonel Gorst, but—'

'Bremer.' *I might as well die with one person in the world who knows me by my first name.*

Jalenhorm's eyes went even wider. Then he gave a faint smile. 'Truly touching, Bremer, but I am afraid I could not consider it. His Majesty expects—'

Fuck his Majesty. 'You are a good man.' *A floundering incompetent, but still.* 'War is no place for good men.'

'I respectfully disagree, on both counts. War is a wonderful thing for redemption.' Jalenhorm narrowed his eyes at the Heroes, seeming so close now, just across the water. 'If you smile in the face of danger, acquit yourself well, stand your ground, then, live or die, you are made new. Battle can make a man . . . clean, can't it?' *No. Wash yourself in blood and you come out bloody.* 'Only look at you. I may or may not be a good man, but you are without doubt a hero.'

'Me?'

'Who else? Two days ago, here at these very shallows, you charged the enemy alone and saved my division. An established fact, I witnessed part of the action myself. And yesterday you were at the Old Bridge?' Gorst frowned at nothing. 'You forced a crossing when Mitterick's men were mired in the filth, a crossing that may very well win this battle for us today. You are an inspiration, Bremer. You prove that one man still can be worth something in the midst of . . . all this. You do not need to fight here today, and yet you stand ready to give your life for king and country.' *To toss it away for a king who does not care and a country which cannot.* 'Heroes are a great deal rarer than good men.'

'Heroes are quickly fashioned from the basest materials. Quickly fashioned, and quickly replaced. If I qualify, they are worthless.'

'I beg to differ.'

'Differ, by all means, but please . . . remain behind the lines.'

Jalenhorm gave a sad little smile, and he reached out, and tapped at Gorst's dented shoulder-plate with his fist. 'Your concern for my safety really is touching, Bremer. But I'm afraid I cannot do it. I cannot do it any more than you can.'

'No.' Gorst frowned up towards the hill, a black mass against the stained sky. 'A shame.'

Calder squinted through his father's eyeglass. Beyond the circle of light cast by all the lamps, the fields faded into shifting blackness. Down towards the Old Bridge he could pick out spots of brightness, perhaps the odd glint of metal, but not much more. 'Do you think they're ready?'

'I can see horses,' said Pale-as-Snow. 'A lot of horses.'

'You can? I can't see a bloody thing.'

'They're there.'

'You think they're watching?'

'I reckon they are.'

'Mitterick watching?'

'I would be.'

Calder squinted up at the sky, starting to show grey between the fast-moving clouds. Only the most committed optimist could've called it dawn, and he wasn't one. 'Guess it's time, then.'

He took one more swig from the flask, rubbed at his aching bladder, then passed it over to Pale-as-Snow and clambered up the stack of crates, blinking into the lamplight, conspicuous as a shooting star. He took a look over his shoulder at the ranks of men ranged behind him, dark shapes in front of the long wall. He didn't really understand them, or like them, and they felt the same about him, but they had one powerful thing in common. They'd all basked in his father's glory. They'd been great men because of who they served. Because they'd sat at the big table in Skarling's Hall, in the places of honour. They'd all fallen a long way when Calder's father died. It looked like none of them could stand to fall any further, which was a relief, since a Chief without soldiers is just a very lonely man in a big bloody field.

He was very much aware of all those eyes on him as he

unlaced. The eyes of a couple of thousand of his boys behind, and a fair few of Tenways' too, and the eyes of a few thousand Union cavalry ahead, he hoped, General Mitterick among them, ready to pop his skull with anger.

Nothing. Try to relax or try to push? Bloody typical, that would be, all this effort and he found he couldn't go. To make matters worse the wind was keen and it was freezing the end of his prick. The man holding up the flag on his left, a grizzled old Carl with a great scar right across one cheek, was watching his efforts with a slightly puzzled expression.

'Can you not look?' snapped Calder.

'Sorry, Chief.' And he cleared his throat and almost daintily averted his eyes.

Maybe it was being called Chief that got him over the hump. Calder felt that hint of pain down in his bladder, and he grinned, let it build, let his head drop back, looked up at the bruised sky.

'Hah.' Piss showered out, drops shining in the lamplight, and spattered all over the first flag with a sound like rain on the daisies. Behind Calder, a wave of laughter swept down the lines. Easily pleased, maybe, but large bodies of fighting men don't tend to go for subtle jokes. They go for shit, and piss, and people falling over.

'And some for you too.' He sent a neat arc across the other flag, and he smirked towards the Union as wide as he could. Behind him men started to jump up, and dance about, and jeer across the barley. He might not be much of a warrior, or a leader, but he knew how to make men laugh, and how to make them angry. With his free hand he pointed up at the sky, and he gave a great whoop, and he shook his hips around and sent piss shooting all over the place. 'I'd shit on 'em too,' he shouted over his shoulder, 'but I'm all bound up from White-Eye's stew!'

'I'll shit on 'em!' someone shrieked, to a scattering of shrill chuckles.

'Save it for the Union, you can shit on them when they get here!'

And the men whooped and laughed, shook their weapons at the sky and clattered them against their shields and sent up quite the happy din. A couple had even climbed up on the wall and were pissing at the Union lines themselves. Maybe they found it a good deal funnier because they knew what was coming, just across the other side of the barley, but still Calder smiled to hear it. At least he'd stood up, and done one thing worth singing about. At least he'd given his father's men a laugh. His brother's men. His men.

Before they all got fucking murdered.

Beck thought he could hear laughter echoing on the wind, but he'd no idea what anyone might have to laugh about. It was getting light enough to see across the valley now. Light enough to get an idea of the Union's numbers. To begin with Beck hadn't believed those faint blocks on the other side of the shallows could be solid masses of men. Then he'd tried to make himself believe they weren't. Now there was no denying it.

'There are thousands of 'em,' he breathed.

'I know!' Whirrun was nearly jumping with happiness. 'And the more there are, the more our glory, right, Craw?'

Craw took a break from chewing his nails. 'Oh, aye. I wish there were twice as many.'

'By the dead, so do I!' Whirrun dragged in a long breath and blew it through a beaming smile. 'But you never know, maybe they've got more out of sight!'

'We can hope,' grunted Yon out of the corner of his mouth.

'I fucking love war!' squeaked Whirrun. 'I fucking love it, though, don't you?'

Beck didn't say anything.

'The smell of it. The feel of it.' He rubbed one hand up and down the stained sheath of his sword, making a faint swishing sound. 'War is honest. There's no lying to it. You don't have to say sorry here. Don't have to hide. You cannot. If you die? So what? You die among friends. Among worthy foes. You die looking the Great Leveller in the eye. If you live? Well, lad, that's living, isn't it? A man isn't truly alive until he's facing death.' Whirrun stamped his foot into the sod. 'I love war! Just a shame Ironhead's down there on the Children. Do you reckon they'll even get all the way up here, Craw?'

'Couldn't say.'

'I reckon they will. I hope they will. Better come before the rain starts, though. That sky looks like witch's work, eh?' It was true there was a strange colour to the first hint of sunrise, great towers of sullen-looking cloud marching in over the fells to the north. Whirrun bounced up and down on his toes. 'Oh, bloody hell, I can't wait!'

'Ain't they people too, though?' muttered Beck, thinking of the face of that Union man lying dead in the shack yesterday. 'Just like us?'

Whirrun squinted across at him. 'More than likely they are. But if you start thinking like that, well . . . you'll get no one killed at all.'

Beck opened his mouth, then closed it. Didn't seem much he could say to that. Made about as much sense as anything else had happened the last few days.

'It's easy enough for you,' grunted Craw. 'Shoglig told you the time and place of your death and it ain't here.'

Whirrun's grin got bigger. 'Well, that's true and I'll admit it's a help to my courage, but if she'd told me here and she'd told me now, do you really reckon that'd make any difference to me?'

Wonderful snorted. 'You might not be yapping about it so bloody loud.'

'Oh!' Whirrun wasn't even listening. 'They're off already, look! That's early!' He pointed the Father of Swords at arm's length to the west, towards the Old Bridge, flinging his other arm around Beck's shoulders. The strength in it was fearsome, he nearly lifted Beck without even trying. 'Look at the pretty horses!' Beck couldn't see much down there but dark land, the glimmer of the river and a speckling of lights. 'That's fresh of 'em, isn't it, though? That's cheeky! Getting started and it's hardly dawn!'

'Too dark for riding,' said Craw, shaking his head.

'They must be as bloody eager as I am. Reckon they mean business today, eh, Craw? Oh, by the dead,' and he shook his sword towards the valley, dragging Beck back and forth and nearly right off his feet, 'I reckon there'll be some songs sung about today!'

'I daresay,' grunted Wonderful through gritted teeth. 'Some folk'll sing about any old shit.'

The Riddle of the Ground

'Here they come,' said Pale-as-Snow, utterly deadpan, as if there was nothing more worrying than a herd of sheep on its way. It hardly needed an announcement. Calder could hear them, however dark it was. First the long note of a trumpet, then the whispering rustle of horses through crops, far off but closing, sprinkled with calls, whinnies, jingles of harness that seemed to tickle at Calder's clammy skin. All faint, but all crushingly inevitable. They were coming, and Calder hardly knew whether to be smug or terrified. He settled on a bit of both.

'Can't believe they fell for it.' He almost wanted to laugh it was so ridiculous. Laugh or be sick. 'Those arrogant fucks.'

'If you can rely on one thing in a battle, it's that men rarely do what's sensible.' Good point. If Calder had any sense he'd have been on horseback himself, spurring hard for somewhere a long, long way away. 'That's what made your father the great man. Always kept a cold head, even in the fire.'

'Would you say we're in the fire now?'

Pale-as-Snow leaned forward and carefully spat. 'I'd say we're about to be. Reckon you'll keep a cold head?'

'Can't see why.' Calder's eyes darted nervously to either side, across the snaking line of torches before the wall. The line of his men, following the gentle rise and fall of the earth. 'The ground is a puzzle to be solved,' his father used to say, 'the bigger your army, the harder the puzzle.' He'd been a master at using it. One look and he'd known where to put every man, how to make each slope, and tree, and stream, and fence fight on his side. Calder had done what he could, used each tump and hummock and ranged his archers behind Clail's Wall, but he doubted that ribbon of waist-high farmer's drystone would give a warhorse anything more than a little light exercise.

The sad fact was a flat expanse of barley didn't offer much help. Except to the enemy, of course. No doubt they were delighted.

It was an irony Calder hadn't missed that his father was the one who'd smoothed off this ground. Who'd broken up the little farms in this valley and a lot of others. Pulled up the hedgerows and filled in the ditches so there could be more crops grown, and taxes paid, and soldiers fed. Rolled out a golden carpet of welcome to the matchless Union cavalry.

Calder could just make out, against the dim fells on the far side of the valley, a black wave through the black sea of barley, sharpened metal glimmering at the crest. He found himself thinking about Seff. Her face coming up so sharp it caught his breath. He wondered if he'd see that face again, if he'd live to kiss his child. Then the soft thoughts were crushed under the drumming of hooves as the enemy broke into a trot. The shrill calls of officers as they struggled to keep the ranks closed, to keep hundreds of tons of horseflesh lined up in one unstoppable mass.

Calder glanced over to the left. Not too far off the ground sloped up towards Skarling's Finger, the crops giving way to thin grass. Much better ground, but it belonged to that flaking bastard Tenways. He glanced over to the right. A gentler upward slope, Clail's Wall hugging the middle, then disappearing out of sight as the ground dropped away to the stream. Beyond the stream, he knew, were woods full of more Union troops, eager to charge into the flank of his threadbare little line and rip it to tatters. But enemies Calder couldn't see were far from his most pressing problem. It was the hundreds, if not thousands, of heavily armed horsemen bearing down from dead ahead, whose treasured flags he'd just pissed on, that were demanding his attention. His eyes flickered over that tide of cavalry, details starting from the darkness now, hints of faces, of shields, lances, polished armour.

'Arrows?' grunted White-Eye, leaning close beside him.

Best to look like he had some idea how far bowshot was, so he waited a moment longer before he snapped his fingers. 'Arrows.'

White-Eye roared the order and Calder heard the bowstrings behind him, shafts flickering overhead, flitting down into the crops between them and the enemy, into the enemy themselves.

Could little bits of wood and metal really do any damage to all that armoured meat, though?

The sound of them was like a storm in his face, pressing him back as they closed and quickened, streaming north towards Clail's Wall and the feeble line of Calder's men. The hooves battered the shaking land, threshed crops flung high. Calder felt a sudden need to run. A shock through him. Found he was edging back despite himself. To stand against that was mad as standing under a falling mountain.

But he found he was less afraid with every moment, and more excited. All his life he'd been dodging this, ferreting out excuses. Now he was facing it, and finding it not so terrible as he'd always feared. He bared his teeth at the dawn. Almost smiling. Almost laughing. Him, leading Carls into battle. Him, facing death. And suddenly he was standing, and spreading his arms in welcome, and roaring nothing at the top of his lungs. Him, Calder, the liar, the coward, playing the hero. You never can tell who'll be called on to fill the role.

The closer the riders came the lower they leaned over their horses, lances swinging down. The faster they moved, stretching to a lethal gallop, the slower time seemed to crawl. Calder wished he'd listened to his father when he'd talked about the ground. Talked about it with a far-off look like a man remembering a lost love. Wished he'd learned to use it like a sculptor uses stone. But he'd been busy showing off, fucking and making enemies that would dog him for the rest of his life. So yesterday evening, when he'd looked at the ground and seen it thoroughly stacked against him, he'd done what he did best.

Cheat.

The horsemen had no chance of seeing the first pit, not in that darkness and those crops. It was only a shallow trench, no more than a foot deep and a foot wide, zigzagging through the barley. Most horses went clean over it without even noticing. But a couple of unlucky ones put a hoof right in, and they went down. They went down hard, a thrashing mass of limbs, tangled straps, breaking weapons, flying dust. And where one went down, more went down behind, caught up in the wreck.

The second pit was twice as wide and twice as deep. More horses fell, snatched away as the front rank ploughed into it, one flailing man flung high, lance still in his hand. The order of the rest, already crumbling in their eagerness to get at the enemy, started to come apart altogether. Some plunged onwards. Others tried to check as they realised something was wrong, spreading confusion as another flight of arrows fell among them. They became a milling mass, almost as much of a threat to each other as they were to Calder and his men. The terrible thunder of hooves became a sorry din of scrapes and stumbles, screams and whinnies, desperate shouting.

The third pit was the biggest of all. Two of them, in fact, about as straight as a Northman could dig by darkness and angling roughly inwards. Funnelling Mitterick's men on both sides towards a gap in the centre where the precious flags were set. Where Calder was standing. Made him wonder, as he gaped at the mob of plunging horses converging on him, whether he should have found somewhere else to stand, but it was a bit late for that.

'Spears!' roared Pale-as-Snow.

'Aye,' muttered Calder, brandishing his sword as he took a few cautious steps back. 'Good idea.'

And Pale-as-Snow's picked men, who'd fought for Calder's brother and his father at Uffrith and Dunbrec, at the Cumnur and in the High Places, came up from behind the wind-blown barley five ranks deep, howling their high war cry, and their long spears made a deadly thicket, points glittering as the first sunlight crept into the valley.

Horses screamed and skidded, tumbled over, tossed their riders, driven onto the spears by the weight of those behind. A crazy chorus of shrieking steel and murdered men, tortured wood and tortured flesh. Spear shafts bent and shattered, splinters flying. A new gloom of kicked-up dirt and trampled barley dust and Calder coughing in the midst of it, sword dangling from his limp hand.

Wondering what strange convergence of mischances could have allowed this madness to happen. And what other one might allow him to get out of it alive.

Onwards and Upwards

'**D**o you suppose we could call that dawn?' asked General
Jalenhorm.

Colonel Gorst shrugged his great shoulders, battered
armour rattling faintly.

The general looked down at Retter. 'Would you call that
dawn, boy?'

Retter blinked at the sky. Over in the east, where he imagined
Osrung was though he'd never been there, the heavy clouds had
the faintest ominous tinge of brightness about their edges. 'Yes,
General.' His voice was a pathetic squeak and he cleared his
throat, rather embarrassed.

General Jalenhorm leaned close and patted his shoulder.
'There's no shame in being scared. Bravery is being scared, and
doing it anyway.'

'Yes, sir.'

'Just stay close beside me. Do your duty, and everything will
be well.'

'Yes, sir.' Though Retter was forced to wonder how doing his
duty might stop an arrow. Or a spear. Or an axe. It seemed a
mad thing to him to be climbing a hill as big as that one, with
slavering Northmen waiting for them on the slopes. Everyone
said they were slavering. But he was only thirteen, and had been
in the army for six months, and didn't know much but polishing
boots and how to sound the various manoeuvres. He wasn't even
entirely sure what the word manoeuvres meant, just pretended.
And there was nowhere safer to be than close by the general and a
proper hero like Colonel Gorst, albeit he looked nothing like a
hero and sounded like one less. There wasn't the slightest glitter
about the man, but Retter supposed if you needed a battering
ram at short notice he'd make a fair substitute.

'Very well, Retter.' Jalenhorm drew his sword. 'Sound the advance.'

'Yes, sir.' Retter carefully wet his lips with his tongue, took a deep breath and lifted his bugle, suddenly worried that he'd fumble it in his sweaty hand, that he'd blow a wrong note, that it would somehow be full of mud and produce only a miserable fart and a shower of dirty water. He had nightmares about that. Maybe this would be another. He very much hoped it would be.

But the advance rang out bright and true, tooting away as bravely as it ever had on the parade ground. 'Forward!' the bugle sang, and forward went Jalenhorm's division, and forward went Jalenhorm himself, and Colonel Gorst, and a clump of the general's staff, pennants snapping. So, with some reluctance, Retter gave his pony his heels, and clicked his tongue, and forward he went himself, hooves crunching down the bank then slopping out into the sluggish water.

He supposed he was one of the lucky ones since he got to ride. At least he'd come out of this with dry trousers. Unless he wet himself. Or got wounded in the legs. Either one of which seemed quite likely, come to think of it.

A few arrows looped over from the far bank. Exactly from where, Retter couldn't say. He was more interested in where they were going. A couple plopped harmlessly into the channels ahead. Others were lost among the ranks where they caused no apparent damage. Retter flinched as one pinged off a helmet and spun in among the marching soldiers. Everyone else had armour. General Jalenhorm had what looked like the most expensive armour in the world. It hardly seemed fair that Retter didn't have any, but the army wasn't the place for fair, he supposed.

He snatched a look back as his pony scrambled from the water and up onto a little island of sand, driftwood gathered in a pale tangle at one end. The shallows were filled with soldiers, marching up to ankles, or knees, or even waists in places. Behind them the whole long bank was covered by ranks of men waiting to follow, still more appearing over the brow behind them. It made Retter feel brave, to be one among so many. If the Northmen killed a hundred, if they killed a thousand, there would still be thousands more. He wasn't honestly sure how many a thousand was, but it was a lot.

Then it occurred to him that was all very well unless you were one of the thousand flung in a pit, in which case it wasn't very good at all, especially since he'd heard only officers got coffins, and he really didn't want to lie pressed up cold against the mud. He looked nervously towards the orchards, flinched again as an arrow clattered from a shield a dozen strides away.

'Keep up, lad!' called Jalenhorm, spurring his horse onto the next bar of shingle. They were half way across the shallows now, the great hill looming up ever steeper beyond the trees ahead.

'Sir!' Retter realised he was hunching his shoulders, pressing himself down into his saddle to make a smaller target, realised he looked a coward and forced himself straight. Over on the far bank he saw men scurrying from a patch of scrubby bushes. Ragged men with bows. The enemy, he realised. Northern skirmishers. Close enough to shout at, and be heard. So close it seemed a little silly. Like the games of chase he used to play behind the barn. He sat up taller, forced his shoulders back. They looked every bit as scared as he was. One with a shock of blond hair knelt to shoot an arrow which came down harmlessly in the sand just ahead of the front rank. Then he turned and hurried off towards the orchards.

Curly ducked into the trees along with the rest, rushed through the apple-smelling darkness bent low, heading uphill. He hopped over the felled logs and came up kneeling on the other side, peering off to the south. The sun was barely risen and the orchards were thick with shadows. He could see the metal gleaming to either side, men hidden in a long line through the trees.

'They coming?' someone asked. 'They here?'

'They're coming,' said Curly. Maybe he'd been the last to run but that was nothing much to take pride in. They'd been rattled by the sheer number of the bastards. It was like the land was made of men. Seething with 'em. Hardly seemed worth sitting there on the bank, no cover but a scraggy bush or two, just a few dozen shooting arrows at all that lot. Pointless as going at a swarm of bees with a needle. Here in the orchard was a better place to give 'em a test. Ironhead would understand that. Curly hoped to hell he would.

447

They'd got all mixed up with some folks he didn't know on the way back. A tall old-timer with a red hood was squatting by him in the dappled shadows. Probably one of Golden's boys. There was no love lost between Golden's lot and Ironhead's most of the time. Not much more'n there was between Golden and Ironhead themselves, which was less than fuck all. But right now they had other worries.

'You see the number of 'em?' someone squeaked.

'Bloody hundreds.'

'Hundreds and hundreds and hundreds and—'

'We ain't here to stop 'em,' growled Curly. 'We slow 'em, we put a couple down, we give 'em something to think about. Then, when we have to, we pull back to the Children.'

'Pull back,' someone said, sounding like it was the best idea he'd ever heard.

'When we have to!' snapped Curly over his shoulder.

'They got Northmen with 'em too,' someone said, 'some o' the Dogman's boys, I reckon.'

'Bastards,' someone grunted.

'Aye, bastards. Traitors.' The man with the red hood spat over their log. 'I heard the Bloody-Nine was with 'em.'

There was a nervy silence. That name did no favours for anyone's courage.

'The Bloody-Nine's back to the mud!' Curly wriggled his shoulders. 'Drowned. Black Dow killed him.'

'Maybe.' The man with the red hood looked grim as a gravedigger. 'But I heard he's here.'

A bowstring went right by Curly's ear and he spun around. 'What the—'

'Sorry!' A young lad, bow trembling in his hand. 'Didn't mean to, just—'

'The Bloody-Nine!' It came echoing out of the trees on their left, a mad yell, slobbering, terrified. 'The Bloody—' It cut off in a shriek, long drawn out and guttering away into a sob. Then a burst of mad laughter in the orchard ahead, making the collar prickle at Curly's sweaty neck. An animal sound. A devil sound. They all crouched there for a stretched-out moment – staring, silent, disbelieving.

'Shit on this!' someone shouted, and Curly turned just in time to see one of the lads running off through the trees.

'I ain't fighting the Bloody-Nine! I ain't!' A boy scrambling back, kicking up fallen leaves.

'Get back here, you bastards!' Curly snarled, waving his bow about, but it was too late. His head snapped around at another blubbering scream. Couldn't see where it came from but it sounded like hell, right enough.

'The Bloody-Nine!' came roaring again out of the gloom on the other side. He thought he could see shadows in the trees, flashes of steel, maybe. There were others running, right and left. Giving up good spots behind their logs without a shaft shot or a blade drawn. When he turned back, most of his lads were showing their backs. One even left his quiver behind, snagged on a bush.

'Cowards!' But there was naught Curly could do. A Chief can kick one or two boys into line, but when the lot of 'em just up and run he's helpless. Being in charge can seem like a thing iron-forged, but in the end it's just an idea everyone agrees to. By the time he ducked back behind the log everyone had stopped agreeing, and far as he could tell it was just him and the stranger with the red hood.

'There he is!' he hissed, stiffening up all of a sudden. 'It's him!'

That madman's laughter echoed through the trees again, bouncing around, coming from everywhere and nowhere. Curly nocked an arrow, his hands sticky, his bow sticky in 'em. Eyes jerking around, catching one slice of slashed-up shade then another, jagged branches and the shadows of jagged branches. The Bloody-Nine was dead, everyone knew that. What if he weren't, though?

'I don't see nothing!' His hands were shaking, but shit on it, the Bloody-Nine was just a man, and an arrow would kill him as dead as anyone else. Just a man is all he was, and Curly weren't running from one man no matter how fucking hard, no matter if the rest of 'em were running, no matter what. 'Where is he?'

'There!' hissed the man with the red hood, catching him by the shoulder and pointing off into the trees. 'There he is!'

Curly raised his bow, peering into the darkness. 'I don't— Ah!' There was a searing pain in his ribs and he let go of the string, arrow spinning off harmless into the dirt. Another searing pain, and he looked down, and he saw the man with the red hood had stabbed him. Knife hilt right up against his chest, and the hand dark with blood.

Curly grabbed a fistful of the man's shirt, twisted it. 'Wha . . .' But he didn't have the breath in him to finish, and he didn't seem to be able to take another.

'Sorry,' said the man, wincing as he stabbed him again.

Red Hat took a quick look about, make sure no one was watching, but it looked like Ironhead's boys were all too busy legging it out of the orchards and uphill towards the Children, a lot of 'em with brown trousers, more'n likely. He'd have laughed to see it if it weren't for the job he'd just had to do. He laid down the man he'd killed, patting him gently on his bloody chest as his eyes went dull, still with that slightly puzzled, slightly upset look.

'Sorry 'bout that.' A hard reckoning for a man who'd just been doing his job the best he could. Better'n most, since he'd chosen to stick when the rest had run. But that's how war is. Sometimes you're better off doing a worse job. This was the black business and there was no use crying about it. Tears'll wash no one clean, as Red Hat's old mum used to tell him.

'The Bloody-Nine!' he shrieked, broken and horror-struck as he could manage. 'He's here! He's here!' Then he gave a scream as he wiped his knife on the lad's jerkin, still squinting into the shadows for signs of other holdouts, but signs there were none.

'The Bloody-Nine!' someone roared, no more'n a dozen strides behind. Red Hat turned and stood up.

'You can stop. They've gone.'

The Dogman's grey face slid from the shadows, bow and arrows loose in one hand. 'What, all of 'em?'

Red Hat pointed down at the corpse he'd just made. 'All but a few.'

'Who'd have thought it?' The Dogman squatted beside him, a few more of his lads creeping out from the trees behind. 'The work you can get done with a dead man's name.'

'That and a dead man's laugh.'

'Colla, get back there and tell the Union the orchards are clear.'

'Aye.' And one of the others scurried off through the trees.

'How does it look up ahead?' Dogman slid over the logs and stole towards the treeline, keeping nice and low. Always careful, the Dogman, always sparing with men's lives. Sparing o' lives on both sides. Rare thing in a War Chief, and much to be applauded, for all the big songs tended to harp on spilled guts and what have you. They squatted there in the brush, in the shadows. Red Hat wondered how long the pair of 'em had spent squatting in the brush, in the shadows, in one damp corner of the North or another. Weeks on end, more'n likely. 'Don't look great, does it?'

'Not great, no,' said Red Hat.

Dogman eased his way closer to the edge of the trees and hunkered down again. 'And it looks no better from here.'

'Wasn't going to, really, was it?'

'Not really. But a man needs hope.'

The ground weren't offering much. A couple more fruit trees, a scrubby bush or two, then the bare hillside sloped up sharp ahead. Some runners were still struggling up the grass and beyond them, as the sun started throwing some light onto events, the ragged line of some digging in. Above that the tumbledown wall that ringed the Children, and above that the Children themselves.

'All crawling with Ironhead's boys, no doubt,' muttered the Dogman, speaking Red Hat's very thoughts.

'Aye, and Ironhead's a stubborn bastard. Always been tricky to shift, once he gets settled.'

'Like the pox,' said Dogman.

'And about as welcome.'

'Reckon the Union'll need more'n dead heroes to get up there.'

'Reckon they'll need a few living ones too.'

'Aye.'

'Aye.' Red Hat shielded his eyes with one hand, realised too late he'd got blood stuck all over the side of his face. He thought he could see a big man standing up on the diggings below the Children, shouting at the stragglers as they fled. Could just hear his bellowing voice. Not quite the words, but the tone spoke plenty.

Dogman was grinning. 'He don't sound happy.'

'Nope,' said Red Hat, grinning too. As his old mum used to say, there's no music so sweet as an enemy's despair.

'You fucking coward bastards!' snarled Irig, and he kicked the last of 'em on the arse as he went past, bent over and gasping from the climb, knocked him on his face in the muck. Better'n he deserved. Lucky he only got Irig's boot, rather'n his axe.

'Fucking bastard cowards!' sneered Temper at a higher pitch, and kicked the coward in the arse again as he started to get up.

'Ironhead's boys don't run!' snarled Irig, and he kicked the coward in the side and rolled him over.

'Ironhead's boys never run!' And Temper kicked the lad in the fruits as he tried to scramble off and made him squeal.

'But the Bloody-Nine's down there!' shouted another, his face milk pale and his eyes wide as shit-pits, cringing like a babe. A worried muttering followed the name, rippling through the boys all waiting behind the ditch. 'The Bloody-Nine. The Bloody-Nine? The Bloody-Nine. The—'

'*Fuck*,' snarled Irig, 'the Bloody-Nine!'

'Aye,' hissed Temper. 'Fuck him. Fucking fuck him!'

'Did you even see him?'

'Well . . . no, I mean, not myself, but—'

'If he ain't dead, which he is, and if he's got the bones, which he don't, he can come up here.' And Irig leaned close to the lad, and tickled him under the chin with the spike on the end of his axe. 'And he can deal with me.'

'Aye!' Temper was nearly shrieking it, veins popping out his head. 'He can come up here and deal with . . . with him! With Irig! That's right! Ironhead's going to hang you bastards for running! Like he hung Crouch, and cut his guts out for treachery, he'll fucking do the same to you, he will, and we'll—'

'You think you're helping?' snapped Irig.

'Sorry, Chief.'

'You want names? We got Cairm Ironhead up there at the Children. And at his back on the Heroes, we got Cracknut Whirrun, and Caul Shivers, and Black Dow his bloody self, for that matter—'

'Up there,' someone muttered.

'Who said that?' shrieked Temper. 'Who fucking well said—'

'Any man who stands now,' Irig held up his axe and gave it a shake with each word, since he'd often found a shaken axe adds an edge to the bluntest of arguments, 'and does his part, he'll get his place at the fire and his place in the songs. Any man runs from this spot here, well,' and Irig spat onto the curled-up coward next to his boot. 'I won't put Ironhead to the trouble o' passing judgement, I'll just give you to the axe, and there's an end on it.'

'An end!' shrieked Temper.

'Chief.' Someone was tugging at his arm.

'Can't you see I'm trying to—' snarled Irig, spinning around. 'Shit.'

Never mind the Bloody-Nine. The Union were coming.

'Colonel, you must dismount.'

Vinkler smiled. Even that was an effort. 'Couldn't possibly.'

'Sir, really, this is no time for heroics.'

'Then . . .' Vinkler glanced across the massed ranks of men emerging from the fruit trees to either side. 'When is the time, exactly?'

'Sir—'

'The bloody leg just won't manage it.' Vinkler winced as he touched his thigh. Even the weight of his hand on it was agonising now.

'Is it bad, sir?'

'Yes, Sergeant, I think it's quite bad.' He was no surgeon, but he was twenty years a soldier and well knew the meaning of stinking dressings and a mottling of purple-red bruises about a wound. He had, in all honesty, been surprised to wake at all this morning.

'Perhaps you should retire and see the surgeon, sir—'

'I have a feeling the surgeons will be very busy today. No, Sergeant, thank you, but I'll press on.' Vinkler turned his horse with a twitch of the reins, worried that the man's concern would cause his courage to weaken. He needed all the courage he had. 'Men of his Majesty's Thirteenth!' He drew his sword and directed its point towards the scattering of stones high above them. 'Forward!' And with his good heel he urged his horse up onto the slope.

He was the only mounted man in the whole division now, as far as he could tell. The rest of the officers, General Jalenhorm and Colonel Gorst among them, had left their horses in the orchard and were proceeding on foot. Only a complete fool would have chosen to ride up a hill as steep as this one, after all. Only a fool, or the hero from an unlikely storybook, or a dead man.

The irony was that it hadn't even been much of a wound. He'd been run through at Ulrioch, all those years ago, and Lord Marshal Varuz had visited him in the hospital tent, and pressed his sweaty hand with an expression of deep concern, and said something about bravery which Vinkler had often wished he could remember. But to everyone's surprise, his own most of all, he had lived. Perhaps that was why he had thought nothing of a little nick on the thigh. Now it gave every appearance of having killed him.

'Bloody appearances,' he forced through gritted teeth. The only thing for it was to smile through the agony. That's what a soldier was meant to do. He had written all the necessary letters and supposed that was something. His wife had always worried there would be no goodbye.

Rain was starting to flit down. He could feel the odd spot against his face. His horse's hooves were slipping on the short grass and it tossed and snorted, making him grimace as his leg was jolted. Then a flight of arrows went up ahead. A great number of arrows. Then they began to curve gracefully downwards, falling from on high.

'Oh, bloody hell.' He narrowed his eyes and hunched his shoulders instinctively as a man might stepping from a porch into a hailstorm. Some of them dropped down around him, sticking silently into the turf to either side. He heard clanks and rattles behind as they bounced from shields or armour. He heard a shriek, followed by another. Shouting. Men hit.

Damned if he was going to just sit there. 'Yah!' And Vinkler gave his horse the spurs, wincing as it lurched up the hill, well ahead of his men. He stopped perhaps twenty strides from the enemy's earthworks. He could see the archers peering down, their bows picked out black against the sky, which was starting to darken again, drizzle prickling at Vinkler's helmet. He was terribly close. An absurdly easy target. More arrows whizzed past him. With a great effort he turned in his saddle and, lips curled back against the pain, stood in his stirrups, raising his sword.

'Men of the Thirteenth! At the double now! Have you somewhere else to be?'

A few soldiers fell as more arrows whipped past into the front rank, but the rest gave a hearty roar and broke into something close to a run, which was a damned fine testament to their spirit after the march they'd already had.

Vinkler became aware of an odd sensation in his throbbing leg, looked down, and was surprised to see an arrow poking from his dead thigh. He burst out laughing. 'That's my least vulnerable spot, you bloody arseholes!' he roared at the Northmen on the earthworks. The foremost of his charging men were level with him now, pounding up the hill, yelling.

An arrow stuck deep into his horse's neck. It reared, and Vinkler bounced in his saddle, only just keeping hold of the reins, which proved a waste of time anyway as his mount tottered sideways, twisted, fell. There was an almighty thud.

Vinkler tried to shake the dizziness from his head. He tried to look about him but was trapped beneath his horse. Worse yet, it seemed he had crushed one of his soldiers and the man's spear had run him through as he fell. The bloody blade of it was poking through Vinkler's hip now, just under his breastplate. He gave a helpless sigh. It seemed that, wherever you put armour, you never had it where you needed it.

'Dear, dear,' he said, looking down at the broken arrow-shaft protruding from his leg, the spear-point from his hip. 'What a mess.' It hardly hurt, that was the strange thing. Maybe that was a bad sign, though. Probably. Boots were thumping at the dirt all around him as his men charged up the hill. 'On you go, boys,' waving one hand weakly. They would have to make it the rest of the way without him. He looked towards the earthworks, not far off. Not far off at all. He saw a wild-haired man perched there, bow levelled at him.

'Oh, damn,' he said.

Temper shot at the bastard who'd been on the horse. He was flattened under it, and no danger to no one, but a man acting

455

that bloody fearless within shot of Temper's bow was an insult to his aim. As luck had it, luck being a fickle little shit, his elbow got jogged just as he was letting go the string and he shot his shaft off high into the air.

He snatched at another arrow, but by then things were getting a bit messy. A bit more'n a bit. The Union were up to the ditch they'd dug and the earth wall they'd thrown up, and Temper wished now they'd dug it a deal deeper and thrown it up a deal higher, 'cause there were a bloody lot of Southerners crowding round it, and plenty more on the way.

Irig's boys were packed in on the packed earth, jabbing down with spears, doing a lot of shouting. Temper saw a fair few spears jabbing the other way too. He went up on tiptoes trying to see, then lurched out the way of Irig's axe as it flashed past his nose. Once his blood was going that big bastard didn't care much who got caught on the backswing.

A Northman staggered past, tangling with Temper and nearly dragging him over, scrabbling at his chest as blood bubbled through his torn chain mail. A Union man sprang up onto the earth-wall in the gap he'd left like he was on a bloody spring. A neckless bastard with a great heavy jaw and hard brows wrinkled over hard little eyes. No helmet but thick plates of scuffed armour on the rest of him, shield in one hand, heavy sword in the other already dark with blood.

Temper stumbled away from him, since he only had his bow to hand and had always liked to keep fighting at a polite distance anyway, making way for a more willing Carl whose sword was already swinging. Neckless seemed off balance, the blade sure to take his head right off, but in one quick movement he blocked it with a clang of steel, and blood showered, and the Carl reeled back onto his face. Before he was still, Neckless had hit another man so hard he took him right off his feet, turned him over in the air and sent him tumbling down the hillside.

Temper scrambled back up the slope, mouth wide open and salty with someone's blood, sure he was looking the Great Leveller in the face at last, and an ugly face it was, too. Then Irig came rushing from the side, axe following close behind.

Neckless went down hard, a great dent smashed into his shield. Temper hooted with laughter but the Union man only went down as far as his knees would bend then burst straight back up, flinging Irig's great bulk away and slicing him across the guts all in one motion, sending him staggering, blood spraying from his chain mail coat, eyes popping more with shock than pain. Just couldn't believe he'd been done so easy, and neither could Temper. How could a man run up that hill and still move so hard and so fast at the top of it?

'It's the Bloody-Nine!' someone wailed, though it bloody obviously weren't the Bloody-Nine at all. He was causing quite a bloody panic all the same. Another Carl went at him with a spear and he slid around it, sword crashing down and leaving a mighty dent in the middle of the Carl's helmet, folding him on his face, arms and legs thrashing mindless in the mud.

Temper gritted his teeth, raised his bow, took a careful bead on the neckless bastard, but just as Temper let go the string Irig pushed himself up, clutching his bloody guts with one hand while he raised his axe in the other. Luck being luck, he got himself right in the way of the arrow and it took him in the shoulder, made him grunt.

The Union man's eyes flicked sideways, and his sword flicked out with 'em and took Irig's arm off just like that, and almost before the blood began to spurt from the stump the blade lashed back the other way and ripped a bloody gash in his chest, back the other way and laid Irig's head wide open between his mouth and his nose, top teeth snatched through the air and off down the hill.

Neckless crouched there still, dented shield up in front, sword up behind, big face all spotted with red and his eyes ahead, calm as a fisherman waiting for a tug on the line. Four carved Northmen dead as ever a man could be at his feet and Irig toppling gently sideways and into the ditch, even deader.

He might as well have been the Bloody-Nine, this neckless bastard, Carls falling over 'emselves to get away from him. More Union men started to pull themselves up to either side, over the earth wall in numbers, and the shift backwards became a run.

Temper went with 'em, as eager as any. He caught an elbow in the neck from someone, slipped over and slapped his chin on the grass, gave his tongue an awful bite, scrambled up and ran on, men shouting and shrieking all around. He snatched one desperate look back, saw Neckless hack down a running Carl calmly as you might swat a fly. Beside him a tall Union man in a bright breastplate was pointing towards Temper with a drawn blade, shouting at the top of his voice.

'On!' roared Jalenhorm, waving his sword towards the Children. Bloody hell, he was out of breath. 'Up! Up!' They had to keep the momentum. Gorst had opened the gate a crack, and they had to push through before it closed. 'On! On!' He bent down, offering his hand to haul men over the ditch and slapping them on the back as they laboured off uphill again.

It looked as if the fleeing Northmen were causing chaos at the drystone wall above, tangling with the defenders there, spreading panic, letting the foremost of Jalenhorm's men clamber up after them without resistance. As soon as he had the breath to do it he followed himself, lurching up the steep slope. He had to push on.

Bodies. Bodies, and wounded men scattered on the grass. A Northman stared at him, bloody hands clapped to the top of his head. A Union soldier clutched dumbly at his oozing thigh. A soldier running just beside him made a hiccupping sound and fell on his back, and when Jalenhorm glanced over his shoulder he saw the man had an arrow in his face. He could not stop for him. Could only press on, swallowing a sudden wave of nausea. His own thudding heartbeat and his own whooshing breath damped the war cries and the clashes of metal down to an endless nagging rattle. The thickening drizzle was far from helping, turning the trampled grass slippery slick. The world jumped and wobbled, full of running men, slipping and sliding men, occasional whirring arrows, flying grass and mud.

'On,' he grunted, 'on.' No one could have heard him. It was himself he was ordering. 'On.' This was his one chance at redemption. If they could only capture the summit. Break the Northmen where they were strongest. 'Up. Up.' Then nothing else would matter. He would be no longer the king's incompetent old drinking partner, who fumbled his command on the first day. He would have finally earned his place. 'On,' he wheezed, 'up!'

He pushed on, bent over, clawing at the wet grass with his free hand, so intent on the ground that the wall caught him by surprise. He stood, waving his sword uncertainly, not sure whether it would be held by his men or the enemy, or what he should do about it in either case. Someone reached down with a gloved hand. Gorst. Jalenhorm found himself hauled up with shocking ease, scrambled over the damp stones and onto the flat top of the spur.

The Children stood just ahead. Much larger at close quarters than he had imagined, a circle of rough-hewn rocks a little higher than a man. There were more bodies here, but fewer than on the slopes below. It seemed resistance had been light and, for the moment at least, had disappeared altogether. Union soldiers stood about in various stages of exhausted confusion. Beyond them the hill sloped up towards the summit. Towards the Heroes themselves. A gentler incline, and covered with retreating Northmen. More of an organised withdrawal than a rout this time, from what Jalenhorm could gather at a glance.

A glance was all he could manage. With no immediate peril, his body sagged. He stood for a moment, hands on his knees, chest heaving, belly squeezing uncomfortably against the inside of his wondrous breastplate with every in-breath. Damn thing didn't bloody fit him any more. It had never bloody fit him.

'The Northmen are falling back!' Gorst's weird falsetto jangled in Jalenhorm's ears. 'We must pursue!'

'General! We should regroup.' One of Jalenhorm's staff, his armour beaded with wet. 'We're well ahead of the second wave. Too far ahead.' He gestured towards Osrung, shrouded now in the thickening rain. 'And Northern cavalry have attacked the Stariksa Regiment, they're bogged down on our right—'

Jalenhorm managed to straighten up. 'The Aduan Volunteers?'

'Still in the orchard, sir!'

'We're getting split up from our support—' chimed in another.

Gorst waved them angrily away, his piping voice making a ludicrous contrast with his blood-spotted aspect. He barely even looked out of breath. 'Damn the support! We press on!'

'General, sir, Colonel Vinkler is dead, the men are exhausted, we must pause!'

Jalenhorm stared up at the summit, chewing at his lip. Seize the moment, or wait for support? He saw the spears of the

Northmen against the darkening sky. Gorst's eager, red-speckled face. The clean, nervous ones of his staff. He winced, looked at the handful of men to hand, then shook his head. 'We will hold here a little while for reinforcements. Secure this position and gather our strength.'

Gorst had the expression of a boy who had been told he could not have a puppy this year. 'But, General—'

Jalenhorm put a hand on his shoulder. 'I share your eagerness, Bremer, believe me, but not everyone can run for ever. Black Dow is ready, and cunning, and this retreat might only be a ruse. I do not intend to be fooled by him a second time.' He squinted up, the clouds getting steadily angrier above them. 'The weather is against us. As soon as we have the numbers, we must attack.' They might not be resting long. Union soldiers were flooding over the wall now, choking the stone circle.

'Where's Retter?'

'Here, sir,' called the lad. He looked pale, and scared, but so did they all.

Jalenhorm smiled to see him. There, indeed, was a hero. 'Sound the assembly, boy, and ready on the advance.'

They could not be reckless, but nor could they afford to waste the initiative. This was their one chance at redemption. Jalenhorm stared yearningly up at the Heroes, rain tinkling on his helmet. So very near. The last Northmen were swarming up the slopes towards the top. One stood, looking back through the rain.

Ironhead frowned back towards the Children, already riddled with Union soldiers.

'Shit,' he hissed.

Hurt him to do this. He'd a hard-won name for never giving ground, but he hadn't won it in fights he was sure to lose. He wasn't about to face the might of the Union on his own just so men could blow their noses and say Cairm Ironhead died bravely. He'd no plans to follow after Whitesides, or Littlebone, or Old Man Yawl. They'd all died bravely, and who sang about those bastards these days?

'Pull back!' he bellowed at the last of his men, urging 'em between the planted stakes and up towards the Heroes. A shameful thing to show your back to the enemy, but better their eyes on your back than their spears in your front. If Black Dow wanted to fight for this worthless hill and these worthless stones he could do it his worthless self.

He strode up frowning through the thickening rain, through the gap in the mossy wall that ringed the Heroes. He walked slow, shoulders back and head high, hoping folk would think this was all well planned and he'd done nothing the least bit cowardly—

'Well, well, well. Who should I find running away from the Union but Cairm Ironhead?' Who else but Glama Golden, the swollen prick, leaning against one of the great stones with a big, fat smile on his big, bruised face.

By the dead, how Ironhead hated this bastard. Those big puffy cheeks. That moustache, like a pair of yellow slugs on his fat top lip. Ironhead's skin crawled at the sight of him. The sight of him smug made him want to tear his own eyes out. 'Pulling back,' he growled.

'Showing back, I'd call it.'

That got a few laughs, but they sputtered out as Ironhead came forwards, baring his teeth. Golden took a careful step back, narrowed eyes flickering down to Ironhead's drawn sword, hand dropping to his own axe, making ready.

Then Ironhead stopped himself. He hadn't got his name by letting anger tug him about by the nose. There was a right time to settle this, and a right way, and it wasn't now, standing on even terms with all kinds of witnesses. No. He'd wait for his moment, and make sure he enjoyed it too. So he forced his face into a smile of his own. 'We can't all have your record of bravery, Glama Golden. Takes some bones to batter a man's fist with your face the way you did.'

'Least I fucking fought, didn't I?' snarled Golden, his Carls bristling up around him.

'If you can call it fighting when a man just falls off his horse then runs away.'

Golden's turn to bare his teeth. 'You dare talk to me about running away, you cowardly—'

'Enough.' Black Dow had Curnden Craw on his left, Caul Shivers on his right and Cracknut Whirrun just behind. That and a whole crowd of heavy-armed, heavy-scarred, heavy-scowled Carls. A fearsome company, but the look on Dow's face was more fearsome still. He was rigid with rage, eyes bulging as if they might burst. 'This what you call Named Men these days? A pair o' great big names with a pair o' sulking *children* hiding inside?' Dow curled his tongue and blew spit onto the mud between Ironhead and Golden. 'Rudd Threetrees was a stubborn bastard, and Bethod a sly bastard, and the Bloody-Nine an evil bastard, the dead know that, but there are times I miss 'em. Those were *men!*' He roared the word in Ironhead's face, spraying spit and making everyone flinch. 'They said a thing, they *did a fucking thing!*'

Ironhead thought it best to make a second quick retreat, eyes on Black Dow's ready weapons just in case an even quicker one was needful. He was no keener on that fight than he was on the one with the Union. Even less, if anything, but luckily Golden couldn't resist sticking his broken nose in.

'I'm with you, Chief!' he piped up. 'With you all the way!'

'Is that right?' Dow turned to him, mouth curling with contempt. 'Oh, lucky *fucking* me!' And he shouldered Golden out of his way and led his men towards the wall.

When Ironhead turned back he found Curnden Craw giving him a look from under his grey brows. 'What?' he snapped.

Craw just kept giving him that look. 'You know what.'

He shook his head as he brushed between Ironhead and Golden. They were a sorry excuse for a pair of War Chiefs. For a pair of men, for that matter, but Craw had seen worse. Selfishness, cowardice and greed never surprised him these days. Those were the times.

'Pair o' fucking worms!' Dow hissed into the drizzle as Craw came up beside him. He clawed at the old drystone, tore loose a rock and stood, every muscle flexed, lips twisting and moving with no sound as if he didn't know whether to fling it down the slope or stave in someone's skull with it or smash his own face with it or what. In the end he just gave a frustrated snarl, and put it helplessly back on top of the wall. 'I should kill 'em. Maybe I will. Maybe I will. Burn the fucking pair.'

Craw winced. 'Don't know they'd take a flame in this weather,

Chief.' He peered down through the shroud of rain towards the Children. 'And I reckon there'll be killing enough for everyone soon.' The Union had fearsome numbers down there and, from what he could tell, they were finding their order. Forming ranks. Lots and lots of close-packed ranks. 'Looks like they're coming on.'

'Why wouldn't they? Ironhead good as invited the bastards.' Dow took a scowling breath and snorted it out like a bull ready to charge, breath smoking in the wet. 'You'd think it'd be easy being Chief.' He shifted his shoulders like the chain sat too heavy on 'em. 'But it's like dragging a fucking mountain through the muck. Threetrees told me that. Told me every leader stands alone.'

'Ground's still with us.' Craw thought he should have a stab at building up the positive. 'And this rain'll help too.'

Dow only frowned down at his free hand, fingers spread. 'Once they're bloody . . .'

'Chief!' Some lad was forcing his way through the crowd of sodden Carls, shoulders of his jerkin dark with damp. 'Chief! Reachey's hard pressed down in Osrung! They're over the bridge and fighting in the streets and he needs someone to lend a— Gah!'

Dow grabbed him around the back of his neck, jerked him roughly forward and steered his face towards the Children and the Union men swarming over 'em like ants on a trodden nest. 'Do I look like I've got fucking men to spare? Well? What do you reckon?'

The lad swallowed. 'No, Chief.'

Dow shoved him tottering back and Craw managed to stick out a hand and catch him 'fore he fell. 'Tell Reachey to hold on best he can,' Dow tossed over his shoulder. 'Might be some help will come along.'

'I'll tell him.' And the lad backed off quick and was soon lost in the press.

The Heroes was left a strange, funeral quiet. Only the odd mutter, the faint clatter of gear, the soft ping and patter of rain on metal. Down at the Children, someone was tooting on a horn. Seemed a mournful little tune, somehow, floating up out of the rain. Or maybe it was just a tune, and Craw was the mournful one. Wondering who out of all these men around him would kill before the sun was set, and who get killed. Wondering which of them had the Great Leveller's cold hand on their shoulder. Wondering if he did. He closed his eyes, and made himself a promise that if he got through this he'd retire. Just like he had a dozen times before.

'Looks like it's time.' Wonderful was holding out her hand.

'Aye.' Craw took it, and shook it, and looked her in the face, her jaw set hard, her stubbly hair black in the wet, line of the long scar white down the side. 'Don't die, eh?'

'I'm not planning on it. Stick close and I'll try not to let you die either.'

'Deal.' And they were all grabbing each other's hands, and slapping each other's shoulders, that last moment of comradeship before the blood, when you feel bound together closer than with your own family. Craw clasped hands with Flood, and with Scorry, and with Drofd, and Shivers, even, and he found himself seeking among strangers for Brack's big paw to shake, then realised he was under the sod behind 'em.

'Craw.' Jolly Yon, and clear from his sorry look what he was after.

'Aye, Yon. I'll tell 'em. You know I will.'

'I know.' And they clasped hands, and Yon had a twitch to the corner of his mouth might've been a smile for him. All the while Beck just stood there, dark hair plastered to pale forehead, staring down towards the Children like he was staring at nothing.

Craw took the lad's hand and gave it a squeeze. 'Just do what's right. Stand with your crew, stand with your Chief.' He leaned a little closer. 'Don't get killed.'

Beck squeezed back. 'Aye. Thanks, Chief.'

'Where's Whirrun?'

'Never fear!' And he came shouldering through the wet and unhappy throng. 'Whirrun of Bligh stands among you!'

For reasons known only to himself he'd taken his shirt off and was standing stripped to his waist, Father of Swords over one shoulder. 'By the dead,' muttered Craw. 'Every time we fight you're bloody wearing less.'

Whirrun tipped his head back and blinked into the rain. 'I'm not wearing a shirt in this. A wet shirt only chafes my nipples.'

Wonderful shook her head. 'All part of the hero's mystery.'

'That too.' Whirrun grinned. 'How about it, Wonderful? Does a wet shirt chafe your nipples? I need to know.'

She shook his hand. 'You worry about your nipples, Cracknut, I'll handle mine.'

Everything was bright now, and still, and quiet. Water gleaming on armour, furs curled up with wet, bright painted shields beaded with dew. Faces flashed at Craw, known and unknown. Grinning, stern, crazy, afraid. He held out his hand, and Whirrun pressed it in his own, grinning with every tooth. 'You ready?'

Craw always had his doubts. Ate 'em, breathed 'em, lived 'em twenty years or more. Hardly a moment free of the bastards. Every day since he buried his brothers.

But now was no time for doubts. 'I'm ready.' And he drew his sword, and looked down towards the Union men, hundreds upon hundreds, blurring in the rain to spots and splashes and glints of colour, and he smiled. Maybe Whirrun was right, and a man ain't really alive until he faces death. Craw raised his sword up high, and he gave a howl, and all around him men did the same.

And they waited for the Union to come.

More Tricks

The sun had to be up somewhere but you'd never have known it. The angry clouds had thickened and the light was still poor. Positively beggarly, in fact. As far as Corporal Tunny could tell, and somewhat to his surprise, no one had moved. The helmets and spears still showed above the stretch of wall that he could see, shifting a little from time to time but going nowhere fast. Mitterick's attack was well underway. That much they could hear. But on this forgotten far end of the battle, the Northmen waited.

'Are they still there?' asked Worth. Waiting for action like this got most men shitting themselves. Worth was unique, in that it seemed it was the one thing that could stop him.

'They're still there.'

'Not moving?' squeaked Yolk.

'If they were moving we'd be moving, wouldn't we?' Tunny peered through his eyeglass once again. 'No. They're not moving.'

'Is that fighting I can hear?' muttered Worth, as a gust of wind brought the echoing of angry men, horses and metal across the stream.

'It's that or it's a serious disagreement in a stable. Do you think it's a disagreement in a stable?'

'No, Corporal Tunny.'

'No. Neither do I.'

'Then what's going on?' asked Yolk. A riderless horse appeared from over the rise, stirrups flapping at its flanks, trotted down towards the water, stopped and started nibbling at the grass.

Tunny lowered his eyeglass. 'Honestly, I'm not sure.' All around them, rain tapped at the leaves.

*

The trampled barley was scattered with dead and dying horses, dead and dying men. In front of Calder and his stolen standards they were heaped up in a bloody tangle. Only a few strides away, three Carls were arguing with each other as they tried to free their spears, all impaled in the same Union rider. A few boys had been sent scurrying out to gather spent arrows. A couple more had been unable to resist clambering into the third pit to get an early start at picking over the bodies there, and White-Eye was roaring at them to get back into line.

The Union cavalry were all done. A brave effort, but a stupid one. It seemed to Calder the two often went together. To make matters worse, having failed once they'd insisted on giving it another try, still more doomed. Three score or so had jumped the third pit on the right, managed to get over Clail's Wall and kill a few archers before they were shot or speared themselves. All pointless as mopping a beach. That was the trouble with pride, and courage, and all those clench-jawed virtues bards love to harp on. The more you have, the more likely you are to end up bottom in a pile of dead men. All the Union's bravest had achieved was to give Calder's men the biggest boost to their spirits they'd had since Bethod was King of the Northmen.

They were letting the Union know it, now, as the survivors rode, or limped, or crawled back towards their lines. They danced about, and clapped and whooped into the drizzle. They shook each others' hands, and thumped each other's backs, and clashed their shields together. They chanted Bethod's name, and Scale's, and even quite frequently Calder's, which was gratifying. The comradeship of warriors, who would've thought? He grinned around as men cheered and brandished their weapons at him, held up his sword and gave it a wave in return. He wondered whether it was too late to smear a bit of blood on the blade, since he hadn't quite got around to swinging it. There was plenty of blood about and he doubted its previous owners would miss it now.

'Chief?'

'Eh?'

Pale-as-Snow was pointing off to the south. 'Might want to pull 'em back into position.'

The rain was getting weightier, fat drops leaving the earth

spattered with dark spots, pinging from the armour of the living and the dead. It had drawn a misty haze across the battlefield to the south, but beyond the riderless horses aimlessly wandering, and the horseless riders stumbling back towards the Old Bridge, Calder thought he could see shapes moving in the barley.

He shielded his eyes with one hand. More and more emerged from the rain, turning from ghosts to flesh and metal. Union foot. Vast blocks of them, trampling forward in carefully measured, well-ordered, dreadfully purposeful ranks, pole-arms held high, flags struck limp by the wet.

Calder's men had seen them too, and their triumphant jeering was already a memory. The barking voices of Named Men rang through the rain, bringing them grimly back to their places behind the third pit. White-Eye was marshalling some of the lightly wounded to fight as a reserve and plug any holes. Calder wondered if they'd be plugging holes in him before the day was out. It looked a good bet.

'Don't suppose you've got any more tricks?' asked Pale-as-Snow.

'Not really.' Unless you counted running like hell. 'You?'

'Just the one.' And the old warrior carefully wiped the blood from his sword with a rag and held it up.

'Oh.' Calder looked down at his own clean blade, glistening with beads of water. 'That.'

The Tyranny of Distance

'**I** can't see a damn thing!' hissed Finree's father, taking a stride forwards and peering through his eyeglass again, presumably to no more effect than before. 'Can you?'

'No, sir,' grumbled one of his staff, unhelpfully.

They had witnessed Mitterick's premature charge in stunned silence. Then, as the first light crawled across the valley, the start of Jalenhorm's advance. Then the drizzle had begun. First Osrung had disappeared in the grey pall on the right, then Clail's Wall on the left, then the Old Bridge and the nameless inn where Finree had almost died yesterday. Now even the shallows were half-remembered ghosts. Everyone stood silent, paralysed with anxiety, straining for sounds that would occasionally tickle at the edge of hearing, over the damp whisper of the rain. For all that they could see now, there might as well have been no battle at all.

Finree's father paced back and forth, the fingers of one hand fussing at nothing. He came to stand beside her, staring off into the featureless grey. 'I sometimes think there isn't a person in the world more powerless than a supreme commander on a battle-field,' he muttered.

'How about his daughter?'

He gave her a tight smile. 'Are you all right?'

She thought about smiling back but gave up on it. 'I'm fine,' she lied, and quite transparently too. Apart from the very real pain through her neck whenever she turned her head, down her arm whenever she used her hand, and across her scalp all the time, she still felt a constant, suffocating worry. Time and again she would startle, staring about like a miser for his lost purse, but with no idea what she was even looking for. 'You have far more important things to worry about—'

As if to prove her point he was already striding away to meet a messenger, riding up towards the barn from the east. 'News?'

'Colonel Brock reports that his men have begun their attack on the bridge in Osrung!' Hal was in the fight, then. Leading from the front, no doubt. She felt herself sweating more than ever under her clothes, the damp beneath Hal's coat meeting the damp leaking through from above in a crescendo of chafing discomfort. 'Colonel Brint, meanwhile, is leading an assault against the savages who yesterday . . .' His eyes flickered nervously to Finree, and back. 'Against the savages.'

'And?' asked her father.

'That is all, Lord Marshal.'

He grimaced. 'My thanks. Please, bring further news when you are able.'

The messenger saluted, turned his horse and galloped off through the rain.

'No doubt your husband is distinguishing himself enormously in the assault.' Bayaz leaned beside her on his staff, bald pate glistening with moisture. 'Leading from the front, in the style of Harod the Great. A latter-day hero! I've always had the greatest admiration for men of that stamp.'

'Perhaps you should try it yourself.'

'Oh, I have. I was quite the firebrand in my youth. But an unquenchable thirst for danger is unseemly in the old. Heroes have their uses, but someone has to point them the right way. And clean up afterwards. They always raise a cheer from the public, but they leave a hell of a mess.' Bayaz thoughtfully patted his stomach. 'No, a cup of tea at the rear is more my style. Men like your husband can gather the plaudits.'

'You are far too generous.'

'Few indeed would agree.'

'But where is your tea now?'

Bayaz frowned at his empty hand. 'My servant has . . . more important errands to run this morning.'

'Can there be anything more important than attending to your whims?'

'Oh, my whims stretch beyond the kettle . . .'

Hoofbeats echoed out of the rain, a lone rider thumping up

the track from the west, everyone straining breathlessly to see as a chinless frown emerged from the wet gloom.

'Felnigg!' snapped Finree's father. 'What's happening on the left?'

'Mitterick bloody well went off half-drawn!' frothed Felnigg as he swung from the saddle. 'Sent his cavalry across the barley in the dark! Pure bloody recklessness!'

Knowing the state of the relationship between the two men, Finree suspected Felnigg had made his own contribution to the fiasco.

'We saw,' her father forced through tight lips, evidently coming to a similar conclusion.

'The man should be bloody drummed out!'

'Perhaps later. What was the outcome?'

'It was . . . still in doubt when I left.'

'So you haven't the slightest idea what's going on over there?'

Felnigg opened his mouth, then closed it. 'I thought it best to return at once—'

'And report Mitterick's mistake, rather than inform me of its consequences. My thanks, Colonel, but I am already amply supplied with ignorance.' And her father turned his back before Felnigg had the chance to speak, striding across the hillside again to look fruitlessly to the north. 'Shouldn't have sent them,' she heard him mutter as he squelched past. 'Should never have sent them.'

Bayaz sighed, the sound niggling at her sweaty shoulders like a corkscrew. 'I sympathise most deeply with your father.'

Finree was finding that her admiration for the First of the Magi was steadily fading, while her dislike only sharpened with time. 'Do you,' she said, in the same way one would say, 'Shut up,' and with the same meaning.

If Bayaz took it he ignored it. 'Such a shame we cannot see the little people struggle from afar. There is nothing quite like looking down upon a battle, and this is a large one, even in my experience. But the weather answers to no one.' Bayaz grinned up into the increasingly solemn heavens. 'A veritable storm! What drama, eh? What better accompaniment to a clash of arms?'

'Did you call it up yourself just for the atmosphere?'

'I wish I had the power. Only imagine, there could be thunder whenever I approached! In the Old Time my master, great Juvens, could call down lightning with a word, make a river flood with a gesture, summon a hoar frost with a thought. Such was the power of his Art.' And he spread his hands wide, tipping his face into the rain and raising his staff towards the streaming heavens. 'But that was long ago.' He let his arms drop. 'These days the winds blow their own way. Like battles. We who remain must work in a more . . . roundabout fashion.'

More hoofbeats, and a dishevelled young officer cantered from the murk ahead.

'Report!' demanded Felnigg at great volume, making Finree wonder how he had lasted so long without being punched in the face.

'Jalenhorm's men have flushed the enemy from the orchards,' answered the messenger breathlessly, 'and are climbing the slope at the double!'

'How far have they gone?' asked Finree's father.

'When I last saw them they were well on the way up to the smaller stones. The Children. But whether or not they were able to take them—'

'Heavy resistance?'

'Becoming heavier.'

'When did you leave them?'

'I rode here with all despatch, sir, so perhaps a quarter of an hour ago?'

Finree's father bared his teeth at the downpour. The outline of the hill the Heroes stood on was little more than a darker smudge in a curtain of grey. She could follow his thoughts. By now they might have captured the summit in glory, be engaged in furious combat, or have been bloodily driven off. Anyone or no one alive or dead, victorious or defeated. He spun on his heel. 'Saddle my horse!'

Bayaz' smugness was snuffed out like a candle flame. 'I would advise against it. There is nothing you can do down there, Marshal Kroy.'

'There is certainly nothing I can do up here, Lord Bayaz,' said her father curtly, stepping past him and towards the horses. His staff followed, along with several guards, Felnigg snapping out orders in every direction, the headquarters suddenly alive with rattling activity.

'Lord Marshal!' shouted Bayaz. 'I deem this unwise!'

Her father did not even turn. 'By all means remain here, then.' And he planted one boot in the stirrup and pulled himself up.

'By the dead,' hissed Bayaz under his breath.

Finree gave him a sickly smile. 'It seems you may be called to the front after all. Perhaps you can see the little people struggle at first hand.'

The First of the Magi did not appear amused.

Blood

'They're coming!'

That much Beck knew already, but men were packed so tight into the Heroes he didn't know much else. Wet furs, wet armour, weapons gleaming with rain, scowling faces running with water. The stones themselves were streaky shadows, ghosts beyond a forest of jagged spears. Spit and splattering whisper of drops on metal. Crash and clang of steel echoing from the slopes, shouts of battle muffled by the downpour.

A great surge went through the crowd and Beck was lifted right off his feet, kicking at nothing, dumped in a mass of punching, jostling, shouting men. Took him a moment to realise they weren't the enemy, but there were a lot of blades poking every which way even so and it didn't have to be a Union one to stick you in the fruits. Hadn't been a Union sword killed Reft, had it?

Someone elbowed him in the head and he staggered sideways, was knocked by someone else and onto his knees, a trampling boot squashed his hand into the mud. Dragged himself up by a shield with a dragon's head painted on it, owner not best pleased. Man with a beard roaring at him. Battle sounds were louder. Men struggling to get away or get towards. Men clutching at wounds, blood run pink in the rain, clutching at weapons, all dripping wet and mad on fear and anger.

By the dead, he wanted to run. He wasn't sure if he was crying. Just knew he couldn't fail again. Stand with his crew, that's what Craw said, weren't it? Stand with his Chief. He blinked into the storm, saw a flash of Black Dow's black standard flapping, soaked through. Knew Craw had to be near it. Pressed towards it between the jerking bodies, boots slithering in the churned-up slop. Thought he caught a glimpse of Drofd's snarling face.

474

Heard a roar and a spear came at him. Not even fast. He moved his head to the side, far as he could, straining with everything he had, and the point slid past his ear. Someone squealed in the other one, dropped against him, warm on his shoulder. Grunting and gurgling. Hot and wet all down his arm. He gasped, wriggled his shoulders, shrugging the corpse off, working it down towards the mud.

Another surge in the crowd and Beck was dragged sliding to the left, mouth open as he fought to stay upright. Warm rain spattered his cheek, the man in front of him suddenly whisked away and he was left blinking at space. A strip of mud, covered with sprawled bodies, and rain-pocked puddles, and broken spears.

And on the other side of it, the enemy.

Dow roared something over his shoulder but Craw couldn't hear him. Could hardly hear anything over the hissing of the rain and the clamour of rough voices, loud as a storm themselves. Too late for orders. Time comes a man just has to stick with the orders he's given, trust in his men to do the right thing, and fight. He thought maybe he saw the hilt of the Father of Swords waving between the spears. Should've been with his dozen. Stood with his crew. Why had he said yes to being Dow's Second? Maybe 'cause he'd been Threetrees' Second once, and he'd somehow thought if he had the place he used to have the world would be like it used to be. An old fool, grabbing at ghosts. Way too late. Should've married Colwen when he had the chance. Asked her, anyway. Given her the chance to turn him down.

He closed his eyes for a moment, breathed in the wet, cold air. 'Should've stayed a carpenter,' he whispered. But the sword had been the easier choice. To work wood you need all manner of tools – chisels and saws, axes great and small, nails and hammers, awls and planes. To be a killer you just need two. A blade and the will. Only Craw wasn't sure he had the will any more. He squeezed his fist tight around his sword's wet grip, the roar of battle growing louder and louder, binding with the roar of his own breath in his ears, the roar of his own heart pumping. Choices made. And he gritted his teeth, and snapped his eyes open.

The crowd split apart like timber down the grain and the Union boiled from the gap. One barrelled into Craw before he could swing, their shields locked together, boots slithering in the mud. A glimpse of a snarling face, managed to tip his shield forward so the metal rim dug up into a nose, and back, and up, gurgling, whimpering. Dragging at the shield strap with all his strength, jabbing with it, stabbing with it, growling and spitting with it, grinding it into the man's head. It caught the buckle on his helmet, half-tore it off. Craw tried to twist his sword free, a blade whipped past him and took a great chunk out of the man's face. Craw left sliding in the muck, nothing to push against.

Black Dow spun his axe around, brought the pick side down on someone's helmet, punching right through to the haft. Left it buried in the corpse's head as it toppled backwards, arms wide.

A mud-splattered Northman tangled with a spear, his arm twisted over it and his war-hammer wafting about uselessly, a clawing hand on his face, forcing his head up while he peered down at the fingers.

A Union soldier came at Craw. Someone tripped him and he went down on one knee in the muck. Craw hit him across the back of the head with a dull clonk and put a dent in his helmet. Hit him again and knocked him sprawling. Hit him again, and again, hammering his face into the mud, spitting curses.

Shivers smashed at someone with his shield, smiling, rain turned the great scar on his face bright red like a fresh wound. War tips everything upside down. Men who are a menace in peacetime become your best hope once the steel starts swinging.

A corpse kicked over from front to back, back to front again. Blood curling out into dirty water, plopping rain. The Father of Swords swung down and split someone open like a chisel splitting a carving of a man. Craw ducked behind his shield again as blood showered across it, rain spattered against it, mist of drops.

Spears pushing every way, a random, rattling, slippery mass. The point of one slid slowly down wood and into a hand, and through it, skewering it into someone's chest and pushing him down into the muck, shaking his head, no, no, fumbling at the shaft with the other hand as the merciless boots thumped over him.

Craw prodded a spear-point away with his shield, stabbing

back with his sword, caught someone under the jaw and sent his head jerking up, blood gushing as he fell, making a honking note like the first note of a song he used to know.

Behind him was a Union officer wearing the most beautiful armour Craw ever saw, carved all over with gleaming golden designs. He was beating away stupidly at Black Dow with a muddy sword, had managed to drive him to his knees. *Stand by your Chief.* Craw stepped up, roaring, boot hammering down in a puddle and showering muddy water. Cut mindlessly across that lovely breastplate, edge scoring a bright groove through all that craftsmanship and sending its owner lurching. Forward again, stabbing as the Union man turned, Craw's blade grating against the bottom edge of his armour, sliding right through him and carrying him backwards.

Craw struggled with the grip of his sword, hot blood sticky all over his hand, up his arm. Holding this bastard up as he wrestled to twist the blade out of him, staggering together in the muck in a mad hug. Face against Craw's cheek, stubble scratching, breath rasping in his ear, and Craw realised he never even got this close to Colwen. *Choices made, eh? Choices—*

Wanting is not always enough, and however much Gorst wanted to, he could not get there. Too many straining bodies in his way. By the time he had hacked the leg from the last of them and flung him aside, the old Northman had already run Jalenhorm right through the guts. Gorst could see the bloody point of the sword under the gilded rim of his rain-dewed breastplate. The general had the oddest expression as his killer struggled to pull the blade out of him. Almost a smile.

Redeemed.

The old Northman twisted around as he heard Gorst's howl, eyes going wide, bringing his shield up. The long steel chopped deep into it, splitting the timbers, wrenching it around on his arm, driving the metal rim into his head and tossing him tumbling sideways.

Gorst stepped up to finish the job but again there was some-one in his way. *As always.* Hardly more than a boy, swinging a hatchet, shouting. *The usual stuff, probably, die, die, blah, blah, blah.* Gorst was happy to die, of course. *But not for this fool's convenience.* He jerked his head sideways, let the hatchet bounce harmlessly from his shoulder-plate, spun about, long steel curving after him through the wet air. The boy tried desperately to block it but the heavy blade snatched the hatchet from his hand and split his face wide open, spraying brains.

The point of a sword whispered at him and Gorst whipped back from the waist, felt the wind of it across his cheek, a niggling discomfort under his eye. A space had opened in the screaming crowd, the battle blooming from a single press to mindless clumps of sodden combat at the very centre of the Heroes. All concepts of lines, tactics, directions, orders, of sides even, vanished as though they had never been. *And good riddance, they only confuse things.*

For some reason a half-naked Northman stood facing him, with the biggest sword Gorst had ever seen. *And I have seen a lot.* Absurdly long, as if it had been forged for a giant's use, dull grey metal gleaming with rain, a single letter stamped near the hilt.

He looked like some lurid painting by an artist who never saw a battlefield, but silly-looking people can be just as deadly as silly-sounding ones, and Gorst had coughed out all his arrogance in the smoke of Cardotti's House of Leisure. *A man must treat every fight as though it is his last. Will this be my last? We can hope.*

He rocked back, cautious, as the man's elbow twitched up for a sideways blow, shifted his shield to meet it, steel ready to counter. But instead of swinging the Northman lunged, using the great blade like a spear, the point darting past the edge of Gorst's shield and squealing down his breastplate, sending him stumbling. *A feint.* The instinct to jump back was powerful but he forced himself to keep his eyes fixed on the blade, watched its path curve through the rain, an arc of glistening droplets following after.

Gorst wrenched himself sideways and the great sword hissed past, caught the armour on his elbow and ripped it flapping off. He was already thrusting but the point of his steel caught only falling water as his half-naked opponent slid away. Gorst switched back for a savage head-height cut but the man snaked under it, hefted the great sword up with shocking speed as Gorst's steel swept down, blades ringing together with a finger-numbing clang.

They broke apart, watchful, the Northman's eyes calmly focused on Gorst in spite of the hammering rain.

His weapon might have looked like a prop from a bad comedy, but this man was no jester. The stance, the balance, the angle of the long blade gave him all manner of options both in defence and attack. The technique was hardly what one would find in Rubiari's *Forms of Swordsmanship*, but then neither was the sword itself. *We both are masters, nonetheless.*

A Union soldier came tottering between them before Gorst could move, bent over around a wound in his stomach, hands full of his own blood. Gorst smashed him impatiently out of the way with his shield, sprang at the half-naked Northman with a thrust and a slash, but he dodged the thrust and parried the cut faster than Gorst would have thought possible with that weight of metal. Gorst feinted right, switched left, swinging low. The Northman was ready, sprang out of the way, Gorst's steel feathering the mud then hacking a leg out from under a struggling man and bringing him down with a shriek. *Don't stand in the way, then, fool.*

Gorst recovered just in time to see the great sword coming, gasped as he ducked behind his shield. The blade crashed into it, leaving a huge dent in the already battered metal, bending it hard over Gorst's forearm and driving his fist into his mouth. But he kept his feet, drove back, tasting blood, crashed into the Northman's body shield-first and flung him away, lashed backhand and forehand with his steel, high and low. The Northman dodged the high but the low caught him across the leg with the very point, sent blood flying and made his knee buckle. *One to me. And now to finish it.*

Gorst whipped his steel across on the backhand, saw movement at the limit of his vision, changed the angle of his swing and let it go wide, roaring, opening his shoulder, hit a Carl in the side of the helmet so hard he was ripped off his feet and pitched upside down into a tangle of spears. Gorst snapped back, bringing the steel scything over, but the Northman rolled away as nimbly as a squirrel and came up ready even as Gorst's sword sent up a spray of dirty water beside them.

Gorst found he was smiling as they faced each other again, the battle a sodden nightmare around them. *When did I last live like this? Have I ever?* His heart was pumping fire, his skin singing as the rain trickled down it. *All the disappointments, the embarrassments, the failures are nothing now.* Every detail standing out like a flame in the blackness, every moment lasting an age, every tiniest movement of him or his opponent a story of its own. *There is only win or die.* The Northman smiled back as Gorst shook the ruined shield from his arm and into the mud, and nodded. *And we recognise each other, and understand each other, and meet as equals. As brothers.* There was respect, but there would be no mercy. The slightest hesitation on either side would be an insult to the skill of the other. So Gorst nodded back, but before he was done he was already springing forward.

The Northman caught the sword on his but Gorst still had his free hand, shrieking as he swung it, gloved fist thudding into bare ribs, the Northman twisted grunting sideways. Gorst aimed another lashing punch at his face but he jerked away, the pommel of the great sword shot out of nowhere and Gorst only just wrenched his chin back far enough, the lump of metal missing his nose by a whisker. He looked up to see the Northman leaping at him, sword raised high and already coming down. Gorst forced his aching legs to spring one more time, notched steel gripped in both hands, and caught the long blade with his own. Metal screeched, that grey edge biting into his Calvez-made steel and, with impossible keenness, peeling a bright shaving from the blade.

Gorst was sent sliding back by the force of it, the huge sword held just short of his face, his crossed eyes fixed on the rain-dewed edge. He got purchase as his heels hit a corpse and brought the two of them to a wobbling halt. He tried to kick the Northman's leg away but he blocked it with his knee, lurching closer, only getting them further tangled. They gasped and spat in each other's faces, locked together, blades scraping and squealing as they shifted their balance one way or another, twisted their grips one way or another, jerked with one muscle or another, both searching desperately for some tiniest advantage, neither one able to find it.

The perfect moment. Gorst knew nothing about this man, not even his name. *But we are still bound closer than lovers, because we share this one sublime splinter of time.* Facing each other. *And facing death, the ever-present third in our little party.* Knowing it might all be over in a bloody instant. *Victory and defeat, glory and oblivion, in absolute balance.*

The perfect moment. And though he strained with every sinew to bring it to an end, Gorst wished it would go on for ever. *And we will join the stones, two more Heroes to add to the circle, frozen in conflict, and the grass will grow up around us, a monument to the glory of war, to the dignity of single combat, an eternal meeting of champions on the noble field of—*

'Oh,' said the Northman. The pressure released. The blades slid apart. He stumbled back through the rain, blinking at Gorst, and then down, mouth hanging stupidly open. He still held the great sword in one hand, its point dragging through the mud and leaving a watery groove behind. With the other he reached up and gently touched the spear stuck through his chest, the blood already running down the shaft.

'Wasn't expecting that,' he said. Then he dropped like a stone.

Gorst stood, frowning down. It felt like a while, but probably it was only an instant. No telling from where the spear had come. *It is a battle. There is no shortage of them.* He heaved out a misty sigh. *Ah, well. The dance goes on.* The old man who had killed Jalenhorm was floundering in the muck just a step and a sword-swing away.

He took the step, raising his notched steel.

Then his head exploded with light.

Beck saw it all happen, through the straining bodies, barged and battered from all sides, his whole body numb with fear. Saw Craw go down, rolling in the mud. Saw Drofd step over him and be hacked down in turn. Saw Whirrun fight that mad bull of a Union soldier, a fight that only seemed to take a few savage moments, too fast for him to follow. Saw Whirrun fall.

He remembered Craw pointing him out in front of Dow's Carls. Pointing him out as an example of what to do. A man dropped screaming in front of him and a space opened. Just do what's right. Stand by your Chief. Keep your head. As the Union man stepped towards Craw, Beck stepped towards the Union man from his blind side.

Do what's right.

481

At the last moment he twisted his wrist, and it was the flat of Beck's sword that hit him on the side of his head and knocked him flopping in the muck. And that was the last Beck saw of him before the trampling boots, tangled weapons, snarling faces surged in again.

Craw blinked, shook his head, then, as puke burned the back of his throat, decided that wasn't helping. He rolled over, groaning like the dead in hell.

His shield was a shattered wreck, timbers splintered, bloody rim bent over his throbbing arm. He dragged it off. Scraped blood out of one eye.

Boom, boom, boom went his skull, like someone was hammering a great nail into it. Other'n that, it was oddly quiet. Seemed the Northmen had driven the Union off the hill, or the other way around, and Craw found he hardly cared which. The pounding feet had shuffled on, left the hilltop a sea of blood-sprinkled, rain-lashed, boot-churned filth, dead and wounded scattered tight as autumn leaves, the Heroes themselves standing their same useless watch over it all.

'Ah, shit.' Drofd was lying just a stride or two off, pale face turned towards him. Craw tried to stand and nearly puked again. Chose to crawl instead, dragging himself through the muck. 'Drofd, you all right? You—' The other side of the lad's head was all hacked away, Craw couldn't tell where the black mess inside met the black mess outside.

He patted Drofd on his chest. 'Ah. Shit.' He saw Whirrun. On his back, the Father of Swords half-buried in the mud beside him, pommel not far from his right hand. There was a spear through him, bloody shaft sticking straight up.

'Ah, shit,' said Craw again. Didn't know what else to say.

Whirrun grinned up as he crawled close, teeth pink with blood. 'Craw! Hey! I would get up, but . . .' He lifted his head to peer down at the spear-shaft. 'I'm fucked.' Craw had seen a lifetime of wounds, and he knew right off there was no help for this one.

'Aye.' Craw slowly sat back, hands heavy as anvils in his lap. 'I reckon.'

'Shoglig was talking shit. That old bitch didn't know when I

482

was going to die at all. If I'd known that I'd surely have worn more armour.' Whirrun made a sound somewhere between a cough and a laugh, then winced, coughed, laughed again, winced again. 'Fuck, it hurts. I mean, you know it will, but, fuck, it really does hurt. Guess you showed me my destiny anyway, eh, Craw?'

'Looks that way.' Wasn't much of a destiny the way Craw saw it. Not one anyone would pick out from a set.

'Where's the Father of Swords?' grunted Whirrun, trying to twist around to look for it.

'Who cares?' Blood was tickling at Craw's eyelid, making it flicker.

'Got to pass it on. Those are the rules. Like Daguf Col passed it on to me, and Yorweel the Mountain to him, and I think it was Four-Faces before that? I'm getting sketchy on the details.'

'All right.' Craw leaned over him, head thumping, dug the hilt out of the muck and pressed it into Whirrun's hand. 'Who do you want to give it to?'

'You'll make sure it's done?'

'I'll make sure.'

'Good. There ain't many I'd trust it to, but you're a straight edge, Craw, like they say. A straight edge.' Whirrun smiled up at him. 'Put it in the ground.'

'Eh?'

'Bury it with me. Time was I thought it was a blessing and a curse. But it's only a curse, and I ain't about to curse some other poor bastard with it. Time was I thought it was reward and punishment both. But this is the only reward for men like us.' And Whirrun nodded down towards the bloody spear-shaft. 'This or . . . just living long enough to become nothing worth talking of. Put it in the mud, Craw.' And he winced as he heaved the grip into Craw's limp hand and pressed his dirty fingers around it.

'I will.'

'Least I won't have to carry it no more. You see how bloody heavy it is?'

'Every sword's a weight to carry. Men don't see that when they pick 'em up. But they get heavier with time.'

'Good words.' Whirrun bared his bloody teeth for a moment. 'I really should've thought out some good words for this. Words

483

to get folk all damp about the eye. Something for the songs. Thought I had years still, though. Can you think of any?'

'What, words?'

'Aye.'

Craw shook his head. 'Never been any good with 'em. As for the songs . . . I daresay the bards just make up their own.'

'Daresay they do at that, the bastards.' Whirrun blinked up, past Craw's face into the sky. The rain was finally slacking off. 'Sun's coming out, at least.' He shook his head, still smiling. 'What do you know? Shoglig was talking shit.'

Then he was still.

Pointed Metal

The rain was hammering down and Calder could hardly see fifty paces. Ahead of him his men were in a mindless tangle with the Union's, spears and pole-arms locked together, arms, legs, faces all crushed up against each other. Roaring, howling, boots sliding in the puddled muck, hands slipping on slick grips, slick pikestaffs, bloody metal, the dead and wounded shoved up like corks in a flood or trampled into the mud beneath. From time to time shafts would flap down, no way of knowing from which side, bounce from helmets or spin from shields and into the slop.

The third pit, or what Calder could see of it, had become a nightmare bog in which filth-caked devils stabbed and wrestled at floundering half-speed. The Union were across it in quite a few places. More than once they'd made it through and over the wall, and only been pushed back by a desperate effort from White-Eye and his growing mob of fighting wounded.

Calder's throat was raw from shouting and still he couldn't make himself heard. Every man who could hold a weapon was fighting and still the Union kept coming, wave after wave, tramping on endlessly. He'd no idea where Pale-as-Snow had got to. Dead, maybe. A lot of men were. A hand-to-hand fight like this, the enemy close enough to spit in your face, couldn't last long. Men weren't made to stand it. Sooner or later one side would give and, like a dam crumbling, dissolve all at once. That moment wasn't far away now, Calder could feel it. He looked nervously behind him. A few wounded, and a few archers, and beyond them the faint shape of the farm. His horse was there. Probably not too late to—

Men were clambering out of the pit on his left and struggling towards him. For a moment he thought they were his own men, doing the sensible thing and running for their lives. Then, with a cold shock, he realised that under the muck they were Union soldiers, slipped through a gap in the shifting fight.

He stood open-mouthed as they lumbered at him. Too late to run. The leading man was on him, a Union officer who'd lost his helmet, tongue hanging out as he panted for breath. He swung a muddy blade and Calder lurched out of the way, splashing through a puddle. He managed to block the next swing, numbing impact twisting the sword in his grip, making his arm buzz to the shoulder.

He wanted to scream something manly, but what he shouted was, 'Help! Fuck! Help!' All rough and throaty and nobody could hear him or cared a shit, they were all fighting for their own lives.

No one could have guessed that Calder had been dragged into the yard every morning as a boy to train with spear and blade. He remembered none of it. He poked away with both hands like some old matron poking at a spider with a broom, mouth hanging wide, eyes full of wet hair. Should've cut his damn—

He gasped as the officer's sword jabbed at him again, his ankle caught and he tottered, one arm grabbing at nothing, and went down on his arse. It was one of the stolen flags that had tripped him. Oh, the irony. His sodden Styrian boots kicked up mud as he tried to scramble back. The officer took a tired step, sword up, then gave a breathless squeal and fell onto his knees. His head flew off sideways and his body toppled into Calder's lap, squirting blood, leaving him gasping, spitting, blinking.

'Thought I might help you out.' Who should be standing behind, sword in hand, but Brodd Tenways, nasty-looking grin on his rashy face and his chain mail gleaming with rainwater. An unlikely saviour if ever there was one. 'Couldn't leave you to snatch all the glory on your own, could I?'

Calder kicked the leaking body away and floundered up. 'I've half a mind to tell you to get fucked!'

'What about the other half?'

'Shitting itself.' No joke. He wouldn't have been at all surprised if his was the next head Tenways' sword whipped off.

But Tenways only gave him a rotten smile. 'Might be the first honest thing I've ever heard you say.'

'Probably that's fair.'

Tenways nodded towards the soaked melee. 'You coming?'

'Damn right.' Calder wondered for a moment whether he should charge in, roaring like a madman, and turn the tide of battle. That's what Scale would've done. But it would hardly have been playing to his strengths. The enthusiasm he'd felt when he saw the cavalry routed had long ago leached away leaving him wet, cold, sore and exhausted. He feigned a grimace as he took a step, clutching at his knee. 'Ah! Shit! I'll have to catch you up.'

Tenways grinned. ''Course. Why wouldn't you? With me, you bastards!' And he led a glowering wedge of his Carls towards the gap in the lines, more of them pouring over the wall on the left and adding their weight to the straining combat.

The rain was thinning. Calder could see a little further and, to his great relief, it looked as if Tenways' arrival might have shifted the balance back their way. Might have. A few more Union soldiers on the other side of the scales and it could all still come apart. The sun peeped through the clouds for a moment, brought out a faint rainbow that curved down above the heaving mass of wet metal on the right and gently touched the bare rise beyond, and the low wall on top of it.

Those bastards beyond the stream. How long would they just sit still?

Peace in Our Time

There were wounded men everywhere on the slopes of the hill. Dying men. Dead men. Finree thought she saw faces she knew among them, but could not be sure whether they really were dead friends, or dead acquaintances, or just corpses with familiar hair. More than once she saw Hal's slack face leering, gaping, grinning. It hardly seemed to matter. The truly frightening thing about the dead, once she realised it, was that she was used to them.

They passed through a gap in a low wall and into a circle of stones, casualties sprawled on every spare stretch of grass. A man was trying to hold a great wound in his leg together, but when he clamped one end shut the other sagged open, blood welling out. Her father climbed down from his horse, his officers following him, she following them, a pale lad with a bugle clutched in one muddy fist watching her in silence. They picked their way through the madness in a pale procession, virtually ignored, her father staring about him, jaw clenched tight.

A junior officer trampled heedlessly past, waving a bent sword. 'Form up! Form *up*! You! Where the hell—'

'Lord Marshal.' An unmistakable high voice. Gorst stood, somewhat unsteadily, from a group of tattered soldiers, and gave Finree's father a tired-looking salute. Without doubt he had seen a great deal of action. His armour was battered and stained. His scabbard was empty and drooped about his legs in a manner that might have been comical on another day. He had a long, black-scabbed cut under one eye, his cheek, his jaw, the side of his thick neck streaked and crusted with drying blood. When he turned his head Finree saw the white of the other eye was bruised a sickly red, bandages above it soaked through.

'Colonel Gorst, what happened?'

'We attacked.' Gorst blinked, noticed Finree and seemed to falter, then silently raised his hands and let them fall. 'We lost.'

'The Northmen still hold the Heroes?'

He nodded slowly.

'Where is General Jalenhorm?' asked her father.

'Dead,' piped Gorst.

'Colonel Vinkler?'

'Dead.'

'Who is in command?'

Gorst stood in silence. Finree's father turned away, frowning towards the summit. The rain was slackening off, the long slope leading up to the Heroes starting to take shape out of the grey, and with each stride of trampled grass that became visible, so did more corpses. Dead of both sides, broken weapons and armour, shattered stakes, spent arrows. Then the wall that ringed the summit, rough stones turned black by the storm. More bodies below it, the spears of the Northmen above. Still holding. Still waiting.

'Marshal Kroy!' The First of the Magi had not bothered to dismount. He sat, wrists crossed over the saddle-bow and his thick fingers dangling. As he took in the carnage he had the discerning, slightly disappointed air of a man who has paid for his garden to be weeded but on inspecting the grounds finds there is still a nettle or two about. 'A minor reverse, but re-inforcements are arriving all the time and the weather is clearing. Might I suggest you reorganise and prepare your men for another attack? It would appear General Jalenhorm made it all the way up to the Heroes, so a second effort might—'

'No,' said Finree's father.

Bayaz gave the slightest puzzled frown. As at a normally reliable hound who refused to come to heel today. 'No?'

'No. Lieutenant, do you have a flag of parley with you?'

Her father's standard-bearer looked nervously over at Bayaz, then back, then swallowed. 'Of course, Lord Marshal.'

'I would like you to attach it to your flagstaff, ride carefully up towards the Heroes and see if the Northmen can be prevailed upon to talk.'

A strange mutter went through the men within earshot. Gorst

489

took a step forward. 'Marshal Kroy, with another effort I think—'

'You are the king's observer. Observe.'

Gorst stood frozen for a moment, glanced at Finree, then snapped his mouth shut and stepped back.

The First of the Magi watched the white flag raised, his frown growing ever more thunderous even as the skies cleared. He nudged his horse forwards, causing a couple of exhausted soldiers to scramble from his path.

'His Majesty will be greatly dismayed, Lord Marshal.' He managed to project an aura of fearsomeness utterly disproportionate to a thickset old bald man in a soggy coat. 'He expects every man to do his duty.'

Finree's father stood before Bayaz' horse, chest out and chin raised, the overpowering weight of the Magus' displeasure on him. 'My duty is to care for the lives of these men. I simply cannot countenance another attack. Not while I am in command.'

'And how long do you suppose that will be?'

'Long enough. Go!' he snapped at his standard-bearer and the man spurred away, his white flag snapping.

'Lord Marshal.' Bayaz leaned forward, each syllable dropping like a mighty stone. 'I earnestly hope that you have weighed the consequences—'

'I have weighed them and I am content.' Finree's father was leaning forward slightly himself, eyes narrowed as if he was facing into a great wind. She thought she could see his hand trembling, but his voice emerged calm and measured. 'I suspect my great regret will be that I allowed things to go so far.'

The Magus' brows drew in further, his hissing voice almost painful to the ear. 'Oh, a man can have greater regrets than that, Lord Marshal—'

'If I may?' Bayaz' servant was striding jauntily through the chaos towards them. He was wet through, as though he had swum a river, dirt-caked as though he had waded a bog, but he showed not the slightest discomfort. Bayaz leaned down towards him and the servant whispered in his ear through a cupped hand. The Magus' frown slowly faded as he first listened, then sat slowly back in his saddle, considering, and finally shrugged.

'Very well, Marshal Kroy,' he said. 'Yours is the command.'

Finree's father turned away. 'I will need a translator. Who speaks the language?'

An officer with a heavily bandaged arm stepped up. 'The Dogman and some of his Northmen were with us at the start of the attack, sir, but . . .' He squinted into the milling crowd of wounded and worn-out soldiery. Who could possibly know where anyone was now?

'I have a smattering,' said Gorst.

'A smattering might cause misunderstandings. We cannot afford any.'

'It should be me,' said Finree.

Her father stared at her, as if astonished to find her there, let alone volunteering for duty. 'Absolutely not. I cannot—'

'Afford to wait?' she finished for him. 'I spoke with Black Dow only yesterday. He knows me. He offered me terms. I am the best suited. It should be me.'

He looked at her for a moment longer, then gave the slightest smile. 'Very well.'

'I will accompany you,' piped Gorst with a show of chivalry sickeningly inappropriate among so many dead men. 'Might I borrow your sword, Colonel Felnigg? I left mine at the summit.'

So they set off, the three of them, through the thinning drizzle, the Heroes jutting clearly now from the hilltop ahead. Not far up the slope her father slipped, gasped as he fell awkwardly, catching at the grass. Finree started forward to help him up. He smiled, and patted her hand, but he looked suddenly old. As if his confrontation with Bayaz had sucked ten years out of him. She had always been proud of her father, of course. But she did not think she had ever been so proud of him as she was at that moment. Proud and sad at once.

Wonderful slipped the needle through, pulled the thread after and tied it off. Normally it would've been Whirrun doing it, but Cracknut had sewed his last stitches, more was the pity. 'Just as well you've got a thick head.'

'Served me well my whole life.' Craw made the joke without thinking, no laughter given or expected, just as shouting came up from the wall that faced the Children. Where shouting would come from if the Union came again. He stood, the world see-sawed wildly for a moment and his skull felt like it was going to burst.

Yon grabbed his elbow. 'You all right?'

'Aye, all things considered.' And Craw swallowed his urge to spew and pushed through the crowd, the valley opening out in front of him, sky stained strange colours as the storm passed off. 'They coming again?' He wasn't sure they could stand another go. He was sure he couldn't.

Dow was all grin, though. 'In a manner of speaking.' He pointed out three figures making their way up the slope towards the Heroes. The very same route Hardbread had taken a few days before when he came to ask for his hill back. When Craw had still had the best part of a dozen, all looking to him to keep 'em safe. 'Reckon they want to talk.'

'Talk?'

'Let's go.' And Dow tossed his blood-crusted axe to Shivers, straightened the chain about his shoulders and strode through the gap in the mossy wall and down the hillside.

'Not too fast,' called Craw as he set off after. 'Don't reckon my knees'll take it!'

The three figures came closer. Craw felt just the slightest bit happier when he realised one was the woman he'd taken across the bridge yesterday, wearing a soldier's coat. The relief leaked quick when he saw who the third was, though. The big Union man who'd nearly killed him, a bandage around his thick skull.

They met about half way between the Heroes and the Children. Where the first arrows were prickling the ground. The old man stood with shoulders back, one fist clasped behind him in the other. Clean-shaven, with short grey hair and a sharp look, like he missed nothing. He wore a black coat, stitched with leaves at the collar in silver thread, a sword at his side with a pommel made from some jewel, looked like it had never been drawn. The girl stood at his elbow, the neckless soldier a little further back, his eyes on Craw, the white of one turned all bloody red and a black cut under the other. Looked like he'd left his sword in the mud up on the hill, but he'd found another. You didn't have to look far for a blade around here. Those were the times.

Dow stopped a couple of paces above them and Craw stopped a pace behind that, hands crossed in front of him. Close enough to get at his sword quick, though he doubted he'd have had the strength to draw the damn thing. Standing up was enough of a challenge. Dow was chirpier.

'Well, well.' Grinning down at the girl with every tooth and spreading his arms in greeting. 'Never expected to be seeing you again so soon. Do you want to hold me?'

'No,' she said. 'This is my father, Lord Marshal Kroy, commander of his Majesty's—'

'I guessed. And you lied.'

She frowned up at him. 'Lied?'

'He's shorter'n me.' Dow's grin spread even wider. 'Or he looks it from where I'm standing, anyway. Quite the day we're having, ain't it? Quite the red day.' He lifted a fallen Union spear with the toe of his boot, then nudged it away. 'So what can I do for you?'

'My father would like to end the fighting.'

Craw felt such a wave of relief his swollen knees almost went out from under him. Dow was cagier. 'Could've done that yesterday when I offered, given us all a lot less bloody digging to do.'

'He's offering now.'

Dow looked across at Craw, and Craw just about managed to shrug. 'Better tardy than not at all.'

'Huh.' Dow narrowed his eyes at the girl, and at the soldier, and at the marshal, like he was thinking of saying no. Then he put his hands on his hips, and sighed. 'All right. Can't say I wanted any of this in the first place. There's people of my own I could've been killing, 'stead o' wasting my sweat on you bastards.'

The girl said a few words to her father, he said a few back. 'My father is greatly relieved.'

'Then my life's worth living. I've a few things to tidy up before we hammer out the details.' He cast an eye over the carnage on the Children. 'Probably you have too. We'll talk tomorrow. Let's say after lunch, I can't do business with a hollow belly.'

The girl passed it on to her father in Union, and while she did it Craw looked down at the red-eyed soldier, and he looked back. He had a long smear of blood down his neck. His, or Craw's, or one of Craw's dead friends'? Not even an hour ago they'd struggled with every shred of strength and will to murder each other. Now there was no need. Made him wonder why there ever had been.

'He's a right fucking killer, your man there,' said Dow, more or less summing up Craw's thoughts.

The girl looked over her shoulder. 'He is . . .' searching for the right words. 'The king's watcher.'

Dow snorted. 'He did a bit more'n fucking watch today. He's got a devil in him, and I mean that as a compliment. Man like him could do well over on our side o' the Whiteflow. He was a Northman he'd be in all the songs. Shit, might be he'd be a king instead o' just watching one.' Dow smiled that killing smile he had. 'Ask him if he wants to work for me.'

The girl opened her mouth but the neckless one spoke first, with a thick accent and the strangest, high, girlish little voice Craw had ever heard on a man. 'I am happy where I am.'

Dow raised one brow. ''Course you are. Real happy. Must be why you're so damn good at killing men.'

'What about my friend?' asked the girl. 'The one who was captured with me—'

'Don't give up, do you?' Dow showed his teeth again. 'You really think anyone'll want her back, now?'

She looked him right in the eye. 'I want her back. Didn't I get what you asked for?'

'Too late for some.' Dow ran a careless eye over the carnage scattered across the slope, took in a breath, and blew it out. 'But that's war, eh? There have to be losers. Might be an idea to send some messengers, let everyone know they can all stop fighting and have a big sing-song instead. Be a shame to carry on butchering each other for nothing, wouldn't it?'

The woman blinked, then rendered it into Union again. 'My father would like to recover our dead.'

But the Protector of the North was already turning away. 'Tomorrow. They won't run off.'

Black Dow walked off up the slope, the older man giving her the faintest, apologetic grin before he followed.

Finree took a long breath, held it, then let it out. 'I suppose that's it.'

'Peace is always an anticlimax,' said her father, 'but no less desirable for that.' He started stiffly back towards the Children and she walked beside him.

A throwaway conversation, a couple of bad jokes that half the gathering of five could not even have understood, and it was done. The battle was over. The war was over. Could they have had that conversation at the start, and would all those men – all these men – still be alive? Still have their arms, or legs? However she turned it around, she could not make it fit. Perhaps she should have been angry at the stupendous waste, but she was too tired, too irritated by the way her damp clothes were chafing her back. And at least it was over now after—

Thunder rolled across the battlefield. Terribly, frighteningly loud. For a moment she thought it must be lightning striking the Heroes. A last, petulant stroke of the storm. Then she saw the mighty ball of fire belching up from Osrung, so large she fancied she could feel the heat of it on her face. Specks flew about it, spun away from it, streaks and spirals of dust following them high into the sky. Pieces of buildings, she realised. Beams, blocks. Men. The flame vanished and a great cloud of black smoke shot up after it, spilling into the sky like a waterfall reversed.

'Hal,' she muttered, and before she knew it, she was running.

'Finree!' shouted her father.

'I'll go.' Gorst's voice.

She took no notice, charging on downhill as fast as she could with the tails of Hal's coat snatching at her legs.

'What the hell—' muttered Craw, watching the column of smoke crawl up, the wind already dragging it billowing out towards them, the orange of fires flickering at its base, licking at the jagged wrecks that used to be buildings.

'Oops,' said Dow. 'That'll be Ishri's surprise. Shitty timing for all concerned.'

Another day Craw might've been horror-struck, but today it was hard to get worked up. A man can only feel so sorry and he was way past his limit. He swallowed, and turned from the giant tree of dirt spreading its branches over the valley, and struggled back up the hillside after Dow.

'You couldn't call it a win, exactly,' he was saying, 'but not a bad result, all in all. Best send someone off to Reachey, tell him tools down. Tenways and Calder too, if they're still—'

'Chief.' Craw stopped on the wet slope, next to the face-down corpse of a Union soldier. A man has to do the right thing. Has to stand by his Chief, whatever his feelings. He'd stuck to that all his life, and they say an old horse can't jump new fences.

'Aye?' Dow's grin faded as he looked into Craw's face. 'What's to frown about?'

'There's something I need to tell you.'

The Moment of Truth

The deluge had finally come to an end but the leaves were still dripping relentlessly on the soaked, sore, unhappy soldiers of his Majesty's First. Corporal Tunny was the most soaked, sore and unhappy of the lot. Still crouching in the bushes. Still staring towards that same stretch of wall he'd been staring at all day and much of the day before. His eye chafed raw from the brass end of his eyeglass, his neck chafed raw from his constant scratching, his arse and armpits chafed raw from his wet clothes. He'd had some shitty duties in his chequered career, but this was down there among the worst, somehow combining the two awful constants of the army life – terror and tedium. For some time the wall had been lost in the hammering rain but now had taken shape again. The same mossy pile slanting down towards the water. And the same spears bristling above it.

'Can we see yet?' hissed Colonel Vallimir.

'Yes, sir. They're still there.'

'Give me that!' Vallimir snatched the eyeglass, peered towards the wall for a moment, then sulkily let it fall. 'Damn it!' Tunny had mild sympathy. About as much as he could ever have for an officer. Going meant disobeying the letter of Mitterick's order. Staying meant disobeying the tone of it. Either way there was a good chance he'd suffer. Here, if one was needed, was a compelling argument against ever rising beyond corporal.

'We go anyway!' snapped Vallimir, desire for glory evidently having tipped the scales. 'Get the men ready to charge!'

Forest saluted. 'Sir.'

So there it was. No stratagems for delay, no routes to light duty, no feigning of illness or injuries. It was time to fight, and Tunny had to admit he was almost relieved as he did up the buckle on his helmet. Anything but crouching in the bloody bushes any longer. There was a whispering as the order was passed down the line, a rattling and scraping as men stood, adjusted their armour, drew their weapons.

'That it, then?' asked Yolk, eyes wide.

'That's it.' Tunny was strangely light-headed as he undid the ties and slid the canvas cover from the standard. He felt that old, familiar tightness in his throat as he gently unfurled the precious square of red material. Not fear. Not fear at all. That other, much more dangerous thing. The one Tunny had tried over and over to smother, but always sprouted up again as powerful as ever when he wanted it least.

'Oh, here we go,' he whispered. The golden sun of the Union slipped out of hiding as the cloth unrolled. The number one embroidered on it. The standard of Corporal Tunny's regiment, which he'd served with since a boy. Served with in the desert and the snow. The names of a score of old battles stitched in gold thread, glittering in the shadows. The names of battles fought and won by better men than him.

'Oh, here we bloody go.' His nose hurt. He looked up at the branches, at the black leaves and the bright cracks of sky between them, at the glittering beads of water at their edges. His eyelids fluttered, blinking back tears. He stepped forward to the very edge of the trees, trying to swallow the dull pain behind his breastbone as men gathered around him in a long line. His limbs were tingling. Yolk and Worth behind him, the last of his little flock of recruits, both pale as they faced towards the water, and the wall beyond it. As they faced—

'Charge!' roared Forest, and Tunny was away. He burst from the trees and down the long slope, threading between old tree stumps, bounding from one to another. He heard men shouting behind him, men running, but he was too busy holding the standard high in both hands, the wind taking the cloth and dragging it out straight above his head, tugging hard at his hands, his arms, his shoulders.

He splashed out into the stream, floundered through the slow water to the middle, no more than thigh deep. He turned, waving the standard back and forth, its golden sun flashing. 'On, you bastards!' he roared at the crowd of running men behind him.

'On, the First! Forward! Forward!' Something whipped past in the air, just seen out of the corner of his eye.

'I'm hit!' shrieked Worth, staggering in the stream, helmet twisted across his stricken face, clutching at his breastplate.

'By birdshit, idiot!' Tunny took the standard in one hand and wedged the other under Worth's armpit, dragged him along a few steps until he had his balance back then plunged on himself, lifting his knees up high, spraying water with every step.

He hauled himself up the mossy bank, free hand clutching at roots, wet boots wrestling at the loose earth, finally clambering onto the overhanging turf. He snatched a look back, all he could hear his own whooping breath echoing in his helmet. The whole regiment, or the few hundred who remained, at any rate, were flooding down the slope and across the stream after him, kicking up sparkling drops.

He shoved the snapping standard high into the air, gave a meaningless roar as he drew his sword and ran on, face locked into a snarling mask, thumping towards the wall, spear-tips showing above it. Two more great strides and he sprang up onto the drystone, screaming like a madman, swinging his sword wildly one way and the other to clatter against the spears and knock them toppling . . .

There was no one there.

Just old pole-arms leaning loose against the wall, and damp barley shifting in the wind, and the calm, wooded fells rising faint at the north side of the valley very much like they did at the south side.

No one to fight.

No doubt there had been fighting, and plenty of it too. Over to the right the crops were flattened, the ground before the wall trampled to a mass of mud, littered with the bodies of men and horses, the ugly rubbish of victory and defeat.

But the fighting was over now.

Tunny narrowed his eyes. A few hundred strides away, off to the north and east, figures were jogging across the fields, chinks of sunlight through the heavy clouds glinting on armour. The Northmen, presumably. And since no one appeared to be pursuing them, pulling back in their own time, and on their own terms.

'Yah!' shrieked Yolk as he ran up, a war cry that could hardly have made a duck nervous. 'Yah!' Leaning over the wall to poke away wildly with his sword. 'Yah?'

'No one here,' said Tunny, letting his own blade slowly fall.

'No one here?' muttered Worth, trying to straighten his twisted helmet.

Tunny sat down on the wall, the standard between his knees. 'Only him.' Not far away a scarecrow had been planted, a spear nailed to each stick arm, a brightly polished helmet on its sack-head. 'And I reckon the whole regiment can take him.' It all looked a pathetic ruse now. But then ruses always do, once you've seen through them. Tunny ought to have known that. He'd played more than a few himself, though usually on his own officers rather than the enemy.

More soldiers were reaching the wall. Wet through, tired out, mixed up. One clambered over it, walked up to the scarecrow and levelled his sword.

'Lay down your arms in the name of his Majesty!' he roared. There was a smattering of laughter, quickly cut off as Colonel Vallimir clambered up onto the drystone with a face like fury, Sergeant Forest beside him.

A horseman was pounding over from the empty gap in the wall on their right. The gap where they'd been sure a furious battle was taking place. A battle they would gloriously turn the tide of. A battle that was already over. He reined in before them, he and his horse breathing hard, dashed with mud from a full gallop.

'Is General Mitterick here?' he managed to gasp.

'Afraid not,' said Tunny.

'Do you know where he is?'

'Afraid not,' said Tunny.

'What's the matter, man?' snapped Vallimir, getting tangled with his scabbard as he hopped down from the wall and nearly falling on his face.

The messenger snapped out a salute. 'Sir. Lord Marshal Kroy orders all hostilities to cease at once.' He smiled, teeth gleaming white in his muddy face. 'We've made peace with the North-men!' He turned his horse smartly and rode off, past a pair of stained and tattered flags drooping forgotten from leaning poles and south, towards a line of Union foot advancing across the ruined fields.

'Peace?' mumbled Yolk, soaked and shivering.

'Peace,' grunted Worth, trying to rub the birdshit from his breastplate.

'Fuck!' snarled Vallimir, flinging down his sword.

Tunny raised his brows, and stuck his own blade point-first in the earth. He couldn't say he felt anywhere near as strongly as Vallimir about it, but he had to admit to feeling a mite disappointed at the way things had turned out.

'But that's war, eh, my beauty?' He started to roll up the standard of his Majesty's First, smoothing out the kinks with his thumb the way a woman might put away her wedding shawl when the big day was over.

'That was quite some standard-bearing, Corporal!' Forest was a stride or two away, foot up on the wall, a grin across his scarred face. 'Up front, leading the men, in the place of most danger and most glory. "Forward!" cried brave Corporal Tunny, hurling his courage in the teeth of the enemy! I mean, there was no enemy, as it turned out, but still, I always knew you'd come through. You always do. Can't help yourself, can you? Corporal Tunny, hero of the First!'

'Fuck yourself, Forest.'

Tunny started to work the standard carefully back into its cover. Looking across the flat land to the north and east, watching the last of the Northmen hurrying away through the sunlit fields.

Luck. Some men have it. Some don't. Calder could not but conclude, as he bounded through the barley behind his men, exhausted and muddy but very much alive, that he had it. By the dead, he had it.

Mad luck, that Mitterick had done the apparently insane, chosen to charge without checking the ground or waiting for light and doomed his cavalry. Impossible luck, that Brodd Tenways, of all people, would have lent a helping hand, the worst of his many enemies saving his life at the last moment. Even the rain had fought on his side, swept over at just the time to ruin the order of the Union foot and turn their dream ground into a nightmare of mud.

Even then, the men in the woods could still have done for him, but they'd been put off by a bundle of dead men's spears, a scarecrow and a few boys each slipped a coin to wear a helmet twice too big and stick their heads up once in a while. Deal with them, Dow had said, and somehow bold Prince Calder had found a way.

When he thought of all the luck he'd had that day he felt dizzy. Felt as if the world must've chosen him for something. Must have great plans for him. How else could he have lurched through all this with his life? Him, Calder, who deserved it so bloody little?

There was an old ditch running through the fields up ahead with a low hedgerow behind. A boundary his father hadn't quite managed to tear up, and the perfect place to form a new line. Another little slice of luck. He found himself wishing that Scale had lived to see this. To hug him and thump his back and say how proud he was at last. He'd fought, and what was even more surprising, he'd won. Calder was laughing as he jumped the ditch, slid sideways through a gap in the bushes— And stopped.

A few of his lads were scattered around, most of them sitting or even lying, weapons tossed aside, all the way knackered from a day's hard fighting and a run across the fields. Pale-as-Snow was with them, but they weren't alone. A good score of Dow's Carls stood in a frowning crescent ahead. A grim-looking set of bastards, and the shitty jewel in the midst was Caul Shivers, his one eye fixed on Calder.

There was no reason for them to be there. Unless Curnden Craw had done what he said he would, and told Black Dow the truth. And Curnden Craw was a man famous for always doing what he said he would. Calder licked his lips. Seemed a bit of a foolish decision now, to have gambled against the inevitable. Seemed he was such a good liar he'd managed to trick himself on his chances.

'Prince Calder,' whispered Shivers, taking a step forward.

Way too late to run. He'd only be running at the Union anyway. A mad hope tickled the back of his mind that his father's closest might leap to his defence. But they hadn't lasted as long as they had by pissing into the wind. He glanced at Pale-as-Snow and the old warrior offered him the tiniest shrug. Calder had given them a day to be proud of, but he'd get no suicidal gestures of loyalty and he deserved none. They weren't going to set themselves on fire for his benefit any more than Caul Reachey was. You have to be realistic, as the Bloody-Nine had been so bloody fond of saying.

So Calder could only give a hopeless smile, and stand there trying to get his breath as Shivers took another step towards him, then another. That terrible scar loomed close. Close enough almost to kiss. Close enough so all Calder could see was his own distorted, unconvincing grin reflected in that dead metal ball of an eye.

'Dow wants you.'

Luck. Some men have it. Some don't.

Spoils

The smell, first. Of a kitchen mishap, perhaps. Then of a bonfire. Then more. An acrid note that niggled at the back of Gorst's throat. The smell of buildings aflame. Adua had smelled that way, during the siege. So had Cardotti's House of Leisure, as he reeled through the smoke-filled corridors.

Finree rode like a madwoman and, dizzy and aching as he was, she pulled away from him, sending men hopping from the road. Ash started to flutter down as they passed the inn, black snow falling. Rubbish was dotted about as the fence of Osrung loomed from the smoky murk. Scorched wood, broken slates, scraps of cloth raining from the sky.

More wounded here, dotted haphazardly about the town's south gate, burned as well as hacked, stained with soot as well as blood, but the sounds were the same as they had been on the Heroes. As they always were. Gorst gritted his teeth against it. *Help them or kill them, but someone please put an end to their damned bleating.*

Finree was already down from her horse and making for the town. He scrambled after, head pounding, face burning, and caught up with her just inside the gate. He thought the sun might be dropping in the sky, but it hardly mattered. In Osrung it was choking twilight. Fires burned among the wooden buildings. Flames rearing up, the heat of them drying the spit in Gorst's mouth, sucking the sweat out of his face, making the air shimmer. A house hung open like a man gutted, missing one of its walls, floorboards jutting into air, windows from nowhere to nowhere.

Here is war. Here it is, shorn of its fancy trappings. None of the polished buttons, the jaunty bands, the stiff salutes. None of the clenched jaws and clenched buttocks. None of the speeches, the bugles, the lofty ideals. Here it is, stripped bare.

Just ahead someone bent over a man, helping him. He glanced up, sooty-faced. Not helping. He had been trying to get his boots off. As Gorst came close he startled and dashed away into the strange dusk. Gorst looked down at the soldier he left behind, one bare foot pale against the mud. *Oh, flower of our manhood! Oh, the brave boys! Oh, send them to war no more until next time we need a fucking distraction.*

'Where should we look?' he croaked.

Finree stared at him for a moment, hair tangled across her face, soot stuck under her nose, eyes wild. *But still as beautiful as ever. More. More.* 'Over there! Near the bridge. He'd have been at the front.' *Such nobility! Such heroism! Lead on, my love, to the bridge!*

They went beneath a row of trees on fire, burning leaves fluttering down around them like confetti. *Sing! All sing for the happy couple!* People called out, voices muffled in the gloom. People looking for help, or looking for men to help, or men to rob. Figures shambled past, leaning on one another, carrying stretchers between them, casting about as though for something they had mislaid, digging at the wreckage with their hands. *How could you find one man in this? Where would you find one man? A whole one, anyway.*

There were bodies all about. There were parts of bodies. Strangely robbed of meaning. Bits of meat. *Someone scrape them up and pack them in gilt coffins back to Adua so the king can stand to attention as they pass and the queen can leave glistening tear-tracks through her powder and the people can tear their hair and ask why, why, while they wonder what to have for dinner or whether they need a new pair of shoes or whatever the fuck.*

'Over here!' shouted Finree, and he hurried to her, hauled a broken beam aside, two corpses underneath, neither one an officer. She shook her head, biting her lip, put one hand on his shoulder. He had to stop himself smiling. Could she know the thrill that touch sent through him? He was wanted. Needed. And by her.

Finree picked her way from one ruined shell to another, coughing, eyes watering, tearing at rubbish with her fingernails, turning over bodies, and he followed. Searching every bit as feverishly as she did. More, even. But for different reasons. *I will drag aside some fallen trash and there will be his ruined, gaping corpse, not half so fucking handsome now, and she will see it. Oh no! Oh yes. Cruel, vicious, lovely fate. And she will turn to me in her misery, and weep upon my uniform and perhaps thump my chest lightly with her fist, and I will hold her, and whisper insipid consolations, and be the rock for her to founder upon, and we will be together, as we should have been, and would have been had I had the courage to ask her.*

Gorst grinned to himself, teeth bared as he rolled over another body. Another dead officer, arm so broken it was wrapped right around his back. *Taken too soon with all his young life ahead of him and blah, blah, blah. Where is Brock? Show me Brock.*

A few splinters of stone and a great crater, flooded by churning river water, were all that remained to show where Osrung's bridge once stood. Most of the buildings around it were little more than heaps of rubbish, but one stone-built was largely intact, its roof stripped off and some of the bare rafters aflame. Gorst struggled towards it while Finree picked at some bodies, one arm over her face. A doorway with a heavy lintel, and in the doorway a thick door twisted from its hinges, and just showing beneath the door, a boot. Gorst reached down and heaved the door up like the lid of a coffin.

And there was Brock. He did not seem badly injured at a first glance. His face was streaked with blood, but not smashed to pulp as Gorst might have hoped. One leg was folded underneath him at an unnatural angle, but his limbs were all attached.

Gorst bent over him, placed a hand over his mouth. Breath. *Still alive.* He felt a surge of disappointment so strong that his knees nearly buckled, closely followed by a sobering rage. *Cheated. Gorst, the king's squeaking clown, why should he have what he wants? What he needs? What he deserves? Dangle it in his fat face and laugh! Cheated. Just as I was in Sipani. Just as I was at the Heroes. Just as I always am.*

Gorst raised one brow, and he blew out a long, soft breath, and he shifted his hand down, down to Brock's neck. He slid his thumb and his middle finger around it, feeling out the narrowest point, then gently, firmly squeezed.

What's the difference? Fill a hundred pits with dead Northmen, congratulations, have a parade! Kill one man in the same uniform as you? A crime. A murder. Worse than despicable. Are we not all men? All blood and bone and dreams?

He squeezed a little harder, impatient to be done. Brock did not complain. Did not so much as twitch. He was so nearly dead anyway. *Nothing more than nudging fate in the right direction.*

So much easier than all the others. No steel and screams and mess, just a little pressure and a little time. So much more point than all the others. They had nothing I needed, they simply faced the other way. I should be ashamed of their deaths. But this? This is justice. This is righteous. This is—

'Have you found anything?'

Gorst's hand sprang open and he shifted it slightly so two fingers were pressed up under Brock's jaw, as if feeling for a pulse. 'He's alive,' he croaked.

Finree leaned down beside him, touched Brock's face with a trembling hand, the other pressed to her mouth, gave a gasp of relief that might as well have been a dagger in Gorst's face. He slid one arm under Brock's knees, the other under his back, and scooped him up. *I have failed even at killing a man. It seems my only choice is to save him.*

A surgeon's tent stood near the south gate, canvas turned muddy grey by the falling ash. Wounded waited outside for attention, clutching at assorted injuries, moaning, or whimpering, or silent, eyes empty. Gorst stomped through them and up to the tent. *We can jump the queue, because I am the king's observer, and she is the marshal's daughter, and the wounded man is a colonel of the most noble blood, and so it is only fitting that any number of the rank and file can die before bastards like us are inconvenienced.*

Gorst pushed through the flap and set Brock down ever so gently on a stained table, and a tight-faced surgeon listened at his chest and proclaimed him alive. *And all my silly, pretty little hopes strangled. Again.* Gorst stepped back as the assistants crowded in, Finree bending over her husband, holding his sooty hand, looking eagerly down into his face, her eyes shining with hope, and fear, and love.

Gorst watched. *If it was me dying on that table, would anyone care? They would shrug and tip me out with the slops. And why shouldn't they? It would be better than I deserve.* He left them to it, trudged outside and stood there, frowning at the wounded, he did not know how long for.

'They say he is not too badly hurt.'

He turned to look at her. Forcing the smile onto his face was harder work than climbing the Heroes had been. 'I am . . . so glad.'

'They say it is amazing luck.'

'Too true.'

They stood there in silence a moment longer. 'I don't know how I can ever repay you . . .'

Easy. Abandon that pretty fool and be mine. That's all I want. That one little thing. Just kiss me, and hold me, and give yourself to me, utterly and completely. That's all. 'It's nothing,' he whispered.

But she had already turned and hurried into the tent, leaving him alone. He stood for a moment as the ash gently fluttered down, settled across the ground, settled across his shoulders. Beside him a boy lay on a stretcher. On the way to the tent, or while waiting for the surgeon, he had died.

Gorst frowned down at the body. *He is dead and I, self-serving coward that I am, still live.* He sucked in air through his sore nose, blew it out through his sore mouth. *Life is not fair. There is no pattern. People die at random.* Obvious, perhaps. Something that everyone knows. *Something that everyone knows, but no one truly believes. They think when it comes to them there will be a lesson, a meaning, a story worth telling. That death will come to them as a dread scholar, a fell knight, a terrible emperor.* He poked at the boy's corpse with a toe, rolled it onto its side, then let it flop back. *Death is a bored clerk, with too many orders to fill. There is no reckoning. No profound moment. It creeps up on us from behind, and snatches us away while we shit.*

He stepped over the corpse and walked back towards Osrung, past the shambling grey ghosts that clogged the road. He was no more than a dozen steps inside the gate when he heard a voice calling to him.

'Over here! Help!' Gorst saw an arm sticking from a heap of charred rubbish. Saw a desperate, ash-smeared face. He clambered carefully up, undid the buckle under the man's chin, removed his helmet and tossed it away. The lower half of his body was trapped under a splintered beam. Gorst took one end, heaved it up and swung it away, lifted the soldier as gently as a father might a sleeping child and carried him back towards the gate.

'Thank you,' he croaked, one hand pawing at Gorst's soot-stained jacket. 'You're a hero.'

Gorst said nothing. *But if only you knew, my friend. If only you knew.*

Desperate Measures

Time to celebrate.

No doubt the Union would have their own way of looking at it, but Black Dow was calling this a victory and his Carls were minded to agree. So they'd dug new fire-pits, and cracked the kegs, and poured the beer, and every man was looking forward to a double gild, and most of 'em to heading home to plough their fields, or their wives, or both.

They chanted, laughed, staggered about in the gathering darkness, tripping through fires and sending sparks showering, drunker'n shit. All feeling twice as alive for facing death and coming through. They sang old songs, and made up new ones with the names of today's heroes where yesterday's used to be. Black Dow, and Caul Reachey, and Ironhead and Tenways and Golden raised up on high while the Bloody-Nine, and Bethod, and Threetrees and Littlebone and even Skarling Hoodless sank into the past like the sun sinking in the west, the midday glory of their deeds dimming just to washed-out memories, a last flare among the stringy clouds before night swallowed 'em. You didn't hear much about Whirrun of Bligh even. About Shama Heartless, not a peep. Names turned over by time, like the plough turning the soil. Bringing up the new while the old were buried in the mud.

'Beck.' Craw lowered himself stiffly down beside the fire, a wooden ale cup in one hand, and gave Beck's knee an encouraging pat.

'Chief. How's your head?'

The old warrior touched a finger to the fresh stitches above his ear. 'Sore. But I've had worse. Very nearly had a lot worse today, in fact, as you might've noticed. Scorry told me you saved my life. Most folk wouldn't place a high value on that particular article but I must admit I'm quite attached to it. So. Thanks, I guess. A lot of thanks.'

'Just trying to do the right thing. Like you said.'

'By the dead. Someone was listening. Drink?' And Craw offered out his wooden mug.

'Aye.' Beck took it and a good swallow too. Taste of beer, sour on his tongue.

'You did good today. Bloody good, far as I'm concerned. Scorry told me it was you put that big bastard down. The one who killed Drofd.'

'Did I kill him?'

'No. He's alive.'

'Didn't kill no one today, then.' Beck wasn't sure whether he should be disappointed by that or glad. He wasn't up to feeling much about anything either way. 'I killed a man yesterday,' he found he'd said.

'Flood said you killed four.'

Beck licked his lips. Trying to lick away the sour taste, but it was going nowhere. 'Flood got it wrong and I was too much the coward to put him right. Lad called Reft killed those men.' He took another swallow, too fast, made his voice spill out breathless. 'I hid in a cupboard while they were fighting. Hid in a cupboard and pissed my pants. There's Red Beck for you.'

'Huh.' Craw nodded, his lips pressed thoughtfully together. He didn't seem all that bothered. He didn't seem all that surprised. 'Well, it don't change what you did today. There's far worse a man can do in a battle than hide in a cupboard.'

'I know,' muttered Beck, and his mouth hung open, ready to let it spill. It was like his body needed to say it, to spit out the rot like a sick man might need to puke. His mouth had to do it, however much he might want to keep it hid. 'I need to tell you something, Chief,' his dried-out tongue wrestling with the words.

'I'm listening,' said Craw.

He cast about for the best way to put it, like the sick man casting about for the best thing to spew into. As though there were words pretty enough to make it less ugly. 'The thing is—'

'Bastard!' someone shouted, knocked Beck so bad he spilled the dregs of the cup into the fire.

511

'Oy!' growled Craw, wincing as he got up, but whoever it was had already gone. There was a current through the crowd, of a sudden. A new mood, angry, jeering at someone being dragged through their midst. Craw followed on and Beck followed him, more relieved than upset at the distraction, like the sick man realising he don't have to puke into his wife's hat after all.

They shouldered through the crowd to the biggest fire-pit, in the centre of the Heroes, where the biggest men were. Black Dow sat in the midst of 'em in Skarling's Chair, one dangling hand twisting the pommel of his sword round and round. Shivers was there, on the far side of the fire, pushing someone down onto his knees.

'Shit,' muttered Craw.

'Well, well, well.' And Dow licked his teeth and sat back, grinning. 'If it ain't Prince Calder.'

Calder tried to look as comfortable as he could on his knees with his hands tied and Shivers looming over him. Which wasn't all that comfortable. 'The invitation was hard to refuse,' he said.

'I'll bet,' answered Dow. 'Can you guess why I made it?'

Calder took a look around the gathering. All the great men of the North were there. All the bloated fools. Glama Golden, sneering over from the far side of the fire. Cairm Ironhead, watching, one brow raised. Brodd Tenways, a bit less scornful than usual, but a long way from friendly. Caul Reachey, with a 'My hands are tied' sort of a wince, and Curnden Craw, with a 'Why didn't you run?' sort of a one. Calder gave the pair of them a sheepish nod. 'I've an inkling.'

'For anyone who hasn't an inkling, Calder here tried to prevail on my new Second to kill me.' Some muttering ran through the firelit crowd, but not that much. No one was overly surprised. 'Ain't that right, Craw?'

Craw looked at the ground. 'That's right.'

'You going to deny it, even?' asked Dow.

'If I did, could we forget the whole thing?'

Dow grinned. 'Still joking. I like that. Not that the faithlessness surprises me, you're known for a schemer. The stupidity does, though. Curnden Craw's a straight edge, everyone knows that.' Craw winced even harder, and looked away. 'Stabbing men in the back ain't his style.'

'I'll admit it wasn't my brightest moment,' said Calder. 'How about we notch it up to youthful folly and let it slide?'

'Don't see how I can. You've pushed my patience too far, and it's got a spike on the end. Haven't I treated you like a son?' A few chuckles ran along both sides of the fire-pit. 'I mean, not a favourite son. Not a firstborn or nothing. A runty one, down near the end o' the litter, but still. Didn't I let you take charge when your brother died, though you haven't the experience or the name for it? Didn't I let you have your say around the fire? And when you said too much didn't I clear you off to Carleon with your wife to cool your head rather than just cut your head off and worry later on the details? Your father weren't so forgiving to those who disagreed with him, as I recall.'

'True,' said Calder. 'You've been generosity itself. Oh. Apart from trying to kill me, of course.'

Dow's forehead wrinkled. 'Eh?'

'Four nights past, at Caul Reachey's weapontake? Bringing anything back? No? Three men tried to murder me, and when I put one to the question he dropped Brodd Tenways' name. And everyone knows Brodd Tenways wouldn't do a thing without your say-so. You denying it?'

'I am, in fact.' Dow looked over at Tenways and he gave a little shake of his rashy head. 'And Tenways too. Might be he's lying, and has his own reasons, but I can tell you one thing for a fact – any man here can tell I had no part in it.'

'How's that?'

Dow leaned forwards. 'You're still fucking breathing, boy. You think if I'd a mind to kill you there's a man could stop me?' Calder narrowed his eyes. He had to admit there was something to that argument. He looked for Reachey, but the old warrior was steadfastly looking elsewhere.

'But it don't much matter who didn't die yesterday,' said Dow. 'I can tell you who'll die tomorrow.' Silence stretched out, and never had the word to end it been so horribly clear. 'You.' Seemed like everyone was smiling. Everyone except Calder, and Craw, and maybe Caul Shivers, but that was probably just because his face was so scarred he couldn't get his mouth to curl. 'Anyone got any objections to this?' Aside from the crackling of the fire, there wasn't a sound. Dow stood up on his seat and shouted it. 'Anyone want to speak up for Calder?' None spoke.

How silly his whispers in the dark seemed now. All his seeds had fallen on stony ground all right. Dow was firmer set in Skarling's Chair than ever and Calder hadn't a friend to his name. His brother was dead and he'd somehow found a way to make Curnden Craw his enemy. Some spinner of webs he was.

'No one? No?' Slowly, Dow sat back down. 'Anyone here not happy about this?'

'I'm not fucking delighted,' said Calder.

Dow burst out laughing. 'You got bones, lad, whatever they say. Bones of a rare kind. I'll miss you. You got a preference when it comes to method? We could hang you, or cut your head off, or your father was partial to the bloody cross though I couldn't advise it—'

Maybe the fighting today had gone to Calder's head, or maybe he was sick of treading softly, or maybe it was the cleverest thing to do right then. 'Fuck yourself!' he snarled, and spat into the fire. 'I'd sooner die with a sword in my hand! You and me, Black Dow, in the circle. A challenge.'

Slow, scornful silence. 'Challenge?' sneered Dow. 'Over what? You make a challenge to decide an issue, boy. There's no issue here. Just you turning on your Chief and trying to talk his Second into stabbing him in the back. Would your father have taken a challenge?'

'You're not my father. You're not a fucking shadow of him! He made that chain you're wearing. Forged it link by link, like he forged the North new. You stole it from the Bloody-Nine, and you had to stab him in the back to get it.' Calder smirked like his life depended on it. Which it did. 'All you are is a thief, Black Dow, and a coward, and an oath-breaker, and a fucking idiot besides.'

'That a fact?' Dow tried to smile himself, but it looked more like a scowl. Calder might be a beaten man, but that was just the point. Having a beaten man fling shit at him was souring his day of victory.

'Haven't you got the bones to face me, man to man?'

'Show me a man and we'll see.'

'I was man enough for Tenways' daughter.' Calder got a flutter of laughter of his own. 'But what?' And he nodded up to Shivers. 'You get harder men to do your black work now, do you, Black Dow? Lost your taste for it? Come on! Fight me! The circle!'

Dow had no real reason to say yes. He'd nothing to win. But sometimes it's more about how it looks than how it is. Calder was famous as the biggest coward and piss-poorest fighter in any given company. Dow's name was all built on being the very opposite. This was a challenge to everything he was, in front of all the great men of the North. He couldn't turn it down. Dow saw it, and he slouched back in Skarling's Chair like a man who'd argued with his wife over whose turn it was to muck out the pigpen, and lost.

'All right. You want it the hard way you can have it the fucking hard way. Tomorrow at dawn. And no pissing about spinning the shield and choosing weapons. Me and you. A sword each. To the death.' He angrily waved his hand. 'Take this bastard somewhere I don't have to look at him smirk.'

Calder gasped as Shivers jerked him to his feet, twisted him around and marched him off. The crowd closed in behind them. Songs started up again, and laughter, and bragging, and all the business of victory and success. His imminent doom was a distraction hardly worth stopping the party for.

'I thought I told you to run.' Craw's familiar voice in his ear, the old man pushing through the press beside him.

Calder snorted. 'I thought I told you not to say anything. Seems neither of us can do as we're told.'

'I'm sorry it had to be this way.'

'It didn't have to be this way.'

He saw Craw's grimace etched by firelight. 'You're right. I'm sorry this is what I chose, then.'

'Don't be. You're a straight edge, everyone knows it. And let's face the facts, I've been hurtling towards the grave ever since my father died. Just a surprise it's taken me this long to hit mud. Who knows, though?' he called as Shivers dragged him between two of the Heroes, giving Craw one last smirk over his shoulder. 'Maybe I'll beat Dow in the circle!'

He could tell from Craw's sorry face he didn't think it likely.

Neither did Calder, if he was honest for once. The very reasons for the success of his little plan were also its awful shortcomings. Calder was the biggest coward and piss-poorest fighter in any given company. Black Dow was the very opposite. They hadn't earned their reputations by accident.

He'd about as much chance in the circle as a side of ham, and everyone knew it.

Stuff Happens

'I've a letter for General Mitterick,' said Tunny, hooding his lantern as he walked up out of the dusk to the general's tent. Even in the limited light, it was plain the guard was a man who nature had favoured better below the neck than above it. 'He's with the lord marshal. You'll have to wait.'

Tunny displayed his sleeve. 'I'm a full corporal, you know. Don't I get precedence?'

The guard did not take the joke. 'Press-a-what?'

'Never mind.' Tunny sighed, and stood beside him, and waited. Voices burbled from the tent, gaining in volume.

'I demand the right to attack!' one boomed out. Mitterick. There weren't many soldiers in the army who had the good fortune not to recognise that voice. The guard frowned across at Tunny as though to say, you shouldn't be listening to this. Tunny held up the letter and shrugged. 'We've forced them back! They're teetering, exhausted! They've no stomach left for it.' Shadows moved on the side of the tent, perhaps a shaken fist. 'The slightest push now . . . I have them just where I want them!'

'You thought you had them there yesterday and it turned out they had you.' Marshal Kroy's more measured tones. 'And the Northmen aren't the only ones who've run out of stomach.'

'My men deserve the chance to finish what they've started! Lord Marshal, I deserve the—'

'No!' Harsh as a whip cracking.

'Then, sir, I demand the right to resign—'

'No to that too. No even more to that.' Mitterick tried to say something but Kroy spoke over him. 'No! Must you argue every point? You will swallow your damn pride and do your damn duty! You will stand down, you will bring your men back across the bridge and you will prepare your division for the journey south to Uffrith as soon as we have completed negotiations. Do you understand me, General?'

There was a long pause and then, very quietly, 'We lost.' Mitterick's voice, but hardly recognisable. Suddenly shrunk very small, and weak, sounding almost as if there were tears in it. As if some cord held vibrating taut had suddenly snapped, and all Mitterick's bluster had snapped with it. 'We lost.'

'We drew.' Kroy's voice was quiet now, but the night was quiet, and few men could drop eaves like Tunny when there was something worth hearing. 'Sometimes that's the most one can hope for. The irony of the soldier's profession. War can only ever pave the way for peace. And it should be no other way. I used to be like you, Mitterick. I thought there was but one right thing to do. One day, probably very soon, you will replace me, and you will learn the world is otherwise.'

Another pause. 'Replace you?'

'I suspect the great architect has tired of this particular mason. General Jalenhorm died at the Heroes. You are the only reasonable choice. One that I support in any case.'

'I am speechless.'

'If I had known I could achieve that simply by resigning I would have done it years ago.'

A pause. 'I would like Opker promoted to lead my division.'

'I see no objection.'

'And for General Jalenhorm's I thought—'

'Colonel Felnigg has been given the command,' said Kroy. 'General Felnigg, I should say.'

'Felnigg?' came Mitterick's voice, with a tinge of horror.

'He has the seniority, and my recommendation to the king is already sent.'

'I simply cannot work with that man—'

'You can and you will. Felnigg is sharp, and cautious, and he will balance you out, as you have balanced me. Though you were often, frankly, a pain in my arse, by and large it has been an honour.' There was a sharp crack, as of polished boot heels snapping together.

Then another. 'Lord Marshal Kroy, the honour has been entirely mine.'

Tunny and the guard both flung themselves to the most rigid

attention as the two biggest hats in the army suddenly strode from the tent. Kroy made sharply off into the gathering gloom. Mitterick stayed there, looking after him, one hand opening and closing by his side.

Tunny had a pressing appointment with a bottle and a bedroll. He cleared his throat. 'General Mitterick, sir!'

Mitterick turned, very obviously wiping away a tear while pretending to be clearing dust from his eye. 'Yes?'

'Corporal Tunny, sir, standard-bearer of his Majesty's First Regiment.'

Mitterick frowned. 'The same Tunny who was made colour sergeant after Ulrioch?'

Tunny puffed out his chest. 'The same, sir.'

'The same Tunny who was demoted after Dunbrec?'

Tunny's shoulders slumped. 'The same, sir.'

'The same Tunny who was court-martialled after that business at Shricta?'

And further yet. 'The same, sir, though I hasten to point out that the tribunal found no evidence of wrongdoing, sir.'

Mitterick snorted. 'So much for tribunals. What brings you here, Tunny?'

He held out the letter. 'I have come in my official capacity as standard-bearer, sir, with a letter from my commanding officer, Colonel Vallimir.'

Mitterick looked down at it. 'What does it say?'

'I wouldn't—'

'I do not believe a soldier with your experience of tribunals would carry a letter without a good idea of the contents. What does it say?'

Tunny conceded the point. 'Sir, I believe the colonel lays out at some length the reasons behind his failure to attack today.'

'Does he.'

'He does, sir, and he furthermore apologises most profusely to you, sir, to Marshal Kroy, to his Majesty, and in fact to the people of the Union in general, and he offers his immediate resignation, sir, but also demands the right to explain himself before a court martial – he was rather vague on that point, sir – he goes on to praise the men and to shoulder the blame entirely himself, and—'

Mitterick took the letter from Tunny's hand, crumpled it up in his fist and tossed it into a puddle.

'Tell Colonel Vallimir not to worry.' He watched the letter for a moment, drifting in the broken reflection of the evening sky, then shrugged. 'It's a battle. We all made mistakes. Would it be pointless, Corporal Tunny, to tell you to stay out of trouble?'

'All advice gratefully considered, sir.'

'What if I make it an order?'

'All orders considered too, sir.'

'Huh. Dismissed.'

Tunny snapped out his most sycophantic salute, turned and quick-marched off into the night before anyone decided to court-martial him.

The moments after a battle are a profiteer's dream. Corpses to be picked over, or dug up and picked over, trophies to be traded, booze, and chagga, and husk to be sold to the celebrating or the commiserating at equally outrageous mark-ups. He'd seen men without a bit to their names in the year leading up to an engagement make their fortunes in the hour after. But most of Tunny's stock was still on his horse, which was who knew where, and, besides, his heart just wasn't in it.

So he kept his distance from the fires and the men around them, strolling along behind the lines, heading north across the trampled battlefield. He passed a pair of clerks booking the dead by lamplight, one making notes in a ledger while the other twitched up shrouds to look for corpses worth noting and shipping back to Midderland, men too noble to go in the Northern dirt. As though one dead man's any different from another. He clambered over the wall he'd spent all day watching, become again the unremarkable farmer's folly it had been before the battle, and picked his way through the dusk towards the far left of the line where the remains of the First were stationed.

'I didn't know, I just didn't know, I just didn't see him!'

Two men stood in barley patched with little white flowers, maybe thirty strides from the nearest fire, staring down at something. One was a nervous-looking young lad Tunny didn't recognise, holding an empty flatbow. A new recruit, maybe. The other was Yolk, a torch in one hand, stabbing at the lad with a pointed finger.

'What's to do?' growled Tunny as he walked up, already developing a bad feeling. It got worse when he saw what they were looking at. 'Oh, no, no.' Worth lay in a bald patch of earth, his eyes open and his tongue hanging out, a flatbow bolt right through his breastbone.

'I thought it was Northmen!' said the lad.

'The Northmen are on the north side of the lines, you fucking idiot!' snapped Yolk at him.

'I thought he had an axe!'

'A shovel.' Tunny dug it out of the barley, just beyond the limp fingers of Worth's left hand. 'Reckon he'd been off doing what he did best.'

'I should fucking kill you!' snarled Yolk, reaching for his sword. The lad gave a helpless squeak, holding his flatbow up in front of him.

'Leave it.' Tunny stepped between them, put a restraining palm on Yolk's chest and gave a long, painful sigh. 'It's a battle. We all made mistakes. I'll go to Sergeant Forest, see what's to be done.' He pulled the flatbow from the lad's limp hands and pushed the shovel into them. 'In the meantime, you'd better get digging.' For Worth, the Northern dirt would have to do.

AFTER THE BATTLE

'You never have to wait long, or look far,
to be reminded of how thin the line is
between being a hero or a goat'

Mickey Mantle

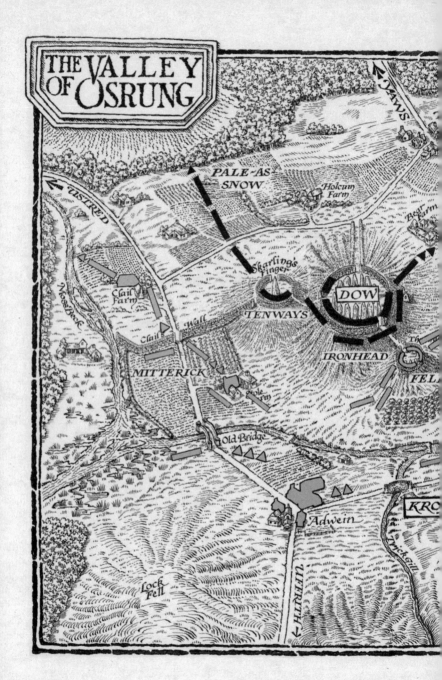

THE VALLEY OF OSRUNG

YAWS

PALE-AS SNOW

USTRED

Holcum Farm

Bear Farm

Clail Farm

Moss Beck

Skarling's Finger

DOW

TENWAYS

Wall

Clail

IRONHEAD

Th

FEL

MITTERICK

Cole Barn

Old Bridge

KRO

Adwein

UFFRITH

Brick Hill

Lock Fell

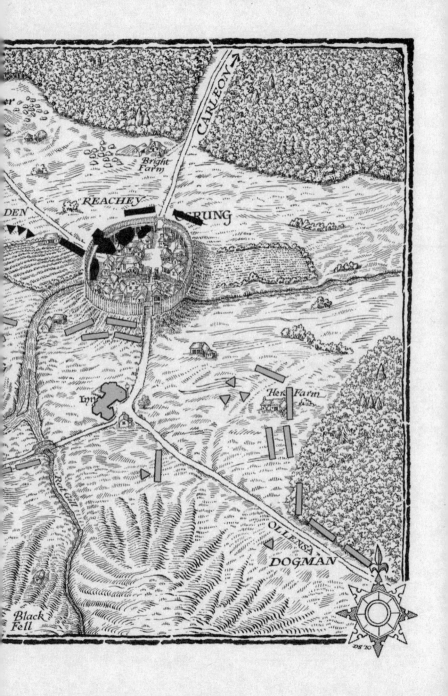

End of the Road

'He in there?'

Shivers gave one slow nod. 'He's there.'

'Alone?' asked Craw, putting his hand on the rotten handle.

'He went in alone.'

Meaning, more'n likely, he was with the witch. Craw wasn't keen to renew his acquaintance with her, especially after seeing her surprise yesterday, but dawn was on the way, and it was past time he was too. About ten years past time. He had to tell his Chief first. That was the right thing to do. He blew out through his puffed cheeks, grimaced at his stitched face, then turned the handle and went in.

Ishri stood in the middle of the dirt floor, hands on her hips, head hanging over on one side. Her long coat was scorched about the hem and up one sleeve, part of the collar burned away, the bandages underneath blackened. But her skin was still so perfect the torch flames were almost reflected in her cheek, like a black mirror.

'Why fight this fool?' she was sneering, one long finger pointing up towards the Heroes. 'There is nothing you can win from him. If you step into the circle I cannot protect you.'

'Protect me?' Dow slouched by the dark window, hard face all in shadow, his axe held loose just under the blade. 'I've handled men ten times harder'n Prince bloody Calder in the circle.' And he gave it a long, screeching lick with a whetstone.

'Calder.' Ishri snorted. 'There are other forces at work here. Ones beyond your understanding—'

'Ain't really beyond my understanding. You're in a feud with this First of the Magi, so you're using my feud with the Union as a way to fight each other. Am I close to it? Feuds I understand,

527

believe me. You witches and whatever think you live in a world apart, but you've got both feet in this one, far as I can tell.'

She lifted her chin. 'Where there is sharp metal there are risks.'

''Course. It's the appeal o' the stuff.' And the whetstone ground down the blade again.

Ishri narrowed her eyes, lip curling. 'What is it with you damn pink men, and your damn fighting, and your damn pride?'

Dow only grinned, teeth shining as his face tipped out of the darkness. 'Oh, you're a clever woman, no doubt, you know all kinds o' useful things.' One more lick of the stone, and he held the axe up to the light, edge glittering. 'But you know less'n naught about the North. I gave my pride up years ago. Didn't fit me. Chafed all over. This is about my name.' He tested the edge, sliding his thumb-tip down it gently as you might down a lover's neck, then shrugged. 'I'm Black Dow. I can't get out o' this any more'n I can fly to the moon.'

Ishri shook her head in disgust. 'After all the effort I have gone to—'

'If I get killed your wasted effort will be my great fucking regret, how's that?'

She scowled at Craw, and then at Dow as he set his axe down by the wall, and gave an angry hiss. 'I will not miss your weather.' And she took hold of her singed coat-tail and jerked it savagely in front of her face. There was a snapping of cloth and Ishri was gone, only a shred of blackened bandage fluttering down where she'd stood.

Dow caught it between finger and thumb. 'She could just use the door, I guess, but it wouldn't have quite the . . . drama.' He blew the scrap of cloth away and watched it twist through the air. 'Ever wish you could just disappear, Craw?'

Only every day for the last twenty years. 'Maybe she's got a point,' he grunted. 'You know. About the circle.'

'You too?'

'There's naught to gain. Bethod always used to say there's nothing shows more power than—'

'*Fuck* mercy,' growled Dow, sliding his sword from its sheath, fast enough to make it hiss. Craw swallowed, had to stop himself taking a step back. 'I've given that boy all kinds o' chances and he's made me look a prick and a half. You know I've got to kill him.' Dow started polishing the dull, grey blade with a rag, muscles working on the side of his head. 'I got to kill him bad. I got to kill him so much no one'll think to make me look a prick for a hundred years. Got to teach a lesson. That's how this works.' He looked up and Craw found he couldn't meet his eye. Found he was looking down at the dirt floor, and saying nothing. 'Take it you won't be sticking about to hold a shield for me?'

'Said I'd stick 'til the battle's done.'

'You did.'

'The battle's done.'

'The battle ain't ever done, Craw, you know that.' Dow watched him, half his face in the light, the other eye just a gleam in the dark, and Craw started spilling reasons even though he hadn't been asked.

'There are better men for the task. Younger men. Men with better knees, and stronger arms, and harder names.' Dow just kept watching. 'Lost a lot o' my friends the last few days. Too many. Whirrun's dead. Brack's gone.' Desperate not to say he'd no stomach for seeing Dow butcher Calder in the circle. Desperate not to say his loyalty might not stand it. 'Times have changed. Men the likes o' Golden and Ironhead, they got no respect for me in particular, and I got less for them. All that, and . . . and . . .'

'And you've had enough,' said Dow.

Craw's shoulders sagged. Hurt him to admit, but that summed it all up pretty well. 'I've had enough.' Had to clench his teeth and curl back his lips to stop the tears. As if saying it made it all catch up with him at once. Whirrun, and Drofd, and Brack, and Athroc and Agrick and all those others. An accusing queue of the dead, stretching back into the gloom of memory. A queue of battles fought, and won, and lost. Of choices made, right and wrong, each one a weight to carry.

Dow just nodded as he slid his sword carefully back into its sheath. 'We all got a limit. Man o' your experience needn't ever be shamed. Not ever.'

Craw just gritted his teeth, and swallowed his tears, and managed to find some dry words to say. 'Daresay you'll soon find someone else to do the job—'

'Already have.' And Dow jerked his head towards the door. 'Waiting outside.'

'Good.' Craw reckoned Shivers could handle it, probably better'n he had. He reckoned the man weren't as far past redemption as folk made out.

'Here.' Dow tossed something across the room and Craw caught it, coins snapping inside. 'A double gild and then some. Get you started, out there.'

'Thanks, Chief,' said Craw, and meant it. He'd expected a knife in his back before a purse in his hand.

Dow stood his sword up on its end. 'What you going to do?'

'I was a carpenter. A thousand bloody years ago. Thought I might go back to it. Work some wood. You might shape a coffin or two, but you don't bury many friends in that trade.'

'Huh.' Dow twisted the pommel gently between finger and thumb, the end of the sheath twisting into the dirt. 'Already buried all mine. Except the ones I made my enemies. Maybe that's where every fighter's road leads, eh?'

'If you follow it far enough.' Craw stood there a moment longer but Dow didn't answer. So he took a breath, and he turned to go.

'It was pots for me.'

Craw stopped, hand on the doorknob, hairs prickling all the way up his neck. But Black Dow was just stood there, looking down at his hand. His scarred, and scabbed, and calloused hand.

'I was apprentice to a potter.' Dow snorted. 'A thousand bloody years ago. Then the wars came, and I took up a sword instead. Always thought I'd go back to it, but . . . things happen.' He narrowed his eyes, gently rubbing the tip of his thumb against the tips of his fingers. 'The clay . . . used to make my hands . . . so soft. Imagine that.' And he looked up, and he smiled. 'Good luck, Craw.'

'Aye,' said Craw, and went outside, and shut the door behind him, and breathed out a long breath of relief. A few words and it was done. Sometimes a thing can seem an impossible leap, then when you do it you find it's just been a little step all along. Shivers was standing where he had been, arms folded, and Craw clapped him on the shoulder. 'Reckon it's up to you, now.'

'Is it?' Someone else came forward into the torchlight, a long scar through shaved-stubble hair.

'Wonderful,' muttered Craw.

'Hey, hey,' she said. Somewhat of a surprise to see her here, but it saved him some time. It was her he had to tell next.

'How's the dozen?' he asked.

'All four of 'em are great.'

Craw winced. 'Aye. Well. I need to tell you something.' She raised one brow at him. Nothing for it but just to jump. 'I'm done. I'm quitting.'

'I know.'

'You do?'

'How else would I be taking your place?'

'My place?'

'Dow's Second.'

Craw's eyes opened up wide. He looked at Wonderful, then at Shivers, then back to her. 'You?'

'Why not me?'

'Well, I just thought—'

'When you quit the sun would stop rising for the rest of us? Sorry to disappoint you.'

'What about your husband, though? Your sons? Thought you were going to—'

'Last time I went to the farm was four years past.' She tipped her head back, and there was a hardness in her eye Craw wasn't used to seeing. 'They were gone. No sign o' where.'

'But you went back not a month ago.'

'Walked a day, sat by the river and fished. Then I came back to the dozen. Couldn't face telling you. Couldn't face the pity. This is all there is for the likes of us. You'll see.' She took his hand, and squeezed it, but his stayed limp. 'Been an honour fighting with you, Craw. Look after yourself.' And she pushed her way through the door, and shut it with a clatter, and left him behind, blinking at the silent wood.

'You reckon you know someone, and then . . .' Shivers clicked his tongue. 'No one knows anyone. Not really.'

Craw swallowed. 'Life's riddled with surprises all right.' And he turned his back on the old shack and was off into the gloom.

*

He'd daydreamed often enough about the grand farewell. Walking down an aisle of well-wishing Named Men and off to his bright future, back sore from all the clapping on it. Striding through a passageway of drawn swords, twinkling in the sunlight. Riding away, fist held high in salute as Carls cheered for him and women wept over his leaving, though where the women might have sprung from was anyone's guess.

Sneaking away in the chill gloom as dawn crept up, unremarked and unremembered, not so much. But it's 'cause real life is what it is that a man needs daydreams.

Most anyone with a name worth knowing was up at the Heroes, waiting to see Calder get slaughtered. Only Jolly Yon, Scorry Tiptoe and Flood were left to see him off. The remains of Craw's dozen. And Beck, dark shadows under his eyes, the Father of Swords held in one pale fist. Craw could see the hurt in their faces, however they tried to plaster smiles over it. Like he was letting 'em down. Maybe he was.

He'd always prided himself on being well liked. Straight edge and that. Even so, his dead friends long ago got his living ones outnumbered, and they'd worked the advantage a good way further the last few days. Three of those that might've given him the warmest send-off were back to the mud at the top of the hill, and two more in the back of his cart.

He tried to drag the old blanket straight, but no tugging at the corners was going to make this square. Whirrun's chin, and Drofd's, and their noses, and their feet making sorry little tents of the threadbare old cloth. Some hero's shroud. But the living could use the good blankets. The dead there was no warming.

'Can't believe you're going,' said Scorry.

'Been saying for years I would.'

'Exactly. You never did.'

Craw could only shrug. 'Now I am.'

In his head saying goodbye to his own crew had always been like pressing hands before a battle. That same fierce tide of comradeship. Only more, because they all knew it was the last time, rather than just fearing it might be. But aside from the feeling of squeezing flesh, it was nothing like that. They seemed strangers, almost. Maybe he was like the corpse of a dead comrade, now. They just wanted him buried, so they could get on.

For him there wouldn't even be the worn-down ritual of heads bowed about the fresh-turned earth. There'd just be a goodbye that felt like a betrayal on both sides.

'Ain't staying for the show, then?' asked Flood.

'The duel?' Or the murder, as it might be better put. 'I seen enough blood, I reckon. The dozen's yours, Yon.'

Yon raised an eyebrow at Scorry, and at Flood, and at Beck. 'All of 'em?'

'You'll find more. We always have. Few days time you won't even notice there's aught missing.' Sad fact was it was more'n likely true. That's how it had always been, when they lost one man or another. Hard to imagine it'd be the same with yourself. That you'd be forgotten the way a pond forgets a stone tossed in. A few ripples and you're gone. It's in the nature of men to forget.

Yon was frowning at the blanket, and what was underneath. 'If I die,' he muttered, 'who'll find my sons for me—'

'Maybe you should find 'em yourself, you thought o' that? Find 'em yourself, Yon, and tell 'em what you are, and make amends, while you've got breath still to do it.'

Yon looked down at his boots. 'Aye. Maybe.' A silence comfortable as a spike up the arse. 'Well, then. We got shields to hold, I reckon, up there with Wonderful.'

'Right y'are,' said Craw. Yon turned and walked off up the hill, shaking his head. Scorry gave a last nod then followed him.

'So long, Chief,' said Flood.

'I guess I'm no one's Chief no more.'

'You'll always be mine.' And he limped off after the other two, leaving just Craw and Beck beside the cart. A lad he hadn't even known two days before to say the last goodbye.

Craw sighed, and he hauled himself up into the seat, wincing at all the bruises he'd gained the last few days. Beck stood below, Father of Swords in both hands, sheathed point on the dirt. 'I've got to hold a shield for Black Dow,' he said. 'Me. You ever done that?'

'More'n once. There's nothing to it. Just hold the circle, make sure no one leaves it. Stand by your Chief. Do the right thing, like you did yesterday.'

'Yesterday,' muttered Beck, staring down at the wheel of the cart, like he was staring right through the ground and didn't like what he saw on the other side. 'I didn't tell you everything, yesterday. I wanted to, but . . .'

Craw frowned over his shoulder at the two shapes under the blanket. He could've done without hearing anyone's confessions. He was carting enough weight around with his own mistakes. But Beck was already talking. Droning, flat, like a bee trapped in a hot room. 'I killed a man, in Osrung. Not a Union one, though. One of ours. Lad called Reft. He stood, and fought, and I ran, and hid, and I killed him.' Beck was still staring at the cartwheel, wet glistening in his eyes. 'Stabbed him right through with my father's sword. Took him for a Union man.'

Craw wanted just to snap those reins and go. But maybe he could help, and all his years wasted might be some use to someone. So he gritted his teeth, and leaned down, and put his hand on Beck's shoulder. 'I know it burns at you. Probably it always will. But the sad fact is, I've heard a dozen stories just like it in my time. A score. Wouldn't raise much of an eyebrow from any man who's seen a battle. This is the black business. Bakers make bread, and carpenters make houses, and we make dead men. All you can do is take each day as it comes. Try and do the best you can with what you're given. You won't always do the right thing, but you can try. And you can try to do the right thing next time. That, and stay alive.'

Beck shook his head. 'I killed a man. Shouldn't I pay?'

'You killed a man?' Craw raised his arms, helplessly let them drop. 'It's a battle. Everyone's at it. Some live, some die, some pay, some don't. If you've come through all right, be thankful. Try to earn it.'

'I'm a fucking coward.'

'Maybe.' Craw jerked his thumb over his shoulder at Whirrun's corpse. 'There's a hero. Tell me who's better off.'

Beck took a shuddering breath. 'Aye. I guess.' He held up the Father of Swords and Craw took it under the crosspiece, hefted the great length of metal up and slid it carefully down in the back, next to Whirrun's body. 'You taking it now, then? He left it to you?'

'He left it to the ground.' Craw twitched the blanket across so it was out of sight. 'Wanted it buried with him.'

'Why?' asked Beck. 'Ain't it God's sword, fell from the sky? I thought it had to be passed on. Is it cursed?'

Craw took up the reins and turned back to the north. 'Every sword's a curse, boy.' And he gave 'em a snap, and the wagon trundled off.

Away up the road.

Away from the Heroes.

By the Sword

alder sat, and watched the guttering flames.

It was looking very much as if he'd used up all his cunning for the sake of another few hours alive. And cold, hungry, itchy, increasingly terrified hours at that. Sitting, staring across a fire at Shivers, bound wrists chafed and crossed legs aching and the damp working up through the seat of his trousers and making his arse clammy-cold.

But when a few hours is all you can get, you'll do anything for them. Probably he would've done anything for a few more. Had anyone been offering. They weren't. Like his brilliant ambitions the diamond-bright stars had slowly faded to nothing, crushed out as the first merciless signs of day slunk from the east, behind the Heroes. His last day.

'How long 'til dawn?'

'It'll come when it comes,' said Shivers.

Calder stretched out his neck and wriggled his shoulders, sore from slumping into twisted half-sleep with his hands tied, twitching through nightmares which, when he jerked awake, he felt faintly nostalgic for. 'Don't suppose you could see your way to untying my hands, at least?'

'When it comes.'

How bloody disappointing it all was. What lofty hopes his father had held. 'All for you,' he used to say, a hand on Calder's shoulder and a hand on Scale's. 'You'll rule the North.' What an ending, for a man who'd spent his life dreaming of being king. He'd be remembered, all right. For dying the bloodiest death in the North's bloody history.

Calder sighed, ragged. 'Things don't tend to work out the way we imagine, do they?'

With a faint clink, clink, Shivers tapped his ring against his metal eye. 'Not often.'

'Life is, basically, fucking shit.'

'Best to keep your expectations low. Maybe you'll be pleasantly surprised.'

Calder's expectations had plunged into an abyss but a pleasant surprise still didn't seem likely. He flinched at the memory of the duels the Bloody-Nine had fought for his father. The blood-mad shriek of the crowd. The ring of shields about the edge of the circle. The ring of grim Named Men holding them. Making sure no one could leave until enough blood was spilled. He'd never dreamed he'd end up fighting in one. Dying in one.

'Who's holding the shields for me?' he muttered, as much to fill the silence as anything.

'I heard Pale-as-Snow offered, and old White-Eye Hansul. Caul Reachey too.'

'He can hardly get out of it, can he, since I'm married to his daughter?'

'He can hardly get out of it.'

'Probably they've only asked for a shield so they don't get sprayed with too much of my gore.'

'Probably.'

'Funny thing, gore. A sour annoyance to those it goes on and a bitter loss to those it comes out of. Where's the upside, eh? Tell me that.'

Shivers shrugged. Calder worked his wrists against the rope, trying to keep the blood flowing to his fingers. It would be nice if he could hold on to his sword long enough to get killed with it in his hand, at least. 'Got any advice for me?'

'Advice?'

'Aye, you're some fighter.'

'If you get a chance, don't hesitate.' Shivers frowned down at the ruby on his little finger. 'Mercy and cowardice are the same.'

'My father always used to say that nothing shows greater power than mercy.'

'Not in the circle.' And Shivers stood.

Calder held up his wrists. 'It's time?'

The knife glimmered pink with the dawn as it darted out and neatly slit the cord. 'It's time.'

'We just wait?' grunted Beck.

Wonderful turned her frown on him. 'Unless you fancy doing a little dance out there. Get everyone warmed up.'

Beck didn't fancy it. The circle of raked-over mud in the very centre of the Heroes looked a lonely place to be right then. Very bare, and very empty, while all about its pebble-marked edge folk were packed in tight. It was in a circle like this one his father had fought the Bloody-Nine. Fought, and died, and bad.

A lot of the great names of the North were holding shields for this one. Beside the leftovers of Craw's dozen there was Brodd Tenways, Cairm Ironhead and Glama Golden on Dow's half of the circle, and plenty of their Named Men around 'em.

Caul Reachey stood on the opposite side of the case, a couple of other old boys, none of 'em looking happy to be there. Would've been a sorry lot compared to Dow's side if it hadn't been for the biggest bastard Beck had ever seen, towering over the rest like a mountain peak above the foothills.

'Who's the monster?' he muttered.

'Stranger-Come-Knocking,' Flood whispered back. 'Chief of all the lands east of the Crinna. Bloody savages out there, and I hear he's the worst.'

It was a savage pack the giant had at his back. Men all wild hair and wild twitching, pierced with bone and prickled with paint, dressed in skulls and tatters. Men who looked like they'd sprung straight from an old song, maybe the one about how Shubal the Wheel stole the crag lord's daughter. How had it gone?

'Here they come,' grunted Yon. A disapproving mutter, a few sharp words, but mostly thick silence. The men on the other side of the circle parted and Shivers came through, dragging Calder under the arm.

He looked a long stretch less smug than when Beck first saw him, riding up to Reachey's weapontake on his fine horse, but he was still grinning. A wonky, pale-faced, pink-eyed grin, but a grin still. Shivers let go of him, squelched heedless across the seven strides of empty muck leaving a trail of gently filling boot-prints, fell in beside Wonderful and took a shield from a man behind her.

Calder nodded across the circle at each man, like they were a set of old friends. He nodded to Beck. When Beck had first seen that smirk it'd looked full of pride, full of mockery, but maybe they'd both changed since. If Calder was laughing now it looked like he was only laughing at himself. Beck nodded back, solemn. He knew what it was to face your death, and he reckoned it took some bones to smile at a time like that. Some bones.

Calder was so scared the faces across the circle were just a dizzying smear. But he was set on meeting the Great Leveller as his father had, and his brother too. With some pride. He kept that in front of him, and he clung on to his smirk, nodding at faces too blurred to recognise as if they'd turned out for his wedding rather than his burial.

He had to talk. Fill the time with blather. Anything to stop him thinking. Calder grabbed Reachey's hand, the one without the battered shield on it. 'You came!'

The old man hardly met his eye. 'Least I could do.'

'Most you could do, far as I'm concerned. Tell Seff for me . . . well, tell her I'm sorry.'

'I will.'

'And cheer up. This isn't a funeral.' He nudged the old man in the ribs. 'Yet.' The scatter of chuckles he got for that made him feel a little less like shitting his trousers. There was a soft, low laugh among them, too. One that came from very high up. Stranger-Come-Knocking, and by all appearances on Calder's side. 'You're holding a shield for me?'

The giant tapped the tiny-looking circle of wood with his club of a forefinger. 'I am.'

'What's your interest?'

'In the clash of vengeful steel and the blood watering the thirsty earth? In the roar of the victor and the scream of the slaughtered? What could interest me more than seeing men give all and take all, life and death balanced on the edge of a blade?'

Calder swallowed. 'Why on my side, though?'

'There was room.'

'Right.' That was about all he had to offer now. A good spot to watch his own murder. 'Did you come for the room?' he asked Pale-as-Snow.

'I came for you, and for Scale, and for your father.'

'And me,' said White-Eye Hansul.

After all the hate he'd shrugged off, that bit of loyalty almost cracked his smirk wide open. 'Means a lot,' he croaked. The really sad thing was that it was true. He thumped White-Eye's shield with his fist, squeezed Pale-as-Snow's shoulder. 'Means a lot.'

But the time for hugs and damp eyes was fading rapidly into the past. There was noise in the crowd across the circle, then movement, then the shield-carriers stood aside. The Protector of the North strolled through the gap, easy as a gambler who'd already won the big bet, his black standard looming behind him like the shadow of death indeed. He'd stripped down to a leather vest, arms and shoulders heavy with branched vein and twisted sinew, the chain Calder's father used to wear hanging around his neck, diamond winking.

Hands clapped, weapons rattled, metal clanged on metal, everyone straining to get the faintest approving glance from the man who'd seen off the Union. Everyone cheering, even on Calder's side of the circle. He could hardly blame them. They'd still have to scratch a living when Dow had carved him into weeping chunks.

'You made it, then.' Dow jerked his head towards Shivers. 'I was worried my dog might've eaten you in the night.' There was a good deal more laughter than the joke deserved but Shivers didn't so much as twitch, his scarred face a dead blank. Dow grinned around at the Heroes, their lichen-spotted tops peering over the heads of the crowd, and opened his arms, fingers spread. 'Looks like we got a circle custom made for the purpose, don't it? Quite the venue!'

'Aye,' said Calder. That was about all the bravado he could manage.

'Normally there's a form to follow.' Dow turned one finger round and round. 'Laying out the matter to decide, listing the pedigree of the champions and so on, but I reckon we can skip that. We all know the matter. We all know you got no pedigree.' Another laugh, and Dow spread his arms again. 'And if I start naming all the men I've put back in the mud we'll never get started!'

A flood of thigh-slapping manly amusement. Seemed Dow

was intent on proving himself the better wit as well as the better fighter, and it was no fairer a contest. Winners always get the louder laughs and, for once, Calder was out of jokes. Dead men aren't that funny, maybe. So he just stood as the crowd quieted and left only the gentle wind over the muck, the flapping of the black standard, a bird chirruping from the top of one of the stones.

Dow heaved out a sigh. 'Sorry to say I've had to send to Carleon for your wife. She stood hostage for you, didn't she?'

'Let her be, you bastard!' barked Calder, nearly choking on a surge of anger. 'She's got no part in this!'

'You're in no place to tell me what's what, you little shit.' Dow turned his head without taking his eyes off Calder, and spat into the mud. 'I've half a mind to burn her. Give her the bloody cross, just for the fucking lesson. Wasn't that the way your father liked to do it, back in the old days?' Dow held up his open palm. 'But I can afford to be generous. Reckon I'll let it pass. Out of respect to Caul Reachey, since he's the one man in the North who still does what he fucking says he will.'

'I'm right grateful for it,' grunted Reachey, still not meeting Calder's eye.

''Spite of my reputation, I don't much care for hanging women. I get any softer they'll have to call me White Dow!' Another round of laughter, and Dow let go a flurry of punches at the air, so fast Calder could hardly count how many. 'Reckon I'll just have to kill you twice as much to make up for it.'

Something poked him in the ribs. The pommel of his sword, Pale-as-Snow handing it over with a look that said sorry, belt wrapped around the sheath.

'Oh, right. You got any advice?' asked Calder, hoping the old warrior would narrow his eyes and spout some razor observations about how Dow led with the point too much, or dipped his shoulder too low, or was awfully vulnerable to a middle cut.

All he did was puff out his cheeks. 'It's fucking Black Dow,' he muttered.

'Right.' Calder swallowed sour spit. 'Thanks for that.' It was all so disappointing. He drew his sword, held the sheath uncertainly for a moment, then handed it back. Couldn't see why he'd have any need for it again. There was no talking his way out of this. Sometimes you have to fight. He took a long breath and a step forwards, his worn-out Styrian boot squelching into the muck. Only a little step over a ring of pebbles, but still the hardest he'd ever taken.

Dow stretched his head one way, then the other, then drew his own blade, taking his time about it, metal hissing softly. 'This was the Bloody-Nine's sword. I beat him, man against man. You know. You were there. So what do you reckon your fucking chances are?' Looking at that long grey blade, Calder didn't reckon his chances were very good at all. 'Didn't I warn you? If you tried to play your own games things'd get ugly.' Dow swept the faces around the circle with his scowl. It was true, there were few pretty ones among them. 'But you had to preach peace. Had to spread your little lies around. You had to—'

'Shut your fucking hole and get *on* with it!' screamed Calder. 'You boring old cunt!'

A mutter went up, then some laughter, then another, bowel-loosening round of clattering metal. Dow shrugged, and took his own step forwards.

There was a rattle as men eased inwards, rims of their shields scraping, locking together. Locking them in. A round wall of bright painted wood. Green trees, dragon heads, rivers running, eagles flying, some scarred and beaten from the work of the last few days. A ring of hungry faces, teeth bared in snarls and grins, eyes bright with expectation. Just Calder, and Black Dow, and no way out but blood.

Calder probably should've been thinking about how he might beat the long, long odds, and get out of this alive. Opening gambits, thrust or feint, footwork, all the rest. Because he had a chance, didn't he? Two men fight, there's always a chance. But all he could think about was Seff's face, and how beautiful it was. He wished he'd been able to see it one more time. Tell her that he loved her, or not to worry, or to forget him and live her life or some other useless shit. His father always told him, 'You find out what a man really is, when he's facing death.' It seemed, after all, he was a sentimental little prick. Maybe we all are at the end.

Calder raised his sword, open hand out in front, the way he thought he remembered being taught. Had to attack. That's what

Scale would've said. If you're not attacking you're losing. He realised too late his hand was trembling.

Dow looked him up and down, his own blade hanging carelessly at his side, and snorted a joyless chuckle. 'I guess not every duel's worth singing about.' And he darted forwards, lashing out underhand with a flick of his wrist.

Calder really shouldn't have been surprised to see a sword coming at him. That was what a duel was all about, after all. But even so he was pitifully unprepared. He lurched a pace back and Dow's sword crashed into his with numbing force, near ripping it from his hand, sending the blade flapping sideways and him stumbling, spare arm flailing for balance, all thought of attacking barged away by the overwhelming need to survive just one more moment.

Fortunately White-Eye Hansul's shield caught his back and spared him the indignity of sprawling in the mud, pushed him up straight in time to reel sideways as Dow sprang again, sword catching Calder's with a clang and wrenching his wrist the other way, a hearty cheer going up. Calder floundered back, cold with terror, trying to put as much space between them as he could, but the ring of shields was only so big. That was the point of it.

They slowly circled each other, Dow strutting with easy grace, sword swinging loose, as cocky and comfortable in a duel to the death as Calder might've been in his own bedchamber. Calder took the doddery, uncertain steps of a child just learning to walk, mouth hanging open, already breathing hard, cringing and stumbling at Dow's every tiniest taunting movement. The noise was deafening, breath going up in smoky puffs as the onlookers roared and hissed and hooted their support and their hatred and their—

Calder blinked, blinded for a moment. Dow had worked him around so the rising sun stabbed past the ragged edge of the standard and right in Calder's eyes. He saw metal glint, waved his sword helplessly, felt something thud into his left shoulder and spin him sideways, making a breathless squeal, waiting for the agony. He slid, righted himself, was shocked to see none of his own blood spraying. Dow had only slapped him with the flat. Toying with him. Making a show of it.

Laughter swept through the crowd, enough to sting some

anger up in Calder. He gritted his teeth, hefting his sword. If he wasn't attacking he was losing. He lunged at Dow but it was so slippery underfoot he couldn't get any snap in it. Dow just turned sideways and caught Calder's wobbling sword as he laboured past, blades scraping together, hilts locking.

'Fucking weak,' hissed Dow, and flung Calder away like a man might swat away a fly, heels kicking hopelessly at the slop as he reeled across the circle.

The men on Dow's side were less helpful than Hansul had been. A shield cracked Calder in the back of the skull and sent him sprawling. For a moment he couldn't see, couldn't breathe, skin fizzing all over. Then he was dragging himself up, limbs feeling like they weighed a ton a piece, the circle of mud tipping wildly about, jeering voices all booming and burbling.

He didn't have his sword. Reached for it. A boot came down and squashed his hand into the cold mud, spraying flecks of it in his face. He gave a gasp, more shock than pain. Then another, definitely pain as Dow twisted his heel, crushing Calder's fingers deeper.

'Prince of the North?' The point of Dow's sword pricked into Calder's neck, twisting his head towards the bright sky, making him slither helplessly up onto all fours. 'You're a fucking embarrassment, boy.' And Calder gasped as the point flicked his head back and left a burning cut up the middle of his chin.

Dow was trotting away, arms up, dragging out the show, a half-circle of leering, gurning, sneering faces showing above the shields behind him, all shouting. 'Black . . . Dow . . . Black . . . Dow . . .' Tenways chanting gleefully along, and Golden, and Shivers just frowning, weapons thrusting at the air behind them in time.

Calder worked his hand trembling out of the mud. From what he could tell as red-black spots pattered onto it from his chin, not all of his finger-joints were where they used to be.

'Get up!' An urgent voice behind him. Pale-as-Snow, maybe. 'Get up!'

'Why?' he whispered at the ground. The shame of it. Butchered by an old thug for the amusement of baying morons. He couldn't say it was undeserved, but that made it no more appealing, and no less painful either. His eyes flickered around the circle, desperately seeking a way out. But there was no way through the thicket of stomping boots, punching fists, twisted mouths, rattling shields. No way out but blood.

He took a few breaths until the world stopped spinning, then fished his sword from the mud with his left hand and got ever so slowly to his feet. Probably he should've been feigning weakness, but he didn't know how he could look any weaker than he felt. He tried to shake the fuzz from his head. He had a chance, didn't he? Had to attack. But by the dead, he was tired. Already. By the dead, his broken hand hurt, cold all the way to his shoulder.

Dow flicked his sword spinning into the air with a flourish. Left himself open for a moment in a show of warrior's arrogance. The moment for Calder to strike, and save himself, and earn a place in the songs besides. He tensed his leaden legs to spring, but by then Dow had already snatched the sword from the air with his left hand and was standing ready, his warrior's arrogance well deserved. They faced each other as the crowd slowly quieted, and the blood ran from Calder's slit chin and worked its way tickling down his neck.

'Your father died badly, as I remember,' Dow called to him. 'Head smashed to pulp in the circle.' Calder stood in silence, saving his breath for another lunge, trying to judge the space between them. 'Hardly had a face at all once the Bloody-Nine was done with him.' A big step and a swing. Now, while Dow was busy boasting. Two men fight, there's always a chance. Dow grinned. 'A bad death. Don't worry, though—'

Calder sprang, teeth rattling as his left boot thumped down and sprayed wet dirt, his sword going high and slicing hard towards Dow's skull. There was a slapping of skin as Dow caught Calder's left hand in his right, crushing Calder's fist around the hilt of his sword, blade wrenched up to waggle harmlessly at the sky.

'—I'll make sure yours is worse,' Dow finished.

Calder pawed at Dow's shoulder with his broken hand, fingers flopping uselessly at his father's chain. The thumb still worked, though, and he scraped at Dow's pitted cheek with the nail, drawing a little bead of blood, growling as he tried to force it into the hole where Dow's ear used to be along with all his disappointment, and his desperation, and his anger, finding that flap of scar with the tip, baring his teeth as—

The pommel of Dow's sword drove into his ribs with a hollow thud and pain flashed through him to the roots of his hair. He probably would've screamed if he'd had any breath in him, but it was all gone in one ripping, vomiting wheeze. He tottered, bent over, bile washing into his frozen mouth and dangling in a string from his bloody lip.

'Thought you were the big *thinker*.' Dow dragged him up by his left hand so he could hiss it right in his face. 'Thought you could get the better o' me? In the *circle*? Don't look too clever now, do you?' The pommel crunched into Calder's ribs just as he was taking a shuddering breath and drove it whimpering out again, left him limp as a wet sheepskin. 'Does he?' The crowd heckled and cackled and spat, rattled their shields and shrieked for blood. 'Hold this.' Dow tossed his sword through the air and Shivers caught it by the hilt.

'Stand up, fucker.' Dow's hand thumped shut around Calder's throat, quick and final as a bear trap. 'For once in your life, stand up.' And Dow hauled Calder straight, not able to stand by himself, not able to move his one good hand or the sword still uselessly stuck in it, not able even to breathe. Singularly unpleasant, having your windpipe squeezed shut. Calder squirmed helplessly. His mouth tasted of sick. His face was burning, burning. It always catches people by surprise, the moment of their death, even when they should see it coming. They always think they're special, somehow expect a reprieve. But no one's special. Dow squeezed harder, making the bones in Calder's neck click. His eyes felt like they were going to pop. Everything was getting bright.

'You think this is the end?' Dow grinned as he lifted Calder higher, feet almost leaving the mud. 'I'm just getting started, you fu—'

There was a sharp crack and blood sprayed up, dark streaks against the sky. Calder lurched back clumsily, gasping as his throat and his sword hand came free, near slipping over as Dow fell against him then flopped face down in the filth.

Blood gushed from his split skull, spattering Calder's ruined boots.

Time stopped.

Every voice sputtered out, coughed off, leaving the circle in sudden, breathless silence. Every eye fixed on the bubbling wound in the back of Black Dow's head. Caul Shivers stood glowering down in the midst of those gaping faces, the sword that had been the Bloody-Nine's in his fist, the grey blade dashed and speckled with Black Dow's blood.

'I'm no dog,' he said.

Calder's eyes flicked to Tenways', just as his flicked to Calder's. Both their mouths open, both doing the sums. Tenways was Black Dow's man. But Black Dow was dead, and everything was changed. Tenways' left eye twitched, just a fraction.

You get a chance, don't hesitate. Calder flung himself forward, not much more than falling, his sword coming down as Tenways reached for the hilt of his, eyes going wide. He tried to bring his shield up, got it tangled with the man beside him, and Calder's blade split his rashy face open right down to his nose, blood showering out across the men beside him.

Just goes to show, a poor fighter can beat a great one easily, even with his left hand. As long as he's the one with the drawn sword.

Beck looked around as he felt Shivers move. Saw the blade flash over and stared, skin prickling, as Dow hit the muck. Then he went for his sword. Wonderful caught his wrist before it got there.

'No.'

Beck flinched as Calder lurched at him, blade swinging. There was a hollow click and blood spattered around them, a spot on Beck's face. He tried to shake Wonderful off, get at his sword, but Scorry's hand was on his shield arm, dragging him back. 'The right thing's a different thing for every man,' hissed in his ear.

Calder stood swaying, his mouth wide open, his heart pounding so hard it was on the point of blowing his head apart, his eyes flickering from one stricken face to another. Tenways' blood-speckled Carls. Golden, and Ironhead, and their Named Men. Dow's own guards, Shivers in the midst of them, the sword that had split Dow's head still in his hand. Any moment now the circle would erupt into an orgy of carnage and it was anyone's guess who'd come out of it alive. Only certain thing seemed to be that he wouldn't.

'Come on!' he croaked, taking a wobbling step towards Tenways' men. Just to get it over with. Just to get it done.

But they stumbled back as if Calder was Skarling himself. He couldn't understand why. Until he felt a shadow fall across him, then a great weight on his shoulder. So heavy it almost made his knees buckle.

The huge hand of Stranger-Come-Knocking. 'This was well done,' said the giant, 'and fairly done too, for anything that wins is fair in war, and the greatest victory is the one that takes the fewest blows. Bethod was King of the Northmen. So should his son be. I, Stranger-Come-Knocking, Chief of a Hundred Tribes, stand with Black Calder.'

Whether the giant thought whoever was in charge stuck Black before his name, or whether he thought Calder claimed it having won, or whether he just thought it suited, who could say? Either way it stuck.

'And I.' Reachey's hand slapped down on Calder's other shoulder, his grinning, grizzled face beside it. 'I stand with my son. With Black Calder.' Now the proud father, nothing but support. Dow was dead, and everything was changed.

'And I.' Pale-as-Snow stepped up on the other side, and suddenly all those words Calder had thought wasted breath, all those seeds he'd thought dead and forgotten, sprouted forth and bore amazing blooms.

'And I.' Ironhead was next, and as he stepped from his men he gave Calder the faintest nod.

'And I.' Golden, desperate not to let his rival get ahead of him. 'I'm for Black Calder!'

'Black Calder!' men were shouting all around, urged on by their Chiefs. 'Black Calder!' All competing to shout it loudest, as though loyalty to this sudden new way of doing things could be proved through volume. 'Black Calder!' As though this had been what everyone wanted all along. What they'd expected.

Shivers squatted down and dragged the tangled chain over Dow's ruined head. He offered it to Calder, dangling from one finger, the diamond his father had worn swinging gently, made half a ruby by blood.

'Looks like you win,' said Shivers.

In spite of the very great pain, Calder found it in himself to smirk. 'Doesn't it, though?'

What was left of Craw's dozen slipped unnoticed back through the press even as most of the crowd were straining forwards.

Wonderful still had Beck's arm, Scorry at his shoulder. They bundled him away from the circle, past a set of wild-eyed men already busy tearing Dow's standard down and ripping it up between 'em, Yon and Flood behind. They weren't the only ones sloping off. Even as Black Dow's War Chiefs were stumbling over his corpse to kiss Black Calder's arse, other men were drifting away. Men who could feel which way the wind was blowing, and thought if they stuck about it might blow 'em right into the mud. Men who'd stood tight with Dow, or had scores with Bethod and didn't fancy testing his son's mercy.

They stopped in the long shadow of one of the stones, and Wonderful set her shield down against it and took a careful look around. Folk had their own worries though, and no one was paying 'em any mind.

She reached into her coat, pulled something out and slapped it into Yon's hand. 'There's yours.' Yon even had something like a grin as he closed his big fist around it, metal clicking inside. She slipped another into Scorry's hand, a third for Flood. Then she offered one to Beck. A purse. And with plenty in it too, by the way it was bulging. He stood, staring at it, until Wonderful shoved it under his nose. 'You get a half-share.'

'No,' said Beck.

'You're new, boy. A half-share is more'n fair—'

'I don't want it.'

They were all frowning at him now. 'He don't want it,' muttered Scorry.

'We should've done . . .' Beck weren't at all sure what they should've done. 'The right thing,' he finished, lamely.

'The *what*?' Yon's face screwed up with scorn. 'I hoped to have heard the last of that shit! Spend twenty years in the black business and have naught to show for it but scars, then you can preach to me about the right fucking thing, you little bastard!' He took a step at Beck but Wonderful held her arm out to stop him.

'What kind of right ends up with more men dead than less?' Her voice was soft, no anger in it. 'Well? D'you know how many friends I lost the last few days? What's right about that? Dow was done. One way or another, Dow was done. So we should've fought for him? Why? He's nothing to me. No better'n Calder or anyone else. You saying we should've died for that, Red Beck?'

Beck paused for a moment, mouth open. 'I don't know. But I don't want the money. Whose is it, even?'

'Ours,' she said, looking him right in the eye.

'This ain't right.'

'Straight edge, eh?' She slowly nodded, and her eyes looked tired. 'Well. Good luck with that. You'll need it.'

Flood looked a patch guilty, but he wasn't giving aught back. Scorry had a little smile as he dropped his shield on the grass and sank cross-legged onto it, humming some tune in which noble deeds were done. Yon was frowning as he rooted through the purse, working out how much he'd got.

'What would Craw have made o' this?' muttered Beck.

Wonderful shrugged. 'Who cares? Craw's gone. We got to make our own choices.'

'Aye.' Beck looked from one face to another. 'Aye.' And he walked off.

'Where you going?' Flood called after him.

He didn't answer.

He passed by one of the Heroes, shoulder brushing the ancient rock, and kept moving. He hopped over the drystone wall, heading north down the hillside, shook the shield off his arm and left it in the long grass. Men stood about, talking fast. Arguing. One pulled a knife, another backing off, hands up. Panic spreading along with the news. Panic and anger, fear and delight.

'What happened?' someone asked him, grabbing at his cloak. 'Did Dow win?'

Beck shook his hand off. 'I don't know.' He strode on, almost breaking into a run, down the hill and away. He only knew one thing. This life weren't for him. The songs might be full of heroes, but the only ones here were stones.

The Currents of History

Finree had gone where the wounded lay, to do what women were supposed to do when a battle ended. To soothe parched throats with water tipped to desperate lips. To bind wounds with bandages torn from the hems of their dresses. To calm the dying with soft singing that reminded them of Mother.

Instead of which she stood staring. Appalled by the mindless chorus of weeping, whining, desperate slobbering. By the flies, and the shit, and the blood-soaked sheets. By the calmness of the nurses, floating among the human wreckage as serene as white ghosts. Appalled more than anything else by the numbers. Laid out in ranks on pallets or sheets or cold ground. Companies of them. Battalions.

'There are more than a dozen,' a young surgeon told her.

'There are scores,' she croaked back, struggling not to cover her mouth at the stink.

'No. More than a dozen of these tents. Do you know how to change a dressing?'

If there was such a thing as a romantic wound there was no room for them here. Every peeled-back bandage a grotesque striptease with some fresh oozing nightmare beneath. A hacked-open arse, a caved-in jaw with most of the teeth and half the tongue gone, a hand neatly split leaving only thumb and fore-finger, a punctured belly leaking piss. One man had been cut across the back of the neck and could not move, only lie on his face, breath softly wheezing. His eyes followed her as she passed and the look in them made her cold all over. Bodies skinned, burned, ripped open at strange angles, their secret insides laid open to the world in awful violation. Wounds that would ruin men as long as they lived. Ruin those who loved them.

She tried to keep her eyes on her work, such as it was, chewing her tongue, trembling fingers fumbling with knots and pins. Trying not to listen to the whispers for help that she did not know how to give. That no one could give. Red spots appearing on the new bandages even before she finished, and growing, and growing, and she was forcing down tears, and forcing down sick, and on to the next, who was missing his left arm above the elbow, the left side of his face covered by bandages, and—

'Finree.'

She looked up and realised, to her cold horror, that it was Colonel Brint. They stared at each other for what felt like for ever, in awful silence, in that awful place.

'I didn't know . . .' There was so much she did not know she hardly knew how to continue.

'Yesterday,' he said, simply.

'Are you . . .' She almost asked him if he was all right, but managed to bite the words off. The answer was horribly obvious. 'Do you need—'

'Have you heard anything? About Aliz?' The name alone was enough to make her guts cramp up even further. She shook her head. 'You were with her. Where were you held?'

'I don't know. I was hooded. They took me away and sent me back.' And oh, how glad she was that Aliz had been left behind in the dark, and not her. 'I don't know where she'll be now . . .' Though she could guess. Perhaps Brint could too. Perhaps he was spending all his time guessing.

'Did she say anything?'

'She was . . . very brave.' Finree managed to force her face into the sickly semblance of a smile. That was what you were supposed to do, wasn't it? Lie? 'She said she loved you.' She put a halting hand on his arm. The one he still had. 'She said . . . not to worry.'

'Not to worry,' he muttered, staring at her with one bloodshot eye. Whether he was comforted, or outraged, or simply did not believe a word of her blame-shirking platitudes she could not tell. 'If I could just *know*.'

Finree did not think it would help him to know. It was not helping her. 'I'm so sorry,' she whispered, unable even to look at him any longer. 'I tried . . . I did everything I could, but . . .'

That, at least, was true. Wasn't it? She gave Brint's limp arm one last squeeze. 'I have to . . . get some more bandages—'

'Will you come back?'

'Yes,' she said, lurching up, not sure if she was still lying, 'of course I will.' And she almost tripped over her feet in her haste to escape that nightmare, thanking the Fates over and over and over that they had chosen her for saving.

Sick of penance, she wandered up the hillside path towards her father's headquarters. Past a pair of corporals dancing a drunken jig to the music of a squeaky fiddle. Past a row of women washing shirts in a brook. Past a row of soldiers queuing eagerly for the king's gold, gleaming metal in the paymaster's fingers glimpsed through the press of bodies. A small crowd of yammering sales-men, conmen and pimps had already gathered about the far end of the line like gulls about a patch of crumbs, realising, no doubt, that peace would soon put them out of business and give honest men the chance to thrive.

Not far from the barn she passed General Mitterick, chaper-oned by a few of his staff, and he gave her a solemn nod. Right away she felt something was wrong. Usually his intolerable smugness was reliable as the dawn. Then she saw Bayaz step from the low doorway, and the feeling grew worse. He stood aside to let her pass with all the smugness Mitterick had been missing.

'Fin.' Her father stood alone in the middle of the dim room. He gave her a puzzled smile. 'Well, there it is.' Then he sat down in a chair, gave a shuddering sigh and undid his top button. She had not seen him do that during the day in twenty years.

She strode back into the open air. Bayaz had made it no more than a few dozen strides, speaking softly to his curly-headed henchman.

'You! I want to speak to you!'

'And I to you, in fact. What a happy chance.' The Magus turned to his servant. 'Take him the money, then, as we agreed, and . . . send for the plumbers.' The servant bowed and backed respectfully away. 'Now, what can I—'

'You cannot replace him.'

'And we are speaking of?'

'My father!' she snapped. 'As you well know!'

'I did not replace him.' Bayaz looked almost amused. 'Your father had the good grace, and the good sense, to resign.'

'He is the best man for the task!' It was an effort to stop herself from grabbing the Magus' bald head and biting it. 'The one man who did a thing to limit this pointless bloody slaughter! That puffed-up fool Mitterick? He charged half his division to their deaths yesterday! The king needs men who—'

'The king needs men who obey.'

'You do not have the authority!' Her voice was cracking. 'My father is a lord marshal with a chair on the Closed Council, only the king himself can remove him!'

'Oh, the shame! Undone by the very rules of government I myself drafted!' Bayaz stuck out his bottom lip as he reached into his coat pocket and slid out a scroll with a heavy red seal. 'Then I suppose this carries no weight either.' He gently unrolled it, thick parchment crackling faintly. Finree found herself suddenly breathless as the Magus cleared his throat.

'By royal decree, Harod dan Brock is to be restored to his father's seat on the Open Council. Some of the family estates near Keln will be returned, along with lands near Ostenhorm from which, it will be hoped, your husband will attend to his new responsibilities as lord governor of Angland.' Bayaz turned the paper around and brought it closer, her eyes darting over the blocks of masterful calligraphy like a miser's over a chest of jewels.

'How could the king not be moved by such loyalty, such bravery, such sacrifice as the young *Lord* Brock displayed?' Bayaz leaned close. 'Not to mention the courage and tenacity of his wife who, captured by the Northmen, mark you, poked Black Dow in the eye and demanded the release of sixty prisoners! Why, his August Majesty would have to be made of *stone*. He is not, in case you were wondering. Few men less so, indeed. He wept when he read the despatch that described your husband's heroic assault upon the bridge. *Wept*. Then he ordered this paper drawn up, and signed it within the hour.' The Magus leaned closer yet, so she could almost feel his breath upon her face. 'I daresay . . . if one were closely to inspect this document . . . one could see the marks of his Majesty's earnest tears . . . staining the vellum.'

For the first time since it had been produced, Finree shifted her eyes from the scroll. She was close enough to see each grey hair of Bayaz' beard, each brown liver spot on his bald pate, each deep, hard crease in his skin. 'It would take a week for the despatch to reach him and another week for the edict to return. It has only been a day since—'

'Call it magic. His Majesty's carcass may be a week away in Adua, but his right hand?' Bayaz held his own up between them. 'His right hand is a little closer by. But none of that matters now.' He stepped back, sighing, and started to roll the parchment up. 'Since you say I have not the authority. I shall burn this worthless paper, shall I?'

'No!' She had to stop herself snatching it from his hand. 'No.'

'You no longer object to your father's replacement?'

She bit her lip for a moment. War is hell, and all that, but it presents opportunities. 'He resigned.'

'Did he?' Bayaz smiled wide, but his green eyes stayed glittering hard. 'You impress me once again. My earnest congratulations on your husband's meteoric rise to power. And your own, of course . . . Lady Governess.' He held out the scroll by one handle. She took it by the other. He did not let go.

'Remember this, though. People love heroes, but new ones can always be found. With one finger of one hand I make you. With one finger of one hand . . .' He put his finger under her chin and pushed it up, sending a stab of pain through her stiff neck. 'I can unmake you.'

She swallowed. 'I understand.'

'Then I wish you good day!' And Bayaz released her and the scroll, all smiles again. 'Please convey the happy news to your husband, though I must ask that you keep it between yourselves for the time being. People might not appreciate, as you do, quite how the magic works. I shall convey your husband's acceptance to his Majesty along with the news that he made the offer. Shall I?'

Finree cleared her throat. 'By all means.'

'My colleagues on the Closed Council will be delighted that the matter has been put to rest so swiftly. You must visit Adua when your husband is recovered. The formalities of his appointment. A parade, or some such. Hours of pomp in the Lords' Round. Breakfast with the queen.' Bayaz raised one eyebrow as he turned away. 'You really should procure some better clothes. Something with a heroic air.'

The room was clean and bright, light streaming in through a window and across the bed. No sobbing. No blood. No missing limbs. No awful not knowing. The luck of it. One arm was bound under the covers, the other lying pale on the sheet, knuckles scabbed over, gently rising and falling with his breath.

'Hal.' He grunted, eyelids flickering open. 'Hal, it's me.'

'Fin.' He reached up and touched her cheek with his fingertips. 'You came.'

'Of course.' She folded his hand in hers. 'How are you?'

He shifted, winced, then gave a weak smile. 'Bit stiff, honestly, but lucky. Damn lucky to have you. I heard you dragged me out of the rubble. Shouldn't I be the one rushing to your rescue?'

'If it helps it was Bremer dan Gorst who found you and carried you back. I just ran around crying, really.'

'You've always cried easily, it's one thing I love about you.' His eyes started to drift shut. 'I suppose I can live with Gorst . . . doing the saving . . .'

She squeezed his hand tighter. 'Hal, listen to me, something has happened. Something wonderful.'

'I heard.' His eyelids moved lazily. 'Peace.'

She shrugged it off. 'Not that. Well, yes, that, but . . .' She leaned over him, wrapping her other hand around his. 'Hal, listen to me. You're getting your father's seat in the Open Council.'

'What?'

'Some of his lands, too. They want us . . . you . . . the king wants you to take Meed's place.'

Hal blinked. 'As general of his division?'

'As lord governor of Angland.'

For a moment he looked simply stunned then, as he studied her face, worried. 'Why me?'

'Because you're a good man.' And a good compromise. 'A hero, apparently. Your deeds have come to the notice of the king.'

'Hero?' He snorted. 'How did you do it?' He tried to get up

onto his elbows but she put a hand on his chest and held him gently down.

Now was the opportunity to tell him the truth. The idea barely crossed her mind. 'You did it. You were right after all. Hard work and loyalty and all those things. Leading from the front. That's how you get on.'

'But—'

'Shhhh.' And she kissed him on one side of the lips, and on the other, and in the middle. His breath was foul, but she did not care. She was not about to let him ruin this. 'We can talk about it later. You rest, now.'

'I love you,' he whispered.

'I love you too.' Gently stroking his face as he slipped back into sleep. It was true. He was a good man. One of the best. Honest, brave, loyal to a fault. They were well matched. Optimist and pessimist, dreamer and cynic. And what is love anyway, but finding someone who suits you? Someone who makes up for your shortcomings?

Someone you can work with. Work on.

Terms

'They're late,' grumbled Mitterick.

The table had six chairs around it. His Majesty's new lord marshal occupied one, stuffed into a dress uniform swaddled with braid and too tight about his neck. Bayaz occupied another, drumming his thick fingers upon the tabletop. The Dogman slumped in the third, frowning up towards the Heroes, a muscle on the side of his head occasionally twitching.

Gorst stood a pace behind Mitterick's chair, arms folded. Beside him was Bayaz' servant, a map of the north rolled up in his hands. Behind them, posed stiffly within the ring of stones but out of earshot, were a handful of the most senior remaining officers of the army. *A sadly denuded complement. Meed, and Wetterlant, and Vinkler, and plenty more besides could not be with us. Jalenhorm too.* Gorst frowned up towards the Heroes. *Standing on first-name terms with me is as good as a death sentence, it seems.* His Majesty's Twelfth Regiment were all in attendance, though, arrayed in parade-ground order just outside the Children on the south side, their forest of shouldered halberds glittering in the chilly sun. *A little reminder that we seek peace today, but are more than prepared for the alternative.*

In spite of his battered head, burning cheek, a score of other cuts and scrapes and the countless bruises outside and in, Gorst was more than prepared for the alternative as well. Itching for it, in fact. *What employment would I find in peacetime, after all? Teach swordsmanship to sneering young officers? Lurk about the court like a lame dog, hoping for scraps? Sent as royal observer to the sewers of Keln? Or give up training, and run to fat, and become an embarrassing drunk trading on old stories of almost-glory. You know that's Bremer dan Gorst, who was once the king's First Guard? Let's buy the squeaking joke a drink! Let's buy him ten so we can watch him piss himself!*

Gorst felt his frown grow deeper. *Or . . . should I take up Black Dow's offer? Should I go where they sing songs about men like me instead of sniggering at their disgrace? Where peace need never come at all? Bremer dan Gorst, hero, champion, the most feared man in the North—*

'Finally,' grunted Bayaz, bringing a sharp end to the fantasy.

There was the unmistakable sound of soldiers on the move and a body of Northmen began to tramp down the long slope from the Heroes, the rims of their painted shields catching the light. *It seems the enemy are prepared for the alternative, too.* Gorst gently loosened his spare long steel in its sheath, watchful for any sign of an ambush. Itching for it, in fact. A single Northern toe too close and he would draw. *And peace would simply be one more thing in my life that failed to happen.*

But to his disappointment the great majority halted on the gently sloping ground outside the Children, no nearer to the centre than the soldiers of the Twelfth. Several more stopped just inside the stones, balancing out the officers on the Union side. A truly vast man, black hair shifting in the breeze, was conspicuous among them. So was the one in gilded armour whose face Gorst had so enthusiastically beaten on the first day of the battle. He clenched his fist at the memory, fervently hoping for the chance to do it again.

Four men approached the table, but of Black Dow there was no sign. The foremost among them had a fine cloak, a very handsome face and the slightest mocking smile. In spite of a bandaged hand and a fresh scar down the middle of his chin, no one had ever looked more carelessly, confidently in charge. *And I hate him already.*

'Who is that?' muttered Mitterick.

'Calder.' The Dogman's frown had grown deeper than ever. 'Bethod's youngest son. And a snake.'

'More of a worm,' said Bayaz, 'but it is Calder.'

Two old warriors flanked him, one pale-skinned, pale-haired, a pale fur around his shoulders, the other heavyset with a broad, weathered face. A fourth followed, axe at his belt, terribly scarred on one cheek. His eye gleamed as if made of metal, but that was not what made Gorst blink. He felt a creeping sense of recognition. *Did I see him in the battle yesterday? Or the day before? Or was it somewhere before that . . .*

'You must be Marshal Kroy.' Calder spoke the common tongue with only a trace of the North.

'Marshal Mitterick.'

'Ah!' Calder's smile widened. 'How nice to finally meet you! We faced each other yesterday, across the barley on the right of the battlefield.' He waved his bandaged hand to the west. 'Your left, I should say, I really am no soldier. That charge of yours was . . . magnificent.'

Mitterick swallowed, his pink neck bulging over his stiff collar.

'In fact, do you know, I think . . .' Calder rooted through an inside pocket, then positively beamed as he produced a scrap of crumpled, muddied paper. 'I have something of yours!' He tossed it across the table. Gorst saw writing over Mitterick's shoulder as he opened it up. An order, perhaps. Then Mitterick crumpled it again, so tightly his knuckles went white.

'And the First of the Magi! The last time we spoke was a humbling experience for me. Don't worry, though, I've had many others since. You won't find a more humbled man anywhere.' Calder's smirk said otherwise, though, as he pointed out the grizzled old men at his back. 'This is Caul Reachey, my wife's father. And Pale-as-Snow, my Second. Not forgetting my respected champion—'

'Caul Shivers.' The Dogman gave the man with the metal eye a solemn nod. 'It's been a while.'

'Aye,' he whispered back, simply.

'The Dogman, we all know, of course!' said Calder. 'The Bloody-Nine's bosom companion, in all those songs along with him! Are you well?'

The Dogman ignored the question with a masterpiece of slouching disdain. 'Where's Dow?'

'Ah.' Calder grimaced, though it looked feigned. *Everything about him looks feigned.* 'I'm sorry to say he won't be coming. Black Dow is . . . back to the mud.'

There was a silence that Calder gave every indication of greatly enjoying. 'Dead?' The Dogman slumped back in his chair. *As if he had been informed of the loss of a dear friend rather than a bitter enemy. Truly, the two can sometimes be hard to separate.*

'The Protector of the North and I had . . . a disagreement. We settled it in the traditional way. With a duel.'

'And you won?' asked the Dogman.

Calder raised his brows and rubbed gently at the stitches on his chin with a fingertip, as if he could not quite believe it either. 'Well, I'm alive and Dow's dead so . . . yes. It's been a strange morning. They've taken to calling me Black Calder.'

'Is that a fucking fact?'

'Don't worry, it's just a name. I'm all for peace.' Though Gorst fancied the Carls ranged on the long slope had different feelings. 'This was Dow's battle, and a waste of everyone's time, money and lives as far as I'm concerned. Peace is the best part of any war, if you're asking me.'

'I heartily concur.' Mitterick might have had the new uniform, but it was Bayaz who did the talking now. 'The settlement I propose is simple.'

'My father always said that simple things stick best. You remember my father?'

The Magus hesitated for the slightest moment. 'Of course.' He snapped his fingers and his servant slipped forward, unrolling the map across the table with faultless dexterity. Bayaz pointed out the curl of a river. 'The Whiteflow shall remain the northern boundary of Angland. The northern frontier of the Union, as it has for hundreds of years.'

'Things change,' said Calder.

'This one will not.' The Magus' thick finger sketched another river, north of the first. 'The land between the Whiteflow and the Cusk, including the city of Uffrith, shall come under the governorship of the Dogman. It shall become a protectorate of the Union, with six representatives on the Open Council.'

'All the way to the Cusk?' Calder gave a sharp little in-breath. 'Some of the best land in the North.' He gave the Dogman a pointed look. 'Sitting on the Open Council? Protected by the Union? What would Skarling Hoodless have said to that? What would my father have said?'

'Who cares a shit what dead men might have said?' The Dogman stared evenly back. 'Things change.'

'Stabbed with my own knife!' Calder clutched at his chest, then gave a resigned shrug. 'But the North needs peace. I am content.'

'Good.' Bayaz beckoned to his servant. 'Then we can sign the articles—'

'You misunderstand me.' There was an uneasy pause as Calder shuffled forwards in his chair, as if they at the table were all friends together and the real enemy was at his back, and straining to hear their plans. '*I* am content, but I am not alone in this. Dow's War Chiefs are . . . a jealous set.' Calder gave a helpless laugh. 'And they have all the swords. I can't just agree to anything or . . .' He drew a finger across his bruised throat with a squelching of his tongue. 'Next time you want to talk you might find some stubborn blowhard like Cairm Ironhead, or some tower of vanity like Glama Golden in this chair. Good luck finding terms then.' He tapped the map with a fingertip. 'I'm all for this myself. All for it. But let me take it away and convince my surly brood, then we can meet again to sign the whatevers.'

Bayaz frowned, ever so sourly, at the Northmen standing just inside the Children. 'Tomorrow, then.'

'The day after would be better.'

'Don't push me, Calder.'

Calder was the picture of injured helplessness. 'I don't want to push at all! But I'm not Black Dow. I'm more . . . spokesman than tyrant.'

'Spokesman,' muttered the Dogman, as though the word tasted of piss.

'That will not be good enough.'

But Calder's smirk was made of steel. Bayaz' every effort bounced right off. 'If only you knew how hard I've worked for peace, all this time. The risks I've taken for it.' Calder pressed his injured hand against his heart. 'Help me! Help me to help us all.' *Help you to help yourself, more likely.*

As Calder stood he reached across the map and offered his good hand to the Dogman. 'I know we've been on different sides for a long time, one way or another, but if we're to be neighbours there should be no chill between us.'

'Different sides. That happens. Time comes you got to bury it.' The Dogman stood, looking Calder in the eye all the way.

562

'But you killed Forley the Weakest. Never did no harm to no one, that lad. Came to give you a warning, and you killed him for it.'

Calder's smile had turned, for the first time, slightly lopsided. 'There isn't a morning comes I don't regret it.'

'Then here's another.' The Dogman leaned forward, extended his forefinger, pressed one nostril closed with it and blew snot out of the other straight into Calder's open palm. 'Set foot south o' the Cusk, I'll cut the bloody cross in you. Then there'll be no chill.' And he gave a scornful sniff, and stalked past Gorst and away.

Mitterick nervously cleared his throat. 'We will reconvene soon, then?' Looking to Bayaz for support that did not arrive.

'Absolutely.' Calder regained most of his grin as he wiped the Dogman's snot off on the edge of the table. 'In three days.' And he turned his back and went to talk to the man with the metal eye. The one called Shivers.

'This Calder seems a slippery bastard,' Mitterick muttered to Bayaz as they left the table. 'I'd rather have dealt with Black Dow. At least with him you knew what you were getting.' Gorst was hardly listening. He was too busy staring at Calder and his scarred henchman. *I know him. I know that face. But from where . . . ?*

'Dow was a fighter,' Bayaz was murmuring. 'Calder is a politician. He realises we are keen to leave, and that when the troops go home we will have nothing to bargain with. He knows he can win far more by sitting still and smirking than Dow ever did with all the steel and fury in the North . . .'

Shivers turned the ruined side of his face away as he spoke to Calder, the unburned side moving into the sun . . . and Gorst's skin prickled with recognition, and his mouth came open.

Sipani.

That face, in the smoke, before he was sent tumbling down the stairs. *That face.* How could it be the same man? And yet he was almost sure.

Bayaz' voice faded behind him as Gorst strode around the table, jaw clenched, and onto the Northmen's side of the Children. One of Calder's old retainers grunted as Gorst shouldered him out of the way. Probably this was extremely poor, if not potentially fatal, etiquette for peace negotiations. *And I could not care less.* Calder glanced up, and took a worried step back. Shivers turned to look. Not angry. Not afraid.

'Colonel Gorst!' someone shouted, but Gorst ignored it, his hand closing around Shivers' arm and pulling him close. The War Chiefs about the edge of the Children were all frowning. The giant took a huge step forwards. The man with the golden armour was calling out to the body of Carls. Another had put his hand to the hilt of his sword.

'Calm, everyone!' Calder shouted in Northern, one restraining palm up behind him. 'Calm!' But he looked nervous. *As well he should. All our lives are balanced on a razor's edge. And I could not care less.*

Shivers did not look as if he cared overmuch himself. He glanced down at Gorst's gripping hand, then back up at his face, and raised the brow over his good eye.

'Can I help you?' His voice was the very opposite of Gorst's. A gravelly whisper, harsh as millstones grinding. Gorst looked at him. Really looked. As though he could drill into his head with his eyes. That face, in the smoke. He had glimpsed it only for a moment, and masked, and without the scar. *But still.* He had seen it every night since, in his dreams, and in his waking, and in the twisted space between, every detail stamped into his memory. *And I am almost sure.*

He could hear movement behind him. Excited voices. The officers and men of his Majesty's Twelfth. *Probably upset to have missed out on the battle. Probably almost as keen to become involved in a new chapter of it as I am myself.*

'Colonel Gorst!' came Bayaz' warning growl.

Gorst ignored him. 'Have you ever been . . .' he hissed, 'to Styria?' Every part of him tingling with the desire to do violence.

'Styria?'

'Yes,' snarled Gorst, gripping even harder. Calder's two old men were creeping back in fighting crouches. 'To Sipani.'

'Sipani?'

'Yes.' The giant had taken another immense step, looming taller than the tallest of the Children. *And I could not care less.* 'To Cardotti's House of Leisure.'

'Cardotti's?' Shivers' good eye narrowed as he studied Gorst's face. Time stretched out. All around them tongues licked nervously at lips, hands hovered ready to give their fatal signals, fingertips tickled at the grips of weapons. Then Shivers leaned close. Close enough almost for Gorst to kiss. Closer even than they had been to each other four years ago, in the smoke.

If they had been.

'Never heard of it.' And he slipped his arm out of Gorst's slack grip and strode out of the Children without a backward glance. Calder swiftly followed, and the two old men, and the War Chiefs. All letting their hands drop from their weapons with some relief or, in the case of the giant, great reluctance.

They left Gorst standing there, in front of the table, alone. Frowning up towards the Heroes.

Almost sure.

Family

In many ways the Heroes hadn't changed since the previous night. The old stones were just as they had been, and the lichen crusted to them, and the trampled, muddied, bloodied grass inside their circle. The fires weren't much different, nor the darkness beyond them, nor the men who sat about them. But as far as Calder was concerned, there'd been some big-arsed changes.

Rather than dragging him in shame to his doom, Caul Shivers followed at a respectful distance, watching over his life. There was no scornful laughter as he strolled between the fires, no heckling and no hate. All changed the moment Black Dow's face hit the dirt. The great War Chiefs, and their fearsome Named Men, and their hard-handed, hard-hearted, hard-headed Carls all smiled upon him as if he was the sun rising after a bastard of a winter. How soon they'd adjusted. His father always said men rarely change, except in their loyalties. Those they'll shrug off like an old coat when it suits them.

In spite of his splinted hand and his stitched chin, Calder didn't have to work too hard to get the smirk onto his face now. He didn't have to work at all. He might not have been the tallest man about, but still he was the biggest in the valley. He was the next King of the Northmen, and anyone he told to eat his shit would be doing it with a smile. He'd already decided who'd be getting the first serving.

Caul Reachey's laughter echoed out of the night. He sat on a log beside a fire, pipe in his hand, spluttering smoke at something some woman beside him had said. She looked around as Calder walked up and he nearly tripped over his own feet.

'Husband.' She stood, awkward from the weight of her belly, and held out one hand.

He took it in his and it felt small, and soft, and strong. He guided it over his shoulder, and slid his arms around her, hardly feeling the pain in his battered ribs as they held each other tight, tight. For a moment it seemed as if there was no one in the Heroes but them. 'You're safe,' he whispered.

'No thanks to you,' rubbing her cheek against his.

His eyelids were stinging. 'I . . . made some mistakes.'

'Of course. I make all your good decisions.'

'Don't leave me alone again, then.'

'I think I can say it'll be the last time I stand hostage for you.'

'So can I. That's a promise.' He couldn't stop the tears coming. Some biggest man in the valley, stood weeping in front of Reachey and his Named Men. He would've felt a fool if he hadn't been so glad to see her he couldn't feel anything else. He broke away long enough to look at her face, light on one side, dark on the other, eyes with a gleam of firelight to them. Smiling at him, two little moles near the corner of her mouth he'd never noticed before. All he could think was that he didn't deserve this.

'Something wrong?' she asked.

'No. Just . . . wasn't long ago I thought I'd never see your face again.'

'And are you disappointed?'

'I never saw anything so beautiful.'

She bared her teeth at him. 'Oh, they were right about you. You are a liar.'

'A good liar tells as much truth as he can. That way you never know what you're getting.'

She took his bandaged hand in hers, turning it over, stroking it with her fingertips. 'Are you hurt?'

'Nothing to a famous champion like me.'

She pressed his hand tighter. 'I mean it. Are you hurt?'

Calder winced. 'Doubt I'll be fighting any more duels for a while, but I'll heal. Scale's dead.'

'I heard.'

'You're all my family, now.' And he laid his good hand on her swollen belly. 'Still—'

'Like a sack of oats on my bladder all the way from Carleon in a lurching bloody cart? Yes.'

He smiled through his tears. 'The three of us.'

'And my father too.'

He looked over at Reachey, grinning at them from his log. 'Aye. And him.'

'You haven't put it on, then?'

'What?'

'Your father's chain.'

He slid it from his inside pocket, warm from being pressed close to his heart, and the diamond dropped to one side, full of the colours of fire. 'Waiting for the right moment, maybe. Once you put it on . . . you can't take it off.' He remembered his father telling him what a weight it was. Near the end.

'Why would you take it off? You're king, now.'

'Then you're queen.' He slipped the chain over her head. 'And it looks better on you.' He let the diamond drop against her chest while she dragged her hair free.

'My husband goes away for a week and all he brings me is the North and everything in it?'

'That's just half your gift.' He moved as if to kiss her and held back at the last moment, clicking his teeth together just short of her mouth. 'I'll give you the rest later.'

'Promises, promises.'

'I need to talk to your father, just for a moment.'

'Talk, then.'

'Alone.'

'Men and their bloody chatter. Don't keep me waiting too long.' She leaned close, her lip tickling at his ear, her knee rubbing up against the inside of his leg, his father's chain brushing against his shoulder. 'I've a mind to kneel before the King of the Northmen.' One fingertip brushed the scab on his chin as she stepped away, keeping his face towards her, watching him over her shoulder, waddling just a little with the weight of her belly but none the worse for that. None the worse at all. All he could think was that he didn't deserve this.

He shook himself and clambered to the fire, somewhat bent over since his prick was pressing up hard against the inside of his trousers, and poking a tent in Reachey's face was no way to start a conversation. His wife's father had shooed his grey-bearded henchmen away and was sitting alone, pressing a fresh lump of chagga down into his pipe with one thick thumb. A private little chat. Just like the one they'd had a few nights before. Only now Dow was dead, and everything was changed.

Calder wiped the wet from his eyes as he sat beside the fire-pit. 'She's one of a kind, your daughter.'

'I've heard you called a liar, but there was never a truer word said than that.'

'One of a kind.' As Calder watched her disappear into the darkness.

'You're a lucky man to have her. Remember what I told you? Wait long enough by the sea, everything you want'll just wash up on the beach.' Reachey tapped at the side of his head. 'I've been around a while. You ought to listen to me.'

'I'm listening now, aren't I?'

Reachey wriggled down the log, a little closer to him. 'All right, then. A lot of my boys are restless. Had their swords drawn a long time. I could do with letting some of 'em get home to their own wives. You got a mind to take this wizard's offer?'

'Bayaz?' Calder snorted. 'I've a mind to let the lying bastard simmer. He had a deal with my father, a long time ago, and betrayed him.'

'So it's a question of revenge?'

'A little, but mostly it's good sense. If the Union had pushed on yesterday they might've finished us.'

'Maybe. So?'

'So the only reason I can see for stopping is if they had to. The Union's a big place. Lots of borders. I reckon they've got other worries. I reckon every day I let that bald old fuck sit his terms'll get better.'

'Huh.' Reachey fished a burning stick from the fire, pressed it to the bowl of his pipe, starting to grin as he got it lit. 'You're a clever one, Calder. A thinker. Like your father. Always said you'd make quite a leader.'

Calder had never heard him say it. 'Didn't help me get here, did you?'

'I told you I'd burn if I had to, but I wouldn't set myself on fire. What was it the Bloody-Nine used to say?'

'You have to be realistic.'

'That's right. Realistic. Thought you'd know that better'n most.' Reachey's cheeks went hollow as he sucked at his pipe, let the brown smoke curl from his mouth. 'But now Dow's dead, and you've got the North at your feet.'

'You must be almost as pleased as I am with how it's all come out.'

''Course,' as Reachey handed the pipe over.

'Your grandchildren can rule the North,' as Calder took it.

'Once you're finished with it.'

'I plan not to finish for a while.' Calder sucked, bruised ribs aching as he breathed deep and felt the smoke bite.

'Doubt I'll live to see it.'

'Hope not.' Calder grinned as he blew out, and they both chuckled, though there might've been the slightest edge on their laughter. 'You know, I've been thinking about something Dow said. How if he'd wanted me dead I'd have been dead. The more I think on it, the more sense it makes.'

Reachey shrugged. 'Maybe Tenways tried it on his own.'

Calder frowned at the bowl of the pipe as if thinking it over, though he'd already thought it over and decided it didn't add. 'Tenways saved my life in the battle yesterday. If he hated me that much he could've let the Union kill me and no one would've grumbled.'

'Who knows why anyone does anything? The world's a complicated bloody place.'

'Everyone has their reasons, my father used to tell me. It's just a question of knowing what they are. Then the world's simple.'

'Well, Black Dow's back to the mud. And from the look o' your sword in his head, Tenways too. I guess we'll never know now.'

'Oh, I reckon I've worked it out.' Calder handed the pipe back and the old man leaned to take it. 'It was you said Dow wanted me dead.' Reachey's eyes flicked up to his, just for an instant, but long enough for Calder to be sure. 'That wasn't altogether true, was it? It was what you might call a lie.'

Reachey slowly sat back, puffing out smoke rings. 'Aye, a little bit, I'll admit. My daughter has a loving nature, Calder, and she loves you. I've tried explaining what a pain in the arse you are but she just ain't hearing it. There's naught she wouldn't do for you. But it was getting so you and Dow weren't seeing things at all the same way. All your talk of bloody peace making things hard for everyone. Then my daughter up and stands hostage for you? Just couldn't have my only child at risk like that. Out of you and Dow, one had to go.' He looked evenly at Calder, through the smoke of his pipe. 'I'm sorry, but there it is. If it was you, well, that's a shame, but Seff would've found a new man. Better still, there was always the chance you'd come out on top o' Dow. And I'm happy to say that's how it happened. All I wanted was the best for my blood. So I'm ashamed to admit it, but I stirred the pot between the two o' you.'

'Hoping all along I'd get the better of Dow.'

'Of course.'

'So it wasn't you at all who sent those boys to kill me at your weapontake?'

The pipe froze half way to Reachey's mouth. 'Why would I do a thing like that?'

'Because Seff was standing hostage, and I was talking big about dealing with Dow, and you decided to stir the pot a bit harder.'

Reachey pressed the end of his tongue between his teeth, lifted the pipe the rest of the way, sucked at it again, but it was dead. He tapped the ashes out on the stones by the fire. 'If you're going to stir the pot, I've always believed in doing it . . . firmly.'

Calder slowly shook his head. 'Why not just get your old pricks to kill me when we were sat around the fire? Make sure of it?'

'I got a reputation to think on. When it comes to knives in the dark I hire out, keep my name free of it.' Reachey didn't look guilty. He looked annoyed. Offended, even. 'Don't sit there like you're disappointed. Don't pretend you haven't done worse. What about Forley the Weakest, eh? Killed him for nothing, didn't you?'

'I'm me!' said Calder. 'Everyone knows me for a liar! I guess I just . . .' Sounded stupid now he said it. 'Expected better from you. I thought you were a straight edge. Thought you did things the old way.'

Reachey gave a scornful grunt. 'The old way? Hah! People are apt to get all misty-eyed over how things used to be. Age o' Heroes, and all. Well, I remember the old way. I was there, and it was no different from the new.' He leaned forward, stabbing at Calder with the stem of his pipe. 'Grab what you can, however you can! Folk might like to harp on how your father changed everything. They like someone to blame. But he was just better at it than the rest. It's the winners sing the songs. And they can pick what tune they please.'

'I'm just picking out what tune they'll play on you!' hissed Calder, the anger flaring up for a moment. But, 'Anger's a luxury the man in the big chair can't afford.' That's what his father used to say. Mercy, mercy, always think about mercy. Calder took in a long, sore breath, and heaved out resignation. 'But maybe I'd have done no different, wearing your coat, and I've too few friends by far. The fact is I need your support.'

Reachey grinned. 'You'll have it. To the death, don't worry about that. You're family, lad. Family don't always get on but, in the end, they're the only ones you can trust.'

'So my father used to tell me.' Calder slowly stood and gave another aching sigh, right from his gut. 'Family.' And he made his way off through the fires, towards the tent that had been Black Dow's.

'And?' croaked Shivers, falling into step beside him.

'You were right. The old fuck tried to kill me.'

'Shall I return the favour?'

'By the dead, no!' He forced his voice softer as they headed away. 'Not until my child's born. I don't want my wife upset. Let things settle then do it quietly. Some way that'll point the finger at someone else. Glama Golden, maybe. Can you do that?'

'When it comes to killing, I can do it any way you want it.'

'I always said Dow should've made better use of you. Now my wife's waiting. Go and have some fun.'

'I just might.'

'What do you do for fun, anyway?'

There was a glint in Shivers' eye as he turned away, but then there always was. 'I sharpen my knives.'

Calder wasn't quite sure if he was joking.

New Hands

*D*ear Mistress Worth,
    With the greatest regret, I must inform you of the death of your son in action on the battlefield near Osrung.

    It is usual for the commanding officer to write such letters, but I requested the honour as I knew your son personally, and have but rarely in a long career served with so willing, pleasant, able, and courageous a comrade. He embodied all those virtues that one looks for in a soldier. I do not know if it can provide you with any satisfaction in the face of a loss so great, but it is not stretching the truth to say that your son died a hero. I feel honoured to have known him.

    With the deepest condolences,
    Your obedient servant,
    Corporal Tunny, Standard-Bearer of His Majesty's First Regiment.

Tunny gave a sigh, folded the letter ever so carefully and pressed two neat creases into it with his thumbnail. Might be the worst letter the poor woman ever got, he owed it to her to put a decent crease in the damn thing. He tucked it inside his jacket next to Mistress Klige's, unscrewed the cap from Yolk's flask and took a nip, then dipped the pen in the ink bottle and started on the next.

Dear Mistress Lederlingen,
    With the greatest regret, I must inform you of the death of your son in—

'Corporal Tunny!' Yolk was approaching with a cocky strut somewhere between that of a pimp and a labourer. His boots were caked with dirt, his stained jacket was hanging open showing a strip of sweaty chest, his sunburned face sported several days' worth of patchy stubble and instead of a spear over his shoulder he had a worn shovel. He looked, in short, like a proud veteran of his August Majesty's army. He came to a stop not far from Tunny's hammock, looking down at the papers. 'Working out all the debts you're owed?'

'The ones I owe, as it goes.' Tunny seriously doubted Yolk could read, but he pushed a sheet of paper over the unfinished letter even so. If this got out it could ruin his reputation. 'Everything all right?'

'Everything's well enough,' said Yolk as he set down his shovel, though under his good humour he looked, in fact, a little pensive. 'The colonel's had us doing some burying.'

'Uh.' Tunny worked the stopper back into the ink bottle. He'd done a fair amount of burying himself and it was never a desirable duty. 'Always some cleaning up to do after a battle. A lot to put right, here and at home. Might take years to clean up what takes a day or three to dirty.' He cleaned off his pen on a bit of rag. 'Might never happen.'

'Why do it, then?' asked Yolk, frowning off across the sunlit barley towards the hazy hills. 'I mean to say, all the effort, and all the men dead, and what've we got done here?'

Tunny scratched his head. Never had Yolk down as a philosopher, but he guessed every man has his thoughtful moments. 'Wars don't often change much, in my considerable experience. Bit here, bit there, but overall there have to be better ways for men to settle their differences.' He thought about it for a moment. 'Kings, and nobles, and Closed Councils, and so forth, I never have quite understood why they keep at it, given how the lessons of history do seem to stack up powerfully against. War is damned uncomfortable work, for minimal rewards, and it's the soldiers who always bear the worst.'

'Why be a soldier, then?'

Tunny found himself temporarily at a loss for words. Then he shrugged. 'Best job in the world, isn't it.'

A group of horses were being led without urgency up the track nearby, hooves clopping at the mud, a few soldiers trudging along with them. One detached himself and strolled over, chewing at an apple. Sergeant Forest, and grinning broadly.

'Oh, bloody hell,' muttered Tunny under his breath, quickly clearing the last evidence of letter writing and tossing the shield he'd been leaning on under his hammock.

'What is it?' whispered Yolk.

'When First Sergeant Forest smiles there's rarely good news on the way.'

'When is there good news on the way?'

Tunny had to admit Yolk had a point.

'Corporal Tunny!' Forest stripped his apple and flicked away the core. 'You're awake.'

'Sadly, Sergeant, yes. Any news from our esteemed commanders?'

'Some.' Forest jerked a thumb towards the horses. 'You'll be delighted to learn we're getting our mounts back.'

'Marvellous,' grunted Tunny. 'Just in time to ride them back the way we came.'

'Let it never be said that his August Majesty does not provide his loyal soldiers with everything needful. We're pulling out in the morning. Or the following morning, at the latest. Heading for Uffrith, and a nice warm boat.'

Tunny found a smile of his own. He'd had about enough of the North. 'Homewards, eh? My favourite direction.'

Forest saw Tunny's grin and raised him a tooth on each side. 'Sorry to disappoint you. We're shipping for Styria.'

'Styria?' muttered Yolk, hands on hips.

'For beautiful Westport!' Forest flung an arm around Yolk's shoulders and pushed his other hand out in front of them, as if showing off a magnificent civic vista where there was, in fact, a stand of rotting trees. 'Crossroads of the world! We're to stand alongside our bold allies in Sipani, and take righteous arms against that notorious she-devil Monzcarro Murcatto, the Snake of Talins. She is, by all reports, a fiend in human form, an enemy to freedom and the greatest threat ever to face the Union!'

'Since Black Dow.' Tunny rubbed at the bridge of his nose, his smile a memory. 'Who we made peace with yesterday.'

Forest slapped Yolk on the shoulder. 'The beauty of the

soldier's profession, trooper. The world never runs out of villains. And Marshal Mitterick's just the man to make 'em quake!'

'Marshal . . . Mitterick?' Yolk looked baffled. 'What happened to Kroy?'

'He's done,' grunted Tunny.

'How many have you outlasted now?' asked Forest.

'I'm thinking . . . eight, at a quick guess.' Tunny counted them off on his fingers. 'Frengen, then Altmoyer, then that short one . . .'

'Krepsky.'

'Krepsky. Then the other Frengen.'

'The other Frengen,' snorted Forest.

'A notable fool even for a commander-in-chief. Then there was Varuz, then Burr, then West—'

'He was a good man, West.'

'Gone too early, like most good men. Then we had Kroy . . .'

'Lord marshals are temporary in nature,' explained Forest, gesturing at Tunny, 'but corporals? Corporals are eternal.'

'Sipani, you say?' Tunny slid slowly back in his hammock, putting one boot up and rocking himself gently back and forth with the other. 'Never been there myself.' Now that he was thinking about it, he was starting to see the advantages. A good soldier always keeps an eye on the advantages. 'Fine weather, I expect?'

'Excellent weather,' said Forest.

'And I hear they have the best bloody whores in the world.'

'The ladies of the city have been mentioned once or twice since the orders came down.'

'Two things to look forward to.'

'Which is two more than you get in the North.' Forest was smiling bigger than ever. Bigger than seemed necessary. 'And in the meantime, since your detail stands so sadly reduced, here's another.'

'Oh, no,' groaned Tunny, all hopes of whores and sunshine quickly wilting.

'Oh, yes! Up you come, lads!'

And up they came indeed. Four of them. New recruits, fresh off the boat from Midderland by their looks. Seen off at the docks with kisses from Mummy or sweetheart or both. New uniforms pressed, buckles gleaming, and ready for the noble soldiering life, indeed. They stared open-mouthed at Yolk, who could hardly have presented a greater contrast, his face pinched and rat-like, his jacket frayed and mud-smeared from grave-digging, one strap on his pack broken and repaired with string. Forest gestured towards Tunny like a showman towards his freak, and trotted out that same little speech he always gave.

'Boys, this here is the famous Corporal Tunny, one of the longest-serving non-commissioned officers in General Felnigg's division.' Tunny gave a long, hard sigh, right from his stomach. 'A veteran of the Starikland Rebellion, the Gurkish War, the last Northern War, the Siege of Adua, the recent climactic Battle of Osrung and a quantity of peacetime soldiering that would have bored a keener mind to death.' Tunny unscrewed the cap of Yolk's flask, took a pull, then handed it over to its original owner, who shrugged and had a swig of his own. 'He has survived the runs, the rot, the grip, the autumn shudders, the caresses of Northern winds, the buffets of Southern women, thousands of miles of marching, many years of his Majesty's rations and even a tiny bit of actual fighting to stand – or sit – before you now . . .'

Tunny crossed one ruined boot over the other, sank slowly back into his hammock and closed his eyes, the sun glowing pink through his lids.

Old Hands

It was near sunset when he made it back. Midges swirling in clouds over the marshy little brook, yellowing leaves casting dappled shadows onto the path, boughs stirring in the breeze, low enough he had to duck.

The house looked smaller'n he remembered. It looked small, but it looked beautiful. Looked so beautiful it made him want to cry. The door creaked as he pushed it wide, almost as scared for some reason as he had been in Osrung. There was no one inside. Just the same old smoke-smelling dimness. His cot was packed away to make more space, slashes of pale sunlight across the boards where it had been.

No one here, and his mouth went sour. What if they had packed up and left? Or what if men had come when he was away, deserters turned bandit—

He heard the soft *clock* of an axe splitting logs. He ducked back out into the evening, hurrying past the pen and the staring goats and the five big tree stumps all hacked and scarred from years of his blade practice. Practice that hadn't helped much, as it went. He knew now stabbing a stump ain't much preparation for stabbing a man.

His mother was just over the rise, leaning on the axe by the old chopping block, arching her back while Festen gathered up the split halves and tossed 'em onto the pile. Beck stood there for a moment, watching 'em. Watching his mother's hair stirring in the breeze. Watching the boy struggling with the chunks of wood.

'Ma,' he croaked.

She looked around, blinked at him for a moment. 'You're back.'

'I'm back.'

He walked over to her, and she stuck one corner of the axe in the block for safe keeping and met him half way. Even though she was so much smaller than him she still held his head against her shoulder. Held it with one hand and pressed it to her, wrapped her other arm tight around him, strong enough to make it hard to breathe.

'My son,' she whispered.

He broke away from her, sniffing back his tears, looking down. Saw his cloak, or her cloak, and how muddied, and bloodied, and torn it was. 'I'm sorry. Reckon I got your cloak ruined.'

She touched his face. 'It's a bit of cloth.'

'Guess it is at that.' He squatted down, and ruffled Festen's hair. 'You all right?' He could hardly keep his voice from cracking.

'I'm fine!' Slapping Beck's hand away from his head. 'Did you get yourself a name?'

Beck paused. 'I did.'

'What is it?'

Beck shook his head. 'Don't matter. How's Wenden?'

'Same,' said Beck's mother. 'You weren't gone more'n a few days.'

He hadn't expected that. Felt like years since he was last here. 'I guess I was gone long enough.'

'What happened?'

'Can we . . . not talk about it?'

'Your father talked about nothing else.'

He looked up at her. 'If there's one thing I learned it's that I'm not my father.'

'Good. That's good.' She patted him gently on the side of the face, wet glimmering in her eyes. 'I'm glad you're here. Don't have the words to tell you how glad I am. You hungry?'

He stood, straightening his legs feeling like quite the effort, and wiped away more tears on the back of his wrist. Realised he hadn't eaten since he left the Heroes, yesterday morning. 'I could eat.'

'I'll get the fire lit!' And Festen trotted off towards the house.

'You coming in?' asked Beck's mother.

Beck blinked out towards the valley. 'Reckon I might stay out here a minute. Split a log or two.'

'All right.'

'Oh.' And he slid his father's sword from his belt, held it for a moment, then offered it out to her. 'Can you put this away?'

'Where?'

'Anywhere I don't have to look at it.'

She took it from him, and it felt like a weight he didn't have to carry no more. 'Seems like good things can come back from the wars,' she said.

'Coming back's the only good thing I could see.' He leaned down and set a log on the block, spat on one palm and took up the wood axe. The haft felt good in his hands. Familiar. It fitted 'em better than the sword ever had, that was sure. He swung it down and two neat halves went tumbling. He was no hero, and never would be.

He was made to chop logs, not to fight.

And that made him lucky. Luckier'n Reft, or Stodder, or Brait. Luckier'n Drofd or Whirrun of Bligh. Luckier'n Black Dow, even. He worked the axe clear of the block and stood back. They don't sing many songs about log-splitters, maybe, but the lambs were bleating, up on the fells out of sight, and that sounded like music. Sounded a sweeter song to him then than all the hero's lays he knew.

He closed his eyes and breathed in the smell of grass and woodsmoke. Then he opened 'em, and looked across the valley. Skin all tingling with the peace of that moment. Couldn't believe he used to hate this place.

Didn't seem so bad, now. Didn't seem so bad at all.

Everyone Serves

'**S**o you're standing with me?' asked Calder, breezy as a spring morning.

'If there's still room.'

'Loyal as Rudd Threetrees, eh?'

Ironhead shrugged. 'I won't take you for a fool and say yes. But I know where my best interest lies and it's at your heels. I'd also point out loyalty's a dangerous foundation. Tends to wash away in a storm. Self-interest stands in any weather.'

Calder had to nod at that. 'A sound principle.' He glanced up at Foss Deep, lately returned to his service following the end of hostilities and an apt display of the power of self-interest in the flesh. Despite his stated distaste for battles he'd somehow acquired, gleaming beneath his shabby coat, a splendid Union breastplate engraved with a golden sun. 'A man should have some, eh, Deep?'

'Some what?'

'Principles.'

'Oh, I'm a big, big, big believer in 'em. My brother too.'

Shallow took a quick break from furiously picking his finger-nails with the point of his knife. 'I like 'em with milk.'

A slightly uncomfortable silence. Then Calder turned back to Ironhead. 'Last time we spoke you told me you'd stick with Dow. Then you pissed on my boots.' He lifted one up, even more battered, gouged and stained from the events of the past few days than Calder was himself. 'Best bloody boots in the North a week ago. Styrian leather. Now look.'

'I'll be more'n happy to buy you a new pair.'

Calder winced at his aching ribs as he stood. 'Make it two.'

'Whatever you say. Maybe I'll get a pair myself and all.'

'You sure something in steel wouldn't be more your style?'

Ironhead shrugged. 'No call for steel boots in peacetime. Anything else?'

'Just keep your men handy, for now. We need to put a good show on 'til the Union get bored of waiting and slink off. Shouldn't be long.'

'Right y'are.'

Calder took a couple of steps away, then turned back. 'Get a gift for my wife, too. Something beautiful, since my child's due soon.'

'Chief.'

'And don't feel too bad about it. Everyone serves someone.'

'Very true.' Ironhead didn't so much as twitch. A little disappointing, in fact – Calder had hoped to watch him sweat. But there'd be time for that later, once the Union were gone. There'd be time for all kinds of things. So he gave a lordly nod and smirked off, his two shadows trailing after.

He had Reachey on-side, and Pale-as-Snow. He'd had a little word with Wonderful, and she'd had the same little word with Dow's Carls, and their loyalty had washed with the rainwater, all right. Most of Tenways' men had drifted off, and White-Eye Hansul had made his own appeal to self-interest and argued the rest around. Ironhead and Golden still hated each other too much to pose a threat and Stranger-Come-Knocking, for reasons beyond Calder's ken, was treating him like an old and honoured friend.

Laughing stock to king of the world in the swing of a sword. Luck. Some men have it, some don't.

'Time to plumb the depth of Glama Golden's loyalty,' said Calder happily. 'Or his self-interest, anyway.'

They walked down the hillside in the gathering darkness, stars starting to peep out from the inky skies, Calder smirking at the thought of how he'd make Golden squirm. How he'd have that puffed-up bastard tripping over his own tongue trying to ingratiate himself. How much he'd enjoy twisting the screw. They reached a fork in the path and Deep strolled off to the left, around the foot of the Heroes.

'Golden's camp is on the right,' grunted Calder.

'True,' said Deep, still walking. 'You've an unchallenged grasp on your rights and lefts, which puts you a firm rung above my brother on the ladder of learning.'

'They look the bloody same,' snapped Shallow, and Calder felt something prick at his back. A cold and surprising something, not quite painful but certainly not pleasant. It took him a moment to realise what it was, but when he did all his smugness drained away as though that jabbing point had already made a hole.

How flimsy is arrogance. It only takes a bit of sharp metal to bring it all crashing down.

'We're going left.' Shallow's point prodded again and Calder set off, hands up, his smirk abandoned in the gloom.

There were plenty of people about. Fires surrounded by half-lit faces. One set playing at dice, another making up ever more bloated lies about their high deeds in the battle, another slapping out stray embers on someone's cloak. A drunken group of Thralls lurched past but they barely even looked over. No one rushed to Calder's rescue. They saw nothing to comment on and even if they had, they didn't care a shit. People don't, on the whole.

'Where are we going?' Though the only real question was whether they'd dug his grave already, or were planning to argue over it after.

'You'll find out.'

'Why?'

'Because we'll get there.'

'No. Why are you doing this?'

They burst out laughing together, as though that was quite the joke. 'Do you think we were watching you by accident, over at Caul Reachey's camp?'

'No, no, no,' hummed Shallow. 'No.'

They were moving away from the Heroes, now. Fewer people, fewer fires. Hardly any light but the circle of crops picked out by Deep's torch. Any hope of help fading into the black behind them along with the bragging and the songs. If Calder was going to be saved he'd have to do it himself. They hadn't even bothered to take his sword away from him. But who was he fooling? Even if his right hand hadn't been useless, Shallow could've cut his throat a dozen times before he got it drawn. Across the darkened fields he could pick out the line of trees far to the north. Maybe if he ran—

'No.' Shallow's knife pricked at Calder's side again. 'No nee no no no.'

'Really no,' said Deep.

'Look, maybe we can come to an arrangement. I've got money—'

'There's no pockets deep enough to outbid our employer. Your best bet is just to follow along like a good boy.' Calder rather doubted that but, clever as he liked to think he was, he had no better ideas. 'We're sorry about this, you know. We've naught but respect for you just as we'd naught but respect for your father.'

'What good is your sorry going to do me?'

Deep's shoulders shrugged. 'A little less than none, but we always make a point of saying it.'

'He thinks that lends us class,' said Shallow.

'A noble air.'

'Oh, aye,' said Calder. 'You're a right pair of fucking heroes.'

'It's a pitiable fellow who ain't a hero to someone,' said Deep. 'Even if it's only himself.'

'Or Mummy,' said Shallow.

'Or his brother.' Deep grinned over his shoulder. 'How did your brother feel about you, my lordling?'

Calder thought about Scale, fighting against the odds on that bridge, waiting for help that never came. 'I'm guessing he went off me at the end.'

'Wouldn't cry too many tears about it. It's a rare fine fellow who ain't a villain to someone. Even if it's only himself.'

'Or his brother,' whispered Shallow.

'And here we are.'

A ramshackle farmhouse had risen out of the darkness. Large and silent, stone covered with rustling creeper, flaking shutters slanting in the windows. Calder realised it was the same one he'd slept in for two nights, but it looked a lot more sinister now. Everything does with a knife at your back.

'This way, if you please.' To the porch on the side of the house, lean-to roof missing slates, a rotten table under it, chairs lying on their sides. A lamp swung gently from a hook on one of the flaking columns, its light shifting across a yard scattered with weeds, a slumping fence beyond separating the farm from its fields.

There were a lot of tools leaning against the fence. Shovels, axes, pickaxes, caked in mud, as though they'd been hard used that day by a team of workmen and left there to be used again tomorrow. Tools for digging. Calder felt his fear, faded slightly on the walk, shoot up cold again. Through a gap in the fence and the light of Deep's torch flared out across trampled crops and fell on fresh-turned earth. A knee-high heap of it, big as the foundations of a barn. Calder opened his mouth, maybe to make some desperate plea, strike some last bargain, but he had no words any more.

'They been working hard,' said Deep, as another mound crept from the night beside the first.

'Slaving away,' said Shallow, as the torchlight fell on a third.

'They say war's an awful affliction, but you'll have a hard time finding a gravedigger to agree.'

The last one hadn't been filled in yet. Calder's skin crawled as the torch found its edges, five strides across, maybe, its far end lost in the sliding shadows. Deep made it to the corner and peered over the edge. 'Phew.' He wedged his torch in the earth, turned and beckoned. 'Up you come, then. Walking slow ain't going to make the difference.'

Shallow gave him a nudge and Calder plodded on, throat tightening with each drawn-out breath, more and more of the sides of the pit crawling into view with each unsteady step.

Earth, and pebbles, and barley roots. Then a pale hand. Then a bare arm. Then corpses. Then more. The pit was full of them, heaped up in a grisly tangle. The refuse of battle.

Most were naked. Stripped of everything. Would some gravedigger end up with Calder's good cloak? The dirt and the blood looked the same in the torchlight. Black smears on dead white skin. Hard to say which twisted legs and arms belonged to which bodies.

Had these been men a couple of days before? Men with ambitions, and hopes, and things they cared for? A mass of stories, cut off in the midst, no ending. The hero's reward.

He felt a warmth down his leg and realised he'd pissed himself.

'Don't worry.' Deep's voice was soft, like a father to a scared child. 'That happens a lot.'

'We've seen it all.'

'And then a little more.'

'You stand here.' Shallow took him by the shoulders and turned him to face the pit, limp and helpless. You never think you'll just meekly do what you're told when you're facing your death. But everyone does. 'A little to the left.' Guiding him a step to the right. 'That's left, right?'

'That's right, fool.'

'Fuck!' Shallow gave him a harder yank and Calder slipped at the edge, boot heel sending a few lumps of earth down onto the bodies. Shallow pulled him back straight. 'There?'

'There,' said Deep. 'All right, then.'

Calder stood, looking down, silently starting to cry. Dignity no longer seemed to matter much. He'd have even less soon enough. He wondered how deep the pit was. How many bodies he'd share it with when they picked those tools up in the morning and heaped the earth on top. Five score? Ten score? More?

He stared at the nearest of them, right beneath him, a great black wound in the back of its head. *His* head, Calder supposed, though it was hard to think of it as a man. It was a thing, robbed of all identity. Robbed of all . . . unless . . .

The face had been Black Dow's. His mouth was open, half-full of dirt, but it was the Protector of the North, no doubt. He looked almost as if he was smiling, one arm flung out to welcome Calder, like an old friend, to the land of the dead. Back to the mud indeed. So quickly it can happen. Lord of all to meat in a hole.

Tears crept down Calder's hot face, glistened in the torchlight as they pattered into the pit, making fresh streaks through the grime on Black Dow's cold cheek. Death in the circle would've been a disappointment. How much worse was this? Tossed in a nameless hole, unmarked by those that loved or even those that hated him.

He was blubbing like a baby, sore ribs heaving, the pit and the corpses glistening through the salt water.

When would they do it? Surely, now, here it came. A breeze

wafted up, chilling the tears on his face. He let his head drop back, squeezing his eyes shut, wincing, grunting, as if he could feel the knife sliding into his back. As if the metal was already in him. When would they do it? Surely now . . .

The wind dropped away, and he thought he heard clinking. Voices from behind him, from the direction of the house. He stood for a while longer, making a racking sob with every breath.

'Fish to start,' someone said.

'Excellent.'

Trembling, cringing, every movement a terrifying effort, Calder slowly turned.

Deep and Shallow had vanished, their torch flickering abandoned at the edge of the pit. Beyond the ramshackle fence, under the ramshackle porch, the old table had been covered with a cloth and set for dinner. A man was unpacking dishes from a large basket. Another sat in one of the chairs. Calder wiped his eyes on the back of his wildly trembling hand, not sure whether to believe the evidence of his senses. The man in the chair was the First of the Magi.

Bayaz smiled over. 'Why, Prince Calder!' As if they'd run into each other by accident in the market. 'Pray join me!'

Calder wiped snot from his top lip, still expecting a knife to dart from the darkness. Then ever so slowly, his knees wobbling so much he could hear them flapping against the inside of his wet trousers, he picked his way back through the gap in the fence and over to the porch.

The servant righted the fallen chair, dusted it off and held his open palm towards it. Calder sagged into it, numb, eyes still gently leaking by themselves, and watched Bayaz fork a piece of fish into his mouth and slowly, deliberately, thoroughly chew, and swallow.

'So. The Whiteflow shall remain the northern boundary of Angland.'

Calder sat for a moment, aware of a faint snorting at the back of his nose with every quick breath but unable to stop it. Then he blinked, and finally nodded.

'The land between the Whiteflow and the Cusk, including the city of Uffrith, shall come under the governorship of the

Dogman. It shall become a protectorate of the Union, with six representatives on the Open Council.'

Calder nodded again.

'The rest of the North as far as the Crinna is yours.' Bayaz popped the last piece of fish into his mouth and waved his fork around. 'Beyond the Crinna it belongs to Stranger-Come-Knocking.'

Yesterday's Calder might've snapped out some defiant jibe, but all he could think of now was how very lucky he felt not to be gushing blood into the mud, and how very much he wanted to carry on not gushing blood. 'Yes,' he croaked.

'You don't need time to . . . chew it over?'

Eternity in a pit full of corpses, perhaps? 'No,' whispered Calder.

'Pardon me?'

Calder took a shuddering breath. 'No.'

'Well.' Bayaz dabbed his mouth with a cloth, and looked up. 'This is much better.'

'A very great improvement.' The curly-headed servant had a pouty smile as he whisked Bayaz' plate away and replaced it with a clean one. Probably much the same as Calder's habitual smirk, but he enjoyed seeing it on another man about as much as he might have enjoyed seeing another man fuck his wife. The servant whipped the cover from a dish with a flourish.

'Ah, the meat, the meat!' Bayaz watched the knife flash and flicker as wafer slices were carved with blinding skill. 'Fish is all very well, but dinner hasn't really started until you're served something that bleeds.' The servant added vegetables with the dexterity of a conjuror, then turned his smirk on Calder.

There was something oddly, irritatingly familiar about him. Like a name at the tip of Calder's tongue. Had he seen him visit his father once, in a fine cloak? Or at Ironhead's fire with a Carl's helmet on? Or at the shoulder of Stranger-Come-Knocking, with paint on his face and splinters of bone through his ear? 'Meat, sir?'

'No,' whispered Calder. All he could think of was all the meat in the pits just a few strides away.

'You really should try it!' said Bayaz. 'Go on, give him some! And help the prince, Yoru, he has an injured right hand.'

The servant doled meat onto Calder's plate, bloody gravy gleaming in the gloom, then began to cut it up at frightening speed, making Calder flinch with each sweep of the knife.

Across the table, the Magus was already happily chewing. 'I must admit, I did not entirely enjoy the tenor of our last conversation. It reminded me somewhat of your father.' Bayaz paused as if expecting a response, but Calder had none to give. 'That is meant as a very small compliment and a very large warning. For many years your father and I had . . . an understanding.'

'Some good it did him.'

The wizard's brows went up. 'How short your family's memory! Indeed it did! Gifts he had of me, and all manner of help and wise counsel and oh, how he thrived! From piss-pot chieftain to King of the Northmen! Forged a nation where there were only squabbling peasants and pigshit before!' The edge of Bayaz' knife screeched against the plate and his voice sharpened with it. 'But he became arrogant in his glory, and forgot the debts he owed, and sent his puffed-up sons to make demands of me. *Demands,*' hissed the Magus, eyes glittering in the shadows of their sockets. 'Of *me.*'

Calder's throat felt uncomfortably tight as Bayaz sat back. 'Bethod turned his back on our friendship, and his allies fell away, and all his great achievements withered, and he died in blood and was buried in an unmarked grave. There is a lesson there. Had your father paid his debts, perhaps he would be King of the Northmen still. I have high hopes you will learn from his mistake, and remember what you owe.'

'I've taken nothing from you.'

'Have . . . you . . . not?' Bayaz bit off each word with a curl of his lip. 'You will never know, nor could you even understand, the many ways in which I have interceded on your behalf.'

The servant arched one brow. 'The account is lengthy.'

'Do you suppose things run your way because you think yourself charming? Or cunning? Or uncommonly lucky?'

Calder had, in fact, thought exactly that.

'Was it charm that saved you from Reachey's assassins at his weapontake, or the two colourful Northmen I sent to watch over you?'

Calder had no answer.

'Was it cunning that saved you in the battle, or my instructions to Brodd Tenways that he should keep you from harm?'

Even less to that. 'Tenways?' he whispered.

'Friends and enemies can sometimes be difficult to tell apart. I asked him to act like Black Dow's man. Perhaps he was too good an actor. I heard he died.'

'It happens,' croaked Calder.

'Not to you.' The 'yet' was unsaid, but still deafening. 'Even though you faced Black Dow in a duel to the death! And was it luck that tipped the balance towards you when the Protector of the North lay dead at your feet, or was it my old friend Stranger-Come-Knocking?'

Calder felt as if he was up to his chest in quicksand, and had only just realised. 'He's your man?'

Bayaz did not gloat or cackle. He looked almost bored. 'I knew him when he was still called Pip. But big men need big names, eh, Black Calder?'

'Pip,' he muttered, trying to square the giant with the name.

'I wouldn't use it to his face.'

'I don't reach his face.'

'Few do. He wants to bring civilisation to the fens.'

'I wish him luck.'

'Keep it for yourself. I gave it to you.'

Calder was too busy trying to think his way through it. 'But . . . Stranger-Come-Knocking fought for Dow. Why not have him fight for the Union? You could have won on the second morning and saved us all a—'

'He was not content with my first offer.' Bayaz sourly speared some greens with his fork. 'He demonstrated his value, and so I made a better one.'

'This was all a disagreement over prices?'

The Magus let his head tip to one side. 'Just what do you think a war is?' That sank slowly into the silence between them like a ship with all hands. 'There are many others who have debts.'

'Caul Shivers.'

'No,' said the servant. 'His intervention was a happy accident.'

Calder blinked. 'Without him . . . Dow would've torn me apart.'

'Good planning does not prevent accidents,' said Bayaz, 'it allows for them. It makes sure every accident is a happy one. I am not so careless a gambler as to make only one bet. But the North has ever been short of good material, and I admit you are my preference. You are no hero, Calder. I like that. You see what men are. You have your father's cunning, and ambition, and ruthlessness, but not his pride.'

'Pride always struck me as a waste of effort,' murmured Calder. 'Everyone serves.'

'Keep that in mind and you will prosper. Forget it, well . . .' Bayaz forked a slice of meat into his mouth and noisily chewed. 'My advice would be to keep that pit of corpses always at your feet. The feeling as you stared down into it, waiting for death. The awful helplessness. Skin tickling with the expectation of the knife. The regret for everything left undone. The fear for those you leave behind.' He gave a bright smile. 'Start every morning and end every day at the brink of that pit. Remember, because forgetfulness is the curse of power. And you may find yourself once again staring into your own grave, this time with less happy results. You need only defy me.'

'I've spent the last ten years kneeling to one man or another.' Calder didn't have to lie. Black Dow had let him live, then demanded obedience, then made threats. Look how that turned out. 'My knees bend very easily.'

The Magus smacked his lips as he swallowed the last piece of carrot and tossed his cutlery on the plate. 'That gladdens me. You cannot imagine how many similar conversations I have had with stiff-kneed men. I no longer have the slightest patience for them. But I can be generous to those who see reason. It may be that at some point I will send someone to you requesting . . . favours. When that day comes, I hope you will not disappoint me.'

'What sort of favours?'

'The sort that will prevent you from ever again being taken down the wrong path by men with knives.'

Calder cleared his throat. 'Those kinds of favours I will always be willing to grant.'

'Good. In return you will have gold from me.'

'That's the generosity of Magi? Gold?'

'What were you expecting, a magic codpiece? This is no

children's storybook. Gold is everything and anything. Power, love, safety. Sword and shield together. There is no greater gift. But I do, as it happens, have another.' Bayaz paused like a jester about to deliver the joke. 'Your brother's life.'

Calder felt his face twitch. Hope? Or disappointment? 'Scale's dead.'

'No. He lost his right hand at the Old Bridge but he lives. The Union are releasing all prisoners. A gesture of goodwill, as part of the historic peace accord that you have so gratefully agreed to. You can collect the pinhead at midday tomorrow.'

'What should I do with him?'

'Far be it from me to tell you what to do with your gift, but you do not get to be a king without making some sacrifices. You do want to be king, don't you?'

'Yes.' Things had changed a great deal since the evening began, but of that Calder was more sure than ever.

The First of the Magi stood, taking up his staff as his servant began nimbly to clear away the dishes. 'Then an elder brother is a dreadful encumbrance.'

Calder watched him for a moment, looking calmly off across the darkened fields as though they were full of flowers rather than corpses. 'Have you eaten here, within a long piss of a mass grave . . . just to show me how ruthless you are?'

'Must everything have some sinister motive? I have eaten here because I was hungry.' Bayaz tipped his head to one side as he looked down at Calder. Like the bird looks at the worm. 'Graves mean nothing to me either way.'

'Knives,' muttered Calder, 'and threats, and bribes, and war?'

Bayaz' eyes shone with the lamplight. 'Yes?'

'What kind of a fucking wizard are you?'

'The kind you obey.'

The servant reached for his plate but Calder caught him by the wrist before he got there. 'Leave it. I might get hungry later.'

The Magus smiled at that. 'What did I say, Yoru? He has a stronger stomach than you'd think.' He waved over his shoulder as he walked away. 'I believe, for now, the North is in safe hands.'

Bayaz' servant took up the basket, took down the lamp, and followed his master.

'Where's dessert?' Calder shouted after them.

The servant gave him one last smirk. 'Black Dow has it.'

The glimmer of the lamp followed them around the side of the house and they were gone, leaving Calder to sink into his rickety chair in the darkness, eyes closed, breathing hard, with a mixture of crushing disappointment and even more crushing relief.

Just Deserts

My dear and trusted friend,
     It gives me great pleasure to tell you that the
     circumstances have arisen in which I can invite you
back to Adua, to once again take up your position among the
Knights of the Body, and your rightful place as my First Guard.
     You have been greatly missed. During your absence your letters
have been a constant comfort and delight. For any wrong on your
part, I long ago forgave you. For any wrong on mine, I earnestly
hope that you can do the same. Please, let me know that we can
continue as we were before Sipani.
     Your sovereign,
     The High King of Angland, Starikland, and Midderland,
Protector of Westport and Dagoska, His August Majesty . . .

Gorst could read no further. He closed his eyes, tears stinging
at the inside of the lids, and pressed the crumpled paper against
his chest as one might embrace a lover. How often had poor,
scorned, exiled Bremer dan Gorst dreamed of this moment? *Am I
dreaming now?* He bit his sore tongue and the sweet taste of blood
was a relief. Prised his eyelids open again, tears running freely,
and stared at the letter through the shimmering water.

*Dear and trusted friend . . . rightful place as First Guard . . .
comfort and delight . . . as we were before Sipani. As we were before
Sipani . . .*

He frowned. Brushed his tears on the back of his wrist and
peered down at the date. The letter had been despatched six days
ago. *Before I fought at the fords, on the bridge, at the Heroes. Before
the battle even began.* He hardly knew whether to laugh or cry
more and in the end did both, shuddering with weepy giggles,
spraying the letter with happy specks of spit.

What did it matter why? *I have what I deserve.*

He burst from the tent and it was as if he had never felt the sunlight before. The simple joy of the life-giving warmth on his face, the caress of the breeze. He gazed about in damp-eyed wonder. The patch of ground sloping down to the river, a mud-churned, rubbish-strewn midden when he trudged inside, had become a charming garden, filled with colour. With hopeful faces and pleasing chatter. With laughter and birdsong.

'You all right?' Rurgen looked faintly concerned, as far as Gorst could tell through the wet.

'I have a letter from the king,' he squeaked, no longer caring a damn how he sounded.

'What is it?' asked Younger. 'Bad news?'

'Good news.' And he grabbed Younger around the shoulders and made him groan as he hugged him tight. 'The best.' He gathered up Rurgen with the other arm, lifting their feet clear of the ground, squeezing the pair of them like a loving father might squeeze his sons. 'We're going home.'

Gorst walked with an unaccustomed bounce. Armour off, he felt so light he might suddenly spring into the sunny sky. The very air smelled sweeter, even if it did still carry the faint tang of latrines, and he dragged it in through both nostrils. All his injuries, all his aches and pains, all his petty disappointments, faded in the all-conquering glow.

I am born again.

The road to Osrung – or to the burned-out ruin that had been Osrung a few days before – brimmed with smiling faces. A set of whores blew kisses from the seat of a wagon and Gorst blew them back. A crippled boy gave excited hoots and Gorst jovially ruffled his hair. A column of walking wounded shuffled past, one on crutches at the front nodded and Gorst hugged him, kissed him on the forehead and walked on, smiling.

'Gorst! It's Gorst!' Some cheering went up, and Gorst grinned and shook one scabbed fist in the air. *Bremer dan Gorst, hero of the battlefield! Bremer dan Gorst, confidant of the monarch! Knight of the Body, First Guard to the High King of the Union, noble, righteous, loved by all!* He could do anything. He could have anything.

Joyous scenes were everywhere. A man with sergeant's stripes was being married by the colonel of his regiment to a pudding-faced woman with flowers in her hair while a gathering of his comrades gave suggestive whistles. A new ensign, absurdly young-looking, beamed in the sunlight as he carried the colours of his regiment by way of initiation, the golden sun of the Union snapping proudly. *Perhaps one of the very flags that Mitterick so carelessly lost only a day ago? How soon some trespasses are forgotten. The incompetent rewarded along with the wronged.*

As if to illustrate that very point, Gorst caught sight of Felnigg beside the road in his new uniform, staff officers in a crowing crowd around him, giving hell to a tearful young lieutenant beside a tipped-over cart, gear, weapons and for some reason a full-sized harp spilled from its torn awning like the guts from a dead sheep.

'General Felnigg!' called Gorst jauntily. 'Congratulations on your promotion!' *It could not have happened to a less deserving drunken pedant.* He briefly considered the possibility of challenging the man to the duel he had been too cowardly to demand a few evenings before. Then to the possibility of backhanding him into the ditch as he passed. *But I have other business.*

'Thank you, Colonel Gorst. I wished to let you know how very much I admire your—'

Gorst could not even be bothered to make excuses. He simply barged past, scattering Felnigg's staff – most of whom had recently been Marshal Kroy's staff – like a plough through muck and left them clucking and puffing in his wake. *And away to fuck with the lot of you, I'm free. Free!* He sprang up and punched the air.

Even the wounded near the charred gates of Osrung looked happy as he passed, tapping shoulders with his fist, muttering banal encouragements. *Share my joy, you crippled and dying! I have plenty to spare!*

And there she stood, among them, giving out water. *Like the Goddess of mercy. Oh, soothe my pain.* He had no fear now. He knew what he had to do.

'Finree!' he called, then cleared his throat and tried again, a little deeper. 'Finree.'

'Bremer. You look . . . happy.' She lifted one enquiring

eyebrow, as though a smile on his face was as incongruous as on a horse, or a rock, or a corpse. *But get used to this smile, for it is here to stay!*

'I am very happy. I wanted to say . . .' *I love you.* 'Goodbye. I am returning to Adua this evening.'

'Really? So am I.' His heart leaped. 'Well, as soon as my husband is well enough to be moved.' And plummeted back down. 'But they say that won't be long.' She looked annoyingly delighted about it too.

'Good. Good.' *Fuck him.* Gorst realised his fist was clenched, and forced it open. *No, no, forget him. He is nothing. I am the winner, and this is my moment.* 'I received a letter from the king this morning.'

'Really? So did we!' She blurted it out, seizing him by the arm, eyes bright. His heart leaped again, as though her touch was a second letter from his Majesty. 'Hal is being restored to his seat on the Open Council.' She looked furtively around, then whispered it in a husky rush. 'They're making him lord governor of Angland!'

There was a long, uncomfortable pause while Gorst took that in. *Like a sponge soaking up a puddle of piss.* 'Lord . . . governor?' It seemed a cloud had moved across the sun. It was no longer quite so warm upon his face as it had been.

'I know! There will be a parade, apparently.'

'A parade.' *Of cunts.* A chilly breeze blew up and flapped his loose shirt. 'He deserves it.' *He presided over a blown-up bridge and so he gets a parade?* 'You deserve it.' *Where's my fucking parade?*

'And your letter?'

My letter? My pathetic embarrassment of a letter? 'Oh . . . the king has asked me to take up my old position as First Guard.' Somehow he could no longer muster quite the enthusiasm he had when he opened it. *Not lord governor, oh no! Nothing like lord governor. The king's first hand-holder. The king's first cock-taster. Pray don't wipe your own arse your Majesty, let me!*

'That's wonderful news.' Finree smiled as though everything had turned out just right. 'War is full of opportunities, after all, however terrible it may be.'

It is pedestrian news. My triumph is all spoiled. My garlands rotted. 'I thought . . .' His face twitched. He could not cling on to his smile any longer. 'My success seems quite meagre now.'

'Meagre? Well, of course not, I didn't mean—'

'I'll never have anything worth the having, will I?'

She blinked. 'I—'

'I'll never have you.'

Her eyes went wide. 'You'll— What?'

'I'll never have you, or anyone like you.' Colour burned up red under her freckled cheeks. 'Then let me be honest. War is terrible, you say?' He hissed it right in her horrified face. '*Shit*, I say! I fucking *love* war.' The unsaid words boiled out of him. He could not stop them, did not want to. 'In the dreamy yards, and drawing rooms, and pretty parks of Adua, I am a squeaking fucking joke. A falsetto embarrassment. A ridiculous clown-man.' He leaned even closer, enjoying it that she flinched. *Only this way will she know that I exist. Then let it be this way.* 'But on the battlefield? On the battlefield I am a *god*. I love war. The steel, the smell, the corpses. I wish there were more. On the first day I drove the Northmen back alone at the ford. Alone! On the second I carried the bridge! Me! Yesterday I climbed the Heroes! I *love* war! I . . . I wish it wasn't over. I wish . . . I wish . . .'

But far sooner than he had expected, the well had run dry. He was left standing there, breathing hard, staring down at her. Like a man who has throttled his wife and come suddenly to his senses, he had no idea what to do next. He turned to make his escape, but Finree's hand was still on his arm and now her fingers dug into him, pulling him back.

The blush of shock was fading now, her face hard with growing anger, jaw muscles clenched. 'What happened in Sipani?'

And now it was his cheeks that burned. As if the name was a slap. 'I was betrayed.' He tried to make the last word stab at her as it stabbed him, but his voice had lost all its edge. 'I was made the scapegoat.' A goat's plaintive bleating, indeed. 'After all my loyalty, all my diligence . . .' He fumbled for more words but his voice was not used to making them, fading into a squeaky whine as she bared her teeth.

'I heard when they came for the king you were passed out drunk with a whore.' Gorst swallowed. But he could hardly deny it. Stumbling from that room, head spinning, struggling to fasten his belt and draw his sword at once. 'I heard it was not the first time you had disgraced yourself, and that the king had forgiven you before, and that the Closed Council would not let him do it again.' She looked him up and down, and her lip curled. 'God of the battlefield, eh? Gods and devils can look much alike to us little people. You went to a ford, and a bridge, and a hill, and what did you do there except kill? What have you made? Who have you helped?'

He stood there for a moment, all his bravado slithering out. *She is right. And no one knows it better than me.* 'Nothing and no one,' he whispered.

'So you love war. I used to think you were a decent man. But I see now I was mistaken.' She stabbed at his chest with her forefinger. 'You're a *hero*.'

She turned with one last look of excruciating contempt and left him standing among the wounded. They no longer looked so happy for him as they had done. They looked, on the whole, to be in very great pain. The birdsong was half-dead crowing once more. His elation was a charming sandcastle, washed away by the pitiless tide of reality. He felt as if he was cast from lead.

Am I doomed always to feel like this? A most uncomfortable thought occurred. *Did I feel like this . . . before Sipani?* He frowned after Finree as she vanished back into the hospital tent. *Back to her pretty young dolt of a lord governor.* He realised far too late he should have pointed out that he had been the one to save her husband. *One never says the right things at the right time.* A stupendous understatement if ever there was one. He gave an epic, grinding sigh. *This is why I keep my fucking mouth shut.*

Gorst turned and trudged away into the gloomy afternoon, fists clenched, frowning up towards the Heroes, black teeth against the sky at the top of their solemn hill.

By the Fates, I need to fight someone. Anyone.

But the war was over.

Black Calder

'Just give me the nod.'

'The nod?'

Shivers turned to look at him, and nodded. 'The nod. And it's done.'

'Simple as that,' muttered Calder, hunching in his saddle.

'Simple as that.'

Easy. Just nod, and you can be king. Just nod, and kill your brother.

It was hot, a few shreds of cloud hanging in the blue over the fells, bees floating about some yellow flowers at the edge of the barley, the river glittering silver. The last hot day, maybe, before autumn shooed the summer off and beckoned winter on. It should've been a day for lazy dreams and trailing hot toes in the shallows. Perhaps a hundred strides downstream a few Northmen had stripped off and were doing just that. A little further along the opposite bank and a dozen Union soldiers were doing the same. The laughter of both sets would occasionally drift to Calder's ear over the happy chattering of the water. Sworn enemies one day, now they played like children, close enough almost to splash.

Peace. And that had to be a good thing.

For months he'd been preaching for it, hoping for it, plotting for it, with few allies and fewer rewards, and here it was. If ever there was a day to smirk it was this one, but Calder could've lifted one of the Heroes more easily than the corners of his mouth. His meeting with the First of the Magi had been weighing them down all through a sleepless night. That and the thought of the meeting that was coming.

'Ain't that him?' asked Shivers.

'Where?' There was only one man on the bridge, and not one he recognised.

'It is. That's him.'

Calder narrowed his eyes, then shaded them against the glare. 'By the . . .'

Until last night he'd thought his brother killed. He hadn't been so far wrong. Scale was a ghost, crept from the land of the dead and ready to be snatched back by a breath of wind. Even at this distance he looked withered, shrunken, greasy hair plastered to one side of his head. He'd long had a limp but now he shuffled sideways, left boot dragging over the old stones. He had a threadbare blanket around his shoulders, left hand clutching two corners at his throat while the others flapped about his legs.

Calder slid from his saddle, tossing the reins over his horse's neck, bruised ribs burning as he hurried to help his brother.

'Just give me the nod,' came Shivers' whisper.

Calder froze, guts clenching. Then he went on.

'Brother.'

Scale squinted up like a man who hadn't seen the sun for days, sunken face covered with scabby grazes on one side, a black cut across the swollen bridge of his nose. 'Calder?' He gave a weak grin and Calder saw he'd lost his two front teeth, blood dried to his cracked lips. He let go of his blanket to take Calder's hand and it slid off, left him hunched around the stump of his right arm like a beggar woman around her baby. Calder found his eyes drawn to that horrible absence of limb. Strangely, almost comically shortened, bound to the elbow with grubby bandages, spotted brown at the end.

'Here.' He unclasped his cloak and slipped it around his brother's shoulders, his own broken hand tingling unpleasantly in sympathy.

Scale looked too pained and exhausted even to gesture at stopping him. 'What happened to your face?'

'I took your advice about fighting.'

'How did it work out?'

'Painfully for all concerned,' said Calder, fumbling the clasp shut with one hand and one thumb.

Scale stood, swaying as if he might drop at any moment, blinking out across the shifting barley. 'The battle's over, then?' he croaked.

'It's over.'

'Who won?'

Calder paused. 'We did.'

'Dow did, you mean?'

'Dow's dead.'

Scale's bloodshot eyes went wide. 'In the battle?'

'After.'

'Back to the mud.' Scale wriggled his hunched shoulders under the cloak. 'I guess it was coming.'

All Calder could think of was the pit opening up at the toes of his boots. 'It's always coming.'

'Who's taken his place?'

Another pause. The swimming soldiers' laughter drifted over, then faded back into the rustling crops. 'I have.' Scale's scabbed mouth hung gormlessly open. 'They've taken to calling me Black Calder, now.'

'Black . . . Calder.'

'Let's get you mounted.' Calder led his brother over to the horses, Shivers watching them all the way.

'Are you two on the same side now?' asked Scale.

Shivers put a finger on his scarred cheek and pulled it down so his metal eye bulged from the socket. 'Just keeping an eye out.'

Scale reached for the saddle-bow with his right arm, stopped himself and took it awkwardly with his left. He found one stirrup with a fishing boot and started to drag himself up. Calder hooked a hand under his knee to help him. When Calder had been a child Scale used to lift him up into the saddle. Fling him up sometimes, none too gently. How things had changed.

The three of them set off up the track. Scale slumped in the saddle, reins dangling from his limp left hand and his head nodding with each hoof-beat. Calder rode grimly beside him. Shivers followed, like a shadow. The Great Leveller, waiting at their backs. Through the fields they went, at an interminable walk, towards the gap in Clail's Wall where Calder had faced the Union charge a few days before.

His heart was beating just as fast as it had then. The Union had pulled back behind the river that morning and Pale-as-Snow's boys were up north behind the Heroes, but there were still eyes around. A few nervous pickers combing through the trampled barley, searching for some trifle others might have missed. Scrounging up arrowheads or buckles or anything that could turn a copper. A couple of men thrashing through the crops off to the east, one with a fishing rod over his shoulder. Strange, how quickly a battlefield turned back to being just a stretch of ground. One day every finger's breadth of it is something men can die over. The next it's just a path from here to there. As he looked about Calder caught Shivers' eye and the killer lifted his chin, silently asking the question. Calder jerked his head away like a hand from a boiling pot.

He'd killed men before. He'd killed Brodd Tenways with his own sword hours after the man had saved his life. He'd ordered Forley the Weakest dead for nothing but his own vanity. Killing a man when Skarling's Chair was the prize shouldn't have made his hand shake on the reins, should it?

'Why didn't you help me, Calder?' Scale had eased his stump out from the gap in the cloak and was frowning down at it, jaw set hard. 'At the bridge. Why didn't you come?'

'I wanted to.' Liar, liar. 'Found out there were Union men in the woods across that stream. Right on our flank. I wanted to go but I couldn't. I'm sorry.' That much was true. He was sorry. For what good that did.

'Well.' Scale's face was a grimacing mask as he slid the stump back under his cloak. 'Looks like you were right. The world needs more thinkers and fewer heroes.' He glanced over for an instant and the look in his eye made Calder wince. 'You always were the clever one.'

'No. It was you who was right. Sometimes you have to fight.'

This was where he'd made his little stand and the land still bore the scars. Crops trodden, broken arrow shafts scattered, scraps of ruined gear around the remains of the trenches. Before Clail's Wall the ground had been churned to mud then baked hard again, smeared bootprints, hoofprints, handprints stamped into it, all that was left of the men who died there.

'Get what you can with words,' muttered Calder, 'but the words of an armed man ring that much sweeter. Like you said. Like our father said.' And hadn't he said something about family, as well? How nothing is more important? And mercy? Always think about mercy?

'When you're young you think your father knows everything,'

said Scale. 'Now I'm starting to realise he might've been wrong on more than one score. Look how he ended up, after all.'

'True.' Every word said was like lifting a great stone. How long had Calder lived with the frustration of having this thick-headed heap of brawn in his way? How many knocks, and mocks, and insults had he endured from him? His fist closed tight around the metal in his pocket. His father's chain. His chain. Is nothing more important than family? Or is family the lead that weighs you down?

They'd left the pickers behind, and the scene of the fighting too. Down the quiet track near the farmhouse where Scale had woken him a few mornings before. Where Bayaz had given him an even harsher awakening the previous night. Was this a test? To see whether Calder was ruthless enough for the wizard's tastes? He'd been accused of many things, but never too little ruthlessness.

How long had he dreamed of taking back his father's place? Even before his father lost it, and now there was only one last little fence to jump. All it would take was a nod. He looked sideways at Scale, wrung-out wreck that he was. Not much of a fence to trip a man with ambition. Calder had been accused of many things, but never too little ambition.

'You were the one took after our father,' Scale was saying. 'I tried, but . . . couldn't ever do it. Always thought you'd make a better king.'

'Maybe,' whispered Calder. Definitely.

Shivers was close behind, one hand on the reins, the other resting on his hip. He looked as relaxed as ever a man could, swaying gently with the movements of his horse. But his fingertips just so happened to be brushing the grip of his sword, sheathed beside the saddle in easy reach. The sword that had been Black Dow's. The sword that had been the Bloody-Nine's. Shivers raised one brow, asking the question.

The blood was surging behind Calder's eyes. Now was the time. He could have everything he wanted.

Bayaz had been right. You don't get to be a king without making some sacrifices.

Calder took an endless breath in, and held it. Now.

And he gently shook his head.

Shivers' hand slid away. His horse dropped ever so slowly back.

'Maybe I'm the better brother,' said Calder, 'but you're the elder.' He brought his horse up close, and he pulled their father's chain from his pocket and slipped it over Scale's neck, arranged it carefully across his shoulders. Patted him on the back and left his hand there, wondering when he got to love this stupid bastard. When he got to love anyone besides himself. He lowered his head. 'Let me be the first to bow before the new King of the Northmen.'

Scale blinked down at the diamond on his grubby shirt. 'Never thought things would end up this way.'

Neither had Calder. But he found he was glad they had. 'End?' He smirked across at his brother. 'This is the beginning.'

Retired

The house wasn't by the water. It didn't have a porch. It did have a bench outside with a view of the valley, but when he sat on it of an evening with his pipe he didn't tend to smile, just thought of all the men he'd buried. It leaked somewhat around the western eaves when the rain came down, which it had in quite some measure lately. It had just the one room, and a shelf up a ladder for sleeping on, and when it came to the great divide between sheds and houses, was only just on the right side of the issue. But it was a house, still, with good oak bones and a good stone chimney. And it was his. Dreams don't just spring up by themselves, they need tending to, and you've got to plant that first seed somewhere. Or so Craw told himself.

'Shit!' Hammer and nail clattered to the boards and he was off around the room, spitting and cursing and shaking his hand about.

Working wood was a tough way to earn a living. He might not have been chewing his nails so much, but he'd taken to hammering the bastards into his fingers instead. The sad fact was, now the wounds all over Craw's hands had forced him to face it, he wasn't much of a carpenter. In his dreams of retirement he'd always seen himself crafting things of beauty. Probably while light streamed in through coloured windows and sawdust went up in artful puffs. Gables carved with gilded dragon heads, so lifelike they'd be the wonder of the North, folk flocking from miles around to get a look. But it turned out wood was just as full of split, and warp, and splinters as people were.

'Bloody hell.' Rubbing the life back into his thumb, nail already black from where he caught it yesterday.

They smiled at him in the village, brought him odd jobs, but he reckoned more'n one of the farmers was a good stretch better

606

with a hammer than he was. Certainly they'd got that new barn up without calling on his skills and he had to admit it was likely a finer building for it. He'd started to think they wanted him in the valley more for his sword than his saw. While the war was on, the North's ready supply of scum had the Southerners to kill and rob. Now they just had their own kind, and were taking every chance at it. A Named Man to hand was no bad thing. Those were the times. Those were still the times, and maybe they always would be.

He squatted beside the stricken chair, latest casualty in his war against furniture. He'd split the joint he'd spent the last hour chiselling out and now the new leg stuck at an angle, an ugly gouge where he'd been hammering. Served him right for working as the light was going, but if he didn't get this done tonight he'd—

'Craw!'

His head jerked up. A man's voice, deep and rough.

'You in there, Craw?'

His skin went cold all over. Might be he'd played the straight edge most of his life, but you don't walk free of the black business without some scores however you play it.

He sprang up, or as close to springing as he could get these days, snatched his sword from the bracket above the door, fumbled it and nearly dropped it on his head, hissing more curses. If it was someone come to kill him it didn't seem likely they'd have given him a warning by calling his name. Not unless they were idiots. Idiots can be just as vengeful as anyone else, though, if not more so.

The shutters of the back window were open. He could slip out and off into the wood. But if they were serious they'd have thought of that, and with his knees he'd be outrunning no one. Better to come out the front way and look 'em in the eye. The way he would've done when he was young. He sidled up, swallowing as he drew his sword. Turned the knob, wedged the blade into the gap and gently levered the door open while he peered around the frame.

He'd go out the front way, but he wasn't painting a target on his shirt.

He counted eight at a glance, spread out in a crescent on the damp patch of dirt in front of his house. A couple had torches, light catching mail and helm and spear's tip and making 'em twinkle in the damp twilight. Carls, and battle-toughened by their looks, though there weren't many men left in the North you couldn't say that about. They all had plenty of weapons, but no blades drawn that he could see. That gave him some measure of comfort.

'That you, Craw?' He got a big measure more when he saw who was in charge, standing closest to the house with palms up.

'That it is.' Craw let his sword point drop and poked his head out a bit further. 'Here's a surprise.'

'Pleasant one, I hope.'

'I guess you'll tell me. What're you after, Hardbread?'

'Can I come in?'

Craw sniffed. 'You can. Your crew might have to enjoy the night air for now.'

'They're used to it.' And Hardbread ambled up to the house alone. He looked prosperous. Beard trimmed back. New mail. Silver on the hilt of his sword. He climbed the steps and ducked past Craw, strolled to the centre of the one room, which didn't take long to get to, and cast an appraising eye around. Took in Craw's pallet on the shelf, his workbench and his tools, the half-finished chair, the broken wood and the shavings scattering the boards. 'This what retirement looks like?' he asked.

'No, I've a fucking palace out back. Why you here?'

Hardbread took a breath. 'Because mighty Scale Ironhand, King of the Northmen, has gone to war with Glama Golden.'

Craw snorted. 'Black Calder has, you mean. Why?'

'Golden killed Caul Reachey.'

'Reachey's dead?'

'Poisoned. And Golden did the deed.'

Craw narrowed his eyes. 'That a fact?'

'Calder says it is, so Scale says it is, so it's close to a fact as anyone's going to get. All the North's lining up behind Bethod's sons, and I've come to see if you want to line up too.'

'Since when did you fight for Calder and Scale?'

'Since the Dogman hung up his sword and stopped paying staples.'

Craw frowned at him. 'Calder would never take me.'

'It was Calder sent me. He's got Pale-as-Snow, and Cairm Ironhead, and your old friend Wonderful as his War Chiefs.'

'Wonderful?'

'Canny woman, that one. But Calder's lacking a Name to stand Second and lead his own Carls. He's in need of a straight edge, apparently.' Hardbread cocked a brow at the chair. 'So I don't reckon he'll be hiring you as a carpenter.'

Craw stood there, trying to get his head around it. Offered a place, and a high one. Back among folk he understood, and admired him. Back to the black business, and trying to juggle the right thing, and finding words over graves.

'Sorry to bring you all this way for nothing, Hardbread, but the answer's no. Pass my apologies on to Calder. My apologies for this and . . . for whatever else. But tell him I'm done. Tell him I'm retired.'

Hardbread gave a sigh. 'All right. It's a shame, but I'll pass it on.' He paused in the doorway, looking back. 'Look after yourself, eh, Craw? Ain't many of us left know the difference between the right thing and the wrong.'

'What difference?'

Hardbread snorted. 'Aye. Look after yourself, anyway.' And he stomped down the steps and out into the gathering dark.

Craw looked after him for a moment, wondering whether he was happy the thumping of his heart was softening or sad. Weighing his sword in his hand, remembering how it felt to hold it. Different from a hammer, that was sure. He remembered Threetrees giving it to him. The pride he'd felt, like a fire in him. Smiled in spite of himself to remember what he used to be. How prickly and wild and hungry for glory, not a straight edge on him anywhere.

He looked around at that one room, and the few things in it. He'd always thought retiring would be going back to his life after some nightmare pause. Some stretch of exile in the land of the dead. Now it came to him that all his life worth living had happened while he was holding a sword.

Standing alongside his dozen. Laughing with Whirrun, and Brack, and Wonderful. Clasping hands with his crew before the fight, knowing he'd die for them and they for him. The trust, the brotherhood, the love, knit closer than family. Standing by

609

Threetrees on the walls of Uffrith, roaring their defiance at Bethod's great army. The day he charged at the Cumnur. And at Dunbrec. And in the High Places, even though they lost. Because they lost. The day he earned his name. Even the day he got his brothers killed. Even when he'd stood at the top of the Heroes as the rain came down, watching the Union come, knowing every dragged-out moment might be the last.

Like Whirrun had said – you can't live more'n that. Certainly not by fixing a chair.

'Ah, shit,' he muttered, and he grabbed his sword-belt and his coat, threw 'em over his shoulder and strode out, slapping the door shut. Didn't even bother to lock it behind him.

'Hardbread! Wait up!'

Acknowledgements

As always, four people without whom:

Bren Abercrombie, whose eyes are sore from reading it.
Nick Abercrombie, whose ears are sore from hearing about it.
Rob Abercrombie, whose fingers are sore from turning the pages.
Lou Abercrombie, whose arms are sore from holding me up.

Then, my heartfelt thanks:

To all the lovely and talented folks at my UK Publisher, Gollancz, and their parent Orion, particularly Simon Spanton, Jo Fletcher, Jon Weir, Mark Stay and Jon Wood. Then, of course, all those who've helped make, publish, publicise, translate and above all *sell* my books wherever they may be around the world.

To the artists responsible for somehow making me look classy: Didier Graffet, Dave Senior and Laura Brett.

To editors across the Pond: Devi Pillai and Lou Anders.

To other hard-bitten professionals who've provided various mysterious services: Robert Kirby, Darren Turpin, Matthew Amos, Lionel Bolton.

To all the writers whose paths have crossed mine either electronically or in the actual flesh, and who've provided help, laughs and a few ideas worth stealing, including but by no means limited to: James Barclay, Mark Billingham, Peter V. Brett, Stephen Deas, Roger Levy, Tom Lloyd, Joe Mallozzi, George R. R. Martin, John Meaney, Richard Morgan, Mark Charan Newton, Garth Nix, Adam Roberts, Pat Rothfuss, Marcus Sakey, Wim Stolk and Chris Wooding.

'Joe Abercrombie's *Best Served Cold* is a bloody and relentless epic of vengeance and obsession in the grand tradition, a kind of splatter-punk sword 'n sorcery *Count of Monte Cristo*, Dumas by way of Moorcock. His cast features tyrants and torturers, a pair of poisoners, a serial killer, a treacherous drunk, a red-handed warrior and a blood-soaked mercenary captain. And those are the good guys . . . The battles are vivid and visceral, the action brutal, the pace headlong, and Abercrombie piles the betrayals, reversals, and plot twists one atop another to keep us guessing how it will all come out. This is his best book yet'   George RR Martin

'A satisfyingly brutal fantasy quest. Best served cold? Modern fantasy doesn't get much hotter than this'   *SFX*

'Joe Abercrombie is probably the brightest star among the new generation of British fantasy writers . . . Abercrombie never underestimates the horrors that people are prepared to inflict on one another, or their longlasting, often unexpected, consequences. Abercrombie writes a vivid, well-paced tale that never loosens its grip. His action scenes are cinematic in the best sense, and the characters are all distinct and interesting'   *The Times*

'Spiked with cynicism, and indeed spikes, *Best Served Cold* has as much in common with a classic Hollywood caper as it does with the rest of the genre. Moral ambiguity, hard violence, and that weaving of laughter, horror and pathos make it breathe, though the brilliant characters are what really make this soar. This is the highest grade of adult, commercial fantasy we have seen for quite a while'   *Deathray*

'Abercrombie is both fiendishly inventive and solidly convincing, especially when sprinkling his appallingly vivid combat scenes with humour so dark that it's almost ultraviolet'   *Publishers' Weekly*

'Storms along at a breakneck pace. Each character has a history of betrayal and a wobbly moral compass, giving further realism and depth to Abercrombie's world. The violence is plentiful, the methods of exacting revenge are eye-wateringly inventive and the characters well fleshed out. A fan of Bernard Cornwell's historical escapades could easily fall for it. Believe the hype'

Waterstone's Book Quarterly

'All in all, we can't say enough good things about Mr Abercrombie's latest addition to the genre. It's intelligent, measure, thoughtful, well paced and considered, but retains a sense of fun that has flavoured the rest of his excellent biography. We can't recommend it enough'

Sci Fi Now

'This is deep, dark stuff but it's a mark of that nice Mr Abercrombie's talent that he can wrap such complex themes in the kind of rip-roaring adventure that is so utterly compelling that, from the first page, it is impossible to put down'   *Sci-Fi London*

'Abercrombie weaves a dense plot, but not at the expense of the pace, and casts an ensemble of gritty, odd but always interesting characters to undertake Murcatto's revenge. Fans of Abercrombie's work will not be disappointed by his latest offering, which features all his usual hallmarks: cold steel, black comedy, fully realised characters and internecine struggles, both personal and epic'

Dreamwatch

'Abercrombie writes dark, adult fantasy, by which I mean there's a lot of stabbing in it, and after people stab each other they sometimes have sex with each other. His tone is morbid and funny and hardboiled, not wholly dissimilar to that of Iain Banks . . . Like Fritz Leiber you can see in your head where the blades are going, what is clanging off what, the sweat, the blood, the banter. And like George R. R. Martin Abercrombie has the will and the cruelty to actually kill and maim his characters'   *Time Magazine*

BEST
SERVED
COLD

Also by Joe Abercrombie from Gollancz:

THE FIRST LAW TRILOGY
The Blade Itself
Before They Are Hanged
Last Argument of Kings

Best Served Cold

BEST
SERVED
COLD

JOE ABERCROMBIE

The right of Joe Abercrombie to be identified as the author
of this work has been asserted by him in accordance with
the Copyright, Designs and Patents Act 1988.

First published in Great Britain in 2009 by
Gollancz
An imprint of the Orion Publishing Group
Orion House, 5 Upper St Martin's Lane,
London WC2H 9EA
An Hachette UK Company

This edition published in Great Britain in 2010
by Gollancz

11

A CIP catalogue record for this book
is available from the British Library.

ISBN 978 0 575 08248 9

Typeset at The Spartan Press Ltd,
Lymington, Hants

Printed and bound by
CPI Group (UK) Ltd, Croydon, CR0 4YY

The Orion Publishing Group's policy is to use papers
that are natural, renewable and recyclable products and
made from wood grown in sustainable forests. The logging
and manufacturing processes are expected to conform to
the environmental regulations of the country of origin.

www.joeabercrombie.com
www.orionbooks.co.uk

For Grace
One day you will read this
And be slightly worried

Benna Murcatto Saves a Life

The sunrise was the colour of bad blood. It leaked out of the east and stained the dark sky red, marked the scraps of cloud with stolen gold. Underneath it the road twisted up the mountainside towards the fortress of Fontezarmo – a cluster of sharp towers, ash-black against the wounded heavens. The sunrise was red, black and gold.

The colours of their profession.

'You look especially beautiful this morning, Monza.'

She sighed, as if that was an accident. As if she hadn't spent an hour preening herself before the mirror. 'Facts are facts. Stating them isn't a gift. You only prove you're not blind.' She yawned, stretched in her saddle, made him wait a moment longer. 'But I'll hear more.'

He noisily cleared his throat and held up one hand, a bad actor preparing for his grand speech. 'Your hair is like to . . . a veil of shimmering sable!'

'You pompous cock. What was it yesterday? A curtain of midnight. I liked that better, it had some poetry to it. Bad poetry, but still.'

'Shit.' He squinted up at the clouds. 'Your eyes, then, gleam like piercing sapphires, beyond price!'

'I've got stones in my face, now?'

'Lips like rose petals?'

She spat at him, but he was ready and dodged it, the phlegm clearing his horse and falling on the dry stones beside the track. 'That's to make your roses grow, arsehole. You can do better.'

'Harder every day,' he muttered. 'That jewel I bought looks wonderful well on you.'

She held up her right hand to admire it, a ruby the size of an almond, catching the first glimmers of sunlight and glistening like an open wound. 'I've had worse gifts.'

'It matches your fiery temper.'

She snorted. 'And my bloody reputation.'

'Piss on your reputation! Nothing but idiots' chatter! You're a dream. A vision. You look like . . .' He snapped his fingers. 'The very Goddess of War!'

'Goddess, eh?'

'Of War. You like it?'

'It'll do. If you can kiss Duke Orso's arse half so well, we might even get a bonus.'

Benna puckered his lips at her. 'I love nothing more of a morning than a faceful of his Excellency's rich, round buttocks. They taste like . . . power.'

Hooves crunched on the dusty track, saddles creaked and harness rattled. The road turned back on itself, and again. The rest of the world dropped away below them. The eastern sky bled out from red to butchered pink. The river crept slowly into view, winding through the autumn woods in the base of the steep valley. Glittering like an army on the march, flowing swift and merciless towards the sea. Towards Talins.

'I'm waiting,' he said.

'For what?'

'My share of the compliments, of course.'

'If your head swells any further it'll fucking burst.' She twitched her silken cuffs up. 'And I don't want your brains on my new shirt.'

'Stabbed!' Benna clutched one hand to his chest. 'Right here! Is this how you repay my years of devotion, you heartless bitch?'

'How dare *you* presume to be devoted to *me*, peasant? You're like a tick devoted to a tiger!'

'Tiger? Hah! When they compare you to an animal they usually pick a snake.'

'Better than a maggot.'

'Whore.'

'Coward.'

'Murderer.'

She could hardly deny that one. Silence settled on them again. A bird trilled from a thirsty tree beside the road.

Benna's horse drew gradually up beside hers, and ever so gently he murmured, 'You look especially beautiful this morning, Monza.'

That brought a smile to the corner of her mouth. The corner he couldn't see. 'Well. Facts are facts.'

She spurred round one more steep bend, and the outermost wall of the citadel thrust up ahead of them. A narrow bridge crossed a dizzy ravine to the gatehouse, water sparkling as it fell away beneath. At the far end an archway yawned, welcoming as a grave.

'They've strengthened the walls since last year,' muttered Benna. 'I wouldn't fancy trying to storm the place.'

'Don't pretend you'd have the guts to climb the ladder.'

'I wouldn't fancy telling someone else to storm the place.'

'Don't pretend you'd have the guts to give the orders.'

'I wouldn't fancy watching you tell someone else to storm the place.'

'No.' She leaned gingerly from her saddle and frowned down at the plummeting drop on her left. Then she peered up at the sheer wall on her right, battlements a jagged black edge against the brightening sky. 'It's almost as if Orso's worried someone might try to kill him.'

'He's got enemies?' breathed Benna, eyes round as saucers with mock amazement.

'Only half of Styria.'

'Then . . . we've got enemies?'

'More than half of Styria.'

'But I've tried so hard to be popular . . .' They trotted between two dour-faced soldiers, spears and steel caps polished to a murderous glint. Hoofbeats echoed in the darkness of the long tunnel, sloping gradually upwards. 'You have that look, now.'

'What look?'

'No more fun today.'

'Huh.' She felt the familiar frown gripping her face. 'You can afford to smile. You're the good one.'

It was a different world beyond the gates, air heavy with lavender, shining green after the grey mountainside. A world of close-clipped lawns, of hedges tortured into wondrous shapes, of fountains throwing up glittering spray. Grim guardsmen, the black cross of Talins stitched into their white surcoats, spoiled the mood at every doorway.

'Monza . . .'

'Yes?'

'Let's make this the last season on campaign,' Benna wheedled. 'The last summer in the dust. Let's find something more comfortable to do. Now, while we're young.'

'What about the Thousand Swords? Closer to ten thousand now, all looking to us for orders.'

'They can look elsewhere. They joined us for plunder and we've given them plenty. They've no loyalty beyond their own profit.'

She had to admit the Thousand Swords had never represented the best of mankind, or even the best of mercenaries. Most of them were a step above the criminal. Most of the rest were a step below. But that wasn't the point. 'You have to stick at something in your life,' she grunted.

'I don't see why.'

'That's you all over. One more season and Visserine will fall, and Rogont will surrender, and the League of Eight will be just a bad memory. Orso can crown himself King of Styria, and we can melt away and be forgotten.'

'We deserve to be remembered. We could have our own city. You could be the noble Duchess Monzcarro of . . . wherever—'

'And you the fearless Duke Benna?' She laughed at that. 'You stupid arse. You can scarcely govern your own bowels without my help. War's a dark enough trade, I draw the line at politics. Orso crowned, then we retire.'

Benna sighed. 'I thought we were mercenaries. Cosca never stuck to an employer like this.'

'I'm not Cosca. And anyway, it's not wise to say no to the Lord of Talins.'

'You just love to fight.'

'No. I love to win. Just one more season, then we can see the world. Visit the Old Empire. Tour the Thousand Isles. Sail to Adua and stand in the shadow of the House of the Maker. Everything we talked about.' Benna pouted, just as he always did when he didn't get his way. He pouted, but he never said no. It scratched at her, sometimes, that she always had to make the choices. 'Since we've clearly only got one pair of balls between us, don't you ever feel the need to borrow them yourself?'

'They look better on you. Besides, you've got all the brains. It's best they stay together.'

4

'What do you get from the deal?'

Benna grinned at her. 'The winning smile.'

'Smile, then. For one more season.' She swung down from her saddle, jerked her sword belt straight, tossed the reins at the groom and strode for the inner gatehouse. Benna had to hurry to catch up, getting tangled with his own sword on the way. For a man who earned his living from war, he'd always been an embarrassment where weapons were concerned.

The inner courtyard was split into wide terraces at the summit of the mountain, planted with exotic palms and even more heavily guarded than the outer. An ancient column said to come from the palace of Scarpius stood tall in the centre, casting a shimmering reflection in a round pool teeming with silvery fish. The immensity of glass, bronze and marble that was Duke Orso's palace towered around it on three sides like a monstrous cat with a mouse between its paws. Since the spring they'd built a vast new wing along the northern wall, its festoons of decorative stonework still half-shrouded in scaffolding.

'They've been building,' she said.

'Of course. How could Prince Ario manage with only ten halls for his shoes?'

'A man can't be fashionable these days without at least twenty rooms of footwear.'

Benna frowned down at his own gold-buckled boots. 'I've no more than thirty pairs all told. I feel my shortcomings most keenly.'

'As do we all,' she muttered. A half-finished set of statues stood along the roofline. Duke Orso giving alms to the poor. Duke Orso gifting knowledge to the ignorant. Duke Orso shielding the weak from harm.

'I'm surprised he hasn't got one of the whole of Styria tonguing his arse,' whispered Benna in her ear.

She pointed to a partly chiselled block of marble. 'That's next.'

'Benna!'

Count Foscar, Orso's younger son, rushed around the pool like an eager puppy, shoes crunching on fresh-raked gravel, freckled face all lit up. He'd made an ill-advised attempt at a beard since Monza had last seen him but the sprinkling of sandy hairs only made him look more boyish. He might have inherited all the honesty in his family, but the looks had gone elsewhere. Benna grinned, threw one arm around Foscar's shoulders and ruffled his hair. An insult from anyone else, from Benna it was effortlessly charming. He had a knack of making people happy that always seemed like magic to Monza. Her talents lay in the opposite direction.

'Your father here yet?' she asked.

'Yes, and my brother too. They're with their banker.'

'How's his mood?'

'Good, so far as I can tell, but you know my father. Still, he's never angry with you two, is he? You always bring good news. You bring good news today, yes?'

'Shall I tell him, Monza, or—'

'Borletta's fallen. Cantain's dead.'

Foscar didn't celebrate. He hadn't his father's appetite for corpses. 'Cantain was a good man.'

That was a long way from the point, as far as Monza could see. 'He was your father's enemy.'

'A man you could respect, though. There are precious few of them left in Styria. He's really dead?'

Benna blew out his cheeks. 'Well, his head's off, and spiked above the gates, so unless you know one hell of a physician . . .'

They passed through a high archway, the hall beyond dim and echoing as an emperor's tomb, light filtering down in dusty columns and pooling on the marble floor. Suits of old armour stood gleaming to silent attention, antique weapons clutched in steel fists. The sharp clicking of boot heels snapped from the walls as a man in a dark uniform paced towards them.

'Shit,' Benna hissed in her ear. 'That reptile Ganmark's here.'

'Leave it be.'

'There's no way that cold-blooded bastard's as good with a sword as they say—'

'He is.'

'If I was half a man, I'd—'

'You're not. So leave it be.'

General Ganmark's face was strangely soft, his moustaches limp, his pale grey eyes always watery, lending him a look of perpetual sadness. The rumour was he'd been thrown out of the Union army for a sexual indiscretion involving another officer, and crossed the sea to find a more broad-minded master. The breadth of Duke Orso's mind was infinite where his servants were concerned, provided they were effective. She and Benna were proof enough of that.

Ganmark nodded stiffly to Monza. 'General Murcatto.' He nodded stiffly to Benna. 'General Murcatto. Count Foscar, you are keeping to your exercises, I hope?'

'Sparring every day.'

'Then we will make a swordsman of you yet.'

Benna snorted. 'That, or a bore.'

'Either one would be something,' droned Ganmark in his clipped Union accent. 'A man without discipline is no better than a dog. A soldier without discipline is no better than a corpse. Worse, in fact. A corpse is no threat to his comrades.'

Benna opened his mouth but Monza talked over him. He could make an arse of himself later, if he pleased. 'How was your season?'

'I played my part, keeping your flanks free of Rogont and his Osprians.'

'Stalling the Duke of Delay?' Benna smirked. 'Quite the challenge.'

'No more than a supporting role. A comic turn in a great tragedy, but one appreciated by the audience, I hope.'

The echoes of their footsteps swelled as they passed through another archway and into the towering rotunda at the heart of the palace. The curving walls were vast panels of sculpture showing scenes from antiquity. Wars between demons and magi, and other such rubbish. High above, the great dome was frescoed with seven winged women against a stormy sky – armed, armoured and angry-looking. The Fates, bringing destinies to earth. Aropella's greatest work. She'd heard it had taken him eight years to finish. Monza never got over how tiny, weak, utterly insignificant this space made her feel. That was the point of it.

The four of them climbed a sweeping staircase, wide enough for twice as many to walk abreast. 'And where have your comic talents taken you?' she asked Ganmark.

'Fire and murder, to the gates of Puranti and back.'

Benna curled his lip. 'Any actual fighting?'

7

'Why ever would I do that? Have you not read your Stolicus? "An animal fights his way to victory—"'

'"A general marches there,"' Monza finished for him. 'Did you raise many laughs?'

'Not for the enemy, I suppose. Precious few for anyone, but that is war.'

'I find time to chuckle,' threw in Benna.

'Some men laugh easily. It makes them winning dinner companions.' Ganmark's soft eyes moved across to Monza's. 'I note you are not smiling.'

'I will. Once the League of Eight are finished and Orso is King of Styria. Then we can all hang up our swords.'

'In my experience swords do not hang comfortably from hooks. They have a habit of finding their way back into one's hands.'

'I daresay Orso will keep you on,' said Benna. 'Even if it's only to polish the tiles.'

Ganmark did not give so much as a sharp breath. 'Then his Excellency will have the cleanest floors in all of Styria.'

A pair of high doors faced the top of the stairs, gleaming with inlaid wood, carved with lions' faces. A thick-set man paced up and down before them like a loyal old hound before his master's bedchamber. Faithful Carpi, the longest-serving captain in the Thousand Swords, the scars of a hundred engagements marked out on his broad, weathered, honest face.

'Faithful!' Benna seized the old mercenary's big slab of a hand. 'Climbing a mountain, at your age? Shouldn't you be in a brothel somewhere?'

'If only.' Carpi shrugged. 'But his Excellency sent for me.'

'And you, being an obedient sort . . . obeyed.'

'That's why they call me Faithful.'

'How did you leave things in Borletta?' asked Monza.

'Quiet. Most of the men are quartered outside the walls with Andiche and Victus. Best if they don't set fire to the place, I thought. I left some of the more reliable ones in Cantain's palace with Sesaria watching over them. Old-timers, like me, from back in Cosca's day. Seasoned men, not prone to impulsiveness.'

Benna chuckled. 'Slow thinkers, you mean?'

'Slow but steady. We get there in the end.'

'Going in, then?' Foscar set his shoulder to one of the doors and heaved it open. Ganmark and Faithful followed. Monza paused a moment on the threshold, trying to find her hardest face. She looked up and saw Benna smiling at her. Without thinking, she found herself smiling back. She leaned and whispered in his ear.

'I love you.'

'Of course you do.' He stepped through the doorway, and she followed.

Duke Orso's private study was a marble hall the size of a market square. Lofty windows marched in bold procession along one side, standing open, a keen breeze washing through and making the vivid hangings twitch and rustle. Beyond them a long terrace seemed to hang in empty air, overlooking the steepest drop from the mountain's summit.

The opposite wall was covered with towering panels, painted by the foremost artists of Styria, displaying the great battles of history. The victories of Stolicus, of Harod the Great, of Farans and Verturio, all preserved in sweeping oils. The message that Orso was the latest in a line of royal winners was hard to miss, even though his great-grandfather had been a usurper, and a common criminal besides.

The largest painting of them all faced the door, ten strides high at the least. Who else but Grand Duke Orso? He was seated upon a rearing charger, his shining sword raised high, his piercing eye fixed on the far horizon, urging his men to victory at the Battle of Etrea. The painter seemed to have been unaware that Orso hadn't come within fifty miles of the fighting.

But then fine lies beat tedious truths every time, as he had often told her.

The Duke of Talins himself sat crabbed over a desk, wielding a pen rather than a sword. A tall, gaunt, hook-nosed man stood at his elbow, staring down as keenly as a vulture waiting for thirsty travellers to die. A great shape lurked near them, in the shadows against the wall. Gobba, Orso's bodyguard, fat-necked as a great hog. Prince Ario, the duke's eldest son and heir, lounged in a gilded chair nearer at hand. He had one leg crossed over the other, a wine glass dangling carelessly, a bland smile balanced on his blandly handsome face.

'I found these beggars wandering the grounds,' called Foscar, 'and thought I'd commend them to your charity, Father!'

'Charity?' Orso's sharp voice echoed around the cavernous room. 'I am not a great admirer of the stuff. Make yourselves comfortable, my friends, I will be with you shortly.'

'If it isn't the Butcher of Caprile,' murmured Ario, 'and her little Benna too.'

'Your Highness. You look well.' Monza thought he looked an indolent cock, but kept it to herself.

'You too, as ever. If all soldiers looked as you did, I might even be tempted to go on campaign myself. A new bauble?' Ario waved his own jewel-encrusted hand limply towards the ruby on Monza's finger.

'Just what was to hand when I was dressing.'

'I wish I'd been there. Wine?'

'Just after dawn?'

He glanced heavy-lidded towards the windows. 'Still last night as far as I'm concerned.' As if staying up late was a heroic achievement.

'I will.' Benna was already pouring himself a glass, never to be outdone as far as showing off went. Most likely he'd be drunk within the hour and embarrass himself, but Monza was tired of playing his mother. She strolled past the monumental fireplace held up by carven figures of Juvens and Kanedias, and towards Orso's desk.

'Sign here, and here, and here,' the gaunt man was saying, one bony finger hovering over the documents.

'You know Mauthis, do you?' Orso gave a sour glance in his direction. 'My leash-holder.'

'Always your humble servant, your Excellency. The Banking House of Valint and Balk agrees to this further loan for the period of one year, after which they regret they must charge interest.'

Orso snorted. 'As the plague regrets the dead, I'll be bound.' He scratched out a parting swirl on the last signature and tossed down his pen. 'Everyone must kneel to someone, eh? Make sure you extend to your superiors my infinite gratitude for their indulgence.'

'I shall do so.' Mauthis collected up the documents. 'That

concludes our business, your Excellency. I must leave at once if I mean to catch the evening tide for Westport—'

'No. Stay a while longer. We have one other matter to discuss.'

Mauthis' dead eyes moved towards Monza, then back to Orso. 'As your Excellency desires.'

The duke rose smoothly from his desk. 'To happier business, then. You do bring happy news, eh, Monzcarro?'

'I do, your Excellency.'

'Ah, whatever would I do without you?' There was a trace of iron grey in his black hair since she'd seen him last, perhaps some deeper lines at the corners of his eyes, but his air of complete command was impressive as ever. He leaned forwards and kissed her on both cheeks, then whispered in her ear, 'Ganmark can lead soldiers well enough, but for a man who sucks cocks he hasn't the slightest sense of humour. Come, tell me of your victories in the open air.' He left one arm draped around her shoulders and guided her, past the sneering Prince Ario, through the open windows onto the high terrace.

The sun was climbing now, and the bright world was full of colour. The blood had drained from the sky and left it a vivid blue, white clouds crawling high above. Below, at the very bottom of a dizzy drop, the river wound through the wooded valley, autumn leaves pale green, burned orange, faded yellow, angry red, light glinting silver on fast-flowing water. To the east, the forest crumbled away into a patchwork of fields – squares of fallow green, rich black earth, golden crop. Further still and the river met the grey sea, branching out in a wide delta choked with islands. Monza could just make out the suggestion of tiny towers there, buildings, bridges, walls. Great Talins, no bigger than her thumbnail.

She narrowed her eyes against the stiff breeze, pushed some stray hair out of her face. 'I never tire of this view.'

'How could you? It's why I built this damn place. Here I can keep one eye always on my subjects, as a watchful parent should upon his children. Just to make sure they don't hurt themselves while they play, you understand.'

'Your people are lucky to have such a just and caring father,' she lied smoothly.

'Just and caring.' Orso frowned thoughtfully towards the

distant sea. 'Do you think that is how history will remember me?'

Monza thought it incredibly unlikely. 'What did Bialoveld say? "History is written by the victors."'

The duke squeezed her shoulder. 'All this, and well read into the bargain. Ario is ambitious enough, but he has no insight. I'd be surprised if he could read to the end of a signpost in one sitting. All he cares about is whoring. And shoes. My daughter Terez, meanwhile, weeps most bitterly because I married her to a king. I swear, if I had offered great Euz as the groom she would have whined for a husband better fitting her station.' He gave a heavy sigh. 'None of my children understand me. My great-grandfather was a mercenary, you know. A fact I do not like to advertise.' Though he told her every other time they met. 'A man who never shed a tear in his life, and wore on his feet whatever was to hand. A low-born fighting man, who seized power in Talins by the sharpness of his mind and sword together.' More by blunt ruthlessness and brutality, the way Monza had heard the tale. 'We are from the same stock, you and I. We have made ourselves, out of nothing.'

Orso had been born to the wealthiest dukedom in Styria and never done a hard day's work in his life, but Monza bit her tongue. 'You do me too much honour, your Excellency.'

'Less than you deserve. Now tell me of Borletta.'

'You heard about the battle on the High Bank?'

'I heard you scattered the League of Eight's army, just as you did at Sweet Pines! Ganmark says Duke Salier had three times your number.'

'Numbers are a hindrance if they're lazy, ill-prepared and led by idiots. An army of farmers from Borletta, cobblers from Affoia, glass-blowers from Visserine. Amateurs. They camped by the river, thinking we were far away, scarcely posted guards. We came up through the woods at night and caught them at sunrise, not even in their armour.'

'I can see Salier now, the fat pig, waddling from his bed to run!'

'Faithful led the charge. We broke them quickly, captured their supplies.'

'Turned the golden cornfields crimson, I was told.'

'They hardly even fought. Ten times as many drowned trying to swim the river as died fighting. More than four thousand prisoners. Some ransoms were paid, some not, some men were hanged.'

'And few tears shed, eh, Monza?'

'Not by me. If they were so keen to live, they could've surrendered.'

'As they did at Caprile?'

She stared straight back into Orso's black eyes. 'Just as they did at Caprile.'

'Borletta is besieged, then?'

'Fallen already.'

The duke's face lit up like a boy's on his birthday. 'Fallen? Cantain surrendered?'

'When his people heard of Salier's defeat, they lost hope.'

'And people without hope are a dangerous crowd, even in a republic.'

'Especially in a republic. A mob dragged Cantain from the palace, hanged him from the highest tower, opened the gates and threw themselves on the mercy of the Thousand Swords.'

'Hah! Slaughtered by the very people he laboured to keep free. There's the gratitude of the common man, eh, Monza? Cantain should have taken my money when I offered. It would have been cheaper for both of us.'

'The people are falling over themselves to become your subjects. I've given orders they should be spared, where possible.'

'Mercy, eh?'

'Mercy and cowardice are the same,' she snapped out. 'But you want their land, not their lives, no? Dead men can't obey.'

Orso smiled. 'Why can my sons not mark my lessons as you have? I entirely approve. Hang only the leaders. And Cantain's head above the gates. Nothing encourages obedience like a good example.'

'Already rotting, with those of his sons.'

'Fine work!' The Lord of Talins clapped his hands, as though he never heard such pleasing music as the news of rotting heads. 'What of the takings?'

The accounts were Benna's business, and he came forwards now, sliding a folded paper from his chest pocket. 'The city was scoured, your Excellency. Every building stripped, every floor dug up, every person searched. The usual rules apply, according to our terms of engagement. Quarter for the man that finds it, quarter for his captain, quarter for the generals,' and he bowed low, unfolding the paper and offering it out, 'and quarter for our noble employer.'

Orso's smile broadened as his eyes scanned down the figures. 'My blessing on the Rule of Quarters! Enough to keep you both in my service a little longer.' He stepped between Monza and Benna, placed a gentle hand on each of their shoulders and led them back through the open windows. Towards the round table of black marble in the centre of the room, and the great map spread out upon it. Ganmark, Ario and Faithful had already gathered there. Gobba still lurked in the shadows, thick arms folded across his chest. 'What of our one-time friends and now our bitter enemies, the treacherous citizens of Visserine?'

'The fields round the city are burned up to the gates, almost.' Monza scattered carnage across the countryside with a few waves of her finger. 'Farmers driven off, livestock slaughtered. It'll be a lean winter for fat Duke Salier, and a leaner spring.'

'He will have to rely on the noble Duke Rogont and his Osprians,' said Ganmark, with the faintest of smiles.

Prince Ario snickered. 'Much talk blows down from Ospria, always, but little help.'

'Visserine is poised to drop into your lap next year, your Excellency.'

'And with it the heart is torn from the League of Eight.'

'The crown of Styria will be yours.'

The mention of crowns teased Orso's smile still wider. 'And we have you to thank, Monzcarro. I do not forget that.'

'Not only me.'

'Curse your modesty. Benna has played his part, and our good friend General Ganmark, and Faithful too, but no one could deny this is your work. Your commitment, your single-mindedness, your swiftness to act! You shall have a great triumph, just as the heroes of ancient Aulcus did. You shall ride through the streets of Talins and my people will shower you with flower petals in honour of your many victories.' Benna was grinning, but Monza couldn't join him. She'd never had much taste for congratulations. 'They will cheer far louder for you, I think, than they ever will for my own sons. They will cheer far louder even than they do for me, their rightful lord, to whom they owe so much.' It seemed that Orso's smile slipped, and his face looked tired, and sad, and worn without it. 'They will cheer, in fact, a little too loudly for my taste.'

There was the barest flash of movement at the corner of her eye, enough to make her bring up her hand on an instinct.

The wire hissed taut around it, snatching it up under her chin, crushing it chokingly tight against her throat.

Benna started forwards. 'Mon—' Metal glinted as Prince Ario stabbed him in the neck. He missed his throat, caught him just under the ear.

Orso carefully stepped back as blood speckled the tiles with red. Foscar's mouth fell open, wine glass dropping from his hand, shattering on the floor.

Monza tried to scream, but only spluttered through her half-shut windpipe, made a sound like a honking pig. She fished at the hilt of her dagger with her free hand but someone caught her wrist, held it fast. Faithful Carpi, pressed up tight against her left side.

'Sorry,' he muttered in her ear, pulling her sword from its scabbard and flinging it clattering across the room.

Benna stumbled, gurgling red drool, one hand clutched to the side of his face, black blood leaking out between white fingers. His other hand fumbled for his sword while Ario watched him, frozen. He drew a clumsy foot of steel before General Ganmark stepped up and stabbed him, smoothly and precisely – once, twice, three times. The thin blade slid in and out of Benna's body, the only sound the soft breath from his gaping mouth. Blood shot across the floor in long streaks, began to leak out into his white shirt in dark circles. He tottered forwards, tripped over his own feet and crashed down, half-drawn sword scraping against the marble underneath him.

Monza strained, every muscle trembling, but she was held helpless as a fly in honey. She heard Gobba grunting with effort in her ear, his stubbly face rubbing against her cheek, his great body warm against her back. She felt the wire cut slowly into the sides of her neck, deep into the side of her hand, caught fast against her throat. She felt the blood running down her forearm, into the collar of her shirt.

One of Benna's hands crawled across the floor, reaching out for her. He lifted himself an inch or two, veins bulging from his neck. Ganmark leaned forwards and calmly ran him through the heart from behind. Benna quivered for a moment, then sagged down and was still, pale cheek smeared with red. Dark blood crept out from under him, worked its way along the cracks between the tiles.

'Well.' Ganmark leaned down and wiped his sword on the back of Benna's shirt. 'That's that.'

Mauthis watched, frowning. Slightly puzzled, slightly irritated, slightly bored. As though examining a set of figures that wouldn't quite add.

Orso gestured at the body. 'Get rid of that, Ario.'

'Me?' The prince's lip curled.

'Yes, you. And you can help him, Foscar. The two of you must learn what needs to be done to keep our family in power.'

'No!' Foscar stumbled away. 'I'll have no part of this!' He turned and ran from the room, his boots slapping against the marble floor.

'That boy is soft as syrup,' muttered Orso at his back. 'Ganmark, help him.'

Monza's bulging eyes followed them as they dragged Benna's corpse out through the doors to the terrace, Ganmark grim and careful at the head end, Ario cursing as he daintily took one boot, the other smearing a red trail after them. They heaved Benna up onto the balustrade and rolled him off. Like that he was gone.

'Ah!' squawked Ario, waving one hand. 'Damn it! You scratched me!'

Ganmark stared back at him. 'I apologise, your Highness. Murder can be a painful business.'

The prince looked around for something to wipe his bloody hands on. He reached for the rich hangings beside the window.

'Not there!' snapped Orso. 'That's Kantic silk, at fifty scales a piece!'

'Where, then?'

'Find something else, or leave them red! Sometimes I wonder if your mother told the truth about your paternity, boy.' Ario wiped his hands sulkily on the front of his shirt while Monza stared, face burning from lack of air. Orso frowned over at her, a blurred black figure through the wet in her eyes, the hair tangled across her face. 'Is she still alive? Whatever are you about, Gobba?'

'Fucking wire's caught on her hand,' hissed the bodyguard.

'Find another way to be done with her, then, lackwit.'

'I'll do it.' Faithful pulled the dagger from her belt, still pinning her wrist with his other hand. 'I really am sorry.'

'Just get to it!' growled Gobba.

The blade went back, steel glinting in a shaft of light. Monza stomped down on Gobba's foot with all the strength she had left. The bodyguard grunted, grip slipping on the wire, and she dragged it away from her neck, growling, twisting hard as Carpi stabbed at her.

The blade went well wide of the mark, slid in under her bottom rib. Cold metal, but it felt burning hot, a line of fire from her stomach to her back. It slid right through and the point pricked Gobba's gut.

'Gah!' He let go the wire and Monza whooped in air, started shrieking mindlessly, lashed at him with her elbow and sent him staggering. Faithful was caught off guard, fumbled the knife as he pulled it out of her and sent it spinning across the floor. She kicked at him, missed his groin and caught his hip, bent him over. She snatched at a dagger on his belt, pulled it from its sheath, but her cut hand was clumsy and he caught her wrist before she could ram the blade into him. They wrestled with it, teeth bared, gasping spit in each other's faces, lurching back and forth, their hands sticky with her blood.

'Kill her!'

There was a crunch and her head was full of light. The floor cracked against her skull, slapped her in the back. She spat blood, mad screams guttering to a long drawn croak, clawing at the smooth floor with her nails.

'Fucking bitch!' The heel of Gobba's big boot cracked down on her right hand and sent pain lancing up her forearm, tore a sick gasp from her. His boot crunched again across her knuckles, then her fingers, then her wrist. At the same time Faithful's foot was thudding into her ribs, over and over, making her cough and shudder. Her shattered hand twisted, turned sideways on. Gobba's heel crashed down and crushed it flat into the cold marble with a splintering of bone. She flopped back, hardly able to breathe, the room turning over, history's painted winners grinning down.

'You stabbed me, you dumb old bastard! You stabbed me!'

'You're hardly even cut, fathead! You should've kept a hold on her!'

'I should stab the useless pair of you!' hissed Orso's voice. 'Just get it done!'

Gobba's great fist came down, dragged Monza up by her throat. She tried to grab at him with her left hand but all her strength had leaked out through the hole in her side, the cuts in her neck. Her clumsy fingertips only smeared red traces across his stubbly face. Her arm was dragged away, twisted sharply behind her back.

'Where's Hermon's gold?' came Gobba's rough voice. 'Eh, Murcatto? What did you do with the gold?'

Monza forced her head up. 'Lick my arse, cocksucker.' Not clever, perhaps, but from the heart.

'There never was any gold!' snapped Faithful. 'I told you that, pig!'

'There's this much.' One by one, Gobba twisted the battered rings from her dangling fingers, already bloating, turning angry purple, bent and shapeless as rotten sausages. 'Good stone, that,' he said, peering at the ruby. 'Seems a waste of decent flesh, though. Why not give me a moment with her? A moment's all it would take.'

Prince Ario tittered. 'Speed isn't always something to be proud of.'

'For pity's sake!' Orso's voice. 'We're not animals. Off the terrace and let us be done. I am late for breakfast.'

She felt herself dragged, head lolling. Sunlight stabbed at her. She was lifted, limp boots scraping on stone. Blue sky turning. Up onto the balustrade. The breath scraped at her nose, shuddered in her chest. She twisted, kicked. Her body, struggling vainly to stay alive.

'Let me make sure of her.' Ganmark's voice.

'How sure do we need to be?' Blurry through the bloody hair

across her eyes she saw Orso's lined face. 'I hope you understand. My great-grandfather was a mercenary. A low-born fighting man, who seized power by the sharpness of his mind and sword together. I cannot allow another mercenary to seize power in Talins.'

She meant to spit in his face, but all she did was blow bloody drool down her own chin. 'Fuck yourse—'

Then she was flying.

Her torn shirt billowed and flapped against her tingling skin. She turned over, and over, and the world tumbled around her. Blue sky with shreds of cloud, black towers at the mountain top, grey rock face rushing past, yellow-green trees and sparkling river, blue sky with shreds of cloud, and again, and again, faster, and faster.

Cold wind ripped at her hair, roared in her ears, whistled between her teeth along with her terrified breath. She could see each tree, now, each branch, each leaf. They surged up towards her. She opened her mouth to scream—

Twigs snatched, grabbed, lashed at her. A broken branch knocked her spinning. Wood cracked and tore around her as she plunged down, down, and crashed into the mountainside. Her legs splintered under her plummeting weight, her shoulder broke apart against firm earth. But rather than dashing her brains out on the rocks, she only shattered her jaw against her brother's bloody chest, his mangled body wedged against the base of a tree.

Which was how Benna Murcatto saved his sister's life.

She bounced from the corpse, three-quarters senseless, and down the steep mountainside, over and over, flailing like a broken doll. Rocks, and roots, and hard earth clubbed, punched, crushed her, as if she was battered apart with a hundred hammers.

She tore through a patch of bushes, thorns whipping and clutching. She rolled, and rolled, down the sloping earth in a cloud of dirt and leaves. She tumbled over a tree root, crumpled on a mossy rock. She slid slowly to a stop, on her back, and was still.

'Huuuurrrrhhh . . .'

Stones clattered down around her, sticks and gravel. Dust slowly settled. She heard wind, creaking in the branches, crackling in the leaves. Or her own breath, creaking and crackling in her broken throat. The sun flickered through black trees, jabbing at one eye. The other was dark. Flies buzzed, zipping and swimming in the warm morning air. She was down with the waste from Orso's kitchens. Sprawled out helpless in the midst of the rotten vegetables, and the cooking slime, and the stinking offal left over from the last month's magnificent meals. Tossed out with the rubbish.

'Huuurrhhh . . .'

A jagged, mindless sound. She was embarrassed by it, almost, but couldn't stop making it. Animal horror. Mad despair. The groan of the dead, in hell. Her eye darted desperately around. She saw the wreck of her right hand, a shapeless, purple glove with a bloody gash in the side. One finger trembled slightly. Its tip brushed against torn skin on her elbow. The forearm was folded in half, a broken-off twig of grey bone sticking through bloody silk. It didn't look real. Like a cheap theatre prop.

'Huurrhhh . . .'

The fear had hold of her now, swelling with every breath. She couldn't move her head. She couldn't move her tongue in her mouth. She could feel the pain, gnawing at the edge of her mind. A terrible mass, pressing up against her, crushing every part of her, worse, and worse, and worse.

'Huurhh . . . uurh . . .'

Benna was dead. A streak of wet ran from her flickering eye and she felt it trickle slowly down her cheek. Why was she not dead? How could she not be dead?

Soon, please. Before the pain got any worse. Please, let it be soon.

'Uurh . . . uh . . . uh.'

Please, death.

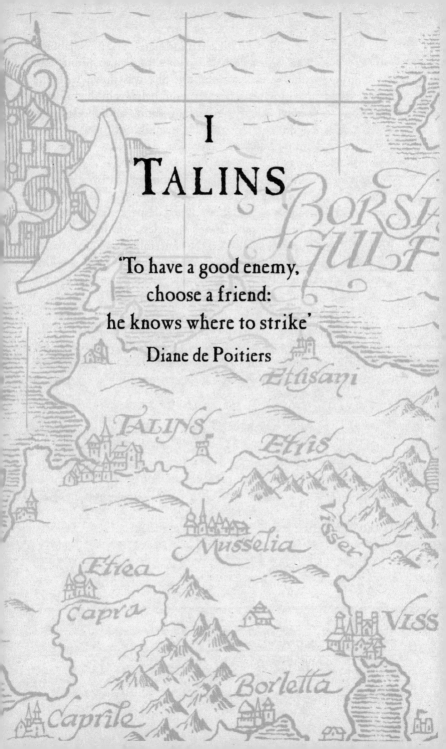

I
TALINS

"To have a good enemy,
choose a friend:
he knows where to strike"
Diane de Poitiers

*J*appo Murcatto never said why he had such a good sword, but he knew well how to use it. Since his son was by five years his younger child and sickly too, from a tender age he passed on the skill to his daughter. Monzcarro had been her father's mother's name, in the days when her family had pretended at nobility. Her own mother had not cared for it in the least, but since she had died giving birth to Benna that scarcely mattered.

Those were peaceful years in Styria, which were as rare as gold. At ploughing time Monza would hurry behind her father while the blade scraped through the dirt, weeding any big stones from the fresh black earth and throwing them into the wood. At reaping time she would hurry behind her father while his scythe-blade flashed, gathering the cut stalks into sheaves.

'Monza,' he would say, smiling down at her, 'what would I do without you?'

She helped with the threshing and tossed the seed, split logs and drew water. She cooked, swept, washed, carried, milked the goat. Her hands were always raw from some kind of work. Her brother did what he could, but he was small, and ill, and could do little. Those were hard years, but they were happy ones.

When Monza was fourteen, Jappo Murcatto caught the fever. She and Benna watched him cough, and sweat, and wither. One night her father seized Monza by her wrist, and stared at her with bright eyes.

'Tomorrow, break the ground in the upper field, or the wheat won't rise in time. Plant all you can.' He touched her cheek. 'It's not fair that it should fall to you, but your brother is so small. Watch over him.' And he was dead.

Benna cried, and cried, but Monza's eyes stayed dry. She was thinking about the seed that needing planting, and how she would do it. That night Benna was too scared to sleep alone, and so they *slept together in her narrow bed, and held each other for comfort. They had no one else now.*

The next morning, in the darkness, Monza dragged her father's corpse from the house, through the woods behind and rolled it into the river. Not because she had no love in her, but because she had no time to bury him.

By sunrise she was breaking the ground in the upper field.

Land of Opportunity

First thing Shivers noticed as the boat wallowed in towards the wharves, it was nothing like as warm as he'd been expecting. He'd heard the sun always shone in Styria. Like a nice bath, all year round. If Shivers had been offered a bath like this he'd have stayed dirty, and probably had a few sharp words to say besides. Talins huddled under grey skies, clouds bulging, a keen breeze off the sea, cold rain speckling his cheek from time to time and reminding him of home. And not in a good way. Still, he was set on looking at the sunny side of the case. Probably just a shitty day was all. You get 'em everywhere.

There surely was a seedy look about the place, though, as the sailors scuttled to make the boat fast to the dock. Brick buildings lined the grey sweep of the bay, narrow windowed, all squashed in together, roofs slumping, paint peeling, cracked-up render stained with salt, green with moss, black with mould. Down near the slimy cobbles the walls were plastered over with big papers, slapped up at all angles, ripped and pasted over each other, torn edges fluttering. Faces on them, and words printed. Warnings, maybe, but Shivers weren't much of a reader. Specially not in Styrian. Speaking the language was going to be enough of a challenge.

The waterfront crawled with people, and not many looked happy. Or healthy. Or rich. There was quite the smell. Or to be more precise, a proper reek. Rotten salt fish, old corpses, coal smoke and overflowing latrine pits rolled up together. If this was the home of the grand new man he was hoping to become, Shivers had to admit to being more'n a touch disappointed. For the briefest moment he thought about paying over most of what he had left for a trip straight back home to the North on the next tide. But he shook it off. He was done with war, done with leading men to death, done with killing and all that went along

25

with it. He was set on being a better man. He was going to do the right thing, and this was where he was going to do it.

'Right, then.' He gave the nearest sailor a cheery nod. 'Off I go.' He got no more'n a grunt in return, but his brother used to tell him it was what you gave out that made a man, not what you got back. So he grinned like he'd got a merry send-off, strode down the clattering gangplank and into his brave new life in Styria.

He'd scarcely taken a dozen paces, staring up at looming buildings on one side, swaying masts on the other, before someone barged into him and near knocked him sideways.

'My apologies,' Shivers said in Styrian, keeping things civilised. 'Didn't see you there, friend.' The man kept going, didn't even turn. That prickled some at Shivers' pride. He had plenty of it still, the one thing his father had left him. He hadn't lived through seven years of battles, skirmishes, waking with snow on his blanket, shit food and worse singing so he could come down here and get shouldered.

But being a bastard was crime and punishment both. Let go of it, his brother would've told him. Shivers was meant to be looking on the sunny side. So he took a turn away from the docks, down a wide road and into the city. Past a clutch of beggars on blankets, waving stumps and withered limbs. Through a square where a great statue stood of a frowning man, pointing off to nowhere. Shivers didn't have a clue who he was meant to be, but he looked pretty damn pleased with himself. The smell of cooking wafted up, made Shivers' guts grumble. Drew him over to some kind of stall where they had sticks of meat over a fire in a can.

'One o' them,' said Shivers, pointing. Didn't seem much else needed saying, so he kept it simple. Less chance of mistakes. When the cook told him the price he near choked on his tongue. Would've got him a whole sheep in the North, maybe even a breeding pair. The meat was half fat and the rest gristle. Didn't taste near so good as it had smelled, but by that point it weren't much surprise. It seemed most things in Styria weren't quite as advertised.

The rain had started up stronger now, flitting down into Shivers' eyes as he ate. Not much compared to storms he'd laughed through in the North, but enough to damp his mood a touch, make him wonder where the hell he'd rest his head tonight. It trickled from mossy eaves and broken gutters, turned the cobbles dark, made the people hunch and curse. He came from the close buildings and onto a wide river bank, all built up and fenced in with stone. He paused a moment, wondering which way to go.

The city went on far as he could see, bridges upstream and down, buildings on the far bank even bigger than on this side – towers, domes, roofs, going on and on, half-shrouded and turned dreamy grey by the rain. More torn papers flapping in the breeze, letters daubed over 'em too with bright coloured paint, streaks running down to the cobbled street. Letters high as a man in places. Shivers peered over at one set, trying to make some sense of it.

Another shoulder caught him, right in the ribs, made him grunt. This time he whipped round snarling, little meat stick clutched in his fist like he might've clutched a blade. Then he took a breath. Weren't all that long ago Shivers had let the Bloody-Nine go free. He remembered that morning like it was yesterday, the snow outside the windows, the knife in his hand, the rattle as he'd let it fall. He'd let the man who killed his brother live, passed up revenge, all so he could be a better man. Step away from blood. Stepping away from a loose shoulder in a crowd was nothing to sing about.

He forced half a smile back on and walked the other way, up onto the bridge. Silly thing like the knock of a shoulder could leave you cursing for days, and he didn't want to poison his new beginning 'fore it even got begun. Statues stood on either side, staring off above the water, monsters of white stone streaky with bird droppings. People flooded past, one kind of river flowing over the other. People of every type and colour. So many he felt like nothing in the midst of 'em. Bound to have a few shoulders catch you in a place like this.

Something brushed his arm. Before he knew it he'd grabbed someone round the neck, was bending him back over the parapet twenty strides above the churning water, gripping his throat like he was strangling a chicken. 'Knock me, you bastard?' he snarled in Northern. 'I'll cut your fucking eyes out!'

He was a little man, and he looked bloody scared. Might've

been a head shorter'n Shivers, and not much more than half his weight. Getting over the first red flush of rage, Shivers realised this poor fool had barely even touched him. No malice in it. How come he could shrug off big wrongs then lose his temper over nothing? He'd always been his own worst enemy.

'Sorry, friend,' he said in Styrian, and meaning it too. He let the man slither down, brushed the crumpled front of his coat with a clumsy hand. 'Real sorry about that. Little . . . what do you call it . . . mistake is all. Sorry. Do you want . . .' Shivers found he was offering the stick, one last shred of fatty meat still clinging to it. The man stared. Shivers winced. 'Course he didn't want that. Shivers hardly wanted it himself. 'Sorry . . .' The man turned and dashed off into the crowd, looking once over his shoulder, scared, like he'd just survived being attacked by a madman. Maybe he had. Shivers stood on the bridge, frowned down at that brown water churning past. Same sort of water they had in the North, it had to be said.

Seemed being a better man might be harder work than he'd thought.

The Bone-Thief

When her eyes opened, she saw bones.

Bones long and short, thick and thin, white, yellow, brown. Covering the peeling wall from floor to ceiling. Hundreds of them. Nailed up in patterns, a madman's mosaic. Her eyes rolled down, sore and sticky. A tongue of fire flickered in a sooty hearth. On the mantelpiece above, skulls grinned emptily at her, neatly stacked three high.

Human bones, then. Monza felt her skin turn icy cold.

She tried to sit up. The vague sense of numb stiffness flared into pain so suddenly she nearly puked. The darkened room lurched, blurred. She was held fast, lying on something hard. Her mind was full of mud, she couldn't remember how she'd got here.

Her head rolled sideways and she saw a table. On the table was a metal tray. On the tray was a careful arrangement of instruments. Pincers, pliers, needles and scissors. A small but very businesslike saw. A dozen knives at least, all shapes and sizes. Her widening eyes darted over their polished blades – curved, straight, jagged edges cruel and eager in the firelight. A surgeon's tools?

Or a torturer's?

'Benna?' Her voice was a ghostly squeak. Her tongue, her gums, her throat, the passages in her nose, all raw as skinned meat. She tried to move again, could scarcely lift her head. Even that much effort sent a groaning stab through her neck and into her shoulder, set off a dull pulsing up her legs, down her right arm, through her ribs. The pain brought fear with it, the fear brought pain. Her breath quickened, shuddering and wheezing through her sore nostrils.

Click, click.

She froze, silence prickling at her ears. Then a scraping, a key in a lock. Frantically now she squirmed, pain bursting in every joint, ripping at every muscle, blood battering behind her eyes, thick tongue wedged into her teeth to stop herself screaming. A door creaked open and banged shut. Footsteps on bare boards, hardly making a sound, but each one still a jab of fear in her throat. A shadow reached out across the floor – a huge shape, twisted, monstrous. Her eyes strained to the corners, nothing she could do but wait for the worst.

A figure came through the doorway, walked straight past her and over to a tall cupboard. A man no more than average height, in fact, with short fair hair. The misshapen shadow was caused by a canvas sack over one shoulder. He hummed tunelessly to himself as he emptied it, placing each item carefully on its proper shelf, then turning it back and forth until it faced precisely into the room.

If he was a monster, he seemed an everyday sort of one, with an eye for the details.

He swung the doors gently shut, folded his empty bag once, twice, and slid it under the cupboard. He took off his stained coat and hung it from a hook, brushed it down with a brisk hand, turned and stopped dead. A pale, lean face. Not old, but deeply lined, with harsh cheekbones and eyes hungry bright in bruised sockets.

They stared at each other for a moment, both seeming equally shocked. Then his colourless lips twitched into a sickly smile.

'You are awake!'

'Who are you?' A terrified scratch in her dried-up throat.

'My name is not important.' He spoke with the trace of a Union accent. 'Suffice it to say I am a student of the physical sciences.'

'A healer?'

'Among other things. As you may have gathered, I am an enthusiast, chiefly, for bones. Which is why I am so glad that you . . . fell into my life.' He grinned again, but it was like the skulls' grins, never touching his eyes.

'How did . . .' She had to wrestle with the words, jaw stiff as rusted hinges. It was like trying to talk with a turd in her mouth, and hardly better tasting. 'How did I get here?'

'I need bodies for my work. They are sometimes to be found

where I found you. But I have never before found one still alive. I would judge you to be a spectacularly lucky woman.' He seemed to think about it for a moment. 'It would have been luckier still if you had not fallen in the first place but . . . since you did—'

'Where's my brother? Where's Benna?'

'Benna?'

Memory flooded back in a blinding instant. Blood pumping from between her brother's clutching fingers. The long blade sliding through his chest while she watched, helpless. His slack face, smeared with red.

She gave a croaking scream, bucked and twisted. Agony flashed up every limb and made her squirm the more, shudder, retch, but she was held fast. Her host watched her struggle, waxy face empty as a blank page. She sagged back, spitting and moaning as the pain grew worse and worse, gripping her like a giant vice, steadily tightened.

'Anger solves nothing.'

All she could do was growl, snatched breaths slurping through her gritted teeth.

'I imagine you are in some pain, now.' He pulled open a drawer in the cupboard and took out a long pipe, bowl stained black. 'I would try to get used to it, if you can.' He stooped and fished a hot coal from the fire with a set of tongs. 'I fear that pain will come to be your constant companion.'

The worn mouthpiece loomed at her. She'd seen husk-smokers often enough, sprawling like corpses, withered to useless husks themselves, caring for nothing but the next pipe. Husk was like mercy. A thing for the weak. For the cowardly.

He smiled his dead-man's smile again. 'This will help.'

Enough pain makes a coward of anyone.

The smoke burned at her lungs and made her sore ribs shake, each choke sending new shocks to the tips of her fingers. She groaned, face screwing up, struggling again, but more weakly, now. One more cough, and she lay limp. The edge was gone from the pain. The edge was gone from the fear and the panic. Everything slowly melted. Soft, warm, comfortable. Someone made a long, low moan. Her, maybe. She felt a tear run down the side of her face.

'More?' This time she held the smoke as it bit, blew it tickling out in a shimmering plume. Her breath came slower, and slower, the surging of blood in her head calmed to a gentle lapping.

'More?' The voice washed over her like waves on the smooth beach. The bones were blurred now, glistening in haloes of warm light. The coals in the grate were precious jewels, sparkling every colour. There was barely any pain, and what there was didn't matter. Nothing did. Her eyes flickered pleasantly, then even more pleasantly drifted shut. Mosaic patterns danced and shifted on the insides of her eyelids. She floated on a warm sea, honey sweet . . .

'Back with us?' His face flickered into focus, hanging limp and white as a flag of surrender. 'I was worried, I confess. I never expected you to wake, but now that you have, it would be a shame if—'

'Benna?' Monza's head was still floating. She grunted, tried to work one ankle, and the grinding ache brought the truth back, crushed her face into a hopeless grimace.

'Still sore? Perhaps I have a way to lift your spirits.' He rubbed his long hands together. 'The stitches are all out, now.'

'How long did I sleep?'

'A few hours.'

'Before that?'

'Just over twelve weeks.' She stared back, numb. 'Through the autumn, and into winter, and the new year will soon come. A fine time for new beginnings. That you have woken at all is nothing short of miraculous. Your injuries were . . . well, I think you will be pleased with my work. I know I am.'

He slid a greasy cushion from under the bench and propped her head up, handling her as carelessly as a butcher handles meat, bringing her chin forwards so she could look down at herself. So there was no choice but to. Her body was a lumpy outline under a coarse grey blanket, three leather belts across chest, hips and ankles.

'The straps are for your own protection, to prevent you rolling from the bench while you slept.' He hacked out a sudden chuckle. 'We wouldn't want you breaking anything, would we? Ha . . . ha! Wouldn't want to break anything.' He unbuckled the last of the belts, took the blanket between thumb and forefinger while she stared down, desperate to know, and desperate not to know at once.

He whipped it away like a showman displaying his prize exhibit.

She hardly recognised her own body. Stark naked, gaunt and withered as a beggar's, pale skin stretched tight over ugly knobbles of bone, stained all over with great black, brown, purple, yellow blooms of bruise. Her eyes darted over her own wasted flesh, steadily widening as she struggled to take it in. She was slit all over with red lines. Dark and angry, edged with raised pink flesh, stippled with the dots of pulled stitches. There were four, one above the other, following the curves of her hollow ribs on one side. More angled across her hips, down her legs, her right arm, her left foot.

She'd started to tremble. This butchered carcass couldn't be her body. Her breath hissed through her rattling teeth, and the blotched and shrivelled ribcage heaved in time. 'Uh . . .' she grunted. 'Uh . . .'

'I know! Impressive, eh?' He leaned forwards over her, following the ladder of red marks on her chest with sharp movements of his hand. 'The ribs here and the breastbone were quite shattered. It was necessary to make incisions to repair them, you understand, and to work on the lung. I kept the cutting to the minimum, but you can see that the damage—'

'Uh . . .'

'The left hip I am especially pleased with.' Pointing out a crimson zigzag from the corner of her hollow stomach down to the inside of her withered leg, surrounded on both sides by trails of red dots. 'The thighbone, here, unfortunately broke into itself.' He clicked his tongue and poked a finger into his clenched fist. 'Shortening the leg by a fraction, but, as luck would have it, your other shin was shattered, and I was able to remove the tiniest section of bone to make up the difference.' He frowned as he pushed her knees together, then watched them roll apart, feet flopping hopelessly outwards. 'One knee slightly higher than the other, and you won't stand quite so tall but, considering—'

'Uh . . .'

'Set, now.' He grinned as he squeezed gently at her shrivelled legs from the tops of her thighs down to her knobbly ankles. She watched him touching her, like a cook kneading at a plucked chicken, and hardly felt it. 'All quite set, and the screws removed. A wonder, believe me. If the doubters at the academy could see this now they wouldn't be laughing. If my old master could see this, even he—'

'Uh . . .' She slowly raised her right hand. Or the trembling mockery of a hand that dangled from the end of her arm. The palm was bent, shrunken, a great ugly scar where Gobba's wire had cut into the side. The fingers were crooked as tree roots, squashed together, the little one sticking out at a strange angle. Her breath hissed through gritted teeth as she tried to make a fist. The fingers scarcely moved, but the pain still shot up her arm and made bile burn the back of her throat.

'The best I could do. Small bones, you see, badly damaged, and the tendons of the little finger were quite severed.' Her host seemed disappointed. 'A shock, of course. The marks will fade . . . somewhat. But really, considering the fall . . . well, here.' The mouthpiece of the husk-pipe came towards her and she sucked on it greedily. Clung to it with her teeth as if it was her only hope. It was.

He tore a tiny piece from the corner of the loaf, the kind you might feed birds with. Monza watched him do it, mouth filling with sour spit. Hunger or sickness, there wasn't much difference. She took it dumbly, lifted it to her lips, so weak that her left hand trembled with the effort, forced it between her teeth and down her throat.

Like swallowing broken glass.

'Slowly,' he murmured, 'very slowly, you have eaten nothing but milk and sugar-water since you fell.'

The bread caught in her craw and she retched, gut clamping up tight around the knife-wound Faithful had given her.

'Here.' He slid his hand round her skull, gentle but firm, lifted her head and tipped a bottle of water to her lips. She swallowed, and again, then her eyes flicked towards his fingers. She could feel unfamiliar lumps there, down the side of her head. 'I was forced to remove several pieces of your skull. I replaced them with coins.'

'Coins?'

'Would you rather I had left your brains exposed? Gold does not rust. Gold does not rot. An expensive treatment, of course, but if you had died, I could always have recouped my investment, and since you have not, well . . . I consider it money well spent. Your scalp will feel somewhat lumpy, but your hair will grow back. Such beautiful hair you have. Black as midnight.'

He let her head fall gently back against the bench and his hand lingered there. A soft touch. Almost a caress.

'Normally I am a taciturn man. Too much time spent alone, perhaps.' He flashed his corpse-smile at her. 'But I find you . . . bring out the best in me. The mother of my children is the same. You remind me of her, in a way.'

Monza half-smiled back, but in her gut she felt a creeping of disgust. It mingled with the sickness she was feeling every so often, now. That sweating need.

She swallowed. 'Could I—'

'Of course.' He was already holding the pipe out to her.

'Close it.'

'It won't close!' she hissed, three of the fingers just curling, the little one still sticking out straight, or as close to straight as it ever came. She remembered how nimble-fingered she used to be, how sure, and quick, and the frustration and the fury were sharper even than the pain. 'They won't close!'

'For weeks you have been lying here. I did not mend you so you could smoke husk and do nothing. Try harder.'

'Do you want to fucking try?'

'Very well.' His hand closed relentlessly around hers and forced the bent fingers into a crunching fist. Her eyes bulged from her head, breath whistling too fast for her to scream.

'I doubt you understand how much I am helping you.' He squeezed tighter and tighter. 'One cannot grow without pain. One cannot improve without it. Suffering drives us to achieve great things.' The fingers of her good hand plucked and scrabbled uselessly at his fist. 'Love is a fine cushion to rest upon, but only hate can make you a better person. There.' He let go of her and she sagged back, whimpering, watched her trembling fingers come gradually halfway open, scars standing out purple.

She wanted to kill him. She wanted to shriek every curse she knew. But she needed him too badly. So she held her tongue, sobbed, gasped, ground her teeth, smacked the back of her head against the bench.

'Now, close your hand.' She stared into his face, empty as a fresh-dug grave. 'Now, or I must do it for you.'

She growled with the effort, whole arm throbbing to the shoulder. Gradually, the fingers inched closed, the little one still sticking straight. 'There, you fucker!' She shook her numb, knobbly, twisted fist under his nose. 'There!'

'Was that so hard?' He held the pipe out to her and she snatched it from him. 'You need not thank me.'

'And we will see if you can take the—'

She squealed, knees buckling, would have fallen if he hadn't caught her.

'Still?' He frowned. 'You should be able to walk. The bones are knitted. Pain, of course, but . . . perhaps a fragment within one of the joints, still. Where does it hurt?'

'Everywhere!' she snarled at him.

'I trust this is not simply your stubbornness. I would hate to open the wounds in your legs again unnecessarily.' He hooked one arm under her knees and lifted her without much effort back onto the bench. 'I must go for a while.'

She clutched at him. 'You'll be back soon?'

'Very soon.'

His footsteps vanished down the corridor. She heard the front door click shut, the sound of the key scraping in the lock.

'Son of a fucking whore.' And she swung her legs down from the bench. She winced as her feet touched the floor, bared her teeth as she straightened up, growled softly as she let go of the bench and stood on her own feet.

It hurt like hell, and it felt good.

She took a long breath, gathered herself and began to waddle towards the far side of the room, pains shooting through her ankles, knees, hips, into her back, arms held out wide for balance. She made it to the cupboard and clung to its corner, slid open the drawer. The pipe lay inside, a jar of bubbly green glass beside it with some black lumps of husk in the bottom. How she wanted it. Her mouth was dry, her palms sticky with sick need. She slapped the drawer closed and hobbled back to the bench. Everything was still pierced with cold aches, but she was getting stronger each day. Soon she'd be ready. But not yet.

Patience is the parent of success, Stolicus wrote.

Across the room, and back, growling through her clenched teeth. Across the room and back, lurching and grimacing. Across the room and back, whimpering, wobbling, spitting. She leaned against the bench, long enough to get her breath.

Across the room and back again.

The mirror had a crack across it, but she wished it had been far more broken.

Your hair is like a curtain of midnight!

Shaved off down the left side of her head, grown back to a scabby stubble. The rest hung lank, tangled and greasy as old seaweed.

Your eyes gleam like piercing sapphires, beyond price!

Yellow, bloodshot, lashes gummed to clumps, rimmed red-raw in sockets purple-black with pain.

Lips like rose petals?

Cracked, parched, peeling grey with yellow scum gathered at the corners. There were three long scabs across her sucked-in cheek, sore brown against waxy white.

You look especially beautiful this morning, Monza . . .

On each side of her neck, withered down to a bundle of pale cords, the red scars left by Gobba's wire. She looked like a woman just dead of the plague. She looked scarcely better than the skulls stacked on the mantelpiece.

Beyond the mirror, her host was smiling. 'What did I tell you? You look well.'

The very Goddess of War!

'I look a fucking carnival curiosity!' she sneered, and the ruined crone in the mirror sneered back at her.

'Better than when I found you. You should learn to look on the happy side of the case.' He tossed the mirror down, stood and pulled on his coat. 'I must leave you for the time being, but I will be back, as I always am. Continue working the hand, but keep your strength. Later I must cut into your legs and establish the cause of your difficulty in standing.'

37

She forced a sickly smile onto her face. 'Yes. I see.'

'Good. Soon, then.' He threw his canvas bag over his shoulder. His footsteps creaked down the corridor, the lock closed. She counted slowly to ten.

Off the bench and she snatched up a pair of needles and a knife from the tray. She limped to the cupboard, ripped open the drawer, stuffed the pipe into the pocket of the borrowed trousers hanging from her hip bones, the jar with it. She lurched down the hall, boards creaking under bare feet. Into the bedroom, grimacing as she fished the old boots from under the bed, grunting as she pulled them on.

Out into the corridor again, her breath hissing with effort, and pain, and fear. She knelt down by the front door, or at least lowered herself by creaking degrees until her burning knees were on the boards. It was a long time since she'd worked a lock. She fished and stabbed with the needles, twisted hand fumbling.

'Turn, you bastard. Turn.'

Luckily the lock wasn't good. The tumblers caught, turned with a satisfying clatter. She grabbed the knob and hauled the door open.

Night, and a hard one. Cold rain lashed an overgrown yard, rank weeds edged with the slightest glimmer of moonlight, crumbling walls slick with wet. Beyond a leaning fence bare trees rose up, darkness gathered under their branches. A rough night for an invalid to be out of doors. But the chill wind whipping at her face, the clean air in her mouth, felt almost like being alive again. Better to freeze free than spend another moment with the bones. She ducked out into the rain, hobbled across the garden, nettles snatching at her. Into the trees, between their glistening trunks, and she struck away from the track and didn't look back.

Up a long slope, bent double, good hand dragging at the muddy ground, pulling her on. She grunted at each slipping footfall, every muscle screeching at her. Black rain dripped from black branches, pattered on fallen leaves, crept through her hair and plastered it across her face, crept through her stolen clothes and stuck them to her sore skin.

'One more step.'

She had to make some distance from the bench, and the

knives, and that slack, white, empty face. That face, and the one in the mirror.

'One more step . . . one more step . . . one more step.'

The black ground lurched past, her hand trailing against the wet mud, the tree roots. She followed her father as he pushed the plough, long ago, hand trailing through the turned earth for stones.

What would I do without you?

She knelt in the cold woods beside Cosca, waiting for the ambush, her nose full of that damp, crisp smell of trees, her heart bursting with fear and excitement.

You have a devil in you.

She thought of whatever she needed to so she could keep going, memories rushing on ahead of her clumsy boots.

Off the terrace and let us be done.

She stopped, stood bent over, shuddering smoky breaths into the wet night. No idea how far she'd come, where she'd started, where she was going. For now, it hardly mattered.

She wedged her back against a slimy tree-trunk, prised at her belt buckle with her good hand, shoved at it with the side of the other one. It took her a teeth-gritted age to finally get the damn thing open. At least she didn't have to pull her trousers down. They sagged off her bony arse and down her scarred legs under their own weight. She paused a moment, wondering how she'd get them back up.

One battle at a time, Stolicus wrote.

She grabbed a low branch, slick with rain, lowered herself under it, right hand cradled against her wet shirt, bare knees trembling.

'Come on,' she hissed, trying to make her knotted bladder unclench. 'If you need to go, just go. Just go. Just—'

She grunted with relief, piss spattering into the mud along with the rain, trickling down the hillside. Her right leg was burning worse than ever, wasted muscles quivering. She winced as she tried to move her hand down the branch, shift her weight to her other leg. In a sick instant one foot flew out from under her and she went over backwards, breath whooping in, reason all blotted out by the dizzy memory of falling. She bit her tongue as her head cracked down in the mud, slid a stride or two, flailed to a stop in a wet hollow full of rotting leaves. She lay in the tapping rain, trousers tangled round her ankles, and wept.

It was a low moment, no doubt of that.

She bawled like a baby. Helpless, heedless, desperate. Her sobs racked her, choked her, made her mangled body shake. She didn't know the last time she'd cried. Never, maybe. Benna had done the weeping for both of them. Now all the pain and fear of a dozen black years and more came leaking out of her screwed-up face. She lay in the mud, and tortured herself with everything she'd lost.

Benna was dead, and everything good in her was dead with him. The way they made each other laugh. That understanding that comes from a life together, gone. He'd been home, family, friend and more, all killed at once. All snuffed out carelessly as a cheap candle. Her hand was ruined. She held the aching, mocking remnant of it to her chest. The way she used to draw a sword, use a pen, firmly shake a hand, all crushed under Gobba's boot. The way she used to walk, run, ride, all scattered broken down the mountainside under Orso's balcony. Her place in the world, ten years' work, built with her own sweat and blood, struggled for, sweated for, vanished like smoke. All she'd worked for, hoped for, dreamed of.

Dead.

She worked her belt back up, dead leaves dragged up with it, and fumbled it shut. A few last sobs, then she snorted snot down, wiped the rest from under her nose on her cold hand. The life she'd had was gone. The woman she'd been was gone. What they'd broken could never be mended.

But there was no point weeping about it now.

She knelt in the mud, shivering in the darkness, silent. These things weren't just gone, they'd been stolen from her. Her brother wasn't just dead, he'd been murdered. Slaughtered like an animal. She forced her twisted fingers closed until they made a trembling fist.

'I'll kill them.'

She made herself see their faces, one by one. Gobba, the fat hog, lounging in the shadows. *A waste of decent flesh.* Her face twitched as she saw his boot stomp down across her hand, felt the bones splinter. Mauthis, the banker, his cold eyes staring down at her brother's corpse. Inconvenienced. Faithful Carpi. A man who'd walked beside her, eaten beside her, fought beside her, year upon year. *I really am sorry.* She saw his arm go back, ready to stab her through, felt the wound niggling at her side, pressed at it through her wet shirt, dug her fingers into it back and front until it burned like fury.

'I'll kill them.'

Ganmark. She saw his soft, tired face. Flinched as his sword punched through Benna's body. *That's that.* Prince Ario, lounging in his chair, wine glass dangling. His knife cut Benna's neck open, blood bubbling between his fingers. She made herself see each detail, remember each word said. Foscar, too. *I'll have no part of this.* But that changed nothing.

'I'll kill them all.'

And Orso, last. Orso, who she'd fought for, struggled for, killed for. Grand Duke Orso, Lord of Talins, who'd turned on them over a rumour. Murdered her brother, left her broken for nothing. For a fear they'd steal his place. Her jaw ached, her teeth were clenched so hard. She felt his fatherly hand on her shoulder and her shivering flesh crawled. She saw his smile, heard his voice echoing in her pounding skull.

What would I do without you?

Seven men.

She dragged herself up, chewing at her sore lip, and lurched off through the dark trees, water trickling from her sodden hair and down her face. The pain gnawed through her legs, her sides, her hand, her skull, but she bit down hard and forced herself on.

'I'll kill them . . . I'll kill them . . . I'll kill them . . .'

It hardly needed to be said. She was done with crying.

The old track was grown over, almost past recognition. Branches thrashed at Monza's aching body. Brambles snatched at her burning legs. She crept through a gap in the overgrown hedgerow and frowned down at the place where she'd been born. She wished she'd been able to make the stubborn soil bear a crop as well as it bloomed thorn and nettle now. The upper field was a patch of dead scrub. The lower was a mass of briar. The remains of the mean farmhouse peered sadly over from the edge of the woods, and she peered sadly back.

It seemed that time had given both of them a kicking.

She squatted, gritting her teeth as her withered muscles stretched around her crooked bones, listening to a few birds cawing at the sinking sun, watching the wind twitch the wild grass and snatch at the nettles. Until she was sure the place was every bit as abandoned as it looked. Then she gently worked the life back into her battered legs and limped for the buildings. The house where her father died was a tumbled-down shell and a rotted beam or two, its outline so small it was hard to believe she could ever have lived there. She, and her father, and Benna too. She turned her head and spat into the dry dirt. She hadn't come here for bitter-sweet remembrances.

She'd come for revenge.

The shovel was where she'd left it two winters ago, blade still bright under some rubbish in the corner of the roofless barn. Thirty strides into the trees. Hard to imagine how easily she'd taken those long, smooth, laughing steps as she waddled through the weeds, spade dragging behind her. Into the quiet woods, wincing at every footfall, broken patterns of sunlight dancing across the fallen leaves as the evening wore down.

Thirty strides. She hacked the brambles away with the edge of the shovel, finally managed to drag the rotten tree-trunk to one side and began to dig. It would've been some task with both her hands and both her legs. As she was now, it was a groaning, sweating, teeth-grinding ordeal. But Monza had never been one to give up halfway, whatever the costs. *You have a devil in you*, Cosca used to tell her, and he'd been right. He'd learned it the hard way.

Night was coming on when she heard the hollow clomp of metal against wood. She scraped the last soil away, prised the iron ring from the dirt with broken fingernails. She strained, growled, stolen clothes stuck cold to her scarred skin. The trapdoor came open with a squealing of metal and a black hole beckoned, a ladder half-seen in the darkness.

She worked her way down, painstakingly slow since she'd no interest in breaking any more bones. She fumbled in the black until she found the shelf, wrestled with the flint in her bad joke of a hand and finally got the lamp lit. Light flared out weakly around the vaulted cellar, glittering along the metal edges of Benna's precautions, sitting safe, just as they'd left them.

He always had liked to plan ahead.

Keys hung from a row of rusted hooks. Keys to empty buildings, scattered across Styria. Places to hide. A rack along the left-hand wall bristled with blades, long and short. She opened a chest beside it. Clothes, carefully folded, never worn. She doubted they'd even fit her wasted body now. She reached out to touch one of Benna's shirts, remembering him picking out the silk for it, caught sight of her own right hand in the lamplight. She snatched up a pair of gloves, threw one away and shoved the maimed thing into the other, wincing as she worked the fingers, the little one still sticking out stubbornly straight.

Wooden boxes were stacked at the back of the cellar, twenty of them all told. She hobbled to the nearest one and pushed back the lid. Hermon's gold glittered at her. Heaps of coins. A small fortune in that box alone. She touched her fingertips gingerly to the side of her skull, felt the ridges under her skin. Gold. There's so much more you can do with it than just hold your head together.

She dug her hand in and let coins trickle between her fingers. The way you somehow have to if you find yourself alone with a box of money. These would be her weapons. These, and . . .

She let her gloved hand trail across the blades on the rack, stopped and went back one. A long sword of workmanlike grey steel. It didn't have much in the way of ornamental flourishes, but there was a fearsome beauty about it still, to her eye. The beauty of a thing fitted perfectly to its purpose. It was a Calvez, forged by the best swordsmith in Styria. A gift from her to Benna, not that he'd have known the difference between a good blade and a carrot. He'd worn it for a week then swapped it for an overpriced length of scrap metal with stupid gilt basketwork.

The one he'd been trying to draw when they killed him.

She curled her fingers round the cold grip, strange in her left hand, and slid a few inches of steel from the sheath. It shone bright and eager in the lamplight. Good steel bends, but never breaks. Good steel stays always sharp and ready. Good steel feels no pain, no pity and, above all, no remorse.

She felt herself smile. The first time in months. The first time since Gobba's wire hissed tight around her neck.

Vengeance, then.

Fish out of Water

The cold wind swept in from the sea and gave the docks of Talins a damn good blasting. Or a damn bad one, depending how well dressed you were. Shivers weren't that well dressed at all. He pulled his thin coat tight round his shoulders, though he might as well not have bothered, for all the good it did him. He narrowed his eyes and squinted miserably into the latest gust. He was earning his name today, alright. He had been for weeks.

He remembered sitting warm by the fire, up in the North in a good house in Uffrith, with a belly full of meat and a head full of dreams, talking to Vossula about the wondrous city of Talins. He remembered it with some bitterness, because it was that bloody merchant, with his dewy eyes and his honey tales of home, who'd talked him into this nightmare jaunt to Styria.

Vossula had told him that the sun always shone in Talins. That was why Shivers had sold his good coat before he set off. Didn't want to end up sweating, did he? Seemed now, as he shivered like a curled-up autumn leaf only just still clinging to its branch, that Vossula had been doing some injury to the truth.

Shivers watched the restless waves chew at the quay, throwing icy spray over the few rotting skiffs stirring at their rotting wharves. He listened to the hawsers creaking, to the ill seabirds croaking, to the wind making a loose shutter rattle, to the grunts and grumbles of the men around him. All of 'em huddled on the docks for the sniff of a chance at work, and there'd never been in one place such a crowd of sad stories. Grubby and gaunt, ragged clothes and pinched-in faces. Desperate men. Men just like Shivers, in other words. Except they'd been born here. He'd been stupid enough to choose this.

He slid the last hard heel of bread from his inside pocket as carefully as a miser breaking out his hoard, took a nibble from

45

the end, making sure to taste every crumb of it. Then he caught the man nearest to him staring, licking his pale lips. Shivers felt his shoulders slump, broke some off and handed it over.

'Thanks, friend,' as he wolfed it down.

'No bother,' said Shivers, though he'd spent hours chopping logs for it. Quite a lot of painful bother, in fact. The rest of 'em were all looking now, big sad eyes like pups needed feeding. He threw up his hands. 'If I had bread for everyone, why the fuck would I be stood here?'

They turned away grumbling. He snorted cold snot up and spat it out. Aside from some stale bread it was the only thing to have passed his lips that morning, and going in the wrong direction. He'd come with a pocketful of silver, and a faceful of smiles, and a swelling chestful of happy hope. Ten weeks in Styria, and all three of those were emptied to the bitter dregs.

Vossula had told him the people of Talins were friendly as lambs, welcomed foreigners like guests. He'd found nothing but scorn, and a lot of folk keen to use any rotten trick to relieve him of his dwindling money. They weren't just handing out second chances on the street corners here. No more'n they had been in the North.

A boat had come in now, was tying off at the quay, fishers scurrying over and around it, hauling at ropes and cursing at sailcloth. Shivers felt the rest of the desperate perking up, wondering if there might be a shift of work for one of 'em. He felt a dismal little flair of hope in his own chest, however hard he tried to keep it down, and stood up keen on tiptoes to watch.

Fish slid from the nets onto the dockside, squirming silver in the watery sun. It was a good, honest trade, fishing. A life on the salty brine where no sharp words are spoken, all men set together against the wind, plucking the shining bounty from the sea, and all that. A noble trade, or so Shivers tried to tell himself, in spite of the stink. Any trade that'd have him seemed pretty noble about then.

A man weathered as an old gatepost hopped down from the boat and strutted over, all self-importance, and the beggars jostled each other to catch his eye. The captain, Shivers guessed.

'Need two hands,' he said, pushing his battered cap back and looking those hopeful, hopeless faces over. 'You, and you.'

Hardly needed saying Shivers weren't one of 'em. His head sagged along with the rest as he watched the lucky pair hurrying back to the boat after its captain. One was the bastard he gave his bread to, didn't so much as look round, let alone put in a word for him. Maybe it was what you gave out that made a man, not what you got back, like Shivers' brother used to say, but getting back's a mighty good thing to stop you starving.

'Shit on this.' And he started after them, picking his way between the fishers sorting their flapping catch into buckets and barrows. Wearing the friendliest grin he could muster, he walked up to where the captain was busying himself on the deck. 'Nice boat you got here,' he tried, though it was a slimy tub of shit far as he could see.

'And?'

'Would you think of taking me on?'

'You? What d'you know about fish?'

Shivers was a proven hand with axe, blade, spear and shield. A Named Man who'd led charges and held lines across the North and back. Who'd taken a few bad wounds and given out a lot of worse. But he was set on doing better'n that, and he was clinging to the notion tight as a drowning man to driftwood.

'I used to fish a lot, when I was a boy. Down by the lake, with my father.' His bare feet crunching in the shingle. The light glistening on the water. His father's smile, and his brother's.

But the captain didn't come over nostalgic. 'Lake? Sea-fishing's what we do, boy.'

'Sea-fishing, I've got to say, I've had no practice at.'

'Then why you wasting my bloody time? I can get plenty of Styrian fishers for my measure, the best hands, all with a dozen years at sea.' He waved at the idle men lining the dock, looked more like they'd spent a dozen years in an ale-cup. 'Why should I give work to some Northern beggar?'

'I'll work hard. Had some bad luck is all. I'm just asking for a chance.'

'So are we all, but I'm not hearing why I should be the one to give it you.'

'Just a chance is—'

'Away from my boat, you big pale bastard!' The captain snatched up a length of rough wood from the deck and had himself a step forwards, as if he was set to beat a dog. 'Get off, and take your bad luck with you!'

'I may be no kind of fisher, but I've always had a talent for making men bleed. Best put that stick down before I make you fucking eat it.' Shivers gave a look to go with the warning. A killing look, straight out of the North. The captain faltered, stopped, stood there grumbling. Then he tossed his stick away and started shouting at one of his own people.

Shivers hunched his shoulders and didn't look back. He trudged to the mouth of an alley, past the torn bills pasted on the walls, the words daubed over 'em. Into the shadows between the crowded buildings, and the sounds of the docks went muffled at his back. It had been the same story with the smiths, and with the bakers, and with every damn trade in this damn city. There'd even been a cobbler who'd looked like a good enough sort until he told Shivers to fuck himself.

Vossula had said there was work everywhere in Styria, all you had to do was ask. It seemed, for reasons he couldn't fathom, that Vossula had been lying out of his arse the whole way. Shivers had asked him all kinds of questions. But it occurred to him now, as he sank down on a slimy doorstep with his worn-out boots in the gutter and some fish-heads for company, he hadn't asked the one question he should've. The one question staring him in the face ever since he got here.

Tell me, Vossula – if Styria's such a slice of wonder, why the hell are you up here in the North?

'Fucking Styria,' he hissed in Northern. He had that pain behind his nose meant he was close to weeping, and he was that far gone he was scarcely even shamed. Caul Shivers. Rattleneck's son. A Named Man who'd faced death in all weathers. Who'd fought beside the biggest names in the North – Rudd Threetrees, Black Dow, the Dogman, Harding Grim. Who'd led the charge against the Union near the Cumnur. Who'd held the line against a thousand Shanka at Dunbrec. Who'd fought seven days of murder up in the High Places. He almost felt a smile tugging at his mouth to think of the wild, brave times he'd come out alive from. He knew he'd been shitting himself the whole way, but what happy days those seemed now. Least he hadn't been alone.

He looked up at the sound of footsteps. Four men were

ambling into the alley from the docks, the way he'd come. They had that sorry look men can get when they've got mischief in mind. Shivers hunched into his doorway, hoping whatever mischief they were planning didn't include him.

His heart took a downward turn as they gathered in a half-circle, standing over him. One had a bloated-up red nose, the kind you get from too much drinking. Another was bald as a boot-toe, had a length of wood held by his leg. A third had a scraggy beard and a mouthful of brown teeth. Not a pretty set of men, and Shivers didn't reckon they had anything pretty in mind.

The one at the front grinned down, a nasty-looking bastard with a pointed rat-face. 'What you got for us?'

'I wish I'd something worth the taking. But I've not. You might as well just go your way.'

Rat Face frowned at his bald mate, annoyed they might get nothing. 'Your boots, then.'

'In this weather? I'll freeze.'

'Freeze. See if I care a shit. Boots, now, before we give you a kicking for the sport of it.'

'Fucking Talins,' mouthed Shivers under his breath, the ashes of self-pity in his throat suddenly flaring up hot and bloody. It gnawed at him to come this low. Bastards had no use for his boots, just wanted to make themselves feel big. But it'd be a fool's fight four against one, and with no weapon handy. A fool's choice to get killed for some old leather, however cold it was.

He crouched down, muttering as he started to pull his boots off. Then his knee caught Red Nose right in his fruits and doubled him over with a breathy sigh. Surprised himself as much as he did them. Maybe going barefoot was more'n his pride would stretch to. He smashed Rat Face on the chin, grabbed him by the front of his coat and rammed him back into one of his mates, sent them sprawling over together, yelping like cats in a rainstorm.

Shivers dodged the bald bastard's stick as it came down and shrugged it off his shoulder. The man came stumbling past, off balance, mouth wide open. Shivers planted a punch right on the point of his hanging chin and snapped his head up, then hooked his legs away with one boot, sent him squawking onto his back and followed him down. Shivers' fist crunched into his face – two, three, four times, and made a right mess of it, spattering blood up the arm of Shivers' dirty coat.

He scrambled away, leaving Baldy spitting teeth into the gutter. Red Nose was still curled up wailing with his hands between his legs. But the other two had knives out now, sharp metal glinting. Shivers crouched, fists clenched, breathing hard, eyes flicking from one of 'em to the other and his anger wilting fast. Should've just given his boots over. Probably they'd be prising them off his cold, dead feet in a short and painful while. Bloody pride, that rubbish only did a man harm.

Rat Face wiped blood from under his nose. 'Oh, you're a dead man now, you Northern fuck! You're good as a—' His leg suddenly went from underneath him and he fell, shrieking, knife bouncing from his hand.

Someone slid out of the shadows behind him. Tall and hooded, sword held loose in a pale left fist, long, thin blade catching such light as there was in the alley and glinting murder. The last of the boot-thieves still standing, the one with the shitty teeth, stared at that length of steel with eyes big as a cow's, his knife looking a piss-poor tool all of a sudden.

'You might want to run for it.' Shivers frowned, caught off guard. A woman's voice. Brown Teeth didn't need telling twice. He turned and sprinted off down the alley.

'My leg!' Rat Face was yelling, clutching at the back of his knee with one bloody hand. 'My fucking leg!'

'Stop whining or I'll slit the other one.'

Baldy was lying there, saying nothing. Red Nose had finally fought his way moaning to his knees.

'Want my boots, do you?' Shivers took a step and kicked him in the fruits again, lifted him up and put him back down mewling on his face. 'There's one of 'em, bastard!' He watched the newcomer, blood swoosh-swooshing behind his eyes, not sure how he came through that without getting some steel in his guts. Not sure if he might not still. This woman didn't have the look of good news. 'What d'you want?' he growled at her.

'Nothing you'll have trouble with.' He could see the corner of a smile inside her hood. 'I might have some work for you.'

*

A big plate of meat and vegetables in some kind of gravy, slabs of doughy bread beside. Might've been good, might not have been, Shivers was too busy ramming it into his face to tell. Most likely he looked a right animal, two weeks unshaved, pinched and greasy from dossing in doorways, and not even good ones. But he was far past caring how he looked, even with a woman watching.

She still had her hood up, though they were out of the weather now. She stayed back against the wall, where it was dark. She tipped her head forwards when folk came close, tar-black hair hanging across one cheek. He'd worked out a notion of her face anyway, in the moments when he could drag his eyes away from his food, and he reckoned it was a good one.

Strong, with hard bones in it, a fierce line of jaw and a lean neck, a blue vein showing up the side. Dangerous, he reckoned, though that wasn't such a clever guess since he'd seen her slit the back of a man's knee with small regret. Still, there was something in the way her narrow eyes held him that made him nervous. Calm and cold, as if she'd already got his full measure, and knew just what he'd do next. Knew better'n he did. She had three long marks down one cheek, old cuts still healing. She had a glove on her right hand, and scarcely used it. A limp too he'd noticed on the way here. Caught up in some dark business, maybe, but Shivers didn't have so many friends he could afford to be picky. Right then, anyone who fed him had the full stretch of his loyalty.

She watched him eat. 'Hungry?'

'Somewhat.'

'Long way from home?'

'Somewhat.'

'Had some bad luck?'

'More'n my share. But I made some bad choices, too.'

'The two go together.'

'That is a fact.' He tossed knife and spoon clattering down onto the empty plate. 'I should've thought it through.' He wiped up the gravy with the last slice of bread. 'But I've always been my own worst enemy.' They sat facing each other in silence as he chewed it. 'You've not told me your name.'

'No.'

'Like that, is it?'

'I'm paying, aren't I? It's whatever way I say it is.'

'Why are you paying? A friend of mine . . .' He cleared his throat, starting to doubt whether Vossula had been any kind of friend. 'A man I know told me to expect nothing for free in Styria.'

'Good advice. I need something from you.'

Shivers licked at the inside of his mouth and it tasted sour. He had a debt to this woman, now, and he wasn't sure what he'd have to pay. By the look of her, he reckoned it might cost him dear. 'What do you need?'

'First of all, have a bath. No one's going to deal with you in that state.'

Now the hunger and the cold were gone, they'd left a bit of room for shame. 'I'm happier not stinking, believe it or not. I got some fucking pride left.'

'Good for you. Bet you can't wait to get fucking clean, then.'

He worked his shoulders around, uncomfortable. He had this feeling like he was stepping into a pool with no idea how deep it might be. 'Then what?'

'Not much. You go into a smoke-house and ask for a man called Sajaam. You say Nicomo demands his presence at the usual place. You bring him to me.'

'Why not do that yourself?'

'Because I'm paying you to do it, fool.' She held up a coin in her gloved fist. Silver glinted in the firelight, design of weighing scales stamped into the bright metal. 'You bring Sajaam to me, you get a scale. You decide you still want fish, you can buy yourself a barrelful.'

Shivers frowned. For some fine-looking woman to come out of nowhere, more'n likely save his life, then make him a golden offer? His luck had never been anywhere near that good. But eating had only reminded him how much he used to enjoy doing it. 'I can do that.'

'Good. Or you can do something else, and get fifty.'

'Fifty?' Shivers' voice was an eager croak. 'This a joke?'

'You see me laughing? Fifty, I said, and if you still want fish you can buy your own boat and have change for some decent tailoring, how's that?'

Shivers tugged somewhat shamefacedly at the frayed edge of

his coat. With that much he could hop the next boat back to Uffrith and kick Vossula's skinny arse from one end of the town to the other. A dream that had been his one source of pleasure for some time. 'What do you want for fifty?'

'Not much. You go into a smoke-house and ask for a man called Sajaam. You say Nicomo demands his presence at the usual place. You bring him to me.' She paused for a moment. 'Then you help me kill a man.'

It was no surprise, if he was honest with himself for once. There was only one kind of work that he was really good at. Certainly only one kind that anyone would pay him fifty scales for. He'd come here to be a better man. But it was just like the Dogman had told him. Once your hands are bloody, it ain't so easy to get 'em clean.

Something poked his thigh under the table and he near jumped out of his chair. The pommel of a long knife lay between his legs. A fighting knife, steel crosspiece gleaming orange, its sheathed blade in the woman's gloved hand.

'Best take it.'

'I didn't say I'd kill anyone.'

'I know what you said. The blade's just to show Sajaam you mean business.'

He had to admit he didn't much care for a woman surprising him with a knife between his thighs. 'I didn't say I'd kill anyone.'

'I didn't say you did.'

'Right then. Just as long as you know.' He snatched the blade from her and slid it down inside his coat.

The knife pressed against his chest as he walked up, nuzzling at him like an old lover back for more. Shivers knew it was nothing to be proud of. Any fool can carry a knife. But even so, he wasn't sure he didn't like the weight of it against his ribs. Felt like being someone again.

He'd come to Styria looking for honest work. But when the purse runs empty, dishonest work has to do. Shivers couldn't say he'd ever seen a place with a less honest look about it than this one. A heavy door in a dirty, bare, windowless wall, with a big man standing guard on each side. Shivers could tell it in the way they stood – they had weapons, and were right on the edge of putting 'em to use. One was a dark-skinned Southerner, black hair hanging around his face.

'Need something?' he asked, while the other gave Shivers the eyeball.

'Here to see Sajaam.'

'You armed?' Shivers slid out the knife, held it up hilt first, and the man took it off him. 'With me, then.' The hinges creaked as the door swung open.

The air was thick on the other side, hazy with sweet smoke. It scratched at Shivers' throat and made him want to cough, prickled at his eyes and made them water. It was dim and quiet, too sticky warm for comfort after the nip outside. Lamps of coloured glass threw patterns across the stained walls – green, and red, and yellow flares in the murk. The place was like a bad dream.

Curtains hung about, dirty silk rustling in the gloom. Folk sprawled on cushions, half-dressed and half-asleep. A man lay on his back, mouth wide open, pipe dangling from his hand, trace of smoke still curling from the bowl. A woman was pressed against him, on her side. Both their faces were beaded with sweat, slack as corpses. Looked like an uneasy cross between delight and despair, but tending towards the latter.

'This way.' Shivers followed his guide through the haze and down a shadowy corridor. A woman leaning in a doorway watched him pass with dead eyes, saying nothing. Someone was grunting somewhere, 'Oh, oh, oh,' almost bored.

Through a curtain of clicking beads and into another big room, less smoky but more worrying. Men were scattered about it, an odd mix of types and colours. Judging by their looks, all used to violence. Eight were sitting at a table strewn with glasses, bottles and small money, playing cards. More lounged about in the shadows. Shivers' eye fell right away on a nasty-looking hatchet in easy reach of one, and he didn't reckon it was the only weapon about. A clock was nailed up on the wall, innards dangling, swinging back and forth, tick, tock, tick, loud enough to set his nerves jangling even worse.

A big man sat at the head of the table, the chief's place if this had been the North. An old man, face creased like leather past its best. His skin was oily dark, short hair and beard dusted with iron grey. He had a gold coin he was fiddling with, flipping it across his knuckles from one side of his hand back to the other. The guide leaned down to whisper in his ear, then handed across the knife. His eyes and the eyes of the others were on Shivers, now. A scale was starting to seem a small reward for the task, all of a sudden.

'You Sajaam?' Louder than Shivers had in mind, voice squeaky from the smoke.

The old man's smile was a yellow curve in his dark face. 'Sajaam is my name, as all my sweet friends will confirm. You know, you can tell an awful lot about a man from the style of weapon he carries.'

'That so?'

Sajaam slid the knife from its sheath and held it up, candle-light glinting on steel. 'Not a cheap blade, but not expensive either. Fit for the job, and no frills at the edges. Sharp, and hard, and meaning business. Am I close to the mark?'

'Somewhere round it.' It was plain he was one of those who loved to prattle on, so Shivers didn't bother to mention that it weren't even his knife. Less said, sooner he could be on his way.

'What might your name be, friend?' Though the friend bit didn't much convince.

'Caul Shivers.'

'Brrrr.' Sajaam shook his big shoulders around like he was cold, to much chuckling from his men. Easily tickled, by the look of things. 'You are a long, long way from home, my man.'

'Don't I fucking know it. I've a message for you. Nicomo demands your presence.'

The good humour drained from the room quick as blood from a slit throat. 'Where?'

'The usual place.'

'Demands, does he?' A couple of Sajaam's people were moving away from the walls, hands creeping in the shadows. 'Awfully bold of him. And why would my old friend Nicomo send a big white Northman with a blade to talk to me?' It came to Shivers about then that, for reasons unknown, the woman might've landed him right in the shit. Clearly she weren't this Nicomo character. But he'd swallowed his fill of scorn these last few weeks, and the dead could have him before he tongued up any more.

'Ask him yourself. I didn't come here to swap questions, old man. Nicomo demands your presence in the usual place, and that's all. Now get off your fat black arse before I lose my temper.'

There was a long and ugly pause, while everyone had a think about that.

'I like it,' grunted Sajaam. 'You like that?' he asked one of his thugs.

'It's alright, I guess, if that style o' thing appeals.'

'On occasion. Large words and bluster and hairy-chested manliness. Too much gets boring with great speed, but a little can sometimes make me smile. So Nicomo demands my presence, does he?'

'He does,' said Shivers, no choice but to let the current drag him where it pleased, and hope to wash up whole.

'Well, then.' The old man tossed his cards down on the table and slowly stood. 'Let it never be said old Sajaam reneged on a debt. If Nicomo is calling . . . the usual place it is.' He pushed the knife Shivers had brought through his belt. 'I'll keep hold of this though, hmmm? Just for the moment.'

It was late when they got to the place the woman had showed him and the rotten garden was dark as a cellar. Far as Shivers could tell it was empty as one too. Just torn papers twitching on the night air, old news hanging from the slimy bricks.

'Well?' snapped Sajaam. 'Where's Cosca?'

'Said she'd be here,' Shivers muttered, half to himself.

'She?' His hand was on the hilt of the knife. 'What the hell are you—'

'Over here, you old prick.' She slid out from behind a tree-trunk and into a scrap of light, hood back. Now Shivers saw her clearly, she was even finer-looking than he'd thought, and harder-looking too. Very fine, and very hard, with a sharp red line down the side of her neck, like the scars you see on hanged men. She had this frown – brows drawn in hard, lips pressed tight, eyes narrowed and fixed in front. Like she'd decided to break a door down with her head, and didn't care a shit for the results.

Sajaam's face had gone slack as a soaked shirt. 'You're alive.'

'Still sharp as ever, eh?'

'But I heard—'

'No.'

Didn't take long for the old man to scrape himself together. 'You shouldn't be in Talins, Murcatto. You shouldn't be within a hundred miles of Talins. Most of all, you shouldn't be within a hundred miles of me.' He cursed in some language Shivers didn't know, then tipped his face back towards the dark sky. 'God, God, why could you not have sent me an honest life to lead?'

The woman snorted. 'Because you haven't the guts for it. That and you like money too much.'

'All true, regrettably.' They might've talked like old friends, but Sajaam's hand hadn't left the knife. 'What do you want?'

'Your help killing some men.'

'The Butcher of Caprile needs my help killing, eh? As long as none of them are too close to Duke Orso—'

'He'll be the last.'

'Oh, you mad bitch.' Sajaam slowly shook his head. 'How you love to test me, Monzcarro. How you always loved to test us all. You'll never do it. Never, not if you wait until the sun burns out.'

'What if I could, though? Don't tell me it hasn't been your fondest wish all these years.'

'All these years when you were spreading fire and murder across Styria in his name? Happy to take his orders and his coin, lick his arse like a puppy dog with a new bone? Is it those years you mean? I don't recall you offering your shoulder for me to weep upon.'

'He killed Benna.'

'Is that so? The bills said Duke Rogont's agents got you both.' Sajaam was pointing out some old papers stirring on the wall behind her shoulder. A woman's face on 'em, and a man's. Shivers realised, and with a sharp sinking in his gut, the woman's face was hers. 'Killed by the League of Eight. Everyone was so very upset.'

'I'm in no mood for jokes, Sajaam.'

'When were you ever? But it's no joke. You were a hero round these parts. That's what they call you when you kill so many people the word murderer falls short. Orso gave the big speech, said we all had to fight harder than ever to avenge you, and everyone wept. I am sorry about Benna. I always liked the boy. But I made peace with my devils. You should do the same.'

'The dead can forgive. The dead can be forgiven. The rest of us have better things to do. I want your help, and I'm owed. Pay up, bastard.'

They frowned at each other for a long moment. Then the old man heaved up a long sigh. 'I always said you'd be the death of me. What's your price?'

'A point in the right direction. An introduction here or there. That's what you do, now, isn't it?'

'I know some people.'

'Then I need to borrow a man with a cold head and a good arm. A man who won't get flustered at blood spilled.'

Sajaam seemed to think about that. Then he turned his head and called over his shoulder. 'You know a man like that, Friendly?'

Footsteps scraped out of the darkness from the way Shivers had come. Seemed there'd been someone following them, and doing it well. The woman slid into a fighting crouch, eyes narrowed, left hand on her sword hilt. Shivers would've reached for a weapon too, if he'd had one, but he'd sold all his own in Uffrith and given the knife over to Sajaam. So he settled for a nervous twitching of his fingers, which wasn't a scrap of use to anyone.

The new arrival trudged up, stooped over, eyes down. He was a half-head or more shorter than Shivers but had a fearsome solid look to him, thick neck wider than his skull, heavy hands dangling from the sleeves of a heavy coat.

'Friendly,' Sajaam was all smiles at the surprise he'd pulled, 'this is an old friend of mine, name of Murcatto. You're going to work for her a while, if you have no objection.' The man shrugged his weighty shoulders. 'What did you say your name was, again?'

'Shivers.'

Friendly's eyes flickered up, then back to the floor, and stayed there. Sad eyes and strange. Silence for a moment.

'Is he a good man?' asked Murcatto.

'This is the best man I know of. Or the worst, if you stand on his wrong side. I met him in Safety.'

'What had he done to be locked in there with the likes of you?'

'Everything and more.'

More silence. 'For a man called Friendly, he's not got much to say.'

'My very thoughts when I first met him,' said Sajaam. 'I suspect the name was meant with some irony.'

'Irony? In a prison?'

'All kinds of people end up in prison. Some of us even have a sense of humour.'

'If you say so. I'll take some husk as well.'

'You? More your brother's style, no? What do you want husk for?'

'When did you start asking your customers why they want your goods, old man?'

'Fair point.' He pulled something from his pocket, tossed it to her and she snatched it out of the air.

'I'll let you know when I need something else.'

'I shall tick off the hours! I always swore you'd be the death of me, Monzcarro.' Sajaam turned away. 'The death of me.'

Shivers stepped in front of him. 'My knife.' He didn't understand the fine points of what he'd heard, but he could tell when he was caught up in something dark and bloody. Something where he was likely to need a good blade.

'My pleasure.' Sajaam slapped it back into Shivers' palm, and it weighed heavy there. 'Though I advise you to find a larger blade if you plan on sticking with her.' He glanced round at them, slowly shaking his head. 'You three heroes, going to put an end to Duke Orso? When they kill you, do me a favour? Die quickly and keep my name out of it.' And with that cheery thought he ambled off into the night.

When Shivers turned back, the woman called Murcatto was looking him right in the eye. 'What about you? Fishing's a bastard of a living. Almost as hard as farming, and even worse-smelling.' She held out her gloved hand and silver glinted in the palm. 'I can still use another man. You want to take your scale? Or you want fifty more?'

Shivers frowned down at that shining metal. He'd killed men

for a lot less, when he thought about it. Battles, feuds, fights, in all settings and all weathers. But he'd had reasons, then. Not good ones, always, but something to make it some kind of right. Never just murder, blood bought and paid for.

'This man we're going to kill . . . what did he do?'

'He got me to pay fifty scales for his corpse. Isn't that enough?'

'Not for me.'

She frowned at him for a long moment. That straight-ahead look that was already giving him the worries, somehow. 'So you're one of them, eh?'

'One o' what?'

'One of those men that like reasons. That need excuses. You're a dangerous crowd, you lot. Hard to predict.' She shrugged. 'But if it helps. He killed my brother.'

Shivers blinked. Hearing those words, from her mouth, brought that day right back somehow, sharper than he'd remembered it for years. Seeing his father's grey face, and knowing. Hearing his brother was killed, when he'd been promised mercy. Swearing vengeance over the ashes in the long hall, tears in his eyes. An oath he'd chosen to break, so he could walk away from blood and be a better man.

And here she was, out of nowhere, offering him another chance at vengeance. He killed my brother. Felt as if he would've said no to anything else. But maybe he just needed the money.

'Shit on it, then,' he said. 'Give me the fifty.'

Six and One

The dice came up six and one. The highest dice can roll and the lowest. A fitting judgement on Friendly's life. The pit of horror to the heights of triumph. And back.

Six and one made seven. Seven years old, when Friendly committed his first crime. But six years later that he was first caught, and given his first sentence. When they first wrote his name in the big book, and he earned his first days in Safety. Stealing, he knew, but he could hardly remember what he stole. He certainly could not remember why. His parents had worked hard to give him all he needed. And yet he stole. Some men are born to do wrong, perhaps. The judges had told him so.

He scooped the dice up, rattled them in his fist, then let them free across the stones again, watched them as they tumbled. Always that same joy, that anticipation. Dice just thrown can be anything until they stop rolling. He watched them turning, chances, odds, his life and the life of the Northman. All the lives in the great city of Talins turning with them.

Six and one.

Friendly smiled, a little. The odds of throwing six and one a second time were one in eighteen. Long odds, some would say, looking forward into the future. But looking into the past, as he was now, there was no chance of any other numbers. What was coming? Always full of possibilities. What was past? Done, and hardened, like dough turned to bread. There was no going back.

'What do the dice say?'

Friendly glanced up as he gathered the dice with the edge of his hand. He was a big man, this Shivers, but with none of that stringiness tall men sometimes get. Strong. But not like a farmer, or a labourer. Not slow. He understood the work. There were clues, and Friendly knew them all. In Safety, you have to reckon

61

the threat a man poses in a moment. Reckon it, and deal with it, and never blink.

A soldier, maybe, and fought in battles, by his scars, and the set of his face, and the look in his eye as they waited to do violence. Not comfortable, but ready. Not likely to run or get carried away. They are rare, men that keep a sharp head when the trouble starts. There was a scar on his thick left wrist that, if you looked at it a certain way, was like the number seven. Seven was a good number today.

'Dice say nothing. They are dice.'

'Why roll 'em, then?'

'They are dice. What else would I do with them?'

Friendly closed his eyes, closed his fist around the dice and pressed them to his cheek, feeling their warm, rounded edges against his palm. What numbers did they hold for him now, waiting to be released? Six and one again? A flicker of excitement. The odds of throwing six and one for a third time were three hundred and twenty-four to one. Three hundred and twenty-four was the number of cells in Safety. A good omen.

'They're here,' whispered the Northman.

There were four of them. Three men and a whore. Friendly could hear the vague tinkling of her night-bell on the chill air, one of the men laughing. They were drunk, shapeless outlines lurching down the darkened alley. The dice would have to wait.

He sighed, wrapped them carefully in their soft cloth, once, twice, three times, and he tucked them up tight, safe into the darkness of his inside pocket. He wished that he was tucked up tight, safe in the darkness, but things were what they were. There was no going back. He stood and brushed the street scum from his knees.

'What's the plan?' asked Shivers.

Friendly shrugged. 'Six and one.'

He pulled his hood up and started walking, hunched over, hands thrust into his pockets. Light from a high window cut across the group as they came closer. Four grotesque carnival masks, leering with drunken laughter. The big man in the centre had a soft face with sharp little eyes and a greedy grin. The painted woman tottered on her high shoes beside him. The man on the left smirked across at her, lean and bearded. The one on the right was wiping a tear of happiness from his grey cheek.

'Then what?' he shrieked through his gurgling, far louder than there was a need for.

'What d'you think? I kicked him 'til he shat himself.' More gales of laughter, the woman's falsetto tittering a counterpoint to the big man's bass. 'I said, Duke Orso likes men who say yes, you lying—'

'Gobba?' asked Friendly.

His head snapped round, smile fading from his soft face. Friendly stopped. He had taken forty-one steps from the place where he rolled the dice. Six and one made seven. Seven times six was forty-two. Take away the one . . .

'Who're you?' growled Gobba.

'Six and one.'

'What?' The man on the right made to shove Friendly away with a drunken arm. 'Get out of it, you mad fu—'

The cleaver split his head open to the bridge of his nose. Before his mate on the left's mouth had fallen all the way open, Friendly was across the road and stabbing him in the body. Five times the long knife punched him through the guts, then Friendly stepped back and slashed his throat on the backhand, kicked his legs away and brought him tumbling to the cobbles.

There was a moment's pause as Friendly breathed out, long and slow. The first man had the single great wound yawning in his skull, a black splatter of brains smeared over his crossed eyes. The other had the five stab wounds in his body, and blood pouring from his cut throat.

'Good,' said Friendly. 'Six and one.'

The whore started screaming, spots of dark blood across one powdered cheek.

'You're a dead man!' roared Gobba, taking a stumbling step back, fumbling a bright knife from his belt. 'I'll kill you!' But he did not come on.

'When?' asked Friendly, blades hanging loose from his hands. 'Tomorrow?'

'I'll—'

Shivers' stick cracked down on the back of Gobba's skull. A good blow, right on the best spot, crumpling his knees easily as paper. He flopped down, slack cheek thumping against the cobbles, knife clattering from his limp fist, out cold.

'Not tomorrow. Not ever.' The woman's shriek sputtered out. Friendly turned his eyes on her. 'Why aren't you running?' She fled into the darkness, teetering on her high shoes, whimpering breath echoing down the street, her night-bell jangling after.

Shivers frowned down at the two leaking corpses in the road. The two pools of blood worked their way along the cracks between the cobblestones, touched, mingled and became one. 'By the dead,' he muttered in his Northern tongue.

Friendly shrugged. 'Welcome to Styria.'

Bloody Instructions

Monza stared down at her gloved hand, lips curled back hard from her teeth, and flexed the three fingers that still worked – in and out, in and out, gauging the pattern of clicks and crunches that came with every closing of her fist. She felt oddly calm considering that her life, if you could call it a life, was balanced on a razor's edge.

Never trust a man beyond his own interests, Verturio wrote, and the murder of Grand Duke Orso and his closest was no one's idea of an easy job. She couldn't trust this silent convict any further than she could trust Sajaam, and that was about as far as she could piss. She had a creeping feeling the Northman was halfway honest, but she'd thought that about Orso, with results that had hardly been happy. It would've been no great surprise to her if they'd brought Gobba in smiling, ready to drag her back to Fontezarmo so they could drop her down the mountain a second time.

She couldn't trust anyone. But she couldn't do it alone.

Hurried footsteps scuffled up outside. The door banged open and three men came through. Shivers was on the right, Friendly on the left. Gobba hung between them, head dangling, an arm over each of their shoulders, his boot-toes scraping through the sawdust scattered across the ground. So it seemed she could trust the pair of them this far, at least.

Friendly dragged Gobba to the anvil – a mass of scarred black iron bolted down in the centre of the floor. Shivers had a length of chain, a manacle on each end, looping it round and round the base. All the while he had this fixed frown. As if he'd got some morals, and they were stinging.

Nice things, morals, but prone to chafe at times like this.

The two men worked well together for a beggar and a convict. No time or movement wasted. No sign of nerves, given they were going about a murder. But then Monza had always had a knack for picking the right men for a job. Friendly snapped the manacles shut on the bodyguard's thick wrists. Shivers reached out and turned the knob on the lamp, the flame fluttering up behind the glass, light spilling out around the grubby forge.

'Wake him up.'

Friendly flung a bucket of water in Gobba's face. He coughed, dragged in a breath, shook his head, drops flicking from his hair. He tried to stand and the chain rattled, snatching him back down. He glared around, little eyes hard.

'You stupid bastards! You're dead men, the pair of you! Dead! Don't you know who I am? Don't you know who I work for?'

'I know.' Monza did her best to walk smoothly, the way she used to, but couldn't quite manage it. She limped into the light, pushing back her hood.

Gobba's fat face crinkled up. 'No. Can't be.' His eyes went wide. Then wider still. Shock, then fear, then horror. He lurched back, chains clinking. 'No!'

'Yes.' And she smiled, in spite of the pain. 'How fucked are you? You've put weight on, Gobba. More than I've lost, even. Funny, how things go. Is that my stone you've got there?'

He had the ruby on his little finger, red glimmer on black iron. Friendly reached down, twisted it off and tossed it over to her. She snatched it out of the air with her left hand. Benna's last gift. The one they'd smiled at together as they rode up the mountain to see Duke Orso. The thick band was scratched, bent a little, but the stone still sparkled bloodily as ever, the colour of a slit throat.

'Somewhat damaged when you tried to kill me, eh, Gobba? But weren't we all?' It took her a while to fumble it onto her left middle finger, but in the end she twisted it past the knuckle. 'Fits this hand just as well. Piece of luck, that.'

'Look! We can make a deal!' There was sweat beading Gobba's face now. 'We can work something out!'

'I already did. Don't have a mountain to hand, I'm afraid.' She slid the hammer from the shelf – a short-hafted lump hammer with a block of heavy steel for a head – and felt her knuckles shift as she closed her gloved hand tight around it. 'So I'm going to break you apart with this, instead. Hold him, would you?' Friendly folded Gobba's right arm and forced it onto the anvil, clawing fingers spread out pale on the dark metal. 'You should've made sure of me.'

'Orso'll find out! He'll find out!'

'Of course he will. When I throw him off his own terrace, if not before.'

'You'll never do it! He'll kill you!'

'He already did, remember? It didn't stick.'

Veins stood out on Gobba's neck as he struggled, but Friendly had him fast, for all his bulk. 'You can't beat him!'

'Maybe not. I suppose we'll see. There's only one thing I can tell you for sure.' She raised the hammer high. 'You won't.'

The head came down on his knuckles with a faintly metallic crunch – once, twice, three times. Each blow jarred her hand, sent pain shooting up her arm. But a lot less pain than shot up Gobba's. He gasped, yelped, trembled, Friendly's slack face pressed up against his taut one. Gobba jerked back from the anvil, his hand turning sideways on. Monza felt herself grinning as the hammer hissed down and crushed it flat. The next blow caught his wrist and turned it black.

'Looks worse even than mine did.' She shrugged. 'Well. When you pay a debt, it's only good manners to add some interest. Get the other hand.'

'No!' squealed Gobba, dribbling spit. 'No! Think of my children!'

'Think of my brother!'

The hammer smashed his other hand apart. She aimed each blow carefully, taking her time, both eyes on the details. Finger-tips. Fingers. Knuckles. Thumb. Palm. Wrist.

'Six and six,' grunted Friendly, over Gobba's roars of pain.

The blood was surging in Monza's ears. She wasn't sure she'd heard him right. 'Eh?'

'Six times, and six times.' He let go of Orso's bodyguard and stood, brushing his palms together. 'With the hammer.'

'And?' she snapped at him, no clue how that mattered.

Gobba was bent over the anvil, legs braced, dragging on the manacles and spraying spit as he tried vainly to shift the great thing with all his strength, blackened hands flopping.

She leaned towards him. 'Did I tell you to get up?' The hammer split his kneecap with a sharp bang. He crumpled onto the floor on his back, was dragging in the air to scream when the hammer crunched into his leg again and snapped it back the wrong way.

'Hard work, this.' She winced at a twinge in her shoulder as she dragged her coat off. 'But then I'm not as limber as I was.' She rolled her black shirtsleeve up past the long scar on her forearm. 'You always did tell me you knew how to make a woman sweat, eh, Gobba? And to think I laughed at you.' She wiped her face on the back of her arm. 'Shows you what I know. Unhook him.'

'You sure?' asked Friendly.

'Worried he'll bite your ankles? Let's make a chase of it.' The convict shrugged, then leaned down to unlock the cuffs around Gobba's wrists. Shivers was frowning at her from the darkness. 'Something wrong?' she snapped at him.

He stayed silent.

Gobba dragged himself to nowhere through the dirty sawdust with his elbows, broken leg slithering along behind. He made a kind of mindless groan while he did it. Something like the ones she'd made when she lay broken at the foot of the mountain beneath Fontezarmo.

'Huuuurrrrhhhh . . .'

Monza wasn't enjoying this half as much as she'd hoped, and it was making her angrier than ever. Something about those groans was intensely annoying. Her hand was pulsing with pain. She forced a smile onto her face and limped after him, pretended to enjoy it more.

'I've got to say I'm disappointed. Didn't Orso always like to boast about what a hard man he had for a bodyguard? I suppose now we'll find out how hard you really are. Softer than this hammer, I'd—'

Her foot slipped and she yelped as she went over on her ankle, tottered against the brick-lined side of a furnace, put her left hand down to steady herself. It took her a moment to realise the thing was still scalding hot.

'Shit!' Stumbling back the other way like a clown, kicking a bucket and sending dirty water showering up the side of her leg. 'Fuck!'

She leaned down over Gobba and lashed petulantly at him with the hammer, suddenly, stupidly angry she'd embarrassed herself. 'Bastard! Bastard!' He grunted and gurgled as the steel head thudded into his ribs. He tried to curl up and half-dragged her over on top of him, twisting her leg.

Pain lanced up her hip and made her screech. She dug at the side of his head with the haft of the hammer until she'd torn his ear half-off. Shivers took a step forwards but she'd already wrenched herself free. Gobba blubbered, somehow dragged himself up to sitting, back against a big water butt. His hands had swollen up to twice the size they had been. Purple, flopping mittens.

'Beg!' she hissed. 'Beg, you fat fucker!'

But Gobba was too busy staring at the mincemeat on the end of his arms, and screaming. Hoarse, short, slobbery screams.

'Someone might hear.' Friendly looked like he didn't care much either way.

'Better shut him up, then.'

The convict leaned over the barrel from behind with a wire between his fists, hooked Gobba under the neck and dragged him up hard, cutting his bellows down to slippery splutters.

Monza squatted in front of him so their faces were level, her knees burning as she watched the wire cut into his fat neck. Just the way it had cut into hers. The scars it had left on her itched. 'How does it feel?' Her eyes flickered over his face, trying to squeeze some sliver of satisfaction from it. 'How does it feel?' Though no one knew better than her. Gobba's eyes bulged, his jowls trembled, turning from pink, to red, to purple. She pushed herself up to standing. 'I'd say it's a waste of good flesh. But it isn't.'

She closed her eyes and let her head drop back, sucked a long breath in through her nose as she tightened her grip on the hammer, lifted it high.

'Betray me and leave me alive?'

It came down between Gobba's piggy eyes with a sharp bang like a stone slab splitting. His back arched, his mouth yawned wide but no sound came out.

'Take my hand and leave me alive?'

The hammer hit him in the nose and caved his face in like a broken egg. His body crumpled, shattered leg jerking, jerking.

'Kill my brother and leave me alive?'

The last blow broke his skull wide open. Black blood bubbled down his purple skin. Friendly let go the wire and Gobba slid sideways. Gently, gracefully almost, he rolled over onto his front, and was still.

Dead. You didn't have to be an expert to see that. Monza winced as she forced her aching fingers open and the hammer clattered down, its head gleaming red, a clump of hair stuck to one corner.

One dead. Six left.

'Six and one,' she muttered to herself. Friendly stared at her, eyes wide, and she wasn't sure why.

'What's it like?' Shivers, watching her from the shadows.

'What?'

'Revenge. Does it feel good?'

Monza wasn't sure she felt much of anything beyond the pain pulsing through her burned hand and her broken hand, up her legs and through her skull. Benna was still dead, she was still broken. She stood there frowning, and didn't answer.

'You want me to get rid of this?' Friendly waved an arm at the corpse, a heavy cleaver gleaming in his other hand.

'Make sure he won't be found.'

Friendly grabbed Gobba's ankle and started dragging him back towards the anvil, leaving a bloody trail through the sawdust. 'Chop him up. Into the sewers. Rats can have him.'

'Better than he deserves.' But Monza felt the slightest bit sick. She needed a smoke. Getting to that time of day. A smoke would settle her nerves. She pulled out a small purse, the one with fifty scales in it, and tossed it to Shivers.

Coins snapped together inside as he caught it. 'That's it?'

'That's it.'

'Right.' He paused, as though he wanted to say something but couldn't think what. 'Sorry about your brother.'

She looked at his face in the lamplight. Really looking, trying to guess him out. He knew next to nothing about her or Orso. Next to nothing about anything, at a first glance. But he could fight, she'd seen that. He'd walked into Sajaam's place alone, and that took courage. A man with courage, with morals, maybe. A man with pride. That meant he might have some loyalty too, if she could get a grip on it. And loyal men were a rare commodity in Styria.

She'd never spent much time alone. Benna had always been beside her. Or behind her, at any rate. 'You're sorry.'

'That's right. I had a brother.' He started to turn for the door.

'You need more work?' She kept her eyes fixed on his as she came forwards, and while she did it she slid her good hand around behind her back and found the handle of the knife there. He knew her name, and Orso's, and Sajaam's, and that was enough to get them all killed ten times over. One way or another, he had to stay.

'More work like this?' He frowned down at the bloodstained sawdust under her boots.

'Killing. You can say it.' She thought about whether to stab him down into the chest or up under the jaw, or wait until he'd turned and take his back. 'What did you think it'd be? Milking a goat?'

He shook his head, long hair swaying. 'Might sound foolish to you, but I came here to be a better man. You got your reasons, sure, but this feels like a bastard of a stride in the wrong direction.'

'Six more men.'

'No. No. I'm done.' As if he was trying to convince himself. 'I don't care how much—'

'Five thousand scales.'

His mouth was already open to say no again, but this time the word didn't come. He stared at her. Shocked at first, then thoughtful. Working out how much money that really was. What it might buy him. Monza had always had a knack for reckoning a man's price. Every man has one.

She took a step forwards, looking up into his face. 'You're a good man, I see that, and a hard man too. That's the kind of man I need.' She let her eyes flick down to his mouth, and then back up. 'Help me. I need your help, and you need my money. Five thousand scales. Lot easier to be a better man with that much money behind you. Help me. I daresay you could buy half the North with that. Make a king of yourself.'

'Who says I want to be a king?'

'Be a queen, if you please. I can tell you what you won't be doing, though.' She leaned in, so close she was almost breathing on his neck. 'Begging for work. You ask me, it's not right, a proud man like you in that state. Still.' And she looked away. 'I can't force you.'

He stood there, weighing the purse. But she'd already taken her hand off her knife. She already knew his answer. *Money is a different thing to every man*, Bialoveld wrote, *but always a good thing.*

When he looked up his face had turned hard. 'Who do we kill?'

The time was she'd have smirked sideways to see Benna smirking back at her. *We won again.* But Benna was dead, and Monza's thoughts were on the next man to join him. 'A banker.'

'A what?'

'A man who counts money.'

'He makes money counting money?'

'That's right.'

'Some strange fashions you folk have down here. What did he do?'

'He killed my brother.'

'More vengeance, eh?'

'More vengeance.'

Shivers gave a nod. 'Reckon I'm hired, then. What do you need?'

'Give Friendly a hand taking out the rubbish, then we're gone tonight. No point loitering in Talins.'

Shivers looked towards the anvil, and he took a sharp breath. Then he pulled out the knife she'd given him, walked over to where Friendly was starting work on Gobba's corpse.

Monza looked down at her left hand, rubbed a few specks of blood from the back. Her fingers were trembling some. From killing a man earlier, from not killing one just now, or from needing a smoke, she wasn't sure.

All three, maybe.

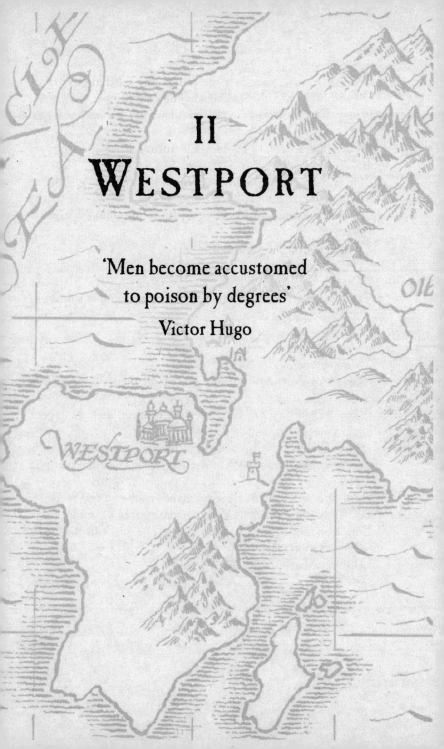

II
WESTPORT

'Men become accustomed
to poison by degrees'

Victor Hugo

The first year they were always hungry, and Benna had to beg in the village while Monza worked the ground and scavenged in the woods.

The second year they took a better harvest, and grew roots in a patch by the barn, and got some bread from old Destort the miller when the snows swept in and turned the valley into a place of white silence.

The third year the weather was fine, and the rain came on time, and Monza raised a good crop in the upper field. As good a crop as her father had ever brought in. Prices were high because of troubles over the border. They would have money, and the roof could be mended, and Benna could have a proper shirt. Monza watched the wind make waves in the wheat, and she felt that pride at having made something with her own hands. That pride her father used to talk about.

A few days before reaping time, she woke in the darkness and heard sounds. She shook Benna from his sleep beside her, one hand over his mouth. She took her father's sword, eased open the shutters, and together they stole through the window and into the woods, hid in the brambles behind a tree-trunk.

There were black figures in front of the house, torches flickering in the darkness.

'Who are they?'

'Shhhh.'

She heard them break the door down, heard them crashing through the house and the barn.

'What do they want?'

'Shhhh.'

They spread out around the field and set their torches to it, and the fire ate through the wheat until it was a roaring blaze. She heard someone cheering. Another laughing.

75

Benna stared, face dim-lit with shifting orange, tear-tracks glistening on his thin cheeks. 'But why would they . . . why would they . . . ?'

'Shhhh.'

Monza watched the smoke rolling up into the clear night. All her work. All her sweat and pain. She stayed there long after the men had gone, and watched it burn.

In the morning more men came. Folk from around the valley, hard-faced and vengeful, old Destort at their head with a sword at his hip and his three sons behind him.

'Came through here too then, did they? You're lucky to be alive. They killed Crevi and his wife, up the valley. Their son too.'

'What are you going to do?'

'We're going to track them, then we're going to hang them.'

'We'll come.'

'You might be better—'

'We'll come.'

Destort had not always been a miller, and he knew his business. They caught up with the raiders the next night, working their way back south, camped around fires in the woods without even a proper guard. More thieves than soldiers. Farmers among them too, just from one side of the border rather than the other, chosen to settle some made-up grievance while their lords were busy settling theirs.

'Anyone ain't ready to kill best stay here.' Destort drew his sword and the others made their cleavers, and their axes, and their make-shift spears ready.

'Wait!' hissed Benna, clinging at Monza's arm.

'No.'

She ran quiet and low, her father's sword in her hand, fires dancing through the black trees. She heard a cry, a clash of metal, the sound of a bowstring.

She came out from the bushes. Two men crouched by a campfire, a pot steaming over it. One had a thick beard, a wood-axe in his fist. Before he lifted it halfway Monza slashed him across the eyes and he fell down, screaming. The other turned to run and she spitted him through the back before he got a stride. The bearded man roared and roared, hands clutching at his face. She stabbed him in the chest, and he groaned out a few wet breaths, then stopped.

She frowned down at the two corpses while the sounds of fighting

76

slowly petered out. Benna crept from the trees, and he took the bearded man's purse from his belt, and he tipped a heavy wedge of silver coins out into his palm.

'He has seventeen scales.'

It was twice as much as the whole crop had been worth. He held the other man's purse out to her, eyes wide. 'This one has thirty.'

'Thirty?' Monza looked at the blood on her father's sword, and thought how strange it was that she was a murderer now. How strange it was that it had been so easy to do. Easier than digging in the stony soil for a living. Far, far easier. Afterwards, she waited for the remorse to come upon her. She waited for a long time.

It never came.

Poison

I t was just the kind of afternoon that Morveer most enjoyed. Crisp, even chilly, but perfectly still, immaculately clear. The bright sun flashed through the bare black branches of the fruit trees, found rare gold among dull copper tripod, rods and screws, struck priceless sparks from the tangle of misted glassware. There was nothing finer than working out of doors on a day like this, with the added advantage that any lethal vapours released would harmlessly dissipate. Persons in Morveer's profession were all too frequently despatched by their own agents, after all, and he had no intention of becoming one of their number. Quite apart from anything else, his reputation would never recover.

Morveer smiled upon the rippling lamp flame, nodded in time to the gentle rattling of condenser and retort, the soothing hiss of escaping steam, the industrious pop and bubble of boiling reagents. As the drawing of the blade to the master swordsman, as the jingle of coins to the master merchant, so were these sounds to Morveer. The sounds of his work well done. It was with comfortable satisfaction, therefore, that he watched Day's face, creased with concentration, through the distorting glass of the tapered collection flask.

It was a pretty face, undoubtedly: heart-shaped and fringed with blonde curls. But it was an unremarkable and entirely unthreatening variety of prettiness, further softened by a disarming aura of innocence. A face that would attract a positive response, but excite little further comment. A face that would easily slip the mind. It was for her face, above all, that Morveer had selected her. He did nothing by accident.

A jewel of moisture formed at the utmost end of the condenser. It stretched, bloated, then finally tore itself free, tumbled sparkling through space and fell silently to the bottom of the flask.

'Excellent,' muttered Morveer.

More droplets swelled and broke away in solemn procession. The last of them clung reluctantly at the edge, and Day reached out and gently flicked the glassware. It fell, and joined the rest, and looked, for all the world, like a little water in the bottom of a flask. Barely enough to wet one's lips.

'And carefully, now, my dear, so very, *very* carefully. Your life hangs by a filament. Your life, and mine too.'

She pressed her tongue into her lower lip, ever so carefully twisted the condenser free and set it down on the tray. The rest of the apparatus followed, piece by slow piece. She had fine, soft hands, Morveer's apprentice. Nimble yet steady, as indeed they were required to be. She pressed a cork carefully into the flask and held it up to the light, the sunshine making liquid diamonds of that tiny dribble of fluid, and she smiled. An innocent, a pretty, yet an entirely forgettable smile. 'It doesn't look much.'

'That is the *entire* point. It is without colour, odour or taste. And yet the most infinitesimal drop consumed, the softest mist inhaled, the gentlest touch upon the skin, even, will kill a man in minutes. There is no antidote, no remedy, no immunity. Truly . . . this is the King of Poisons.'

'The King of Poisons,' she breathed, with suitable awe.

'Keep this knowledge close to your heart, my dear, to be used only in the *extreme* of need. Only against the most dangerous, suspicious and cunning of targets. Only against those *intimately* acquainted with the poisoner's art.'

'I understand. Caution first, always.'

'Very good. That is the most valuable of lessons.' Morveer sat back in his chair, making a steeple of his fingers. 'Now you know the deepest of my secrets. Your apprenticeship is over, but . . . I hope you will continue, as my assistant.'

'I'd be honoured to stay in your service. I still have much to learn.'

'So do we all, my dear.' Morveer jerked his head up at the sound of the gate bell tinkling in the distance. 'So do we *all*.'

Two figures were approaching the house down the long path through the orchard, and Morveer snapped open his eyeglass and

79

trained it upon them. A man and a woman. He was very tall, and powerful-looking with it, wearing a threadbare coat, long hair swaying. A Northman, from his appearance.

'A primitive,' he muttered, under his breath. Such men were prone to savagery and superstition, and he held them in healthy contempt.

He trained the eyeglass on the woman, now, though she was dressed much like a man. She looked straight towards the house, unwavering. Straight towards him, it almost seemed. A beautiful face, without doubt, edged with coal-black hair. But it was a hard and unsettling variety of beauty, further sharpened by a brooding appearance of grim purpose. A face that at once issued a challenge and a threat. A face that, having been glimpsed, one would not quickly forget. She did not compare with Morveer's mother in beauty, of course, but who could? His mother had almost transcended the human in her goodly qualities. Her pure smile, kissed by the sunlight, was etched for ever into Morveer's memory as if it were a—

'Visitors?' asked Day.

'The Murcatto woman is here.' He snapped his fingers towards the table. 'Clear all this away. With the *very* greatest care, mark you! Then bring wine and cakes.'

'Do you want anything in them?'

'Only plums and apricots. I mean to welcome my guests, not kill them.' Not until he had heard what they had to say, at least.

While Day swiftly cleared the table, furnished it with a cloth and drew the chairs back in around it, Morveer took some elementary precautions. Then he arranged himself in his chair, highly polished knee-boots crossed in front of him and hands clasped across his chest, very much the country gentleman enjoying the winter air of his estate. Had he not earned it, after all?

He rose with his most ingratiating smile as his visitors came in close proximity to the house. The Murcatto woman walked with the slightest hint of a limp. She covered it well, but over long years in the trade Morveer had sharpened his perceptions to a razor point, and missed no detail. She wore a sword on her right hip, and it appeared to be a good one, but he paid it little mind. Ugly, unsophisticated tools. Gentlemen might wear them, but only the coarse and wrathful would stoop to actually use one. She wore a glove on her right hand, suggesting she had something she was keen to hide, because her left was bare, and sported a blood-red stone big as his thumbnail. If it was, as it certainly appeared to be, a ruby, it was one of promisingly great value.

'I am—'

'You are Monzcarro Murcatto, once captain general of the Thousand Swords, recently in the service of Duke Orso of Talins.' Morveer thought it best to avoid that gloved hand, and so he offered out his left, palm upwards, in a gesture replete with humbleness and submission. 'A Kantic gentleman of our mutual acquaintance, one Sajaam, told me to expect your visit.' She gave it a brief shake, firm and businesslike. 'And your name, my friend?' Morveer leaned unctuously forwards and folded the Northman's big right hand in both of his.

'Caul Shivers.'

'Indeed, indeed, I have always found your Northern names *delightfully* picturesque.'

'You've found 'em what now?'

'Nice.'

'Oh.'

Morveer held his hand a moment longer, then let it free. '*Pray* have a seat.' He smiled upon Murcatto as she worked her way into her chair, the barest phantom of a grimace on her face. 'I must confess I was expecting you to be considerably less beautiful.'

She frowned at that. 'I was expecting you to be less friendly.'

'Oh, I can be *decidedly* unfriendly when it is called for, believe me.' Day silently appeared and slid a plate of sweet cakes onto the table, a tray with a bottle of wine and glasses. 'But it is hardly called for now, is it? Wine?'

His visitors exchanged a loaded glance. Morveer grinned as he pulled the cork and poured himself a glass. 'The two of you are mercenaries, but I can only assume you do not rob, threaten and extort from *everyone* you meet. Likewise, I do not poison my every acquaintance.' He slurped wine noisily, as though to advertise the total safety of the operation. 'Who would pay me then? You are safe.'

'Even so, you'll forgive us if we pass.'

Day reached for a cake. 'Can I—'

'Gorge yourself.' Then to Murcatto. 'You did not come here for my wine, then.'

'No. I have work for you.'

Morveer examined his cuticles. 'The deaths of Grand Duke Orso and sundry others, I presume.' She sat in silence, but it suited him to speak as though she had demanded an explanation. 'It scarcely requires a towering intellect to make the deduction. Orso declares you and your brother killed by agents of the League of Eight. Then I hear from your friend and mine Sajaam that you are less deceased than advertised. Since there has been no tearful reunion with Orso, no happy declaration of your miraculous survival, we can assume the Osprian assassins were in fact . . . *a fantasy*. The Duke of Talins is a man of notoriously jealous temper, and your many victories made you too popular for your master's taste. Do I come close to the mark?'

'Close enough.'

'My heartfelt condolences, then. Your brother, it would appear, could not be with us, and I understood you were inseparable.' Her cold blue eyes had turned positively icy now. The Northman loomed grim and silent beside her. Morveer carefully cleared his throat. Blades might be unsophisticated tools, but a sword through the guts killed clever men every bit as thoroughly as stupid ones. 'You understand that I am the *very* best at my trade.'

'A fact,' said Day, detaching herself from her sweetmeat for a moment. 'An unchallengeable fact.'

'The many persons of quality upon whom I have utilised my skills would so testify, were they able, but, of course, they are not.'

Day sadly shook her head. 'Not a one.'

'Your point?' asked Murcatto.

'The best costs money. More money than you, having lost your employer, can, perhaps, afford.'

'You've heard of Somenu Hermon?'

'The name is familiar.'

'Not to me,' said Day.

Morveer took it upon himself to explain. 'Hermon was a destitute Kantic immigrant who rose to become, supposedly, the richest merchant in Musselia. The luxury of his lifestyle was notorious, his largesse legendary.'

'And?'

'Alas, he was in the city when the Thousand Swords, in the pay of Grand Duke Orso, captured Musselia by stealth. Loss of life was kept to a minimum, but the city was plundered, and Hermon never heard from again. Nor was his money. The assumption was that this merchant, as merchants often do, greatly exaggerated his wealth, and beyond his gaudy and glorious accoutrements possessed . . . precisely . . . *nothing*.' Morveer took a slow sip of wine, peering at Murcatto over the rim of his glass. 'But others would know far better than I. The commanders of that particular campaign were . . . what were the names now? A brother and sister . . . I believe?'

She stared straight back at him, eyes undeviating. 'Hermon was far wealthier than he pretended to be.'

'Wealthier?' Morveer wriggled in his chair. '*Wealthier?* Oh my! The advantage to Murcatto! See how I *squirm* at the mention of so infinite a sum of bountiful gold! Enough to pay my meagre fees two dozen times and more, I do not doubt! Why . . . my *overpowering* greed has left me quite . . .' He lifted his open hand and slapped it down against the table with a bang. '*Paralysed*.'

The Northman toppled slowly sideways, slid from his chair and thumped onto the patchy turf beneath the fruit trees. He rolled gently over onto his back, knees up in the air in precisely the form he had taken while sitting, body rigid as a block of wood, eyes staring helplessly upwards.

'Ah,' observed Morveer as he peered over the table. 'The advantage to Morveer, it would seem.'

Murcatto's eyes flicked sideways, then back. A flurry of twitches ran up one side of her face. Her gloved hand trembled on the tabletop by the slightest margin, and then lay still.

'It worked,' murmured Day.

'How could you doubt me?' Morveer, liking nothing better than a captive audience, could not resist explaining how it had been managed. 'Yellowseed oil was first applied to my hands.' He held them up, fingers outspread. 'In order to prevent the agent affecting me, you understand. I would not want to find myself suddenly paralysed, after all. That would be a *decidedly* unpleasant experience!' He chuckled to himself, and Day joined him at a higher pitch while she bent down to check the Northman's pulse, second cake wedged between her teeth. 'The active ingredient was a distillation of spider venom. Extremely effective, even on touch. Since I held his hand for longer, your friend has taken a much heavier dose. He'll be lucky to move today . . . if I choose to let him move again, of course. You should have retained the power of speech, however.'

'Bastard,' Murcatto grunted through frozen lips.

'I see that you have.' He rose, slipped around the table and perched himself beside her. 'I really must apologise, but you understand that I am, as you have been, a person at the precarious *summit* of my profession. We of extraordinary skills and achievements are obliged to take extraordinary precautions. Now, unimpeded by your ability to move, we can speak with absolute candour on the subject of . . . Grand Duke Orso.' He swilled around a mouthful of wine, watched a little bird flit between the branches. Murcatto said nothing, but it hardly mattered. Morveer was happy to speak for them both.

'You have been done a terrible wrong, I see that. Betrayed by a man who owed you so much. Your beloved brother killed and you rendered . . . less than you were. My own life has been *littered* with painful reverses, believe me, so I entirely empathise. But the world is brimming with the awful and we humble individuals can only alter it by . . . small degrees.' He frowned over at Day, munching noisily.

'What?' she grunted, mouth full.

'Quietly if you must, I am trying to expound.' She shrugged, licking her fingers with entirely unnecessary sucking sounds. Morveer gave a disapproving sigh. 'The carelessness of youth. She will learn. Time marches in only one direction for us all, eh, Murcatto?'

'Spare me the fucking philosophy,' she forced through tight lips.

'Let us confine ourselves to the practical, then. With your notable assistance, Orso has made himself the most powerful man in Styria. I would never pretend to have your grasp of all things military, but it scarcely takes Stolicus himself to perceive that, following your glorious victory at the High Bank last year, the League of Eight are on the verge of collapse. Only a miracle will save Visserine when summer comes. The Osprians will treat for peace or be crushed, depending on Orso's mood, which, as you know far better than most, tends towards crushings. By the close of the year, barring accidents, Styria will have a king at last. An end to the Years of Blood.' He drained his glass and waved it expansively. 'Peace and prosperity for all and sundry! A better world, surely? Unless one is a mercenary, I suppose.'

'Or a poisoner.'

'On the contrary, we find more than ample employment in peacetime too. In any case, my point is that killing Grand Duke Orso – quite apart from the apparent impossibility of the task – seems to serve nobody's interests. Not even yours. It will not bring your brother back, or your hand, or your legs.' Her face did not flicker, but that might merely have been due to paralysis. 'The attempt will more than likely end in your death, and possibly even in mine. My point is that you have to stop this madness, my *dear* Monzcarro. You have to stop it *at once*, and give it no further thought.'

Her eyes were pitiless as two pots of poison. 'Only death will stop me. Mine, or Orso's.'

'No matter the cost? No matter the pain? No matter who's killed along the path?'

'No matter,' she growled.

'I find myself *entirely* convinced as to your level of commitment.'

'Everything.' The word was a snarl.

Morveer positively beamed. 'Then we can do business. On that basis, and no other. What do I never deal in, Day?'

'Half-measures,' his assistant murmured, eyeing the one cake left on the plate.

'Correct. How many do we kill?'

'Six,' said Murcatto, 'including Orso.'

'Then my rate shall be ten thousand scales per secondary, payable upon proof of their demise, and fifty thousand for the Duke of Talins himself.'

Her face twitched slightly. 'Poor manners, to negotiate while your client is helpless.'

'Manners would be *ludicrous* in a conversation about murder. In any case, I never haggle.'

'Then we have a deal.'

'I am so glad. Antidote, please.'

Day pulled the cork from a glass jar, dipped the very point of a thin knife into the syrupy reduction in its bottom and handed it to him, polished handle first. He paused, looking into Murcatto's cold blue eyes.

Caution first, always. This woman they called the Serpent of Talins was dangerous in the extreme. If Morveer had not known it from her reputation, from their conversation, from the employment she had come to engage him for, he could have seen it at a single glance. He most seriously considered the possibility of giving her a fatal jab instead, throwing her Northern friend in the river and forgetting the whole business.

But to kill Grand Duke Orso, the most powerful man in Styria? To shape the course of history with one deft twist of his craft? For his deed, if not his name, to echo through the ages? What finer way to crown a career of achieving the impossible? The very thought made him smile the wider.

He gave a long sigh. 'I hope I will not come to regret this.' And he jabbed the back of Murcatto's hand with the point of the knife, a single bead of dark blood slowly forming on her skin.

Within a few moments the antidote was already beginning to take effect. She winced as she turned her head slowly one way, then the other, worked the muscles in her face. 'I'm surprised,' she said.

'Truly? How so?'

'I was expecting a Master Poisoner.' She rubbed at the mark on the back of her hand. 'Who'd have thought I'd get such a little prick?'

Morveer felt his grin slip. It only took him a moment to regain his composure, of course. Once he had silenced Day's giggle with a sharp frown. 'I hope your temporary helplessness was not too great an inconvenience. I am forgiven, am I not? If the two of us are to cooperate, I would hate to have to labour beneath a shadow.'

'Of course.' She worked the movement back into her

shoulders, the slightest smile at one corner of her mouth. 'I need what you have, and you want what I have. Business is business.'

'Excellent. Magnificent. Un . . . *paralleled*.' And Morveer gave his most winning smile.

But he did not believe it for a moment. This was a most deadly job, and with a most deadly employer. Monzcarro Murcatto, the notorious Butcher of Caprile, was not a person of the forgiving variety. He was not forgiven. He was not even in the neighbourhood. From now on it would have to be caution first, second and third.

Science and Magic

Shivers pulled his horse up at the top of the rise. The country sloped away, a mess of dark fields with here or there a huddled farm or village, a stand of bare trees. No more'n a dozen miles distant, the line of the black sea, the curve of a wide bay, and along its edge a pale crust of city. Tiny towers clustered on three hills above the chilly brine, under an iron-grey sky.

'Westport,' said Friendly, then clicked his tongue and moved his horse on.

The closer they came to the damn place the more worried Shivers got. And the more sore, cold and bored besides. He frowned at Murcatto, riding on her own ahead, hood up, a black figure in a black landscape. The cart's wheels clattered round on the road. The horses clopped and snorted. Some crows caw-cawed from the bare fields. But no one was talking.

They'd been a grim crowd all the way here. But then they'd a grim purpose in mind. Nothing else but murder. Shivers wondered what his father would've made of that. Rattleneck, who'd stuck to the old ways tight as a barnacle to a boat and always looked for the right thing to do. Killing a man you never met for money didn't seem to fit that hole however you twisted it around.

There was a sudden burst of high laughter. Day, perched on the cart next to Morveer, a half-eaten apple in her hand. Shivers hadn't heard much laughter in a while, and it drew him like a moth to flame.

'What's funny?' he asked, starting to grin along at the joke.

She leaned towards him, swaying with the cart. 'I was just wondering, when you fell off your chair like a turtle tipped over, if you soiled yourself.'

'I was of the opinion you probably did,' said Morveer, 'but doubted we could have smelled the difference.'

Shivers' smile was stillborn. He remembered sitting in that orchard, frowning across the table, trying to look dangerous. Then he'd felt twitchy, then dizzy. He'd tried to lift his hand to his head, found he couldn't. He'd tried to say something about it, found he couldn't. Then the world tipped over. He didn't remember much else.

'What did you do to me?' He lowered his voice. 'Sorcery?'

Day sprayed bits of apple as she burst out laughing. 'Oh, this just gets better.'

'And I said he would be an uninspiring travelling companion.' Morveer chuckled. '*Sorcery*. I swear. It's like one of those stories.'

'Those big, thick, stupid books! Magi and devils and all the rest!' Day was having herself quite the snigger. 'Stupid stories for children!'

'Alright,' said Shivers. 'I think I get it. I'm slow as a fucking trout in treacle. Not sorcery. What, then?'

Day smirked. 'Science.'

Shivers didn't much care for the sound of it. 'What's that? Some other kind of magic?'

'No, it most *decidedly* is not,' sneered Morveer. 'Science is a system of rational thought devised to investigate the world and establish the laws by which it operates. The scientist uses those laws to achieve an effect. One which might easily appear magical in the eyes of the primitive.' Shivers struggled with all the long Styrian words. For a man who reckoned himself clever, Morveer had a fool's way of talking, seemed meant to make the simple difficult. 'Magic, conversely, is a system of lies and nonsense devised to fool idiots.'

'Right y'are. I must be the stupidest bastard in the Circle of the World, eh? It's a wonder I can hold my own shit in without paying mind to my arse every minute.'

'The thought had occurred.'

'There is magic,' grumbled Shivers. 'I've seen a woman call up a mist.'

'Really? And how did it differ from ordinary mist? Magic coloured? Green? Orange?'

Shivers frowned. 'The usual colour.'

'So a woman called, and there was mist.' Morveer raised one eyebrow at his apprentice. 'A wonder *indeed*.' She grinned, teeth crunching into her apple.

'I've seen a man marked with letters, made one half of him proof against any blade. Stabbed him myself, with a spear. Should've been a killing blow, but didn't leave a mark.'

'Ooooooh!' Morveer held both hands up and wiggled his fingers like a child playing ghost. 'Magic letters! First, there was no wound, and then . . . *there was no wound*? I recant! The world is *stuffed* with miracles.' More tittering from Day.

'I know what I've seen.'

'No, my mystified friend, you *think* you know. There is no such thing as magic. Certainly not here in Styria.'

'Just treachery,' sang Day, 'and war, and plague, and money to be made.'

'Why did you favour Styria with your presence, anyway?' asked Morveer. 'Why not stay in the North, swaddled in the magic mists?'

Shivers rubbed slowly at the side of his neck. Seemed a strange reason, now, and he felt even more of a fool saying it. 'I came here to be a better man.'

'Starting from where you are, I hardly think that would prove too difficult.'

Shivers had some pride still, and this prick's sniggering was starting to grate on it. He'd have liked to just knock him off his cart with an axe. But he was trying to do better, so he leaned over instead and spoke in Northern, nice and careful. 'I think you've got a head full of shit, which is no surprise because your face looks like an arse. You little men are all the same. Always trying to prove how clever y'are so you've something to be proud of. But it don't matter how much you laugh at me, I've won already. You'll never be tall.' And he grinned right round his face. 'Seeing across a crowded room will always be a dream to you.'

Morveer frowned. 'And what is that jabber supposed to mean?'

'You're the fucking scientist. You work it out.'

Day snorted with high laughter until Morveer caught her with a hard glance. She was still smiling, though, as she stripped the apple core to the pips and tossed it away. Shivers dropped back and watched the empty fields slither by, turned earth half-frozen with a morning frost. Made him think of home. He gave a sigh, and it smoked out against the grey sky. The friends Shivers had made in his life had all been fighters. Carls and Named Men, comrades in the line, most back in the mud, now, one way or another. He reckoned Friendly was the closest thing he'd get to that in the midst of Styria, so he gave his horse a nudge in the flanks and brought it up next to the convict.

'Hey.' Friendly didn't say a word. He didn't even move his head to show he'd heard. Silence stretched out. Looking at that brick wall of a face it was hard to picture the convict a bosom companion, chuckling away at his jokes. But a man's got to clutch at some hope, don't he? 'You were a soldier, then?'

Friendly shook his head.

'But you fought in battles?'

And again.

Shivers ploughed on as if he'd said yes. Not much other choice, now. 'I fought in a few. Charged in the mist with Bethod's Carls north of the Cumnur. Held the line next to Rudd Threetrees at Dunbrec. Fought seven days in the mountains with the Dogman. Seven desperate days, those were.'

'Seven?' asked Friendly, one heavy brow twitching with interest.

'Aye,' sighed Shivers. 'Seven.' The names of those men and those places meant nothing to no one down here. He watched a set of covered carts coming the other way, men with steel caps and flatbows in their hands frowning at him from their seats. 'Where did you learn to fight, then?' he asked, the smear of hope at getting some decent conversation drying out quick.

'In Safety.'

'Eh?'

'Where they put you when they catch you for a crime.'

'Why keep you safe after that?'

'They don't call it Safety because you're safe there. They call it Safety because everyone else is safe from you. They count out the days, months, years they'll keep you. Then they lock you in, deep down, where the light doesn't go, until the days, months, years have all rubbed past, and the numbers are all counted down to nothing. Then you say thank you, and they let you free.'

Sounded like a barbaric way of doing things to Shivers. 'You do a crime in the North, you pay a gild on it, make it right. That, or if the chieftain decides, they hang you. Maybe put the bloody cross in you, if you've done murders. Lock a man in a hole? That's a crime itself.'

Friendly shrugged. 'They have rules there that make sense. There's a proper time for each thing. A proper number on the great clock. Not like out here.'

'Aye. Right. Numbers, and that.' Shivers wished he'd never asked.

Friendly hardly seemed to hear him. 'Out here the sky is too high, and every man does what he pleases when he likes, and there are no right numbers for anything.' He was frowning off towards Westport, still just a sweep of hazy buildings round the cold bay. 'Fucking chaos.'

They got to the city walls about midday, and there was already a long line of folk waiting to get in. Soldiers stood about the gate, asking questions, going through a pack or a chest, poking half-hearted at a cart with their spear-butts.

'The Aldermen have been nervous since Borletta fell,' said Morveer from his seat. 'They are checking everyone who enters. I will do the talking.' Shivers was happy enough to let him, since the prick loved the sound of his own voice so much.

'Your name?' asked the guard, eyes infinitely bored.

'Reevrom,' said the poisoner, with a massive grin. 'A humble merchant from Puranti. And these are my associates—'

'Your business in Westport?'

'Murder.' An uncomfortable silence. 'I hope to make a verit-able *killing* on the sale of Osprian wines! Yes, indeed, I hope to make a *killing* in your city.' Morveer chuckled at his own joke and Day tittered away beside him.

'This one doesn't look like the kind we need.' Another guard was frowning up at Shivers.

Morveer kept chuckling. 'Oh, no need to worry on his account. The man is practically a retard. Intellect of a child. Still, he is good for shifting a barrel or two. I keep him on out of sentiment as much as anything. What am I, Day?'

'Sentimental,' said the girl.

'I have too much heart. Always have had. My mother died when I was very young, you see, a wonderful woman—'

'Get on with it!' someone called from behind them.

Morveer took hold of the canvas sheet covering the back of the wagon. 'Do you want to check—'

'Do I look like I want to, with half of Styria to get through my bloody gate? On.' The guard waved a tired hand. 'Move on.'

The reins snapped, the cart rolled into the city of Westport, and Murcatto and Friendly rode after. Shivers came last, which seemed about usual lately.

Beyond the walls it was crushed in tight as a battle, and not much less frightening. A paved road struck between high buildings, bare trees planted on either side, crammed with a shuffling tide of folk every shape and colour. Pale men in sober cloth, narrow-eyed women in bright silks, black-skinned men in white robes, soldiers and sell-swords in chain mail and dull plate. Servants, labourers, tradesmen, gentlemen, rich and poor, fine and stinking, nobles and beggars. An awful lot of beggars. Walkers and riders came surging up and away in a blur, horses and carts and covered carriages, women with a weight of piled-up hair and an even greater weight of jewellery, carried past on teetering chairs by pairs of sweating servants.

Shivers had thought Talins was rammed full with strange variety. Westport was way worse. He saw a line of animals with great long necks being led through the press, linked by thin chains, tiny heads swaying sadly about on top. He squeezed his eyes shut and shook his head, but when he opened them the monsters were still there, heads bobbing over the milling crowd, not even remarked upon. The place was like a dream, and not the pleasant kind.

They turned down a narrower way, hemmed in by shops and stalls. Smells jabbed at his nose one after another – fish, bread, polish, fruit, oil, spice and a dozen others he'd no idea of – and they made his breath catch and his stomach lurch. Out of nowhere a boy on a passing cart shoved a wicker cage in Shivers' face and a tiny monkey inside hissed and spat at him, near knocking him from his saddle in surprise. Shouts battered at his ears in a score of different tongues. A kind of a chant came floating up over the top of it, louder and louder, strange but beautiful, made the hairs on his arms bristle.

A building with a great dome loomed over one side of a square, six tall turrets sprouting from its front wall, golden spikes gleaming on their roofs. It was from there the chanting was coming. Hundreds of voices, deep and high together, mingling into one.

'It's a temple.' Murcatto had dropped back beside him, her hood still up, not much more of her face showing than her frown.

If Shivers was honest, he was more'n a bit feared of her. It was bad enough that he'd watched her break a man apart with a hammer and give every sign of enjoying it. But he'd had this creeping feeling afterwards, when they were bargaining, that she was on the point of stabbing him. Then there was that hand she always kept a glove on. He couldn't remember ever being scared of a woman before, and it made him shamed and nervous at once. But he could hardly deny that, apart from the glove, and the hammer, and the sick sense of danger, he liked the looks of her. A lot. He wasn't sure he didn't like the danger a bit more than was healthy too. All added up to not knowing what the hell to say from one moment to the next.

'Temple?'

'Where the Southerners pray to God.'

'God, eh?' Shivers' neck ached as he squinted up at those spires, higher than the tallest trees in the valley where he was born. He'd heard some folk down South thought there was a man in the sky. A man who'd made the world and saw everything. Had always seemed a mad kind of a notion, but looking at this Shivers weren't far from believing it himself. 'Beautiful.'

'Maybe a hundred years ago, when the Gurkish conquered Dawah, a lot of Southerners fled before them. Some crossed the water and settled here, and they raised up temples in thanks for their salvation. Westport is almost as much a part of the South as it's a part of Styria. But then it's part of the Union too, since the Aldermen finally had to pick a side, and bought the High King his victory over the Gurkish. They call this place the Crossroads of the World. Those that don't call it a nest of liars, anyway. There are people settled here from across the Thousand Isles,

94

from Suljuk and Sikkur, from Thond and the Old Empire. Northmen even.'

'Anything but those stupid bastards.'

'Primitives, to a man. I hear some of them grow their hair long like women. But they'll take anyone here.' Her gloved finger pointed out a long row of men on little platforms at the far end of the square. A strange bloody crowd, even for this place. Old and young, tall and short, fat and bony, some with strange robes or headgear, some half-naked and painted, one with bones through his face. A few had signs behind 'em in all kinds of letters, beads or baubles hanging. They danced and capered, threw their arms up, stared at the sky, dropped on their knees, wept, laughed, raged, sang, screamed, begged, all blathering away over each other in more languages than Shivers had known about.

'Who the hell are these bastards?' he muttered.

'Holy men. Or madmen, depending who you ask. Down in Gurkhul, you have to pray how the Prophet tells you. Here each man can worship as he pleases.'

'They're praying?'

Murcatto shrugged. 'More like they're trying to convince everyone else that they know the best way.'

People stood watching 'em. Some nodding along with what they were saying. Some shaking their heads, laughing, shouting back even. Some just stood there, bored. One of the holy men, or the madmen, started screaming at Shivers as he rode past in words he couldn't make a smudge of sense from. He knelt, stretching out his arms, beads round his neck rattling, voice raw with pleading. Shivers could see it in his red-rimmed eyes – he thought this was the most important thing he'd ever do.

'Must be a nice feeling,' said Shivers.

'What must?'

'Thinking you know all the answers . . .' He trailed off as a woman walked past with a man on a lead. A big, dark man with a collar of shiny metal, carrying a sack in either hand, his eyes kept on the ground. 'You see that?'

'In the South most men either own someone or are owned themselves.'

95

'That's a bastard custom,' muttered Shivers. 'I thought you said this was part o' the Union, though.'

'And they love their freedom over in the Union, don't they? You can't make a man a slave there.' She nodded towards some more, being led past meek and humble in a line. 'But if they pass through no one's freeing them, I can tell you that.'

'Bloody Union. Seems those bastards always want more land. There's more of 'em than ever in the North. Uffrith's full of 'em, since the wars started up again. And what do they need more land for? You should see that city they've got already. Makes this place look a village.'

She looked sharply across at him. 'Adua?'

'That's the one.'

'You've been there?'

'Aye. I fought the Gurkish there. Got me this mark.' And he pulled back his sleeve to show the scar on his wrist. When he looked back she had an odd look in her eye. You might almost have called it respect. He liked seeing it. Been a while since anyone looked at him with aught but contempt.

'Did you stand in the shadow of the House of the Maker?' she asked.

'Most of the city's in the shadow of that thing one time o' day or another.'

'What was it like?'

'Darker'n outside it. Shadows tend to be, in my experience.'

'Huh.' The first time Shivers had seen anything close to a smile on her face, and he reckoned it suited her. 'I always said I'd go.'

'To Adua? What's stopping you?'

'Six men I need to kill.'

Shivers puffed out his cheeks. 'Ah. That.' A surge of worry went through him, and he wondered afresh just why the hell he'd ever said yes. 'I've always been my own worst enemy,' he muttered.

'Stick with me, then.' Her smile had widened some. 'You'll soon have worse. We're here.'

Not all that heartening, as a destination. A narrow alley, dim as dusk. Crumbling buildings crowded in, shutters rotten and peeling, sheets of plaster cracking away from damp bricks. He led his horse after the cart and through a dim archway while

Murcatto swung the creaking doors shut behind them and shot the rusted bolt. Shivers tethered his horse to a rotting post in a yard strewn with weeds and fallen tiles.

'A palace,' he muttered, staring up towards the square of grey sky high above, the walls all round coated with dried-up weeds, the shutters hanging miserable from their hinges. 'Once.'

'I took it for the location,' said Murcatto, 'not the décor.'

They made for a gloomy hall, empty doorways leading into empty chambers. 'Lot of rooms,' said Shivers.

Friendly nodded. 'Twenty-two.'

Their boots thump, thumped on the creaking staircase as they made their way up through the rotten guts of the building.

'How are you going to begin?' Murcatto was asking Morveer.

'I already have. Letters of introduction have been sent. We have a *sizeable* deposit to entrust to Valint and Balk tomorrow morning. Sizeable enough to warrant the attention of their most senior officer. I, my assistant and your man Friendly will infiltrate the bank disguised as a merchant and his associates. We will meet with – then seek out an opportunity to kill – Mauthis.'

'Simple as that?'

'Seizing an opportunity is more often than not the key in these affairs, but if the moment does not present itself, I will be laying the groundwork for a more . . . structured approach.'

'What about the rest of us?' asked Shivers.

'Our employer, obviously, is possessed of a memorable visage and might be recognised, while *you*,' and Morveer sneered back down the stairs at him, 'stand out like a cow among the wolves, and would be no more useful than one. You are far too tall and far too scarred and your clothes are far too rural for you to belong in a bank. As for that hair—'

'Pfeeesh,' said Day, shaking her head.

'What's that supposed to mean?'

'Exactly how it sounded. You are simply far, far too . . .' Morveer swirled one hand around. '*North.*'

Murcatto unlocked a flaking door at the top of the last flight of steps and shoved it open. Muddy daylight leaked through and Shivers followed the others out blinking into the sun.

'By the dead.' A jumble of mismatched roofs every shape and pitch stretched off all round – red tiles, grey slates, white lead, rotting thatch, bare rafters caked with moss, green copper streaked with dirt, patched with canvas and old leather. A tangle of leaning gables, garrets, beams, paint peeling and sprouting with weeds, dangling gutters and crooked drains, bound up with chains and sagging washing lines, built all over each other at every angle and looking like the lot might slide off into the streets any moment. Smoke belched up from countless chimneys, cast a haze that made the sun a sweaty blur. Here and there a tower poked or a dome bulged above the chaos, the odd tangle of bare wood where some trees had beaten the odds and managed to stick out a twig. The sea was a grey smudge in the distance, the masts of ships in the harbour a far-off forest, shifting uneasily with the waves.

From up here the city seemed to make a great hiss. Noise of work and play, of men and beasts, calls of folk selling and buying, wheels rattling and hammers clanging, splinters of song and scraps of music, joy and despair all mixed up together like stew in a great pot.

Shivers edged to the lichen-crusted parapet beside Murcatto and peered over. People trickled up and down a cobbled lane far below, like water in the bottom of a canyon. A monster of a building loomed up on the other side.

Its wall was a sheer cliff of smooth-cut pale stone, with a pillar every twenty strides that Shivers couldn't have got both arms around, crusted at the top with leaves and faces carved out of stone. There was a row of small windows at maybe twice the height of a man, then another above, then a row of much bigger ones, all blocked by metal grilles. Above that, all along the line of the flat roof, about level with where Shivers was standing, a hedge of black iron spikes stuck out, like the spines on a thistle.

Morveer grinned across at it. 'Ladies, gentlemen and savages, I give you the Westport branch . . . of the Banking House . . . of Valint and Balk.'

Shivers shook his head. 'Place looks like a fortress.'

'Like a prison,' murmured Friendly.

'Like a *bank*,' sneered Morveer.

The Safest Place in the World

The banking hall of the Westport office of Valint and Balk was an echoing cavern of red porphyry and black marble. It had all the gloomy splendour of an emperor's mausoleum, the minimum light necessary creeping in through small, high windows, their thick bars casting cross-hatched shadows across the shining floor. A set of huge marble busts stared smugly down from on high: great merchants and financiers of Styrian history, by the look of them. Criminals made heroes by colossal success. Morveer wondered whether Somenu Hermon was among them, and the thought that the famous merchant might indirectly be paying his wages caused his smirk to expand by the slightest margin.

Sixty clerks or more attended identical desks loaded with identical heaps of papers, each with a huge, leather-bound ledger open before him. All manner of men, with all colours of skin, some sporting the skullcaps, turbans or characteristic hairstyles of one Kantic sect or other. The only prejudice here was in favour of those who could turn the fastest coin. Pens rattled in ink bottles, nibs scratched on heavy paper, pages crackled as they were turned. Merchants stood in clumps and haggles, conversing in whispers. Nowhere was a single coin in evidence. The wealth here was made of words, of ideas, of rumours and lies, too valuable to be held captive in gaudy gold or simple silver.

It was a setting intended to awe, to amaze, to intimidate, but Morveer was not a man to be intimidated. He belonged here perfectly, just as he did everywhere and nowhere. He swaggered past a long queue of well-dressed supplicants with the air of studied self-satisfaction that always accompanied new money. Friendly lumbered in his wake, strongbox held close, and Day tiptoed demurely at the rear.

Morveer snapped his fingers at the nearest clerk. 'I have an appointment with . . .' He consulted his letter for effect. 'One Mauthis. On the subject of a sizeable deposit.'

'Of course. If you would wait for one moment.'

'One, but no more. Time and money are the same.'

Morveer inconspicuously studied the arrangements for security. It would have been an understatement to call them daunting. He counted twelve armed men stationed around the hall, as comprehensively equipped as the King of the Union's bodyguard. There had been another dozen outside the towering double-doors.

'The place is a fortress,' muttered Day under her breath.

'But considerably better defended,' replied Morveer.

'How long is this going to take?'

'Why?'

'I'm hungry.'

'Already? For pity's *sake*! You will not starve if you— Wait.'

A tall man had emerged from a high archway, gaunt-faced with a prominent beak of a nose and thinning grey hair, arrayed in sombre robes with a heavy fur collar. 'Mauthis,' murmured Morveer, from Murcatto's exhaustive description. 'Our intended.'

He was walking behind a younger man, curly haired and with a pleasant smile, not at all richly dressed. So unexceptional, in fact, he would have had a fine appearance for a poisoner. And yet Mauthis, though supposedly in charge of the bank, hurried after with hands clasped, as though he was the junior. Morveer sidled closer, bringing them within earshot.

'. . . Master Sulfur, I hope you will inform our superiors that everything is under complete control.' Mauthis had, perhaps, the very slightest note of panic in his voice. 'Absolute and complete—'

'Of course,' answered the one called Sulfur, offhand. 'Though I rarely find our superiors need informing as to how things stand. They are watching. If everything is under complete control, I am sure they will already be satisfied. If not, well . . .' He smiled wide at Mauthis, and then at Morveer, and Morveer noticed he had different-coloured eyes, one blue, one green. 'Good day.' And he strode away and was soon lost in the crowds.

'May I be of assistance?' grated Mauthis. He looked as if he had never laughed in his life. He was running out of time to try it now.

'I certainly hope you may. My name is Reevrom, a merchant of Puranti.' Morveer tittered inwardly at his own joke, as he did whenever he utilised the alias, but his face showed nothing but the warmest bonhomie as he offered his hand.

'Reevrom. I have heard of your house. A privilege to make your acquaintance.' Mauthis disdained to shake it, and kept a carefully inoffensive distance between them. Evidently a cautious man. Just as well, for his sake. The tiny spike on the underside of Morveer's heavy middle-finger ring was loaded with scorpion venom in a solution of Leopard Flower. The banker would have sat happily through their meeting, then dropped dead within the hour.

'This is my niece,' continued Morveer, not in the least down-hearted by his failed attempt. 'I have been entrusted with the responsibility of escorting her to an introduction with a potential suitor.' Day looked up from beneath her lashes with perfectly judged shyness. 'And this is my associate.' He glanced sideways at Friendly and the man frowned back. 'I do him too much credit. My bodyguard, Master Charming. He is not a great conversationalist, but when it comes to bodyguarding, he is . . . barely adequate in truth. Still, I promised his old mother that I would take him under my—'

'You have come here on a matter of business?' droned Mauthis.

Morveer bowed. 'A *sizeable* deposit.'

'I regret that your associates must remain behind, but if you would care to follow me we would, of course, be happy to accept your deposit and prepare a receipt.'

'Surely my niece—'

'You must understand that, in the interests of security, we can make no exceptions. Your niece will be perfectly comfortable here.'

'Of course, of course you will, my dear. Master Charming! The strongbox!' Friendly handed the metal case over to a be-spectacled clerk, left tottering under its weight. 'Now wait here, and get up to no mischief!' Morveer gave a heavy sigh as he followed Mauthis into the depths of the building, as though he had insurmountable difficulties securing competent help. 'My money will be safe here?'

'The bank's walls are at no point less than twelve feet in thickness. There is only one entrance, guarded by a dozen well-armed men during the day, sealed at night with three locks, made by three different locksmiths, the keys kept by three separate employees. Two parties of men constantly patrol the exterior of the bank until morning. Even then the interior is kept under watch by a most sharp-eyed and competent guard.' He gestured towards a bored-looking man in a studded leather jerkin, seated at a desk to the side of the hallway.

'He is locked in?'

'All night.'

Morveer worked his mouth with some discomfort. '*Most* comprehensive arrangements.'

He pulled out his handkerchief and pretended to cough daintily into it. The silk was soaked in Mustard Root, one of an extensive range of agents to which he had himself long since developed an immunity. He needed only a few moments un-observed, then he could clasp it to Mauthis' face. The slightest inhalation and the man would cough himself to bloody death within moments. But the clerk laboured along between them with the strongbox in his arms, and not the slightest opportunity was forthcoming. Morveer was forced to tuck the lethal cloth away, then narrow his eyes as they turned into a long hallway lined with huge paintings. Light poured in from above, the very roof, far overhead, fashioned from a hundred thousand diamond panes of glass.

'A ceiling of windows!' Morveer turned slowly round and round, head back. 'Truly a wonder of architecture!'

'This is an entirely modern building. Your money could not be more secure anywhere, believe me.'

'The depths of ruined Aulcus, perhaps?' joked Morveer, as an overblown artist's impression of the ancient city passed by on their left.

'Not even there.'

'And making a withdrawal would be *considerably* more testing, I imagine! Ha ha. Ha ha.'

'Quite so.' The banker did not display even the inkling of a smile. 'Our vault door is a foot thickness of solid Union steel. We do not exaggerate when we say this is the safest place in the Circle of the World. This way.'

Morveer was ushered into a voluminous chamber panelled with oppressively dark wood, ostentatious yet still uncomfortable, tyrannised by a desk the size of a poor man's house. A sombre oil was set above a looming fireplace: a heavyset bald man glowering down as though he suspected Morveer of being up to no good. Some Union bureaucrat of the dusty past, he suspected. Zoller, maybe, or Bialoveld.

Mauthis took up a high, hard seat and Morveer found one opposite while the clerk lifted the lid of the strongbox and began to count out the money, using a coin-stacker with practised efficiency. Mauthis watched, scarcely blinking. At no stage did he touch either case or coins himself. A cautious man. Damnably, infuriatingly cautious. His slow eyes slid across the desk.

'Wine?'

Morveer raised an eyebrow at the distorted glassware behind the windows of a towering cabinet. 'Thank you, no. I become quite flustered under its influence, and between the two of us have frequently embarrassed myself. I decided, in the end, to abstain entirely, and stick to selling it to others. The stuff is . . . *poison*.' And he gave a huge smile. 'But don't let me stop you.' He slid an unobtrusive hand into a hidden pocket within his jacket where the vial of Star Juice was waiting. It would be a small effort to mount a diversion and introduce a couple of drops to Mauthis' glass while he was—

'I too avoid it.'

'Ah.' Morveer released the vial and instead plucked a folded paper from his inside pocket quite as if that had been his intention from the first. He unfolded it and pretended to read while his eyes darted about the office. 'I counted five thousand . . .' He took in the style of lock upon the door, the fashion of its construction, the frame within which it was set. 'Two hundred . . .' The tiles from which the floor was made, the panels on the walls, the render of the ceiling, the leather of Mauthis' chair, the coals on the unlit fire. 'And twelve scales.' Nothing seemed promising.

Mauthis showed no emotion at the number. Fortunes and

small change, all one. He opened the heavy cover of a huge ledger upon his desk. He licked one finger and flicked steadily through the pages, paper crackling. Morveer felt a warm satisfaction spread out from his stomach to every extremity at the sight, and it was only with an effort that he prevented himself from whooping with triumph. He settled for a prim smile. 'Takings from my last trip to Sipani. Wine from Ospria is always a profitable venture, even in these uncertain times. Not everyone has our temperance, Master Mauthis, I am happy to say!'

'Of course.' The banker licked his finger once again as he turned the last few pages.

'Five thousand, two hundred and eleven,' said the clerk.

Mauthis' eyes flickered up. 'Trying to get away with something?'

'Me?' Morveer passed it off with a false chuckle. 'Damn that man Charming, he can't count for anything! I swear he has no feel for numbers whatsoever.'

The nib of Mauthis' pen scratched across the ledger; the clerk hurried over and blotted the entry as his master neatly, precisely, emotionlessly prepared the receipt. The clerk carried it to Morveer and offered it to him along with the empty strongbox.

'A note for the full amount in the name of the Banking House of Valint and Balk,' said Mauthis. 'Redeemable at any reputable mercantile institution in Styria.'

'Must I sign anything?' asked Morveer hopefully, his fingers closing around the pen in his inside pocket. It doubled as a highly effective blowgun, the needle concealed within containing a lethal dose of—

'No.'

'Very well.' Morveer smiled as he folded the paper and slid it away, taking care that it did not catch on the deadly edge of his scalpel. 'Better than gold, and a great deal lighter. For now, then, I take my leave. It has been a *decided* pleasure.' And he held out his hand again, poisoned ring glinting. No harm in making the effort.

Mauthis did not move from his chair. 'Likewise.'

Evil Friends

It had been Benna's favourite place in Westport. He'd dragged her there twice a week while they were in the city. A shrine of mirrors and cut glass, polished wood and glittering marble. A temple to the god of male grooming. The high priest – a small, lean barber in a heavily embroidered apron – stood sharply upright in the centre of the floor, chin pointed to the ceiling, as though he'd been expecting them that very moment to enter.

'Madam! A delight to see you again!' He blinked for a moment. 'Your husband is not with you?'

'My brother.' Monza swallowed. 'And no, he . . . won't be back. I've an altogether tougher challenge for you—'

Shivers stepped through the doorway, gawping about as fearfully as a sheep in a shearing pen. She opened her mouth to speak but the barber cut her off. 'I believe I see the problem.' He made a sharp circuit of Shivers while the Northman frowned down at him. 'Dear, dear. All off?'

'What?'

'All off,' said Monza, taking the barber by the elbow and pressing a quarter into his hand. 'Go gently, though. I doubt he's used to this and he might startle.' She realised she was making him sound like a horse. Maybe that was giving him too much credit.

'Of course.' The barber turned, and gave a sharp intake of breath. Shivers had already taken his new shirt off and was looming pale and sinewy in the doorway, unbuckling his belt.

'He means your hair, fool,' said Monza, 'not your clothes.'

'Uh. Thought it was odd, but, well, Southern fashions . . .' Monza watched him as he sheepishly buttoned his shirt back up. He had a long scar from his shoulder across his chest, pink and twisted. She might've thought it ugly once, but she'd had to change her opinions on scars, along with a few other things.

Shivers lowered himself into the chair. 'Had this hair all my life.'

'Then it is past time you were released from its suffocating embrace. Head forwards, please.' The barber produced his scissors with a flourish and Shivers lurched out of his seat.

'You think I'm letting a man I never met near my face with a blade?'

'I must protest! I trim the heads of Westport's finest gentlemen!'

'You.' Monza caught the barber's shoulder as he backed away and marched him forwards. 'Shut up and cut hair.' She slipped another quarter into his apron pocket and gave Shivers a long look. 'You, shut up and sit still.'

He sidled back into the chair and clung so tight to its arms that the tendons stood from the backs of his hands. 'I'm watching you,' he growled.

The barber gave a long sigh and with lips pursed began to work.

Monza wandered around the room while the scissors snip-snipped behind her. She walked along a shelf, absently pulling the stoppers from the coloured bottles, sniffing at the scented oils inside. She caught a glimpse of herself in the mirror. A hard face, still. Thinner, leaner, sharper even than she used to be. Eyes sunken from the nagging pain up her legs, from the nagging need for the husk that made the pain go away.

You look especially beautiful this morning, Monza . . .

The idea of a smoke stuck in her mind like a bone in her craw. Each day the need crept up on her earlier. More time spent sick, sore and twitchy, counting the minutes until she could creep off and be with her pipe, sink back into soft, warm nothingness. Her fingertips tingled at the thought, tongue working hungrily around her dry mouth.

'Always worn it long. Always.' She turned back into the room. Shivers was wincing like a torture victim as tufts of cut hair tumbled down and built up on the polished boards under the chair. Some men clam up when they're nervous. Some men blather. It seemed Shivers was in the latter camp. 'Guess my brother had long hair and I went and did the same. Used to try and copy him. Looked up to him. Little brothers, you know . . . What was your brother like?'

She felt her cheek twitch, remembering Benna's grinning face in the mirror, and hers behind it. 'He was a good man. Everyone loved him.'

'My brother was a good man. Lot better'n me. My father thought so, anyway. Never missed a chance to tell me . . . I mean, just saying, nothing strange 'bout long hair where I come from. Folk got other things to cut in a war than their hair, I guess. Black Dow used to laugh at me, 'cause he'd always hacked his right off, so as not to get in the way in a fight. But then he'd give a man shit about anything, Black Dow. Hard mouth. Hard man. Only man harder was the Bloody-Nine his self. I reckon—'

'For someone with a weak grip on the language, you like to talk, don't you? You know what I reckon?'

'What?'

'People talk a lot when they've nothing to say.'

Shivers heaved out a sigh. 'Just trying to make tomorrow that bit better than today is all. I'm one of those . . . you've got a word for it, don't you?'

'Idiots?'

He looked sideways at her. 'It was a different one I had in mind.'

'Optimists.'

'That's the one. I'm an optimist.'

'How's it working out for you?'

'Not great, but I keep hoping.'

'That's optimists. You bastards never learn.' She watched Shivers' face emerging from that tangle of greasy hair. Hard-boned, sharp-nosed, with a nick of a scar through one eyebrow. It was a good face, in so far as she cared. She found she cared more than she'd thought she would. 'You were a soldier, right? What do they call them up in the North . . . a Carl?'

'I was a Named Man, as it goes,' and she could hear the pride in his voice.

'Good for you. So you led men?'

'I had some looking to me. My father was a famous man, my brother too. A little some of that rubbed off, maybe.'

'So why throw it away? Why come down here to be nothing?'

He looked at her in the mirror while the scissors clicked round his face. 'Morveer said you were a soldier yourself. A famous one.'

'Not that famous.' It was only half a lie. Infamous was closer to it.

'That'd be a strange job for a woman, where I come from.'

She shrugged. 'Easier than farming.'

'So you know war, am I right?'

'Yes.'

'Daresay you've seen some battles. You've seen men killed.'

'Yes.'

'Then you've seen what goes with it. The marches, the waiting, the sickness. Folk raped, robbed, crippled, burned out who've done nought to deserve it.'

Monza thought of her own field burning, all those years ago. 'You've got a point, you can out and say it.'

'That blood only makes more blood. That settling one score only starts another. That war gives a bastard of a sour taste to any man that's not half-mad, and it only gets worse with time.' She didn't disagree. 'So you know why I'd rather be free of it. Make something grow. Something to be proud of, instead of just breaking. Be . . . a good man, I guess.'

Snip, snip. Hair tumbled down and gathered on the floor. 'A good man, eh?'

'That's right.'

'So you've seen dead men yourself?'

'I've seen my share.'

'You've seen a lot together?' she asked. 'Stacked up after the plague came through, spread out after a battle?'

'Aye, I've seen that.'

'Did you notice some of those corpses had a kind of glow about them? A sweet smell like roses on a spring morning?'

Shivers frowned. 'No.'

'The good men and the bad, then – all looked about the same, did they? They always did to me, I can tell you that.' It was his turn to stay quiet. 'If you're a good man, and you try to think about what the right thing is every day of your life, and you build things to be proud of so bastards can come and burn them in a moment, and you make sure and say thank you kindly each time they kick the guts out of you, do you think when you die, and they stick you in the mud, you turn into gold?'

'What?'

'Or do you turn to fucking shit like the rest of us?'

He nodded slowly. 'You turn to shit, alright. But maybe you can leave something good behind you.'

She barked empty laughter at him. 'What do we leave behind but things not done, not said, not finished? Empty clothes, empty rooms, empty spaces in the ones who knew us? Mistakes never made right and hopes rotted down to nothing?'

'Hopes passed on, maybe. Good words said. Happy memories, I reckon.'

'And all those dead men's smiles you've kept folded up in your heart, they were keeping you warm when I found you, were they? How did they taste when you were hungry? They raise a smile, even, when you were desperate?'

Shivers puffed out his cheeks. 'Hell, but you're a ray of sunshine. Might be they did me some good.'

'More than a pocketful of silver would've?'

He blinked at her, then away. 'Maybe not. But I reckon I'll try to keep thinking my way, just the same.'

'Hah. Good luck, good man.' She shook her head as if she'd never heard such stupidity. *Give me only evil men for friends*, Verturio wrote. *Them I understand.*

A last quick clicking of the scissors and the barber stepped away, dabbing at his own sweaty brow with the back of one sleeve. 'And we are all finished.'

Shivers stared into the mirror. 'I look a different man.'

'Sir looks like a Styrian aristocrat.'

Monza snorted. 'Less like a Northern beggar, anyway.'

'Maybe.' Shivers looked less than happy. 'I daresay that's a better-looking man there. A cleverer man.' He ran one hand through his short dark hair, frowning at his reflection. 'Not sure if I trust that bastard, though.'

'And to finish . . .' The barber leaned forwards, a coloured crystal bottle in his hands, and squirted a fine mist of perfume over Shivers' head.

The Northman was up like a cat off hot coals. 'What the *fuck*?'

he roared, big fists clenched, shoving the man away and making him totter across the room with a squeal.

Monza burst out laughing. 'Looks of a Styrian nobleman, maybe.' She pulled out a couple more quarters and tucked them into the gaping barber's apron pocket. 'The manners might be a while coming, though.'

It was getting dark when they came back to the crumbling mansion, Monza with her hood drawn up and Shivers striding proudly along in his new coat. A cold rain flitted down into the ruined courtyard, a single lamp burned in a window on the first floor. She frowned towards it, and then at Shivers, found the grip of the knife in the back of her belt with her left hand. Best to be ready for every possibility. Up the creaking stairs a peeling door stood ajar, light spilling out across the boards. She stepped up and poked it open with her boot.

A pair of burning logs in the soot-blackened fireplace barely warmed the chamber on the other side. Friendly stood beside the far window, peering through the shutters towards the bank. Morveer had some sheets of paper spread out on a rickety old table, marking his place with an ink-spotted hand. Day sat on the tabletop with her legs crossed, peeling an orange with a dagger. 'Definite improvement,' she grunted, giving Shivers a glance.

'Oh, I cannot but agree.' Morveer grinned. 'A dirty, long-haired idiot left the building this morning. A clean, short-haired idiot has returned. It *must* be magic.'

Monza let go the grip of her knife while Shivers muttered angrily to himself in Northern. 'Since you're not crowing your own praises, I'm guessing the job's not done.'

'Mauthis is a *most* cautious and well-protected man. The bank is far too heavily guarded during the day.'

'On his way to the bank, then.'

'He leaves by an armoured carriage with a dozen guards in attendance. To try and intercept them would be too great a risk.'

Shivers tossed another log on the fire and held his palms out towards it. 'At his house?'

'Pah,' sneered Morveer. 'We followed him there. He lives on a walled island in the bay where several of the city's Aldermen have their estates. The public are not admitted. We have no method of gaining advance access to the building even if we can deduce which one is his. How many guards, servants, family members would be in attendance? All unknown. I *flatly* refuse to attempt a job of this difficulty on conjecture. What do I never take, Day?'

'Chances.'

'Correct. I deal in *certainties*, Murcatto. That is why you came to me. I am hired for a *certain* man most *certainly* dead, not for a butcher's mess and your target slipped away in the chaos. We are not in Caprile, now—'

'I know where we are, Morveer. What's your plan, then?'

'I have gathered the necessary information and devised a sure means of achieving the desired effect. I need only gain access to the bank during the hours of darkness.'

'And how do you plan to do that?'

'How do I plan to do that, Day?'

'Through the rigorous application of observation, logic and method.'

Morveer flashed his smug little smile again. 'Precisely so.'

Monza glanced sideways at Benna. Except Benna was dead, and Shivers was in his place. The Northman raised his eyebrows, blew out a long sigh and looked back to the fire. *Give me only evil men for friends*, Verturio wrote. But there had to be a limit.

Two Twos

The dice came up two twos. Two times two is four. Two plus two is four. Add the dice, or multiply, the same result. It made Friendly feel helpless, that thought. Helpless but calm. All these people struggling to get things done, but whatever they did, it turned out the same. The dice were full of lessons. If you knew how to read them.

The group had formed two twos. Morveer and Day were one pair. Master and apprentice. They had joined together, they stayed together, they laughed together at everyone else. But now Friendly saw that Murcatto and Shivers were forming a pair of their own. They crouched next to each other at the parapet, black outlines against the dim night sky, staring across towards the bank, an immense block of thicker darkness. He had often seen that it was in the nature of people to form pairs. Everyone except him. He was left alone, in the shadows. Maybe there was something wrong with him, the way the judges had said.

Sajaam had chosen him to form a pair with, in Safety, but Friendly had no illusions. Sajaam had chosen him because he was useful. Because he was feared. As feared as anyone in the darkness. But Sajaam had not pretended any differently. He was the only honest man that Friendly knew, and so it had been an honest arrangement. It had worked so well that Sajaam had made enough money in prison to buy his freedom from the judges. But he was an honest man and so, when he was free, he had not forgotten Friendly. He had come back and bought his freedom too.

Outside the walls, where there were no rules, things were different. Sajaam had other business, and Friendly was left alone again. He did not mind, though. He was used to it, and had the dice for company. So he found himself here, in the darkness, on a roof in Westport, in the dead of winter. With these two mis-matched pairs of dishonest people.

The guards came in two twos as well, four at a time, and two groups of four, following each other endlessly around the bank all night. It was raining now, a half-frozen sleet spitting down. Still they followed each other, round, and round, and round through the darkness. One party trudged along the lane beneath, well armoured, polearms shouldered.

'Here they come again,' said Shivers.

'I see that,' sneered Morveer. 'Start a count.'

Day's whisper came through the night, high and throaty. 'One . . . two . . . three . . . four . . . five . . .' Friendly stared open-mouthed at her lips moving, the dice forgotten by his limp hand. His own mouth moved silently along with hers. 'Twenty-two . . . twenty-three . . . twenty-four . . .'

'How to reach the roof?' Morveer was musing. 'How to reach the roof?'

'Rope and grapple?' asked Murcatto.

'Too slow, too noisy, too uncertain. The rope would be left in plain view the entire time, even supposing we could firmly set a grapple. No. We need a method that allows for no accidents.'

Friendly wished they would shut their mouths so he could listen to Day's counting. His cock was aching hard from listening to it. 'One hundred and twelve . . . one hundred and thir-teen . . .' He let his eyes close, let his head fall back against the wall, one finger moving back and forth in time. 'One hundred and eighty-two . . . one hundred and eighty-three . . .'

'No one could climb up there free,' came Murcatto's voice. 'Not anyone. Too smooth, too sheer. And the spikes to worry on.'

'I am in *complete* agreement.'

'Up from inside the bank, then.'

'Impossible. *Entirely* too many eyes. It must be up the walls, then in via the great windows in the roof. At least the lane is deserted during the hours of darkness. That is something in our favour.'

'What about the other sides of the building?'

'The north face is considerably busier and better lit. The east contains the primary entrance, with an additional party of four guards posted all night. The south is identical to this face, but without the advantage of our having access to an adjacent roof. No. This wall is our *only* option.'

Friendly saw the faint flicker of light down below in the lane. The next patrol, two times two guards, two plus two guards, four guards working their steady way around the bank.

'All night they keep this up?'

'There are two other parties of four that relieve them. They maintain their vigil uninterrupted until daybreak.'

'Two hundred and ninety-one . . . two hundred and ninety-two . . . and here comes the next set.' Day clicked her tongue. 'Three hundred, give or take.'

'Three hundred,' hissed Morveer, and Friendly could see his head shaking in the darkness. 'Not enough time.'

'Then how?' snapped Monza.

Friendly swept the dice up again, felt their familiar edges pressing into his palm. It hardly mattered to him how they got into the bank, or even whether they ever did. His hopes mostly involved Day starting to count again.

'There must be a way . . . there *must* be a—'

'I can do it.' They all looked round. Shivers was sitting against the parapet, white hands dangling.

'You?' sneered Morveer. 'How?'

Friendly could just make out the curve of the Northman's grin in the darkness. 'Magic.'

Plans and Accidents

The guards grumbled their way down the lane. Four of 'em – breastplates, steel caps, halberd blades catching the light from their swinging lanterns. Shivers pressed himself deep into the doorway as they clattered past, waited a nervy moment, then padded across the lane and into the shadows beside the pillar he'd chosen. He started counting. Three hundred or so, to make it to the top and onto the roof. He looked up. Seemed a bastard of a long way. Why the hell had he said yes to this? Just so he could slap the smile off that idiot Morveer's face, and show Murcatto he was worth his money?

'Always my own worst enemy,' he whispered. Turned out he'd too much pride. That and a terrible weakness for fine-looking women. Who'd have thought it?

He pulled the rope out, two strides long with an eye at one end and a hook at the other. He cast a glance over the windows in the buildings facing him. Most were shuttered against the cold night, but a few were open, a couple still with lights burning inside. He wondered what the chances were of someone looking out and seeing him shinning up the side of a bank. Higher than he'd like, that was sure.

'Worst fucking enemy.' He got ready to climb up onto the pillar's base.

'Somewhere here.'

'Where, idiot?'

Shivers froze, rope dangling from his hands. Footsteps now, armour jingling. Bastard guards were coming back. They'd never done that in fifty circuits of the place. For all his chat about science, that bloody poisoner had made an arse of it and Shivers was the one left with his fruits dangling in the wind. He squeezed deeper into the shadows, felt the big flatbow on his back scraping stone. How the hell was he going to explain that? Just a midnight stroll, you know, all in black, taking the old bow for a walk.

If he bolted they'd see him, chase him, more'n likely stab him with something. Either way they'd know someone had been trying to creep into the bank and that would be the end of the whole business. If he stayed put . . . same difference, more or less, except the stabbing got a sight more likely.

The voices came closer. 'Can't be far away, all we bloody do is go round and round . . .'

One of 'em must've lost something. Shivers cursed his shitty luck, and not for the first time. Too late to run. He closed his fist round the grip of his knife. Footsteps thumped, just on the other side of the pillar. Why'd he taken her silver? Turned out he'd a terrible weakness for money too. He gritted his teeth, waited for—

'Please!' Murcatto's voice. She walked out across the lane, hood back, long coat swishing. Might've been the first time Shivers had seen her without a sword. 'I'm so, so sorry to bother you. I'm only trying to get home, but I seem to have got myself completely lost.'

One of the guards stepped round the pillar, his back to Shivers, and then another. They were no more than arm's length away, between him and her. He could almost have reached out and touched their backplates.

'Where you staying?'

'With some friends, near the fountain on Lord Sabeldi Street, but I'm new in the city, and,' she gave a hopeless laugh, 'I've quite misplaced it.'

One of the guards pushed back his helmet. 'I'll say you have. Other side of town, that.'

'I swear I've been wandering the city for hours.' She began to move away, drawing the men gently after her. Another guard appeared, and another. All four now, with their backs still to Shivers. He held his breath, heart thumping so loud it was a wonder none of them could hear it. 'If one of you gentlemen could point me in the right direction I'd be so grateful. Stupid of me, I know.'

'No, no. Confusing place, Westport.'

''Specially at night.'

'I get lost here myself, time to time.' The men laughed, and Monza laughed along, still drawing 'em on. Her eye caught Shivers' just for an instant, and they looked right at each other, and then she was gone round the next pillar, and the guards too, and their eager chatter drifted away. He closed his eyes, and slowly breathed out. Just as well he weren't the only man around with a weakness for women.

He swung himself up onto the square base of the pillar, slid the rope around it and under his rump, hooked it to make a loop. No idea what the count was now, just knew he had to get up there fast. He set off, gripping the stone with his knees and the edges of his boots, sliding the loop of rope up, then dragging it tight while he shifted his legs and set 'em again.

It was a trick his brother taught him, when he was a lad. He'd used it to climb the tallest trees in the valley and steal eggs. He remembered how they'd laughed together when he kept falling off near the bottom. Now he was using it to help kill folk, and if he fell off he'd be dead himself. Safe to say life hadn't turned out quite the way he'd hoped.

Still, he went up quick and smooth. Just like climbing a tree, except no eggs at the end of it and less chance of bark-splinters in your fruits. Hard work, though. He was sweating through by the time he made it up the pillar and still had the hardest part to go. He worked one hand into the mess of stonework at the top, unhooked the rope with the other and dragged it over his shoulder. Then he pulled himself up, fingers and toes digging holds out among the carvings, breath hissing, arms burning. He slipped one leg over a sculpture of a woman's frowning face and sat there, high above the lane, clinging to a pair of stone leaves and hoping they were stronger than the leafy kind.

He'd been in some better spots, but you had to look on the sunny side. It was the first time he'd had a woman's face between his legs in a while. He heard a hiss from across the lane, picked out Day's black shape on the roof. She pointed down. The next patrol were on their way.

'Shit.' He pressed himself tight to the stonework, trying to look like rock himself, hands tingling raw from gripping the hemp, hoping no one chose that moment to look up. They clattered by underneath and he let out a long hiss of air, heart pounding in his ears louder than ever. He waited for them to move off round the corner of the building, getting his breath back for the last stretch.

The spikes further along the walls were mounted on poles, could spin round and round. Impossible to get over. At the tops of the pillars, though, they were mortared to the stone. He took his gloves out – heavy smith's gloves, and pulled them on, then he reached up and worked his hands tight around two spikes, took a deep breath. He let go with his legs and swung free, drew himself up, staring a touch cross-eyed at the iron points in front of his face. Just like pulling yourself into the branches, except for the chance of taking your eye out, of course. Be nice to come out of this with both his eyes.

He swung one way, then heaved himself back the other and got one boot up on top. He twisted himself round, felt the spikes scrape against his thick jerkin, digging at his chest as he dragged himself over.

And he was up.

'Seventy-eight . . . seventy-nine . . . eighty . . .' Friendly's lips moved by themselves as he watched Shivers roll over the parapet and onto the roof of the bank.

'He made it,' whispered Day, voice squeaky with disbelief.

'And in good time too.' Morveer chuckled softly. 'Who would have thought he would climb . . . *like an ape.*'

The Northman stood, a darker shape against the dark night sky. He pulled the big flatbow off his back and started to fiddle with it. 'Let's hope he doesn't shoot like an ape,' whispered Day.

Shivers took aim. Friendly heard the soft click of the bow-string. A moment later he felt the bolt thud into his chest. He snatched hold of the shaft, frowning down. It hardly hurt at all.

'A *happy* circumstance that it has no point.' Morveer un-hooked the wire from the flights. 'We would do well to avoid any further mishaps, and your untimely death would seem to qualify.'

Friendly tossed the blunt bolt away and tied the rope off to the end of the wire.

'You sure that thing will take his weight?' muttered Day.

'Suljuk silk cord,' said Morveer smugly. 'Light as down but

strong as steel. It would take all three of us simultaneously, and no one looking up will see a thing.'

'You hope.'

'What do I never take, my dear?'

'Yes, yes.'

The black cord hissed through Friendly's hands as Shivers started reeling the wire back in. He watched it creep out across the space between the roofs, counting the strides. Fifteen and Shivers had the other end. They pulled it tight between them, then Friendly looped it through the iron ring they'd bolted to the roof timbers and began to knot it, once, twice, three times.

'Are you *entirely* sure of that knot?' asked Morveer. 'There is no place in the plan for a lengthy drop.'

'Twenty-eight strides,' said Friendly.

'What?'

'The drop.'

A brief pause. 'That is not helpful.'

A taut black line linked the two buildings. Friendly knew it was there, and still he could hardly see it in the darkness.

Day gestured towards it, curls stirred by the breeze. 'After you.'

Morveer fumbled his way over the balustrade, breathing hard. In truth, the trip across the cord had not been a pleasant excursion by any stretch of the imagination. A chilly wind had blown up halfway and set his heart to hammering. There had been a time, during his apprenticeship to the infamous Moumah-yin-Bek, when he had executed such acrobatic exertions with a feline grace, but he suspected it was dwindling rapidly into his past along with a full head of hair. He took a moment to compose himself, wiped chill sweat from his forehead, then realised Shivers was sitting there, grinning at him.

'Is there some manner of a joke?' demanded Morveer.

'Depends what makes you laugh, I reckon. How long will you be in there?'

'Precisely as long as I need to be.'

'Best move quicker than you did across that rope, then. You might still be climbing in when they open the place tomorrow.' The Northman was still smiling as he slipped over the parapet and back across the cord, swift and sure for all his bulk.

'If there is a God, he has cursed me through my acquaintance.' Morveer gave only the briefest consideration to the notion of cutting the knot while the primitive was halfway across, then crept away down a narrow lead channel between low-pitched slopes of slate towards the centre of the building. The great glass roof glowed ahead of him, faint light glittering through thousands of distorting panes. Friendly squatted beside it, already unwinding a second length of cord from around his waist.

'Ah, the modern age.' Morveer knelt beside Day, pressing his hands gently to the expanse of glass. 'What will they think of next?'

'I feel blessed to live in such exciting times.'

'So should we all, my dear.' He carefully peered down into the bank's interior. 'So should we *all*.' The hallway was barely lit, a single lamp burning at each end, bringing a precious gleam to the gilt frames of the huge paintings but leaving the doorways rich with shadow. 'Banks,' he whispered, a ghost of a smile on his face, 'always trying to economise.'

He pulled out his glazing tools and began to prise away the lead with pliers, lifting each piece of glass out carefully with blobs of putty. The brilliance of his dexterity was quite undimmed by age, and it took him mere moments to remove nine panes, to snip the lead latticework with pincers and peel it back to leave a diamond-shaped hole ample for his purposes.

'Perfect timing,' he murmured. The light from the guard's lantern crept up the panelled walls of the hallway, brought a touch of dawn to the dark canvases. His footsteps echoed as he passed by underneath them, giving vent to a booming yawn, his long shadow stretching out over the marble tiles. Morveer applied the slightest blast of air to his blowpipe.

'Gah!' The guard clapped a hand to the top of his head and Morveer ducked away from the window. There were footsteps below, a scuffling, a gurgle, then the loud thump and clatter of a toppling body. On peering back through the aperture the guard was plainly visible, spreadeagled on his back, lit lamp on its side by one outstretched hand.

'Excellent,' breathed Day.

'Naturally.'

'However much we talk about science, it always seems like magic.'

'We are, one might say, the wizards of the modern age. The rope, if you please, Master Friendly.' The convict tossed one end of the silken cord over, the other still knotted around his waist. 'You are sure you can take my weight?'

'Yes.' There was indeed a sense of terrible strength about the silent man that lent even Morveer a level of confidence. With the rope secured by a knot of his own devising, he lowered first one soft shoe and then the other into the diamond-shaped opening. He worked his hips through, then his shoulders, and he was inside the bank.

'Lower away.' And down he drifted, as swiftly and smoothly as if lowered by a machine. His shoes touched the tiles and he slipped the knot with a jerk of his wrist, slid silently into a shadowy doorway, loaded blowgun ready in one hand. He was expecting but the single guard within the building, but one should never become blinded by expectations.

Caution first, always.

His eyes rolled up and down the darkened hallway, his skin tingling with the excitement of the work under way. There was no movement. Only silence so complete it seemed almost a pressure against his prickling ears.

He looked up, saw Day's face at the gap and beckoned gently to her. She slid through as nimbly as a circus performer and glided down, their equipment folded around her body in a bandolier of black cloth. When her feet touched the ground she slipped free of the rope and crouched there, grinning.

He almost grinned back, then stopped himself. It would not do to let her know the warm admiration for her talents, judgement and character that had developed during their three years together. It would not do to let her even suspect the depth of his regard. It was when he did so that people inevitably betrayed his trust. His time in the orphanage, his apprenticeship, his marriage, his working life – all were scattered with the most poignant betrayals. Truly his heart bore many wounds. He would keep matters entirely professional, and thus protect them both. Him from her, and her from herself.

'Clear?' she hissed.

'As an empty squares board,' he murmured, standing over the stricken guard, 'and all according to plan. What do we most despise, after all?'

'Mustard?'

'And?'

'Accidents.'

'Correct. There are no such things as happy ones. Get his boots.'

With considerable effort they manoeuvred him down the hallway to his desk and into his chair. His head flopped back and he began to snore, long moustache fluttering gently around his lips.

'Ahhhhh, he sleeps like a babe. Props, if you please.'

Day handed him an empty spirits bottle and Morveer placed it carefully on the tiles beside the guard's boot. She passed him a half-full bottle, and he removed the stopper and sloshed a generous measure down the front of the guard's studded leather jerkin. Then he placed it carefully on its side by his dangling fingers, spirits leaking out across the tiles in an acrid puddle.

Morveer stepped back and framed the scene with his hands. 'The tableau . . . is prepared. What employer does not suspect his nightwatchman of partaking, against his express instructions, of a measure or two after dark? Observe the slack features, the reek of strong spirits, the loud snoring. Ample grounds, upon his discovery at dawn, for his immediate dismissal. He will protest his innocence, but in the total absence of any evidence–' he rummaged through the guard's hair with his gloved fingers and plucked the spent needle from his scalp '–no further suspicions will be aroused. All *perfectly* as normal. Except it will not be normal, will it? Oh no. The silent halls of the Westport office . . . of the Banking House of Valint and Balk . . . will conceal *a deadly secret.*' He blew out the flame of the guard's lantern, sinking them into deeper darkness. 'This way, Day, and do not dither.'

They crept together down the hallway, a pair of silent shadows, and stopped beside the heavy door to Mauthis' office. Day's picks gleamed as she bent down to work the lock. It only took a moment for her to turn the tumblers with a meaty clatter, and the door swung silently open.

'Poor locks for a bank,' as she slid her picks away.

'They put the good locks where the money is.'

'And we're not here to steal.'

'Oh no, no, we are rare thieves indeed. We leave *gifts* behind us.' He padded around Mauthis' monstrous desk and swung the heavy ledger open, taking care not to move it so much as a hair from its position. 'The solution, if you please.'

She handed him the jar, full almost to the brim with thin paste, and he carefully twisted the cork out with a gentle thwop. He used a fine paintbrush for the application. The very tool for an artist of his incalculable talents. The pages crackled as he turned them, giving a flick of the brush to the corners of each and every one.

'You see, Day? Swift, smooth and precise, but with every care. With *every* care, most of all. What kills most practitioners of our profession?'

'Their own agents.'

'*Precisely* so.' With every care, therefore, he swung the ledger closed, its pages already close to dry, slid the paintbrush away and pressed the cork back into the jar.

'Let's go,' said Day. 'I'm hungry.'

'Go?' Morveer's smile widened. 'Oh no, my dear, we are *far* from finished. You must still earn your supper. We have a long night's work ahead of us. A *very* long . . . night's . . . work.'

'Here.'

Shivers nearly jumped clean over the parapet, he was that shocked, lurched round, heart in his mouth. Murcatto crouched behind, grinning, breath leaving a touch of smoke about her shadowy face.

'By the dead but you gave me a scare!' he hissed.

'Better than what those guards would've given you.' She crept to the iron ring and tugged at the knot. 'You made it up there, then?' More'n a touch of surprise in her voice.

'You ever doubt I'd do it?'

'I thought you'd break your skull, if you even got high enough to fall.'

He tapped his head with a finger. 'Least vulnerable part o' me. Shake our friends off?'

'Halfway to bloody Lord Sabeldi Street, I did. If I'd known they'd be that easily led I'd have hooked them in the first place.'

Shivers grinned. 'Well, I'm glad you hooked 'em in the end, or they'd most likely have hooked me.'

'Couldn't have that. We've still got a lot of work to do.' Shivers wriggled his shoulders, uncomfortable. It was easy to forget at times that the work they were about was killing a man. 'Cold, eh?'

He snorted. 'Where I come from, this is a summer day.' He dragged the cork from the bottle and held it out to her. 'This might help keep you warm.'

'Well, that's very thoughtful of you.' She took a long swallow, and he watched the thin muscles in her neck shifting.

'I'm a thoughtful man, for one out of a gang of hired killers.'

'I'll have you know that some hired killers are very nice people.' She took another swig, then handed the bottle back. 'None of this crew, of course.'

'Hell, no, we're shits to a man. Or woman.'

'They're in there? Morveer and his little echo?'

'Aye, a while now, I reckon.'

'And Friendly with them?'

'He's with them.'

'Morveer say how long he'd be?'

'Him, tell me anything? I thought I was the optimist.'

They crouched in cold silence, close together by the parapet, looking across at the dark outline of the bank. For some reason he felt very nervy. Even more than you'd expect going about a murder. He stole a sideways glance at her, then didn't look away quite quick enough when she looked at him.

'Not much for us to do but wait and get colder, then,' she said.

'Not much, I reckon. Unless you want to cut my hair any shorter.'

'I'd be scared to get the scissors out in case you tried to strip.'

That brought a laugh from him. 'Very good. Reckon that earns you another pull.' He held out the bottle.

'I'm quite the humorist, for a woman who hires killers.' She came closer to take it. Close enough to give him a kind of tingle in the side that was near her. Close enough that he could feel the breath in his throat all of a sudden, coming quick. He looked away, not wanting to make a fool of himself any more than he'd been doing the last couple of weeks. Heard her tip the bottle, heard her drink. 'Thanks again.'

'Not a worry. Anything I can do, Chief, just let me know.'

When he turned his head she was looking right at him, lips pressed together in a hard line, eyes fixed on his, that way she had, like she was working out how much he was worth. 'There is one other thing.'

Morveer pushed the last lips of lead into position with consummate delicacy and stowed his glazing tools.

'Will that do?' asked Day.

'I doubt it will deflect a rainstorm, but it will serve until tomorrow. By then I suspect they will have *considerably* greater worries than a leaking window.' He rolled the last smudges of putty away from the glass, then followed his assistant across the rooftop to the parapet. Friendly had already negotiated the cord, a squat shape on the other side of a chasm of empty air. Morveer peered over the edge. Beyond the spikes and the ornamental carvings, the smooth stone pillar dropped vertiginously to the cobbled lane. One of the groups of guards slogged past it, lamps bobbing.

'What about the rope?' Day hissed once they were out of earshot. 'When the sun comes up someone will—'

'No detail overlooked.' Morveer grinned as he produced the tiny vial from an inside pocket. 'A few drops will burn through the knot some time after we have crossed. We need only wait at the far side and reel it in.'

As far as could be ascertained by darkness, his assistant appeared unconvinced. 'What if it burns more quickly than—'

'It will not.'

'Seems like an awful chance, though.'

'What do I never take, my dear?'

'Chances, but—'

'You go first, then, by all means.'

'You can count on it.' Day swung quickly under the rope and swarmed across, hand over hand. It took her no longer than a count of thirty to make it to the other side.

Morveer uncorked the little bottle and allowed a few drops to fall onto the knots. Considering it, he allowed a few more. He had no desire to wait until sunup for the cursed thing to come apart. He allowed the next patrol to pass below, then clambered over the parapet with, it had to be admitted, a good deal less grace than his assistant had displayed. Still, there was no need for undue haste. Caution first, always. He took the rope in his gloved hands, swung beneath it, hooked one shoe over the top, lifted the other—

There was a harsh ripping sound, and the wind blew suddenly cold about his knee.

Morveer peered down. His trouser-leg had caught upon a spike bent upwards well above the others, and torn almost as far as his rump. He thrashed his foot, trying to untangle it, but only succeeded in entrapping it more thoroughly.

'Damn it.' Plainly, this had not been part of the plan. Faint smoke was curling now from the balustrade around which the rope was knotted. It appeared the acid was acting more swiftly than anticipated.

'Damn it.' He swung himself back to the roof of the bank and perched beside the smoking knot, gripping the rope with one hand. He slid his scalpel from an inside pocket, reached forwards and cut the flapping cloth away from the spike with a few deft strokes. One, two, three and it was almost done, neat as a surgeon. The final stroke and—

'Ah!' He realised with annoyance, then mounting horror, that he had nicked his ankle with the blade. 'Damn it!' The edge was tainted with Larync tincture and, since the stuff had always given him a swell of nausea in the mornings, he had allowed his resistance to it to fade. It would not be fatal. Not of itself. But it might cause him to drop off a rope, and he had developed no immunity to a flailing plunge onto hard, hard cobblestones. The irony was bitter indeed. Most practitioners of his profession were killed, after all, by their own agents.

He pulled one glove off with his teeth and fumbled through his many pockets for that particular antidote, gurgling curses around the leather, swaying this way and that as the chill wind gusted up and spread gooseflesh all the way down his bare leg. Tiny tubes of glass rattled against his fingertips, each one etched with a mark that enabled him to identify it by touch.

Under the circumstances, though, the operation was still a testing one. He burped and felt a rush of nausea, a sudden painful shifting in his stomach. His fingers found the right mark. He let the glove fall from his mouth, pulled the phial from his coat with a trembling hand, dragged the cork out with his teeth and sucked up the contents.

He gagged on the bitter extract, spluttered sour spit down onto the faraway cobbles. He clung tight to the rope, fighting dizziness, the black street seeming to tip round and around him. He was a child again, and helpless. He gasped, whimpered, clung on with both hands. As desperately as he had clung to his mother's corpse when they came to take him.

Slowly the antidote had its effect. The dark world steadied, his stomach ceased its mad churning. The lane was beneath him, the sky above, back in their customary positions. His attention was drawn sharply to the knots again, smoking more than ever now and making a slight hissing sound. He could distinctly smell the acrid odour as they burned through.

'Damn it!' He hooked both legs over the rope and set off, pitifully weak from the self-administered dose of Larync. The air hissed in his throat, tightened now by the unmistakable grip of fear. If the cord burned through before he reached the other side, what then? His guts cramped up and he had to pause for a moment, teeth gritted, wobbling up and down in empty air.

On again, but he was lamentably fatigued. His arms trembled, his hands shuffled, bare palm and bare leg burning from friction. Well beyond halfway now, and creeping onwards. He let his head hang back, sucking in air for one more effort. He saw Friendly, an arm out towards him, big hand no more than a few strides distant. He saw Day, staring, and Morveer wondered with some annoyance if he could detect the barest hint of a smile on her shadowy face.

Then there was a faint ripping sound from the far end of the rope.

The bottom dropped out of Morveer's stomach and he was falling, falling, swinging downwards, chill air whooshing in through his gaping mouth. The side of the crumbling building plunged towards him. He started to let go a mad wail, just like the one he made when they tore him from his mother's dead hand. There was a sickening impact that drove his breath out, cut his scream off, tore the cord from his grasping hands.

There was a crashing, a tearing of wood. He was falling, clawing at the air, mind a cauldron of mad despair, eyes bulging sightless. Falling, arms flailing, legs kicking helplessly, the world reeling around him, wind rushing at his face. Falling, falling . . . no further than a stride or two. His cheek slapped against floorboards, fragments of wood clattering down around him

'Eh?' he muttered.

He was shocked to find himself snatched around the neck, dragged into the air and rammed against a wall with bowel-loosening force, breath driven out in a long wheeze for the second time in a few moments.

'You! What the fuck?' Shivers. The Northman was, for some reason still obscure, entirely naked. The grubby room behind him was dimly lit by some coals banked up in a grate. Morveer's eyes wandered down to the bed. Murcatto was in it, propped up on her elbows, rumpled shirt hanging open, breasts flattened against her ribs. She peered at him with no more than a mild surprise, as if she'd opened her front door to see a visitor she had not been expecting until later.

Morveer's mind clicked into place. Despite the embarrassment of the position, the residual pulsing of mortal terror and the tingling scratches on his face and hands, he began to chuckle. The rope had snapped ahead of time and, by some freak but hugely welcome chance, he had swung down in a perfect arc and straight through the rotten shutters of one of the rooms in the crumbling house. One had to appreciate the irony.

'It seems there *is* such a thing as a happy accident after all!' he cackled.

Murcatto squinted over from the bed, eyes somewhat un-focused. She had a set of curious scars, he noticed, following the lines of her ribs on one side.

'Why you smoking?' she croaked.

Morveer's eyes slid to the husk-pipe on the boards beside the bed, a ready explanation for her lack of surprise at the unortho-dox manner of his entrance. 'You are confused, but it is easy to see why. I believe it is you that has been smoking. That stuff is absolute *poison*, you realise. Absolute—'

Her arm stretched out, limp finger pointing towards his chest. 'Smoking, idiot.' He looked down. A few acrid wisps were curling up from his shirt.

'Damn it!' he squeaked as Shivers took a shocked step back and let him fall. He tore his jacket off, fragments of glass from the shattered acid bottle tinkling to the boards. He scrabbled with his shirt, the front of which had begun to bubble, ripped it open and flung it on the floor. It lay there, smoking noticeably and filling the grubby chamber with a foul reek. The three of them stared at it, by a turn of fate that surely no one could have anticipated, all now at least half-naked.

'My apologies.' Morveer cleared his throat. 'Plainly, this was not part of the plan.'

Repaid in Full

Monza frowned at the bed, and she frowned at Shivers in it. He lay flat out, blanket rumpled across his stomach. One big long arm hung off the edge of the mattress, white hand lying limp on its back against the floorboards. One big foot stuck from under the blanket, black crescents of dirt under the nails. His face was turned towards her, peaceful as a child's, eyes shut, mouth slightly open. His chest, and the long scar across it, rose and fell gently with his breathing.

By the light of day, it all seemed like a serious error.

She tossed the coins at Shivers and they jingled onto his chest and scattered across the bed. He jerked awake, blinking around.

'Whassis?' He stared blearily down at the silver stuck to his chest.

'Five scales. More than a fair price for last night.'

'Eh?' He pushed sleep out of his eye with two fingers. 'You're paying me?' He shoved the coins off his skin and onto the blanket. 'I feel something like a whore.'

'Aren't you one?'

'No. I've got some pride.'

'So you'll kill a man for money, but you won't suck a cunt for it?' She snorted. 'There's morals for you. You want my advice? Take the five and stick to killing in future. That you've got a talent for.'

Shivers rolled over and dragged the blanket up around his neck. 'Shut the door on your way out, eh? It's dreadful cold in here.'

The blade of the Calvez slashed viciously at the air. Cuts left and right, high and low. She spun in the far corner of the courtyard, boots shuffling across the broken paving, lunging with her left arm, bright point darting out chest-high. Her quick breath smoked around her face, shirt stuck to her back in spite of the cold.

Her legs were a little better each day. They still burned when she moved quickly, were stiff as old twigs in the morning and ached like fury by evening time, but at least she could almost walk without grimacing. There was some spring in her knees even, for all their clicking. Her shoulder and her jaw were loosening. The coins under her scalp barely hurt when she pressed them.

Her right hand was as ruined as ever, though. She tucked Benna's sword under her arm and pulled the glove off. Even that was painful. The twisted thing trembled, weak and pale, the scar from Gobba's wire lurid purple round the side. She winced as she forced the crooked fingers closed, little one still stubbornly straight. The thought that she'd be cursed with this hideous liability for the rest of her life brought on a sudden rush of fury.

'Bastard,' she hissed through gritted teeth, and dragged the glove back on. She remembered her father giving her a sword to hold for the first time, no more than eight years old. She remembered how heavy it had felt, how strange and unwieldy in her right hand. It hardly felt much better now, in her left. But she had no choice but to learn.

To start from nothing, if that was what it took.

She faced a rotten shutter, blade out straight towards it, wrist turned flat to the ground. She snapped out three jabs and the point tore three slats from the frame, one above the other. She snarled as she twisted her wrist and slashed downwards, splitting it clean in two, splinters flying.

Better. Better each day.

'*Magnificent.*' Morveer stood in a doorway, a few fresh scratches across one cheek. 'There is not a shutter in Styria that will dare oppose us.' He ambled forwards into the courtyard, hands clasped behind him. 'I daresay you were even more impressive when your right hand still functioned.'

'I'll worry about that.'

'A great deal, I should think. Recovered from your . . . *exertions* of last night with our Northern acquaintance?'

'My bed, my business. And you? Recovered from your little drop through my window?'

'No more than a scratch or two.'

'Shame.' She slapped the Calvez back into its sheath. 'Is it done?'

'It will be.'

'He's dead?'

'He will be.'

'When?'

Morveer grinned up at the square of pale sky above them. 'Patience is the first of virtues, General Murcatto. The bank has only just opened its doors, and the agent I used takes some time to work. Jobs done well are rarely done quickly.'

'But it will work?'

'Oh, absolutely so. It will be . . . *masterful*.'

'I want to see it.'

'Of course you do. Even in my hands the science of death is never utterly precise, but I would judge about an hour's time to be the best moment. I strongly caution you to touch nothing within the bank, however.' He turned away, wagging one finger at her over his shoulder. 'And take care you are not recognised. Our work together is only just commencing.'

The banking hall was busy. Dozens of clerks worked at heavy desks, bent over great ledgers, their pens scratching, rattling, scratching again. Guards stood bored about the walls, watching half-heartedly or not watching at all. Monza weaved between primped and pretty groups of wealthy men and women, slid between their oiled and bejewelled rows, Shivers shouldering his way through after. Merchants and shopkeepers and rich men's wives, bodyguards and lackeys with strongboxes and money bags. As far as she could tell it was an ordinary day's monumental profits for the Banking House of Valint and Balk.

The place Duke Orso got his money.

Then she caught a glimpse of a lean man with a hook nose, speaking to a group of fur-trimmed merchants and with a clerk flanking him on either side, ledgers tucked under their arms. That vulture face sprang from the crowds like a spark in a cellar, and set a fire in her. Mauthis. The man she'd come to Westport to kill. And it hardly needed saying that he looked very much alive.

Somebody called out over in the corner of the hall but Monza's eyes were fixed ahead, jaw suddenly clenched tight. She started to push through the queues towards Orso's banker.

'What're you doing?' Shivers hissed in her ear, but she shook him off, shoved a man in a tall hat out of her way.

'Give him some air!' somebody shouted. People were looking around, muttering, craning up to see something, the orderly queues starting to dissolve. Monza kept going, closer now, and closer. Closer than was sensible. She had no idea what she'd do when she got to Mauthis. Bite him? Say hello? She was less than ten paces away – as near as she'd been when he peered down at her dying brother.

Then the banker gave a sudden wince. Monza slowed, easing carefully through the crowd. She saw Mauthis double over as if he'd been punched in the stomach. He coughed, and again – hard, retching coughs. He took a lurching step and clutched at the wall. People were moving all around, the place echoing with curious whispers, the odd strange shout.

'Stand back!'

'What is it?'

'Turn him over!'

Mauthis' eyes shimmered with wet, veins bulging from his thin neck. He clawed at one of the clerks beside him, knees buckling. The man staggered, guiding his master slowly to the floor.

'Sir? Sir?'

An atmosphere of breathless fascination seemed to have gripped the whole hall, teetering on the brink of fear. Monza edged closer, peering over a velvet-clad shoulder. Mauthis' starting eyes met hers, and they stared straight at each other. His face was stretched tight, skin turning red, fibres of muscle standing rigid. One quivering arm raised up towards her, one bony finger pointing.

'Muh,' he mouthed, 'Muh . . . Muh . . .'

His eyes rolled back and he started to dance, legs flopping, back arching, jerking madly around on the marble tiles like a landed fish. The men about him stared down, horrified. One of them was doubled up by a sudden coughing fit. People were shouting all over the banking hall.

'Help!'

'Over here!'

'Somebody!'

'Some air, I said!'

A clerk lurched up from his desk, chair clattering over, hands at his throat. He staggered a few steps, face turning purple, then crashed down, a shoe flying off one kicking foot. One of the clerks beside Mauthis was on his knees, fighting for breath. A woman gave a piercing scream.

'By the dead—' came Shivers' voice.

Pink foam frothed from the banker's wide-open mouth. His thrashing settled to a twitching. Then to nothing. His body sagged back, empty eyes goggling up over Monza's shoulder, towards the grinning busts ranged round the walls.

Two dead. Five left.

'Plague!' somebody shrieked, and as if a general had roared for the charge on a battlefield, the place was plunged instantly into jostling chaos. Monza was nearly barged over as one of the merchants who'd been talking to Mauthis turned to run. Shivers stepped up and gave him a shove, sent him sprawling on top of the banker's corpse. A man with skewed eyeglasses clutched at her, bulging eyes horribly magnified in his pink face. She punched on an instinct with her right hand, gasped as her twisted knuckles jarred against his cheek and sent a jolt of pain to her shoulder, chopped at him with the heel of her left and knocked him over backwards.

No plague spreads quicker than panic, Stolicus wrote, *nor is more deadly.*

The veneer of civilisation was peeled suddenly away. The rich and self-satisfied were transformed into animals. Those in the way were flung aside. Those that fell were given no mercy. She saw a fat merchant punch a well-dressed lady in the face and she collapsed with a squeal, was kicked to the wall, wig twisted across her bloody face. She saw an old man huddled on the floor, trampled by the mob. A strongbox banged down, silver coins spilling, ignored, kicked across the floor by milling shoes. It was like the madness of a rout. The screaming and the jostling, the swearing and the stink of fear, the scattering of bodies and broken junk.

Someone shoved at her and she lashed out with an elbow, felt something crunch, spots of blood on her cheek. She was caught up by the crush like a twig in a river, jabbed at, twisted, torn and tangled. She was carried snarling through the doorway and into the street, feet scarcely touching the ground, people pressing, thrashing, wriggling up against her. She was swept sideways, slipped from the steps, twisted her leg on the cobbles and lurched against the wall of the bank.

She felt Shivers grab her by the elbow and half-lead, half-carry her off. A couple of the bank's guards stood, trying ineffectually to stem the flow of panic with the hafts of their halberds. There was a sudden surge in the crowd and Monza was carried back. Between flailing arms she saw a man quivering on the ground, coughing red foam onto the cobbles. A wall of horrified, fascinated faces twitched and bobbed as people fought to get away from him.

Monza felt dizzy, mouth sour. Shivers strode beside her, breathing fast through his nose, glancing back over his shoulder. They rounded the corner of the bank and made for the crumbling house, the maddened clamour fading behind them. She saw Morveer, standing at a high window like a wealthy patron enjoying the theatre from his private box. He grinned down, and waved with one hand.

Shivers growled something in his own tongue as he heaved the heavy door open and Monza came after him. She snatched up the Calvez and made straight for the stairs, taking them two at a time, hardly noticing the burning in her knees.

Morveer still stood by the window when she got there, his assistant cross-legged on the table, munching her way through half a loaf of bread. 'There seems to be *quite* the ruckus down in the street!' The poisoner turned into the room, but his smile vanished as he saw Monza's face. 'What? He's alive?'

'He's dead. Dozens of them are.'

Morveer's eyebrows went up by the slightest fraction. 'An establishment of that nature, the books will be in constant movement around the building. I could not take the risk that Mauthis would end up working from another. What do I never take, Day?'

'Chances. Caution first, always.' Day tore off another

mouthful of bread, and mumbled around it. 'That's why we poisoned them all. Every ledger in the place.'

'This isn't what we agreed,' Monza growled.

'I rather think it is. Whatever it takes, you told me, no matter who gets killed along the way. Those are the only terms under which I work. Anything else allows for *misunderstandings*.' Morveer looked somewhat puzzled, somewhat amused. 'I am well aware that some individuals are uncomfortable with whole-sale murder, but I certainly never anticipated that you, Monzcarro Murcatto, the Serpent of Talins, the Butcher of Caprile, would be one. You need not worry about the money. Mauthis will cost you ten thousand, as we agreed. The rest are free of—'

'It's not a question of money, fool!'

'Then what *is* the question? I undertook a piece of work, as commissioned by you, and was successful, so how can I be at fault? You say you never had in mind any such result, and did not undertake the work yourself, so how can you be at fault? The responsibility seems to drop between us, then, like a *turd* straight from a beggar's *arse* and into an open sewer, to be lost from sight for ever and cause nobody any further discomfort. An unfortunate misunderstanding, shall we say? An accident? As if a sudden wind blew up, and a great tree fell, and caught every little insect in that place and squashed . . . them . . . *dead*!'

'Squashed 'em,' chirped Day.

'If your conscience nags at you—'

Monza felt a stab of anger, gloved hand gripping the sword's scabbard painfully hard, twisted bones clicking as they shifted. 'Conscience is an excuse not to do what needs doing. This is about keeping control. We'll stick to one dead man at a time from now on.'

'Will we indeed?'

She took a sudden stride into the room and the poisoner edged away, eyes flickering nervously down to her sword, then back. 'Don't test me. Not ever. One . . . at a time . . . I said.'

Morveer carefully cleared his throat. 'You are the client, of course. We will proceed as you dictate. There really is no cause to get angry.'

'Oh, you'll know if I get angry.'

He gave a pained sigh. 'What is the tragedy of our profession, Day?'

'No appreciation.' His assistant popped the last bit of crust into her mouth.

'*Precisely* so. Come, we will take a turn about the city while our employer decides which name on her little list next merits our attentions. The atmosphere in here feels somewhat tainted by *hypocrisy*.' He marched out with an air of injured innocence. Day looked up from under her sandy lashes, shrugged, stood, brushed crumbs from the front of her shirt, then followed her master.

Monza turned back to the window. The crowds had mostly broken up. Groups of nervous city watch had appeared, blocking off the street before the bank, keeping a careful distance from the still shapes sprawled out on the cobbles. She wondered what Benna would've said to this. Told her to calm down, most likely. Told her to think it through.

She grabbed a chest with both hands and snarled as she flung it across the room. It smashed into the wall, sending lumps of plaster flying, clattered down and sagged open, clothes spilling out across the floor.

Shivers stood there in the doorway, watching her. 'I'm done.'

'No!' She swallowed. 'No. I still need your help.'

'Standing up and facing a man, that's one thing . . . but this—'

'The rest will be different. I'll see to it.'

'Nice, clean murders? I doubt it. You set your mind to killing, it's hard to pick the number of the dead.' Shivers slowly shook his head. 'Morveer and his fucking like might be able to step away from it and smile, but I can't.'

'So what?' She walked slowly to him, the way you might walk to a skittish horse, trying to stop it bolting with your eyes. 'Back to the North with fifty scales for the journey? Grow your hair and go back to bad shirts and blood on the snow? I thought you had pride. I thought you wanted to be better than that.'

'That's right. I wanted to be better.'

'You can be. Stick. Who knows? Maybe you can save some lives, that way.' She laid her left hand gently on his chest. 'Steer me down the righteous path. Then you can be good and rich at once.'

'I'm starting to doubt a man can be both.'

'Help me. I have to do this . . . for my brother.'

'You sure? The dead are past helping. Vengeance is for you.'

'For me then!' She forced her voice to drop soft again. 'There's nothing I can do to change your mind?'

His mouth twisted. 'Going to toss me another five, are you?'

'I shouldn't have done that.' She slid her hand up, traced the line of his jaw, trying to judge the right words, pitch the right bargain. 'You didn't deserve it. I lost my brother, and he's all I had. I don't want to lose someone else . . .' She let it hang in the air.

There was a strange look in Shivers' eye, now. Part angry, part hungry, part ashamed. He stood there silent for a long moment, and she felt the muscles clenching and unclenching on the side of his face.

'Ten thousand,' he said.

'Six.'

'Eight.'

'Done.' She let her hand fall, and they stared at each other. 'Get packed, we leave within the hour.'

'Right.' He slunk guiltily out of the door without meeting her eye and left her there, alone.

And that was the trouble with good men. Just so damned expensive.

III
SIPANI

'The belief in a supernatural source
of evil is not necessary; men alone
are quite capable of every wickedness'

Joseph Conrad

Not two weeks later, men came over the border looking to even the tally, and they hanged old Destort and his wife, and burned the mill. A week after that his sons set out for vengeance, and Monza took down her father's sword and went with them, Benna snivelling along behind. She was glad to go. She had lost the taste for farming.

They left the valley to settle a score, and for two years they did not stop. Others joined them, men who had lost their work, their farms, their families. Before too long it was them burning crops, breaking into farmhouses, taking what they could find. Before too long it was them doing the hangings. Benna grew up quickly, and sharpened to a merciless edge. What other choice? They avenged killings, then thefts, then slights, then the rumours of slights. There was war, so there was never any shortage of wrongs to avenge.

Then, at the end of summer, Talins and Musselia made peace with nothing gained on either side but corpses. A man with a gold-edged cloak rode into the valley with soldiers behind him and forbade reprisals. Destort's sons and the rest split up, took their spoils with them, went back to what they had been doing before the madness started or found new madness to take a hand in. By then, Monza's taste for farming had grown back.

They made it as far as the village.

A vision of martial splendour stood at the edge of the broken fountain in a breastplate of shining steel, a sword hilt set with glinting gemstones at his hip. Half the valley had gathered to listen to him speak.

'My name is Nicomo Cosca, captain of the Company of the Sun – a noble brotherhood fighting with the Thousand Swords, greatest mercenary brigade in Styria! We have a Paper of Engagement from the young Duke Rogont of Ospria and are looking for men! Men with experience of war, men with courage, men with a love of *adventure and a taste for money! Are any of you sick of grubbing in the mud for a living? Do any of you hope for something better? For honour? For glory? For riches? Join us!'*

'We could do that,' Benna hissed.

'No,' said Monza, 'I'm done with fighting.'

'There will be little fighting!' shouted Cosca, as if he could guess her thoughts. 'That I promise you! And what there is you will be well paid for thrice over! A scale a week, plus shares of booty! And there will be plenty of booty, lads, believe me! Our cause is just . . . or just enough, and victory is a certainty.'

'We could do that!' hissed Benna. 'You want to go back to tossing mud? Broken down tired every night and dirt under your fingernails? I won't!'

Monza thought of the work she would have just to clear the upper field, and how much she might make from doing it. A line had formed of men keen to join the Company of the Sun, beggars and farmers mostly. A black-skinned notary took their names down in a ledger.

Monza shoved past them.

'I am Monzcarro Murcatto, daughter of Jappo Murcatto, and this is my brother Benna, and we are fighters. Can you find work for us in your company?'

Cosca frowned at her, and the black-skinned man shook his head. 'We need men with experience of war. Not women and boys.' He tried to move her away with his arm.

She would not be moved. 'We've experience. More than these scrapings.'

'I've work for you,' said one of the farmers, made bold by signing his mark on the paper. 'How about you suck my cock?' He laughed at that. Until Monza knocked him down in the mud and made him swallow half his teeth with the heel of her boot.

Nicomo Cosca watched this methodical display with one eyebrow slightly raised. 'Sajaam, the Paper of Engagement. Does it specify men, exactly? What is the wording?'

The notary squinted at a document. 'Two hundred cavalry and two hundred infantry, those to be persons well equipped and of quality. Persons is all it says.'

'And quality is such a vague term. You, girl! Murcatto! You are hired, and your brother too. Make your marks.'

She did so, and so did Benna, and as simply as that they were soldiers of the Thousand Swords. Mercenaries. The farmer clutched at Monza's leg.

'My teeth.'

'Pick through your shit for them,' she said.

Nicomo Cosca, famed soldier of fortune, led his new hirings from the village to the sound of a merry pipe, and they camped under the stars that night, gathered round fires in the darkness, talking of making it rich in the coming campaign.

Monza and Benna huddled together with their blanket around their shoulders. Cosca came out of the murk, firelight glinting on his breastplate. 'Ah! My war-children! My lucky mascots! Cold, eh?' He swept his crimson cloak off and tossed it down to them. 'Take this. Might keep the frost from your bones.'

'What d'you want for it?'

'Take it with my compliments, I have another.'

'Why?' she grunted, suspicious.

'"A captain looks first to the comfort of his men, then to his own," Stolicus said.'

'Who's he?' asked Benna.

'Stolicus? Why, the greatest general of history!' Monza stared blankly at him. 'An emperor of old. The most famous of emperors.'

'What's an emperor?' asked Benna.

Cosca raised his brows. 'Like a king, but more so. You should read this.' He slid something from a pocket and pressed it into Monza's hand. A small book, with a red cover scuffed and scarred.

'I will.' She opened it and frowned at the first page, waiting for him to go.

'Neither of us can read,' said Benna, before Monza could shut him up.

Cosca frowned, twisting one corner of his waxed moustache between finger and thumb. Monza was waiting for him to tell them to go back to the farm, but instead he lowered himself slowly and sat cross-legged beside them. 'Children, children.' He pointed at the page. 'This here is the letter "A".'

Fogs and Whispers

Sipani smelled of rot and old salt water, of coal smoke, shit and piss, of fast living and slow decay. Made Shivers feel like puking, though the smell mightn't have mattered so much if he could've seen his hand before his face. The night was dark, the fog so thick that Monza, walking close enough to touch, weren't much more than a ghostly outline. His lamp scarcely lit ten cobbles in front of his boots, all shining with cold dew. More than once he'd nearly stepped straight off into water. It was easily done. In Sipani, water was hiding round every corner.

Angry giants loomed up, twisted, changed to greasy buildings and crept past. Figures charged from the mist like the Shanka did at the Battle of Dunbrec, then turned out to be bridges, railings, statues, carts. Lamps swung on poles at corners, torches burned by doorways, lit windows glowed, hanging in the murk, treacherous as marsh-lights. Shivers would set his course by one set, squinting through the mist, only to see a house start drifting. He'd blink, and shake his head, the ground shifting dizzily under his boots. Then he'd realise it was a barge, sliding past in the water beside the cobbled way, bearing its lights off into the night. He'd never liked cities, fog or salt water. The three together were like a bad dream.

'Bloody fog,' Shivers muttered, holding his lamp higher, as though that helped. 'Can't see a thing.'

'This is Sipani,' Monza tossed over her shoulder. 'City of Fogs. City of Whispers.'

The chill air was full of strange sounds, alright. Everywhere the slap, slop of water, the creaking of ropes as rowing boats squirmed on the shifting canals. Bells tolling in the darkness, folk calling out, all kinds of voices. Prices. Offers. Warnings. Jokes and threats spilling over each other. Dogs barked, cats hissed, rats skittered, birds croaked. Snatches of music, lost in the mist. Ghostly laughter fluttered past on the other side of the seething water, lamps bobbing through the gloom as some revel wended into the night from tavern, to brothel, to gambling den, to smoke-house. Made Shivers' head spin, and left him sicker than ever. Felt like he'd been sick for weeks. Ever since Westport.

Footsteps echoed from the darkness and Shivers pressed himself against the wall, right hand on the haft of the hatchet tucked in his coat. Men loomed up and away, brushing past him. Women too, one holding a hat to her piled-up hair as she ran. Devil faces, smeared with drunken smiles, reeling past in a flurry and gone into the night, mist curling behind their flapping cloaks.

'Bastards,' hissed Shivers after them, letting go his axe and peeling himself away from the sticky wall. 'Lucky I didn't split one of 'em.'

'Get used to it. This is Sipani. City of Revels. City of Rogues.'

Rogues were in long supply, alright. Men slouched around steps, on corners, beside bridges, dishing out hard looks. Women too, black outlines in doorways, lamps glowing behind, some of 'em hardly dressed in spite of the cold. 'A scale!' one called at him from a window, letting one thin leg dangle in the murk. 'For a scale you get the night of your life! Ten bits then! Eight!'

'Selling themselves,' Shivers grunted.

'Everyone's selling themselves,' came Monza's muffled voice. 'This is—'

'Yes, yes. This is fucking Sipani.'

Monza stopped and he nearly walked into her. She pushed her hood back and squinted at a narrow doorway in a wall of crumbling brickwork. 'This is it.'

'You take a man to all the finest places, eh?'

'Maybe later you'll get the tour. For now we've got business. Look dangerous.'

'Right y'are, Chief.' Shivers stood up tall and fixed his hardest frown. 'Right y'are.'

She knocked, and not long after the door wobbled open. A woman stared out from a dim-lit hallway, long and lean as a spider. She had a way of standing, hips loose and tilted to one side, arm up on the doorframe, one thin finger tapping at the wood. Like the fog was hers, and the night, and them too. Shivers brought his lamp up a touch closer. A hard, sharp face with a knowing smile, spattered with freckles, short red hair sprouting all ways from her head.

'Shylo Vitari?' asked Monza.

'You'll be Murcatto, then.'

'That's right.'

'Death suits you.' She narrowed her eyes at Shivers. Cold eyes, with a hint of a cruel joke in 'em. 'Who's your man?'

He spoke for himself. 'Name's Caul Shivers, and I'm not hers.'

'No?' She grinned at Monza. 'Whose is he, then?'

'I'm my own.'

She gave a sharp laugh at that. Seemed everything about her had an edge on it. 'This is Sipani, friend. Everyone belongs to someone. Northman, eh?'

'That a problem?'

'Got tossed down a flight of stairs by one once. Haven't been entirely comfortable around them since. Why Shivers?'

She caught him off balance with that one. 'What?'

'Up in the North, the way I heard it, a man earns his name. Great deeds done, and all that. Why Shivers?'

'Er . . .' The last thing he needed was to look the fool in front of Monza. He was still hoping to make it back into her bed at some point. 'Because my enemies shiver with fear when they face me,' he lied.

'That so?' Vitari stood back from the door, giving him a mocking grin as he ducked under the low lintel. 'You must have some cowardly bloody enemies.'

'Sajaam says you know people here,' said Monza as the woman led them into a narrow sitting room, barely lit by some smoky coals on a grate.

'I know everyone.' She took a steaming pot off the fire. 'Soup?'

'Not me,' said Shivers, leaning against the wall and folding his arms over his chest. He'd been a lot more careful about hospitality since he met Morveer.

'Nor me,' said Monza.

'Suit yourselves.' Vitari poured a mug out for herself and sat, folding one long leg over the other, pointed toe of her black boot rocking backwards and forwards.

Monza took the only other chair, wincing a touch as she lowered herself into it. 'Sajaam says you can get things done.'

'And just what is it that the two of you need doing?'

Monza glanced across at Shivers, and he shrugged back at her. 'I hear the King of the Union is coming to Sipani.'

'So he is. Seems he's got it in mind that he's the great statesman of the age.' Vitari smiled wide, showing two rows of clean, sharp teeth. 'He's going to bring peace to Styria.'

'Is he now?'

'That's the rumour. He's brought together a conference to negotiate terms, between Grand Duke Orso and the League of Eight. He's got all their leaders coming – those who are still alive, at least, Rogont and Salier at the front. He's got old Sotorius to play host – neutral ground here in Sipani, is the thinking. And he's got his brothers-in-law on their way, to speak for their father.'

Monza craned forwards, eager as a buzzard at a carcass. 'Ario and Foscar both?'

'Ario and Foscar both.'

'They're going to make peace?' asked Shivers, and soon regretted saying anything. The two women each gave him their own special kind of sneer.

'This is Sipani,' said Vitari. 'All we make here is fog.'

'And that's all anyone will be making at this conference, you can depend on that.' Monza eased herself back into her chair, scowling. 'Fogs and whispers.'

'The League of Eight is splitting at the seams. Borletta fallen. Cantain dead. Visserine will be under siege when the weather breaks. No talk's going to change that.'

'Ario will sit, and smirk, and listen, and nod. Scatter a little trail of hopes that his father will make peace. Right up until Orso's troops appear outside the walls of Visserine.'

Vitari lifted her cup again, narrow eyes on Monza. 'And the Thousand Swords alongside them.'

'Salier and Rogont and all the rest will know that well enough. They're no fools. Misers and cowards, maybe, but no fools. They're only playing for time to manoeuvre.'

'Manoeuvre?' asked Shivers, chewing on the strange word.

'Wriggle,' said Vitari, showing him her teeth again. 'Orso

won't make peace, and the League of Eight aren't looking for it. The only man who's come here hoping for anything but fog is his August Majesty, but they say he's got a talent for self-deception.'

'Comes with the crown,' said Monza, 'but he's nothing to me. Ario and Foscar are my business. What will they be about, other than feeding lies to their brother-in-law?'

'There's going to be a masked ball in honour of the king and queen at Sotorius' palace on the first night of the conference. Ario and Foscar will be there.'

'That'll be well guarded,' said Shivers, doing his best to keep up. Didn't help that he thought he could hear a child crying somewhere.

Vitari snorted. 'A dozen of the best-guarded people in the world, all sharing a room with their bitterest enemies? There'll be more soldiers than at the Battle of Adua, I'll be bound. Hard to think of a spot where the brothers would be less vulnerable.'

'What else, then?' snapped Monza.

'We'll see. I'm no friend of Ario's, but I know someone who is. A close, close friend.'

Monza's black brows drew in. 'Then we should be talking to—'

The door creaked suddenly open and Shivers spun round, hatchet already halfway out.

A child stood in the doorway. A girl maybe eight years old, dressed in a too-long shift with bony ankles and bare feet sticking out the bottom, red hair poking from her head in a tangled mess. She stared at Shivers, then Monza, then Vitari with wide blue eyes. 'Mama. Cas is crying.'

Vitari knelt down and smoothed the little girl's hair. 'Never you mind, baby, I hear. Try and soothe him. I'll be up soon as I can, and sing to you all.'

'Alright.' The girl gave Shivers another look, and he pushed his axe away, somewhat shamefaced, and tried to make a grin. She backed off and pulled the door shut.

'My boy's got a cough,' said Vitari, her voice with its hard edge again. 'One gets ill, then they all get ill, then I get ill. Who'd be a mother, eh?'

Shivers lifted his brows. 'Can't say I've got the equipment.'

'Never had much luck with family,' said Monza. 'Can you help us?'

Vitari's eyes flickered over to Shivers, and back. 'Who else you got along with you?'

'A man called Friendly, as muscle.'

'Good, is he?'

'Very,' said Shivers, thinking of the two men hacked bloody on the streets of Talins. 'Bit strange, though.'

'You need to be in this line of work. Who else?'

'A poisoner and his assistant.'

'A good one?'

'According to him. Name of Morveer.'

'Gah!' Vitari looked as if she'd the taste of piss in her mouth. 'Castor Morveer? That bastard's about as trustworthy as a scorpion.'

Monza looked back, hard and level. 'Scorpions have their uses. Can you help us, I asked?'

Vitari's eyes were two slits, shining in the firelight. 'I can help you, but it'll cost. If we can get the job done, something tells me I won't be welcome in Sipani any more.'

'Money isn't a problem. Just as long as you can get us close. You know someone who can help with that?'

Vitari drained her mug, then tossed the dregs hissing onto the coals. 'Oh, I know all kinds of people.'

The Arts of Persuasion

It was early, and the twisting streets of Sipani were quiet. Monza hunched in a doorway, coat wrapped tight around her, hands wedged under her armpits. She'd been hunched there for an hour at least, steadily getting colder, breathing fog into the foggy air. The edges of her ears and her nostrils tingled unpleasantly. It was a wonder the snot hadn't frozen in her nose. But she could be patient. She had to be.

Nine-tenths of war is waiting, Stolicus wrote, and she felt he'd called it low.

A man wheeled past a barrow heaped with straw, tuneless whistling deadened by the thinning mist, and Monza's eyes slid after him until he became a murky outline and was gone. She wished Benna was with her.

And she wished he'd brought his husk pipe with him.

She shifted her tongue in her dry mouth, trying to push the thought out of her mind, but it was like a splinter under her thumbnail. The painful, wonderful bite at her lungs, the taste of the smoke as she let it curl from her mouth, her limbs growing heavy, the world softening. The doubt, the anger, the fear all leaking away . . .

Footsteps clapped on wet flagstones and a pair of figures rose out of the gloom. Monza stiffened, fists clenching, pain flashing through her twisted knuckles. A woman in a bright red coat edged with gold embroidery. 'Hurry up!' Snapped in a faint Union accent to a man lumbering along behind with a heavy trunk on one shoulder. 'I do not mean to be late again—'

Vitari's shrill whistle cut across the empty street. Shivers slid from a doorway, loomed up behind the servant and pinned his arms. Friendly came out of nowhere and sank four heavy punches into his gut before he could even shout, sent him to the cobbles blowing vomit.

Monza heard the woman gasp, caught a glimpse of her wide-eyed face as she turned to run. Before she'd gone a step Vitari's voice echoed out of the gloom ahead. 'Carlot dan Eider, unless I'm much mistaken!'

The woman in the red coat backed towards the doorway where Monza was standing, one hand held up. 'I have money! I can pay you!'

Vitari sauntered out of the murk, loose and easy as a mean cat in her own garden. 'Oh, you'll pay alright. I must say I was surprised when I learned Prince Ario's favourite mistress was in Sipani. I heard you could hardly be dragged from his bedchamber.' Vitari herded her towards the doorway and Monza backed off, into the dim corridor, wincing at the sharp pains through her legs as she started to move.

'Whatever the League of Eight are paying, I'll—'

'I don't work for them, and I'm hurt by the assumption. Don't you remember me? From Dagoska? Don't you remember trying to sell the city to the Gurkish? Don't you remember getting caught?' And Monza saw her let something drop and clatter against the cobbles – a cross-shaped blade, dancing and rattling on the end of a chain.

'Dagoska?' Eider's voice had a note of strange terror in it now. 'No! I've done everything he asked! Everything! Why would he—'

'Oh, I don't work for the Cripple any more.' Vitari leaned in close. 'I've gone freelance.'

The woman in the red coat stumbled back over the threshold and into the corridor. She turned and saw Monza waiting, gloved hand slack on the pommel of her sword. She stopped dead, ragged breath echoing from the damp walls. Vitari shut the door behind them, latch dropping with a final-sounding click.

'This way.' She gave Eider a shove and she nearly fell over her own coat-tails. 'If it please you.' Another shove as she found her feet and she sprawled through the doorway on her face. Vitari dragged her up by one arm and Monza followed them slowly into the room beyond, jaw clenched tight.

Like her jaw, the room had seen better days. The crumbling plaster was stained with black mould, bubbling up with damp, the stale air smelled of rot and onions. Day leaned back in one corner, a carefree smile on her face as she buffed a plum the colour of a fresh bruise against her sleeve. She offered it to Eider.

'Plum?'

'What? No!'

'Suit yourself. They're good though.'

'Sit.' Vitari shoved Eider into the rickety chair that was the only furniture. Usually a good thing, getting the only seat. But not now. 'They say history moves in circles but who'd ever have thought we'd meet like this again? It's enough to bring tears to our eyes, isn't it? Yours, anyway.'

Carlot dan Eider didn't look like crying any time soon, though. She sat upright, hands crossed in her lap. Surprising composure, under the circumstances. Dignity, almost. She was past the first flush of youth, but a most striking woman still, and everything carefully plucked, painted and powdered to make the best show of it. A necklace of red stones flashed around her throat, gold glittered on her long fingers. She looked more like a countess than a mistress, as out of place in the rotting room as a diamond ring in a rubbish heap.

Vitari prowled slowly around the chair, leaning down to hiss in her ear. 'You're looking well. Always did know how to land on your feet. Quite the tumble, though, isn't it? From head of the Guild of Spicers to Prince Ario's whore?'

Eider didn't even flinch. 'It's a living. What do you want?'

'Just to talk.' Vitari's voice purred low and husky as a lover's. 'Unless we don't get the answers we want. Then I'll have to hurt you.'

'No doubt you'll enjoy that.'

'It's a living.' She punched Ario's mistress suddenly in the ribs, hard enough to twist her in the chair. She doubled up, gasping, and Vitari leaned over her, bringing her fist up again. 'Another?'

'No!' Eider held her hand up, teeth bared, eyes flickering round the room then back to Vitari. 'No . . . ah . . . I'll be helpful. Just . . . just tell me what you need to know.'

'Why are you down here, ahead of your lover?'

'To make arrangements for the ball. Costumes, masks, all kinds of—'

Vitari's fist thumped into her side in just the same spot, harder than the first time, the sharp thud echoing off the damp walls.

Eider whimpered, arms wrapped around herself, took a shudder-ing breath then coughed it out, face twisted with pain. Vitari leaned down over her like a black spider over a bound-up fly. 'I'm losing patience. Why are you here?'

'Ario's putting on . . . another kind of celebration . . . after-wards. For his brother. For his brother's birthday.'

'What kind of celebration?'

'The kind for which Sipani is famous.' Eider coughed again, turned her head and spat, a few wet specks settling across the shoulder of her beautiful coat.

'Where?'

'At Cardotti's House of Leisure. He's hired the whole place for the night. For him, and for Foscar, and for their gentlemen. He sent me here to make the arrangements.'

'He sent his mistress to hire whores?'

Monza snorted. 'Sounds like Ario. What arrangements?'

'To find entertainers. To make the place ready. To make sure it's safe. He . . . trusts me.'

'More fool him.' Vitari chuckled. 'I wonder what he'd do if he knew who you really worked for, eh? Who you really spy for? Our mutual friend at the House of Questions? Our crippled friend from his Majesty's Inquisition? Keeping an eye on Styrian business for the Union, eh? You must have trouble remembering who you're supposed to betray from week to week.'

Eider glowered back at her, arms still folded around her battered ribs. 'It's a living.'

'A dying, if Ario learns the truth. One little note is all it would take.'

'What do you want?'

Monza stepped from the shadows. 'I want you to help us get close to Ario, and to Foscar. I want you to let us into Cardotti's House of Leisure on the night of this celebration of yours. When it comes to arranging the entertainments, I want you to hire who we say, when we say, how we say. Do you understand?'

Eider's face was very pale. 'You mean to kill them?' No one spoke, but the silence said plenty. 'Orso will guess I betrayed him! The Cripple will know I betrayed him! There aren't two worse enemies in the Circle of the World! You might as well kill me now!'

153

'Alright.' The blade of the Calvez rang gently as she drew it. Eider's eyes went wide.

'Wait—'

Monza reached out, resting the glinting point of the sword in the hollow between Eider's collarbones, and gently pushed. Ario's mistress arched back over the chair, hands opening and closing helplessly.

'Ah! Ah!' Monza twisted her wrist, steel flashing as the slender blade tilted one way and the other, the point grinding, digging, screwing ever so slowly into Eider's neck. A line of dark blood trickled from the wound it made and crept down her breastbone. Her squealing grew more shrill, more urgent, more terrified. 'No! Ah! Please! No!'

'No?' Monza held her there, pinned over the back of the chair. 'Not quite ready to die after all? Not many of us are, when it comes to the moment.' She slid the Calvez free and Eider rocked forwards, touching one trembling fingertip to her bloody neck, breath coming in ragged gasps.

'You don't understand. It isn't just Orso! It isn't just the Union! They're both backed by the bank. By Valint and Balk. Owned by the bank. The Years of Blood are no more than a sideshow to them. A skirmish. You've no idea whose garden you're pissing in—'

'Wrong.' Monza leaned down and made Eider shrink back. 'I don't care. There's a difference.'

'Now?' asked Day.

'Now.'

The girl's hand darted out and pricked Eider's ear with a glinting needle. 'Ah!'

Day yawned as she slipped the splinter of metal into an inside pocket. 'Don't worry, it's slow-working. You've got at least a week.'

'Until what?'

'Until you get sick.' Day took a bite out of her plum and juice ran down her chin. 'Bloody hell,' she muttered, catching it with a fingertip.

'Sick?' breathed Eider.

'Really, really sick. A day after that you'll be deader than Juvens.'

'Help us, you get the antidote, and at least the chance to run.' Monza rubbed the blood from the point of Benna's sword with gloved thumb and forefinger. 'Try and tell anyone what we're planning, here or in the Union, Orso, or Ario, or your friend the Cripple, and . . .' She slid the blade back into its sheath and slapped the hilt home with a sharp snap. 'One way or another, Ario will be short one mistress.'

Eider stared round at them, one hand still pressed to her neck. 'You evil bitches.'

Day gave the plum pit a final suck then tossed it away. 'It's a living.'

'We're done.' Vitari dragged Ario's mistress to her feet by one elbow and started marching her towards the door.

Monza stepped in front of them. 'What will you be telling your battered manservant, when he comes round?'

'That . . . we were robbed?'

Monza held out her gloved hand. Eider's face fell even further. She unclasped her necklace and dropped it into Monza's palm, then followed it with her rings. 'Convincing enough?'

'I don't know. You seem like the kind of woman to put up a struggle.' Monza punched her in the face. She squawked, stumbled, would've fallen if Vitari hadn't caught her. She looked up, blood leaking from her nose and her split lip, and for an instant she had this strange expression. Hurt, yes. Afraid, of course. But more angry than either one. Like the look Monza had herself, maybe, when they threw her from the balcony.

'Now we're done,' she said.

Vitari yanked at Eider's elbow and dragged her out into the hallway, towards the front door, their footsteps scraping against the grubby boards. Day gave a sigh, then pushed herself away from the wall and brushed plaster-dust from her backside. 'Nice and neat.'

'No thanks to your master. Where is he?'

'I prefer employer, and he said there were some errands he had to run.'

'Errands?'

'That a problem?'

'I paid for the master, not the dog.'

Day grinned. 'Woof, woof. There's nothing Morveer can do that I can't.'

'That so?'

'He's getting old. Arrogant. That rope burning through was nearly the death of him, in Westport. I wouldn't want any carelessness like that to interfere with your business. Not for what you're paying. No one worse to have next to you than a careless poisoner.'

'You'll get no argument from me on that score.'

Day shrugged. 'Accidents happen all the time in our line of work. Especially to the old. It's a young person's trade, really.' She sauntered out into the corridor, passed Vitari stalking back the other way. The look of glee was long gone from her sharp face, and the swagger with it. She lifted one black boot and shoved the chair angrily away into one corner.

'There's our way in, then,' she said.

'Seems so.'

'Just what I promised you.'

'Just what you promised.'

'Ario and Foscar, both together, and a way to get to them.'

'A good day's work.'

They looked at each other, and Vitari ran her tongue around the inside of her mouth as if it tasted bitter. 'Well.' She shrugged her bony shoulders. 'It's a living.'

The Life of the Drinker

'**A** drink, a drink, a drink. Where can a man find a drink?' Nicomo Cosca, famed soldier of fortune, tottered against the wall of the alley, rooting through his purse yet again with quivering fingers. There was still nothing in it but a tuft of grey fluff. He dug it out, blew it from his fingertips and watched it flutter gently down. All his fortune.

'Bastard purse!' He flung it in the gutter in a feeble rage. Then he thought better of it and had to stoop to pick it up, groaning like an old man. He was an old man. A lost man. A dead man, give or take a final rattle of breath. He sank slowly to his knees, gazing at his broken reflection in the black water gathered between the cobblestones.

He would have given all he owned for the slightest taste of liquor. He owned nothing, it had to be said. But his body was his, still. His hands, which had raised up princes to the heights of power and flung them down again. His eyes, which had surveyed the turning points of history. His lips, which had softly kissed the most celebrated beauties of the age. His itching cock, his aching guts, his rotting neck, he would happily have sold it all for a single measure of grape spirit. But it was hard to see where he would find a buyer.

'I have become myself . . . an empty purse.' He raised his leaden arms imploringly and roared into the murky night. 'Someone give me a fucking drink!'

'Stop your mouth, arsehole!' a rough voice called back, and then, with the clatter of shutters closing, the alley plunged into deeper gloom.

He had dined at the tables of dukes. He had sported in the beds of countesses. Cities had trembled at the name of Cosca.

'How did it ever come . . . to this?' He clambered up, swallowing the urge to vomit. He smoothed his hair back from his throbbing temples, fumbled with the limp ends of his moustaches. He made for the lane with something approaching his famous swagger of old. Out between the ghostly buildings and into a patch of lamplight in the mist, moist night breeze tickling at his sore face. Footsteps approached and Cosca lurched round, blinking.

'Good sir! I find myself temporarily without funds, and wonder whether you would be willing to advance me a small loan until—'

'Away and piss, beggar.' The man shoved past, barging him against the wall.

Cosca's skin flushed with greasy outrage. 'You address none other than Nicomo Cosca, famed soldier of fortune!' The effect was somewhat spoiled by the brittle cracking of his ravaged voice. 'Captain general of the Thousand Swords! Ex-captain general, that is.' The man made an obscene gesture as he disappeared into the fog. 'I dined . . . at the beds . . . of dukes!' Cosca collapsed into a fit of hacking coughs and was obliged to bend over, shaking hands on his shaking knees, aching ribcage going like a creaky bellows.

Such was the life of the drinker. A quarter on your arse, a quarter on your face, a quarter on your knees and the rest of your time bent over. He finally hawked up a great lump of phlegm, and with one last cough blew it spinning from his sore tongue. Would this be his legacy? Spit in a hundred thousand gutters? His name a byword for petty betrayal, avarice and waste? He straightened with a groan of the purest despair, staring up into nothingness, even the stars denied him by Sipani's all-cloaking fog.

'One last chance. That's all I'm asking.' He had lost count of the number of last chances he had wasted. 'Just one more. God!' He had never believed in God for an instant. 'Fates!' He had never believed in Fates either. 'Anyone!' He had never believed in anything much beyond the next drink. 'Just one . . . more . . . chance.'

'Alright. One more.'

Cosca blinked. 'God? Is that . . . you?'

Someone chuckled. A woman's voice, and a sharp, mocking,

most ungodlike sort of a chuckle. 'You can kneel if you like, Cosca.'

He squinted into the sliding mist, pickled brains spurred into something approaching activity. Someone knowing his name was unlikely to be a good thing. His enemies far outnumbered his friends, and his creditors far outnumbered both. He fished drunkenly for the hilt of his gilded sword, then realised he had pawned it months ago in Ospria and bought a cheap one. He fished drunkenly for the hilt of that instead, then realised he had pawned that one when he first reached Sipani. He let his shaky hand drop. Not much lost. He doubted he could have swung a blade even if he'd had one.

'Who the bloody hell's out there? If I owe you money, make ready—' his stomach lurched and he gave vent to a long, acrid burp '—to die?'

A dark shape rose suddenly from the murk at his side and he spun, tripped over his own feet and went sprawling, head cracking against the wall and sending a blinding flash across his vision.

'So you're alive, still. You are alive, aren't you?' A long, lean woman, a sharp face mostly in shadow, spiky hair tinted orange. His mind fumbled sluggishly to recognition.

'Shylo Vitari, well I never.' Not an enemy, perhaps, but certainly not a friend. He propped himself up on one elbow, but from the way the street was spinning, decided that was far enough. 'Don't suppose you might consent . . . to buy a man a drink, might you?'

'Goat's milk?'

'What?'

'I hear it's good for the digestion.'

'They always said you had a flint for a heart, but I never thought even you would be so cold as to suggest I drink *milk*, damn you! Just one more shot of that old grape spirit.' A drink, a drink, a drink. 'Just one more and I'm done.'

'Oh, you're done alright. How long you been drunk this time?'

'I've a notion it was summer when I started. What is it now?'

'Not the same year, that's sure. How much money have you wasted?'

'All there is and more. I'd be surprised if there's a coin in the world that hasn't been through my purse at some point. But I seem to be out of funds right now, so if you could just spare some change—'

'You need to make a change, not spend some.'

He drew himself up, as far as his knees at least, and jabbed at his chest with a crabbing finger. 'Do you suppose the shrivelled, piss-soaked, horrified better part of me, the part that screams to be released from this torture, doesn't know that?' He gave a helpless shrug, aching body collapsing on itself. 'But for a man to change he needs the help of good friends, or, better yet, good enemies. My friends are all long dead, and my enemies, I am forced to admit . . . have better things to do.'

'Not all of us.' Another woman's voice, but one that sent a creeping shiver of familiarity down Cosca's back. A figure formed out of the gloom, mist sucked into smoky swirls after her flicking coat-tails.

'No . . .' he croaked.

He remembered the moment he first laid eyes on her: a wild-haired girl of nineteen with a sword at her hip and a bright stare rich with anger, defiance and the slightest fascinating hint of contempt. There was a hollowness to her face now, a twist of pain about her mouth. The sword hung on the other side, gloved right hand resting slack on the pommel. Her eyes still had that un-wavering sharpness, but there was more anger, more defiance and a long stretch more contempt. Who could blame her for that? Cosca was beyond contemptible, and knew it.

He had sworn a thousand times to kill her, of course, if he ever saw her again. Her, or her brother, or Andiche, Victus, Sesaria, Faithful Carpi or any of the other treacherous bastards from the Thousand Swords who had once betrayed him. Stolen his place from him. Sent him fleeing from the battlefield at Afieri with his reputation and his clothes both equally tattered.

He had sworn a thousand times to kill her, but Cosca had broken all manner of oaths in his life, and the sight of her brought no rage. Instead what welled up in him was a mixture of worn-out self-pity, sappy joy and, most of all, piercing shame at seeing in her face how far he had fallen. He felt the ache in his nose, behind his cheeks, tears welling in his stinging eyes. For once he was grateful that they were red as wounds at the best of times. If he wept, no one could tell the difference.

'Monza.' He tried to tug his filthy collar straight, but his hands were shaking too badly to manage it. 'I must confess I heard you were dead. I was meaning to take revenge, of course—'

'On me or for me?'

He shrugged. 'Difficult to remember . . . I stopped on the way for a drink.'

'Smells like it was more than one.' There was a hint of disappointment in her face that pricked at his insides almost worse than steel. 'I heard you finally got yourself killed in Dagoska.'

He managed to lift one arm high enough to wave her words away. 'There have always been false reports of my death. Wishful thinking, on the part of my many enemies. Where is your brother?'

'Dead.' Her face did not change.

'Well. I'm sorry for that. I always liked the boy.' The lying, gutless, scheming louse.

'He always liked you.' They had detested each other, but what did it matter now?

'If only his sister had felt as warmly about me, things might be so much different.'

' "Might be" takes us nowhere. We've all got . . . regrets.'

They looked at each other for a long moment, her standing, him on his knees. Not quite how he had pictured their reunion in his dreams. 'Regrets. The cost of the business, Sazine used to tell me.'

'Perhaps we should put the past behind us.'

'I can hardly remember yesterday,' he lied. The past weighed on him like a giant's suit of armour.

'The future, then. I've a job for you, if you'll take it. Reckon you're up to a job?'

'What manner of job?'

'Fighting.'

Cosca winced. 'You always were far too attached to fighting. How often did I tell you? A mercenary has no business getting involved with that nonsense.'

'A sword is for rattling, not for drawing.'

'There's my girl. I've missed you.' He said it without thinking, had to cough down his shame and nearly coughed up a lung.

'Help him up, Friendly.'

A big man had silently appeared while they were talking, not tall but heavyset, with an air of calm strength about him. He hooked Cosca under his elbow and pulled him effortlessly to his feet.

'That's a strong arm and a good deed,' he gurgled over a rush of nausea. 'Friendly is your name? Are you a philanthropist?'

'A convict.'

'I see no reason why a man cannot be both. My thanks in any case. Now if you could just point us in the direction of a tavern—'

'The taverns will have to wait for you,' said Vitari. 'No doubt causing a slump in the wine industry. The conference begins in a week and we need you sober.'

'I don't do sober any more. Sober hurts. Did someone say conference?'

Monza was still watching him with those disappointed eyes. 'I need a good man. A man with courage and experience. A man who won't mind crossing Grand Duke Orso.' The corner of her mouth curled up. 'You're as close as we could find at short notice.'

Cosca clung to the big man's arm while the misty street tipped around. 'From that list, I have . . . experience?'

'I'll take one of four, if he needs money too. You need money, don't you, old man?'

'Shit, yes. But not as much as I need a drink.'

'Do the job right and we'll see.'

'I accept.' He found he was standing tall, looking down at Monza now, chin held high. 'We should have a Paper of Engagement, just like the old days. Written in swirly script, with all the accoutrements, the way Sajaam used to write them. Signed with red ink and . . . where can a man find a notary this time of night?'

'Don't worry. I'll take your word.'

'You must be the only person in Styria who would ever say that to me. But as you please.' He pointed decisively down the street. 'This way, my man, and try to keep up.' He boldly stepped forwards, his leg buckled and he squawked as Friendly caught him.

'Not that way,' came the convict's slow, deep voice. He slid one hand under Cosca's arm and half-led him, half-carried him in the opposite direction.

'You are a gentleman, sir,' muttered Cosca.

'I am a murderer.'

'I see no reason why a man cannot be both . . .' Cosca strained to focus on Vitari, loping along up ahead, then at the side of Friendly's heavy face. Strange companions. Outsiders. Those no one else would find a use for. He watched Monza walking, the purposeful stride he remembered from long ago turned slightly crooked. Those who were willing to cross Grand Duke Orso. And that meant madmen, or those with no choices. Which was he?

The answer was in easy reach. There was no reason a man could not be both.

Left Out

Friendly's knife flashed and flickered, twenty strokes one way and twenty the other, grazing the whetstone with a sharpening kiss. There was little worse than a blunt knife and little better than a sharp one, so he smiled as he tested the edge and felt that cold roughness against his fingertip. The blade was keen.

'Cardotti's House of Leisure is an old merchant's palace,' Vitari was saying, voice chilly calm. 'Wood-built, like most of Sipani, round three sides of a courtyard with the Eighth Canal right at its rear.'

They had set up a long table in the kitchen at the back of the warehouse, and the six of them sat about it now. Murcatto and Shivers, Day and Morveer, Cosca and Vitari. On the table stood a model of a large wooden building on three sides of a courtyard. Friendly judged that it was one thirty-sixth the size of the real Cardotti's House of Leisure, though it was hard to be precise, and he liked very much to be precise.

Vitari's fingertip trailed along the windows on one side of the tiny building. 'There are kitchens and offices on the ground floor, a hall for husk and another for cards and dice.' Friendly pressed his hand to his shirt pocket and was comforted to feel his own dice nuzzling against his ribs. 'Two staircases in the rear corners. On the first floor thirteen rooms where guests are entertained—'

'Fucked,' said Cosca. 'We're all adults here, let's call it what it is.' His bloodshot eyes flickered up to the two bottles of wine on the shelf, then back. Friendly had noticed they did that a lot.

Vitari's finger drifted up towards the model's roof. 'Then, on the top floor, three large suites for the . . . *fucking* of the most valued guests. They say the Royal Suite in the centre is fit for an emperor.'

'Then Ario might just consider it fit for himself,' growled Murcatto.

The group had grown from five to seven, so Friendly cut each of the two loaves into fourteen slices, the blade hissing through the crust and sending up puffs of flour dust. There would be twenty-eight slices in all, four slices each. Murcatto would eat less, but Day would make up for it. Friendly hated to leave a slice of bread uneaten.

'According to Eider, Ario and Foscar will have three or four dozen guests, some of them armed but not keen to fight, as well as six bodyguards.'

'She telling the truth?' Shivers' heavy accent.

'Chance may play a part, but she won't lie to us.'

'Keeping charge o' that many . . . we'll need more fighters.'

'Killers,' interrupted Cosca. 'Again, let's call them what they are.'

'Twenty, maybe,' came Murcatto's hard voice, 'as well as you three.'

Twenty-three. An interesting number. Heat kissed the side of Friendly's face as he unhooked the door of the old stove and pulled it creaking open. Twenty-three could be divided by no other number, except one. No parts, no fractions. No half-measures. Not unlike Murcatto herself. He hauled the big pot out with a cloth around his hands. Numbers told no lies. Unlike people.

'How do we get twenty men inside without being noticed?'

'It's a revel,' said Vitari. 'There'll be entertainers. And we'll provide them.'

'Entertainers?'

'This is Sipani. Every other person in the city is an entertainer or a killer. Shouldn't be too difficult to find a few who are both.'

Friendly was left out of the planning, but he did not mind. Sajaam had asked him to do what Murcatto said, and that was the end of it. He had learned long ago that life became much easier if you ignored what was not right before you. For now the stew was his only concern.

He dipped in his wooden spoon and took a taste, and it was good. He rated it forty-one out of fifty. The smell of cooking, the sight of the steam rising, the sound of the fizzing logs in the stove, it all put him in comforting mind of the kitchens in Safety. Of the stews, and soups, and porridge they used to make in the great vats. Long ago, back when there was an infinite weight of comforting stone always above his head, and the numbers added, and things made sense.

'Ario will want to drink for a while,' Murcatto was saying, 'and gamble, and show off to his idiots. Then he'll be brought up to the Royal Suite.'

Cosca split a crack-lipped grin. 'Where women will be waiting for him, I take it?'

'One with black hair and one with red.' Murcatto exchanged a hard look with Vitari.

'A surprise fit for an emperor,' chuckled Cosca, wetly.

'When Ario's dead, which will be quickly, we'll move next door and pay Foscar the same kind of visit.' Murcatto shifted her scowl to Morveer. 'They'll have brought guards upstairs to watch things while they're busy. You and Day can handle them.'

'Can we indeed?' The poisoner took a brief break from sneering at his fingernails. 'A *fit* purpose for our talents, I am sure.'

'Try not to poison half the city this time. We should be able to kill the brothers without raising any unwanted attention, but if something goes wrong, that's where the entertainers come in.'

The old mercenary jabbed at the model with a quivery finger. 'Take the courtyard first, the gaming and smoking halls, and from there secure the staircases. Disarm the guests and round them up. Politely, of course, and in the best taste. Keep control.'

'Control.' Murcatto's gloved forefinger stabbed the tabletop. 'That's the word I want at the front of your tiny minds. We kill Ario, we kill Foscar. If any of the rest make trouble, you do what you have to, but keep the murder to a minimum. There'll be trouble enough for us afterwards without a bloodbath. You all got that?'

Cosca cleared his throat. 'Perhaps a drink would help me to commit it all to—'

'I've got it.' Shivers spoke over him. 'Control, and as little blood as possible.'

'Two murders.' Friendly set the pot down in the middle of the table, 'one and one, and no more. Food.' And he began to ladle portions out into the bowls.

He would have liked very much to ensure that everyone had the exact same number of pieces of meat. The same number of pieces of carrot and onion too, the same number of beans. But by the time he had counted them out the food would have been cold, and he had learned that most people found that level of precision upsetting. It had led to a fight in the mess in Safety once, and Friendly had killed two men and cut a hand from another. He had no wish to kill anyone now. He was hungry. So he satisfied himself by giving each one of them the same number of ladles of stew, and coped with the deep sense of unease it left him.

'This is good,' gurgled Day, around a mouthful. 'This is excellent. Is there more?'

'Where did you learn to cook, my friend?' Cosca asked.

'I spent three years in the kitchens in Safety. The man who taught me used to be head cook to the Duke of Borletta.'

'What was he doing in prison?'

'He killed his wife, and chopped her up, and cooked her in a stew, and ate it.'

There was quiet around the table. Cosca noisily cleared his throat. 'No one's wife in this stew, I trust?'

'The butcher said it was lamb, and I've no reason to doubt him.' Friendly picked up his fork. 'No one sells human meat that cheap.'

There was one of those uncomfortable silences that Friendly always seemed to produce when he said more than three words at once. Then Cosca gave a gurgling laugh. 'Depends on the circumstances. Reminds me of when we found those children, do you remember, Monza, after the siege at Muris?' Her scowl grew even harder than usual, but there was no stopping him. 'We found those children, and we wanted to sell them on to some slavers, but you thought we could—'

'Of course!' Morveer almost shrieked. '*Hilarious!* What could possibly be more amusing than orphan children sold into slavery?'

There was another awkward silence while the poisoner and the mercenary gave each other a deadly glare. Friendly had seen men exchange that very look in Safety. When new blood came in, and prisoners were forced into a cell together. Sometimes two men would just catch each other wrong. Hate each other from the moment they met. Too different. Or too much the same. Things were harder to predict out here, of course. But in Safety, when you saw two men look at each other that way you knew, sooner or later, there would be blood.

A drink, a drink, a drink. Cosca's eyes lurched from that preening louse Morveer and down to the poisoner's full wine glass, around the glasses of the others, reluctantly back to his own sickening mug of water and finally to the wine bottle on the table, where his gaze was gripped as if by burning pincers. A quick lunge and he could have it. How much could he swallow before they wrestled it from his hands? Few men could drink faster when circumstances demanded—

Then he noticed Friendly watching him, and there was something in the convict's sad, flat eyes that made him think again. He was Nicomo Cosca, damn it! Or he had been once, at least. Cities had trembled, and so on. He had spent too many years never thinking beyond his next drink. It was time to look further. To the drink after next, at any rate. But change was not easy.

He could almost feel the sweat springing out of his skin. His head was pulsing, booming with pain. He clawed at his itchy neck but that only made it itch the more. He was smiling like a skull, he knew, and talking far too much. But it was smile, and talk, or scream his exploding head off.

'. . . saved my life at the siege of Muris, eh, Monza? At Muris, was it?' He hardly even knew how his cracking voice had wandered onto the subject. 'Bastard came at me out of nowhere. A quick thrust!' He nearly knocked his water cup over with a wayward jab of his finger. 'And she ran him through! Right through the heart, I swear. Saved my life. At Muris. Saved my . . . life . . .'

And he almost wished she had let him die. The kitchen seemed to be spinning, tossing, tipping wildly like the cabin of a ship in a fatal tempest. He kept expecting to see the wine slosh from the glasses, the stew spray from the bowls, the plates slide from the see-sawing table. He knew the only storm was in his head, yet still found himself clinging to the furniture whenever the room appeared to heel with particular violence.

'. . . wouldn't have been so bad if she hadn't done it again the next day. I took an arrow in the shoulder and fell in the damn moat. Everyone saw, on both sides. Making me look a fool in front of my friends is one thing, but in front of my enemies—'

'You've got it wrong.'

Cosca squinted up the table at Monza. 'I have?' Though he had to admit he could hardly remember his last sentence, let alone the events of a siege a dozen drunken years ago.

'It was me in the moat, you that jumped in to pull me out. Risked your life, and took an arrow doing it.'

'Seems astoundingly unlikely I'd have done a thing like that.' It was hard to think about anything beyond his violent need for a drink. 'But I'm finding it somewhat difficult to recall the details, I must confess. Perhaps if one of you could just see your way to passing me the wine I could—'

'Enough.' She had that same look she always used to have when she dragged him from one tavern or another, except even angrier, even sharper and even more disappointed. 'I've five men to kill, and I've no time to be saving anyone any more. Especially from their own stupidity. I've no use for a drunk.' The table was silent as they all watched him sweat.

'I'm no drunk,' croaked Cosca. 'I simply like the taste of wine. So much so that I have to drink some every few hours or become violently ill.' He clung to his fork while the room swayed around him, fixed his aching smile while they chuckled away. He hoped they enjoyed their laughter while they could, because Nicomo Cosca always laughed last. Provided he wasn't being sick, of course.

Morveer was feeling left out. He was a scintillating conversationalist face to face, it hardly needed to be said, but had never been at his ease in large groups. This scenario reminded him unpleasantly of the dining room in the orphanage, where the larger children had amused themselves by throwing food at him, a terrifying prelude to the whisperings, beatings, dunkings and other torments in the nocturnal blackness of the dormitories.

Murcatto's two new assistants, on the hiring of whom he had not been given even the most superficial consultation, were far from putting his mind at ease. Shylo Vitari was a torturer and broker in information, highly competent but possessed of an abrasive personality. He had collaborated with her once before, and the experience had not been a happy one. Morveer found the whole notion of inflicting pain with one's own hands thoroughly repugnant. But she knew Sipani, so he supposed he could suffer her. For now.

Nicomo Cosca was infinitely worse. A notoriously destructive, treacherous and capricious mercenary with no code or scruple but his own profit. A drunkard, dissipater and womaniser with all the self-control of a rabid dog. A self-aggrandising backslider with an epically inflated opinion of his own abilities, he was everything Morveer was not. But now, as well as taking this dangerously unpredictable element into their confidence and involving him intimately in their plans, the group seemed to be paying court to the trembling shell. Even Day, his own assistant, was chortling at his jokes whenever she did not have her mouth full, which, admittedly, was but rarely.

'. . . a group of miscreants hunched around a table in an abandoned warehouse?' Cosca was musing, bloodshot eyes rolling round the table, 'talking of masks, and disguises, and weaponry? I cannot imagine how a man of my high calibre ended up in such company. One would think there was some underhand business taking place!'

'My own thoughts exactly!' Morveer shrilly interjected. 'I could never countenance such a stain upon my conscience. That is why I applied an extract of Widow's Blossom to your bowls. I hope you all enjoy your last few agonising moments!'

Six faces frowned back at him, entirely silent.

'A jest, of course,' he croaked, realising instantly that his conversational foray had suffered a spectacular misfire. Shivers exhaled long and slow. Murcatto curled her tongue sourly around one canine tooth. Day was frowning down at her bowl.

'I've taken more amusing punches in the face,' said Vitari.

'Poisoners' humour.' Cosca glowered across the table, though the effect was somewhat spoiled by the rattling of his fork against his bowl as his right hand vibrated. 'A lover of mine was murdered by poison. I have had nothing but disgust for your profession ever since. And all its members, naturally.'

'You can hardly expect me to take responsibility for the actions of every person in my line of work.' Morveer thought it best not to mention that he had, in fact, been personally responsible, having been hired by Grand Duchess Sefeline of Ospria to murder Nicomo Cosca some fourteen years before. It was becoming a matter of considerable annoyance that he had missed the mark and killed his mistress instead.

'I crush wasps whenever I find them, whether they have stung me or not. To my mind you people – if I can call you people – are all equally worthy of contempt. A poisoner is the filthiest kind of coward.'

'Second only to a drunkard!' returned Morveer with a suitable curling of his upper lip. 'Such human refuse might almost evoke pity were they not so utterly repellent. No animal is more predictable. Like a befouled homing pigeon, the drunk returns ever to the bottle, unable to change. It is their one route of escape from the misery they leave in their wake. For them the sober world is so crowded with old failures and new fears that they suffocate in it. There is a *true* coward.' He raised his glass and took a long, self-satisfied gulp of wine. He was unused to drinking rapidly and felt, in fact, a powerful urge to vomit, but forced a queasy smile onto his face nonetheless.

Cosca's thin hand clutched the table with a white-knuckled intensity as he watched Morveer swallow. 'How little you understand me. I could stop drinking whenever I wish. In fact, I have already resolved to do so. I would prove it to you.' The mercenary held up one wildly flapping hand. 'If I could just get half a glass to settle these damn palsies!'

The others laughed, the tension diffused, but Morveer caught the lethal glare on Cosca's face. The old soak might have seemed harmless as a village dunce, but he had once been counted among the most dangerous men in Styria. It would have been folly to take such a man lightly, and Morveer was nobody's fool. He was no longer the orphan child who had blubbered for his mother while they kicked him.

Caution first, each and every time.

Monza sat still, said no more than she had to and ate less, gloved hand painfully clumsy with the knife. She left herself out, up here at the head of the table. The distance a general needs to keep from the soldiers, an employer from the hirelings, a wanted woman from everyone, if she's got any sense. It wasn't hard to do. She'd been keeping her distance for years and leaving Benna to do the talking, and the laughing, and be liked. A leader can't afford to be liked. Especially not a woman. Shivers kept glancing up the table towards her, and she kept not meeting his eye. She'd let things slip in Westport, made herself look weak. She couldn't let that happen again.

'The pair o' you seem pretty familiar,' Shivers was saying now, eyes moving between her and Cosca. 'Old friends, are you?'

'Family, rather!' The old mercenary waved his fork wildly enough to have someone's eye out. 'We fought side by side as noble members of the Thousand Swords, most famous mercenary brigade in the Circle of the World!' Monza frowned sideways at him. His old bloody stories were bringing back things done and choices made she'd sooner have left in the past. 'We fought across Styria and back, while Sazine was captain general. Those were the days to be a mercenary! Before things started to get . . . complicated.'

Vitari snorted. 'You mean bloody.'

'Different words for the same thing. People were richer back then, and scared more easily, and the walls were all lower. Then Sazine took an arrow in the arm, then lost the arm, then died, and I was voted to the captain general's chair.' Cosca poked his stew around. 'Burying that old wolf, I realised that fighting was too much hard work, and I, like most persons of quality, wished to do as little of it as possible.' He gave Monza a twitchy grin. 'So we split the brigade in two.'

'You split the brigade in two.'

'I took one half, and Monzcarro and her brother Benna took the other, and we spread a rumour we'd had a falling out. We hired ourselves out to both sides of every argument we could find – and we found plenty – and . . . pretended to fight.'

'Pretended?' muttered Shivers.

Cosca's trembling knife and fork jabbed at each other in the air. 'We'd march around for weeks at a time, picking the country clean all the while, mount the odd harmless skirmish for the show of it, then leave off at the end of each season a good deal richer but with no one dead. Well, a few of the rot, maybe. Every bit as profitable as having at the business in earnest, though. We even mounted a couple of fake battles, didn't we?'

'We did.'

'Until Monza took an engagement with Grand Duke Orso of Talins, and decided she was done with fake battles. Until she decided to mount a proper charge, with swords well sharpened and swung in earnest. Until you decided to make a difference, eh, Monza? Shame you never told me we weren't faking any more. I could've warned my boys and saved some lives that day.'

'Your boys.' She snorted. 'Let's not pretend you ever cared for anyone's life but your own.'

'There have been a few others I valued higher. I never profited by it, though, and neither did they.' Cosca hadn't taken his bloodshot eyes from Monza's. 'Which of your own people turned on you? Faithful Carpi, was it? Not so faithful in the end, eh?'

'He was as faithful as you could wish for. Right up until he stabbed me.'

'And now he's taken the captain general's chair, no doubt?'

'I hear he's managed to wedge his fat arse into it.'

'Just as you slipped your skinny one into it after mine. But he couldn't have taken anything without the consent of some other captains, could he? Fine lads, those. That bastard Andiche. That big leech Sesaria. That sneering maggot Victus. Were those three greedy hogs still with you?'

'They still had their faces in the trough. All of them turned on me, I'm sure, just the way they turned on you. You're telling me nothing I don't know.'

'No one thanks you, in the end. Not for the victories you bring them. Not for the money you make them. They get bored. And the first sniff of something better—'

Monza was out of patience. A leader can't afford to look soft. Especially not a woman. 'For such an expert on people, it's a wonder you ended up a friendless, penniless drunk, eh, Cosca? Don't pretend I didn't give you a thousand chances. You wasted them all, like you wasted everything else. The only question that interests me is – are you set on wasting this one too? Can you do as I fucking tell you? Or are you set on being my enemy?'

Cosca only gave a sad smile. 'In our line of work, enemies are things to be proud of. If experience has taught the two of us anything, it's that your friends are the ones you need to watch. My congratulations to the cook.' He tossed his fork down in his bowl, got up and strutted from the kitchen in almost a straight line. Monza frowned at the sullen faces he left around the table.

Never fear your enemies, Verturio wrote, *but your friends, always.*

A Few Bad Men

The warehouse was a draughty cavern, cold light finding chinks in the shutters and leaving bright lines across the dusty boards, across the empty crates piled up in one corner, across the old table in the middle of the floor. Shivers dropped into a rickety chair next to it, felt the grip of the knife Monza had given him pressing at his calf. A sharp reminder of what he'd been hired for. Life was getting way more dark and dangerous than back home in the North. As far as being a better man went, he was going backwards, and quicker every day.

So why the hell was he still here? Because he wanted Monza? He had to admit it, and the fact she'd been cold with him since Westport only made him want her more. Because he wanted her money? That too. Money was a damn good thing for buying stuff. Because he needed the work? He did. Because he was good at the work? He was.

Because he enjoyed the work?

Shivers frowned. Some men aren't stamped out for doing good, and he was starting to reckon he might be one of 'em. He was less and less sure with every day that being a better man was worth all the effort.

The sound of a door banging tugged him from his thoughts, and Cosca came down the creaking wooden steps from the rooms where they were sleeping, scratching slowly at the splatter of red rash up the side of his neck.

'Morning.'

The old mercenary yawned. 'So it seems. I can barely remember the last one of these I saw. Nice shirt.'

Shivers twitched at his sleeve. Dark silk, with polished bone buttons and clever stitching round the cuff. A good stretch fancier than he'd have picked out, but Monza had liked it. 'Hadn't noticed.'

'I used to be one for fine clothes myself.' Cosca dropped into a rickety chair next to Shivers. 'So did Monza's brother, for that matter. He had a shirt just like that one, as I recall.'

Shivers weren't sure what the old bastard was getting at, but he was sure he didn't like it. 'And?'

'Spoken much about her brother, has she?' Cosca had a strange little smile, like he knew something Shivers didn't.

'She told me he's dead.'

'So I hear.'

'She told me she's not happy about it.'

'Most decidedly not.'

'Something else I should know?'

'I suppose we could all be wiser than we are. I'll leave that up to her, though.'

'Where is she?' snapped Shivers, patience drying up.

'Monza?'

'Who else?'

'She doesn't want anyone to see her face that doesn't have to. But not to worry. I have hired fighting men all across the Circle of the World. And my fair share of entertainers too, as it goes. Do you have any issue with my taking charge of the proceedings?'

Shivers had a pile of issues with it. It was plain the only thing Cosca had taken charge of for a good long while was a bottle. After the Bloody-Nine killed his brother, and cut his head off, and had it nailed up on a standard, Shivers' father had taken to drinking. He'd taken to drinking, and rages, and having the shakes. He'd stopped making good choices, and he'd lost the respect of his people, and he'd wasted all he'd built, and died leaving Shivers nought but sour memories.

'I don't trust a man who drinks,' he growled, not bothered about dressing it up. 'A man takes to drinking, then he gets weak, then his mind goes.'

Cosca sadly shook his head. 'You have it back to front. A man's mind goes, then he gets weak, then he takes to drink. The bottle is the symptom, not the cause. But though I am touched to my core by your concern, you need not worry on my account. I feel a great deal steadier today!' He spread his hands out above the tabletop. It was true they weren't shaking as bad as they had been. A gentle quiver rather than a mad jerk. 'I'll be back to my best before you know it.'

'I can hardly wait to see that.' Vitari strutted out from the kitchen, arms folded.

'None of us can, Shylo!' And Cosca slapped Shivers on the arm. 'But enough about me! What criminals, footpads, thugs and other such human filth have you dug from the slimy backstreets of old Sipani? What fighting entertainers have you for our consideration? Musicians who murder? Deadly dancers? Singers with swords? Jugglers who . . . who . . .'

'Kill?' offered Shivers.

Cosca's grin widened. 'Brusque and to the point, as always.'

'Brusque?'

'Thick.' Vitari slid into the last chair and unfolded a sheet of paper on the scarred tabletop. 'First up, there's a band I found playing for bits near the docks. I reckon they make a fair stretch more from robbing passers-by than serenading them, though.'

'Rough-and-tumble fellows, eh? The very type we need.' Cosca stretched out his scrawny neck like a cock about to crow. 'Enter!'

The door squealed open and five men wandered in. Even where Shivers came from they would've been reckoned a rough-looking set. Greasy-haired. Pock-faced. Rag-dressed. Their eyes darted about, narrow and suspicious, dirty hands clutching a set of stained instruments. They shuffled up in front of the table, one of them scratching his groin, another prodding at a nostril with his drumstick.

'And you are?' asked Cosca.

'We're a band,' the nearest said.

'And has your band a name?'

They looked at each other. 'No. Why would it?'

'Your own names, then, if you please, and your specialities both as entertainer and fighter.'

'My name's Solter. I play the drum, and the mace.' Flicking his greasy coat back to show the dull glint of iron. 'I'm better with the mace, if I'm honest.'

'I'm Morc,' said the next in line. 'Pipe, and cutlass.'

'Olopin. Horn, and hammer.'

'Olopin, as well.' Jerking a thumb sideways. 'Brother to this article. Fiddle, and blades.' Whipping a pair of long knives from his sleeves and spinning 'em round his fingers.

The last had the most broken nose Shivers had ever seen, and he'd seen some bad ones. 'Gurpi. Lute, and lute.'

'You fight with your lute?' asked Cosca.

'I hits 'em with it just so.' The man showed off a sideways swipe, then flashed two rows of shit-coloured teeth. 'There's a great-axe hidden in the body.'

'Ouch. A tune, then, if you please, my fellows, and make it something lively!'

Shivers weren't much for music, but even he could tell it was no fine playing. The drum was out of time. The pipe was tuneless tooting. The lute was flat, probably on account of all the ironware inside. But Cosca nodded along, eyes shut, like he'd never heard sweeter music.

'My days, what multi-talented fellows you are!' he shouted after a couple of bars, bringing the din to a stuttering halt. 'You're hired, each one of you, at forty scales per man for the night.'

'Forty . . . scales . . . a man?' gawped the drummer.

'Paid on completion. But it will be tough work. You will undoubtedly be called upon to fight, and possibly even to play. It may have to be a fatal performance, for our enemies. You are ready for such a commitment?'

'For forty scales a man?' They were all grinning now. 'Yes, sir, we are! For that much we're fearless.'

'Good men. We know where to find you.'

Vitari leaned across as the band made their way out. 'Ugly set of bastards.'

'One of the many advantages of a *masked* revel,' whispered Cosca. 'Stick 'em in motley and no one will be any the wiser.'

Shivers didn't much care for the idea of trusting his life to those lot. 'They'll notice the playing, no?'

Cosca snorted. 'People don't visit Cardotti's for the music.'

'Shouldn't we have checked how they fight?'

'If they fight like they play we should have no worries.'

'They play about as well as runny shit.'

'They play like lunatics. With luck they fight the same way.'

'That's no kind of—'

'I hardly thought of you as the fussy type.' Cosca peered at Shivers down his long nose. 'You need to learn to live a little, my friend. All victories worth the winning are snatched with vim and brio!'

'With who?'

'Carelessness,' said Vitari.

'Dash,' said Cosca. 'And seizing the moment.'

'And what do you make of all this?' Shivers asked Vitari. 'Vim and whatever.'

'If the plan goes smoothly we'll get Ario and Foscar away from the others and—' She snapped her fingers with a sharp crack. 'Won't matter much who strums the lute. Time's running out. Four days until the great and good of Styria descend on Sipani for their conference. I'd find better men, in an ideal world. But this isn't one.'

Cosca heaved a throaty sigh. 'It most certainly is not. But let's not be downhearted – a few moments in and we're five men to the good! Now, if I could just get a glass of wine we'd be well on our way to—'

'No wine,' growled Vitari.

'It's coming to something when a man can't even wet his throat.' The old mercenary leaned close enough that Shivers could pick out the broken veins across his cheeks. 'Life is a sea of sorrows, my friend. Enter!'

The next man barely fit through the warehouse door, he was that big. A few fingers taller than Shivers but a whole lot weightier. He had thick stubble across his great chunk of jaw and a mop of grey curls though he didn't seem old. His heavy hands fussed with each other as he came towards the table, a bit stooped like he was shamed of his own size, boards giving a complaining creak every time one of his great boots came down.

Cosca whistled. 'My, my, that is a big one.'

'Found him in a tavern down by the First Canal,' said Vitari, 'drunk as shit but everyone too scared to move him. Hardly speaks a word of Styrian.'

Cosca leaned towards Shivers. 'Perhaps you might take the lead with this one? The brotherhood of the North?'

Shivers didn't remember there being that much brotherhood up there in the cold, but it was worth a try. The words felt strange in his mouth, it was that long since he'd used them. 'What's your name, friend?'

The big man looked surprised to hear Northern. 'Greylock.' He pointed at his hair. 'S'always been this colour.'

'What brought you all the way down here?'

'Come looking for work.'

'What sort o' work?'

'Whatever'll have me, I reckon.'

'Even if it's bloody?'

'Likely it will be. You're a Northman?'

'Aye.'

'You look like a Southerner.'

Shivers frowned, drew his fancy cuffs back and out of sight under the table. 'Well, I'm not one. Name's Caul Shivers.'

Greylock blinked. 'Shivers?'

'Aye.' He felt a flush of pleasure that the man knew his name. He still had his pride, after all. 'You heard o' me?'

'You was at Uffrith, with the Dogman?'

'That's right.'

'And Black Dow too, eh? Neat piece o' work, the way I heard it.'

'That it was. Took the city with no more'n a couple dead.'

'No more'n a couple.' The big man nodded slowly, eyes never leaving Shivers' face. 'That must've been real smooth.'

'It was. He was a good chief for keeping folk alive, the Dogman. Best I took orders from, I reckon.'

'Well, then. Since the Dogman ain't here his self, it'd be my honour to stand shoulder to shoulder with a man like you.'

'Right you are. Likewise. Pleased to have you along. He's in,' said Shivers in Styrian.

'Are you sure?' asked Cosca. 'He has a certain . . . sourness to his eye that worries me.'

'You need to learn to live a little,' grunted Shivers. 'Get some fucking brio in.'

Vitari snorted laughter and Cosca clutched his chest. 'Gah! Run through with my own rapier! Well, I suppose you can have your little friend. What could we do with a pair of Northmen, now?' He threw up one finger. 'We could mount a re-enactment! A rendering of that famous Northern duel – you know the one,

Fenris the Feared, or whatever, and . . . you know, what's-his-name now . . .'

Shivers' back went cold as he said the name. 'The Bloody-Nine.'

'You've heard of it?'

'I was there. Right in the thick. I held a shield at the edge of the circle.'

'Excellent! You should be able to bring a frisson of historical accuracy to the proceedings, then.'

'Frisson?'

'Bit,' grunted Vitari.

'Why not just bloody say bit, then?'

But Cosca was too busy grinning at his own notion. 'A whiff of violence! Ario's gentlemen will lap it up! And what better excuse for weapons in plain sight?' Shivers was a sight less keen. Dressing up as the man who killed his brother, a man he'd nearly killed himself, and pretending to fight. The one thing in its favour was he wouldn't have to strum a lute, at least.

'What's he saying?' rumbled Greylock in Northern.

'The two of us are going to pretend to have a duel.'

'Pretend?'

'I know, but they pretend all kinds o' shit down here. We'll put a show on. Act it out, you know. Entertainment.'

'The circle's no laughing matter,' and the big man didn't look like laughing either.

'Down here it is. First we pretend, then we might have some others to fight for real. Forty scales if you can make it work.'

'Right you are, then. First we pretend. Then we fight for real. Got it.' Greylock gave Shivers a long, slow look, then lumbered away.

'Next!' bellowed Cosca. A skinny man pranced through the doorway in orange tights and a bright red jacket, big bag in one hand. 'Your name?'

'I am none other than—' he gave a fancy bow '—the Incredible Ronco!'

The old mercenary's brows shot up as fast as Shivers' heart sank. 'And your specialities, both as entertainer and fighter?'

'They are one and the same, sirs!' Nodding to Cosca and Shivers. 'My lady!' Then to Vitari. He turned slowly round, reaching stealthily into his bag, then spun about, one hand to his face, cheeks puffed out—

There was a rustle and a blaze of brilliant fire shot from Ronco's lips, close enough for Shivers to feel the heat sting his cheek. He would've dived from his chair if he'd had the time, but instead he was left rooted – blinking, staring, gasping, as his eyes got used to the darkness of the warehouse again. A couple of patches of fire clung to the table, one just beyond the ends of Cosca's trembling fingers. The flames sputtered, in silence, and died, leaving behind a smell that made Shivers want to puke.

The Incredible Ronco cleared his throat. 'Ah. A slightly more . . . vigorous demonstration than I intended.'

'But damned impressive!' Cosca wafted the smoke away from his face. 'Undeniably entertaining, and undeniably deadly. You are hired, sir, at the price of forty scales for the night.'

The man beamed. 'Delighted to be of service!' He bowed even lower this time round. 'Sirs! My lady! I take . . . my leave!'

'You sure about that?' asked Shivers as Ronco strutted to the door. 'Bit of a worry, ain't it? Fire in a wooden building?'

Cosca looked down his nose again. 'I thought you Northmen were all wrath and bad teeth. If things turn sour, fire in a wooden building could be just the equaliser we need.'

'The what we need, now?'

'Leveller,' said Vitari.

That seemed a bad word to pick. They called death the Great Leveller, up in the hills of the North. 'Fire indoors could end up levelling the lot of us, and in case you didn't notice, that bastard weren't too precise. Fire is dangerous.'

'Fire is pretty. He's in.'

'But won't he—'

'Ah.' Cosca held up a silencing hand.

'We should—'

'Ah.'

'Don't tell me—'

'Ah, I said! Do you not have the word "ah" in your country? Murcatto put me in charge of the entertainers and, with the greatest of respect, that means I say who is in. We are not taking votes. You concentrate on mounting a show to make Ario's gentlemen cheer. I'll handle the planning. How does that sound?'

'Like a short cut to disaster,' said Shivers.

'Ah, disaster!' Cosca grinned. 'I can't wait. Who have we to consider in the meantime?'

Vitari cocked one orange brow at her list. 'Barti and Kummel – tumblers, acrobats, knife-artists and walkers on the high wire.'

Cosca nudged Shivers in the ribs with his elbow. 'Walkers on the high wire, there you go. How could *that* end badly?'

The Peacemakers

It was a rare clear day in the City of Fogs. The air was crisp and cold, the sky was perfectly blue and the King of the Union's conference of peace was due to begin its noble work. The ragged rooflines, the dirty windows, the peeling doorways were all thick with onlookers, waiting eagerly for the great men of Styria to appear. They trickled down both gutters of the wide avenue below, a multicoloured confusion, pressing up against the grim grey lines of soldiers deployed to hold them back. The hubbub of the crowd was a weight on the air. Thousands of murmuring voices, stabbed through here and there by the shouts of hawkers, bellowed warnings, squeals of excitement. Like the sound of an army before a battle.

Nervously waiting for the blood to start spilling.

Five more dots, perched on the roof of a crumbling warehouse, were nothing to remark upon. Shivers stared down, big hands dangling over the parapet. Cosca had his boot propped carelessly on the cracked stonework, scratching at his scabby neck. Vitari leaned back against the wall, long arms folded. Friendly stood bolt upright to the side, seeming lost in a world of his own. The fact that Morveer and his apprentice were away on their own business gave Monza scant confidence. When she first met the poisoner, she hadn't trusted him at all. Since Westport, she trusted him an awful lot less. And these were her troops. She sucked in a long, bitter breath, licked her teeth and spat down into the crowd below.

When God means to punish a man, the Kantic scriptures say, *he sends him stupid friends, and clever enemies.*

'That's a lot o' people,' said Shivers, eyes narrowed against the chilly glare. Just the kind of stunning revelation Monza had come to expect from the man. 'An awful lot.'

'Yes.' Friendly's eyes flickered over the crowds, lips moving silently, giving Monza the worrying impression that he was trying to count them.

'This is nothing.' Cosca dismissed half of Sipani with an airy wave. 'You should have seen the throng that packed the streets of Ospria after my victory at the Battle of the Isles! They filled the air with falling flowers! Twice as many, at the least. You should have been there!'

'I was there,' said Vitari, 'and there were half as many at the most.'

'Does pissing on my dreams give you some sick satisfaction?'

'A little.' Vitari smirked at Monza, but she didn't laugh. She was thinking of the triumph they'd put on for her in Talins, after the fall of Caprile. Or the massacre at Caprile, depending on who you asked. She remembered Benna grinning while she frowned, standing in his stirrups and blowing kisses to the balconies. The people chanting her name, even though Orso was riding in thoughtful silence just behind with Ario at his shoulder. She should've seen it coming then . . .

'Here they are!' Cosca shielded his eyes with one hand, leaning out dangerously far over the railing. 'All hail our great leaders!'

The noise of the crowd swelled as the procession came into view. Seven mounted standard-bearers brought up the front, flags on lances all at the exact same angle – the illusion of equality deemed necessary for peace talks. The cockleshell of Sipani. The white tower of Ospria. The three bees of Visserine. The black cross of Talins. The symbols of Puranti, Affoia and Nicante stirred lazily in the breeze alongside them. A man in gilded armour rode behind, the golden sun of the Union drooping from his black lance.

Sotorius, Chancellor of Sipani, was the first of the great and good to appear. Or the mean and evil, depending on who you asked. He was truly ancient, with thin white hair and beard, hunched under the weight of the heavy chain of office he'd worn since long before Monza was born. He hobbled along doggedly with the aid of a cane and with the eldest of his many sons, probably in his sixties himself, at his elbow. Several columns of Sipani's leading citizens followed, sun twinkling on jewels and polished leather, bright silk and cloth of gold.

'Chancellor Sotorius,' Cosca was noisily explaining to Shivers.

'According to tradition, the host goes on foot. Still alive, the old bastard.'

'Looks like he needs a rest though,' muttered Monza. 'Someone get the man a coffin.'

'Not quite yet, I think. Half-blind he may be, but he still has clearer sight than most. The long-established master of the middle ground. One way or another he's kept Sipani neutral for two decades. Right through the Years of Blood. Ever since I gave him a bloody nose at the Battle of the Isles!'

Vitari snorted. 'Didn't stop you taking his coin when it all turned sour with Sefeline of Ospria, as I recall.'

'Why should it have? Paid soldiers can't be too picky over their employers. You have to blow with the wind in this business. Loyalty on a mercenary is like armour on a swimmer.' Monza frowned sideways, wondering whether that was meant for her, but Cosca was blathering on as though it meant nothing to anyone. 'Still, he never suited me much, old Sotorius. It was a wedding of necessity, an unhappy marriage and, once victory was won, a divorce we were both happy to agree to. Peaceful men find little work for mercenaries, and the old Chancellor of Sipani has made a rich and glorious career from peace.'

Vitari sneered down at the wealthy citizens tramping by below. 'Looks like he's hoping to make an export of it.'

Monza shook her head. 'One thing Orso will never be buying.'

The leaders of the League of Eight came next. Orso's bitter enemies, which had meant Monza's too, until her tumble down a mountain. They were attended by a regiment of hangers-on, all decked out in a hundred clashing liveries. Duke Rogont rode at the front on a great black charger, reins in one sure hand, giving the occasional nod to the crowds as someone shouted for him. He was a popular man, and was called on to nod often, almost to the point that his head bobbed like a turkey's. Salier had somehow been wedged into the saddle of a stocky roan beside Rogont, pink jowls bulging out over the gilded collar of his uniform, on one side, then the other, in time to the movement of his labouring mount.

'Who's the fat man?' asked Shivers.

'Salier, Grand Duke of Visserine.'

Vitari sniggered. 'For another month or two, maybe. He

squandered his city's soldiers in the summer.' Monza had charged them down on the High Bank, with Faithful Carpi beside her. 'His city's food in the autumn.' Monza had merrily burned the fields about the walls and driven off the farmers. 'And he's fast running out of allies.' Monza had left Duke Cantain's head rotting on the walls of Borletta. 'You can almost see him sweating from here, the old bastard.'

'Shame,' said Cosca. 'I always liked the man. You should see the galleries in his palace. The greatest collection of art in the world, or so he says. Quite the connoisseur. Kept the best table in Styria too, in his day.'

'It shows,' said Monza.

'One does wonder how they get him in his saddle.'

'Block and tackle,' snapped Vitari.

Monza snorted. 'Or dig a trench and ride the horse up underneath him.'

'What about the other one?' asked Shivers.

'Rogont, Grand Duke of Ospria.'

'He looks the part.' True enough. Tall and broad-shouldered with a handsome face and a mass of dark curls.

'Looks it.' Monza spat again. 'But not much more.'

'The nephew of my one-time employer, now thankfully deceased, the Duchess Sefeline.' Cosca had made his neck bleed with his scratching. 'They call him the Prince of Prudence. The Count of Caution. The Duke of Delay. A fine general, by all accounts, but doesn't like to gamble.'

'I'd be less charitable,' said Monza.

'Few people are less charitable than you.'

'He doesn't like to fight.'

'No good general likes to fight.'

'But every good general has to, from time to time. Rogont's been pitted against Orso throughout the Years of Blood and never fought more than a skirmish. The man's the best withdrawer in Styria.'

'Toughest thing to manage, a retreat. Maybe he just hasn't found his moment yet.'

Shivers gave a faraway sigh. 'We're all of us waiting for our moment.'

'He's wasted all his chances now,' said Monza. 'Once Visserine falls, the way to Puranti is open, and beyond that nothing but Ospria itself, and Orso's crown. No more delays. The sand's run through on caution.'

Rogont and Salier passed underneath them. The two men who, along with honest, honourable, dead Duke Cantain, had formed the League of Eight to defend Styria against Orso's insatiable ambition. Or to frustrate his rightful claims so they could fight among themselves for whatever was left, depending on who you asked. Cosca had a faraway smile on his face as he watched them go. 'You live long enough, you see everything ruined. Caprile, a shell of her former glory.'

Vitari grinned at Monza. 'That was one of yours, no?'

'Musselia most shamefully capitulated to Orso in spite of her impenetrable walls.'

Vitari grinned wider. 'Wasn't that one of yours too?'

'Borletta fallen,' Cosca lamented, 'bold Duke Cantain dead.'

'Yes,' growled Monza, before Vitari could open her mouth.

'The invincible League of Eight has withered to a company of five and will soon dwindle to a party of four, with three of those far from keen on the whole notion.'

Monza could just hear Friendly's whisper, 'Eight . . . five . . . four . . . three . . .'

Those three followed now, glittering households trailing them like the wake behind three ducks. Junior partners in the League – Lirozio, the Duke of Puranti, defiant in elaborate armour and even more elaborate moustaches. The young Countess Cotarda of Affoia – a pasty girl whose pale yellow silks weren't helping her complexion, her uncle and first advisor, some said her first lover, hovering close at her shoulder. Patine came last, First Citizen of Nicante – his hair left wild, dressed in sackcloth with a knotted rope for a belt, to show he was no better than the lowest peasant in his care. The rumour was he wore silken undergarments and slept on a golden bed, and with no shortage of company. So much for the humility of the powerful.

Cosca was already looking to the next chapter in the procession of greatness. 'By the Fates. Who are these young gods?'

They were a magnificent pair, there was no denying that. They rode identical greys with effortless confidence, arrayed in matching white and gold. Her snowy gown clung to her impossibly tall and slender form and spread out behind her, fretted with glittering thread. His gilded breastplate was polished to a mirror-glare, simple crown set with a single stone so big Monza could almost see its facets glittering a hundred strides distant.

'How incredibly fucking regal,' she sneered.

'One can almost smell the majesty,' threw in Cosca. 'I would kneel if I thought my knees could bear it.'

'His August Majesty, the High King of the Union.' Vitari's voice was greasy with irony. 'And his queen, of course.'

'Terez, the Jewel of Talins. She sparkles brightly, no?'

'Orso's daughter,' Monza forced out through clenched teeth. 'Ario and Foscar's sister. Queen of the Union, and a royal cunt into the bargain.'

Even though he was a foreigner on Styrian soil, even though Union ambitions were treated with the greatest suspicion here, even though his wife was Orso's daughter, the crowd found themselves cheering louder for a foreign king than they had for their own geriatric chancellor.

The people far prefer a leader who appears great, Bialoveld wrote, *to one who is.*

'Hardly the most neutral of mediators, you'd think.' Cosca puffed his cheeks out thoughtfully. 'Bound so tight to Orso and his brood you can hardly see the light between them. Husband, and brother, and son-in-law to Talins?'

'No doubt he considers himself above such earthly considerations.' Monza's lip curled as she watched the royal pair approach. It looked as if they'd ridden from the pages of a lurid storybook and out into the drab and slimy city by accident. Wings on their horses were all they needed to complete the fantasy. It was a wonder someone hadn't glued some on. Terez wore a great necklace of huge stones, flashing so brilliantly in the sun they were painful to look at.

Vitari was shaking her head. 'How many jewels can you pile on one woman?'

'Not many more without burying the bitch,' growled Monza. The ruby that Benna had given her seemed a child's trinket by comparison.

'Jealousy is a terrible thing, ladies.' Cosca nudged Friendly in the ribs. 'She seems well enough in my eyes, eh, my friend?' The convict said nothing. Cosca tried Shivers instead. 'Eh?'

The Northman glanced sideways at Monza, then away. 'Don't get the fuss, myself.'

'Well, a pretty pair, the two of you! I never met such cold-blooded fighting men. I may be past my prime but I'm nothing like so withered inside as you set of long faces. My heart can still be moved by a young couple in love.'

Monza doubted there could be that much fire between them, however they might grin at one another. 'Few years ago now, well before she was a queen in anything but her own mind, Benna had a bet with me that he could bed her.'

Cosca raised one brow. 'Your brother always liked to sow his seed widely, as I recall. The results?'

'Turned out he wasn't her type.' It had turned out Monza interested her a great deal more than Benna ever could.

A household even grander than the whole League of Eight had fielded followed respectfully behind the royal couple. A score at least of ladies-in-waiting, each one dripping jewels of her own. A smattering of Lords of Midderland, Angland and Starikland, weighty furs and golden chains about their shoulders. Men-at-arms plodded behind, armour stained with dust from the hooves in front. Each man choking on the dirt of his betters. The ugly truth of power.

'King of the Union, eh?' mused Shivers, watching the royal couple move off. 'That there is the most powerful man in the whole Circle of the World?'

Vitari snorted. 'That there is the man he stands behind. Everyone kneels to someone. You don't know too much about politics, do you?'

'About what?'

'Lies. The Cripple rules the Union. That boy with all the gold is the mask he wears.'

Cosca sighed. 'If you looked like the Cripple, I daresay you'd get a mask too . . .'

Such cheering as there was moved off slowly after the king and queen, and left a sullen silence behind it. Quiet enough that Monza could hear the clattering of the wheels as a gilded carriage rattled down the avenue. Several score of grim guardsmen tramped in practised columns to either side, weapons less well polished than the Union's had been, but better used. A crowd of well-dressed and entirely useless gentlemen followed.

Monza closed her right fist tight, crooked bones shifting. The pain crept across her knuckles, through her hand, up her arm, and she felt her mouth twist into a grim smile.

'There they are,' said Cosca.

Ario sat on the right, draped over his cushions, swaying gently with the movement of the carriage, his customary look of lazy contempt smeared across his face. Foscar sat pale and upright beside him, head starting this way and that at every smallest sound. Preening tomcat and eager puppy dog, placed neatly together.

Gobba had been nothing. Mauthis had been just a banker. Orso would scarcely have remarked on the new faces around him when they were replaced. But Ario and Foscar were his sons. His precious flesh. His future. If she could kill them, it would be the next best thing to sticking the blade in Orso's own belly. Her smile grew, imagining his face as they brought him the news.

Your Excellency! Your sons . . . are dead . . .

A sudden shriek split the silence. 'Murderers! Scum! Orso's bastards!' Some limbs flailed down in the crowd below, someone trying to break through the cordon of soldiers. 'You're a curse on Styria!' There was a swell of angry mutterings, a nervous ripple spread out through the onlookers. Sotorius might have called himself neutral, but the people of Sipani had no love for Orso or his brood. They knew when he broke the League of Eight, they'd be next. Some men always want more.

A couple of the mounted gentlemen drew steel. Metal gleamed at the edge of the crowd, there was a thin scream. Foscar was almost standing in the carriage, staring off into the heaving mass of people. Ario pulled him down and slouched back in his seat, careless eyes fixed on his fingernails.

The disturbance was finished. The carriage rattled off, gentlemen finding their formation again, soldiers in the livery of Talins tramping behind. The last of them passed under the roof of the warehouse, and off down the avenue.

'And the show is over,' sighed Cosca, pushing himself from the railing and making for the door that led to the stairs.

'I wish it could've gone on for ever,' sneered Vitari as she turned away.

'One thousand eight hundred and twelve,' said Friendly.

Monza stared at him. 'What?'

'People. In the parade.'

'And?'

'One hundred and five stones in the queen's necklace.'

'Did I fucking ask?'

'No.' Friendly followed the others back to the stairs.

She stood there alone, frowning into the stiffening wind for a moment longer, glaring off up the avenue as the crowd began to disperse, her fist and her jaw still clenched aching tight.

'Monza.' Not alone. When she turned her head, Shivers was looking her in the eye, and from closer than she'd have liked. He spoke as if finding the words was hard work. 'Seems like we haven't . . . I don't know. Since Westport . . . I just wanted to ask—'

'Best if you don't.' She brushed past him and away.

Cooking up Trouble

Nicomo Cosca closed his eyes, licked his smiling lips, breathed in deep through his nose in anticipation and raised the bottle. A drink, a drink, a drink. The familiar promise of the tap of glass against his teeth, the cooling wetness on his tongue, the soothing movement of his throat as he swallowed . . . if only it hadn't been water.

He had crept from his sweat-soaked bed and down to the kitchen in his clammy nightshirt to hunt for wine. Or any old piss that could make a man drunk. Something to make his dusty bedroom stop shaking like a carriage gone off the road, banish the ants he felt were crawling all over his skin, sponge away his pounding headache, whatever the costs. Shit on change, and Murcatto's vengeance too.

He had hoped that everyone would be in bed, and squirmed with trembling frustration when he had seen Friendly at the stove, making porridge for breakfast. Now, though, he had to admit, he was strangely glad to have found the convict here. There was something almost magical about Friendly's aura of calmness. He had the utter confidence to stay silent and simply not care what anyone thought. Enough to take Cosca a rare step towards calmness himself. Not silence, though. Indeed he had been talking, virtually uninterrupted, since the first light began to creep through the chinks in the shutters and turn to dawn.

'. . . why the hell am I doing this, Friendly? Fighting, at my age? Fighting! I've never enjoyed that part of the business. And on the same side as that self-congratulating vermin Morveer! A poisoner? Stinking way to kill a man, that. And I am acutely aware, of course, that I am breaking the soldier's first rule.'

Friendly cocked one eyebrow a fraction as he slowly stirred the porridge. Cosca strongly suspected the convict knew exactly why he had come here, but if he did, he had better manners than to bring it up. Convicts, in the main, are wonderfully polite. Bad manners can be fatal in prison. 'First?' he asked.

'Never fight for the weaker side. Much though I have always despised Duke Orso with a flaming passion, there is a huge and potentially fatal gulf between hating the man and actually doing anything about it.' He thumped his fist gently against the table-top and made the model of Cardotti's rattle gently. 'Particularly on behalf of a woman who already betrayed me once . . .'

Like a homing pigeon drawn endlessly back to its loved and hated cage, his mind was dragged back through nine wasted years to Afieri. He pictured the horses thundering down the long slope, sun flashing behind them, as he had so many times since in a hundred different stinking rooms, and bone-cheap boarding houses, and broken-down slum taverns across the Circle of the World. A fine pretence, he had thought as the cavalry drew closer, smiling through the haze of drink to see it done so well. He remembered the cold dismay as the horsemen did not slow. The sick lurch of horror as they crashed into his own slovenly lines. The mixture of fury, hopelessness, disgust and dizzy drunkenness as he scrambled onto his horse to flee, his ragtag brigade ripped apart around him and his reputation with it. That mixture of fury, hopelessness, disgust and dizzy drunkenness that had followed him as tightly as his shadow ever since. He frowned at the distorted reflection of his wasted face in the bubbly glass of the water bottle.

'The memories of our glories fade,' he whispered, 'and rot away into half-arsed anecdotes, thin and unconvincing as some other bastard's lies. The failures, the disappointments, the regrets, they stay raw as the moments they happened. A pretty girl's smile, never acted on. A petty wrong we let another take the blame for. A nameless shoulder that knocked us in a crowd and left us stewing for days, for months. For ever.' He curled his lip. 'This is the stuff the past is made of. The wretched moments that make us what we are.'

Friendly stayed silent, and it drew Cosca out better than any coaxing.

'And none more bitter than the moment Monzcarro Murcatto turned on me, eh? I should be taking my revenge on her, instead of helping her take hers. I should kill her, and Andiche, and

Sesaria, and Victus, and all my other one-time bastard friends from the Thousand Swords. So what the *shit* am I doing here, Friendly?'

'Talking.'

Cosca snorted. 'As ever. I always had poor judgement where women were concerned.' He barked with sudden laughter. 'In truth, I always had dire judgement on every issue. That is what has made my life such a series of thrills.' He slapped the bottle down on the table. 'Enough penny philosophy! The fact is I need the chance, I need to change and, much more importantly, I desperately need the money.' He stood up. 'Fuck the past. I am Nicomo Cosca, damn it! I laugh in the face of fear!' He paused for a moment. 'And I am going back to bed. My earnest thanks, Master Friendly, you make as fine a conversation as any man I've known.'

The convict looked away from his porridge for just a moment. 'I've hardly said a word.'

'Exactly.'

Morveer's morning repast was arranged upon the small table in his small bedchamber, once perhaps an upstairs storeroom in an abandoned warehouse in an insalubrious district of Sipani, a city he had always despised. Refreshment consisted of a misshapen bowl of cold oatmeal, a battered cup of steaming tea, a chipped glass of sour and lukewarm water. Beside them, in a neat row, stood seventeen various vials, bottles, jars and tins, each filled with its own pastes, liquids or powders in a range of colours from clear, to white, through dull buff to the verdant blue of the scorpion oil.

Morveer reluctantly spooned in a mouthful of mush. While he worked it around his mouth with scant relish, he removed the stoppers from the first four containers, slid a glinting needle from its packet, dipped it in the first and pricked the back of his hand. The second, and the same. The third, and the fourth, and he tossed the needle distastefully away. He winced as he watched a tiny bead of blood well from one of the prick-marks, then dug another spoonful from the bowl and sat back, head hanging, while the wave of dizziness swept over him.

'Damn Larync!' Still, it was far preferable that he should

endure a tiny dose and a little unpleasantness every morning, than that a large dose, administered by malice or misadventure, should one day burst every blood vessel in his brain.

He forced down another mouthful of salty slop, opened the tin next in line, scooped out a tiny pinch of Mustard Root, held one nostril closed and snorted it up the other. He shivered as the powder burned at his nasal passages, licked at his teeth as his mouth turned unpleasantly numb. He took a mouthful of tea, found it unexpectedly scalding as he swallowed and nearly coughed it back up.

'Damn Mustard Root!' That he had employed it against targets with admirable efficacy on several occasions gave him no extra love for consuming the blasted stuff himself. Quite the opposite. He gargled a mouthful of water in a vain attempt to sluice away the acrid taste, knowing full well that it would be creeping from the back of his nose for hours to come.

He lined up the next six receptacles, unscrewed, uncorked, uncapped them. He could have swallowed their contents one at a time, but long years of such breakfasts had taught him it was better to dispose of them all at once. So he squirted, flicked and dripped the appropriate amounts into his glass of water, mixed them carefully with his spoon, gathered himself and forced it back in three ugly swallows.

Morveer set the glass down, wiped the tears from under his eyes and gave vent to a watery burp. He felt a momentary nudge of nausea, but it swiftly calmed. He had been doing this every morning for twenty years, after all. If he was not accustomed to it by—

He dived for the window, flung the shutters open and thrust his head through just in time to spray his meagre breakfast into the rotten alley beside the warehouse. He gave a bitter groan as he slumped back, dashed the burning snot from his nose and picked his way unsteadily to the washstand. He scooped water from the basin and rubbed it over his face, stared at his reflection in the mirror as moisture dripped from his brows. The worst of it was that he would now have to force more oatmeal into his rebellious guts. One of the many unappreciated sacrifices he was forced to make, simply in order to excel.

The other children at the orphanage had never appreciated his special talents. Nor had his master, the infamous Moumah-yin-Bek. His wife had not appreciated him. His many apprentices had not. And now it seemed his latest employer, also, had no appreciation for his selfless, for his discomforting, for his – no, no, it was no exaggeration – *heroic* efforts on her behalf. That dissolute old wineskin Nicomo Cosca was afforded greater respect than he.

'I am doomed,' he murmured disconsolately. 'Doomed to give, and give, and get *nothing* in return.'

A knock at the door, and Day's voice. 'You ready?'

'Soon.'

'They're getting everyone together downstairs. We need to be off to Cardotti's. Lay the groundwork. The importance of preparation and all that.' It sounded as if she was talking with her mouth full. It would, in fact, have been a surprise had she not been.

'I will catch up with you!' He heard her footsteps moving off. There, at least, was one person with the requisite admiration for his magisterial skills, who rendered him the fitting respect, exceeded his lofty expectations. He was coming to rely on her a great deal, he realised, both practically and emotionally. More than was cautious, perhaps.

But even a man of Morveer's extraordinary talents could not manage everything himself. He gave a long sigh, and turned from the mirror.

The entertainers, or the killers, for they were both, were scattered around the warehouse floor. Twenty-five of them, if Friendly counted himself. The three Gurkish dancers sat crossed-legged – two with their ornate cat-face masks pushed up on their oiled black hair. The last had her mask down, eyes glistening darkly behind the slanted eyeholes, rubbing carefully at a curved dagger. The band were already dressed in smart black jackets and tights striped grey and yellow, their silvered masks in the shape of musical notes, practising a jig they had finally managed to play half-decently.

Shivers stood nearby in a stained leather tunic with balding fur on the shoulders, a big round wooden shield on his arm and a heavy sword in the other hand. Greylock loomed opposite, an iron mask covering his whole face, a great club set with iron studs in his fists. Shivers was talking fast in Northern, showing how he was going to swing his sword, how he wanted Greylock to react, practising the show they would put on.

Barti and Kummel, the acrobats, wore tight-fitting chequered motley, arguing with each other in the tongue of the Union, one of them passionately waving a short stabbing sword. The Incredible Ronco watched from behind a mask painted vivid red, orange and yellow, like dancing flames. Beyond him the three jugglers were filling the air with a cascade of shining knives, flashing and flickering in the half-darkness. Others lounged against crates, sat cross-legged on the floor, capered about, sharpened blades, tinkered with costumes.

Friendly hardly recognised Cosca himself, dressed in a velvet coat heavy with silver embroidery, a tall hat on his head and a long black cane in his hand with a heavy golden knob on the end. The rash on his neck was disguised with powder. His greying moustaches were waxed to twinkling curves, his boots were polished to a glistening shine, his mask was crusted with splinters of sparkling mirror, but his eyes sparkled more.

He swaggered towards Friendly with the smirk of a ringmaster at a circus. 'My friend, I hope you are well. My thanks again for your ear this morning.'

Friendly nodded, trying not to grin. There was something almost magical about Cosca's aura of good humour. He had the utter confidence to talk, and talk, and know he would be listened to, laughed with, understood. It almost made Friendly want to talk himself.

Cosca held something out. A mask in the shape of a pair of dice, showing double one with eyeholes where the spots should have been. 'I hoped you might do me the favour of minding the dice table tonight.'

Friendly took the mask from him with a trembling hand. 'I would like that very much.'

Their mad crew wound through the twisting streets as the morning mists were clearing – down grey alleys, over narrow bridges, through hazy, rotting gardens and along damp tunnels, footfalls hollow in the gloom. The treacherous water was never far off, Shivers wrinkling his nose at the salt stink of the canals.

Half the city was masked and in costume, and it seemed they all had something to celebrate. Folk who weren't invited to the great ball in honour of Sipani's royal visitors had their own revels planned, and a lot of 'em were getting started good and early. Some hadn't gone too wild with their costumes – holiday coats and dresses with a plain mask around their eyes. Some had gone wild, then further still – huge trousers, high shoes, gold and silver faces locked up in animal snarls and madman grins. Put Shivers in mind of the Bloody-Nine's face when he fought in the circle, devil smile spattered with blood. That did nothing for his nerves. Didn't help he was wearing fur and leather like he used to in the North, carrying a heavy sword and shield not much different from ones he'd used in earnest. A crowd poured past all covered in yellow feathers, masks with great beaks, squawking like a flock of crazy seagulls. That did nothing for his nerves either.

Off in the mist, half-glimpsed round corners and across hazy squares, there were stranger shapes still, their hoots and warbles echoing down the wooden alleyways. Monsters and giants. Made Shivers' palms itch, thinking of the way the Feared rose out of the mist up at Dunbrec, bringing death with him. These were just silly bastards on stilts, of course, but still. You put a mask on a person, something weird happens. Changes the way they act along with the way they look. Sometimes they don't seem like people at all no more, but something else.

Shivers wouldn't have liked the flavour of it even if they hadn't been planning murder. Felt like the city was built on the borders of hell and devils were spilling out into the streets, mixing with the everyday and no one acting like there was much special about it. He had to keep reminding himself that, of all the strange and dangerous-seeming crowds, his was much the strangest and most dangerous they were likely to happen across. If there were devils in the city, he was one of the worst. Wasn't actually that comforting a thought, once it'd taken root.

'This way, my friends!' Cosca led them across a square planted with four clammy, leafless trees and a building loomed up from the gloom – a large wooden building on three sides of a court-yard. The same building that had been sitting on the kitchen table at the warehouse the last few days. Four well-armed guards were frowning around a gate of iron bars, and Cosca sprang smartly up the steps towards them, heels clicking. 'A fine morning to you, gentlemen!'

'Cardotti's is closed today,' the nearest growled back, 'and tonight too.'

'Not to us.' Cosca took in the mismatched troupe with a sweep of his cane. 'We are the entertainers for this evening's private function, selected and hired especially for the purpose by Prince Ario's consort, Carlot dan Eider. Now open that gate quick sharp, we have a great deal of preparation to attend to. In we come, my children, and don't dally! People must be entertained!'

The yard was bigger'n Shivers had been expecting, and a lot more of a disappointment too, since this was supposed to be the best brothel in the world. A stretch of mossy cobbles with a couple of rickety tables and chairs, painted in flaking gilt. Lines were strung from upstairs windows, sheets flapping sluggishly as they dried. A set of wine-barrels were badly stacked in one corner. A bent old man was sweeping with a worn-out broom, a fat woman was giving what might've been some underwear a right thrashing on a washboard. Three skinny women sat about a table, bored. One had an open book in her hand. Another frowned at her nails as she worked 'em with a file. The last slouched in her chair, watching the entertainers file in while she blew smoke from a little clay chagga pipe.

Cosca sighed. 'There's nothing more mundane, or less arousing, than a whorehouse in the daytime, eh?'

'Seems not.' Shivers watched the jugglers find a space over in one corner and start to unpack their tools, gleaming knives among 'em.

'I've always thought it must be a fine enough life, being a whore. A successful one, at any rate. You get the days off, and when finally you are called upon to work you can get most of it done lying down.'

'Not much honour in it,' said Shivers.

'Shit at least makes flowers grow. Honour isn't even that useful.'

'What happens when you get old, though, and no one wants

you no more? Seems to me all you're doing is putting off the despair and leaving a pack of regrets behind you.'

Below Cosca's mask, his smile had a sad twist. 'That's all any of us are doing, my friend. Every business is the same, and ours is no different. Soldiering, killing, whatever you want to call it. No one wants you when you get old.' He strutted past Shivers and into the courtyard, cane flicking backwards and forwards with each stride. 'One way or another, we're all of us whores!' He snatched a fancy cloth from a pocket, waved it at the three women as he passed and gave a bow. 'Ladies. A most profound honour.'

'Silly old cock,' Shivers heard one of them mutter in Northern, before she went back to her pipe. The band were already tuning up, making almost as sour a whine as when they were actually playing.

Two tall doorways led from the yard – left to the gaming hall, right to the smoking hall, from those to the two staircases. His eyes crept up the ivy-covered wall, herringbone planks of weather-darkened wood, to the row of narrow windows on the first floor. Rooms for the entertainment of guests. Higher still, to bigger windows of coloured glass, just under the roofline. The Royal Suite, where the most valued visitors were welcomed. Where they planned to welcome Prince Ario and his brother Foscar in a few hours.

'Oy.' A touch on his shoulder, and he turned, and stood blinking.

A tall woman stood behind him, a shining black fur draped around her shoulders, long black gloves on her long arms, black hair scraped over to one side and hanging soft and smooth across her white face. Her mask was scattered with chips of crystal, eyes gleaming through the narrow slots and set on him.

'Er . . .' Shivers had to make himself look away from her chest, the shadow between her tits drawing his eyes like a bear's to a beehive. 'Something I can . . . you know . . .'

'I don't know, is there?' Her painted lips twisted up at one corner, part sneer and part smile. Seemed as if there was something familiar about that voice. Through the slit in her skirts he could just see the end of a long pink scar on her thigh.

'Monza?' he whispered.

'Who else as fine as this would have anything to say to the likes of you?' She eyed him up and down. 'This brings back memories. You look almost as much of a savage as when I first met you.'

'That's the idea, I reckon. You look, er . . .' He struggled for the word.

'Like a whore?'

'A damn pricey one, maybe.'

'I'd hate to look a cheap one. I'm headed upstairs, to wait for our guests. All goes well, I'll see you at the warehouse.'

'Aye. If all goes well.' Shivers' life had a habit of not going well. He frowned up at those stained-glass windows. 'You going to be alright?'

'Oh, I can handle Ario. I've been looking forward to it.'

'I know, but, I'm just saying . . . if you need me closer—'

'Stick your tiny mind to keeping things under control down here. Let me worry about me.'

'I'm worried enough that I can spare some.'

'Thought you were an optimist,' she tossed over her shoulder as she walked away.

'Maybe you talked me out of it,' he muttered at her back. He didn't like it much when she spoke to him that way, but he liked it a lot better'n when she wouldn't speak to him at all. He saw Greylock glowering at him as he turned, and stabbed an angry finger at the big bastard. 'Don't just stand there! Let's get this damn fake circle marked out, 'fore we get old!'

Monza was a long way from comfortable as she teetered through the gambling hall, Cosca beside her. She wasn't used to the high shoes. She wasn't used to the draught around her legs. Corsets were torture at the best of times, and it hardly helped that this one had two of the bones removed and replaced with long, thin knives, the points up between her shoulder blades and the grips hidden in the small of her back. Her ankles, and her knees, and her hips were already throbbing. The notion of a smoke tickled at the back of her mind, just like always, but she forced it away. She'd endured enough pain, these past few months. A little more was a light price to pay if it got her close to Ario. Close enough to stick a blade in his sneering face. The thought alone put some swagger back into her step.

Carlot dan Eider waited for them at the end of the room, standing with regal superiority between two card tables covered with grey sheets, wearing a red dress fit for an empress of legend.

'Will you look at the two of us?' sneered Monza as she came close. 'A general dressed like a whore and a whore dressed like a queen. Everyone's pretending to be someone else tonight.'

'That's politics.' Ario's mistress frowned over at Cosca. 'Who's this?'

'Magister Eider, what a delightful and unexpected honour.' The old mercenary bowed as he swept his hat off, exposing his scabrous, sweat-beaded bald patch. 'I never dreamed the two of us would meet again.'

'You!' Eider stared coldly back at him. 'I might have known you'd be caught up in this. I thought you died in Dagoska!'

'So did I, but it turned out I was only very, *very* drunk.'

'Not so drunk you couldn't fumble your way to betraying me.'

The old mercenary shrugged. 'It's always a crying shame when honest people are betrayed. When it happens to the treacherous, though, one cannot avoid a certain sense of . . . cosmic justice.' Cosca grinned from Eider, to Monza, and back. 'Three people as loyal as us all on one side? I can hardly wait to see how this turns out.'

Monza's guess was that it would turn out bloody. 'When will Ario and Foscar get here?'

'When Sotorius' grand ball begins to break up. Midnight, or just before.'

'We'll be waiting.'

'The antidote,' snapped Eider. 'I've done my part.'

'You'll get it when I get Ario's head on a plate. Not before.'

'What if something goes wrong?'

'You'll die along with the rest of us. Better hope things run smoothly.'

'What's to stop you from letting me die anyway?'

'My dazzling reputation for fair play and good behaviour.'

Unsurprisingly, Eider didn't laugh. 'I tried to do the right thing in Dagoska.' She jabbed at her chest with a finger. 'I tried to do the right thing! I tried to save people! Look what it's cost me!'

'There might be a lesson in there about doing the right thing.' Monza shrugged. 'I've never had that problem.'

'You can joke! Do you know what it's like, to live in fear every moment?'

Monza took a quick step towards her and she shrank back against the wall. 'Living in fear?' she snarled, their masks almost scraping together. 'Welcome to *my* fucking life! Now quit whining and smile for Ario and the other bastards at the ball tonight!' She dropped her voice to a whisper. 'Then bring him to us. Him and his brother. Do as I tell you, and you might still get a happy ending.'

She knew that neither one of them thought that very likely. There'd be precious few happy endings to tonight's festivities.

Day turned the drill one last time, bit squealing through wood, then eased it gently free. A chink of light peeped up into the darkness of the attic and brightly illuminated a circular patch of her cheek. She grinned across at Morveer, and he was touched by a sudden bitter-sweet memory of his mother's smiling face by candlelight. 'We're through.'

Now was hardly the time for nostalgia. He swallowed the upwelling of emotion and crept over, taking the greatest care to set his feet only upon the rafters. A black-clad leg bursting through the ceiling and kicking wildly would no doubt give Orso's sons and their guards some cause for concern. Peering down through the hole, doubtless invisible among the thick mouldings, Morveer could see an opulent stretch of panelled corridor with a rich Gurkish carpet and two high doorways. A crown was carved into the wood above the nearest one.

'*Perfect* positioning, my dear. The Royal Suite.' From here they had an unobstructed view of guards stationed by either door. He reached into his jacket, and frowned. He patted at his other pockets, panic stabbing at him.

'Damn it! I forgot my spare blowpipe! What if—'

'I brought two extra, just in case.'

Morveer pressed one hand to his chest. 'Thank the Fates. No! Damn the Fates. Thank your prudent planning. Where would I be without you?'

Day grinned her innocent little grin. 'About where you are now, but with less charming company. Caution first, always.'

'*So* true.' He dropped his voice back to a whisper. 'And here they come.' Murcatto and Vitari appeared, both masked, powdered and dressed, or rather undressed, like the many female employees of the establishment. Vitari opened the door beneath the crown and entered. Murcatto glanced briefly up at the ceiling, nodded, then followed her. 'They are within. So far all proceeds according to plan.' But there was ample time yet for disasters. 'The yard?'

Day wriggled on her stomach to the far edge of the attic where roof met rafters, and peered through the holes they had drilled overlooking the building's central courtyard. 'Looks as if they're ready to welcome our guests. What now?'

Morveer crept to the minuscule, grubby window and brushed some cobwebs away with the side of one hand. The sun was sinking behind the ragged rooftops, casting a muddy flare over the City of Whispers. 'The masked ball should soon be under way at Sotorius' palace.' On the far side of the canal, behind Cardotti's House of Leisure, the torches were being lit, lamplight spilling from the windows in the black residences and into the blue evening. Morveer flicked the cobwebs from his fingers with some distaste. 'Now we sit here in this mouldering attic, and wait for his Highness Prince Ario to arrive.'

Sex and Death

By darkness, Cardotti's House of Leisure was a different world. A fantasy land, as far removed from drab reality as the moon. The gaming hall was lit by three hundred and seventeen flickering candles. Friendly had counted them as they were hoisted up on tinkling chandeliers, bracketed to gleaming sconces, twisted into glittering candlesticks.

The sheets had been flung back from the gaming tables. One of the dealers was shuffling his cards, another was sitting, staring into space, a third carefully stacking up his counters. Friendly counted silently along with him. At the far end of the room an old man was oiling the lucky wheel. Not too lucky for those that played it, by Friendly's assessment of the odds. That was the strange thing about games of chance. The chances were always against the player. You might beat the numbers for a day, but you could never beat them in the end.

Everything shone like hidden treasure, and the women most of all. They were dressed now, and masked, transformed by warm candlelight into things barely human. Long, thin limbs oiled and powdered and dusted with glitter, eyes shining darkly through the eyeholes of gilded masks, lips and nails painted black-red like blood from a fatal wound.

The air was full of strange, frightening smells. There had been no women in Safety, and Friendly felt greatly on edge. He calmed himself by rolling the dice over and over, and adding the scores one upon another. He had reached already four thousand two hundred and . . .

One of the women swept past, her ruffled dress swishing against the Gurkish carpet, one long, bare leg sliding out from the blackness with each step. Two hundred and . . . His eyes seemed glued to that leg, his heart beating very fast. Two hundred and . . . twenty-six. He jerked his eyes away and back to the dice.

Three and two. Utterly normal, and nothing to worry about. He straightened, and stood waiting. Outside the window, in the courtyard, the guests were beginning to arrive.

'Welcome, my friends, welcome to Cardotti's! We have everything a growing boy needs! Dice and cards, games of skill and chance are this way! For those who relish the embrace of mother husk, that door! Wine and spirits on demand. Drink deep, my friends! There will be various entertainments mounted here in the yard throughout the evening! Dancing, juggling, music . . . even perhaps a little violence, for those with a taste for blood! As for female companionship, well . . . that you will find throughout the building . . .'

Men were pouring into the courtyard in a masked and powdered flow. The place was already heaving with expensively tailored bodies, the air thick with their braying chatter. The band were sawing out a merry tune in one corner of the yard, the jugglers flinging a stream of sparkling glasses high into the air in another. Occasionally one of the women would strut through, whisper to someone, lead him away into the building. And upstairs, no doubt. Cosca could not help wondering . . . could he be spared for a few moments?

'Quite utterly charmed,' he murmured, tipping his hat at a willowy blonde as she swayed past.

'Stick to the guests!' she snarled viciously in his face.

'Only trying to lift the mood, my dear. Only trying to help.'

'You want to help, you can suck a prick or two! I've enough to get through!' Someone touched her on the shoulder and she turned, smiling radiantly, took him by the arm and swept away.

'Who are all these bastards?' Shivers, muttering in his ear. 'Three or four dozen, weren't we told, a few armed but not keen to fight? There must be twice that many in already!'

Cosca grinned as he clapped the Northman on the shoulder. 'I know! Isn't it a thrill when you throw a party and you get more guests than you expected? Somebody's popular!'

Shivers did not look amused. 'I don't reckon it's us! How do we keep control of all this?'

'What makes you think I have the answers? In my experience, life rarely turns out the way you expect. We must bend with the circumstances, and simply do our best.'

'Maybe six guards, weren't we told? So who are they?' The Northman jerked his head towards a grim-looking knot of men gathered in one corner, all with polished breastplates over their padded black jackets, with serious masks of plain steel, serious swords and long knives at their hips, serious frowns on their chiselled jaws. Their eyes darted carefully about the yard as though looking for threats.

'Hmmm,' mused Cosca. 'I was wondering the same thing.'

'Wondering?' The Northman's big fist was uncomfortably tight round Cosca's arm. 'When does wondering turn into shitting yourself?'

'I've often wondered.' Cosca peeled the hand away. 'But it's a funny thing. I simply don't get scared.' He made off through the crowd, clapping backs, calling for drinks, pointing out attractions, spreading good humour wherever he went. He was in his element, now. Vice, and high living, but danger too.

He feared old age, failure, betrayal and looking a fool. Yet he never feared before a fight. Cosca's happiest moments had been spent waiting for battles to begin. Watching the countless Gurkish march upon the walls of Dagoska. Watching the forces of Sipani deploy before the Battle of the Isles. Scrambling onto his horse by moonlight when the enemy sallied from the walls of Muris. Danger was the thing he most enjoyed. Worries for the future, purged. Failures of the past, erased. Only the glorious now remained. He closed his eyes and sucked in air, felt it tingling pleasantly in his chest, heard the excited babbling of the guests. He scarcely even felt the need for a drink any more.

He snapped his eyes open to see two men stepping through the gate, others scraping away to make grovelling room for them. His Highness Prince Ario was dressed in a scarlet coat, silken cuffs drooping from his embroidered sleeves in a manner that implied he would never have to grip anything for himself. A spray of multicoloured feathers sprouted from the top of his golden mask, thrashing like a peacock's tail as he looked about him, unimpressed.

'Your Highness!' Cosca swept off his hat and bowed low. 'We are truly, *truly* honoured by your presence.'

'Indeed you are,' said Ario. 'And by the presence of my brother.' He wafted a languid hand at the man beside him, dressed all in spotless white with a mask in the form of half a golden sun, somewhat twitchy and reluctant-seeming, Cosca rather thought. Foscar, no doubt, though he had grown a beard which very much suited him. 'Not to mention that of our mutual friend, Master Sulfur.'

'Alas, I cannot stay.' A nondescript fellow had slipped in behind the two brothers. He had a curly head of hair, a simple suit and a faint smile. 'So much to do. Never the slightest peace, eh?' And he grinned at Cosca. Inside the holes of his plain mask, his eyes were different colours: one blue, one green. 'I must to Talins tonight, and speak to your father. We cannot allow the Gurkish a free hand.'

'Of course not. Damn those Gurkish bastards. Good journey to you, Sulfur.' Ario gave the slightest bow of his head.

'Good journey,' growled Foscar, as Sulfur turned for the gate.

Cosca jammed his hat back on his head. 'Well, your two honours are certainly most welcome! Please, enjoy the entertainments! Everything is at your disposal!' He sidled closer, flashing his most mischievous grin. 'The top floor of the building has been reserved for you and your brother. Your Highness will find, I rather think, a particularly surprising diversion in the Royal Suite.'

'There, brother. Let us see if, in due course, we can divert you from your cares.' Ario frowned towards the band. 'By the heavens, could that woman not have found some better music?'

The thickening throng parted to let the brothers pass. Several sneering gentlemen followed in their wake, as well as four more of the grim men with their swords and armour. Cosca frowned after their shining backplates as they stepped through the door into the gaming hall.

Nicomo Cosca felt no fear, that was a fact. But a measure of sober concern at all these well-armed men seemed only prudent. Monza had asked for control, after all. He hopped over to the entrance and touched one of the guards outside upon his arm. 'No more in tonight. We are full.' He shut the gate in the man's surprised face, turned the key in the lock and slipped it into his waistcoat pocket. Prince Ario's friend Master Sulfur would have the honour of being the last man to pass through the front gate tonight.

He flung one arm up at the band. 'Something livelier lads, strike up a tune! We are here to entertain!'

Morveer knelt, hunched in the darkness of the attic, peering from the eaves of the roof into the courtyard far below. Men in ostentatious attire formed knots that swelled, dissolved, shifted and flowed in and out through the two doors that led into the building. They glittered and gleamed in pools of lamplight. Ribald exclamations and hushed chatter, poor music and good-natured laughter floated up through the night, but Morveer was not inclined to celebrate.

'Why so many?' he whispered. 'We were anticipating less than half this number. Something . . . is *awry*.'

A gout of incandescent flame went up into the frigid night and there was an eruption of clapping. That imbecile Ronco, endangering his own existence and that of every other person in the yard. Morveer slowly shook his head. If that was a good idea then he was the Emperor of—

Day hissed at him, and he fumbled his way back across the rafters, old wood creaking gently, and applied his eye to one of the holes. 'Someone's coming.'

A group of eight persons emerged from the stairway, all of them masked. Four were evidently guards, armoured in highly polished breastplates. Two were even more evidently women employed by Cardotti's. It was the final two men that were of interest to Morveer.

'Ario and Foscar,' whispered Day.

'So it would *undoubtedly* appear.' Orso's sons exchanged a brief word while their guards took up positions flanking the two doors. Then Ario bowed low, his snigger echoing faintly around the attic. He swaggered down the corridor to the second door, one of the women on each arm, leaving his brother to approach the Royal Suite.

Morveer frowned. 'Something is most seriously *awry*.'

*

It was an idiot's idea of what a king's bedchamber might look like. Everything was overpatterned, gaudy with gold and silver thread. The bed was a monstrous four-poster suffocated with swags of crimson silk. An obese cabinet burst with coloured liquor bottles. The ceiling was crusted with shadowy mouldings and an enormous, tinkling chandelier that hung too low. The fireplace was carved like a pair of naked women holding up a plate of fruit, all in green marble.

There was a huge canvas in a gleaming frame on one wall – a woman with an improbable bosom bathing in a stream, and seeming to enjoy it a lot more than was likely. Monza never had understood why getting out a tit or two made for a better painting. But painters seemed to think it did, so tits is what you got.

'That bloody music's giving me a headache,' Vitari grumbled, hooking a finger under her corset and scratching at her side.

Monza jerked her head sideways. 'That fucking bed's giving me a headache. Especially against that wallpaper.' A particularly vile shade of azure blue and turquoise stripes with gilt stars splashed across them.

'Enough to drive a woman to smoking.' Vitari prodded at the ivory pipe lying on the marbled table beside the bed, a lump of husk in a cut-glass jar beside it. Monza hardly needed it drawn to her attention. For the last hour her eyes had rarely been off it.

'Mind on the job,' she snapped, jerking her eyes away and back towards the door.

'Always.' Vitari hitched up her skirt. 'Not easy with these bloody clothes. How does anyone—'

'Shhh.' Footsteps, coming down the corridor outside.

'Our guests. You ready?'

The grips of the two knives jabbed at the small of Monza's back as she shifted her hips. 'Bit late for second thoughts, no?'

'Unless you've decided you'd rather fuck them instead.'

'I think we'll stick to murder.' Monza slid her right hand up the window frame in what she hoped was an alluring pose. Her heart was thumping, the blood surging painfully loud in her ears.

The door creaked ever so slowly open, and a man stepped through into the room. He was tall and dressed all in white, his golden mask in the shape of half a rising sun. He had an impeccably trimmed beard, which failed to disguise a ragged scar down his chin. Monza blinked at him. He wasn't Ario. He wasn't even Foscar.

'Shit,' she heard Vitari breathe.

Recognition hit Monza like spit in the face. It wasn't Orso's son, but his son-in-law. None other than the great peacemaker himself, his August Majesty, the High King of the Union.

'Ready?' asked Cosca.

Shivers cleared his throat one more time. It had felt like there was something stuck in it ever since he'd walked into this damn place. 'Bit late for second thoughts, no?'

The old mercenary's mad grin spread even wider. 'Unless you've decided you'd rather fuck them instead. Gentlemen! Ladies! Your attention, please!' The band stopped playing and the violin began to hack out a single, sawing note. It didn't make Shivers feel much better.

Cosca jabbed with his cane, clearing the guests out of the circle they'd marked in the middle of the yard. 'Step back, my friends, for you are in the gravest danger! One of the great moments of history is about to be acted out before your disbelieving eyes!'

'When do I get a fuck?' someone called, to ragged laughter.

Cosca leaped forwards, nearly took the man's eye out on the end of his cane. 'Once someone dies!' The drum had joined in now, whack, whack, whack. Folk pressed round the circle by flickering torchlight. A ring of masks – birds and beasts, soldiers and clowns, leering skulls and grinning devils. Men's faces underneath – drunk, bored, angry, curious. At the back, Barti and Kummel teetered on each other's shoulders, whichever was on top clapping along with the drumbeats.

'For your education, edification and enjoyment . . .' Shivers hadn't a clue what that meant. 'Cardotti's House of Leisure presents to you . . .' He took a rough breath, hefting sword and shield, and pushed through into the circle. 'The infamous duel between Fenris the Feared . . .' Cosca flicked his cane out towards Greylock as he lumbered into the circle from the other side. 'And Logen Ninefingers!'

'He's got ten fingers!' someone called, making a ripple of drunken laughter.

Shivers didn't join 'em. Greylock might've been a long way less frightening than the real Feared had been, but he was a long way clear of a comforting sight still, big as a house with that mask of black iron over his face, left side of his shaved head and his great left arm painted blue. His club looked awful heavy and very dangerous, right then, clutched in those big fists. Shivers had to keep telling himself they were on the same side. Just pretending was all. Just pretending.

'You gentlemen would be well advised to make room!' shouted Cosca, and the three Gurkish dancers pranced round the edge of the circle, black-cat masks over their black faces, herding the guests towards the walls. 'There may be blood!'

'There'd better be!' Another wave of laughter. 'I didn't come here to watch a pair of idiots dance with each other!'

The onlookers whooped, whistled, booed. Mostly booed. Shivers somehow doubted his plan – hop around the circle for a few minutes flailing at the air, then stab Greylock between his arm and his side while the big man burst a bladder of pig blood – was going to get these fuckers clapping. He remembered the real duel, outside the walls of Carleon with the fate of all the North hanging on the outcome. The cold morning, the breath smoking on the air, the blood in the circle. The Carls gathered round the edge, shaking their shields, screaming and roaring. He wondered what those men would've made of this nonsense. Life took you down some strange paths, alright.

'Begin!' shouted Cosca, springing back into the crowd.

Greylock gave a mighty roar and came charging forwards, swinging the club and swinging it hard. Gave Shivers the bastard of a shock. He got his shield up in time, but the weight of the blow knocked him clean over, sliding across the ground on his arse, left arm struck numb. He sprawled out, all tangled up with his sword, nicked his eyebrow on the edge. Lucky not to get the point in his eye. He rolled, the club crashing down where he'd lain a moment before and sending stone chips flying. Even as he was clambering up, Greylock was at him again, looking like he meant deadly business, and Shivers had to scramble away with all the dignity of a cat in a wolf-pen. He didn't remember this being what they discussed. Seemed the big man meant to give these bastards a show to remember after all.

'Kill him!' Someone laughed.

'Give us some blood, you idiots!'

Shivers tightened his hand round the grip of the sword. He suddenly had a bad feeling. Even worse'n before.

Rolling dice normally made Friendly feel calm, but not tonight. He had a bad feeling. Even worse than before. He watched them tumble, clatter, spin, their clicking seeming to dig at his clammy skin, and come to rest.

'Two and four,' he said.

'We see the numbers!' snapped the man with the mask like a crescent moon. 'Damn dice hate me!' He tossed them angrily over, bouncing against the polished wood.

Friendly frowned as he scooped them up and rolled them gently back. 'Five and three. House wins.'

'It seems to be making a habit of it,' growled the one with the mask like a ship, and some of their friends muttered angrily. They were all of them drunk. Drunk and stupid. The house always makes a habit of winning, which is why it hosts games of chance in the first place. But it was hardly Friendly's job to educate them on that point. Someone at the far end of the room cried out with shrill delight as the lucky wheel brought up their number. A few of the card players clapped with mild disdain.

'Bloody dice.' Crescent Moon slurped from his glass of wine as Friendly carefully gathered up the counters and added them to his own swelling stacks. He was having trouble breathing, the air was so thick with strange smells – perfume, and sweat, and wine, and smoke. He realised his mouth was hanging open, and snapped it shut.

The King of the Union looked from Monza, to Vitari, and back – handsome, regal and most extremely unwelcome. Monza realised her mouth was hanging open, and snapped it shut.

'I mean no disrespect, but one of you will be more than adequate and I have . . . always had a weakness for dark hair.' He gestured to the door. 'I hope I will not offend by asking you to leave us. I will make sure you are paid.'

'How generous.' Vitari glanced sideways and Monza gave her the tiniest shrug, her mind flipping around like a frog in hot water as it sought desperately for a way clear of this self-made trap. Vitari pushed herself away from the wall and strutted to the door. She brushed the front of the king's coat with the back of her hand on the way past. 'Curse my red-haired mother,' she sneered. The door clicked shut.

'A most . . .' The king cleared his throat. 'Pleasing room.'

'You're easily pleased.'

He snorted with laughter. 'My wife would not say so.'

'Few wives say good things about their husbands. That's why they come to us.'

'You misunderstand. I have her blessing. My wife is expecting our third child and therefore . . . well, that hardly interests you.'

'I'll seem interested whatever you say. That's what I'm paid for.'

'Of course.' The king rubbed his hands somewhat nervously together. 'Perhaps a drink.'

She nodded towards the cabinet. 'There they are.'

'Do you need one?'

'No.'

'No, of course, why would you?' Wine gurgled from the bottle. 'I suppose this is nothing new for you.'

'No.' Though in fact it was hard to remember the last time she'd been disguised as a whore in a room with a king. She had two choices. Bed him, or murder him. Neither one held much appeal. Killing Ario would make trouble enough. To kill a king – even Orso's son-in-law – would be asking for a great deal more.

When faced with two dark paths, Stolicus wrote, *a general should always choose the lighter.* She doubted these were quite the circumstances he'd had in mind, but that changed nothing. She slid one hand around the nearest bedpost, lowered herself until she was sitting awkwardly on the garish covers. Then her eye fell on the husk pipe.

When faced with two dark paths, Farans wrote, *a general should always find a third.*

'You seem nervous,' she murmured.

The king had made it as far as the foot of the bed. 'I must confess it's been a long time since I visited . . . a place like this one.'

'Something to calm you, then.' She turned her back on him

before he had the chance to say no, and began to fill the pipe. It didn't take her long to make it ready. She did it every night, after all.

'Husk? I'm not sure that I—'

'You need your wife's blessing for this too?' She held it out to him.

'Of course not.'

She stood, lifting the lamp, holding his eye, and set the flame to the bowl. His first breath in he coughed out straight away. The second not much later. The third he managed to hold, then blow out in a plume of white smoke.

'Your turn,' he croaked, pressing the pipe back into her hand as he sank down on the bed, smoke still curling up from the bowl and tickling her nose.

'I . . .' Oh, how she wanted it. She was trembling with her need for it. 'I . . .' Right there, right in her hand. But this was no time to indulge herself. She needed to stay in control.

His mouth curled up in a gormless grin. 'Whose blessing do you need?' he croaked. 'I promise I won't tell a . . . oh.'

She was already setting the flame to the grey-brown flakes, sucking the smoke in deep, feeling it burn at her lungs.

'Damn boots,' the king was saying as he tried to drag his highly polished footwear off. 'Don't bloody fit me. You pay . . . a hundred marks . . . for some boots . . . you expect them to—' One flew off and clattered into the wall, leaving a bright trace behind it. Monza was finding it hard to stand up.

'Again.' She held the pipe out.

'Well . . . where's the harm?' Monza stared at the lamp flame as it flared up. Shimmering, shining, all the colours of a hoard of priceless jewels, the crumbs of husk glowing orange, turning from sweet brown to blazing red to used-up grey ash. The king breathed a long plume of sweet-smelling smoke in her face and she closed her eyes and sucked it in. Her head was full of it, swelling with it, ready to burst open.

'Oh.'

'Eh?'

He stared around. 'That is . . . rather . . .'

'Yes. Yes it is.' The room was glowing. The pains in her legs had become pleasurable tickles. Her bare skin fizzed and tingled.

She sank down, mattress creaking under her rump. Just her and the King of the Union, perched on an ugly bed in a whorehouse. What could've been more comfortable?

The king licked lazily at his lips. 'My wife. The queen. You know. Did I mention that? Queen. She does not always—'

'Your wife likes women,' Monza found she'd said. Then she snorted with laughter, and had to wipe some snot off her lip. 'She likes them a lot.'

The king's eyes were pink inside the eyeholes of his mask. They crawled lazily over her face. 'Women? What were we talking of?' He leaned forwards. 'I don't feel . . . nervous . . . any more.' He slid one clumsy hand up the side of her leg. 'I think . . .' he muttered, working his tongue around his mouth. 'I . . . think . . .' His eyes rolled up and he flopped back on the bed, arms outspread. His head tipped slowly sideways, mask skewing across his face, and he was still, faint snoring echoing in Monza's ears.

He looked so peaceful there. She wanted to lie down. She was always thinking, thinking, worrying, thinking. She needed to rest. She deserved to. But there was something nagging at her – something she needed to do first. What was it? She drifted to her feet, swaying uncertainly.

Ario.

'Uh. That's it.' She left his Majesty sprawled across the bed and made for the door, the room tipping one way and then the other, trying to catch her out. Tricky bastard. She bent down and tore one of the high shoes off, tottered sideways and nearly fell. She flung the other away and it floated gently through the air, like an anchor sinking through water. She had to force her eyes open wide as she looked at the door, because there was a mosaic of blue glass between her and the world, candle flames beyond it leaving long, blinding smears across her sight.

Morveer nodded to Day, and she nodded back, a deeper black shape crouched in the fizzing darkness of the attic, the slightest strip of blue light across her grin. Behind her, the joists, the laths, the rafters were all black outlines touched down the edges with the faintest glow. 'I will deal with the pair beside the Royal Suite,' he whispered. 'You . . . take the others.'

'Done, but when?'

When was the question of paramount importance. He put his eye to the hole, blowpipe in one hand, fingertips of the other rubbing nervously against his thumb. The door to the Royal Suite opened and Vitari emerged from between the guards. She frowned up, then walked away down the corridor. There was no sign of Murcatto, no sign of Foscar, no further sign of anything. This was not part of the plan, of that Morveer was sure. He had still to kill the guards, of course, he had been paid to do so and always followed through on a contracted task. That was one thing among many that separated him from the obscene likes of Nicomo Cosca. But when, when, when . . .

Morveer frowned. He was sure he could hear the vague sound of someone chewing. 'Are you eating?'

'Just a bun.'

'Well stop it! We are at work, for pity's sake, and I am trying to think! Is an *iota* of professionalism too much to ask?'

Time stretched out to the vague accompaniment of the incompetent musicians down in the courtyard, but with the exception of the guards rocking gently from side to side, there was no further sign of movement. Morveer slowly shook his head. In this case, it seemed, as in so many, one moment was much like another. He breathed in deep, lifted the pipe to his lips, taking aim on the furthest of his allotted pair—

The door to Ario's chamber banged open. The two women emerged, one still adjusting her skirts. Morveer held his breath, cheeks puffed out. They pulled the door shut then made off down the corridor. One of the guards said something to the other, and he laughed. There was the most discreet of hisses as Morveer discharged his pipe, and the laughter was cut short.

'Ah!' The nearest guard pressed one hand to his scalp.

'What?'

'Something . . . I don't know, stung me.'

'Stung you? What would've—' It was the other guard's turn to rub at his head. 'Bloody hell!'

The first had found the needle in his hair, and now held it up to the light. 'A needle.' He fumbled for his sword with a clumsy hand, lurched back against the wall and slid down onto his backside. 'I feel all . . .'

The second guard took an unsteady stride into the corridor, reached up at nothing, then pitched over on his face, arm outstretched. Morveer allowed himself the slightest nod of satisfaction, then crept over to Day, crouching over two of the holes with her blowpipe in her hand.

'Success?' he asked.

'Of course.' She held the bun in the other, and now took a bite from it. Through the hole Morveer saw the two guards beside Ario's suite slumped motionless.

'Fine work, my dear. But that, *alas*, is all the work with which we were trusted.' He began to gather up their equipment.

'Should we stay, see how it goes?'

'I see no reason so to do. The best we can hope for is that men will die, and that I have witnessed before. Frequently. Take it from me. One death is *much* like another. You have the rope?'

'Of course.'

'Never too soon to secure the means of escape.'

'Caution first, always.'

'*Precisely* so.'

Day uncoiled the cord from her pack and made one end of it fast around a heavy joist. She lifted one foot and kicked the little window from its frame. Morveer heard the sound of it splashing down into the canal behind the building.

'Most neatly done. *What* would I do without you?'

'Die!' And Greylock came charging across the circle with that great lump of wood high over his head. Shivers gasped along with the crowd, only just scrambled clear in time, felt the wind of it ripping at his face. He caught the big man in a clumsy hug and they tottered together round the outside of the circle.

'What the fuck are you after?' Shivers hissed in his ear.

'Vengeance!' Greylock dealt him a knee in the side then flung him off.

Shivers stumbled away, finding his balance, picking his brains for some slight he'd given the man. 'Vengeance? For what, you mad bastard?'

'For Uffrith!' He slapped his great foot down, feinting, and Shivers hopped back, peering over the top of his shield.

'Eh? No one got killed there!'

'You sure?'

'A couple o' men down on the docks, but—'

'My brother! No more'n fourteen years old!'

'I had no part o' that, you great turd! Black Dow did them killings!'

'Black Dow ain't before me now, and I swore to my mother I'd make someone pay. You'd a big enough part for me to knock it out o' you, fucker!' Shivers gave a girlish kind of squeak as he ducked back from another great sweep, heard men cheering around him, as keen for blood as the watchers might be at a real duel.

Vengeance, then. A double-edged blade if ever there was one. You never could tell when that bastard was going to cut you. Shivers stood, blood creeping down the side of his face from a knock he took just before, and all he could think was how fucking unfair it was. He'd tried to do the right thing, just the way his brother had always told him he should. He'd tried to be a better man. Hadn't he? This was where good intentions put you. Right in the shit.

'But I just . . . I done my best!' he bellowed in Northern.

Greylock sent spit spinning through the mouth-hole of his mask. 'So did my brother!' He came on, club coming down in a blur. Shivers ducked round it, jerked his shield up hard and smashed the rim under the big man's jaw, sent him staggering back, spluttering blood.

Shivers still had his pride. That much he'd kept for himself. He was damned if he was going to be put in the mud by some great thick bastard who couldn't tell a good man from a bad. He felt the fury boiling up his throat, the way it used to back home in the North, when the battle was joined and he was in the thick of it.

'Vengeance, is it?' he screamed. 'I'll show you fucking vengeance!'

Cosca winced as Shivers caught a blow on his shield and staggered sideways. He snarled something extremely angry-sounding in Northern, lashed at the air with his sword and missed Greylock by no more than the thickness of a finger, almost chopping deep into the onlookers on the backswing and making them shuffle nervously away.

'Amazing stuff!' someone frothed. 'It looks almost real! I must hire them for my daughter's wedding . . .'

It was true, the Northmen were mounting a good show. Rather too good. They circled warily, eyes fixed on each other, one of them occasionally jabbing forwards with foot or weapon. The furious, concentrated caution of men who knew the slightest slip could mean death. Shivers had his hair matted to the side of his face with blood. Greylock had a long scratch through the leather on his chest and a cut under his chin where the shield-rim had cracked him.

The onlookers had stopped yelling obscenities, cooing and gasping instead, eyes locked hungrily on the fighters, caught between wanting to press forwards to see, and press back when the weapons were swung. They felt something on the air in the courtyard. Like the weight of the sky before a great storm. Genuine, murderous rage.

The band had more than got the trick of the battle music, the fiddle stabbing as Shivers slashed with the sword, drum booming whenever Greylock heaved his great club, adding significantly to the near-unbearable tension.

Quite clearly they were trying to kill each other, and Cosca had not the ghost of a notion how to stop them. He winced as the club crashed into Shivers' shield again and nearly knocked him off his feet. He glanced worriedly up towards the stained-glass windows high above the yard.

Something told him they were going to leave more than two corpses behind tonight.

The corpses of the two guards lay beside the door. One was sitting up, staring at the ceiling. The other lay on his face. They hardly looked dead. Just sleeping. Monza slapped her own face, tried to shake the husk out of her head. The door wobbled towards her and a hand in a black glove reached out and grabbed the knob. Damn it. She needed to do that. She stood there, swaying, waiting for the hand to let go.

'Oh.' It was her hand. She turned it and the door came suddenly open. She fell through, almost pitched on her face.

The room swam around her, walls flowing, melting, streaming waterfalls. Flames crackled, sparkling crystal in a fireplace. One window was open and music floated in, men shouting from down below. She could see the sounds, happy smears curling in around the glass, reaching across the changing space between, tickling at her ears.

Prince Ario lay on the bed, stark naked, body white on the rumpled cover, legs and arms spread out wide. His head turned towards her, the spray of feathers on his mask making long shadows creep across the glowing wall behind.

'More?' he murmured, taking a lazy swallow from a wine bottle.

'I hope we haven't . . . tired you out . . . already.' Monza's own voice seemed to boom out of a faraway bucket as she padded towards the bed, a ship tossing on a choppy red sea of soft carpet.

'I daresay I can rise to the occasion,' said Ario, fumbling with his cock. 'You seem to have the advantage of me, though.' He waved a finger at her. 'Too many clothes.'

'Uh.' She shrugged the fur from her shoulders and it slithered to the floor.

'Gloves off.' He swatted with his hand. 'Don't care for them.'

'Nor me.' She pulled them off, tickling at her forearms. Ario was staring at her right hand. She held it up in front of her eyes, blinked at it. There was a long, pink scar down her forearm, the hand a blotchy claw, palm squashed, fingers twisted, little one sticking out stubbornly straight.

'Ah.' She'd forgotten about that.

'A crippled hand.' Ario wriggled eagerly down the bed towards her, his cock and the feathers sprouting from his head waggling from side to side with the movements of his hips. 'How terribly . . . exotic.'

'Isn't it?' The memory of Gobba's boot crunching down across it flashed through her mind and snatched her into the cold moment. She felt herself smile. 'No need for this.' She took hold of the feathers and plucked the mask from his head, tossed it away into the corner.

Ario grinned at her, pink marks around his eyes where the mask had sat. She felt the glow of the husk leaking from her mind as she stared into his face. She saw him stabbing her brother in the neck, heaving him off the terrace, complaining at being cut. And here he was, before her now. Orso's heir.

'How rude.' He clambered up from the bed. 'I must teach you a lesson.'

'Or maybe I'll teach you one.'

He came closer, so close that she could smell his sweat. 'Bold, to bandy words with me. Very bold.' He reached out and ran one finger up her arm. 'Few women are as bold as that.' Closer, and he slipped his other hand into the slit in her skirts, up her thigh, squeezing at her arse. 'I almost feel as if I know you.'

Monza took hold of the corner of her mask with her ruined right hand as Ario drew her closer still. 'Know me?' She slid her other fist gently behind her back, found the grip of one of the knives. 'Of course you know me.'

She pulled her mask away. Ario's smile lingered for a moment longer as his eyes flickered over her face. Then they went staring wide.

'Somebody—!'

'A hundred scales on this next throw!' Crescent Moon bellowed, holding the dice up high. The room grew quiet as people turned to watch.

'A hundred scales.' It meant nothing to Friendly. None of it was his money, and money only interested him as far as counting it went. Losses and gains were exactly the same.

Crescent Moon rattled the dice in his hand. 'Come on, you shits!' The man flung them recklessly across the table, bouncing and tumbling.

'Five and six.'

'Hah!' Moon's friends whooped, chuckled, slapped him on the back as though he had achieved something fine by throwing one number instead of another.

The one with the mask like a ship threw his arms in the air. 'Have that!'

The one with the fox mask made an obscene gesture.

The candles seemed to have grown uncomfortably bright. Too bright to count. The room was very hot, close, crowded. Friendly's shirt was sticking to him as he scooped up the dice and tossed them gently back. A few gasps round the table. 'Five and six. House wins.' People often forgot that any one score is just as likely as any other, even the same score. So it was not entirely a shock that Crescent Moon lost his sense of perspective.

'You cheating bastard!'

Friendly frowned. In Safety he would have cut a man who spoke to him like that. He would have had to, so that others would have known not to try. He would have started cutting him and not stopped. But they were not in Safety now, they were outside. Control, he had been told. He made himself forget the warm handle of his cleaver, pressing into his side. Control. He only shrugged. 'Five and six. The dice don't lie.'

Crescent Moon grabbed hold of Friendly's wrist as he began to sweep up the counters. He leaned forwards and poked him in the chest with a drunken finger. 'I think your dice are loaded.'

Friendly felt his face go slack, the breath hardly moving in his throat, it had constricted so painfully tight. He could feel every drop of sweat tickling at his forehead, at his back, at his scalp. A calm, cold, utterly unbearable rage seared through every part of him. 'You think my dice are what?' he could barely whisper.

Poke, poke, poke. 'Your dice are liars.'

'My dice . . . are *what*?' Friendly's cleaver split the crescent mask in half and the skull underneath it wide open. His knife stabbed the man with the ship over his face through his gaping mouth and the point emerged from the back of his head. Friendly stabbed him again, and again, squelch, squelch, the grip of the blade turning slippery. A woman gave a long, shrill scream.

Friendly was vaguely aware that everyone in the hall was gaping at him, four times three times four of them, or more, or less. He flung the dice table over, sending glasses, counters, coins flying. The man with the fox mask was staring, eyes wide inside the eyeholes, spatters of dark brains across his pale cheek.

Friendly leaned forwards into his face. 'Apologise!' he roared at the very top of his lungs. 'Apologise to my fucking dice!'

'Somebody—!'

Ario's cry turned to a breathy wheeze of an in-breath. He stared down, and she did too. Her knife had gone in the hollow where his thigh met his body, just beside his wilting cock, and was buried in him to the grip, blood running out all over her fist. For the shortest moment he gave a hideous, high-pitched shriek, then the point of Monza's other knife punched in under his ear and slid out of the far side of his neck.

Ario stayed there, eyes bulging, one hand plucking weakly at her bare shoulder. The other crept trembling up and fumbled at the handle of the blade. Blood leaked out of him thick and black, oozing between his fingers, bubbling down his legs, running down his chest in dark, treacly streaks, leaving his pale skin all smeared and speckled with red. His mouth yawned, but his scream was nothing but a soft farting sound, breath squelching around the wet steel in his throat. He tottered back, his other arm fishing at the air, and Monza watched him, fascinated, his white face leaving a bright trace across her vision.

'Three dead,' she whispered. 'Four left.'

His bloody thighs slapped against the windowsill and he fell, head smashing against the stained glass and knocking the window wide. He tumbled through and out into the night.

The club came over, a blow that could've smashed in Shivers' skull like an egg. But it was tired, sloppy, left Greylock's side open. Shivers ducked it, already spinning, snarling as he whipped the heavy sword round. It cut into the big man's blue-painted forearm with a meaty thump, hacked it off clean, carried on through and chopped deep into the side of his stomach. Blood showered from the stump and into the faces of the onlookers. The club clattered to the cobbles, hand and wrist along with it. Someone gave a thin shriek. Someone else laughed.

'How'd they do that?'

Then Greylock started squealing like he'd caught his foot in a door. 'Fuck! It hurts! Ah! Ah! What's my . . . by the—'

He reached around with the one hand he had left, fumbling at the gash in his side, dark mush bulging out. He lurched forwards onto one knee, head tipping back, and started to scream. Until Shivers' sword hit his mask right in the forehead and made a clang that cut his roar off dead, left a huge dent between the eyeholes. The big man crashed over on his back, his boots flew up in the air, then thumped down.

And that was the end of the evening's entertainment.

The band spluttered out a last few wobbly notes, then the music died. Apart from some vague yelling leaking from the gaming hall, the yard was silent. Shivers stared down at Greylock's corpse, blood bubbling out from beneath the stoved-in mask. His fury had suddenly melted, leaving him only with a painful arm, a scalp prickling with cold sweat and a healthy sense of creeping horror.

'Why do things like this always happen to me?'

'Because you're a bad, bad man,' said Cosca, peering over his shoulder.

Shivers felt a shadow fall across his face. He was just looking up when a naked body crashed down headfirst into the circle from above, showering the already gaping crowd with blood.

That's Entertainment

All at once, things got confused.

'The king!' someone squealed, for no reason that made any sense. The blood-spattered space that had been the circle was suddenly full of stumbling bodies, running to nowhere. Everyone was bawling, wailing, shouting. Men's voices and women's, a noise fit to deafen the dead. Someone shoved at Shivers' shield and he shoved back on an instinct, sent them sprawling over Greylock's corpse.

'It's Ario!'

'Murder!' A guest started to draw his sword, and one of the band stepped calmly forwards and smashed his skull apart with a sharp blow of a mace.

More screams. Steel rang and grated. Shivers saw one of the Gurkish dancers slit a man's belly open with a curved knife, saw him fumble his sword as he vomited blood, stab the man behind him in the leg. There was a crash of tinkling glass and a flailing body came flying through one of the windows of the gambling hall. Panic and madness spread like fire in a dry field.

One of the jugglers was flinging knives, flying metal clattering about the yard, thudding into flesh and wood, just as deadly to friends as enemies. Someone grabbed hold of Shivers' sword arm and he elbowed them in the face, lifted his sword to hack at them and realised it was Morc, the pipe player, blood running from his nose. There was a loud whomp and a glare of orange through the heaving bodies. The screaming went up a notch, a mindless chorus.

'Fire!'

'Water!'

'Out of my way!'

'The juggler! Get the—'

'Help! Help!'

'Knights of the Body, to me! To me!'

'Where's the prince? Where's Ario?'

'Somebody help!'

'Back!' shouted Cosca.

'Eh?' Shivers called at him, not sure who was howling at who. A knife flickered past in the darkness, rattled away between the thrashing bodies.

'Back!' Cosca sidestepped a sword-thrust, whipped his cane around, a long, thin blade sliding free of it, ran a man through the neck with a swift jab. He slashed at someone else, missed and almost stabbed Shivers as he lurched past. One of Ario's gentlemen, mask like a squares board, nearly caught Cosca with a sword. Gurpi loomed up behind and smashed his lute over the man's head. The wooden body shattered, the axe blade inside split his shoulder right down to his chest and crushed his butchered wreckage into the cobbles.

Another surge of flame went up, people stumbled away, shoving madly, a ripple through the straining crowd. They suddenly parted and the Incredible Ronco came thrashing straight at Shivers, white fire wreathing him like some devil burst out of hell. Shivers tottered back, smashed him away with his shield. Ronco reeled into the wall, bounced off it and into another, showering globs of liquid fire, folk scrambling away, steel stabbing about at random. The flames spread up the dry ivy, first a crackle, then a roar, leaped to the wooden wall, bathing the heaving courtyard in wild, flickering light. A window shattered. The locked gates clattered as men clutched at 'em, screaming to be let out. Shivers beat the flames on his shield against the wall. Ronco was rolling on the ground, still burning, making a thin screech like a boiling kettle, the flames casting a crazy glare across the bobbing masks of guests and entertainers – twisted monsters' faces, everywhere Shivers looked.

There was no time to make sense of any of it. All that mattered was who lived and who died, and he'd no mind to join the second lot. He backed off, keeping close to the wall, shoving men away with his scorched shield as they grabbed at him.

A couple of the guards in breastplates were forcing their way through the press. One of 'em chopped Barti or Kummel down with his sword, hard to say which, caught one of Ario's gentlemen on the backswing and took part of his skull off. He staggered round, squealing, one hand clapped to his head, blood running out between his fingers, over his golden mask and down his face in black streaks. Barti or Kummel, whichever was left, stabbed a knife into the top of the swordsman's head, right up to the hilt, then hooted as the point of a blade slid out of the front of his chest.

Another armoured guard shouldered his way towards Shivers, sword held high, shouting something, sounded like the Union tongue. Didn't much matter where he was from, he had a mind for killing, that was clear, and Shivers didn't plan on giving him the first blow. He snarled as he swung, full-blooded, but the guard lurched back out of the way and Shivers' sword chopped into something else with a meaty thwack. A woman's chest, just happened to be stumbling past. She fell against the wall, scream turning to a gurgle as she slid down through the ivy, mask half-torn off, one eye staring at him, blood bubbling from her nose, from her mouth, pouring down her white neck.

The courtyard was a place of madness, lit by spreading flames. A fragment of a night-time battlefield, but a battle with no sides, no purpose, no winners. Bodies were kicked around under the panicking crowd – living, dead, split and bloodied. Gurpi was flailing, all tangled up with the wreckage of his lute, not even able to swing his axe for the broken strings and bits of wood. While Shivers watched, one of the guards hacked him down, sent blood showering black in the firelight.

'The smoking hall!' hissed Cosca, chopping someone out of their way with his sword. Shivers thought it might've been one of the jugglers, there was no way of telling. He dived through the open doorway after the old mercenary, together they started to heave the door shut. A hand came through and got caught against the frame, clutching wildly. Shivers bashed at it with the pommel of his sword until it slithered back trembling through the gap. Cosca wrestled the door closed and the latch dropped, then he tore the key around and flung it jingling away across the boards.

'What now?'

The old mercenary stared at him, eyes wild. 'What makes you think I've got the fucking answers?'

The hall was long and low, scattered with cushions, split up by billowing curtains, lit by guttering lamps, smelling of sweet husk-smoke. The sounds of violence out in the yard were muffled. Someone snored. Someone else giggled. A man sat against the wall opposite, a beaked mask and a broad smile on his face, pipe dangling from his hand.

'What about the others?' hissed Shivers, squinting into the half-light.

'I think we've reached the point of every man for himself, don't you?' Cosca was busy trying to drag an old chest in front of the door, already shuddering from blows outside. 'Where's Monza?'

'They'll get in by the gaming hall, no? Won't they—' Something crashed against a window and it burst inwards, spraying twinkling glass into the room. Shivers shuffled further into the murk, heart thumping hard as a hammer at the inside of his skull. 'Cosca?' Nought but smoke and darkness, flickering light through the windows, flickering lamps on tables. He got tangled with a curtain, tore it down, fabric ripping from the rail above. Smoke was scratching at his throat. Smoke from the husk in here, smoke from the fire out there, more and more. The air was hazy with it.

He could hear voices. Crashing and screaming on his left like a bull going mad in the burning building. 'My dice! My dice! Bastards!'

'Help!'

'Somebody send for . . . somebody!'

'Upstairs! The king! Upstairs!'

Someone was beating at a door with something heavy, he could hear the wood shuddering under the blows. A figure loomed at him. 'Excuse me, could you—' Shivers smashed him in the face with his shield and knocked him flying, stumbled past, a vague idea he was after the stairs. Monza was upstairs. Top floor. He heard the door burst open behind him, shifting light, brown smoke, writhing figures began to pour through into the smoking hall, blades shining in the gloom. One of 'em pointed at him. 'There! There he is!'

Shivers snatched a lamp up in his shield hand and flung it, missed the man at the front and hit the wall. It burst apart, showering burning oil across a curtain. People scattered, one of them screaming, arm on fire. Shivers ran the other way, deeper into the building, half-falling as cushions and tables tripped him in the darkness. He felt a hand grab his ankle and hacked at it with his sword. He staggered through the choking shadows to a doorway, a faint chink of light down the edge, shouldered it open, sure he'd get stabbed between the shoulder blades any moment.

He started up a set of spiral steps two at a time, panting with effort, legs burning as he climbed up towards the rooms where guests were entertained. Or fucked, depending how you looked at it. A panelled corridor met the stairway and a man came barrelling out of it just as Shivers got there, almost ran straight into him. They ended up staring into each other's masks. One of the bastards with the polished breastplates. He clutched at Shivers' shoulder with his free hand, showing his teeth, tried to pull his sword back for a thrust but got his elbow caught on the wall behind.

Shivers butted him in the face on an instinct, felt the man's nose crunch under his forehead. No room for the sword. Shivers chopped him in the hip with the edge of his shield, gave him a knee in the fruits that made him whoop, then swung him round and bundled him down the stairs, watched him flop over and over around the corner, sword clattering away. He kept going, upwards, not stopping for breath, starting to cough.

He could hear more shouting behind him, crashing, screaming. 'The king! Protect the king!' He staggered on, one step at a time now, sword aching heavy in his hand, shield dangling from his limp arm. He wondered who was still alive. He wondered about the woman he'd killed in the courtyard, the hand he'd smashed in the doorway. He tottered into the hallway at the top of the stairs, wafting his shield in front of his face to try and clear the haze.

There were bodies here, black shapes sprawled under the wide windows. Maybe she was dead. Anyone could've been dead. Everyone. He heard coughing. Smoke rolled around near the ceiling, pouring into the corridor over the tops of the doors. He squinted into it. A woman, bent over, bare arms stretched out in front of her, black hair hanging.

Monza.

He ran towards her, trying to hold his breath, keep down low under the smoke. He caught her round the waist, she grabbed his neck, snarling. She had blood spotted across her face, soot around her nose and her mouth.

'Fire,' she croaked at him.

'Over here.' He turned back the way he came, and stopped still.

Down at the end of the corridor, two men with breastplates were getting to the top of the steps. One of them pointed at him.

'Shit.' He remembered the model. Cardotti's backs onto the Eighth Canal. He lifted one boot and kicked the window wide. A long way down below, beyond the blowing smoke, water shifted, busy with the reflections of fire.

'My own worst fucking enemy,' he forced through his gritted teeth.

'Ario's dead,' Monza drawled in his ear. Shivers dropped his sword, grabbed hold of her. 'What're you—' He threw her out of the window, heard her choking shriek as she started falling. He tore his shield from his arm and flung it at the two men as they ran down the corridor towards him, climbed up on the window ledge and jumped.

Smoke washed and billowed around him. The rushing air tore at his hair, his stinging eyes, his open mouth. He hit the water feet first and it dragged him down. Bubbles rushed in the blackness. The cold gripped him, almost forced him to suck in a breath of water. He hardly knew which way was up, flailing about, struck his head on something.

A hand grabbed him under the jaw, pulled at it, his face burst into the night and he gasped in cold air and cold water. He was dragged along through the canal, choking on the smoke he'd breathed, on the water he'd breathed, on the stink of the rotten water he was breathing now. He thrashed and jerked, wheezing, gasping.

'Still, you bastard!'

A shadow fell across his face, his shoulder scraped on stone. He fished around and his hand closed on an old iron ring, enough to hold his head above the water while he coughed up a lungful of canal. Monza was pressed to him, treading water, arm around his back, holding him tight. Her quick, scared, desperate breathing and his own hissed out together, merged with the slapping of the water and echoed under the arch of a bridge.

Beyond its black curve he could see the back of Cardotti's House of Leisure, the fire shooting high into the sky above the buildings around it, flames crackling and roaring, showers of sparks fizzing and popping, ash and splinters flying, smoke pouring up in a black-brown cloud. Light flickered and danced on the water and across one half of Monza's pale face – red, orange, yellow, the colours of fire.

'Shit,' he hissed, shivering at the cold, at the aching lag-end of battle, at what he'd done back there in the madness. He felt tears burning at his eyes. Couldn't stop himself crying. He started to shake, to sob, only just managing to keep his grip on the ring. 'Shit . . . shit . . . shit . . .'

'Shhh.' Monza's hand clapped over his mouth. Footsteps snapped against the road above, shouted voices echoing back and forth. They shrank back together, pressing against the slimy stonework. 'Shhh.' Few hours ago he'd have given a lot to be pressed up against her like this. Somehow, right then, he didn't feel much in the way of romance, though.

'What happened?' she whispered.

Shivers couldn't even look at her. 'I've no fucking idea.'

What Happened

Nicomo Cosca, infamous soldier of fortune, skulked in the shadows and watched the warehouse. All seemed quiet, shutters dark in their rotting frames. No vengeful mob, no clamour of guards. His instincts told him simply to walk off into the night, and pay no further mind to Monzcarro Murcatto and her mad quest for vengeance. But he needed her money, and his instincts had never been worth a runny shit. He shrank back into the doorway as a woman in a mask ran down the lane, skirts held up, giggling. A man chased after her. 'Come back! Kiss me, you bitch!' Their footsteps clattered away.

Cosca strutted across the street as if he owned it, into the alley behind the warehouse, then plastered himself to the wall. He sidled up to the back door. He slid the sword from his cane with a faint ring of steel, blade coldly glittering in the night. The knob turned, the door crept open. He eased his way through into the darkness—

'Far enough.' Metal kissed his neck. Cosca opened his hand and let the sword clatter to the boards.

'I am undone.'

'Cosca, that you?' The blade came away. Vitari, pressed into the shadows behind the door.

'Shylo, you changed? I much preferred the clothes you had at Cardotti's. More . . . ladylike.'

'Huh.' She pushed past him and down the dark passageway. 'That underwear, such as it was, was torture.'

'I shall have to content myself with seeing it in my dreams.'

'What happened at Cardotti's?'

'What happened?' Cosca bent over stiffly and fished his sword up between two fingers. 'I believe the word "bloodbath" would fit the circumstances. Then it caught fire. I must confess . . . I made a quick exit.' He was, in truth, disgusted with himself for

234

having fled and saved his own worthless skin. But the decided habits of a whole life, especially a wasted life, were hard to change. 'Why don't you tell me what happened?'

'The King of the Union happened.'

'The what?' Cosca remembered the man in white, with the mask like the rising sun. The man who had not looked very much like Foscar. 'Aaaaaah. That would explain all the guards.'

'What about your entertainers?'

'Hugely expendable. None of them have shown their faces here?'

Vitari shook her head. 'Not so far.'

'Then, I would guess, they are largely, if not entirely, expended. So it always is with mercenaries. Easily hired, even more easily discharged and never missed once they are gone.'

Friendly sat in the darkened kitchen, hunched over the table, rolling his dice gently in the light from a single lamp. A heavy and extremely threatening cleaver gleamed on the wood beside it.

Cosca came close, pointing to the dice. 'Three and four, eh?'

'Three and four.'

'Seven. A most ordinary score.'

'Average.'

'May I?'

Friendly looked sharply up at him. 'Yes.'

Cosca gathered the dice and gently rolled them back. 'Six. You win.'

'That's my problem.'

'Really? Losing is mine. What happened? No trouble in the gaming hall?'

'Some.'

There was a long streak of half-dried blood across the convict's neck, dark in the lamplight. 'You've got something . . . just here,' said Cosca.

Friendly wiped it off, looked down at his red-brown fingertips with all the emotion of an empty sink. 'Blood.'

'Yes. A lot of blood, tonight.' Now Cosca was back to something approaching safety, the giddy rush of danger was starting to recede, and all the old regrets crowded in behind it. His hands were shaking again. A drink, a drink, a drink. He wandered through the doorway into the warehouse.

'Ah! The ringmaster for tonight's circus of murder!' Morveer leaned against the rail of the stairs, sneering down, Day not far behind, her dangling hands slowly peeling an orange.

'Our poisoners! I'm sorry to see you made it out alive. What happened?'

Morveer's lip curled still further. 'Our allotted role was to remove the guards on the top floor of the building. That we accomplished with *absolute* speed and secrecy. We were not asked to remain in the building thereafter. Indeed we were ordered not to. Our employer does not entirely trust us. She was concerned that there be no *indiscriminate slaughter*.'

Cosca shrugged. 'Slaughter, by its very definition, would not appear to discriminate.'

'Either way, your responsibility is over. I doubt anyone will object if you take this, now.'

Morveer flicked his wrist and something sparkled in the darkness. Cosca snatched it from the air on an instinct. A metal flask, liquid sloshing inside. Just like the one he used to carry. The one he sold . . . where was it now? That sweet union of cold metal and strong liquor lapped at his memory, brought the spit flooding into his dry mouth. A drink, a drink, a drink—

He was halfway through unscrewing the cap before he stopped himself. 'It would seem a sensible life lesson never to swallow gifts from poisoners.'

'The only poison in there is the same kind you have been swallowing for years. The same kind you will never stop swallowing.'

Cosca lifted the flask. 'Cheers.' He upended it and let the spirit inside spatter over the warehouse floor, then tossed it clattering away into a corner. He made sure he noted where it ended up, though, in case there was a trickle left inside. 'No sign of our employer?' he called to Morveer, 'or her Northern puppy?'

'None. We should give some consideration to the possibility that there may never be any.'

'He's right.' Vitari was a black shape in the lamplit doorway to the kitchen. 'Chances are good they're dead. What do we do then?'

Day looked at her fingernails. 'I, for one, will weep a river.'

Morveer had other plans. 'We should have a scheme for dividing such money as Murcatto has here—'

'No,' said Cosca, for some reason intensely irritated at the thought. 'I say we wait.'

'This place is not safe. One of the entertainers could have been captured by the authorities, could even now be divulging its location.'

'Exciting, isn't it? I say we wait.'

'Wait if you please, but I—'

Cosca whipped his knife out in one smooth motion. The blade whirred shining through the darkness and thumped, vibrating gently, into the wood no more than a foot or two from Morveer's face. 'A little gift of my own.'

The poisoner raised one eyebrow at it. 'I do not appreciate drunks throwing knives at me. What if your aim had been off?'

Cosca grinned. 'It was. We wait.'

'For a man of *notoriously* fickle loyalties, I find your attachment to a woman who once betrayed you . . . perplexing.'

'So do I. But I've always been an unpredictable bastard. Perhaps I'm changing my ways. Perhaps I've made a solemn vow to be sober, loyal and diligent in all my dealings from now on.'

Vitari snorted. 'That'll be the day.'

'And how long do we wait?' demanded Morveer.

'I suppose you'll know when I say you can leave.'

'And suppose . . . I choose . . . to leave before?'

'You're nothing like as clever as you think you are.' Cosca held his eye. 'But you're cleverer than that.'

'Everyone be calm,' snarled Vitari, in the most uncalming voice imaginable.

'I don't take orders from you, you pickled *remnant*!'

'Maybe I need to teach you how—'

The warehouse door banged open and two figures burst through. Cosca whipped his sword from his stick, Vitari's chain rattled, Day had produced a small flatbow from somewhere and levelled it at the doorway. But the new arrivals were not representatives of the authorities. They were none other than Shivers and Monza, both wet through, stained with dirt and soot and panting for breath as though they had been pursued through half the streets of Sipani. Perhaps they had.

Cosca grinned. 'You need only mention her name and up she springs! Master Morveer was just now discussing how we should divide your money if it turned out you were burned to a cinder in the shell of Cardotti's.'

'Sorry to disappoint you,' she croaked.

Morveer gave Cosca a deadly glare. 'I am by *no* means disappointed, I assure you. I have a vested interest in your survival to the tune of many thousands of scales. I was simply considering . . . a contingency.'

'Best to be prepared,' said Day, lowering the bow and sucking the juice from her orange.

'Caution first, *always*.'

Monza lurched across the warehouse floor, one bare foot dragging, jaw muscles clenched tight against evident pain. Her clothes, which had not left too much to the imagination in the first instance, were badly ripped. Cosca could see a long red scar up one thin thigh, more across her shoulder, down her forearm, pale and prickly with gooseflesh. Her right hand was a mottled, bony claw, pressed against her hip as though to keep it out of sight.

He felt an unexpected stab of dismay at the sight of those marks of violence. Like seeing a painting one had always admired wilfully defaced. A painting one had secretly hoped to own, perhaps? Was that it? He shrugged his coat off and held it out to her as she came past him. She ignored it.

'Do we gather you are less than satisfied with tonight's endeavours?' asked Morveer.

'We got Ario. It could've been worse. I need some dry clothes. We leave Sipani right away.' She limped up the steps, torn skirts dragging in the dust behind her, and shouldered past Morveer. Shivers swung the warehouse door shut and leaned against it, head back.

'That is one stone-hearted bitch,' muttered Vitari as she watched her go.

Cosca pursed his lips. 'I always said she had a devil in her. But of the two, her brother was the truly ruthless one.'

'Huh.' Vitari turned back into the kitchen. 'It was a compliment.'

Monza managed to shut the door and make it a few steps into her room before her insides clenched up as if she'd been punched in the guts. She retched so hard she could hardly breathe, a long string of bitter drool dangling from her lip and spattering against the boards.

She shivered with revulsion, started trying to twist her way out of the whore's clothes. Her flesh crept at the touch of them, her guts cramped at the rotten canal stink of them. Numb fingers wrestled with hooks and eyes, clawed at buttons and buckles. Gasping and grunting, she tore the damp rags off and flung them away.

She caught sight of herself in the mirror, in the light of the one lamp. Hunched like a beggar, shivering like a drunk, red scars standing out from white skin, black hair hanging lank and loose. A drowned corpse, standing. Just about.

You're a dream. A vision. The very Goddess of War!

She was doubled over by another stab of sickness, stumbled to her chest and started dragging fresh clothes on with trembling hands. The shirt had been one of Benna's. For a moment it was almost like having his arms around her. As close as she could ever get, now.

She sat on the bed, her own arms clamped around herself, bare feet pressed together, rocking back and forth, willing the warmth to spread. Another rush of nausea dragged her up and had her spitting bile. Once it passed she shoved Benna's shirt down behind her belt, bent to drag her boots on, grimacing at the cold aches through her legs.

She delved her hands into the washbasin and threw cold water on her face, started to scrape away the traces of paint and powder, the smears of blood and soot, digging at her ears, at her hair, at her nose.

'Monza!' Cosca's voice outside the door. 'We have a distinguished visitor.'

She pulled the leather glove back over her twisted joke of a hand, winced as she worked her bent fingers into it. She took a long, shuddering breath, then slid the Calvez out from under her mattress and into the clasp on her belt. It made her feel better just having it there. She pulled the door open.

Carlot dan Eider stood in the middle of the warehouse floor, gold thread gleaming in her red coat, watching Monza as she came down the steps, trying not to limp, Cosca following after.

'What in hell happened? Cardotti's is still burning! The city's in uproar!'

'What happened?' barked Monza. 'Why don't you tell me what happened? His August fucking Majesty was where Foscar was supposed to be!'

The black scab on Eider's neck shifted as she swallowed. 'Foscar wouldn't go. He said he had a headache. So Ario took his brother-in-law along in his place.'

'And he happened to bring a dozen Knights of the Body with him,' said Cosca. 'The king's own bodyguards. As well as a far greater volume of guests than anyone anticipated. The results were not happy. For anyone.'

'Ario?' muttered Eider, face pale.

Monza stared into her eyes. 'Deader than *fuck*.'

'The king?' she almost whispered.

'Alive. When I left him. But the building did tend to burn down after that. Maybe they got him out.'

Eider looked at the floor, rubbing at one temple with her gloved hand. 'I'd hoped you might fail.'

'No such luck.'

'There will be consequences now. You do a thing like this, there are consequences. Some you see coming, and some you don't.' She held out one hand. 'My antidote.'

'There isn't one.'

'I kept my side of the bargain!'

'There was no poison. Just a jab with a dry needle. You're free.'

Eider barked despairing laughter at her. 'Free? Orso won't rest until he's fed me to his dogs! Perhaps I can keep ahead of him, but I'll never keep ahead of the Cripple. I let him down, and put his precious king in harm's way. He won't let that pass. He never lets anything pass. Are you happy now?'

'You talk as if there was a choice. Orso and the rest die, or I do, and that's all. Happy isn't part of the sum.' Monza shrugged as she turned away. 'You'd better start running.'

'I sent a letter.'

She stopped, then turned back. 'Letter?'

'Earlier today. To Grand Duke Orso. It was written in some passion, so I forget exactly what was said. The name Shylo Vitari was mentioned, though. And the name Nicomo Cosca.'

Cosca waved it away with one hand. 'I've always had a lot of powerful enemies. I consider it a point of pride. Listing them makes excellent dinner conversation.'

Eider turned her sneer from the old mercenary back to Monza. 'Those two names, and the name of Murcatto as well.'

Monza frowned. 'Murcatto.'

'How much of a fool do you take me for? I know who you are, and now Orso will know too. That you're alive, and that you killed his son, and that you had help. A petty revenge, perhaps, but the best I could manage.'

'Revenge?' Monza nodded slowly. 'Well. Everyone's at it. It would've been better if you hadn't done that.' The Calvez rattled gently as she rested her hand on its hilt.

'Why, will you kill me for it? Hah! I'm good as dead already!'

'Then why should I bother? You're not on my list. You can go.' Eider stared at her for a moment, mouth slightly open as though she was about to speak, then she snapped it shut and turned for the door. 'Aren't you going to wish me luck?'

'What?'

'The way I see it, your best hope now is that I kill Orso.'

Ario's one-time mistress paused in the doorway. 'Some fucking chance of that!' And she was gone.

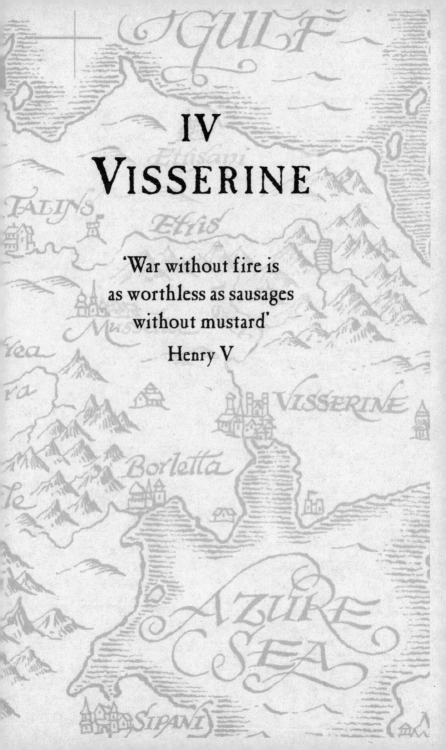

IV
VISSERINE

'War without fire is
as worthless as sausages
without mustard'

Henry V

The Thousand Swords fought for Ospria against Muris. They fought for Muris against Sipani. They fought for Sipani against Muris, then for Ospria again. Between contracts, they sacked Oprile on a whim. A month later, judging they had perhaps not been thorough enough, they sacked it again, and left it in smouldering ruins. They fought for everyone against no one, and no one against everyone, and all the while they hardly did any fighting at all.

But robbery and plunder, arson and pillage, rape and extortion, yes.

Nicomo Cosca liked to surround himself with the curious that he might seem strange and romantic. A nineteen-year-old swordswoman inseparable from her younger brother seemed to qualify, so he kept them close. At first he found them interesting. Then he found them useful. Then he found them indispensable.

He and Monza would spar together in the cold mornings – the flicker and scrape of steel, the hiss and smoke of snatched breath. He was stronger, and she quicker, and so they were well matched. They would taunt each other, and spit at each other, and laugh. Men from the company would gather to watch them, laugh to see their captain bested by a girl half his age, often as not. Everyone laughed, except Benna. He was no swordsman.

He had a trick for numbers, though, and he took charge of the company's books, and then the buying of the stocks, and then the management and resale of the booty and the distribution of the proceeds. He made money for everyone, and had an easy manner, and soon was well loved.

Monza was a quick study. She learned what Stolicus wrote, and Verturio, and Bialoveld, and Farans. She learned all that Nicomo Cosca had to teach. She learned tactics and strategy, manoeuvre and logistics, how to read the ground and how to read an enemy. She *learned by watching, then she learned by doing. She learned all the arts and all the sciences that were of use to the soldier.*

'You have a devil in you,' Cosca told her, when he was drunk, which was not rarely. She saved his life at Muris, then he saved hers. Everyone laughed, except Benna, again. He was no lifesaver.

Old Sazine died of an arrow, and the captains of the companies that made up the Thousand Swords voted Nicomo Cosca to the captain general's chair. Monza and Benna went with him. She carried Cosca's orders. Then she told him what his orders should be. Then she gave orders while he was passed out drunk and pretended they were his. Then she stopped pretending they were his, and no one minded because her orders were better than his would have been, even had he been sober.

As the months passed and turned to years, he was sober less and less. The only orders he gave were in the tavern. The only sparring he did was with a bottle. When the Thousand Swords had picked one part of the country clean and it came time to move on, Monza would search for him through the taverns, and the smoke-houses, and the brothels, and drag him back.

She hated to do it, and Benna hated to watch her do it, but Cosca had given them a home and they owed him, so she did it still. As they wended their way to camp in the dusk, him stumbling under the weight of drink, and her stumbling under the weight of him, he would whisper in her ear.

'Monza, Monza. What would I do without you?'

Vengeance, Then

General Ganmark's highly polished cavalry boots click-clicked against the highly polished floor. The chamberlain's shoes squeak-squeaked along behind. The echoes of both snap-snapped from the glittering walls and around the great, hollow space, their hurry setting lazy dust motes swirling through bars of light. Shenkt's own soft work boots, scuffed and supple from long use, made no sound whatsoever.

'Upon entering the presence of his Excellency,' the chamberlain's words frothed busily out, 'you advance towards him, without undue speed, looking neither right nor left, your eyes tilted down towards the ground and at no point meeting those of his Excellency. You stop at the white line upon the carpet. Not before the line and under no circumstances beyond it but *precisely* at the line. You then kneel—'

'I do not kneel,' said Shenkt.

The chamberlain's head rotated towards him like an affronted owl's. 'Only the heads of state of foreign powers are excepted! Everyone must—'

'I do not kneel.'

The chamberlain gasped with outrage, but Ganmark snapped over him. 'For pity's sake! Duke Orso's son and heir has been murdered! His Excellency does not give a damn whether a man kneels if he can bring him vengeance. Kneel or not, as it suits you.' Two white-liveried guardsmen lifted their crossed halberds to let them pass, and Ganmark shoved the double doors wide open.

The hall beyond was dauntingly cavernous, opulent, grand. Fit for the throne room of the most powerful man in Styria. But Shenkt had stood in greater rooms, before greater men, and had no awe left in him. A thin red carpet stretched away down the mosaic floor, a white line at its lonely end. A high dais rose beyond it, a dozen men in full armour standing guard in front. Upon the dais was a golden chair. Within the chair was Grand Duke Orso of Talins. He was dressed all in black, but his frown was blacker yet.

A strange and sinister selection of people, three score or more, of all races, sizes and shapes, knelt before Orso and his retinue in a wide arc. They carried no weapons now, but Shenkt guessed they usually carried many. He knew some few of them by sight. Killers. Assassins. Hunters of men. Persons in his profession, if the whitewasher could be said to be in the same profession as the master painter.

He advanced towards the dais, without undue speed, looking neither right nor left. He passed through the half-circle of assorted murderers and stopped precisely at the line. He watched General Ganmark stride past the guards and up the steps to the throne, lean to whisper in Orso's ear while the chamberlain took up a disapproving pose at his other elbow.

The grand duke stared at Shenkt for a long moment and Shenkt stared back, the hall cloaked all the while in that oppressive silence that only great spaces can produce. 'So this is he. Why is he not kneeling?'

'He does not kneel, apparently,' said Ganmark.

'Everyone else kneels. What makes you special?'

'Nothing,' said Shenkt.

'But you do not kneel.'

'I used to. Long ago. No more.'

Orso's eyes narrowed. 'And what if a man tried to make you?'

'Some have tried.'

'And?'

'And I do not kneel.'

'Stand, then. My son is dead.'

'You have my sorrow.'

'You do not sound sorrowful.'

'He was not my son.'

The chamberlain nearly choked on his tongue, but Orso's sunken eyes did not deviate. 'You like to speak the truth, I see. Blunt counsel is a valuable thing to powerful men. You come to me with the highest recommendations.'

Shenkt said nothing.

'That business in Keln. I understand that was your work. All of that, your work alone. It is said that the things that were left could hardly be called corpses.'

Shenkt said nothing.

'You do not confirm it.'

Shenkt stared into Duke Orso's face, and said nothing.

'You do not deny it, though.'

More nothing.

'I like a tight-lipped man. A man who says little to his friends will say less than nothing to his enemies.'

Silence.

'My son is murdered. Thrown from the window of a brothel like rubbish. Many of his friends and associates, my citizens, were also killed. My son-in-law, his Majesty the King of the Union, no less, only just escaped the burning building with his life. Sotorius, the half-corpse Chancellor of Sipani who was their host, wrings his hands and tells me he can do nothing. I am betrayed. I am bereaved. I am . . . *embarrassed*. Me!' he screamed suddenly, making the chamber ring, and every person in it flinch.

Every person except Shenkt. 'Vengeance, then.'

'Vengeance!' Orso smashed the arm of his chair with his fist. 'Swift and terrible.'

'Swift I cannot promise. Terrible – yes.'

'Then let it be slow, and grinding, and merciless.'

'It may be necessary to cause some harm to your subjects and their property.'

'Whatever it takes. Bring me their heads. Every man, woman or child involved in this, to the slightest degree. Whatever is necessary. Bring me their heads.'

'Their heads, then.'

'What will be your advance?'

'Nothing.'

'Not even—'

'If I complete the job, you will pay me one hundred thousand scales for the head of the ringleader, and twenty thousand for each assistant to a maximum of one quarter of a million. That is my price.'

'A very high one!' squeaked the chamberlain. 'What will you do with so much money?'

'I will count it and laugh, while considering how a rich man need not answer the questions of idiots. You will find no employer, anywhere, unsatisfied with my work.' Shenkt moved his eyes slowly to the half-circle of scum at his back. 'You can pay less to lesser men, if you please.'

'I will,' said Orso. 'If one of them should find the killers first.'

'I would accept no other arrangement, your Excellency.'

'Good,' growled the duke. 'Go, then. All of you, go! Bring . . . me . . . revenge!'

'You are dismissed!' screeched the chamberlain. There was a rustling, rattling, clattering as the assassins rose to leave the great chamber. Shenkt turned and walked back down the carpet towards the great doors, without undue speed, looking neither right nor left.

One of the killers blocked his path, a dark-skinned man of average height but wide as a door, lean slabs of muscle showing through the gap in his brightly coloured shirt. His thick lip curled. 'You are Shenkt? I expected more.'

'Pray to whatever god you believe in that you never see more.'

'I do not pray.'

Shenkt leaned close, and whispered in his ear. 'I advise you to start.'

Although a large room by most standards, General Ganmark's study felt cluttered. An oversized bust of Juvens frowned balefully from above the fireplace, his stony bald spot reflected in a magnificent mirror of coloured Visserine glass. Two monumental vases loomed either side of the desk almost to shoulder height. The walls were crowded with canvases in gilded frames, two of them positively vast. Fine paintings. Far too fine to be squeezed.

'A most impressive collection,' said Shenkt.

'That one is by Coliere. It would have burned in the mansion in which I found it. And these two are Nasurins, that by Orhus.' Ganmark pointed them out with precise jabs of his forefinger. 'His early period, but still. Those vases were made as tribute to the first Emperor of Gurkhul, many hundreds of years ago, and somehow found their way to a rich man's house outside Caprile.'

'And from there to here.'

'I try to rescue what I can,' said Ganmark. 'Perhaps when the

Years of Blood end, Styria will still have some few treasures worth keeping.'

'Or you will.'

'Better I have them than the flames. The campaign season begins, and I will be away to Visserine in the morning, to take the city under siege. Skirmishes, sacks and burnings. March and counter-march. Famine and pestilence, naturally. Maim and murder, of course. All with the awful randomness of a stroke from the heavens. Collective punishment. Of everyone, for nothing. War, Shenkt, war. And to think I once dreamed of being an honourable man. Of doing good.'

'We all dream of that.'

The general raised one eyebrow. 'Even you?'

'Even me.' Shenkt slid out his knife. A Gurkish butcher's sickle, small but sharp as fury.

'I wish you joy of it, then. The best I can do is strive to keep the waste to the merely . . . epic.'

'These are wasteful times.' Shenkt took the little lump of wood from his pocket, dog's head already roughly carved into the front.

'Aren't they all? Wine? It is from Cantain's own cellar.'

'No.'

Shenkt worked carefully with his knife while the general filled his own glass, woodchips scattering across the floor between his boots, the hindquarters of the dog slowly taking shape. Hardly a work of art like those around him, but it would serve. There was something calming in the regular movements of the curved blade, in the gentle fluttering down of the shavings.

Ganmark leaned against the mantel, drew out the poker and gave the fire a few unnecessary jabs. 'You have heard of Monzcarro Murcatto?'

'The captain general of the Thousand Swords. A most successful soldier. I heard she was dead.'

'Can you keep a secret, Shenkt?'

'I keep many hundreds.'

'Of course you do. Of course.' He took a long breath. 'Duke Orso ordered her death. Hers and her brother's. Her victories had made her popular in Talins. Too popular. His Excellency feared she might usurp his throne, as mercenaries can do. You are not surprised?'

'I have seen every kind of death, and every kind of motive.'

'Of course you have.' Ganmark frowned at the fire. 'This was not a good death.'

'None of them are.'

'Still. This was not a good one. Two months ago Duke Orso's bodyguard vanished. No great surprise, he was a foolish man, took little care over his safety, was prone to vice and bad company and had made many enemies. I thought nothing of it.'

'And?'

'A month later, the duke's banker was poisoned in Westport, along with half his staff. This was a different matter. He took a very great deal of care over his safety. To poison him was a task of the greatest difficulty, carried out with a formidable profession-alism and an exceptional lack of mercy. But he dabbled widely in the politics of Styria, and the politics of Styria is a fatal game with few merciful players.'

'True.'

'Valint and Balk themselves suspected a long enmity with Gurkish rivals might be the motive.'

'Valint and Balk.'

'You are familiar with the institution?'

Shenkt paused. 'I believe they employed me once. Go on.'

'But now Prince Ario, murdered.' The general pushed one fingertip under his ear. 'Stabbed in the very spot in which he stabbed Benna Murcatto, then thrown down from a high window?'

'You think Monzcarro Murcatto is still alive?'

'A week after his son's death, Duke Orso received a letter. From one Carlot dan Eider, Prince Ario's mistress. We had long suspected she was here to spy for the Union, but Orso tolerated the affair.'

'Surprising.'

Ganmark shrugged. 'The Union is our confirmed ally. We helped them win the latest round of their endless wars against the Gurkish. We both enjoy the backing of the Banking House of Valint and Balk. Not to mention the fact that the King of the Union is Orso's son-in-law. Naturally we send each other spies, by way of neighbourly good manners. If one must entertain a spy, she might as well be a charming one, and Eider was, undeniably, charming. She was with Prince Ario in Sipani. After his death she disappeared. Then the letter.'

'And it said?'

'That she was compelled through poison to assist Prince Ario's murderers. That they included among their number a mercenary named Nicomo Cosca and a torturer named Shylo Vitari, and were led by none other than Murcatto herself. Very much alive.'

'You believe it?'

'Eider had no reason to lie to us. No letter will save her from his Excellency's wrath if she is found, and she must know it. Murcatto was alive when she went over the balcony, that much I am sure of. I have not seen her dead.'

'She is seeking revenge.'

Ganmark gave a joyless chuckle. 'These are the Years of Blood. Everyone is seeking revenge. The Serpent of Talins, though? The Butcher of Caprile? Who loved nothing in the world but her brother? If she lives, she is on fire with it. There are few more single-minded enemies a man could find.'

'Then I should find this woman Vitari, this man Cosca and this serpent Murcatto.'

'No one must learn she might still live. If it was known in Talins that Orso was the one who planned her death . . . there could be unrest. Revolt, even. She was much loved among the people. A talisman. A mascot. One of their own, risen through merit. As the wars drag on and the taxes mount, his Excellency is . . . less well liked than he could be. I can trust you to keep silent?'

Shenkt kept silent.

'Good. There are associates of Murcatto's still in Talins. Perhaps one of them knows where she is.' The general looked up, the orange glow of the fire splashed across one side of his tired face. 'But what am I saying? It is your business to find people. To find people, and to . . .' He stabbed again at the glowing coals and sent up a shower of dancing sparks. 'I need not tell you your business, need I?'

Shenkt put away his half-finished carving, and his knife, and turned for the door. 'No.'

Downwards

They came upon Visserine as the sun was dropping down behind the trees and the land was turning black. You could see the towers even from miles distant. Dozens of 'em. Scores. Sticking up tall and slim as lady's fingers into the cloudy blue-grey sky, pricks of light scattered where lamps burned in high windows.

'Lot o' towers,' Shivers muttered to himself.

'There always was a fashion for them in Visserine.' Cosca grinned sideways at him. 'Some date all the way back to the New Empire, centuries old. The greatest families compete to build the tallest ones. It is a point of pride. I remember when I was a boy, one fell before it was finished, not three streets from where I lived. A dozen poor dwellings were destroyed in the collapse. It's always the poor who are crushed under rich men's ambitions. And yet they rarely complain, because . . . well . . .'

'They dream of having towers o' their own?'

Cosca chuckled. 'Why, yes, I suppose they do. They don't see that the higher you climb, the further you have to fall.'

'Men rarely see that 'til the ground's rushing at 'em.'

'All too true. And I fear many of the rich men of Visserine will be tumbling soon . . .'

Friendly lit a torch, Vitari too, and Day a third, set at the front of the cart to light the way. Torches were lit all round them, 'til the road was a trickle of tiny lights in the darkness, winding through the dark country towards the sea. Would've made a pretty picture, at another time, but not now. War was coming, and no one was in a pretty mood.

The closer they came to the city, the more choked the road got with people, and the more rubbish was scattered either side of it. Half of 'em seemed desperate to get into Visserine and find some walls to hide behind, the other half to get out and find some open country to run through. It was a bastard of a choice for farmers, when war was on the way. Stick to your land and get a dose of fire and robbery for certain, with rape or murder more'n likely. Make for a town on the chance they'll find room for you, risk being robbed by your protectors, or caught up in the sack if the place falls. Or run for the hills to hide, maybe get caught, maybe starve, maybe just die of an icy night.

War killed some soldiers, sure, but it left the rest with money, and songs to sing, and a fire to sit around. It killed a lot more farmers, and left the rest with nought but ashes.

Just to lift the mood rain started flitting down through the darkness, spitting and hissing as it fell on the flickering torches, white streaks through the circles of light around 'em. The road turned to sticky mud. Shivers felt the wet tickle his scalp, but his thoughts were far off. Same place they'd tended to stray to these last few weeks. Back to Cardotti's, and the dark work he'd done there.

His brother had always told him it was about the lowest thing a man could do, kill a woman. Respect for womenfolk, and children, sticking to the old ways and your word, that was what set men apart from animals, and Carls from killers. He hadn't meant to do it, but when you swing steel in a crowd you can't duck the blame for the results. The good man he'd come here to be should've been gnawing his nails to the bloody quick over what he'd done. But all he could get in his head when he thought of his blade chopping a bloody chunk out of her ribs, the hollow sound it made, her staring face as she slid dying down the wall, was relief he'd got away with it.

Killing a woman by mistake in a brothel was murder, evil as it got, but killing a man on purpose in a battle was all kinds of noble? A thing to take pride in, sing songs of? Time was, gathered round a fire up in the cold North, that had seemed simple and obvious. But Shivers couldn't see the difference so sharp as he'd used to. And it wasn't like he'd got himself confused. He'd suddenly got it clear. You set to killing folk, there's no right place to stop that means a thing.

'You look as if you've dark thoughts in mind, my friend,' said Cosca.

'Don't seem the time for jokes.'

The mercenary chuckled. 'My old mentor Sazine once told me you should laugh every moment you live, for you'll find it decidedly difficult afterwards.'

'That so? And what became of him?'

'Died of a rotten shoulder.'

'Poor punchline.'

'Well, if life's a joke,' said Cosca, 'it's a black one.'

'Best not to laugh, then, in case the joke's on you.'

'Or trim your sense of humour to match.'

'You'd need a twisted sense of humour to make laughs o' this.'

Cosca scratched at his neck as he looked towards the walls of Visserine, rising up black out of the thickening rain. 'I must confess, for now I'm failing to see the funny side.'

You could tell from the lights there was an ugly press at the gate, and it got no prettier the closer they came. Folk were coming out from time to time – old men, young men, women carrying children, gear packed up on mules or on their backs, cartwheels creaking round through the sticky mud. Folk were coming out, easing nervous through the angry crowd, but there weren't many being let the other way. You could feel the fear, heavy on the air, and the thicker they all crowded the worse it got.

Shivers swung down from his horse, stretched his legs and made sure he loosened his sword in its sheath.

'Alright.' Under her hood, Monza's hair was stuck black to the side of her scowling face. 'I'll get us in.'

'You are *absolutely* convinced that we should enter?' demanded Morveer.

She gave him a long look. 'Orso's army can't be more than two days behind us. That means Ganmark. Faithful Carpi too, maybe, with the Thousand Swords. Wherever they are is where we need to be, and that's all.'

'You are my employer, of course. But I feel duty-bound to point out that there is such a thing as being *too* determined. Surely we can devise a less perilous alternative to trapping ourselves in a city that will soon be surrounded by hostile forces.'

'We'll do no good waiting out here.'

'No good will be done if we are all *killed*. A plan too brittle to bend with circumstance is worse than no—' She turned before he'd finished and made off towards the archway, shoving her way between the bodies. 'Women,' Morveer hissed through gritted teeth.

'What about them?' growled Vitari.

'Present company entirely excepted, they are prone to think with heart rather than head.'

'For what she's paying she can think with her arse for all I care.'

'Dying rich is still dying.'

'Better'n dying poor,' said Shivers.

Not long after, a half-dozen guards came shoving through the crowd, herding folk away with their spears, clearing a muddy path to the gate. An officer came frowning with 'em, Monza just behind his shoulder. No doubt she'd sown a few coins, and this was the harvest.

'You six, with the cart there.' The officer pointed a gloved finger at Shivers and the rest. 'You're coming in. You six and no one else.'

There were some angry mutters from the rest stood about the gate. Somebody gave the cart a kick as it started moving. 'Shit on this! It ain't right! I paid my taxes to Salier all my life, and I get left out?' Someone snatched at Shivers' arm as he tried to lead his horse after. A farmer, from what he could tell in the torchlight and the spitting rain, even more desperate than most. 'Why should these bastards be let through? I've got my family to—'

Shivers smashed his fist into the farmer's face. He caught him by his coat as he fell and dragged him up, followed the first punch with another, knocked him sprawling on his back in the ditch by the road. Blood bubbled down his face, black in the dusk as he tried to push himself up. You start some trouble, it's best to start it and finish it all at once. A bit of sharp violence can save you a lot worse down the line. That's the way Black Dow would've handled it. So Shivers stepped forwards quick, planted his boot on the man's chest and shoved him back into the mud.

'Best stay where y'are.' A few others stood behind, dark outlines of men, a woman with two children around her legs. One lad looking straight at him, bent over like he was thinking of doing something about it all. The farmer's son, maybe. 'I do this shit for a living, boy. You feel a pressing need to lie down?'

The lad shook his head. Shivers took hold of his horse's bridle again, clicked his tongue and made for the archway. Not too fast. Good and ready in case anyone was fool enough to test him. But they were already back to shouting before he'd got a stride or two, calling out how they were special, why they should be let in while the rest were left to the wolves. A man getting his front teeth knocked out was nothing to cry about in all this. Those that hadn't seen far worse guessed they'd be seeing it soon enough, and all their care was to make sure they weren't on the sharp end of it. He followed the others, blowing on his skinned knuckles, under the archway and into the darkness of the long tunnel.

Shivers tried to remember what the Dogman had told him, a hundred years ago it seemed now, back in Adua. Something about blood making more blood, and it not being too late to be better'n that. Not too late to be a good man. Rudd Threetrees had been a good man, none better. He'd stuck to the old ways all his life, never took the easy path, if he thought it was the wrong one. Shivers was proud to say he'd fought beside the man, called him chief, but in the end, what had Threetrees' honour got him? A few misty-eyed mentions around the fire. That, and a hard life, and a place in the mud at the end of it. Black Dow had been as cold a bastard as Shivers ever knew. A man who never faced an enemy if he could take him in the back, burned villages without a second thought, broke his own oaths and spat on the results. A man as merciful as the plague, and with a conscience the size of a louse's cock. Now he sat in Skarling's chair with half the North at his feet and the other half feared to say his name.

They came out from the tunnel and into the city. Water spattered from broken gutters and onto worn cobbles. A wet procession of men, women, mules, carts, waiting to get out, watching them as they tramped the other way. Shivers tipped his head back, eyes narrowed against the rain flitting down into his face as they went under a great tower, soaring up into the black night. Must've been three times the height of the tallest thing in Carleon, and it weren't even the biggest one around.

He glanced sideways at Monza, the way he'd got so good at doing. She had her usual frown, eyes fixed right ahead, light from passing torches shifting across the hard bones in her face. She set her mind to a thing, and did whatever it took. Shit on conscience and consequences both. Vengeance first, questions later.

He moved his tongue around in his mouth and spat. The more he saw, the more he saw she was right. Mercy and cowardice were the same. No one was giving prizes for good behaviour. Not here, not in the North, not anywhere. You want a thing, you have to take it, and the greatest man is the one that snatches most. Maybe it would've been nice if life was another way.

But it was how it was.

Monza was stiff and aching, just like always. She was angry and tired, just like always. She needed a smoke, worse than ever. And just to sprinkle some spice on the evening, she was getting wet, cold and saddle-sore besides.

She remembered Visserine as a beautiful place, full of twinkling glass and graceful buildings, fine food, laughter and freedom. She'd been in a rare good mood when she last visited, true, in a warm summer rather than a chill spring, with no one but Benna looking to her for leadership and no four men she had to kill.

But even so, the place was a long way from the bright pleasure garden of her memory.

Where there was a lamp burning the shutters were closed tight, light just leaking out around the edges, catching the little glass figures in their niches above the doors and making them twinkle. Household spirits, a tradition from long ago, before the time of the New Empire even, put there to bring prosperity and drive off evil. Monza wondered what good those chunks of glass would be when Orso's army broke through into the city. Not much. The streets were thick with fear, the sense of threat so heavy it seemed to stick to Monza's clammy skin and make the hairs on her neck prickle.

Not that Visserine wasn't crawling with people. Some were running, making for docks or gates. Men and women with packs, everything they could save on their backs, children in tow, elders shuffling behind. Wagons rattled along stacked with sacks and boxes, with mattresses and chests of drawers, with all manner of useless junk that would no doubt end up abandoned, lining one road or another out of Visserine. A waste of time and effort, trying to save anything but your lives at a time like this.

You chose to run, you'd best run fast.

But there were plenty who'd chosen to run into the city for refuge, and found to their great dismay it was a dead end. They lined the streets in places. They filled the doorways, huddled under blankets against the rain. They crammed the shadowy arcades of an empty market in their dozens, cowering as a column of soldiers tramped past, armour beaded up with moisture, gleaming by torchlight. Sounds came echoing through the murk. Crashes of breaking glass or tearing wood. Angry shouts, or fearful. Once or twice an outright scream.

Monza guessed a few of the city's own people were making an early start on the sacking. Settling a score or two, or snatching a few things they'd always envied while the eyes of the powerful were fixed on their own survival. This was one of those rare moments when a man could get something for free, and there'd be more and more taking advantage of it as Orso's army gathered outside the city. The stuff of civilisation, already starting to dissolve.

Monza felt eyes following her and the rest of the merry band as they rode slowly through the streets. Fearful eyes, suspicious eyes, and the other kind – trying to judge if they were soft enough or rich enough to be worth robbing. She kept the reins in her right hand, for all it hurt her to tug at them, so her left could rest on her thigh, close to the hilt of her sword. The only law in Visserine now was at the edge of a blade. And the enemy hadn't even arrived yet.

I have seen hell, Stolicus wrote, *and it is a great city under siege*.

Up ahead the road passed under a marble arch, a long rivulet of water spattering from its high keystone. A mural was painted on the wall above. Grand Duke Salier sat enthroned at the top, optimistically depicted as pleasantly plump rather than massively obese. He held one hand up in blessing, a heavenly light radiating from his fatherly smile. Beneath him an assortment of Visserine's citizens, from the lowest to the highest, humbly enjoyed the benefits of his good governance. Bread, wine, wealth. Under them, around the top of the archway, the words *charity, justice, courage* were printed in gold letters high as a man. Someone with an appetite for truth had managed to climb up there and part daub over them in streaky red, *greed, torture, cowardice*.

'The arrogance of that fat fucker Salier.' Vitari grinned sideways at her, orange hair black-brown with rain. 'Still, I reckon he's made his last boast, don't you?'

Monza only grunted. All she could think about as she looked into Vitari's sharp-boned face was how far she could trust her. They might be in the middle of a war, but the greatest threats were still more than likely from within her own little company of outcasts. Vitari? Here for the money – ever a risky motivation since there's always some bastard with deeper pockets. Cosca? How can you trust a notoriously treacherous drunk you once betrayed yourself? Friendly? Who knew how the hell that man's mind worked?

But they were all tight as family beside Morveer. She stole a glance over her shoulder, caught him frowning at her from the seat of his cart. The man was poison, and the moment he could profit by it he'd murder her easily as crushing a tick. He was already suspicious of the choice to come into Visserine, but the last thing she wanted was to share her reasoning. That Orso would have Eider's letter by now. Would have offered a king's ransom of Valint and Balk's money for her death and got half the killers in the Circle of the World scouring Styria hoping to put her head in a bag. Along with the heads of anyone who'd helped her, of course.

The chances were high they'd be safer in the middle of a battle than outside it.

Shivers was the only one she could even halfway trust. He rode hunched over, big and silent beside her. His babble had been quite the irritation in Westport, but now it had dried up, strange to say, it had left a gap. He'd saved her life, in foggy Sipani. Monza's life wasn't all it had been, but a man saving it still raised him a damn sight higher in her estimation.

'You're quiet, all of a sudden.'

She could hardly see his face in the darkness, just the hard set of it, shadows in his eye sockets, in the hollows under his cheeks. 'Don't reckon I've much to say.'

'Never stopped you before.'

'Well. I'm starting to see all kinds o' things different.'

'That so?'

'You might think it comes easy to me, but it's an effort, trying to stay hopeful. An effort that don't ever seem to pay off.'

'I thought being a better man was its own reward.'

'I guess it ain't reward enough for all the work. In case you hadn't noticed, we're in the middle of a war.'

'Believe me, I know what a war looks like. I've been living in one most of my life.'

'Well, what are the odds o' that? Me too. From what I've seen, and I've seen plenty, a war ain't really the place for bettering yourself. I'm thinking I might try it your way, from now on.'

'Pick out a god and praise him! Welcome to the real world!' She wasn't sure she didn't feel a twinge of disappointment though, for all her grinning. Monza might have given up on being a decent person long ago, but somehow she liked the idea that she could have pointed one out. She pulled on her reins and eased her horse up, the cart clattering to a halt behind her. 'We're here.'

The place she and Benna had bought in Visserine was an old one, built before the city had good walls, and rich men each took their own care to guard what was theirs. A stone tower-house on five storeys, hall and stables to one side, with slit windows on the ground floor and battlements on the high roof. It stood big and black against the dark sky, a very different beast from the low brick-and-timber houses that crowded in close around it. She lifted the key to the studded door, then frowned. It was open a crack, light gathering on the rough stone down its edge. She put her finger to her lips and pointed towards it.

Shivers raised one big boot and kicked it shuddering open, wood clattering on the other side as something was barged out of the way. Monza darted in, left hand on the hilt of her sword. The kitchen was empty of furniture and full of people. Grubby and tired-looking, every one of them staring at her, shocked and fearful, in the light of one flickering candle. The nearest, a stocky man with one arm in a sling, stumbled up from an empty barrel and caught hold of a length of wood.

'Get back!' he screamed at her. A man in a dirty farmer's smock took a stride towards her, waving a hatchet.

Shivers stepped around Monza's shoulder, ducking under the lintel and straightening up, big shadow shifting across the wall behind him, his heavy sword drawn and gleaming down by his leg. 'You get back.'

The farmer did as he was told, scared eyes fixed on that length of bright metal. 'Who the hell are you?'

'Me?' snapped Monza. 'This is my house, bastard.'

'Eleven of them,' said Friendly, slipping through the doorway on the other side.

As well as the two men there were two old women and a man even older, bent right over, gnarled hands dangling. There was a woman about Monza's age, a baby in her arms and two little girls sat near her, staring with big eyes, like enough to be twins. A girl of maybe sixteen stood by the empty fireplace. She had a rough-forged knife out that she'd been gutting a fish with, her other arm across a boy, might've been ten or so, pushing him behind her shoulder.

Just a girl, looking out for her little brother.

'Put your sword away,' Monza said.

'Eh?'

'No one's getting killed tonight.'

Shivers raised one heavy brow at her. 'Now who's the optimist?'

'Lucky for you I bought a big house.' The one with his arm in a sling looked like the head of the family, so she fixed her eye on him. 'There's room for all of us.'

He let his club drop. 'We're farmers from up the valley, just looking for somewhere safe. Place was like this when we found it, we didn't steal nothing. We'll be no trouble—'

'You'd better not be. This all of you?'

'My name's Furli. That's my wife—'

'I don't need your names. You'll stay down here, and you'll stay out of our way. We'll be upstairs, in the tower. You don't come up there, you understand? That way no one gets hurt.'

He nodded, fear starting to mix with relief. 'I understand.'

'Friendly, get the horses stabled, and that cart off the street.' Those farmers' hungry faces – helpless, weak, needy – made Monza feel sick. She kicked a broken chair out of the way then started up the stairs, winding into the darkness, her legs stiff from a day in the saddle. Morveer caught up with her on the fourth landing, Cosca and Vitari just behind him, Day at the back, a trunk in her arms. Morveer had brought a lamp with him, light pooling on the underside of his unhappy face.

'Those peasants are a decided threat to us,' he murmured. 'A problem easily solved, however. It will hardly be necessary to utilise the King of Poisons. A charitable contribution of a loaf of bread, dusted with Leopard Flower of course, and they would cease to—'

'No.'

He blinked. 'If your intention is to leave them at liberty down there, I must most strongly protest at—'

'Protest away. Let's see if I care a shit. You and Day can take that room.' As he turned to peer into the darkness, Monza snatched the lamp out of his hand. 'Cosca, you're on the second floor with Friendly. Vitari, seems like you get to sleep alone next door.'

'Sleeping alone.' She kicked some fallen plaster away across the boards. 'Story of my life.'

'I will to my cart, then, and bring my equipment into the Butcher of Caprile's hostel for *displaced peasantry*.' Morveer was shaking his head with disgust as he turned for the stairs.

'Do that,' snapped Monza at his back. She loitered for a moment, until she'd heard his boots scrape down a few flights and out of earshot. Until, apart from Cosca's voice burbling away endlessly to Friendly downstairs, it was quiet on the landing. Then she followed Day into her room and gently pushed the door closed. 'We need to talk.'

The girl had opened her trunk and was just getting a chunk of bread out of it. 'What about?'

'The same thing we talked about in Westport. Your employer.'

'Picking at your nerves, is he?'

'Don't tell me he isn't picking at yours.'

'Every day for three years.'

'Not an easy man to work for, I reckon.' Monza took a step into the room, holding the girl's eye. 'Sooner or later a pupil has to step out from her master's shadow, if she's ever going to become the master herself.'

'That why you betrayed Cosca?'

That gave Monza a moment's pause. 'More or less. Sometimes you have to take a risk. Grasp the nettle. But then you've got much better reasons even than I had.' Said offhand, as though it was obvious.

Day's turn to pause. 'What reasons?'

Monza pretended to be surprised. 'Well . . . because sooner or later Morveer will betray me, and go over to Orso.' She wasn't sure of it, of course, but it was high time she guarded herself against the possibility.

'That so?' Day wasn't smiling any longer.

'He doesn't like the way I do things.'

'Who says I like the way you do things?'

'You don't see it?' Day only narrowed her eyes, food, for once, forgotten in her hand. 'If he goes to Orso, he'll need someone to blame. For Ario. A scapegoat.'

Now she got the idea. 'No,' she snapped. 'He needs me.'

'How long have you been with him? Three years, did you say? Managed before, didn't he? How many assistants do you think he's had? See a lot of them around, do you?'

Day opened her mouth, blinked, then thoughtfully shut it.

'Maybe he'll stick, and we'll stay a happy family and part friends. Most poisoners are good sorts, when you get to know them.' Monza leaned down close to whisper. 'But when he tells you he's going over to Orso, don't say I didn't warn you.'

She left Day frowning at her chunk of bread, slipped quietly through the door and brushed it shut with her fingertips. She peered down the stairwell, but there was no sign of Morveer, only the handrail spiralling down into the shadows. She nodded to herself. The seed was planted now, she'd have to see what sprouted from it. She pushed her tired legs up the narrow steps to the top of the tower, through the creaking door and into the high chamber under the roof, faint sound of rain drumming above.

The room where she and Benna had spent a happy month together, in the midst of some dark years. Away from the wars. Laughing, talking, watching the world from the wide windows. Pretending at how life might have been if they'd never taken up warfare, and somehow made it rich some other way. She found she was smiling, despite herself. The little glass figure still gleamed in its niche above the door. Their household spirit. She remembered Benna grinning over his shoulder as he pushed it up there with his fingertips.

So it can watch over you while you sleep, the way you've always watched over me.

Her smile leaked away, and she walked to the window and dragged open one of the flaking shutters. Rain had thrown a grey veil across the dark city, pelting down now, spattering against the sill. A stroke of distant lightning picked out the tangle of wet roofs below for an instant, the grey outlines of other towers looming from the murk. A few moments later the thunder crackled sullen and muffled across the city.

'Where do I sleep?' Shivers stood in the doorway, arm up on the frame and some blankets over one shoulder.

'You?' She glanced up to the little glass statue above his head, then back to Shivers' face. Maybe she'd had high standards, long ago, but back then she'd had Benna, and both her hands, and an army behind her. She had nothing behind her now but six well-paid misfits, a good sword and a lot of money. A general should keep her distance from her troops, maybe, and a wanted woman from everyone, but Monza wasn't a general any more. Benna was dead, and she needed something. You can weep over your misfortunes, or you can pick yourself up and make the best of things, shit though they may be. She elbowed the shutter closed, sank down wincing on the bed and set the lamp on the floor.

'You're in here, with me.'

His brows went up. 'I am?'

'That's right, optimist. Your lucky night.' She leaned back on her elbows, old bed-frame creaking, and stuck one foot up at him. 'Now shut the door and help me get my fucking boots off.'

Rats in a Sack

Cosca squinted as he stepped out onto the roof of the tower. Even the sunlight seemed set on tormenting him, but he supposed he richly deserved it. Visserine was spread out around him: jumbles of brick-and-timber houses, villas of cream-coloured stone, the green tops of leafing trees where the parks and broad avenues were laid out. Everywhere windows glinted, statues of coloured glass on the rooflines of the grandest buildings catching the morning sun and shining like jewels. Other towers were widely scattered, dozens of them, some far taller than the one he stood on, each casting its own long shadow across the sprawl.

Southwards the grey-blue sea, the smoke of industry still rising from the city's famous glass-working district on its island just offshore, the gliding specks of seabirds circling above it. To the east the Visser was a dark snake glimpsed through the buildings, four bridges linking the two halves of the city. Grand Duke Salier's palace squatted jealously on an island in its midst. A place where Cosca had spent many enjoyable evenings, an honoured guest of the great connoisseur himself. When he had still been loved, feared and admired. So long ago it seemed another man's life.

Monza stood motionless at the parapet, framed by the blue sky. The blade of her sword and her sinewy left arm made a line, perfectly straight, from shoulder to point. The steel shone bright, the ruby on her middle finger glittered bloody, her skin gleamed with sweat. Her vest stuck to her with it. She let the sword drop as he came closer, as he lifted the wine jug and took a long, cool swallow.

'I wondered how long it would take you.'

'Only water in it, more's the pity. Did you not witness my solemn oath never to touch wine again?'

She snorted. 'That I've heard before, with small results.'

'I am in the slow and agonising process of mending my ways.'

'I've heard that too, with even smaller ones.'

Cosca sighed. 'Whatever must a man do to be taken seriously?'

'Keep his word once in his life?'

'My fragile heart, so often broken in the past! Can it take such a buffeting?' He wedged one boot up on the battlements beside her. 'I was born in Visserine, you know, no more than a few streets away. A happy childhood but a wild youth, full of ugly incidents. Including the one that obliged me to flee the city to seek my fortune as a paid soldier.'

'Your whole life has been full of ugly incidents.'

'True enough.' He had few pleasant memories, in fact. And most of those, Cosca realised as he peered sideways at Monza, had involved her. Most of the best moments of his life, and the very worst of all. He took a sharp breath and shielded his eyes with a hand, looking westwards, past the grey line of the city walls and out into the patchwork of fields beyond. 'No sign of our friends from Talins yet?'

'Soon. General Ganmark isn't a man to turn up late to an engagement.' She paused for a moment, frowning, as always. 'When are you going to say you told me?'

'Told you what?'

'About Orso.'

'You know what I told you.'

'Never trust your own employer.' A lesson he had learned at great cost from Duchess Sefeline of Ospria. 'And now I'm the one paying your wages.'

Cosca made an effort at a grin, though it hurt his sore lips to do it. 'But we are fittingly suspicious in all our dealings with each other.'

'Of course. I wouldn't trust you to carry my shit to the stream.'

'A shame. Your shit smells sweet as roses, I am sure.' He leaned back against the parapet and blinked into the sun. 'Do you remember how we used to spar, in the mornings? Before you got too good.'

'Before you got too drunk.'

'Well, I could hardly spar afterwards, could I? There is a limit to how much a man should be willing to embarrass himself before breakfast. Is that a Calvez you have there?'

She lifted the sword, sun's gleam gliding along its edge. 'I had it made for Benna.'

'For Benna? What the hell would he do with a Calvez? Use it as a spit and cook apples on it?'

'He didn't even do that much, as it goes.'

'I used to have one, you know. Damn good sword. Lost it in a card game. Drink?' He held out the jug.

She reached for it. 'I could—'

'Hah!' He flung the water in her face and she yelped, stumbling back, drops flying. He ripped his sword from its sheath and as the jug shattered against the roof he was already swinging. She managed to parry the first cut, ducked desperately under the second, slipped, sprawled, rolled away as Cosca's blade squealed down the roofing lead where she had been a moment before. She came up in a crouch, sword at the ready.

'You're getting soft, Murcatto.' He chuckled as he paced out into the centre of the roof. 'You'd never have fallen for the old water in the face ten years ago.'

'I didn't fall for it just now, idiot.' She wiped her brow slowly with her gloved hand, water dripping from the ends of her wet hair, never taking her eyes from his. 'You got anything more than water in the face, or is that as far as your swordsmanship reaches these days?'

Not much further, if he was honest. 'Why don't we find out?'

She sprang forwards and their blades feathered together, metal ringing and scraping. She had a long scar on her bare right shoulder, another curving round her forearm and into her black glove.

He waved his sword at it. 'Fighting left-handed, eh? Hope you're not taking pity on an old man.'

'Pity? You know me better than that.' He flicked away a jab, but another came so quickly behind it he only just got out of the way, the blade punching a ragged hole in his shirt before it whipped back out.

He raised his brows. 'Good thing I lost some weight during my last binge.'

'You could lose more, if you're asking me.' She circled him, the point of her tongue showing between her teeth.

'Trying to get the sun behind you?'

'You never should've taught me all those dirty tricks. Care to use your left, even things up a little?'

'Give up an advantage? You know me better than that!' He feinted right then went the other way and left her lunging at nothing. She was quick, but not near as quick as she had been with her right hand. He trod on her boot as she passed, made her stumble, the point of his sword left a neat scratch across the scar on her shoulder, and made a cross of it.

She peered down at the little wound, a bead of blood forming at its corner. 'You old bastard.'

'A little something to remember me by.' And he twirled his sword around and slashed ostentatiously at the air. She lunged at him again and their swords rang together, cut, cut, jab and parry. All a touch clumsy, like sewing with gloves on. The time was they had given exhibitions, but it seemed time had done nothing for either of them. 'One question . . .' he murmured, keeping his eyes on hers. 'Why did you betray me?'

'I got tired of your fucking jokes.'

'I deserved to be betrayed, of course. Every mercenary ends up stabbed in the front or the back. But by you?' He jabbed at her, followed it with a cut that made her shuffle back, wincing. 'After all I taught you? All I gave you? Safety, and money, and a place to belong? I treated you like my own daughter!'

'Like your mother, maybe. You've left out getting so drunk you'd shit in your clothes. I owed you, but there's a limit.' She circled him, looking for an opening, no more than the thickness of a finger between the points of their swords. 'I might've followed you to hell, but I wasn't taking my brother there with me.'

'Why not? He'd have been right at home.'

'Fuck yourself!' She tricked him with a feint, switched angle and forced him to hop away with all the grace of a dying frog. He had forgotten how much work swordplay required. His lungs were burning already, shoulder, forearm, wrist, hand, all aching with a vengeance. 'If it hadn't been me it would've been one of the other captains. Sesaria! Victus! Andiche!' She pushed home each hated name with a sharp cut, jarring the sword in his hand. 'They were all falling over themselves to be rid of you at Afieri!'

'Can we not mention that *damn place*!' He parried her next effort and switched smartly to the attack with something close to his old vigour, driving her back towards the corner of the roof. He needed to bring this to a close before he died of exhaustion. He lunged again and caught her sword on his. He drove her off balance against the parapet, bent her back over the battlements, guards scraping together until their faces were no more than a few inches apart, the long drop to the street looming into view behind her head. He could feel her quick breath on his cheek. For the briefest moment he almost kissed her, and he almost pushed her off the roof. Perhaps it was only because he could not decide which to do that he did neither one.

'You were better with your right hand,' he hissed.

'You were better ten years ago.' She slid from under his sword and her gloved little finger came from nowhere and poked him in the eye.

'Eeeee!' he squealed, free hand clapped to his face. Her knee thudded almost silently into his fruits and sent a lance of pain through his belly as far as his neck. 'Oooooof . . .' He tottered, blade clattering from his clutching fingers, bent over, unable to breathe. 'A little something to remember me by.' And the glittering point of Monza's sword left him a burning scratch across his cheek.

'Gah!' He sank down slowly to the roofing lead. Back on his knees. There really is no place like home . . .

Through the savage pain he heard slow clapping coming from the stairway. 'Vitari,' he croaked, squinting over at her as she ambled out into the sunlight. 'Why is it . . . you always find me . . . at my lowest moments?'

'Because I enjoy them so.'

'You bitches don't know your luck . . . that you'll never feel the pain . . . of a blow to the fruits.'

'Try childbirth.'

'A charming invitation . . . if I were a little less bruised in the relevant areas, I would definitely take you up on it.'

But, as so often, his wit was wasted. Vitari's attention was already fixed far beyond the battlements, and Monza's too. Cosca dragged himself up, bow-legged. A long column of horsemen had crested a rise to the west of the city, framed between two nearby towers, a cloud of dust rising from the hooves of their horses and leaving a brown smear across the sky.

'They're here,' said Vitari. From somewhere behind them a bell began to ring, soon joined by others.

'And there,' said Monza. A second column had appeared. And a pillar of smoke, drifting up beyond a hill to the north.

Cosca stood as the sun slowly rose into the blue sky, no doubt administering a healthy dose of sunburn to his spreading bald patch, and watched Duke Orso's army steadily deploy in the fields outside the city. Regiment after regiment smoothly found their positions, well out of bowshot from the walls. A large detachment forded the river to the north and completed the encirclement. The horse screened the foot as they formed neat lines, then fell back behind them, no doubt to set about the business of ravaging anything carelessly left unravaged last season.

Tents began to appear, and carts too as the supplies came up, stippling the muddy land behind the lines. The tiny defenders at the walls could do nothing but watch as the Talinese dug in around them, as orderly as the workings of a gigantic clock. Not Cosca's style, of course, even when sober. More engineering than artistry, but one had to admire the discipline.

He spread his arms wide. 'Welcome, one and all, to the siege of Visserine!'

The others had all gathered on the roof to watch Ganmark's grip on the city tighten. Monza stood with her left hand on her hip, gloved right slack on the pommel of her sword, black hair stirring around her scowl. Shivers was on Cosca's other side, staring balefully out from under his brows. Friendly sat near the door to the stairs, rolling his dice between his crossed legs. Day and Vitari muttered to each other further along the parapet. Morveer looked even more sour than usual, if that was possible.

'Can no one's sense of humour withstand so small a thing as a siege? Cheer up, my comrades!' Cosca gave Shivers a hearty clap on his broad back. 'It isn't every day you get to see so large an army handled so well! We should all congratulate Monza's friend General Ganmark on his exceptional patience and discipline. Perhaps we should pen him a letter.'

'My dear General Ganmark.' Monza worked her mouth, curled her tongue and blew spit over the battlements. 'Yours ever, Monzcarro Murcatto.'

'A simple missive,' observed Morveer, 'but no doubt he will treasure it.'

'Lot o' soldiers down there,' Shivers grunted.

Friendly's voice drifted gently over. 'Thirteen thousand four hundred, or thereabouts.'

'Mostly Talinese troops.' Cosca waved at them with the eyeglass. 'Some regiments from Orso's older allies – flags of Etrisani on the right wing, there, near the water, and some others of Cesale in the centre. All regulars, though. No sign of our old comrades-in-arms, the Thousand Swords. Shame. It would be fine to renew some old friendships, wouldn't it, Monza? Sesaria, Victus, Andiche. Faithful Carpi too, of course.' Renew old friendships . . . and be revenged on old friends.

'The mercenaries will be away to the east.' Monza jerked her head across the river. 'Holding off Duke Rogont and his Osprians.'

'Great fun for all involved, no doubt. But we, at least, are here.' Cosca gestured towards the crawling soldiers outside the city. 'General Ganmark, one presumes, is there. The plan, to bring us all together in a happy reunion? We presume you have a plan?'

'Ganmark is a cultured man. He has a taste for art.'

'And?' demanded Morveer.

'No one has more art than Grand Duke Salier.'

'His collection is impressive.' Cosca had admired it on several occasions, or at any rate pretended to, while admiring his wine.

'The finest in Styria, they say.' Monza strode to the opposite parapet, looking towards Salier's palace on its island in the river. 'When the city falls, Ganmark will make straight for the palace, eager to rescue all those priceless works from the chaos.'

'To steal them for himself,' threw in Vitari.

Monza's jaw was set even harder than usual. 'Orso will want to be done with this siege quickly. Leave as much time as possible to put an end to Rogont. Finish the League of Eight for good and claim his crown before winter comes. That means breaches, and assaults, and bodies in the streets.'

'Marvellous!' Cosca clapped his hands. 'Streets may boast noble trees, and stately buildings, but they never feel complete without a dusting of corpses, do they?'

'We take armour, uniforms, weapons from the dead. When the city falls, which will be soon, we disguise ourselves as Talinese. We find our way into the palace, and while Ganmark is going about the rescue of Salier's collection and his guard is down . . .'

'Kill the bastard?' offered Shivers.

There was a pause. 'I believe I perceive the most *minute* of flaws in the scheme.' Morveer's whining words were like nails driven into the back of Cosca's skull. 'Grand Duke Salier's palace will be among the best-guarded locations in Styria at the present moment, and *we* are not in it. Nor likely to receive an invitation.'

'On the contrary, I have one already.' Cosca was gratified to find them all staring at him. 'Salier and I were quite close some years ago, when he employed me to settle his boundary issues with Puranti. We used to dine together once a week and he assured me I was welcome whenever I found myself in the city.'

The poisoner's face was a caricature of contempt. 'Would this, by any chance, have been *before* you became a wine-ravaged sot?'

Cosca waved one careless hand while filing that slight carefully away with the rest. 'During my long and most enjoyable transformation into one. Like a caterpillar turning into a beautiful butterfly. In any case, the invitation still stands.'

Vitari narrowed her eyes at him. 'How the hell do you plan to make use of it?'

'I imagine I will address the guards at the palace gate, and say something along the lines of – "I am Nicomo Cosca, famed soldier of fortune, and I am here for dinner." '

There was an uncomfortable silence, quite as if he had contributed a giant turd rather than a winning idea.

'Forgive me,' murmured Monza, 'but I doubt your name opens doors the way it used to.'

'*Latrine* doors, maybe.' Morveer gave a sneering shake of his head. Day chuckled softly into the wind. Even Shivers had a dubious curl to his lip.

'Vitari and Morveer, then,' snapped Monza. 'That's your job. Watch the palace. Find us a way in.' The two of them gave each other an unenthusiastic frown. 'Cosca, you know something about uniforms.'

He sighed. 'Few men more. Every employer wants to give you one of their own. I had one from the Aldermen of Westport cut from cloth of gold, about as comfortable as a lead pipe up the—'

'Something less eye-catching might be better suited to our purpose.'

Cosca drew himself up and snapped out a vibrating salute. 'General Murcatto, I will do my straining utmost to obey your orders!'

'Don't strain. Man of your age, you might rupture something. Take Friendly with you, once the assaults begin.' The convict shrugged, and went back to his dice.

'We will most nobly strip the dead to their naked arses!' Cosca turned towards the stairs, but was brought up short by the sight in the bay. 'Ah! Duke Orso's fleet has joined the fun.' He could just see ships moving on the horizon, white sails marked with the black cross of Talins.

'More guests for Duke Salier,' said Vitari.

'He always was a conscientious host, but I'm not sure even he can be prepared for so many visitors at once. The city is entirely cut off.' And Cosca grinned into the wind.

'A prison,' said Friendly, and almost with a smile of his own.

'We are helpless as rats in a sack!' snapped Morveer. 'You speak quite as if that were a *good thing*.'

'Five times I have been under siege, and always quite relished the experience. It has a wonderful way of limiting the options. Of freeing the mind.' Cosca took a long breath in through his nose and blew it happily out. 'When life is a cell, there is nothing more liberating than captivity.'

The Forlorn Hope

Fire.

Visserine by night had become a place of flame and shadow. An endless maze of broken walls, fallen roofs, jutting rafters. A nightmare of disembodied cries, ghostly shapes flitting through the darkness. Buildings loomed, gutted shells, the eyeless gaps of window and doorway screaming open, fire spurting out, licking through, tickling at the darkness. Charred beams stabbed at the flames and they stabbed back. Showers of white sparks climbed into the black skies, and a black snow of ash fell softly the other way. The city had new towers now, crooked towers of smoke, glowing with the light of the fires that gave them birth, smudging out the stars.

'How many did we get the last time?' Cosca's eyes gleamed yellow from the flames across the square. 'Three was it?'

'Three,' croaked Friendly. They were safe in the chest in his room: the armour of two Talinese soldiers, one with the square hole left by a flatbow bolt, and the uniform of a slight young lieutenant he had found crushed under a fallen chimney. Bad luck for him, but then Friendly supposed it was his side throwing the fire everywhere.

They had catapults beyond the walls, five on the west side of the river, and three on the east. They had catapults on the twenty-two white-sailed ships in the harbour. The first night, Friendly had stayed up until dawn watching them. They had thrown one hundred and eighteen burning missiles over the walls, scattering fires about the city. Fires shifted, and burned out, and split, and merged one with another, and so they could not be counted. The numbers had deserted Friendly, and left him alone and afraid. It had taken but six short days, three nights times two, for peaceful Visserine to turn to this.

The only part of the city untouched was the island on which

Duke Salier's palace stood. There were paintings there, Murcatto said, and other pretty things that Ganmark, the leader of Orso's army, the man they were here to kill, wished to save. He would burn countless houses, and countless people in them, and order murder night and day, but these dead things of paint had to be protected. Friendly thought this was a man who should be put in Safety, so that the world outside could be a safer place. But instead he was obeyed, and admired, and the world burned. It seemed all turned around, all wrong. But then Friendly could not tell right from wrong, the judges had told him so.

'You ready?'

'Yes,' lied Friendly.

Cosca flashed a crazy grin. 'Then to the breach, dear friend, once more!' And he trotted off down the street, one hand on the hilt of his sword, the other clasping his hat to his head. Friendly swallowed, then followed, lips moving silently as he counted the steps he took. He had to count something other than the ways he could die.

It only grew worse the closer they got to the city's western edge. The fires rose up in terrible magnificence, creaking and roaring, towering devils, gnawing at the night. They burned Friendly's eyes and made them weep. Or perhaps he wept anyway, to see the waste of it. If you wanted a thing, why burn it? And if you did not want it, why fight to take it from someone else? Men died in Safety. They died there all the time. But there was no waste like this. There was not enough there to risk destroying what there was. Each thing was valued.

'Bloody Gurkish fire!' Cosca cursed as they gave another roaring blaze a wide berth. 'Ten years ago no one had dreamed of using that stuff as a weapon. Then they made Dagoska an ash-heap with it, knocked holes in the walls of the Agriont with it. Now no sooner does a siege begin than everyone's clamouring to blow things up. We liked to torch a building or two in my day, just to get things moving, but nothing like this. War used to be about making money. Some degree of modest misery was a regrettable side effect. Now it's just about destroying things, and the more thoroughly the better. Science, my friend, science. Supposed to make life easier, I thought.'

Lines of sooty soldiers tramped by, armour gleaming orange

with reflected flames. Lines of sooty civilians passed buckets of water from hand to hand, desperate faces half-lit by the glow of unquenchable fires. Angry ghosts, black shapes in the sweltering night. Behind them, a great mural on a shattered wall. Duke Salier in full armour, sternly pointing the way to victory. He had been holding a flag, Friendly thought, but the top part of the building had collapsed, and his raised arm along with it. Dancing flames made it look as if his painted face was twitching, as if his painted mouth was moving, as if the painted soldiers around him were charging onwards to the breach.

When Friendly was young, there had been an old man in the twelfth cell on his corridor who had told tales of long ago. Tales of the time before the Old Time, when this world and the world below were one, and devils roamed the earth. The inmates had laughed at that old man, and Friendly had laughed at him too, since it was wise in Safety to do just as others did and never to stand out. But he had gone back when no one else was near, to ask how many years, exactly, it had been since the gates were sealed and Euz shut the devils out of the world. The old man had not known the number. Now it seemed the world below had broken through the gates between again, flooding out into Visserine, chaos spreading with it.

They hurried past a tower in flames, fire flickering in its windows, pluming up from its broken roof like a giant's torch. Friendly sweated, coughed, sweated more. His mouth was endlessly dry, his throat endlessly rough, his fingertips chalky with soot. He saw the toothed outline of the city's walls at the end of a street strangled with rubble.

'We're getting close! Stay with me!'

'I . . . I . . .' Friendly's voice croaked to nothing on the smoky air. He could hear a noise, now, as they sidled down a narrow alley, red light flickering at its end. A clattering and clashing, a surging tide of furious voices. A noise like the great riot had made in Safety, before the six most feared convicts, Friendly among them, had agreed to put a stop to the madness. Who would stop the madness here? There was a boom that made the earth shudder, and a ruddy glare lit the night sky.

Cosca slipped up to the trunk of a scorched tree, keeping low, and crouched against it. The noise grew louder as Friendly crept after, terribly loud, but his heart pounding in his ears almost drowned it out.

The breach was no more than a hundred strides off, a ragged black patch of night torn from the city wall and clogged with heaving Talinese troops. They crawled like ants over the nightmare of fallen masonry and broken timbers that formed a ragged ramp down into a burned-out square at the city's edge. There might have been an orderly battle when the first assault came, but now it had dissolved into a shapeless, furious mêlée, defenders crowding in from barricades thrown up before the gutted buildings, attackers fumbling their way on, on through the breach, adding their mindless weight to the fight, their breathless corpses to the carnage.

Axe and sword blades flashed and glinted, pikes and spears waved and tangled, a torn flag or two hung limp over the press. Arrows and bolts flitted up and down, from the Talinese crowding outside the walls, from defenders at their barricades, from a crumbling tower beside the breach. While Friendly watched, a great chunk of masonry was sent spinning down from the top of the wall and into the boiling mass below, tearing a yawning hole through them. Hundreds of men, struggling and dying by the hellish glare of burning torches, of burning missiles, of burning houses. Friendly could hardly believe it was real. It all looked false, fake, a model staged for a lurid painting.

'The breach at Visserine,' he whispered to himself, framing the scene with his hands and imagining it hanging on some rich man's wall.

When two men set out to kill each other, there is a pattern to it. A few men, for that matter. A dozen, even. With a situation like that, Friendly had always been entirely comfortable. There is a form to be followed, and by being faster, stronger, sharper, you can come out alive. But this was otherwise. The mindless press. Who could know when you would be pushed, by the simple pressure of those behind, onto a pike? The awful randomness. How could you predict an arrow, or a bolt, or a falling rock from above? How could you see death coming, and how could you avoid it? It was one colossal game of chance with your life as the stake. And like the games of chance at Cardotti's House of Leisure, in the long run, the players could only lose.

'Looks like a hot one!' Cosca screamed in his ear.

'Hot?'

'I've been in hotter! The breach at Muris looked like a slaughter yard when we were done!'

Friendly could hardly bring himself to speak, his head was spinning so much. 'You've been . . . in that?'

Cosca waved a dismissive hand. 'A few times. But unless you're mad you soon tire of it. Looks like fun, maybe, but it's no place for a gentleman.'

'How do they know who's on whose side?' hissed Friendly.

Cosca's grin gleamed in his soot-smeared face. 'Guesswork, mostly. You just try to stay pointed in the right direction and hope for the . . . ah.'

A fragment had broken from the general mêlée and was flowing forwards, bristling with weapons. Friendly could not even tell whether they were the besiegers or the besieged, they hardly seemed like men at all. He turned to see a wall of spears advancing down the street from the opposite direction, shifting light gleaming on dull metal, across stony faces. Not individual men, but a machine for killing.

'This way!' Friendly felt a hand grab his arm, shove him through a broken doorway in a tottering piece of wall. He stumbled and slipped, pitched over on his side. He half-ran, half-slid down a great heap of rubble, through a cloud of choking ash, and lay on his belly beside Cosca, staring up towards the combat in the street above. Men crashed together, killed and died, a formless soup of rage. Over their screams, their bellows of anger, the clash and squeal of metal, Friendly could hear something else. He stared sideways. Cosca was bent over on his knees, shaking with ill-suppressed mirth.

'Are you laughing?'

The old mercenary wiped his eyes with a sooty finger. 'What's the alternative?'

They were in a kind of darkened valley, choked with rubble. A street? A drained canal? A sewer? Ragged people picked through the rubbish. Not far away a dead man lay face down. A woman crouched over the corpse with a knife out, in the midst of cutting the fingers from one limp hand for his rings.

'Away from that body!' Cosca lurched up, drawing his sword.

'This is ours!' A scrawny man with tangled hair and a club in his hand.

'No.' Cosca brandished the blade. 'This is ours.' He took a step forwards and the scavenger stumbled back, falling through a scorched bush. The woman finally got through the bone with her knife, pulled the ring off and stuffed it in her pocket, flung the finger at Cosca along with a volley of abuse, then scuttled off into the darkness.

The old mercenary peered after them, weighing his sword in his hand. 'He's Talinese. His gear, then!'

Friendly crept numbly over and began to unbuckle the dead man's armour. He pulled the backplate away and slid it into his sack.

'Swiftly, my friend, before those sewer rats return.'

Friendly had no mind to delay, but his hands were shaking. He was not sure why. They did not normally shake. He pulled the soldier's greaves off, and his breastplate, rattling into the sack with the rest. Four sets, this would be. Three plus one. Three more and they would have one each. Then perhaps they could kill Ganmark, and be done, and he could go back to Talins, and sit in Sajaam's place, counting the coins in the card game. What happy times those seemed now. He reached out and snapped off the flatbow bolt in the man's neck.

'Help me.' Hardly more than a whisper. Friendly wondered if he had imagined it. Then he saw the soldier's eyes were wide open. His lips moved again. 'Help me.'

'How?' whispered Friendly. He undid the hooks and eyes on the man's padded jacket and, as gently as he could, stripped it from him, dragging the sleeve carefully over the oozing stumps of his severed fingers. He stuffed his clothes into the sack, then gently rolled him back over onto his face, just as he had found him.

'Good!' Cosca pointed towards a burned-out tower leaning precariously over a collapsed roof. 'That way, maybe?'

'Why that way?'

'Why not that way?'

Friendly could not move. His knees were trembling. 'I don't want to go.'

'Understandable, but we should stay together.' The old

mercenary turned and Friendly caught his arm, words starting to burble out of his mouth.

'I'm losing count! I can't . . . I can't think. What number are we up to, now? What . . . what . . . have I gone mad?'

'You? No, my friend.' Cosca was smiling as he clapped his hand down on Friendly's shoulder. 'You are entirely sane. This. All this!' He swept his hat off and waved it wildly around. 'This is insanity!'

Mercy and Cowardice

Shivers stood at the window, one half open and the other closed, the frame around him like the frame around a painting, watching Visserine burn. There was an orange edge to his black outline from the fires out towards the city walls – down the side of his stubbly face, one heavy shoulder, one long arm, the twist of muscle at his waist and the hollow in the side of his bare arse.

If Benna had been there he'd have warned her she was taking some long chances, lately. Well, first he'd have asked who the big naked Northman was, then he'd have warned her. Putting herself in the middle of a siege, death so close she could feel it tickling at her neck. Letting her guard down even this much with a man she was meant to be paying, walking the soft line with those farmers downstairs. She was taking risks, and she felt that tingling mix of fear and excitement that a gambler can't do without. Benna wouldn't have liked it. But then she'd never listened to his warnings when he was alive. If the odds stand long against you, you have to take long chances, and Monza had always had a knack for picking the right ones.

Up until they killed Benna and threw her down the mountain, at least.

Shivers' voice came out of the darkness. 'How'd you come by this place, anyway?'

'My brother bought it. Long time ago.' She remembered him standing at the window, squinting into the sun, turning to her and smiling. She felt a grin tug at the corner of her own mouth, just for a moment.

Shivers didn't turn, now, and he didn't smile either. 'You were close, eh? You and your brother.'

'We were close.'

'Me and my brother were close. Everyone that knew him felt

close to him. He had that trick. He got killed, by a man called the Bloody-Nine. He got killed when he'd been promised mercy, and his head nailed to a standard.'

Monza didn't much care for this story. On the one hand it was boring her, on the other it was making her think of Benna's slack face as they tipped him over the parapet. 'Who'd have thought we had so much in common? Did you take revenge?'

'I dreamed of it. My fondest wish, for years. I had the chance, more'n once. Vengeance on the Bloody-Nine. Something a lot of men would kill for.'

'And?'

She saw the muscles working on the side of Shivers' head. 'The first time I saved his life. The second I let him go, and chose to be a better man.'

'And you've been wandering round like a tinker with his cart ever since, pedalling mercy to anyone who'll take? Thanks for the offer, but I'm not buying.'

'Not sure I'm selling any more. I been acting the good man all this time, talking up the righteous path, hoping to convince myself I done the right thing walking away. Breaking the circle. But I didn't, and that's a fact. Mercy and cowardice are the same, just like you told me, and the circle keeps turning, whatever you try. Taking vengeance . . . it might not answer no questions. It sure won't make the world a fairer place or the sun shine warmer. But it's better'n not taking it. It's a damn stretch better.'

'I thought you were all set on being Styria's last good man.'

'I've tried to do the right thing when I could, but you don't get a name in the North without doing some dark work, and I done my share. I fought beside Black Dow, and Crummock-i-Phail, and the Bloody-Nine his self, for that matter.' He gave a snort. 'You think you got cold hearts down here? You should taste the winters where I come from.' There was something in the set of his face she hadn't seen before, and hadn't expected to. 'I'd like to be a good man, that's true. But you need it the other way, then I know how.'

There was silence for a moment, while they looked at each other. Him leaning against the window frame, her sprawled on the bed with one hand behind her head.

'If you really are such a snow-hearted bastard, why did you come back for me? In Cardotti's?'

'You still owe me money.'

She wasn't sure if he was joking. 'I feel warm all over.'

'That and you're about the best friend I've got in this mad fucking country.'

'And I don't even like you.'

'I'm still hoping you'll warm to me.'

'You know what? I might just be getting there.'

She could see his grin in the light from beyond the window. 'Letting me in your bed. Letting Furli and the rest stay in your house. If I didn't know better I'd be thinking I'd pedalled you some mercy after all.'

She stretched out. 'Maybe beneath this harsh yet beautiful shell I'm really still a soft-hearted farmer's daughter, only wanting to do good. You think of that?'

'Can't say I did.'

'Anyway, what's my choice? Put them out on the street, they might start talking. Safer here, where they owe us something.'

'They're safest of all in the mud.'

'Why don't you go downstairs and put all our minds at rest, then, killer? Shouldn't be a problem for the hero that used to carry Black Now's luggage.'

'Dow.'

'Whoever. Best put some trousers on first, though, eh?'

'I'm not saying we should've killed 'em or nothing, I'm just pointing out the fact. Mercy and cowardice are the same, I heard.'

'I'll do what needs doing, don't worry. I always have. But I'm not Morveer. I'm not murdering eleven farmers just for my convenience.'

'Nice to hear, I guess. All those little people dying in the bank didn't seem to bother you none, long as one of 'em was Mauthis.'

She frowned. 'That wasn't the plan.'

'Nor the folk at Cardotti's.'

'Cardotti's didn't go quite the way I had in mind either, in case you didn't notice.'

'I noticed pretty good. The Butcher of Caprile, they call you, no? What happened there?'

'What needed doing.' She remembered riding up in the dusk, the stab of worry as she saw the smoke over the city. 'Doing it and liking it are different things.'

'Same results, no?'

'What the hell would you know about it? I don't remember you being there.' She shook the memory off and slid from the bed. The careless warmth of the last smoke was wearing through and she felt strangely awkward in her own scarred skin, crossing the room with his eyes on her, stark naked but for the glove still on her right hand. The city, and its towers, and its fires spread out beyond the window, blurred through the bubbly glass panes in the closed half. 'I didn't bring you up here to remind me of my mistakes. I've made enough of the bastards.'

'Who hasn't? Why did you bring me up here?'

'Because I've an awful weakness for big men with tiny minds, what do you think?'

'Oh, I try not to think much, makes my tiny mind hurt. But I'm starting to get the feeling you might not be quite so hard as you make out.'

'Who is?' She reached out and touched the scar on his chest. Fingertip trailing through hair, over rough, puckered skin.

'We've all got our wounds, I guess.' He slid his hand down the long scar on her hip bone, and her stomach clenched up tight. That gambler's mix of fear and excitement still, with a trace of disgust mixed in.

'Some worse than others.' The words sour in her mouth.

'Just marks.' His thumb slid across the scars on her ribs, one by one. 'They don't bother me any.'

She pulled the glove off her crooked right hand and stuck it in his face. 'No?'

'No.' His big hands closed gently around her ruined one, warm and tight. She stiffened up at first, almost dragged it away, breath catching with ugly shock, as if she'd caught him caressing a corpse. Then his thumbs started to rub at her twisted palm, at the aching ball of her thumb, at her crooked fingers, all the way to the tips. Surprisingly tender. Surprisingly pleasant. She let her eyes close and her mouth open, stretched her fingers out as wide as they'd go, and breathed.

She felt him closer, the warmth of him, his breath on her face.

Not much chance to wash lately and he had a smell – sweat and leather and a hint of bad meat. Sharp, but not entirely unpleasant. She knew she had a smell herself. His face brushed hers, rough cheek, hard jaw, nudging against her nose, nuzzling at her neck. She was half-smiling, skin tingling in the draught from the window, carrying that familiar tickle of burning buildings to her nose.

One of his hands still held hers, out to the side now, the other slid up her flank, over the knobble of her hip bone, slid under her breast, thumb rubbing back and forth over her nipple, slightly pleasant, slightly clumsy. Her free hand brushed against his cock, already good and hard, up, and down, damp skin sticky on her palm. She lifted one foot, heel scraping loose plaster from the wall, wedged it on the windowsill so her legs were spread wide. His fingers slid back and forth between them with a soft squelch, squelch.

Her right hand was round under his jaw, twisted fingers pulling at his ear, turning his head sideways, thumb dragging his mouth open so she could push her tongue into it. It tasted of the cheap wine they'd been drinking, but hers probably did too, and who cared a shit anyway?

She drew him close, pressing up against him, skin sliding against skin. Not thinking about her dead brother, not thinking about her crippled hand, not thinking about the war outside, or needing a smoke, or the men she had to kill. Just his fingers and her fingers, his cock and her cunt. Not much, maybe, but something, and she needed something.

'Get on and fuck me,' she hissed in his ear.

'Right,' he croaked at her, hooked her under one knee, lifted her to the bed and dumped her on her back, frame creaking. She wriggled away, making room, and he knelt down between her open knees, working his way forwards, fierce grin on his face as he looked down at her. Same grin she had, keen to get on with it. She felt the end of his cock sliding around between her thighs, one side, then the other. 'Where the fuck . . .'

'Bloody Northmen, couldn't find your arse with a chair.'

'My arse ain't the hole I'm looking for.'

'Here.' She dragged some spit off her tongue with her fingers, propped herself up on one elbow, reached down and took hold of him, working his cock around until she found the spot.

'Ah.'

'Ah,' she grunted back. 'That's it.'

'Aye.' He moved his hips in circles, easing deeper with each one. 'That . . . is . . . it.' He ran his hands up her thighs, fingers into the short hair, started rubbing at her with his thumb.

'Gently!' She slapped his hand away and slid her own down in its place, middle finger working slowly round and round. 'You're not trying to crack a nut, fool.'

'Your nut, your business, I reckon.' His cock slid out as he worked his way forwards, onto his arms above her, but she slid it back in easy enough. They started finding a rhythm, patient but building, bit by bit.

She kept her eyes open, looking in his face, and she could see the gleam of his in the darkness looking back. Both of them with teeth bared, breathing hard. He opened his mouth to meet hers, then moved his head away as she craned up to kiss him, always just out of reach until she had to slump back flat with a gasp that sent a warm shiver through her.

She slid her right hand onto his backside, squeezing at one buttock as it tensed and relaxed, tensed and relaxed. Faster now, damp skin slap-slapping, and she pushed her twisted hand round further, down into the crack of his arse. She strained her head up off the bed again, biting at his lips, at his teeth, and he nipped at her, grunting in his throat and her grunting back. He came down onto one elbow, his other hand sliding up over her ribs, squeezing hard at one breast then the other, almost painful.

Creak, creak, creak, and her feet were off the bed and in the air, his hand tangled in her hair, fingers rubbing at the coins under her skin, dragging her head back, her face up against his, and she sucked his tongue out of his mouth and into hers, bit at it, licked at it. Deep, slobbery, hungry, snarling kisses. Hardly kisses at all. She pushed her finger into his arsehole, up to the first knuckle.

'What the fuck?' He broke clear of her as if she'd slapped him in the face, stopped moving, still and tense above her. She jerked her right hand back, left still busy between her legs.

'Alright,' she hissed. 'Doesn't make you less of a man, you know. Your arse, your business. I'll keep clear of it in—'

'Not that. D'you hear something?'

Monza couldn't hear anything but her own fast breath and the faint sound of her fingers still sliding wetly up and down. She pushed her hips back up against him. 'Come on. There's nothing but—'

The door crashed open, wood flying from the splintered lock. Shivers scrambled from the bed, tangled with the blanket. Monza was dazzled by lamplight, caught a glimpse of bright metal, armour, a shout and a sword swung.

There was a metallic thud, Shivers gave a squawk and went down hard on the boards. Monza felt spots of blood patter on her cheek. She had the hilt of the Calvez in her hand. Right hand, stupidly, by force of habit, blade a few inches drawn.

'No you don't.' A woman coming through the ruins of the door, loaded flatbow levelled, hair scraped back from a soft-looking round face. A man turned from standing over Shivers and towards Monza, sword in hand. She could scarcely see more of him than the outline of his armour, his helmet. Another soldier stomped through the door, lantern in one fist and an axe in the other, curved blade gleaming. Monza let her twisted fingers open and the Calvez clattered down beside the bed half-drawn.

'That's better,' said the woman.

Shivers gave a groan, tried to push himself up, eyes narrowed against the light, blood trickling down his face from a cut in his hair. Must have been clubbed with the flat. The one with the axe stepped forwards and swung a boot into his ribs, thud, thud, made him grunt, curled up naked against the wall. A fourth soldier walked in, some dark cloth over one arm.

'Captain Langrier.'

'What did you find?' asked the woman, handing him the flatbow.

'This, and some others.'

'Looks like a Talinese uniform.' She held the jacket up so Monza could see it. 'Got anything to say about this?'

The jolt of cold shock was fading, and an even frostier fear was pressing in fast behind it. These were Salier's soldiers. She'd been so fixed on killing Ganmark, so fixed on Orso's army, she hadn't spared a thought for the other side. They'd got her attention now, alright. She felt a sudden need for another smoke, so bad she was nearly sick. 'It's not what you think,' she managed to croak out, acutely aware she was stark naked and smelled sharply of fucking.

'How do you know what I think?'

Another soldier with a big drooping moustache appeared in the doorway. 'A load of bottles and suchlike in one of the rooms. Didn't fancy touching 'em. Looked like poison to me.'

'Poison, you say, Sergeant Pello?' Langrier stretched her head to one side and rubbed at her neck. 'Well, that is damn suspicious.'

'I can explain it.' Monza's mouth was dry. She knew she couldn't. Not in any way these bastards would believe.

'You'll get your chance. Back at the palace, though. Bind 'em up.'

Shivers grimaced as the axeman dragged his wrists behind his back and snapped manacles shut on them, hauled him to his feet. One of the others grabbed Monza's arm, twisted it roughly behind her as he jammed the cuffs on.

'Ah! Mind my hand!' One of them dragged her off the bed, shoved her stumbling towards the door and she nearly slipped, getting her balance back without much dignity. There wasn't much dignity to be had in all of this. Benna's little glass statue watched from its niche. So much for household spirits. 'Can we get some clothes at least?'

'I don't see why.' They hauled her out onto the landing, into the light of another lantern. 'Wait there.' Langrier squatted down, frowning at the zigzag scars on Monza's hip and along her thigh, neat pink dots of the pulled stitches almost faded. She prodded at them with one thumb as though she was checking a joint of meat in a butcher's for rot. 'You ever seen marks like that before, Pello?'

'No.'

She looked up at Monza. 'How did you get these?'

'I was shaving my cunt and the razor slipped.'

The woman spluttered with laughter. 'I like that. That's funny.'

Pello was laughing too. 'That is funny.'

'Good thing you've got a sense of humour.' Langrier stood up, brushing dust from her knees. 'You'll need that later.' She thumped Monza on the side of the head with an open hand and sent her tumbling down the stairs. She fell on her shoulder with a jarring impact, the steps battered her back, skinned her knees, her legs went flying over. She squealed and grunted as the wood drove the air out of her, then the wall cracked her in the nose and knocked her sprawling, one leg buckled against the plaster. She lifted her head, groggy as a drunkard, the stairway still reeling. Her mouth tasted of blood. She spat it out. It filled up again.

'Fuh,' she grunted.

'No more jokes? We've got a few more flights if you're still' feeling witty.'

She wasn't. She let herself be dragged up, grunting as pain ground at her battered shoulder-joint.

'What's this?' She felt the ring pulled roughly off her middle finger, saw Langrier smiling as she held her hand up to the light, ruby glinting.

'Looks good on you,' said Pello. Monza kept her silence. If the worst she lost out of this was Benna's ring, she'd count herself lucky indeed.

There were more soldiers on the floors below, rooting through the tower, dragging gear from the chests and boxes. Glass crunched and tinkled as they upended one of Morveer's cases onto the floor. Day was sitting on a bed nearby, yellow hair hanging over her face, hands bound behind her. Monza met her eye for a moment, and they stared at each other, but there wasn't much pity to spare. At least she'd been lucky enough to have her shift on when they came.

They shoved Monza down into the kitchen and she leaned against the wall, breathing fast, stark naked but past caring. Furli was down there, and his brother too. Langrier walked over to them and pulled a purse from her back pocket.

'Looks like you were right. Spies.' She counted coins out into the farmer's waiting palm. 'Five scales for each of them. Duke Salier thanks you for your diligence, citizen. You say there were more?'

'Four others.'

'We'll keep a watch on the tower and pick them up later. You'd better find somewhere else for your family.'

Monza watched Furli take the money, licking at the blood running out of her nose and thinking this was where charity got you. Sold for five scales. Benna would probably have been upset by the size of the bounty, but she had far bigger worries. The farmer gave her a last look as they dragged her stumbling out through the door. There was no guilt in his eyes. Maybe he felt he'd done the best thing for his family, in the midst of a war. Maybe he was proud that he'd had the courage to do it. Maybe he was right to be.

Seemed it was as true now as it had been when Verturio wrote the words. *Mercy and cowardice are the same.*

The Odd Couple

It was Morveer's considered opinion that he was spending entirely too much of his time in lofts, of late. It did not help in the slightest that this one was exposed to the elements. Large sections of the roof of the ruined house were missing, and the wind blew chill into his face. It reminded him most unpleasingly of that crisp spring night, long ago, when two of the prettiest and most popular girls had lured him onto the roof of the orphanage then locked him up there in his nightshirt. He was found in the morning, grey-lipped and shivering, close to having frozen to death. How they had all laughed.

The company was far from warming him. Shylo Vitari crouched in the darkness, her head a spiky outline with the night sky behind, one eye shut, her eyeglass to the other. Behind them in the city, fires burned. War might be good for a poisoner's business, but Morveer had always preferred to keep it at arm's length. Considerably beyond, in fact. A city under siege was no place for a civilised man. He missed his orchard. He missed his good goose-down mattress. He attempted to shift the collars of his coat even higher around his ears, and transferred his attention once again to the palace of Grand Duke Salier, brooding on its long island in the midst of the fast-flowing Visser.

'Why ever a man of my talents should be called upon to survey a scene of this nature is entirely beyond me. I am no general.'

'Oh no. You're a murderer on a much smaller scale.'

Morveer frowned sideways. 'As are you.'

'Surely, but I'm not the one complaining.'

'I resent being dropped into the centre of a war.'

'It's Styria. It's spring. Of course there's a war. Let's just come up with a plan and get back out of the night.'

'Huh. Back to Murcatto's charitable institution for the

housing of displaced agricultural workers, do you mean? The stench of self-righteous hypocrisy in that place causes my bile to rise.'

Vitari blew into her cupped hands. 'Better than out here.'

'Is it? Downstairs, the farmer's brats wail into the night. Upstairs, our employer's profoundly unsubtle erotic adventures with our barbarian companion keep the floorboards groaning at all hours. I ask you, is there anything more unsettling than the sound of other . . . people . . . *fucking*?'

Vitari grinned. 'You've got a point there. They'll have that floor in before they're done.'

'They'll have my skull in before that. I ask you, is an iota of professionalism too much to ask for?'

'Long as she's paying, who cares?'

'I care if her carelessness leads to my untimely demise, but I suppose we must make do.'

'Less whining and more work, then, maybe? A way in.'

'A way in, because the noble leaders of Styrian cities are trusting folk, always willing to welcome uninvited guests into their places of residence . . .'

Morveer moved his eyeglass carefully across the front of the sprawling building, rising up sheer from the frothing waters of the river. For the home of a renowned aesthete, it was an edifice of minimal architectural merit. A confusion of ill-matched styles awkwardly mashed together into a jumble of roofs, turrets, cupolas, domes and dormers, its single tower thrusting up into the heavens. The gatehouse was comprehensively fortified, complete with arrow loops, bartizans, machicolations and gilded portcullis facing the bridge into the city. A detachment of fifteen soldiers were gathered there in full armour.

'The gate is far too well guarded, the front elevation far too visible to climb, either to roof or window.'

'Agreed. The only spot we'd have a chance of getting in without being seen is the north wall.'

Morveer swung his eyeglass towards the narrow northern face of the building, a sheer expanse of mossy grey stone pierced by darkened stained-glass windows and with a begargoyled parapet above. Had the palace been a ship sailing upriver, that would have been its prow, and fast-flowing water foamed with particular energy around its sloping base. 'Unobserved, perhaps, but also the most difficult to reach.'

'Scared?' Morveer lowered his eyeglass with some irritation to see Vitari grinning at him.

'Let us say rather that I am dubious as to our chances of success. Though I confess I feel some warmth at the prospect of your *plunging* from a rope into the frothing river, I am far from attracted by the prospect of following you.'

'Why not just say you're scared?'

Morveer refused to rise to such ham-fisted taunting. It had not worked in the orphanage; it would most certainly not work now. 'We would require a boat, of course.'

'Shouldn't be too hard to find something upriver.'

He pursed his lips as he weighed the benefits. 'The plan would have the added advantage of providing a means of egress, an aspect of the venture by which Murcatto seems decidedly untroubled. Once Ganmark has been put paid to, we might hope to reach the roof, still disguised, and back down the rope to the boat. Then we could simply float out to sea and—'

'Look at that.' Vitari pointed at a group moving briskly along the street below, and Morveer trained his eyeglass upon them. Perhaps a dozen armoured soldiers marched on either side of two stumbling figures, entirely naked, hands bound behind them. A woman and a large man.

'Looks like they've caught some spies,' said Vitari. 'Bad luck for them.'

One of the soldiers jabbed the man with the butt of his spear and knocked him over in the road, bare rump sticking into the air. Morveer chuckled. 'Oh yes, indeed, even among Styrian prisons, the dungeons beneath Salier's palace enjoy a black reputation.' He frowned through the eyeglass. 'Wait, though. The woman looks like—'

'Murcatto. It's fucking them!'

'Can nothing run smoothly?' Morveer felt a mounting sense of horror he had in no way expected. Stumbling along at the back in her nightshirt, hands bound behind her, was Day. 'Curse it all! They have my assistant!'

'Piss on your assistant. They have our employer! That means they have my pay!'

Morveer could do nothing but grind his teeth as the prisoners were herded across the bridge and into the palace, the heavy gates tightly sealed behind them. 'Damn it! The tower-house is no longer safe! We cannot return there!'

'An hour ago you couldn't stand the thought of going back to that den of hypocrisy and erotic adventure.'

'But my equipment is there!'

'I doubt it.' Vitari nodded her spiky head towards the palace. 'It'll be with all the boxes they carried in there.'

Morveer slapped petulantly at the bare rafter by his head, winced as he took a splinter in his forefinger and was forced to suck it. 'Damn and shitting *blast*!'

'Calm, Morveer, calm.'

'I am calm!' The sensible thing to do was undeniably to find a boat, to float silently up to Duke Salier's palace, then past it and out to sea, writing off his losses, return to the orchard and train another assistant, leaving Murcatto and her imbecile Northman to reap the consequences of their stupidity. Caution first, always, but . . .

'I cannot leave my assistant behind in there,' he barked. 'I simply *cannot*!'

'Why?'

'Well, because . . .' He was not sure why. 'I *flatly* refuse to go through the trouble of instructing another!'

Vitari's irritating grin had grown wider. 'Fine. You need your girl and I need my money. You want to cry about it or work on a way in? I still say boat down the river to the north wall, then rope and grapple to the roof.'

Morveer squinted unhopefully towards the sheer stonework. 'You can truthfully secure a grapple up there?'

'I could get a grapple through a fly's arse. It's you getting the boat into position that worries me.'

He was not about to be outdone. 'I challenge you to find a more accomplished oarsman! I could hold a boat steady in a deluge twice as fierce, but it will not be needful. I can drive a hook into that stonework and anchor the boat against those rocks all night.'

'Good for you.'

'Good. Excellent.' His heart was beating with considerable

urgency at the argument. He might not have liked the woman, but her competence was in no doubt. Given the circumstances he could not have selected a more suitable companion. A most handsome woman, too, in her own way, and no doubt every bit as firm a disciplinarian as the sternest nurse at the orphanage had been . . .

Her eyes narrowed. 'I hope you're not going to make the same suggestion you made last time we worked together.'

Morveer bristled. 'There will be no repetition of that *whatsoever*, I can assure you!'

'Good. Because I'd still rather fuck a hedgehog.'

'You made your preferences *quite* clear on that occasion!' he answered shrilly, then moved with all despatch to shift the topic. 'There is no purpose in delay. Let us find a vessel appropriate to our needs.' He took one last look down as he slithered back into the attic, and paused. 'Who's this now?' A single figure was striding boldly towards the palace gates. Morveer felt his heart sink even lower. There was no mistaking the flamboyant gait. '*Cosca*. What ever is that horrible old drunkard about?'

'Who knows what goes through that scabby head?'

The mercenary strode towards the guards quite as if it was his palace rather than Duke Salier's, waving one arm. Morveer could just hear his voice in between the sighing of the wind, but had not the slightest notion of the words. 'What are they saying?'

'You can't read lips?' Vitari muttered.

'No.'

'Nice to find there's one subject you're not the world's greatest expert on. The guards are challenging him.'

'Of course!' That much was clear from the halberds lowered at Cosca's chest. The old mercenary swept off his hat and bowed low.

'He is replying . . . my name is Nicomo Cosca . . . famed soldier of fortune . . . and I am here . . .' She lowered the eyeglass, frowning.

'Yes?'

Vitari's eyes slid towards him. 'And I am here for dinner.'

Darkness

Utter dark. Monza opened her eyes wide, squinted and stared, and saw nothing but fizzing, tingling blackness. She wouldn't have been able to see her hand before her face. But she couldn't move her hand there anyway, or anywhere else.

They'd chained her to the ceiling by her wrists, to the floor by her ankles. If she hung limp, her feet just brushed the clammy stones. If she stretched up on tiptoe, she could ease the throbbing ache through her arms, through her ribs, through her sides, a merciful fraction. Soon her calves would start to burn, though, worse and worse until she had to ease back down, teeth gritted, and swing by her skinned wrists. It was agonising, humiliating, terrifying, but the worst of it was, she knew – this was as good as things were going to get.

She wasn't sure where Day was. Probably she'd blinked those big eyes, shed a single fat tear and said she knew nothing, and they'd believed her. She had the sort of face that people believed. Monza never had that sort of face. But then she probably didn't deserve one. Shivers was struggling somewhere in the inky black, metal clinking as he twisted at his chains, cursing in Northern, then Styrian. 'Fucking Styria. Fucking Vossula. Shit. Shit.'

'Stop!' she hissed at him. 'Might as well . . . I don't know . . . keep your strength.'

'Strength going to help us, you reckon?'

She swallowed. 'Couldn't hurt.' Couldn't help. Nothing could.

'By the dead, but I need to piss.'

'Piss, then,' she snapped into the darkness. 'What's the difference?

A grunt. The sound of liquid spattering against stone. She might've joined him if her bladder hadn't been knotted up tight with fear. She pushed up on her toes again, legs aching, wrists, arms, sides burning with every breath.

'You got a plan?' Shivers' words sank away and died on the buried air.

'What fucking plan do you think I'd have? They think we're spies in their city, working for the enemy. They're sure of it! They're going to try and get us to talk, and when we don't have anything to say they want to hear, they're going to fucking kill us!' An animal growl, more rattles. 'You think they didn't plan for you struggling?'

'What d'you want me to do?' His voice was strangled, shrill, as if he was on the verge of sobbing. 'Hang here and wait for them to start cutting us?'

'I . . .' She felt the unfamiliar thickness of tears at the back of her own throat. She didn't have the shadow of an idea of a way clear of this. Helpless. How could you get more helpless than chained up naked, deep underground, in the pitch darkness? 'I don't know,' she whispered. 'I don't know.'

There was the clatter of a lock turning and Monza jerked her head up, skin suddenly prickling. A door creaked open and light stabbed at her eyes. A figure came down stone steps, boots scraping, a torch flickering in his hand. Another came behind him.

'Let's see what we're doing, shall we?' A woman's voice. Langrier, the one who'd caught them in the first place. The one who'd knocked Monza down the stairs and taken her ring. The other one was Pello, with the moustache. They were both dressed like butchers, stained leather aprons and heavy gloves. Pello went around the room, lighting torches. They didn't need torches, they could've had lamps. But torches are that bit more sinister. As if, at that moment, Monza needed scaring. Light crept out across rough stone walls, slick with moisture, splattered with green moss. There were a couple of tables about, heavy cast-iron implements on them. Unsubtle-looking implements.

She'd felt better when it was dark.

Langrier bent over a brazier and got it lit, blowing patiently on the coals, orange glow flaring across her soft face with each breath.

Pello wrinkled his nose. 'Which one of you pissed?'

'Him,' said Langrier. 'But what's the difference?' Monza watched her slide a few lengths of iron into the furnace, and felt her throat close up tight. She looked sideways at Shivers, and he looked back at her, and said nothing. There was nothing to say. 'More than likely they'll both be pissing soon enough.'

'Alright for you, you don't have to mop it up.'

'I've mopped up worse.' She looked at Monza, and her eyes were bored. No hate in them. Not much of anything. 'Give them some water, Pello.'

The man offered a jug. She would've liked to spit in his face, scream obscenities, but she was thirsty, and it was no time for pride. So she opened her mouth and he stuck the spout in it, and she drank, and coughed, and drank, and water trickled down her neck and dripped to the cold flags between her bare feet.

Langrier watched her get her breath back. 'You see, we're just people, but I have to be honest, that's probably the last kindness you'll be getting out of us if you're not helpful.'

'It's a war, boy.' Pello offered the jug to Shivers. 'A war, and you're on the other side. We don't have the time to be gentle.'

'Just give us something,' said Langrier. 'Just a little something I can give to my colonel, then we can leave you be, for now, and we'll all be a lot happier.'

Monza looked her right in the eye, unwavering, and did her best to make her believe. 'We're not with Orso. The opposite. We're here—'

'You had his uniforms, didn't you?'

'Only so we could drop in with them if they broke into the city. We're here to kill Ganmark.'

'Orso's Union general?' Pello raised his brows at Langrier and she shrugged back.

'It's either what she said, or they're spies, working with the Talinese. Here to assassinate the duke, maybe. Now which of those seems the more likely?'

Pello sighed. 'We've been in this game a long time, and the obvious answer, nine times out of ten, is the right one.'

'Nine times out of ten.' Langrier spread her hands in apology. 'So you might have to do better than that.'

'I can't do any fucking better,' Monza hissed through gritted teeth, 'that's all I—'

Langrier's gloved fist thudded suddenly into her ribs. 'The truth!' Her other fist into Monza's other side. 'The truth!' A punch in the stomach. 'The truth! The truth! The truth!' She sprayed spit in Monza's face as she screamed it, knocking her back and forth, the sharp thumps and Monza's wheezing grunts echoing dully from the damp walls of the place.

She couldn't do any of the things her body desperately needed to do – bring her arms down, or fold up, or fall over, or breathe even. She was helpless as a carcass on a hook. When Langrier got tired of pounding the guts out of her she shuddered silently for a moment, eyes bulging, every muscle cramped up bursting tight, creaking back and forth by her wrists. Then she coughed watery puke into her armpit, heaved half a desperate, moaning breath in and drooled out some more. She dropped limp as a wet sheet on a drying line, hair tangled across her face, heard that she was whimpering like a beaten dog with every shallow breath but couldn't stop it and didn't care.

She heard Langrier's boots scraping over to Shivers. 'So she's a fucking idiot, that's proven. Let's give you a chance, big man. I'll start with something simple. What's your name?'

'Caul Shivers,' voice high and tight with fear.

'Shivers.' Pello chuckled.

'Northerners. Who dreams up all these funny names? What about her?'

'Murcatto, she calls herself. Monzcarro Murcatto.' Monza slowly shook her head. Not because she blamed him for saying her name. Just because she knew the truth couldn't help.

'What do you know? The Butcher of Caprile herself in my little cell! Murcatto's dead, idiot, months ago, and I'm getting bored. You'd think none of us would ever die, the way you're wasting our time.'

'You reckon they're very stupid,' asked Pello, 'or very brave?'

'What's the difference?'

'You want to hold him?'

'You mind doing it?' Langrier winced as she worked one elbow around. 'Damn shoulder's aching today. Wet weather always gets it going.'

'You and your bloody shoulder.' Metal rattled as Pello let a stride of chain out through the pulley above and Shivers' hands dropped down around his head. Any relief he felt was short lived, though. Pello came up behind and kicked him in the back of his legs, sent him lurching onto his knees, arms stretched out again, kept him there by planting one boot on the back of his calves.

'Look!' It was cold but Shivers' face was all beaded up with sweat. 'We're not with Orso! I don't know nothing about his army. I just . . . I just don't know!'

'It's the truth,' Monza croaked, but so quiet no one could hear her. Even that started her coughing, each heave stabbing through her battered ribs.

Pello slid one arm around Shivers' head, elbow under his jaw, his other hand firm behind, tilting his face back.

'No!' squawked Shivers, the one bulging eye Monza could see rolling towards her. 'It was her! Murcatto! She hired me! To kill seven men! Vengeance, for her brother! And . . . and—'

'You've got him?' asked Langrier.

'I've got him.'

Shivers' voice rose higher. 'It was her! She wants to kill Duke Orso!' He was trembling now, teeth chattering together. 'We did Gobba, and a banker! A banker . . . called Mauthis! Poisoned him, and then . . . and then . . . Prince Ario, in Sipani! At Cardotti's! And now—'

Langrier stuck a battered wooden dowel between his jaws, putting a quick end to his wasted confession. 'Wouldn't want you to chew your tongue off. Still need you to tell me something worth hearing.'

'I've got money!' croaked Monza, her voice starting to come back.

'What?'

'I've got money! Gold! Boxes full of it! Not with me, but . . . Hermon's gold! Just—'

Langrier chuckled. 'You'd be amazed how everyone remembers buried treasure at a time like this. Doesn't often work out.'

Pello grinned. 'If I had just a tenth of what I've been promised in this room I'd be a rich man. I'm not, in case you're wondering.'

'But if you did have boxes full of gold, where the hell would I spend it now? You came a few weeks too late to bribe us. The Talinese are all around the city. Money's no use here.' Langrier

302

rubbed at her shoulder, winced, worked her arm in a circle, then dragged an iron from the brazier. It squealed out with the sound of metal on metal, sent up a drifting shower of orange sparks and a sick twist of fear through Monza's churning guts.

'It's true,' she whispered. 'It's true.' But all the strength had gone out of her.

' 'Course it is.' And Langrier stepped forwards and pressed the yellow-hot metal into Shivers' face. It made a sound like a slice of bacon dropped into a pan, but louder, and with his mindless, blubbering screech on top of it, of course. His back arched, his body thrashed and trembled like a fish on a line, but Pello kept his grip on him, grim-faced.

Greasy steam shot up, a little gout of flame that Langrier blew out with a practised puff of air through pursed lips, grinding the iron one way then the other, into his eye. While she did it, she had the same look she might have had wiping a table. A tedious, distasteful chore that had fallen to her and unfortunately had to be done.

The sizzling grew quieter. Shivers' scream had become a moaning hiss, the last air in his lungs being dragged out of him, spit spraying from his stretched-back lips, frothing from the wood between his bared teeth. Langrier stepped away. The iron had cooled to dark orange, smeared down one side with smoking black ash. She tossed it clattering back into the coals with some distaste.

Pello let go and Shivers' head dropped forwards, breath bubbling in his throat. Monza didn't know if he was awake or not, aware or not. She prayed not. The room smelled of charred meat. She couldn't look at his face. Couldn't look. Had to look. A glimpse of a great blackened stripe across his cheek and through his eye, raw-meat-red around it, bubbled and blistered, shining oily with fat cooked from his face. She jerked her eyes back to the floor, wide open, the air crawling in her throat, all her skin as clammy-cold as a corpse dragged from a river.

'There we go. Aren't we all better off for that, now? All so you could keep your secrets for a few minutes longer? What you won't tell us, we'll just get out of that little yellow-haired bitch later.' She waved a hand in front of her face. 'Damn, that stinks. Drop her down, Pello.'

The chains rattled and she went down. Couldn't stand, even. Too scared, too hurting. Her knees grazed the stone. Shivers' breath crackled. Langrier rubbed at her shoulder. Pello clicked his tongue softly as he made the chains fast. Monza felt the sole of his boot dig into the backs of her calves.

'Please,' she whispered, whole body shivering, teeth rattling. Monzcarro Murcatto, the dreaded Butcher of Caprile, the fearsome Serpent of Talins, that monster who'd washed herself in the Years of Blood, all that was a distant memory. 'Please.'

'You think we enjoy doing this? You think we wouldn't rather get on with people? I'm well liked mostly, aren't I, Pello?'

'Mostly.'

'For pity's sake, give me something I can use. Just tell me . . .' Langrier closed her eyes and rubbed at them with the back of her wrist. 'Just tell me who you get your orders from, at least. Let's just start with that.'

'Alright, alright!' Monza's eyes were stinging. 'I'll talk!' She could feel tears running down her face. 'I'm talking!' She wasn't sure what she was saying. 'Ganmark! Orso! Talins!' Gibberish. Nothing. Anything. 'I . . . I work for Ganmark!' Anything to keep the irons in the brazier for a few more moments. 'I take my orders from him!'

'From him directly?' Langrier frowned over at Pello, and he took a break from picking at the dry skin on one palm to frown back. 'Of course you do, and his Excellency Grand Duke Salier is constantly down here checking how we're getting along. Do you think I'm a fucking idiot?' She cuffed Monza across the face, one way and back the other, turned her mouth bloody and set her skin burning, made the room jerk and sway. 'You're making this up as you go along!'

Monza tried to shake the mud out of her head. 'Wha' d'you wan' me to tell you?' Words all mangled in her swollen mouth.

'Something that fucking helps me!'

Monza's bloody lip moved up and down, but nothing came out except a string of red drool. Lies were useless. The truth was useless. Pello's arm snaked around her head from behind, tight as a noose, dragged her face back towards the ceiling.

'No!' she squawked. 'No! N—' The piece of wood was wedged into her mouth, wet with Shivers' spit.

Langrier loomed into Monza's blurry vision, shaking one arm out. 'My damn shoulder! I swear I'm in more pain than anyone, but no one has mercy on me, do they?' She dragged a fresh iron clear of the coals, held it up, yellow-white, casting a faint glow across her face, making the beads of sweat on her forehead glisten. 'Is there anything more boring than other people's pain?'

She raised the iron, Monza's weeping eye jammed wide open and fixed on its white tip as it loomed towards her, fizzing ever so softly. The breath wheezed and shuddered in her throat. She could almost feel the heat from it on her cheek, almost feel the pain already. Langrier leaned forwards.

'Stop.' Out of the corner of her eye, she saw a blurry figure in the doorway. She blinked, eyelids fluttering. A great fat man, standing at the top of the steps in a white dressing gown.

'Your Excellency!' Langrier shoved the iron back into the brazier as though it was her it was burning. The grip round Monza's neck was suddenly released, Pello's boot came off the back of her calves.

Grand Duke Salier's eyes shifted slowly in his great expanse of pale face, from Monza, to Shivers, and back to Monza. 'Are these they?'

'Indeed they are.' Nicomo Cosca peered over the duke's shoulder and down into the room. Monza couldn't remember ever in her life being so glad to see someone. The old mercenary winced. 'Too late for the Northman's eye.'

'Early enough for his life, at least. But whatever have you done to her skin, Captain Langrier?'

'The scars she had already, your Excellency.'

'Truly? Quite the collection.' Salier slowly shook his head. 'A most regrettable case of mistaken identity. For the time being, these two people are my honoured guests. Some clothes for them, and do what you can for his wound.'

'Of course.' She snatched the dowel out of Monza's mouth and bowed her head. 'I deeply regret my mistake, your Excellency.'

'Quite understandable. This is war. People get burned.' The duke gave a long sigh. 'General Murcatto, I hope you will accept a bed in my palace, and join us for breakfast in the morning?'

The chains rattled free and her limp hands fell down into her lap. She thought she managed to gasp out a 'yes' before she started sobbing so hard she couldn't speak, tears running free down her face.

Terror, and pain, and immeasurable relief.

The Connoisseur

Anyone would have supposed it was an ordinary morning of peace and plenty in Duke Salier's expansive dining chamber, a room in which his Excellency no doubt spent much of his time. Four musicians struck up sweet music in a far-distant corner, all smiling radiantly, as though serenading the doomed in a palace surrounded by enemies was all they had ever wished for. The long table was stacked high with delicacies: fish and shellfish, breads and pastries, fruits and cheeses, sweets, meats and sweetmeats, all arranged as neatly on their gilded plates as medals on a general's chest. Too much food for twenty, and there were but three to dine, and two of those not hungry.

Monza did not look well. Both of her lips were split, her face was ashen in the centre, swollen and bruised shiny pink on both sides, the white of one eye red with bloodshot patches, fingers trembling. Cosca felt raw to look at her, but he supposed it might have been worse. Small help to their Northern friend. He could have sworn he could hear the groans through the walls all night long.

He reached out with his fork, ready to spear a sausage, well-cooked meat striped black from the grill. An image of Shivers' well-cooked, black-striped face drifted through his mind, and he cleared his throat and caught himself instead a hard-boiled egg. It was only when it was halfway to his plate that he noticed its similarity to an eyeball. He shook it hastily off his fork and into its dish with a rumbling of nausea, and contented himself with tea, silently pretending it was heavily laced with brandy.

Duke Salier was busy reminiscing on past glories, as men are prone to do when their glories are far behind them. One of Cosca's own favourite pastimes, and, if it was even a fraction as boring when he did it, he resolved to give it up. '. . . Ah, but the banquets I have held in this very room! The great men and women who have enjoyed my hospitality at this table! Rogont, Cantain, Sotorius, Orso himself, for that matter. I never trusted that weasel-faced liar, even back then.'

'The courtly dance of Styrian power,' said Cosca. 'Partners never stay together long.'

'Such is politics.' The roll of fat around Salier's jaw shifted softly as he shrugged. 'Ebb and flow. Yesterday's hero, tomorrow's villain. Yesterday's victory . . .' He frowned at his empty plate. 'I fear the two of you will be my last guests of note and, if you will forgive me, you both have seen more notable days. Still! One takes the guests one has, and makes the merry best of it!' Cosca gave a weary grin. Monza did not stretch herself even that far. 'No mood for levity? Anyone would think my city was on fire by your long faces! We will do no more good at the breakfast table, anyway. I swear I've eaten twice what the two of you have combined.' Cosca reflected that the duke undoubtedly weighed more than twice what the two of them did combined. Salier reached for a glass of white liquid and raised it to his lips.

'Whatever are you drinking?'

'Goat's milk. Somewhat sour, but wondrous for the digestion. Come, friends – and enemies, of course, for there is nothing more valuable to a powerful man than a good enemy – take a turn with me.' He struggled from his chair with much grunting, tossed his glass away and led them briskly across the tiled floor, one plump hand waving in time to the music. 'How is your companion, the Northman?'

'Still in very great pain,' murmured Monza, looking in some herself.

'Yes . . . well . . . a terrible business. Such is war, such is war. Captain Langrier tells me there were seven of you. The blonde woman with the child's face is with us, and your man, the quiet one who brought the Talinese uniforms and has apparently been counting every item in my larder since the crack of dawn this morning. One does not need his uncanny facility with numbers to note that two of your band are still . . . at large.'

'Our poisoner and our torturer,' said Cosca. 'A shame, it's so hard to find good ones.'

'Fine company you keep.'

'Hard jobs mean hard company. They'll be out of Visserine by now, I daresay.' They would be halfway to being out of Styria by now, if they had any sense, and Cosca was far from blaming them.

'Abandoned, eh?' Salier gave a grunt. 'I know the feeling. My allies have abandoned me, my soldiers, my people. I am distraught. My sole remaining comfort is my paintings.' One fat finger pointed to a deep archway, heavy doors standing open and bright sunlight spilling through.

Cosca's trained eye noted a deep groove in the stonework, metal points gleaming in a wide slot in the ceiling. A portcullis, unless he was much mistaken. 'Your collection is well protected.'

'Naturally. It is the most valuable in Styria, long years in the making. My great-grandfather began it.' Salier ushered them into a long hallway, a strip of gold-embroidered carpet beckoning them down the centre, many-coloured marble gleaming in the light from huge windows. Vast and brooding oils crowded the opposite wall in long procession, gilt frames glittering.

'This hall is given over to the Midderland masters, of course,' Salier observed. There was a snarling portrait of bald Zoller, a series of Kings of the Union – Harod, Arnault, Casimir, and more. One might have thought they all shat molten gold, they looked so smug. Salier paused a moment before a monumental canvas of the death of Juvens. A tiny, bleeding figure lost in an immensity of forest, lightning flaring across a lowering sky. 'Such brushwork. Such colouring, eh, Cosca?'

'Astounding.' Though one daub looked much like another to his eye.

'The happy days I have spent in profound contemplation of these works. Seeking the hidden meanings in the minds of the masters.' Cosca raised his brows at Monza. More time in profound contemplation of the campaign map and less on dead painters and perhaps Styria would not have found itself in the current fix.

'Sculptures from the Old Empire,' murmured the duke as they passed through a wide doorway and into a second airy gallery, lined on both sides with ancient statues. 'You would not believe the cost of shipping them from Calcis.' Heroes, emperors, gods. Their missing noses, missing arms, scarred and pitted bodies gave them a look of wounded surprise. The forgotten winners of ten centuries ago, reduced to confused amputees. Where am I? And for pity's sake, where are my arms?

'I have been wondering what to do,' said Salier suddenly, 'and would value your opinion, General Murcatto. You are renowned across Styria and beyond for your ruthlessness, single-mindedness and commitment. Decisiveness has never been my greatest talent. I am too prone to think on what is lost by a certain course of action. To look with longing at all those doors that will be closed, rather than the possibilities presented by the one that I must open.'

'A weakness in a soldier,' said Monza.

'I know it. I am a weak man, perhaps, and a poor soldier. I have relied on good intentions, fair words and righteous causes, and it seems I and my people now will pay for it.' Or for that and his avarice, betrayals and endless warmongering, at least. Salier examined a sculpture of a muscular boatman. Death poling souls to hell, perhaps. 'I could flee the city, by small boat in the hours of darkness. Down the river and away, to throw myself upon the mercy of my ally Grand Duke Rogont.'

'A brief sanctuary,' grunted Monza. 'Rogont will be next.'

'True. And a man of my considerable dimensions, fleeing? Terribly undignified. Perhaps I could surrender myself to your good friend General Ganmark?'

'You know what would follow.'

Salier's soft face turned suddenly hard. 'Perhaps Ganmark is not so utterly bereft of mercy as some of Orso's other dogs have been?' Then he seemed to sink back down, face settling into the roll of fat under his chin. 'But I daresay you are right.' He peered significantly sideways at a statue that had lost its head some time during the last few centuries. 'My fat head on a spike would be the best that I could hope for. Just like good Duke Cantain and his sons, eh, General Murcatto?'

She looked evenly back at him. 'Just like Cantain and his sons.' Heads on spikes, Cosca reflected, were still as fashionable as ever.

Around a corner and into another hall, still longer than the first, walls crowded with canvases. Salier clapped his hands. 'Here hang the Styrians! Greatest of our countrymen! Long after we are dead and forgotten, their legacy will endure.' He paused before a scene of a bustling marketplace. 'Perhaps I could bargain with

Orso? Curry favour by delivering to him a mortal enemy? The woman who murdered his eldest son and heir, perhaps?'

Monza did not flinch. She never had been the flinching kind. 'The best of luck.'

'Bah. Luck has deserted Visserine. Orso would never negotiate, even if I could give him back his son alive, and you have put well and truly paid to that possibility. We are left with suicide.' He gestured at a huge, dark-framed effort, a half-naked soldier offering his sword to his defeated general. Presumably so they could make the last sacrifice that honour demanded. That was where honour got a man. 'To plunge the mighty blade into my bared breast, as did the fallen heroes of yesteryear!'

The next canvas featured a smirking wine merchant leaning on a barrel and holding a glass up to the light. Oh, a drink, a drink, a drink. 'Or poison? Deadly powders in the wine? Scorpion in the bedsheets? Asp down one's undergarments?' Salier grinned round at them. 'No? Hang myself? I understand men often spend, when they are hanged.' And he flapped his hands away from his groin in demonstration, as though they had been in any doubt as to his meaning. 'Sounds like more fun than poison, anyway.' The duke sighed and stared glumly at a painting of a woman surprised while bathing. 'Let us not pretend I have the courage for such exploits. Suicide, that is, not spending. That I still manage once a day, in spite of my size. Do you still manage it, Cosca?'

'Like a fucking fountain,' he drawled, not to be outdone in vulgarity.

'But what to do?' mused Salier. 'What to—'

Monza stepped in front of him. 'Help me kill Ganmark.' Cosca felt his brows go up. Even beaten, bruised and with the enemy at the gates, she could not wait to draw the knives again. Ruthlessness, single-mindedness and commitment indeed.

'And why ever would I wish to do that?' .

'Because he'll be coming for your collection.' She had always had a knack for tickling people where they were most ticklish. Cosca had seen her do it often. To him, among others. 'Coming to box up all your paintings, and your sculptures, and your jars, and ship them back to Fontezarmo to adorn Orso's latrines.' A nice touch, his latrines. 'Ganmark is a connoisseur, like yourself.'

'That Union cocksucker is nothing like me!' Anger suddenly

flared red across the back of Salier's neck. 'A common thief and braggart, a degenerate man-fucker, tramping blood across the sweet soil of Styria as though its mud were not fit for his boots! He can have my life, but he'll never have my paintings! I will see to it!'

'I can see to it,' hissed Monza, stepping closer to the duke. 'He'll come here, when the city falls. He'll rush here, keen to secure your collection. We can be waiting, dressed as his soldiers. When he enters,' she snapped her fingers, 'we drop your portcullis, and we have him! You have him! Help me.'

But the moment had passed. Salier's veneer of heavy-lidded carelessness had descended again. 'These are my two favourites, I do believe,' gesturing, all nonchalance, towards two matching canvases. 'Parteo Gavra's studies of the woman. They were intended always as a pair. His mother, and his favourite whore.'

'Mothers and whores,' sneered Monza. 'A curse on fucking artists. We were talking of Ganmark. Help me!'

Salier blew out a tired sigh. 'Ah, Monzcarro, Monzcarro. If only you had sought my help five seasons ago, before Sweet Pines. Before Caprile. Even last spring, before you spiked Cantain's head above his gate. Even then, the good we could have done, the blows we could have struck together for freedom. Even—'

'Forgive me if I'm blunt, your Excellency, but I spent the night being beaten like a sack of *meat*.' Monza's voice cracked slightly on the last word. 'You ask for my opinion. You've lost because you're too weak, too soft and too slow, not because you're too good. You fought alongside Orso happily enough when you shared the same goals, and smiled happily enough at his methods, as long as they brought you more land. Your men spread fire, rape and murder when it suited you. No love of freedom then. The only open hand the farmers of Puranti had from you back in those days was the one that crushed them flat. Play the martyr if you must, Salier, but not with me. I feel sick enough already.'

Cosca felt himself wincing. There was such a thing as too much truth, especially in the ears of powerful men.

The duke's eyes narrowed. 'Blunt, you say? If you spoke to Orso in such a manner it is small wonder he threw you down a mountain. I almost wish I had a long drop handy. Tell me, since candour seems the fashion, what did you do to anger Orso so? I thought he loved you like a daughter? Far more than his own children, not that any of those three ever were so very lovable – fox, shrew and mouse.'

Her bruised cheek twitched. 'I became too popular with his people.'

'Yes. And?'

'He was afraid I might steal his throne.'

'Indeed? And I suppose your eyes were never turned upon it?'

'Only to keep him in it.'

'Truly?' Salier grinned sideways at Cosca. 'It would hardly have been the first chair your loyal claws tore from under its owner, would it?'

'I did nothing!' she barked. 'Except win his battles, make him the greatest man in Styria. Nothing!'

The Duke of Visserine sighed. 'I have a fat body, Monzcarro, not a fat head, but have it your way. You are all innocence. Doubtless you handed out cakes at Caprile as well, rather than slaughter. Keep your secrets if you please. Much good may they do you now.'

Cosca narrowed his eyes against the sudden glare as they stepped out of an open doorway, through an echoing arcade and into the pristine garden at the centre of Salier's gallery. Water trickled in pools at its corners. A pleasant breeze made the new flowers nod, stirred the leaves of the topiary, plucked specks of blossom from Suljuk cherry trees, no doubt torn from their native soil and brought across the sea for the amusement of the Duke of Visserine.

A magnificent sculpture towered over them in the midst of a cobbled space, twice life-size or more, carved from perfectly white, almost translucent marble. A naked man, lean as a dancer and muscular as a wrestler, one arm extended and with a bronze sword, turned dark and streaked with green, thrust forwards in the fist. As if directing a mighty army to storm the dining room. He had a helmet pushed back on the top of his head, a frown of stern command on his perfect features.

'The Warrior,' murmured Cosca, as the shadow of the great

blade fell across his eyes, the glare of sunlight blazing along its edge.

'Yes, by Bonatine, greatest of all Styrian sculptors, and this perhaps his greatest work, carved at the height of the New Empire. It originally stood on the steps of the Senate House in Borletta. My father took it as an indemnity after the Summer War.'

'He fought a war?' Monza's split lip curled. 'For this?'

'Only a small one. But it was worth it. Beautiful, is it not?'

'Beautiful,' Cosca lied. To the starving man, bread is beautiful. To the homeless man, a roof is beautiful. To the drunkard, wine is beautiful. Only those who want for nothing else need find beauty in a lump of rock.

'Stolicus was the inspiration, I understand, ordering the famous charge at the Battle of Darmium.'

Monza raised an eyebrow. 'Leading a charge, eh? You'd have thought he'd have put some trousers on for work like that.'

'It's called artistic licence,' snapped Salier. 'It's a fantasy, one can do as one pleases.'

Cosca frowned. 'Really? I always felt a man makes more points worth making if he steers always close to the truth . . .'

Hurried boot heels cut him off and a nervous-looking officer rushed across the garden, face touched with sweat, a long smear of black mud down the left side of his jacket. He came to one knee on the cobbles, head bowed.

'Your Excellency.'

Salier did not even look at him. 'Speak, if you must.'

'There has been another assault.'

'So close to breakfast time?' The duke winced as he placed a hand on his belly. 'A typical Union man, this Ganmark, he has no more regard for mealtimes than you did, Murcatto. With what result?'

'The Talinese have forced a second breach, towards the harbour. We drove them back, but with heavy losses. We are greatly outnumbered—'

'Of course you are. Order your men to hold their positions as long as possible.'

The colonel licked his lips. 'And then . . . ?'

314

'That will be all.' Salier did not take his eyes from the great statue.

'Your Excellency.' The man retreated towards the door. And no doubt to a heroic, pointless death at one breach or another. The most heroic deaths of all were the pointless ones, Cosca had always found.

'Visserine will soon fall.' Salier clicked his tongue as he stared up at the great image of Stolicus. 'How profoundly . . . depressing. Had I only been more like this.'

'Thinner waisted?' murmured Cosca.

'I meant warlike, but while we are wishing, why not a thin waist too? I thank you for your . . . almost uncomfortably honest counsel, General Murcatto. I may have a few days yet to make my decision.' To delay the inevitable at the cost of hundreds of lives. 'In the meantime, I hope the two of you will remain with us. The two of you, and your three friends.'

'Your guests,' asked Monza, 'or your prisoners?'

'You have seen how my prisoners are treated. Which would be your choice?'

Cosca took a deep breath, and scratched slowly at his neck. A choice that more or less made itself.

Vile Jelly

Shivers' face was near healed. Faint pink stripe left across his forehead, through his brow, across his cheek. More'n likely it would fade altogether in a few days more. His eye still ached a bit, but he'd kept his looks alright. Monza lay in the bed, sheet round her waist, skinny back turned towards him. He stood a moment, grinning, watching her ribs shift gently as she breathed, patches of shadow between them shrinking and growing. Then he padded from the mirror across to the open window, looking out. Beyond it the city was burning, fires lighting up the night. Strange thing though, he wasn't sure which city, or why he was there. Mind was moving slowly. He winced, rubbing at his cheek.

'Hurts,' he grunted. 'By the dead it hurts.'

'Oh, *that* hurts?' He whipped round, stumbling back against the wall. Fenris the Feared loomed over him, bald head brushing the ceiling, half his body tattooed with tiny letters, the rest all cased in black metal, face writhing like boiling porridge.

'You're . . . you're fucking dead!'

The giant laughed. 'I'll say I'm fucking dead.' He had a sword stuck right through his body, the hilt above one hip, point of the blade sticking out under his other arm. He jerked one massive thumb at the blood dripping from the pommel and scattering across the carpet. 'I mean, this *really* hurts. Did you cut your hair? I liked you better before.'

Bethod pointed to his smashed-in head, a twisted mess of blood, brains, hair, bone. 'Shuth uth, the pair o' youth.' He couldn't speak right because his mouth was all squashed in on itself. 'Thith ith whath hurts lookth like!' He gave the Feared a pointless shove. 'Why couldn't you win, you thtupid half-devil bathtard?'

'I'm dreaming,' Shivers said to himself, trying to think his way through it, but his face was throbbing, throbbing. 'I must be dreaming.'

Someone was singing. 'I . . . am made . . . of death!' Hammer banging on a nail. 'I am the Great Leveller!' Bang, bang, bang, each time sending a jolt of pain through Shivers' face. 'I am the storm in the High Places!' The Bloody-Nine hummed to himself as he cut the corpse of Shivers' brother into bits, stripped to the waist, body a mass of scars and twisted muscle all daubed-up with blood. 'So you're the good man, eh?' He waved his knife at Shivers, grinning. 'You need to fucking toughen up, boy. You should've killed me. Now help me get his arms off, optimist.'

'The dead know I don't like this bastard any, but he's got a point.' Shivers' brother's head peered down at him from its place nailed to Bethod's standard. 'You need to toughen up. Mercy and cowardice are the same. You reckon you could get this nail out?'

'You're a fucking embarrassment!' His father, slack face streaked with tears, waving his jug around. 'Why couldn't you be the one dead, and your brother lived? You useless little fuck! You useless, gutless, disappointing speck o' shit!'

'This is rubbish,' snarled Shivers through gritted teeth, sitting down on his crossed legs by the fire. His whole head was pulsing. 'This is just . . . just rubbish!'

'What's rubbish?' gurgled Tul Duru, blood leaking from his cut throat as he spoke.

'All this. Faces from the past, saying meaningful stuff. Bit fucking obvious, ain't it? Couldn't you do better'n this shit?'

'Uh,' said Grim.

Black Dow looked a bit put out. 'Don't blame us, boy. Your dream, no? You cut your hair?'

Dogman shrugged. 'If you was cleverer, maybe you'd have cleverer dreams.'

He felt himself grabbed from behind, face twisted round. The Bloody-Nine was there beside him, hair plastered to his head with blood, scarred face all dashed with black. 'If you was cleverer, maybe you wouldn't have got your eye burned out.' And he ground his thumb into Shivers' eye, harder and harder. Shivers thrashed, and twisted, and screamed, but there was no way free. It was already done.

*

He woke up screaming, 'course. He always did now. You could hardly call it a scream any more, his voice was worn down to a grinding stub, gravel in his raw throat.

It was dark. Pain tore at his face like a wolf at a carcass. He thrashed free of the blankets, reeled to nowhere. Like the iron was still pressed against him, burning. He crashed into a wall, fell on his knees. Bent over, hands squeezing the sides of his skull like they might stop his head from cracking open. Rocking, every muscle flexed to bursting. He groaned and moaned, whimpered and snarled, spat and blubbered, drooled and gibbered, mad from it, mindless with it. Touch it, press it. He held his quivering fingers to the bandages.

'Shhhh.' He felt a hand. Monza, pawing at his face, pushing back his hair.

Pain split his head where his eye used to be like an axe splitting a log, split his mind too, broke it open, thoughts all spilling out in a mad splatter. 'By the dead . . . make it stop . . . shit, shit.' He grabbed her hand and she winced, gasped. He didn't care. 'Kill me! Kill me. Just make it stop.' He wasn't even sure what tongue he was talking. 'Kill me. By the . . .' He was sobbing, tears stinging the eye he still had. She tore her hand away and he was rocking again, rocking, pain ripping through his face like a saw through a tree-stump. He'd tried to be a good man, hadn't he?

'I tried, I fucking tried. Make it stop . . . please, please, please, please—'

'Here.' He snatched hold of the pipe and sucked at it, greedy as a drunkard at the bottle. He hardly even marked the smoke biting, just heaved in air until his lungs were full, and all the while she held him, arms tight around him, rocking him back and forward. The darkness was full of colours, now. Covered with glittering smears. The pain was a step away, 'stead of pressed burning against him. His breathing had softened to a whimper, aching body all washed out.

She helped him up, dragging him to his feet, pipe clattering from his limp hand. The open window swayed, a painting of another world. Hell maybe, red and yellow spots of fire leaving long brushstrokes through the dark. The bed came up and

318

swallowed him, sucked him down. His face throbbed still, pulsed a dull ache. He remembered, remembered why.

'The dead . . .' he whispered, tears running down his other cheek. 'My eye. They burned my eye out.'

'Shhhh,' she whispered, gently stroking the good side of his face. 'Quiet now, Caul. Quiet.'

The darkness was reaching for him, wrapping him up. Before it took him he twisted his fingers clumsily in her hair and dragged her face towards his, close enough almost to kiss his bandages.

'Should've been you,' he whispered at her. 'Should've been you.'

Other People's Scores

'**T**hat's his place,' said the one with the sore on his cheek. 'Sajaam's place.'

A stained door in a stained wall, pasted with fluttering old bills decrying the League of Eight as villains, usurpers and common criminals. A pair of caricature faces stared from each one, a bloated Duke Salier and a sneering Duke Rogont. A pair of common criminals stood at the doorway, scarcely less caricatures themselves. One dark-skinned, the other with a heavy tattoo down one arm, both sweeping the street with identical scowls.

'Thank you, children. Eat, now.' Shenkt pressed a scale into each grubby hand, twelve pairs of eyes wide in smudged faces to have so much money. Once a few days had passed, let alone a few years, he knew it would have done them little good. They were the beggars, thieves, whores, early dead of tomorrow. But Shenkt had done much harm in his life, and so he tried, wherever possible, to be kind. It put nothing right, he knew that. But perhaps a coin could tip the scales of life by that vital degree, and one among them would be spared. It would be a good thing, to spare even one.

He hummed quietly to himself as he crossed the street, the two men at the door frowning at him all the way. 'I am here to speak to Sajaam.'

'You armed?'

'Always.' He and the dark-skinned guard stared at each other for a moment. 'My ready wit could strike at any moment.'

Neither one of them smiled, but Shenkt had not expected them to, and did not care into the bargain. 'What've you got to say to Sajaam?'

' "Are you Sajaam?" That shall be my opening gambit.'

'You mocking us, little man?' The guard put one hand on the mace hanging at his belt, no doubt thinking himself fearsome.

'I would not dare. I am here to enjoy myself, and have money to spend, nothing more.'

'Maybe you came to the right place after all. With me.'

He led Shenkt through a hot, dim room, heavy with oily smoke and shadows. Lit blue, green, orange, red by lamps of coloured glass. Husk-smokers sprawled around it, pale faces twisted with smiles, or hanging slack and empty. Shenkt found that he was humming again, and stopped himself.

A greasy curtain pushed aside into a large back room that smelled of unwashed bodies, smoke and vomit, rotten food and rotten living. A man covered in tattoos sat cross-legged upon a sweat-stained cushion, an axe leaning against the wall beside him. Another man sat on the other side of the room, digging at an ugly piece of meat with a knife, a loaded flatbow beside his plate. Above his head an old clock hung, workings dangling from its underside like the intestines from a gutted corpse, pendulum swinging, tick, tick, tick.

Upon a long table in the centre of the room were the chattels of a card game. Coins and counters, bottles and glasses, pipes and candles. Men sat about it, six of them in all. A fat man at Shenkt's right hand, a scrawny one at the left, stuttering out a joke to his neighbour.

'. . . he fuh, fuh, fucked her!'

Harsh laughter, harsh faces, cheap lives of cheap smoke, cheap drink, cheap violence. Shenkt's guide walked around to the head of the table, leaned down to speak to a broad-shouldered man, black-skinned, white-haired, with the smile of comfortable owner-ship on his lined face. He toyed with a golden coin, flipping it glinting across the tops of his knuckles.

'You are Sajaam?' asked Shenkt.

He nodded, entirely at his ease. 'Do I know you?'

'No.'

'A stranger, then? We do not entertain many strangers here, do we, my friends?' A couple of them grinned half-heartedly. 'Most of my customers are well known to us. What can Sajaam do for you, stranger?'

'Where is Monzcarro Murcatto?'

Like a man plunging through thin ice, the room was sucked

into sudden, awful silence. That heavy quiet before the heavens split. That pregnant stillness, bulging with the inevitable.

'The Snake of Talins is dead,' murmured Sajaam, eyes narrowing.

Shenkt felt the slow movement of the men around him. Their smiles creeping off, their feet creeping to the balance for killing, their hands creeping to their weapons. 'She is alive and you know where. I want only to talk to her.'

'Who the shuh, shit does this bastard thuh, think he is?' asked the scrawny card player, and some of the others laughed. Tight, fake laughs, to hide their tension.

'Only tell me where she is. Please. Then no one's conscience need grow any heavier today.' Shenkt did not mind pleading. He had given up his vanity long ago. He looked each man in the eyes, gave each a chance to give him what he needed. He gave everyone a chance, where he could. He wished more of them took it.

But they only smiled at him, and at each other, and Sajaam smiled widest of all. 'I carry my conscience lightly enough.'

Shenkt's old master might have said the same. 'Some of us do. It is a gift.'

'I tell you what, we'll toss for it.' Sajaam held his coin up to the light, gold flashing. 'Heads, we kill you. Tails, I tell you where Murcatto is . . .' His smile was all bright teeth in his dark face. 'Then we kill you.' There was the slightest ring of metal as he flicked his coin up.

Shenkt sucked in breath through his nose, slow, slow.

The gold crawled into the air, turning, turning.

The clock beat deep and slow as the oars of a great ship.

Boom . . . boom . . . boom . . .

Shenkt's fist sank into the great gut of the fat man on his right, almost to the elbow. Nothing left to scream with, he gave the gentlest fragment of a sigh, eyes popping. An instant later the edge of Shenkt's open hand caved his astonished face in and ripped his head half-off, bone crumpling like paper. Blood sprayed across the table, black spots frozen, the expressions of the men around it only now starting to shift from rage to shock.

Shenkt snatched the nearest of them from his chair and flung him into the ceiling. His cry was barely begun as he crashed into a pair of beams, wood bursting, splinters spinning, mangled body falling back down in a languid shower of dust and broken plaster. Long before he hit the floor, Shenkt had seized the next player's head and rammed his face through the table, through the floor beneath it. Cards, and broken glasses, chunks of planking, fragments of wood and flesh made a swelling cloud. Shenkt ripped the half-drawn hatchet from his fist as he went down, sent it whirling across the room and into the chest of the tattooed man, halfway up from his cushion and the first note of a war cry throbbing from his lips. It hit him haft first, so hard it scarcely mattered, spun him round and round like a child's top, ripped wide open, blood gouting from his body in all directions.

The flatbow twanged, deep and distorted, string twisting as it pushed the bolt towards him, swimming slowly through the dust-filled air as if through treacle, shaft flexing lightly back and forth. Shenkt snatched it from its path and drove it clean through a man's skull, his face folding into itself, meat bursting from torn skin. Shenkt caught him under the jaw and sent his corpse hurtling across the room with a flick of his wrist. He crashed into the archer, the two bodies mashed together, flailing bone-lessly into the wall, through the wall, out into the alley on the other side, leaving a ragged hole in the shattered planks behind them.

The guard from the door had his mace raised, mouth open, air rushing in as he made ready to roar. Shenkt leaped the ruins of the table and slapped him backhanded across the chest, burst his ribcage and sent him reeling, twisting up like a corkscrew, mace flying from his lifeless hand. Shenkt stepped forwards and snatched Sajaam's coin from the air as it spun back down, metal slapping into his palm.

He breathed out, and time flowed again.

The last couple of corpses tumbled across the floor. Plaster dropped, settled. The tattooed man's left boot rattled against the boards, leg quivering as he died. One of the others was groaning, but not for much longer. The last spots of blood rained softly from the air around them, misting across the broken glass, the broken wood, the broken bodies. One of the cushions had burst, the feathers still fluttering down in a white cloud.

Shenkt's fist trembled before Sajaam's slack face. Steam hissed from it, then molten gold, trickling from between his fingers, running down his forearm in shining streaks. He opened his hand and showed it, palm forwards, daubed with black blood, smeared with glowing metal.

'Neither heads nor tails.'

'Fuh . . . fuh . . . fuh . . .' The stuttering man still sat at his place, where the table had been, cards clutched in his rigid hand, every part of him spattered, spotted, sprayed with blood.

'You,' said Shenkt. 'Stuttering man. You may live.'

'Fuh . . . fuh . . .'

'You alone are spared. Out, before I reconsider.'

The mumbling beggar dropped his cards, fled whimpering for the door and tumbled through it. Shenkt watched him go. A good thing, even to spare one.

As he turned back, Sajaam was swinging his chair over his head. It burst apart across Shenkt's shoulder, broken pieces bouncing from the floor and clattering away. A futile gesture, Shenkt scarcely even felt it. The edge of his hand chopped into the man's big arm, snapped it like a dead twig, spun him around and sent him rolling over and over across the floor.

Shenkt walked after him, his scuffed work boots making not the slightest sound as they found the gaps between the debris. Sajaam coughed, shook his head, started to worm away on his back, gurgling through gritted teeth, hand dragging behind him the wrong way up. The heels of his embroidered Gurkish slippers kicked at the floor, leaving stuttering trails though the detritus of blood, dust, feathers and splinters that had settled across the whole room like leaves across a forest floor in autumn.

'A man sleeps through most of his life, even when awake. You get so little time, yet still you spend it utterly oblivious. Angry, frustrated, fixated on meaningless nothings. That drawer does not close flush with the front of my desk. What cards does my opponent hold, and how much money can I win from him? I wish I were taller. What will I have for dinner, for I am not fond of parsnips?' Shenkt rolled a mangled corpse out of his way with the toe of one boot. 'It takes a moment like this to jerk us to our senses, to draw our eyes from the mud to the heavens, to root our attention in the present. Now you realise how precious is each moment. That is my gift to you.'

Sajaam reached the back wall and propped himself up against it, worked himself slowly to standing, broken arm hanging limp.

'I despise violence. It is the last tool of feeble minds.' Shenkt stopped a stride away. 'So let us have no more foolishness. Where is Monzcarro Murcatto?'

To give the man his due for courage, he made for the knife at his belt.

Shenkt's pointed finger sank into the hollow where chest met shoulder, just beneath his collarbone. It punched through shirt, skin, flesh, and as the rest of his fist smacked hard against Sajaam's chest and drove him back against the wall, his fingernail was already scraping against the inside surface of his shoulder blade, buried in his flesh right to the knuckles. Sajaam screamed, knife clattering from his dangling fingers.

'No more foolishness, I said. Where is Murcatto?'

'In Visserine the last I heard!' His voice was hoarse with pain. 'In Visserine!'

'At the siege?' Sajaam nodded, bloody teeth clenched tight together. If Visserine had not fallen already, it would have by the time Shenkt got there. But he never left a job half-done. He would assume she was still alive, and carry on the chase. 'Who does she have with her?'

'Some Northman beggar, called himself Shivers! A man of mine named Friendly! A convict! A convict from Safety!'

'Yes?' Shenkt twisted his finger in the man's flesh, blood trickling from the wound and down his hand, around the streaks of gold dried to his forearm, dripping from his elbow, tap, tap, tap.

'Ah! Ah! I put her in touch with a poisoner called Morveer! In Westport, and in Sipani with a woman called Vitari!' Shenkt frowned. 'A woman who can get things done!'

'Murcatto, Shivers, Friendly, Morveer . . . Vitari.'

A desperate nod, spit flying from Sajaam's gritted teeth with every heaving, agonised breath.

'And where are these brave companions bound next?'

'I'm not sure! Gah! She said seven men! The seven men who killed her brother! Ah! Puranti, maybe! Keep ahead of Orso's army! If she gets Ganmark, maybe she'll try for Faithful next, for Faithful Carpi!'

'Maybe she will.' Shenkt jerked his finger free with a faint sucking sound and Sajaam collapsed, sliding down until his rump hit the floor, his shivering, sweat-beaded face twisted with pain.

'Please,' he grunted. 'I can help you. I can help you find her.'

Shenkt squatted down in front of him, blood-smeared hands dangling on the knees of his blood-smeared trousers. 'But you have helped. You can leave the rest to me.'

'I have money! I have money.'

Shenkt said nothing.

'I was planning on turning her in to Orso, sooner or later, once the price was high enough.'

More nothing.

'That doesn't make any difference, does it?'

Silence.

'I told that bitch she'd be the death of me.'

'You were right. I hope that is a comfort.'

'Not much of one. I should have killed her then.'

'But you saw money to be made. Have you anything to say?'

Sajaam stared at him. 'What would I say?'

'Some people want to say things, at the end. Do you?'

'What are you?' he whispered.

'I have been many things. A student. A messenger. A thief. A soldier in old wars. A servant of great powers. An actor in great events. Now?' Shenkt puffed out an unhappy breath as he gazed around at the mangled corpses hunched, sprawled, huddled across the room. 'Now, it seems, I am a man who settles other people's scores.'

The Fencing Master

Monza's hands were shaking again, but that was no surprise. The danger, the fear, not knowing if she was going to live out the next moment. Her brother murdered, herself broken, everything she'd worked for gone. The pain, the withering need for husk, trusting no one, day after day, week after week. Then there was all the death she'd been the cause of, in Westport, in Sipani, gathering on her shoulders like a great weight of lead.

The last few months had been enough to make anyone's hands shake. But maybe it was just watching Shivers have his eye burned out and thinking she'd be next.

She looked nervously towards the door between her room and his. He'd be awake soon. Screaming again, which was bad enough, or silent, which was worse. Kneeling there, looking at her with his one eye. That accusing look. She knew she should have been grateful, should have cared for him the way she used to for her brother. But a growing part of her just wanted to kick him and not stop. Maybe when Benna died everything warm, or decent, or human in her had been left rotting on the mountainside with his corpse.

She pulled her glove off and stared at the thing inside. At the thin pink scars where the shattered bones had been put back together. The deep red line where Gobba's wire had cut into her. She curled the fingers into a fist, or something close, except the little one, still pointing off like a signpost to nowhere. It didn't hurt as badly as it used to, but more than enough to bring a grimace to her face, and the pain cut through the fear, crushed the doubts.

'Revenge,' she whispered. Kill Ganmark, that was all that mattered now. His soft, sad face, his weak, watery eyes. Calmly stabbing Benna through the stomach. Rolling his corpse off the terrace. *That's that.* She squeezed her fist tighter, bared her teeth at it.

'Revenge.' For Benna and for herself. She was the Butcher of Caprile, merciless, fearless. She was the Snake of Talins, deadly as the viper and no more regretful. Kill Ganmark, and then . . .

'Whoever's next.' And her hand was steady.

Running footsteps slapped hard along the hallway outside and away. She heard someone shout in the distance, couldn't make out the words, but couldn't miss the edge of fear in the voice. She crossed to the window and pulled it open. Her room, or her cell, was high up on the north face of the palace. A stone bridge spanned the Visser upstream, tiny dots moving fast across it. Even from this distance she could tell people running for their lives.

A good general gets to know the smell of panic, and suddenly it was reeking. Orso's men must have finally carried the walls. The sack of Visserine had begun. Ganmark would be on his way to the palace, even now, to take possession of Duke Salier's renowned collection.

The door creaked open and Monza spun about. Captain Langrier stood in the doorway in a Talinese uniform, a bulging sack in one hand. She had a sword at one hip and a long dagger at the other. Monza had nothing of the kind, and she found herself acutely aware of the fact. She stood, hands by her sides, trying to look as if every muscle wasn't ready to fight. And die, more than likely.

Langrier moved slowly into the room. 'So you really are Murcatto, eh?'

'I'm Murcatto.'

'Sweet Pines? Musselia? The High Bank? You won all those battles?'

'That's right.'

'You ordered all those folk killed at Caprile?'

'What the fuck do you want?'

'Duke Salier says he's decided to do it your way.' Langrier dumped the sack on the floor and it sagged open. Metal gleamed inside. The Talinese armour Friendly had stolen out near the breach. 'Best put this on. Don't know how long we'll have before your friend Ganmark gets here.'

Alive, then. For now. Monza dragged a lieutenant's jacket from the sack and pulled it on over her shirt, started to button it up. Langrier watched her for a minute, then started talking.

'I just wanted to say . . . while there's a chance. Well. That I always admired you, I guess.'

Monza stared at her. 'What?'

'A woman. A soldier. Getting where you've been. Doing what you've done. You might've stood on the other side from us, but you always were something of a hero to—'

'You think I care a shit?' Monza didn't know which sickened her more – being called a hero or who was saying it.

'Can't blame me for not believing you. Woman with your reputation, thought you'd be harder in a fix like that—'

'You ever watched someone have their eye burned out of their head and thought you'd be next?'

Langrier worked her mouth. 'Can't say I've sat on that side of the issue.'

'You should try it, see how fucking hard you end up.' Monza pulled some stolen boots on, not so bad a fit.

'Here.' Langrier was holding Benna's ring out to her, big stone gleaming the colour of blood. 'Doesn't suit me anyway.'

Monza snatched it from her hand, twisted it onto her finger. 'What? Give me back what you stole in the first place and think that makes us even?'

'Look, I'm sorry about your man's eye and the rest, but it isn't about you, understand? Someone's a threat to my city, I have to find out how. I don't like it, it's just what has to be done. Don't pretend you haven't done worse. I don't expect we'll ever share any jokes. But for now, while we've got this task to be about, we'll need to put it behind us.'

Monza kept her silence as she dressed. It was true enough. She'd done worse, alright. Watched it done, anyway. Let it be done, which was no better. She buckled on the breastplate, must've come from some lean young officer and fitted her well enough, pulled the last strap through. 'I need something to kill Ganmark with.'

'Once we get to the garden you can have a blade, not—'

Monza saw a hand close around the grip of Langrier's dagger. She started to turn, surprised. 'Wha—' The point slid out of the front of her neck. Shivers' face loomed up beside hers, white and wasted, bandages bound tight over one whole side of it, a pale stain through the cloth where his eye used to be. His left arm slid around Langrier's chest from behind and drew her tight against him. Tight as a lover.

'It ain't about you, understand?' He was almost kissing at her ear as blood began to run from the point of the knife and down her neck in a thick black line. 'You take my eye, I've got to take your life.' She opened her mouth, and her tongue flopped out, and blood started to trickle from the tip of it and down her chin. 'I don't like it.' Her face turned purple, eyes rolling up. 'Just what has to be done.' Her legs kicked, her boot heels clattering against the boards as he lifted her up in the air. 'Sorry about your neck.' The blade ripped sideways and opened her throat up wide, black blood showering out across the bedclothes, spraying up the wall in an arc of red spots.

Shivers let her drop and she crumpled, sprawling face down as if her bones had turned to mud, another gout of blood spurting sideways. Her boots moved, toes scraping. One set of nails scratched at the floor. Shivers took a long breath in through his nose, then he blew it out, and he looked up at Monza, and he smiled. A friendly little grin, as if they'd shared some private joke that Langrier just hadn't got.

'By the dead but I feel better for that. Ganmark's in the city, did she say?'

'Uh.' Monza couldn't speak. Her skin was flushed and burning.

'Then I reckon we got work ahead of us.' Shivers didn't seem to notice the rapidly spreading slick of blood creep between his toes, around the sides of his big bare feet. He dragged the sack up and peered inside. 'Armour in here, then? Guess I'd better get dressed, eh, Chief? Hate to arrive at a party in the wrong clothes.'

The garden at the centre of Salier's gallery showed no signs of imminent doom. Water trickled, leaves rustled, a bee or two floated lazily from one flower to another. White blossom occasionally filtered down from the cherry trees and dusted the well-shaved lawns.

Cosca sat cross-legged and worked the edge of his sword with a whetstone, metal softly ringing. Morveer's flask pressed into his thigh, but he felt no need for it. Death was at the doorstep, and so he was at peace. His blissful moment before the storm. He tipped his head back, eyes closed, sun warm on his face, and wondered why he could never feel this way unless the world was burning down around him.

Calming breezes washed through the shadowy colonnades, through doorways into hallways lined with paintings. Through one open window Friendly could be seen, in the armour of a Talinese guardsman, counting every soldier in Nasurin's colossal painting of the Second Battle of Oprile. Cosca grinned. He tried always to be forgiving of other men's foibles. He had enough of his own, after all.

Perhaps a half-dozen of Salier's guards had remained, disguised as soldiers from Duke Orso's army. Men loyal enough to die beside their master at the last. He snorted as he ran the whetstone once more down the edge of his sword. Loyalty had always sat with honour, discipline and self-restraint on his list of incomprehensible virtues.

'Why so happy?' Day sat beside him on the grass, a flatbow across her knees, chewing at her lip. The uniform she wore must have come from some dead drummer-boy, it fit her well. Very well. Cosca wondered if it was wrong of him to find something peculiarly alluring about a pretty girl in a man's clothes. He wondered furthermore if she might be persuaded to give a comrade-in-arms . . . a little help sharpening his weapon before the fighting started? He cleared his throat. Of course not. But a man could dream.

'Perhaps something is wrong in my head.' He rubbed a blemish from the steel with his thumb. 'Getting out of bed.' Metal rang. 'A day of honest work.' Whetstone scraped. 'Peace. Normality. Sobriety.' He held the sword up to the light and watched the metal gleam. 'These are the things that terrify me. Danger, by contrast, has long been my only relief. Eat something. You'll need your strength.'

'I've no appetite,' she said glumly. 'I've never faced certain death before.'

'Oh, come, come, don't say such a thing.' He stood, brushed the blossom from the captain's insignia on the sleeves of his stolen uniform. 'If there is one thing I have learned in all my many last stands, it is that death is never certain, only . . . extremely likely.'

'Truly inspirational words.'

'I try. Indeed I do.' Cosca slapped his sword into its sheath, picked up Monza's Calvez and ambled away towards the statue of The Warrior. His Excellency Duke Salier stood in its muscular shadow, arrayed for a noble death in a spotless white uniform festooned with gold braid.

'How did it end like this?' he was musing. The very same question Cosca had so often asked himself, while sucking the last drop from one cheap bottle or another. Waking baffled in one unfamiliar doorway, or another. Carrying out one hateful, poorly paid act of violence. Or another. 'How did it end . . . like this?'

'You underestimated Orso's venomous ambition and Murcatto's ruthless competence. Don't feel too badly, though, we've all done it.'

Salier's eyes rolled sideways. 'The question was intended to be rhetorical. But you are right, of course. It seems I have been guilty of arrogance, and the penalty will be harsh. No less than everything. But who could have expected a young woman would win one unlikely victory over us after another? How I laughed when you made her your second, Cosca. How we all laughed when Orso gave her command. We were already planning our triumphs, dividing his lands between us. Our chuckles are become sobs now, eh?'

'I find chuckles have a habit of doing so.'

'I suppose that makes her a very great soldier and me a very poor one. But then I never aspired to be a soldier, and would have been perfectly happy as merely a grand duke.'

'Now you are nothing, instead, and so am I. Such is life.'

'Time for one last performance, though.'

'For both of us.'

The duke grinned back. 'A pair of dying swans, eh, Cosca?'

'A brace of old turkeys, maybe. Why aren't you running, your Excellency?'

'I must confess I am wondering myself. Pride, I think. I have spent my life as the Grand Duke of Visserine, and insist on dying the same way. I refuse to be simply fat Master Salier, once of importance.'

'Pride, eh? Can't say I ever had much of the stuff.'

'Then why aren't you running, Cosca?'

'I suppose . . .' Why was he not running? Old Master Cosca, once of importance, who always kept his last thought for his own skin? Foolish love? Mad bravery? Old debts to pay? Or simply so that merciful death could spare him from further shame? 'But look!' He pointed to the gate. 'Only think of her and she appears.'

She wore a Talinese uniform, hair gathered up under a helmet, jaw set hard. Just like a serious young officer, clean-shaven this morning and keen to get stuck into the manly business of war. If Cosca had not known, he swore he would never have guessed. A tiny something in the way she walked, perhaps? In the set of her hips, the length of her neck? Again, the women in men's clothes. Did they have to torture him so?

'Monza!' he called. 'I was worried you might not make it!'

'And leave you to die gloriously alone?' Shivers came behind her wearing breastplate, greaves and helmet stolen from a big corpse out near the breach. Bandages stared accusingly from one blind eyehole. 'From what I can hear, they're at the palace gate already.'

'So soon?' Salier's tongue darted over his plump lips. 'Where is Captain Langrier?'

'She ran. Seems glory didn't appeal.'

'Is there no loyalty left in Styria?'

'I never noticed any before.' Cosca tossed the Calvez over in its scabbard and Monza snatched it smartly from the air. 'Unless you count each man for himself. Is there any plan, besides wait for Ganmark to come calling?'

'Day!' She pointed up to the narrower windows on the floor above. 'I want you up there. Drop the portcullis once we've had a try at Ganmark. Or once he's had a try at us.'

The girl looked greatly relieved to be put at least temporarily out of harm's way, though Cosca feared it would be no more than temporary. 'Once the trap's sprung. Alright.' She hurried off towards one of the doorways.

'We wait here. When Ganmark arrives we tell him we've

captured Grand Duke Salier. We bring your Excellency close, and then . . . you realise we may well all die today?'

The duke smiled weakly, jowls trembling. 'I am not a fighter, General Murcatto, but nor am I a coward. If I am to die, I might as well spit from my grave.'

'I couldn't agree more,' said Monza.

'Oh, nor me,' Cosca threw in. 'Though a grave's a grave, spit or no. You are quite sure he'll come?'

'He'll come.'

'And when he does?'

'Kill,' grunted Shivers. Someone had given him a shield and a heavy studded axe with a long pick on the reverse. Now he took a brutal-looking practice swipe with it.

Monza's neck shifted as she swallowed. 'I guess we just wait and see.'

'Ah, wait and see.' Cosca beamed. 'My kind of plan.'

A crash came from somewhere in the palace, distant shouting, maybe even the faint clash and clatter of steel. Monza worked her left hand nervously around the hilt of the Calvez, hanging drawn beside her leg.

'Did you hear that?' Salier's soft face was pale as butter beside her. His guards, scattered about the garden fingering their borrowed weapons, looked hardly more enthusiastic. But that was the thing about facing death, as Benna had often pointed out. The closer it gets, the worse an idea it seems. Shivers didn't look like he had any doubts. Hot iron had burned them out of him, maybe. Cosca neither, his happy grin widening with each moment. Friendly sat cross-legged, rolling his dice across the cobbles.

He looked up at her, face blank as ever. 'Five and four.'

'That a good thing?'

He shrugged. 'It's nine.' Monza raised her brows. A strange group she'd gathered, surely, but when you have a half-mad plan you need men at least half-mad to see it through.

Sane ones might be tempted to look for a better idea.

Another crash, and a thin scream, closer this time. Ganmark's soldiers, working their way through the palace towards the garden at its centre. Friendly threw his dice once more, then gathered them up and stood, sword in hand. Monza tried to stay still, eyes fixed on the open doorway ahead, the hall lined with paintings beyond it, beyond that the archway that led into the rest of the palace. The only way in.

A helmeted head peered round the side of the arch. An armoured body followed. A Talinese sergeant, sword and shield raised and ready. Monza watched him creep carefully under the portcullis, across the marble tiles. He stepped cautiously out into the sunlight, frowning about at them.

'Sergeant,' said Cosca brightly.

'Captain.' The man straightened up, letting his sword point drop. More men followed him. Well-armed Talinese soldiers, watchful and bearded veterans tramping into the gallery with weapons at the ready. They looked surprised, at first, to see their own side already in the garden, but not unhappy. 'That him?' asked the sergeant, pointing to Salier.

'This is him,' said Cosca, grinning back.

'Well, well. Fat fucker, ain't he?'

'That he is.'

More soldiers were coming through the entrance now, and behind them a knot of staff officers in pristine uniforms, with fine swords but no armour. Striding at their head with an air of unchallengeable authority came a man with a soft face and sad, watery eyes.

Ganmark.

Monza might have felt some grim satisfaction that she'd predicted his actions so easily, but the swell of hatred at the sight of him crowded it away. He had a long sword at his left hip, a shorter one at his right. Long and short steels, in the Union style.

'Secure the gallery!' he called in his clipped accent as he marched out into the garden. 'Above all, ensure no harm comes to the paintings!'

'Yes, sir!' Boots clattered as men moved to follow his orders. Lots of men. Monza watched them, jaw set aching hard. Too many, maybe, but there was no use weeping about it now. Killing Ganmark was all that mattered.

'General!' Cosca snapped out a vibrating salute. 'We have Duke Salier.'

'So I see. Well done, Captain, you were quick off the mark, and shall be rewarded. Very quick.' He gave a mocking bow. 'Your Excellency, an honour. Grand Duke Orso sends his brotherly greetings.'

'Shit on his greetings,' barked Salier.

'And his regrets that he could not be here in person to witness your utter defeat.'

'If he was here, I'd shit on him too.'

'Doubtless. He was alone?'

Cosca nodded. 'Just waiting here, sir, looking at this.' And he jerked his head towards the great statue in the centre of the garden.

'Bonatine's Warrior.' Ganmark paced slowly towards it, smiling up at the looming marble image of Stolicus. 'Even more beautiful in person than by report. It shall look very well in the gardens of Fontezarmo.' He was no more than five paces away. Monza tried to keep her breath slow, but her heart was hammering. 'I must congratulate you on your wonderful collection, your Excellency.'

'I shit on your congratulations,' sneered Salier.

'You shit on a great many things, it seems. But then a person of your size no doubt produces a vast quantity of the stuff. Bring the fat man closer.'

Now was the moment. Monza gripped the Calvez tight, stepped forwards, gloved right hand on Salier's elbow, Cosca moving up on his other side. Ganmark's officers and guards were spreading out, staring at the statue, at the garden, at Salier, peering through the windows into the hallways. A couple still stuck close to their general, one with his sword drawn, but they didn't look worried. Didn't look ready. All comrades together.

Friendly stood, still as a statue, sword in hand. Shivers' shield hung loose, but she saw his knuckles white on the haft of his axe, saw his good eye flickering from one enemy to another, judging the threat. Ganmark's grin spread as they led Salier forwards.

'Well, well, your Excellency. I still remember the text of that rousing speech, the one you made when you formed the League of Eight. What was it you said? That you'd rather die than kneel to a dog like Orso? I'd very much like to see you kneel, now.' He grinned at Monza as she came closer, no more than a couple of strides between them. 'Lieutenant, could you—' His pale eyes narrowed for an instant, and he knew her. She sprang at him, barging his nearest guard out of the way, lunging for his heart.

She felt the familiar scrape of steel on steel. In that flash Ganmark had somehow managed to get his sword half-drawn, enough to send her thrust wide by a hair. He jerked his head to one side and the point of the Calvez left him a long cut across his cheek before he flicked it away, his sword ringing clear from its sheath.

Then it was chaos in the garden.

Monza's blade left a long scratch down Ganmark's face. The nearest officer gave Friendly a puzzled look. 'But—'

Friendly's sword hacked deep into his head. The blade stuck in his skull as he fell, and Friendly let it go. A clumsy weapon, he preferred to work closer. He slid out the cleaver, the knife from his belt, felt the comfort of the familiar grips in his fists, the overwhelming relief that things were now simple. Kill as many as possible while they were surprised. Even the odds. Eleven against twenty-six were not good ones.

He stabbed a red-haired officer in the stomach before he could draw his sword, shoved him back into a third and sent his arm wide, crowded in close and hacked the cleaver into his shoulder, heavy blade splitting cloth and flesh. He dodged a spear-thrust and the soldier who held it stumbled past. Friendly sank the knife into his armpit, and out, blade scraping against the edge of his breastplate.

There was a screeching, rattling sound as the portcullis dropped. Two soldiers were standing in the archway. The gate came down just behind one, sealing him into the gallery with everyone else. The other must have leaned back, trying to get out of the way. The plummeting spikes caught him in the stomach and crushed him helpless into the floor, stoving in his breastplate, one leg folded underneath him, the other kicking wildly. He began to scream, but it hardly mattered. By then everyone was screaming.

The fight spread out across the garden, spilled into the four beautiful hallways surrounding it. Cosca dropped a guard with a slash across the backs of his thighs. Shivers had cut one man near in half when the fight began, and now was hemmed in by three more, backing towards the hall full of statues, swinging wildly, making a strange noise between a laugh and a roar.

The red-haired officer Friendly had stabbed limped away, groaning, through the doorway into the first hall, leaving a scattering of bloody spots across the polished floor. Friendly sprang after, rolled under a panicky sweep of his sword, came up and took the back of his head off with the cleaver. The soldier pinned under the portcullis gibbered, gurgled, tore pointlessly at the bars. The other one, only just now working out what was happening, pointed his halberd at Friendly. A confused-looking officer with a birthmark across one cheek turned from contemplation of one of the seventy-eight paintings in the hall and drew his sword.

Two of them. One and one. Friendly almost smiled. This he understood.

Monza slashed at Ganmark again but one of his soldiers got in her way, bundled into her with his shield. She slipped, rolled sideways and scrambled up, the fight thrashing around her.

She saw Salier give a bellow, whip out a narrow small-sword from behind his back and cut one astonished officer down with a slash across the face. He thrust at Ganmark, surprisingly agile for a man of his size, but nowhere near agile enough. The general sidestepped and calmly ran the Grand Duke of Visserine right through his big belly. Monza saw a bloody foot of metal slide out from the back of his white uniform. Just as it had slid out through the back of Benna's white shirt.

'Oof,' said Salier. Ganmark raised a boot and shoved him off, sent him stumbling back across the cobbles and into The Warrior's marble pedestal. The duke slid down it, plump hands clutched to the wound, blood soaking through the soft white cloth.

'Kill them all!' bellowed Ganmark. 'But mind the pictures!'

Two soldiers came at Monza. She hopped sideways so they got in each other's way, slid round a careless overhead chop from one, lunged and ran him through the groin, just under his breastplate. He made a great shriek, falling to his knees, but before she could find her balance again the other was swinging at her. She only just parried, the force almost jarring the Calvez from her hand. He slammed her in the chest with his shield and the rim of her breastplate dug into her stomach and drove her breath out, left her helpless. He raised his sword again, squawked, lurched sideways. One knee buckled and he pitched on his face, sliding forwards. The flights of a flatbow bolt stuck from the nape of his neck. Monza saw Day leaning from a window above, bow in her hands.

Ganmark pointed up towards her. 'Kill the blonde woman!' She vanished inside, and the last of the Talinese soldiers hurried obediently after her.

Salier stared down at the blood leaking out over his plump hands, eyes slightly unfocused. 'Whoever would've thought . . . I'd die fighting?' And his head dropped back against the statue's pedestal.

'Is there no end to the surprises the world throws up?' Ganmark undid the top button of his jacket and pulled a handkerchief from inside it, dabbed at the bleeding cut on his face, then carefully wiped Salier's blood from the blade of his sword. 'It's true, then. You are still alive.'

Monza had her breath back now, and her brother's sword up. 'It's true, cocksucker.'

'I always did admire the subtlety of your rhetoric.' The one Monza had stabbed through the groin was groaning as he tried to drag himself towards the entrance. Ganmark stepped carefully over him on his way towards her, tucking the bloody handkerchief into a pocket and doing his top button up again with his free hand. The crash, scrape, cry of fighting leaked from the halls beyond the colonnades, but for now they were alone in the garden. Unless you counted all the corpses scattered around the entrance. 'Just the two of us, then? It's been a while since I drew steel in earnest, but I'll endeavour not to disappoint you.'

'Don't worry about that. Your death will be entirely satisfying.'

He gave his weak smile, and his damp eyes drifted down to her sword. 'Fighting left-handed?'

'Thought I'd give you some kind of chance.'

'The least I can do is extend to you the same courtesy.' He

flicked his sword smartly from one palm into the other, switched his guard and pointed the blade towards her. 'Shall we—'

Monza had never been one to wait for an invitation. She lunged at him but he was ready, sidestepped it, came back at her with a sharp pair of cuts, high and low. Their blades rang together, slid and scraped, darting back and forth, glittering in the strips of sunlight between the trees. Ganmark's immaculately polished cavalry boots glided across the cobbles as nimbly as a dancer's. He jabbed at her, lightning fast. She parried once, twice, then nearly got caught and only just twisted away. She had to stumble back a few quick steps, take a breath and set herself afresh.

It is a deplorable thing to run from the enemy, Farans wrote, *but often better than the alternative.*

She watched Ganmark as he paced forwards, gleaming point of his sword moving in gentle little circles. 'You keep your guard too low, I am afraid. You are full of passion, but passion without discipline is no more than a child's tantrum.'

'Why don't you shut your fucking mouth and fight?'

'Oh, I can talk and cut pieces from you both at once.' He came at her in earnest, pushing her from one side of the garden to the other, parrying desperately, jabbing weakly back when she could, but not often, and to no effect.

She'd heard it said he was one of the greatest swordsmen in the world, and it wasn't hard to believe, even with his left hand. A good deal better than she'd been at her best, and her best was squashed under Gobba's boot and scattered down the mountainside beneath Fontezarmo. Ganmark was quicker, stronger, sharper. Which meant her only chance was to be cleverer, trickier, dirtier. Angrier.

She screeched as she came at him, feinted left, jabbed right. He sprang back, and she pulled her helmet off and flung it in his face. He saw it just in time to duck, it bounced from the top of his head and made him grunt. She came in after it but he twisted sideways and she only nicked the gold braid on the shoulder of his uniform. She jabbed and he parried, well set again.

'Tricky.'

'Get your arse fucked.'

'I think I might be in the mood, once I've killed you.' He

slashed at her, but instead of backing off she came in close, caught his sword, their hilts scraping. She tried to trip him but he stepped around her boot, just kept his balance. She kicked at him, caught his knee, his leg buckled for the briefest moment. She cut viciously, but Ganmark had already slid away and she only hacked a chunk from some topiary, little green leaves fluttering.

'There are easier ways to trim hedges, if that's your aim.' Almost before she knew it he was on her with a series of cuts, driving her across the cobbles. She hopped over the bloody corpse of one of his guards, ducked behind the great legs of the statue, keeping it between them, trying to think out some way to come at him. She undid the buckles on one side of her breastplate, pulled it open and let it clatter down. It was no protection against a swordsman of his skill, and the weight of it was only tiring her.

'No more tricks, Murcatto?'

'I'll think of something, bastard!'

'Think fast, then.' Ganmark's sword darted between the statue's legs and missed by a hair as she jerked out of its way. 'You don't get to win, you know, simply because you think yourself aggrieved. Because you believe yourself justified. It is the best swordsman who wins, not the angriest.'

He seemed about to slide around The Warrior's huge right leg, but came instead the other way, jumping over Salier's corpse slumped against the pedestal. She saw it coming, knocked his sword wide then hacked at his head with small elegance but large force. He ducked just in time. The blade of the Calvez clanged against Stolicus' well-muscled calf and sent chips of marble flying. She only just kept a hold on the buzzing grip, left hand aching as she reeled away.

Ganmark frowned, gently touched the crack in the statue's leg with his free hand. 'Pure vandalism.' He leaped at her, caught her sword and drove her back, once, then twice, her boots sliding from the cobbles and up onto the turf beside, fighting all the while to tease, or trick, or bludgeon out some opening she could use. But Ganmark saw everything well before it came, handled it with the simple efficiency of masterful skill. He was scarcely even breathing hard. The longer they fought the more he had her measure, and the slimmer dwindled her chances.

'You should mind that backswing,' he said. 'Too high. It limits your options and leaves you open.' She cut at him, and again, but he flicked them dismissively away. 'And you are prone to tilt your steel to the right when extended.' She jabbed and he caught the blade on his, metal sliding on metal, his sword whipping around hers. With an effortless twist of his wrist he tore the Calvez from her hand and sent it skittering across the cobbles. 'See what I mean?'

She took a shocked step back, saw the gleam of light as Ganmark's sword darted out. The blade slid neatly through the palm of her left hand, point passing between the bones and pricking her in the shoulder, bending her arm back and holding it pinned like meat and onions on a Gurkish skewer. The pain came an instant later, making her groan as Ganmark twisted the sword and drove her helplessly down onto her knees, bent backwards.

'If that feels undeserved from me, you can tell yourself it's a gift from the townsfolk of Caprile.' He twisted his sword the other way and she felt the point grind into her shoulder, the steel scrape against the bones in her hand, blood running down her forearm and into her jacket.

'Fuck you!' she spat at him, since it was that or scream.

His mouth twitched into that sad smile. 'A gracious offer, but your brother was more my type.' His sword whipped out of her and she lurched onto all fours, chest heaving. She closed her eyes, waiting for the blade to slide between her shoulder blades and through her heart, just the way it had through Benna's.

She wondered how much it would hurt, how long it would hurt for. A lot, most likely, but not for long.

She heard boot heels clicking away from her on cobbles, and slowly raised her head. Ganmark hooked his foot under the Calvez and flicked it up into his waiting hand. 'One touch to me, I rather think.' He tossed the sword arrow-like and it thumped into the turf beside her, wobbling gently back and forth. 'What do you say? Shall we make it the best of three?'

The long hall that housed Duke Salier's Styrian masterpieces was now further adorned by five corpses. The ultimate decoration for any palace, though the discerning dictator needs to replace them regularly if he is to avoid an odour. Especially in warm weather. Two of Salier's disguised soldiers and one of Ganmark's officers all sprawled bloodily in attitudes of scant dignity, though one of the general's guards had managed to die in a position approaching comfort, curled around an occasional table with an ornamental vase on top.

Another guard was dragging himself towards the far door, leaving a greasy red trail across the polished floor as he went. The wound Cosca had given him was in his stomach, just under his breastplate, and it was tough to crawl and hold your guts in all at once.

That left two young staff officers, bright swords drawn and bright eyes full of righteous hate, and Cosca. Probably they would both have been nice enough people under happier circumstances. Probably their mothers loved them and probably they loved their mothers back. Certainly they did not deserve to die here in this gaudy temple to greed simply for choosing one self-serving side over another. But what choice for Cosca other than to do his very best to kill them? The lowest slug, weed, slime struggle always to stay alive. Why should Styria's most infamous mercenary hold himself to another standard?

The two officers moved apart, one heading for the tall windows, the other for the paintings, herding Cosca towards the end of the room and, more than likely, the end of his life. He was prickly with sweat under the Talinese uniform, the breath burning his lungs. Fighting to the death was undeniably a young man's game.

'Now, now, lads,' he muttered, weighing his sword. 'How about you face me one at a time? Have you no honour?'

'No honour?' sneered one. 'Us?'

'You disguised yourself in order to launch a cowardly attack upon our general by stealth!' hissed the other, face pinking with outrage.

'True. True.' Cosca let the point of his sword drop. 'And the shame of it stabs at me. I surrender.'

The one on the left was not taken in for a moment. The one on the right looked somewhat puzzled, though, lowered his sword for an instant. It was him that Cosca flung his knife at.

It twittered through the air and thudded into the young man's side, doubling him over. Cosca charged in behind it, aiming for the chest. Perhaps the boy leaned forwards, or perhaps Cosca's aim was wayward, but the blade caught the officer's neck and, in a spectacular justification of all the sharpening, took his head clean off. It spun away, spraying spots of blood, bounced from one of the paintings with a hollow clonk and a flapping of canvas. The body keeled forwards, blood welling from the severed neck in long spurts and creeping out across the floor.

Even as Cosca yelped with surprised triumph, the other officer was on him, slashing away like a man beating a carpet. Cosca ducked, weaved, parried, jerked helplessly back from a savage cut, tripped over the headless corpse and went sprawling in the slick of blood around it.

The officer gave a shriek as he sprang to finish the work. Cosca's flailing hand clutched for the nearest thing, gripped it, flung it. The severed head. It caught the young man in the face and sent him stumbling. Cosca floundered to his blade and snatched it up, spun about, hand, sword, face, clothes all daubed with red. Strangely fitting, for a man who had lived the life he had.

The officer was already at him again with a flurry of furious cuts. Cosca gave ground as fast as he could without falling over, sword drooping, pretending at complete exhaustion and not having to pretend all that much. He collided with the table, nearly fell, his free hand fished behind him, found the rim of the ornamental jar. The officer came forwards, lifting his sword with a yelp of triumph. It turned to a gurgle of shock as the jar came flying at him. He managed to smash it away with the hilt of his sword, fragments of pottery bursting across one side of him, but that left his blade wide for a moment. Cosca made one last desperate lunge, felt a gentle resistance as his blade punched through the officer's cheek and out through the back of his head with textbook execution.

'Oh.' The officer wobbled slightly as Cosca whipped his sword back and capered sharply away. 'Is that . . .' His look was one of bleary-eyed surprise, like a man who had woken up drunk to find himself robbed and tied naked to a post. Cosca could not quite remember whether it was in Etrisani or Westport that had happened to him, those years all rather blended into one.

'Whasappenah?' The officer slashed with exaggerated slowness and Cosca stepped out of the way, let him spin round in a wide circle and sprawl over onto his side. He laboriously rolled, clambered up, blood running gently from the neat little slit beside his nose. The eye above it was flickering now, face on that side gone slack as old leather.

'Sluviduviduther,' he drooled.

'Your pardon?' asked Cosca.

'Slurghhh!' And he raised his quivering sword and charged. Directly sideways into the wall. He crashed into the painting of the girl surprised while bathing, tore a great gash through it with his flailing sword arm, brought the great canvas keeling down on top of him as he fell, one boot sticking out from underneath the gilded frame. He did not move again.

'The lucky bastard,' Cosca whispered. To die beneath a naked woman. It was the way he had always wanted to go.

The wound in Monza's shoulder burned. The one through her left hand burned far worse. Her palm, her fingers, sticky with blood. She could barely make a fist, let alone grip a blade. No choice, then. She dragged the glove from her right hand with her teeth, reached out and took hold of the Calvez' hilt with it, feeling the crooked bones shift as her twisted fingers closed around the grip, little one still painfully straight.

'Ah. Right-handed?' Ganmark flicked his sword spinning into the air, snatched it back with his own right hand as nimbly as a circus trickster. 'I always did admire your determination, if not the goals on which you trained it. Revenge, now, eh?'

'Revenge,' she snarled.

'Revenge. If you could even get it, what good would it do you? All this expenditure of effort, pain, treasure, blood, for what? Who is ever left better off for it?' His sad eyes watched her slowly stand. 'Not the avenged dead, certainly. They rot on, regardless. Not those who are avenged upon, of course. Corpses all. And what of the ones who take vengeance, what of them? Do they sleep easier, do you suppose, once they have heaped murder on murder? Sown the bloody seeds of a hundred other retributions?'

She circled around, trying to think of some trick to kill him with. 'All those dead men at that bank in Westport, that was your righteous work, I suppose? And the carnage at Cardotti's, a fair and proportionate reply?'

'What had to be done!'

'Ah, what had to be done. The favourite excuse of unexamined evil echoes down the ages and slobbers from your twisted mouth.' He danced at her, their swords rang together, once, twice. He jabbed, she parried and jabbed back. Each contact sent a jolt of pain up her arm. She ground her teeth together, forced the scowl to stay on her face, but there was no disguising how much it hurt her, or how clumsy she was with it. If she'd had small chances with her left, she had none at all with her right, and he knew it already.

'Why the Fates chose you for saving I will never guess, but you should have thanked it kindly and slunk away into obscurity. Let us not pretend you and your brother did not deserve precisely what you received.'

'Fuck yourself! I didn't deserve that!' But even as she said it, she had to wonder. 'My brother didn't!'

Ganmark snorted. 'No one is quicker to forgive a handsome man than I, but your brother was a vindictive coward. A charming, greedy, ruthless, spineless parasite. A man of the very lowest character imaginable. The only thing that lifted him from utter worthlessness, and utter inconsequence, was you.' He sprang at her with lethal speed and she reeled away, fell against a cherry tree with a grunt and stumbled back through the shower of white blossom. He could surely have spitted her but he stayed still as a statue, sword at the ready, smiling faintly as he watched her thrash her way clear.

'And let us face the facts, General Murcatto. You, for all your undeniable talents, have hardly been a paragon of virtue. Why, there must be a hundred thousand people with just reasons to fling your hated carcass from that terrace!'

'Not Orso. Not him!' She came low, jabbing sloppily at his hips, wincing as he flicked her sword aside and jarred the grip in her twisted palm.

'If that's a joke, it's not a funny one. Quibble with the judge, when the sentence is self-evidently more than righteous?' He placed his feet with all the watchful care of an artist applying paint to a canvas, steering her back onto the cobbles. 'How many deaths have you had a hand in? How much destruction? You are a bandit! A glorified profiteer! You are a maggot grown fat on the rotting corpse of Styria!' Three more blows, rapid as a sculptor's hammer on his chisel, snapping her sword this way and that in her aching grip. 'Did not deserve, you say to me, *did not deserve*? That excuse for a right hand is embarrassing enough. Pray do not shame yourself further.'

She made a tired, pained, clumsy lunge. He deflected it disdainfully, already stepping around her and letting her stumble past. She expected his sword in her back; instead she felt his boot thud into her arse and send her sprawling across the cobbles, Benna's sword bouncing from her numb fingers one more time. She lay there a moment, panting for breath, then slowly rolled over, came up to her knees. There hardly seemed much point standing. She'd be back here soon enough, once he ran her through. Her right hand throbbed, trembled. The shoulder of her stolen uniform was dark with blood, the fingers of her left hand were dripping with it.

Ganmark flicked his wrist, whipped the head from a flower and into his waiting palm. He lifted it to his face and breathed in deep. 'A beautiful day, and a good place to die. We should have finished you up at Fontezarmo, along with your brother. But now will do.'

She couldn't think of much in the way of sharp last words, so she just tipped her head back and spat at him. It spattered against his neck, his collar, the pristine front of his uniform. Not much vengeance, maybe, but something. Ganmark peered down at it. 'A perfect lady to the end.'

His eyes flickered sideways and he jerked away as something flashed past him, twittered into a flower bed behind. A thrown knife. There was a snarl and Cosca was on him, barking like a mad dog as he harried the general back across the cobbles.

'Cosca!' Fumbling her sword up. 'Late, as ever.'

'I was somewhat occupied next door,' growled the old mercenary, pausing to catch his breath.

'Nicomo Cosca?' Ganmark frowned at him. 'I thought you were dead.'

'There have always been false reports of my death. Wishful thinking—'

'On the part of his many enemies.' Monza stood, shaking the weakness out of her limbs. 'You've got a mind to kill me, you should get it done instead of talking about it.'

Ganmark backed slowly away, sliding his short steel from its sheath with his left hand, pointing it towards her, the long towards Cosca, his eyes flitting back and forth between them. 'Oh, there's still time.'

Shivers weren't himself. Or maybe he finally was. The pain had turned him mad. Or the eye they'd left him wasn't working right. Or he was still all broken up from the husk he'd been sucking at the past few days. Whatever the reasons, he was in hell.

And he liked it.

The long hall pulsed, glowed, swam like a rippling pool. Sunlight burned through the windows, stabbing and flashing at him through a hundred hundred glittering squares of glass. The statues shone, smiled, sweated, cheered him on. He might've had one eye less than before, but he saw things clearer. The pain had swept away all his doubts, his fears, his questions, his choices. All that shit had been dead weight on him. All that shit was weakness, and lies, and a waste of effort. He'd made himself think things were complicated when they were beautifully, awfully simple. His axe had all the answers he needed.

Its blade caught the sunlight and left a great white, fizzing smear, hacked into a man's arm sending black streaks flying. Cloth flapping. Flesh torn. Bone splintered. Metal bent and twisted. A spear squealed across Shivers' shield and he could taste the roar in his mouth, sweet as he swung the axe again. It crashed into a breastplate and left a huge dent, sent a body flailing into a pitted urn, burst it apart, writhing on the floor in a mass of shattered pottery.

The world was turned inside out, like the glistening innards of the officer he'd gutted a few moments before. He used to get tired when he fought. Now he got stronger. The rage boiled up in him, leaked out of him, set his skin on fire. With every blow he struck it got worse, better, muscles burning until he had to scream it out, laugh it out, weep, sing, thrash, dance, shriek.

He smashed a sword away with his shield, tore it from a hand, was on the soldier behind it, arms around him, kissing his face, licking at him. He roared as he ran, ran, legs pounding, rammed him into one of the statues, sent it over, crashing into another, and another beyond that, tipping, smashing on the floor, breaking apart into chunks in a cloud of dust.

The guard groaned, sprawling in the ruins, tried to roll over. Shivers' axe stoved the top of his helmet in deep with a hollow clonk, drove the metal rim right down over his eyes and squashed his nose flat, blood running out from underneath.

'Fucking die!' Shivers bashed in the side of the helmet and sent his head one way. 'Die!' Swung back and crumpled the other side, neck crunching like a sock full of gravel. 'Die! Die!' Bonk, bonk, like pots and pans clattering in the river after mealtime. A statue looked on, disapproving.

'Look at me?' Shivers smashed its head off with his axe. Then he was on top of someone, not knowing how he got there, ramming the edge of his shield into a face until it was nothing but a shapeless mess of red. He could hear someone whispering, whispering in his ear. Mad, hissing, croaking voice.

'I am made of death. I am the Great Leveller. I am the storm in the High Places.' The Bloody-Nine's voice, but it came from his own throat. The hall was strewn with fallen men and fallen statues, scattered with bits of both. 'You.' Shivers pointed his bloody axe at the last of them, cringing at the far end of the dusty hallway. 'I see you there, fucker. No one gets away.' He realised he was talking in Northern. The man couldn't understand a word he said. Hardly mattered, though.

He reckoned he got the gist.

Monza forced herself on down the arcade, wringing the last strength from her aching legs, snarling as she lunged, jabbed, cut clumsily, not letting up for a moment. Ganmark was on the retreat, dropping back through sunlight, then shadow, then sunlight again, frowning with furious concentration. His eyes flickered from side to side, parrying her blade and Cosca's as it jabbed at him from between the pillars on her right, their hard breathing, their shuffling footsteps, the quick scraping of steel echoing from the vaulted ceiling.

She cut at him, then back the other way, ignoring the burning pain in her fist as she tore the short steel from his hand and sent it clattering into the shadows. Ganmark lurched away, only just turned one of Cosca's thrusts wide with his long steel, left his unguarded side facing her. She grinned, was pulling her arm back to lunge when something crashed into the window on her left, sent splinters of glass flying into her face. She thought she heard Shivers' voice, roaring in Northern from the other side. Ganmark slipped between two pillars as Cosca slashed at him and away across the lawn, backing off into the centre of the garden.

'Could you get on and kill this bastard?' wheezed Cosca.

'Doing my best. You go left.'

'Left it is.' They moved apart, herding Ganmark towards the statue. He looked spent now, blowing hard, soft cheeks turned blotchy pink and shining with sweat. She smiled as she feinted at him, sensing victory, felt her smile slip as he suddenly sprang to meet her. She dodged his first thrust, slashed at his neck, but he caught it and pushed her away. He was a lot less spent than she'd thought, and she was a lot more. Her foot came down badly and she tottered sideways. Ganmark darted past and his sword left a burning cut across her thigh. She tried to turn, screeched as her leg crumpled, fell and rolled, the Calvez tumbling from her limp fingers and bouncing away.

Cosca sprang past with a hoarse cry, swinging wildly. Ganmark dropped under his cut, lunged from the ground and ran him neatly through the stomach. Cosca's sword clanged hard into The Warrior's shin and flew from his hand, stone chips spinning. The general whipped his blade free and Cosca dropped to his knees, sagged sideways with a long groan.

'And that's that.' Ganmark turned towards her, Bonatine's greatest work looming up behind him. A few flakes of marble trickled from the statue's ankle, already cracked where Monza's sword had chopped into it. 'You've given me some exercise, I'll grant you that. You are a woman – or have been a woman – of remarkable determination.' Cosca dragged himself across the cobbles, leaving spotty smears of blood behind him. 'But in keeping your eyes always ahead, you blinded yourself to everything around you. To the nature of the great war you fight in. To the natures of the people closest to you.' Ganmark flicked out his handkerchief again, dabbed sweat from his forehead, carefully wiped blood from his steel. 'If Duke Orso and his state of Talins are no more than a sword in the hand of Valint and Balk, then you were never more than that sword's ruthless point.' He flicked the shining point of his own sword with his forefinger. 'Always stabbing, always killing, but never considering why.' There was a gentle creaking, and over his shoulder The Warrior's own great sword wobbled ever so slightly. 'Still. It hardly matters now. For you the fight is over.' Ganmark still wore his sad smile as he came to a stop a stride from her. 'Any pithy last words?'

'Behind you,' growled Monza through gritted teeth, as The Warrior rocked ever so gently forwards.

'You must take me for—' There was a loud bang. The statue's leg split in half and the whole vast weight of stone toppled inexorably forwards.

Ganmark was just beginning to turn as the point of Stolicus' giant sword pinned him between the shoulder blades, drove him onto his knees, burst out through his stomach and crashed into the cobbles, spraying blood and rock chips in Monza's stinging face. The statue's legs broke apart as they hit the ground, noble feet left on the pedestal, the rest cracking into muscular chunks and rolling around in a cloud of white marble dust. From the hips up, the proud image of the greatest soldier of history stayed in one magnificent piece, staring sternly down at Orso's general, impaled on his monstrous sword beneath him.

Ganmark made a sucking sound like water draining from a broken bath, and coughed blood down the front of his uniform. His head fell forwards, steel clattering from his dangling hand.

There was a moment of stillness.

'Now that,' croaked Cosca, 'is what I call a happy accident.'

Four dead, three left. Monza saw someone creep out from one of the colonnades, grimaced as she shuffled to her sword and dragged it up for the third time, hardly sure which ruined hand to hold it in. It was Day, loaded flatbow levelled. Friendly trudged along behind her, knife and cleaver hanging from his fists.

'You got him?' asked the girl.

Monza looked at Ganmark's corpse, kneeling spitted on the great length of bronze. 'Stolicus did.'

Cosca had kicked his way as far as one of the cherry trees and sat with his back against the trunk. He looked just like a man relaxing on a summer's day. Apart from the bloody hand pressed to his stomach. She limped up to him, stuck the Calvez point-first into the turf and knelt down.

'Let me have a look.' She fumbled with the buttons on Cosca's jacket, but before she got the second one undone he reached up, gently took her bloody hand and her twisted one in his.

'I've been waiting years for you to tear my clothes off, but I think I'll have politely to decline. I'm finished.'

'You? Never.'

He squeezed her hands tighter. 'Right through the guts, Monza. It's over.' His eyes rolled towards the gate, and she could hear the faint clattering as soldiers on the other side struggled to lever the portcullis open. 'And you'll have other problems soon enough. Four of seven, though, girl.' He grinned. 'Never thought you'd make four of seven.'

'Four of seven,' muttered Friendly, behind her.

'I wish I could've made Orso one of them.'

'Well.' Cosca raised his brows. 'It's a noble calling, but I guess you can't kill everyone.'

Shivers was walking slowly over from one of the doorways. He barely even glanced at Ganmark's impaled corpse as he passed. 'None left?'

'Not in here.' Friendly nodded towards the gate. 'Some out there, though.'

'Reckon so.' The Northman stopped not far away. His hanging axe, his dented shield, his pale face and the bandages across one half of it were all dashed and speckled dark red.

'You alright?' asked Monza

'Don't rightly know what I am.'

'Are you hurt, I'm asking?'

He touched one hand to the bandages. 'No worse'n before we started . . . reckon I must be beloved o' the moon today, as the hillmen say.' His eye rolled down to her bloody shoulder, her bloody hand. 'You're bleeding.'

'My fencing lesson turned ugly.'

'You need a bandage?'

She nodded towards the gateway, the noise of the Talinese

soldiers on the other side getting louder with every moment. 'We'll be lucky if we get the time to bleed to death.'

'What now, then?'

She opened her mouth, but nothing came out. There was no use fighting, even if she'd had the strength. The palace would be swarming with Orso's soldiers. There was no use surrendering, even if she'd been the type. They'd be lucky if they made it back to Fontezarmo to be killed. Benna had always warned her she didn't think far enough ahead, and it seemed he'd had a point—

'I've an idea.' Day's face had broken out in an unexpected smile. Monza followed her pointing finger, up to the roofline above the garden, and squinted into the sun. A black figure crouched there against the bright sky.

'A *fine* afternoon to you!' She never thought she'd be glad to hear Castor Morveer's scraping whine. 'I was hoping to view the Duke of Visserine's famous collection and I appear to have become entirely lost! I don't suppose any of you kind gentlefolk know where I might find it? I hear he has Bonatine's greatest work!'

Monza jerked her bloody thumb at the ruined statue. 'Not all it's cracked up to be!'

Vitari had appeared beside the poisoner now, was smoothly lowering a rope. 'We're rescued,' grunted Friendly, in just the same tone as he might have said, 'We're dead.'

Monza hardly had the energy even to feel pleased. She hardly knew if she was pleased. 'Day, Shivers, get up there.'

'No doubt.' Day tossed her bow away and ran for it. The Northman frowned at Monza for a moment, then followed.

Friendly was looking down at Cosca. 'What about him?' The old mercenary seemed to have dozed off for a moment, eyelids flickering.

'We'll have to pull him up. Get a hold.'

The convict slid one arm around his back and started to lift him. Cosca woke with a jolt, grimaced. 'Dah! No, no, no, no, no.' Friendly let him carefully back down and Cosca shook his scabby head, breathing ragged. 'I'm not screaming my way up a rope just so I can die on a roof. Here's as good a place as any, and this as good a time. I've been promising to do it for years. Might as well keep my word this once.'

She squatted down beside him. 'I'd rather call you a liar one more time, and keep you watching my back.'

'I only stayed there . . . because I like looking at your arse.' He bared his teeth, winced, gave a long growl. The clanging at the gate was getting louder.

Friendly offered Cosca's sword to him. 'They'll be coming. You want this?'

'Why would I? It was messing with those things got me into this fix in the first place.' He tried to shift, winced and sagged back, his skin already carrying that waxy sheen that corpses have.

Vitari and Morveer had bundled Shivers over the gutter and onto the roof. Monza jerked her head at Friendly. 'Your turn.'

He crouched there for a moment, not moving, then looked to Cosca. 'Do you want me to stay?'

The old mercenary took Friendly's big hand and smiled as he gave it a squeeze. 'I am touched beyond words to hear you make the offer. But no, my friend. This I had better handle alone. Give your dice a roll for me.'

'I will.' Friendly stood and strode off towards the rope without a backward glance. Monza watched him go. Her hands, her shoulder, her leg burned, her battered body ached. Her eyes slunk over the bodies scattered across the garden. Sweet victory. Sweet vengeance. Men turned into meat.

'Do me one favour.' Cosca had a sad smile, almost as if he guessed her thoughts.

'You came back for me, didn't you? I can stretch to one.'

'Forgive me.'

She made a sound – half-snort, half-retch. 'I thought I was the one betrayed you?'

'What does it matter now? Treachery is commonplace. Forgiveness is rare. I'd rather go without any debts. Except all the money I owe in Ospria. And Adua. And Dagoska.' He weakly waved one bloody hand. 'Let's say no debts to you, anyway, and leave it at that.'

'That I can do. We're even.'

'Good. I lived like shit. Glad to see at least I got the dying right. Get on.'

Part of her wanted to stay with him, to be with him when Orso's men broke through the gate, make sure there really were no debts. But not that big a part. She'd never been prone to sentiment. Orso had to die, and if she was killed here, who'd get it done? She pulled the Calvez from the ground, slid it back into its sheath and turned without another word. Words are poor tools at a time like that. She limped to the rope, tied it off under her hips the best she could, twisted it around her wrist.

'Let's go!'

From the roof Monza could see right across the city. The wide curve of the Visser and its graceful bridges. The many towers poking at the sky, dwarfed by pillars of smoke still rising from the scattered fires. Day had already got a pear from somebody and was biting happily into it, yellow curls blowing on the breeze, juice gleaming on her chin.

Morveer raised one eyebrow at the carnage down in the garden. 'I am relieved to observe that, in my absence, you succeeded in keeping the slaughter under tight control.'

'Some things never change,' she snapped at him.

'Cosca?' asked Vitari.

'Not coming.'

Morveer gave a sickening little grin. 'He failed to save his own skin this time? So a drunkard can change after all.'

Rescue or not, Monza would have stabbed him at that moment if she'd had a good hand to do it with. From the way Vitari scowled at the poisoner, she was feeling much the same. She jerked her spiky head towards the river instead. 'We should have the tearful reunion down in the boat. The city's full of Orso's troops. High time we were floating out to sea.'

Monza took one last look back. All was still down in the garden. Salier had slid from the fallen statue's pedestal and rolled onto his back, arms outstretched as if welcoming a dear old friend. Ganmark knelt in a wide slick of blood, impaled on The Warrior's great bronze blade, head dangling. Cosca's eyes were closed, hands resting in his lap, a slight smile still on his tipped-back face. Cherry blossom wafted down and settled across his stolen uniform.

'Cosca, Cosca,' she murmured. 'What will I do without you?'

V
PURANTI

'For mercenaries are disunited, thirsty for power, undisciplined, and disloyal; they are brave among their friends and cowards before the enemy; they have no fear of God, they do not keep faith with their fellow men; they avoid defeat just as long as they avoid battle; in peacetime you are despoiled by them and in wartime by the enemy'

Niccolò Machiavelli

For two years, half the Thousand Swords pretended to fight the other half. Cosca, when he was sober enough to speak, boasted that never before in history had men made so much for doing so little. They sucked the coffers of Nicante and Affoia bone dry, then turned north when their hopes were dashed by the sudden outbreak of peace, seeking new wars to profit from, or ambitious employers to begin them.

No employer was more ambitious than Orso, the new Grand Duke of Talins, kicked to power after his elder brother was kicked by his favourite horse. He was all too eager to sign a Paper of Engagement with the well-known mercenary Monzcarro Murcatto. Especially since his enemies in Etrea had but lately hired the infamous Nicomo Cosca to lead their troops.

It proved difficult to bring the two to battle, however. Like two cowards circling before a brawl, they spent a whole season in ruinously expensive manoeuvrings, doing much harm to the farmers of the region but little to each other. They were finally urged together in ripe wheat-fields near the village of Afieri, where a battle seemed sure to follow. Or something that looked very like one.

But that evening Monza had an unexpected visitor to her tent. None other than Duke Orso himself.

'Your Excellency, I had not expected—'

'No need for pleasantries. I know what Nicomo Cosca has planned for tomorrow.'

Monza frowned. 'I imagine he plans to fight, and so do I.'

'He plans no such thing, and neither do you. The pair of you have been making fools of your employers for the past two years. I do not care to be made a fool of. I can see fake battles in the theatre at a fraction of the cost. That is why I will pay you twice to fight him in earnest.'

Monza had not been expecting this. 'I . . .'

'You have loyalty to him, I know. I respect that. Everyone must stick at something in their lives. But Cosca is the past, and I have decided that you are the future. Your brother agrees with me.'

Monza had certainly not been expecting that. She stared at Benna, and he grinned back. 'It's better like this. You deserve to lead.'

'I can't . . . the other captains will never—'

'I spoke to them already,' said Benna. 'All except Faithful, and that old dog will follow along when he sees how the wind's blowing. They're sick of Cosca, and his drinking, and his foolishness. They want a long contract and a leader they can be proud of. They want you.'

The Duke of Talins was watching. She could not afford to seem reluctant. 'Then I accept, of course. You had me at paid twice,' she lied.

Orso smiled. 'I have a feeling you and I will do well for one another, General Murcatto. I will look forward to news of your victory tomorrow.' And he left.

When the tent flap dropped Monza cuffed her brother across the face and knocked him to the ground. 'What have you done, Benna? What have you done?'

He looked sullenly up at her, one hand to his bloody mouth. 'I thought you'd be pleased.'

'No you fucking didn't! You thought you'd be. I hope you are.'

But there was nothing she could do but forgive him, and make the best of it. He was her brother. The only one who really knew her. And Sesaria, Victus, Andiche and most of the other captains had agreed. They were tired of Nicomo Cosca. So there could be no turning back. The next day, as dawn slunk out of the east and they prepared for the coming battle, Monza ordered her men to charge in earnest. What else could she do?

By evening she was sitting in Cosca's chair, with Benna grinning beside her and her newly enriched captains drinking to her first victory. Everyone laughed but her. She was thinking of Cosca, and all he had given her, what she had owed him and how she had paid him back. She was in no mood to celebrate.

Besides, she was captain general of the Thousand Swords. She could not afford to laugh.

Sixes

The dice came up a pair of sixes.

In the Union they call that score suns, like the sun on their flag. In Baol they call it twice won, because the house pays double on it. In Gurkhul they call it the Prophet or the Emperor, depending where a man's loyalty lies. In Thond it is the golden dozen. In the Thousand Isles, twelve winds. In Safety they call two sixes the jailer, because the jailer always wins. All across the Circle of the World men cheer for that score, but to Friendly it was no better than any other. It won him nothing. He turned his attention back to the great bridge of Puranti, and the men crossing it.

The faces of the statues on their tall columns might have worn to pitted blobs, the roadway might have cracked with age and the parapet crumbled, but the six arches still soared tall and graceful, scornful of the dizzy drop below. The great piers of rock from which they sprang, six times six strides high, still defied the battering waters. Six hundred years old and more, but the Imperial bridge was still the only way across the Pura's deep gorge at this time of year. The only way to Ospria by land.

The army of Grand Duke Rogont marched across it in good order, six men abreast. The regular tramp, tramp of their boots was like a mighty heartbeat, accompanied by the jingle and clatter of arms and harness, the occasional calls of officers, the steady murmur of the watching crowd, the rushing throb of the river far below. They had been marching across it all morning, now, by company, by battalion, by regiment. Moving forests of spear tips, gleaming metal and studded leather. Dusty, dirty, determined faces. Proud flags hanging limp on the still air. Their six-hundredth rank had passed not long before. Some four thousand men across already and at least as many more to follow. Six, by six, by six, they came.

'Good order. For a retreat.' Shivers' voice had withered to a throaty whisper in Visserine.

Vitari snorted. 'If there's one thing Rogont knows how to manage it's a retreat. He's had enough practice.'

'One must appreciate the irony,' observed Morveer, watching the soldiers pass with a look of faint scorn. 'Today's proud legions march over the last vestiges of yesterday's fallen empire. So it always is with military splendour. Hubris made flesh.'

'How incredibly profound.' Murcatto curled her lip. 'Why, travelling with the great Morveer is both pleasure and education.'

'I am philosopher and poisoner all in one. I *pray* you not to worry, though, my fee covers both. Remunerate me for my bottomless insights, the poison comes free of charge.'

'Does our luck have no end?' she grated back.

'Does it even have a beginning?' murmured Vitari.

The group was down to six, and those more irritable than ever. Murcatto, hood drawn up, black hair hanging lank from inside, only her pointed nose and chin and hard mouth visible. Shivers, half his head still bandaged and the other half milk-pale, his one eye sunk in a dark ring. Vitari, sitting on the parapet with her legs stretched out and her shoulders propped against a broken column, freckled face tipped back towards the bright sun. Morveer, frowning down at the churning water, his apprentice leaning nearby. And Friendly, of course. Six. Cosca was dead. In spite of his name, Friendly rarely kept friends long.

'Talking of remuneration,' Morveer droned on, 'we should visit the nearest bank and have a note drawn up. I hate to have debts outstanding between myself and an employer. It leaves a sour taste on our otherwise honey-sweet relationship.'

'Sweet,' grunted Day, around a mouthful, though whether she was talking about her cake or the relationship, it was impossible to say.

'You owe me for my part in General Ganmark's demise, a peripheral yet vital one, since it prevented you from partaking in a demise of your own. I have also to replace the equipment so carelessly lost in Visserine. Need I once again point out that, had you allowed me to remove our problematic farmers as I desired, there would have been no—'

'Enough,' hissed Murcatto. 'I don't pay you to be reminded of my mistakes.'

'I imagine that service too is free of charge.' Vitari slid down from the parapet. Day swallowed the last of her cake and licked her fingers. They all made ready to move, except for Friendly. He stayed, looking down at the water.

'Time to move,' said Murcatto.

'Yes. I am going back to Talins.'

'You're what?'

'Sajaam was sending word to me here, but there is no letter.'

'It's a long way to Talins. There's a war—'

'This is Styria. There's always a war.'

There was a pause while she looked at him, her eyes almost hidden in her hood. The others watched, none showing much feeling at his going. People rarely did, when he went, and nor did he. 'You're sure?' she asked.

'Yes.' He had seen half of Styria – Westport, Sipani, Visserine and much of the country in between, and hated it all. He had felt shiftless and scared sitting in Sajaam's smoke-house, dreaming of Safety. Now those long days, the smell of husk, the endless cards and posturing, the routine rounds of the slums collecting money, the occasional moments of predictable and well-structured violence, all seemed like some happy dream. There was nothing for him out here, where every day was under a different sky. Murcatto was chaos, and he wanted no more of her.

'Take this then.' She pulled a purse out from her coat.

'I am not here for your money.'

'Take it anyway. It's a lot less than you deserve. Might make the journey easier.' He let her press it into his hand.

'Luck be at your back,' said Shivers.

Friendly nodded. 'The world is made of six, today.'

'Six be at your back, then.'

'It will be, whether I want it or not.' Friendly swept up the dice with the side of his hand, wrapped them carefully in their cloth and tucked them down inside his jacket. Without a backward glance he slipped off through the crowds lining the bridge, against the endless current of soldiers, over the endless current of water. He left both behind, struck on into the smaller, meaner part of the city on the river's western side. He would pass the time by counting the number of strides it took him to reach Talins. Since he said his goodbyes he had made already three hundred and sixty-six—

'Master Friendly!' He jerked round, frowning, hands itching ready to move to knife and cleaver. A figure leaned lazily in a doorway off the street, arms and boots crossed, face all in shadow. 'Whatever are the odds of meeting you here?' The voice sounded terribly familiar. 'Well, you would know the odds better than me, I'm sure, but a happy chance indeed, on that we can agree.'

'We can,' said Friendly, beginning to smile as he realised who it was.

'Why, I feel almost as if I threw a pair of sixes . . .'

The Eye-Maker

A bell tinkled as Shivers shoved the door open and stepped through into the shop, Monza at his shoulder. It was dim inside, light filtering through the window in a dusty shaft and falling across a marble counter, shadowy shelves down one wall. At the back, under a hanging lamp, was a big chair with a leather pad to rest your head on. Might've looked inviting, except for the straps to hold the sitter down. On a table beside it a neat row of instruments were laid out. Blades, needles, clamps, pliers. Surgeon's tools.

That room might've given him a cold tremble fit to match his name once, but no more. He'd had his eye burned out of his face, and lived to learn the lessons. The world hardly seemed to have any horrors left. Made him smile, to think how scared he'd always been before. Scared of everything and nothing. Smiling tugged at the great wound under his bandages and made his face burn, so he stopped.

The bell brought a man creeping through a side door, hands rubbing nervously together. Small and dark-skinned with a sorry face. Worried they were here to rob him, more'n likely, what with Orso's army not far distant. Everyone in Puranti seemed worried, scared they'd lose what they had. Apart from Shivers himself. He hadn't much to lose.

'Sir, madam, can I be of assistance?'

'You're Scopal?' asked Monza. 'The eye-maker?'

'I am Scopal,' he bent a nervous bow, 'scientist, surgeon, physician, specialising in all things relating to the vision.'

Shivers undid the knot at the back of his head. 'Good enough.' And he started unwinding the bandages. 'Fact is I've lost an eye.'

That perked the surgeon up. 'Oh, don't say lost, my friend!' He came forwards into the light from the window. 'Don't say lost until I have had a chance to view the damage. You would be amazed at what can be achieved! Science is leaping forwards every day!'

'Springy bastard, ain't it.'

Scopal gave an uncertain chuckle. 'Ah . . . most elastic. Why, I have returned a measure of sight to men who thought themselves blind for life. They called me a magician! Imagine that! They called me . . . a . . .'

Shivers peeled away the last bandages, the air cold against his tingling skin, and he stepped up closer, turning the left side of his face forwards. 'Well? What do you reckon? Can science make that big a jump?'

The man gave a polite nod. 'My apologies. But even in the area of replacement I have made great discoveries, never fear!'

Shivers took a half-step further, looming over the man. 'Do I look feared to you?'

'Not in the least, of course, I merely meant . . . well . . .' Scopal cleared his throat and sidled to the shelves. 'My current process for an ocular prosthesis is—'

'The fuck?'

'Fake eye,' said Monza.

'Oh, much, much more than that.' Scopal slid out a wooden rack. Six metal balls sat on it, gleaming silver-bright. 'A perfect sphere of the finest Midderland steel is inserted into the orbit where it will, one hopes, remain permanently.' He brought down a round board, flipped it towards them with a showy twist. It was covered with eyes. Blue ones, green ones, brown ones. Each had the colour of a real eye, the gleam of a real eye, some of the whites even had a red vein or two in 'em. And still they looked about as much like a real eye as a boiled egg might've.

Scopal waved at his wares with high smugness. 'A curved enamel such as these, painted with care to match perfectly your other eye, is then inserted between metal ball and eyelid. These are prone to wear, and must therefore be regularly changed, but, believe me, the results can be uncanny.'

The fake eyes stared, unblinking, at Shivers. 'They look like dead men's eyes.'

An uncomfortable pause. 'When glued upon a board, of course, but properly fitted within a living face—'

'Reckon it's a good thing. Dead men tell no lies, eh? We'll have no more lies.' Shivers strode to the back of the shop, dropped down into the chair, stretched out and crossed his legs. 'Get to it, then.'

'At once?'

'Why not?'

'The steel will take an hour or two to fit. Preparing a set of enamels usually requires at least a fortnight—' Monza tossed a stack of silver coins onto the counter and they jingled as they spilled across the stone. Scopal humbly bowed his head. 'I will fit the closest I have, and have the rest ready by tomorrow evening.' He turned the lamp up so bright Shivers had to shield his good eye with one hand. 'It will be necessary to make some incisions.'

'Some whats, now?'

'Cuts,' said Monza.

' 'Course it will. Nothing in life worth doing that doesn't need a blade, eh?'

Scopal shuffled the instruments around on the little table. 'Followed by some stitches, the removal of the useless flesh—'

'Dig out the dead wood? I'm all for it. Let's have a fresh start.'

'Might I suggest a pipe?'

'Fuck, yes,' he heard Monza whisper.

'Suggest away,' said Shivers. 'I'm getting bored o' pain the last few weeks.'

The eye-maker bowed his head, eased off to charge the pipe. 'I remember you getting your hair cut,' said Monza. 'Nervous as a lamb at its first shearing.'

'Heh. True.'

'Now look at you, keen to be fitted for an eye.'

'A wise man once told me you have to be realistic. Strange how fast we change, ain't it, when we have to?'

She frowned back at him. 'Don't change too far. I've got to go.'

'No stomach for the eye-making business?'

'I've got to renew an acquaintance.'

'Old friend?'

'Old enemy.'

Shivers grinned. 'Dearer yet. Watch you don't get killed, eh?' And he settled back in the chair, pulled the strap tight round his forehead. 'We've still got work to do.' He closed his good eye, the lamplight glowing pink through the lid.

Prince of Prudence

Grand Duke Rogont had made his headquarters in the Imperial Bath-Hall. The building was still one of the greatest in Puranti, casting half the square at the east end of the old bridge into shadow. But like the rest of the city, it had seen better centuries. Half its great pediment and two of the six mighty pillars that once held it up had collapsed lifetimes before, the stone pilfered for the mismatched walls of newer, meaner buildings. The stained masonry sprouted with grass, with dead ivy, with a couple of stubborn little trees, even. Probably baths had been a higher priority when it was built, before everyone in Styria started trying to kill each other. Happy times, when keeping the water hot enough had been anyone's biggest worry. The crumbling building might have whispered of the glories of a lost age, but made a sad comment on Styria's long decline.

If Monza had cared a shit.

But she had other things on her mind. She waited for a gap to appear between one tramping company of Rogont's retreating army and the next, then she forced her shoulders back and strode across the square. Up the cracked steps of the Bath-Hall, trying to walk with all her old swagger while her crooked hip bone clicked back and forth in its socket and sent stings right through her arse. She pushed her hood back, keeping her eyes fixed on the foremost of the guards, a grizzled-looking veteran wide as a door with a scar down one colourless cheek.

'I need to speak to Duke Rogont,' she said.

'Of course.'

'I'm Mon . . . what?' She'd been expecting to explain herself. Probably to be laughed at. Possibly to be strung up from one of the pillars. Certainly not to be invited in.

'You're General Murcatto.' The man had a twist to his grey mouth that came somewhere near a smile. 'And you're expected.

I'll need the sword, though.' She frowned as she handed it over, liking the feel of this less than if they'd kicked her down the street.

There was a great pool in the marble hall beyond, surrounded by tall columns, murky water smelling strongly of rot. Her old enemy Grand Duke Rogont was poring over a map on a folding table, in a sober grey uniform, lips thoughtfully pursed. A dozen officers clustered about him, enough gold braid between them to rig a carrack. A couple looked up as she made her way around the fetid pond towards them.

'It's her,' she heard one say, his lip well curled.

'Mur . . . cat . . . to,' another, as if the very name was poison. No doubt it was to them. She'd been making fools of these very men for the past few years and the more of a fool a man is, the less he cares to look like one. Still, *the general with the smallest numbers should remain always on the offensive*, Stolicus wrote. So she walked up unhurried, the thumb of her bandaged left hand hooked carelessly in her belt, as if this was her bath and she was the one with all the swords.

'If it isn't the Prince of Prudence, Duke Rogont. Well met, your Cautiousness. A proud-looking set of comrades you've got here, for men who've spent seven years retreating. Still, at least you're not retreating today.' She let it sink in for a moment. 'Oh, wait. You are.'

That forced a few chins to haughtily rise, a nostril or two to flare. But the dark eyes of Rogont himself shifted up from the map without any rush, a little tired, perhaps, but still irritatingly handsome and at ease. 'General Murcatto, what a pleasure! I wish we could have met after a great battle, preferably with you as a crestfallen prisoner, but my victories have been rather thin on the ground.'

'Rare as summer snows.'

'And you, so cloaked in glories. I feel quite naked under your victorious glare.' He peered towards the back of the hall. 'But wherever are your all-conquering Thousand Swords now?'

Monza sucked her teeth. 'Faithful Carpi's borrowed them from me.'

'Without asking? How . . . rude. I fear you are too much soldier and not enough politician. I fear I am the opposite.

Words may hold more power than swords, as Juvens said, but I have discovered to my cost that there are times when there is no substitute for pointy metal.'

'These are the Years of Blood.'

'Indeed they are. We are all the prisoners of circumstance, and circumstances have left me once again with no other choice but bitter retreat. The noble Lirozio, Duke of Puranti and owner of this wonderful bath, was as staunch and warlike an ally as could be imagined when Duke Orso's power was long leagues away on the other side of the great walls of Musselia. You should have heard him gnash his teeth, his sword never so eager to spring forth and spill hot blood.'

'Men love to talk about fighting.' Monza let her eyes wander over the sullen faces of Rogont's advisors. 'Some like to dress for it, too. Getting blood on the uniforms is a different matter.'

A couple of angry head-tosses from the peacocks, but Rogont only smiled. 'My own sad realisation. Now Musselia's great walls are breached, thanks to you, Borletta fallen, thanks to you, and Visserine burned too. The army of Talins, ably assisted by your erstwhile comrades, the Thousand Swords, are picking the country clean on Lirozio's very doorstep. The brave duke finds his enthusiasm for drum and bugle much curtailed. Powerful men are as inconstant as the shifting water. I should have picked weaker allies.'

'Bit late for that.'

The duke puffed out his cheeks. 'Too late, too late, shall be my epitaph. At Sweet Pines I arrived but two days tardy, and rash Salier had fought and lost without me. So Caprile was left helpless before your well-documented wrath.' That was a fool's version of the story, but Monza kept it to herself, for now. 'At Musselia I arrived with all my power, prepared to hold the great walls and block the Gap of Etris against you, and found you had stolen the city the day before, picked it clean already and now held the walls against me.' More injury to the truth, but Monza kept her peace. 'Then at the High Bank I found myself unavoidably detained by the late General Ganmark, while the also late Duke Salier, quite determined not to be fooled by you a second time, was fooled by you a second time and his army scattered like chaff on a stiff wind. So Borletta . . .' He stuck his tongue between his lips, jerked his thumb towards the floor and blew a loud farting sound. 'So brave Duke Cantain . . .' He drew one finger across his throat and blew another. 'Too late, too late. Tell me, General Murcatto, how come you are always first to the field?'

'I rise early, shit before daybreak, check I'm pointed in the right direction and let nothing stop me. That and I actually try to get there.'

'Your meaning?' demanded a young man at Rogont's elbow, his face even sourer than the rest.

'My meaning?' she parroted, goggling like an idiot, and then to the duke himself, 'Is that you could have reached Sweet Pines on time but chose to dither, knowing proud, fat Salier would piss before his trousers were down and more than likely waste all his strength whether he won or not. He lost, and looked the fool, and you the wiser partner, just as you hoped.' It was Rogont's turn to stay carefully silent. 'Two seasons later you could have reached the Gap in time and held it against the world, but it suited you to delay, and let me teach the proud Musselians the lesson you wanted them to learn. Namely to be humble before your prudent Excellency.'

The whole chamber was very still as her voice grated on. 'When did you realise time was running out? That you'd delayed so much you'd let your allies wane too weak, let Orso wax too strong? No doubt you would have liked to make it to the High Bank for once on time, but Ganmark got in your way. As far as playing the good ally, by that time it was . . .' She leaned forwards and whispered it. '*Too late.* All your policy was making sure you were the strongest partner when the League of Eight won, so you could be the first among them. A grand notion, and carefully managed. Except, of course, Orso has won, and the League of Eight . . .' She stuck her tongue between her lips and blew a long fart at the assembled flower of manhood. 'So much for too late, fuckers.'

The shrillest of the brood stepped towards her, fists clenched. 'I will not listen to one word more of this, you . . . you devil! My father died at Sweet Pines!'

It seemed everyone had their own wrongs to avenge, but

Monza had too many wounds of her own to be much stung by other people's. 'Thank you,' she said.

'What?'

'Since your father was presumably among my enemies, and the aim of a battle is to kill them, I take his death as a compliment. I shouldn't have to explain that to a soldier.'

His face had turned a blotchy mixture of pink and white. 'If you were a man I'd kill you where you stand.'

'If you were a man, you mean. Still, since I took your father, it's only fair I give you something in trade.' She curled her tongue and blew spit in his face.

He came at her clumsily, and with his hands, just as she'd guessed he would. Any man who needs to be worked up to it that hard isn't likely to be too fearful when he finally gets there. She was ready, dodged around him, grabbed the top and bottom rims of his gilded breastplate, used his own weight to swing him, caught his toe with one well-placed boot. She grabbed the hilt of his sword as he stumbled helplessly past, bent almost double, part running and part falling, and whipped it from his belt. He squawked as he splashed into the pool, sending up a fountain of shining spray, and she spun round, blade at the ready.

Rogont rolled his eyes. 'Oh, for pity's—' His men bundled past, all fumbling their swords out, cursing, nearly knocking the table over in their haste to get at her. 'Less steel, gentlemen, if you please, less steel!' The officer had surfaced now, or at least was fighting to, splashing and floundering, hauled down by the weight of his ornamental armour. Two of Rogont's other attendants hurried to drag him from the pool while the rest shuffled towards Monza, jostling at each other in their efforts to stab her first.

'Shouldn't you be the ones retreating?' she hissed as she backed away past the pillars.

The nearest jabbed at her. 'Die, you damned—'

'Enough!' roared Rogont. 'Enough! Enough!' His men scowled like naughty children called to account. 'No swordplay in the bath, for pity's sake! Will my shame never end?' He gave a long sigh, then waved an arm. 'Leave us, all of you!'

His foremost attendant's moustache bristled with horror. 'But, your Excellency, with this . . . foul creature?'

'Never fear, I will survive.' He arched one eyebrow at them. 'I can swim. Now out, before someone hurts themselves. Shoo! Go!'

Reluctantly they sheathed their swords and grumbled their way from the hall, the soaked man leaving a squelching trail of wet fury behind him. Monza grinned as she tossed his gilded sword into the pool, where it vanished with a splash. A small victory, maybe, but she had to enjoy the ones she got these days.

Rogont waited in silence until they were alone, then gave a heavy sigh. 'You told me she would come, Ishri.'

'It is well that I never tire of being right.' Monza started. A dark-skinned woman lay on her back on a high windowsill, a good stride or two above Rogont's head. Her legs were crossed, up against the wall, one arm and her head hanging off the back of the narrow ledge so that her face was almost upside down. 'For it happens often.' She slid off backwards, flipped over at the last moment and dropped silently to all fours, nimble as a lizard.

Monza wasn't sure how she'd missed her in the first place, but she didn't like that she had. 'What are you? An acrobat?'

'Oh, nothing so romantic as an acrobat. I am the East Wind. You can think of me as but one of the many fingers on God's right hand.'

'You talk enough rubbish to be a priest.'

'Oh, nothing so dry and dusty as a priest.' Her eyes rolled to the ceiling. 'I am a passionate believer, in my way, but only men may take the robe, thanks be to God.'

Monza frowned. 'An agent of the Gurkish Emperor.'

'Agent sounds so very . . . underhanded. Emperor, Prophet, Church, State. I would call myself a humble representative of Southern Powers.'

'What's Styria to them?'

'A battlefield.' And she smiled wide. 'Gurkhul and the Union may be at peace, but . . .'

'The fighting goes on.'

'Always. Orso's allies are our enemies, so his enemies are our allies. We find ourselves with common cause.'

'The downfall of Grand Duke Orso of Talins,' muttered Rogont. 'Please God.'

Monza curled her lip at him. 'Huh. Praying to God now, Rogont?'

'To whoever will listen, and most fervently.'

The Gurkish woman stood, stretching up on tiptoe to the ends of her long fingers. 'And you, Murcatto? Are you the answer to this poor man's desperate prayers?'

'Maybe.'

'And he to yours, perhaps?'

'I've been often disappointed by the powerful, but I can hope.'

'You'd hardly be the first friend I've disappointed.' Rogont nodded towards the map. 'They call me the Count of Caution. The Duke of Delay. The Prince of Prudence. Yet you would make an ally of me?'

'Look at me, Rogont, I'm almost as desperate as you are. "Great tempests," Farans said, "wash up strange companions."'

'A wise man. How can I help my strange companion, then? And, more importantly, how can she help me?'

'I need to kill Faithful Carpi.'

'Why would we care for treacherous Carpi's death?' Ishri sauntered forwards, head falling lazily onto one side, then further still. Too far to look at comfortably, let alone to do. 'Are there not other captains among the Thousand Swords? Sesaria, Victus, Andiche?' Her eyes were pitch black, as empty and dead as the eye-maker's replacements. 'Will not one of those infamous vultures fill your old chair, keen to pick at the corpse of Styria?'

Rogont pouted. 'And so my weary dance continues, but with a fresh partner. I win only the most fleeting reprieve.'

'Those three have no loyalty to Orso beyond their pockets. They were persuaded easily enough to betray Cosca for me, and me for Faithful, when the price was right. If the price is right, with Faithful gone I can bring them back to me, and from Orso's service to yours.'

A slow silence. Ishri raised her fine black brows. Rogont tipped his head thoughtfully back. The two of them exchanged a lingering glance. 'That would go a long way towards evening the odds.'

'You are sure you can buy them?' asked the Gurkish woman.

'Yes,' Monza lied smoothly. 'I never gamble.' An even bigger lie, so she delivered it with even greater confidence. There was no certainty where the Thousand Swords were concerned, and even less with the faithless bastards who commanded them. But there might be a chance, if she could kill Faithful. Get Rogont's help with that, then they'd see.

'How high would be the price?'

'To turn against the winning side? Higher than I can afford, that's sure.' Even if she'd had the rest of Hermon's gold to hand, and most of it was still buried thirty strides from her dead father's ruined barn. 'But you, the Duke of Ospria—'

Rogont gave a sorry chuckle. 'Oh, the bottomless purse of Ospria. I am in hock up to my neck and beyond. I'd sell my arse if I thought I could get more than a few coppers for it. No, you will coax no gold from me, I fear.'

'What about your Southern Powers?' asked Monza. 'I hear the mountains of Gurkhul are made of gold.'

Ishri wriggled back against one of the pillars. 'Of mud, like everyone else's. But there may be much gold in them, if one knows where to dig. How do you plan to put an end to Faithful?'

'Lirozio will surrender to Orso's army as soon as it arrives.'

'Doubtless,' said Rogont. 'He is every bit as proficient at surrender as I am at retreat.'

'The Thousand Swords will push on southwards towards Ospria, picking the country clean, and the Talinese will follow.'

'I need no military genius to tell me this.'

'I'll find a place, somewhere between, and bring Carpi out. With two-score men I can get him killed. Small risk for either one of you.'

Rogont cleared his throat. 'If you can bring that loyal old hound out of his kennel, then I can surely spare some men to put him down.'

Ishri watched Monza, just as Monza might have watched an ant. 'And once he is at peace, if you can buy the Thousand Swords then I can furnish the money.'

If, if, if. But that was more than Monza had any right to hope for here. She could just as easily have left the meeting feet first. 'Then it's as good as done. To strange companions, eh?'

'Indeed. God has truly blessed you.' Ishri gave an extravagant yawn. 'You came looking for one friend, and you leave with two.'

'Lucky me,' said Monza, far from sure she was leaving with any. She turned towards the gate, boot heels scraping against the worn marble, hoping she didn't start shaking before she got there.

'One more thing, Murcatto!' She looked back to Rogont, standing alone now by his maps. Ishri had vanished as suddenly as she'd appeared. 'Your position is weak, and so you are obliged to play at strength. I see that. You are what you are, bold beyond recklessness. I would not have it any other way. But I am what I am, also. Some more respect, in future, will make our marriage of mutual desperation run ever so much more smoothly.'

Monza gave an exaggerated curtsey. 'Your Resplendence, I am not only weak, but abject with regret.'

Rogont slowly shook his head. 'That officer of mine really should have drawn and run you through.'

'Is that what you'd have done?'

'Oh, pity, no.' He looked back to his charts. 'I'd have asked for more spit.'

Neither Rich nor Poor

Shenkt hummed to himself as he walked down the shabby corridor, his footfalls making not the slightest sound. The exact tune always somehow eluded him. A nagging fragment of something his sister sang when he was a child. He could see the sunlight still, through her hair, the window at her back, face in shadow. All long ago, now. All faded, like cheap paints in the sun. He had never been much of a singer himself. But he hummed, at least, and imagined his sister's voice singing along with him, and that was some comfort.

He put his knife away, and the carved bird too, almost finished now, though the beak was giving him some trouble and he did not wish to break it by rushing. Patience. As vital to the wood-carver as it is to the assassin. He stopped before the door. Soft, pale pine, full of knots, badly jointed, light shining through a split. He wished, sometimes, that his work took him to better places. He raised one boot, and burst the lock apart with a single kick.

Eight sets of hands leaped to weapons as the door splintered from its hinges. Eight hard faces snapped towards him, seven men and a woman. Shenkt recognised most of them. They had been among the kneeling half-circle in Orso's throne room. Killers, sent after Prince Ario's murderers. Comrades, of a kind, in the hunt. If the flies on a carcass can be said to be comrades to the lion that made the kill. He had not expected such as these to beat him to his quarry, but he was long past being surprised by the turns life took. His twisted like a snake in its death throes.

'Have I come at a bad time?' he asked.

'It's him.'

'The one who wouldn't kneel.'

'Shenkt.' This last from the man who had blocked his path in Orso's throne room. The one he had advised to pray. Shenkt hoped he had taken the advice, but did not think it likely. A couple of them relaxed when they recognised his face, pushed back their half-drawn blades, thinking him one of their number.

'Well, well.' A man with a pockmarked face and long, black hair seemed to be in charge. He reached out and gently pushed the woman's bow towards the floor with one finger. 'My name's Malt. You're just in time to help us bring them in.'

'Them?'

'The ones his Excellency Duke Orso's paying us to find, who do you think? Over there, in the smoke-house yonder.'

'All of them?'

'The leader, anyway.'

'How do you know you have the right man?'

'Woman. Pello knows, don't you, Pello?'

Pello was possessed of a ragged moustache and a look of sweaty desperation. 'It's Murcatto. The same one who led Orso's army at Sweet Pines. She was in Visserine, not but a month ago. Took her prisoner. Questioned her myself. That's where the Northman lost his eye.' The Northman called Shivers, that Sajaam had spoken of. 'In Salier's palace. She killed Ganmark there, that general of Orso's, few days afterward.'

'The Snake of Talins herself,' said Malt proudly, 'and still alive. What do you think of that?'

'I am all amaze.' Shenkt walked slowly to the window and peered out across the street. A shabby-looking place for a famous general, but such was life. 'She has men with her?'

'Just this Northman. Nothing we can't deal with. Lucky Nim and two of her boys are waiting in the alley at the back. When the big clock next chimes, we go in the front. They won't be getting away.'

Shenkt looked slowly round at each suspicious face, and gave each man a chance. 'You all are determined to do this? All of you?'

'Of fucking course we are. You'll find no faint hearts here, my friend.' Malt looked at him through narrowed eyes. 'You want to come in with us?'

'With you?' Shenkt took a long breath, then sighed. 'Great tempests wash up strange companions.'

'I'll take that as a yes.'

'We don't need this fucker.' The one Shenkt had told to pray, again, making a great show of a curved knife. A man of small patience, evidently. 'I say we cut his throat, and one less share to pay.'

Malt gently pushed his knife down. 'Come now, no need to be greedy. I've been on jobs like that before, everyone stuck on the money not the work, watching their backs every minute. Bad for your health and your business. We'll do this civilised, or not at all. What do you say?'

'I say civilised,' said Shenkt. 'For pity's sake, let's kill like honest men.'

'Exactly so. With what Orso's paying, there'll be enough for everyone. Equal shares all round, and we can all be rich.'

'Rich?' Shenkt smiled sadly as he shook his head. 'The dead are neither rich nor poor.' The look of mild surprise was just forming on Malt's face when Shenkt's pointing finger split it neatly in half.

Shivers sat on the greasy bed, back pressed to the dirty wall, with Monza sprawled on top of him. Her head lay in his lap, breath hissing shallow, in and out. The pipe was still in her bandaged left hand, smoke twisting from the embers in a brown streak. He frowned at it creeping through the shafts of light, rippling, spreading, filling the room with sweet haze.

Husk was good stuff for pain. Too good, to Shivers' mind. So good you always needed more. So good that after a while stubbing your toe seemed like excuse enough. Took your edge off, all that smoking, left you soft. Maybe Monza had more edge than she wanted, but he didn't trust it. The smoke was tickling at his nose, making him feel sick and needy both together. His eye was itching under the bandages. Would've been easy to do it. Where was the harm . . . ?

He had a sudden panic, wriggling out from under her like he was buried alive. Monza gave an irritated burble then fell back, eyelids flickering, hair stuck across her clammy face. Shivers ripped back the bolt on the window and pulled the wonky shutters open, getting a nice view of the rotting alley behind the building and a face full of cold, piss-smelling air. At least that smell was honest.

There were two men down there by a back door, and a woman holding one hand up. A bell rang out, from a high clock tower in the next street. The woman nodded, the men pulled out a bright sword and a heavy mace. She opened the door and they hurried in.

'Shit,' hissed Shivers, hardly able to believe it. Three of 'em and, from the way they'd been waiting, most likely more coming in the front. Too late to run. But then Shivers was sick of running anyway. He had his pride, still, didn't he? Running from the North and down here to fucking Styria was what landed him in this one-eyed mess in the first place.

He reached towards Monza, but stopped short. State she was in she'd be no use. So he let her be, slid out the heavy knife she'd given him the first day they met. The grip was firm in his hand and he squeezed it tight. They were better armed, maybe, but big weapons and small rooms don't mix. Surprise was on his side, and that's the best weapon a man can have. He pressed himself into the shadows behind the door, feeling his heart thumping, the breath burning in his throat. No fear, no doubt, just furious readiness.

He heard their soft steps on the stairs and had to stop himself laughing. A bit of a giggle crept out all the same, and he didn't know why, 'cause there was nothing funny. A creak and a muttered curse. Not the sharpest assassins in the whole Circle of the World. He bit on his lip, trying to stop his ribs shaking. Monza stirred, stretched out smiling on the greasy blanket.

'Benna . . .' she murmured. The door was yanked open and the swordsman sprang in. Monza's eyes came blearily open. 'Whathe—'

The second man barged in like a fool, knocking his mate off balance, lifting his mace over his head, tip scraping a little shower of plaster from the low ceiling. It was almost like he was offering it up. Would've seemed rude to turn it down, so Shivers snatched it from his hand while he stabbed the first one in the back.

The blade slid in and out of him. Quick, quiet scrapes, up to the hilt. Shivers growled through his teeth, half-sniggering with the leftover shreds of laughter, arm pumping in and out. The stabbed man made a shocked little hoot each time, not sure what was happening yet, twisted round, jerking the knife out of Shivers' hand.

The other one turned, eyes wide, too close to swing at. 'Wha—'

Shivers thumped him in the nose with the butt of the mace and felt it pop, sent him reeling towards the empty fireplace. The stabbed man's knees went, he caught his sword point on the wall above Monza and pitched on top of her. No need to worry about him. Shivers took a short stride, dropping onto his knees so the mace wouldn't hit the ceiling, roaring as he swung the big lump of metal. It hit its previous owner in the forehead with a meaty crunch, stove his skull in, spattered the ceiling with spots of blood.

He heard a scream behind, twisted round. The woman sprang through the door, a short blade in each hand. Monza's kicking leg tripped her as she struggled out from under the dying swordsman. Happy chance, the woman's scream switching from fury to shock as she blundered into Shivers' arms, fumbling one of her knives. He grabbed her other wrist as he went down under her, on top of the maceman's corpse, his head smacking against the side of the fireplace and leaving him blinded for a moment.

He kept his grip on her wrist, felt her nails tearing at his bandages. They growled stupidly at each other, her hair hanging down and tickling at him, tongue stuck between her teeth with the effort as she tried to push the blade into his neck with all her weight. Her breath smelled of lemons. He wrenched himself round and punched her under the jaw, snapped her head up, teeth sinking deep into her tongue.

Same moment the sword hacked clumsily into her arm, the point almost catching Shivers' shoulder, making him jerk back. Monza's white face behind her, eyes hardly focused. The woman howled, tried to drag herself free. Another fumbling sword blow caught the top of her head with the flat and knocked her sideways. Monza floundered into the wall, tripped over the bed, almost stabbing herself as the sword clattered from her hand. Shivers twisted the blade from the woman's limp grip and stabbed her under the jaw right to the hilt, blood spraying out across Monza's shirt and up the wall.

He kicked himself free of the tangle of limbs, scrabbling up the mace, pulling his knife from the dead swordsman's back and pushing it into his belt, stumbling for the door. The corridor outside was empty. He grabbed Monza's wrist and dragged her up. She was staring down at herself, soaked with the woman's blood.

'Wha . . . wha . . .'

He pulled her limp arm over his shoulder and hauled her through the door, bundled her down the stairs, her boots clattering against the treads. Out through the open back door into sunlight. She tottered a step and blew thin vomit down the wall. Groaned and heaved again. He pushed the haft of the mace up his sleeve, the bloody head in his fist, ready to let it drop if he needed to. He realised he was sniggering again as he did it. Couldn't see why. Still nothing funny. Quite the opposite, far as he could tell. Still laughing, though.

Monza took a drunken step or two, bent almost double. 'I got stop smoking,' she muttered, spitting bile.

''Course. Just as soon as my eye grows back.' He grabbed her elbow, pulled her after him towards the end of the alley, folk moving in the sunlit street. He paused at the corner, took a quick look both ways, then dragged her arm around his shoulder again, and away.

Aside from the three corpses, the room was empty. Shenkt padded to the window, stepping carefully around the slick of blood across the boards, and peered out. Of Murcatto and the one-eyed Northman there was no sign. But it was better they should escape than someone else should find them before he did. That he would not allow. When Shenkt took on a job, he always saw it through.

He squatted down, forearms resting on his knees, hands dangling. He had hardly made a worse mess of Malt and his seven friends than Murcatto and her Northman had of these three. The walls, the floor, the ceiling, the bed, all spattered and smeared with red. One man lay by the fireplace, his skull roundly pulped. The other was face down, the back of his shirt ripped with stab-wounds, soaked through with blood. The woman had a yawning gash in her neck.

Lucky Nim, he presumed. It seemed her luck had deserted her.

'Just Nim, then.'

Something gleamed in the corner, by the wall. He stooped and picked it up, held it to the light. A golden ring with a large, blood-red ruby. Far too fine a ring for any of these scum to wear. Murcatto's ring, even? Still warm from her finger? He slid it onto his own, then took hold of Nim's ankle and dragged her corpse up onto the bed, humming to himself as he stripped it bare.

Her right leg had a patch of scaly rash across the thigh, so he took the left instead, cut it free, buttock and all, with three practised movements of his butcher's sickle. He popped the bone from the hip joint with a sharp twist of his wrists, took the foot off with two jerks of the curved blade, wrapped her belt around the neatly butchered leg to hold it folded and slid it into his bag.

A rump steak, then, thick-cut and pan-fried. He always carried a special mix of Suljuk four-spice with him, crushed to his taste, and the oil native to the region around Puranti had a wonderful nutty flavour. Then salt, and crushed pepper. Good meat was all in the seasoning. Pink in the centre, but not bloody. Shenkt had never been able to understand people who liked their meat bloody, the notion disgusted him. Onions sizzling alongside. Perhaps then dice the shank and make stew, with roots and mushrooms, a broth from the bones, a dash of that old Muris vinegar to give it . . .

'Zing.'

He nodded to himself, carefully wiped the sickle clean, shouldered the bag, turned for the door and . . . stopped.

He had passed a baker's earlier, and thought what fine, crusty, new-baked loaves they had in the window. The smell of fresh bread. That glorious scent of honesty and simple goodness. He would very much have liked to be a baker, had he not been . . . what he was. Had he never been brought before his old master. Had he never followed the path laid out for him, and had he never rebelled against it. How well that bread would be, he now thought, sliced and thickly smeared with a coarse pâté. Perhaps with a quince jelly, or some such, and a good glass of wine. He drew his knife again and went in through Lucky Nim's back for her liver.

After all, it was no use to her now.

Heroic Efforts, New Beginnings

The rain stopped, and the sun came out over the farmland, a faint rainbow stretching down from the grey heavens. Monza wondered if there was an elf-glade where it touched the ground, the way her father used to tell her. Or if there was just shit, like everywhere else. She leaned from her saddle and spat into the wheat.

Elf shit, maybe.

She pushed her wet hood back and scowled to the west, watching the showers roll off towards Puranti. If there was any justice they'd dump a deluge on Faithful Carpi and the Thousand Swords, their outriders probably no more than a day's ride behind. But there was no justice, and Monza knew it. The clouds pissed where they pleased.

The damp winter wheat was spattered with patches of red flowers, like smears of blood across the tawny country. It would be ready to harvest soon, except there'd be no one here to do the reaping. Rogont was doing what he was best at – pulling back, and the farmers were taking everything they could carry and pulling back with him towards Ospria. They knew the Thousand Swords were coming, and knew better than to be there when they did. There were no more infamous foragers in the world than the men Monza used to lead.

Forage, Farans wrote, *is robbery so vast that it transcends mere crime, and enters the arena of politics.*

She'd lost Benna's ring. She kept fussing at her middle finger with her thumb, endlessly disappointed to find it wasn't there. A pretty piece of rock hadn't changed the fact Benna was dead. But still it felt as if she'd lost some last little part of him she'd managed to cling on to. One of the last little parts of herself worth keeping.

She was lucky a ring was all she'd lost back in Puranti, though.

She'd been careless, and it had nearly been the end of her. She had to stop smoking. Make a new beginning. Had to, and yet she was smoking more than ever. Each time she woke from sweet oblivion she told herself it would have to be the last, but a few hours later and she'd be sweating desperation from every pore. Waves of sick need, like an incoming tide, each one higher than the last. Each one resisted took a heroic effort, and Monza was no hero, however the people of Talins might once have cheered for her. She'd thrown her pipe away, then in a sticky panic bought another. She wasn't sure how many times she'd hidden the dwindling lump of husk down at the bottom of one bag or another. But she'd found there's a problem with hiding a thing yourself.

You always know where it is.

'I do not care for this country.' Morveer stood from his swaying seat and peered out across the flat land. 'This is good country for an ambush.'

'That's why we're here,' Monza growled back. Hedgerows, the odd stand of trees, brown houses and barns alone or in groups away across the fields – plenty of hiding places. Scarcely a thing moved. Scarcely a sound but for the crows, the wind flapping the canvas on the cart, the wheels rattling, splattering through an occasional puddle.

'Are you sure it is prudent to put your faith in Rogont?'

'You don't win battles with prudence.'

'No, one plans murders with it. Rogont is *notoriously* untrust-worthy even for a grand duke, and an old enemy of yours besides.'

'I can trust him as far as what's in his own interest.' The question was all the more irritating as it was one she'd been asking herself ever since they left Puranti. 'Small risk for him killing Faithful Carpi, but a hell of a pay-off if I can bring him the Thousand Swords.'

'But it would hardly be your first miscalculation. What if we are *marooned* out here in the path of an army? You are paying me to kill one man at a time, not fight a war single—'

'I paid you to kill one man in Westport, and you murdered fifty at a throw. I need no lessons from you in taking care.'

'Scarcely more than forty, and that was due to too much care to get your man, not too little! Was your butcher's bill any shorter at Cardotti's House of Leisure? Or in Duke Salier's palace? Or at Caprile, for that matter? Forgive me if I have *scant* faith in your ability to keep violence contained!'

'Enough!' she snarled at him. 'You're like a goat that won't stop bleating! Do the job I pay you for, and that's the end of it!'

Morveer pulled up the cart suddenly with a haul on the reins and Day squawked as she nearly fumbled her apple. 'Is this the thanks I get for your timely rescue in Visserine? After you so *pointedly* ignored my sage advice?'

Vitari, sprawling among the supplies on the back of the cart, stuck up one long arm. 'That rescue was as much my doing as his. No one's thanked me.'

Morveer ignored her. 'Perhaps I should find a more grateful employer!'

'Perhaps I should find a more obedient fucking poisoner!'

'Perhaps . . . ! But wait.' Morveer held up a finger, squeezing his eyes shut. 'But wait.' He puckered his lips and sucked in a deep breath, held it for a moment, then slowly blew it out. And again. Shivers rode up, raised his one eyebrow at Monza. One more breath, and Morveer's eyes came open, and he gave a chuckle of sickening falseness. 'Perhaps . . . I should most *sincerely* apologise.'

'What?'

'I realise I am . . . not always the easiest company.' A sharp burst of laughter from Vitari and Morveer winced, but carried on. 'If I seem always contrary it is because I want only the best for you and your venture. It has ever been a failing of mine to be too *intransigent* in my pursuit of excellence. There is no more important characteristic than *pliability* in a man who must, perforce, be your *humble* servant. Can I entreat you to make with me . . . a heroic effort? To put this unpleasantness behind us?' He snapped the reins and moved the cart on, still smiling thinly over his shoulder. 'I feel it! A new beginning!'

Monza caught Day's eye as she passed, rocking gently on her seat. The blonde girl lifted her brows, stripped her apple to the last fragment of stalk and flicked it away into the field. Vitari was on the back of the cart, just pulling off her coat and sprawling out on the canvas in the sunlight. 'Sun's coming out. New

387

beginning.' She pointed across the country, one hand pressed to her chest. 'And aaaaaaw, a rainbow! You know, they say there's an elf-glade where it touches the ground!'

Monza scowled after them. Seemed more likely they'd stumble on an elf-glade than that Morveer would make a new beginning. She trusted this sudden obedience even less than his endless carping.

'Maybe he just wants to be loved,' came Shivers' whispery voice as they set off again.

'If men can change like that.' And Monza snapped her fingers in his face.

'That's the only way they do change, ain't it?' His one eye stayed on her. 'If things change enough around 'em? Men are brittle, I reckon. They don't bend into new shapes. They get broken into them. Crushed into them.'

Burned into them, maybe. 'How's your face?' she muttered.

'Itchy.'

'Did it hurt, at the eye-maker's?'

'On a scale between stubbing your toe and having your eye burned out, it was down near the bottom.'

'Most everything is.'

'Falling down a mountain?'

'Not that bad, as long as you lie still. It's when you try to get up it starts to sting some.' That got a grin from him, though he was grinning a lot less than he used to. Small surprise after what he'd been through, maybe. What she'd put him through. 'I suppose . . . I should be thanking you for saving my life, again. It's getting to be a habit.'

'What you're paying me for, ain't it, Chief? Work well done is its own reward, my father always used to tell me. Fact is I'm good at it. As a fighter I'm a man you need to respect. As anything else I'm just a big shiftless fuck wasted a dozen years in the wars, with nothing to show for it but bloody dreams and one less eye than most. I've got my pride, still. Man's got to be what he is, I reckon. Otherwise what is he? Just pretending, no? And who wants to spend all the time they're given pretending to be what they ain't?'

Good question. Luckily they crested a rise, and she was spared having to think of an answer. The remains of the Imperial road stretched away, an arrow-straight stripe of brown through the fields. Eight centuries old, and still the best road in Styria. A sad comment on the leadership since. There was a farm not far from it. A stone house of two storeys, windows shuttered, roof of red tiles turned mossy brown with age, a small stable-block beside. A waist-high wall of lichen-splattered drystone round a muddy yard, a couple of scrawny birds pecking at the dirt. Opposite the house a wooden barn, roof slumping in the middle. A weather vane in the shape of a winged snake flapped limply on its leaning turret.

'That's the place!' she called out, and Vitari stuck her arm up to show she'd heard.

A stream wound past the buildings and off towards a mill-house a mile or two distant. The wind came up, shook the leaves on a hedgerow, made soft waves in the wheat, drove the ragged clouds across the sky, their shadows flowing over the land beneath.

It reminded Monza of the farm where she was born. She thought of Benna, a boy running through the crop, just the top of his head showing above the ripening grain, hearing his high laughter. Long ago, before their father died. Monza shook herself and scowled. Maudlin, self-indulgent, nostalgic shit. She'd hated that farm. The digging, the ploughing, the dirt under her nails. And all for what? There weren't many things you worked so hard at to make so little.

The only other one she could think of right off was revenge.

Since his earliest remembrances, Morveer seemed always to have had an uncanny aptitude for saying the wrong thing. When he meant to contribute, he would find he was complaining. When he intended to be solicitous, he would discover he was insulting. When he sought earnestly to provide support, he would be construed as undermining. He wanted only to be valued, respect-ed, included, and yet somehow every attempt at good fellowship only made matters worse.

He was almost starting to believe, after thirty years of failed relationships – a mother who had left him, a wife who had left him, apprentices who had left, robbed or attempted to kill him, usually by poison but on one memorable occasion with an axe – that he simply was not very good with people. He should have been glad, at least, that the loathsome drunk Nicomo Cosca was dead, and indeed he had at first felt some relief. But the dark clouds had soon rolled back to re-establish the eternal baseline of mild depression. He found himself once more squabbling with his troublesome employer over every detail of their business.

Probably it would have been better if he had simply retired to the mountains and lived as a hermit, where he could injure nobody's feelings. But the thin air had never suited his delicate constitution. So he had resolved, once more, to make a heroic effort at camaraderie. To be more compliant, more graceful, more indulgent of the shortcomings of others. He had taken the first step, therefore, while the rest of the party were out surveying the land for signs of the Thousand Swords, by pretending at a headache and preparing a pleasant surprise, in the form of his mother's recipe for mushroom soup. Perhaps the only tangible thing which she had left her only son.

He nicked his finger while slicing, singed his elbow upon the hot stove, both of which events almost caused him to forsake his new beginning in a torrent of unproductive rage. But by the time he heard the horses returning to the farm, just as the sun was sinking and the shadows in the yard outside were stretching out, he had the table set, two stubs of candle casting a welcoming glow, two loaves of bread sliced and the pot of soup at the ready, exuding a wholesome fragrance.

'Excellent.' His rehabilitation was assured.

His new vein of optimism did not survive the arrival of the diners, however. When they entered, incidentally without removing their boots and therefore treading mud across his gleaming floor, they looked towards his lovingly cleaned kitchen, his carefully laid table, his laboriously prepared potage with all the enthusiasm of convicts being shown the executioner's block.

'What's this?' Murcatto's lips were pushed out and her brows drawn down in even deeper suspicion than usual.

Morveer did his best to float over it. 'This is an apology. Since our number-obsessed cook has returned to Talins, I thought I might occupy the vacuum and prepare dinner. My mother's recipe. Sit, sit, pray sit!' He hurried round dragging out chairs and, notwithstanding some uncomfortable sideways glances, they all found seats.

'Soup?' Morveer advanced on Shivers with pan and ladle at the ready.

'Not for me. You did, what do you call it . . .'

'Paralyse,' said Murcatto.

'Aye. You paralysed me that time.'

'You mistrust me?' he snapped.

'Almost by definition,' said Vitari, watching him from under her ginger brows. 'You're a poisoner.'

'After all we have been through together? You mistrust me, over a little *paralysis*?' He was making heroic efforts to repair the foundering ship of their professional relationship, and nobody appreciated it one whit. 'If my intention was to poison you, I would simply sprinkle Black Lavender on your pillow and lull you to a sleep that would *never end*. Or put Amerind thorns in your boots, Larync on the grip of your axe, Mustard Root in your water flask.' He leaned down towards the Northman, knuckles white around the ladle. 'There are a thousand thousand ways that I could kill you and you would never suspect the merest *shadow* of a thing. I would not go to all the trouble of *cooking* you *dinner*!'

Shivers' one eye stared levelly back into his for what seemed a very long time. Then the Northman reached out, and for the briefest moment Morveer wondered if he was about to receive his first punch in the face for many years. But instead Shivers only folded his big hand round Morveer's with exaggerated care, tipping the pan so soup spilled out into his bowl. He picked up his spoon, dipped it in his soup, blew delicately on it and slurped up the contents. 'It's good. Mushroom, is it?'

'Er . . . yes, it is.'

'Nice.' Shivers held Morveer's eye a moment longer before letting go his hand.

'Thank you.' Morveer hefted the ladle. 'Now, does anyone *not* want soup?'

'Me!' The voice barked out of nowhere like boiling water squirted in Morveer's ear. He jerked away, the pan tumbling, hot soup flooding out across the table and straight into Vitari's lap. She leaped up with a screech, wet cutlery flying. Murcatto's chair went clattering over as she lurched out of it, fumbling for her sword. Day dropped a half-eaten slice of bread as she took a shocked step back towards the door. Morveer whipped around, dripping ladle clutched pointlessly in one fist—

A Gurkish woman stood smiling beside him, arms folded. Her skin was smooth as a child's, flawless as dark glass, eyes midnight black.

'Wait!' barked Murcatto, one hand up. 'Wait. She's a friend.'

'She's no friend of mine!' Morveer was still desperately trying to understand how she could have appeared from nothing in such a manner. There was no door near her, the window was tightly shuttered and barred, the floor and ceiling intact.

'You have no friends, poisoner,' she purred at him. Her long, brown coat hung open. Underneath, her body seemed to be swaddled entirely in white bandages.

'Who are you?' demanded Day. 'And where the hell did you come from?'

'They used to call me the East Wind.' The woman displayed two rows of utterly perfect white teeth as she turned one finger gracefully round and round. 'But now they call me Ishri. I come from the sun-bleached South.'

'She meant—' began Morveer.

'Magic,' murmured Shivers, the only member of the party who had remained in his seat. He calmly raised his spoon and slurped up another mouthful. 'Pass the bread, eh?'

'Damn your bread!' he snarled back. 'And your magic too! How did you get in here?'

'One of them.' Vitari had a table-knife in her fist, eyes narrowed to deadly slits as the remains of the soup dripped from the table and tapped steadily on the floor. 'An Eater.'

The Gurkish woman pushed one fingertip through the spilled soup and curled her tongue around it. 'We must all eat something, no?'

'I don't care to be on the menu.'

'You need not worry. I am very picky about my food.'

'I tangled with your kind before, in Dagoska.' Morveer did not fully understand what was being said, a sensation which was among his least favourite, but Vitari seemed worried, and that made him worried. She was by no means a woman prone to

392

high-blown fancies. 'What deals have you been making, Murcatto?'

'The ones that needed making. She works for Rogont.'

Ishri let her head fall to one side, so far that it was almost horizontal. 'Or perhaps he works for me.'

'I don't care who's the rider and who's the donkey,' snapped Murcatto, 'as long as one or the other of you is sending men.'

'He is sending them. Two score of his best.'

'In time?'

'Unless the Thousand Swords come early, and they will not. Their main body are camped six miles distant still. They were held up picking a village clean. Then they just had to burn the place. A destructive little crowd.' Her gaze fell on Morveer. Those black eyes made him unnecessarily nervous. He did not like the fact that she was wrapped up in bandages. He found himself curious as to why—

'They keep me cool,' she said. He blinked, wondering whether he might have spoken the question out loud. 'You did not.' He felt himself turn cold to the roots of his hair. Just as he had when the nurses uncovered his secret materials at the orphanage, and guessed their purpose. He could not escape the irrational conclusion that this Gurkish devil somehow knew his private thoughts. Knew the things he had done, that he had thought no one would ever know . . .

'I will be in the barn!' he screeched, voice far more shrill than he had intended. He dragged it down with difficulty. 'I must prepare, if we are to have visitors tomorrow. Come, Day!'

'I'll just finish this.' She had quickly grown accustomed to their visitor, and was busy buttering three slices of bread at once.

'Ah . . . yes . . . I see.' He stood twitching for a moment, but there was nothing he could achieve by staying but further embarrassment. He stalked towards the door.

'You need your coat?' asked Day.

'I will be more than warm enough!'

It was only when he was through the door of the farmhouse and into the darkness, the wind sighing chill across the wheat and straight through his shirt, that he realised he would not be warm enough by any stretch of the imagination. It was too late to return without looking entirely the fool, and that he steadfastly refused to do.

'Not *me*.' He cursed most bitterly as he picked his way across the darkened farmyard, wrapping his arms around himself and already beginning to shiver. He had allowed some Gurkish charlatan to unnerve him with simple parlour tricks. 'Bandaged *bitch*.' Well, they would all see. 'Oh *yes*.' He had got the better of the nurses at the orphanage, in the end, for all the whippings. 'We'll see who whips who *now*.' He peered over his shoulder to make sure he was unobserved. 'Magic!' he sneered. 'I'll show you a trick or—'

'Eeee!' His boot squelched, slid, and he went over on his back in a patch of mud. 'Bah! Damn it to your bastard *arse*!' So much for heroic efforts, and new beginnings too.

The Traitor

Shivers reckoned it was an hour or two short of dawn. The rain had slacked right off but water still drip-dripped from the new leaves, pattering in the dirt. The air was weighty with chill damp. A swollen stream gurgled near the track, smothering the muddy falls of his horse's hooves. He knew he was close, could see the faintest ruddy campfire glow at the edges of the slick tree-trunks.

Dark times are the best for dark business, Black Dow always used to say, and he should've known.

Shivers nudged his horse through the wet night, hoping some drunk sentry didn't get nervous and serve him up an arrow through the guts. One of those might hurt less than having your eye burned out, but it was nought to look forward to. Luckily, he saw the first guard before the guard saw him, pressed up against a tree, spear resting on his shoulder. He had an oilskin draped right over his head, couldn't have seen a thing, even if he'd been awake.

'Oy!' The man jerked round, dropped his spear in the muck. Shivers grinned as he watched him fumbling for it in the dark, arms crossed loose on his saddle-bow. 'You want to give me a challenge, or shall I just head on and leave you to it?'

'Who goes there?' he growled, tearing his spear up along with a clump of wet grass.

'My name's Caul Shivers, and Faithful Carpi's going to want to talk to me.'

The Thousand Swords' camp looked pretty much like camps always do. Men, canvas, metal and mud. Mud in particular. Tents scattered every which way. Horses tethered to trees, breath smoking in the darkness. Spears stacked up one against the other. Campfires, some burning, some down to fizzling embers, the air sharp with their smoke. A few men still awake, wrapped in blankets mostly, on guard or still drinking, frowning as they watched Shivers pass.

Reminded him of all the cold, wet nights he'd spent in camps across the North and back. Huddled around fires, hoping to the dead the rain didn't get heavier. Roasting meat, spitted on dead men's spears. Curled up shivering in the snow under every blanket he could find. Sharpening blades for dark work on the morrow. He saw faces of men dead and gone back to the mud, that he'd shared drink and laughter with. His brother. His father. Tul Duru, that they'd called the Thunderhead. Rudd Threetrees, the Rock of Uffrith. Harding Grim, quieter than the night. Brought up a swell of unexpected pride, those memories. Then a swell of unexpected shame at the work he was about now. More feeling than he'd had since he lost his eye, or he'd expected to have again.

He sniffed, and his face stung underneath the bandages, and the soft moment slipped away and left him cold again. They stopped at a tent big as a house, lamplight leaking out into the night round the edges of its flap.

'Now you'd best behave yourself in here, you Northern bastard.' The guard jabbed at Shivers with his own axe. 'Or I'll—'

'Fuck yourself, idiot.' Shivers brushed him out of the way with one arm and pushed on through. Inside it smelled of stale wine, mouldy cloth, unwashed men. Ill-lit by flickering lamps, hung round the edges with slashed and tattered flags, trophies from old battlefields.

A chair of dark wood set with ivory, stained, scarred and polished with hard use, stood on a pair of crates up at the far end. The captain general's chair, he guessed. The one that had been Cosca's, then Monza's, and now was Faithful Carpi's. Didn't look much more than some battered rich man's dining chair. Surely didn't look like much to kill folk over, but then small reasons often serve for that.

There was a long table set up in the midst, men sat down each side. Captains of the Thousand Swords. Rough-looking men, scarred, stained and battered as the chair, and with quite a collection of weapons too, between 'em. But Shivers had smiled in harder company, and he smiled now. Strange thing was, he felt more at home with these lot than he had in months. He knew the rules here, he reckoned, better'n he did with Monza. Seemed as if they'd started out doing some planning, by the maps that were spread across the wood, but some time in the middle of the night the strategy had turned to dice. Now the maps were weighted down with scattered coins, with half-full bottles, with old cups, chipped glasses. One great chart was soaked red with spilled wine.

A big man stood at the head of the table – a faceful of scars, short hair grey and balding. He had a bushy moustache, the rest of his thick jaw covered in white stubble. Faithful Carpi himself, from what Monza had said. He was shaking the dice in one chunk of fist. 'Come on, you shits, come on and give me nine!' They came up one and three, to a few sighs and some laughter. 'Damn it!' He tossed some coins down the table to a tall, pock-faced bastard with a hook-nose and the ugly mix of long black hair and a big bald patch. 'One of these days I'll work your trick out, Andiche.'

'No trick. I was born under a lucky star.' Andiche scowled at Shivers, about as friendly a look as a fox spares for a chicken. 'Who the hell's this bandaged arsehole?'

The guard pushed in past Shivers, giving him a dirty look sideways. 'General Carpi, sir, this Northman says he needs to speak to you.'

'That a fact?' Faithful spared Shivers a quick glance, then went back to stacking up his coins. 'And why would I want to speak to the likes of him? Toss me the dice there, Victus, I ain't done.'

'That's the problem with generals.' Victus was bald as an egg and gaunt as famine, bunches of rings on his fingers and chains round his neck doing nothing to make him look prettier. 'They never do know when they're done.' And he tossed the dice back down the table, couple of his fellows chuckling.

The guard swallowed. 'He says he knows who killed Prince Ario!'

'Oh, you do, do you? And who was that?'

'Monzcarro Murcatto.' Every hard face in the tent turned sharp towards Shivers. Faithful carefully set the dice down, eyes narrowed. 'Looks like you know the name.'

'Should we hire him for a jester or hang him for a liar?' Victus grated out.

'Murcatto's dead,' another.

'That so? I wonder who it is I been fucking for the past month, then?'

'If you've been fucking Murcatto I'd advise you to get back to it.' Andiche grinned around him. 'From what her brother told me, no one here can suck a cock as well as she could.'

A good few chuckles at that. Shivers wasn't sure what he meant about her brother, but it didn't matter none. He'd already undone the bandages, and now he dragged the lot off in one go, turned his face towards the lamplight. Such laughter as there was mostly sputtered out. He had the kind of face now put a sharp end to mirth. 'Here's what she's cost me so far. For a handful of silver? Shit on that, I ain't half the fool she takes me for, and I've got my pride, still. I'm done with the bitch.'

Faithful Carpi was frowning at him. 'Describe her.'

'Tall, lean, black hair, blue eyes, frowns a lot. Sharp tongue on her.'

Victus waved one jewel-crusted hand at him. 'Common knowledge!'

'She's got a broken right hand, and marks all over. From falling down a mountain, she says.' Shivers pushed his finger into his stomach, keeping his eyes on Faithful. 'Got a scar just here, and one matching in her back. Says a friend of hers gave it to her. Stabbed her through with her own dagger.'

Carpi's face had turned grim as a gravedigger's. 'You know where she is?'

'Hold up just a trice, there.' Victus looked even less happy than his chief. 'You saying Murcatto's alive?'

'I'd heard a rumour,' said Faithful.

A huge black-skinned man with long ropes of iron-grey hair stood up sharp from the table. 'I'd heard all kinds of rumours,' voice slow and deep as the sea. 'Rumours and facts are two different things. When were you planning to fucking tell us?'

'When you fucking needed to know, Sesaria. Where is she?'

'At a farm,' said Shivers. 'Maybe an hour's hard ride distant.'

'How many does she have with her?'

'Just four. A whining poisoner and his apprentice, hardly

more'n a girl. A red-haired woman name of Vitari and some brown bitch.'

'Where exactly?'

Shivers grinned. 'Well, that's why I'm here, ain't it? To sell you the where exactly.'

'I don't like the smell of this shit,' snarled Victus. 'If you're asking me—'

'I'm not,' growled Faithful, without looking round. 'What's your price for it?'

'A tenth part of what Duke Orso's offering on the head o' Prince Ario's killer.'

'Just a tenth?'

'I reckon a tenth is plenty more'n I'll get from her, but not enough to get me killed by you. I want no more'n I can carry away alive.'

'Wise man,' said Faithful. 'Nothing we hate more than greed, is there, boys?' A couple of chuckles, but most were still looking far from happy at their old general's sudden return from the land of the dead. 'Alright, then, a tenth part is fair. You've a deal.' And Faithful stepped forwards and slapped his hand into Shivers', looking him right in the face. 'If we get Murcatto.'

'You need her dead or alive?'

'Sorry to say, I'd prefer dead myself.'

'Good, so would I. Last thing I want is a running score with that crazy bitch. She don't forget.'

Faithful nodded. 'So it seems. I reckon we can do business, you and me. Swolle?'

'General?' A man with a heavy beard stepped up.

'Get three-score horsemen ready to ride, and quick, those with the fastest—'

'Might be best to keep it to fewer,' said Shivers.

'That so? And how would fewer men be better?'

'The way she tells it, she's got friends here still.' Shivers let his eye wander round the hard faces in the tent. 'The way she tells it, there's plenty o' men in this camp wouldn't say no to having her back in charge. The way she tells it, they won victories to be proud of with her, and with you they skulk around and scout, while Orso's men get all the prizes.' Faithful's eyes darted sideways, then back. Enough to let Shivers know he'd touched a wound. There's no chief in the world so sure of himself he don't worry some. No chief of men like these, leastways. 'Best keep it to a few, and them ones you're sure of. I've no problem stabbing Murcatto in the back, I reckon she's got it coming. Getting stabbed by one o' these is another matter.'

'Five all told, and four of 'em women?' Swolle grinned. 'A dozen should do it.'

Faithful kept his eyes on Shivers. 'Still. Make it three score, like I said, just in case there's more at the party than we're expecting. I'd be all embarrassed to arrive at a job short-handed.'

'Sir.' And Swolle shouldered his way out through the tent flap.

Shivers shrugged. 'Have it your way.'

'Why, that I will. You can depend on it.' Faithful turned to his frowning captains. 'Any of you old bastards want to come out on the hunt?'

Sesaria shook his big head, long hair swaying. 'This is your mess, Faithful. You can swing the broom.'

'I've foraged enough for one night.' Andiche was already pushing out through the flap, a few others following in a muttering crowd, some looking suspicious, some looking careless, some looking drunk.

'I too must take my leave, General Carpi.' The speaker stood out among all these rough, scarred, dirty men, if only 'cause nothing much about him stood out. He had a curly head of hair, no weapon Shivers could see, no scar, no sneer, no fighter's air of menace in the least. But Faithful still chuckled up to him like he was a man needed respect.

'Master Sulfur!' Folding his hand in both of his big paws and giving it a squeeze. 'My thanks for stopping by. You're always welcome here.'

'Oh, I am loved wherever I go. Easy to remain on good terms with the man who brings the money.'

'Tell Duke Orso, and your people at the bank, they've nothing to worry on here. It'll all be taken care of, like we discussed. Just as soon as I've dealt with this little problem.'

'Life does love to throw up problems, doesn't it?' Sulfur gave Shivers a splinter of a smile. He had odd-coloured eyes, one blue, one green. 'Happy hunting, then.' And he ambled out into the dawn.

Faithful was back in Shivers' face right away. 'An hour's ride, you said?'

'If you move quick for your age.'

'Huh. How do you know she won't have missed you by then, slipped away?'

'She's asleep. Husk sleep. She smokes more o' that shit every day. Half her time drooling with it, the rest drooling for it. She won't be waking any time soon.'

'Best to waste no time, though. That woman can cause unpleasant surprises.'

'That's a fact. And she's expecting help. Two-score men from Rogont, coming by tomorrow afternoon. They're planning to shadow you, lay an ambush as you turn south.'

'No better feeling than flipping a surprise around, eh?' Faithful grinned. 'And you'll be riding at the front.'

'For a tenth part o' the take I'll ride at the front side-saddle.'

'Just in front will do. Right next to me and you can point out the ground. We honest men need to stick together.'

'That we do,' said Shivers. 'No doubt.'

'Alright.' Faithful clapped his big hands and rubbed them together. 'A piss, then I'm getting my armour on.'

King of Poisons

'Boss?' came Day's high voice. 'You awake?'

Morveer exhaled a racking sigh. 'Merciful slumber has indeed released me from her soft bosom . . . and back into the *frigid* embrace of an uncaring world.'

'What?'

He waved it bitterly away. 'Never mind. My words fall like seeds . . . on stony ground.'

'You said to wake you at dawn.'

'Dawn? Oh, harsh mistress!' He threw back his one thin blanket and struggled up from the prickling straw, truly a humble repose for a man of his matchless talents, stretched his aching back and clambered stiffly down the ladder to the floor of the barn. He was forced to concede that he had long been too advanced in years, not to mention too refined in tastes, for haylofts.

Day had assembled the apparatus during the hours of darkness and now, as the first anaemic flicker of dawn niggled at the narrow windows, the burners were alight. Reagents happily simmered, steam carelessly condensed, distillations merrily dripped into the collecting flasks. Morveer processed around the makeshift table, rapping his knuckles against the wood as he passed, making the glassware clink and tinkle. Everything appeared to be entirely in order. Day had learned her business from a master, after all, perhaps the greatest poisoner in all the wide Circle of the World, who would say nay? But even the sight of the good work well done could not coax Morveer from his maudlin mood.

He puffed out his cheeks and gave vent to a weary sigh. 'No one understands me. I am *doomed* to be misunderstood.'

'You're a complex person,' said Day.

'Exactly! *Exactly* so! *You* see it!' Perhaps she alone appreciated that beneath his stern and masterful exterior there were reservoirs of feeling deep as mountain lakes.

'I've made tea.' She held a battered metal mug out to him, steam curling from within. His stomach grumbled unpleasantly.

'No. I am grateful for your kind attentions, of course, but no. My digestion is unsettled this morning, *terribly* unsettled.'

'Our Gurkish visitor making you nervous?'

'Absolutely and entirely *not*,' he lied, suppressing a shiver at the very remembrance of those midnight eyes. 'My dyspepsia is the result of my ongoing difference of opinion with our employer, the notorious Butcher of Caprile, the ever-contrary Murcatto! I simply cannot seem to find the correct approach with that woman! However cordially I behave, however spotless my intentions, she bears it *ill*!'

'She's somewhat prickly, true.'

'In my opinion she passes beyond prickly and enters the arena of . . . sharp,' he finished, lamely.

'Well, the betrayal, the being thrown down the mountain, the dead brother and all—'

'Explanations, not excuses! We all have suffered painful reverses! I declare, I am half-tempted to abandon her to her inevitable fate and seek out fresh employment.' He snorted with laughter at a sudden thought. 'With *Duke Orso*, perhaps!'

Day looked up sharply. 'You're joking.'

It had, in fact, been intended as a witticism, for Castor Morveer was not the man to abandon an employer once he had accepted a contract. Certain standards of behaviour had to be observed, in his business more than any other. But it amused him to explore the notion further, counting off the points one by one upon his outstretched digits. 'A man who can undoubtedly afford my services. A man who undoubtedly *requires* my services. A man who has proved himself unencumbered by the slightest troublesome moral qualm.'

'A man with a record of pushing his employees down mountains.'

Morveer dismissed it. 'One should never be foolish enough to trust the sort of person who would hire a poisoner. In that he is no worse an employer than any other. Why, it is a profound wonder the thought did not occur sooner!'

'But . . . we killed his son.'

'Bah! Such difficulties are easily explained away when two men find they need each other.' He airily waved one hand. 'Some invention will suffice. Some wretched scapegoat can always be found to shoulder the blame.'

She nodded slowly, mouth set hard. 'A scapegoat. Of course.'

'A *wretched* one.' One less mutilated Northman in the world would be no loss to posterity. Nor one less insane convict or abrasive torturer, for that matter. He was almost warming to the notion. 'But I daresay for the time being we are stuck with Murcatto and her futile quest for revenge. *Revenge.* I swear, is there a more pointless, destructive, unsatisfying motive in all the world?'

'I thought motives weren't our business,' observed Day, 'only jobs and the pay.'

'Correct, my dear, very correct, every motive is a pure one that necessitates our services. You see straight to the heart of the matter as always, as though the matter were entirely *transparent.* Whatever would I do without you?' He came smiling around the apparatus. 'How are our preparations proceeding?'

'Oh, I know what to do.'

'Good. Very good. Of course you do. You learned from a master.'

She bowed her head. 'And I marked your lessons well.'

'Most *excellent* well.' He leaned down to flick at a condenser, watched the Larync essence dripping slowly down into the retort. 'It is vital to be exhaustively prepared for any and every eventuality. Caution first, always, of— Ah!' He frowned down at his forearm. A tiny speck of red swelled, became a dot of blood. 'What . . .' Day backed slowly away from him, an expression of the most peculiar intensity on her face. She held a mounted needle in her hand.

'Someone to take the blame?' she snarled at him. 'Scapegoat, am I? Fuck yourself, bastard!'

'Come on, come on, come on.' Faithful was pissing again, stood by his horse, back to Shivers, shaking his knees around. 'Come on, come on. Bloody years catching up on me, that's what this is.'

'That or your dark deeds,' said Swolle.

'I've done nothing black enough to deserve this shit, surely. You feel like you never had to go so bad in your life, then when you finally get your prick out, you end up stood here in the wind for an age of . . . ah . . . ah . . . there's the fucker!' He leaned backwards, showing off his big bald spot. A brief spatter, then another. One more, he worked his shoulders around as he shook the drips off, and started lacing up again.

'That's it?' asked Swolle.

'What's your interest?' snapped the general. 'To bottle it? Years catching up on me is all it is.' He picked his way up the slope bent over, heavy red cloak held out of the mud in one hand, and squatted down next to Shivers. 'Right then. Right then. That's the place?'

'That's the place.' The farm sat at the end of an open paddock, in the midst of a sea of grey wheat, under the grey sky, clouds smudged with watery dawn. Faint light flickered at the narrow windows of the barn, but no more signs of life. Shivers rubbed his fingers slowly against his palms. He'd never done much treachery. Nothing so sharply cut as this, leastways, and it was making him nervy.

'Looks peaceful enough.' Faithful ran a slow hand over his white stubble. 'Swolle, you get a dozen men and take 'em round the side, out of sight, into that stand of trees down there, get on the flank. Then if they see us and make a run for it you can finish up.'

'Right y'are, General. Nice and simple, eh?'

'Nothing worse than too much plan. More there is to remember, more there is to make a shit of. Don't need to tell you not to make a shit of it, do I, Swolle?'

'Me? No, sir. Into the trees, then if I see anyone running, charge. Just like at the High Bank.'

'Except Murcatto's on the other side now, right?'

'Right. Fucking evil bitch.'

'Now, now,' said Faithful. 'Some respect. You were happy enough to clap for her when she brought you victories, you can clap for her now. Shame things have come to this, is all. Nothing else for it. Don't mean there can't be some respect.'

'Right. Sorry.' Swolle paused for a moment. 'Sure it wouldn't be better to try and creep down there on foot? I mean, we can't ride into that farmhouse, can we?'

Faithful gave him a long look. 'Did they pick a new captain general while I was away, and are you it?'

'Well, no, 'course not, just—'

'Creeping up ain't my style, Swolle. Knowing how often you wash, more than likely Murcatto'd fucking smell you before we got within a hundred strides, and be ready. No, we'll ride down there and spare my knees the wear. We can always get down once we've given the place the check over. And if she's got any surprises for us, well, I'd rather be in my saddle.' He frowned sideways at Shivers. 'You see a problem with that, boy?'

'Not me.' From what Shivers had seen he reckoned Faithful was one o' those men make a good second and a poor chief. Lots of bones but no imagination. Looked like he'd got stuck to one way of doing things over the years and had to do it now whether it fit the job or not. But he weren't about to say so. Strong leaders might like it when someone brings 'em a better idea, but weak ones never do. 'You reckon I could get my axe back, though?'

Faithful grinned. ''Course you can. Just as soon as I see Murcatto's dead body. Let's go.' He nearly tripped on his cloak as he turned for the horses, angrily dragged it up and tossed it over his shoulder. 'Bloody thing. Knew I should've got a shorter one.'

Shivers took one last look at the farm before he followed, shaking his head. There's nothing worse'n too much plan, that's true. But too little comes in close behind.

Morveer blinked. 'But . . .' He took a slow step towards Day. His ankle wobbled and he slumped sideways against the table, knocking over a flask and making the fizzing contents spill across the wood. He clutched one hand to his throat, his skin flushing, burning. He knew already what she must have done, the realisation spreading out frigid through his veins. He knew already what the consequences would have to be. 'The King . . .' he rasped, 'of Poisons?'

'What else? Caution first, always.'

He grimaced, at the meagre pain of the tiny prick in his arm, and at the far deeper wound of bitter betrayal besides. He coughed, fell forwards onto his knees, one hand stretching, trembling upwards. 'But—'

Day kicked his hand away with the toe of one shoe. 'Doomed to be misunderstood?' Her face was twisted with contempt. With hatred, even. The pleasing mask of obedience, of admiration, of innocence too, finally dropped. 'What do you think there is to understand about you, you swollen-headed parasite? You're thin as tissue paper!' There was the deepest cut of all – ingratitude, after all he had given her! His knowledge, his money, his . . . fatherly affection! 'The personality of a baby in the body of a murderer! Bully and coward in one. Castor Morveer, greatest poisoner in the world? Greatest bore in the world, maybe, you—'

He sprang forwards with consummate nimbleness, nicked her ankle with his scalpel as he passed, rolled under the table and came up on the other side, grinning at her through the complexity of apparatus, the flickering flames of the burners, the distorting shapes of twisted tubes, the glinting surfaces of glass and metal.

'Ha *ha*!' He shouted, entirely alert and not dying in the least. '*You*, poison *me*? The *great* Castor Morveer, undone by his *assistant*? I think *not*!' She stared down at her bleeding ankle, and then up at him, eyes wide. 'There is no King of Poisons, fool!' he cackled. 'The method I showed you, that produces a liquid that smells, tastes and looks like water? It makes water! Entirely *harmless*! Unlike the concoction with which I just now pricked you, which was enough to kill a dozen horses!'

He slipped his hand inside his shirt, deft fingertips unerringly selecting the correct vial and sliding it out into the light. Clear fluid gleamed inside. 'The antidote.' She winced as she saw it, made to dive one way around the table then came the other, but her feet were clumsy and he evaded her with negligible effort. '*Most* undignified, my dear! Chasing each other around our apparatus, in a barn, in the middle of rural Styria! Most *terribly* undignified!'

'Please,' she hissed at him. 'Please, I'll . . . I'll—'

'Don't embarrass us both! You have displayed your true nature now you . . . you ingrate *harpy*! You are unmasked, you treacherous *cuckoo*!'

'I didn't want to take the blame is all! Murcatto said sooner or later you'd go over to Orso! That you'd want to use me as the scapegoat! Murcatto said—'

'*Murcatto?* You listen to *Murcatto* over *me*? That degenerate, husk-addled and notorious *butcher* of the *bloody battlefield*? Oh, *commendable* guiding *light*! Curse me for an imbecile to trust either one of you! It seems you were correct, at least, that I am like to a baby. All *unspoiled innocence*! All *undeserved mercy*!' He flicked the vial through the air at Day. 'Let it never again be said,' as he watched her fumbling through the straw for it, 'that I am not,' as she clawed it up and ripped out the cork, 'as generous, merciful and forgiving as any poisoner,' as she sucked down the contents, 'within the *entire* Circle of the World.'

Day wiped her mouth and took a shuddering breath. 'We need . . . to talk.'

'We certainly do. But not for long.' She blinked, then a strange spasm passed over her face. Just as he had known it would. He wrinkled his nose as he tossed his scalpel clattering across the table. 'The blade carried no poison, but you have just consumed a vial of undiluted Leopard Flower.'

She flopped over, eyes rolling back, skin turning pink, began to jerk around in the straw, froth gurgling from her mouth.

Morveer stepped forwards, leaned down over her, baring his teeth, stabbing at his chest with a clawing finger. 'Kill *me*, would you? *Poison* me? Castor *Morveer*?' The heels of her shoes drummed out a rapid beat on the hard-packed earth, sending up puffs of straw-dust. '*I* am the only King of Poisons, you . . . you child-faced *fool*!' Her thrashing became a locked-up trembling, back arched impossibly far. 'The simple *insolence* of you! The *arrogance*! The *insult*! The, the, the . . .' He fumbled breathlessly for the right word, then realised she was dead. There was a long, slow silence as her corpse gradually relaxed.

'Shit!' he barked. 'Entirely *shit*!' The scant satisfaction of victory was already fast melting, like an unseasonable flurry of snow on a warm day, before the crushing disappointment, wounding betrayal and simple inconvenience of his new, assistant-less, employer-less situation. For Day's final words had left him in no doubt that Murcatto was to blame. That after all his thankless, selfless toil on her behalf she had plotted his death. Why had he not anticipated this development? How could he not have expected it, after all the painful reverses he had suffered in his life? He was simply too soft a personage for this harsh land, this unforgiving epoch. Too trusting and too comradely for his own good. He was prone to see the world in the rosy tones of his own benevolence, cursed always to expect the best from people.

'Thin as paper, am I? Shit! You . . . *shit*!' He kicked Day's corpse petulantly, his shoe thudding into her body over and over and making it shudder again. '*Swollen-headed?*' he near shrieked it. '*Me?* Why, I am *humility* . . . its . . . fucking . . . *self*!' He realised suddenly that it ill befit a man of his boundless sensitivity to kick a person already dead, especially one he had cared for almost as a daughter. He felt a sudden bubbling-up of melodramatic regret.

'I'm sorry! So sorry.' He knelt beside her, gently pushed her hair back, touched her face with trembling fingers. That vision of innocence, never more to smile, never more to speak. 'I'm so sorry, but . . . but why? I will always remember you, but— Oh . . . urgh!' There was a sharp smell of urine. The corpse voiding itself, an inevitable side effect of a colossal dose of Leopard Flower that a man of his experience really should have seen coming. The pool had already spread out through the straw and soaked the knees of his trousers. He tottered up, wincing with disgust.

'Shit! Shit!' He snatched up a flask and flung it against the wall in a fury, fragments of glass scattering. 'Bully and coward in one?' He gave Day's body another petulant kick, bruised his toes and set off limping around the barn at a great pace.

'Murcatto!' That evil witch had incited his apprentice to treachery. The best and most loved apprentice he had trained since he was obliged to pre-emptively poison Aloveo Cray back in Ostenhorm. He knew he should have killed Murcatto in his orchard, but the scale, the importance and the apparent impossibility of the work she offered had appealed to his vanity. 'Curse my vanity! The *one* flaw in my character!'

But there could be no vengeance. '*No.*' Nothing so base and uncivilised, for that was not Morveer's way. He was no savage, no animal like the Serpent of Talins and her ilk, but a refined and cultured gentleman of the highest ethical standards. He was considerably out of pocket, now, after all his hard and loyal work, so he would have to find a proper contract. A proper employer and an entirely orderly and clean-motived set of murders, resulting in 'a proper, honest *profit.*'

And who would pay him to murder the Butcher of Caprile and her barbaric cronies? The answer was not so very difficult to fathom.

He faced a window and practised his most sycophantic bow, the one with the full finger twirl at the end. 'Grand Duke Orso, an incom . . . parable *honour.*' He straightened, frowning. At the top of the long rise, silhouetted against the grey dawn, were several dozen riders.

'For honour, glory and, above all, a decent pay-off!' A scattering of laughter as Faithful drew his sword and held it up high. 'Let's go!' And the long line of horsemen started moving, keeping loosely together as they thrashed through the wheat and out into the paddock, upping the pace to a trot.

Shivers went along with 'em. There wasn't much choice since Faithful was right at his side. Hanging back would've seemed poor manners. He would've liked his axe to hand, but hoping for a thing often brought on the opposite. Besides, as they picked up speed to a healthy canter, keeping both hands on the reins seemed like an idea with some weight to it.

Maybe a hundred strides out now, and all still looking peaceful. Shivers frowned at the farmhouse, at the low wall, at the barn, gathering himself, making ready. It all seemed like a bad plan, now. It had seemed a bad plan at the time, but having to do it made it seem a whole lot worse. The ground rushed past hard under his horse's hooves, the saddle jolted at his sore arse, the wind nipped at his narrowed eye, tickled at the raw scars on the other side of his face, bitter cold without the bandages. Faithful rode on his right, sitting up tall, cloak flapping behind him, sword still raised, shouting, 'Steady! Steady!' On his left the line shifted and buckled, eager faces of men and horses in a twisting row, spears jolting up and down at all angles. Shivers worked his boots free of the stirrups.

Then the shutters of the farmhouse flew open all together with an echoing bang. Shivers saw the Osprians at the windows, first light glinting on their steel caps as a long row of 'em came up from behind the wall together, flatbows levelled. Comes a time you just have to do a thing, shit on the consequences. The air whooped in his throat as he sucked in a great breath and held it, then threw himself sideways and tumbled from the saddle. Over the batter of hooves, the clatter of metal, the rushing of wind he heard Monza's sharp cry.

Then the dirt struck him, jarred his teeth together. He rolled, grunting, over and over, took a mouthful of mud. The world spun, all dark sky and flicking soil, flying horses, falling men. Hooves thudded around him, mud spattered in his eyes. He heard screams, fought his way up as far as his knees. A corpse dropped, flailing, crashed into Shivers and knocked him on his back again.

Morveer made it to the double doors of the barn and wrestled one wide enough to stick his head through, just in time to see the Osprian soldiers rise from behind the farmyard wall and deliver a disciplined and deadly volley of flatbow fire.

Out in the grassy paddock men jerked and tumbled from their saddles, horses fell and threw their riders. Flesh plunged down, ploughed into the wet dirt, limbs flailing. Beasts and men roared and wailed in shock and fury, pain and fear. Perhaps a dozen riders dropped, but the rest broke into a full charge without the slightest hint of reluctance, weapons raised and gleaming, releasing war cries to match the death screams of their fallen comrades.

Morveer whimpered, shoved the door shut and pressed his back against it. Red-edged battle. Rage and randomness. Pointed metal moving at great speed. Blood spilled, brains dashed, soft bodies ripped open and their innards laid sickeningly bare. A most uncivilised way to carry on, and decidedly not his area of expertise. His own guts, thankfully still within his abdomen, shifted with a first stab of bestial terror and revulsion, then constricted with a more reasoned wash of fear. If Murcatto won, her lethal intentions towards him had already been clearly displayed. She had not balked for a moment at engineering the death of his innocent apprentice, after all. If the Thousand Swords won, well, he was an accomplice of Prince Ario's killer. In either case his life would undoubtedly be painfully forfeit.

'Damn it!'

Beyond the one doorway the farmyard was rapidly becoming a slaughteryard, but the windows were too narrow to squeeze through. Hide in the hayloft? No, no, what was he, five years old? Lay down beside poor Day and play dead? What? Lie down in urine? Never! He dashed to the back of the barn with all despatch, poked desperately at the planking for a way through. He found a loose board and began kicking at it.

'Break, you wooden *bastard*! Break! Break! *Break!*' The sounds of mortal combat were growing ever more intense in the yard behind him. Something crashed against the side of the barn and made him startle, dust filtering down from the rafters with the force of it. He turned back to the carpentry, whimpering now with fear and frustration, face prickling with sweat. One last kick and the wood tore free. Wan daylight slunk in through a narrow gap between two ragged-edged planks. He knelt, turning sideways on, forced his head through the crack, splinters digging at his scalp, gained a view of flat country, brown wheat, a stand of trees perhaps two hundred strides distant. Safety. He worked one arm through into the free air, clutching vainly at the weathered outside of the barn. One shoulder, half his chest, and then he stuck fast.

It had been optimistic of him, to say the least, to imagine that he might have effortlessly slipped through that gap. Ten years ago he had been slender as a willow-swatch, could have glided through a space half the width with the grace of a dancer. Too many pastries in the interim had rendered such an operation impossible, however, and there appeared to be a growing prospect that they might have cost him his life. He wriggled, squirmed, sharp wood digging at his belly. Is this how they would find him? Is this the tale that they would snigger over in after years? Would that be his legacy? The great Castor Morveer, death without a face, most feared of all poisoners, finally brought to book, wedged in a crack in the back of a barn while fleeing?

'Damn *pastries*!' he screamed, and with one last effort tore himself through, teeth gritted as a rogue nail ripped his shirt half-off and left him a long and painful cut down his ribs. 'Damn it! Shit!' He dragged his aching legs through after him. Finally liberated from the clawing embrace of poor-quality joinery and riddled with splinters, he began to dash towards the proffered safety of the trees, waist-high wheat stalks tripping him, thrashing him, snatching at his legs.

He had progressed no further than five wobbly strides when he fell headlong, sprawling in the damp crop with a squeal. He struggled up, cursing. One of his shoes had been snatched off by the jealous wheat as he went down. 'Damn *wheat*!' He was just beginning to cast about for it when he became aware of a loud drumming sound. To his disbelieving horror, a dozen horsemen had burst from the trees towards which he had been fleeing, and were even now bearing down on him at full gallop, spears lowered.

He gave vent to a breathless squeak, spun, slipped on his bare foot, began to limp back to the crack that had so mauled him on their first acquaintance. He wedged one leg through, whimpered at a stab of agony as he accidentally squashed his fruits against a plank. His back prickled as the hammering of hooves grew louder. The riders were no more than fifty strides from him, eyes of men and beasts starting, teeth of men and beasts bared, brightening morning sun catching warlike metal, chaff flying from threshing hooves. He would never tear his bleeding body back through the narrow gap in time. Would he be thrashed, now? Poor, humble Castor Morveer, who only ever wanted to be—

The corner of the barn exploded in a gout of bright flame. It made no sound beyond the crack and twang of shattering wood. The air suddenly swarmed with spinning debris: a tumbling chunk of flaming beam, ripped planks, bent nails, a scouring cloud of splinters and sparks. A cone of wheat was flattened in one great rustling wave, sucking up a rippling swell of dust, stalk, grain, embers. Two not insignificant barrels were suddenly exposed, standing proud in the midst of the levelled crop, directly in the path of the charging horsemen. Flames leaped up from them, black char spreading spontaneously across their sides.

The right-hand barrel exploded with a blinding flash, the left almost immediately after. Two great fountains of soil were hurled into the sky. The lead horse, trapped between them, seemed to stop, frozen, twist, then burst apart along with its rider. Most of the rest were enveloped in the spreading clouds of dust and, presumably, reduced to flying mincemeat.

A wave of wind flattened Morveer against the side of the barn, tearing at his ripped shirt, his hair, his eyes. A moment later the thunderous double detonation reached his ears and made his teeth rattle. A couple of horses at either end of the line remained largely in one piece, flapping bonelessly as they were tossed through the air like an angry toddler's toys, one mount turned mostly inside out, crashing down to leave bloody scars through the crop near the trees from which they had first emerged.

Clods of earth rattled against the plank wall. Dust began to settle. Patches of damp wheat burned reluctantly around the edges of the blast, sending up smudges of acrid smoke. Charred splinters of wood, blackened chaff, smouldering fragments of men and beasts still rained from the sky. Ash wafted softly down on the breeze.

Morveer stood, still wedged in the side of the barn, struck to the heart with cold amazement. Gurkish fire, it seemed, or something darker, more . . . magical? A figure appeared around the smouldering corner of the barn just as he wrenched himself free and dived into the wheat, peering up between the stalks.

The Gurkish woman, Ishri. One arm and the hem of her brown coat were thoroughly on fire. She seemed suddenly to notice as the flames licked up around her face, shrugged the burning garment off without rush and tossed it aside, standing bandaged from neck to toe, unburned and pristine as the body of some ancient desert queen embalmed and ready for burial. She took one long look towards the trees, then smiled and slowly shook her head.

She said something happily in Kantic. Morveer's mastery of the tongue was not supreme, but it sounded like, 'You still have it, Ishri.' She swept the wheat where Morveer was hiding with her black eyes, at which he ducked down with the greatest alacrity, then she turned and disappeared behind the shattered corner of the barn from whence she came. He heard her faintly chuckling to herself.

'You still have it.'

Morveer was left only with an overpowering – but in his opinion entirely justifiable – desire to flee, and never look back.

So he wormed his way through the gore-spattered crops on his belly. Towards the trees, inch by painful inch, breath wheezing in his burning chest, terror pricking at his arse all the long way.

No Worse

Monza jerked the Calvez back and the man gave a wheezing grunt, face all squeezed up with shock, clutching at the little wound in his chest. He took a tottering step forwards, hauling up his short-sword as if it weighed as much as an anvil. She stepped out to the left and ran him through the side, just under his ribs, a foot of well-used blade sliding through his studded leather jerkin. He turned his head in her direction, face pink and trembling, veins bulging in his stretched-out neck. When she pulled the sword out, he dropped as if it had been the only thing holding him up. His eyes rolled towards her.

'Tell my . . .' he whispered.

'What?'

'Tell . . . her—' He strained up from the boards, dust caked across one side of his face, then coughed black vomit and stopped moving.

Monza placed him, all of a sudden. Baro, his name had been, or Paro, something with an 'o' on the end. Some cousin of old Swolle's. He'd been there at Musselia, after the siege, after they sacked the town. He'd laughed at one of Benna's jokes. She remembered because it hadn't seemed the time for jokes, after they'd murdered Hermon and stolen his gold. She hadn't felt much like laughing, she knew that.

'Varo?' she muttered, trying to think what that joke had been. She heard a board creak, saw movement just in time to drop down. Her head jolted, the floor hit her in the face. She got up, the room tipped over and she ploughed into the wall, put one elbow out of the window, almost fell right through it. Roaring outside, clatter and clash of combat.

Through a head full of lights she saw something come at her and she tumbled out of the way, heard it smash into plaster. Splinters in her face. She screamed, reeling off balance, slashed at a black shape with the Calvez, saw her hand was empty. Dropped it already. There was a face at the window.

'Benna?' And some blood trickled from her mouth.

No time for jokes. Something clattered into her back and drove her breath out. She saw a mace, dull metal gleaming. Saw a man's face, snarling. A chain whipped around his neck and jerked him up. The room was settling, blood whooshing in her head, she tried to stand and only rolled onto her back.

Vitari had him round the throat and they lurched together about the dim room. He elbowed at her, other hand fiddling at the chain, but she dragged it tight, eyes ground to two furious little slits. Monza struggled up, made it to her feet, wobbled towards them. He fished at his belt for a knife but Monza got there first, pinned his free arm with her left hand, drew the blade with her right and started stabbing him with it.

'Uh, uh, uh.' Squelch, scrape, thud, honking and spitting in each other's faces, her stuttering moan, and his squealing grunts, and Vitari's low growl all mingling together into an echoing, animal mess. Pretty much the same sounds they would have made if they were fucking rather than killing each other. Scrape, thud, squelch. 'Uh, ah, uh.'

'Enough!' hissed Vitari. 'He's done!'

'Uh.' She let the knife clatter to the boards. Her arm was sticky wet inside her coat all the way to her elbow, gloved hand locked up into a burning claw. She turned to the door, narrowing her stinging eyes against the brightness, stepped clumsily over the corpse of an Osprian soldier and through the broken wood in the doorway.

A man with blood down his cheek clawed at her, near dragged her over as he fell, smearing gore across her coat. A mercenary was stabbed from behind as he tried to stagger up from the yard, went down thrashing on his face. Then the Osprian soldier who'd speared him got kicked in the head by a horse, his steel cap flying right off and him toppling sideways like a felled tree. Men and mounts strained all around – a deadly storm of thumping boots, hooves, clattering metal, swinging weapons and flying dirt.

And not ten strides from her, through the mass of writhing bodies, Faithful Carpi sat on his big warhorse, roaring like a madman. He hadn't much changed – the same broad, honest, scarred face. The bald pate, the thick white moustache and the white stubble round it. He'd got himself a shiny breastplate and a long red cloak better suited to a duke than a mercenary. He had a flatbow bolt sticking from his shoulder, right arm hanging useless, the other raised to point a heavy sword towards the house.

The strange thing was that she felt a rush of warmth when she first laid eyes on him. That happy pang you get when you see a friend's face in a crowd. Faithful Carpi, who'd led five charges for her. Who'd fought for her in all weathers and never let her down. Faithful Carpi, who she would've trusted with her life. Who she had trusted with her life, so he could sell it cheap for Cosca's old chair. Sell her life, and sell her brother's too.

The warmth didn't last long. The dizziness faded with it, left her a dose of anger scalding her guts and a stinging pain down the side of her head where the coins held her skull together.

The mercenaries could be bitter fighters when they had no other choice, but they much preferred foraging to fighting and they'd been withered by that first volley, rattled by the shock of men where they hadn't expected them. They had spears ahead, enemies in the buildings, archers at the windows and on the flat stable roof, shooting down at their leisure. A rider shrieked as he was dragged from his saddle, spear tumbling from his hand and clattering at Monza's feet.

A couple of his comrades turned their horses to run. One made it back into the paddock. The other was poked wailing from his saddle with a sword, foot caught in one stirrup, dancing upside down while his horse thrashed about. Faithful Carpi was no coward, but you don't last thirty years as a mercenary without knowing when to make a dash for it. He wheeled his horse around, chopping an Osprian soldier down and laying his skull wide open in the mud. Then he was gone round the side of the farmhouse.

Monza clawed up the fallen spear in her gloved hand, snatched hold of the bridle of the riderless horse with the other and dragged herself into the saddle, her sudden bitter need to kill Carpi putting some trace of the old spring back into her lead-filled legs. She pulled the horse around to face the farmyard wall, gave it her heels and jumped it, an Osprian soldier flinging his flatbow down and diving out of her way with a cry. She thumped down on the other side, jolting in the saddle and near stabbing herself in the face, crashed out into the wheat, stalks thrashing at the legs of her stolen horse as it struggled up the long slope. She fumbled the spear across into her left hand, took the reins in her right, crouched down and drummed up a jagged canter with her heels. She saw Carpi stop at the top of the rise, a black outline against the bright eastern sky, then turn his horse and tear away.

She burst out from the wheat and across a field spotted with thorny bushes, downhill now, clods of mud flying from the soft ground as she dug her mount to a full gallop. Not far ahead of her Carpi jumped a hedgerow, greenery thrashing at his horse's hooves. He landed badly, flailing in the saddle to keep his balance. Monza picked her spot better, cleared the hedge easily, gaining on him all the time. She kept her eyes ahead, always ahead. Not thinking of the speed, or the danger, or the pain in her hand. All that was in her mind was Faithful Carpi, and his horse, and the overpowering need to stick her spear into one or the other.

They thundered across an unplanted field, hooves hammering at the thick mud, towards a crease in the ground that looked like a stream. A whitewashed building gleamed beside it in the brightening morning sun, a mill-house from what Monza could tell with the world shaking, wobbling, rushing around her. She strained forwards over her horse's neck, gripping hard at the spear couched under her arm, wind rushing at her narrowed eyes. Willing herself closer to Faithful Carpi. Willing herself closer to vengeance. It looked as though his horse might have picked up a niggle when he spoiled that jump, she was making ground on him now, making ground fast.

There were just three lengths between them, then two, specks of mud from the hooves of Carpi's warhorse flicking in her face. She drew herself up in the saddle, pulling back the spear, sun twinkling on the tip for a moment. She caught a glimpse of Faithful's familiar face as he jerked his head round to look over his shoulder, one grey eyebrow thick with blood, streaks down his stubbly cheek from a cut on his forehead. She heard him growl, digging hard with his spurs, but his horse was a heavy beast, better suited to charging than fleeing. The bobbing head of her mount crept slowly closer and closer to the streaming tail of Carpi's, the ground a brown blur rushing by between the two.

She screamed as she rammed the spear point into the horse's rump. It jerked, twisted, head flailing, one eye rolling wild, foam on its bared teeth. Faithful jolted in the saddle, one boot torn from the stirrup. The warhorse carried on for a dizzy moment, then its wounded leg twisted underneath it and all at once it went down, pitching forwards, head folding under its hurtling weight, hooves flailing, mud flying. She heard Carpi squeal as she flashed past, heard the thumping behind her as his horse tumbled over and over across the muddy field.

She hauled on the reins with her right hand, pulled her horse up, snorting and tossing, legs shaky from the hard ride. She saw Carpi pushing himself drunkenly from the ground, tangled with his long red cloak, all spattered and streaked with dirt. She was surprised to see him still alive, but not unhappy. Gobba, Mauthis, Ario, Ganmark, they'd had their part in what Orso had done to her, done to her brother, and they'd paid their price for it. But none of them had been her friends. Faithful had ridden beside her. Eaten with her. Drunk from her canteen. Smiled, and smiled, then stabbed her when it suited him, and stolen her place.

She had a mind to stretch this out.

He took a dizzy step, mouth hanging open, eyes wide in his bloody face. He saw her and she grinned, held the spear up high and gave a whoop. Like a hunter might do, seeing the fox in the open. He started limping desperately away towards the edge of the field, wounded arm cradled against his chest, the shaft of the flatbow bolt jutting broken from his shoulder.

The smile tugged hard at her face as she trotted up closer, close enough to hear his wheezing breath as he struggled pointlessly towards the stream. The sight of that treacherous bastard crawling for his life made her happier than she'd been in a long while. He hauled his sword from its scabbard with his left hand, floundering desperately forwards, using it as a crutch.

'Takes time,' she called to him, 'to learn to use the wrong hand! I should know! You don't have that much fucking time, Carpi!' He was close to the stream, but she'd be on him before he got there, and he knew it.

He turned, clumsily raising the blade. She jerked the reins and sent her mount sideways so he hacked nothing but air. She stood in the stirrups, stabbed down with the spear, caught him in the shoulder and tore the armour from it, ripped a gash in his cloak and knocked him to his knees, sword left stuck in the earth. He moaned through gritted teeth, blood trickling down his breast-plate, struggling to get up again. She pulled one boot from the stirrup, brought her horse closer and kicked him in the face, snapped his head back and sent him rolling down the bank and into the stream.

She tossed the spear point-first into the soil, swung her leg over the saddle and slid down. She stood a moment, watching Carpi floundering, shaking the life back into her stiff legs. Then she snatched the spear up, took a long, slow breath and started picking her way down the bank to the water's edge.

Not far downstream the mill-house stood, waterwheel clatter-ing as it slowly turned. The far bank had been walled up with rough stone, all bearded with moss. Carpi was fumbling at it, cursing, trying to drag himself up onto the far side. But weighed down with armour, his cloak heavy with water, a flatbow bolt in one shoulder and a spear wound in the other, he had less than no chance. So he waded doggedly along, up to his waist in the stream, while she shadowed him on the other bank, grinning, spear levelled.

'You keep on going, Carpi, I'll give you that. No one could call you a coward. Just an idiot. Stupid Carpi.' She forced out a laugh. 'I can't believe you fell for this shit. All those years taking my orders, you should've known me better. Thought I'd be sitting waiting, did you, weeping over my misfortunes?'

He edged back through the water, eyes fixed on the point of her spear, breathing hard. 'That fucking Northman lied to me.'

'Almost as if you can't trust anyone these days, eh? You should've stabbed me in the heart, Faithful, instead of the guts.'

'Heart?' he sneered. 'You don't have one!' He floundered through the water at her, sending up a shower of glittering spray, dagger in his fist. She thrust at him, felt the spear's shaft jolt in her aching right hand as the point took him in the hip, twisted him round and sent him over backwards. He struggled up again, snarling through his gritted teeth. 'I'm better'n you at least, you murdering scum!'

'If you're so much better than me, how come you're the one in the stream and I'm the one with the spear, fucker?' She moved the point in slow circles, shining with wet. 'You keep on coming, Carpi, I'll give you that. No one could call you a coward. Just a fucking liar. Traitor Carpi.'

'Me a traitor?' he dragged himself down the wall towards the slowly clattering waterwheel. 'Me? After all those years I stuck with you? I wanted to be loyal to Cosca! I *was* loyal to him. I'm Faithful!' He thumped his wet breastplate with his bloody hand. 'That's what I am. What I was. You stole that from me! You and your fucking brother!'

'I didn't throw Cosca down a mountain, bastard!'

'You think I wanted to do it? You think I wanted any of this?' There were tears in the old mercenary's eyes as he struggled away from her. 'I'm not made to lead! Ario comes to me, says Orso's decided you can't be trusted! That you have to go! That you're the past and I'm the future, and the rest of the captains already agreed. So I took the easy way. What was my choice?'

Monza wasn't enjoying herself any more. She remembered Orso standing smiling in her tent. *Cosca is the past, and I have decided that you are the future.* Benna smiling beside him. *It's better like this. You deserve to lead.* She remembered taking the easy way. What had been her choice? 'You could've warned me, given me a chance to—'

'Like you warned Cosca? Like you warned me? Fuck yourself, Murcatto! You pointed out the path and I followed, that's all! You sow bloody seeds, you'll reap a bloody harvest, and you sowed seeds across Styria and back! You did this to yourself! You did this to— Gah!' He twisted backwards, fumbling weakly at his neck. That fine cloak of his had floated back and got all caught up in the gears of the waterwheel. Now the red cloth was winding tighter and tighter, dragging him hard against the slowly turning wood.

'Fucking . . .' He fumbled with his one half-good arm at the mossy slats, at the rusted bolts of the great wheel, but there was no stopping it. Monza watched, mouth half-open but no words to say, spear hanging slack from her hands as he was dragged down, down under the wheel. Down, down, into the black water. It surged and bubbled around his chest, then around his shoulders, then around his neck.

His bulging eyes rolled up towards her. 'I'm no worse'n you, Murcatto! Just did what I had to!' He was fighting to keep his mouth above the frothing water. 'I'm . . . no worse . . . than—'

His face disappeared.

Faithful Carpi, who'd led five charges for her. Who'd fought for her in all weathers and never let her down. Faithful Carpi, who she'd trusted with her life.

Monza floundered down into the stream, cold water closing around her legs. She caught hold of Faithful's clutching hand, felt his fingers grip hers. She pulled, teeth gritted, growling with the effort. She lifted the spear, rammed it into the gears hard as she could, felt the shaft jam there. She hooked her gloved hand under his armpit, up to her neck in surging water, fighting to drag him out, straining with every burning muscle. She felt him starting to come up, arm sliding out of the froth, elbow, then shoulder, she started fumbling at the buckle on his cloak with her gloved hand but she couldn't make the fingers work. Too cold, too numb, too broken. There was a crack as the spear shaft splintered. The waterwheel started turning, slowly, slowly, metal squealing, cogs grating, and dragged Faithful back under.

The stream kept on flowing. His hand went limp, and that was that.

Five dead, two left.

She let it go, breathing hard. She watched as his pale fingers slipped under the water, then she waded out of the stream and limped up onto the bank, soaked to the skin. There was no strength left in her, legs aching deep in the bones, right hand throbbing all the way up her forearm and into her shoulder, the wound on the side of her head stinging, blood pounding hard as a club behind her eyes. It was all she could manage to get one foot in the stirrup and drag herself into the saddle.

She took a look back, felt her guts clench and double her over, spat a mouthful of scalding sick into the mud, then another. The wheel had pulled Faithful right under and now it was dragging him up on the other side, limbs dangling, head lolling, eyes wide open and his tongue hanging out, some waterweed tangled around his neck. Slowly, slowly, it hoisted him up into the air, like an executed traitor displayed as an example to the public.

She wiped her mouth on the back of her arm, scraped her tongue over her teeth and tried to spit the bitterness away while her sore head spun. Probably she should have cut him down from there, given him some last shred of dignity. He'd been her friend, hadn't he? No hero, maybe, but who was? A man who'd wanted to be loyal in a treacherous business, in a treacherous world. A man who'd wanted to be loyal and found it had gone out of fashion. Probably she should have dragged him up onto the bank at least, left him somewhere he could lie still. But instead she turned her horse back towards the farm.

Dignity wasn't much help to the living, it was none to the dead. She'd come here to kill Faithful, and he was killed.

No point weeping about it now.

Harvest Time

Shivers sat on the steps of the farmhouse, trimming some loose skin from the big mass of grazes on his forearm and watching some man weep over a corpse. Friend. Brother, even. He weren't trying to hide it, just sat slumped over, tears dripping off his chin. A moving sight, most likely, if you were that way inclined.

And Shivers always had been. His brother had called him pig-fat when he was a boy on account of his being that soft. He'd cried at his brother's grave and at his father's. When his friend Dobban got stabbed through with a spear and took two days going back to the mud. The night after the fight at Dunbrec, when they buried half his crew along with Threetrees. After the battle in the High Places, even, he'd gone off and found a spot on his own, let fall a full puddle of salt water. Though that might've been relief the fighting was done, rather than sorrow some lives were.

He knew he'd wept all those times, and he knew why, but he couldn't remember for the life of him how it had felt to do it. He wondered if there was anyone left in the world he'd cry for now, and he wasn't sure he liked the answer.

He took a swig of sour water from his flask, and watched a couple of Osprian soldiers picking over the bodies. One rolled a dead man over, some bloody guts slithering out of his split side, wrestled his boot off, saw it had a hole in the sole, tossed it away. He watched another pair, shirtsleeves rolled up, one with a shovel over his shoulder, arguing the toss over where'd be easiest to start digging. He watched the flies, floating about in the soupy air, already gathering round the open mouths, the open eyes, the open wounds. He looked at ragged gashes and broken bone, cut-off limbs and spilled innards, blood in sticky streaks, drying spots and spatters, red-black pools across the stony yard, and felt no pleasure at a job well done, but no disgust either, no guilt and no sorrow. Just the stinging of his grazes, the uncomfortable stickiness of the heat, the tiredness in his bruised limbs and a niggling trace of hunger, since he'd missed breakfast.

There was a man screaming inside the farmhouse, where they were dealing with the wounded. Screaming, screaming, hoarse and blubbery. But there was a bird tweeting happily from the eaves of the stable too, and Shivers found without too much effort he could concentrate on one and forget the other. He smiled and nodded along with the bird, leaned back against the door frame and stretched his leg out. Seemed a man could get used to anything, in time. And he was damned if he was going to let some screaming shift him off a good spot on the doorstep.

He heard hoofbeats, looked round. Monza, trotting slowly down the slope, a black figure with the bright-blue sky behind her. He watched her pull her lathered horse up in the farmyard, frowning at the bodies. Her clothes were sodden wet, as if she'd been dunked in a stream. Her hair was matted with blood on one side, her pale cheek streaked with it.

'Aye aye, Chief. Good to see you.' Should've been true but it felt like some kind of a lie, still. He felt not much of anything either way. 'Faithful dead, is he?'

'He's dead.' She slid stiffly down. 'Have any trouble getting him here?'

'Not much. He wanted to bring more friends than we'd planned for, but I couldn't bring myself to turn 'em down. You know how it is when folk hear about a party. They looked so eager, poor bastards. Have any trouble killing him?'

She shook her head. 'He drowned.'

'Oh aye? Thought you'd have stabbed him.' He picked her sword up and offered it to her.

'I stabbed him a bit.' She looked at the blade for a moment, then took it from his hand and sheathed it. 'Then I let him drown.'

Shivers shrugged. 'Up to you. Drowning'll do it, I reckon.'

'Drowning did it.'

'Five of seven, then.'

'Five of seven.' Though she didn't look like celebrating. Hardly any more than the man crying over his dead friend. It

426

weren't much of a joyous occasion for anyone, even on the winning side. There's vengeance for you.

'Who's that screaming?'

'Someone. No one.' Shivers shrugged. 'Listen to the bird instead.'

'What?'

'Murcatto!' Vitari stood, arms folded, in the open doorway of the barn. 'You'll want to see this.'

It was cool and dim inside, sunlight coming in through a ragged hole in the corner, through the narrow windows, throwing bright stripes across the darkened straw. One fell over Day's corpse, yellow hair tangled across her face, body twisted awkwardly. No blood. No marks of violence at all.

'Poison,' muttered Monza.

Vitari nodded. 'Oh, the irony.'

A hellish-looking mess of copper rods, glass tubes and odd-shaped bottles was stood on the table beside the body, a couple of lamps with yellow-blue flames flickering underneath, stuff bubbling away inside, trickling, dripping. Shivers liked the look of the poisoner's equipment even less than the look of the poisoner's corpse. Bodies he was good and familiar with, science was all unknown.

'Fucking science,' he muttered. 'Even worse'n magic.'

'Where's Morveer?' asked Monza.

'No sign.' The three of them looked hard at each other for a moment.

'Not among the dead?'

Shivers slowly shook his head. 'It's a shame, but I didn't see him.'

Monza took a worried step back. 'Best not touch anything.'

'You think?' growled Vitari. 'What happened?'

'Difference of opinion between master and apprentice, by the look of things.'

'Serious difference,' muttered Shivers.

Vitari slowly shook her spiky head. 'That's it. I'm finished.'

'You're what?' asked Monza.

'I'm out. In this business you have to know when to quit. It's war now, and I try not to get involved with that. Too hard to pick the outcome.' She nodded towards the yard where, out in

427

the sunshine, they were piling up the corpses. 'Visserine was a step too far for me, and this is a step further. That and I've no taste for being on the wrong side of Morveer. I could do without looking over my shoulder every day of my life.'

'You'll still be looking over your shoulder for Orso,' said Monza.

'Knew it when I took the job. Needed the money.' Vitari held out her open palm. 'Talking of which . . .'

Monza frowned at her hand, then her face. 'You've only come halfway. Halfway, half what we agreed.'

'Seems fair. All the money and dead is no kind of payment. I'll settle for half and live.'

'I'd sooner keep you on. I can use you. And you won't be safe as long as Orso's alive—'

'Then you'd best get on and kill the bastard, hadn't you? But without me.'

'Your choice.' Monza reached inside her coat and pulled out a flat leather pouch, a little stained with water. She unfolded it twice and slid a paper from inside, damp at one corner, covered with fancy-looking script. 'More than half what we agreed. Five thousand two hundred and twelve scales, in fact.' Shivers frowned at it. He still couldn't see how you could turn such a weight of silver into a scrap of paper.

'Fucking banking,' he murmured. 'Even worse'n science.'

Vitari took the bill from Monza's gloved hand, gave it a quick look over. 'Valint and Balk?' Her eyes went even narrower than usual, which was some achievement. 'This paper better pay. If not, there's no place in the Circle of the World you'll be safe from—'

'It'll pay. If there's one thing I don't need it's more enemies.'

'Then let's part friends.' Vitari folded the paper and pushed it down into her shirt. 'Maybe we'll work together again some time.'

Monza stared right into her face, that way she had. 'I'll count the minutes.'

Vitari backed off for a few steps, then turned towards the sunlit square of the doorway.

'I fell in a river!' Shivers called after her.

'What?'

428

'When I was young. First time I went raiding. I got drunk, and I went for a piss, and I fell in the river. Current sucked my trousers off, dumped me half a mile downstream. Time I got back to camp I'd more or less turned blue with cold, shivering so bad I near shook my fingers off.'

'And?'

'That's why they called me Shivers. You asked. Back in Sipani.' And he grinned. Seemed like he could see the funny side of it, these days. Vitari stood there for a moment, a lean black outline, then slid out through the door. 'Well, Chief, looks like it's just you and me—'

'And me!' He snapped round, reaching for his axe. Beside him Monza crouched, sword already half-drawn, both straining into the darkness. Ishri's grinning face hung on one side, over the edge of the hayloft. 'And a fine afternoon to my two heroes.' She slid down the ladder face first, as smooth as if her bandaged body had no bones in it. Up onto her feet, looking impossibly thin without her coat, and she sauntered across the straw towards Day's corpse. 'One of your killers killed the other. There's killers for you.' She looked at Shivers, eyes black as coal, and he gripped his axe tight.

'Fucking magic,' he mumbled. 'Even worse'n banking.'

She crept up, all white-toothed, hungry grin, touched one finger to the pick on the back of his axe and pushed it gently down towards the floor. 'Do I take it you murdered your old friend Faithful Carpi to your satisfaction?'

Monza slapped her sword back into its sheath. 'Faithful's dead, if that's the point of your fucking performance.'

'You have a strange manner of celebration.' She lifted her long arms to the ceiling. 'Vengeance is yours! Praise be to God!'

'Orso still lives.'

'Ah, yes.' Ishri opened her eyes very wide, so wide Shivers wondered if they might drop out. 'When Orso dies you will smile.'

'What do you care whether I smile?'

'I, care? Not a particle. You Styrians have a habit of boasting, and boasting, and never following through. I am pleased to find one who can get the job done. Do the job, scowl by all means.' She ran her fingers across the table-top then casually snuffed the flames of the burners out with the palm of her hand. 'Speaking of which, you told our mutual friend Duke Rogont you could bring the Thousand Swords over to his side, as I recall?'

'If the Emperor's gold is forthcoming—'

'In your shirt pocket.'

Monza frowned as she pulled something from her pocket and held it up to the light. A big red-gold coin, shining with that special warmth gold has that somehow makes you want to hold it. 'Very nice, but it'll take more than one.'

'Oh, there'll be more. The mountains of Gurkhul are made of gold, I hear.' She peered at the charred edges of the hole in the corner of the barn, then happily clicked her tongue. 'I still have it.' And she twisted her body through the gap like a fox through a fence and was gone.

Shivers left it a moment, then leaned close to Monza. 'Can't put my finger on it, but there's something odd about her.'

'You've got this amazing sense for people, haven't you?' She turned without smiling and followed Vitari out of the barn.

Shivers stood there a moment longer, frowning down at Day's body, working his face around, feeling the scars on the left side stretching, shifting, itching. Cosca dead, Day dead, Vitari gone, Friendly gone, Morveer fled and, by the look of things, turned against them. So much for the merry company. He should've been all nostalgic for the happy friends of long ago, the bands of brothers he'd been a part of. United in a common cause, even if it was no more'n staying alive. Dogman, and Harding Grim, and Tul Duru. Black Dow, even, all men with a code. All faded into the past, and left him alone. Down here in Styria, where no one had any code that meant a thing.

Even then, his right eye was about as close to crying as his left.

He scratched at the scar on his cheek. Ever so gently, just with his fingertips. He winced, scratched harder. And harder still. He stopped himself, hissing through his teeth. Now it itched worse than ever, and hurt into the bargain. He'd yet to work out a way to scratch that itch that didn't make matters worse.

There's vengeance for you.

The Old New Captain General

Monza had seen wounds past counting, in all their wondrous variety. The making of them had been her profession. She'd witnessed bodies ruined in every conceivable manner. Men crushed, slashed, stabbed, burned, hanged, skinned, gutted, gored. But Caul Shivers' scar might well have been the worst she'd ever seen on the face of a living man.

It started as a pink mark near the corner of his mouth, became a ragged groove thick as a finger below his cheekbone, then widened, a stream of mottled, melted flesh flowing towards his eye. Streaks and spots of angry red spread out from it across his cheek, down the side of his nose. There was a thin mark to match slanting across his forehead and taking off half his eyebrow. Then there was the eye itself. It was bigger than the other. Lashes gone, lids shrivelled, the lower one drooping. When he blinked with his right eye, the left only twitched, and stayed open. He'd sneezed a while back, and it had puckered up like a swallowing throat, the dead enamelled pupil still staring at her through the pink hole. She'd had to will herself not to spew, and yet she was gripped with a horrified fascination, constantly looking to see if it would happen again, and it hardly helped that she knew he couldn't see her looking.

She should have felt guilt. She'd been the cause of it, hadn't she? She should have felt sympathy. She'd scars of her own, after all, and ugly enough. But disgust was as close as she could get. She wished she'd started off riding on the other side of him, but it was too late now. She wished he'd never taken the bandages off, but she could hardly tell him to put them back on. She told herself it might heal, might get better, and maybe it would.

But not much, and she knew it.

He turned suddenly, and she realised why he'd been staring at his saddle. His right eye was on her. His left, in the midst of all that scar, still looked straight downwards. The enamel must have slipped, and now his mismatched eyes gave him a look of skewed confusion.

'What?'

'Your, er . . .' She pointed at her face. 'It's slipped . . . a bit.'

'Again? Fucking thing.' He put his thumb in his eye and slid it back up. 'Better?' Now the false one was fixed straight ahead while the real one glared at her. It was almost worse than it had been.

'Much,' she said, doing her best to smile.

Shivers spat something in Northern. 'Uncanny results, did he say? If I happen back through Puranti I'll give that eye-making bastard a visit . . .'

The mercenaries' first picket came into view around a curve in the track – a scattering of shady-looking men in mismatched armour. She knew the one in charge by sight. She'd made it her business to know every veteran in the Thousand Swords, and what he was good for. Secco was this one's name, a tough old wolf who'd served as a corporal for six years or more.

He pointed his spear at her as they brought their horses to a walk, his fellows around him, flatbows, swords, axes at the ready. 'Who goes—'

She pushed her hood back. 'Who do you think, Secco?'

The words froze on his lips and he stood, spear limp, as she rode past. On into the camp, men going about their morning rituals, eating their breakfasts, getting ready to march. A few looked up as she and Shivers passed on the track, or at any rate the widest stretch of mud between the tents. A few of them started staring. Then a few more, watching, following at a distance, gathering along the way.

'It's her.'

'Murcatto.'

'She's alive?'

She rode through them the way she used to, shoulders back, chin up, sneer locked on her mouth, not even bothering to look. As if they were nothing to her. As if she was a better kind of animal than they were. And all the while she prayed silently they didn't work out what they'd never worked out yet, but what she was always afraid to the pit of her stomach they would.

That she didn't know what the hell she was doing, and a knife would kill her just as dead as anyone else.

But none of them spoke to her, let alone tried to stop her. Mercenaries are cowards, on the whole, even more so than most people. Men who'll kill because it's the easiest way they've found to make a living. Mercenaries have no loyalty in them, on the whole, by definition. Not much to their leaders, even less to their employers.

That was what she was counting on.

The captain general's tent was pitched on a rise in a big clearing, red pennant hanging limp from its tallest pole, well above the jumble of badly pitched canvas around it. Monza kicked her horse up, making a couple of men scurry out of her way, trying not to let the nerves that were boiling up her throat show. It was a long enough gamble as it was. Show one grain of fear and she'd be done.

She swung down from her horse, tossed the reins carelessly round a sapling trunk. She had to sidestep a goat someone had tethered there, then strode up towards the flap. Nocau, the Gurkish outcast who'd guarded the tent during the daylight since way back in Sazine's time, stood staring, his big scimitar not even drawn.

'You can shut your mouth now, Nocau.' She leaned in close and pushed his slack jaw shut with her gloved finger so his teeth snapped together. 'Wouldn't want a bird nesting in there, eh?' And she pushed through the flap.

The same table, even if the charts on it were of a different stretch of ground. The same flags hanging about the canvas, some of them that she'd added, won at Sweet Pines and the High Bank, at Musselia and Caprile. And the same chair, of course, that Sazine had supposedly stolen from the Duke of Cesale's dining table the day he formed the Thousand Swords. It stood empty on a pair of crates, waiting for the arse of the new captain general. For her arse, if the Fates were kind.

Though she had to admit they weren't usually.

The three most senior captains left in the great brigade stood close to the improvised dais, muttering to each other. Sesaria,

Victus, Andiche. The three Benna had persuaded to make her captain general. The three who'd persuaded Faithful Carpi to take her place. The three she needed to persuade to give it back to her. They looked up, and they saw her, and they straightened.

'Well, well,' rumbled Sesaria.

'Well, well, well,' muttered Andiche. 'If it isn't the Serpent of Talins.'

'The Butcher of Caprile herself,' whined Victus. 'Where's Faithful?'

She looked him right in the eye. 'Not coming. You boys need a new captain general.'

The three of them swapped glances, and Andiche sucked noisily at his yellowed teeth. A habit Monza had always found faintly disgusting. One of many disgusting things about the lank-haired rat of a man. 'As it happens, we'd reached the same conclusion on our own.'

'Faithful was a good fellow,' rumbled Sesaria.

'Too good for the job,' said Victus.

'A decent captain general needs to be an evil shit at best.'

Monza showed her teeth. 'Any one of you three is more than evil enough, I reckon. There aren't three bigger shits in Styria.' It was no kind of joke. She should've murdered these three rather than Faithful. 'Too big a set of shits to work for each other, though.'

'True enough,' said Victus sourly.

Sesaria tipped his head back and stared at her down his flat nose. 'We need someone new.'

'Or someone old,' said Monza.

Andiche grinned at his two fellows. 'As it happens, we'd reached the same conclusion on our own,' he said again.

'Good for you.' This was going more smoothly even than she'd hoped. Eight years she'd led the Thousand Swords, and she knew how to handle the likes of these three. Greed, nice and simple. 'I'm not the type to let a little bad blood get in the way of a lot of good money, and I damn well know that none of you are.' She held Ishri's coin up to the light, a Gurkish double-headed coin, Emperor on one side, Prophet on the other. She flicked it to Andiche. 'There'll be plenty more like that, to go over to Rogont.'

Sesaria stared at her from under his thick grey brows. 'Fight for Rogont, against Orso?'

'Fight all the way back across Styria?' The chains round Victus' neck rattled as he tossed his head. 'The same ground we've fought over the past eight years?'

Andiche looked up from the coin to her, and puffed out his acne-scarred cheeks. 'Sounds like an awful lot of fighting.'

'You've won against longer odds, with me in charge.'

'Oh, that's a fact.' Sesaria gestured at the tattered flags. 'We've won all kinds of glory with you in the chair, all kinds of pride.'

'But try paying a whore with that.' Victus was grinning, and that weasel never grinned. Something was wrong about their smiles, something mocking in them.

'Look.' Andiche rested one lazy hand on the arm of the captain general's chair and dusted the seat off with the other. 'We don't doubt for a moment that when it comes to a fight, you're the best damn general a man could ask for.'

'Then what's the problem?'

Victus' face twisted into a snarl. 'We don't want to fight! We want to make . . . fucking . . . money!'

'Who ever brought you more money than me?'

'Ahem,' came a voice right in her ear. Monza jerked round, and froze, hand halfway to the hilt of her sword. Standing just behind her, with a faintly embarrassed smile, was Nicomo Cosca.

He'd shaved off his moustache, and all his hair besides, left only a black and grey stubble over his knobbly skull, his sharp jaw. The rash had faded to a faint pink splash up the side of his neck. His eyes were less sunken, his face no longer trembling or beaded with sweat. But the smile was the same. The faint little smile and the playful gleam in his dark eyes. The same he used to have, when she first met him.

'A delight to see you both well.'

'Uh,' grunted Shivers. Monza found she'd made a kind of strangled cough, but no words came with it.

'I am in resplendent health, your concern for my welfare is most touching.' Cosca strolled past, slapping a puzzled-looking Shivers on the back, more captains of the Thousand Swords pushing their way through the flap after him and spreading out around the edges of the tent. Men whose names, faces, qualities, or lack of them, she knew well. A thick-set man with a stoop, a worn coat and almost no neck came at the rear. He raised his heavy brows at her as he passed.

'Friendly?' she hissed. 'I thought you were going back to Talins!'

He shrugged, as if it was nothing. 'Didn't make it all the way.'

'So I fucking see!'

Cosca stepped up onto the packing cases and turned to the assembly with a self-satisfied flourish. He'd acquired a grand black breastplate with golden scrollwork from somewhere, a sword with a gilded hilt, fine black boots with shining buckles. He settled himself into the captain general's chair with as much pomp as an Emperor into his throne, Friendly standing watchful beside the cases, arms crossed. As Cosca's arse touched the wood the tent broke into polite applause, every captain tapping their fingers against their palms as daintily as fine ladies attending the theatre. Just as they had for Monza, when she stole the chair. If she hadn't felt suddenly so sick she might almost have laughed.

Cosca waved away the applause while obviously encouraging it. 'No, no, really, entirely undeserved. But it's good to be back.'

'How the hell—'

'Did I survive? The wound, it appears, was not quite so fatal as we all supposed. The Talinese took me, on account of my uniform, for one of their own, and bore me directly to an excellent surgeon, who was able to staunch the bleeding. I was two weeks abed, then slipped out of a window. I made contact in Puranti with my old friend Andiche, who I had gathered might be desirous of a change in command. He was, and so were all his noble fellows.' He gestured to the captains scattered about the tent, then to himself. 'And here I am.'

Monza snapped her mouth shut. There was no planning for this. Nicomo Cosca, the very definition of an unpredictable development. Still, a plan too brittle to bend with circumstances is worse than no plan at all. 'My congratulations, then, General Cosca,' she managed to grate. 'But my offer still stands. Gurkish gold in return for your services to Duke Rogont—'

'Ah.' Cosca winced, sucking air through his teeth. 'Tiny little problem there, unfortunately. I already signed a new engagement with Grand Duke Orso. Or with his heir, to be precise, Prince

Foscar. A promising young man. We'll be moving against Ospria just as Faithful Carpi planned, prior to his untimely demise.' He poked at the air with his forefinger. 'Putting paid to the League of Eight! Taking the fight to the Duke of Delay! There's plenty to sack in Ospria. It was a good plan.' Agreeing mutters from the captains. 'Why work out another?'

'But you hate Orso!'

'Oh, I despise him utterly, that's well known, but I've nothing against his money. It's the exact same colour as everybody else's. You should know. He paid you enough of it.'

'You old cunt,' she said.

'You really shouldn't talk to me that way.' Cosca stuck his lips out at her. 'I am a mature forty-eight. Besides, I gave my life for you!'

'You didn't fucking die!' she snarled.

'Well. Rumours of my death are often exaggerated. Wishful thinking, on the part of my many enemies.'

'I'm beginning to know how they feel.'

'Oh, come, come, whatever were you thinking? A noble death? Me? Very much not my style. I mean to go with my boots off, a bottle in my hand and a woman on my cock.' His eyebrows went up. 'It's not that job you've come for, is it?'

Monza ground her teeth. 'If it's a question of money—'

'Orso has the full support of the Banking House of Valint and Balk, and you'll find no deeper pockets anywhere. He's paying well, and better than well. But it's not about the money, actually. I signed a contract. I gave my solemn word.'

She stared at him. 'When have you ever cared a shit about your word?'

'I'm a changed man.' Cosca pulled a flask from a back pocket, unscrewed it and took a long swig, never taking his amused eyes from her face. 'And I must admit I owe it all to you. I've put the past behind me. Found my principles.' He grinned at his captains, and they grinned back. 'Bit mossy, but they should polish up alright. You forged a good relationship with Orso. Loyalty. Honesty. Stability. Hate to toss all your hard work down the latrine. Besides, there's the soldier's first rule to consider, isn't there, boys?'

Victus and Andiche spoke in unison, just the way they'd used to, before she took the chair. 'Never fight for the losing side!'

Cosca's grin grew wider. 'Orso holds the cards. Find a good hand of your own, my ears are always open. But we'll stick with Orso for now.'

'Whatever you say, General,' said Andiche.

'Whatever you say,' echoed Victus. 'Good to have you back.'

Sesaria leaned down, muttering something in Cosca's ear. The new captain general recoiled as though stung. 'Give them over to Duke Orso? Absolutely not! Today is a happy day! A joyous occasion for one and all! There'll be no killing here, not today.' He wafted a hand at her as though he was shooing a cat out of the kitchen. 'You can go. Better not come back tomorrow, though. We might not be so joyous, then.'

Monza took a step towards him, a curse half-out of her mouth. There was a rattling of metal as the assorted captains began to draw their weapons. Friendly blocked her path, arms coming uncrossed, hands dropping to his sides, expressionless face turned towards her. She stopped still. 'I need to kill Orso!'

'And if you manage it, your brother will live again, yes?' Cosca cocked his head to one side. 'You'll get your hand back? No?'

She was cold all over, skin prickling. 'He deserves what's coming!'

'Ah, but most of us do. All of us will get it regardless. How many others will you suck into your little vortex of slaughter in the meantime?'

'For Benna—'

'No. For you. I know you, don't forget. I've stood where you stand now, beaten, betrayed, disgraced, and come out the other side. As long as you have men to kill you are still Monzcarro Murcatto, the great and fearsome! Without that, what are you?' Cosca's lip curled. 'A lonely cripple with a bloody past.'

The words were strangled in her throat. 'Please, Cosca, you have to—'

'I don't have to do a thing. We're even, remember? More than even, say I. Out of my sight, snake, before I pack you off back to Duke Orso in a jar. You need a job, Northman?'

Shivers' good eye crept across to Monza, and for a moment she

438

was sure he'd say yes. Then he slowly shook his head. 'I'll stick with the chief I've got.'

'Loyalty, eh?' Cosca snorted. 'Be careful with that nonsense, it can get you killed!' A scattering of laughter. 'The Thousand Swords is no place for loyalty, eh, boys? We'll have none of that childishness here!' More laughter, a score or more hard grins all aimed at Monza.

She felt dizzy. The tent seemed too bright and too dark at once. Her nose caught a waft of something – sweaty bodies, or strong drink, or stinking cooking, or a latrine pit too close to the headquarters, and her stomach turned over, set her mouth to watering. A smoke, oh please, a smoke. She turned on her heel, somewhat unsteadily, shoved her way between a couple of chuckling men and through the flap, out of the tent and into the bright morning.

Outside it was far worse. Sunlight stabbed at her. Faces, dozens of them, blurred together into a mass of eyes, all fixed on her. A jury of scum. She tried to look ahead, always ahead, but she couldn't stop her lids from flickering. She tried to walk in the old way, head back, but her knees were trembling so hard she was sure they must be able to hear them slapping against the insides of her trousers. It was as if she'd been putting off the fear, the weakness, the pain. Putting it off, storing it up, and now it was breaking on her in one great wave, sweeping her under, helpless. Her skin was icy with cold sweat. Her hand was aching all the way to her neck. They saw what she really was. Saw she'd lost. A lonely cripple with a bloody past, just like Cosca said. Her guts shifted and she gagged, an acid tickle at the back of her throat. The world lurched.

Hate only keeps you standing so long.

'Can't,' she whispered. 'Can't.' She didn't care what happened, as long as she could stop. Her leg buckled and she started to fall, felt Shivers grab hold of her arm and drag her up.

'Walk,' he hissed in her ear.

'Can't—'

His fist dug hard into her armpit, and the pain stopped the world spinning for a moment. 'Fucking walk, or we're finished.'

Enough strength, with Shivers' help, to make it to the horses. Enough to put a boot in a stirrup. Enough, with an aching groan, to get herself into the saddle, pull her horse around and get it facing the right way. As they rode from the camp she could hardly see. The great captain general, Duke Orso's would-be nemesis, sagging in her saddle like dead meat.

You make yourself too hard, you make yourself brittle too. Crack once, crack all to pieces.

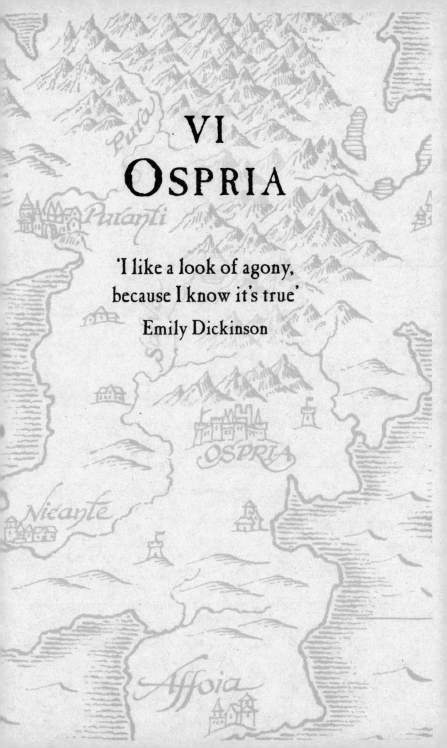

VI
OSPRIA

'I like a look of agony,
because I know it's true'
Emily Dickinson

I t seemed a little gold could spare a lot of blood.

Musselia could not be captured without an indefinite siege, this was well known. It had once been a great fortress of the New Empire, and its inhabitants placed great pride in their ancient walls. Too much pride in walls, perhaps, and not enough gold in the pockets of their defenders. It was for a sum almost disappointing that Benna arranged for a small side gate to be left unlocked.

Even before Faithful and his men had taken possession of the defences, and long before the rest of the Thousand Swords spilled out into the city to begin the sack, Benna was leading Monza through the darkened streets. Him leading her was unusual enough in itself.

'Why did you want to be at the front?'

'You'll see.'

'Where are we going?'

'To get our money back. Plus interest.'

Monza frowned as she hurried after him. Her brother's surprises tended always to have a sting in them. Through a narrow archway in a narrow street. A cobbled courtyard inside, lit by two flickering torches. A Kantic man in simple travelling clothes stood beside a canvas-covered cart, horse hitched and ready. Monza did not know him, but he knew Benna, coming forwards, hands out, his smile gleaming in the darkness.

'Benna, Benna. It is good to see you!' They embraced like old comrades.

'And you, my friend. This is my sister, Monzcarro.'

The man bowed to her. 'The famous and fearsome. An honour.'

'Somenu Hermon,' said Benna, smiling wide. 'Greatest merchant of Musselia.'

'No more than a humble trader, like any other. There are only a few last . . . things . . . to move. My wife and children have already left.'

'Good. That makes this much easier.'

Monza frowned at her brother. 'What's going—'

Benna snatched her dagger from her belt and stabbed Hermon overhand in his face. It happened so fast that the merchant was still smiling as he fell. Monza drew her sword on an instinct, staring into the shadows around the courtyard, out into the street, but all was quiet.

'What the hell have you done?' she snarled at him. He was up on the cart, ripping back the canvas, a mad, eager look on his face. He fumbled open the lid of a box underneath, delved inside and let coins slowly drop with the jingling rattle of falling money.

Gold.

She hopped up beside him. More gold than she had ever seen at once. With a sickly widening of her eyes she realised there were more boxes. She pushed the canvas back with trembling hands. Many more.

'We're rich!' squeaked Benna. 'We're rich!'

'We were already rich.' She was looking down at her knife stuck through Hermon's eye, blood black in the lamplight. 'Did you have to kill him?'

He stared at her as if she had gone mad. 'Rob him and leave him alive? He would have told people we had the money. This way we're safe.'

'Safe? This much gold is the opposite of safe, Benna!'

He frowned, as though he was hurt by her. 'I thought you'd be pleased. You of all people, who slaved in the dirt for nothing.' As though he was disappointed in her. 'This is for us. For us, do you understand?' As though he was disgusted with her. 'Mercy and cowardice are the same, Monza! I thought you knew that.'

What could she do? Unstab Hermon's face?

It seemed a little gold could cost a lot of blood.

His Plan of Attack

The southernmost range of the Urval Mountains, the spine of Styria, all shadowy swales and dramatic peaks bathed in golden evening light, marched boldly southwards, ending at the great rock into which Ospria itself was carved. Between the city and the hill on which the headquarters of the Thousand Swords had been pitched, the deep and verdant valley was patched with wild flowers in a hundred colours. The Sulva wound through its bottom and away towards the distant sea, touched by the setting sun and turned the orange of molten iron.

Birds twittered in the olive trees of an ancient grove, grasshoppers chirped in the waving long grass, the wind kissed at Cosca's face and made the feather on his hat, held gently in one hand, heroically thrash and flutter. Vineyards were planted on the slopes to the north of the city, green rows of vines on the dusty hillsides that drew Cosca's eye and made his mouth water with an almost painful longing. The best vintages in the Circle of the World were trampled out on that very ground . . .

'Sweet mercy, a drink,' he mouthed.

'Beautiful,' breathed Prince Foscar.

'You never before looked upon fair Ospria, your Highness?'

'I had heard stories, but . . .'

'Breathtaking, isn't she?' The city was built upon four huge shelves cut into the cream-coloured rock of the steep hillside, each one surrounded by its own smooth wall, crammed with lofty buildings, stuffed with a tangle of roofs, domes, turrets. The ancient Imperial aqueduct curved gracefully down from the mountains to meet its outermost rampart, fifty arches or more, the tallest of them twenty times the height of a man. The citadel clung impossibly to the highest crag, four great towers picked out against the darkening azure sky. The lamps were being lit in the windows as the sun sank, the outline of the city dusted with pinprick points of light. 'There can be no other place quite like this one.'

A pause. 'It seems almost a shame to spoil it with fire and sword,' observed Foscar.

'Almost, your Highness. But this is war, and those are the tools available.'

Cosca had heard that Count Foscar, now Prince Foscar following his brother's mishap in a famous Sipanese brothel, was a boyish, callow, weak-nerved youth, and was therefore pleasantly impressed by what he had seen thus far. The lad was fresh-faced, true, but every man begins young, and he seemed thoughtful rather than weak, sober rather than bloodless, polite rather than limp. A young man very much like Cosca himself had been at that age. Only the absolute reverse in every particular, of course.

'They appear to be most powerful fortifications . . .' murmured the prince, scanning the towering walls of the city with his eyeglass.

'Oh, indeed. Ospria was the furthest outpost of the New Empire, built as a bastion to hold back the restless Baolish hordes. Parts of the walls have been standing firm against the savage for more than five hundred years.'

'Then will Duke Rogont not simply retreat behind them? He does seem prone to avoid battle whenever possible . . .'

'He'll give battle, your Highness,' said Andiche.

'He must,' rumbled Sesaria, 'or we'll just camp in his pretty valley and starve him out.'

'We outnumber him three to one or more,' whined Victus.

Cosca could not but agree. 'Walls are only useful if one expects help, and no help is coming to the League of Eight now. He must fight. He will fight. He is desperate.' If there was one thing he understood, it was desperation.

'I must confess I have some . . . concerns.' Foscar nervously cleared his throat. 'I understood that you always hated my father with a passion.'

'Passion. Hah.' Cosca dismissed it with a wave. 'As a young man I let my passion lead me by the nose, but I have learned numerous harsh lessons in favour of a cool head. I and your father have had our disagreements but I am, above all else, a mercenary. To let my personal feelings reduce the weight of my purse would be an act of criminal unprofessionalism.'

'Hear, hear.' Victus wore an unsightly leer. Even more so than usual.

'Why, my own three closest captains,' and Cosca took them in with a theatrical sweep of his hat, 'betrayed me utterly and put Murcatto in my chair. They fucked me to their balls, as they say in Sipani. To their balls, your Highness. If I had a taste for vengeance, it would be on these three heaps of human shit.' Then Cosca chuckled, and they chuckled, and the vaguely uncomfortable atmosphere was swiftly dispelled. 'But we can all be useful to each other, and so I have forgiven them everything, and your father too. Vengeance brings no man a brighter tomorrow, and when placed on the scales of life, does not outweigh a single . . . scale. You need not worry on that score, Prince Foscar, I am all business. Bought and paid for, and entirely your man.'

'You are generosity itself, General Cosca.'

'I am avarice itself, which is not quite the same, but will do in a pinch. Now, perhaps, for dinner. Would any of you gentlemen care for a drink? We came by a crate of a very fine vintage in a manor house upstream only yesterday, and—'

'It might be best if we were to discuss our strategy before the levity begins.' Colonel Rigrat's shrill voice was as a file applied directly to Cosca's sensitive back teeth. He was a sharp-faced, sharp-voiced, sharply self-satisfied man in his late thirties and a well-pressed uniform, previously General Ganmark's second in command and now Foscar's. Presumably the military brains behind the Talinese operation, such as they were. 'Now, while everyone still has their wits close to hand.'

'Believe me, young man,' though he was neither young, nor yet a man as far as Cosca was concerned, 'my wits and I are not easily parted. You have a plan in mind?'

'I do!' Rigrat produced his baton with a flourish. Friendly loomed out from under the nearest olive tree, hands moving to his weapons. Cosca sent him melting back into the shadows with the faintest smile and shake of his head. No one else even noticed.

Cosca had been a soldier all his life, of a kind, and had yet to understand what the purpose of a baton truly was. You could not kill a man with one, or even look like you might. You could not hammer in a tent peg, cook a good side of meat or even pawn it for anything worthwhile. Perhaps they were intended for scratching those hard-to-reach places in the small of the back? Or stimulating the anus? Or perhaps simply for marking a man out as a fool? For that purpose, he reflected as Rigrat pointed self-importantly towards the river with his baton, they served admirably.

'There are two fords across the Sulva! Upper . . . and lower! The lower is much the wider and more reliable crossing.' The colonel indicated the point where the dirty stripe of the Imperial road met the river, glimmering water flaring out in the gently sloping bottom of the valley. 'But the upper, perhaps a mile upstream, should also be usable at this time of year.'

'Two fords, you say?' It was a fact well known there were two damn fords. Cosca himself had crossed in glory by one when he came into Ospria to be toasted by Grand Duchess Sefeline and her subjects, and fled by another just after the bitch had tried to poison him. Cosca slid his battered flask from his jacket pocket. The one that Morveer had flung at him back in Sipani. He unscrewed the cap.

Rigrat gave him a sharp glance. 'I thought we agreed that we would drink once we had discussed strategy.'

'You agreed. I just stood here.' Cosca closed his eyes, took a deep breath, tilted up the flask and took a long swallow, then another, felt the coolness fill his mouth, wash at his dry throat. A drink, a drink, a drink. He gave a happy sigh. 'Nothing like a drink of an evening.'

'May I continue?' hissed Rigrat, riddled with impatience.

'Of course, my boy, take your time.'

'The day after tomorrow, at dawn, you will lead the Thousand Swords across the lower ford—'

'Lead? From the front, do you mean?'

'Where else would a commander lead from?'

Cosca exchanged a baffled glance with Andiche. 'Anywhere else. Have you ever been at the front of a battle? The chances of being killed there really are very high.'

'Extremely high,' said Victus.

Rigrat ground his teeth. 'Lead from what position pleases you, but the Thousand Swords will cross the lower ford, supported by our allies from Etrisani and Cesale. Duke Rogont will have no choice but to engage you with all his power, hoping to crush your forces while you are still crossing the river. Once he is committed, our Talinese regulars will break from hiding and cross the upper ford. We will take the enemy in the flank, and—' He snapped his baton into his waiting palm with a smart crack.

'You'll hit them with a stick?'

Rigrat was not amused. Cosca had to wonder whether he ever had been. 'With steel, sir, with steel! We will rout them utterly and put them to flight, and thus put an end to the troublesome League of Eight!'

There was a long pause. Cosca frowned at Andiche, and Andiche frowned back. Sesaria and Victus shook their heads at one another. Rigrat tapped his baton impatiently against his leg. Prince Foscar cleared his throat once more, nervously pushed his chin forwards. 'Your opinion, General Cosca?'

'Hmm.' Cosca gloomily shook his head, eyeing the sparkling river with the weightiest of frowns. 'Hmm. Hmm. Hmmmm.'

'Hmmm.' Victus tapped his pursed lips with one finger.

'Humph.' Andiche puffed out his cheeks.

'Hrrrrrm.' Sesaria's unconvinced voice throbbed at a deeper pitch.

Cosca removed his hat, scratched his head and placed it back with a flick at the feather. 'Hmmmmmmmmmmmmmm—'

'Are we to take it that you disapprove?' asked Foscar.

'I somehow let slip my misgivings? Then I cannot in good conscience suppress them. I am not convinced that the Thousand Swords are well suited to the task you have assigned.'

'Not convinced,' said Andiche.

'Not well suited,' said Victus.

Sesaria was a silent mountain of reluctance.

'Have you not been well paid for your services?' demanded Rigrat.

Cosca chuckled. 'Of course, and the Thousand Swords will fight, you may depend on that!'

'They will fight, every man!' asserted Andiche.

'Like devils!' added Victus.

'But it is how they are to be made to fight best that concerns me as their captain general. They have lost two leaders in a brief space.' He hung his head as if he regretted the fact, and had in no way benefited hugely himself.

'Murcatto, then Faithful.' Sesaria sighed as if he had not been one of the prime agents in the changes of command.

'They have been relegated to support duties.'

'Scouting,' lamented Andiche.

'Clearing the flanks,' growled Victus.

'Their morale is at a terribly low ebb. They have been paid, but money is never the best motivation for a man to risk his life.' Especially a mercenary, it needed hardly to be said. 'To throw them into a pitched mêlée against a stubborn and desperate enemy, toe to toe . . . I'm not saying they might break, but . . . well . . .' Cosca winced, scratching slowly at his neck. 'They might break.'

'I hope this is not an example of your notorious reluctance to fight,' sneered Rigrat.

'Reluctance . . . to fight? Ask anyone, I am a tiger!' Victus snorted snot down his chin but Cosca ignored him. 'This is a question of picking the right tool for the task. One does not employ a rapier to cut down a stubborn tree. One employs an axe. Unless one is a complete arse.' The young colonel opened his mouth to retort but Cosca spoke smoothly over him. 'The plan is sound, in outline. As one military man to another I congratulate you upon it unreservedly.' Rigrat paused, unbalanced, not sure if he was being taken for a fool or not, though he most obviously was.

'But it would be wiser counsel for your regular Talinese troops – tried and tested recently in Visserine, then Puranti, committed to their cause, used to victory and with the very firmest of morale – to cross the lower ford and engage the Osprians, supported by your allies of Etrisani and Cesale, and so forth.' He waved his flask towards the river, a far more useful implement to his mind than a baton, since a baton makes no man drunk. 'The Thousand Swords would be far better deployed concealed upon the high ground. Waiting to seize the moment! To drive across the upper ford, with dash and vigour, and take the enemy in the rear!'

'Best place to take an enemy,' muttered Andiche. Victus sniggered.

Cosca finished with a flourish of his flask. 'Thus, your earthy courage and our fiery passion are used where they are best suited. Songs will be sung, glory will be seized, history will be made, Orso will be king . . .' He gave Foscar a gentle bow. 'And yourself, your Highness, in due course.'

Foscar frowned towards the fords. 'Yes. Yes, I see. The thing is, though—'

'Then we are agreed!' Cosca flung an arm around his shoulders and guided him back towards the tent. 'Was it Stolicus who said great men march often in the same direction? I believe it was! Let us march now towards dinner, my friends!' He pointed one finger back towards the darkening mountains, where Ospria glimmered in the sunset. 'I swear, I am so hungry I could eat a city!' Warm laughter accompanied him back into the tent.

Politics

Shivers sat there frowning, and drank.

Duke Rogont's great dining hall was the grandest room he'd ever got drunk in by quite a stretch. When Vossula told him Styria was packed with wonders it was this type of thing, rather than the rotting docks of Talins, that Shivers had in mind. It must've had four times the floor of Bethod's great hall in Carleon and a ceiling three times as high or more. The walls were pale marble with stripes of blue-black stone through it, all fretted with veins of glitter, all carved with leaves and vines, all grown up and crept over with ivy so the real plants and the sculpted tangled together in the dancing shadows. Warm evening breezes washed in through open windows wide as castle gates, made the orange flames of a thousand hanging lamps flicker and sway, striking a precious gleam from everything.

A place of majesty and magic, built by gods for the use of giants.

Shame the folk gathered there fell a long way short of either. Women in gaudy finery, brushed, jewelled and painted to look younger, or thinner, or richer than they were. Men in bright-coloured jackets who wore lace at their collars and little gilded daggers at their belts. They looked at him first with mild disdain on their powdered faces, like he was made of rotting meat. Then, once he'd turned the left side of his face forwards, with a sick horror that gave him three parts grim satisfaction and one part sick horror of his own.

Always at every feast there's some stupid, ugly, mean bastard got a big score to settle with no one in particular, drinks way too much and makes the night a worry for everyone. Seemed tonight it was him, and he was taking to the part with a will. He hawked up phlegm and spat it noisily across the gleaming floor.

A man at the next table in a yellow coat with long tails to it looked round, the smallest sneer on his puffed-up lips. Shivers leaned towards him, grinding the point of his knife into the polished table-top. 'Something to say to me, piss-coat?' The man paled and turned back to his friends without a word. 'Bunch o' bastard cowards,' Shivers growled into his quickly emptying wine-cup, good and loud enough to be heard three tables away. 'Not a single bone in the whole fucking crowd!'

He thought about what the Dogman might've made of this crew of tittering dandies. Or Rudd Threetrees. Or Black Dow. He gave a grim snort to think of it, but his laughter choked off short. If there was a joke, it was on him. Here he was, in the midst of 'em, after all, leaning on their charity without a friend to his name. Or so it seemed.

He scowled towards the high table, up on a raised dais at the head of the room. Rogont sat in the midst of his most favoured guests, grinning around as though he was a star shining from the night sky. Monza sat beside him. Hard to tell from where Shivers was, specially with everything smeared up with anger and too much wine, but he thought he saw her laughing. Enjoying herself, no doubt, without her one-eyed errand boy to drag her down.

He was a fine-looking bastard, the Prince of Prudence. Had both his eyes, anyway. Shivers would've liked to break his smooth, smug face open. With a hammer, like Monza had broken Gobba's head. Or just with his fists. Crush it in his hands. Pound it to red splinters. He gripped his knife trembling tight, spinning out a whole mad story of how he'd go about it. Picking over all the bloody details, shifting them about until they made him look as big a man as possible, Rogont wailing for mercy and pissing himself, twisting it into crazy shapes where Monza wanted him more'n ever at the end of it. And all the while he watched the two of 'em through one twitching, narrowed eye.

He goaded himself with the notion they were laughing at him, but he knew that was foolishness. He didn't matter enough to laugh at, and that made him stew hotter than ever. He was still clinging to his pride, after all, like a drowning man to a twig way too small to keep him afloat. He was a maimed embarrassment, after he'd saved her life how many times? Risked his life how many times? And after all the bloody steps he'd climbed to get to

453

the top of this bastard mountain too. Might've hoped for something better'n scorn at the end of it.

He jerked his knife from the split wood. The knife Monza had given him the first day they met. Back when he had both his eyes and a lot less blood on his hands. Back when he had it in mind to leave killing behind him, and be a good man. He could hardly remember what that had felt like.

Monza sat there frowning, and drank.

She hadn't much taste for food lately, had less for ceremony, and none at all for tonguing arses, so Rogont's banquet of the doomed came close to a nightmare. Benna had been the one for feasting, form and flattery. He would have loved this – pointing, laughing, slapping backs with the worst of them. If he'd found a moment clear of soaking up the flattery of people who despised him, he would have leaned over, and touched her arm with a soothing hand, and whispered in her ear to grin and take it. Baring her teeth in a rictus snarl was about as close as she could come.

She had a bastard of a headache, pulsing away down the side where the coins were screwed, and the genteel rattle of cutlery might as well have been nails hammered into her face. Her guts seemed to have been cramping up ever since she left Faithful drowned on the millwheel. It was the best she could do not to turn to Rogont and spew, and spew, and spew all over his gold-embroidered white coat.

He leaned towards her with polite concern. 'Why so glum, General Murcatto?'

'Glum?' She swallowed the rising acid enough to speak. 'Orso's army are on their way.'

Rogont turned his wine glass slowly round and round by the stem. 'So I hear. Ably assisted by your old mentor Nicomo Cosca. The scouts of the Thousand Swords have already reached Menzes Hill, overlooking the fords.'

'No more delays, then.'

'It would appear not. My designs on glory will soon be ground into the dust. As such designs often are.'

'You sure the night before your own destruction is the best time to celebrate?'

'The day after might be too late.'

'Huh.' True enough. 'Perhaps you'll get a miracle.'

'I've never been a great believer in divine intervention.'

'No? What are they here for, then?' Monza jerked her head towards a knot of Gurkish just below the high table, dressed in the white robes and skullcaps of the priesthood.

The duke peered down at them. 'Oh, their help goes well beyond the spiritual. They are emissaries of the Prophet Khalul. Duke Orso has his allies in the Union, the backing of their banks. I must find friends of my own. And even the Emperor of Gurkhul kneels before the Prophet.'

'Everyone kneels to someone, eh? I guess Emperor and Prophet can console each other after their priests bring news of your head on a spike.'

'They'll soon get over it. Styria is a sideshow to them. I daresay they're already preparing the next battlefield.'

'I hear the war never ends.' She drained her glass and slung it rattling back across the wood. Maybe they pressed the best wine in the world in Ospria, but it tasted of vomit to her. Everything did. Her life was made of sick. Sick and frequent, painful, watery shits. Raw-gummed, saw-tongued, rough-toothed, sore-arsed. A horse-faced servant in a powdered wig flowed around her shoulder and let fall a long stream of wine into the empty glass, as though flourishing the bottle as far above her as possible would make it taste better. He retreated with consummate ease. Retreat was the speciality down in Ospria, after all. She reached for the glass again. The most recent smoke had stopped her hand shaking, but nothing more.

So she prayed for mindless, shameful, stupefying drunkenness to swarm over and blot out the misery.

She let her eyes crawl over Ospria's richest and most useless citizens. If you really looked for it, the banquet had an edge of shrill hysteria. Drinking too much. Talking too fast. Laughing too loud. Nothing like a dash of imminent annihilation to lower the inhibitions. The one consolation of Rogont's coming rout was that a good number of these fools would lose everything along with him.

'You sure I should be up here?' she grunted.

'Someone has to be.' Rogont glanced sideways at the girlish

Countess Cotarda of Affoia without great enthusiasm. 'The noble League of Eight, it seems, has become a League of Two.' He leaned close. 'And to be entirely honest I'm wondering if it's not too late for me to get out of it. The sad fact is I'm running short of notable guests.'

'So I'm an exhibit to stiffen your wilting prestige, am I?'

'Exactly so. A perfectly charming one, though. And those stories about my wilting are all scurrilous rumours, I assure you.' Monza couldn't find the strength even to be irritated, let alone amused, and settled for a weary snort. 'You should eat something.' He gestured at her untouched plate with his fork. 'You look thin.'

'I'm sick.' That and her right hand hurt so badly she could scarcely hold the knife. 'I'm always sick.'

'Really? Something you ate?' Rogont forked meat into his mouth with all the relish of a man likely to live out the week. 'Or something you did?'

'Maybe it's just the company.'

'I wouldn't be at all surprised. My Aunt Sefeline was always revolted by me. She was a woman much prone to nausea. You remind me of her in a way. Sharp mind, great talents, will of iron, but a weaker stomach than might have been expected.'

'Sorry to disappoint you.' The dead knew she disappointed herself enough.

'Me? Oh, quite the reverse, I assure you. We are none of us made from flint, eh?'

If only. Monza gagged down more wine and scowled at the glass. A year ago, she'd had nothing but contempt for Rogont. She remembered laughing with Benna and Faithful over what a coward he was, what a treacherous ally. Now Benna was dead, she'd murdered Faithful and she'd run to Rogont for shelter like a wayward child to her rich uncle. An uncle who couldn't even protect himself, in this case. But he was far better company than the alternative. Her eyes were dragged reluctantly towards the bottom of the long table on the right, where Shivers sat alone.

The hard fact was he sickened her. It was an effort just to stand beside him, let alone touch him. It was far more than the simple ugliness of his maimed face. She'd seen enough that was ugly, and done enough too, to have no trouble at least pretending to be comfortable around it. It was the silences, when before she couldn't shut him up. They were full of debts she couldn't pay. She'd see that skewed, dead ruin of an eye and remember him whispering at her, *It should've been you.* And she'd know it should have been. When he did talk he said nothing about doing the right thing any more, nothing about being a better man. Maybe it should have pleased her to have won that argument. She'd tried hard enough. But all she could think was that she'd taken a halfway decent man and somehow made a halfway evil one. She wasn't only rotten herself, she rotted everything she touched.

Shivers sickened her, and the fact she was disgusted when she knew she should have been grateful only sickened her even more.

'I'm wasting time,' she hissed, more at her glass than anyone else.

Rogont sighed. 'We all are. Just passing the ugly moments until our ignominious deaths in the least horrible manner we can find.'

'I should be gone.' She tried to make a fist of her gloved hand, but the pain only made her weaker now. 'Find a way . . . find a way to kill Orso.' But she was so tired she could hardly find the strength to say it.

'Revenge? Truly?'

'Revenge.'

'I would be crushed if you were to leave.'

She could hardly be bothered to take care what she said. 'Why the hell would you want me?'

'I, want you?' Rogont's smile slipped for a moment. 'I can delay no longer, Monzcarro. Soon, perhaps tomorrow, there will be a great battle. One that will decide the fate of Styria. What could be more valuable than the advice of one of Styria's greatest soldiers?'

'I'll see if I can find you one,' she muttered.

'And you have many friends.'

'Me?' She couldn't think of a single one alive.

'The people of Talins love you still.' He raised his eyebrows at the gathering, some of them still glowering at her with scant friendliness. 'Less popular here, of course, but that only serves to prove the point. One man's villain is another's hero, after all.'

'They think I'm dead in Talins, and don't care into the bargain.' She hardly cared herself.

'On the contrary, agents of mine are in the process of making the citizens well aware of your triumphant survival. Bills posted at every crossroads dispute Duke Orso's story, charge him with your attempted murder and proclaim your imminent return. The people care deeply, believe me, with that bottomless passion common folk sometimes have for great figures they have never met, and never will. If nothing else, it turns them further against Orso, and gives him difficulties at home.'

'Politics, eh?' She drained her glass. 'Small gestures, when war is knocking at your gates.'

'We all make the gestures we can. But in war and politics both you are still an asset to be courted.' His smile was back now, and broader than ever. 'Besides, what extra reason should a man require to keep cunning and beautiful women close at hand?'

She scowled sideways. 'Fuck yourself.'

'When I must.' He looked straight back at her. 'But I'd much rather have help.'

'You look almost as bitter as I feel.'

'Eh?' Shivers prised his scowl from the happy couple. 'Ah.' There was a woman talking to him. 'Oh.' She was very good to look at, so much that she seemed to have a glow about her. Then he saw everything had a glow. He was drunk as shit.

She seemed different from the rest, though. Necklace of red stones round her long neck, white dress that hung loose, like the ones he'd seen black women wearing in Westport, but she was very pale. There was something easy in the way she stood, no stiff manners to her. Something open in her smile. For a moment, it almost had him smiling with her. First time in a while.

'Is there space here?' She spoke Styrian with a Union accent. An outsider, like him.

'You want to sit . . . with me?'

'Why not, do you carry the plague?'

'With my luck I wouldn't be surprised.' He turned the left side of his face towards her. 'This seems to keep most folk well clear o' me by itself, though.'

Her eyes moved over it, then back, and her smile didn't flicker. 'We all have our scars. Some of us on the outside, some of us—'

'The ones on the inside don't take quite such a toll on the looks, though, eh?'

'I've found that looks are overrated.'

Shivers looked her slowly up and down, and enjoyed it. 'Easy for you to say, you've plenty to spare.'

'Manners.' She puffed out her cheeks as she looked round the hall. 'I'd despaired of finding any among this crowd. I swear, you must be the only honest man here.'

'Don't count on it.' Though he was grinning wide enough. There was never a bad time for flattery from a fine-looking woman, after all. He had his pride. She held out one hand to him and he blinked at it. 'I kiss it, do I?'

'If you like. It won't dissolve.'

It was soft and smooth. Nothing like Monza's hand – scarred, tanned, calloused as any Named Man's. Even less like her other one, twisted as a nettle root under that glove. Shivers pressed his lips to the woman's knuckles, caught a giddy whiff of scent. Like flowers, and something else that made the breath sharpen in his throat.

'I'm, er . . . Caul Shivers.'

'I know.'

'You do?'

'We've met before, though briefly. Carlot dan Eider is my name.'

'Eider?' Took him a moment to place it. A half-glimpsed face in the mist. The woman in the red coat, in Sipani. Prince Ario's lover. 'You're the one that Monza—'

'Beat, blackmailed, destroyed and left for dead? That would be me.' She frowned up towards the high table. 'Monza, is it? Not only first-name terms, but an affectionate shortening. The two of you must be very close.'

'Close enough.' Nowhere near as close as they had been, though, in Visserine. Before they took his eye.

'And yet she sits up there, with the great Duke Rogont, and you sit down here, with the beggars and the embarrassments.'

Like she knew his own thoughts. His fury flickered up again

and he tried to steer the talk away from it. 'What brings you here?'

'After the carnage in Sipani I had no other choices. Duke Orso is doubtless offering a pretty price for my head. I've spent the last three months expecting every person I passed to stab me, poison me, throttle me, or worse.'

'Huh. I know that feeling.'

'Then you have my sympathy.'

'The dead know I could do with some.'

'You can have all mine, for what that's worth. You're just as much a piece in this sordid little game as I am, no? And you've lost even more than I. Your eye. Your face.'

She didn't seem to move, but she seemed to keep getting closer. Shivers hunched his shoulders. 'I reckon.'

'Duke Rogont is an old acquaintance. A somewhat unreliable man, though undoubtedly a handsome one.'

'I reckon,' he managed to grate out.

'I was forced to throw myself upon his mercy. A hard landing, but some succour, for a while. Though it seems he has found a new diversion now.'

'Monza?' The fact he'd been thinking it himself all night didn't help any. 'She ain't like that.'

Carlot dan Eider gave a disbelieving snort. 'Really? Not a treacherous, murdering liar who'll use anyone and anything to get her way? She betrayed Nicomo Cosca, no, and stole his chair? Why do you think Duke Orso tried to kill her? Because it was his chair she was planning to steal next.' The drink had made him half-stupid, he couldn't think of a thing to say to it. 'Why not use Rogont to get her way? Or is she in love with someone else?'

'No,' he growled. 'Well . . . how would I know— Fucking no! You've got it twisted!'

She touched one hand to her pale chest. 'I have it twisted? There's a reason why they call her the Snake of Talins! A snake loves nothing but itself!'

'You'd say anything. She used you in Sipani. You hate her!'

'I'd shed no tears over her corpse, that's true. The man who put a blade in her could have my gratitude and more besides. But that doesn't make me a liar.' She was halfway to whispering in his ear. 'Monzcarro Murcatto, the Butcher of Caprile? They murdered children there.' He could almost feel her breath on him, his skin tingling with having her so near, anger and lust all mangled hot together. 'Murdered! In the streets! She wasn't even faithful to her brother, from what I hear—'

'Eh?' Shivers wished he'd drunk less, the hall was getting some spin to it.

'You didn't know?'

'Know what?' An odd mix of curiosity, and fear, and disgust creeping up on him.

Eider laid one hand on his arm, close enough that he caught another waft of scent – sweet, dizzying, sickening. 'She and her brother were *lovers*.' She purred the last word, dragging it out long.

'What?' His scarred cheek was burning like he'd been slapped.

'Lovers. They used to sleep together, like husband and wife. They used to *fuck* each other. It's no kind of secret. Ask anyone. Ask her.'

Shivers found he could hardly breathe. He should've known it. Few things made sense now had tripped him at the time. He had known it, maybe. But still he felt tricked. Betrayed. Laughed at. Like a fish tickled from a stream and left choking. After all he'd done for her, after all he'd lost. The rage boiled up in him so hot he could hardly keep hold of himself.

'Shut your fucking mouth!' He flung Eider's hand off. 'You think I don't see you goading me?' He was up from his bench somehow, standing over her, hall tipping around him, blurred lights and faces swaying. 'You take me for a fool, woman? D'you set me at nothing?'

Instead of cringing back she came forwards, pressing against him almost, eyes seeming big as dinner plates. 'Me? You've made no sacrifices for me! Am *I* the one who's cut you off? Am *I* the one who sets you at nothing?'

Shivers' face was on fire. The blood was battering at his skull, so hard it felt like it might pop his eye right out. Except it was burned out already. He gave a strangled sort of a yelp, throat closed up with fury. He staggered back, since it was that or throttle her, lurched straight into a servant, knocking his silver tray from his hands, glasses falling, bottle shattering, wine spraying.

'Sir, I most humbly—'

Shivers' left fist thudded into his ribs and twisted him sideways, right crunched into the man's face before he could fall. He bounced off the wall and sprawled in the wreckage of his bottles. There was blood on Shivers' fist. Blood, and a white splinter between his fingers. A piece of tooth. What he wanted, more'n anything, was to kneel over this bastard, take his head in his hands and smash it against the beautiful carvings on the wall until his brains came out. He almost did it.

But instead he made himself turn. Made himself turn and stumble away.

Time crawled.

Monza lay on her side, back to Shivers, at the very edge of the bed. Keeping as much space between them as she possibly could without rolling onto the floor. The first traces of dawn were creeping from between the curtains now, turning the room dirty grey. The wine was wearing through and leaving her more nauseous, weary, hopeless than ever. Like a wave washing up on a dirty beach that you hope will wash it clean, but only sucks back out and leaves a mass of dead fish behind it.

She tried to think what Benna would have said. What he'd have done, to make her feel better. But she couldn't remember what his voice had sounded like any more. He was leaking away, and taking the best of her with him. She thought of him a boy, long ago, small and sickly and helpless. Needing her to take care of him. She thought of him a man, laughing, riding up the mountain to Fontezarmo. Still needing her to take care of him. She knew what colour his eyes had been. She knew there had been creases at their corners, from smiling often. But she couldn't see his smile.

Instead the faces that came to her in all their bloodied detail were the five men she'd killed. Gobba, fumbling at Friendly's garrotte with his great bloated, ruined hands. Mauthis, flapping around on his back like a puppet, gurgling pink foam. Ario, hand to his neck as black blood spurted from him. Ganmark, grinning up at her, stuck through the back with Stolicus' outsize sword. Faithful, drowned and dripping, dangling from his waterwheel, no worse than her.

The faces of the five men she'd killed, and of the two she hadn't. Eager little Foscar, barely even a man himself. And Orso, of course. Grand Duke Orso, who'd loved her like a daughter.

Monza, Monza, what would I do without you . . .

She tore the blankets back and swung her sweaty legs from the bed, dragged her trousers on, shivering though it was too hot, head pounding with worn-out wine.

'What you doing?' came Shivers' croaky voice.

'Need a smoke.' Her fingers were trembling so badly she could hardly turn the lamp up.

'Maybe you should be smoking less, think of that?'

'Thought of it.' She fumbled with the lump of husk, wincing as she moved her ruined fingers. 'Decided against.'

'It's the middle of the night.'

'Go to sleep, then.'

'Shitty fucking habit.' He was sitting up on the side of the bed, broad back to her, head turned so he was frowning out of the corner of his one good eye.

'You're right. Maybe I should take up knocking servants' teeth out instead.' She picked up her knife and started hacking husk into the bowl of the pipe, scattering dust. 'Rogont wasn't much impressed, I can tell you that.'

'Wasn't long ago you weren't much impressed with him, as I recall. Seems your feelings about folk change with the wind, though, don't it?'

Her head was splitting. She'd no wish to talk to him, let alone argue. But it's at times like those people bite each other hardest. 'What's eating at you?' she snapped, knowing full well already and not wanting to hear about it either.

'What d'you think?'

'You know what, I've my own problems.'

'You leaving me, is what!'

She'd have jumped at the chance. 'Leaving you?'

'Tonight! Down with the shit while you sat up there lording it with the Duke of Delay!'

'You think I was in charge of the fucking *seating*?' she sneered at him. 'He put me there to make him look good, is all.'

There was a pause. He turned his head away from her,

shoulders hunching. 'Well. I guess looking good ain't something I can help with these days.'

She twitched — awkward, annoyed. 'Rogont can help me. That's all. Foscar's out there, with Orso's army. Foscar's out there . . .' And he had to die, whatever the costs.

'Vengeance, eh?'

'They killed my brother. I shouldn't have to explain it to you. You know how I feel.'

'No. I don't.'

She frowned. 'What about your brother? Thought you said the Bloody-Nine killed him? I thought—'

'I hated my fucking brother. Folk called him Skarling reborn, but the man was a bastard. He'd show me how to climb trees, and fish, nick me under the chin and laugh when our father was there. When he was gone, he used to kick me 'til I couldn't breathe. He said I'd killed our mother. All I did was be born.' His voice was hollow, no anger left in it. 'When I heard he was dead, I wanted to laugh, but I cried instead because everyone else was. I swore vengeance on his killer and all the rest 'cause, well, there's a form to be followed, ain't there? Wouldn't want to fall short. But when I heard the Bloody-Nine nailed my bastard of a brother's head up, I didn't know whether I hated the man for doing it, or hated that he'd robbed me o' the chance, or wanted to kiss him for the favour like you'd kiss . . . a brother, I guess . . .'

For a moment she was about to get up, go to him, put her hand on his shoulder. Then his one eye moved towards her, cold and narrow. 'But you'd know all about that, I reckon. Kissing your brother.'

The blood pounded suddenly behind her eyes, worse than ever. 'What my brother was to me is my fucking business!' She realised she was stabbing at him with the knife, tossed it away across the table. 'I'm not in the habit of explaining myself. I don't plan to start with the men I hire!'

'That's what I am to you, is it?'

'What else would you be?'

'After what I've done for you? After what I've lost?'

She flinched, hands trembling worse than ever. 'Well paid, aren't you?'

464

'Paid?' He leaned towards her, pointing at his face. 'How much is my eye worth, you evil cunt?'

She gave a strangled growl, jerked up from the chair, snatched up the lamp, turned her back on him and made for the door to the balcony.

'Where you going?' His voice had turned suddenly wheedling, as if he knew he'd stepped too far.

'Clear of your self-pity, bastard, before I'm sick!' She ripped the door open and stepped out into the cold air.

'Monza—' He was sitting slumped on the bed, the saddest sort of look on his face. On the half of it that still worked, anyway. Broken. Hopeless. Desperate. Fake eye pointing off sideways. He looked as if he was about to weep, to fall down, to beg to be forgiven.

She slammed the door shut. It suited her to have an excuse. She preferred the passing guilt of turning her back on him to the endless guilt of facing him. Much, much preferred it.

The view from the balcony might well have been among the most breathtaking in the world. Ospria dropped away below, a madman's maze of streaky copper roofs, each one of the four tiers of the city surrounded by its own battlemented walls and towers. Tall buildings of old, pale stone crowded tight behind them, narrow-windowed and striped with black marble, pressed in alongside steeply climbing streets, crooked alleys of a thousand steps, deep and dark as the canyons of mountain streams. A few early lights shone from scattered windows, flickering dots of sentries' torches moved on the walls. Beyond them the valley of the Sulva was sunk in the shadows of the mountains, only the faintest glimmer of the river in its bottom. At the summit of the highest hill on the other side, against the dark velvet of the sky, perhaps the pinpricks of the campfires of the Thousand Swords.

Not a place for anyone with a fear of heights.

But Monza had other things on her mind. All that mattered was to make nothing matter, and as fast as she could. She crabbed down into the deepest corner, hunched jealously over her lamp and her pipe like a freezing man over a last tongue of fire. She gripped the mouthpiece in her teeth, lifted the rattling hood with trembling hands, leaned forwards—

A sudden gust came up, swirled into the corner, whipped her

greasy hair in her eyes. The flame fluttered and went out. She stayed there, frozen, staring at the dead lamp in achy confusion, then sweaty disbelief. Her face went slack with horror as the implications fumbled their way into her thumping head.

No flame. No smoke. No way back.

She sprang up, took a step towards the parapet and flung the lamp out across the city with all her strength. She tilted her head back, taking a great breath, grabbed the parapet, rocked forwards and screamed her lungs out. Screamed her hatred at the lamp as it tumbled down, at the wind that had blown it out, at the city spread out below her, at the valley beyond it, at the world and everyone in it.

In the distance, the angry sun was beginning to creep up behind the mountains, staining the sky around their darkened slopes with blood.

No More Delays

Cosca stood before the mirror, making the final adjustments to his fine lace collar, turning his five rings so the jewels faced precisely outwards, adjusting each bristle of his beard to his satisfaction. It had taken him an hour and a half, by Friendly's calculation, to make ready. Twelve passes of the razor against the sharpening strap. Thirty-one movements to trim away the stubble. One tiny nick left under his jaw. Thirteen tugs of the tweezers to purge the nose hairs. Forty-five buttons done up. Four pairs of hooks and eyes. Eighteen straps to tighten and buckles to fasten.

'And all is ready. Master Friendly, I wish you to take the post of first sergeant of the brigade.'

'I know nothing about war.' Nothing except that it was madness, and threw him out of all compass.

'You need know nothing. The role would be to keep close to me, to keep silent but sinister, to support and follow my lead where necessary and most of all to watch my back and yours. The world is full of treachery, my friend! The odd bloody task too, and on occasion to count out sums of money paid and received, to take inventory of the numbers of men, weapons and sundries at our disposal . . .'

That was, to the letter, what Friendly had done for Sajaam, in Safety then outside it. 'I can do that.'

'Better than any man alive, I never doubt! Could you begin by fastening this buckle for me? Bloody armourers. I swear they only put it there to vex me.' He jerked his thumb at the side strap on his gilded breastplate, stood tall and held his breath, sucking in his gut as Friendly tugged it closed. 'Thank you, my friend, you are a rock! An anchor! An axle of calm about which I madly spin. Whatever would I do without you?'

Friendly did not understand the question. 'The same things.'

'No, no. Not the same. Though we are not long acquainted, I feel there is . . . an understanding between us. A bond. We are much alike, you and I.'

Friendly sometimes felt he feared every word he had to speak, every new person and every new place. Only by counting everything and anything could he claw by his fingernails from morning to night. Cosca, by sharp contrast, drifted effortlessly through life like blossom on the wind. The way that he could talk, smile, laugh, make others do the same seemed like magic as surely as when Friendly had seen the Gurkish woman Ishri form from nowhere. 'We are nothing alike.'

'You see my point exactly! We are entire opposites, like earth and air, yet we are both . . . missing something . . . that others take for granted. Some part of that machinery that makes a man fit into society. But we each miss different cogs on the wheel. Enough that we may make, perhaps, between the two of us, one half-decent human.'

'One whole from two halves.'

'An extraordinary whole, even! I have never been a reliable man – no, no, don't try to deny it.' Friendly had not. 'But you, my friend, are constant, clear-sighted, single-minded. You are . . . *honest* enough . . . to make me more honest.'

'I've spent most of my life in prison.'

'Where you did more to spread honesty among Styria's most dangerous convicts than all the magistrates in the land, I do not doubt!' Cosca slapped Friendly on his shoulder. 'Honest men are so very rare, they are often mistaken for criminals, for rebels, for madmen. What were your crimes, anyway, but to be different?'

'Robbery the first time, and I served seven years. When they caught me again there were eighty-four counts, with fourteen murders.'

Cosca cocked an eyebrow. 'But were you truly guilty?'

'Yes.'

He frowned for a moment, then waved it away. 'Nobody's perfect. Let's leave the past behind us.' He gave his feather a final flick, jammed his hat onto his head at its accustomed rakish angle. 'How do I look?'

Black pointed knee-boots set with huge golden spurs in the likeness of bull's heads. Breastplate of black steel with golden adornments. Black velvet sleeves slashed with yellow silk, cuffs of Sipanese lace hanging at the wrists. A sword with flamboyant gilded basketwork and matching dagger, slung ridiculously low. An enormous hat, its yellow feather threatening to brush the ceiling. 'Like a pimp who lost his mind in a military tailor's.'

Cosca broke out in a radiant grin. 'Precisely the look I was aiming at! So to business, Sergeant Friendly!' He strode forwards, flung the tent flap wide and stepped through into the bright sunlight.

Friendly stuck close behind. It was his job, now.

The applause began the moment he stepped up onto the big barrel. He had ordered every officer of the Thousand Swords to attend his address, and here they were indeed; clapping, whooping, cheering and whistling to the best of their ability. Captains to the fore, lieutenants crowding further back, ensigns clustering at the rear. In most bodies of fighting men these would have been the best and brightest, the youngest and highest born, the bravest and most idealistic. This being a brigade of mercenaries, they were the polar opposite. The longest serving, the most steeped in vice, the slyest back-stabbers, most practised grave-robbers and fastest runners, the men with fewest illusions and most betrayals under their belts. Cosca's very own constituency, in other words.

Sesaria, Victus and Andiche lined up beside the barrel, all three clapping gently, the biggest, blackest crooks of the lot. Unless you counted Cosca himself, of course. Friendly stood not far behind, arms tightly folded, eyes darting over the crowd. Cosca wondered if he was counting them, and decided it was a virtual certainty.

'No, no! No, no! You do me too much honour, boys! You shame me with your fond attentions!' And he waved the adulation down, fading into an expectant silence. A mass of scarred, pocked, sunburned and diseased faces turned towards him, waiting. As hungry as a gang of bandits. They were one.

'Brave heroes of the Thousand Swords!' His voice rang out into the balmy morning. 'Well, let us say brave men of the Thousand Swords, at least. Let us say men, anyway!' Scattered laughter, a whoop of approval. 'My boys, you all know my stamp! Some of you have fought beside me . . . or at any rate in front.' More laughter. 'The rest of you know my . . . spotless reputation.' And more yet. 'You all know that I, above all, am one of you. A soldier, yes! A fighter, of course! But one who would much prefer to sheathe his weapon.' And he gave a gentle cough as he adjusted his groin. 'Than draw his blade!' And he slapped the hilt of his sword to widespread merriment.

'Let it never be said that we are not masters and journeymen of the glorious profession of arms! As much so as any lapdog at some noble's boots! Men strong of sinew!' And he slapped Sesaria's great arm. 'Men sharp of wits!' And he pointed at Andiche's greasy head. 'Men hungry for glory!' He jerked his thumb towards Victus. 'Let it never be said we will not brave risks for our rewards! But let the risks be kept as lean as possible, and the rewards most hearty!' Another swell of approval.

'Your employer, the young Prince Foscar, was keen that you carry the lower ford and meet the enemy head on in pitched battle . . .' Nervous silence. 'But I declined! Though you are paid to fight, I told him, you are far keener on the pay than the fighting!' A rousing cheer. 'We'll wet our boots higher up, therefore, and with considerably lighter opposition! And whatever occurs today, however things may seem, you may always depend upon it that I have your . . . best interests closest to my own heart!' And he rubbed his fingers against his thumb to an even louder cheer.

'I will not insult you by calling for courage, for steadfastness, for loyalty and honour! All these things I already know you possess in the highest degree!' Widespread laughter. 'So to your units, officers of the Thousand Swords, and await my order! May Mistress Luck be always at your side and mine! She is drawn, after all, to those who least deserve her! May darkness find us victorious! Uninjured! And above all – rich!'

There was a rousing cheer. Shields and weapons, mailed and plated arms, gauntleted fists shaken in the air.

'Cosca!'

'Nicomo Cosca!'

'The captain general!'

He hopped smiling down from his barrel as the officers began to disperse, Sesaria and Victus going with them to make their regiments – or their gangs of opportunists, criminals and thugs – ready for action. Cosca strolled away towards the brow of the hill, the beautiful valley opening out before him, shreds of misty cloud clinging to the hollows in its sides. Ospria looked proudly down on all from her mountain, fairer than ever by daylight, all cream-coloured stone banded with blue-black stripes of masonry, roofs of copper turned pale green by the years or, on a few buildings recently repaired, shining brilliantly in the morning glare.

'Nice speech,' said Andiche. 'If your taste runs to speeches.'

'Most kind. Mine does.'

'You've still got the trick of it.'

'Ah, my friend, you have seen captain generals come and go. You well know there is a happy time, after a man is elevated to command, in which he can say and do no wrong in the eyes of his men. Like a husband in the eyes of his new wife, just following the marriage. Alas, it cannot last. Sazine, myself, Murcatto, ill-fated Faithful Carpi, our tides all flowed out with varying speed and left each one of us betrayed or dead. And so shall mine again. I will have to work harder for my applause in future.'

Andiche split a toothy grin. 'You could always appeal to the cause.'

'Hah!' Cosca lowered himself into the captain general's chair, set out in the dappled shade of a spreading olive tree with a fine view of the glittering fords. 'My curse on fucking causes! Nothing but big excuses. I never saw men act with such ignorance, violence and self-serving malice as when energised by a just cause.' He squinted at the rising sun, brilliant in the bright blue sky. 'As we will no doubt witness, in the coming hours . . .'

Rogont drew his sword with a faint ring of steel.

'Free men of Ospria! Free men of the League of Eight! Great hearts!'

Monza turned her head and spat. Speeches. Better to move fast and hit hard than waste time talking about it. If she'd found herself with time for a speech before a battle she would have reckoned she'd missed her moment, pulled back and looked for another. It took a man with a bloated sense of himself to think his words might make all the difference.

So it was no surprise that Rogont had his all well worked out.

'Long have you followed me! Long have you waited for the day you would prove your mettle! My thanks for your patience! My thanks for your courage! My thanks for your faith!' He stood in his stirrups and raised his sword high above his head. 'Today we fight!'

He cut a pretty picture, there was no denying that. Tall, strong and handsome, dark curls stirred by the breeze. His armour was studded with glittering gems, steel polished so bright it was almost painful to look at. But his men had made an effort too. Heavy infantry in the centre, well armoured under a forest of polearms or clutching broadswords in their gauntleted fists, shields and blue surcoats all stitched with the white tower of Ospria. Light infantry on the wings, all standing to stiff attention in studded leather, pikes kept carefully vertical. Archers too, steel-capped flatbowmen, hooded longbowmen. A detachment of Affoians on the far right slightly spoiled the pristine organisation, weapons mismatched and their ranks a little skewed, but still a good stretch neater than any men Monza had ever led.

And that was before she turned to the cavalry lined up behind her, a gleaming row in the shadow of the outermost wall of Ospria. Every man noble of birth and spirit, horses in burnished bardings, helmets with sculpted crests, lances striped, polished and ready to be steeped in glory. Like something out of a badly written storybook.

She snorted some snot from the back of her nose, and spat again. In her experience, and she had plenty, clean men were the keenest to get into battle and the keenest to get clear of it.

Rogont was busy cranking up his rhetoric to new heights. 'We stand now upon a battlefield! Here, in after years, men will say heroes fought! Here, men will say the fate of Styria was decided! Here, my friends, here, on our own soil! In sight of our own homes! Before the ancient walls of proud Ospria!' Enthusiastic cheering from the companies drawn up closest to him. She doubted the rest could hear a word of it. She doubted most could even see him. For those that could, she doubted the sight of a shiny speck in the distance would do much for their morale.

'Your fate is in your own hands!' Their fate had been in Rogont's hands, and he'd frittered it away. Now it was in Cosca's and Foscar's, and it was likely to be a bloody one.

'Now for freedom!' Or at best a better-looking brand of tyranny.

'Now for glory!' A glorious place in the mud at the bottom of the river.

Rogont jerked on the reins with his free hand and made his chestnut charger rear, lashing at the air with its front hooves. The effect was only slightly spoiled by a few heavy clods of shit that happened to fall from its rear end at the same moment. It sped off past the massed ranks of infantry, each company cheering Rogont as he passed, lifting their spears in unison and giving a roar. It might have been an impressive sight. But Monza had seen it all before, with grim results. A good speech wasn't much compensation for being outnumbered three to one.

The Duke of Delay trotted up towards her and the rest of his staff, the same gathering of heavily decorated and lightly experienced men she'd made fools of in the baths at Puranti, arrayed for battle now rather than the parade ground. Safe to say they hadn't warmed to her. Safe to say she didn't care.

'Nice speech,' she said. 'If your taste runs to speeches.'

'Most kind.' Rogont turned his horse and drew it up beside her. 'Mine does.'

'I'd never have guessed. Nice armour too.'

'A gift from the young Countess Cotarda.' A knot of ladies had gathered to observe at the top of the slope in the shade of the city walls. They sat side-saddle in bright dresses and twinkling jewels, as if they were expecting to attend a wedding rather than a slaughter. Cotarda herself, milk-pale in flowing yellow silks, gave a shy wave and Rogont returned it without much vigour. 'I think her uncle has it in mind that we might marry. If I live out the day, of course.'

'Young love. My heart is all aglow.'

'Damp down your sentimental soul, she's not at all my type. I like a woman with a little . . . bite. Still, it is a fine armour. An impartial observer might mistake me for some kind of hero.'

'Huh. "Desperation bakes heroes from the most rotten flour," Farans wrote.'

Rogont blew out a heavy sigh. 'We are running short of time for this particular loaf to rise.'

'I thought that talk about you having trouble rising was all scurrilous rumours . . .' There was something familiar about one of the ladies in Countess Cotarda's party, more simply dressed than the others, long-necked and elegant. She turned her head and then her horse, began to ride down the grassy slope towards them. Monza felt a cold twinge of recognition. 'What the hell is she doing here?'

'Carlot dan Eider? You know her?'

'I know her.' If punching someone in the face in Sipani counted.

'An old . . . friend.' He said the word in a way that implied more than that. 'She came to me in peril of her life, begging for protection. Under what circumstances could I possibly refuse?'

'If she'd been ugly?'

Rogont shrugged with a faint rattling of steel. 'I freely admit it, I'm every bit as shallow as the next man.'

'Far shallower, your Excellency.' Eider nudged her horse up close to them, and gracefully inclined her head. 'And who is this? The Butcher of Caprile! I thought you were but a thief, black-mailer, murderer of innocents and keen practiser of incest! Now it seems you are a soldier too.'

'Carlot dan Eider, such a surprise! I thought this was a battle but now it smells more like a brothel. Which is it?'

Eider raised one eyebrow at the massed regiments. 'Judging by all the swords I'd guess . . . the former? But I suppose you'd be the expert. I saw you at Cardotti's and I see you here, equally comfortable dressed as warrior or whore.'

'Strange how it goes, eh? I wear the whore's clothes and you do the whore's business.'

'Perhaps I should turn my hand to murdering children in-stead?'

'For pity's sake, enough!' snapped Rogont. 'Am I doomed to be always surrounded by women, showing off? Have the two of you not noticed I have a battle to lose? All I need now is for that vanishing devil Ishri to spring out of my horse's arse and give me my death of shock to complete the trio! My Aunt Sefeline was the same, always trying to prove she had the biggest cock in the

474

chamber! If all your purpose is to posture, the two of you can get that done behind the city walls and leave me out here to ponder my downfall alone.'

Eider bowed her head. 'Your Excellency, I would hate to intrude. I am here merely to wish you the best of fortune.'

'Sure you wouldn't care to fight?' snapped Monza at her.

'Oh, there are other ways of fighting than bloody in the mud, Murcatto.' She leaned from her saddle and hissed it. 'You'll see!'

'Your Excellency!' A shrill call, soon joined by others, a ripple of excitement spreading through the horsemen. One of Rogont's officers was pointing over the river, towards the ridge on the far side of the valley. There was movement there against the pale sky. Monza nudged her horse towards it, sliding out a borrowed eyeglass and scanning across the ridge.

A scattering of horsemen came first. Outriders, officers and standard-bearers, banners held high, white flags carrying the black cross of Talins, the names of battles stitched along their edges in red and silver thread. It hardly helped that a good number of the victories she'd had a hand in herself. A wide column of men tramped into view behind them, marching steadily down the brown stripe of the Imperial road towards the lower ford, spears shouldered.

The foremost regiment stopped and began to spread out about a half-mile from the water. Other columns began to spill from the road, forming battle lines across the valley. There was nothing clever about the plan, as far as she could see.

But they had the numbers. They didn't need to be clever.

'The Talinese have arrived,' murmured Rogont, pointlessly.

Orso's army. Men she'd fought alongside this time last year, led to victory at Sweet Pines. Men Ganmark had led until Stolicus fell on him. Men Foscar was leading now. That eager young lad with the fluff moustache who'd laughed with Benna in the gardens of Fontezarmo. That eager young lad she'd sworn to kill. She chewed her lip as she moved the eyeglass across the dusty front ranks, more men and more flooding over the hill behind them.

'Regiments from Etrisani and Cesale on their right wing, some Baolish on their left.' Ragged-marching men in fur and heavy chain mail, savage fighters from the hills and the mountains in the far east of Styria.

'The great majority of Duke Orso's regular troops. But where, oh where, are your comrades of the Thousand Swords?'

Monza nodded up towards Menzes Hill, a green lump speckled with olive groves above the upper ford. 'I'd bet my life they're there, behind the brow. Foscar will cross the lower ford in strength and give you no choice but to meet him head on. Once you're committed, the Thousand Swords will cross the upper ford unopposed and take you in the flank.'

'Very likely. What would be your advice?'

'You should've turned up to Sweet Pines on time. Or Musselia. Or the High Bank.'

'Alas, I was late for those battles then. I am extremely late for them now.'

'You should have attacked long before this. Taken a gamble as they marched down the Imperial road from Puranti.' Monza frowned at the valley, the great number of soldiers on both sides of the river. 'You have the smaller force.'

'But the better position.'

'To get it you gave up the initiative. Lost your chance at surprise. Trapped yourself. The general with the smallest numbers is well advised to stay always on the offensive.'

'Stolicus, is it? I never had you down for book learning.'

'I know my business, Rogont, books and all.'

'My epic thanks to you and your friend Stolicus for explaining my failures. Perhaps one of you might furnish an opinion on how I might now achieve success?'

Monza let her eyes move over the landscape, judging the angles of the slopes, the distances from Menzes Hill to the upper ford, from the upper to the lower, from the striped walls of the city to the river. The position seemed better than it was. Rogont had too much ground to cover and not enough men for the job.

'All you can do now is the obvious. Hit the Talinese with all your archers as they cross, then all your foot as soon as their front ranks touch dry land. Keep the cavalry here to at least hold up the Thousand Swords when they show. Hope to break Foscar quickly, while his feet are in the river, then turn to the mercenaries. They won't stick if they see the game's against them. But breaking Foscar . . .' She watched the great body of men forming up into lines as wide as the wide ford, more columns belching from the Imperial road to join them. 'If Orso thought you had a chance at it he'd have picked a commander more experienced and less valuable. Foscar's got more than twice your numbers on his own, and all he has to do is hold you.' She peered up the slope. The Gurkish priests sat observing the battle not far from the Styrian ladies, their white robes bright in the sunlight, their dark faces grim. 'If the Prophet sent you a miracle, now might be the time.'

'Alas, he sent only money. And kind words.'

Monza snorted. 'You'll need more than kind words to win today.'

'*We'll* need,' he corrected, 'since you fight beside me. Why do you fight beside me, by the way?'

Because she was too tired and too sick to fight alone any more. 'Seems I can't resist pretty men in lots of trouble. When you held all the cards I fought for Orso. Now look at me.'

'Now look at us both.' He took in a long breath, and gave a happy sigh.

'What the hell are you so pleased about?'

'Would you rather I despaired?' Rogont grinned at her, handsome and doomed. Maybe the two went together. 'If the truth be known, I'm relieved the waiting is over, whatever odds we face. Those of us who carry great responsibilities must learn patience, but I have never had much taste for it.'

'That's not your reputation.'

'People are more complicated than their reputations, General Murcatto. You should know that. We will settle our business here, today. No more delays.' He twitched his horse away to confer with one of his aides, and left Monza slumped in her saddle, arms limp across the bow, frowning up towards Menzes Hill.

She wondered if Nicomo Cosca was up there, squinting towards them through his eyeglass.

Cosca squinted through his eyeglass towards the mass of soldiery on the far side of the river. The enemy, though he held no personal rancour towards them. The battlefield was no place for rancour. Blue flags carrying the white tower of Ospria fluttered above them, but one larger than the others, edged with gold. The standard of the Duke of Delay himself. Horsemen were scattered about it, a group of ladies too, by the look of things, ridden out to watch the battle, all in their best. Cosca fancied he could even see some Gurkish priests, though he could not imagine what their interest might be. He wondered idly whether Monzcarro Murcatto was there. The notion of her sitting side-saddle in floating silks fit for a coronation gave him a brief moment of amusement. The battlefield was most definitely a place for amusement. He lowered his eyeglass, took a swig from his flask and happily closed his eyes, feeling the sun flicker through the branches of the old olive trees.

'Well?' came Andiche's rough voice.

'What? Oh, you know. Still forming up.'

'Rigrat sends word the Talinese are beginning their attack.'

'Ah! So they are.' Cosca sat forwards, training his eyeglass on the ridge to his right. The front ranks of Foscar's foot were close to the river now, spread out across the flower-dotted sward in orderly lines, the hard dirt of the Imperial road invisible beneath that mass of men. He could faintly hear the tramping of their feet, the disembodied calls of their officers, the regular thump, thump of their drums floating on the warm air, and he waved one hand gently back and forth in time. 'Quite the spectacle of military splendour!'

He moved his round window on the world down the road to the glittering, slow-flowing water, across it to the far bank and up the slope. The Osprian regiments were deploying to meet them, perhaps a hundred strides above the river. Archers had formed a long line behind them on higher ground, kneeling, making ready their bows. 'Do you know, Andiche . . . I have a feeling we will shortly witness some bloodshed. Order the men forwards, up behind us here. Fifty strides, perhaps, beyond the brow of the hill.'

'But . . . they'll be seen. We'll lose the surprise—'

'Shit on the surprise. Let them see the battle, and let the battle see them. Give them a taste for it.'

'But General—'

'Give the orders, man. Don't fuss.'

Andiche turned away, frowning, and beckoned over one of his sergeants. Cosca settled back with a satisfied sigh, stretched his legs out and crossed one highly polished boot over the other. Good boots. How long had it been since he'd last worn good boots? The front rank of Foscar's men were in the river. Wading forwards with grim determination, no doubt, up to their knees in cold water, looking without relish at the considerable body of soldiers drawn up in good order on the high ground to their front. Waiting for the arrows to start falling. Waiting for the charge to come. An unenviable task, forcing that ford. He had to admit to being damn pleased he had talked his way clear of it.

He raised Morveer's flask and wet his lips, just a little.

Shivers heard the faint cries of the orders, the rattling rush of a few hundred shafts loosed together. The first volley went up from Rogont's archers, black splinters drifting, and rained down on the Talinese as they waded on through the shallows.

Shivers shifted in his saddle, rubbed gently at his itching scar as he watched the lines twist and buckle, holes opening up, flags drooping. Some men slowing, wanting to get back, others moving faster, wanting to press on. Fear and anger, two sides to the same coin. No one's favourite job, trying to march tight over bad terrain while men shoot arrows at you. Stepping over corpses. Friends, maybe. The horrible chance of it, knowing a little gust might be the difference between an arrow in the earth by your boot or an arrow through your face.

Shivers had seen battles enough, of course. A lifetime of 'em. He'd watched them play out or listened to the sounds in the distance, waiting to hear the call and take his own part, fretting on his chances, trying to hide his fear from those he led and those he followed. He remembered Black Well, running through the mist, heart pounding, startling at shadows. The Cumnur, where he'd screamed the war cry with five thousand others as they thundered down the long slope. Dunbrec, where he'd followed Rudd Threetrees in a charge against the Feared, damn near given his life to hold the line. The battle in the High Places, Shanka boiling up out of the valley, mad Easterners trying to climb the wall, fighting back to back with the Bloody-Nine, stand or die.

Memories sharp enough to cut himself on – the smells, the sounds, the feel of the air on his skin, the desperate hope and mad anger.

He watched another volley go up, watched the great mass of Talinese coming on through the water, and felt nothing much but curious. No kinship with either side. No sorrow for the dead. No fear for himself. He watched men dropping under the hail of fire, and he burped, and the mild burning up his throat gave him a sight more worry than if the river had suddenly flooded and washed every one of those bastards down there out to the ocean. Drowned the fucking world. He didn't care a shit about the outcome. It wasn't his war.

Which made him wonder why he was ready to fight in it, and more'n likely on the losing side.

His eye twitched from the brewing battle to Monza. She clapped Rogont on the shoulder and Shivers felt his face burn like he'd been slapped. Each time they spoke it stung at him. Her black hair blew back for a moment, showed him the side of her face, jaw set hard. He didn't know if he loved her, or wanted her, or just hated that she didn't want him. She was the scab he couldn't stop picking, the split lip he couldn't stop biting at, the loose thread he couldn't stop tugging 'til his shirt came all to pieces.

Down in the valley the front rank of the Talinese had worse troubles, floundering from the river and up onto the bank, lost their shape from slogging across the ford under fire. Monza shouted something at Rogont, and he called to one of his men. Shivers heard the cries creep up from the slopes below. The order to charge. The Osprian foot lowered their spears, blades a glittering wave as they swung down together, then began to move. Slow at first, then quicker, then breaking into a jog, pouring away from the archers, still loading and firing fast as they could, down the long slope towards the sparkling water, and the Talinese trying to form some kind of line on the bank.

Shivers watched the two sides come together, merge. A moment later he heard the contact, faint on the wind. That rattling, clattering, jangling din of metal, like a hailstorm on a lead roof. Roars, wails, screams from nowhere floating with it. Another volley fell among the ranks still struggling through the water. Shivers watched it all, and burped again.

Rogont's headquarters was quiet as the dead, everyone staring down towards the ford, mouths and eyes wide, faces pale and reins clenched tight with worry. The Talinese had flatbowmen of their own ready now, sent a wave of bolts up from the water, flying flat and hissing among the archers. More'n one fell. Someone started squealing. A rogue bolt thudded into the turf not far from one of Rogont's officers, made his horse startle and near dumped him from the saddle. Monza urged her own mount a pace or two forwards, standing in the stirrups to get a better view, borrowed armour gleaming dully in the morning sun. Shivers frowned.

One way or another, he was here for her. To fight for her. Protect her. Try to make things right between them. Or maybe just hurt her like she'd hurt him. He closed his fist, nails digging into his palm, knuckles sore from knocking that servant's teeth out. They weren't done yet, that much he knew.

All Business

The upper ford was a patch of slow-moving water, sparkling in the morning sun as it broke up in the shallows. A faint track led from the far bank between a few scattered buildings, then through an orchard and up the long slope to a gate in the black-banded outermost wall of Ospria. All seemingly deserted. Rogont's foot were mostly committed to the savage fight at the lower ford. Only a few small units hung back to guard the archers, loading and firing into the mass of men in the midst of the river as fast as they possibly could.

The Osprian cavalry were waiting in the shadow of the walls as a last reserve, but too few, and too far away. The Thousand Swords' path to victory appeared unguarded. Cosca stroked gently at his neck. In his judgement, now was the perfect moment to attack.

Andiche evidently agreed. 'Getting hot down there. Should I tell the men to mount up?'

'Let's not trouble them quite yet. It's still early.'

'You sure?'

Cosca turned to look evenly back at him. 'Do I look unsure?' Andiche puffed out his pitted cheeks, then stomped off to confer with some of his own officers. Cosca stretched out, hands clasped behind his head, and watched the battle slowly develop. 'What was I saying?'

'A chance to leave all this behind,' said Friendly.

'Ah yes! I had the chance to leave all this behind. Yet I chose to come back. Change is not a simple thing, eh, Sergeant? I entirely see and understand the pointlessness and waste of it all, yet I do it anyway. Does that make me worse or better than the man who does it thinking himself ennobled by a righteous cause? Or the man who does it for his own profit, without the slightest grain of thought for right or wrong? Or are we all the same?'

Friendly only shrugged.

'Men dying. Men maimed. Lives destroyed.' He might as well have been reciting a list of vegetables for all the emotion he felt. 'I have spent half my life in the business of destruction. The other half in the dogged pursuit of self-destruction. I have created nothing. Nothing but widows, orphans, ruins and misery, a bastard or two, perhaps, and a great deal of vomit. Glory? Honour? My piss is worth more, that at least makes nettles grow.' But if his aim was to prick his own conscience into wakefulness it still slumbered on regardless. 'I have fought in many battles, Sergeant Friendly.'

'How many?'

'A dozen? A score? More? The line between battle and skirmish is a fuzzy one. Some of the sieges dragged on, with many engagements. Do those count as one, or several?'

'You're the soldier.'

'And even I don't have the answers. In war, there are no straight lines. What was I saying?'

'Many battles.'

'Ah, yes! Many! And though I have tried always to avoid becoming closely involved in the fighting, I have often failed. I am fully aware of what it's like in the midst of that mêlée. The flashing blades. Shields cloven and spears shattered. The crush, the heat, the sweat, the stink of death. The tiny heroics and the petty villainies. Proud flags and honourable men crushed underfoot. Limbs lopped off, showers of blood, split skulls, spilled guts, and all the rest.' He raised his eyebrows. 'Reasonable to suppose some drownings too, under the circumstances.'

'How many, would you say?'

'Difficult to be specific.' Cosca thought of the Gurkish drowning in the channel at Dagoska, brave men swept out to sea, their corpses washed up on every tide, and gave a long sigh. 'Still, I find I can watch without much sentiment. Is it ruthlessness? Is it the fitting detachment of command? Is it the configuration of the stars at my birth? I find myself always sanguine in the face of death and danger. More so than at any other time. Happy when I should be horrified, fearful when I should be calm. I am a riddle, to be sure, even to myself. I am a back-to-front man, Sergeant

Friendly!' He laughed, then chuckled, then sighed, then was silent. 'A man upside down and inside out.'

'General.' Andiche was leaning over him again, lank hair hanging.

'What, for pity's sake? I am trying to philosophise!'

'The Osprians are fully engaged. All their foot are tackling Foscar's troops. They've no reserves but a few horse.'

Cosca squinted down towards the valley. 'I see that, Captain Andiche. We all quite clearly see that. There is no need to state the obvious.'

'Well . . . we'll sweep those bastards away, no trouble. Give me the order and I'll see to it. We'll get no easier chance.'

'Thank you, but it looks dreadfully hot out there now. I am quite comfortable where I am. Perhaps later.'

'But why not—'

'It amazes me, that after so long on campaign, the whole business of the chain of command still confounds you! You will find it far less worrisome if, rather than trying to anticipate my orders, you simply wait for me to give them. It really is the simplest of military principles.'

Andiche scratched his greasy head. 'I understand the concept.'

'Then act according to it. Find a shady spot, man, take the weight from your feet. Stop running to nowhere. Take a lesson from my goat. Do you see her fussing?'

The goat lifted her head from the grass between the olive trees for a moment, and bleated.

Andiche put his hands on his hips, winced, stared down at the valley, up at Cosca, frowned at the goat, then turned away and walked off, shaking his head.

'Everyone rushing, rushing, Sergeant Friendly, do we get no peace? Is a quiet moment out of the sun really too much to ask? What was I saying?'

'Why isn't he attacking?'

When Monza had seen the Thousand Swords easing onto the brow of the hill, the tiny shapes of men, horses, spears black against the blue morning sky, she'd known they were about to charge. To splash happily across the upper ford and take Rogont's men in the flank, just the way she'd said they would.

Just the way she'd have done. To put a bloody end to the battle, to the League of Eight, to her hopes, such as they were. No man was quicker to pluck the easy fruit than Nicomo Cosca, and none quicker to wolf it down than the men she used to lead.

But the Thousand Swords only sat there, in plain view, on top of Menzes Hill, and waited. Waited for nothing. Meanwhile Foscar's Talinese struggled on the banks of the lower ford, at push of pike with Rogont's Osprians, water, ground and slope all set against them, arrows raining down on the men behind the front line with punishing regularity. Bodies were carried by the current, limp shapes washing up on the bank of the river, bobbing in the shallows below the ford.

Still the Thousand Swords didn't move.

'Why show himself in the first place, if he doesn't mean to come down?' Monza chewed at her lip, not trusting it. 'Cosca's no fool. Why give away the surprise?'

Duke Rogont only shrugged. 'Why complain about it? The longer he waits, the better for us, no? We have enough to worry on with Foscar.'

'What's he up to?' Monza stared up at the mass of horsemen ranged across the crest of the hill, beside the olive grove. 'What's that old bastard about?'

Colonel Rigrat whipped his well-lathered horse between the tents, sending idle mercenaries scattering, and reined the beast in savagely not far away. He slid from the saddle, nearly fell, tore his boot from the stirrup and stormed up, ripping off his gloves, face flushed with sweaty fury. 'Cosca! Nicomo Cosca, damn you!'

'Colonel Rigrat! A fine morning, my young friend! I hope all is well?'

'Well? Why are you not attacking?' He stabbed one finger down towards the river, evidently having misplaced his baton. 'We are engaged in the valley! Most hotly engaged!'

'Why, so you are.' Cosca rocked forwards and rose smoothly from the captain general's chair. 'Perhaps it would be better if we were to discuss this away from the men. Not good form, to bicker. Besides, you're scaring my goat.'

'What?'

Cosca patted the animal gently on the back as he passed. 'She's the only one who truly understands me. Come to my tent. I have fruit there! Andiche! Come join us!'

He strode off, Rigrat blustering after, Andiche falling into puzzled step behind. Past Nocau, on guard before the flap with his great scimitar drawn, and into the cool, dim interior of the tent, draped all around with the victories of the past. Cosca ran the back of his hand affectionately down one swathe of thread-bare cloth, edges blackened by fire. 'The flag that hung upon the walls of Muris, during the siege . . . was it truly a dozen years ago?' He turned to see Friendly sidle through the flap after the others and lurk near the entrance. 'I brought it down from the highest parapet with my own hand, you know.'

'After you tore it from the hand of the dead hero who was up there first,' said Andiche.

'Whatever is the purpose of dead heroes, if not to pass on stolen flags to more prudent fellows in the rank behind?' He snatched the bowl of fruit from the table and shoved it under Rigrat's nose. 'You look ill, Colonel. Have a grape.'

The man's trembling face was rapidly approaching grape colour. 'Grape? Grape?' He lashed at the flap with his gloves. 'I demand that you attack at once! I flatly demand it!'

'Attack.' Cosca winced. 'Across the upper ford?'

'Yes!'

'According to the excellent plan you laid out to me last night?'

'Yes, damn it! Yes!'

'In all honesty, nothing would please me more. I love a good attack, ask anyone, but the problem is . . . you see . . .' Pregnant silence stretched out as he spread his hands wide. 'I took such an enormous sum of money from Duke Rogont's Gurkish friend not to.'

Ishri came from nowhere. Solidified from the shadows at the edges of the tent, slid from the folds in the ancient flags and strutted into being. 'Greetings,' she said. Rigrat and Andiche both stared at her, equally stunned.

Cosca peered up at the gently flapping roof of the tent, tapping at his pursed lips with one finger. 'A dilemma. A moral quandary. I want so badly to attack, but I cannot attack Rogont. And I can scarcely attack Foscar, when his father has also paid me so handsomely. In my youth I jerked this way and that just as the wind blew me, but I am trying earnestly to change, Colonel, as I explained to you the other evening. Really, in all good conscience, the only thing I can do is sit here.' He popped a grape into his mouth. 'And do nothing.'

Rigrat gave a splutter and made a belated grab for his sword, but Friendly's big fist was already around the hilt, knife gleaming in his other hand. 'No, no, no.' The colonel froze as Friendly slid his sword carefully from its sheath and tossed it across the tent.

Cosca snatched it from the air and took a couple of practice swipes. 'Fine steel, Colonel, I congratulate you on your choice of blades, if not of strategy.'

'You were paid by both? To fight neither?' Andiche was smiling ear to ear as he draped one arm around Cosca's shoulders. 'My old friend! Why didn't you tell me? Damn, but it's good to have you back!'

'Are you sure?' Cosca ran him smoothly through the chest with Rigrat's sword, right to the polished hilt. Andiche's eyes bulged, his mouth dropped open and he dragged in a great long wheeze, his pockmarked face twisted, trying to scream. But all that came out was a gentle cough.

Cosca leaned close. 'You think a man can turn on me? Betray me? Give my chair to another for a few pieces of silver, then smile and be my friend? You mistake me, Andiche. Fatally. I may make men laugh, but I'm no clown.'

The mercenary's coat glistened with dark blood, his trembling face had turned bright red, veins bulging in his neck. He clawed weakly at Cosca's breastplate, bloody bubbles forming on his lips. Cosca let go the hilt, wiped his hand on Andiche's sleeve and shoved him over. He fell on his side, spitted, gave a gentle groan and stopped moving.

'Interesting.' Ishri squatted over him. 'I am rarely surprised. Surely Murcatto is the one who stole your chair. You let her go free, no?'

'On reflection, I doubt the facts of my betrayal quite match the story. But in any case, a man can forgive all manner of faults in beautiful women that in ugly men he finds entirely beyond sufferance. And if there's one thing I absolutely cannot abide, it's disloyalty. You have to stick at something in your life.'

'Disloyalty?' screeched Rigrat, finally finding his voice. 'You'll pay for this, Cosca, you treacherous—'

Friendly's knife thumped into his neck and out, blood showered across the floor of the tent and spattered the Musselian flag that Sazine had taken the day the Thousand Swords were formed.

Rigrat fell to his knees, one hand clutched to his throat, blood pouring down the sleeve of his jacket. He flopped forwards onto his face, trembled for a moment, then was still. A dark circle bloomed out through the material of the groundsheet and merged with the one already creeping from Andiche's corpse.

'Ah,' said Cosca. He had been planning to ransom Rigrat back to his family. It did not seem likely now. 'That was . . . ungracious of you, Friendly.'

'Oh.' The convict frowned at his bloody knife. 'I thought . . . you know. Follow your lead. I was being first sergeant.'

'Of course you were. I take all the blame myself. I should have been more specific. I have ever suffered from . . . unspecificity? Is that a word?'

Friendly shrugged. So did Ishri.

'Well.' Cosca scratched gently at his neck as he looked down at Rigrat's body. 'An annoying, pompous, swollen-headed man, from what I saw. But if those were capital crimes I daresay half the world would hang, and myself first to the gallows. Perhaps he had many fine qualities of which I was unaware. I'm sure his mother would say so. But this is a battle. Corpses are a sad inevitability.' He crossed to the tent flap, took a moment to compose himself, then clawed it desperately aside. 'Some help here! For pity's sake, some help!'

He hurried back to Andiche's body and squatted beside it, knelt one way and then another, found what he judged to be the most dramatic pose just as Sesaria burst into the tent.

'God's breath!' as he saw the two corpses, Victus bundling in behind, eyes wide.

'Andiche!' Cosca gestured at Rigrat's sword, still where he had left it. 'Run through!' He had observed that people often state the obvious when distressed.

'Someone get a surgeon!' roared Victus.

'Or better yet a priest.' Ishri swaggered across the tent towards them. 'He's dead.'

'What happened?'

'Colonel Rigrat stabbed him.'

'Who the hell are you?'

'Ishri.'

'He was a great heart!' Cosca gently touched Andiche's staring-eyed, gape-mouthed, blood-spattered face. 'A true friend. He stepped before the thrust.'

'Andiche did?' Sesaria did not look convinced.

'He gave his life . . . to save mine.' Cosca's voice almost croaked away to nothing at the end, and he dashed a tear from the corner of his eye. 'Thank the Fates Sergeant Friendly moved as quickly as he did or I'd have been done for too.' He beat at Andiche's chest, fist squelching on his warm, blood-soaked coat. 'My fault! My fault! I blame myself!'

'Why?' snarled Victus, glaring down at Rigrat's corpse. 'I mean, why did this bastard do it?'

'My fault!' wailed Cosca. 'I took money from Rogont to stay out of the battle!'

Sesaria and Victus exchanged a glance. 'You took money . . . to stay out?'

'A huge amount of money! There will be shares by seniority, of course.' Cosca waved his hand as though it was a trifle now. 'Danger pay for every man, in Gurkish gold.'

'Gold?' rumbled Sesaria, eyebrows going up as though Cosca had pronounced a magic word.

'But I would sink it all in the ocean for one minute longer in my old friend's company! To hear him speak again! To see him smile. But never more. Forever . . .' Cosca swept off his hat, laid it gently over Andiche's face and hung his head. 'Silent.'

Victus cleared his throat. 'How much gold are we talking about, exactly?'

'A . . . huge . . . quantity.' Cosca gave a shuddering sniff. 'As much again as Orso paid us to fight on his behalf.'

'Andiche dead. A heavy price to pay.' But Sesaria looked as if he perceived the upside.

'Too heavy a price. Far too heavy.' Cosca slowly stood. 'My friends . . . could you bring yourselves to make arrangements for the burial? I must observe the battle. We must stumble on. For him. There is one consolation, I suppose.'

'The money?' asked Victus.

Cosca slapped down a hand on each captain's shoulder. 'Thanks to my bargain we will not need to fight. Andiche will be the only casualty the Thousand Swords suffer today. You could say he died for all of us. Sergeant Friendly!' And Cosca turned and pushed past into the bright sunlight. Ishri glided silently at his elbow.

'Quite the performance,' she murmured. 'You really should have been an actor rather than a general.'

'There's not so much air between the two as you might imagine.' Cosca walked to the captain general's chair and leaned on the back, feeling suddenly tired and irritable. Considering the long years he had dreamed of taking revenge for Afieri, it was a disappointing pay-off. He was in terrible need of a drink, fumbled for Morveer's flask, but it was empty. He frowned down into the valley. The Talinese were engaged in a desperate battle perhaps half a mile wide at the bank of the lower ford, waiting for help from the Thousand Swords. Help that would never come. They had the numbers, but the Osprians were still holding their ground, keeping the battle narrow, choking them up in the shallows. The great mêlée heaved and glittered, the ford crawling with men, bobbing with bodies.

Cosca gave a long sigh. 'You Gurkish think there's a point to it all, don't you? That God has a plan, and so forth?'

'I've heard it said.' Ishri's black eyes flicked from the valley to him. 'And what do you think God's plan is, General Cosca?'

'I have long suspected that it might be to annoy me.'

She smiled. Or at least her mouth curled up to show sharp white teeth. 'Fury, paranoia and epic self-centredness in the space of a single sentence.'

'All the fine qualities a great military leader requires . . .' He shaded his eyes, squinting off to the west, towards the ridge behind the Talinese lines. 'And here they are. Perfectly on schedule.' The first flags were showing there. The first glittering spears. The first of what appeared to be a considerable body of men.

The Fate of Styria

'Up there.' Monza's gloved forefinger, and her little finger too, of course, pointed towards the ridge.

More soldiers were coming over the crest, a mile or two to the south of where the Talinese had first appeared. A lot more. It seemed Orso had kept a few surprises back. Reinforcements from his Union allies, maybe. Monza worked her sore tongue around her sour mouth and spat. From faint hopes to no hopes. A small step, but one nobody ever enjoys taking. The leading flags caught a gust of wind and unfurled for a moment. She peered at them through her eyeglass, frowned, rubbed her eye and peered again. There was no mistaking the cockleshell of Sipani.

'Sipanese,' she muttered. Until a few moments ago, the world's most neutral men. 'Why the hell are they fighting for Orso?'

'Who says they are?' When she turned to Rogont, he was smiling like a thief who'd whipped the fattest purse of his career. He spread his arms out wide. 'Rejoice, Murcatto! The miracle you asked for!'

She blinked. 'They're on our side?'

'Most certainly, and right in Foscar's rear! And the irony is that it's all your doing.'

'Mine?'

'Entirely yours! You remember the conference in Sipani, arranged by that preening mope the King of the Union?'

The great procession through the crowded streets, the cheering as Rogont and Salier led the way, the jeering as Ario and Foscar followed. 'What of it?'

'I had no more intention of making peace with Ario and Foscar than they had with me. My only care was to talk old Chancellor Sotorius over to my side. I tried to convince him that if the League of Eight lost then Duke Orso's greed would not end at Sipani's borders, however neutral they might be. That once my young head was off, his ancient one would be next on the block.'

More than likely true. Neutrality was no better defence against Orso than it was against the pox. His ambitions had never stopped at one river or the next. One reason why, until the moment he'd tried to kill her, he'd made Monza such a fine employer.

'But the old man clung to his cherished neutrality, tight as a captain to the wheel of his sinking ship, and I despaired of dislodging him. I am ashamed to admit I began to despair entirely, and was seriously considering fleeing Styria for happier climes.' Rogont closed his eyes and tilted his face towards the sun. 'And then, oh, happy day, oh, serendipity . . .' He opened them and looked straight at her. 'You murdered Prince Ario.'

Black blood pumping from his pale throat, body tumbling through the open window, fire and smoke as the building burned. Rogont grinned with all the smugness of a magician explaining the workings of his latest trick.

'Sotorius was the host. Ario was under his protection. The old man knew Orso would never forgive him for the death of his son. He knew the doom of Sipani was sounded. Unless Orso could be stopped. We came to an agreement that very night, while Cardotti's House of Leisure was still burning. In secret, Chancellor Sotorius brought Sipani into the League of Nine.'

'Nine,' muttered Monza, watching the Sipanese host march steadily down the gentle hillside towards the fords, and Foscar's almost undefended rear.

'My long retreat from Puranti, which you thought so ill-advised, was intended to give him time to prepare. I backed willingly into this little trap so I could play the bait in a greater one.'

'You're cleverer than you look.'

'Not difficult. My aunt always told me I looked a dunce.'

She frowned across the valley at the motionless host on top of Menzes Hill. 'What about Cosca?'

'Some men never change. He took a very great deal of money from my Gurkish backers to keep out of the battle.'

It suddenly seemed she didn't understand the world nearly as well as she'd thought. 'I offered him money. He wouldn't take it.'

'Imagine that, and negotiation so very much your strong point. He wouldn't take the money from *you*. Ishri, it seems, talks more sweetly. "War is but the pricking point of politics. Blades can kill men, but only words can move them, and good neighbours are the surest shelter in a storm." I quote from Juvens' *Principles of Art*. Flim-flam and superstition mostly, but the volume on the exercise of power is quite fascinating. You should read more widely, General Murcatto. Your book-learning is narrow in scope.'

'I came to reading late,' she grunted.

'You may enjoy the full use of my library, once I've butchered the Talinese and conquered Styria.' He smiled happily down towards the bottom of the valley, where Foscar's army were in grave danger of being surrounded. 'Of course, if Orso's troops had a more seasoned leader today than the young Prince Foscar, things might have been very different. I doubt a man of General Ganmark's abilities would have fallen so completely into my trap. Or even one of Faithful Carpi's long experience.' He leaned from his saddle and brought his self-satisfied smirk a little closer. 'But Orso has suffered some unfortunate losses in the area of command, lately.'

She snorted, turned her head and spat. 'So glad to be of help.'

'Oh, I couldn't have done it without you. All we need do is hold the lower ford until our brave allies of Sipani reach the river, crush Foscar's men between us, and Duke Orso's ambitions will be drowned in the shallows.'

'That all?' Monza frowned towards the water. The Affoians, an untidy red-brown mass on the neglected far right of the battle, had been forced back from the bank. No more than twenty paces of churned-up mud, but enough to give the Talinese a foothold. Now it looked as if some Baolish had waded through the deeper water upstream and got around their flank.

'It is, and it appears that we are already well on our way to . . . ah.' Rogont had seen it too. 'Oh.' Men were beginning to break from the fighting, struggling up the hillside towards the city.

'Looks as if your brave allies of Affoia have tired of your hospitality.'

The mood of smug jubilation that had swept through Rogont's headquarters when the Sipanese appeared was fading rapidly as more and more dots crumbled from the back of the bulging Affoian lines and began to scatter in every direction. Above them the companies of archers grew ragged as bowmen looked nervously up towards the city. No doubt they weren't keen to get closer acquainted with the men they'd been shooting arrows down at for the last hour.

'If those Baolish bastards break through they'll take your people in the flank, roll your whole line up. It'll be a rout.'

Rogont chewed at his lip. 'The Sipanese are less than half an hour away.'

'Excellent. They'll turn up just in time to count our corpses. Then theirs.'

He glanced nervously back towards the city. 'Perhaps we should retire to our walls—'

'You haven't the time to disengage from that mess. Even as skilled a withdrawer as you are.'

The duke's face had lost its colour. 'What do we do?'

It suddenly seemed she understood the world perfectly. Monza drew her sword with a faint ringing of steel. A cavalry sword she'd borrowed from Rogont's armoury – simple, heavy and murderously well-sharpened. His eyes rolled down to it. 'Ah. That.'

'Yes. That.'

'I suppose there comes a time when a man must truly cast prudence to one side.' Rogont set his jaw, muscles working on the side of his head. 'Cavalry. With me . . .' His voice died to a throaty croak.

A loud voice to a general, Farans wrote, *is worth a regiment.*

Monza stood in her stirrups and screamed at the top of her lungs. 'Form the horse!'

The duke's staff began to screech, point, wave their swords. Mounted men drew in all around, forming up in long ranks. Harness rattled, armour clanked, lances clattered against each other, horses snorted and pawed at the ground. Men found their places, tugged their restless mounts around, cursed and bellowed, strapped on helmets and slapped down visors.

The Baolish were breaking through in earnest, boiling out of the widening gaps in Rogont's shattered right wing like the rising tide through a wall of sand. Monza could hear their shrill war cries as they streamed up the slope, see their tattered banners waving, the glitter of metal on the move. The lines of archers above them dissolved all at once, men tossing away their bows and running for the city, mixed up with fleeing Affoians and a few Osprians who were starting to think better of the whole business. It had always amazed her how quickly an army could come apart once the panic started to spread. Like pulling out the keystone of a bridge, the whole thing, so firm and ordered one minute, could be nothing but ruins the next. They were on the brink of that moment of collapse now, she could feel it.

Monza felt a horse pull up beside her and Shivers met her eye, axe in one hand, reins and a heavy shield in the other. He hadn't bothered with armour. Just wore the shirt with the gold thread on the cuffs. The one she'd picked out for him. The one that Benna might have worn. It didn't seem to suit him much now. Looked like a crystal collar on a killing dog.

'Thought maybe you'd headed back North.'

'Without all that money you owe me?' His one eye shifted down into the valley. 'Never yet turned my back on a fight.'

'Good. Glad to have you.' It was true enough, at that moment. Whatever else, he had a handy habit of saving her life. She'd already looked away by the time she felt him look at her. And by that time, it was time to go.

Rogont raised his sword, and the noon sun caught the mirror-bright blade and struck flashing fire from it. Just like in the stories.

'Forward!'

Tongues clicked, heels kicked, reins snapped. Together, as if they were one animal, the great line of horsemen started to move. First at a walk, horses stirring, snorting, jerking sideways. The ranks twisted and flexed as eager men and mounts broke ahead. Officers bellowed, bringing them back into formation. Faster they moved, and faster, armour and harness clattering, and Monza's heart beat faster with them. That tingling mix of fear and joy that comes when the thinking's done and there's nothing left but to do. The Baolish had seen them, were struggling to form some kind of line. Monza could see their snarling faces in the moments when the world held still, wild-haired men in tarnished chain mail and ragged fur.

The lances of the horsemen around her began to swing down, points gleaming, and they broke into a trot. The breath hissed cold in Monza's nose, sharp in her dry throat, burned hot in her chest. Not thinking about the pain or the husk she needed for it. Not thinking about what she'd done or what she'd failed to do. Not thinking about her dead brother or the men who'd killed him. Just gripping with all her strength to her horse and to her sword. Just staying fixed on the scattering of Baolish on the slope in front of her, already wavering. They were tired out and ragged from fighting in the valley, running up the hill. And a few hundred tons of horseflesh bearing down on a man could tax his nerve at the best of times.

Their half-formed line began to crumble.

'Charge!' roared Rogont. Monza screamed with him, heard Shivers bellowing beside her, shouts and wails from every man in the line. She dug her heels in hard and her horse swerved, righted itself, sprang down the hill at a bone-cracking gallop. Hooves thudded at the ground, mud and grass flicked and flew, Monza's teeth rattled in her head. The valley bounced and shuddered around her, the sparkling river rushed up towards her. Her eyes were full of wind, she blinked back wet, the world turned to a blurry, sparkling smear then suddenly, mercilessly sharp again. She saw the Baolish scattering, flinging down weapons as they ran. Then the cavalry were among them.

A horse ahead of the pack was impaled on a spear, shaft bending, shattering. It took spearman and rider with it, tumbling over and over down the slope, straps and harness flailing in the air.

She saw a lance take a running man in the back, rip him open from his arse to his shoulders and send the corpse reeling. The fleeing Baolish were spitted, hacked, trampled, broken.

One was flung spinning from the chest of a horse in front, chopped across the back with a sword, clattered shrieking against Monza's leg and was broken apart under the hooves of Rogont's charger.

Another dropped his spear, turning away, his face a pale blur of fear. She swung her sword down, felt the jarring impact up her arm as the heavy blade stoved his helmet deep in with a hollow clonk.

Wind rushed in her ears, hooves pounded. She was screaming still, laughing, screaming. Cut another man down as he tried to run, near taking his arm off at the shoulder and sending blood up in a black gout. Missed another with a full-blooded sweep and only just kept her saddle as she was twisted round after her sword. Righted herself just in time, clinging to the reins with her aching hand.

They were through the Baolish now, had left their torn and bloody corpses in their wake. Shattered lances were flung aside, swords were drawn. The slope levelled off as they plunged on, closer to the river, the ground spotted with Affoian bodies. The battle was a tight-packed slaughter ahead, brought out in greater detail now, more and more Talinese crossing the ford, adding their weight to the mindless press on the banks. Polearms waved and glittered, blades flashed, men struggled and strained. Over the wind and her own breath Monza could hear it, like a distant storm, metal and voices mangled together. Officers rode behind the lines, screaming vainly, trying to bring some trace of order to the madness.

A fresh Talinese regiment had started to push through the gap the Baolish had made on the far right – heavy infantry, well armoured. They'd wheeled and were pressing at the end of the Osprian line, the men in blue straining to hold them off but sorely outnumbered now, more men coming up from the river every moment and forcing the gap wider.

Rogont, shining armour streaked with blood, turned in his saddle and pointed his sword towards them, screamed something no one could hear. It hardly mattered. There was no stopping now.

The Talinese were forming a wedge around a white battle flag, black cross twisting in the wind, an officer at the front stabbing madly at the air as he tried to get them ready to meet the charge. Monza wondered briefly whether she'd ever met him. Men knelt, a mass of glittering armour at the point of the wedge, bristling with polearms, waving and rattling further back, half still caught up with the Osprians, tangled together every which way, a thicket of blades.

Monza saw a cloud of bolts rise from the press in the ford. She winced as they flickered towards her, held her breath for no reason that made any sense. Held breath won't stop an arrow. Rattle and whisper as they showered down, clicking into turf, pinging from heavy armour, thudding into horseflesh.

A horse took a bolt in the neck, twisted, went over on its flank. Another careered into it and its rider came free of the saddle, thrashing at the air, his lance tumbling down the hillside, digging up clods of black soil. Monza wrenched her horse around the wreckage. Something rattled off her breastplate and spun up into her face. She gasped, rolling in her saddle, pain down her cheek. Arrow. The flights had scratched her. She opened her eyes to see an armoured man clutching at a bolt in his shoulder, jolting, jolting, then tumbling sideways, dragged clanking after his madly galloping horse, foot still caught in one stirrup. The rest of them plunged on, horses flowing round the fallen or over them, leaving them trampled.

She'd bitten her tongue somewhere. She spat blood, digging her spurs in again and forcing her mount on, lips curled right back, wind rushing cold at her mouth.

'We should've stuck to farming,' she whispered. The Talinese came pounding up to meet her.

Shivers never had understood where the eager fools came from in every battle, but there were always enough of the bastards to make a show. These ones drove their horses straight for the white flag, at the point of the wedge where the spears were well set. The front horse checked before it got there, skidded and reared, rider just clinging on. The horse behind crashed into it and sent beast and man both onto the gleaming points, blood and splinters flying. Another bucked behind, pitching its rider forwards over its head and tumbling into the muck where the front rank gratefully stabbed at him.

Calmer-headed horsemen broke to the sides, flowing round the wedge like a stream round a rock and into its softer flanks where the spears weren't set. Squealing soldiers clambered over each other as the riders bore down, fighting to be anywhere but the front, spears wobbling at all angles.

Monza went left and Shivers followed, his eye fixed on her. Up ahead a couple of horses jumped the milling front rank and into the midst, riders lashing about with swords and maces. Others crashed into the scrambling men, crushing them, trampling them, sending them spinning, screaming, begging, driving through 'em towards the river. Monza chopped some stumbling fool down as she passed and was into the press, hacking away with her sword. A spearman jabbed at her and caught her in the backplate, near tore her from the saddle.

Black Dow's words came to mind – there's no better time to kill a man than in a battle, and that goes double when he's on your own side. Shivers gave his horse the spurs and urged it up beside Monza, standing tall in his stirrups, bringing his axe up high above her head. His lips curled back. He swung it down with a roar and right into the spearman's face, burst it wide open and sent his corpse tumbling. He heaved the axe all the way over to the other side and it crashed into a shield and left a great dent in it, knocked the man who held it under the threshing hooves of the horse beside. Might've been one of Rogont's people, but it was no time to be thinking on who was who.

Kill everyone not on a horse. Kill anyone on a horse who got in his way.

Kill everyone.

He screamed his war cry, the one he'd used outside the walls of Adua, when they scared the Gurkish off with screams alone. The high wail, out of the icy North, though his voice was cracked and creaking now. He laid about him, hardly looking what he was chopping at, axe blade clanking, banging, thudding, voices crying, blubbering, screeching.

A broken voice roared in Northern. 'Die! Die! Back to the mud, fuckers!' His ears were full of mindless roar and rattle. A shifting sea of jabbing weapons, squealing shields, shining metal, bone shattered, blood spattered, furious, terrified faces washing all round him, squirming and wriggling, and he hacked and chopped and split them like a mad butcher going at a carcass.

His muscles were throbbing hot, his skin was on fire to the tips of his fingers, damp with sweat in the burning sun. Forwards, always forwards, part of the pack, towards the water, leaving a bloody path of broken bodies, dead men and dead horses behind them. The battle opened up and he was through, men scattering in front of him. He spurred his horse between two of them, jolting down the bank and into the shallow river. He hacked one between the shoulders as they fled then chopped deep into the other's neck on the backswing, sent him spinning into the water.

There were riders all round him now, splashing into the ford, hooves sending up showers of bright spray. He caught a glimpse of Monza, still ahead, horse struggling through deeper water, sword blade twinkling as it went up and cut down. The charge was spent. Lathered horses floundered in the shallows. Riders leaned down, chopping, barking, soldiers stabbed back at them with spears, cut at their legs and their mounts with swords. A horseman floundered desperately in the water, crest of his helmet skewed while men battered at him with maces, knocking him this way and that, leaving great dents in his heavy armour.

Shivers grunted as something grabbed him round the stomach, was bent back, shirt ripping. He flailed with his elbow but couldn't get a good swing. A hand clutched at his head, fingers dug at the scarred side of his face, nails scraping at his dead eye. He roared, kicked, squirmed, tried to swing his left arm but someone had hold of that too. He let go his shield, was dragged back, off his horse and down, twisting into the shallows, rolling sideways and up onto his knees.

A young lad in a studded leather jacket was right next to him in the river, wet hair hanging round his face. He was staring down at something in his hand, something flat and glinting. Looked like an eye. The enamel that'd been in Shivers' face until a moment before. The boy looked up, and they stared at each other. Shivers felt something beside him, ducked, wind on his wet hair as his own shield swung past his head. He spun, axe following him in a great wide circle and thudding deep into someone's ribs, blood showering out. It bent him sideways and snatched him howling off his feet, flung him splashing down a stride or two away.

When he turned, the lad was coming at him with a knife. Shivers twisted sideways, managed to catch his forearm and hold it. They staggered, tangled together, went over, cold water clutching. The knife nicked Shivers' shoulder but he was far bigger, far stronger, rolled out on top. They wrestled and clawed, snorting in each other's faces. He let the axe shaft drop through his fist until he was gripping it right under the blade, the lad caught his wrist with his free hand, water washing around his head, but he didn't have the strength to stop it. Shivers gritted his teeth, twisted the axe until the heavy blade slid up across his neck.

'No,' whispered the boy.

The time to say no was before the battle. Shivers pushed with all his weight, growling, moaning. The lad's eyes bulged as the metal bit slowly into his throat, deeper, deeper, the red wound opening wider and wider. Blood squirted out in sticky spurts, down Shivers' arm, over his shirt, into the river and washed away. The lad trembled for a moment, red mouth wide open, then he went limp, staring at the sky.

Shivers staggered up. His rag of a shirt was trapping him, heavy with blood and water. He tore it off, hand so clumsy from gripping his shield hard as murder that he clawed hair from his chest while he did it. He stared about, blinking into the ruthless sun. Men and horses thrashed in the glittering river, blurred and smeary. He bent down and jerked his axe from the boy's half-severed neck, leather twisted round the grip finding the grooves in his palm like a key finds its lock.

He sloshed on through the water on foot, looking for more. Looking for Murcatto.

The dizzy surge of strength the charge had given her was fading fast. Monza's throat was raw from screaming, her legs were aching from gripping her horse. Her right hand was a crooked mass of pain on the reins, her sword arm burned from fingers to shoulder, the blood pounded behind her eyes. She twisted about, not sure any more which was east or west. It hardly mattered now.

In war, Verturio wrote, *there are no straight lines.*

There were no lines at all down in the ford, just horsemen and soldiers all tangled up into a hundred murderous, mindless little fights. You could hardly tell friend from enemy and, since no one was checking too closely, there wasn't much difference between the two. Your death could come from anywhere.

She saw the spear, but too late. Her horse shuddered as the point sank into its flank just beside her leg. Its head twisted, one eye rolling wild, foam on its bared teeth. Monza clung to the saddle-bow as it lurched sideways, spear rammed deeper, her leg hot with horse blood. She gave a helpless shriek as she went over, feet still in the stirrups, sword tumbling from her hand as she clutched at nothing. Water hit her in the side, the saddle dug her in the stomach and drove her breath out.

She was under, head full of light, bubbles rushing round her face. Cold clutched at her, and cold fear too. She thrashed her way up for a moment, out of the darkness and suddenly into the glare, the sound of battle crashing at her ears again. She gasped in a breath, shipped some water, coughed it out, gasped in another. She clawed at the saddle with her left hand, tried to drag herself free, but her leg was trapped under her horse's thrashing body.

Something cracked against her forehead and she was under for a moment, dizzy, floppy. Her lungs were burning, her arms were made of mud. Fought her way up again, but weaker this time, only far enough to snatch one breath. Blue sky reeling, shreds of white cloud, like the sky as she tumbled down from Fontezarmo.

The sun flickered at her, searing bright along with her whooping breath, then blurred and sparkling with muffled gurgles as the river washed over her face. No strength left to twist herself out of the water. Was this what Faithful's last moments had been like, drowned on the mill-wheel?

Here was justice.

A black shape blotted out the sun. Shivers, seeming ten feet tall as he stood over her. Something gleamed bright in the socket of his blinded eye. He lifted one boot slowly clear of the river, frowning hard, water trickling from the edges of the sole and into her face. For a moment she was sure he was going to plant that foot on her neck and push her under. Then it splashed down beside her. She heard him growling, straining at the corpse of her horse. She felt the weight across her leg release a little, then a little more. She squirmed, groaned, breathed in water and coughed it out, finally dragged her leg free and floundered up.

She trembled on hands and knees, up to her elbows in the river, babbling water sparkling and flickering in front of her, drips falling from her wet hair. 'Shit,' she whispered, every breath shuddering in her sore ribs. 'Shit.' She needed a smoke.

'They're coming,' came Shivers' voice. She felt his hand rammed into her armpit, dragging her up. 'Get a blade.'

She staggered under the weight of wet clothes and wet armour to a bobbing corpse caught on a rock. A heavy mace with a metal shaft was still hanging by its strap from his wrist, and she dragged it free with fumbling fingers, pulled a long knife from his belt.

Just in time. An armoured man was bearing down on her, planting his feet carefully, peering at her with hard little eyes over the top of his shield, sword beaded with wet sticking out sideways. She backed off a step or two, pretending to be finished. Didn't take much pretending. As he took another step she came at him. Couldn't have called it a spring. More of a tired half-dive, hardly able to shove her feet through the water fast enough to keep up with the rest of her body.

She swung at him mindlessly with the mace and it clanged off his shield, made her arm sing to the shoulder. She grunted, wrestled with him, stabbed at him with her knife, but it caught the side of his breastplate and scraped off harmless. The shield barged into her and sent her stumbling. She saw one swing of his sword coming and just had the presence of mind to duck it. She flailed with the mace and caught air, reeled off balance, hardly any strength left, gulping for air. His sword went up again.

She saw Shivers' mad grin behind him, a flash as the red blade of his axe caught the sun. It split the man's armoured shoulder down to his chest with a heavy thud, sent blood spraying in Monza's face. She reeled away, ears full of his gargling shriek, nose full of his blood, trying to scrape her eyes clear on the back of one hand.

First thing she saw was another soldier, open helmet with a bearded face inside, stabbing with a spear. She tried to twist away but it caught her hard in the chest, point shrieked down her breastplate, sent her toppling, head snapping forwards. She was on her back in the ford and the soldier stumbled past, floundering into a crack in the river bed, sending water showering in her eyes. She fought her way up to one knee, bloody hair tangled across her face. He turned, lifting the spear to stab at her again. She twisted round and rammed the knife between two plates of armour, into the side of his knee right to the crosspiece.

He bent down over her, eyes bulging, opened his mouth wide to scream. She snarled as she jerked the mace up and smashed it into the bottom of his jaw. His head snapped back, blood and teeth and bits of teeth flew high. He seemed to stay there for a moment, hands dangling, then she clubbed his stretched-out throat with the mace, sprawled on top of him as he fell, rolled about in the river and came up spitting.

There were men around her still, but none of them fighting. Standing or sitting in their saddles, staring about. Shivers stood watching her, axe hanging from one hand. For some reason he was stripped half-naked, his white skin dashed and spattered with red. The enamel was gone from his eye and the bright metal ball behind it gleamed in the socket with the midday sun, dewy with beads of wet.

'Victory!' She heard someone scream. Blurry, quivering, wet-eyed, she saw a man on a brown horse, in the midst of the river, standing in his stirrups, shining sword held high. 'Victory!'

She took a wobbling step towards Shivers and he dropped his scarred axe, caught her as she fell. She clung on to him, right arm around his shoulder, left dangling, still just gripping the mace, if only because she couldn't make the fingers open.

'We won,' she whispered at him, and she felt herself smiling.

'We won,' he said, squeezing her tight, half-lifting her off her feet.

'We won.'

Cosca lowered his eyeglass, blinked and rubbed his eyes, one half-blind from being shut for the best part of the hour, the other half-blind from being jammed into the eyepiece for the same period. 'Well, there we are.' He shifted uncomfortably in the captain general's chair. His trousers had become wedged in the sweaty crack of his arse and he wriggled as he tugged them free. 'God smiles on results, do you Gurkish say?'

Silence. Ishri had melted away as swiftly as she had appeared. Cosca swivelled the other way, towards Friendly. 'Quite the show, eh, Sergeant?'

The convict looked up from his dice, frowned down into the valley and said nothing. Duke Rogont's timely charge had plugged the gaping hole in his lines, crushed the Baolish, driven deep into the Talinese ranks and left them broken. Not at all what the Duke of Delay was known for. In fact, Cosca was oddly pleased to perceive the audacious hand, or perhaps the fist, of Monzcarro Murcatto all over it.

The Osprian infantry, the threat on their right wing extinguished, had blocked off the eastern bank of the lower ford entirely. Their new Sipanese allies had well and truly joined the fray, won a brief engagement with Foscar's surprised rearguard and were close to sealing off the western bank. A good half of Orso's army – or of those that were not now scattered dead on the slopes, on the banks downstream or floating face-down out to sea – were trapped hopelessly in the shallows between the two, and were laying down their arms. The other half were fleeing, dark specks scattered across the green slopes on the valley's western side. The very slopes down which they had so proudly marched but a few short hours ago, confident of victory. Sipanese cavalry moved in clumps around their edges, armour gleaming in the fierce noon sun, rounding up the survivors.

'All done now, though, eh, Victus?'

'Looks that way.'

'Everyone's favourite part of a battle. The rout.' Unless you were in it, of course. Cosca watched the tiny figures spilling from the fords, spreading out across the trampled grass, and had to shake off a sweaty shiver at the memory of Afieri. He forced the carefree grin to stay on his face. 'Nothing like a good rout, eh, Sesaria?'

'Who'd have thought it?' The big man slowly shook his head. 'Rogont won.'

'Grand Duke Rogont would appear to be a most unpredictable and resourceful gentleman.' Cosca yawned, stretched, smacked his lips. 'One after my own heart. I look forward to having him as an employer. Probably we should help with the mopping up.' The searching of the dead. 'Prisoners to be taken and ransomed.' Or murdered and robbed, depending on social station. 'Unguarded baggage that should be confiscated, lest it spoil in the open air.' Lest it be plundered or burned before they could get their gauntlets on it.

Victus split a toothy grin. 'I'll make arrangements to bring it all in from the cold.'

'Do so, brave Captain Victus, do so. I declare the sun is on its way back down and it is past time the men were on the move. I would be ashamed if, in after times, the poets said the Thousand Swords were at the Battle of Ospria . . . and did nothing.' Cosca smiled wide, and this time with feeling. 'Lunch, perhaps?'

To the Victors . . .

Black Dow used to say the only thing better'n a battle was a battle then a fuck, and Shivers couldn't say he disagreed. Seemed she didn't either. She was waiting there for him, after all, when he stalked into the darkened room, bare as a baby, stretched out on the bed, her hands behind her head and one long, smooth leg pointing out towards him.

'What kept you?' she asked, rocking her hips from one side to the other.

Time was he'd reckoned himself a quick thinker but the only thing moving fast right then was his cock. 'I was . . .' He was having trouble thinking much beyond the patch of dark hair between her legs, his anger all leaked away like beer from a broken jar. 'I was . . . well . . .' He kicked the door shut and walked slowly to her. 'Don't matter much, does it?'

'Not much.' She slipped off the bed, started undoing his borrowed shirt, going about it as if it was something they'd arranged.

'Can't say I was expecting . . . this.' He reached out, almost scared to touch her in case he found he was dreaming it. Ran his fingertips down her bare arms, skin rough with gooseflesh. 'Not after last time we spoke.'

She pushed her fingers into his hair and pulled his head down towards her, breath on his face. She kissed his neck, then his chin, then his mouth. 'Shall I go?' She sucked gently at his lips again.

'Fuck, no,' his voice hardly more'n a croak.

She had his belt open now, dug inside and pulled his cock free, started working at it with one hand while his trousers sagged slowly down, catching on his knees, belt buckle scraping on the floor.

Her lips were cool on his chest, on his stomach, her tongue tickled his belly. Her hand slid under his fruits, cold and ticklish and he squirmed, gave a womanly kind of a squeak. He heard a quiet slurp as she wrapped her lips around him and he stood there, bent over some, knees weak and trembling and his mouth hanging open. Her head started bobbing slowly in and out, and he moved his hips in time without thinking, grunting to himself like a pig got the swill.

Monza wiped her mouth on the back of her arm, squirmed her way onto the bed, pulling him after, kissing at her neck, at her breastbone, nipping at her chest, growling to himself like a dog got the bone.

She brought her knee up and flipped him over onto his back. He frowned, left side of his face all in darkness, right side full of shadows from the shifting lamplight, running his fingertips gently along the scars on her ribs. She slapped his hand away. 'Told you. I fell down a mountain. Get your trousers off.'

He wriggled eagerly free of them, got them tangled around his ankles. 'Shit, damn, bastard— Ah!' He finally kicked them off and she shoved him down onto his back, clambered on top of him, one of his hands sliding up her thigh, wet fingers working between her legs. She stayed there a while, crouched over him, growling in his face and feeling his breath coming quick back at her, grinding her hips against his hand, feeling his prick rubbing up against the inside of her thigh—

'Ah, wait!' He wriggled away, sitting up, winced as he fiddled with the skin at the end of his cock. 'Got it. Go!'

'I'll tell you when to go.' She worked her way forwards on her knees, finding the spot and then nudging her cunt against him softly, gently, not in and not out, halfway between.

'Oh.' He wriggled his way up onto his elbows, straining vainly up against her.

'Ah.' She leaned down over him, her hair tickling his face, and he smiled, snapped his teeth at it.

'Oh-urgh.' She pushed her thumb into his mouth, dragged his head sideways and he sucked at it, bit at it, catching her wrist, licking at her hand, then her chin, then her tongue.

'Ah.' She started to push down on him, smiling herself, grunting in her throat and him grunting back at her.

'Oh.'

She had the root of his cock in one hand, rubbing herself against the end of it, not in and not out, always halfway between. She had the other round the back of Shivers' head, holding his face against her tits while he gathered them up, squeezed them, bit at them.

Her fingers worked under his jaw, thumb-tip sliding ever so gently onto his ruined cheek, tickling, teasing, scratching. He felt a sudden stab of fury, snatched hold of her wrist, hard, twisted it round, twisted her off him and onto her knees, twisted her arm behind her, face pushed down into the sheet, making her gasp.

He was grunting something in Northern and even he didn't know what. He felt a burning need to hurt her. Hurt himself. He tangled his free hand in her hair and shoved her head hard against the wall, growling and whimpering at her from behind while she groaned, gasped, mouth wide open, hair across her face fluttering with her breath. He still had her arm twisted behind her and her hand curled round, gripping his wrist hard while he gripped hers, dragging him down over her.

Uh, uh, their mindless grunting. Creak, creak, the bed moaning along with them. Squelch, squelch, his skin slapping hard against her arse.

Monza worked her hips against him a few more times, and with each one he gave a little hoot, head back, veins standing from his stretched-out neck. With each one she gave a snarl through gritted teeth, muscles all clenched aching tight, then slowly going soft. She stayed there for a moment, hunched over, limp as wet leaves, hard breath catching in the back of her throat. She winced and he shivered as she ground herself against him one last time. Then she slid off, gathered up a handful of sheet and wiped herself on it.

He lay there on his back, sweaty chest rising and falling fast, arms spread out wide, staring at the gilded ceiling. 'So this is what victory feels like. If I'd known I'd have taken some gambles sooner.'

'No, you wouldn't. You're the Duke of Delay, remember?'

He peered down at his wet cock, nudged it to one side, then the other. 'Well, some things it's best to take your time with . . .'

Shivers prised his fingers open, scuffed, scabbed, scratched and clicking from gripping his axe all the long day. They left white marks across her wrist, turning slowly pink. He rocked back on his haunches, body sagging, aching muscles loose, heaving in air. His lust all spent and his rage spent with it. For now.

Her necklace of red stones rattled as she rolled over towards him. Onto her back, tits flattened against her ribs, the knobbles of her hip bones sticking sharp from her stomach, of her collarbones sticking sharp from her shoulders. She winced, working her hand around, rubbing at her wrist.

'Didn't mean to hurt you,' he grunted, lying badly, and not much caring either.

'Oh, I'm nothing like that delicate. And you can call me Carlot.' She reached up and brushed his lips gently with a fingertip. 'I think we know each other well enough for that . . .'

Monza clambered off the bed and walked to the desk, legs weak and aching, feet flapping against the cool marble. The husk lay on it, beside the lamp. The knife blade gleamed, the polished stem of the pipe shone. She sat down in front of it. Yesterday she wouldn't have been able to keep her trembling hands away from it. Today, even with a legion of fresh aches, cuts, grazes from the battle, it didn't call to her half so loud. She held her left hand up, knuckles starting to scab over, and frowned at it. It was firm.

'I never really thought I could do it,' she muttered.

'Eh?'

'Beat Orso. I thought I might get three of them. Four, maybe, before they killed me. Never thought I'd live this long. Never thought I could actually do it.'

'And now one would say the odds favour you. How quickly hope can flicker into life once more.' Rogont drew himself up before the mirror. A tall one, crusted with coloured flowers of Visserine glass. She could hardly believe, watching him pose, that she'd once been every bit as vain. The hours she'd wasted preening before the mirror. The fortunes she and Benna had spent on clothes. A fall down a mountain, a body scarred, a hand ruined and six months living like a hunted dog seemed to have cured her of that, at least. Perhaps she should've suggested the same remedy to Rogont.

The duke lifted his chin in a regal gesture, chest inflated. He frowned, sagged, pressed at a long scratch just below his collarbone. 'Damn it.'

'Nick yourself on your nail-file, did you?'

'A savage sword-cut like this could easily have been the death of a lesser man, I'll have you know! But I braved it, without complaint, and fought on like a tiger, blood streaming, *streaming* I say, down my armour! I am beginning to suspect it could even leave a mark.'

'No doubt you'll wear it with massive pride. You could have a hole cut in all your shirts to display it to the public.'

'If I didn't know better I'd suspect I was being mocked. You do realise, if things unfold according to my plans – and they have so far, I might observe – you will soon be directing your sarcasm at the King of Styria. I have already, in fact, commissioned my crown, from Zoben Casoum, the world-famous master jeweller of Corontiz—'

'Cast from Gurkish gold, no doubt.'

Rogont paused for a moment, frowning. 'The world is not as simple as you think, General Murcatto. A great war rages.'

She snorted. 'You think I missed that? These are the Years of Blood.'

He snorted back. 'The Years of Blood are only the latest skirmish. This war began long before you or I were born. A struggle between the Gurkish and the Union. Or between the forces that control them, at least, the church of Gurkhul and the banks of the Union. Their battlefields are everywhere, and every man must pick his side. The middle ground contains only corpses. Orso stands with the Union. Orso has the backing of the banks. And so I have my . . . backers. Every man must kneel to someone.'

'Perhaps you didn't notice. I'm not a man.'

Rogont's smile broke out again. 'Oh, I noticed. It was the second thing that attracted me to you.'

'The first?'

'You can help me unite Styria.'

'And why should I?'

'A united Styria . . . she could be as great as the Union, as great as the Empire of Gurkhul. Greater, even! She could free herself from their struggle, and stand alone. Free. We have never been closer! Nicante and Puranti fall over themselves to re-enter my good graces. Affoia never left them. Sotorius is my man, with certain trifling concessions to Sipani, no more than a few islands and the city of Borletta—'

'And what do the citizens of Borletta have to say to it?'

'Whatever I tell them to say. They are a changeable crowd, as you discovered when they scrambled to offer you their beloved Duke Cantain's head. Muris bowed to Sipani long ago, and Sipani now bows to me, in name at least. The power of Visserine is broken. As for Musselia, Etrea and Caprile, well. You and Orso between you, I suspect, have quite crushed their independent temper out of them.'

'Westport?'

'Details, details. Part of the Union or of Kanta, depending on who you ask. No, it is Talins that concerns us now. Talins is the key in the lock, the hub of the wheel, the missing piece in my majestic jigsaw.'

'You love to listen to your own voice, don't you?'

'I find it talks a lot of good sense. Orso's army is scattered, and with it his power is vanished, like smoke on the wind. He has ever resorted first to the sword, as certain others are wont to do, in fact . . .' He raised his brows significantly at her, and she waved him on. 'He finds, now his sword is broken, that he has no friends to sustain him. But it will not be enough to destroy Orso. I need someone to replace him, someone to guide the trouble-some citizens of Talins into my gracious fold.'

'Let me know when you find the right shepherd.'

'Oh, I already have. Someone of skill, cunning, matchless resilience and fearsome reputation. Someone loved in Talins far more than Orso himself. Someone he tried to kill, in fact . . . for stealing his throne . . .'

She narrowed her eyes at him. 'I didn't want his throne then. I don't want it now.'

'But since it is there for the taking . . . what comes once you have your revenge? You deserve to be remembered. You deserve to shape the age.' Benna would have said so, and Monza had to admit that part of her was enjoying the flattery. Enjoying being so close to power again. She'd been used to both, and it had been a long time since she'd had a taste of either. 'Besides, what better revenge could you have than making Orso's greatest fear come to pass?' That struck a fine note with her, and Rogont gave her a sly grin to show he knew it. 'Let me be honest. I need you.'

'Let me be honest. I need you.' That rested easily on Shivers' pride, and she gave him a sly smile to show she knew it. 'I scarcely have a friend left in all the wide Circle of the World.'

'Seems you've a knack for making new ones.'

'It's harder than you'd think. To be always the outsider.' He didn't need to be told that after the few months he'd had. She didn't lie, from what he could tell, just led the truth by the nose whichever way it suited her. 'And sometimes it can be hard to tell your friends from your enemies.'

'True enough.' He didn't need to be told that either.

'I daresay where you come from loyalty is considered a noble quality. Down here in Styria, a man has to bend with the wind.' Hard to believe anyone who smiled so sweetly could have anything dark in mind. But everything was dark to him now. Everything had a knife hidden in it. 'Your friends and mine General Murcatto and Grand Duke Rogont, for example.' Carlot's two eyes drifted up to his one. 'I wonder what they're about, right now?'

'Fucking!' he barked at her, the fury boiling out of him so sharp she flinched away, like she was expecting him to smash her head into the wall. Maybe he nearly did. That or smash his own. But her face soon smoothed out and she smiled some more, like murderous rage was her favourite quality in a man.

'The Snake of Talins and the Worm of Ospria, all stickily entwined together. Well matched, that treacherous pair. Styria's greatest liar and Styria's greatest murderer.' She gently traced the scar on his chest with one fingertip. 'What comes once she has her revenge? Once Rogont has raised her up and dangled her like a child's toy for the people of Talins to stare at? Will you have a place when the Years of Blood are finally ended? When the war is over?'

'I don't have a place anywhere without a war. That much I've proved.'

'Then I fear for you.'

Shivers snorted. 'I'm lucky to have you watching my back.'

'I wish I could do more. But you know how the Butcher of Caprile solves her problems, and Duke Rogont has scant regard for honest men . . .'

'I have nothing but the highest regard for honest men, but fighting stripped to the waist? It's so . . .' Rogont grimaced as though he'd tasted off milk. 'Cliché. You wouldn't catch me doing it.'

'What, fighting?'

'How dare you, woman, I am Stolicus reborn! You know what I mean. Your Northern accomplice, with the . . .' Rogont waved a lazy hand at the left side of his face. 'Eye. Or lack thereof.'

'Jealous, already?' she muttered, sick at even coming near the subject.

'A little. But it's his jealousy that concerns me. This is a man much prone to violence.'

'It's what I took him on for.'

'Perhaps the time has come to lay him off. Mad dogs savage their owner more often than their owner's enemies.'

'And their owner's lovers first of all.'

Rogont nervously cleared his throat. 'We certainly would not want that. He seems firmly attached to you. When a barnacle is firmly attached to the hull of a ship, it is sometimes necessary to remove it with a sudden, unexpected and . . . decisive force.'

'No!' Her voice stabbed out far sharper than she'd had in mind. 'No. He's saved my life. More than once, and risked his life to do it. Just yesterday he did it, and today have him killed? No. I owe him.' She remembered the smell as Langrier pushed the brand into his face, and she flinched. *It should've been you.* 'No! I'll not have him touched.'

'Think about it.' Rogont padded slowly towards her. 'I understand your reluctance, but you must see it's the safe thing to do.'

'The prudent thing?' she sneered at him. 'I'm warning you. Leave him be.'

'Monzcarro, please understand, it's your safety I'm— Oooof!'

She sprang up from the chair, kicking his foot away, caught his arm as he lurched onto his knees and twisted his wrist behind his shoulder blade, forced him down until she was squatting over his back, his face squashed against the cool marble.

'Didn't you hear me say no? If it's sudden, unexpected and decisive force I want . . .' She twisted his hand a little further and he squeaked, struggled helplessly. 'I can manage it myself.'

'Yes! Ah! Yes! I quite clearly see that!'

'Good. Don't bring him up again.' She let go of his wrist and he lay there for a moment, breathing hard. He wriggled onto his back, rubbing gently at his hand, looking up with a hurt frown as she straddled his stomach.

'You didn't have to do that.'

'Maybe I enjoyed doing it.' She looked over her shoulder. His cock was half-hard, nudging at the back of her leg. 'I'm not sure you didn't.'

'Now that you mention it . . . I must confess I rather relish being looked down on by a strong woman.' He brushed her knees with his fingertips, ran his hands slowly up the insides of her scarred thighs to the top, and then gently back down. 'I don't suppose . . . you could be persuaded . . . to piss on me, at all?'

Monza frowned. 'I don't need to go.'

'Perhaps . . . some water, then? And afterwards—'

'I think I'll stick to the pot.'

'Such a waste. The pot will not appreciate it.'

'Once it's full you can do what you like with it, how's that?'

'Ugh. Not at all the same thing.'

Monza slowly shook her head as she stepped off him. 'A pretend grand duchess, pissing on a would-be king. You couldn't make it up.'

'Enough.' Shivers was covered with bruises, grazes, scratches. A bastard of a gash across his back, just where it was hardest to scratch. Now his cock was going soft they were all niggling at him again in the sticky heat, stripping his patience. He was sick of talking round and round it, when it was lying between 'em, plain as a rotting corpse in the bed. 'You want Murcatto dead, you can out and say it.'

She paused, mouth half-open. 'You're surprisingly blunt.'

'No, I'm about as blunt as you'd expect for a one-eyed killer. Why?'

'Why what?'

'Why do you need her dead so bad? I'm an idiot, but not that big an idiot. I don't reckon a woman like you is drawn to my pretty face. Nor my sense of humour neither. Maybe you want yourself some revenge for what we did to you in Sipani. Everyone likes revenge. But that's just part of it.'

'No small part . . .' She let one fingertip trail slowly up his leg. 'As far as being drawn to you, I was always more interested in honest men than pretty faces, but I wonder . . . can I trust you?'

'No. If you could I wouldn't be much suited to the task, would I?' He caught hold of her trailing finger and twisted it towards him, dragged her wincing face close. 'What's in it for you?'

'Ah! There's a man in the Union! The man I work for, the one who sent me to Styria in the first place, to spy on Orso!'

'The Cripple?' Vitari had said the name. The man who stood behind the King of the Union.

'Yes! Ah! Ah!' She squealed as he twisted her finger further, then he let it go and she snatched it back, holding it to her chest, bottom lip stuck out at him. 'You didn't have to do that.'

'Maybe I enjoyed doing it. Go on.'

'When Murcatto made me betray Orso . . . she made me betray the Cripple too. Orso I can live with as an enemy, if I must—'

'But not this Cripple?'

She swallowed. 'No. Not him.'

'A worse enemy than the great Duke Orso, eh?'

'Far worse. Murcatto is his price. She threatens to rip apart all his carefully woven plans to bring Talins into the Union. He wants her dead.' The smooth mask had slipped and she had this look, shoulders slumped, staring down wide-eyed at the sheet. Hungry, and sick, and very, very scared. Shivers liked seeing it. Might've been the first honest look he'd seen since he landed in Styria. 'If I can find a way to kill her, I get my life,' she whispered.

'And I'm your way.'

She looked back up at him, and her eyes were hard. 'Can you do it?'

'I could've done it today.' He'd thought of splitting her head with his axe. He'd thought of planting his boot on her face and shoving her under the water. Then she'd have had to respect him. But instead he'd saved her. Because he'd been hoping. Maybe he still was . . . but hoping had made a fool of him. And Shivers was good and sick of looking the fool.

How many men had he killed? In all those battles, skirmishes, desperate fights up in the North? Just in the half-year since he came to Styria, even? At Cardotti's, in the smoke and the madness? Among the statues in Duke Salier's palace? In the battle just a few hours back? It might've been a score. More. And women among 'em. He was steeped in blood, deep as the Bloody-Nine himself. Didn't seem likely that adding one more to the tally would cost him a place among the righteous. His mouth twisted.

'I could do it.' It was plain as the scar on his face that Monza cared nothing for him. Why should he care anything for her? 'I could do it easily.'

'Then do it.' She crept forwards on her hands and knees, mouth half-open, pale tits hanging heavy, looking him right in his one eye. 'For me.' Her nipples brushed against his chest, one way then the other as she crawled over him. 'For you.' Her necklace of blood-red stones clicked gently against his chin. 'For us.'

'I'll need to pick my moment.' He slid his hand down her back and up onto her arse. 'Caution first, eh?'

'Of course. Nothing done well is ever . . . rushed.'

His head was full of her scent, sweet smell of flowers mixed with the sharp smell of fucking. 'She owes me money,' he growled, the last objection.

'Ah, money. I used to be a merchant, you know. Buying. Selling.' Her breath was hot on his neck, on his mouth, on his face. 'And in my long experience, when people begin to talk prices, the deal is already done.' She nuzzled at him, lips brushing the mass of scar down his cheek. 'Do this thing for me, and I promise you'll get all you could ever spend.' The cool tip of her tongue lapped gently at the raw flesh round his metal eye, sweet and soothing. 'I have an arrangement . . . with the Banking House . . . of Valint and Balk . . .'

So Much for Nothing

Silver gleamed in the sunlight with that special, mouth-watering twinkle that somehow only money has. A whole strongbox full of it, stacked in plain sight, drawing the eyes of every man in the camp more surely than if a naked countess had been sprawled suggestively upon the table. Piles of sparking, sparkling coins, freshly minted. Some of the cleanest currency in Styria, pressed into some of its grubbiest hands. A pleasing irony. The coins carried the scales on one side, of course, traditional symbol of Styrian commerce since the time of the New Empire. On the other, the stern profile of Grand Duke Orso of Talins. An even more pleasing irony, to Cosca's mind, that he was paying the men of the Thousand Swords with the face of the man they had but lately betrayed.

In a pocked and spattered, squinting and scratching, coughing and slovenly line the soldiers and staff of the first company of the first regiment of the Thousand Swords passed by the makeshift table to receive their unjust deserts. They were closely supervised by the chief notary of the brigade and a dozen of its most reliable veterans, which was just as well, because during the course of the morning Cosca had witnessed every dispiriting trick imaginable.

Men approached the table on multiple occasions in different clothes, giving false names or those of dead comrades. They routinely exaggerated, embellished or flat-out lied in regards to rank or length of service. They wept for sick mothers, children or acquaintances. They delivered a devastating volley of complaints about food, drink, equipment, runny shits, superiors, the smell of other men, the weather, items stolen, injuries suffered, injuries given, perceived slights on non-existent honour and on, and on, and on. Had they demonstrated the same audacity and persistence in combat that they did in trying to prise the slightest dishonest pittance from their commander they would have been the greatest fighting force of all time.

But First Sergeant Friendly was watching. He had worked for years in the kitchens of Safety, where dozens of the world's most infamous swindlers vied daily with each other for enough bread to survive, and so he knew every low trick, con and stratagem practised this side of hell. There was no sliding around his basilisk gaze. The convict did not permit a single shining portrait of Duke Orso to be administered out of turn.

Cosca shook his head in deep dismay as he watched the last man trudge away, the unbearable limp for which he had demanded compensation miraculously healed. 'By the Fates, you would have thought they'd be glad of the bonus! It isn't as if they had to fight for it! Or even steal it themselves! I swear, the more you give a man, the more he demands, and the less happy he becomes. No one ever appreciates what he gets for nothing. A pox on charity!' He slapped the notary on the shoulder, causing him to scrawl an untidy line across his carefully kept page.

'Mercenaries aren't all they used to be,' grumbled the man as he sourly blotted it.

'No? To my eye they seem very much as violent-tempered and mean-spirited as ever. "Things aren't what they used to be" is the rallying cry of small minds. When men say things used to be better, they invariably mean they were better for them, because they were young, and had all their hopes intact. The world is bound to look a darker place as you slide into the grave.'

'So everything stays the same?' asked the notary, looking sadly up.

'Some men get better, some get worse.' Cosca heaved a weighty sigh. 'But on the grand scale, I have observed no significant changes. How many of our heroes have we paid now?'

'That's all of Squire's company, of Andiche's regiment. Well, Andiche's regiment that was.'

Cosca put a hand over his eyes. 'Please, don't speak of that brave heart. His loss still stabs at me. How many have we paid?'

The notary licked his fingers, flipped over a couple of crackling leaves of his ledger, started counting the entries. 'One, two, three—'

'Four hundred and four,' said Friendly.

'And how many persons in the Thousand Swords?'

The notary winced. 'Counting all ancillaries, servants and tradesmen?'

'Absolutely.'

'Whores too?'

'Counting them first, they're the hardest workers in the whole damned brigade!'

The lawyer squinted skywards. 'Er . . .'

'Twelve thousand, eight-hundred and nineteen,' said Friendly.

Cosca stared at him. 'I've heard it said a good sergeant is worth three generals, but you may well be worth three dozen, my friend! Thirteen thousand, though? We'll be here tomorrow night still!'

'Very likely,' grumbled the notary, flipping over the page. 'Crapstane's company of Andiche's regiment will be next. Andiche's regiment . . . as was . . . that is.'

'Meh.' Cosca unscrewed the cap of the flask Morveer had thrown at him in Sipani, raised it to his lips, shook it and realised it was empty. He frowned at the battered metal bottle, remembering with some discomfort the poisoner's sneering assertion that a man never changes. So much discomfort, in fact, that his need for a drink was sharply increased. 'A brief interlude, while I obtain a refill. Get Crapstane's company lined up.' He stood, grimacing as his aching knees crunched into life, then cracked a smile. A large man was walking steadily towards him through the mud, smoke, canvas and confusion of the camp.

'Why, Master Shivers, from the cold and bloody North!' The Northman had evidently given up on fine dressing, wearing a leather jack and rough-spun shirt with sleeves rolled to the elbows. His hair, neat as any Musselian dandy's when Cosca first laid eyes upon the man, had grown back to an unkempt tangle, heavy jaw fuzzed with a growth between beard and stubble. None of it did anything to disguise the mass of scar covering one side of his face. It would take more than hair to hide that. 'My old partner in adventure!' Or murder, as was in fact the case. 'You have a twinkle in your eye.' Literally he did, for bright metal in the Northman's empty socket was catching the noon sun and shining with almost painful brightness. 'You look well, my friend, most well!' Though he looked, in fact, a mutilated savage.

'Happy face, happy heart.' The Northman showed a lopsided smile, burned flesh shifting only by the smallest margin.

'Quite so. Have a smile for breakfast, you'll be shitting joy by lunch. Were you in the battle?'

'That I was.'

'I thought as much. You have never struck me as a man afraid to roll up his sleeves. Bloody, was it?'

'That it was.'

'Some men thrive on blood, though, eh? I daresay you've known a few who were that way.'

'That I have.'

'And where is your employer, my infamous pupil, replacement and predecessor, General Murcatto?'

'Behind you,' came a sharp voice.

He spun about. 'God's teeth, woman, but you haven't lost the knack of creeping up on a man!' He pretended at shock to smother the sentimental welling-up that always accompanied her appearance, and threatened to make his voice crack with emotion. She had a long scratch down one cheek, some bruising on her face, but otherwise looked well. Very well. 'My joy to see you alive knows no bounds, of course.' He swept off his hat, feather drooping apologetically, and kneeled in the dirt in front of her. 'Say you forgive me my theatrics. You see now I was thinking only of you all along. My fondness for you is undiminished.'

She snorted at that. 'Fondness, eh?' More than she could ever know, or he would ever tell her. 'So this pantomime was for my benefit? I may swoon with gratitude.'

'One of your most endearing features was always your readiness to swoon.' He cranked himself back up to standing. 'A consequence of your sensitive, womanly heart, I suppose. Walk with me, I have something to show you.' He led her off through the trees towards the farmhouse, its whitewashed walls gleaming in the midday sun, Friendly and Shivers trailing them like bad memories. 'I must confess that, as well as doing you a favour, and the sore temptation of placing my boot in Orso's arse at long last, there were some trifling issues of personal gain to consider.'

'Some things never change.'

'Nothing ever does, and why should it? A considerable

quantity of Gurkish gold was on offer. Well, you know it was, you were the first to offer it. Oh, and Rogont was kind enough to promise me, in the now highly likely event that he is crowned King of Styria, the Grand Duchy of Visserine.'

He was deeply satisfied by her gasp of surprise. 'You? Grand fucking Duke of Visserine?'

'I probably won't use the word *fucking* on my decrees, but otherwise, correct. Grand Duke Nicomo sounds rather well, no? After all, Salier is dead.'

'That much I know.'

'He had no heirs, not even distant ones. The city was plundered, devastated by fire, its government collapsed, much of the populace fled, killed or otherwise taken advantage of. Visserine is in need of a strong and selfless leader to restore her to her glories.'

'And instead they'll have you.'

He allowed himself a chuckle. 'But who better suited? Am I not a native of Visserine?'

'A lot of people are. You don't see them helping themselves to its dukedom.'

'Well, there's only one, and it's mine.'

'Why do you even want it? Commitments? Responsibilities? I thought you hated all that.'

'I always thought so, but my wandering star led me only to the gutter. I have not had a productive life, Monzcarro.'

'You don't say.'

'I have frittered my gifts away on nothing. Self-pity and self-hatred have led me by unsavoury paths to self-neglect, self-injury and the very brink of self-destruction. The unifying theme?'

'Yourself?'

'Precisely so. Vanity, Monza. Self-obsession. The mark of infancy. I need, for my own sake and those of my fellow men, to be an adult. To turn my talents outwards. It is just as you always tried to tell me – the time comes when a man has to stick. What better way than to commit myself wholeheartedly to the service of the city of my birth?'

'Your wholehearted commitment. Alas for the poor city of Visserine.'

'They'll do better than they did with that art-thieving gourmand.'

'Now they'll have an all-thieving drunk.'

'You misjudge me, Monzcarro. A man can change.'

'I thought you just said nothing ever does?'

'Changed my mind. And why not? In one day I bagged myself a fortune, and one of the richest dukedoms in Styria too.'

She shook her head in combined disgust and amazement. 'And all you did was sit here.'

'Therein lies the real trick. Anyone can *earn* rewards.' Cosca tipped his head back, smiled up at the black branches and the blue sky beyond them. 'Do you know, I think it highly unlikely that ever in history has one man gained so much for doing absolutely nothing. But I am hardly the only one to profit from yesterday's exploits. Grand Duke Rogont, I daresay, is happy with the outcome. And you are a great stride nearer to your grand revenge, are you not?' He leaned close to her. 'Speaking of which, I have a gift for you.'

She frowned at him, ever suspicious. 'What gift?'

'I would hate to spoil the surprise. Sergeant Friendly, could you take your ex-employer and her Northern companion into the house, and show her what we found yesterday? For her to do with as she pleases, of course.' He turned away with a smirk. 'We're all friends now!'

'In here.' Friendly pushed the low door creaking open. Monza gave Shivers a look. He shrugged back. She ducked under the lintel and into a dim room, cool after the sun outside, with a ceiling of vaulted brick and patches of light across a dusty stone floor. As her eyes adjusted to the gloom she saw a figure wedged into the furthest corner. He shuffled forwards, chain between his ankles rattling faintly, and criss-cross shadows from the grubby window panes fell across one half of his face.

Prince Foscar, Duke Orso's younger son. Monza felt her whole body stiffen.

It seemed he'd finally grown up since she last saw him, running from his father's hall in Fontezarmo, wailing that he wanted no part in her murder. He'd lost the fluff on his top lip, gained a bloom of bruises ringing one eye and swapped the apologetic look for a fearful one. He stared at Shivers, then at Friendly as they stepped through into the room behind her. Not two men to give a prisoner hope, on the whole. He met Monza's eye, finally, reluctantly, with the haunted look of a man who knows what's coming.

'It's true then,' he whispered. 'You're alive.'

'Unlike your brother. I stabbed him through his throat then threw him out of the window.' The sharp knobble in Foscar's neck bobbed up and down as he swallowed. 'I had Mauthis poisoned. Ganmark run through with a ton of bronze. Faithful's stabbed, slashed, drowned and hung from a waterwheel. Still turning on it, for all I know. Gobba was lucky. I only smashed his hands, and his knees, and his skull to bonemeal with a hammer.' The list gave her grim nausea rather than grim satisfaction, but she forced her way through it. 'Of the seven men who were in that room when they murdered Benna, there's just your father left.' She slid the Calvez from its sheath, the gentle scraping of the blade as ugly as a child's scream. 'Your father . . . and you.'

The room was close, stale. Friendly's face was empty as a corpse's. Shivers leaned back against the wall beside her, arms folded, grinning.

'I understand.' Foscar came closer. Small, unwilling steps, but towards her still. He stopped no more than a stride away, and sank to his knees. Awkwardly, since his hands were tied behind him. The whole time his eyes were on hers. 'I'm sorry.'

'You're fucking *sorry*?' she squeezed through gritted teeth.

'I didn't know what was going to happen! I loved Benna!' His lip trembled, a tear ran down the side of his face. Fear, or guilt, or both. 'Your brother was like . . . a brother to me. I would never have wanted . . . that, for either of you. I'm sorry . . . for my part in it.' He'd had no part in it. She knew that. 'I just . . . I want to live!'

'So did Benna.'

'Please.' More tears trickled, leaving glistening trails down his cheeks. 'I just want to live.'

Her stomach churned, acid burning her throat and washing up into her watering mouth. Do it. She'd come all this way to do it, suffered all this and made all those others suffer just so she could do it. Her brother would have had no doubts, not then. She could almost hear his voice.

Do what you have to. Conscience is an excuse. Mercy and cowardice are the same.

It was time to do it. He had to die.

Do it now.

But her stiff arm seemed to weigh a thousand tons. She stared at Foscar's ashen face. His big, wide, helpless eyes. Something about him reminded her of Benna. When he was young. Before Caprile, before Sweet Pines, before they betrayed Cosca, before they joined up with the Thousand Swords, even. When she'd wanted just to make things grow. Long ago, that boy laughing in the wheat.

The point of the Calvez wobbled, dropped, tapped against the floor.

Foscar took a long, shuddering breath, closed his eyes, then opened them again, wet glistening in the corners. 'Thank you. I always knew you had a heart . . . whatever they said. Thank—'

Shivers' big fist crunched into his face and knocked him on his back, blood bubbling from his broken nose. He got out a shocked splutter before the Northman was on top of him, hands closing tight around his throat.

'You want to fucking live, eh?' hissed Shivers, teeth bared in a snarling grin, the sinews squirming in his forearms as he squeezed tighter and tighter. Foscar kicked helplessly, struggled silently, twisted his shoulders, face turning pink, then red, then purple. Shivers dragged up Foscar's head with both his hands, lifted it towards him, close enough to kiss, almost, then rammed it down against the stone flags with a sharp crack. Foscar's boots jerked, the chain between them rattling. Shivers worked his head to one side then the other as he shifted his hands around Foscar's neck for a better grip, tendons standing stark from their scabbed backs. He dragged him up again, no hurry, and rammed his head back down with a dull crunch. Foscar's tongue lolled out, one eyelid flickering, black blood creeping down from his hairline.

Shivers growled something in Northern, words she couldn't understand, lifted Foscar's head, smashed it down with all the care of a stonemason getting the details right. Again, and again. Monza watched, her mouth half-open, still holding weakly onto her sword, doing nothing. Not sure what she could do, or should do. Whether to stop him or help him. Blood dashed the rendered walls and the stone flags in spots and spatters. Over the pop and crackle of shattering bone she could hear a voice. Benna's voice, she thought for a minute, still whispering at her to do it. Then she realised it was Friendly, calmly counting the number of times Foscar's skull had been smashed into the stones. He got up to eleven.

Shivers lifted the prince's mangled head once more, hair all matted glistening black, then he blinked, and let it drop.

'Reckon that's got it.' He came slowly up to standing, one boot planted on either side of Foscar's corpse. 'Heh.' He looked at his hands, looked around for something to wipe them on, ended up rubbing them together, smearing black streaks of blood dry brown to his elbows. 'One more to the good.' He looked sideways at her with his one eye, corner of his mouth curled up in a sick smile. 'Six out o' seven, eh, Monza?'

'Six and one,' Friendly grunted to himself.

'All turning out just like you hoped.'

She stared down at Foscar, flattened head twisted sideways, crossed eyes goggling up at the wall, blood spreading out across the stone floor in a black puddle from his broken skull. Her voice seemed to come from a long way off, reedy thin. 'Why did you—'

'Why not?' whispered Shivers, coming close. She saw her own pale, scabbed, pinched-in face reflected, bent and twisted in that dead metal ball of an eye. 'What we came here for, ain't it? What we fought for all the day, down in the mud? I thought you was all for never turning back? Mercy and cowardice the same and all that hard talk you gave me. By the dead, Chief.' He grinned, the mass of scar across his face squirming and puckering, his good cheek all dotted with red. 'I could almost swear you ain't half the evil bitch you pretend to be.'

Shifting Sands

With the greatest of care not to attract undue attention, Morveer insinuated himself into the back of Duke Orso's great audience chamber. For such a vast and impressive room, it numbered but a few occupants. Perhaps a function of the difficult circumstances in which the great man found himself. Having catastrophically lost the most important battle in the history of Styria was bound to discourage visitors. Still, Morveer had always been drawn to employers in difficult circumstances. They tended to pay handsomely.

The Grand Duke of Talins was without doubt still a majestic presence. He sat upon a gilded chair, on a high dais, all in sable velvet trimmed with gold, and frowned down with regal fury over the shining helmets of half a dozen no less furious guardsmen. He was flanked by two men who could not have been more polar opposites. On the left a plump, ruddy-faced old fellow stood with a respectful but painful-looking bend to his hips, gold buttons about his chubby throat fastened to the point of uncomfortable tightness and, indeed, considerably beyond. He had ill-advisedly attempted to conceal his utter and obvious baldness by combing back and forth a few sad strands of wiry grey hair, cultivated to enormous length for this precise purpose. Orso's chamberlain. On the right, a curly-haired young man slouched with unexpected ease in travel-stained clothes, resting upon what appeared to be a long stick. Morveer had the frustrating sensation of having seen him somewhere before, but could not place him, and his relationship to the duke was, for now, a slightly worrying mystery.

The only other occupant of the chamber had his well-dressed back to Morveer, prostrate upon one knee on the strip of crimson carpet, clutching his hat in one hand. Even from the very back of the hall the gleaming sheen of sweat across his bald patch was most evident.

'What help from my son-in-law,' Orso was demanding in stentorian tones, 'the High King of the Union?'

The voice of the ambassador, for it appeared to be none other, had the whine of a well-whipped dog expecting further punishment. 'Your son-in-law sends his earnest regrets—'

'Indeed? But no soldiers! What would he have me do? Shoot his regrets at my enemies?'

'His armies are all committed in our unfortunate Northern wars, and a revolt in the city of Rostod causes further difficulties. The nobles, meanwhile, are reluctant. The peasantry are again restless. The merchants—'

'The merchants are behind on their payments. I see. If excuses were soldiers he would have sent a mighty throng indeed.'

'He is beset by troubles—'

'*He* is beset? He is? Are his sons murdered? Are his soldiers butchered? Are his hopes all in ruins?'

The ambassador wrung his hands. 'Your Excellency, he is spread thin! His regrets have no end, but—'

'But his help has no beginning! High King of the Union! A fine talker, and a goodly smile when the sun is up, but when the clouds come in, look not for shelter in Adua, eh? My intervention on his behalf was timely, was it not? When the Gurkish horde clamoured at his gates! But now I need his help . . . forgive me, Father, I am spread *thin*. Out of my sight, bastard, before your master's regrets cost you your tongue! Out of my sight, and tell the Cripple that I see his hand in this! Tell him I will whip the price from his twisted hide!' The grand duke's furious screams echoed out over the hurried footsteps of the ambassador, edging backwards as quickly as he dared, bowing profusely and sweating even more. 'Tell him I will be revenged!'

The ambassador genuflected his way past Morveer, and the double doors were heaved booming shut upon him.

'Who is that skulking at the back of the chamber?' Orso's voice was no more reassuring for its sudden calmness. Quite the reverse.

Morveer swallowed as he processed down the blood-red strip of carpet. Orso's eye held a look of the most withering command.

It reminded Morveer unpleasantly of his meeting with the head-master of the orphanage, when he was called to account for the dead birds. His ears burned with shame and horror at the memory of that interview, more even than his legs burned at the memory of his punishment. He swept out his lowest and most sycophantic bow, unfortunately spoiling the effect by rapping his knuckles against the floor in his nervousness.

'This is one Castor Morveer, your Excellency,' intoned the chamberlain, peering down his bulbous nose.

Orso leaned forwards. 'And what manner of a man is Castor Morveer?'

'A poisoner.'

'*Master* . . . Poisoner,' corrected Morveer. He could be as obsequious as the next man, when it was required, but he flatly insisted on his proper title. Had he not earned it, after all, with sweat, danger, deep wounds both physical and emotional, long study, short mercy and many, many painful reverses?

'Master, is it?' sneered Orso. 'And what great notables have you poisoned to earn the prefix?'

Morveer permitted himself the faintest of smiles. 'Grand Duchess Sefeline of Ospria, your Excellency. Count Binardi of Etrea, and both his sons, though their boat subsequently sank and they were never found. Ghassan Maz, Satrap of Kadir, and then, when further problems presented themselves, his successor Souvon-yin-Saul. Old Lord Isher, of Midderland, he was one of mine. Prince Amrit, who would have been heir to the throne of Muris—'

'I understood he died of natural causes.'

'What could be a more natural death for a powerful man than a dose of Leopard Flower administered into the ear by a dangling thread? Then Admiral Brant, late of the Murisian fleet, and his wife. His cabin boy too, alas, who happened by, a young life cut regrettably short. I would hate to prevail upon your Excellency's valuable time, the list is long indeed, most distinguished and . . . entirely *dead*. With your permission I will add only the most recent name upon it.'

Orso gave the most minute inclination of his head, sneering no longer, Morveer was pleased to note. 'One Mauthis, head of the Westport office of the Banking House of Valint and Balk.'

The duke's face had gone blank as a stone slab. 'Who was your employer for that last?'

'I make it a point of professionalism never to mention the names of my employers . . . but I believe these are *exceptional* circumstances. I was hired by none other than Monzcarro Murcatto, the Butcher of Caprile.' His blood was up now, and he could not resist a final flourish. 'I believe you are acquainted.'

'Some . . . what,' whispered Orso. The duke's dozen guards stirred ominously as if controlled directly by their master's mood. Morveer became aware that he might have gone a flourish too far, felt his bladder weaken and was forced to press his knees together. 'You infiltrated the offices of Valint and Balk in Westport?'

'Indeed,' croaked Morveer.

Orso glanced sideways at the man with the curly hair. 'I congratulate you on the achievement. Though it has been the cause of some considerable discomfort to me and my associates. Pray explain why I should not have you killed for it.'

Morveer attempted to pass it off with a vivacious chuckle, but it died a slow death in the chilly vastness of the hall. 'I . . . er . . . had no notion, of course, that you were in *any* way to be discomfited. None. Really, it was all due to a regrettable failing, or indeed a wilful oversight, deliberate dishonesty, *a lie*, even, on the part of my cursed assistant that I took the job in the first place. I should never have trusted that greedy bitch . . .' He realised he was doing himself no good by blaming the dead. Great men want living people to hold responsible, that they might have them tortured, hanged, beheaded and so forth. Corpses offer no recompense. He swiftly changed tack. 'I was but the tool, your Excellency. Merely the weapon. A weapon I now offer for your own hand to wield, as you see fit.' He bowed again, even lower this time, muscles in his rump, already sore from climbing the cursed mountainside to Fontezarmo, trembling in their efforts to prevent him from pitching on his face.

'You seek a new employer?'

'Murcatto proved as treacherous towards me as she did towards your illustrious Lordship. The woman is a snake indeed. Twisting, poisonous and . . . *scaly*,' he finished lamely. 'I was lucky to escape her toxic clutches with my life, and now seek redress. I am prepared to seek it *most* earnestly, and will not be denied!'

'Redress would be a fine thing for us all,' murmured the man with the curly hair. 'News of Murcatto's survival spreads through Talins like wildfire. Papers bearing her face on every wall.' A fact, Morveer had seen them as he passed through the city. 'They say you stabbed her through the heart but she lived, your Excellency.'

The duke snorted. 'Had I stabbed her, I would never have aimed for her heart. Without doubt her least vulnerable organ.'

'They say you burned her, drowned her, cut her into quarters and tossed them from your balcony, but she was stitched back together and lived again. They say she killed two hundred men at the fords of the Sulva. That she charged alone into your ranks and scattered them like chaff on the wind.'

'The stamp of Rogont's theatrics,' hissed the duke through gritted teeth. 'That bastard was born to be an author of cheap fantasies rather than a ruler of men. We will hear next that Murcatto has sprouted wings and given birth to the second coming of Euz!'

'I wouldn't be at all surprised. Bills are posted on every street corner proclaiming her an instrument of the Fates, sent to deliver Styria from your tyranny.'

'Tyrant, now?' The duke barked a grim chuckle. 'How quickly the wind shifts in the modern age!'

'They say she cannot be killed.'

'Do . . . they . . . indeed?' Orso's red-rimmed eyes swivelled to Morveer. 'What do you say, poisoner?'

'Your Excellency,' and he plunged down into the lowest of bows once more, 'I have fashioned a successful career upon the principle that there is *nothing* that lives that cannot be deprived of life. It is the remarkable ease of killing, rather than the impossibility of it, that has always caused me astonishment.'

'Do you care to prove it?'

'Your Excellency, I humbly entreat only the *opportunity*.' Morveer swept out another bow. It was his considered opinion that one could never bow too much to men of Orso's stamp, though he did reflect that persons of huge ego were a great drain on the patience of bystanders.

'Then here it is. Kill Monzcarro Murcatto. Kill Nicomo

Cosca. Kill Countess Cotarda of Affoia. Kill Duke Lirozio of Puranti. Kill First Citizen Patine of Nicante. Kill Chancellor Sotorius of Sipani. Kill Grand Duke Rogont, before he can be crowned. Perhaps I will not have Styria, but I will have revenge. On that you can depend.'

Morveer had been warmly smiling as the list began. By its end he was smiling no longer, unless one could count the fixed rictus he maintained across his trembling face only by the very greatest of efforts. It appeared his bold gambit had spectacularly over-succeeded. He was forcibly reminded of his attempt to dis-comfort four of his tormentors at the orphanage by placing Lankam salts in the water, which had ended, of course, with the untimely deaths of all the establishment's staff and most of the children too.

'Your Excellency,' he croaked, 'that is a significant quantity of murder.'

'And some fine names for your little list, no? The rewards will be equally significant, on that you can rely, will they not, Master Sulfur?'

'They will.' Sulfur's eyes moved from his fingernails to Morveer's face. Different-coloured eyes, Morveer now noticed, one green, one blue. 'I represent, you see, the Banking House of Valint and Balk.'

'Ah.' Suddenly, and with profound discomfort, Morveer placed the man. He had seen him talking with Mauthis in the banking hall in Westport but a few short days before he had filled the place with corpses. 'Ah. I really had not the *slightest* notion, you understand . . .' How he wished now that he had not killed Day. Then he could have noisily denounced her as the culprit and had something tangible with which to furnish the duke's dungeons. Fortunately, it seemed Master Sulfur was not seeking scapegoats. Yet.

'Oh, you were but the weapon, as you say. If you can cut as sharply on our behalf you have nothing to worry about. And besides, Mauthis was a terrible bore. Shall we say, if you are successful, the sum of one million scales?'

'One . . . million?' muttered Morveer.

'There is nothing that lives that cannot be deprived of life.'

Orso leaned forwards, eyes fixed on Morveer's face. 'Now get about it!'

Night was falling when they came to the place, lamps lit in the grimy windows, stars spilled out across the soft night sky like diamonds on a jeweller's cloth. Shenkt had never liked Affoia. He had studied there, as a young man, before he ever knelt to his master and before he swore never to kneel again. He had fallen in love there, with a woman too rich, too old and far too beautiful for him, and been made a whining fool of. The streets were lined not only with old pillars and thirsty palms, but with the bitter remnants of his childish shame, jealousy, weeping injustice. Strange, that however tough one's skin becomes in later life, the wounds of youth never close.

Shenkt did not like Affoia, but the trail had led him here. It would take more than ugly memories to make him leave a job half-done.

'That is the house?' It was buried in the twisting backstreets of the city's oldest quarter, far from the thoroughfares where the names of men seeking public office were daubed on the walls along with their great qualities and other, less complimentary words and pictures. A small building, with slumping lintels and a slumping roof, squeezed between a warehouse and a leaning shed.

'That's the house.' The beggar's voice was soft and stinking as rotten fruit.

'Good.' Shenkt pressed five scales into his scabby palm. 'This is for you.' He closed the man's fist around the money then held it with his own. 'Never come back here.' He leaned closer, squeezed harder. 'Not ever.'

He slipped across the cobbled street, over the wall before the house. His heart was beating unusually fast, sweat prickling his scalp. He crept across the overgrown front garden, old boots finding the silent spaces between the weeds, and to the lighted window. Reluctant, almost afraid, he peered through. Three children sat on a worn red carpet beside a small fire. Two girls and a boy, all with the same orange hair. They were playing with a brightly painted wooden horse on wheels. Clambering onto it, pushing each other around on it, pushing each other off it, to faint squeals of amusement. He squatted there, fascinated, and watched them.

Innocent. Unformed. Full of possibilities. Before they began to make their choices, or had their choices made for them. Before the doors began to close, and sent them down the only remaining path. Before they knelt. Now, for this briefest spell, they could be anything.

'Well, well. What have we here?'

She was crouching above him on the low roof of the shed, her head on one side, a line of light from a window across the way cutting hard down her face, strip of spiky red hair, red eyebrow, narrowed eye, freckled skin, corner of a frowning mouth. A chain hung gleaming down from one fist, cross of sharpened metal swinging gently on the end of it.

Shenkt sighed. 'It seems you have the better of me.'

She slid from the wall, dropped to the dirt and thumped smoothly down on her haunches, chain rattling. She stood, tall and lean, and took a step towards him, raising her hand.

He breathed in, slow, slow.

He saw every detail of her face: lines, freckles, faint hairs on her top lip, sandy eyelashes crawling down as she blinked.

He could hear her heart beating, heavy as a ram at a gate.

Thump . . . thump . . . thump . . .

She slid her hand around his head, and they kissed. He wrapped his arms about her, pressed her thin body tight against him, she tangled her fingers in his hair, chain brushing against his shoulders, dangling metal knocking lightly against the backs of his legs. A long, gentle, lingering kiss that made his body tingle from his lips to his toes.

She broke away. 'It's been a while, Cas.'

'I know.'

'Too long.'

'I know.'

She nodded towards the window. 'They miss you.'

'Can I . . .'

'You know you can.'

She led him to the door, into the narrow hallway, unbuckling the chain from her wrist and slinging it over a hook, cross-shaped

534

knife dangling. The oldest girl dashed out from the room, stopped dead when she saw him.

'It's me.' He edged slowly towards her, his voice strangled. 'It's me.' The other two children came out from the room, peering around their sister. Shenkt feared no man, but before these children, he was a coward. 'I have something for you.' He reached into his coat with trembling fingers.

'Cas.' He held out the carved dog, and the little boy with his name snatched it from his hand, grinning. 'Kande.' He put the bird in the cupped hands of the littlest girl, and she stared dumbly at it. 'For you, Tee,' and he offered the cat to the oldest girl.

She took it. 'No one calls me that any more.'

'I'm sorry it's been so long.' He touched the girl's hair and she flinched away, he jerked his hand back, awkward. He felt the weight of the butcher's sickle in his coat as he moved, and he stood sharply, took a step back. The three of them stared up at him, carved animals clutched in their hands.

'To bed now,' said Shylo. 'He'll still be here tomorrow.' Her eyes were on him, hard lines across the freckled bridge of her nose. 'Won't you, Cas?'

'Yes.'

She brushed their complaints away, pointed to the stairs. 'To bed.' They filed up slowly, step by step, the boy yawning, the younger girl hanging her head, the other complaining that she wasn't tired. 'I'll come sing to you later. If you're quiet until then, maybe your father will even hum the low parts.' The youngest of the two girls smiled at him, between the banisters at the top of the stairs, until Shylo pushed him into the living room and shut the door.

'They got so big,' he muttered.

'That's what they do. Why are you here?'

'Can't I just—'

'You know you can, and you know you haven't. Why are you . . .' She saw the ruby on his forefinger and frowned. 'That's Murcatto's ring.'

'She lost it in Puranti. I nearly caught her there.'

'Caught her? Why?'

He paused. 'She has become involved . . . in my revenge.'

'You and your revenge. Did you ever think you might be happier forgetting it?'

'A rock might be happier if it was a bird, and could fly from the earth and be free. A rock is not a bird. Were you working for Murcatto?'

'Yes. So?'

'Where is she?'

'You came here for that?'

'That.' He looked towards the ceiling. 'And them.' He looked her in the eye. 'And you.'

She grinned, little lines cutting into the skin at the corners of her eyes. It took him by surprise, how much he loved to see those lines. 'Cas, Cas. For such a clever bastard you're a stupid bastard. You always look for all the wrong things in all the wrong places. Murcatto's in Ospria, with Rogont. She fought in the battle there. Any man with ears knows that.'

'I didn't hear.'

'You don't listen. She's tight with the Duke of Delay, now. My guess is he'll be putting her in Orso's place, keep the people of Talins alongside when he reaches for the crown.'

'Then she'll be following him. Back to Talins.'

'That's right.'

'Then I will follow them. Back to Talins.' Shenkt frowned. 'I could have stayed there these past weeks, and simply waited for her.'

'That's what happens if you're always chasing things. Works better if you wait for what you want to come to you.'

'I was sure you'd have found another man by now.'

'I found a couple. They didn't stick.' She held out her hand to him. 'You ready to hum?'

'Always.' He took her hand, and she pulled him from the room, and through the door, and up the stairs.

VII
TALINS

'Revenge is a dish
best served cold'

Pierre Choderlos de Laclos

Rogont of Ospria was late to the field at Sweet Pines, but Salier of Visserine still enjoyed the weight of numbers and was too proud to retreat. Especially when the enemy was commanded by a woman. He fought, he lost, he ended up retreating anyway, and left the city of Caprile defenceless. Rather than face a certain sack, the citizens opened their gates to the Serpent of Talins in the hope of mercy.

Monza rode in, but most of her men she left outside. Orso had made allies of the Baolish, convinced them to fight with the Thousand Swords under their ragged standards. Fierce fighters, but with a bloody reputation. Monza had a bloody reputation of her own, and that only made her trust them less.

'I love you.'

'Of course you do.'

'I love you, but keep the Baolish out of town, Benna.'

'You can trust me.'

'I do trust you. Keep the Baolish out of town.'

She rode three hours as the sun went down, back to the rotting battlefield at Sweet Pines, to dine with Duke Orso and learn his plans for the close of the season.

'Mercy for the citizens of Caprile, if they yield to me entirely, pay indemnities and acknowledge me their rightful ruler.'

'Mercy, your Excellency?'

'You know what it is, yes?' She knew what it was. She had not thought he did. 'I want their land, not their lives. Dead men cannot obey. You have won a famous victory here. You shall have a great triumph, a procession through the streets of Talins.'

That would please Benna, at least. 'Your Excellency is too kind.'

'Hah. Few would agree with that.'

She laughed as she rode back in the cool dawn, and Faithful

539

laughed beside her. They talked of how rich the soil was, on the banks of the Capra, watching the good wheat shift in the wind.

Then she saw the smoke above the city, and she knew.

The streets were full of dead. Men, women, children, young and old. Birds gathered on them. Flies swarmed. A confused dog limped along beside their horses. Nothing else living showed itself. Empty windows gaped, empty doorways yawned. Fires still burned, whole rows of houses nothing but ash and tottering chimney stacks.

Last night, a thriving city. This morning, Caprile was hell made real.

It seemed Benna had not been listening. The Baolish had begun it, but the rest of the Thousand Swords — drunk, angry, fearing they would miss out on the easy pickings — had eagerly joined in. Darkness and dark company make it easy for even half-decent men to behave like animals, and there were few half-decent men among the scum Monza commanded. The boundaries of civilisation are not the impregnable walls civilised men take them for. As easily as smoke on the wind, they can dissolve.

Monza flopped down from her horse and puked Duke Orso's fine breakfast over the rubbish-strewn cobbles.

'Not your fault,' said Faithful, one big hand on her shoulder.

She shook him off. 'I know that.' But her rebellious guts thought otherwise.

'It's the Years of Blood, Monza. This is what we are.'

Up the steps to the house they'd taken, tongue rough with sick. Benna lay on the bed, fast asleep, husk pipe near one hand. She dragged him up, made him squawk, cuffed him one way and the other.

'Keep them out of town, I told you!' And she forced him to the window, forced him to look down into the bloodstained street.

'I didn't know! I told Victus . . . I think . . .' He slid to the floor, and wept, and her anger leaked away and left her empty. Her fault, for leaving him in charge. She could not let him shoulder the blame. He was a good man, and sensitive, and would not have borne it well. There was nothing she could do but kneel beside him, and hold him, and whisper soothing words while the flies buzzed outside the window.

'Orso wants to give us a triumph . . .'

Soon afterwards the rumours spread. The Serpent of Talins had ordered the massacre that day. Had urged the Baolish on and screamed for more. The Butcher of Caprile, they called her, and she did not deny it. People would far rather believe a lurid lie than a sorry string of accidents. Would far rather believe the world is full of evil than full of bad luck, selfishness and stupidity. Besides, the rumours served a purpose. She was more feared than ever, and fear was useful.

In Ospria they denounced her. In Visserine they burned her image. In Affoia and Nicante they offered a fortune to any man who could kill her. All around the Azure Sea they rang out the bells to her shame. But in Etrisani they celebrated. In Talins they lined the streets to chant her name, to shower her with flower petals. In Cesale they raised a statue in her honour. A gaudy thing, smothered with gold leaf that soon peeled. She and Benna, as they never looked, seated on great horses, frowning boldly towards a noble future.

That was the difference between a hero and a villain, a soldier and a murderer, a victory and a crime. Which side of a river you called home.

Return of the Native

Monza was far from comfortable.

Her legs ached, her arse was chafed raw from riding, her shoulder had stiffened up again so she was constantly twisting her head to one side like a demented owl in a futile attempt to loosen it. Whenever one source of sweaty agony would ease for a moment, another would flare up to plug the gap. Her prodding joke of a little finger seemed attached to a cord of cold pain, tightening relentlessly right to her elbow if she tried to use the hand. The sun was merciless in the clear blue sky, making her squint, niggling at the headache leaking from the coins that held her skull together. Sweat tickled her scalp, ran down her neck, gathered in the scars Gobba's wire had left and made them itch like fury. Her crawling skin was prickly, clammy, sticky. She cooked in her armour like offal in a can.

Rogont had her dressed up like some simpleton's notion of the Goddess of War, an unhappy collision of shining steel and embroidered silk that offered the comfort of full plate and the protection of a nightgown. It might all have been made to measure by Rogont's own armourer, but there was a lot more room for chest in her gold-chased breastplate than there was a need for. This, according to the Duke of Delay, was what people wanted to see.

And enough of them had turned out for the purpose.

Crowds lined the narrow streets of Talins. They squashed into windows and onto roofs to catch a glimpse of her. They packed into the squares and gardens in dizzying throngs, throwing flowers, waving banners, boiling over with hope. They shouted, bellowed, roared, squealed, clapped, stamped, hooted, competing with each other to be the first to burst her skull with their clamour. Sets of musicians had formed at street corners, would strike up martial tunes as she came close, brassy and blaring, clanging away behind her, merging with the off-key offering of the next impromptu band to form a mindless, murderous, patriotic din.

It was like the triumph after her victory at Sweet Pines, only she was older and even more reluctant, her brother was rotting in the mud instead of basking in the glory and her old enemy Rogont was at her back rather than her old friend Orso. Perhaps that was what history came down to, in the end. Swapping one sharp bastard for another was the best you could hope for.

They crossed the Bridge of Tears, the Bridge of Coins, the Bridge of Gulls, looming carvings of seabirds glaring angrily down at the procession as it crawled past, brown waters of the Etris sluggishly churning beneath them. Each time she rounded a corner another wave of applause would break upon her. Another wave of nausea. Her heart was pounding. Every moment, she expected to be killed. Blades and arrows seemed more likely than flowers and kind words, and far more deserved. Agents of Duke Orso, or his Union allies, or a hundred others with a private grudge against her. Hell, if she'd been in the crowd and seen some woman ride past dressed like this, she'd have killed her on general principle. But Rogont must have spread his rumours well. The people of Talins loved her. Or loved the idea of her. Or had to look like they did.

They chanted her name, and her brother's name, and the names of her victories. Afieri. Caprile. Musselia. Sweet Pines. The High Bank. The fords of the Sulva too. She wondered if they knew what they were cheering for. Places she'd left trails of corpses behind her. Cantain's head rotting on the gates of Borletta. Her knife in Hermon's eye. Gobba, hacked to pieces, pulled apart by rats in the sewers beneath their feet. Mauthis and his clerks with their poisoned ledgers, poisoned fingers, poisoned tongues. Ario and all his butchered revellers at Cardotti's, Ganmark and his slaughtered guards, Faithful dangling from the wheel, Foscar's head broken open on the dusty floor. Corpses by the cartload. Some of it she didn't regret, some of it she did. But none of it seemed like anything to cheer about. She winced up towards the happy faces at the windows. Maybe that was where she and these folk differed.

Maybe they just liked corpses, so long as they weren't theirs.

She glanced over her shoulder at her so-called allies, but they hardly gave her comfort. Grand Duke Rogont, the king-in-waiting, smiling to the crowds from a knot of watchful guards, a man whose love would last exactly as long as she was useful. Shivers, steel eye glinting, a man who'd turned under her tender touch from likeable optimist to maimed murderer. Cosca winked back at her – the world's least reliable ally and most unpredictable enemy, and he could still prove to be either one. Friendly . . . who knew what went on behind those dead eyes?

Further back rode the other surviving leaders of the League of Eight. Or Nine. Lirozio of Puranti, fine moustaches bristling, who'd slipped nimbly back into Rogont's camp after the very briefest of alliances with Orso. Countess Cotarda, her watchful uncle never far behind. Patine, First Citizen of Nicante, with his emperor's bearing and his ragged peasant's clothes, who had declined to share in the battle at the fords but seemed more than happy to share in the victory. There were even representatives of cities she'd sacked on Orso's behalf – citizens of Musselia and Etrea, a sly-eyed young niece of Duke Cantain's who'd suddenly found herself Duchess of Borletta, and appeared to be greatly enjoying the experience.

People she'd thought of as her enemies for so long she was having trouble making the adjustment, and by the looks on their faces when her eyes met theirs, so were they. She was the spider they had to suffer in their larder to rid them of their flies. And once the flies are dealt with, who wants a spider in their salad?

She turned back, sweaty shoulders prickling, tried to fix her eyes ahead. They passed along the endless curve of the seafront, gulls sweeping, circling, calling above. All the way her nose was full of that rotten salt tang of Talins. Past the boatyards, the half-finished hulls of two great warships sitting on the rollers like the skeletons of two beached and rotted whales. Past the rope-makers and the sail-weavers, the lumber-yards and the wood-turners, the brass-workers and the chain-makers. Past the vast and reeking fish-market, its flaking stalls empty, its galleries quiet for the first time maybe since the victory at Sweet Pines last emptied the buildings and filled the streets with savagely happy crowds.

Behind the multicoloured splatters of humanity the buildings were smothered with bills, as they had been in Talins more or less since the invention of the press. Old victories, warnings, incitements, patriotic bluster, endlessly pasted over by the new. The latest set carried a woman's face – stern, guiltless, coldly beautiful. Monza realised with a sick turning of her guts that it was meant to be hers, and beneath it, boldly printed: *Strength, Courage, Glory.* Orso had once told her that the way to turn a lie into the truth was to shout it often enough, and here was her self-righteous face, repeated over and over, plastered torn and dog-eared across the salt-stained walls. On the side of the next crumbling façade another set of posters, badly drawn and smudgily printed, had her awkwardly holding high a sword, beneath the legend: *Never Surrender, Never Relent, Never Forgive.* Daubed across the bricks above them in letters of streaky red paint tall as a man was one simple word:

Vengeance.

Monza swallowed, less comfortable than ever. Past the endless docks where fishing vessels, pleasure vessels, merchant vessels of every shape and size, from every nation beneath the sun, stirred on the waves of the great bay, cobwebs of rigging spotted with sailors up to watch the Snake of Talins take the city for her own.

Just as Orso had feared she would.

Cosca was entirely comfortable.

It was hot, but there was a soothing breeze wafting off the glittering sea, and one of his ever-expanding legion of new hats was keeping his eyes well shaded. It was dangerous, the crowd very likely containing more than one eager assassin, but for once there were several more hated targets than himself within easy reach. A drink, a drink, a drink, of course, that drunkard's voice in his head would never be entirely silent. But it was less a desperate scream now than a grumpy murmur, and the cheering was very definitely helping to drown it out.

Aside from the vague smell of seaweed it was just as it had been in Ospria, after his famous victory at the Battle of the Isles. When he had stood tall in his stirrups at the head of the column, acknowledging the applause, holding his hands up and shouting, 'Please, no!' when he meant, 'More, more!' It was Grand Duchess Sefeline, Rogont's aunt, who had basked in his reflected glory then, mere days before she tried to have him poisoned. Mere months before the tide of battle turned against her and she was poisoned herself. That was Styrian politics for you. It made him wonder, just briefly, why he was getting into it.

'The settings change, the people age, the faces swap one with another, but the applause is just the same – vigorous, infectious and so very short-lived.'

'Uh,' grunted Shivers. It seemed to be most of the Northman's conversation, now, but that suited Cosca well enough. In spite of occasional efforts to change, he had always vastly preferred talking to listening.

'I always hated Orso, of course, but I find little pleasure in his fall.' A towering statue of the fearsome Duke of Talins could be seen down a side street as they passed. Orso had ever been a keen patron to sculptors, provided they used him as their subject. Scaffolding had been built up its front, and now men clustered around the face, battering its stern features away gleefully with hammers. 'So soon, yesterday's heroes are shuffled off. Just as I was shuffled off myself.'

'Seems you've shuffled back.'

'My point precisely! We all are washed with the tide. Listen to them cheer for Rogont and his allies, so recently the most despicable slime on the face of the world.' He pointed out the fluttering papers pasted to the nearest wall, on which Duke Orso was displayed having his face pushed into a latrine. 'Only peel back this latest layer of bills and I'll wager you'll find others denouncing half this procession in the filthiest ways imaginable. I recall one of Rogont shitting onto a plate and Duke Salier tucking into the results with a fork. Another of Duke Lirozio trying to mount his horse. And when I say "mount" . . .'

'Heh,' said Shivers.

'The horse was not impressed. Dig through a few layers more and – I blush to admit – you'll find some condemning me as the blackest-hearted rogue in the Circle of the World, but now . . .' Cosca blew an extravagant kiss towards some ladies on a balcony, and they smiled, pointed, showed every sign of regarding him as their delivering hero.

The Northman shrugged. 'People got no weight to 'em down here. Wind blows 'em whatever way it pleases.'

'I have travelled widely,' if fleeing one war-torn mess after another qualified, 'and in my experience people are no heavier elsewhere.' He unscrewed the cap from his flask. 'Men can have all manner of deeply held beliefs about the world in general that they find most inconvenient when called upon to apply to their own lives. Few people let morality get in the way of expediency. Or even convenience. A man who truly believes in a thing beyond the point where it costs him is a rare and dangerous thing.'

'It's a special kind o' fool takes the hard path just 'cause it's the right one.'

Cosca took a long swallow from his flask, winced and scraped his tongue against his front teeth. 'It's a special kind of fool who can even tell the right path from the wrong. I've certainly never had that knack.' He stood in his stirrups, swept off his hat and waved it wildly in the air, whooping like a boy of fifteen. The crowds roared their approval back. Just as if he was a man worth cheering for. And not Nicomo Cosca at all.

So quietly that no one could possibly have heard, so softly that the notes were almost entirely in his mind, Shenkt hummed.

'Here she is!'

The pregnant silence gave birth to a storm of applause. People danced, threw up their arms, cheered with hysterical enthusiasm. People laughed and wept, celebrated as if their own lives might be changed to any significant degree by Monzcarro Murcatto being given a stolen throne.

It was a tide Shenkt had often observed in politics. There is a brief spell after a new leader comes to power, however it is achieved, during which they can do no wrong. A golden period in which people are blinded by their own hopes for something better. Nothing lasts for ever, of course. In time, and usually with alarming speed, the leader's flawless image grows tarnished with their subjects' own petty disappointments, failures, frustrations. Soon they can do no right. The people clamour for a new leader, that they might consider themselves reborn. Again.

But for now they cheered Murcatto to the heavens, so loud that, even though he had seen it all a dozen times before, Shenkt almost allowed himself to hope. Perhaps this would be a great day, the first of a great era, and he would be proud in after years to have had his part in it. Even if his part had been a dark one. Some men, after all, can only play dark parts.

'The Fates.' Beside him, Shylo's lip curled up with scorn. 'What does she look like? A fucking gold candlestick. A gaudy figurehead, gilded up to hide the rot.'

'I think she looks well.' Shenkt was glad to see her still alive, riding a black horse at the head of the sparkling column. Duke Orso might have been all but finished, his people hailing a new leader, his palace at Fontezarmo surrounded and under siege. None of that made the slightest difference. Shenkt had his work, and he would see it through to the end, however bitter. Just as he always did. Some stories, after all, are only suited to bitter endings.

Murcatto rode closer, eyes fixed ahead in an expression of the most bloody-minded resolve. Shenkt would have liked very much to step forwards, to brush the crowds aside, to smile, to hold out his hand to her. But there were altogether too many onlookers, altogether too many guards. The moment was coming when he would greet her, face to face.

For now he stood, as her horse passed by, and hummed.

So many people. Too many to count. If Friendly tried, it made him feel strange. Vitari's face jumped suddenly from the crowd, beside her a gaunt man with short, pale hair and a washed-out smile. Friendly stood in the stirrups but a waving banner swept across his sight and they were gone. A thousand other faces in a blinding tangle. He watched the procession instead.

If this had been Safety, and Murcatto and Shivers had been convicts, Friendly would have known without doubt from the look on the Northman's face that he wanted to kill her. But this was not Safety, more was the pity, and there were no rules here that Friendly understood. Especially once women entered the case, for they were a foreign people to him. Perhaps Shivers loved her, and that look of hungry rage was what love looked like. Friendly knew they had been fucking in Visserine, he had heard them at it enough, but then he thought she might have been fucking the Grand Duke of Ospria lately, and had no idea what difference that might make. Here was the problem.

Friendly had never really understood fucking, let alone love.

When he came back to Talins, Sajaam had sometimes taken him to whores, and told him it was a reward. It seemed rude to turn down a reward, however little he wanted it. To begin with he had trouble keeping his prick hard. Even later, the most enjoyment he ever got from the messy business was counting the number of thrusts before it was all over.

He tried to settle his jangling nerves by counting the hoofbeats of his horse. It seemed best that he avoid embarrassing confusions, keep his worries to himself and let things take the course they would. If Shivers did kill her, after all, it meant little enough to Friendly. Probably lots of people wanted to kill her. That was what happened when you made yourself conspicuous.

Shivers was no monster. He'd just had enough.

Enough of being treated like a fool. Enough of his good intentions fucking him in the arse. Enough of minding his conscience. Enough worrying on other people's worries. And most of all enough of his face itching. He grimaced as he dug at his scars with his fingernails.

Monza was right. Mercy and cowardice were the same. There were no rewards for good behaviour. Not in the North, not here, not anywhere. Life was an evil bastard, and gave to those who took what they wanted. Right was on the side of the most ruthless, the most treacherous, the most bloody, and the way all these fools cheered for her now was the proof of it. He watched her riding slowly up at the front, on her black horse, black hair stirring in the breeze. She'd been right about everything, more or less.

And he was going to murder her, pretty much just for fucking someone else.

He thought of stabbing her, cutting her, carving her ten different ways. He thought of the marks on her ribs, of sliding a blade gently between them. He thought of the scars on her neck, and how his hands would fit just right against them to throttle her. He guessed it would be good to be close to her one last time. Strange, that he should've saved her life so often, risked his own to do it, and now be thinking out the best way to put an end on it. It was like the Bloody-Nine told him once – love and hate have just a knife's edge between 'em.

Shivers knew a hundred ways to kill a woman that'd all leave her just as dead. It was where and when that were the problems. She was watchful all the time, now, expecting knives. Not from him, maybe, but from somewhere. There were plenty of 'em aimed at her besides his, no doubt. Rogont knew it, and was careful with her as a miser with his hoard. He needed her to bring all these people over to his side, always had men watching. So Shivers would have to wait, and pick his time. But he could show some patience. It was like Carlot said. Nothing done well is ever . . . rushed.

'Keep closer to her.'

'Eh?' None other than the great Duke Rogont, ridden up on his blind side. It took an effort for Shivers not to smash his fist right into the man's sneering, handsome face.

'Orso still has friends out there.' Rogont's eyes jumped nervously over the crowds. 'Agents. Assassins. There are dangers everywhere.'

'Dangers? Everyone seems so happy, though.'

'Are you trying to be funny?'

'Wouldn't know how to begin.' Shivers kept his face so slack Rogont couldn't tell whether he was being mocked or not.

'Keep closer to her! You are supposed to be her bodyguard!'

'I know what I am.' And Shivers gave Rogont his widest grin. 'Don't worry yourself on that score.' He dug his horse's flanks and urged on ahead. Closer to Monza, just like he'd been told. Close enough that he could see her jaw muscles clenched tight on the side of her face. Close enough, almost, that he could have pulled out his axe and split her skull.

'I know what I am,' he whispered. He was no monster. He'd just had enough.

The procession finally came to an end in the heart of the city, the square before the ancient Senate House. The mighty building's roof had collapsed centuries ago, its marble steps cracked and rooted with weeds. The carvings of forgotten gods on the colossal pediment had faded to a tangle of blobs, perches for a legion of chattering gulls. The ten vast pillars that supported it looked alarmingly out of true, streaked with droppings, stuck with flapping fragments of old bills. But the mighty relic still dwarfed the meaner buildings that had flourished around it, proclaiming the lost majesty of the New Empire.

A platform of pitted blocks thrust out from the steps and into the sea of people crowding the square. At one corner stood the weathered statue of Scarpius, four times the height of a man, holding out hope to the world. His outstretched hand had broken off at the wrist several hundred years ago and, in what must have been the most blatant piece of imagery in Styria, no one had yet bothered to replace it. Guardsmen stood grimly before the statue, on the steps, at the pillars. They wore the cross of Talins on their coats but Monza knew well enough they were Rogont's men. Perhaps Styria was meant to be one family now, but soldiers in Osprian blue might not have been well received here.

She slid from her saddle, strode down the narrow valley through the crowds. People strained against the guardsmen, calling to her, begging for blessings. As though touching her might do them any good. It hadn't done much to anyone else. She kept her eyes ahead, always ahead, jaw aching from being clenched tight, waiting for the blade, the arrow, the dart that would be the end of her. She'd happily have killed for the sweet oblivion of a smoke, but she was trying to cut back, on the killing and the smoking both.

Scarpius towered over her as she started up the steps, peering down out of the corners of his lichen-crusted eyes as if to say, *Is this bitch the best they could do?* The monstrous pediment loomed behind him, and she wondered if the hundred tons of rock balanced on those pillars might finally choose that moment to crash down and obliterate the entire leadership of Styria, herself along with them. No small part of her hoped that it would, and bring this sticky ordeal to a swift end.

A gaggle of leading citizens – meaning the sharpest and the greediest – had clustered nervously in the centre of the platform, sweating in their most expensive clothes, looking hungrily towards her like geese at a bowl of crumbs. They bowed as she and Rogont came closer, heads bobbing together in a way that suggested they'd been rehearsing. That somehow made her more irritated than ever.

'Get up,' she growled.

Rogont held his hand out. 'Where is the circlet?' He snapped his fingers. 'The circlet, the circlet!'

The foremost of the citizens looked like a bad caricature of wisdom – all hooked nose, snowy beard and creaky deep voice under a green felt hat like an upended chamber pot. 'Madam, my name is Rubine, nominated to speak for the citizens.'

'I am Scavier.' A plump woman whose azure bodice exposed a terrifying immensity of cleavage.

'And I am Grulo.' A tall, lean man, bald as an arse, not quite shouldering in front of Scavier but very nearly.

'Our two most senior merchants,' explained Rubine.

It carried little weight with Rogont. 'And?'

'And, with your permission, your Excellency, we were hoping to discuss some details of the arrangements—'

'Yes? Out with it!'

'As regards the title, we had hoped perhaps to steer away from nobility. Grand duchess smacks rather of Orso's tyranny.'

'We hoped . . .' ventured Grulo, waving a vulgar finger-ring, 'something to reflect the mandate of the common people.'

Rogont winced at Monza, as though the phrase 'common people' tasted of piss. 'Mandate?'

'President elect, perhaps?' offered Scavier. 'First citizen?'

'After all,' added Rubine, 'the previous grand duke is still, technically . . . alive.'

Rogont ground his teeth. 'He is besieged two dozen miles away in Fontezarmo like a rat in his hole! Only a matter of time before he is brought to justice.'

'But you understand the legalities may prove troublesome—'

'Legalities?' Rogont spoke in a furious whisper. 'I will soon be King of Styria, and I mean to have the Grand Duchess of Talins among those who crown me! I will be king, do you understand? Legalities are for other men to worry on!'

'But, your Excellency, it might not be seen as appropriate—'

For a man with a reputation for too much patience, Rogont's had grown very short over the last few weeks. 'How appropriate would it be if I was to, say, have you hanged? Here. Now. Along with every other reluctant bastard in the city. You could argue the legalities to each other while you dangle.'

The threat floated between them for a long, uncomfortable

moment. Monza leaned towards Rogont, acutely aware of the vast numbers of eyes fixed upon them. 'What we need here is a little unity, no? I've a feeling hangings might send the wrong message. Let's just get this done, shall we? Then we can all lie down in a dark room.'

Grulo carefully cleared his throat. 'Of course.'

'A long conversation to end where we began!' snapped Rogont. 'Give me the damn circlet!'

Scavier produced a thin golden band. Monza turned slowly to face the crowd.

'People of Styria!' Rogont roared behind her. 'I give you the Grand Duchess Monzcarro of Talins!' There was a slight pressure as he lowered the circlet onto her head.

And that simply she was raised to the giddy heights of power.

With a faint rustling, everyone knelt. The square was left silent, enough that she could hear the birds flapping and squawking on the pediment above. Enough that she could hear the spatters as some droppings fell not far to her right, daubing the ancient stones with spots of white, black and grey.

'What are they waiting for?' she muttered to Rogont, doing her best not to move her lips.

'Words.'

'Me?'

'Who else?'

A wave of dizzy horror broke over her. By the look of the crowd, she might easily have been outnumbered five thousand to one. But she had the feeling that, for her first action as head of state, fleeing the platform in terror might send the wrong message. So she stepped slowly forwards, as hard a step as she'd ever taken, struggling to get her tumbling thoughts in order, dig up words she didn't have in the splinter of time she did. She passed through Scarpius' great shadow and out into the daylight, and a sea of faces opened up before her, tilted up towards her, wide-eyed with hope. Their scattered muttering dropped to nervous whispering, then to eerie silence. She opened her mouth, still hardly knowing what might come out of it.

'I've never been one . . .' Her voice was a reedy squeak. She had to cough to clear it, spat the results over her shoulder then realised she definitely shouldn't have. 'I've never been one for speeches!' That much was obvious. 'Rather get right to it than talk about it! Born on a farm, I guess. We'll deal with Orso first! Rid ourselves of that bastard. Then . . . well . . . then the fighting's over.' A strange kind of murmur went through the kneeling crowd. No smiles, exactly, but some faraway looks, misty eyes, a few heads nodding. She was surprised by a longing tug in her own chest. She'd never really thought before that she'd wanted the fighting to end. She'd never known much else.

'Peace.' And that needy murmur rippled across the square again. 'We'll have ourselves a king. All Styria, marching one way. An end to the Years of Blood.' She thought of the wind in the wheat. 'Try to make things grow, maybe. Can't promise you a better world because, well, it is what it is.' She looked down awkwardly at her feet, shifted her weight from one leg to another. 'I can promise to do my best at it, for what that's worth. Let's aim at enough for everyone to get by, and see how we go.' She caught the eye of an old man, staring at her with teary-eyed emotion, lip quivering, hat clasped to his chest.

'That's all!' she snapped.

Any normal person would have been lightly dressed on a day so sticky warm, but Murcatto, with characteristic contrariness, had opted for full and, as it happened, ludicrously flamboyant armour. Morveer's only option, therefore, was to take aim at her exposed face. Still, a smaller target only presented the greater and more satisfying challenge for a marksman of his sublime skills. He took a deep breath.

To his horror she shifted at the crucial moment, looking down at the platform, and the dart missed her face by the barest whisker and glanced from one of the pillars of the ancient Senate House behind her.

'Damn it!' he hissed around the mouthpiece of his blowpipe, already fumbling in his pocket for another dart, removing its cap, sliding it gently into the chamber.

It was a stroke of ill fortune of the variety that had tormented Morveer since birth that, just as he was applying his lips to the pipe, Murcatto terminated her incompetent rhetoric with a perfunctory, 'That's all!' The crowd broke into rapturous applause, and his elbow was jogged by the enthusiastic clapping of a peasant beside the deep doorway in which he had secreted himself.

The lethal missile went well wide of its target and vanished into the heaving throng beside the platform. The man whose wild gesticulations had been responsible for his wayward aim looked about, his broad, greasy face puckering with suspicion. He had the appearance of a labourer, hands like rocks, the flame of human intellect barely burning behind his piggy eyes.

'Here, what are you—'

Curse the proletariat, Morveer's attempt was now quite foiled. 'My *profound* regrets, but could I prevail upon you to hold this for just a moment?'

'Eh?' The man stared down at the blowpipe pressed suddenly into his calloused hands. 'Ah!' As Morveer jabbed him in the wrist with a mounted needle. 'What the hell?'

'Thank you *ever* so much.' Morveer reclaimed the pipe and slid it into one of his myriad of concealed pockets along with the needle. It takes the vast majority of men a great deal of time to become truly incensed, usually following a predictable ritual of escalating threats, insults, posturing, jostling and so forth. Instantaneous action is entirely foreign to them. So the elbow-jogger was only now beginning to look truly angry.

'Here!' He seized Morveer by the lapel. 'Here . . .' His eyes took on a faraway look. He wobbled, blinked, his tongue hung out. Morveer took him under the arms, gasped at the sudden dead weight as the man's knees collapsed, and wrestled him to the ground, suffering an unpleasant twinge in his back as he did so.

'He alright?' someone grunted. Morveer looked up to see a half-dozen not dissimilar men frowning down at him.

'*Altogether* too much beer!' Morveer shouted over the noise, adding a false little chuckle. 'My companion here has become *quite* inebriated!'

'Inebri-what?' said one.

'Drunk!' Morveer leaned close. 'He was so very, *very* proud to have the great Serpent of Talins as the mistress of our fates! Are not we all?'

'Aye,' one muttered, utterly confused but partially mollified.

''Course. Murcatto!' he finished lamely, to grunts of approval from his simian comrades.

'Born among us!' shouted another, shaking his fist.

'Oh, *absolutely* so. Murcatto! Freedom! Hope! Deliverance from coarse stupidity! Here we are, friend!' Morveer grunted with effort as he wriggled the big man, now a big corpse, into the shadows of the doorway. He winced as he arched his aching back. Then, since the others were no longer paying attention, he slid away into the crowds, boiling with resentment all the way. It really was insufferable that these imbeciles should cheer so very enthusiastically for a woman who, far from being born among them, had been born on a patch of scrub on the very edge of Talinese territory where the border was notoriously flexible. A ruthless, scheming, lying, apprentice-seducing, mass-murdering, noisily fornicating peasant thief without a filigree shred of conscience, whose only qualifications for command were a sulky manner, a few victories against incompetent opposition, the aforementioned propensity to swift action, a fall down a mountain and the accident of a highly attractive face.

He was forced to reflect once again, as he had so often, that life was rendered immeasurably easier for the comely.

The Lion's Skin

A lot had changed since Monza last rode up to Fontezarmo, laughing with her brother. Hard to believe it was only a year ago. The darkest, maddest, most bloody year in a life made of them. A year that had taken her from dead woman to duchess, and might well still shove her back the other way.

It was dusk instead of dawn, the sun sinking behind them in the west as they climbed the twisting track. To either side of it, wherever the ground was anything close to flat, men had pitched tents. They sat in front of them in lazy groups by the flickering light of campfires – eating, drinking, mending boots or polishing armour, staring slack-faced at Monza as she clattered past.

She'd had no honour guard a year ago. Now a dozen of Rogont's picked men followed eagerly as puppies wherever she went. It was a surprise they didn't all try to tramp into the latrine after her. The last thing the king-in-waiting wanted was for her to get pushed off a mountain again. Not before she'd had the chance to help crown him, anyway. It was Orso she'd been helping to his crown twelve months ago, and Rogont her bitter enemy. For a woman who liked to stick, she'd slid around some in four seasons.

Back then she'd had Benna beside her. Now it was Shivers. That meant no talk at all, let alone laughter. His face was just a hard black outline, blind eye gleaming with the last of the fading light. She knew he couldn't see a thing through it, but still she felt like it was always fixed right on her. Even though he scarcely spoke, still he was always saying, *It should've been you.*

There were fires burning at the summit. Specks of light on the slopes, a yellow glow behind the black shapes of walls and towers, smudges of smoke hanging in the deep evening sky. The road switched back once more, then petered away altogether at a barricade made from three upended carts. Victus sat there on a field chair, warming his hands at a campfire, his collection of stolen chains gleaming round his neck. He grinned as she reined up her horse, and flourished out an absurd salute.

'The Grand Duchess of Talins, here in our slovenly camp! Your Excellency, we're all shame! If we'd had more time to prepare for your royal visit, we'd have done something about all the dirt.' And he spread his arms wide at the sea of churned-up mud, bare rock, broken bits of crate and wagon scattered around the mountainside.

'Victus. The embodiment of the mercenary spirit.' She clambered down from her saddle, trying not to let the pain show. 'Greedy as a duck, brave as a pigeon, loyal as a cuckoo.'

'I always modelled myself on the nobler birds. Afraid you'll have to leave the horses, we'll be going by trench from here. Duke Orso's a most ungracious host – he's taken to shooting catapults at any of his guests who show themselves.' He sprang up, slapping dust from the canvas he'd been sitting on, then holding one ring-encrusted hand out towards it. 'Perhaps I could have some of the lads carry you up?'

'I'll walk.'

He gave her a mocking leer. 'And a fine figure you'll appear, I've no doubt, though I would've thought you could've stretched to silk, given your high station.'

'Clothes don't make the person, Victus.' She gave his jewellery a mocking leer of her own. 'A piece of shit is still a piece of shit, however much gold you stick on it.'

'Oh, how we've missed you, Murcatto. Follow on, then.'

'Wait here,' she snapped at Rogont's guards. Having them behind her all the time made her look weak. Made her look like she needed them.

Their sergeant winced. 'His Excellency was most—'

'Piss on his Excellency. Wait here.'

She creaked down some steps made of old boxes and into the hillside, Shivers at her shoulder. The trenches weren't much different from the ones they'd dug around Muris, years ago – walls of hard-packed earth held back by odds and ends of timber, with that same smell of sickness, mould, damp earth and boredom. The trenches they'd lived in for the best part of six months, like rats in a sewer. Where her feet had started to rot, and Benna got the running shits so bad he lost a quarter of his weight and all his sense of humour. She even saw a few familiar faces as they threaded their way through ditch, tunnel and dugout – veterans who'd been fighting with the Thousand Swords for years. She nodded to them just as she used to when she was in charge, and they nodded back.

'You sure Orso's inside?' she called to Victus.

'Oh, we're sure. Cosca spoke to him, first day.'

Monza didn't draw much comfort from that idea. When Cosca started talking to an enemy he usually ended up richer and on the other side. 'What did those two bastards have to say to each other?'

'Ask Cosca.'

'I will.'

'We've got the place surrounded, don't worry about that. Trenches on three sides.' Victus slapped the earth beside them. 'If you can trust a mercenary to do one thing, it's dig himself a damn good hole to hide in. Then there's pickets down in the woods at the bottom of the cliff.' The woods where Monza had slid to a halt in the rubbish, broken to pulp, groaning like the dead in hell. 'And a wide selection of Styria's finest soldiery further out. Osprians, Sipanese, Affoians, in numbers. All set on seeing our old employer dead. There ain't a rat getting out without our say-so. But then if Orso wanted to run, he could've run weeks ago. He didn't. You know him better than anyone, don't you? You reckon he'll try and run now?'

'No,' she had to admit. He'd sooner die, which suited her fine. 'How about us getting in?'

'Whoever designed the bastard place knew what they were doing. Ground around the inner ward's way too steep to try anything.'

'I could've told you that. North side of the outer ward's your best chance at an assault, then try the inner wall from there.'

'Our very thoughts, but there's a gulf between thinking and doing, specially when high walls are part of the case. No luck yet.' Victus clambered up on a box and beckoned to her. Between two wicker screens, beyond a row of sharpened stakes pointing up the broken slope, she could see the nearest corner of the fortress. One of the towers was on fire, its tall roof fallen in leaving only a cone of naked beams wreathed in flames, notches of battlements picked out in red and yellow, black smoke belching into the dark blue sky. 'We set that tower to burning,' he pointed proudly towards it, 'with a catapult.'

'Beautiful. We can all go home.'

'Something, ain't it?' He led them through a long dugout smelling of damp and sour sweat, men snoring on pallets down both sides. ' "Wars are won not by one great action," ' intoning the words like a bad actor, ' "but many small chances." Weren't you always telling us that? Who was it? Stalicus?'

'Stolicus, you dunce.'

'Some dead bastard. Anyway, Cosca's got a plan, but I'll let him tell you himself. You know how the old man loves to put on a show.' Victus stopped at a hollow in the rock where four trenches came together, sheltered by a roof of gently flapping canvas and lit by a single rustling torch. 'The captain general said he'd be along. Feel free to make use of the facilities while you wait.' Facilities which amounted to dirt. 'Unless there's anything else, your Excellency?'

'Just one more thing.' He flinched in surprise as her spit spattered softly across his eye. 'That's from Benna, you treacherous little fuck.'

Victus wiped his face, eyes creeping shiftily to Shivers, then back to her. 'I didn't do nothing you wouldn't have done. Nothing your brother wouldn't have done, that's certain. Nothing you didn't both do to Cosca, and you owed him more than I owed you—'

'That's why you're wiping your face instead of trying to hold your guts in.'

'You ever think you might have brought this on yourself? Big ambitions mean big risks. All I've done is float with the current—'

Shivers took a sudden step forwards. 'Off you float, then, 'fore you get your throat cut.' Monza realised he had a knife out in one big fist. The one she'd given him the first day they met.

'Whoah there, big man.' Victus held up his palms, rings glittering. 'I'm on my way, don't worry.' He made a big show of turning and strutting off into the night. 'You two need to work on your tempers,' wagging one finger over his shoulder. 'No point getting riled up over every little thing. That'll only end in blood, believe me!'

It wasn't so hard for Monza to believe. Everything ended in blood, whatever she did. She realised she was left alone with Shivers, something she'd spent the last few weeks avoiding like the rot. She knew she should say something, take some sort of step towards making things square with him. They had their problems, but at least he was her man, rather than Rogont's. She might have need of someone to save her life in the coming days, and he was no monster, however he might look.

'Shivers.' He turned to her, knife still clutched tight, steel blade and steel eye catching the torch flame and twinkling the colours of fire. 'Listen—'

'No, you listen.' He bared his teeth, taking a step towards her.

'Monza! You came!' Cosca emerged from one of the trenches, arms spread wide. 'And with my favourite Northman!' He ignored the knife and shook Shivers warmly by his free hand, then grabbed Monza's shoulders and kissed her on both cheeks. 'I haven't had a chance to congratulate you on your speech. Born on a farm. A nice touch. Humble. And talk of peace. From you? It was like seeing a farmer express his hopes for famine. Even this old cynic couldn't help but be moved.'

'Fuck yourself, old man.' But she was secretly glad she didn't have to find the hard words now.

Cosca raised his brows. 'You try and say the right thing—'

'Some folk don't like the right thing,' said Shivers in his gravelly whisper, sliding his knife away. 'You ain't learned that yet?'

'Every day alive is a lesson. This way, comrades! Just up ahead we can get a fine view of the assault.'

'You're attacking? Now?'

'We tried in daylight. Didn't work.' It didn't look like darkness was working any better. There were wounded men lining the next trench – grimaces, groans, bloody bandages. 'Wherever is my noble employer, his Excellency Duke Rogont?'

'In Talins.' And Monza spat into the dirt. There was plenty of it for the purpose. 'Preparing for his coronation.'

'So soon? He is aware Orso's still alive, I suppose, and by all indications will be for some time yet? Isn't there a saying about selling the lion's skin before he's killed?'

'I've mentioned it. Many times.'

'I can only imagine. The Serpent of Talins, counselling caution to the Duke of Delay. Sweet irony!'

'Some good it's done. He's got every carpenter, clothier and jeweller in the city busy at the Senate House, making it ready for the ceremony.'

'Sure the bloody place won't fall in on him?'

'We can hope,' muttered Shivers.

'It will bring to mind proud shadows of Styria's Imperial past, apparently,' said Monza.

Cosca snorted. 'That or the shameful collapse of Styria's last effort at unity.'

'I've mentioned that too. Many times.'

'Ignored?'

'Getting used to it.'

'Ah, hubris! As a long-time sufferer myself I quickly recognise the symptoms.'

'You'll like this one, then.' Monza couldn't stop herself sneering. 'He's importing a thousand white songbirds from distant Thond.'

'Only a thousand?'

'Symbol of peace, apparently. They'll be released over the crowd when he rises to greet them as King of Styria. And admirers from all across the Circle of the World – counts, dukes, princes and the God of the fucking Gurkish too for all I know – will applaud his gigantic opinion of himself, and fall over themselves to lick his fat arse.'

Cosca raised his brows. 'Do I detect a souring of relations between Talins and Ospria?'

'There's something about crowns that makes men act like fools.'

'One takes it you've mentioned that too?'

'Until my throat's sore, but surprisingly enough, he doesn't want to hear it.'

'Sounds quite the event. Shame I won't be there.'

Monza frowned. 'You won't?'

'Me? No, no, no. I'd only lower the tone. There are concerns about some shady deal done for the Dukedom of Visserine, would you believe.'

'Never.'

'Who knows how these far-fetched rumours get started? Besides, someone needs to keep Duke Orso company.'

She worked her tongue sourly round her mouth and spat again. 'I hear the two of you have been chatting already.'

'No more than small talk. Weather, wine, women, his impending destruction, you know the sort of thing. He said he would have my head. I replied I quite understood his enthusiasm, as I find it hugely useful myself. I was firm yet amusing throughout, in fact, while he was, in all honesty, somewhat peevish.' Cosca waved one long finger around. 'The siege, possibly, has him out of sorts.'

'Nothing about you changing sides, then?'

'Perhaps that would have been his next topic, but we were somewhat interrupted by some flatbow fire and an abortive assault upon the walls. Perhaps it will come up when we next take tea together?'

The trench opened into a dugout mostly covered with a plank ceiling, almost too low to stand under. Ladders leaned against the right-hand wall, ready for men to climb and join the attack. A good three score of armed and armoured mercenaries knelt ready to do just that. Cosca went bent over between their ranks, slapping backs.

'Glory, boys, glory, and a decent pay-off!'

Their frowns turned to grins, they tapped their weapons against their shields, their helmets, their breastplates, sending up an approving rattle.

'General!'

'The captain general!'

'Cosca!'

'Boys, boys!' He chuckled, thumping arms, shaking hands, giving out lazy salutes. All as far from her style of command as could've been. She'd had to stay cold, hard, untouchable, or there would have been no respect. A woman can't afford the luxury of being friendly with the men. So she'd let Benna do the laughing for her. Probably why the laughter had been thin on the ground since Orso killed him.

'And up here is my little home from home.' Cosca led them up a ladder and into a kind of shed built from heavy logs, lit by a pair of flickering lamps. There was a wide opening in one wall, the setting sun casting its last glare over the dark, flat country to the west. Narrow windows faced towards the fortress. A stack of crates took up one corner, the captain general's chair sat in another. Beside it a table was covered with a mess of scattered cards, half-eaten sweetmeats and bottles of varying colour and fullness. 'How goes the fight?'

Friendly sat cross-legged, dice between his knees. 'It goes.'

Monza moved to one of the narrow windows. It was almost night, now, and she could barely see any sign of the assault. Perhaps the odd flicker of movement at the tiny battlements, the odd glint of metal in the light of the bonfires scattered across the rocky slopes. But she could hear it. Vague shouting, faint screaming, clattering metal, floating indistinctly on the breeze.

Cosca slid into the battered captain general's chair and rattled the bottles by putting his muddy boots up on the table. 'We four, together again! Just like Cardotti's House of Leisure! Just like Salier's gallery! Happy times, eh?'

There was the creaking swoosh of a catapult released and a blazing missile sizzled overhead, shattered against the great foremost tower of the fortress, sending up a gout of flame, shooting out arcs of glittering embers. The dull flare illuminated ladders against the stonework, tiny figures crawling up them, steel glimmering briefly then fading back into the black.

'You sure this is the best time for jokes?' Monza muttered.

'Unhappy times are the best for levity. You don't light candles in the middle of the day, do you?'

Shivers was frowning up the slope towards Fontezarmo. 'You really think you've a chance of carrying those walls?'

'Those? Are you mad? They're some of the strongest in Styria.'

'Then why—'

'Bad form to just sit outside and do nothing. They have ample stocks of food, water, weapons and, worst of all, loyalty. They might last months in there. Months during which Orso's daughter, the Queen of the Union, might prevail upon her reluctant husband to send aid.' Monza wondered whether the king learning that his wife preferred women would make any difference . . .

'How's watching your men fall off a wall going to help?' asked Shivers.

Cosca shrugged. 'It will wear down the defenders, deny them rest, keep them guessing and distract them from any other efforts we might make.'

'Lot of corpses for a distraction.'

'Wouldn't be much of a distraction without them.'

'How do you get men to climb the ladders for that?'

'Sazine's old method.'

'Eh?'

Monza remembered Sazine displaying the money to the new boys, all laid out in sparkling stacks. 'If the walls fall, a thousand scales to the first man on the battlements, a hundred each to the next ten who follow him.'

'Provided they survive to collect the bounty,' Cosca added. 'If the task's impossible, they'll never collect, and if they do, well, you achieved the impossible for two thousand scales. It ensures a steady flow of willing bodies up the ladders, and has the added benefit of weeding the bravest men out of the company to boot.'

Shivers looked even more baffled. 'Why would you want to do that?'

' "Bravery is the dead man's virtue," ' Monza muttered. ' "The wise commander never trusts it." '

'Verturio!' Cosca slapped one leg. 'I do love an author who can make death funny! Brave men have their uses but they're damned unpredictable. Worrying to the herd. Dangerous to bystanders.'

'Not to mention potential rivals for command.'

'Altogether safest to cream them off,' and Cosca mimed the action with a careless flick of two fingers. 'The moderately cowardly make infinitely better soldiers.'

Shivers shook his head in disgust. 'You people got a pretty fucking way of making war.'

'There is no pretty way of making war, my friend.'

'You said a distraction,' cut in Monza.

'I did.'

'From what?'

There was a sudden fizzing sound and Monza saw fire out of

the corner of her eye. A moment later the heat of it washed across her cheek. She spun, the Calvez already part-drawn. Ishri was draped across the crates behind them, sprawled out lazily as an old cat in the sun, head back, one long, thin, bandaged leg dangling from the edge of the boxes and swinging gently back and forth.

'Can't you ever just say hello?' snapped Monza.

'Where would be the fun in that?'

'Do you have to answer every question with another?'

Ishri pressed one hand to her bandaged chest, black eyes opening wide. 'Who? Me?' She rolled something between her long finger and thumb, a little black grain, and flicked it with uncanny accuracy into the lamp beside Shivers. It went up with a flash and sizzle, cracking the glass hood and spraying sparks. The Northman stumbled away, cursing, flicking embers off his shoulder.

'Some of the men have taken to calling it Gurkish sugar.' Cosca smacked his lips. 'Sounds sweeter, to my ear, than Gurkish fire.'

'Two dozen barrels,' murmured Ishri, 'courtesy of the Prophet Khalul.'

Monza frowned. 'For a man I've never met he likes us a lot.'

'Better yet . . .' The dark-skinned woman slithered from the boxes like a snake, waves running through her body from shoulders down to hips as if she had no bones in her, arms trailing after. 'He hates your enemies.'

'No better basis for an alliance than mutual loathing.' Cosca watched her contortions with an expression stuck between distrust and fascination. 'It's a brave new age, my friends. Time was you had to dig for months, hundreds of strides of mine, tons of wood for props, fill it up with straw and oil, set it on fire, run like merry hell, then half the time it wouldn't even bring the walls down. This way, all you need do is sink a shaft deep enough, pack the sugar in, strike a spark and—'

'Boom,' sang Ishri, up on her toes and stretching to her fingertips.

'Ker-blow,' returned Cosca. 'It's how everyone's conducting sieges these days, apparently, and who am I to ignore a trend . . .' He flicked dust from his velvet jacket. 'Sesaria's a genius at mining. He brought down the bell tower at Gancetta, you know. Somewhat before schedule, admittedly, and a few men did get caught in the collapse. Did I ever tell you—'

'If you bring the wall down?' asked Monza.

'Well, then our men pour through the breach, overwhelm the stunned defenders and the outer ward will be ours. From the gardens within we'll have level ground to work with and room to bring our numbers to bear. Carrying the inner wall should be a routine matter of ladders, blood and greed. Then storm the palace and, you know, keep it traditional. I'll get my plunder and you'll get—'

'My revenge.' Monza narrowed her eyes at the jagged outline of the fortress. Orso was in there, somewhere. Only a few hundred strides away. Perhaps it was the night, the fire, the heady mixture of darkness and danger, but some of that old excitement was building in her now. That fierce fury she'd felt when she hobbled from the bone-thief's crumbling house and into the rain. 'How long until the mine's ready?'

Friendly looked up from his dice. 'Twenty-one days and six hours. At the rate they're going.'

'A shame.' Ishri pushed out her bottom lip. 'I so love fireworks. But I must go back to the South.'

'Tired of our company already?' asked Monza.

'My brother was killed.' Her black eyes showed no sign of emotion. 'By a woman seeking vengeance.'

Monza frowned, not sure if she was being mocked or not. 'Those bitches find a way of doing damage, don't they?'

'But always to the wrong people. My brother is the lucky one, he is with God. Or so they tell me. It is the rest of my family that suffer. We must work the harder now.' She swung herself smoothly down onto the ladder, let her head fall sideways. Uncomfortably far, until it was resting on the top rung. 'Try not to get yourselves killed. I do not intend that my hard work here be wasted.'

'Your wasted work will be my first concern when they cut my throat.' Nothing but silence. Ishri was gone.

'Looks like you've run out of brave men,' came Shivers' croak.

Cosca sighed. 'We didn't have many to begin with.' The remnants of the assault were scrambling back down the rocky mountainside in the flickering light of the fires above. Monza could just make out the last ladder toppling down, perhaps a dot or two flailing as they fell from it. 'But don't worry. Sesaria's still digging. Just a matter of time until Styria stands united.' He slid a metal flask from his inside pocket and unscrewed the cap. 'Or until Orso sees sense, and offers me enough to change sides again.'

She didn't laugh. Perhaps she wasn't meant to. 'Maybe you should try sticking to one side or the other.'

'Why ever would anyone do that?' Cosca raised his flask, took a sip and smacked his lips in satisfaction. 'It's a war. There is no right side.'

Preparation

Regardless of the nature of a great event, the key to success is always preparation. For three weeks, all Talins had been preparing for the coronation of Grand Duke Rogont. Meanwhile, Morveer had been preparing for an attempt to murder him and his allies. So much work had been put into both schemes that, now the day for their consummation had finally arrived, Morveer almost regretted that the success of one could only mean the spectacular failure of the other.

In all honesty, he had been having little success achieving even the smallest part of Duke Orso's immensely ambitious commission to murder no fewer than six heads of state and a captain general. His abortive attempt on the life of Murcatto the day of her triumphant return to Talins, resulting in nothing more than at least one poisoned commoner and a sore back, had been but the first of several mishaps.

Gaining entrance to one of Talins' finest dressmakers through a loose rear window, he had secreted a lethal Amerind thorn within the bodice of an emerald-green gown meant for Countess Cotarda of Affoia. Alas, Morveer's expertise in dressmaking was most limited. Had Day been there she would no doubt have pointed out that the garment was twice too large for their waifish victim. The countess emerged resplendent at a soirée that very evening, her emerald-green gown a sensation. Morveer afterwards discovered, much to his chagrin, that the exceedingly large wife of one of Talins' leading merchants had also commissioned a green gown from that dressmaker, but was prevented from attending the event by a mysterious illness. She swiftly deteriorated and, alas, expired within hours.

Five nights later, after an uncomfortable afternoon spent hiding inside a heap of coal and breathing through a tube, he had succeeded in loading Duke Lirozio's oysters with spider venom.

Had Day been with him in the kitchen she might have suggested they aim for a more basic foodstuff, but Morveer could not resist the most noteworthy dish. The duke, alas, had felt queasy after a heavy lunch and took only a little bread. The shellfish were administered to the kitchen cat, now deceased.

The following week, posing once more as the Purantine wine-merchant Rotsac Reevrom, he insinuated himself into a meeting to discuss trade levies chaired by Chancellor Sotorius of Sipani. During the meal he struck up lively conversation with one of the ancient statesman's aides on the subject of grapes and was able, much to his delight, deftly to brush the top of Sotorius' withered ear with a solution of Leopard Flower. He had sat back with great enthusiasm to observe the rest of the meeting, but the chancellor had steadfastly refused to die, showing, in fact, every sign of being in the most rude health. Morveer could only assume that Sotorius observed a morning routine not dissimilar to his own, and possessed immunities to who knew how many agents.

But Castor Morveer was not a man to be put off by a few reverses. He had suffered many in life, and saw no reason to alter his formula of commendable stoicism simply because the task seemed impossible. With the coronation almost upon him, he had therefore chosen to focus on the principal targets: Grand Duke Rogont and his lover, Morveer's hated ex-employer, now the Grand Duchess of Talins, Monzcarro Murcatto.

It would have been a rank understatement to say that no expense had been spared to ensure the coronation lived long in Styria's collective memory. The buildings enclosing the square had all been freshly painted. The stone platform where Murcatto had administered her fumbling speech, and where Rogont planned to soak up the adulation of his subjects as King of Styria, had been surfaced with gleaming new marble and adorned with a gilded rail. Workmen crawled on ropes and scaffolds across the looming frontage of the Senate House, garlanding the ancient stonework with fresh-cut white flowers, transforming the sullen edifice into a mighty temple to the Grand Duke of Ospria's vanity.

Working in dispiriting solitude, Morveer had appropriated the clothes, toolbox and documentation of a journeyman carpenter who had arrived in the city looking for piecework, and hence would be missed by nobody. Yesterday he had infiltrated the Senate House in this ingenious disguise to reconnoitre the scene and formulate a plan. While doing so, just as a bonus, he had carried out some challenging jointing work to a balustrade with almost conspicuous skill. Truly, he was a loss to carpentry, but he had in no way lost sight of the fact that his primary profession remained murder. Today he had returned to execute his audacious scheme. And to execute Grand Duke Rogont, both together.

'Afternoon,' he grunted to one of the guards as he passed through the vast doorway along with the rest of the labourers returning from lunch, crunching carelessly at an apple with the surly manner he had often observed in common men on their way to labour. Caution first, always, but when attempting to fool someone, supreme confidence and simplicity was the approach that bore the ripest fruit. He excited, in fact, no attention whatsoever from the guards, either at the gate or at the far end of the vestibule. He stripped the core of his apple and tossed it into his workbox, with only the faintest maudlin moment spent reflecting on how much Day would have enjoyed it.

The Senate House was open to the sky, the great dome having collapsed long centuries ago. Three-quarters of the tremendous circular space was filled with concentric arcs of seating, enough for two thousand or more of the world's most honoured spectators. Each marble step was lower than the one behind, so that they formed a kind of theatre, with a space before them where the senators of old had once risen to make their grand addresses. A round platform had been built there now, of inlaid wood painted in meticulous detail with gilded wreaths of oak leaves about a gaudy golden chair.

Great banners of vividly coloured Suljuk silk hung down the full height of the walls, some thirty strides or more, at a cost Morveer hardly dared contemplate, one for each of the great cities of Styria. The azure cloth of Ospria, marked with the white tower, had pride of place, directly behind the central platform. The cross of Talins and the cockleshell of Sipani flanked it upon either side. Arranged evenly about the rest of the circumference were the bridge of Puranti, the red banner of Affoia, the three bees of Visserine, the six rings of Nicante, and the giant flags of Muris, Etrisani, Etrea, Borletta and Caprile besides. No one, it seemed, was to be excluded from the proud new order, whether they desired membership or not.

The whole space crawled with men and women hard at work. Tailors plucked at the hangings and the miles of white cushions provided for the comfort of the most honoured guests. Carpenters sawed and hammered at the platform and the stairways. Flower-sellers scattered the unused floor with a carpet of white blossom. Chandlers carefully positioned their waxen wares in endless rows, teetered on ladders to reach a hundred sconces. All overseen by a regiment of Osprian guardsmen, halberds and armour buffed to mirror brightness.

For Rogont to choose to be crowned here, in the ancient heart of the New Empire? The arrogance was incalculable, and if there was one quality Morveer could not abide, it was arrogance. Humility, after all, cost nothing. He concealed his profound disgust and made his way nonchalantly down the steps, affecting the self-satisfied swagger of the working commoner, weaving through the other tradesmen busy among the curving banks of seating.

At the back of the great chamber, perhaps ten strides above the ground, were two small balconies in which, he believed, scribes had once recorded the debates beneath. Now they were adorned by two immense portraits of Duke Rogont. One showed him stern and manful, heroically posed with sword and armour. The other depicted his Excellency in pensive mood, attired as a judge, holding book and compass. The master of peace and war. Morveer could not suppress a mocking smirk. Up there, in one of those two balconies, would be the fitting spot from which to shoot a dart lethal enough to deflate that idiot's swollen head and puncture his all-vaulting ambitions. They were reached by narrow stairways from a small, unused chamber, where records had been kept in ancient—

He frowned. Though it stood open, a heavy door, thick oak intricately bound and studded with polished steel, had been installed across the entrance of the anteroom. He in no way cared for such an alteration at this late stage. Indeed his first instinct was simply to place caution first and quietly depart, as he had often done before when circumstances appeared to shift. But men did not secure their place in history with caution alone. The venue, the challenge, the potential rewards were too great to let slip on account of a new door. History was breathing upon his neck. For tonight only his name would be audacity.

He strode past the platform, where a dozen decorators were busily applying gilt paint, and to the door. He swung it one way then the other, lips pursed discerningly as if checking the smooth workings of its hinges. Then, with the swiftest and least conspicuous of glances to ensure he was unobserved, he slipped through.

There were neither windows nor lamps within, the only light in the vaulted chamber crept through the door or down the two coiling stairways. Empty boxes and barrels were scattered in disorderly heaps about the walls. He was just deciding which balcony to choose as his shooting position when he heard voices approaching the door. He slid quickly on his side into the narrow space behind a stack of crates, squeaked as he picked up a painful splinter in his elbow, remembered his workbox just in time and fished it after him with one foot. A moment later the door squealed open and scraping boots entered the room, men groaning as though under a dolorous load.

'By the Fates, it's heavy!'

'Set it here!' A noisy clatter and squeal of metal on stone. 'Bastard thing.'

'Where's the key?'

'Here.'

'Leave it in the lock.'

'And what, pray, is the purpose of a lock with the key in it?'

'To present no obstacle, idiot. When we bring the damn case out there in front of three thousand people, and his Excellency tells us to open it up, I don't want to be looking at you and asking where the key is, and you find you dropped the fucker somewhere. See what I mean?'

'You've a point.'

'It'll be safer in here, in a barred room with a dozen guards at the door, than in your dodgy pockets.'

'I'm convinced.' There was a gentle rattle of metal. 'There. Satisfied?'

Several sets of footsteps clattered away. There was the heavy clunk of the door being swung shut, the clicking of locks turned, the squealing of a bar, then silence. Morveer was sealed into a room with a dozen guards outside. But that alone struck no fear into a man of his exceptional fortitude. When the vital moment came, he would lower a cord from one of the balconies and hope to slip away while every eye was focused on Rogont's spectacular demise. With the greatest of care to avoid any further splinters, he wriggled out from behind the crates.

A large case had been placed in the centre of the floor. A work of art in itself, fashioned from inlaid wood, bound with bands of filigree silver, glimmering in the gloom. Plainly it contained something of great importance to the coming ceremony. And since chance had provided him the key . . .

He knelt, turned it smoothly in the lock and with gentle fingers pushed back the lid. It took a great deal to impress a man of Morveer's experience, but now his eyes widened, his jaw dropped and sweat prickled at his scalp. The yellow sheen of gold almost warmed his skin, yet there was something more in his reaction than appreciation of the beauty, the symbolic significance or even the undoubted value of the object before him. Something teasing at the back of his mind . . .

Inspiration struck like lightning, making every hair upon his body suddenly stand tall. An idea of such scintillating brilliance, yet such penetrating simplicity, that he found himself almost in fear of it. The magnificent daring, the wonderful economy, the perfectly fitting irony. He only wished Day had lived to appreciate his genius.

Morveer triggered the hidden catch in his workman's box and removed the tray carrying the carpenter's equipment, revealing the carefully folded silken shirt and embroidered jacket in which he would make his escape. His true tools lay beneath. He carefully pulled on the gloves – lady's gloves of the finest calfskin, for they offered the least resistance to the dextrous operation of his fingers – and reached for the brown glass jar. He reached for it with some trepidation, for it contained a contact venom of his own devising which he called Preparation Number Twelve. There would be no repetition of his error with Chancellor

Sotorius, for this was a poison so deadly that not even Morveer himself could develop the slightest immunity to it.

He carefully unscrewed the cap – caution first, always – and, taking up an artist's brush, began to work.

Rules of War

Cosca crept down the tunnel, knees and back aching fiercely from bending almost double, snatched breath echoing on the stale air. He had become far too accustomed to no greater exertions than sitting around and working his jaw over the last few weeks. He swore a silent oath to take exercise every morning, knowing full well he would never keep it even until tomorrow. Still, it was better to swear an oath and never follow through than not even to bother with the oath. Wasn't it?

His trailing sword scratched soil from the dirt walls with every step. Should have left the bloody thing behind. He peered down nervously at the glittering trail of black powder that snaked off into the shadows, holding his flickering lamp as far away as possible, for all it was made of thick glass and weighty cast iron. Naked flames and Gurkish sugar made unhappy companions in a confined space.

He saw flickering light ahead, heard the sounds of someone else's laboured breath, and the narrow passageway opened out into a chamber lit by a pair of guttering lamps. It was no bigger than a good-sized bedroom, walls and ceiling of scarred rock and hard-packed earth, held up by a web of suspect-looking timbers. More than half the room, or the cave, was taken up by large barrels. A single Gurkish word was painted on the side of each one. Cosca's Kantic did not extend far beyond ordering a drink, but he recognised the characters for fire. Sesaria was a great dark shape in the gloom, long ropes of grey hair hanging about his face, beads of sweat glistening on his black skin as he strained at a keg.

'It's time,' said Cosca, his voice falling flat in the dead air under the mountain. He straightened up with great relief, was hit with a dizzy rush of blood to the head and stumbled sideways.

'Watch!' screeched Sesaria. 'What you're doing with that lamp, Cosca! A spark in the wrong place and the pair of us'll be blown to heaven!'

'Don't let that worry you.' He regained control of his feet. 'I'm not a religious man, but I very much doubt anyone will be letting either of us near heaven.'

'Blown to hell, then.'

'A much stronger possibility.'

Sesaria grunted as he ever so gingerly shifted the last of the barrels up tight to the rest. 'All the others out?'

'They should be back in the trenches by now.'

The big man wiped his hands on his grimy shirt. 'Then we're ready, General.'

'Excellent. These last few days have positively crawled. It's a crime, when you think about how little time we get, that a man should ever be bored. When you're lying on your deathbed, I expect you regret those weeks wasted more than your worst mistakes.'

'You should have said if you had nothing pressing. We could have used your help digging.'

'At my age? The only place I'll be moving soil is on the latrine. And even that's a lot more work than it used to be. What happens now?'

'I hear it only gets harder.'

'Very good. I meant with the mine.'

Sesaria pointed to the trail of black powder, grains gleaming in the lamplight, stopping well short of the nearest keg. 'That leads to the entrance to the mine.' He patted a bag at his belt. 'We join it up to the barrels, leave plenty of extra at the end to make sure it takes. We get to the mouth of the tunnel, we set a spark to one end, then—'

'The fire follows it all the way to the barrels and . . . how big will the explosion be?'

Sesaria shook his head. 'Never seen a quarter as much powder used at one time. That and they keep mixing it stronger. This new stuff . . . I have a worry it might be too big.'

'Better a grand gesture than a disappointing one.'

'Unless it brings the whole mountain down on us.'

'It could do that?'

'Who knows what it'll do?'

Cosca considered the thousands of tons of rock above their heads without enthusiasm. 'It's a little late for second thoughts. Victus has his picked men ready for the assault. Rogont will be king tonight, and he's expecting to honour us with his majestic presence at dawn, and very much inside the fortress so he can order the final attack. I'm damned if I'm going to spend my morning listening to that fool whine at me. Especially with a crown on.'

'You think he'll wear it, day to day?'

Cosca scratched thoughtfully at his neck. 'Do you know, I've no idea. But it's somewhat beside the point.'

'True.' Sesaria frowned at the barrels. 'Doesn't seem right, somehow. You dig a hole, you touch a torch to some dust, you run and—'

'Pop,' said Cosca.

'No need for thinking. No need for courage. No way to fight, if you're asking me.'

'The only good way to fight is the one that kills your enemy and leaves you with the breath to laugh. If science can simplify the process, well, so much the better. Everything else is flimflam. Let's get started.'

'I hear my captain general and obey.' Sesaria pulled the bag from his belt, bent down and started carefully tipping powder out, joining the trail up to the barrels. 'Got to think about how you'd feel, though, haven't you?'

'Have you?'

'One moment you're going about your business, the next you're blasted to bits. Never get to even look your killer in his face.'

'No different from giving others the orders. Is killing a man with powder any worse than getting someone else to stab him with a spear? When exactly did you last look a man in the face?' Not when he'd happily helped stab Cosca in the back at Afieri, that was sure.

Sesaria sighed, powder trickling out across the ground. 'True, maybe. But sometimes I miss the old days, you know. Back when Sazine was in charge. Seemed like a different world, then. A more honest world.'

Cosca snorted. 'You know as well as I do there wasn't a dirty trick this side of hell Sazine would have balked at using. That old miser would have blown the world up if he thought a penny would fall out.'

'Daresay you've the truth of it. Doesn't seem fair, though.'

'I never realised you were such an enthusiast for fair.'

'It's no deal-breaker, but I'd rather win a fair fight than an unfair one.' He upended the bag, the last powder sliding out and leaving a glittering heap right against the side of the nearest barrel. 'Leaves a better taste, somehow, fighting by some kind of rules.'

'Huh.' Cosca clubbed him across the back of the head with his lamp, sending up a shower of sparks and knocking Sesaria sprawling on his face. 'This is war. There are no rules.' The big man groaned, shifted, struggled weakly to push himself up. Cosca leaned down, raised the lamp high and bashed him on the skull again with a crunching of breaking glass, knocked him flat, embers sizzling in his hair. A little closer to the powder than was comfortable, perhaps, but Cosca had always loved to gamble.

He had always loved triumphant rhetoric too, but time was a factor. So he turned for the shadowy passageway and hurried down it. A dozen cramped strides and he was already breathing hard again. A dozen more and he thought he caught the faintest glimmer of daylight up the tunnel. He knelt down, chewing at his lip. He was far from sure how fast the trail would burn once it was lit.

'Good thing I always loved to gamble . . .' He carefully began to unscrew the broken cage around the lamp. It was stuck.

'Shit.' He strained at it, fingers slipping, but it must have got bent when he clubbed Sesaria. 'Bastard thing!' He shifted his grip, growled as he twisted with all his force. The top popped off suddenly, he fumbled both halves, the lamp dropped, he tried to catch it, missed, it hit the floor, bounced, guttered and went out, sinking the passageway into inky darkness.

'Fucking . . . shit!' His only option was to retrace his steps and get one of the lamps from the end of the tunnel. He took a few steps, one hand stretched out in front of him, fishing in the black. A beam caught him right in the face, snapped his head back, mouth buzzing, salty with blood. 'Gah!'

He saw light, shook his throbbing head, strained into the darkness. Lamplight, catching the grain of the props, the stones and roots in the walls, making the snaking trail of powder glisten. Lamplight, and unless he had completely lost his bearings, it was coming from where he had left Sesaria.

Bringing his sword seemed suddenly to have been a stroke of genius. He slid it gently from its sheath with a reassuring ring of metal, had to work his elbow this way and that in the narrow space to get it pointing forwards, accidentally stuck the ceiling with the point and caused a long rivulet of soil to pour gently down onto his bald patch. All the while the light crept closer.

Sesaria appeared around the bend, lamp in one big fist, a line of blood creeping down his forehead. They faced one other for a moment, Cosca crouching, Sesaria bent double.

'Why?' grunted the big man.

'Because I make a point of never letting a man betray me twice.'

'I thought you were all business.'

'Men change.'

'You killed Andiche.'

'Best moment of the last ten years.'

Sesaria shook his head, as much puzzled as angry and in pain. 'Murcatto was the one took your chair, not us!'

'Entirely different matter. Women can betray me as often as they please.'

'You always did have a blind spot for that mad bitch.'

'I'm an incurable romantic. Or maybe I just never liked you.'

Sesaria slid a heavy knife out in his free hand. 'You should've stabbed me back there.'

'I'm glad I didn't. Now I get to use another clever line.'

'Don't suppose you'd consider putting that sword away and fighting knife to knife?'

Cosca gave a cackle. 'You're the one who likes things fair. I tried to kill you by clubbing you from behind then blowing you up, remember? Stabbing you with a sword will give me no sleepless nights.' And he lunged.

In such a confined space, being a big man was a profound disadvantage. Sesaria almost entirely filled the narrow tunnel, which made him, fortunately, more or less impossible to miss.

He managed to steer the clumsy jab away with his knife, but it still pricked him in the shoulder. Cosca pulled back for another thrust, squawked as he caught his knuckles on the earth wall. Sesaria swung his heavy lamp at him and Cosca flopped away, slipped and went over on one knee. The big man scrambled forwards, raising the knife. His fist scraped on the ceiling, bringing down a shower of earth, his knife thudded deep into a beam above. He mouthed some curse in Kantic, wincing as he struggled to drag the blade free. Cosca righted himself and made another clumsy lunge. Sesaria's eyes bulged as the point punctured his shirt and slid smoothly through his chest.

'There!' Cosca snarled in his face. 'Do you get . . . my point?'

Sesaria lurched forwards, groaning bloody drool, face locked in a desperate grimace, the blade sliding inexorably through him until the hilt got tangled with his sticky shirt. He seized hold of Cosca and toppled over, bearing him down on his back, the pommel of the sword digging savagely into his stomach and driving all his breath out in a creaking, 'Ooooooooof.'

Sesaria curled back his lips to show red teeth. 'You call . . . *that* . . . a clever line?' He smashed his lamp down into the trail of powder beside Cosca's face. Glass shattered, flame leaped up, there was a fizzling pop as the powder caught, the heat of it near to burning Cosca's cheek. He struggled with Sesaria's great limp body, struggled to untwist his fingers from the gilded basketwork of his sword, desperately tried to wrestle the big corpse sideways. His nose was full of the acrid reek of Gurkish sugar, snapping sparks moving off slowly down the passage.

He finally dragged himself free, clambered up and ran for the entrance, breath wheezing in his chest, one hand trailing along the dirt wall, knocking against the props. An oval of daylight appeared, wobbled steadily closer. He gave vent to a foolish giggle as he wondered whether it would be this moment or the next that saw the rock he was tottering through a mile in the sky. He burst out into open air.

'Run!' he screeched at no one, flinging his hands wildly around. 'Run!' He pounded down the hillside, tripped, fell, rolled head over heels, bounced painfully from a rock, struggled up and carried on scrambling in a cloud of dust, loose stones clattering around him. The wicker shields that marked the nearest trench crept closer and he charged towards them, screaming madly at the top of his voice. He flung himself onto his face, slid along in the dirt, crashed between two screens and headlong down into the trench in a shower of loose soil.

Victus stared at him as he struggled to right himself. 'What the—'

'Take cover!' wailed Cosca. All around him armour rattled as men shrank down into their trenches, raised their shields over their heads, clapped their gauntleted hands over their ears, squeezed their eyes tight shut in anticipation of an explosion to end the world. Cosca jammed himself back against the hard-packed earth, teeth squeezed together, clasping his hands around his skull.

The silent moments stretched out.

Cosca prised one eye open. A bright-blue butterfly fluttered heedlessly down, circled widdershins around the cowering mercenaries and came peacefully to rest on the blade of a spear. Victus himself had his helmet pushed right down over his face. Now he slowly tipped it back to display an expression of some confusion.

'What the hell happened? Is the fuse lit? Where's Sesaria?'

A sudden image formed in Cosca's mind of the trail of powder sputtering out, of Victus' men creeping into the murky darkness, lamps raised, their light falling across Sesaria's corpse, impaled on a sword with unmistakable gilded basketwork. 'Erm . . .'

The very faintest of tremors touched the earth at Cosca's back. A moment later there was a thunderous detonation, so loud that it sent pain lancing through his head. The world went suddenly, entirely silent but for a faint, high-pitched whine. The earth shook. Wind ripped and eddied along the trench, tearing at his hair and nearly dragging him over. A cloud of choking dust filled the air, nipping at his lungs and making him cough. Gravel rained down from the sky, he gasped as he felt it sting at his arms, at his scalp. He cowered like a man caught out in a hurricane, every muscle tensed. For how long, he was not sure.

Cosca opened his eyes, dumbly uncurled his aching limbs and got weakly to his feet. The world was a ghost-place of silent fog. The land of the dead, surely, men and equipment no more than phantoms in the murk. The mist began to clear. He rubbed at his ears but the whining continued. Others got up, staring around, faces caked with grey dirt. Not far away someone lay still in a puddle in the bottom of a trench, his helmet stoved in by a chunk of rock, steered by the fickle Fates directly onto his head. Cosca peered over the lip of the trench, blinked up towards the summit of the mountain, straining through the gradually settling dust.

'Oh.' The wall of Fontezarmo appeared undamaged, the outline of towers and battlements still very much present against the lead-white sky. A vast crater had been blown from the rock, but the great round tower directly above it still clung stubbornly to the edge, even slightly overhanging empty space. It seemed for a moment to be perhaps the most crushing anticlimax of Cosca's life, and there had been many.

Then, in dreamlike silence and with syrupy slowness, that central tower leaned, buckled, fell in on itself and collapsed into the yawning crater. A huge section of wall to either side of it was dragged after, all folding up and dissolving into rubble under its own weight. A man-made landslide of hundreds of tons of stone rolled, bounced, crashed down towards the trenches.

'Ah,' said Cosca, silently.

For a second time men flung themselves on their faces, covered their heads, prayed to the Fates or whichever of a range of gods and spirits they did or did not believe in for deliverance. Cosca stayed standing, staring fascinated as a giant chunk of masonry perhaps ten tons in weight hurtled down the slope directly towards him, bouncing, spinning, flinging pieces of stone high into the air, all without the slightest sound but for perhaps a vague crunching, like footsteps on gravel. It came to an eventual stop no more than ten strides distant, rocked gently to one side and the other, and was still.

A second cloud of dust had plunged the trench into choking gloom, but as it gradually faded Cosca could see the vast breach left in the outer wall of Fontezarmo, no fewer than two hundred strides across, the crater beneath it now choked with settling rubble. A second tower at its edge leaned at an alarming angle, like a drunken man peering over a cliff, ready at any moment to topple into emptiness.

He saw Victus stand beside him, raise his sword and scream. The word didn't sound much louder than if he had spoken it.

'Charge.'

Men clambered, somewhat dazed, from the trenches. One took a couple of wobbling steps and fell on his face. Others stood there, blinking. Still others began to head uncertainly uphill. More followed, and soon there were a few hundred men scrambling through the rubble towards the breach, weapons and armour shining dully in the watery sun.

Cosca was left alone in the trench with Victus, both of them coated with grey dust.

'Where's Sesaria?' The words thudding dully through the whine in Cosca's ears.

His own voice was a weird burble. 'He wasn't behind me?'

'No. What happened?'

'An accident. An accident . . . as we came out.' It wasn't difficult to force out a tear, Cosca was covered head to toe in knocks and bruises. 'I dropped my lamp! Dropped it! Set off the trail of powder halfway down!' He seized Victus by his fluted breastplate. 'I told him to run with me, but he stayed! Stayed . . . to put it out.'

'He stayed?'

'He thought he could save us both!' Cosca put one hand over his face, voice choked with emotion. 'My fault! All my fault. He truly was the best of us.' He wailed it at the sky. 'Why? Why? Why do the Fates always take the best?'

Victus' eyes flickered down to Cosca's empty scabbard, then back up to the great crater in the hillside, the yawning breach above it. 'Dead, eh?'

'Blown to hell,' whispered Cosca. 'Baking with Gurkish sugar can be a dangerous business.' The sun had come out. Above them, Victus' men were clambering up the sides of the crater and into the breach in a twinkling tide, apparently entirely unopposed. If any defenders had survived the blast, they were in no mood to fight. It seemed the outer ward of Fontezarmo was theirs. 'Victory. At least Sesaria's sacrifice was not in vain.'

'Oh, no.' Victus looked sideways at him through narrowed eyes. 'He'd have been proud.'

One Nation

The echoing grumble of the crowd on the other side of the doors grew steadily louder, and the churning in Monza's guts grew with it. She tried to rub away the niggling tension under her jaw. It did no good.

But there was nothing to do except wait. Her entire role in tonight's grand performance was to stand there with a straight face and look like the highest of nobility, and Talins' best dressmakers had done all the hard work in making that ludicrous lie seem convincing. They'd given her long sleeves to cover the scars on her arms, a high collar to cover the scars on her neck, gloves to render her ruined hand presentable. They'd been greatly relieved they could keep her neckline low without horrifying Rogont's delicate guests. It was a wonder they hadn't cut a great hole out of the back to show her arse – it was about the only other patch of her skin without a mark across it.

Nothing could be seen that might spoil the perfection of Duke Rogont's moment of history. No sword, certainly, and she missed the weight of it like a missing limb. She wondered when was the last time she'd stepped out without a blade in easy reach. Not in the meeting of the Council of Talins she'd attended the day after being lifted to her new station.

Old Rubine had suggested she had no need to wear a sword in the chamber. She replied she'd worn one every day for twenty years. He'd politely pointed out that neither he nor his colleagues carried arms, though they were all men and hence better suited. She asked him what she'd use to stab him with if she left her sword behind. No one was sure whether she was joking or not. But they didn't ask again.

'Your Excellency.' One of the attendants had oozed over and now offered her a silky bow. 'Your Grace,' and another to Countess Cotarda. 'We are about to begin.'

'Good,' snapped Monza. She faced the double doors, shifted her shoulders back and her chin up. 'Let's get this fucking pantomime over with.'

She had no time to spare. Every waking moment of the last three weeks – and she'd scarcely slept since Rogont jammed the circlet on her head – she'd spent struggling to drag the state of Talins out of the cesspit she'd fought so hard to shove it into.

Keeping in mind Bialoveld's maxim – *any successful state is supported by pillars of steel and gold* – she'd dug out every cringing bureaucrat she could find who wasn't besieged in Fontezarmo along with their old master. There'd been discussions about the Talinese army. There wasn't one. Discussions about the treasury. It was empty. The system of taxation, the maintenance of public works, the preservation of security, the administration of justice, all dissolved like cake in a stream. Rogont's presence, or that of his soldiers anyway, was all that was keeping Talins from anarchy.

But Monza had never been put off by a wind in the wrong direction. She'd always had a knack for reckoning a man's qualities, and picking the right one for a given job. Old Rubine was pompous as a prophet, so she made him high magistrate. Grulo and Scavier were the two most ruthless merchants in the city. She didn't trust either, so she made them joint chancellors, and set each one to dream up new taxes, compete in their collection while keeping one jealous eye on the other.

Already they were wringing money from their unhappy colleagues, and already Monza had spent it on arms.

Three long days into her unpromising rule, an old sergeant called Volfier had arrived in the city, a man almost laughably hardbitten, and nearly as scarred as she was. Refusing to surrender, he'd led the twenty-three survivors of his regiment back from the rout at Ospria and all the way across Styria with arms and honour intact. She could always use a man that bloody-minded, and set him to rounding up every veteran in the city. Paying work was thin on the ground and he already had two companies of volunteers, their glorious charge to escort the tax collectors and make sure not a copper went missing.

She'd marked Duke Orso's lessons well. Gold, to steel, to more gold – such was the righteous spiral of politics. Resistance, apathy and scorn from all quarters only made her shove harder. She took a perverse satisfaction in the apparent impossibility of the task, the work pushed the pain to one side, and the husk with it, and kept her sharp. It had been a long, long time since she'd made anything grow.

'You look . . . very beautiful.'

'What?' Cotarda had glided up silently beside her and was offering a nervous smile. 'Oh. Likewise,' grunted Monza, barely even looking.

'White suits you. They tell me I'm too pale for white.' Monza winced. Just the kind of mindless twittering she had no stomach for tonight. 'I wish I was like you.'

'Some time in the sun would do it.'

'No, no. Brave.' Cotarda looked down at her pale fingers, twisting them together. 'I wish I was brave. They tell me I'm powerful. One would have thought being powerful would mean one need not be scared of anything. But I'm afraid all the time. Especially at *events*.' The words spilled out of her to Monza's mounting discomfort. 'Sometimes I can't move for the weight of it. All the fear. I'm such a disappointment. What can I do about that? What would you do?'

Monza had no intention of discussing her own fears. That would only feed them. But Cotarda blathered on regardless.

'I've no character at all, but where does one get character from? Either you have it or you don't. You have. Everyone says you have. Where did you get it? Why don't I have any? Sometimes I think I'm cut out of paper, just acting like a person. They tell me I'm an utter coward. What can I do about that? Being an utter coward?'

They stared at each other for a long moment, then Monza shrugged. 'Act like you're not.'

The doors were pulled open.

Musicians somewhere out of sight struck up a stately refrain as she and Cotarda stepped out into the vast bowl of the Senate House. Though there was no roof, though the stars would soon show in the blue-black sky above, it was hot. Hot, and clammy as a tomb, and the perfumed stink of flowers caught at Monza's tight throat and made her want to retch. Thousands of candles burned in the darkness, filling the great arena with creeping

587

shadows, making gilt glimmer, gems glitter, turning the hundreds upon hundreds of smiling faces that soared up on all sides into leering masks. Everything was outsize – the crowd, the rustling banners behind them, the venue itself. Everything was overdone, like a scene from a lurid fantasy.

A hell of a lot of effort just to watch one man put on a new hat.

The audience were a varied lot. Styrians made up the bulk, rich and powerful men and women, merchants and minor nobility from across the land. A smattering of famous artists, diplomats, poets, craftsmen, soldiers – Rogont wanted no one excluded who might reflect some extra glory onto him. Guests from abroad occupied most of the better seats, down near the front, come to pay their respects to the new King of Styria, or to try to wangle some advantage from his elevation, at least. There were merchant captains of the Thousand Isles with golden hoops through their ears. There were heavy-bearded Northmen, bright-eyed Baolish. There were natives of Suljuk in vivid silks, a pair of priestesses from Thond where they worshipped the sun, heads shaved to yellow stubble. There were three nervous-seeming Aldermen of Westport. The Union, unsurprisingly, was notable by its utter absence, but the Gurkish delegation had willingly spread out to fill their space. A dozen ambassadors from the Emperor Uthman-ul-Dosht, heavy with gold. A dozen priests from the Prophet Khalul, in sober white.

Monza walked through them all as if they weren't there, shoulders back, eyes fixed ahead, the cold sneer on her mouth she'd always worn when she was most terrified. Lirozio and Patine approached with equal pomposity down a walkway opposite. Sotorius waited by the chair that was the golden centrepiece of the entire event, leaning heavily on a staff. The old man had sworn he'd be consigned to hell before he walked down a ramp.

They reached the circular platform, gathering under the expectant gaze of several thousand pairs of eyes. The five great leaders of Styria who'd enjoy the honour of crowning Rogont, all dressed with a symbolism that a mushroom couldn't have missed. Monza was in pearly white, with the cross of Talins across her chest in sparkling fragments of black crystal. Cotarda wore Affoian scarlet. Sotorius had golden cockleshells around the hem of his black gown, Lirozio the bridge of Puranti on his gilded cape. They were like bad actors representing the cities of Styria in some cheap morality play, except at vast expense. Even Patine had shed any pretence at humility, and swapped his rough-spun peasant cloth for green silk, fur and sparkling jewels. Six rings were the symbol of Nicante, but he must have been sporting nine at the least, one with an emerald the size of Friendly's dice.

At close quarters, none of them looked particularly pleased with their role. Like a group who'd agreed, while blind drunk, to jump into the freezing sea in the morning but now, with the sober dawn, were thinking better of it.

'Well,' grunted Monza, as the musicians brought their piece to an end and the last notes faded. 'Here we are.'

'Indeed.' Sotorius swept the murmuring crowd with rheumy eyes. 'Let us hope the crown is large. Here comes the biggest head in Styria.'

An ear-splitting fanfare blasted out from behind. Cotarda flinched, stumbled, would've fallen if Monza hadn't seized her elbow on an instinct. The doors at the very back of the hall were opened, and as the blaring sound of trumpets faded a strange singing began, a pair of voices, high and pure, floating out over the audience. Rogont stepped smiling through into the Senate House, and his guests broke out into well-organised applause.

The king-in-waiting, all in Osprian blue, looked about him with humble surprise as he began to descend the steps. All this, for me? You shouldn't have! When of course he'd planned every detail himself. Monza wondered for a moment, and not for the first time, whether Rogont would turn out to be a far worse king than Orso might've been. No less ruthless, no more loyal, but a lot more vain, and less sense of humour every day. He pressed favoured hands in his, laying a generous palm on a lucky shoulder or two as he passed. The unearthly singing serenaded him as he came through the crowd.

'Can I hear spirits?' muttered Patine, with withering scorn.

'You can hear boys with no balls,' replied Lirozio.

Four men in Osprian livery unlocked a heavy door behind the platform and passed inside, came out shortly afterwards struggling under the weight of an inlaid case. Rogont made a swift pass around the front row, pressing the hands of a few chosen ambassadors, paying particular attention to the Gurkish delegation and stretching the applause to breaking point. Finally he mounted the steps to the platform, smiling the way the winner of a vital hand of cards smiles at his ruined opponents. He held his arms out to the five of them. 'My friends, my friends! The day is finally here!'

'It is,' said Sotorius, simply.

'Happy day!' sang Lirozio.

'Long hoped for!' added Patine.

'Well done?' offered Cotarda.

'My thanks to you all.' Rogont turned to face his guests, silenced their clapping with a gentle motion of his hands, swept his cloak out behind him, lowered himself into his chair and beckoned Monza over. 'No congratulations from you, your Excellency?'

'Congratulations,' she hissed.

'As graceful as always.' He leaned closer, murmuring under his breath. 'You did not come to me last night.'

'Other commitments.'

'Truly?' Rogont raised his brows as though amazed that anything could possibly be more important than fucking him. 'I suppose a head of state has many demands upon her time. Well.' He waved her scornfully away.

Monza ground her teeth. At that moment, she would've been more than willing to piss on him.

The four porters set down their burden behind the throne, one of them turned the key in the lock and lifted the lid with a showy flourish. A sigh went up from the crowd. The crown lay on purple velvet inside. A thick band of gold, set all around with a row of darkly gleaming sapphires. Five golden oak leaves sprouted from it, and at the front a larger sixth curled about a monstrous, flashing diamond, big as a chicken's egg. So large Monza felt a strange desire to laugh at it.

With the expression of a man about to clear a blocked latrine with his hand, Lirozio reached into the case and grasped one of the golden leaves. A resigned shrug of the shoulders and Patine did the same. Then Sotorius and Cotarda. Monza took hold of the last in her gloved right fist, poking little finger looking no better for being sheathed in white silk. She glanced across the faces of her supposed peers. Two forced smiles, a slight sneer and an outright scowl. She wondered how long it would take for these proud princes, so used to being their own masters, to tire of this less favourable arrangement.

By the look of things, the yoke was already starting to chafe.

Together, the five of them lifted the crown and took a few lurching steps forwards, Sotorius having to awkwardly negotiate the case, dragging each other clumsily about by the priceless symbol of majesty. They made it to the chair, and between them raised the crown high over Rogont's head. They paused there for a moment, as if by mutual agreement, perhaps wondering if there was still some way out of this. The whole great space was eerily silent, every man and woman holding their breath. Then Sotorius gave a resigned nod, and together the five of them lowered the crown, seated it carefully on Rogont's skull and stepped away.

Styria, it seemed, was one nation.

Its king rose slowly from the chair and spread his arms wide, palms open, staring straight ahead as though he could see right through the ancient walls of the Senate House and into a brilliant future.

'Our fellow Styrians!' he bellowed, voice ringing from the stones. 'Our humble subjects! And our friends from abroad, all welcome here!' Mostly Gurkish friends, but since the Prophet had stretched to such a large diamond for his crown . . . 'The Years of Blood are at an end!' Or they soon would be, once Monza had spilled Orso's. 'No longer will the great cities of our proud land struggle one against the other!' That remained to be seen. 'But will stand as brothers eternal, bound willingly by happy ties of friendship, of culture, of common heritage. Marching together!' In whatever direction Rogont dictated, presumably. 'It is as if . . . Styria wakes from a nightmare. A nightmare nineteen years long. Some among us, I am sure, can scarcely remember a time without war.' Monza frowned, thinking of her father's plough turning the black earth.

'But now . . . the wars are over! And all of us won! Every one of us.' Some won more than others, it needed hardly to be said. 'Now is the time for peace! For freedom! For healing!' Lirozio noisily cleared his throat, wincing as he tugged at his embroidered collar. 'Now is the time for hope, for forgiveness, for unity!'

And abject obedience, of course. Cotarda was staring at her hand. Her pale palm was mottled pink, almost deep enough to match her scarlet dress. 'Now is the time for us to forge a great state that will be the envy of the world! Now is the time—' Lirozio had started to cough, beads of sweat showing on his ruddy face. Rogont frowned furiously sideways at him. 'Now is the time for Styria to become—' Patine bent forwards and gave an anguished groan, lips curled back from his teeth.

'One nation . . .' Something was wrong, and everyone was beginning to see it. Cotarda lurched backwards, stumbled. She caught the gilded railing, chest heaving, and sank to the floor with a rustling of red silk. The audience gave a stunned collective gasp.

'One nation . . .' whispered Rogont. Chancellor Sotorius sank trembling to his knees, one pink-stained hand clutching at his withered throat. Patine was crouched on all fours now, face bright red, veins bulging from his neck. Lirozio toppled onto his side, back to Monza, his breath a faint wheeze. His right arm stretched out behind him, the twitching hand blotched pink. Cotarda's leg kicked faintly, then she was still. All the while the crowd stayed silent. Transfixed. Not sure if this was some demented part of the show. Some awful joke. Patine sagged onto his face. Sotorius fell backwards, spine arched, heels of his shoes squeaking against the polished wood, then flopped down limp.

Rogont stared at Monza and she stared back, as frozen and helpless as she had been when she watched Benna die. He opened his mouth, raised one hand towards her, but no breath moved. His forehead, beneath the fur-trimmed rim of the crown, had turned angry red.

The crown. They all had touched the crown. Her eyes rolled down to her gloved right hand. All except her.

Rogont's face twisted. He took one step, his ankle buckled and he pitched onto his face, bulging eyes staring sightlessly off to the side. The crown popped from his skull, bounced once, rolled across the inlaid platform to its edge and clattered to the floor below. Someone in the audience gave a single, ear-splitting scream.

There was the whoosh of a counterweight falling, a rattle of wood, and a thousand white songbirds were released from cages concealed around the edge of the chamber, rising up into the clear night air in a beautiful, twittering storm.

It was just as Rogont had planned.

Except that of the six men and women destined to unite Styria and bring an end to the Years of Blood, only Monza was still alive.

All Dust

Shivers took more'n a little satisfaction in the fact Grand Duke Rogont was dead. Maybe it should've been King Rogont, but it didn't matter much which you called him now, and that thought tickled Shivers' grin just a bit wider.

You can be as great a man as you please while you're alive. Makes not a straw of difference once you go back to the mud. And it only takes a little thing. Might happen in a silly moment. An old friend of Shivers' fought all seven days at the battle in the High Places and didn't get a nick. Scratched himself on a thorn leaving the valley next morning, got the rot in his hand, died babbling a few nights after. No point to it. No lesson. Except watch out for thorns, maybe.

But then a noble death like Rudd Threetrees won for himself, leading the charge, sword in his fist as the life left him – that was no better. Maybe men would sing a song about it, badly, when they were drunk, but for him who died, death was death, same for everyone. The Great Leveller, the hillmen called it. Lords and beggars made equal.

All of Rogont's grand ambitions were dirt. His power was mist, blown away on the dawn breeze. Shivers, no more'n a one-eyed killer, not fit to lick the king-in-waiting's boots clean yesterday, this morning was the better man by far. He was still casting a shadow. If there was a lesson, it was this – you have to take what you can while you still have breath. The earth holds no rewards but darkness.

They rode from the tunnel and into the outer ward of Fontezarmo, and Shivers gave a long, soft whistle.

'They done some building work.'

Monza nodded. 'Some knocking down, at least. Seems the Prophet's gift did the trick.'

It was a fearsome weapon, this Gurkish sugar. A great stretch

594

of the walls on their left had vanished, a tower tilted madly at the far end, cracks up its side, looking sure to follow the rest down the mountain any moment. A few leafless shrubs clung to the ragged cliff-edge where the walls had been, clawing at empty air. Shivers reckoned there'd been gardens, but the flaming shot the catapults had been lobbing in the last few weeks had turned 'em mostly to burned-up bramble, split tree-stump and scorched-out mud, all smeared down and puddle-pocked by last night's rain.

A cobbled way led through the midst of this mess, between a half-dozen stagnant fountains and up to a black gate, still sealed tight. A few twisted shapes lay round some wreckage, bristling with arrows. Dead men round a torched ram. Scanning along the battlements above, Shivers' practised eye picked out spears, bows, armour twinkling. Seemed the inner wall was still firm held, Duke Orso no doubt tucked in tight behind it.

They rode around a big heap of damp canvas weighted down with stones, patches of rainwater in the folds. As Shivers passed he saw there were boots sticking out of one end, a few pairs of dirty bare feet, all beaded up with wet.

Seemed one of Volfier's lads was a fresh recruit, went pale when he saw them dead men. Strange, but seeing him all broken up just made Shivers wonder when he got so comfortable around a corpse or two. To him they were just bits of the scenery now, no more meaning than the broken tree-stumps. It was going to take more'n a corpse or two to spoil his good mood that morning.

Monza reined her horse in and slid from the saddle. 'Dismount,' grunted Volfier, and the rest followed her.

'Why do some of 'em have bare feet?' The boy was still staring at the dead.

'Because they had good boots,' said Shivers. The lad looked down at his own foot-leather, then back to those wet bare feet, then put one hand over his mouth.

Volfier clapped the boy on the back and made him start, gave Shivers a wink while he did it. Seemed baiting the new blood was the same the world over. 'Boots or no boots, don't make no difference once they've killed you. Don't worry, boy, you get used to it.'

'You do?'

'If you're lucky,' said Shivers, 'you'll live long enough.'

'If you're lucky,' said Monza, 'you'll find another trade first. Wait here.'

Volfier gave her a nod. 'Your Excellency.' And Shivers watched her pick her way around the wreckage and off.

'Get on top of things in Talins?' he muttered.

'Hope so,' grunted the scarred sergeant. 'Got the fires put out, in the end. Made us a deal with the criminals in the Old Quarter they'd keep an eye on things there for a week, and we wouldn't keep an eye for a month after.'

'Coming to something when you're looking to thieves to keep order.'

'It's a topsy-turvy world alright.' Volfier narrowed his eyes at the inner wall. 'My old master's on the other side o' that. A man I fought my whole life for. Never had any riots when he was in charge.'

'Wish you were with him?'

Volfier frowned sideways. 'I wish we'd won at Ospria, then the choice wouldn't have come up. But then I wish my wife hadn't fucked the baker while I was away in the Union on campaign three years ago. Wishing don't change nothing.'

Shivers grinned, and tapped at his metal eye with a fingernail. 'That there is a fact.'

Cosca sat on his field chair, in the only part of the gardens that was still anything like intact, and watched his goat grazing on the wet grass. There was something oddly calming about her gradual, steady progress across the last remaining bit of lawn. The wriggling of her lips, the delicate nibbling of her teeth, the tiny movements that by patient repetition would soon shave that lawn down to stubble. He stuck a fingertip in his ear and waggled it around, trying to clear the faint ringing that still lurked at the edge of his hearing. It persisted. He sighed, raised his flask, heard footsteps crunching on gravel and stopped. Monza was walking towards him. She looked beyond tired, shoulders hunched, mouth twisted, eyes buried in dark pits.

'Why the hell do you have a goat?'

Cosca took a slow swig from his flask, grimaced and took another. 'Noble beast, the goat. She reminds me, in your absence, to be tenacious, single-minded and hard-working. You have to stick at something in your life, Monzcarro.' The goat looked up, and bleated in apparent agreement. 'I hope you won't take offence if I say you look tired.'

'Long night,' she muttered, and Cosca judged it to be a tremendous understatement.

'I'm sure.'

'The Osprians pulled out of Talins. There was a riot. Panic.'

'Inevitable.'

'Someone spread a rumour that the Union fleet was on its way.'

'Rumours can do more damage than the ships themselves.'

'The crown was poisoned,' she muttered.

'The leaders of Styria, consumed by their own lust for power. There's a message in there, wouldn't you say? Murder and metaphor combined. The poisoner-poet responsible has managed to kill a chancellor, a duke, a countess, a first citizen and a king, and teach the world an invaluable lesson about life all in one evening. Your friend and mine, Morveer?'

She spat. 'Maybe.'

'I never thought that pedantic bastard had such a sense of humour.'

'Forgive me if I don't laugh.'

'Why did he spare you?'

'He didn't.' Monza held up her gloved right hand. 'My glove did.'

Cosca could not help a snort of laughter. 'Just think, one could say that by crushing your right hand, Duke Orso and his cohorts saved your life! The ironies pile one upon the other!'

'I might wait for a more settled moment to enjoy them.'

'Oh, I'd enjoy them now. I've wasted years waiting for more settled moments. In my experience they never come. Only look around you. The Affoians almost all deserted before daybreak. The Sipanese are already splitting into factions, falling back south – to fight each other, would be my guess. The army of Puranti were so keen to get their civil war under way they actually started killing each other in the trenches. Victus had to break it up! Victus, *stopping* a fight, can you imagine? Some of the Osprians are still here, but only because they haven't a clue what else to do.

The lot of them, running around like chickens with their heads cut off. Which I suppose they are. You know, I'm eternally amazed at just how quickly things can fall apart. Styria was united for perhaps the length of a minute and now is plunged into deeper chaos than ever. Who knows who'll seize power, and where, and how much? It seems an end may have been called to the Years of Blood . . .' and Cosca stuck his chin out and gave his neck a scratch, 'somewhat prematurely.'

Monza's shoulders seemed to slump a little lower. 'The ideal situation for a mercenary, no?'

'You'd have thought. But there's such a thing as too much chaos, even for a man like me. I swear, the Thousand Swords are the most coherent and orderly body of troops left up here. Which should give you some idea of the utter disorder that has struck your allies.' He stretched his legs out in front of him, one boot crossed over the other. 'I thought I might take the brigade down towards Visserine, and press my claims there. I very much doubt Rogont will be honouring our agreement now—'

'Stay,' she said, and fixed her eyes on his.

'Stay?'

'Stay.'

There was a long pause while they watched each other. 'You've no right to ask me that.'

'But I am asking. Help me.'

'Help . . . you? It's coming to something when I'm anyone's best hope. What of your loyal subjects, the good people of Talins? Is there no help to be had there?'

'They aren't as keen for a battle as they were for a parade. They won't lift a finger in case they get Orso back in charge and he hangs every man of them.'

'The fickle movements of power, eh? You've raised no soldiers while you had the throne? That hardly seems your style.'

'I raised what I could, but I can't trust them here. Not against Orso. Who knows which way they'll jump?'

'Ah, divided loyalties. I have some experience with them. An unpredictable scenario.' Cosca stuck his finger in his other ear, to no greater effect. 'Have you considered the possibility of . . . perhaps . . . leaving it be?'

She looked at him as if he was speaking in a foreign tongue. 'What?'

'I myself have left a thousand tasks unfinished, unstarted or outright failed across the whole breadth of the Circle of the World. In the end, they bother me considerably less than my successes.'

'I'm not you.'

'No doubt a cause of constant regret for us both. But still. You could forget about revenge. You could compromise. You could . . . be merciful.'

'Mercy and cowardice are the same,' she growled, narrow eyes fixed on the black gate at the far end of the blasted gardens.

Cosca gave a sad smile. 'Are they indeed?'

'Conscience is an excuse not to do what needs doing.'

'I see.'

'No use weeping about it. That's how the world is.'

'Ah.'

'The good get nothing extra. When they die they turn to shit like the rest of us. You have to keep your eyes ahead, always ahead, fight one battle at a time. You can't hesitate, no matter the costs, no matter the—'

'Do you know why I always loved you, Monza?'

'Eh?' Her eyes flickered to him, surprised.

'Even after you betrayed me? More, after you betrayed me?' Cosca leaned slowly towards her. 'Because I know you don't really believe any of that rubbish. Those are the lies you tell yourself so you can live with what you've done. What you've had to do.'

There was a long pause. Then she swallowed as though she was about to puke. 'You always said I had a devil in me.'

'Did I? Well, so do we all.' He waved a hand. 'You're no saint, that much we know. A child of a bloody time. But you're nothing like as dark as you make out.'

'No?'

'I pretend to care for the men, but in truth I don't give a damn whether they live or die. You always did care, but you pretend not to give a damn. I never saw you waste one man's life. And yet they like me better. Hah. There's justice. You always did the right thing by me, Monza. Even when you betrayed me, it was better

599

than I deserved. I've never forgotten that time in Muris, after the siege, when you wouldn't let the slavers have those children. Everyone wanted to take the money. I did. Faithful did. Even Benna. Especially Benna. But not you.'

'Only gave you a scratch,' she muttered.

'Don't be modest, you were ready to kill me. These are ruthless times we live in, and in ruthless times, mercy and cowardice are *entire* opposites. We all turn to shit when we die, Monza, but not all of us are shit while we're alive. Most of us are.' His eyes rolled to heaven. 'God knows I am. But you never were.'

She blinked at him for a moment. 'Will you help me?'

Cosca raised his flask again, realised it was empty and screwed the cap back on. The damn thing needed filling far too often. 'Of course I'll help you. There was never the slightest question in my mind. I have already organised the assault, in fact.'

'Then—'

'I just wanted to hear you ask. I must say I am surprised you did, though. The mere idea that the Thousand Swords would do the hard work of a siege, have one of the richest palaces in Styria at their mercy and walk away without a scrap of booty? Have you lost your reason? I couldn't prise these greedy bastards away with a spade. We're attacking at dawn tomorrow, with or without you, and we'll be picking this place clean. More than likely my boys will have the lead off the roofs by lunchtime. Rule of Quarters, and all that.'

'And Orso?'

'Orso is yesterday's man.' Cosca sat back and patted his goat fondly on her flank. 'Do as you please with him.'

The Inevitable

The dice came up two and one.

Three years ago today, Sajaam bought Friendly's freedom from Safety. Three years he had been homeless. He had followed three people, two men and one woman, all across Styria and back. In that time, the place he had hated least was the Thousand Swords, and not just because it had a number in its name, though that was, of course, a good start.

There was order, here, up to a point. Men had given tasks with given times to do them, knew their places in the big machine. The company was all neatly quantified in the notary's three ledgers. Number of men under each captain, length of service, amount of pay, times reported, equipment hired. Everything could be counted. There were rules, up to a point, explicit and implied. Rules about drinking, gambling and fighting. Rules about use of whores. Rules about who sat where. Who could go where, and when. Who fought and who did not. And the all-important Rule of Quarters, controlling the declaration and assignment of booty, enforced with eagle-eyed discipline.

When rules were broken there were fixed punishments, understood by all. Usually a number of lashes of the whip. Friendly had watched a man whipped for pissing in the wrong place, yesterday. It did not seem such a crime, but Victus had explained to everyone, you start off pissing where you please, then you shit where you please, then everyone dies of the plague. So it had been three lashes. Two and one.

Friendly's favourite place was the mess. There was a comforting routine to mealtimes that put him in mind of Safety. The frowning cooks in their stained aprons. The steam from the great pots. The rattle and clatter of knives and spoons. The slurp and splutter of lips, teeth, tongues. The line of jostling men, all asking for more than their share and never getting it.

The men who would be in the scaling parties this morning got two extra meatballs and an extra spoon of soup. Two and one. Cosca had said it was one thing to get poked off a ladder with a spear, but he could not countenance a man falling off from hunger.

'We'll be attacking within the hour,' he said now.

Friendly nodded.

Cosca took a long breath, pushed it out through his nose and frowned around him. 'Ladders, mainly.' Friendly had watched them being made, over the last few days. Twenty-one of them. Two and one. Each had thirty-one rungs, except for one, which had thirty-two. One, two, three. 'Monza will be going with them. She wants to be the first to Orso. Entirely determined. She's set firm on vengeance.'

Friendly shrugged. She always had been.

'In all honesty, I worry for her.'

Friendly shrugged. He was indifferent.

'A battle is a dangerous place.'

Friendly shrugged. That seemed obvious.

'My friend, I want you to stick near her, in the fighting. Make sure no harm comes to her.'

'What about you?'

'Me?' Cosca slapped Friendly on his shoulder. 'The only shield I need is the universally high regard in which men hold me.'

'You sure?'

'No, but I'll be where I always am. Well behind the fighting with my flask for company. Something tells me she'll need you more. There are enemies still, out there. And Friendly . . .'

'Yes?'

'Watch closely and take great care. The fox is most dangerous when at bay – that Orso will have some deadly tricks in store, well . . .' and he puffed out his cheeks, 'it's inevitable. Watch out, in particular . . . for Morveer.'

'Alright.' Murcatto would have him and Shivers watching her. A party of three, as it had been when they killed Gobba. Two watching one. He wrapped the dice up and slid them down into his pocket. He watched the steam rise as the food was ladled out. Listened to the men grumbling. Counted the complaints.

*

The washed-out grey of dawn was turning to golden daylight, sun creeping over the battlements at the top of the wall they'd all have to climb, its gap-toothed shadow slowly giving ground across the ruined gardens.

They'd be going soon. Shivers shut his eye and grinned into the sun. Tipped his head back and stuck his tongue out. It was getting colder as the year wore down. Felt almost like a fine summer morning in the North. Like mornings he'd fought great battles in. Mornings he'd done high deeds, and a few low ones too.

'You seem happy enough,' came Monza's voice, 'for a man about to risk his life.'

Shivers opened his eye and turned his grin on her. 'I've made peace with myself.'

'Good for you. That's the hardest war of all to win.'

'Didn't say I won. Just stopped fighting.'

'I'm starting to think that's the only victory worth a shit,' she muttered, almost to herself.

Ahead of them, the first wave of mercenaries were ready to go, stood about their ladders, big shields on their free arms, twitchy and nervous, which was no surprise. Shivers couldn't say he much fancied their job. They weren't making the least effort to hide what they had planned. Everyone knew what was coming, on both sides of the wall.

Close round Shivers, the second wave were getting ready too. Giving blades a last stroke with the whetstone, tightening straps on armour, telling a last couple of jokes and hoping they weren't the last they ever told. Shivers grinned, watching them at it. Rituals he'd seen a dozen times before and more. Felt almost like home.

'You ever have the feeling you were in the wrong place?' he asked. 'That if you could just get over the next hill, cross the next river, look down into the next valley, it'd all . . . fit. Be right.'

Monza narrowed her eyes at the inner walls. 'All my life, more or less.'

'All your life spent getting ready for the next thing. I climbed a lot of hills now. I crossed a lot of rivers. Crossed the sea even, left everything I knew and came to Styria. But there I was, waiting for me at the docks when I got off the boat, same man, same life.

Next valley ain't no different from this one. No better anyway. Reckon I've learned . . . just to stick in the place I'm at. Just to be the man I am.'

'And what are you?'

He looked down at the axe across his knees. 'A killer, I reckon.'

'That all?'

'Honestly? Pretty much.' He shrugged. 'That's why you took me on, ain't it?'

She frowned at the ground. 'What happened to being an optimist?'

'Can't I be an optimistic killer? A man once told me – the man who killed my brother, as it goes – that good and evil are a matter of where you stand. We all got our reasons. Whether they're decent ones all depends on who you ask, don't it?'

'Does it?'

'I would've thought you'd say so, of all people.'

'Maybe I would've, once. Now I'm not so sure. Maybe those are just the lies we tell ourselves, so we can live with what we've done.'

Shivers couldn't help himself. He burst out laughing.

'What's funny?'

'I don't need excuses, Chief, that's what I'm trying to tell you. What's the name for it, when a thing's bound to happen? There's a word for it, ain't there, when there's no stopping something? No avoiding it, whatever you try to do?'

'Inevitable,' said Monza.

'That's it. The inevitable.' Shivers chewed happily on the word like a mouthful of good meat. 'I'm happy with what's done. I'm happy with what's coming.'

A shrill whistle cut through the air. All together, with a rattling of armour, the first wave knelt in parties of a dozen and took up their long ladders between them. They started to jog forwards, in piss-poor order if Shivers was honest, slipping and sliding across the slimy gardens. Others followed after, none too eager, sharpshooters with flatbows aiming to keep the archers on the walls busy. There were a few grunts, some calls of 'steady' and the rest, but a quiet rush, on the whole. It wouldn't have seemed right, really, giving your war cry while you ran at a wall. What do you

604

do when you get there? You can't keep shouting all the way up a ladder.

'There they go.' Shivers stood, lifted his axe and shook it above his head. 'Go on! Go on, you bastards!'

They made it halfway across the gardens before Shivers heard a floating shriek of, 'Fire!' A moment later a clicking rattle from the walls. Bolts flitted down into the charging men. There were a couple of screams, sobs, a few boys dropped, but most kept pressing forwards, faster'n ever now. Mercenaries with bows of their own knelt, sent a volley back, pinging from battlements or flying right over.

The whistle went again and the next wave started forwards, the men who'd drawn the happy task of climbing. Light-armoured mostly, so they'd move nice and nimble. The first party had made it to the foot of the walls, were starting to raise their ladder. One of 'em dropped with a bolt in his neck, but the rest managed to push the thing the whole way. Shivers watched it swing over and clatter into the parapet. Other ladders started going up. More movement at the top of the walls, men leaning out with rocks and chucking them down. Bolts fell among the second wave, but most of 'em were getting close to the walls now, crowding round, starting to climb. There were six ladders up, then ten. The next one fell apart when it hit the battlements, bits of wood dropping on the shocked boys who'd raised it. Shivers had to chuckle.

More rocks dropped. A man tumbled from halfway up a ladder, his legs folding every which way underneath him, started shrieking away. There was plenty of shouting all round now, and no mistake. Some defenders on a tower roof upended a big vat of boiling water into the faces of a party trying to raise a ladder below. They made a hell of a noise, ladder toppling, running about clutching their heads like madmen.

Bolts and arrows hissed up and down each way. Stones tumbled, bounced. Men fell at the walls, or on their way to 'em. Others started crawling back through the mud, were dragged back, arms over the shoulders of comrades happy for an excuse to get clear. Mercenaries hacked about madly as they got to the top of the ladders, more'n one poked off by waiting spearmen, taking the quick way back down.

Shivers saw someone at the battlements upending a pot onto a ladder and the men climbing it. Someone else came up with a torch, set light to it, and the whole top half went up in flames. Oil, then. Shivers watched it burn, a couple of the men on it too. After a moment they toppled off, took some others with 'em, more screams. Shivers slid his axe through the loop over his shoulder. Best place for it when you're trying to climb. Unless you slip and it cuts your head off, of course. That thought made him chuckle again. Couple of men around him were frowning, he was chuckling that much, but he didn't care, the blood was pumping fast now. They just made him chuckle more.

Looked like some of the mercenaries had made it to the parapet over on the right. He saw blades twinkling at the battlements. More men pressed up behind. A ladder covered in soldiers was shoved away from the wall with poles. It teetered for a moment, upright, like the best stilt-show in the world. The poor bastards near the top wriggled, clutching at nothing, then it slowly toppled over and mashed them all into the cobbles.

They were up on the left too, just next to the gatehouse. Shivers saw men fighting their way up some steps onto the roof. Five or six of the ladders were down, two were still burning up against the wall, sending up plumes of dark smoke, but most of the rest were crawling with climbing soldiers from top to bottom. Couldn't have been too many men on the defence, and weight of numbers was starting to tell.

The whistle went again and the third wave started to move, heavier-armoured men who'd follow the first up the ladders and press on into the fortress.

'Let's go,' said Monza.

'Right y'are, Chief.' Shivers took a breath and started jogging.

The bows were more or less silenced now, only a few bolts still flitting from arrow-loops in the towers. So it was a happier journey than the folks before had taken, just a morning amble through the corpses scattered across the blasted gardens and over to one of the middle ladders. A couple of men and a sergeant were stood at the foot, boots up on the first rung, gripping it tight. The sergeant slapped each man as he began to climb.

'Up you go now, lads, up you go! Fast but steady! No loitering!

Get up and kill those fuckers! You too, bastard— Oh. Sorry, your . . . er . . . Excellency?'

'Just hold it steady.' And Monza started climbing.

Shivers followed, hands sliding on the rough uprights, boots scraping on the wood, breath hissing through his smile as his muscles worked up an ache. He kept his eyes fixed on the wall in front. No point looking anywhere else. If an arrow came? Nothing you could do. If some bastard dropped a rock on you, or a pot of boiling water? Nothing you could do. If they pushed the ladder off? Shitty luck, alright, but looking out for it would only slow you down and make it the more likely. So he kept on, breathing hard through his clenched teeth.

Soon enough he got to the top, hauled himself over. Monza was there on the walkway, sword already drawn, looking down into the inner ward. He could hear fighting, but not near. There were a few dead men scattered on the walkway, from both sides. A mercenary propped against the stonework had an arm off at the elbow, rope lashed around his shoulder to stop the blood, moaning, 'It fell off the edge, it fell off the edge,' over and over. Shivers didn't reckon he'd last 'til lunch, but he guessed that meant more lunch for everyone else. You have to look at the sunny side, don't you? That's what being an optimist is all about.

He swung his shield off his back and slid his arm through the straps. He pulled his axe out, spun the grip round in his fist. Felt good to do it. Like a smith getting his hammer out, ready for the good work to start. There were more gardens down below, planted on steps cut from the summit of the mountain, nowhere near so battered as the ones further out. Buildings towered over the greenery on three sides. A mass of twinkling windows and fancy stonework, domes and turrets sprouting from the top, crusted with statues and glinting prongs. Didn't take a great mind to spot Orso's palace, which was just as well, 'cause Shivers knew he didn't have a great mind. Just a bloody one.

'Let's go,' said Monza.

Shivers grinned. 'Right behind you, Chief.'

The trenches that riddled the dusty mountainside were empty. The soldiers who had occupied them had dispersed, gone back to their homes, or to play their own small roles in the several power struggles set off by the untimely deaths of King Rogont and his allies. Only the Thousand Swords remained, swarming hungrily around Duke Orso's palace like maggots around a corpse. Shenkt had seen it all before. Loyalty, duty, pride – fleeting motivations on the whole, which kept men smugly happy in good weather but soon washed away when the storm came. Greed, though? On greed you can always rely.

He walked on up the winding track, across the battle-scarred ground before the walls, over the bridge, the looming gatehouse of Fontezarmo drawing steadily closer. A single mercenary sat slouched on a folding chair outside the open gate, spear leaning against the wall beside him.

'What's your business?' Asked with negligible interest.

'Duke Orso commissioned me to kill Monzcarro Murcatto, now the Grand Duchess of Talins.'

'Hilarious.' The guard pulled his collars up around his ears and settled back against the wall.

Often, the last thing men believe is the truth. Shenkt pondered that as he passed through the long tunnel and into the outer ward of the fortress. The rigidly ordered beauty of Duke Orso's formal gardens was entirely departed, along with half the north wall. The mercenaries had made a very great mess of the place. But that was war. There was much confusion. But that was war also.

The final assault was evidently well under way. Ladders stood against the inner wall, bodies scattered in the blasted gardens around their bases. Orderlies wandered among them, offering water, fumbling with splints or bandages, moving men onto stretchers. Shenkt knew few would survive who could not even crawl by themselves. Still, men always clung to the smallest sliver of hope. It was one of the few things to admire in them.

He came to a silent halt beside a ruined fountain and watched the wounded struggling against the inevitable. A man slipped suddenly from behind the broken stonework and almost ran straight into him. An unremarkable balding man, wearing a worn studded-leather jerkin.

'Gah! My most *profound* apologies!'

Shenkt said nothing.

'You are . . . are you . . . that is to say . . . here to participate in the assault?'

'In a way.'

'As am I, as am I. In a way.' Nothing could have been more natural than a mercenary fleeing the fighting, but something did not tally. He was dressed like a thug, this man, but he spoke like a bad writer. His nearest hand flapped around as though to distract attention from the other, which was clearly creeping towards a concealed weapon. Shenkt frowned. He had no desire to draw undue attention. So he gave this man a chance, just as he always did, wherever possible.

'We both have our work, then. Let us delay each other no longer.'

The stranger brightened. 'Absolutely so. To work.'

Morveer gave a false chuckle, then realised he had accidentally strayed into using his accustomed voice. 'To work,' he grunted in an unconvincing commoner's baritone.

'To work,' the man echoed, his bright eyes never wavering.

'Right. Well.' Morveer sidestepped the stranger and walked on, allowing his hand to come free of his mounted needle and drop, inconspicuous, to his side. Without doubt the fellow had been possessed of an unusual manner, but had Morveer's mission been to poison every person with an unusual manner he would never have been halfway done. Fortunately his mission was only to poison seven of the most important persons in the nation, and it was one at which he had only lately achieved spectacular success.

He was still flushed by the sheer scale of his achievement, the sheer audacity of its execution, the unparalleled success of his plan. He was beyond doubt the greatest poisoner ever and had become, indisputably, a great man of history. How it galled him that he could never truly share his grand achievement with the world, never enjoy the adulation his triumph undoubtedly deserved. Oh, if the doubting headmaster at the orphanage could have only witnessed this happy day, he would have been forced to concede that Castor Morveer was indeed prize-winning material! If his wife could have seen it, she would have finally understood him, and never again complained about his unusual habits! If his infamous one-time teacher, Moumah-yin-Bek, could only have been there, he would have finally acknowledged that his pupil had forever eclipsed him. If Day had been alive, she would no doubt have given that silvery giggle in acknowledgement of his genius, smiled her innocent smile and perhaps touched him gently, perhaps even . . . But now was not the time for such fancies. There had been compelling reasons for poisoning all four of them, so Morveer would have to settle for his own congratulations.

It appeared that his murder of Rogont and his allies had quite eliminated any standards at the siege of Fontezarmo. It was not an overstatement to say that the outer ward of the fortress was scarcely guarded at all. He knew Nicomo Cosca for a bloated balloon of braggadocio, a committed drunkard and a rank incompetent to boot, but he had supposed the man would make some provision for security. This was almost disappointingly effortless.

Though the fighting upon the wall seemed largely to have ceased – the gate to the inner ward was now in the hands of the mercenaries and stood wide – the sound of combat still emanated vaguely from the gardens beyond. An utterly distasteful business; he was pleased that he would have no occasion to stray near it. It appeared the Thousand Swords had captured the citadel and Duke Orso's doom was inevitable, but the thought gave Morveer no particular discomfort. Great men come and go, after all. He had a promise of payment from the Banking House of Valint and Balk, and that went beyond any one man, any one nation. That was deathless.

Some wounded had been laid out on a patch of scraggy grass, in the shadow of a tree to which a goat had, inexplicably, been tethered. Morveer grimaced, tiptoed between them, lip wrinkled at the sight of bloody bandages, of ripped and spattered clothing, of torn flesh—

'Water . . .' one of them whispered at him, clutching at his ankle.

'Always it's water!' Tearing his leg free. 'Find your own!' He hurried through an open doorway and into the largest tower in the outer ward where, he was reliably informed, the constable of the fortress had once had his quarters, and Nicomo Cosca now had his.

He slipped through the gloom of narrow passageways, barely

lit by arrow-loops. He crept up a spiral staircase, back hissing against the rough stone wall, tongue pressed into the roof of his mouth. The Thousand Swords were as slovenly and easily fooled as their commander, but he was fully aware that fickle chance might deflate his delight at any moment. Caution first, always.

The first floor had been made a storeroom, filled with shadowy boxes. Morveer crept on. The second floor held empty bunks, no doubt previously utilised by the defenders of the fortress. Twice more around the spiralling steps, he softly tweaked a door open with a finger and applied his eye to the crack.

The circular room beyond contained a large, curtained bed, shelves with many impressive-looking books, writing desk and chests for clothes, an armour stand with suit of polished plate upon it, a sword-rack with several blades, a table with four chairs and a deck of cards, and a large, inlaid cupboard with glasses upon the top. On a row of pegs beside the bed hung several outrageous hats, crystal pins gleaming, gilt bands glinting, a rainbow of different-coloured feathers fluttering in the breeze from an open window. This, without doubt, was the chamber Cosca had taken for his own. No other man would dare to affect such absurd headgear, but for the moment, there was no sign of the great drunkard. Morveer slid inside and eased the door shut behind him. He crossed on silent tiptoes to the cupboard, nimbly avoiding collision with a covered milking-bucket that sat beneath, and with gentle fingers teased open the doors.

Morveer allowed himself the smallest of smiles. Nicomo Cosca would, no doubt, have considered himself a wild and romantic maverick, unfettered by the bonds of routine. In fact he was predictable as the stars, as dully regular as the tide. Most men never change, and a drunk is always a drunk. The chief difficulty appeared to be the spectacular variety of bottles he had collected. There was no way to be certain from which he would drink next. Morveer had no alternative but to poison the entire collection.

He pulled his gloves on, carefully slid the Greenseed solution from his inside pocket. It was lethal only when swallowed, and the timing of its effect varied greatly with the victim, but it gave off only the very slightest fruity odour, entirely undetectable when mingled with wine or spirits. He took careful note of the position of each bottle, the degree to which the cork was inserted, then twisted each free, carefully let fall a drop from his pipette into the neck, replacing cork and bottle precisely as they had been prior to his arrival. He smiled as he poisoned bottles of varying sizes, shapes, colours. This was work as mundane as the poisoned crown had been inspired, but no less noble for that. He would blow through the room like a zephyr of death, undetected, and bring a fitting end to that repulsive drunkard. One more report of Nicomo Cosca's death, and one more only. Few people indeed would consider that anything other than an entirely righteous and public-spirited—

He froze in place. There were footsteps on the stairs. He swiftly pushed the cork back into the final bottle, slid it carefully into position and darted through a narrow doorway into the darkness of a small cell, some kind of—

He wrinkled his nose as he was assailed by a powerful reek of urine. Harsh Mistress Fortune never missed an opportunity to demean him. He might have known he would stumble into a latrine as his hiding place. He had now only to hope that Cosca was not taken with a sudden urge to void his bowels . . .

The battle on the walls appeared to have been settled, and with relatively little difficulty. No doubt the battle continued in the inner ward beyond, through the rich staterooms and echoing marble halls of Duke Orso's palace. But from Cosca's vantage point atop the constable's tower he could not see a blow of it. And even if he could have, what difference? When you've seen one fortress stormed . . .

'Victus, my friend!'

'Uh?' The last remaining senior captain of the Thousand Swords lowered his eyeglass and gave Cosca his usual suspicious squint.

'I rather suspect the day is ours.'

'I rather suspect you're right.'

'The two of us can do no more good up here, even if we could see anything.'

'You speak true, as ever.' Cosca took that for a joke. 'It's all inevitable now. Nothing left but to divide the loot.' Victus absently stroked the many chains around his neck. 'My favourite part of any siege.'

'Cards, then?'

'Why ever not?'

Cosca slapped his eyeglass closed and led the way back down the winding stair to the chamber he had taken for his own. He strode to the cabinet and snatched the inlaid doors open. The many-coloured bottles greeted him like a crowd of old friends. Ah, a drink, a drink, a drink. He took down a glass, pulled the cork from the nearest bottle with a gentle thwop.

'Drink, then?' he called over his shoulder.

'Why ever not?'

There was still fighting, but nothing you could call an organised defence. The mercenaries had swept the walls clean, driven the defenders out of the gardens and were even now breaking into the towers, into the buildings, into the palace. More of them boiled up the ladders every moment, desperate not to miss out on the plunder. No one fought harder or moved faster than the Thousand Swords when they could smell booty.

'This way.' She hurried towards the main gate of the palace, retracing the steps she'd taken the day they killed her brother, past the circular pool, two bodies floating face-down in the shadow of Scarpius' pillar. Shivers followed, that strange smile on his scarred face he'd been wearing all day. They passed an eager clump of men clustered around a doorway, eyes all shining with greed, a couple of them swinging axes at the lock, door wobbling with each blow. They scrambled over each other as it finally came open, screaming, shouting, elbowing to get past. Two of them wrestled each other to the ground, fighting over what they hadn't even stolen yet.

Further on a pair of mercenaries had a servant in a gold-trimmed jacket sitting on the side of a fountain, his shocked face smeared with blood. One would slap him and scream, 'Where's the fucking money?' Then the other would do the same. Back and forth his head went. 'Where's the fucking money, where's the fucking money, where's the fucking money . . .'

A window burst open in a shower of torn lead and broken glass and an antique cabinet tumbled out onto the cobbles, scattering splinters. A whooping mercenary ran past, arms heaped with glinting material. Curtains, maybe. Monza heard a scream, whipped about, saw someone plummet from an upstairs window and headfirst into the garden, drop bonelessly over. She heard shrieking from somewhere. Sounded like a woman's voice, but it was hard to tell when it was that desperate. There was shouting, screaming, laughing everywhere. She swallowed her sickness, tried not to think that she'd made this happen. That this was where her vengeance had led. All she could do was keep her eyes ahead, hope to find Orso first.

Find him and make him pay.

The studded palace doors were still locked, but the mercenaries had found a way round, smashed through one of the great arched windows to one side. Someone must have cut himself in the rush to get in and get rich – there was blood smeared on the windowsill. Monza eased through, boots crunching on broken glass, dropped down into a grand dining room beyond. She'd eaten there once, she realised, Benna beside her, laughing, Faithful too. Orso, Ario, Foscar, Ganmark had all been there, a whole crowd of other officers. It occurred to her that pretty much every guest from that night was dead. The room hadn't fared much better.

It was like a field after the locusts come through. They'd carried off half the paintings, slashed up the rest for the sake of it. The two huge vases beside the fireplace were too big to lift, so they'd smashed them and taken the gilt handles. They'd torn the hangings down, stolen all the plates apart from the ones broken to fragments across the polished floor. Strange, how men are almost as happy to break a thing as steal it, at a time like that. They were still rooting around, ripping drawers from cupboards, chiselling sconces from the walls, dismantling the place for anything worth one bit. One fool had a chair balanced on the bare table and was straining up to reach the chandelier. Another was busy with a knife, trying to prise the crystal doorknobs loose.

A pock-faced mercenary grinned at her, fists bursting with gilded cutlery. 'I got spoons!' he shouted. Monza shoved him out of the way and he tripped, his treasure scattering, other men pouncing on it like ducks on stray crumbs. She pushed through the open doorway, out into a marble hall, Shivers at her shoulder. Sounds of fighting echoed down it. Wails and yells, metal scraping, wood crashing, from everywhere and nowhere. She squinted both ways into the gloom, trying to get her bearings, sweat tickling at her scalp.

'This way.' They passed a vast sitting room, men inside slashing the upholstery of some antique chairs, as if Orso kept his gold in his cushions. The next door was being kicked in by an eager crowd. One man took an arrow in his neck as they broke it open, others poured in past him, whooping, weapons clashed on the other side. Monza kept her eyes ahead, thoughts fixed on Orso. She pushed on up a flight of steps, teeth gritted, hardly feeling the ache in her legs.

Onto a dim gallery at one end of a high, vaulted chamber, its barrelled ceiling crusted with gilded leaves. The whole wall was a great organ, a range of polished pipes sprouting from carved wood, a stool drawn up before the keyboard for the player. Down below, beyond a delicately worked wooden rail, there was a music room. Mercenaries shrieked with laughter, battering a demented symphony from the instruments as they broke them apart.

'We're close,' she whispered over her shoulder.

'Good. Time to get this over with, I reckon.'

Her very thoughts. She crept towards the tall door in the far wall. 'Orso's chambers are up this way.'

'No, no.' She frowned over her shoulder. Shivers stood there, grinning, his metal eye shining in the half-light. 'Not that.'

She felt a cold feeling creeping up her back. 'What, then?'

'You know what.' His smile widened, scars twisting, and he stretched his neck out one way, then the other.

She dropped into a fighting crouch just in time. He snarled as he came at her, axe flashing across. She lurched into the stool and upended it, nearly fell, mind still catching up. His axe thudded into the organ pipes, struck a mad clanging note from them. He wrenched the blade free, leaving a great wound behind in the thin metal. He sprang at her again but the shock had faded now and cold anger leaked in to fill the gap.

'You one-eyed cocksucker!' Not clever, perhaps, but from the heart. She lunged at him but he caught the Calvez on his shield, swung his axe, and she only just hopped away in time, the heavy blade crashing into the organ's surround and sending splinters flying. She dropped back, watchful, keeping her distance. She'd about as much chance of parrying that weight of steel as she did of playing sweet music on that organ.

'Why?' she snarled at him, point of the Calvez moving in little circles. She didn't care a shit about his reasons, really. Just playing for time, looking for an opening.

'Maybe I got sick o' your scorn.' He nudged forwards behind his shield and she backed off again. 'Or maybe Eider offered me more'n you.'

'Eider?' She spat laughter in his face. 'There's your problem! You're a fucking idiot!' She lunged on the last word, trying to catch him off guard, but he wasn't fooled, knocked her jabs calmly away with his shield.

'I'm the idiot? I saved you how many times? I gave up my eye! So you could sneer at me with that empty bastard Rogont? You treat me like a fucking fool and still expect my loyalty, and *I'm* the idiot?' Hard to argue with most of that, now it was stuck under her nose. She should've listened to Rogont, let him put Shivers down, but she'd let guilt get in the way. Mercy might be brave, like Cosca said, but it seemed it wasn't always clever. Shivers shuffled at her and she gave ground again, fast running out of it.

'You should've seen this coming,' he whispered, and she reckoned he had a point. It had been coming a long time. Since she fucked Rogont. Since she turned her back on Shivers. Since he lost his eye in the cells under Salier's palace. Maybe it had been coming from the first moment they met. Before, even. Always.

Some things are inevitable.

Thus the Whirligig . . .

Shivers' axe clanged into the pipes again. He didn't know what the hell they were for but they made a bastard of a racket. Monza had already dodged away though, weighing her sword, narrowed eyes fixed on his. More'n likely he should've just axed her in the back of the skull and put an end to it. But he wanted her to know who'd done it, and why. Needed her to know.

'You don't have to do this,' she hissed at him. 'You could still walk away.'

'I thought the dead could do the forgiving,' he said, circling to cut off her space.

'I'm offering you a chance, Shivers. Back to the North, no one would chase you.'

'They're free to fucking try, but I reckon I'll stay a little longer. A man has to stick at something, don't he? I've got my pride, still.'

'Shit on your pride! You'd be selling your arse in the alleys of Talins if it wasn't for me!' True, more'n likely. 'You knew the risks. You chose to take my money.' True too. 'I made no promises to you and I broke none!' True and all. 'That bitch Eider won't give you a scale!'

Hard to argue with most of that, maybe, but it was too late to go back now, and besides, an axe in the head is the last word in any argument. 'We'll see.' Shivers eased towards her, shield leading the way. 'But this ain't about money. This is about . . . vengeance. Thought you'd understand that.'

'Shit on your vengeance!' She snatched up the stool and flung it at him, underhand. He got his shield in the way and knocked it spinning over the balcony, but she pressed in fast behind it. He managed to catch her sword on the haft of his axe, blade scraping down and just holding on the studs in the wood. She ended up close, pressed against him almost, snarling, point of her sword waving near his good eye.

She spat in his face, made him flinch, threw an elbow and caught him under the jaw, knocked his head sideways. She pulled her sword back for a thrust but he lashed at her first. She dodged, the axe hacked into the railing and broke a great chunk of wood from it. He twisted away, knowing her sword would be coming, felt the steel slide through his shirt and leave a line of hot pain across his stomach as it whipped out. She stumbled towards him, off balance. He shifted his weight, growled as he swung his shield round with all his strength and all his rage behind it. It hit her square in the face, snapped her head about and sent her reeling into the pipes with a dull clang, back of her skull leaving a great dent. She bounced off and pitched over on her back on the wooden floor, sword clattering from her hand.

He stared at her for a moment, blood whacking at his skull, sweat tickling his scarred face. A muscle twitched in her neck. Not a thick neck. He could've stepped up and cut her head off easy as chopping logs. His fingers worked nervously round the grip of his axe at the thought. She coughed out blood, groaned, shook her head. She started to roll over, eyes glassy, dragged herself up onto hands and knees. She reached out woozily for the grip of her sword.

'No, no.' He stepped up close and kicked it into the corner.

She flinched, turned her head away from him, started crawling slowly after the blade, breathing hard, blood from her nose pit-pattering on the wooden floor. He followed, standing over her, talking. Strange, that. The Bloody-Nine had told him once – if you mean to kill, you kill, you don't talk about it – and it was advice he'd always tried to stick to. He could've killed her easily as crushing a beetle, but he didn't. He wasn't sure if he was talking to stretch the moment out or talking to put the moment off. But he was talking, still.

'Let's not pretend like you're the injured party in all this! You've killed half o' Styria so you could get your way! You're a scheming, lying, poisoning, murdering, treacherous, brother-fucking cunt. Aren't you! I'm doing the right thing. S'all about where you stand and that. I'm no monster. So maybe my reasons ain't the noblest. Everyone's got their reasons. The world'll still be better for one less o' you!' He wished his voice hadn't been down to a croak, because that was a fact. 'I'm doing the right thing!' A fact, and he wanted her to admit it. She owed him that. 'Better for one less o' you!' He leaned down over her, lips curling back, heard footsteps hammering up to his side, turned—

Friendly rammed into him full-tilt and took him off his feet. Shivers snarled, caught him round the back with his shield arm, but the best he could do was drag the convict with him. They plunged through the railing with a snapping of wood and went tumbling out into empty air.

Nicomo Cosca came into view, whipping off his hat and flinging it theatrically across the room, where it presumably missed its intended peg since Morveer saw it tumble to the floor not far from the latrine door behind which he had concealed himself. His mouth twisted into a triumphant sneer in the pungent darkness. The old mercenary held in his hand a metal flask. The very one Morveer himself had tossed at Cosca as an offhand insult in Sipani. The wretched old drunk must have gone back and collected it afterwards, no doubt hoping to lick out the barest trickle of grog. How hollow now did his promise seem never to drink again? So much for man's ability to change. Morveer had expected little better, of course, from the world's leading expert on empty bravado, but Cosca's almost pitiable level of debasement surprised even him.

The sound of the cabinet being opened reached his ear. 'Just must fill this up.' Cosca's voice, though he was out of sight. Metal clinked.

Morveer could just observe the weasel-like visage of his companion. 'How can you drink that piss?'

'I have to drink something, don't I? It was recommended to me by an old friend, now, alas, dead.'

'Do you have any old friends who aren't dead?'

'Only you, Victus. Only you.'

A rattling of glass and Cosca swaggered through the narrow strip to which Morveer's vision was reduced, his flask in one hand, a glass and bottle in the other. It was a distinctive purple vessel, which Morveer clearly remembered poisoning but a few moments ago. It seemed he had engineered another fatal irony.

Cosca would be responsible for his own destruction, as he had been so often before. But this time with a fitting finality. He heard the rustling, snapping sound of cards being shuffled.

'Five scales a hand?' came Cosca's voice. 'Or shall we play for honour?'

Both men burst out laughing. 'Let's make it ten.'

'Ten it is.' Further shuffling. 'Well, this is civilised. Nothing like cards while other men fight, eh? Just like old times.'

'Except no Andiche, no Sesaria and no Sazine.'

'Aside from that,' conceded Cosca. 'Now then. Will you deal, or shall I?'

Friendly growled as he dragged himself clear of the wreckage. Shivers was a few strides away, on the other side of the heap of broken wood and ivory, twisted brass and tangled wire that was all that remained of Duke Orso's harpsichord. The Northman rolled onto his knees, shield still on his arm, axe still gripped in his other fist, blood running down the side of his face from a cut just above his gleaming metal eye.

'You counting fuck! I was going to say my quarrel ain't with you. But now it is.'

They slowly stood, together, watching each other. Friendly slid his knife from its sheath, his cleaver out from his jacket, the worn grips smooth and familiar in his palms. He could forget about all the chaos in the gardens, now, all the madness in the palace. One man against one man, the way it used to be, in Safety. One and one. The plainest arithmetic he could ask for.

'Right, then,' said Friendly, and he grinned.

'Right, then,' hissed Shivers through gritted teeth.

One of the mercenaries who had been breaking the room apart took a half-step towards them. 'What the hell is—'

Shivers leaped the wreckage in one bound, axe a shining arc. Friendly dropped away to the right, ducking underneath it, the wind of it snatching at his hair. His cleaver caught the edge of Shivers' shield, the corner of the blade squealed off and dug into the Northman's shoulder. Not hard enough to do more than cut him, though. Shivers twisted round fast, axe flashing down. Friendly slid around it, heard it crash into the wreckage beside him. He stabbed with his knife but the Northman already had his shield in the way, twisted it, jerking the blade out of Friendly's fist, sending it clattering across the polished floor. He hacked with his cleaver but Shivers pressed close and caught Friendly's elbow against his shoulder, the blade flapping at the blind side of his face and leaving him a bloody nick under his ear.

Friendly took a half-step back, cleaver going out for a sideways sweep, not giving Shivers room to use his axe. He charged forwards behind his shield instead, caught Friendly's flailing cleaver against it and lifted him, growling like a mad dog. Friendly punched at his side, struggling to get a good fist around that big circle of wood, but Shivers had more weight and all the momentum. Friendly was bundled through the door, frame thudding against his shoulder, shield digging into his chest, gaining pace all the time. His boots kicked at the floor, then the floor was gone and he was falling. The back of his head hit stone, he jolted, bounced, tumbling over and over, grunting and wheezing, light and darkness spinning round him. Stairs. Falling down stairs, and the worst of it was he couldn't even count them.

He growled again as he slowly picked himself up at the bottom. He was in a long kitchen, a vaulted cellar lit by small windows, high up. Left leg, right shoulder, back of his head all throbbing, blood on his cheek, one sleeve torn back and a long raw scrape down his forearm, blood on his trouser leg where he must have cut himself on his own cleaver as he fell. But everything still moved.

Shivers stood at the top of a flight of fourteen steps, two times seven, a big black shape with light twinkling from one eye. Friendly beckoned to him.

'Down you come.'

She kept crawling. That was all she could do. Drag herself one stride at a time. Keep both eyes ahead, on the hilt of the Calvez in the corner. Crawl, and spit blood, and will the room to stay still. All the slow way her back was itching, tingling, waiting for Shivers' axe to hack into it and give her the ugly ending she deserved.

At least the one-eyed bastard had stopped talking now.

Monza's hand closed around the hilt and she rolled over, snarling, waving the blade out in front of her like a coward might wave a torch into the night. There was no one there. Only a ragged gap in the railing at the edge of the gallery.

She wiped her bloody nose on her gloved hand, came up slowly to her knees. The dizziness was fading now, the roar in her ears had quieted to a steady thump, her face a throbbing mass, everything feeling twice the size it should have. She shuffled to the shattered balustrade and peered down. The three mercenaries who'd been busy destroying the room were still at it, stood staring down at a shattered harpsichord under the gallery. Still no sign of Shivers, still no clue what had happened. But there were other things on Monza's mind.

Orso.

She clenched her aching jaw, crossed to the far door and heaved it open. Down a gloomy corridor, the noise of fighting steadily growing louder. She edged out onto a wide balcony. Above her the great dome was painted with a sky touched by a rising sun, seven winged women brandishing swords. Aropella's grand fresco of the Fates bearing destinies to earth. Below her the two great staircases swept upwards, carved from three different colours of marble. At their top were the double doors, inlaid with rare woods in the pattern of lions' faces. There, in front of those doors, she'd stood beside Benna for the last time, and told him she loved him.

Safe to say things had changed.

On the round mosaic floor of the hall below, and on the wide marble steps, and on the balcony above, a furious battle was being fought. Men from the Thousand Swords struggled to the death with Orso's guards, three score or more of them, a boiling, flailing mass. Swords crashed on shields, maces staved in armour, axes rose and fell, spears jabbed and thrust. Men roared with fury, blubbered with pain, fought and died, hacked down where they stood. The mercenaries were mad on the promise of plunder and the defenders had nowhere to run to. Mercy looked in short supply on both sides. A couple of men in Talinese uniform were kneeling on the balcony not far from her, cranking flatbows. As one of them stood to shoot he caught an arrow in his chest, fell back, coughing, eyes wide with surprise, spattering blood over a fine statue behind him.

Never fight your own battles, Verturio wrote, *if someone else is willing to fight them for you.* Monza eased carefully back into the shadows.

The cork came out with that sucking pop that was Cosca's favourite noise in all the world. He leaned across the table with the bottle and sloshed some of the syrupy contents into Victus' glass.

'Thanks,' he grunted. 'I think.'

To put it politely, Gurkish grape spirit was not to everyone's taste. Cosca had developed if not a love for it then certainly a tolerance, when employed to defend Dagoska. In fact he had developed a powerful tolerance for anything containing alcohol, and Gurkish grape spirit contained a very great deal at a most reasonable cost. The very thought of that gloriously repulsive burned-vomit taste was making his mouth flood with saliva. A drink, a drink, a drink.

He unscrewed the cap of his own flask, shifted in the captain general's chair, fondly stroking the battered wood of one of its arms. 'Well?'

Victus' thin face radiated suspicion, causing Cosca to reflect that no man he had ever met had a shiftier look to his eyes. They slid to his cards, to Cosca's cards, to the money between them, then slithered back to Cosca. 'Alright. Doubles it is.' He tossed some coins into the centre of the table with that delightful jingle that somehow only hard currency can make. 'What are you carrying, old man?'

'Earth!' Cosca smugly spread his cards out.

Victus flung his own hand down. 'Bloody earth! You always did have the luck of a demon.'

'And you the loyalty of one.' Cosca showed his teeth as he swept the coins towards him. 'I shouldn't worry, the boys will be bringing us plenty more silver in due course. Rule of Quarters, and all that.'

'At this rate I'll have lost all my share to you before they get here.'

'We can hope.' Cosca took a sip from his flask and grimaced. For some reason it tasted even more sour than usual. He wrinkled his lips, sucked his gums, then forced another acrid mouthful down and half-screwed the cap back on. 'Now! I am deeply in

623

need of a shit.' He slapped the table with one hand and stood. 'No tampering with the deck while I'm away, you hear?'

'Me?' Victus was all injured innocence. 'You can trust me, General.'

'Of course I can.' Cosca began to walk, his eyes fixed on the dark crack down the edge of the doorway to the latrine, judging the distances, back prickling as he pictured where Victus was sitting. He twisted his wrist, felt his throwing-knife drop into his waiting palm. 'Just like I could trust you at Afieri—' He spun about, and froze. 'Ah.'

Victus had somehow produced a small flatbow, loaded, and now aimed with impressive steadiness at Cosca's heart. 'Andiche took a *sword-thrust* for you?' he sneered. 'Sesaria *sacrificed* himself? I *knew* those two bastards, remember! What kind of a fucking idiot do you take me for?'

Shenkt sprang through the shattered window and dropped silently down into the hall beyond. An hour ago it must have been a grand dining room indeed, but the Thousand Swords had already stripped it of anything that might raise a penny. Only fragments of glass and plate, slashed canvases in shattered frames and the shells of some furniture too big to move remained. Three little flies chased each other in geometric patterns through the air above the stripped table. Near them two men were arguing while a boy perhaps fourteen years old watched nervously.

'I told you I had the fucking spoons!' a pock-faced man screamed at one with a tarnished breastplate. 'But that bitch knocked me down and I lost 'em! Why didn't you get nothing?'

' 'Cause I was watching the door while you got something, you fucking—'

The boy raised a silent finger to point at Shenkt. The other two abandoned their argument to stare at him. 'Who the hell are you?' demanded the spoon-thief.

'The woman who made you lose your cutlery,' asked Shenkt. 'Murcatto?'

'Who the hell are you, I asked?'

'No one. Only passing through.'

'That so?' He grinned at his fellows as he drew his sword. 'Well, this room's ours, and there's a toll.'

'There's a toll,' hissed the one with the breastplate, in a tone no doubt meant to be intimidating.

The two of them spread out, the boy reluctantly following their lead. 'What have you got for us?' asked the first.

Shenkt looked him in the eye as he came close, and gave him a chance. 'Nothing you want.'

'I'll be the judge of that.' His gaze settled on the ruby ring on Shenkt's forefinger. 'What about that?'

'It isn't mine to give.'

'Then it's ours to take.' They closed in, the one with the pocked face prodding at Shenkt with his sword. 'Hands behind your head, bastard, and get on your knees.'

Shenkt frowned. 'I do not kneel.'

The three zipping flies slowed, drifting lazily, then hanging almost still.

Slowly, slowly, the spoon-thief's hungry leer turned into a snarl.

Slowly, slowly, his arm drifted back for a thrust.

Shenkt stepped around his sword, the edge of his hand sank deep into the thief's chest then tore back out. A great chunk of rib and breastbone was ripped out with it, flew spinning through the air to embed itself deep in the ceiling.

Shenkt brushed the sword aside, seized the next man by his breastplate and flung him across the room, his head crumpling against the far wall, blood showering out under such pressure it made a great star of spatters across the gilded wallpaper from floor to ceiling. The flies were sucked from their places by the wind of his passing, dragged through the air in mad spirals. The ear-splitting bang of his skull exploding joined the hiss of blood spraying from his friend's caved-in chest and all over the gaping boy as time resumed its normal flow.

'The woman who made your friend lose his cutlery.' Shenkt flicked the few drops of blood from his hand. 'Murcatto?'

The boy nodded dumbly.

'Which way did she go?'

His wide eyes rolled towards the far door.

'Good.' Shenkt would have liked to be kind. But then this boy might have run and brought more men, and there would have been further entanglements. Sometimes you must take one life to spare more, and when those times come, sentiment helps nobody. One of his old master's lessons that Shenkt had never forgotten. 'I am sorry for this.'

With a sharp crack, his forefinger sank up to the knuckle in the boy's forehead.

They smashed their way through the kitchens, both doing their level worst to kill each other. Shivers hadn't planned on this but his blood was boiling now. Friendly was in his fucking way, and had to be got out of it, simple as that. It had become a point of pride. Shivers was better armed, he had the reach, he had the shield. But Friendly was slippery as an eel and patient as winter. Backing off, dropping away, forcing nothing, giving no openings. All he had was his cleaver, but Shivers knew he'd killed enough men with that alone, and didn't plan on adding his name to the list.

They tangled again, Friendly weaving round an axe-blow and darting in close, hacking with the cleaver. Shivers stepped into it, caught it on his shield then charged on, sent Friendly stumbling back against a table, metal rattling. Shivers grinned, until he saw the table was covered with knives. Friendly snatched up a blade, arm going back to throw. Shivers dropped down behind his shield, felt the thud as the knife buried itself in the wood. He peered over the edge, saw another spinning at him. It bounced from the metal rim and flashed up into Shivers' face, left him a burning scratch across the cheek. Friendly whipped up another knife.

Shivers weren't about to crouch there and be target practice. He roared as he rushed forwards, shield leading the way. Friendly leaped back, rolled across the table, Shivers' axe just missed him, leaving a great wound in the wood and sending knives jumping in the air. He followed while the convict was off balance, punching away with the edge of his shield, swinging wild with his axe, skin burning, sweat tickling, one eye bulging wild, growling through gritted teeth. Plates shattered, pans scattered, bottles broke, splinters flew, a jar of flour burst open and filled the air with blinding dust.

Shivers left a trail of waste through that kitchen the Bloody-Nine himself might've been proud to make, but the convict dodged and danced, nipped and slashed with knife and cleaver, always just out of reach. All Shivers had to show for his fury by the time they'd done their ugly dance the length of the long room was a bleeding cut on his own arm and a reddening mark on the side of Friendly's face where he'd caught him with his shield.

The convict stood ready and waiting, a couple of steps up the flight leading out, knife and cleaver hanging by his sides, sheen of sweat across his flat chunk of face, skin bloody and battered from a dozen different little cuts and kicks, plus a fall off a balcony and a tumble down some stairs, of course. But Shivers hadn't landed nothing telling on him yet. He didn't look halfway to being finished.

'Come 'ere, you tricky fucker!' Shivers hissed, arm aching shoulder to fingers from swinging his axe. 'Let's put an end to you.'

'You come here,' Friendly grunted back at him. 'Let's put an end to you.'

Shivers shrugged his shoulders, shook out his arms, wiped blood off his forehead on the back of his sleeve, twisted his neck one way then the other. 'Right . . . you . . . *fucking* are!' And he came on again. He didn't need asking twice.

Cosca frowned down at his knife. 'If I said I was just going to peel an orange with it, any chance you'd believe me?'

Victus grinned, causing Cosca to reflect that no man he had ever met had a shiftier smile. 'Doubt I'll believe another word you say. But don't worry. You won't be saying many more.'

'Why is it that men pointing loaded flatbows always feel the need to gloat, rather than simply letting fly?'

'Gloating's fun.' Victus reached for his glass, smirking eyes never leaving Cosca, glinting point of the flatbow bolt steady as stone, and quickly tossed back his spirit in one swallow. 'Yeuch.' He stuck his tongue out. 'Damn, that stuff is sour.'

'Sweeter than my situation,' muttered Cosca. 'I suppose now the captain general's chair will be yours.' A shame. He'd only just got used to sitting in it again himself.

Victus snorted. 'Why would I want the fucking thing? Hasn't done much good for the arses on it up to now, has it? Sazine, you, the Murcattos, Faithful Carpi, and you again. Each one ended up dead or close to it, and all the while I've stood behind, and got a lot richer than a nasty little bastard like me deserves.' He winced, put one hand on his stomach. 'No, I'll find some new idiot to sit there, I think, and make me richer'n ever.' He grimaced again. 'Ah, shit on that stuff. Ah!' He staggered up from his chair, clutching the edge of the table, a thick vein bulging from his forehead. 'What've you done to me, you old bastard?' He squinted over, flatbow suddenly wobbling.

Cosca flung himself forwards. The trigger clicked, the bow-string twanged, the bolt clattered against the plaster just to his left. He rolled up beside the table with a whoop of triumph, raising his knife. 'Hah *hah*—' Victus' bow bashed him in the face, just above his eye. 'Gurgh!' Cosca's vision was suddenly filled with light, his knees wobbling wildly. He clutched at the table, waved his knife at nothing. 'Sfup.' Hands closed around his throat. Hands crusted with heavy rings. Victus' pink face loomed up before his, spit spluttering from his twisted mouth.

Cosca's boots went out from under him, the room flipped over, his head crashed into the table. And all was dark.

The battle under the dome was over, and between the two sides they'd made quite a mess of Orso's cherished rotunda. The glittering mosaic floor and the sweeping steps above it were strewn with corpses, scattered with fallen weapons, dashed and spattered, pooled and puddled with dark blood.

The mercenaries had won – if a dozen of them left standing counted as a victory. 'Help me!' one of the wounded was screeching. 'Help me!' But his fellows had other things on their minds.

'Get these fucking things open!' The one taking charge was Secco, the corporal who'd been on guard when she rode into the Thousand Swords' camp only to find Cosca there ahead of her. He dragged a dead Talinese soldier out of the way of the lion-head doors and dumped the corpse down the stairs. 'You! Find an axe!'

Monza frowned. 'Orso'll have more men in there for sure. We'd better wait for help.'

'Wait? And split the takings?' Secco gave her a withering sneer. 'Fuck yourself, Murcatto, you don't give us orders no more! Get it open!' Two men started battering away with axes, splinters of veneer flying. The rest of the survivors jostled dangerously close behind them, breathless with greed. It seemed the doors had been made to impress guests, not keep out armies. They shuddered, loosening on their hinges. A few more blows and one axe broke clean through, a great chunk of wood splintering away. Secco whooped in triumph as he rammed his spear into the gap, levering the bar on the other side out of its brackets. He fumbled with the ragged edge, pulling the doors wide.

Squealing like children on a feast day, tangled up with each other, drunk on blood and avarice, the mercenaries spilled through into the bright hall where Benna died. Monza knew it was a bad idea to follow. She knew Orso might not even be in there, and if he was, he'd be ready.

But sometimes you have to grasp the nettle.

She dashed round the doorframe after them, keeping low. An instant later she heard the rattling of flatbows. The mercenary in front of her fell and she had to duck around him. Another tumbled backwards, clutching at a bolt in his chest. Boots hammered, men bellowed, the grand room with its great windows and its paintings of history's winners wobbled around her as she ran. She saw figures in full armour, glimpses of steel shining. Orso's closest guards.

She saw Secco jabbing away at one with his spear, the blade scraping uselessly off heavy plate. She heard a loud bonk as a mercenary smashed in a helmet with a big mace, then a scream as he was cut down himself, chopped near in half across the back with a two-handed sword, blood jumping. Another bolt snatched a man from his feet as he charged in and sent him sprawling backwards. Monza crouched, setting her shoulder under the edge of a marble table and heaved it over, a vase that had been on top shattering across the floor. She ducked down behind it, flinched as a flatbow bolt glanced off the stone and clattered away.

'No!' she heard someone shout. 'No!' A mercenary flashed past her, running for the door he'd burst through with such enthusiasm a moment before. There was the sound of a bowstring and he stumbled, a bolt sticking from his back, tottered another step and fell, slid along on his face. He tried to push himself up, coughed blood, then sagged down. He died looking right at her.

This was what you got for being greedy. And here she was, wedged in behind a table and all out of friends, more than likely next.

'Grasp the fucking nettle,' she cursed at herself.

Friendly backed up the last of the steps, his boots suddenly striking echoes as a wide space opened up behind him. A great round room under a dome painted with winged women, seven lofty archways leading in. Statues looked down from the walls, sculptures in relief, hundreds of pairs of eyes following him as he moved. The defenders must have made a stand here, there were bodies scattered across the floor and up the two curving stair-cases. Cosca's mercenaries and Orso's guards mixed up together. All on the same side, now. Friendly thought he could hear fighting echoing from somewhere above, but there was still plenty of fight for him down here.

Shivers stepped out from the archway. His hair was dark with blood on one side, plastered to his skull, scarred face streaked red. He was covered with nicks and grazes, right sleeve ripped wide, blood running down his arm. But Friendly hadn't been able to put in that final blow. The Northman still had his axe in one fist, ready to fight, shield criss-crossed with gouges. He nodded as his one eye moved slowly around the room.

'Lot o' corpses,' he whispered.

'Forty-nine,' said Friendly. 'Seven times seven.'

'Fancy that. We add you, we'll make fifty.'

He threw himself forwards, feinting high then swinging his axe in a great low, ankle-chopping sweep. Friendly jumped it, cleaver coming down towards the Northman's head. Shivers jerked his shield up in time and the blade clanged from its dented boss, sending a jolt up Friendly's arm right to his shoulder. He stabbed at Shivers' side as he passed, got his arm tangled with the haft of the axe as it swung back, but still left the Northman a long cut down his ribs. Friendly spun, raising his cleaver to finish the job, got Shivers' elbow in his throat before he could bring it down, staggered back, near tripping over a corpse.

They faced each other again, Shivers bent over, teeth bared, arm pressed to his wounded side, Friendly coughing as he fought to get his breath and his balance back both at once.

'Another?' whispered Shivers.

'One more,' croaked Friendly.

They went at each other again, their snatched breath, squeaking boots, grunting and growling, the scrape of metal on metal, the clang of metal on stone, all echoing from the marble walls and the painted ceiling, as though men were fighting to the death all around them. They chopped, hacked, spat, kicked, stabbed at each other, jumping over bodies, stumbling over weapons, boots slipping and squeaking in black blood on polished stone.

Friendly jerked away from a clumsy axe-swing that hit the wall and sent chips of marble spinning, found he was backing up the steps. They were both tiring now, slowing. A man can only fight, sweat, bleed for so long. Shivers came after him, breathing hard, shield up in front.

Backing up steps is a bad enough idea when they're not scattered with bodies. Friendly was so busy watching Shivers he put his boot down on a corpse's hand, twisted his ankle. Shivers saw it, jabbed with his axe. Friendly couldn't get his leg out of the way in time and the blade tore a gash out of his calf, half-dragged him over. Shivers growled as he lifted his axe high. Friendly lurched forwards, slashed Shivers' forearm with his knife, left a red-black wound, blood running. The Northman grunted, fumbled his axe, the heavy weapon clattering down beside them. Friendly chopped at his skull with the cleaver but Shivers got his shield arm in the way, the two of them getting tangled, the blade only slitting Shivers' scalp, blood bubbling from the wound, pattering over them both. The Northman grabbed Friendly's shoulder with his bloody hand, dragging him close, good eye bulging with crazy rage, steel eye spattered shining red, lips twisted in a mad snarl as he tipped his head backwards.

Friendly drove his knife into Shivers' thigh, felt the metal slide in to the hilt. Shivers gave a kind of squeal, pain and fury together. His forehead smashed into Friendly's mouth with a sick crunch. The hall reeled around, the steps hit Friendly in the back, his skull cracked against marble. He saw Shivers loom over him, thought it would be a good idea to bring the cleaver up. Before he could do it, Shivers rammed his shield down, metal rim clanging against stone. Friendly felt the two bones in his forearm break, cleaver dropping from his numb fingers and clattering down the steps.

Shivers reached down, specks of pink spit flicking from his clenched teeth with each moaning breath, fist closing around the grip of his axe. Friendly watched him do it, feeling no more than a mild curiosity. Everything was bright and blurry, now. He saw the scar on the Northman's thick wrist, in the shape of a number seven. Seven was a good number, today, just as it had been the first day they met. Just as it always was.

'Excuse me.' Shivers froze for a moment, his one eye sliding sideways. He reeled around, axe coming after. A man stood behind him, a lean man with pale hair. It was hard to see what happened. The axe missed, Shivers' shield shattered in a tangle of flying wood, he was snatched off his feet and sent tumbling across the chamber. He crashed into the far wall with a gurgle, bounced off and rolled slowly down the opposite set of steps, flopping over once, twice, three times, and lying still at the bottom.

'Three times,' gurgled Friendly through his split lips.

'Stay,' said the pale man, stepping around him and off up the stairway. It was not so difficult to obey. Friendly had no other plans. He spat a lump of tooth out of his numb mouth, and that was all. He lay there, blinking slowly, staring up at the winged women on the ceiling.

Seven of them, with seven swords.

A rapid spectrum of emotions had swept over Morveer during the past few moments. Triumphant delight, as he had seen Cosca drink from his flask and all unknowing doom himself. Horror and a pointless search for a hiding place as the old mercenary declared his intention to visit the latrine. Curiosity, as he then saw Victus produce a loaded flatbow from beneath the table and train it on his general's back. Triumph once again as he watched Victus consume his own fatal measure of spirit. Finally he was forced to clamp one hand over his mouth to smother his amusement as the poisoned Cosca flung himself clumsily at his poisoned opponent and the two men wrestled, fell to the floor and lay still in a final embrace.

The ironies positively piled one upon the next. Most earnestly they had attempted to kill each other, never realising that Morveer had already done both their jobs for them.

With the smile still on his face he slid his mounted needle from its hidden pocket within the lining of his mercenary's jerkin. Caution first, always. In case any trace of life remained in either of the two murderous old mercenaries, the lightest prick with this shining splinter of metal, coated with his own Preparation Number Twelve, would extinguish it for good and to the general benefit of the world. Morveer carefully eased the latrine door open with the gentlest of creaks, and on pointed toes crept out into the room beyond.

The table was tipped over on its side, coins and cards widely scattered. Cosca lay on his back beside it, left hand hanging nerveless, his flask not far away. Victus was draped on top of him, small flatbow still gripped in one fist, the clasp at its end spotted with red blood. Morveer knelt beside the deceased, hooked his free hand under Victus' corpse and with a grunting effort rolled it off.

Cosca's eyes were closed, his mouth open, blood streaked his cheek from a wound on his forehead. His skin was waxy pale with the unmistakable sheen of death.

'A man can *change*, eh?' sneered Morveer. 'So much for *your* promises!'

To his tremendous shock, Cosca's eyes snapped suddenly open.

To his even more tremendous shock, an indescribably awful pain lanced up through his stomach. He took in a great shuddering breath and gave vent to an unearthly howl. Looking down, he perceived that the old mercenary had driven a knife into his groin. Morveer's breath whooped in again. Desperately he raised his arm.

There was a faint slapping sound as Cosca seized his wrist and wrenched it sharply sideways, causing the needle to sink into Morveer's neck. There was a pregnant pause. They remained frozen, a human sculpture, the knife still in Morveer's groin, the needle in his neck, gripped by his hand, gripped by Cosca's hand. Cosca frowned up. Morveer stared down. His eyes bulged. His body trembled. He said nothing. What could one possibly say? The implications were crushingly obvious. Already the most potent poison of which he was aware, carried swiftly from neck to brain, was causing his extremities to become numb.

'Poisoned the grape spirit, eh?' hissed Cosca.

'Fuh,' gurgled Morveer, unable now to form words.

'Did you forget I promised you never to drink again?' The old mercenary released the knife, reached across the floor with his bloody hand, retrieved his flask, spun the cap off with a practised motion and tipped it up. White liquid splashed out across the floor. 'Goat's milk. I hear it's good for the digestion. The strongest thing I've had since we left Sipani, but it would hardly do to let everyone know it. I have a certain reputation to uphold here. Hence all the bottles.'

Cosca shoved Morveer over. The strength was rapidly fading from his limbs and he was powerless to resist. He flopped limp across Victus' corpse. He could scarcely feel his neck. The agony in his groin had faded to a dull throb. Cosca looked down at him.

'Didn't I promise you I'd stop? What kind of a man do you take me for, that I'd break my word?'

Morveer had no breath left to speak, let alone scream. The pain was fading in any case. He wondered, as he often had, how his life might have differed had he not poisoned his mother, and doomed himself to life in the orphanage. His vision was clouding, blurring, growing dark.

'I need to thank you. You see, Morveer, a man *can* change, given the proper encouragement. And your scorn was the very spur I needed.'

Killed by his own agent. It was the way so many great practitioners of his profession ended their lives. And on the eve of his retirement, too. He was sure there was an irony there somewhere . . .

'Do you know the best thing about all this?' Cosca's voice boomed in his ears, Cosca's grin swam above him. 'Now I can start drinking again.'

One of the mercenaries was pleading, blubbering, begging for his life. Monza sat against the cold marble slab of the tabletop and listened to him, breathing hard, sweating hard, weighing the Calvez in her hand. It would be little better than useless against the heavy armour of Orso's guards, even if she'd fancied taking on that many at once. She heard the damp squelch of a blade rammed into flesh and the pleading was cut off in a long scream and a short gurgle.

Not really a sound to give anyone confidence.

She peered round the edge of the table. She counted seven guards still standing, one ripping his spear free of a dead mercenary's chest, two turning towards her, heavy swords ready, one working an axe from Secco's split skull. Three were kneeling, busily cranking flatbows. Behind them stood the big round table on which the map of Styria was still unrolled. On the map was a crown, a ring of sparkling gold sprouting with gem-encrusted oak leaves, not unlike the one that had killed Rogont and his dream of Styria united. Beside the crown, dressed in black and with his iron-shot black hair and beard as neatly groomed as ever, stood Grand Duke Orso.

He saw her, and she saw him, and the anger boiled up, hot and comforting. One of his guards slipped a bolt into his flatbow and levelled it at her. She was about to duck behind the slab of marble when Orso held out one arm.

'Wait! Stop.' That same voice that she had never disobeyed in eight hard years. 'Is that you, Monzcarro?'

'Damn right it is!' she snarled back. 'Get ready to fucking die!' Though it looked as if she might be going first.

'I've been ready for some time,' he called out softly. 'You've seen to that. Well done! My hopes are all in ruins, thanks to you.'

'You needn't thank me!' she called. 'It was Benna I did it for!'

'Ario is dead.'

'Hah!' she barked back. 'That's what happens when I stab a worthless cunt in the neck and throw him from a window!' A flurry of twitches crawled up Orso's cheek. 'But why pick him out? There was Gobba, and Mauthis, and Ganmark, and Faithful – I've slaughtered the whole crowd! Everyone who was in this room when you murdered my brother!'

'And Foscar? I've heard no word since the defeat at the fords.'

'You can stop listening!' Said with a glee she hardly felt. 'Skull smashed to pulp on a farmhouse floor!'

The anger had all gone from Orso's face and it hung terribly slack. 'You must be happy.'

'I'm not fucking sad, I'll tell you that!'

'Grand Duchess Monzcarro of Talins.' Orso tapped two fingers slowly against his palm, the sharp snaps echoing off the high ceiling. 'I congratulate you on your victory. You have what you wanted after all!'

'What I wanted?' For a moment she could hardly believe what she was hearing. 'You think I wanted *this*? After the battles I fought for you? The victories I won for you?' She was near shrieking, spitting with fury. She ripped her glove off with her teeth and shook her mutilated hand at him. 'I fucking wanted *this*? What reason did we give you to betray us? We were loyal to you! Always!'

'Loyal?' Orso gave a disbelieving gasp of his own. 'Crow your victory if you must, but don't crow your innocence to me! We both know better!'

All three flatbows were loaded and levelled now. 'We were loyal!' she screamed again, voice cracking.

'Can you deny it? That Benna met with malcontents, revolutionaries, traitors among my ungrateful subjects? That he promised them weapons? That he promised you would lead them to glory? Claim my place? Usurp me! Did you think I would not learn of it? Did you think I would stand idly by?'

'What the . . . you fucking *liar*!'

'Still you deny it? I would not believe it myself when they told me! My Monza? Closer to me than my own children? My Monza, betray me? With my own eyes I saw him! With my own eyes!' The echoes of his voice slowly faded, and left the hall almost silent. Only the gentle clanking of the four armoured men as they edged ever so slowly towards her. She could only stare, the realisation creeping slowly through her.

We could have our own city, Benna had said. *You could be the Duchess Monzcarro of . . . wherever*. Of Talins, had been his thought. *We deserve to be remembered*. He'd planned it himself, alone, and given her no choice. Just as he had when he betrayed Cosca. *It's better this way*. Just as he had when he took Hermon's gold. *This is for us*.

He'd always been the one with the big plans.

'Benna,' she mouthed. 'You fool.'

'You didn't know,' said Orso quietly. 'You didn't know, and

now we are come to this. Your brother doomed himself, and both of us, and half of Styria besides.' A sad little chuckle bubbled out of him. 'Just when I think I know it all, life always finds a way to surprise me. You're late, Shenkt.' His eyes flicked to the side. 'Kill her.'

Monza felt a shadow fall across her, lurched around. A man had stolen up while they spoke, his soft work boots making not the slightest sound. Now he stood over her, close enough to touch. He held out his hand. There was a ring in his palm. Benna's ruby ring.

'I believe this is yours,' he said.

A pale, lean face. Not old, but deeply lined, with harsh cheekbones and eyes hungry bright in bruised sockets. Monza's eyes went wide, the chill shock of recognition washing over her like ice water.

'Kill her!' shouted Orso.

The newcomer smiled, but it was like a skull's smile, never touching his eyes. 'Kill her? After all the effort I went to keeping her alive?'

The colour had drained from her face. Indeed she looked almost as pale as she had done when he first found her, broken amongst the rubbish on the slopes of Fontezarmo. Or when she'd first woken after he pulled the stitches, and stared down in horror at her own scarred body.

'Kill her?' he asked again. 'After I carried her from the mountain? After I mended her bones and stitched her back together? After I protected her from your hirelings in Puranti?'

Shenkt turned his hand over and let the ring fall, and it bounced once and tinkled down spinning on the floor beside her twisted right hand. She did not thank him, but he had not expected thanks. It was not for her thanks that he had done it.

'Kill them both!' screamed Orso.

Shenkt was always surprised by how treacherous men could be over trifles, yet how loyal they could be when their lives were forfeit. These last few guards still fought to the death for Orso, even though his day was clearly done. Perhaps they could not comprehend that a man so great as the Grand Duke of Talins might die like any other, and all his power so easily turn to dust.

Perhaps for some men obedience became a habit they could not question. Or perhaps they came to define themselves by their service to a master, and chose to take the short step into death as part of something great, rather than walk the long, hard road of life in insignificance.

If so, then Shenkt would not deny them. Slowly, slowly, he breathed in.

The drawn-out twang of the flatbow string throbbed deep in his ears. He stepped out of the path of the first bolt, let it drift under his raised arm. The aim of the next was good, right for Murcatto's throat. He plucked it from the air between finger and thumb as it crawled past, set it carefully down on a polished table as he crossed the room. He took up an idealised bust of one of Orso's forebears from beside it – his grandfather, Shenkt suspected, the one who had himself been a mercenary. He flung it at the nearest flatbowman, just in the process of lowering his bow, puzzled. It caught him in the stomach, sank deep into his armour, folded him in half in a cloud of stone chips and tore him off his feet towards the far wall, legs and arms stretched out in front of him, his bow spinning high into the air.

Shenkt hit the nearest man on the helmet and stove it deep into his shoulders, blood spraying from the crumpled visor, axe dropping slowly from his twisting hand. The next had an open helm, the look of surprise just forming as Shenkt's fist drove a dent into his breastplate so deep that it bent his backplate out with a groan of twisted metal. He sprang to the table, marble floor splitting under his boots as he came down. The nearest of the two remaining archers slowly raised his flatbow as though to use it as a shield. Shenkt's hand split it in half, string flailing, tore the man's helmet off and sent it hurtling up into the ceiling, his body tumbling sideways, spraying blood, to crumple against the wall in a shower of plaster. Shenkt seized hold of the other archer and tossed him out of one of the high windows, sparkling fragments tumbling down, bouncing, spinning, breaking apart, deep clangour of shattering glass making the air hum.

The last but one had his sword raised, flecks of spit floating from his twisted lips as he gave his war cry. Shenkt caught him by the wrist, hurled him upside-down across the room and into his final comrade. They were mangled together, a tangle of dented armour, crashed into a set of shelves, gilded books ripped open, loose papers spewing into the air, gently fluttering down as Shenkt breathed out, and let time find its course again.

The spinning flatbow fell, bounced from the tiles and clattered away into a corner. Grand Duke Orso stood just where he had before, beside the round table with its map of Styria, the sparkling crown sitting in its centre. His mouth fell open.

'I never leave a job half-done,' said Shenkt. 'But I was never working for you.'

Monza got to her feet, staring at the bodies tangled, scattered, twisted about the far end of the hall. Papers fluttered down like autumn leaves, from a bookcase shattered around a mass of bloody armour, cracks lancing out through the marble walls all about it.

She stepped around the upended table. Past the bodies of mercenaries and guards. Over Secco's corpse, his smeared brains gleaming in one of the long stripes of sunlight from the high windows.

Orso watched her come in silence, the great painting of him proudly claiming victory at the Battle of Etrea looming ten strides high over his shoulder. The little man and his outsized myth.

The bone-thief stood back, hands spattered with blood to the elbow, watching them. She didn't know what he had done, or how, or why. It didn't matter now.

Her boots crunched on broken glass, on splintered wood, ripped paper, shattered pottery. Everywhere black spots of blood were scattered and her soles soaked them up and left bloody footprints behind her. Like the bloody trail she'd left across Styria, to come here. To stand on the spot where they killed her brother.

She stopped, a sword's length away from Orso. Waiting, she hardly knew what for. Now the moment had come, the moment she'd strained for with every muscle, endured so much pain, spent so much money, wasted so many lives to reach, she found it hard to move. What would come after?

Orso raised his brows. He picked up the crown from the table with exaggerated care, the way a mother might pick up a newborn baby. 'This was to be mine. This almost was mine. This is what you fought for, all those years. And this is what you kept from me, in the end.' He turned it slowly around in his hands, the jewels sparkling. 'When you build your life around only one thing, love only one person, dream only one dream, you risk losing everything at a stroke. You built your life around your brother. I built mine around a crown.' He gave a heavy sigh, pursed his lips, then tossed the circle of gold aside and watched it rattle round and round on the map of Styria. 'Now look at us. Both equally wretched.'

'Not equally.' She lifted the scuffed, notched, hard-used blade of the Calvez. The blade she'd had made for Benna. 'I still have you.'

'And when you have killed me, what will you live for then?' His eyes moved from the sword to hers. 'Monza, Monza . . . what will you do without me?'

'I'll think of something.'

The point punctured his jacket with a faint pop, slid effort-lessly through his chest and out of his back. He gave a gentle grunt, eyes widening, and she slid the blade free. They stood there, opposite each other, for a moment.

'Oh.' He touched one finger to dark cloth and it came away red. 'Is that all?' He looked up at her, puzzled. 'I was expecting . . . more.'

He crumpled all at once, knees dropping against the polished floor, then he toppled forwards and the side of his face thumped damply against the marble beside her boot. The one eye she could see rolled slowly towards her, and the corner of his mouth twitched into a smile. Then he was still.

Seven out of seven. It was done.

Seeds

It was a winter's morning, cold and clear, and Monza's breath smoked on the air.

She stood outside the chamber where they killed her brother. On the terrace they threw her from. Her hands resting on the parapet they'd rolled her off. Above the mountainside that had broken her apart. She felt that nagging ache still up the bones of her legs, across the back of her gloved hand, down the side of her skull. She felt that prickling need for the husk-pipe that she knew would never quite fade. It was far from comfortable, staring down that long drop towards the tiny trees that had snatched at her as she fell. That was why she came here every morning.

A good leader should never be comfortable, Stolicus wrote.

The sun was climbing, now, and the bright world was full of colour. The blood had drained from the sky and left it a vivid blue, white clouds crawling high above. To the east, the forest crumbled away into a patchwork of fields – squares of fallow green, rich black earth, golden-brown stubble. Her fields. Further still and the river met the grey sea, branching out in a wide delta, choked with islands. Monza could just make out the suggestion of tiny towers there, buildings, bridges, walls. Great Talins, no bigger than her thumbnail. Her city.

That idea still seemed a madman's ranting.

'Your Excellency.' Monza's chamberlain lurked in one of the high doorways, bowing so low he almost tongued the stone. The same man who'd served Orso for fifteen years, had somehow come through the sack of Fontezarmo unscathed, and now had made the transition from master to mistress with admirable smoothness. Monza had stolen Orso's city, after all, his palace, some of his clothes, even, with a few adjustments. Why not his retainers too? Who knew their jobs better?

'What is it?'

'Your ministers are here. Lord Rubine, Chancellor Grulo, Chancellor Scavier, Colonel Volfier and . . . Mistress Vitari.' He cleared his throat, looking somewhat pained. 'Might I enquire whether Mistress Vitari has a specific title yet?'

'She handles those things no one with a specific title can.'

'Of course, your Excellency.'

'Bring them in.'

The heavy doors were swung open, faced with beaten copper engraved with twisting serpents. Not the works of art Orso's lion-face veneers had been, perhaps, but a great deal stronger. Monza had made sure of that. Her five visitors strutted, strode, bustled and shuffled through, their footsteps echoing around the chill marble of Orso's private audience hall. Two months in, and still she couldn't think of it as hers.

Vitari came first, with much the same dark clothes and smirk she'd worn when Monza first met her in Sipani. Volfier was next, walking stiffly in his braided uniform. Scavier and Grulo competed with each other to follow him. Old Rubine laboured along at the rear, bent under his chain of office, taking his time getting to the point, as always.

'So you still haven't got rid of it.' Vitari frowned at the vast portrait of Orso gazing down from the far wall.

'Why would I? Reminds me of my victories, and my defeats. Reminds me where I came from. And that I have no intention of going back.'

'And it is a fine painting,' observed Rubine, looking sadly about. 'Precious few remain.'

'The Thousand Swords are nothing if not thorough.' The room had lost almost everything not nailed down or carved into the mountainside. Orso's vast desk still crouched grimly at the far end, if somewhat wounded by an axe as someone had searched in vain for hidden compartments. The towering fireplace, held up by monstrous marble figures of Juvens and Kanedias, had proved impossible to remove and now contained a few flaming logs, failing utterly to warm the cavernous interior. The great round table too was still in place, the same map unrolled across it. As it had been the last day that Benna lived, but stained now in one corner with a few brown spots of Orso's blood.

Monza walked to it, wincing at a niggle through her hip, and her ministers gathered around the table in a ring just as Orso's ministers had. They say history moves in circles. 'The news?'

'Good,' said Vitari, 'if you love bad news. I hear the Baolish have crossed the river ten thousand strong and invaded Osprian territory. Muris has declared independence and gone to war with Sipani, again, while Sotorius' sons fight each other in the streets of the city.' Her finger waved over the map, carelessly spreading chaos across the continent. 'Visserine remains leaderless, a plundered shadow of her former glory. There are rumours of plague in Affoia, of a great fire in Nicante. Puranti is in uproar. Musselia is in turmoil.'

Rubine tugged unhappily at his beard. 'Woe is Styria! They say Rogont was right. The Years of Blood are at an end. The Years of Fire are just beginning. In Westport, the holy men are proclaiming the end of the world.'

Monza snorted. 'Those bastards proclaim the end of the world whenever a bird shits. Anywhere without calamities?'

'Talins?' Vitari glanced around the room. 'Though I hear the palace at Fontezarmo did suffer some light looting recently. And Borletta.'

'Borletta?' It wasn't much more than a year since Monza had told Orso, in this very hall, how she'd thoroughly looted that very city. Not to mention spiked its ruler's head above the gates.

'Duke Cantain's young niece foiled a plot by the nobles of the city to depose her. Apparently, she made such a fine speech they all threw aside their swords, fell to their knees and swore undying fealty to her on the spot. Or that's the story they're telling, at any rate.'

'Making armed men fall to their knees is a neat trick, however she managed it.' Monza remembered how Rogont won his great victory. *Blades can kill men, but only words can move them, and good neighbours are the surest shelter in a storm.* 'Do we have such a thing as an ambassador?'

Rubine looked around the table. 'I daresay one could be produced.'

'Produce one and send him to Borletta, with a suitable gift for the persuasive duchess and . . . offers of our sisterly affection.'

'Sisterly . . . affection?' Vitari looked like she'd found a turd in her bed. 'I didn't think that was your style.'

'My style is whatever works. I hear good neighbours are the surest shelter in a storm.'

'Them and good swords.'

'Good swords go without saying.'

Rubine was looking deeply apologetic. 'Your Excellency, your reputation is not . . . all it might be.'

'It never has been.'

'But you are widely blamed for the death of King Rogont, Chancellor Sotorius and their comrades in the League of Nine. Your lone survival was . . .'

Vitari smirked at her. 'Damnably suspicious.'

'In Talins that only makes you better loved, of course. But elsewhere . . . if Styria were not so deeply divided, it would undoubtedly be united against you.'

Grulo frowned across at Scavier. 'We need someone to blame.'

'Let's put the blame where it belongs,' said Monza, 'this once. Castor Morveer poisoned the crown, on Orso's instructions, no doubt. Let it be known. As widely as possible.'

'But, your Excellency . . .' Rubine had moved from apologetic to abject. 'No one knows the name. For great crimes, people must blame great figures.'

Monza's eyes rolled up. Duke Orso smirked triumphantly at her from the painting of a battle he was never at. She found herself smirking back. Fine lies beat tedious truths every time.

'Inflate him, then. Castor Morveer, death without a face, most infamous of Master Poisoners. The greatest and most subtle murderer in history. A poisoner-poet. A man who could slip into the best-guarded building in Styria, murder its monarch and four of its greatest leaders and away unnoticed like a night breeze. Who is safe from the very King of Poisons? Why, I was lucky to escape with my life.'

'Poor innocent that you are.' Vitari slowly shook her head. 'Rubs me wrong to heap fame on that slime of a man.'

'I daresay you live with worse.'

'Dead men make poor scapegoats.'

'Oh, come now, you can breathe some life into him. Bills at every corner, proclaiming his guilt in this heinous crime and offering, let's say, a hundred thousand scales for his head.'

Volfier was looking more worried by the moment. 'But . . . he is dead, isn't he?'

'Buried with the rest when we filled in the trenches. Which means we'll never have to pay. Hell, make it two hundred thousand, then we look rich at the same time.'

'And looking rich is almost as useful as being it,' said Scavier, frowning at Grulo.

'With the tale I'll get told, the name of Morveer will be spoken with hushed awe when we're long dead and gone.' Vitari smiled. 'Mothers will scare their children with it.'

'No doubt he's grinning in his grave at the thought,' said Monza. 'I hear you unpicked a little revolt, by the way.'

'I wouldn't insult the term by applying it to those amateurs. The fools put up bills advertising their meetings! We knew already, but bills? In plain sight? You ask me, they deserve the death penalty just for stupidity.'

'Or there is exile,' offered Rubine. 'A little mercy makes you look just, virtuous and powerful.'

'And I could do with a touch of all three, eh?' She thought about it for a moment. 'Fine them heavily, publish their names, parade them naked before the Senate House, then . . . set them free.'

'Free?' Rubine raised his thick white eyebrows.

'Free?' Vitari raised her thin orange ones.

'How just, virtuous and powerful does that make me? Punish them harshly, we give their friends a wrong to avenge. Spare them, we make resistance seem absurd. Watch them. You said yourself they're stupid. If they plan more treason they'll lead us to it. We can hang them then.'

Rubine cleared his throat. 'As your Excellency commands. I will have bills printed detailing your mercy to these men. The Serpent of Talins forbears to use her fangs.'

'For now. How are the markets?'

A hard smile crossed Scavier's soft face. 'Busy, busy, morning until night. Traders have come to us fleeing the chaos in Sipani, in Ospria, in Affoia, all more than willing to pay our dues if they can bring in their cargoes unmolested.'

'The granaries?'

'The harvest was good enough to see us through the winter

without riots, I hope.' Grulo clicked his tongue. 'But much of the land towards Musselia still lies fallow. Farmers driven out when Rogont's conquering forces moved through, foraging. Then the Thousand Swords left a sweep of devastation almost all the way to the banks of the Etris. The farmers are always the first to suffer in hard times.'

A lesson Monza hardly needed to be taught. 'The city is full of beggars, yes?'

'Beggars and refugees.' Rubine tugged his beard again. He'd tug the bastard out if he told many more sad tales. 'A sign of the times—'

'Give the land away, then, to anyone who can yield a crop, and pay us tax. Farmland without farmers is nothing more than mud.'

Grulo inclined his head. 'I will see to it.'

'You're quiet, Volfier.' The old veteran stood there, glaring at the map and grinding his teeth.

'Fucking Etrisani!' he burst out, bashing his sword-hilt with one big fist. 'I mean, sorry, that is, my apologies, your Excellency, but . . . those bastards!'

Monza grinned. 'More trouble on the border?'

'Three farms burned out.' Her grin faded. 'The farmers missing. Then the patrol who went looking for them was shot at from the woods, one man killed, two wounded. The rest pursued, but mindful of your orders left off at the border.'

'They're testing you,' said Vitari. 'Angry because they were Orso's first allies.'

Grulo nodded. 'They gave up everything in his cause and hoped to reap a golden harvest when he became king.'

Volfier slapped angrily at the table's edge. 'Bastards think we're too weak to stop 'em!'

'Are we?' asked Monza.

'We've three thousand foot and a thousand horse, all armed, drilled, all good men seen action before.'

'Ready to fight?'

'Only give the word, they'll prove it!'

'What about the Etrisanese?'

'All bluster,' sneered Vitari. 'A second-rate power at the best of times, and their best was long ago.'

'We have the advantage in numbers and quality,' growled Volfier.

'Undeniably, we have just cause,' said Rubine. 'A brief sortie across the border to teach a sharp lesson—'

'We have the funds for a more significant campaign,' said Scavier. 'I already have some ideas for financial demands that might leave us considerably enriched—'

'The people will support you,' cut in Grulo. 'And indemnities will more than cover the expense!'

Monza frowned at the map, frowned in particular at those spots of blood in the corner. Benna would have counselled caution. Would have asked for time to think out a plan . . . but Benna was a long time dead, and Monza's taste had always been to move fast, strike hard and worry about the plans afterwards. 'Get your men ready to march, Colonel Volfier. I've a mind to take Etrisani under siege.'

'Siege?' muttered Rubine.

Vitari grinned sideways. 'It's when you surround a city and force its surrender.'

'I am aware of the definition!' snapped the old man. 'But caution, your Excellency, Talins has but lately come through the most painful of upheavals—'

'I have only the greatest respect for your knowledge of the law, Rubine,' said Monza, 'but war is my department, and believe me, once you go to war, there is nothing worse than half measures.'

'But what of making allies—'

'No one wants an ally who can't protect what's theirs. We need to demonstrate our resolve, or the wolves will all be sniffing round our carcass. We need to bring these dogs in Etrisani to heel.'

'Make them pay,' hissed Scavier.

'Crush them,' growled Grulo.

Volfier was grinning wide as he saluted. 'I'll have the men mustered and ready within the week.'

'I'll polish up my armour,' she said, though she kept it polished anyway. 'Anything else?' The five of them stayed silent. 'My thanks, then.'

'Your Excellency.' They bowed each in their own ways,

Rubine with the frown of weighty doubts, Vitari with the slight-est, lingering smirk.

Monza watched them file out. She might have liked to put aside the sword and make things grow. The way she'd wanted to long ago, after her father died. Before the Years of Blood began. But she'd seen enough to know that no battle is ever the last, whatever people might want to believe. Life goes on. Every war carries within it the seeds of the next, and she planned to be good and ready for the harvest.

Get out your plough, by all means, Farans wrote, *but keep a dagger handy, just in case.*

She frowned at the map, left hand straying down to rest on her stomach. It was starting to swell. Three months, now, since her blood had come. That meant it was Rogont's child. Or maybe Shivers'. A dead man's child or a killer's, a king's or a beggar's. All that really mattered was that it was hers.

She walked slowly to the desk, dropped into the chair, pulled the chain from her shirt and turned the key in the lock. She took out Orso's crown, the reassuring weight between her palms, the reassuring pain in her right hand as she lifted it and placed it carefully on the papers scattered across the scuffed leather top. Gold gleamed in the winter sun. The jewels she'd had prised out, sold to pay for weapons. Gold, to steel, to more gold, just as Orso always told her. Yet she found she couldn't part with the crown itself.

Rogont had died unmarried, without heirs. His child, even his bastard, would have a good claim on his titles. Grand Duke of Ospria. King of Styria, even. Rogont had worn the crown, after all, even if it had been a poisoned one, and only for a vainglorious instant. She felt the slightest smile at the corner of her mouth. When you lose all you have, you can always seek revenge. But if you get it, what then? Orso had spoken that much truth. Life goes on. You need new dreams to look to.

She shook herself, snatched the crown up and slid it back inside the desk. Staring at it wasn't much better than staring at her husk-pipe, wondering whether or not to put the fire to it. She was just turning the key in the lock as the doors were swung open and her chamberlain grazed the floor again with his face.

'And this time?'

'A representative of the Banking House of Valint and Balk, your Excellency.'

Monza had known they were coming, of course, but they were no more welcome for that. 'Send him in.'

For a man from an institution that could buy and sell nations, he didn't look like much. Younger than she'd expected, with a curly head of hair, a pleasant manner and an easy grin. That worried her more than ever.

The bitterest enemies come with the sweetest smiles. Verturio. Who else?

'Your Excellency.' He bowed almost as low as her chamberlain, which took some doing.

'Master . . . ?'

'Sulfur. Yoru Sulfur, at your service.' He had different-coloured eyes, she noticed as he drew closer to the desk – one blue, one green.

'From the Banking House of Valint and Balk.'

'I have the honour of representing that proud institution.'

'Lucky you.' She glanced around the great chamber. 'I'm afraid a lot of damage was done in the assault. Things are more . . . functional than they were in Orso's day.'

His smile only widened. 'I noticed a little damage to the walls on my way in. But functional suits me perfectly, your Excellency. I am here to discuss business. To offer you, in fact, the full backing of my employers.'

'I understand you came often to my predecessor, Grand Duke Orso, to offer him your full backing.'

'Quite so.'

'And now I have murdered him and stolen his place, you come to me.'

Sulfur did not even blink. 'Quite so.'

'Your backing moulds easily to new situations.'

'We are a bank. Every change must be an opportunity.'

'And what do you offer?'

'Money,' he said brightly. 'Money to fund armies. Money to fund public works. Money to return glory to Talins, and to Styria. Perhaps even money to render your palace less . . . functional.'

Monza had left a fortune in gold buried near the farm where

649

she was born. She preferred to leave it there still. Just in case. 'And if I like it sparse?'

'I feel confident that we could lend political assistance also. Good neighbours, you know, are the surest shelter in a storm.' She did not like his choice of words, so soon after she'd used them herself, but he went smoothly on. 'Valint and Balk have deep roots in the Union. Extremely deep. I do not doubt we could arrange an alliance between you and their High King.'

'An alliance?' She didn't mention that she'd very nearly consummated an alliance of a different kind with the King of the Union, in a gaudy bedchamber at Cardotti's House of Leisure. 'Even though he's married to Orso's daughter? Even though his sons may have a claim on my dukedom? A better claim than mine, many would say.'

'We strive always to work with what we find, before we strive to change it. For the right leader, with the right backing, Styria is there for the taking. Valint and Balk wish to stand with the victor.'

'Even though I broke into your offices in Westport and murdered your man Mauthis?'

'Your success in that venture only demonstrates your great resourcefulness.' Sulfur shrugged. 'Men are easily replaced. The world is full of them.'

She tapped thoughtfully at the top of her desk. 'Strange that you should come here, making such an offer.'

'How so?'

'Only yesterday I had a very similar visit from a representative of the Prophet of Gurkhul, offering his . . . backing.'

That gave him a moment's pause. 'Whom did he send?'

'A woman called Ishri.'

Sulfur's eyes narrowed by the smallest fraction. 'You cannot trust her.'

'But I can trust you, because you smile so sweetly? So did my brother, and he lied with every breath.'

Sulfur only smiled the more. 'The truth, then. Perhaps you are aware that the Prophet and my employers stand on opposite sides of a great struggle.'

'I've heard it mentioned.'

'Believe me when I say you would not wish to find yourself on the wrong side.'

'I'm not sure I wish to find myself on either side.' She slowly settled back into her chair, faking comfort when she felt like a fraud at a stolen desk. 'But never fear. I told Ishri the price of her support was too high. Tell me, Master Sulfur, what price will Valint and Balk ask for their help?'

'No more than what is fair. Interest on their loans. Preference in their business dealings and those of their partners and associates. That you refuse to deal with the Gurkish and their allies. That you act, when my employers request, in concert with the forces of the Union—'

'Only whenever your employers request?'

'Perhaps once or twice in your lifetime.'

'Or perhaps more, as you see fit. You want me to sell Talins to you and thank you for the privilege. You want me to kneel at your vault door and beg for favours.'

'You over-dramatise—'

'I do not kneel, Master Sulfur.'

It was his turn to pause at her choice of words. But only for a moment. 'May I be candid, your Excellency?'

'I'd like to see you try.'

'You are new to the ways of power. Everyone must kneel to someone. If you are too proud to take our hand of friendship, others will.'

Monza snorted, though behind her scorn her heart was pounding. 'Good luck, to them and to you. May your hand of friendship bring them happier results than it brought to Orso. I believe Ishri was going to start looking for friends in Puranti. Perhaps you should go to Ospria first, or Sipani, or Affoia. I'm sure you'll find someone in Styria to take your money. We're famous for our whores.'

Sulfur's grin twitched even wider. 'Talins owes great debts to my employers.'

'Orso owes great debts to them, you can ask him for your money back. I believe he was thrown out with the kitchen waste, but you should find him if you dig, down there at the bottom of the cliff. I'll happily lend you a trowel for the purpose.'

Still he smiled, but there was no missing his threat. 'It would be a shame if you left us no choice but to yield to the rage of Queen Terez, and let her seek vengeance for her father's death.'

'Ah, vengeance, vengeance.' Monza gave him a smile of her own. 'I don't startle at shadows, Master Sulfur. I'm sure Terez talks a grand war, but the Union is spread thin. They have enemies both North and South and inside their borders too. If your High King's wife wants my little chair, well, she can come and fight me for it. But I rather suspect his August Majesty has other worries.'

'I do not think you realise the dangers that fill the dark corners of the world.' There was no good humour in Sulfur's huge grin now. 'Why, even as we speak you sit here . . . alone.' It had become a hungry leer, filled with sharp, white teeth. 'So very, very fragile.'

She blinked, as if baffled. 'Alone?'

'You are mistaken.' Shenkt had walked up in utter silence until he stood, unobserved, right at Sulfur's shoulder, close as his shadow. Valint and Balk's representative spun about, took a shocked step back and stood frozen, as though he'd turned to see the dead breathing in his ear.

'You,' he whispered.

'Yes.'

'I thought—'

'No.'

'Then . . . this is your doing?'

'I have had my hand in it.' Shenkt shrugged. 'But chaos is the natural state of things, for men pull always in their own directions. It is those who want the world to march all the same way that give themselves the challenge.'

The different-coloured eyes swivelled to Monza, and back. 'Our master will not—'

'*Your* master,' said Shenkt. 'I have none, any more, remember? I told him I was done. I always give a warning when I can, and here is yours. Get you gone. Return, you will not find me in a warning mood. Go back, and tell him you serve. Tell him I used to serve. We do not kneel.'

Sulfur slowly nodded, then his mouth slipped back into the smirk he wore when he came in. 'Die standing, then.' He turned to Monza, gave his graceful bow once more. 'You will hear from us.' And he strutted easily from the room.

Shenkt raised his brows as Sulfur disappeared from sight. 'He took it well.'

She didn't feel like laughing. 'There's a lot you're not telling me.'

'Yes.'

'Who are you, really?'

'I have been many things. An apprentice. An ambassador. A solver of stubborn problems, and a maker of them. Today, it seems, I am a man who settles other people's scores.'

'Cryptic shit. If I want riddles I can visit a fortune-teller.'

'You're a grand duchess. You could probably get one to come to you.'

She nodded towards the doors. 'You knew him.'

'I did.'

'You had the same master?'

'Once. Long ago.'

'You worked for a bank?'

He gave his empty smile. 'In a manner of speaking. They do far more than count coins.'

'So I'm beginning to see. And now?'

'Now, I do not kneel.'

'Why have you helped me?'

'Because they made Orso, and I break whatever they have made.'

'Revenge,' she murmured.

'Not the best of motives, but good outcomes can flow from evil motives, still.'

'And the other way about.'

'Of course. You brought the Duke of Talins all his victories, and so I had been watching you, thinking to weaken him by killing you. As it happened, Orso tried to do it himself. So I mended you instead, thinking to persuade you to kill Orso and take his place. But I underestimated your determination, and you slipped away. As it happened, you set about trying to kill Orso . . .'

She shifted, somewhat uncomfortably, in her ex-employer's chair. 'And took his place.'

'Why dam a river that already flows your way? Let us say we have helped each other.' And he gave his skull's grin one more time. 'We all of us have our scores to settle.'

'In settling yours, it seems you have made me some powerful enemies.'

'In settling yours, it seems you have plunged Styria into chaos.'

That was true enough. 'Not quite my intention.'

'Once you choose to open the box, your intentions mean nothing. And the box is yawning wide as a grave now. I wonder what will spill from it? Will righteous leaders rise from the madness to light the way to a brighter, fairer Styria, a beacon for all the world? Or will we get ruthless shadows of old tyrants, treading circles in the bloody footsteps of the past?' Shenkt's bright eyes did not leave hers. 'Which will you be?'

'I suppose we'll see.'

'I suppose we will.' He turned, his footfalls making not the slightest sound, and pulled the doors silently shut behind him, leaving her alone.

All Change

'**Y**ou need not do this, you know.'

'I know.' But Friendly wanted to do it.

Cosca squirmed in his saddle with frustration. 'If only I could make you see how the world out here . . . swarms with infinite possibilities!' He had been trying to make Friendly see it the entire way from the unfortunate village where the Thousand Swords were camped. He had failed to realise that Friendly saw it with perfect, painful clarity already. And he hated it. As far as he was concerned, fewer possibilities was better. And that meant infinite was far, far too many for comfort.

'The world changes, alters, is born anew and presents a different face each day! A man never knows what each moment will bring!'

Friendly hated change. The only thing he hated more was not knowing what each moment might bring.

'There are all manner of pleasures to sample out here.'

Different men take pleasure in different things.

'To lock yourself away from life is . . . to admit defeat!'

Friendly shrugged. Defeat had never scared him. He had no pride.

'I need you. Desperately. A good sergeant is worth three generals.'

There was a long moment of silence while their horses' hooves crunched on the dry track.

'Well, damn it!' Cosca took a swig from his flask. 'I have made every effort.'

'I appreciate it.'

'But you are resolved?'

'I am.'

Friendly's worst fear had been that they might not let him back in. Until Murcatto had given him a document with a great

655

seal for the authorities of the city of Musselia. It detailed his convictions as an accomplice in the murders of Gobba, Mauthis, Prince Ario, General Ganmark, Faithful Carpi, Prince Foscar and Grand Duke Orso of Talins, and sentenced him to imprisonment for life. Or until such time as he desired to be released. Friendly was confident that would be never. It was the only payment he had asked for, the best gift he had ever been given, and sat now neatly folded in his inside pocket, just beside his dice.

'I will miss you, my friend, I will miss you.'

'And I you.'

'But not so much I can persuade you to remain in my company?'

'No.'

For Friendly, this was a homecoming long anticipated. He knew the number of trees on the road leading to the gate, the warmth welling up in his chest as he counted them off. He stood eagerly in his stirrups, caught a tingling glimpse of the gatehouse, a looming corner of dark brickwork above the greenery. Hardly architecture to fill most convicted men with joy, but Friendly's heart leaped at the sight of it. He knew the number of bricks in the archway, had been waiting for them, longing for them, dreaming of them for so long. He knew the number of iron studs on the great doors, he knew—

Friendly frowned as the track curved about to face the gate. The doors stood open. A terrible foreboding crowded his joy away. What could be more wrong in a prison than that its doors should stand open and unlocked? That was not part of the grand routine.

He slid from his horse, wincing at the pain in his stiff right arm, still healing even though the splints were off. He walked slowly to the gate, almost scared to look inside. A ragged-looking man sat on the steps of the hut where the guards should have been watching, all alone.

'I've done nothing!' He held up his hands. 'I swear!'

'I have a letter signed by the Grand Duchess of Talins.' Friendly unfolded the treasured document and held it out, still hoping. 'I am to be taken into custody at once.'

The man stared at him for a moment. 'I'm no guard, friend. Just using the hut to sleep in.'

'Where are the guards?'

'Gone.'

'Gone?'

'With riots in Musselia I reckon no one was paying 'em, so . . . they up and left.'

Friendly felt a cold prickle of horror on the back of his neck. 'The prisoners?'

'They got free. Most of 'em ran right off. Some of 'em waited. Shut 'emselves into their own cells at night, only imagine that!'

'Only imagine,' said Friendly, with deep longing.

'Didn't know where to run to, I guess. But they got hungry, in the end. Now they've gone too. There's no one here.'

'No one?'

'Only me.'

Friendly looked up the narrow track to the archway in the rocky hillside. All empty. The halls were silent. The circle of sky still looked down into the old quarry, maybe, but there was no rattling of bars as the prisoners were locked up safe and sound each night. No comforting routine, enfolding their lives as tightly as a mother holds her child. No more would each day, each month, each year be measured out into neat little parcels. The great clock had stopped.

'All change,' whispered Friendly.

He felt Cosca's hand on his shoulder. 'The world is all change, my friend. We all would like to go back, but the past is done. We must look forwards. We must change ourselves, however painful it may be, or be left behind.'

So it seemed. Friendly turned his back on Safety, clambered dumbly up onto his horse. 'Look forwards.' But to what? Infinite possibilities? He felt panic gripping him. 'Forwards all depends on which way you face. Which way should I face now?'

Cosca grinned as he turned his own mount about. 'Making that choice is what life is. But if I may make a suggestion?'

'Please.'

'I will be taking the Thousand Swords – or those who have not retired on the plunder of Fontezarmo, at least, or found regular employment with the Duchess Monzcarro – down towards

Visserine to help me press my claims on Salier's old throne.' He unscrewed the cap of his flask. 'My entirely righteous claims.' He took a swig and burped, blasting Friendly with an overpowering reek of strong spirits. 'A title promised me by the King of Styria, after all. The city is in chaos, and those bastards need someone to show them the way.'

'You?'

'And you, my friend, and you! Nothing is more valuable to the ruler of a great city than an honest man who can count.'

Friendly took one last longing look back, the gatehouse already disappearing into the trees. 'Perhaps they'll start it up again, one day.'

'Perhaps they will. But in the meantime I can make noble use of your talents in Visserine. I have entirely rightful claims. Born in the city, you know. There'll be work there. Lots of . . . work.'

Friendly frowned sideways. 'Are you drunk?'

'Ludicrously, my friend, quite ludicrously so. This is the good stuff. The old grape spirit.' Cosca took another swig and smacked his lips. 'Change, Friendly . . . change is a funny thing. Sometimes men change for the better. Sometimes men change for the worse. And often, very often, given time and opportunity . . .' He waved his flask around for a moment, then shrugged. 'They change back.'

Happy Endings

Few days after they'd thrown him in there, they'd set up a gallows just outside. He could see it from the little window in his cell, if he climbed up on the pallet and pressed his face to the bars. A man might wonder why a prisoner would go to all that trouble to taunt himself, but somehow he had to. Maybe that was the point. It was a big wooden platform with a cross-beam and four neat nooses. Trapdoors in the floor so they only had to kick a lever to snap four necks at a go, easy as snapping twigs. Quite a thing. They had machines for planting crops, and machines for printing paper, and it seemed they had machines for killing folk too. Maybe that's what Morveer had meant when he spouted off about science, all those months ago.

They'd hanged a few men right after the fortress fell. Some who'd worked for Orso, given some offence someone needed vengeance for. A couple of the Thousand Swords as well, must've stepped onto some dark ground indeed, since there weren't many rules to break during a sack. But no one had swung for a long time now. Seven weeks, or eight. Maybe he should've counted the days, but what difference would counting 'em have made? It was coming, of that much he was sure.

Every morning when the first light crept into the cell and Shivers woke, he wondered if that would be the morning they'd hang him.

Sometimes he wished he hadn't turned on Monza. But only because it had come out the way it had. Not because he regretted any part of what he'd done. Probably his father wouldn't have approved of it. Probably his brother would've sneered and said he expected no better. No doubt Rudd Threetrees would've shook his head, and said justice would come for it. But Threetrees was dead, and justice with him. Shivers' brother had been a bastard with a hero's face, and his sneers meant nothing no more. And his father had gone back to the mud and left him to work out his own way of doing things. So much for the good men, and the right thing too.

From time to time he wondered whether Carlot dan Eider got away from the mess his failure must've left her in, or whether the Cripple caught up with her. He wondered whether Monza got to kill Orso, and whether it had been all she hoped for. He wondered who that bastard had been who came out of nowhere and knocked him across the hall. Didn't seem likely he'd ever find out the answers now. But that's how life is. You don't always get all the answers.

He was up at the window when he heard keys rattling down the corridor, and he almost smiled at the relief of knowing it was time. He hopped down from his pallet, right leg still stiff where Friendly had stuck his knife in it, stood up tall and faced the metal gate.

He hadn't thought she'd come herself, but he was glad she had. Glad for the chance to look her in the eye one more time, even if they had the jailer and a half-dozen guards for company. She looked well, no doubt of that, not so gaunt as she used to, nor so hard. Clean, smooth, sleek and rich. Like royalty. Hard to believe she ever had aught to do with him.

'Well, look at you,' he said. 'Grand Duchess Monzcarro. How the hell did you come out o' this mess so fine?'

'Luck.'

'There you go. Never had much myself.' The jailer unlocked the gate and pushed it squealing open. Two of the guards came in, snapped manacles shut round Shivers' wrists. He didn't see much purpose in making a fight of it. Would've been just an embarrassment all round. They marched him out into the corridor to face her.

'Quite the trip we've been on, ain't it, Monza, you and I?'

'Quite the trip,' she said. 'You lost yourself, Shivers.'

'No. I found myself. You going to hang me now?' He didn't feel much joy at the thought, but not much sorrow either. Better'n rotting in that cell, he reckoned.

She watched him for a long moment. Blue eyes, and cold.

Looked at him like she did the first time they met. Like nothing he could do would surprise her. 'No.'

'Eh?' Hadn't been expecting that. Left him disappointed, almost. 'What, then?'

'You can go.'

He blinked. 'I can what?'

'Go. You're free.'

'Didn't think you still cared.'

'Who says I ever did? This is for me, not you. I've had enough vengeance.'

Shivers snorted. 'Well, who'd have fucking thought it? The Butcher of Caprile. The Snake of Talins. The good woman, all along. I thought you didn't have much use for the right thing. I thought mercy and cowardice were the same.'

'Mark me down a coward, then. That I can live with. Just don't ever come back here. My cowardice has limits.' She twisted the ring off her finger. The one with the big, blood-red ruby in it, and tossed it in the dirty straw at his feet. 'Take it.'

'Alright.' He bent down and dug it out of the muck, wiped it on his shirt. 'I ain't proud.' Monza turned and walked away, towards the stairway, towards the lamplight spilling from it. 'So that's how this ends, is it?' he called after her. 'That's the ending?'

'You think you deserve something better?' And she was gone.

He slid the ring onto his little finger and watched it sparkle. 'Something worse.'

'Move, then, bastard,' snarled one of the guards, waving a drawn sword.

Shivers grinned back. 'Oh, I'm gone, don't you worry on that score. I've had my fill of Styria.'

He smiled as he stepped out of the darkness of the tunnel and onto the bridge that led away from Fontezarmo. He scratched at his itching face, took in a long breath of cold, free air. All things considered, and well against the run of luck, he reckoned he'd come out alright. Might be he'd lost an eye down here in Styria. Might be he was leaving no richer than when he'd stepped off the boat. But he was a better man, of that he'd no doubt. A wiser man. Used to be he was his own worst enemy. Now he was everyone else's.

He was looking forward to getting back to the North, finding some work that suited him. Maybe he'd make a stop in Uffrith, pay his old friend Vossula a little visit. He set off down the mountain, away from the fortress, boots crunching in the grey dust.

Behind him, the sunrise was the colour of bad blood.

Acknowledgments

As always, four people without whom:

Bren Abercrombie, whose eyes are sore from reading it.
Nick Abercrombie, whose ears are sore from hearing about it.
Rob Abercrombie, whose fingers are sore from turning the pages.
Lou Abercrombie, whose arms are sore from holding me up.

Then, my heartfelt thanks:

To all the lovely and talented folks at my UK Publisher, Gollancz, and their parent Orion, particularly Simon Spanton, Jo Fletcher, Jon Weir, Mark Stay and Jon Wood. Then, of course, all those who've helped make, publish, publicise, translate and above all *sell* my books wherever they may be around the world.

To the artists responsible for somehow making me look classy: Didier Graffet, Dave Senior and Laura Brett.

To editors across the Pond: Devi Pillai and Lou Anders.

To other hard-bitten professionals who've provided various mysterious services: Robert Kirby, Darren Turpin, Matthew Amos, Lionel Bolton.

To all the writers whose paths have crossed mine either electronically or in the actual flesh, and who've provided help, laughs and a few ideas worth stealing, including but by no means limited to: James Barclay, Alex Bell, David Devereux, Roger Levy, Tom Lloyd, Joe Mallozzi, John Meaney, Richard Morgan, Adam Roberts, Pat Rothfuss, Marcus Sakey, Wim Stolk and Chris Wooding.

And lastly, yet firstly:

For unstinting support, advice, food, drink and, you know, *editing* above and beyond the call of duty, my editor, Gillian Redfearn. Long may it continue. I mean, I'm not going to write these damn things on my own . . .

'*The Heroes* is an indictment of war and the duplicity that corrupts men striving for total power: bloody and violent, but never gratuitously so, it's imbued with cutting humour, acute characterisation and world-weary wisdom about the weaknesses of the human race. Brilliant'   *Guardian*

'The futility of settling arguments by violence is the clear message of *The Heroes*, making it an anti-war war story – which I suppose all the best war stories are, really – but it's also a very strong continuation of his excellent previous books. Highly recommended both for fantasy readers and lovers of Cornwell and Iggulden'
Bookgeeks

'[*The Heroes* is a] blood-drenched, thought-provoking dissection of a three-day battle is set in the same world as Abercrombie's *First Law Trilogy* but stands very well alone . . . Abercrombie never glosses over a moment of the madness, passion, and horror of war, nor the tribulations that turn ordinary people into the titular heroes'
Publishers Weekly

'Joe Abercrombie's *Best Served Cold* is a bloody and relentless epic of vengeance and obsession in the grand tradition, a kind of splatterpunk sword 'n sorcery *Count of Monte Cristo*, Dumas by way of Moorcock. His cast features tyrants and torturers, a pair of poisoners, a serial killer, a treacherous drunk, a red-handed warrior and a blood-soaked mercenary captain. And those are the good guys . . . The battles are vivid and visceral, the action brutal, the pace headlong, and Abercrombie piles the betrayals, reversals, and plot twists one atop another to keep us guessing how it will all come out. This is his best book yet'
George R. R. Martin

'Abercrombie writes dark, adult fantasy, by which I mean there's a lot of stabbing in it, and after people stab each other they sometimes have sex with each other. His tone is morbid and funny and hard-boiled, not wholly dissimilar to that of Iain Banks . . .

'And like George R. R. Martin Abercrombie has the will and the cruelty to actually kill and maim his characters . . . Volumetrically speaking, it's hard to think of another fantasy novel in which this much blood gets spilled'   Lev Grossman, *Time Magazine*

'Joe Abercrombie is probably the brightest star among the new generation of British fantasy writers . . . Abercrombie writes a vivid, well-paced tale that never loosens its grip. His action scenes are cinematic in the best sense, and the characters are all distinct and interestingly different'   *The Times*

'Overall this is an immediately rewarding experience. There are reveals in the final third that are unexpected yet satisfyingly logical. The standalone nature of this installment should attract new readers, and its tight, uncompromising focus makes for an absorbing read. *Best Served Cold*? Modern fantasy doesn't get much hotter than this'   *SFX*

'The books are good, really good. They pulled me in. Well-developed world. Unique, compelling characters. I like them so much that when I got to the end of the second book and found out the third book wasn't going to be out in the US for another three months, I experienced a fit of rage, then a fit of depression, then I ate some lunch and had a bit of a lay down'
     Patrick Rothfuss on *The First Law Trilogy*

RED
COUNTRY

Also by Joe Abercrombie

THE FIRST LAW TRILOGY
The Blade Itself
Before They Are Hanged
Last Argument of Kings

Best Served Cold
The Heroes

RED
COUNTRY

JOE ABERCROMBIE

First published in Great Britain in 2012 by Gollancz
An imprint of the Orion Publishing Group
Orion House, 5 Upper St Martin's Lane, London WC2H 9EA
An Hachette UK Company

This edition published in Great Britain in 2013 by Gollancz

A CIP catalogue record for this book is available
from the British Library.

ISBN 978 0 575 09584 7

5 7 9 10 8 6 4

Typeset at The Spartan Press Ltd,
Lymington, Hants

Printed and bound by
CPI Group (UK) Ltd, Croydon, CRO 4YY

The Orion Publishing Group's policy is to use papers that
are natural, renewable and recyclable products and made
from wood grown in sustainable forests. The logging and
manufacturing processes are expected to conform to the
environmental regulations of the country of origin.

www.joeabercrombie.com
www.orionbooks.co.uk
www.gollancz.co.uk

For Teddy

And Clint Eastwood

But since Clint probably ain't that bothered

Mostly Teddy

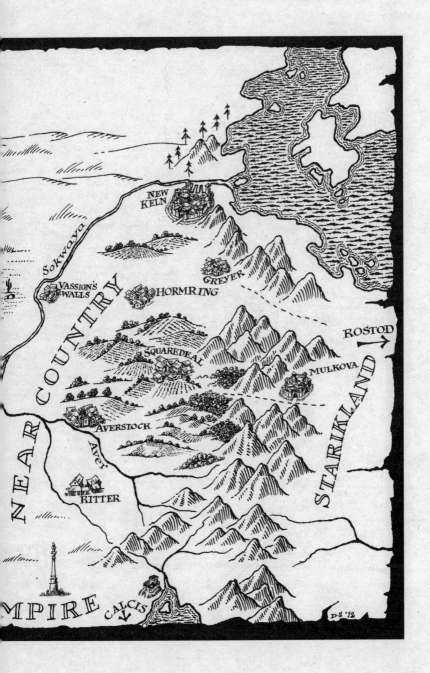

I
TROUBLE

'You, that judge men
by the handle and the sheath,
how can I make you know a good blade?'
Jedediah M. Grant

Some Kind of Coward

'Gold.' Wist made the word sound like a mystery there was no solving. 'Makes men mad.'

Shy nodded. 'Those that ain't mad already.'

They sat in front of Stupfer's Meat House, which might've sounded like a brothel but was actually the worst place to eat within fifty miles, and that with some fierce competition. Shy perched on the sacks in her wagon and Wist on the fence, where he always seemed to be, like he'd such a splinter in his arse he'd got stuck there. They watched the crowd.

'I came here to get away from people,' said Wist.

Shy nodded. 'Now look.'

Last summer you could've spent all day in town and not seen two people you didn't know. You could've spent some days in town and not seen two people. A lot can change with a few months and a gold find. Now Squaredeal was bursting at its ragged seams with bold pioneers. One-way traffic, headed west towards imagined riches, some charging through fast as the clutter would allow, some stopping off to add their own share of commerce and chaos. Wagon-wheels clattered, mules nickered and horses neighed, livestock honked and oxen bellowed. Men, women and children of all races and stations did plenty of their own honking and bellowing too, in every language and temper. It might've been quite the colourful spectacle if everywhere the blown dust hadn't leached each tone to that same grey ubiquity of dirt.

Wist sucked a noisy mouthful from his bottle. 'Quite the variety, ain't there?'

Shy nodded. 'All set on getting something for nothing.'

All struck with a madness of hope. Or of greed, depending on the observer's faith in humanity, which in Shy's case stood less than brim-full. All drunk on the chance of reaching into some freezing pool out there in the great empty and plucking up a new life with both hands.

3

Leaving their humdrum selves behind on the bank like a shed skin and taking a short cut to happiness.

'Tempted to join 'em?' asked Wist.

Shy pressed her tongue against her front teeth and spat through the gap between. 'Not me.' If they made it across the Far Country alive, the odds were stacked high they'd spend a winter up to their arses in ice water and dig up naught but dirt. And if lightning did strike the end of your spade, what then? Ain't like rich folk got no trouble.

There'd been a time Shy thought she'd get something for nothing. Shed her skin and step away smiling. Turned out sometimes the short cut don't lead quite where you hoped, and cuts through bloody country, too.

'Just the rumour o' gold turns 'em mad.' Wist took another swallow, the knobble on his scrawny neck bobbing, and watched two would-be prospectors wrestle over the last pickaxe at a stall while the trader struggled vainly to calm them. 'Imagine how these bastards'll act if they ever close hands around a nugget.'

Shy didn't have to imagine. She'd seen it, and didn't prize the memories. 'Men don't need much beckoning on to act like animals.'

'Nor women neither,' added Wist.

Shy narrowed her eyes at him. 'Why look at me?'

'You're foremost in my mind.'

'Not sure I like being that close to your face.'

Wist showed her his tombstone teeth as he laughed, and handed her the bottle. 'Why don't you got a man, Shy?'

'Don't like men much, I guess.'

'You don't like anyone much.'

'They started it.'

'All of 'em?'

'Enough of 'em.' She gave the mouth of the bottle a good wipe and made sure she took only a sip. She knew how easy she could turn a sip into a swallow, and the swallow into a bottle, and the bottle into waking up smelling of piss with one leg in the creek. There were folk counting on her, and she'd had her fill of being a disappointment.

The wrestlers had been dragged apart and were spitting insults each in their own tongue, neither quite catching the details but both getting the gist. Looked like the pick had vanished in the commotion, more'n likely spirited away by a cannier adventurer while eyes were elsewhere.

'Gold surely can turn men mad,' muttered Wist, all wistful as his

4

name implied. 'Still, if the ground opened and offered me the good stuff I don't suppose I'd be turning down a nugget.'

Shy thought of the farm, and all the tasks to do, and all the time she hadn't got for the doing of 'em, and rubbed her roughed-up thumbs against her chewed-up fingers. For the quickest moment a trek into the hills didn't sound such a mad notion after all. What if there really was gold up there? Scattered on some stream bed in priceless abundance, longing for the kiss of her itchy fingertips? Shy South, luckiest woman in the Near Country . . .

'Hah.' She slapped the thought away like a bothersome fly. High hopes were luxuries she couldn't stretch to. 'In my experience, the ground ain't giving aught away. No more'n the rest of us misers.'

'Got a lot, do you?'

'Eh?'

'Experience.'

She winked as she handed his bottle back. 'More'n you can imagine, old man.' A damn stretch more'n most of the pioneers, that was sure. Shy shook her head as she watched the latest crowd coming through – a set of Union worthies, by their looks, dressed for a picnic rather than a slog across a few hundred miles of lawless empty. Folk who should've been satisfied with the comfortable lives they had, suddenly deciding they'd take any chance at grabbing more. Shy wondered how long it'd be before they were limping back the other way, broken and broke. If they made it back.

'Where's Gully at?' asked Wist.

'Back on the farm, looking to my brother and sister.'

'Haven't seen him in a while.'

'He ain't been here in a while. Hurts him to ride, he says.'

'Getting old. Happens to us all. When you see him, tell him I miss him.'

'If he was here he'd have drunk your bottle dry in one swallow and you'd be cursing his name.'

'I daresay.' Wist sighed. 'That's how it is with things missed.'

By then, Lamb was fording the people-flooded street, shag of grey hair showing above the heads around him for all his stoop, an even sorrier set to his heavy shoulders than usual.

'What did you get?' she asked, hopping down from the wagon.

Lamb winced, like he knew what was coming. 'Twenty-seven?' His rumble of a voice tweaked high at the end to make a question of it, but what he was really asking was, *How bad did I fuck up?*

Shy shook her head, tongue wedged in her cheek, letting him know he'd fucked up middling to bad. 'You're some kind of a bloody coward, Lamb.' She thumped at the sacks and sent up a puff of grain dust. 'I didn't spend two days dragging this up here to give it away.'

He winced a bit more, grey-bearded face creasing around the old scars and laughter lines, all weather-worn and dirt-grained. 'I'm no good with the bartering, Shy, you know that.'

'Remind me what it is y'are good with?' she tossed over her shoulder as she strode for Clay's Exchange, letting a set of piebald goats bleat past then slipping through the traffic sideways-on. 'Except hauling the sacks?'

'That's something, ain't it?' he muttered.

The store was busier even than the street, smelling of sawn wood and spices and hard-working bodies packed tight. She had to shove between a clerk and some blacker'n black Southerner trying to make himself understood in no language she'd ever heard before, then around a washboard hung from the low rafters and set swinging by a careless elbow, then past a frowning Ghost, his red hair all bound up with twigs, leaves still on and everything. All these folk scrambling west meant money to be made, and woe to the merchant who tried to put himself between Shy and her share.

'Clay?' she bellowed, nothing to be gained by whispering. 'Clay!'

The trader frowned up, caught in the midst of weighing flour out on his man-high scales. 'Shy South in Squaredeal. Ain't this my lucky day.'

'Looks that way. You got a whole town full o' saps to *swindle*!' She gave the last word a bit of air, made a few heads turn and Clay plant his big fists on his hips.

'No one's swindling no one,' he said.

'Not while I've got an eye on business.'

'Me and your father agreed on twenty-seven, Shy.'

'You know he ain't my father. And you know you ain't agreed shit 'til I've agreed it.'

Clay cocked an eyebrow at Lamb and the Northman looked straight to the ground, shifting sideways like he was trying and wholly failing to vanish. For all Lamb's bulk he'd a weak eye, slapped down by any glance that held it. He could be a loving man, and a hard worker, and he'd been a fair stand-in for a father to Ro and Pit and Shy too, far as

6

she'd given him the chance. A good enough man, but by the dead he was some kind of coward.

Shy felt ashamed for him, and ashamed of him, and that nettled her. She stabbed her finger in Clay's face like it was a drawn dagger she'd no qualms about using. 'Squaredeal's a strange sort o' name for a town where you'd claw out a business! You paid twenty-eight last season, and you didn't have a quarter of the customers. I'll take thirty-eight.'

'What?' Clay's voice squeaking even higher than she'd predicted. 'Golden grain, is it?'

'That's right. Top quality. Threshed with my own blistered bloody hands.'

'And mine,' muttered Lamb.

'Shush,' said Shy. 'I'll take thirty-eight and refuse to be moved.'

'Don't do me no favours!' raged Clay, fat face filling with angry creases. 'Because I loved your mother I'll offer twenty nine.'

'You never loved a thing but your purse. Anything short of thirty-eight and I'd sooner set up next to your store and offer all this through-traffic just a little less than what you're offering.'

He knew she'd do it, even if it cost her. Never make a threat you aren't at least halfway sure you'll carry through on. 'Thirty-one,' he grated out.

'Thirty-five.'

'You're holding up all these good folk, you selfish bitch!' Or rather she was giving the good folk notice of the profits he was chiselling and sooner or later they'd catch on.

'They're scum to a man, and I'll hold 'em up 'til Juvens gets back from the land of the dead if it means thirty-five.'

'Thirty-two.'

'Thirty-five.'

'Thirty-three and you might as well burn my store down on the way out!'

'Don't tempt me, fat man. Thirty-three and you can toss in a pair o' those new shovels and some feed for my oxen. They eat almost as much as you.' She spat in her palm and held it out.

Clay bitterly worked his mouth, but he spat all the same, and they shook. 'Your mother was no better.'

'Couldn't stand the woman.' Shy elbowed her way back towards the door, leaving Clay to vent his upset on his next customer. 'Not that hard, is it?' she tossed over her shoulder at Lamb.

The big old Northman fussed with the notch out of his ear. 'Think I'd rather have settled for the twenty-seven.'

'That's 'cause you're some kind of a bloody coward. Better to do it than live with the fear of it. Ain't that what you always used to tell me?'

'Time's shown me the downside o' that advice,' muttered Lamb, but Shy was too busy congratulating herself.

Thirty-three was a good price. She'd worked over the sums, and thirty-three would leave something towards Ro's books once they'd fixed the barn's leaking roof and got a breeding pair of pigs to replace the ones they'd butchered in winter. Maybe they could stretch to some seed too, try and nurse the cabbage patch back to health. She was grinning, thinking on what she could put right with that money, what she could build.

You don't need a big dream, her mother used to tell her when she was in a rare good mood, *a little one will do it.*

'Let's get them sacks shifted,' she said.

He might've been getting on in years, might've been slow as an old favourite cow, but Lamb was strong as ever. No weight would bend the man. All Shy had to do was stand on the wagon and heft the sacks one by one onto his shoulders while he stood, complaining less than the wagon had at the load. Then he'd stroll them across, four at a time, and stack them in Clay's yard easy as sacks of feathers. Shy might've been half his weight, but had the easier task and twenty-five years advantage and still, soon enough, she was leaking water faster than a fresh-dug well, vest plastered to her back and hair to her face, arms pink-chafed by canvas and white-powdered with grain dust, tongue wedged in the gap between her teeth while she cursed up a storm.

Lamb stood there, two sacks over one shoulder and one over the other, hardly even breathing hard, those deep laugh lines striking out from the corners of his eyes. 'Need a rest, Shy?'

She gave him a look. 'A rest from your carping.'

'I could shift some o' those sacks around and make a little cot for you. Might be there's a blanket in the back there. I could sing you to sleep like I did when you were young.'

'I'm still young.'

'Ish. Sometimes I think about that little girl smiling up at me.' Lamb looked off into the distance, shaking his head. 'And I wonder – where did me and your mother go wrong?'

'She died and you're useless?' Shy heaved the last sack up and dropped it on his shoulder from as great a height as she could manage.

Lamb only grinned as he slapped his hand down on top. 'Maybe that's it.' As he turned he nearly barged into another Northman, big as he was and a lot meaner-looking. The man started growling some curse, then stopped in the midst. Lamb kept trudging, head down, how he always did from the least breath of trouble. The Northman frowned up at Shy.

'What?' she said, staring right back.

He frowned after Lamb, then walked off, scratching at his beard.

The shadows were getting long and the clouds pink in the west when Shy dumped the last sack under Clay's grinning face and he held out the money, leather bag dangling from one thick forefinger by the drawstrings. She stretched her back out, wiped her forehead on one glove, then worked the bag open and peered inside.

'All here?'

'I'm not going to rob you.'

'Damn right you're not.' And she set to counting it. *You can always tell a thief*, her mother used to say, *on account of all the care they take with their own money.*

'Maybe I should go through every sack, make sure there's grain in 'em not shit?'

Shy snorted. 'If it was shit would that stop you selling it?'

The merchant sighed. 'Have it your way.'

'I will.'

'She does tend to,' added Lamb.

A pause, with just the clicking of coins and the turning of numbers in her head. 'Heard Glama Golden won another fight in the pit up near Greyer,' said Clay. 'They say he's the toughest bastard in the Near Country and there's some tough bastards about. Take a fool to bet against him now, whatever the odds. Take a fool to fight him.'

'No doubt,' muttered Lamb, always quiet when violence was the subject.

'Heard from a man watched it he beat old Stockling Bear so hard his guts came out of his arse.'

'That's entertainment, is it?' asked Shy.

'Beats shitting your own guts.'

'That ain't much of a review.'

9

Clay shrugged. 'I've heard worse ones. Did you hear about this battle, up near Rostod?'

'Something about it,' she muttered, trying to keep her count straight.

'Rebels got beat again, I heard. Bad, this time. All on the run now. Those the Inquisition didn't get a hold on.'

'Poor bastards,' said Lamb.

Shy paused her count a moment, then carried on. There were a lot of poor bastards about but they couldn't all be her problem. She'd enough worries with her brother and sister, and Lamb, and Gully, and the farm without crying over others' self-made misfortunes.

'Might be they'll make a stand up at Mulkova, but they won't be standing long.' Clay made the fence creak as he leaned his soft bulk back on it, hands tucked under his armpits with the thumbs sticking up. 'War's all but over, if you can call it a war, and there's plenty of people shook off their land. Shook off or burned out or lost what they had. Passes are opened up, ships coming through. Lots of folk seeing their fortune out west all of a sudden.' He nodded at the dusty chaos in the street, still boiling over even as the sun set. 'This here's just the first trickle. There's a flood coming.'

Lamb sniffed. 'Like as not they'll find the mountains ain't one great piece of gold and soon come flooding back the other way.'

'Some will. Some'll put down roots. The Union'll be coming along after. However much land the Union get, they always want more, and what with that find out west they'll smell money. That vicious old bastard Sarmis is sitting on the border and rattling his sword for the Empire, but his sword's always rattling. Won't stop the tide, I reckon.' Clay took a step closer to Shy and spoke soft, like he had secrets to share. 'I heard tell there's already been Union agents in Hormring, talking annexation.'

'They're buying folk out?'

'They'll have a coin in one hand, sure, but they'll have a blade in the other. They always do. We should be thinking about how we'll play it, if they come to Squaredeal. We should stand together, those of us been here a while.'

'I ain't interested in politics.' Shy wasn't interested in anything might bring trouble.

'Most of us aren't,' said Clay, 'but sometimes politics takes an interest in us all the same. The Union'll be coming, and they'll bring law with 'em.'

'Law don't seem such a bad thing,' Shy lied.

'Maybe not. But taxes follow law quick as the cart behind the donkey.'

'Can't say I'm an enthusiast for taxes.'

'Just a fancier way to rob a body, ain't it? I'd rather be thieved honest with mask and dagger than have some bloodless bastard come at me with pen and paper.'

'Don't know about that,' muttered Shy. None of those she'd robbed had looked too delighted with the experience, and some a lot less than others. She let the coins slide back into the bag and drew the string tight.

'How's the count?' asked Clay. 'Anything missing?'

'Not this time. But I reckon I'll keep watching just the same.'

The merchant grinned. 'I'd expect no less.'

She picked out a few things they needed – salt, vinegar, some sugar since it only came in time to time, a wedge of dried beef, half a bag of nails which brought the predictable joke from Clay that she was half a bag of nails herself, which brought the predictable joke from her that she'd nail his fruits to his leg, which brought the predictable joke from Lamb that Clay's fruits were so small she might not get a nail through. They had a bit of a chuckle over each other's quick wits.

She almost got carried away and bought a new shirt for Pit which was more'n they could afford, good price or other price, but Lamb patted her arm with his gloved hand, and she bought needles and thread instead so she could make him a shirt from one of Lamb's old ones. She probably could've made five shirts for Pit from one of Lamb's, the boy was that skinny. The needles were a new kind, Clay said were stamped out of a machine in Adua, hundreds at a press, and Shy smiled as she thought what Gully would say to that, shaking his white head at them and saying, needles from a machine, what'll be thought of next, while Ro turned them over and over in her quick fingers, frowning down as she worked out how it was done.

Shy paused in front of the spirits to lick her lips a moment, glass gleaming amber in the darkness, then forced herself on without, haggled harder than ever with Clay over his prices, and they were finished.

'Never come to this store again, you mad bitch!' The trader hurled at her as she climbed up onto the wagon's seat alongside Lamb. 'You've damn near ruined me!'

'Next season?'

He waved a fat hand as he turned back to his customers. 'Aye, see you then.'

She reached to take the brake off and almost put her hand in the beard of the Northman Lamb knocked into earlier. He was standing right beside the wagon, brow all ploughed up like he was trying to bring some foggy memory to mind, thumbs tucked into a sword-belt – big, simple hilt close to hand. A rough style of character, a scar borne near one eye and jagged through his scraggy beard. Shy kept a pleasant look on her face as she eased her knife out, spinning the blade about so it was hidden behind her arm. Better to have steel to hand and find no trouble than find yourself in trouble with no steel to hand.

The Northman said something in his own tongue. Lamb hunched a little lower in his seat, not even turning to look. The Northman spoke again. Lamb grunted something back, then snapped the reins and the wagon rolled off, Shy swaying with the jolting wheels. She snatched a glance over her shoulder when they'd gone a few strides down the rutted street. The Northman was still standing in their dust, frowning after them.

'What'd he want?'

'Nothing.'

She slid her knife into its sheath, stuck one boot on the rail and sat back, settling her hat brim low so the setting sun wasn't in her eyes. 'The world's brimming over with strange people, all right. You spend time worrying what they're thinking, you'll be worrying all your life.'

Lamb was hunched lower than ever, like he was trying to vanish into his own chest.

Shy snorted. 'You're such a bloody coward.'

He gave her a sideways look, then away. 'There's worse a man can be.'

They were laughing when they clattered over the rise and the shallow little valley opened out in front of them. Something Lamb had said. He'd perked up when they left town, as usual. Never at his best in a crowd.

It gave Shy's spirits a lift besides, coming up that track that was hardly more than two faded lines through the long grass. She'd been through black times in her younger years, midnight black times, when she thought she'd be killed out under the sky and left to rot, or caught and hanged and tossed out unburied for the dogs to rip at. More than once, in the midst of nights sweated through with fear, she'd sworn to be grateful every moment of her life if fate gave her the chance to tread this unremarkable path again. Eternal gratitude hadn't quite come about, but that's promises for you. She still felt that bit lighter as the wagon rolled home.

Then they saw the farm, and the laughter choked in her throat and they sat silent while the wind fumbled through the grass around them. Shy couldn't breathe, couldn't speak, couldn't think, all her veins flushed with ice-water. Then she was down from the wagon and running.

'Shy!' Lamb roared at her back, but she hardly heard, head full of her own rattling breath, pounding down the slope, land and sky jolting around her. Through the stubble of the field they'd harvested not a week before. Over the trampled-down fence and the chicken feathers crushed into the mud.

She made it to the yard — what had been the yard — and stood helpless. The house was all dead charred timbers and rubbish and nothing left standing but the tottering chimney-stack. No smoke. The rain must've put out the fires a day or two before. But everything was burned out. She ran around the side of the blacked wreck of the barn, whimpering a little now with each breath.

Gully was hanged from the big tree out back. They'd hanged him over her mother's grave and kicked down the headstone. He was shot through with arrows. Might've been a dozen, might've been more.

Shy felt like she was kicked in the guts and she bent over, arms hugged around herself, and groaned, and the tree groaned with her as the wind shook its leaves and set Gully's corpse gently swinging. Poor old harmless bastard. He'd called to her as they'd rattled off on the wagon. Said she didn't need to worry 'cause he'd look to the children, and she'd laughed at him and said she didn't need to worry 'cause the children would look to him, and she couldn't see nothing for the aching in her eyes and the wind stinging at them, and she clamped her arms tighter, feeling suddenly so cold nothing could warm her.

She heard Lamb's boots thumping up, then slowing, then coming steady until he stood beside her.

'Where are the children?'

They dug the house over, and the barn. Slow, and steady, and numb to begin with. Lamb dragged the scorched timbers clear while Shy scraped through the ashes, sure she'd scrape up Pit and Ro's bones. But they weren't in the house. Nor in the barn. Nor in the yard. Wilder now, trying to smother her fear, and more frantic, trying to smother

her hope, casting through the grass, and clawing at the rubbish, but the closest Shy came to her brother and sister was a charred toy horse Lamb had whittled for Pit years past and the scorched pages of some of Ro's books she let blow through her fingers.

The children were vanished.

She stood there, staring into the wind, back of one raw hand against her mouth and her chest going hard. Only one thing she could think of.

'They're stolen,' she croaked.

Lamb just nodded, his grey hair and his grey beard all streaked with soot.

'Why?'

'I don't know.'

She wiped her blackened hands on the front of her shirt and made fists of them. 'We've got to get after.'

'Aye.'

She squatted down over the chewed-up sod around the tree. Wiped her nose and her eyes. Followed the tracks bent over to another battered patch of ground. She found an empty bottle trampled into the mud, tossed it away. They'd made no effort at hiding their sign. Horse-prints all around, circling the shells of the buildings. 'I'm guessing at about twenty. Might've been forty horses, though. They left the spare mounts over here.'

'To carry the children, maybe?'

'Carry 'em where?'

Lamb just shook his head.

She went on, keen to say anything that might fill the space. Keen to set to work at something so she didn't have to think. 'My way of looking at it, they came in from the west and left going south. Left in a hurry.'

'I'll get the shovels. We'll bury Gully.'

They did it quick. She shinned up the tree, knowing every foot- and handhold. She used to climb it long ago, before Lamb came, while her mother watched and Gully clapped, and now her mother was buried under it and Gully was hanged from it, and she knew somehow she'd made it happen. You can't bury a past like hers and think you'll walk away laughing.

She cut him down, and broke the arrows off, and smoothed his bloody hair while Lamb dug out a hole next to her mother. She closed his popping eyes and put her hand on his cheek and it was cold. He

14

looked so small now, and so thin, she wanted to put a coat on him but there was none to hand. Lamb lowered him in a clumsy hug, and they filled the hole together, and they dragged her mother's stone up straight again and tramped the thrashing grass around it, ash blowing on the cold wind in specks of black and grey, whipping across the land and off to nowhere.

'Should we say something?' asked Shy.

'I've nothing to say.' Lamb swung himself up onto the wagon's seat. Might still have been an hour of light left.

'We ain't taking that,' said Shy. 'I can run faster'n those bloody oxen.'

'Not longer, though, and not with gear, and we'll do no good rushing at this. They've got what? Two, three days' start on us? And they'll be riding hard. Twenty men, you said? We have to be realistic, Shy.'

'Realistic?' she whispered at him, hardly able to believe it.

'If we chase after on foot, and don't starve or get washed away in a storm, and if we catch 'em, what then? We're not armed, even. Not with more'n your knife. No. We'll follow on fast as Scale and Calder can take us.' Nodding at the oxen, grazing a little while they had the chance. 'See if we can pare a couple off the herd. Work out what they're about.'

'Clear enough what they're about!' she said, pointing at Gully's grave. 'And what happens to Ro and Pit while we're fucking *following on*?' She ended up screaming it at him, voice splitting the silence and a couple of hopeful crows taking flight from the tree's branches.

The corner of Lamb's mouth twitched but he didn't look at her. 'We'll follow.' Like it was a fact agreed on. 'Might be we can talk this out. Buy 'em back.'

'Buy 'em? They burn your farm, and they hang your friend, and they steal your children and you want to *pay 'em* for the privilege? You're such a fucking coward!'

Still he didn't look at her. 'Sometimes a coward's what you need.' His voice was rough. Clicking in his throat. 'No shed blood's going to unburn this farm now, nor unhang Gully neither. That's done. Best we can do is get back the little ones, any way we can. Get 'em back safe.' This time the twitch started at his mouth and scurried all the way up his scarred cheek to the corner of his eye. 'Then we'll see.'

Shy took a last look as they lurched away towards the setting sun. Her home. Her hopes. How a day can change things about. Naught left but a few scorched timbers poking at the pinking sky. You don't need a big dream. She felt about as low as she ever had in all her life, and she'd been in some bad, dark, low-down places. Hardly had the strength all of a sudden to hold her head up.

'Why'd they have to burn it all?' she whispered.

'Some men just like to burn,' said Lamb.

Shy looked around at him, the outline of his battered frown showing below his battered hat, the dying sun glimmering in one eye, and thought how strange it was, that he could be so calm. A man who hadn't the guts to argue over prices, thinking death and kidnap through. Being realistic about the end of all they'd worked for.

'How can you sit so level?' she whispered at him. 'Like . . . like you knew it was coming.'

Still he didn't look at her. 'It's always coming.'

The Easy Way

'I have suffered many disappointments.' Nicomo Cosca, captain general of the Company of the Gracious Hand, leaned back stiffly upon one elbow as he spoke. 'I suppose every great man faces them. Abandons dreams wrecked by betrayal and finds new ones to pursue.' He frowned towards Mulkova, columns of smoke drifting from the burning city and up into the blue heavens. 'I have abandoned very many dreams.'

'That must have taken tremendous courage,' said Sworbreck, eye-glasses briefly twinkling as he looked up from his notes.

'Indeed! I lose count of the number of times my death has been prematurely declared by one optimistic enemy or another. Forty years of trials, struggles, challenges, betrayals. Live long enough . . . you see everything ruined.' Cosca shook himself from his reverie. 'But it hasn't been boring, at least! What adventures along the way, eh, Temple?'

Temple winced. He had borne personal witness to five years of occasional fear, frequent tedium, intermittent diarrhoea, failure to avoid the plague, and avoiding fighting as if it was the plague. But he was not paid for the truth. Far from it.

'Heroic,' he said.

'Temple is my notary. He prepares the contracts and sees them honoured. One of the cleverest bastards I ever met. How many languages do you speak, Temple?'

'Fluently, no more than six.'

'Most important man in the whole damn Company! Apart from me, of course.' A breeze washed across the hillside and stirred the wispy white hairs about Cosca's liver-spotted pate. 'I so look forward to telling you my stories, Sworbreck!' Temple restrained another grimace of distaste. 'The Siege of Dagoska!' Which ended in utter disaster. 'The Battle of Afieri!' Shameful debacle. 'The Years of Blood!' Sides changed like shirts. 'The Kadiri Campaign!' Drunken fiasco. 'I even kept a goat for several years. A stubborn beast, but loyal, you'd have to give her that . . .'

Sworbreck achieved the not-inconsiderable feat of performing an obsequious bow while sitting cross-legged against a slab of fallen masonry. 'I have no doubt my readers will thrill to your exploits.'

'Enough to fill twenty volumes!'

'Three will be more than adequate—'

'I was once Grand Duke of Visserine, you know.' Cosca waved down attempts at abasement which had, in fact, not happened. 'Don't worry, you need not call me Excellency – we are all informal here in the Company of the Gracious Hand, are we not, Temple?'

Temple took a long breath. 'We are all informal.' Most of them were liars, all of them were thieves, some of them were killers. Informality was not surprising.

'Sergeant Friendly has been with me even longer than Temple, ever since we deposed Grand Duke Orso and placed Monzcarro Murcatto on the throne of Talins.'

Sworbreck looked up. 'You know the Grand Duchess?'

'Intimately. I consider it no exaggeration to say I was her close friend and mentor. I saved her life at the siege of Muris, and she mine! The story of her rise to power is one I must relate to you at some stage, a noble business. There are precious few persons of quality I have not fought for or against at one time or another. Sergeant Friendly?'

The neckless sergeant looked up, face a blank slab.

'What have you made of your time with me?'

'I preferred prison.' And he returned to rolling his dice, an activity which could fully occupy him for hours at a time.

'He is such a wag, that one!' Cosca waved a bony finger at him, though there was no evidence of a joke. In five years Temple had never heard Sergeant Friendly make a joke. 'Sworbreck, you will find the Company alive with joshing good fun!'

Not to mention simmering feuds, punishing laziness, violence, disease, looting, treachery, drunkenness and debauchery fit to make a devil blush.

'These five years,' said Temple, 'I've hardly stopped laughing.'

'Yes, it's been quite a career. Many proud moments. Many triumphs. But defeats, too. Every great man has them. Regrets are the cost of the business, Sazine always used to say. People have often accused me of inconsistency but I feel that I have always, at any given junction, done the same thing. Exactly what I pleased.' The aged mercenary's fickle attention having wandered back to his imagined glorious past, Temple began to ease away, slipping around a broken column. 'I had a happy childhood but a wild youth, filled with ugly incidents, and at seventeen I left my birthplace to seek my fortune with only my wits, my courage, and my trusty blade . . .'

The sounds of boasting mercifully faded as Temple retreated down the hillside, stepping from the shadow of the ancient ruin and into the sun. Whatever Cosca might say, there was little joshing good fun going on down here.

Temple had seen wretchedness. He had lived through more than his share. But he had rarely seen people so miserable as the Company's latest batch of prisoners: a dozen of the fearsome rebels of Starikland chained naked, bloody, filthy and dead-eyed to a stake in the ground. It was hard to imagine them a threat to the greatest nation in the Circle of the World. It was hard to imagine them as humans. Only the tattoos on their forearms showed some last futile defiance.

Fuck the Union. Fuck the King. Read the nearest, a line of bold script from elbow to wrist. A sentiment with which Temple had increasing sympathy. He was developing a sneaking feeling he had found his way onto the wrong side. Again. But it's not always easy to tell when you're picking. Perhaps, as Kahdia once told him, you are on the wrong side as soon as you pick one. But it had been Temple's observation that it was those caught in the middle that always get the worst of it. And he was done with getting the worst.

Sufeen stood by the prisoners, an empty canteen in one hand.

'What are you about?' asked Temple.

'He is wasting water,' said Bermi, lounging in the sun nearby and scratching at his blond beard.

'On the contrary,' said Sufeen. 'I am trying to administer God's mercy to our prisoners.'

One had a terrible wound in his side, undressed. His eyes flickered, his lips mouthed meaningless orders or meaningless prayers. Once you could smell a wound there was little hope. But the outlook for the others was no better. 'If there is a God, He is a smarmy swindler and never to be trusted with anything of importance,' muttered Temple. 'Mercy would be to kill them.'

Bermi concurred. 'I've been saying so.'

'But that would take courage.' Sufeen lifted his scabbard, offering up the hilt of his sword. 'Have you courage, Temple?'

Temple snorted.

'We await our employers. And the Old Man is feeding his vanity.'

'That's a hell of an appetite to satisfy,' said Bermi, picking daisies and flicking them away.

'Bigger every day. It rivals Sufeen's guilt.'

'This is not guilt,' said Sufeen, frowning towards the prisoners. 'This is righteousness. Did the priests not teach you that?'

'Nothing like a religious education to cure a man of righteousness,' muttered Temple. He thought of Haddish Kahdia speaking the lessons in the plain white room, and his younger self scoffing at them. Charity, mercy, selflessness. How conscience is that piece of Himself that God puts in every man. A splinter of the divine. One that Temple had spent long years struggling to prise out. He caught the eye of one of the rebels. A woman, hair tangled across her face. She reached out as far as the chains would allow. For the water or the sword, he could not say. *Grasp your future!* called the words inked into her skin. He pulled out his own canteen, frowned as he weighed it in his hand.

'Some guilt of your own?' asked Sufeen.

It might have been a while since he wore them, but Temple had not forgotten what chains felt like. 'How long have you been a scout?' he snapped.

'Eighteen years.'

'You should know by now that conscience is a shitty navigator.'

'It certainly doesn't know the country out here,' added Bermi.

Sufeen spread wide his hands. 'Who then shall show us the way?'

'Temple!' Cosca's cracked howl, floating from above.

'Your guide calls,' said Sufeen. 'You will have to give them water later.'

Temple tossed him the canteen as he headed back up the hillside. 'You do it. Later, the Inquisition will have them.'

'Always the easy way, eh, Temple?' called Sufeen after him.

'Always,' muttered Temple. He made no apology for it.

'Welcome, gentlemen, welcome!' Cosca swept off his outrageous hat as their illustrious employers approached, riding in tight formation around a great fortified wagon. Even though the Old Man had, thank God, quit spirits yet again a few months before, he still seemed always slightly drunk. There was a floppy flourish to his knobbly hands, a lazy drooping of his withered eyelids, a rambling music to his speech. That and you could never be entirely sure what he would do or say next. There had been a time Temple had found that constant uncertainty thrilling, like watching the lucky wheel spin and wondering if his number would come up. Now it felt more like cowering beneath a storm-cloud and waiting for the lightning.

Cosca grinned across the valley towards the smouldering city, unintimidated. 'Mulkova burns, I see.'

'Better that it burn in Union hands than prosper under the rebels,' said Inquisitor Lorsen as he got down: tall and gaunt, his eyes bright with zeal. Temple envied him that. To feel certain in the right no matter what wrongs you took part in.

'Quite so,' said Cosca. 'A sentiment with which her citizens no doubt all agree! Sergeant Friendly you know, and this is Master Temple, notary to my company.'

General Brint dismounted last, the operation rendered considerably more difficult since he had lost most of an arm at the Battle of Osrung along with his entire sense of humour, and wore the left sleeve of his crimson uniform folded and pinned to his shoulder. 'You are prepared for legal disagreements, then,' he said, adjusting his sword-belt and eyeing Temple as if he was the morning plague cart.

'The second thing a mercenary needs is a good weapon.' Cosca clapped a fatherly hand on Temple's shoulder. 'The first is good legal advice.'

'And where does an utter lack of moral scruple feature?'

'Number five,' said Temple. 'Just behind a short memory and a ready wit.'

Superior Pike was considering Sworbreck, still scribbling notes. 'And on what does this man advise you?'

'That is Spillion Sworbreck, my biographer.'

'No more than a humble teller of tales!' Sworbreck gave the Superior a flamboyant bow. 'Though I freely confess that my prose has caused grown men to weep.'

'In a good way?' asked Temple.

If he heard, the author was too busy praising himself to respond. 'I compose stories of heroism and adventure to inspire the Union's citizens! Widely distributed now, via the wonders of the new Rimaldi printing press. You have heard, perhaps, of my *Tales of Harod the Great* in five volumes?' Silence. 'In which I mine the mythic splendour of the origin of the Union itself?' Silence. 'Or the eight-volume sequel, *The Life of Casamir, Hero of Angland*?' Silence. 'In which I hold up the mirror of past glories to expose the moral collapse of the present day?'

'No.' Pike's melted face betrayed no emotion.

'I will have copies sent to you, Superior!'

'You could use readings from them to force confessions from your prisoners,' murmured Temple, under his breath.

'Do not trouble yourself,' said Pike.

'No trouble! General Cosca has permitted me to accompany him on his latest campaign while he relates the details of his fascinating career as a soldier of fortune! I mean to make him the subject of my most celebrated work to date!'

The echoes of Sworbreck's words faded into a crushing silence.

'Remove this man from my presence,' said Pike. 'His manner of expression offends me.'

Sworbreck backed down the hillside with an almost reckless speed, shepherded by two Practicals. Cosca continued without the slightest hint of embarrassment.

'General Brint!' and he seized the general's remaining hand in both of his. 'I understand you have some concerns about our participation in the assault—'

'It was the lack of it that bothered me!' snapped Brint, twisting his fingers free.

Cosca pushed out his lips with an air of injured innocence. 'You feel we fell short of our contractual obligations?'

'You've fallen short of honour, decency, professionalism—'

'I recall no reference to them in the contract,' said Temple.

'You were ordered to attack! Your failure to do so cost the lives of several of my men, one a personal friend!'

Cosca waved a lazy hand, as though personal friends were ephemera that could hardly be expected to bear on an adult discussion. 'We were engaged here, General Brint, quite hotly.'

'In a bloodless exchange of arrows!'

'You speak as though a bloody exchange would be preferable.' Temple held out his hand to Friendly. The sergeant produced the contract from an inside pocket. 'Clause eight, I believe.' He swiftly found the place and presented it for inspection. 'Technically, any exchange of projectiles constitutes engagement. Each member of the Company is, in fact, due a bonus as a result.'

Brint looked pale. 'A bonus, too? Despite the fact that not one man was wounded.'

Cosca cleared his throat. 'We do have a case of dysentery.'

'Is that a joke?'

'Not to anyone who has suffered the ravages of dysentery, I assure you!'

'Clause nineteen . . .' Paper crackled as Temple thumbed through the densely written document. ' "Any man rendered inactive by illness during the discharge of his contractual obligations is to be considered a loss to the Company." A further payment is therefore due for the replacement of losses. Not to mention those for prisoners taken and delivered—'

'It all comes down to money, doesn't it?'

Cosca shrugged so high his gilt epaulettes tickled his earlobes. 'What else would it come down to? We are mercenaries. Better motives we leave to better men.'

Brint gazed at Temple, positively livid. 'You must be delighted with your wriggling, you Gurkish worm.'

'You were happy to put your name to the terms, General.' Temple flipped over the back page to display Brint's overwrought signature. 'My delight or otherwise does not enter the case. Nor does my wriggling. And I am generally agreed to be half-Dagoskan, half-Styrian, since you bring my parentage into—'

'You're a brown bastard son of a whore.'

Temple only smiled. 'My mother was never ashamed of her profession – why should I be?'

The general stared at Superior Pike, who had taken a seat on a lichen-splattered block of masonry, produced a haunch of bread and was trying to entice birds down from the crumbling ruin with faint kissing sounds. 'Am I to understand that you approve of this licensed banditry, Superior? This contractual cowardice, this outrageous—'

'General Brint.' Pike's voice was gentle, but somewhere in it had a screeching edge which, like the movement of rusty hinges, enforced wincing silence. 'We all appreciate the diligence you and your men have displayed. But the war is over. We won.' He tossed some crumbs into the grass and watched a tiny bird flit down and begin to peck. 'It is not fitting that we quibble over who did what. You signed the contract. We will honour it. We are not barbarians.'

'*We* are not.' Brint gave Temple, then Cosca, then Friendly a furious glare. They were all, each in his way, unmoved. 'I must get some air. There is a sickening *stench* here!' And with some effort the general hauled himself back into his saddle, turned his horse and thundered away, pursued by several aides-de-camp.

'I find the air quite pleasant,' said Temple brightly, somewhat relieved that confrontation at least was over.

'Pray forgive the general,' said Pike 'He is very much committed to his work.'

'I try always to be forgiving of other men's foibles,' said Cosca. 'I have enough of my own, after all.'

Lorsen stepped forward, evidently relishing his moment. 'The rebellion is at an end. The Inquisition is weeding out all those disloyal to the crown. Some few rebels have escaped, however, scattering through the passes and into the uncivilised west where, no doubt, they will foment new discord.'

'Cowardly bastards!' Cosca slapped at his thigh. 'Could they not stand and be slaughtered like decent men? I'm all for fermentation but fomentation is a damned imposition!'

Lorsen narrowed his eyes as though at a contrary wind, and ploughed on. 'For political reasons, his Majesty's armies are unable to pursue them.'

'Political reasons . . .' offered Temple, 'such as a border?'

'Precisely,' said Lorsen.

Cosca examined his ridged and yellowed fingernails. 'Oh, I've never taken those very seriously.'

'Precisely,' said Pike.

'We want the Company of the Gracious Hand to cross the mountains and pacify the Near Country as far west as the Sokwaya River. This rot of rebellion must be excised once and for all.' Lorsen cut at imaginary filth with the edge of his hand, voice rising as he warmed to his subject. 'We must clean out this sink of depravity which has too long been allowed to fester on our border! This . . . overflowing latrine! This backed-up sewer, endlessly disgorging its ordure of chaos into the Union!'

Temple reflected that, for a man who professed himself opposed to ordure, Inquisitor Lorsen certainly relished a shit-based metaphor.

'Well, no one enjoys a backed-up sewer,' conceded Cosca. 'Except the sewer-men themselves, I suppose, who scratch out their wretched

24

livings in the sludge. Unblocking the drains is a speciality of ours, isn't it, Sergeant Friendly?'

The big man looked up from his dice long enough to shrug.

'Temple is the linguist but perhaps I might in this case interpret?' The Old Man twisted the waxed tips of his grey moustaches between finger and thumb. 'You wish us to visit a plague upon the settlers of the Near Country. You wish us to make stern examples of every rebel sheltered and every person who gives them shelter. You wish us to make them understand that their only future is with the grace and favour of his August Majesty. You wish us to force them into the welcoming arms of the Union. Do I come close to the mark?'

'Close enough,' murmured Superior Pike.

Temple found that he was sweating. When he wiped his forehead his hand trembled. But what could he do?

'The Paper of Engagement is already prepared.' Lorsen produced his own sheaf of crackling documents, a heavy seal of red wax upon its bottom corner.

Cosca waved it away. 'My notary will look it over. All the legal fiddle-faddle quite swims before my eyes. I am a simple soldier.'

'Admirable,' said Pike, his hairless brows raised by the slightest fraction.

Temple's ink-spotted forefinger traced through the blocks of calligraphy, eyes flickering from one point of interest to another. He realised he was picking nervously at the corners of the pages and made himself stop.

'I will accompany you on the expedition,' said Lorsen. 'I have a list of settlements suspected of harbouring rebels. Or rebellious sentiment.'

Cosca grinned. 'Nothing more dangerous than sentiment!'

'In particular, his Eminence the Arch Lector offers a bonus of fifty thousand marks for the capture, alive, of the chief instigator of the insurrection, the one the rebels call Conthus. He goes also under the name of Symok. The Ghosts call him Black Grass. At the massacre in Rostod he used the alias—'

'No further aliases, I beg you!' Cosca massaged the sides of his skull as if they pained him. 'Since suffering a head-wound at the Battle of Afieri I have been cursed with an appalling memory for names. It is a source of constant embarrassment. But Sergeant Friendly has all the details. If your man Conshus—'

'Conthus.'

'What did I say?'

'Conshus.'

'There you go! If he's in the Near Country, he'll be yours.'

'Alive,' snapped Lorsen. 'He must answer for his crimes. He must be made a lesson of. He must be put on display!'

'And he'll make a most educational show, I'm sure!'

Pike flicked another pinch of crumbs to his gathering flock. 'The methods we leave to you, captain general. We would only ask that there be something left in the ashes to annex.'

'As long as you realise a Company of mercenaries is more club than scalpel.'

'An inspirational man, the Arch Lector. We are close friends, you know.'

'His one firm stipulation, clear in the contract, as you see, is that you avoid any Imperial entanglements. Any and all, am I understood?' That grating note entered Pike's voice again. 'Legate Sarmis still haunts the border like an angry phantom. I do not suppose he will cross it but even so he is a man decidedly not to be trifled with, a most bloody-minded and bloody-handed adversary. His Eminence desires no further wars at present.'

'Do not concern yourself, I avoid fighting wherever possible.' Cosca slapped happily at the hilt of his blade. 'A sword is for rattling, not for drawing, eh?'

'We have a gift for you, also.' Superior Pike indicated the fortified wagon, an oaken monster bound in riveted iron and hauled by a team of eight muscular horses. It was halfway between conveyance and castle, with slitted windows and a crenelated parapet about the top, from which defenders might presumably shoot at circling enemies. Far from the most practical of gifts, but then Cosca had never been interested in practicalities.

'For me?' The Old Man pressed his withered hands to his gilded breastplate. 'It shall be my home from home out in the wilderness!'

'There is a . . . *secret* within,' said Lorsen. 'Something his Eminence would very much like to see tested.'

'I love surprises! Ones that don't involve armed men behind me, anyway. You may tell his Eminence it will be my honour.' Cosca stood, wincing as his aged knees audibly clicked. 'How does the Paper of Engagement appear?'

Temple looked up from the penultimate page. 'Er . . .' The contract was closely based on the one he had drawn up for their previous engagement, was watertight in every particular, was even more generous in several. 'Some issues with supply,' he stammered, fumbling for objections. 'Food and weaponry are covered but the clause really should include—'

'Details. No cause for delay. Let's get the papers signed and the men ready to move. The longer they sit idle, the harder to get them off their arses. No force of nature so dangerous to life and commerce as mercenaries without employment.' Except, perhaps, mercenaries with employment.

'It would be prudent to allow me a little longer to—'

Cosca came close, setting his hand on Temple's shoulder again. 'Have you a legal objection?'

Temple paused, clutching for some words which might carry weight with a man with whom nothing carried any weight. 'Not a legal objection, no.'

'A financial objection?' offered Cosca.

'No, General.'

'Then . . . ?'

'Do you remember when we first met?'

Cosca suddenly flashed that luminous smile of which only he was capable, good humour and good intentions radiating from his deep-lined face. 'Of course. I wore that blue uniform, you the brown rags.'

'You said . . .' It hardly felt possible, now. 'You said we would do good together.'

'And haven't we, in the main? Legally *and* financially?' As though the entire spectrum of goodness ranged between those twin poles.

'And . . . morally?'

The Old Man's forehead furrowed as though it was a word in a foreign tongue. 'Morally?'

'General, please.' Temple fixed Cosca with his most earnest expression. And Temple knew he could be earnest, when he truly believed. Or had a great deal to lose. 'I beg you. Do not sign this paper. This will not be war, it will be murder.'

Cosca's brows went up. 'A fine distinction, to the buried.'

'We are not judges! What happens to the people of these towns once the men get among them, hungry for plunder? Women and children, General, who had no part in any rebellion. We are better than this.'

'We are? You did not say so in Kadir. You persuaded me to sign that contract, if I recall.'

'Well—'

'And in Styria, was it not you who encouraged me to take back what was mine?'

'You had a valid claim—'

'Before we took ship to the North, you helped me persuade the men. You can be damned persuasive when you have a mind.'

'Then let me persuade you now. Please, General Cosca. Do not sign.'

There was a long pause. Cosca heaved in a breath, his forehead creasing yet more deeply. 'A *conscientious* objection, then.'

'Conscience is,' muttered Temple hopefully, 'a splinter of the divine?' Not to mention a shitty navigator, and it had led him into some dangerous waters now. He realised he was picking nervously at the hem of his shirt as Cosca gazed upon him. 'I simply have a feeling this job . . .' He struggled for words that might turn the tide of inevitability. 'Will go bad,' he finished, lamely.

'Good jobs rarely require the services of mercenaries.' Cosca's hand squeezed a little tighter at his shoulder and Temple felt Friendly's looming presence behind him. Still, and silent, and yet very much *there*. 'Men of conscience and conviction might find themselves better suited to other lines of work. His Majesty's Inquisition offers a righteous cause, I understand?'

Temple swallowed as he looked across at Superior Pike, who had now attracted a twittering avian crowd. 'I'm not sure I care for their brand of righteousness.'

'Well, that's the thing about righteousness,' murmured Cosca, 'everyone has their own brand. Gold, on the other hand, is universal. In my considerable experience, a man is better off worrying about what is good for his purse than what is simply . . . good.'

'I just—'

Cosca squeezed still more firmly. 'Without wishing to be harsh, Temple, it isn't all about *you*. I have the welfare of the whole company to think of. Five hundred men.'

'Five hundred and twelve,' said Friendly.

'Plus one with dysentery. I cannot inconvenience them for the sake of your *feelings*. That would be . . . *immoral*. I need you, Temple. But if you wish to leave . . .' Cosca issued a weighty sigh. 'In spite of all your promises, in spite of my generosity, in spite of everything we have been through together, well . . .' He held out an arm towards burning Mulkova and raised his brows. 'I suppose the door is always open.'

Temple swallowed. He could have left. He could have said he wanted no part of this. Enough is enough, damn it! But that would have taken courage. That would have left him with no armed men at his back. Alone, and weak, and a victim once again. That would have been hard to do. And Temple always took the easy way. Even when he knew it was the wrong way. Especially then, in fact, since easy and wrong make such good company. Even when he had a damn good notion it would end up being the hard way, even then. Why think about tomorrow when today is such a thorny business?

Perhaps Kahdia would have found some way to stop this. Something involving supreme self-sacrifice, most likely. Temple, it hardly needed to be said, was not Kahdia. He wiped away a fresh sheen of sweat, forced a queasy smile onto his face and bowed. 'I remain always honoured to serve.'

'Excellent!' And Cosca plucked the contract from Temple's limp hand and spread it out to sign upon a sheered-off column.

Superior Pike stood, brushing crumbs from his shapeless black coat and sending birds scattering. 'Do you know what's out there, in the west?'

He let the question hang a moment. Below them the faint jingling, groaning, snapping could be heard of his Practicals dragging the prisoners away. Then he answered himself.

'The future. And the future does not belong to the Old Empire – their time is a thousand years past. Nor does it belong to the Ghosts, savages that they are. Nor does it belong to the fugitives, adventurers and opportunist scum who have put the first grasping roots into its virgin soil. No. The future belongs to the Union. We must seize it.'

'We must not be afraid to do what is necessary to seize it,' added Lorsen.

'Never fear, gentlemen.' Cosca grinned as he scratched out the parting swirl of his signature. 'We will seize the future together.'

Just Men

The rain had stopped. Shy peered through trees alive with the tap-tap of falling water, past a felled trunk abandoned on its trestles, part-stripped, the drawknife left wedged under a curl of bark, and towards the blackened bones of the house.

'Not hard bastards to follow,' muttered Lamb. 'Leave burned-out buildings wherever they go.'

Probably they thought they'd killed anyone cared enough to follow. What might happen once they noticed Lamb and Shy toddling after in their rickety wagon, she was trying not to think about.

Time was she'd thought out everything, every moment of every day – hers, Lamb's, Gully's, Pit and Ro's, too – all parcelled into its proper place with its proper purpose. Always looking forwards, the future better than the now, its shape clear to her as a house already built. Hard to believe since that time it was just five nights spent under the flapping canvas in the back of the cart. Five mornings waking stiff and sore to a dawn like a pit yawning under her feet. Five days following the sign across the empty grassland and into the woods, one eye on her black past, wondering what part of it had crept from the cold earth's clutches and stolen her life while she was grinning at tomorrow.

Her fingertips rubbed nervously against her palm. 'Shall we take a look?' Truth was she was scared what she might find. Scared of looking and scared of not looking. Worn out and scared of everything with a hollow space where her hopes used to be.

'I'll go round the back.' Lamb brushed his knees off with his hat and started circling the clearing, twigs crunching under his boots, a set of startled pigeons yammering into the white sky, giving anyone about fair notice of their arrival. Not that there was anyone about. Leastways, no one living.

There was an overgrown vegetable patch out back, stubborn soil scraped away to make a trench no more than ankle-deep. Next to it a soaked blanket was stretched over something lumpy. From the bottom stuck a pair of boots and a pair of bony bare feet with dirt under the bluish nails.

Lamb squatted down, took one corner and peeled it back. A man's face and a woman's, grey and slack, both with throats cut deep. The woman's head lolled, the wound in her neck yawning wet and purple.

'Ah.' Shy pressed her tongue into the gap between her front teeth and stared at the ground. Would've taken quite the optimist to expect anything else, and she by no means qualified, but those faces still tore at something in her. Worry for Pit and Ro, or worry for herself, or just a sick memory of a sick time when bodies weren't such strange things for her to see.

'Leave 'em be, you bastards!'

First thing Shy took in was the gleam on the arrowhead. Next was the hand that held the drawn bow, knuckles white on dark wood. Last was the face behind – a boy maybe sixteen, a mop of sandy hair stuck to pale skin with the wet.

'I'll kill you! I'll do it!' He eased from the bushes, feet fishing for firm earth to tread on, shadows sliding across his tight face and his hand trembling on the bow.

Shy made herself stay still, some trick to manage with her first two burning instincts to get at him or get away. Her every muscle was itching to do one or the other, and there'd been a time Shy had chased off wherever her instincts led. But since they'd usually led her by an unpleasant route right into the shit, she let the bastards run off without her this time and just stood, looking this boy steady in the eyes. Scared eyes, which was no surprise, open wide and shining in the corners. She kept her voice soft, like they'd met at a harvest dance and had no burned-out buildings, dead folk or drawn bows between them.

'What's your name?'

His tongue darted over his lips, point of the arrow wobbling and making her chest horrible itchy about where it was aimed.

'I'm Shy. This is Lamb.'

The boy's eyes flicked across, and his bow too. Lamb didn't flinch, just put the blanket back how he'd found it and slowly stood. Seeing him with the boy's fresh eyes, he looked anything but harmless. Even with that tangle of grey beard you could tell a man would have to be real careless with his razor to pick up scars like Lamb's by accident.

Shy had always guessed he'd got them in some war up North, but if he'd been a fighter once there was no fight in him now. Some kind of coward like she'd always said. But this boy wasn't to know.

'We been following some men.' Shy kept her voice soft, soft, coaxing the boy's eyes and his arrow's point back to her. 'They burned our farm, up near Squaredeal. They burned it, and they killed a man worked for us, and they took my sister and my little brother . . .' Her voice cracked and she had to swallow and press it out smooth again. 'We been following on.'

'Reckon they been here, too,' said Lamb.

'We been tracking 'em. Maybe twenty men, moving quick.' The arrow-point started to drift down. 'They stopped off at a couple more farms on the way. Same thing. Then we followed 'em into the woods. And here.'

'I'd been hunting,' said the boy quietly.

Shy nodded. 'We were in town. Selling our crop.'

'I came back, and . . .' That point made it right down to the ground, much to Shy's relief. 'Nothing I could've done.'

'No.'

'They took my brother.'

'What was his name?'

'Evin. He was nine years old.'

Silence, with just the trees still dripping and the gentle creak as the boy let his bowstring go slack.

'You know who they were?' asked Lamb.

'I didn't see 'em.'

'You know why they took your brother?'

'I said I wasn't here, didn't I? I wasn't here.'

'All right,' said Shy, calming. 'I know.'

'You following after 'em?' asked the boy.

'We're just about keeping up,' said Lamb.

'Going to get your sister and your brother back?'

'Count on it,' said Shy, as if sounding certain made it certain.

'Can you get mine, too?'

Shy looked at Lamb, and he looked back, and he didn't say nothing. 'We can try,' she said.

'Reckon I'll be coming along with you, then.'

Another silence. 'You sure?' asked Lamb.

'I can do what needs doing, y'old bastard!' screamed the boy, veins popping from his neck.

Lamb didn't twitch a muscle. 'We don't know what'll need doing yet.'

'There's room in the wagon, though, if you want to take your part.' Shy held her hand out to the boy, and he looked at it for a moment, then stepped forward and shook it. He squeezed it too hard, that way men do when they're trying to prove they're tougher than they are.

'My name's Leef.'

Shy nodded towards the two bodies. 'These your folks?'

The boy blinked down at them. 'I been trying to do the burying, but the ground's hard, and I got nothing to dig with.' He rubbed at his broken fingernails with his thumb. 'I been trying.'

'Need some help?' she asked.

His face crushed up, and he hung his head, and he nodded, wet hair dangling.

'We all need some help, time to time,' said Lamb. 'I'll get them shovels down.'

Shy reached out, checked a moment, then gently put her hand on the boy's shoulder. She felt him tense, thought he'd shake it off, but he didn't and she was glad. Maybe she needed it there more than he did.

On they went, gone from two to three but otherwise not much changed. Same wind, same sky, same tracks to be followed, same worried silence between them. The wagon was wearing out on the battered tracks, lurching more with each mile rattled behind those patient oxen. One of the wheels had near shook itself to pieces inside its iron tyre. Shy felt some sympathy, behind her frown she was all shook to pieces herself. They loaded out the gear and let the oxen loose to crop grass, and Lamb lifted one side of the wagon with a grunt and a shrug while Shy did the best she could with the tools she had and her half-sack of nails, Leef eager to do his part but that no more than passing her the hammer when she asked.

The tracks led to a river and forded at a shallow spot. Calder and Scale weren't too keen on the crossing but in the end Shy goaded them over to a tall mill-house, stone-built on three stories. Those they were chasing hadn't bothered to try and burn this one and its wheel still slapped around merrily in the chattering water. Two men and a woman were hanged together in a bunch from the attic window. One had a broken neck stretched out way too long, another feet burned raw, dangling a stride above the mud.

Leef stared up big-eyed. 'What kind o' men do a thing like this?'

'Just men,' said Shy. 'Thing like this don't take no one special.' Though at times it felt to her that they were following something else. Some mad storm blowing mindless through this abandoned country, churning up the dirt and leaving bottles and shit and burned buildings and hanged folk scattered in its wake. A storm that snatched away all the children to who knew where and to what purpose? 'You care to go up there, Leef, and cut these folks down?'

He looked like he didn't much care to, but he drew his knife and went inside to do it anyway.

'Feels like we're doing a lot of burying lately,' she muttered.

'Good thing you got Clay to throw them shovels in,' said Lamb.

She laughed at that, then realised what she was laughing at and turned it into an ugly cough. Leef's head showed at the window and he leaned out, started cutting at the ropes, making the bodies tremble. 'Seems wrong, us having to clean up after these bastards.'

'Someone has to.' Lamb held one of the shovels out to her. 'Or do you want to leave these folks swinging?'

Towards evening, the low sun setting the edges of the clouds to burn and the wind making the trees dance and sweeping patterns in the grass, they came upon a campsite. A big fire had smouldered out under the eaves of a wood, a circle of charred branches and sodden ash three strides across. Shy hopped from the wagon while Lamb was still cooing Scale and Calder to a snorting halt, and she drew her knife and gave the fire a poke, turned up some embers still aglow.

'They were here overnight,' she called.

'We're catching 'em, then?' asked Leef as he jumped down, nocking an arrow loose to his bow.

'I reckon.' Though Shy couldn't help wondering if that was a good thing. She dragged a length of frayed rope from the grass, found a cobweb torn between bushes at the treeline, then a shred of cloth left on a bramble.

'Someone come this way?' asked Leef.

'More'n one. And fast.' Shy slipped through after, keeping low, crept down a muddy slope, slick dirt and fallen leaves treacherous under her boots, trying to keep her balance and peer into the dimness—

She saw Pit, face down by a fallen tree, looking so small there among the knotted roots. She wanted to scream but had no voice, no breath even. She ran, slid on her side in a shower of dead leaves and ran again. She squatted by him, back of his head a clotted mass, hand trembling as she reached out, not wanting to see his face, having to see it. She held her breath as she wrestled him over, his body small but stiff as a board, brushed away the leaves stuck to his face with fumbling fingers.

'Is it your brother?' muttered Leef.

'No.' She was almost sick with relief. Then with guilt that she was relieved, when this boy was dead. 'Is it yours?'

'No,' said Leef.

Shy slid her hands under the dead child and picked him up, struggled up the slope, Leef behind her. Lamb stood staring between the trees at the top, a black shape stamped from the glow of sunset.

'Is it him?' came his cracking voice. 'Is it Pit?'

'No.' Shy laid him on the flattened grass, arms stuck out wide, head tipped back rigid.

'By the dead.' Lamb had his fingers shoved into his grey hair, gripping at his head like it might burst.

'Might be he tried to get away. They made a lesson of him.' She hoped Ro didn't try it. Hoped she was too clever to. Hoped she was cleverer than Shy had been at her age. She leaned on the wagon with her back to the others, squeezed her eyes shut and wiped the tears away. Dug the bastard shovels out and brought them back.

'More fucking digging,' spat Leef, hacking at the ground like it was the one stole his brother.

'Better off digging than getting buried,' said Lamb.

Shy left them to the graves and the oxen to their grazing and spread out in circles, keeping low, fingers combing at the cold grass, trying to read the signs in the fading light. Trying to feel out what they'd done, what they'd do next.

'Lamb.'

He grunted as he squatted beside her, slapping the dirt from his gloves. 'What is it?'

'Looks like three of 'em peeled off here, heading south and east. The rest struck on due west. What do you think?'

'I try not to. You're the tracker. Though when you got so damn good at it, I've no notion.'

'Just a question of thinking it through.' Shy didn't want to admit that chasing men and being chased are sides to one coin, and at being chased she'd two years of the harshest practice.

'They split up?' asked Leef.

Lamb fussed at that notch out of his ear as he looked off south. 'Some style of a disagreement?'

'Could be,' said Shy. 'Or maybe they sent 'em to circle around, check if anyone was following.'

Leef fumbled for an arrow, eyes darting about the horizon.

Lamb waved him down. 'If they'd a mind to check, they'd have seen us by now.' He kept looking south, off along the treeline towards a low ridge, the way Shy thought those three had gone. 'No. I reckon they had enough. Maybe it all went too far for 'em. Maybe they started thinking they might be the next left hanging. Either way we'll follow. Hope to catch 'em before the wheels come off this cart for good. Or off me either,' he added as he dragged himself up wincing into the wagon's seat.

'The children ain't with those three,' said Leef, turning sullen.

'No.' Lamb settled his hat back on. 'But they might point us the right way. We need to get this wagon fixed up proper, find some new oxen or get ourselves some horses. We need food. Might be those three—'

'You fucking old coward.'

There was a pause. Then Lamb nodded over at Shy. 'Me and her spent years chewing over that topic and you got naught worth adding to the conversation.' Shy looked at them, the boy stood on the ground glowering up, the big old man looking down calm and even from his seat.

Leef curled his lip. 'We need to keep after the children or—'

'Get up on the wagon, boy, or you'll be keeping after the children alone.'

Leef opened his mouth again but Shy caught him by the arm first. 'I want to catch 'em just as much as you, but Lamb's right – there's twenty men out there, bad men, and armed, and willing. There's nothing we could do.'

'We got to catch 'em sooner or later, don't we?' snapped Leef, breathing hard. 'Might as well be now while my brother and yours are still alive!'

Shy had to admit he'd a point but there was no help for it. She held his eye and said it to his face, calm but with no give. 'Get on the wagon, Leef.'

This time he did as he was told, and clambered up among their gear and sat there silent with his back to them.

Shy perched her bruised arse next to Lamb as he snapped the reins and got Scale and Calder reluctantly on the move. 'What do we do if we catch these three?' she muttered, keeping her voice down so Leef wouldn't hear it. 'Chances are they're going to be armed and willing, too. Better armed than us, that's sure.'

'Reckon we'll have to be more willing, then.'

Her brows went up at that. This big, gentle Northman who used to run laughing through the wheat with Pit on one shoulder and Ro on the other, used to sit out at sunset with Gully, passing a bottle between them in silence for hours at a time, who'd never once laid a hand on her growing up in spite of some sore provocations, talking about getting red to the elbows like it was nothing.

Shy knew it wasn't nothing.

She closed her eyes and remembered Jeg's face after she stabbed him, bloody hat brim jammed down over his eyes, pitching in the street, still muttering, *Smoke, Smoke*. That clerk in the store, staring at her as his shirt turned black. The look Dodd had as he gawped down at her arrow in his chest. *What did you do that for?*

She rubbed her face hard with one hand, sweating of a sudden, heart banging in her ears hard as it had then, and she twisted inside her greasy clothes like she could twist free of the past. But it had gone and caught her up. For Pit and Ro's sake she had to get her hands red again. She curled her fingers around the grip of her knife, took a hard breath and set her jaw. No choice then. No choice now. And for men the likes of the ones they followed no tears needed shedding.

'When we find 'em,' her voice sounding tiny in the gathering darkness, 'can you follow my lead?'

'No,' said Lamb.

'Eh?' He'd been following her lead so long she'd never thought he might find some other path.

When she looked at him, his old, scarred face was twisted like he was in pain. 'I made a promise to your mother. 'Fore she died. Made a promise to look to her children. Pit and Ro . . . and I reckon it covers you too, don't it?'

'I guess,' she muttered, far from reassured.

'I broke a lot of promises in my life. Let 'em wash away like leaves on the water.' He rubbed at his eyes with the back of one gloved hand. 'I mean to keep that one. So when we find 'em . . . you'll be following my lead. This time.'

'All right.' She could say so, if it helped him.

Then she could do what needed doing.

37

The Best Man

'I believe this is Squaredeal,' said Inquisitor Lorsen, frowning at his map.

'And is Squaredeal on the Superior's list?' asked Cosca.

'It is.' Lorsen made sure there was nothing in his voice that could be interpreted as uncertainty. He was the only man within a hundred miles in possession of anything resembling a cause. He could entertain no doubts.

Superior Pike had said the future was out here in the west, but the town of Squaredeal did not look like the future through Inquisitor Lorsen's eyeglass. It did not look like a present anyone with the choice would want a part in. The people scratching a living out of the Near Country were even poorer than he had expected. Fugitives and outcasts, misfits and failures. Poor enough that supporting a rebellion against the world's most powerful nation was unlikely to be their first priority. But Lorsen could not concern himself with likelihoods. Allowances, explanations and compromises were likewise unaffordable luxuries. He had learned over many painful years managing a prison camp in Angland that people had to be sorted onto the right side or the wrong, and those on the wrong could be given no mercy. He took no pleasure in it, but a better world comes at a price.

He folded his map, scored the sharp crease with the back of his thumbnail and thrust it inside his coat. 'Get your men ready to attack, General.'

'Mmmm.' Lorsen was surprised to see, on glancing sideways, that Cosca was in the midst of sipping from a metal flask.

'Isn't it a little early for spirits?' he forced through clenched teeth. It was, after all, but an hour or two after dawn.

Cosca shrugged. 'A good thing at teatime is surely a good thing at breakfast, too.'

'Likewise a bad thing,' grated Lorsen.

Heedless, Cosca took another taste and noisily smacked his lips. 'Though it might be best if you didn't mention this to Temple. He worries, bless him. He thinks of me almost as a father. He was in some extremity when I came upon him, you know—'

'Fascinating,' snapped Lorsen. 'Get your men *ready*.'

He gave every impression of being a loathsome man, and one who the rude hand of time had in no way improved: inexpressibly vain, trustworthy as a scorpion and an utter stranger to morality. But after a few days with the Company of the Gracious Hand, Inquisitor Lorsen had regretfully concluded that Cosca, or the Old Man as he was fondly known, might be the best among them. His direct underlings offered no counter-arguments. Captain Brachio was a vile Styrian with an eye made always weepy by an old wound. He was a fine rider but fat as a house, and had turned self-serving indolence into a religion. Captain Jubair, a hulking, tar-black Kantic, had done the opposite and turned religion into self-serving madness. Rumour had it he was an ex-slave who had once fought in a pit. Though now far removed, Lorsen suspected some part of the pit remained within him. Captain Dimbik was at least a Union man, but a reject from the army for incompetence and a weak-chinned, petulant one at that who felt the need to affect a threadbare sash as a reminder of past glories. Though balding he had grown his hair long and, rather than merely bald, he now looked both bald and a fool.

As far as Lorsen could tell, none of them truly believed in anything but their own profit. Notwithstanding Cosca's affection, the lawyer, Temple, was the worst of the crew, celebrating selfishness, greed and underhanded manipulation as virtues, a man so slimy he could have found employment as axle grease. Lorsen shuddered as he looked across the other faces swarming about Superior Pike's huge fortified wagon: wretched leavings of every race and mongrel combination, variously scarred, diseased, besmirched, all leering in anticipation of plunder and violence.

But filthy tools can be put to righteous purposes, can they not, and achieve noble ends? He hoped it would prove so. The rebel Conthus was hiding somewhere in this forsaken land, skulking and plotting more sedition and massacre. He had to be rooted out, whatever the costs. He had to be made an example of, so that Lorsen could reap the glory of his capture. He took one last look through his eyeglass towards Squaredeal – all still quiet – before snapping it closed and working his way down the slope.

Temple was talking softly to Cosca at the bottom, a whining note in his voice which Lorsen found especially aggravating. 'Couldn't we, maybe . . . talk to the townspeople?'

'We will,' said Cosca. 'As soon as we've secured forage.'

'Robbed them, you mean.'

Cosca slapped Temple on the arm. 'You lawyers! You see straight to the heart of things!'

'There must be a better way—'

'I have spent my life searching for one and the search has led me here. We signed a contract, Temple, as you well know, and Inquisitor Lorsen means to see us keep our end of the bargain, eh, Inquisitor?'

'I will insist upon it,' grated Lorsen, treating Temple to a poisonous glare.

'If you wanted to avoid bloodshed,' said Cosca, 'you really should have spoken up beforehand.'

The lawyer blinked. 'I did.'

The Old Man raised helpless palms to indicate the mercenaries arming, mounting, drinking and otherwise preparing themselves for violence. 'Not eloquently enough, evidently. How many men have we fit to fight?'

'Four hundred and thirty-two,' said Friendly, instantly. The neckless sergeant appeared to Lorsen to have two uncanny specialities: silent menace and numbers. 'Aside from the sixty-four who chose not to join the expedition, there have been eleven deserters since we left Mulkova, and five taken ill.'

Cosca shrugged them away. 'Some wastage is inevitable. The fewer our numbers, the greater each share of glory, eh, Sworbreck?'

The writer, a ludicrous indulgence on this expedition, looked anything but convinced. 'I . . . suppose?'

'Glory is hard to count,' said Friendly.

'So true,' lamented Cosca. 'Like honour and virtue and all those other desirable intangibles. But the fewer our numbers, the greater each share of the profits too.'

'Profits can be counted.'

'And weighed, and felt, and held up to the light,' said Captain Brachio, rubbing gently at his capacious belly.

'The logical extension of the argument,' Cosca twisted the waxed points of his moustaches sharp, 'would be that all the high ideals in existence are not worth as much as a single bit.'

Lorsen shivered with the most profound disgust. 'That is a world I could not bear to live in.'

The Old Man grinned. 'And yet here you are. Is Jubair in position?'

'Soon,' grunted Brachio. 'We're waiting for his signal.'

Lorsen took a breath through gritted teeth. A crowd of madmen, awaiting the signal of the maddest.

'It is not too late.' Sufeen spoke softly so the others could not hear. 'We could stop this.'

'Why should we?' Jubair drew his sword, and saw the fear in Sufeen's eyes, and felt a pity and a contempt for him. Fear was born of arrogance. Of a belief that everything was not the will of God, and could be changed. But nothing could be changed. Jubair had accepted that many years ago. Since then, he and fear had been entire strangers to each other. 'This is what God wants,' he said.

Most men refused to see the truth. Sufeen stared at him as though he was mad. 'Why would it be God's desire to punish the innocent?'

'Innocence is not for you to judge. Nor is it given to man to understand God's design. If He desires someone saved, He need only turn my sword aside.'

Sufeen slowly shook his head. 'If that is your God, I do not believe in Him.'

'What kind of God would He be if your belief could make the slightest difference? Or mine, or anyone's?' Jubair lifted the blade, patchy sunlight shining down the long, straight edge, glinting in the many nicks and notches. 'Disbelieve this sword, it will still cut you. He is God. We all walk His path regardless.'

Sufeen shook his little head again, as though that might change the way of things. 'What priest taught you this?'

'I have seen how the world is and judged for myself how it must be.' He glanced over his shoulder, his men gathering in the wood, armour and weapons prepared for the work, faces eager. 'Are we ready to attack?'

'I've been down there.' Sufeen pointed through the brush towards Squaredeal. 'They have three constables, and two are idiots. I am not sure anything so vigorous as an attack is really necessary, are you?'

It was true there were few defences. A fence of rough-cut logs had once ringed the town but had been partly torn down to allow for growth. The roof of the wooden watchtower was crusted with moss and someone had secured their washing line to one of its supports.

The Ghosts had long ago been driven out of this country and the townsfolk evidently expected no other threat. They would soon discover their error.

Jubair's eyes slid back to Sufeen. 'I tire of your carping. Give the signal.'

The scout had reluctance in his eyes, and bitterness, but he obeyed, taking out the mirror and crawling to the edge of the treeline to signal Cosca and the others. That was well for him. If he had not obeyed, Jubair would most likely have killed him, and he would have been right so to do.

He tipped his head back and smiled at the blue sky through the black branches, the black leaves. He could do anything and it would be right, for he had made himself a willing puppet of God's purpose and in so doing freed himself. He alone free, surrounded by slaves. He was the best man in the Near Country. The best man in the Circle of the World. He had no fear, for God was with him.

God was everywhere, always.

How could it be otherwise?

Checking he wasn't observed, Brachio tugged the locket from his shirt and snapped it open. The two tiny portraits were blistered and faded 'til anyone else would've seen little more than smudges, but Brachio knew them. He touched those faces with a gentle fingertip and in his mind they were as they'd been when he left – soft, perfect and smiling, too long ago.

'Don't worry, my babies,' he cooed to them. 'I'll be back soon.'

A man has to choose what matters and leave everything else to the dogs. Worry about all of it and you'll do no good at all. He was the only man in the Company with any sense. Dimbik was a preening mope. Jubair and sanity were entire strangers to each other. For all his craft and cunning, Cosca was a dreamer – this shit with the biographer was proof enough of that.

Brachio was the best of them because he knew what he was. No high ideals, no grand delusions. He was a sensible man with sensible ambitions, doing what he had to, and he was content. His daughters were all that mattered. New dresses, and good food, and good dowries, and good lives. Better lives than the hell he'd lived—

'Captain Brachio!' Cosca's braying voice, loud as ever, snatched him back to the now. 'There is the signal!'

Brachio snapped the locket closed, wiped his damp eyes on the back of his fist, and straightened the bandolier that held his knives. Cosca had wedged a boot in one stirrup and now bounced once, twice, three times before dragging on his gilt saddle horn. His bulging eyes came level with it before he froze. 'Could somebody—'

Sergeant Friendly slipped a hand under Cosca's arse and twitched him effortlessly into the saddle. Once there, the Old Man spent a moment getting his wind back, then, with some effort, drew his blade and hefted it high. 'Unsheathe your swords!' He considered that. 'Or cheaper weapons! Let us . . . do some *good!*'

Brachio pointed towards the crest of the hill and bellowed, 'Ride!' With a rousing cheer the front rank spurred their horses and thundered off in a shower of dirt and dry grass. Cosca, Lorsen, Brachio and the rest, as befitted commanders, trotted after.

'That's it?' Brachio heard Sworbreck muttering as the shabby valley, and its patchy fields, and the dusty little settlement came into view below. Maybe he'd been expecting a mile-high fortress with domes of gold and walls of adamant. Maybe it would've become one by the time he'd finished writing the scene. 'It looks . . .'

'Doesn't it?' snapped Temple.

'Look at them go!' Cosca swept off his hat and gave it a wave. 'The brave boys, eh? There's vim and brio for you! How I wish I could still charge in there with the rest of them!'

'Really?' Brachio remembered leading a charge and it had been tough, sore, dangerous work, with vim and brio both conspicuous by their absence.

Cosca thought about it for a moment, then jammed his hat back on his balding head and fumbled his sword back into its sheath. 'No. Not really.'

They made their way down at a walk.

If there had been any resistance, by the time they reached Squaredeal it was over.

A man sat in the dust by the road, bloody hands pressed to his face, blinking at Sworbreck as he rode past. A sheep pen had been broken open and the sheep all needlessly slaughtered, a dog already busy among the fluffy corpses. A wagon had been tipped on its side, one wheel still creaking hopelessly around in the air while a Kantic and a Styrian mercenary argued savagely in terms neither could understand over the scattered contents. Two other Styrians were trying to kick the door of a forge from its hinges. Another had climbed onto the roof and was digging clumsily at it, using his axe like a shovel. Jubair sat on his huge horse in the centre of the street, pointing with his outsize sword and booming orders, along with some incomprehensible utterances about the will of God.

Sworbreck's pencil hovered, his fingertips worrying at its string binding, but he could think of nothing to write. In the end he scratched out, absurdly, *No heroism apparent.*

'What are those idiots up to?' murmured Temple. Several Kantics had roped a team of mules to one of the struts of the town's moss-crusted watchtower and were whipping them into a lather in an attempt to pull it down. So far they had failed.

Sworbreck had observed that many of the men found it enjoyable simply to break things. The greater the effort required in putting them back together, the greater the pleasure. As if to illustrate this rule, four of Brachio's men had knocked someone to the ground and were administering a leisurely beating while a fat man in an apron tried without success to calm them.

Sworbreck had rarely observed violence of even the mildest sort. A dispute over narrative structure between two authors of his acquaintance had turned quite ugly, but that scarcely seemed to qualify now. Finding himself suddenly dropped into the midst of battle, as it were, Sworbreck felt both cold and hot at once. Both terribly fearful and terribly excited. He shied away from the spectacle, yet longed to see more. Was that not what he had come for, after all? To witness blood and ordure and savagery at its most intense? To smell the guts drying and hear the wails of the brutalised? So he could say that he had seen it. So he could bring conviction and authenticity to his work. So he could sit in the fashionable salons of Adua and airily declaim on the dark truths of warfare. Perhaps those were not the highest of motives, but certainly not the lowest on show. He made no claim to be the best man in the Circle of the World, after all.

Merely the best writer.

Cosca swung from his saddle, grunted as he twisted the life into his venerable hips, then, somewhat stiffly, advanced on the would-be peacemaker in the apron. 'Good afternoon! I am Nicomo Cosca, captain general of the Company of the Gracious Hand.' He indicated the four Styrians, elbows and sticks rising and falling as they continued their beating. 'I see you have already met some of my brave companions.'

'Name's Clay,' said the fat man, jowls trembling with fear. 'I own the store here—'

'A store? Excellent! May we browse?' Brachio's men were already carrying supplies out by the armload under the watchful eye of Sergeant Friendly. No doubt ensuring any thieving from the Company remained within acceptable limits. Thieving outside the Company was, it appeared, entirely to be encouraged. Sworbreck shuffled his pencil around. A further note about the lack of heroism seemed superfluous.

'Take whatever you need,' said Clay, showing his flour-dusted palms. 'There's no call for violence.' A pause, broken by the crashing of glass and wood and the whimpering of the man on the ground as he was occasionally and unenthusiastically kicked. 'Might I ask why you're here?'

Lorsen stepped forward. 'We are here to root out disloyalty, Master Clay. We are here to stamp out rebellion.'

'You're . . . from the Inquisition?'

Lorsen said nothing, but his silence spoke volumes.

Clay swallowed. 'There's no rebellion here, I assure you.' Though Sworbreck sensed a falseness in his voice. Something more than understandable nervousness. 'We're not interested in politics—'

'Really?' Lorsen's profession evidently required a keen eye for deception also. 'Roll up your sleeves!'

'What?' The merchant attempted to smile, hoping to defuse the situation with soft movements of his fleshy hands, perhaps, but Lorsen would not be defused. He jerked one hard finger and two of his Practicals hastened forward: burly men, masked and hooded.

'Strip him.'

Clay tried to twist away. 'Wait—'

Sworbreck flinched as one of them punched the merchant soundlessly in his gut and doubled him up. The other ripped his sleeve off and wrenched his bare arm around. Bold script was tattooed from his wrist to his elbow, written in the Old Tongue. Somewhat faded with age, but still legible.

Lorsen turned his head slightly sideways so he could read. '*Freedom and justice*. Noble ideals, with which we could all agree. How do they sit with those innocent citizens of the Union massacred by the rebels at Rostod, do you suppose?'

The merchant was only just reclaiming his breath. 'I never killed anyone in my life, I swear!' His face was beaded with sweat. 'The tattoo was a folly in my youth! Did it to impress a woman! I haven't spoken to a rebel for twenty years!'

'And you supposed you could escape your crimes here, beyond the borders of the Union?' Sworbreck had not seen Lorsen smile before, and he rather hoped he never did again. 'His Majesty's Inquisition has a longer reach than you imagine. And a longer memory. Who else in this miserable collection of hovels has sympathies with the rebels?'

'I daresay if they didn't when we arrived,' Sworbreck heard Temple mutter, 'they'll all have them by the time we leave . . .'

'No one.' Clay shook his head. 'No one means any harm, me least of—'

'Where in the Near Country are the rebels to be found?'

'How would I know? I'd tell you if I knew!'

'Where is the rebel leader Conthus?'

'Who?' The merchant could only stare. 'I don't know.'

'We will see what you know. Take him inside. Fetch my instruments. Freedom I cannot promise you, but there will be some justice here today, at least.'

The two Practicals dragged the unfortunate merchant towards his own store, now entirely plundered of anything of value. Lorsen stalked after, every bit as eager to begin his work as the mercenaries had been to begin theirs. The last of the Practicals brought up the rear, the polished wooden case containing the instruments in one hand. With the other he swung the door quietly shut. Sworbreck swallowed, and considered putting his notebook away. He was not sure he would have anything to write today.

'Why do these rebels tattoo themselves?' he muttered. 'Makes them damned easy to identify.'

Cosca was squinting up at the sky and fanning himself with his hat, making his sparse hairs flutter. 'Ensures their commitment, though. Ensures there can be no turning back. They take pride in them. The more they fight, the more tattoos they add. I saw a man hanged near Rostod with a whole armful.' The Old Man sighed. 'But then men do all manner of things in the heat of the moment that turn out, on sober reflection, to be not especially sensible.'

Sworbreck raised his brows, licked his pencil and copied that down in his notebook. A faint cry echoed from behind the closed door, then another. It made it very difficult to concentrate. Undoubtedly the man was guilty, but Sworbreck could not help placing himself in the merchant's position, and he did not at all enjoy being there. He blinked around at the banal robbery, the careless vandalism, the casual violence, looked for somewhere to wipe his sweaty palms, and ended up wiping them on his shirt. All manner of his standards were rapidly lapsing, it seemed.

'I was expecting it all to be a little more . . .'

'Glorious?' asked Temple. The lawyer had an expression of the most profound distaste on his face as he frowned towards the store.

'Glory in war is rare as gold in the ground, my friend!' said Cosca. 'Or constancy in womenfolk, for that matter! You may use that.'

Sworbreck fingered his pencil. 'Er—'

'But you should have been at the Siege of Dagoska with me! There was glory enough for a thousand tales!' Cosca took him by the shoulder and swept his other arm out as if there were a gilded legion approaching, rather than a set of ruffians dragging furniture from a house. 'The numberless Gurkish marching upon our works! We dauntless few ranged at the battlements of the towering land-walls, hurling our defiance! Then, at the order—'

'General Cosca!' Bermi hurried across the street, lurched back as a pair of horses thundered past, dragging a torn-off door bouncing after them, then came on again, wafting their dust away with his hat. 'We've a problem. Some Northern bastard grabbed Dimbik, put a—'

'Wait.' Cosca frowned. 'Some Northern bastard?'

'That's right.'

'One . . . bastard?'

The Styrian scrubbed at his scruffy golden locks and perched the hat on top. 'A big one.'

'How many men has Dimbik?'

Friendly answered while Bermi was thinking about it. 'One hundred and eighteen men in Dimbik's contingent.'

Bermi spread his palms, absolving himself of all responsibility. 'We do anything he'll kill the captain. He said to bring whoever's in charge.'

Cosca pressed the wrinkled bridge of his nose between finger and thumb. 'Where is this mountainous kidnapper? Let us hope he can be reasoned with before he destroys the entire Company.'

'In there.'

The Old Man examined the weathered sign above the doorway. 'Stupfer's Meat House. An unappetising name for a brothel.'

Bermi squinted up. 'I believe it's an inn.'

'Still less appetising.' With a sharp intake of breath, the Old Man stepped over the threshold, gilt spurs clinking.

It took Sworbreck's eyes a moment to adjust. Brightness glimmered through the gaps in the plank walls. Two chairs and a table had been overturned. Several mercenaries stood about, weapons including two spears, two swords, an axe and two flatbows pointed inwards towards the hostage taker, who sat at a table in the centre of the room.

He was the one man who showed no sign of nervousness. A big Northman indeed, hair hanging about his face and mingling with a patchy fur across his shoulders. He sniffed, and calmly chewed, a plate of meat and eggs before him, a fork held clumsily in his left fist in a strangely childlike manner. His right fist held a knife in a much more practised style. It was pressed against the throat of Captain Dimbik, whose bulge-eyed face was squashed helpless into the tabletop.

Sworbreck snatched a breath. Here, if not heroism, was certainly fearlessness. He had himself published controversial material on occasion, and that took admirable strength of will, but he could scarcely understand how a man could so coolly face such odds as these. To be brave among friends was nothing. To have the world against you and pick your path regardless – there is courage. He licked his pencil to scribble out a note to that effect. The Northman looked over at him and Sworbreck noticed something gleam through the lank hair. He felt a freezing shock. The man's left eye was made of metal, glimmering in the gloom of the benighted eatery, his face disfigured by a giant scar. The other eye held only a terrible willingness. As though he could hardly stop himself from cutting Dimbik's throat just to find out what would happen.

'Well, I never did!' Cosca threw up his arms. 'Sergeant Friendly, it's our old companion-in-arms!'

'Caul Shivers,' said Friendly quietly, never taking his eyes from the Northman. Sworbreck was reasonably sure that looks cannot kill, but even so he was very glad he was not standing between them.

Without taking the blade from Dimbik's throat, Shivers clumsily forked up some eggs, chewed as though none of those present had anything better to do, and swallowed. 'Fucker tried to take my eggs,' he said in a grinding whisper.

'You unmannerly brute, Dimbik!' Cosca righted one of the chairs and dropped into it opposite Shivers, wagging a finger in the captain's flushed face. 'I hope this is a lesson to you. Never take eggs from a metal-eyed man.'

Sworbreck wrote that down, although it struck him as an aphorism of limited application. Dimbik tried to speak, perhaps to make that exact point, and Shivers pressed knuckles and knife a little harder into his throat, cutting him off in a gurgle.

'This a friend of yours?' grunted the Northman, frowning down at his hostage.

Cosca gave a flamboyant shrug. 'Dimbik? He's not without his uses, but I'd hardly say he's the best man in the Company.'

It was difficult for Captain Dimbik to make his disagreement known with the Northman's fist pressed so firmly into his throat he could scarcely breathe, but he did disagree, and most profoundly. He was the only man in the Company with the slightest care for discipline, or dignity, or proper behaviour, and look where it had landed him. Throttled by a barbarian in a wilderness slop-house.

To make matters worse, or at any rate no better, his commanding officer appeared perfectly willing to trade carefree smalltalk with his assailant. 'Whatever are the chances?' Cosca was asking. 'Running into each other after all these years, so many hundreds of miles from where we first met. How many miles, would you say, Friendly?'

Friendly shrugged. 'Wouldn't like to guess.'

'I thought you went back to the North?'

'I went back. I came here.' Evidently Shivers was not a man to embroider the facts.

'Came for what?'

'Looking for a nine-fingered man.'

Cosca shrugged. 'You could cut one off Dimbik and save yourself a search.'

Dimbik spluttered and twisted, tangled with his own sash, and Shivers ground the point of the knife into his neck and forced him helplessly back against the tabletop.

'It's one particular nine-fingered man I'm after,' came his gravelly voice, without the least hint of excitement at the situation. 'Heard a rumour he might be out here. Black Calder's got a score to settle with him. And so have I.'

'You didn't see enough scores settled back in Styria? Revenge is bad for business. And for the soul, eh, Temple?'

'So I hear,' said the lawyer, just visible out of the corner of Dimbik's eye. How Dimbik hated that man. Always agreeing, always confirming, always looking like he knew better, but never saying how.

'I'll leave the souls to the priests,' came Shivers' voice, 'and the business to the merchants. Scores I understand. Fuck!' Dimbik whimpered, expecting the end. Then there was a clatter as the Northman's fumbled fork fell on the table, egg spattering the floor.

'You might find that easier with both hands.' Cosca waved at the mercenaries around the walls. 'Gentlemen, stand down. Shivers is an old friend and not to be harmed.' The various bows, blades and cudgels drifted gradually from readiness. 'Do you suppose you could release Captain Dimbik now? One dies and all the others get restless. Like ducklings.'

'Ducklings got more fight in 'em than this crowd,' said Shivers.

'They're mercenaries. Fighting is the last thing on their minds. Why don't you fall in with us? It would be just like old times. The camaraderie, the laughter, the excitement!'

'The poison, the treachery, the greed? I've found I work better alone.' The pressure on Dimbik's neck was suddenly released. He was taking a whooping breath when he was lifted by the collar and flung reeling across the room. His legs kicked helplessly as he crashed into one of his fellows, the two of them going down tangled with a table.

'I'll let you know if I run into any nine-fingered men,' said Cosca, pressing hands to knees, baring his yellowed teeth and levering himself to his feet.

'Do that.' Shivers calmly turned the knife that had been at the point of ending Dimbik's life to cutting his meat. 'And shut the door on your way out.'

Dimbik slowly stood, breathing hard, one hand to the sore graze left on his throat, glaring at Shivers. He would have greatly liked to kill this animal. Or at any rate to order him killed. But Cosca had said he was not to be harmed and Cosca, for better or worse, though mostly worse, was his commanding officer. Unlike the rest of this chaff, Dimbik was a soldier. He took such things as respect, and obedience, and procedure seriously. Even if no one else did. It was especially important that he take them seriously because no one else did. He wriggled his rumpled sash back into position, noting with disgust that the worn silk was now sullied with egg. What a fine sash it had been once. One would never know. How he missed the army. The real army, not this twisted mockery of the military life.

He was the best man in the Company, and he was treated with scorn. Given the smallest command, the worst jobs, the meanest share of the plunder. He jerked his threadbare uniform smooth, produced his comb and rearranged his hair, then strode from the scene of his shame and out into the street with the stiffest bearing he could manage.

In the lunatic asylum, he supposed, the one sane man looks mad.

Sufeen could smell burning on the air. It put him in mind of other battles, long ago. Battles that had needed fighting. Or so it seemed, now. He had gone from fighting for his country, to fighting for his friends, to fighting for his life, to fighting for a living, to . . . whatever this was. The men who had been trying to demolish the watchtower had abandoned the project and were sitting around it with bad grace, passing a bottle. Inquisitor Lorsen stood near them, with grace even poorer.

'Your business with the merchant is concluded?' asked Cosca as he came down the steps of the inn.

'It has,' snapped Lorsen.

'And what discoveries?'

'He died.'

A pause. 'Life is a sea of sorrows.'

'Some men cannot endure stern questioning.'

'Weak hearts caused by moral decay, I daresay.'

'The outcome is the same,' said the Inquisitor. 'We have the Superior's list of settlements. Next comes Lobbery, then Averstock. Gather the Company, General.'

Cosca's brow furrowed. It was the most concern Sufeen had seen him display that day. 'Can we not let the men stay overnight, at least? Some time to rest, enjoy the hospitality of the locals—'

'News of our arrival must not reach the rebels. The righteous cannot delay.' Lorsen managed to say it without a trace of irony.

Cosca puffed out his cheeks. 'The righteous work hard, don't they?'

Sufeen felt a withering helplessness. He could hardly lift his arms, he was suddenly so tired. If only there had been righteous men to hand, but he was the nearest thing to one. The best man in the Company. He took no pride in that. Best maggot in the midden would have made a better boast. He was the only man there with the slightest shred of conscience. Except Temple, perhaps, and Temple spent his every waking moment trying to convince himself and everyone else that he had no conscience at all. Sufeen watched him, standing slightly behind Cosca, a little stooped as if he was hiding, fingers fussing, trying to twist the buttons off his shirt. A man who could have been anything, struggling to be nothing. But in the midst of this folly and destruction, the waste of one man's potential hardly seemed worth commenting on. Could Jubair be right? Was God a vengeful killer, delighting in destruction? It was hard at that moment to argue otherwise.

The big Northman stood on the stoop in front of Stupfer's Meat House and watched them mount up, great fists clenched on the rail, afternoon sun glinting on that dead metal ball of an eye.

'How are you going to write this up?' Temple was asking.

Sworbreck frowned down at his notebook, pencil hovering, then carefully closed it. 'I may gloss over this episode.'

Sufeen snorted. 'I hope you brought a great deal of gloss.'

Though it had to be conceded, the Company of the Gracious Hand had conducted itself with unusual restraint that day. They put Squaredeal behind them with only mild complaints about the poor quality of plunder, leaving the merchant's body hanging naked from the watchtower, a sign about his neck proclaiming his fate a lesson to the rebels of the Near Country. Whether the rebels would hear the lesson, and if they did what they would learn from it, Sufeen could not say. Two other men hung beside the trader.

'Who were they?' asked Temple, frowning back.

'The young one was shot running away, I think. I'm not sure about the other.'

Temple grimaced, and twitched, and fidgeted with a frayed sleeve. 'What can we do, though?'

'Only follow our consciences.'

Temple rounded on him angrily. 'For a mercenary you talk a lot about conscience!'

'Why concern yourself unless yours bothers you?'

'As far as I can tell, you're still taking Cosca's money!'

'If I stopped, would you?'

Temple opened his mouth, then soundlessly shut it and scowled off at the horizon, picking at his sleeve, and picking, and picking.

Sufeen sighed. 'God knows, I never claimed to be a good man.' A couple of the outlying houses had been set ablaze, and he watched the columns of smoke drift up into the blue. 'Merely the best in the Company.'

All Got a Past

The rain came hard. It had filled the wagon ruts and the deep-sucked prints of boot and hoof until they were one morass and the main street lacked only for a current to be declared a river. It drew a grey curtain across the town, the odd lamp dimmed as through a mist, orange rumours dancing ghostly in the hundred thousand puddles. It fell in mud-spattering streams from the backed-up gutters on the roofs, and the roofs with no gutters at all, and from the brim of Lamb's hat as he hunched silent and soggy on the wagon's seat. It ran in miserable beads down the sign hung from an arch of crooked timbers that proclaimed this leavings of a town to be Averstock. It soaked into the dirt-speckled hides of the oxen, Calder proper lurching lame now in a back leg and Scale not much better off. It fell on the horses tethered to the rail before the shack that excused itself for a tavern. Three unhappy horses, their coats turned dark by the wet.

'That them?' asked Leef. 'Those their horses?'

'That's them,' said Shy, cold and clammy in her leaking coat as a woman buried.

'What we going to do?' Leef was trying to hide the tense note in his voice and falling well short.

Lamb didn't answer him. Not right away. Instead he leaned close to Shy, speaking soft. 'Say you're caught between two promises, and you can't keep one without breaking the other. What do you do?'

To Shy's mind that verged on the whimsical, considering the task in hand. She shrugged, shoulders chafing in her wet shirt. 'Keep the one most needs keeping, I guess.'

'Aye,' he muttered, staring across that mire of a street. 'Just leaves on the water, eh? Never any choices.' They sat a moment longer, no one doing a thing but getting wetter, then Lamb turned in his seat. 'I'll go in first. Get the oxen settled then the two of you follow, keeping easy.' He swung from the wagon, boots splashing into the mud. 'Unless you've a mind to stay here. Might be best all round.'

'I'll do my part,' snapped Leef.

'You know what your part might be? You ever kill a man?'

'Have you?'

'Just don't get in my way.' Lamb was different somehow. Not hunched any more. Bigger. Huge. Rain pattering on the shoulders of his coat, hint of light down one side of his rigid frown, the other all in darkness. 'Stay out of my way. You got to promise me that.'

'All right,' said Leef, giving Shy a funny look.

'All right,' said Shy.

An odd thing for Lamb to say. You could find meaner lambs than him at every lambing season. But men can be strange that way, with their pride. Shy had never had much use for pride herself. So she guessed she could let him talk his talk, and try and work up to it, and go in first. Worked all right when they had crops to sell, after all. Let him draw the eyes while she slipped up behind. She slid her knife into her sleeve, watching the old Northman struggling to make it across the boggy street with both boots still on, arms wide for balance.

When Lamb faltered, she could do what needed doing. Done it before, hadn't she, with lighter reasons and to men less deserving? She checked her knife would slip clear of her wet sleeve all right, heart thumping in her skull. She could do it again. Had to do it again.

The tavern looked a broke-down hovel from outside and a step indoors revealed no grand deception. The place made Shy come over nostalgic for Stupfer's Meat House – a state of mind she'd never thought to entertain. A sorry tongue of fire squirmed in a hearth blackened past the point of rescue, a sour fragrance of woodsmoke and damp and rank bodies unknown to soap. The counter was a slab of old wood full of splits, polished by years of elbows and warped up in the middle. The Tavern-Keep, or maybe in this place the Hovel-Keep, stood over it wiping out cups.

Narrow and low, the place was still far from full, which on a night foul as this was a poor showing. A set of five with two women in the group Shy took for traders, and not prosperous ones, hunched about some stew at the table furthest from her. A bony man sat alone with only a cup and a wore-out look for company. She recognised that from the black-spotted mirror she used to have and figured him for a farmer. Next table a fellow slumped in a fur coat so big it near drowned him, a shock of grey hair above, a hat with a couple of greasy feathers in the band and a half-empty bottle on the wood in front of him. Opposite, upright as a judge at trial, sat an old Ghost woman with a broken sideways nose, grey hair all bound up with what looked like the tatters of an old Imperial flag, and a face so deep-lined you could've used it for a plate rack. If your plates hadn't all been burned up along with your mirror and everything else you owned, that is.

Shy's eyes crawled to the last members of the merry company like she wanted to pretend they weren't there at all. But they were. Three men, huddled to themselves. They looked like Union men, far as you could tell where anyone was born once they were worn down by a few seasons in the dirt and weather of the Near Country. Two were young, one with a mess of red hair and a twitchy way like he'd a fly down his back. The other had a handsome shape to his face, far as Shy could tell standing to his side, a sheepskin coat cinched in with a fancy metal-studded belt. The third was older, bearded and with a tall hat, weather-stained, cocked to the side like he thought a lot of himself. Which most men do, of course, in proportion inverse to their value.

He had a sword – Shy saw the battered brass tip of the sheath poking out the slit in his coat. Handsome had an axe and a heavy knife tucked in his belt along with a coil of rope. Red Hair's back was to her so she couldn't tell for certain, but no doubt he was entertaining a blade or two as well.

She could hardly believe how ordinary they were. How everyday and dirty humdrum and like a thousand other drifters she'd seen floating through Squaredeal. She watched Handsome slide his hand back and tuck the thumb in that fancy belt so his fingers dangled. Just like anyone might, leaning against a counter after a long ride. Except his ride had led right through her burned-out farm, right through her smashed-up hopes, and carried her brother and sister off into who knew what darkness.

She set her jaw hard and eased into the room, sticking to the shadows, not hiding exactly but making no spectacle of herself neither. Wasn't hard, because Lamb was doing the opposite, much against his usual grain. He'd strolled up to the other end of the counter and was leaning over it with his big fists bunched on the split wood.

'Nice night you've laid on for us,' he was saying to the Tavern-Keep, shedding his hat and making a fuss of flapping the water off it so anyone with a mind to look up was watching him. Only the old Ghost's deep-set eyes followed Shy as she slunk around the walls, and she'd nothing to say about it.

'Little on the rainy side, no?' said the Keep.

'Comes down any harder you could have a sideline in a ferry across the street.'

The Keep eyed his guests with scant delight. 'I could do with some sort o' business turns a profit. Hear tell there's crowds coming through the Near Country but they ain't crowding through here. You looking for a drink?'

Lamb pulled his gloves off and tossed them careless on the counter. 'I'll take a beer.'

The tender reached for a metal cup polished bright by his wiping.

'Not that one.' Lamb pointed at a great pottery mug, old-fashioned and dusty on a high shelf. 'I like something I can feel the heft on.'

'We talking about cups or women now?' asked the Keep as he stretched up to fetch it.

'Why not both?' Lamb was grinning. How could he smile, now? Shy's eyes flickered to the three men down the other end of the counter, bent quiet over their drinks.

'Where you in from?' asked the Keep.

'East.' Lamb shrugged his sodden coat off. 'North and east, near Squaredeal.'

One of the three men, the one with the red hair, looked over at Lamb, and sniffed, and looked away.

'That's a distance. Might be a hundred mile.'

'Might be more, the route I've took, and on a bloody ox-cart, too. My old arse is ground to sausage-meat.'

'Well, if you're thinking of heading further west I'd think again. Lots of folks going that way, gold-hungry. I hear they've got the Ghosts all stirred up.'

'That a fact?'

'A certainty, friend,' threw out the man in the fur coat, sticking his head up like a tortoise from its shell. He'd about the deepest, most gravel-throated voice Shy ever heard, and she'd given ear to some worn-down tones in her time. 'They's stirred up all across the Far Country like you trod on an ant's nest. Riled up and banded up and out looking for ears, just like the old days. I heard Sangeed's even got his sword drawn again.'

'Sangeed?' The Keep wriggled his head around like his collar was too tight.

'The Emperor of the Plains his self.' Shy got the sense the old bastard was quite enjoying his scaremongering. 'His Ghosts massacred a whole fellowship o' prospectors out on the dusty not two weeks ago. Thirty men, maybe. Took their ears and their noses and I shouldn't wonder got their cocks besides.'

'What the hell do they *do* with them?' asked the farmer, staring at the old Ghost woman and giving a shudder. She didn't comment. Didn't even move.

'If you're fixed on going west I'd take plenty of company, and make sure that company has a little good humour and a lot o' good steel, so I would.' And the old-timer sank back into his fur coat.

'Good advice.' Lamb lifted that big mug and took a slow swallow. Shy swallowed with him, suddenly desperate for a beer of her own. Hell, but she wanted to get out of there. Get out or get on with it. But somehow Lamb was just as patient now as when he did the ploughing. 'I ain't sure yet exactly where I'm headed, though.'

'What brought you this far?' asked the Keep.

Lamb had started rolling up his damp shirtsleeves, thick muscles in his grey-haired forearms squirming. 'Followed some men out here.'

Red Hair looked over again, a flurry of twitches slinking through his shoulder and up his face, and this time he kept looking. Shy let the knife slide from her sleeve, out of sight behind her arm, fingers hot and tacky round the grip.

'Why'd you do that?' asked the Keep.

'They burned my farm. Stole my children. Hanged my friend.' Lamb spoke like it wasn't much to comment on, then raised his mug.

The place had fallen so silent of a sudden you could hear him swallow. One of the traders had turned to look over, brow all crinkled up with worry. Tall Hat reached for his cup and Shy saw the tendons start from the back of his hand, he was gripping on so tight. Leef picked out that moment to ease through the door and hover on the threshold, wet and pale and not knowing what to do with himself. But everyone was too fixed on Lamb to pay him any mind.

'Bad men, these, with no scruple,' he went on. 'They been stealing children all across the Near Country and leaving folk hanging in their wake. Might be a dozen I've buried the last few days.'

'How many of the bastards?'

'About twenty.'

'Do we need to get a band up and seek 'em out?' Though the Keep looked like he'd far rather stay and wipe his cups some more, and who could blame him?

Lamb shook his head. 'No point. They'll be long gone.'

'Right. Well. Reckon justice'll be catching up with 'em, sooner or later. Justice is always following, they say.'

'Justice can have what's left when I'm done.' Lamb finally had his sleeves rolled how he wanted and turned sideways, leaning easy against the counter, looking straight at those three men at its far end. Shy hadn't known what to expect, but not this, not Lamb just grinning and chatting like he'd never known a worry. 'When I said they've gone that ain't quite all the truth. Three broke off from the rest.'

'That a fact?' Tall Hat spoke up, snatching the conversation from the Keep like a thief snatching a purse.

Lamb caught his eye and held it. 'A certainty.'

'Three men, you say?' Handsome's fussing hand crept round his belt towards his axe. The mood of the place had shifted fast, the weight of coming violence hanging heavy as a storm cloud in that little room.

'Now look,' said the Keep, 'I don't want no trouble in my—'

'I didn't want no trouble,' said Lamb. 'It blew in anyway. Trouble's got a habit that way.' He pushed his wet hair out of his face, and his eyes were wide open and bright, bright, mouth open too, breathing fast, and he was smiling. Not like a man working his way up to a hard task. Like a man enjoying getting to a pleasant one, taking his time about it like you might over a fine meal, and of a sudden Shy saw all those scars anew, and felt this coldness creeping up her arms and down her back and every hair on her standing.

'I tracked those three,' said Lamb. 'Picked up their trail and two days I've followed it.'

Another breathless pause, and the Keep took a step back, cup and cloth still limp in his hands, the ghost of a smile still clinging to his face but the rest all doubt. The three had turned to face Lamb, spreading out a little, backs to Shy, and she found herself easing forwards like she was wading through honey, out of the shadows towards them, tingling fingers shifting around the knife's handle. Every moment was a drawn-out age, breath scratching, catching in every throat.

'Where'd the trail lead?' asked Tall Hat, voice cracking at the end and tailing off.

Lamb's smile spread wider. The smile of a man got exactly what he wanted on his birthday. 'The ends o' your fucking legs.'

Tall Hat twitched his coat back, cloth flapping as he went for his sword.

Lamb flung the big mug at him underhand. It bounced off his head and sent him tumbling in a shower of beer.

A chair screeched as the farmer tried to stumble up and ended tripping over it.

The red-haired lad took a step back, making room or just from shock and Shy slipped her knife around his neck and pressed the flat into it, folding him tight with the other arm.

Someone shouted.

Lamb crossed the room in one spring. He caught Handsome's wrist just as he pulled his axe free, wrenched it up and with the other hand snatched the knife from his fancy belt and rammed it in his groin, dragging up the blade, ripping him wide open, blood spraying the pair of them. He gave a gurgling scream appalling loud in that narrow space and dropped to his knees, eyes goggling as he tried to hold his guts in. Lamb smashed him across the back of the head with the pommel of the knife, cut his scream off and laid him out flat.

One of the trader women jumped up, hands over her mouth.

The red-haired one Shy had a hold of squirmed and she squeezed him tighter and whispered, 'Shush,' grinding the point of her knife into his neck.

Tall Hat floundered up, hat forgotten, blood streaming from the gash the mug had made across his forehead. Lamb caught him around the neck, lifting him easily as if he was made of rags, and smashed his face into the counter, again with a crunch like a breaking pot, again head flopping like a doll's, and blood spotted the Keep's apron, and the wall behind him, and the ceiling, too. Lamb lifted the knife high, flash of his face still stretched wide in that crazy grin, then the blade was a metal blur, through the man's back and with an almighty crack left a split down the length of the bar, splinters flying. Lamb left him nailed there, knees just clear of the floor and his boots scraping at the boards, blood tip-tapping around them like a spilled drink.

All took no longer than Shy would've needed to take three good breaths, if she hadn't been holding hers the while. She was hot now, and dizzy, and the world was too bright. She was blinking. Couldn't quite get a hold on what had happened. She hadn't moved. She didn't move. No one did. Only Lamb, walking forward, eyes gleaming with tears and one side of his face black-dashed and speckled and his bared teeth glistening in his mad smile and each breath a soft growl in his throat like a lover's.

Red Hair whimpered, 'Fuck, fuck,' and Shy pushed the flat of the knife harder into his neck and shushed him up again. He'd a big blade halfway to a sword tucked in his belt and with her free hand she slid that out. Then Lamb was looming over the shrinking pair of them, his head near brushing the low rafters, and he twisted a fistful of the lad's shirt and jerked him out of Shy's limp grip.

'Talk to me.' And he hit the lad across the face, open-handed but hard enough to knock him down if he hadn't been held up.

'I . . .' muttered the lad.

Lamb slapped him again, the sound loud as a clap, the traders up the far end flinching at it but not a one moving. 'Talk.'

'What d'you—'

'Who was in charge?'

'Cantliss. That's his name.' The lad started blathering, words tumbling over each other all slobbery like he couldn't say them fast enough. 'Grega Cantliss. Didn't know how bad a crew they was, just wanted to get from here to there and make a bit of money. I was in the ferrying business back east and one day the rain come up and the ferry got swep' away and—' Slap. 'We didn't want it, you got to believe—' Slap. 'There's some evil ones in with 'em. A Northman called Blackpoint, he shot an old man with arrows. They laughed at it.'

'See me laughing?' said Lamb, cuffing him again.

The red-haired lad held up one useless, shaking hand. 'I didn't laugh none! We didn't want no part of all them killings so we split off! Supposed to be just some robbing, Cantliss told us, but turned out it was children we was stealing, and—'

Lamb cut him off with a slap. 'Why'd he take the children?' And he set him talking with another, the lad's freckled face cut and swelling down one side, blood smearing his nose.

'Said he had a buyer for 'em, and we'd all be rich men if we got 'em there. Said they weren't to be hurt, not a hair on their heads. Wanted 'em perfect for the journey.'

Lamb slapped him again, opening another cut. 'Journey where?'

'To Crease, he said, to begin with.'

'That's up at the head of the Sokwaya,' said Shy. 'Right the way across the Far Country.'

'Cantliss got a boat waiting. Take him upriver . . . upriver . . .'

'To Crease and then where?'

The red-haired lad had slumped in half a faint, lids fluttering. Lamb slapped him again, both sides, shook him by his shirt. 'To Crease and then where?'

'Didn't say. Not to me. Maybe to Taverner.' Looking towards the man nailed to the counter with the knife handle sticking out his back. Shy didn't reckon he'd be telling any tales now.

'Who's buying children?' asked Lamb.

Red Hair drunkenly shook his swollen head. Lamb slapped him again, again, again. One of the trader women hid her face. The other stared, standing rigid. The man beside her dragged her back down into her chair.

'Who's buying?'

'Don't know,' words mangled and bloody drool dangling from his split lip.

'Stay there.' Lamb let the lad go and crossed to Tall Hat, his boots in a bloody puddle, reached around and unbuckled his sword, took a knife from his coat. Then he rolled Handsome over with his foot, left him staring wonky-eyed at the ceiling, a deal less handsome with his insides on the outside. Lamb took the bloody rope from his belt, walked to the red-haired lad and started tying one end around his neck while Shy just watched, numb and weak all over. Weren't clever knots he tied, but good enough, and he jerked the lad towards the door, following along without complaint like a beaten dog.

Then they stopped. The Keep had come around the counter and was standing in the doorway. Just goes to show you never can quite figure what a man will do, or when. He was holding tight to his wiping cloth like it might be a shield against evil. Shy didn't reckon it'd be a very effective one, but she'd some high respect for his guts. Just hoped Lamb didn't end up adding them to Handsome's, scattered bloody on the boards.

'This ain't right,' said the Keep.

'How's you being dead going to make it any righter?' Lamb's voice flat and quiet like it was no kind of threat, just a question. He didn't have to scream it. Those two dead men were doing it for him.

The Keep's eyes darted around but no heroes leaped to his side. All looked scared as if Lamb was death himself come calling. Except the old Ghost woman, sat tall in her chair just watching, and her companion in the fur coat, who still had his boots crossed and, without any quick movements, was pouring himself another drink.

'Ain't right.' But the Keep's voice was weak as watered beer.

'It's right as it's getting,' said Lamb.

'We should put a panel together and judge him proper, ask some—'

Lamb loomed forward. 'All you got to ask is do you want to be in my way.' The Keep shrank back and Lamb dragged the lad past. Shy hurried after, suddenly unfroze, passing Leef loose-jawed in the doorway.

Outside the rain had slacked to a steady drizzle. Lamb was hauling Red Hair across the mired street towards the arch of crooked timbers the sign hung from. High enough for a mounted man to pass under. Or for one on foot to dangle from.

'Lamb!' Shy hopped down from the tavern's porch, boots sinking to the ankles. 'Lamb!' He weighed the rope then tossed it over the crossbar. 'Lamb!' She struggled across the street, mud sucking at her feet. He caught the loose end of the rope and jerked the slack out, the red-haired lad stumbling as the noose went tight under his chin, bloated face showing dumb like he hadn't worked out yet where he was headed.

'Ain't we seen enough folk hanged?' called Shy as she slopped up. Lamb didn't answer, didn't look at her, just wound the free end of the rope about one forearm.

'It ain't right,' she said. Lamb took a sniff and set himself to haul the lad into the air. Shy snatched hold of the rope by the lad's neck and started sawing at it with the short-sword. It was sharp. Didn't take a moment to cut it through.

'Get running.'

The lad blinked at her.

'Run, you fucking idiot!' She kicked the seat of his trousers and he sloshed a few steps and went over on his face, struggled up and floundered away into the darkness, still with his rope collar.

Shy turned back to Lamb. He was staring at her, stolen sword in one hand, loose length of rope in the other. But like he was hardly seeing her. Like he was hardly him, even. How could this be the man who'd bent over Ro when she had the fever, and sung to her? Sung badly, but sung still, face all wrinkled with care? Now she looked in those black eyes and suddenly this dread crept on her like she was looking into the void. Standing on the edge of nothing and it took every grain of courage she had not to run.

'Bring them three horses over!' she snapped at Leef, who'd wandered out onto the porch with Lamb's coat and hat in his hands. 'Bring 'em now!' And he hopped off to do it. Lamb just stood, staring after the red-haired lad, the rain starting to wash the blood off his face. He took hold of the saddle bow when Leef led the biggest horse over, started to swing himself up and the horse shied, and kicked out, and Lamb gave a grunt as he lost his grip and went over backwards, stirrup flapping as he caught it with a clutching hand, splashing down hard in the mud on his side. Shy knelt by him as he struggled to his hands and knees.

'You hurt?'

He looked up at her and there were tears in his eyes, and he whispered, 'By the dead, Shy. By the dead.' She did her best to drag him up, a bastard of a task since he was a corpse-weight of a sudden. When they finally got him standing he pulled her close by her coat. 'Promise me,' he whispered. 'Promise me you won't get in my way again.'

'No.' She laid a hand on his scarred cheek. 'I'll hold your bridle for you, though.' And she did, and the horse's face, too, and whispered calm words to it and wished there was someone to do the same to her while Lamb dragged himself up into the saddle, slow and weary, teeth gritted like it was an effort. When he got up he sat hunched, right hand on the reins, left hand holding his coat closed at his neck. He looked an old man again. Older than ever. An old man with a terrible weight and worry across his hunched shoulders.

'He all right?' Leef's voice not much above a whisper, like he was scared of being overheard.

'I don't know,' said Shy. Lamb didn't seem like he could hear even, wincing off to the black horizon, almost one with the black sky now.

'You all right?' Leef whispered to her.

'Don't know that either.' She felt the world was all broken up and washed away and she was drifting on strange seas, cut loose from land. 'You?'

Leef just shook his head, and looked down at the mud with eyes all round.

'Best get what we need from the wagon and mount up, eh?'

'What about Scale and Calder?'

'They're blown and we've got to move. Leave 'em.'

The wind dashed rain in her face and she pulled her hat-brim down and set her jaw hard. Her brother and her sister, that's what she'd fix on. They were the stars she'd set her course by, two points of light in the black. They were all that mattered.

So she heeled her new horse and led the three of them out into the gathering night. They hadn't gone far when Shy heard noises beyond the wind and slowed to a walk. Lamb brought his horse about and drew the sword. An old cavalry sword, long and heavy, sharpened on one side.

'Someone's following!' said Leef, fumbling with his bow.

'Put that away! You'll more likely shoot yourself in this light. Or worse yet, me.' Shy heard hooves on the track behind them, and a wagon, too, a glimmer of torchlight through tree-trunks. Folk come out from Averstock to chase them? The Keep firmer set on justice than he'd seemed? She slid the short-sword out by its horn handle, metal glinting with the last red touch of twilight. Shy had no notion what to expect any more. If Juvens himself had trotted from the dark and bid them a good evening she'd have shrugged and asked which way he was headed.

'Hold up!' came a voice as deep and rough as Shy ever heard. Not Juvens himself. The man in the fur coat. He came into sight now, riding with a torch in his hand. 'I'm a friend!' he said, slowing to a walk.

'You're no friend o' mine,' she said back.

'Let's put that right as a first step, then.' He delved into a saddlebag and tossed a half-full bottle across to Shy. A wagon trundled up with a pair of horses pulling. The old Ghost woman had the reins, creased face as empty as it had been at the inn, a singed old chagga pipe gripped between her teeth, not smoking it, just chewing it.

They all sat a moment, in the dark, then Lamb said, 'What do you want?'

The stranger reached up slow and tipped his hat back. 'No need to spill more blood tonight, big man, we're no enemies o' yours. And if I was I reckon I'd be reconsidering that position about now. Just want to talk, is all. Make a proposal that might benefit the crowd of us.'

'Speak your piece, then,' said Shy, pulling the cork from the bottle with her teeth but keeping the sword handy.

'Then I will. My name's Dab Sweet.'

'What?' said Leef. 'Like that scout they tell all the stories of?'

'Exactly like. I'm him.'

Shy paused in her drinking. 'You're Dab Sweet? Who was first to lay eyes on the Black Mountains?' She passed the bottle across to Lamb, who passed it straight to Leef, who took a swig, and coughed.

Sweet gave a dry chuckle. 'The mountains saw me first, I reckon, but the Ghosts been there a few hundred years before, and the Imperials before that, maybe, and who knows who back when before the Old Time? Who's to say who's first to anything out in this country?'

'But you killed that great red bear up at the head of the Sokwaya with no more than your hands?' asked Leef, passing the bottle back to Shy.

'I been to the head of the Sokwaya times enough, that's true, but I take some offence at that particular tale.' Sweet grinned, friendly lines spreading out across his weathered face. 'Fighting even a little bear with your hands don't sound too clever to me. My preferred approach to bears – alongside most dangers – is to be where they ain't. But there's all kind of strange water flowed by down the years, and my memory ain't all it was, I'll confess that, too.'

'Maybe you misremembered your name,' said Shy, and took another swig. She had a hell of a thirst on her.

'Woman, I'd accept that for a strong possibility if I didn't have it stamped into my old saddle here.' And he gave the battered leather a friendly pat. 'Dab Sweet.'

'Felt sure from what I've heard you'd be bigger.'

'From what I've heard I should be half a mile high. Folk like to talk. And when they do, ain't really up to me what size I grow to, is it?'

'What's this old Ghost to you?' asked Shy.

So slow and solemn it might've been the eulogy at a funeral, the Ghost said, 'He's my wife.'

Sweet gave his grinding laugh again. 'Sometimes it do feel that way, I'll concede. That there Ghost is Crying Rock. We been up and down every speck o' the Far Country and the Near Country and plenty o' country don't got no names. Right now we're signed on as scouts, hunters and pilots to take a Fellowship of prospectors across the plains to Crease.'

Shy narrowed her eyes. 'That so?'

'From what I heard back there, you'll be headed the same way. You'll be finding no keelboat of your own, not one stopping off to pick you up leastways, and that means out on the lone and level by hoof or wheel or boot. With the Ghosts on the rampage you'll be needing company.'

'Meaning yours.'

'I may not be throttling any bears on the way, but I know the Far Country. Few better. Anyone's going to get you to Crease with your ears still on your head, it's me.'

Crying Rock cleared her throat, shifting her dead pipe from one side of her mouth to the other with her tongue.

'It's me and Crying Rock.'

'And what'd possess you to do us such a favour?' asked Shy. Specially after what they'd just seen.

Sweet scratched at his stubbly beard. 'This expedition got put together before the trouble started on the plains and we've got all sorts along. A few with iron in 'em, but not enough experience and too much cargo.' He was looking over at Lamb with an estimating expression. The way Clay might've sized up a haul of grain. 'Now there's trouble in the Far Country we could use another man don't get sickly at the sight o' blood.' His eyes moved over to Shy. 'And I've a sense you can hold a blade steady too when it's called for.'

She weighed the sword. 'I can just about keep myself from dropping one. What's your offer?'

'Normally folk bring a skill to the company or pay their way. Then everyone shares supplies, helps each other out where they can. The big man—'

'Lamb.'

Sweet raised a brow. 'Really?'

'One name's good as another,' said Lamb.

'I won't deny it, and you go free. I've stood witness to your usefulness. You can pay a half-share, woman, and a full share for the lad, that comes to . . .' Sweet crunched his face up, working the sums.

Shy might've seen two men killed and saved another that night, her stomach still sick and her head still spinning from it, but she wasn't going to let a deal go wandering past.

'We'll all be going free.'

'What?'

'Leef here's the best damn shot with a bow you ever saw. He's an asset.'

Sweet looked less than convinced. 'He is?'

'I am?' muttered Leef.

'We'll all be going free.' Shy took another swig and tossed the bottle back. 'It's that way or no way.'

Sweet narrowed his eyes as he took his own long, slow drink, then he looked over at Lamb again, sat still in the darkness, just the glimmer of the torch in the corners of his eyes, and sighed. 'You like to drive a bargain, don't you?'

'My preferred approach to bad deals is to be where they ain't.'

Sweet gave another chuckle, and he nosed his horse forward, and he stuck the bottle in the crook of his arm, pulled off his glove with his teeth and slapped his hand into hers. 'Deal. Reckon I'm going to like you, girl. What's your name?'

'Shy South.'

Sweet raised that brow again. 'Shy?'

'It's a name, old man, not a description. Now hand me back that bottle.'

And so they headed off into the night, Dab Sweet telling tales in his grinding bass, talking a lot and saying nothing and laughing a fair bit too just as though they hadn't left two men murdered not an hour before, passing the bottle about 'til it was done and Shy tossed it away into the night with a warmth in her belly. When Averstock was just a few lights behind she reined her horse back to a walk and dropped in beside the closest thing she'd ever had to a father.

'Your name hasn't always been Lamb, has it?'

He looked at her, and then away. Hunching down further. Pulling his coat tighter. Thumb slipping out between his fingers over and over, rubbing at the stump of the middle one. The missing one. 'We all got a past,' he said.

Too true, that.

The Stolen

The children were left in a silent huddle each time Cantliss went to round up more. Rounding 'em up, that's what he called it, like they was just unclaimed cattle and no killing was needed. No doing what they'd done at the farm. No laughing about it after when they brought more staring little ones. Blackpoint was always laughing, a lopsided laugh with two of the front teeth missing. Like he'd never heard a joke so funny as murder.

At first Ro tried to guess at where they were. Maybe even leave some sign for those who must be coming after. But the woods and the fields gave way to just a scrubby emptiness in which a bush was quite the landmark. They were headed west, she gathered that much, but no more. She had Pit to think about and the other children too and she tried to keep them fed and cleaned and quiet the best she could.

The children were all kinds, none older than ten. There'd been twenty-one 'til that boy Care had tried to run and Blackpoint came back from chasing him all bloody. So they were down to twenty and no one tried to run after that.

There was a woman with them called Bee who was all right even if she did have scars on her arms from surviving the pox. She held the children sometimes. Not Ro, 'cause she didn't need holding, and not Pit, 'cause he had Ro to hold, but some of the younger ones, and she whispered at them to hush when they cried 'cause she was scared as piss of Cantliss. He'd hit her time to time, and after when she was wiping the blood from her nose she'd make excuses for him. She'd say how he'd had a hard life and been abandoned by his folks and beaten as a child and other such. That sounded to Ro like it should make you slower rather'n quicker to beat others, but she guessed everyone's got their excuses. Even if they're feeble ones.

The way Ro saw it, Cantliss had nothing in him worth a damn. He rode up front in his fancy tailored clothes like he was some big man with important doings to be about, 'stead of a child-thief and murderer and lowest of the low, aiming to make himself look special by gathering even lower scum about him for a backdrop. At night he'd get a great big fire built 'cause he loved to watch things burn, and he'd drink, and once he'd set to drinking his mouth would get a bitter twist and he'd complain. About how life weren't fair and how he'd been tricked out of an inheritance by a banker and how things never seemed to go his way.

They stopped for a day beside wide water flowing and Ro asked him, 'Where are you taking us?' and he just said, 'Upstream.' A keelboat had tied off at the bank and upstream they'd gone, poled and roped and rowed by a set of men all sinew while the flat land slid by, and way, way off north through the haze three blue peaks showed against the sky.

Ro thought at first it would be a mercy, not to have to ride no more, but now all they could do was sit. Sit under a canopy up front and watch the water and the land drift past and feel their old lives dwindle further and further off, the faces of the folks they'd known harder to bring to mind, until the past all felt like a dream and the future an unknown nightmare.

Blackpoint would get off now and again with his bow, a couple of the others with him, and they'd come back later with meat they'd hunted up. Rest of the time he sat smoking, and watched the children, and grinned for hours at a spell. When Ro saw the missing teeth in that grin she thought about him shooting Gully and leaving him swinging there on the tree full of arrows. When she thought about that she wanted to cry, but she knew she couldn't because she was one of the oldest and the little ones were looking to her to be strong and that's what she meant to be. She reckoned if she didn't cry that was her way of beating them. A little victory, maybe, but Shy always said a win's a win.

Few days on the boat and they saw something burning far off across the grass, plumes of smoke trickling up and fading in that vastness of above and the black dots of birds circling, circling. The chief boatman said they should turn back and he was worried about Ghosts and Cantliss just laughed, and shifted the knife in his belt, and said there was things closer at hand for a man to worry on and that was all the conversation.

That evening one of the men had shaken her wakeful and started talking about how she reminded him of someone, smiling though there was something wrong in his eye and his breath sour with spirits, and he'd caught hold of her arm and Pit had hit him hard as he could which wasn't that hard. Bee woke and screamed and Cantliss came and dragged the man away and Blackpoint kicked him 'til he stopped moving and tossed him in the river. Cantliss shouted at the others to leave the goods well alone and just use their fucking hands, 'cause no bastard would be costing him money, you could bet on that.

She knew she should never have said nothing about it but she couldn't help herself then and she'd burst out, 'My sister's following, you can bet on that if you want to bet! She'll find you out!'

She'd thought Cantliss might hit her then but all he'd done was look at her like she was the latest of many afflictions fate had forced upon him and said, 'Little one, the past is gone, like to that water flowing by. The sooner you put it from your pinprick of a mind the happier you'll be. You got no sister now. No one's following.' And he went off to stand on the prow, tutting as he tried to rub the spotted blood out of his fancy clothes with a damp rag.

'Is it true?' Pit asked her. 'Is no one following?'

'Shy's following.' Ro never doubted it because, you'd best believe, Shy was not a person to be told how things would be. But what Ro didn't say was that she half-hoped Shy wasn't following, because she didn't want to see her sister shot through with arrows, and didn't really know what she could do about all this, 'cause even with the three that left, and the two that took most of the horses off to sell when they got on the boat, and the one that Blackpoint killed, Cantliss still had thirteen men. She didn't see what anyone could do about it.

She wished Lamb was with them, though, because he could've smiled and said, 'It's all right. Don't worry none,' like he did when there was a storm and she couldn't sleep. That would've been fine.

II
FELLOWSHIP

'What a wild life, and what
a fresh kind of existence!
But, ah, the discomforts!'
Henry Wadsworth Longfellow

Conscience and the Cock-Rot

'Praying?'

Sufeen sighed. 'No, I am kneeling here with my eyes closed cooking porridge. Yes, I am praying.' He opened one eye a crack and aimed it at Temple. 'Care to join me?'

'I don't believe in God, remember?' Temple realised he was picking at the hem of his shirt again and stopped himself. 'Can you honestly say He ever raised a finger to help you?'

'You don't have to *like* God to believe. Besides, I know I am past help.'

'What do you pray for, then?'

Sufeen dabbed his face with his prayer cloth, eyeing Temple over the fringe. 'I pray for you, brother. You look as if you need it.'

'I've been feeling . . . a little jumpy.' Temple realised he was worrying at his sleeve now, and tore his hand away. For God's sake, would his fingers not be happy until they had unravelled every shirt he possessed? 'Do you ever feel as if there is a dreadful weight hanging over you . . .'

'Often.'

'. . . and that it might fall at any moment . . .'

'All the time.'

'. . . and you just don't know how to get out from under it?'

'But you *do* know.' There was a pause while they watched each other.

'No,' said Temple, taking a step away. 'No, no.'

'The Old Man listens to you.'

'No!'

'You could talk to him, get him to stop this—'

'I tried, he didn't want to hear!'

'Perhaps you didn't try hard enough.' Temple clapped his hands over his ears and Sufeen dragged them away. 'The easy way leads nowhere!'

'You talk to him, then!'

'I'm just a scout!'

'I'm just a lawyer! I never claimed to be a righteous man.'

'No righteous man does.'

Temple tore himself free and strode off through the trees. 'If God wants this stopped, let Him stop it! Isn't He all-powerful?'

'Never leave to God what you can do yourself!' he heard Sufeen call, and hunched his shoulders as though the words were sling-stones. The man was starting to sound like Kahdia. Temple only hoped things didn't end the same way.

Certainly no one else in the Company appeared keen to avoid violence. The woods were alive with eager fighting men, tightening worn-out straps, sharpening weapons, stringing bows. A pair of Northmen were slapping each other to pink-faced heights of excitement. A pair of Kantics were at prayers of their own, kneeling before a blessing stone they had placed with great care on a tree-stump, the wrong way up. Every man takes God for his ally, regardless of which way he faces.

The towering wagon had been drawn up in a clearing, its hardworking horses at their nosebags. Cosca was draped against one of its wheels, outlining his vision for the attack on Averstock to an assembly of the Company's foremost members, switching smoothly between Styrian and common and with expressive gestures of hand and hat for the benefit of those who spoke neither. Sworbreck crouched over a boulder beside him with pencil poised to record the great man at work.

'. . . so that Captain Dimbik's Union contingent can sweep in from the west, alongside the river!'

'Yes, sir,' pronounced Dimbik, sweeping a few well-greased hairs back into position with a licked little finger.

'Brachio will simultaneously bring his men charging in from the east!'

'Simulta what now?' grunted the Styrian, tonguing at a rotten tooth.

'At the same time,' said Friendly.

'Ah.'

'And Jubair will thrust downhill from the trees, completing the encirclement!' The feather on Cosca's hat thrashed as it achieved a metaphorical total victory over the forces of darkness.

'Let no one escape,' ground out Lorsen. 'Everyone must be examined.'

'Of course.' Cosca pushed out his lower jaw and scratched thoughtfully at his neck, where a faint speckling of pink rash was appearing. 'And all plunder declared, assessed and properly noted so that it may be divided according to the Rule of Quarters. Any questions?'

'How many men will Inquisitor Lorsen torture to death today?' demanded Sufeen in ringing tones. Temple stared at him open-mouthed, and he was not alone.

Cosca went on scratching. 'I was thinking of questions relating to our tactics—'

'As many as is necessary,' interrupted the Inquisitor. 'You think I revel in this? The world is a grey place. A place of half-truths. Of half-wrongs and half-rights. Yet there are things worth fighting for, and they must be pursued with all our vigour and commitment. Half-measures achieve nothing.'

'What if there are no rebels down there?' Sufeen shook off Temple's frantic tugging at his sleeve. 'What if you are wrong?'

'Sometimes I will be,' said Lorsen simply. 'Courage lies in bearing the costs. We all have our regrets, but not all of us can afford to be crippled by them. Sometimes it takes small crimes to prevent bigger ones. Sometimes the lesser evil is the greater good. A man of principle must make hard choices and suffer the consequences. Or you could sit and cry over how unfair it all is.'

'Works for me,' said Temple with a laugh of choking falseness.

'It will not work for me.' Sufeen wore a strange expression, as if he was looking through the gathering to something in the far distance, and Temple felt an awful foreboding. Even more awful than usual. 'General Cosca, I want to go down into Averstock.'

'So do we all! Did you not hear my address?'

'Before the attack.'

'Why?' demanded Lorsen.

'To talk to the townsfolk,' said Sufeen. 'To give them a chance to surrender any rebels.' Temple winced. God, it sounded ridiculous. Noble, righteous, courageous and ridiculous. 'To avoid what happened in Squaredeal—'

Cosca was taken aback. 'I thought we were remarkably well behaved in Squaredeal. A company of kittens could have been no gentler! Would you not say so, Sworbreck?'

The writer adjusted his eyeglasses and stammered out, 'Admirable restraint.'

'This is a poor town.' Sufeen pointed into the trees with a faintly shaking finger. 'They have nothing worth taking.'

Dimbik frowned as he scraped at a stain on his sash with a fingernail. 'You can't know that until you look.'

'Just give me a chance. I'm begging you.' Sufeen clasped his hands and looked Cosca in his eye. 'I'm praying.'

'Prayer is arrogance,' intoned Jubair. 'The hope of man to change the will of God. But God's plan is set and His words already spoken.'

'Fuck Him, then!' snapped Sufeen.

Jubair mildly raised one brow. 'Oh, you will find it is God who does the fucking.'

There was a pause, the metallic notes of martial preparations drifting between the tree-trunks along with the morning birdsong.

The Old Man sighed and rubbed at the bridge of his nose. 'You sound determined.'

Sufeen echoed Lorsen's words. 'A man of principle must make hard choices and suffer the consequences.'

'And if I agree to this, what then? Will your conscience continue to prick at our arses all the way across the Near Country and back? Because that could become decidedly tiresome. Conscience can be painful but so can the cock-rot. A grown-up should suffer his afflictions privately and not allow them to become an inconvenience for friends and colleagues.'

'Conscience and the cock-rot are hardly equivalent,' snapped Lorsen.

'Indeed,' said Cosca, significantly. 'The cock-rot is rarely fatal.'

The Inquisitor's face had turned even more livid than usual. 'Am I to understand you are considering this folly?'

'You are, and I am. The town is surrounded, after all, no one is going anywhere. Perhaps this can make all our lives a little easier. What do you think, Temple?'

Temple blinked. 'Me?'

'I am looking at you and using your name.'

'Yes, but . . . me?' There was a good reason why he had stopped making hard choices. He always made the wrong ones. Thirty years of scraping through the poverty and fear between disasters to end up in this fix was proof enough of that. He looked from Sufeen, to Cosca, to Lorsen, and back. Where was the greatest profit? Where the least danger? Who was actually . . . right? It was damned difficult to pick the easy way from this tangle. 'Well . . .'

Cosca puffed out his cheeks. 'The man of conscience and the man of doubts. God help us indeed. You have one hour.'

'I must protest!' barked Lorsen.

'If you must, you must, but I won't be able to hear you with all this noise.'

'What noise?'

Cosca stuck his fingers in his ears. 'Blah-lee-lah-lee-lah-lee-lah-lee-lah . . . !'

He was still doing it as Temple hurried away through the towering trees after Sufeen, their boots crunching on fallen sticks, rotten cones, browned pine needles, the sound of the men fading to leave only the rustling of the branches high above, the twitter and warble of birds.

'Have you gone mad?' hissed Temple, struggling to keep up.

'I have gone sane.'

'What will you do?'

'Talk to them.'

'To who?'

'Whoever will listen.'

'You won't put the world right with talk!'

'What will you use, then? Fire and sword? Papers of Engagement?'

They passed the last group of puzzled sentries, Bermi giving a questioning look from among them and Temple offering only a helpless shrug in return, then they were out into the open, sunlight suddenly bright on their faces. The few dozen houses of Averstock clung to a curve in the river below. 'Houses' was being generous to most of them. They were little better than shacks, with dirt between. They were no better than shacks, with shit between, and Sufeen was already striding purposefully downhill in their direction.

'What the hell is he up to?' hissed Bermi from the shadowy safety of the trees.

'I think he's following his conscience,' said Temple.

The Styrian looked unconvinced. 'Conscience is a shitty navigator.'

'I've often told him so.' Yet Sufeen showed no sign of slowing in his pursuit of it. 'Oh God,' muttered Temple, wincing up at the blue heavens. 'Oh God, oh God.' And he bounded after, grass thrashing about his calves, patched with little white flowers the name of which he did not know.

'Self-sacrifice is not a noble thing!' he called as he caught up. 'I have seen it, and it's an ugly, pointless thing, and nobody thanks you for it!'

'Perhaps God will.'

'If there is a God, He has bigger things to worry about than the likes of us!'

Sufeen pressed on, looking neither left or right. 'Go back, Temple. This is not the easy way.'

'That I fucking realise!' He caught a fistful of Sufeen's sleeve. 'Let's both go back!'

Sufeen shook him off and carried on. 'No.'

'Then I'm coming!'

'Good.'

'Fuck!' Temple hurried to catch up again, the town getting steadily closer and looking less and less like a thing he wished to risk his life for. 'What's your plan? There is a plan, yes?'

'There is . . . part of one.'

'That's not very reassuring.'

'Reassuring you was not my aim.'

'Then you have *fucking* succeeded, my friend.' They passed under the arch of rough-trimmed timbers that served for a gate, a sign creaking beneath it that read *Averstock*. They skirted around the boggiest parts of the boggy main street, between the slumping little buildings, most of warped pine, all on one storey and some barely that.

'God, this is a poor place,' muttered Sufeen.

'It puts me in mind of home,' whispered Temple. Which was far from a good thing. The sun-baked lower city of Dagoska, the seething slums of Styria, the hard-scrabble villages of the Near Country. Every nation was rich in its own way, but poor in the same.

A woman skinned a fly-blown carcass that might have been rabbit or cat and Temple got the feeling she was not bothered which. A pair of half-naked children mindlessly banged wooden swords together in the street. A long-haired ancient whittled a stick on the stoop of one of the few stone-built houses, a sword that was definitely not a toy leaning against the wall behind him. They all watched Temple and Sufeen with sulky suspicion. Some shutters clattered closed and Temple's heart started to pound. Then a dog barked and he nearly shat, sweat standing cold on his brow as a stinking breeze swept past. He wondered if this was the stupidest thing he had ever done in a life littered with idiocy. High on the list, he decided, and still with ample time to bully its way to the top.

Averstock's glittering heart was a shed with a tankard painted on a board above the entrance and a luckless clientele. A pair who looked like a farmer and his son, both red-haired and bony, the boy with a satchel over his shoulder, sat at one table eating bread and cheese far from the freshest. A tragic fellow decked in fraying ribbons was bent over a cup. Temple took him for a travelling bard, and hoped he specialised in sad songs because the sight of him was enough to bring on tears. A woman was cooking over a fire in the blackened hearth, and spared Temple one sour look as he entered.

The counter was a warped slab with a fresh split down its length and a large stain worked into the grain that looked unpleasantly like blood. Behind it the Tavern-Keep was carefully wiping cups with a rag.

'It's not too late,' whispered Temple. 'We could just choke down a cup of whatever piss they sell here, walk straight on through and no harm done.'

'Until the rest of the Company get here.'

'I meant no harm to *us* . . .' But Sufeen was already approaching the counter leaving Temple to curse silently in the doorway for a moment before following with the greatest reluctance.

'What can I get you?' asked the Keep.

'There are some four hundred mercenaries surrounding your town, with every intention of attacking,' said Sufeen, and Temple's hopes of avoiding catastrophe were dealt a shattering blow.

There was a pregnant pause. Heavily pregnant.

'This hasn't been my best week,' grunted the Keep. 'I'm in no mood for jokes.'

'If we were set on laughter I think we could come up with better,' muttered Temple.

Sufeen spoke over him. 'They are the Company of the Gracious Hand, led by the infamous mercenary Nicomo Cosca, and they have been employed by his Majesty's Inquisition to root out rebels in the Near Country. Unless they receive your fullest cooperation, your bad week will get a great deal worse.'

They had the Keep's attention now. They had the attention of every person in the tavern and were not likely to lose it. Whether that was a good thing remained very much to be seen, but Temple was not optimistic. He could not remember the last time he had been.

'And if there is rebels in town?' The farmer leaned against the counter beside them, pointedly rolling up his sleeve. There was a tattoo on his sinewy forearm. *Freedom, liberty, justice.* Here, then, was the scourge of the mighty Union, Lorsen's insidious enemy, the terrifying rebel in the flesh. Temple looked into his eyes. If this was the face of evil, it was a haggard one.

Sufeen chose his words carefully. 'Then they have less than an hour to surrender, and spare the people of this town bloodshed.'

The bony man gave a smile missing several of the teeth and all of the joy. 'I can take you to Sheel. He can choose what to believe.' Clearly he did not believe any of it. Or perhaps even entirely comprehend.

'Take us to Sheel, then,' said Sufeen. 'Good.'

'Is it?' muttered Temple. The feeling of impending disaster was almost choking him now. Or perhaps that was the rebel's breath. He certainly had the breath of evil, if nothing else.

'You'll have to give up your weapons,' he said.

'With the greatest respect,' said Temple, 'I'm not convinced—'

'Hand 'em over.' Temple was surprised to see the woman at the fire had produced a loaded flatbow and was pointing it unwavering at him.

'I am convinced,' he croaked, pulling his knife from his belt between finger and thumb. 'It's only a very small one.'

'Ain't the size,' said the bony man as he plucked it from Temple's hand, 'so much as where you stick it.' Sufeen unbuckled his sword-belt and he took that, too. 'Let's go. And it'd be an idea not to make no sudden moves.'

Temple raised his palms. 'I try always to avoid them.'

'You made one when you followed me down here, as I recall,' said Sufeen.

'And how I regret it now.'

'Shut up.' The bony rebel herded them towards the door, the woman following at a cautious distance, bow levelled. Temple caught the blue of a tattoo on the inside of her wrist. The boy lurched along at the back, one of his legs in a brace and his satchel clutched tight to his chest. It might have been a laughable procession without the threat of death. Temple had always found the threat of death to be a sure antidote to comedy.

Sheel turned out to be the old man who had watched them walk into town a few moments before. What happy times those seemed now. He stiffly stood, waving away a fly, then, almost as an afterthought, even more stiffly bent for his sword before stepping from his porch.

'What's to do, Danard?' he asked in a voice croaky with phlegm.

'Caught these two in the inn,' said the bony man.

'Caught?' asked Temple. 'We walked in and asked for you.'

'Shut up,' said Danard.

'You shut up,' said Sufeen.

Sheel did something between vomiting and clearing his throat, then effortfully swallowed the results. 'Let's all see if we can split the difference between talking too much and not at all. I'm Sheel. I speak for the rebels hereabouts.'

'All four of them?' asked Temple.

'There were more.' He looked sad rather than angry. He looked all squeezed out and, one could only hope, ready to give up.

'My name is Sufeen, and I have come to warn you—'

'We're surrounded, apparently,' sneered Danard. 'Surrender to the Inquisition and Averstock stands another day.'

Sheel turned his watered-down grey eyes on Temple. 'You'd have to agree it's a far-fetched story.'

Easy, hard, it mattered not what crooked path they'd followed here, there was only one way through this now, and that was to convince this man of what they said. Temple fixed him with his most earnest expression. The one with which he had convinced Kahdia he would not steal again, with which he had convinced his wife that everything would be well, with which he had told Cosca he could be trusted. Had they not all believed him?

'My friend is telling you the truth.' He spoke slowly, carefully, as if there were only the two of them there. 'Come with us and we can save lives.'

'He's lying.' The bony man poked Temple in the side with the pommel of Sufeen's sword. 'There ain't no one up there.'

'Why would we come here just to lie?' Temple ignored the prodding and kept his eyes fixed on the old man's wasted face. 'What would we gain?'

'Why do it at all?' asked Sheel.

Temple paused for a moment, his mouth half-open. Why not the truth? At least it was novel. 'We got sick of not doing it.'

'Huh.' That appeared to touch something. The old man's hand drifted from his sword-hilt. Not surrender. A long way from surrender, but something. 'If you're telling the truth and we give up, what then?'

Too much truth is always a mistake. Temple stuck to earnest. 'The people of Averstock will be spared, that I promise you.'

The old man cleared his throat again. God, his lungs sounded bad. Could it be that he was starting to believe? Could it be that this might actually work? Might they not only live out the day, but save lives into the bargain? Might he do something that Kahdia would have been proud of? The thought made Temple proud, just for a moment. He ventured a smile. When did he last feel proud? Had he ever?

Sheel opened his mouth to speak, to concede, to surrender . . . then paused, frowning off over Temple's shoulder.

A sound carried on the wind ever so faintly. Hooves. Horses' hooves. Temple followed the old rebel's gaze and saw, up on the grassy side of the valley, a rider coming down at a full gallop. Sheel saw him, too, and his forehead furrowed with puzzlement. More riders appeared behind the first, pouring down the slope, now a dozen, now more.

'No,' muttered Temple.

'Temple!' hissed Sufeen.

Sheel's eyes widened. 'You bastards!'

Temple held up his hand. 'No!'

He heard grunting in his ear, and when Temple turned to tell Sufeen this was hardly the time saw his friend and Danard lurching about in a snarling embrace. He stared at them, open mouthed.

They should have had an hour.

Sheel clumsily drew his sword, metal scraping, and Temple caught his hand before he could swing it and butted him in the face.

There was no thought, it just happened.

The world jolted, Sheel's crackly breath warm on his cheek. They tussled and tore and a fist hit the side of Temple's face and made his ears ring. He butted again, felt nose-bone pop against his forehead and suddenly Sheel was stumbling back and Sufeen was standing beside Temple with the sword in his hands, and looking very surprised that he had it.

Temple stood a moment, trying to work out how they had got here. Then what they should do now.

He heard a flatbow string, the whisper of a bolt passing, maybe.

Then he saw Danard struggling up. 'You fucking—' And his head came apart.

Temple blinked, blood across his face. Saw Sheel reaching for a knife. Sufeen stabbed at him and the old man gave a croaking cough as the metal slid into his side, clutched at himself, face twisted, blood leaking between his fingers.

He muttered something Temple couldn't understand, and tried to draw his knife again, and the sword caught him just above the eye. 'Oh,' he said, blood washing out of the big slit in his forehead and down his face. 'Oh.' Drops sprinkled the mud as he staggered sideways, bounced off his own porch and fell, rolling over, back arching, one hand flapping.

Sufeen stared down at him. 'We were going to save people,' he muttered. There was blood on his lips. He dropped to his knees and the sword bounced out of his limp hand.

Temple grabbed at him. 'What . . .' The knife he had handed over to Danard was buried in Sufeen's ribs to the grip, his shirt quickly turning black. A very small knife, by most standards. But more than big enough.

That dog was still barking. Sufeen toppled forward onto his face. The woman with the flatbow had gone. Was she reloading somewhere, would she pop up ready to shoot again? Temple should probably have taken cover.

He didn't move.

The sound of hooves grew louder. Blood spread out in a muddy puddle around Sheel's split head. The boy slowly backed away, broke into a waddling trot, dragging his crippled leg after. Temple watched him go.

Then Jubair rounded the side of the inn, mud flicking from the hooves of his great horse, sword raised high. The boy tried to turn again, lurched one more desperate step before the blade caught him in the shoulder and spun him across the street. Jubair tore past, shouting something. More horsemen followed. People were running. Screaming. Faint over the rumble of hooves.

They should have had an hour.

Temple knelt beside Sufeen, reached out to turn him over, check his wounds, tear off a bandage, do those things Kahdia had taught him, long ago. But as soon as he saw Sufeen's face he knew he was dead.

Mercenaries charged through the town, howling like a pack of dogs, waving weapons as though they were the winning cards in a game. He could smell smoke.

Temple picked up Sheel's sword, notched blade red-speckled now, stood and walked over to the lame boy. He was crawling towards the inn, one arm useless. He saw Temple and whimpered, clutching handfuls of muck with his good hand. His satchel had come open and coins were spilling out. Silver scattered in the mud.

'Help me,' whispered the boy. 'Help me!'

'No.'

'They'll kill me! They'll—'

'Shut your fucking mouth!' Temple poked the boy in the back with the sword and he gulped, and cowered, and the more he cowered the more Temple wanted to stick the sword through him. It was surprisingly light. It would have been so easy to do. The boy saw it in his face and whined and cringed more, and Temple poked him again.

'Shut your mouth, fucker! Shut your mouth!'

'Temple! Are you all right?' Cosca loomed over him on his tall grey. 'You're bleeding.'

Temple looked down and saw his shirtsleeve was ripped, blood trickling down the back of his hand. He was not sure how that had happened. 'Sufeen is dead,' he mumbled.

'Why do the Fates always take the best of us . . . ?' But Cosca's attention had been hooked by the glint of money in the mud. He held out a hand to Friendly and the sergeant helped him down from his gilt saddle. The Old Man stooped, fishing one of the coins up between two fingers, eagerly rubbing the muck away, and he produced that luminous smile of which only he was capable, good humour and good intentions radiating from his deep-lined face.

'Yes,' Temple heard him whisper.

Friendly tore the satchel from the boy's back and jerked it open. A faint jingle spoke of more coins inside.

Thump, thump, thump, as a group of mercenaries kicked at the door of the inn. One hopped away cursing, pulling his filthy boot off to nurse his toes. Cosca squatted down. 'Where did this money come from?'

'We went on a raid,' muttered the boy. 'All went wrong.' There was a crash as the inn's door gave, a volley of cheering as men poured through the open doorway.

'All went wrong?'

'Only four of us made it back. So we had two dozen horses to trade. Man called Grega Cantliss bought 'em off us, up in Greyer.'

'Cantliss?' Shutters shattered as a chair was flung through the window of the inn and tumbled across the street beside them. Friendly frowned towards the hole it left but Cosca did not so much as twitch. As though there was nothing in the world but him, and the boy, and the coins. 'What sort of man was this Cantliss? A rebel?'

'No. He had nice clothes. Some crazy-eyed Northman with him. He took the horses and he paid with those coins.'

'Where did he get them?'

'Didn't say.'

Cosca peeled up the sleeve on the boy's limp arm to show his tattoo. 'But he definitely wasn't one of you rebels?'

The boy only shook his head.

'That answer will not make Inquisitor Lorsen happy.' Cosca gave a nod so gentle it was almost imperceptible. Friendly put his hands around the boy's neck. That dog was still barking somewhere. Bark, bark, bark. Temple wished someone would shut it up. Across the street three Kantics were savagely beating a man while a pair of children watched.

'We should stop them,' muttered Temple, but all he did was sit down in the road.

'How?' Cosca had more of the coins in his hand, was carefully sorting through them. 'I'm a general, not a God. Many generals get mixed up on that point, but I was cured of the misapprehension long ago, believe me.' A woman was dragged screaming from a nearby house by her hair. 'The men are upset. Like a flood, it's safer to wash with the current than try to dam it up. If they don't have a channel for their anger, why, it could flow anywhere. Even over me.' He grunted as Friendly helped him up to standing. 'And it's not as though any of this was my fault, is it?'

Temple's head was throbbing. He felt so tired he could hardly move. 'It was mine?'

'I know you meant well.' Flames were already hungrily licking at the eaves of the inn's roof. 'But that's how it is with good intentions. Hopefully we've all learned a lesson here today.' Cosca produced a flask and started thoughtfully unscrewing the cap. 'I, about indulging you. You, about indulging yourself.' And he upended it and steadily swallowed.

'You're drinking again?' muttered Temple.

'You fuss too much. A nip never hurt anyone.' Cosca sucked the last drops out and tossed the empty flask to Friendly for a refill. 'Inquisitor Lorsen! So glad you could join us!'

'I hold you responsible for this debacle!' snapped Lorsen as he reined his horse up savagely in the street.

'It's far from my first,' said the Old Man. 'I shall have to live with the shame.'

'This hardly seems a moment for jokes!'

Cosca chuckled. 'My old commander Sazine once told me you

should laugh every moment you live, for you'll find it decidedly difficult afterward. These things happen in war. I've a feeling there was some confusion with the signals. However carefully you plan, there are always surprises.' As if to illustrate the point, a Gurkish mercenary capered across the street wearing the bard's beribboned jacket. 'But this boy was able to tell us something before he died.' Silver glinted in Cosca's gloved palm. 'Imperial coins. Given to these rebels by a man called . . .'

'Grega Cantliss,' put in Friendly.

'That was it, in the town of Greyer.'

Lorsen frowned hard. 'Are you saying the rebels have Imperial funding? Superior Pike was very clear that we avoid any entanglements with the Empire.'

Cosca held a coin up to the light. 'You see this face? Emperor Ostus the Second. He died some fourteen hundred years ago.'

'I did not know you were such a keen devotee of history,' said Lorsen.

'I am a keen devotee of money. These are ancient coins. Perhaps the rebels stumbled upon a tomb. The great men of old were sometimes buried with their riches.'

'The great men of old do not concern us,' said Lorsen. 'It's today's rebels we're after.'

A pair of Union mercenaries were screaming at a man on his knees. Asking him where the money was. One of them hit him with a length of wood torn from his own shattered door and when he got groggily up there was blood running down his face. They asked him again. They hit him again, slap, slap, slap.

Sworbreck, the biographer, watched them with one hand over his mouth. 'Dear me,' he muttered between his fingers.

'Like everything else,' Cosca was explaining, 'rebellion costs money. Food, clothes, weapons, shelter. Fanatics still need what the rest of us need. A little less of it, since they have their high ideals to nourish them, but the point stands. Follow the money, find the leaders. Greyer appears on Superior Pike's list anyway, does it not? And perhaps this Cantliss can lead us to this . . . Contus of yours.'

Lorsen perked up at that. 'Conthus.'

'Besides.' Cosca gestured at the rebels' corpses with a loose waft of his sword that nearly took Sworbreck's nose off. 'I doubt we'll be getting any further clues from these three. Life rarely turns out the way we expect. We must bend with the circumstances.'

Lorsen gave a disgusted grunt. 'Very well. For now we follow the money.' He turned his horse about and shouted to one of his Practicals. 'Search the corpses for tattoos, damn it, find me any rebels still alive!'

Three doors down, a man had climbed onto the roof of a house and was stuffing bedding down the chimney while others clustered about the door. Cosca, meanwhile, was holding forth to Sworbreck. 'I share your distaste for this, believe me. I have been closely involved in the burning of some of the world's most ancient and beautiful cities. You should have seen Oprile in flames, it lit the sky for miles! This is scarcely a career highlight.'

Jubair had dragged some corpses into a line and was expressionlessly cutting their heads off. Thud, thud, thud, went his heavy sword. Two of his men had torn apart the arch over the road and were whittling the ends of the timbers to points. One was already rammed into the ground and had Sheel's head on it, mouth strangely pouting.

'Dear me,' muttered Sworbreck again.

'Severed heads,' Cosca was explaining, 'never go out of fashion. Used sparingly and with artistic sensibility, they can make a point a great deal more eloquently than those still attached. Make a note of that. Why aren't you writing?'

An old woman had crawled from the burning house, face stained with soot, and now some of the men had formed a circle and were shoving her tottering back and forth.

'What a waste,' Lorsen was bitterly complaining to one of his Practicals. 'How fine this land could be with the proper management. With firm governance, and the latest techniques of agriculture and forestry. They have a threshing machine now in Midderland which can do in a day with one operator what used to take a dozen peasants a week.'

'What do the other eleven do?' asked Temple, his mouth seeming to move by itself.

'Find other employment,' snarled the Practical.

Behind him another head went up on its stick, long hair stirring. Temple did not recognise the face. The smoked-out house was burning merrily now, flames whipping, air shimmering, the men backing off with hands up against the heat, letting the old woman crawl away.

'Find other employment,' muttered Temple to himself.

Cosca had Brachio by the elbow and was shouting in his ear over the noise. 'You need to round up your men! We must head north and east towards Greyer and seek out news of this Grega Cantliss.'

'It might take a while to calm 'em.'

'One hour, then I ask Sergeant Friendly to bring in the stragglers, in pieces if necessary. Discipline, Sworbreck, is vital to a body of fighting men!'

Temple closed his eyes. God, it stank. Smoke, and blood, and fury, and smoke. He needed water. He turned to ask Sufeen for some and saw his corpse in the mud a few strides away. A man of principle must make hard choices and suffer the consequences.

'We brought your horse down,' said Cosca, as though that should make up for at least some of the day's reverses. 'If you want my advice, keep busy. Put this place at your back as swiftly as possible.'

'How do I forget this?'

'Oh, that's too much to ask. The trick is in learning to just . . .' Cosca stepped carefully back as one of the Styrians rode whooping past, a man's corpse bouncing after his horse. 'Not care.'

'I have to bury Sufeen.'

'Yes, I suppose so. But quickly. We have daylight and not a moment to waste. Jubair! Put that down!' And the Old Man started across the street, waving his sword. 'Burn anything that still needs burning and mount up! We're moving east!'

When Temple turned, Friendly was wordlessly offering him a shovel. The dog had finally stopped barking. A big Northman, a tattooed brute from past the Crinna, had spiked its head on a spear beside the heads of the rebels and was pointing up at it, chuckling.

Temple took Sufeen by the wrists and hauled him onto his shoulder, then up and over the saddle of his scared horse. Not an easy task, but easier than he had expected. Living, Sufeen had been big with talk and movement and laughter. Dead he was hardly any weight at all.

'Are you all right?' Bermi, touching him on the arm.

His concern made Temple want to cry. 'I'm not hurt. But Sufeen is dead.' There was justice.

Two of the Northmen had smashed open a chest of drawers and were fighting over the clothes inside, leaving torn cloth scattered across the muddy street. The tattooed man had tied a stick below the dog's head and was carefully arranging a best shirt with a frilly front upon it, face fixed with artist's concentration.

'You sure you're all right?' Bermi called after him from the midst of the rubbish-strewn street.

'Never better.'

Temple led the horse out of town, then off the track, or the two strips of rutted mud that passed for one, the sounds of barked orders, and burning, and the men reluctantly making ready to leave fading behind him to be replaced by chattering water. He followed the river upstream until he found a pleasant enough spot between two trees, their hanging boughs trailing in the water. He slid Sufeen's body down and rolled it over onto its back.

'I'm sorry,' he said, and tossed the shovel into the river. Then he pulled himself up into his saddle.

Sufeen would not have cared where he was laid out, or how. If there was a God, he was with Him now, probably demanding to know why He had so conspicuously failed as yet to put the world to rights. North and east, Cosca had said. Temple turned his horse towards the west, and gave it his heels, and galloped off, away from the greasy pall of smoke rising from the ruins of Averstock.

Away from the Company of the Gracious Hand. Away from Dimbik, and Brachio, and Jubair. Away from Inquisitor Lorsen and his righteous mission.

He had no destination in mind. Anywhere but with Nicomo Cosca.

New Lives

'And there's the Fellowship,' said Sweet, reining in with forearms on saddle horn and fingers dangling.

The wagons were strung out for a mile or so along the bottom of the valley. Thirty or more, some covered with stained canvas, some painted bright colours, dots of orange and purple and twinkling gilt jumping from the dusty brown landscape. Specks of walkers alongside them, riders up ahead. At the back came the beasts – horses, spare oxen, a good-sized herd of cattle – and following hard after a swelling cloud of dust, tugged by the breeze and up into the blue to announce the Fellowship's coming to the world.

'Will you look at that!' Leef kicked his horse forward, standing in his stirrups with a grin all the way across his face. 'D'you see *that*?' Shy hadn't seen him smile before and it made him look young. More boy than man, which he probably was. Made her smile herself.

'I see it,' she said.

'A whole town on the move!'

'True, it's a fair cross section through society,' said Sweet, shifting his old arse in his saddle. 'Some honest, some sharp, some rich, some poor, some clever, some not so much. Lot of prospectors. Some herders and some farmers. Few merchants. All set on a new life out there beyond the horizon. We even got the First of the Magi down there.'

Lamb's head jerked around. 'What?'

'A famous actor. Iosiv Lestek. His Bayaz mesmerised the crowds in Adua, apparently.' Sweet gave his gravelly chuckle. 'About a hundred bloody years ago. He's hoping to bring theatre to the Far Country, I hear, but between you, me and half the population of the Union, his powers are well on the wane.'

'Don't convince as Bayaz any more, eh?' asked Shy.

'He scarcely convinces me as Iosiv Lestek.' Sweet shrugged. 'But what do I know about acting?'

'Even your Dab Sweet's no better'n passable.'

'Let's go down there!' said Leef. 'Get us a better look!'

There was a less romantic feel to the business at close quarters. Isn't there to every business? That number of warm bodies, man and beast, produced a quantity of waste hardly to be credited and certainly not to be smelled without good cause. The smaller and less glamorous animals – dogs and flies, chiefly, though undoubtedly lice, too – didn't stand out from a distance but made double the impression once you were in the midst. Shy was forced to wonder whether the Fellowship might, in fact, be a brave but foolhardy effort to export the worst evils of city-living into the middle of the unspoiled wilderness.

Not blind to this, some of the senior Fellows had removed themselves a good fifty strides from the main body in order to consider the course, meaning argue over it and grab a drink, and were now scratching their heads over a big map.

'Step away from that map 'fore you hurt yourselves!' called Sweet as they rode up. 'I'm back and you're three valleys south o' the course.'

'Only three? Better than I dared hope.' A tall, sinewy Kantic with a fine-shaped skull bald as an egg stepped up, giving Shy and Lamb and Leef a careful look-over on the way. 'You have friends along.'

'This here is Lamb and his daughter Shy.' She didn't bother to correct him on the technicality. 'This lad's name, I must confess, has for the time being slipped from my clutches—'

'Leef.'

'That was it! This here is my . . . *employer*.' Sweet said the word like even admitting its existence was too much cramping of his freedoms. 'An unrepentant criminal by the name of Abram Majud.'

'A pleasure to make your acquaintances.' Majud displayed much good humour and a golden front tooth as he bowed to each of them. 'And I assure you I have been repenting ever since I formed this Fellowship.' His dark eyes took on a faraway look, as though he was gazing back across the long miles travelled. 'Back in Keln along with my partner, Curnsbick. A hard man, but a clever one. He has invented a portable forge, among other things. I am taking it to Crease, with the intention of founding a metalwork business. We might also look into staking some mining claims in the mountains.'

'Gold?' asked Shy.

'Iron and copper.' Majud leaned in to speak softly. 'In my most humble opinion, only fools think there is gold in gold. Are the three of you minded to join up with our Fellowship?'

'That we are,' said Shy. 'We've business of our own in Crease.'

'All are welcome! The rate for buying in—'

'Lamb here is a serious fighting man,' cut in Sweet.

Majud paused, lips pressed into an appraising line. 'Without offence, he looks a little . . . *old*.'

'No one'll be arguing on that score,' said Lamb.

'I lack the freshest bloom myself,' added Sweet. 'You're no toddler if it comes to that. If it's youth you want, the lad with him is well supplied.'

Majud looked still less impressed by Leef. 'I seek a happy medium.'

Sweet snorted. 'Well you won't find many o' them out here. We don't got enough fighters. With the Ghosts fixed on blood it's no time to be cutting costs. Believe me, old Sangeed won't stop to argue prices with you. Lamb's in or I'm out and you can scout your way around in circles 'til your wagons fall apart.'

Majud looked up at Lamb, and Lamb looked back, still and steady. Seemed he'd left his weak eye back in Squaredeal. A few moments to consider, and Majud had seen what he needed to. 'Then Master Lamb goes free. Two paid shares comes to—'

Sweet scratched wincing at the back of his neck. 'I made a deal with Shy they'd all three come free.'

Majud's eyes shifted to her with what might have been grudging respect. 'It would appear she got the better of that particular negotiation.'

'I'm a scout, not a trader.'

'Perhaps you should be leaving the trading to those of us who are.'

'I traded a damn sight better than you've scouted, by all appearances.'

Majud shook his fine-shaped head. 'I have no notion of how I will explain this to my partner Curnsbick.' He walked off, wagging one long finger. 'Curnsbick is not a man to be trifled with on expenses!'

'By the dead,' grumbled Sweet, 'did you ever hear such carping? Anyone would think we'd set out with a company o' women.'

'Looks like you have,' said Shy. One of the brightest of the wagons – scarlet with gilt fixtures – was rattling past with two women in its seat. One was in full whore's get-up, hat clasped on with one hand and a smile gripped no less precariously to her painted face. Presumably advertising her availability for commerce in spite of the ongoing trek.

The other was more soberly dressed for travel, handling the reins calmly as a coachman. A man sat between them in a jacket that matched the wagon, bearded and hard-eyed. Shy took him for the pimp. He had a pimpy look about him, sure enough. She leaned over and spat through the gap in her teeth.

The idea of getting to business in a lurching wagon, half-full of rattling pans and the other of someone else getting to business hardly stoked the fires of passion in Shy. But then those particular embers had been burning so low for so long she'd a notion they'd smouldered out all together. Working a farm with two children and two old men surely can wither the romance in you.

Sweet gave the ladies a wave, and pushed his hat brim up with a knobby knuckle, and under his breath said, 'Bloody hell but nothing's how it used to be. Women, and dandified tailoring, and ploughs and portable forges and who knows what horrors'll be next. Time was there was naught out here but earth and sky and beasts and Ghosts, and far wild spaces you could breathe in. Why, I've spent twelve months at a time with only a horse for company.'

Shy spat again. 'I never in my life felt so sorry for a horse. Reckon I'll take a ride round and greet the Fellowship. See if anyone's heard a whisper of the children.'

'Or Grega Cantliss.' And Lamb frowned hard as he said the name.

'All right,' said Sweet. 'You watch out, though, you hear?'

'I can look after myself,' said Shy.

The old scout's weathered face creased up as he smiled. 'It's everyone else I'm worried for.'

The nearest wagon belonged to a man called Gentili, an ancient Styrian with four cousins along he called the boys, though they weren't much younger than he was and hadn't a word of common between them. He was set stubborn on digging a new life out of the mountains and must've been quite the optimist, since he could scarcely stand up in the dry, let alone to his waist in a freezing torrent. He'd heard of no stolen children. She wasn't even sure he heard the question. As a parting shot he asked Shy if she fancied sharing his new life with him as his fifth wife. She politely declined.

Lord Ingelstad had suffered misfortunes, apparently. When he used the word, Lady Ingelstad – a woman not born to hardships but determined to stomp them all to pieces even so – scowled at him as though she felt she'd suffered all his misfortunes plus one extra, and that her choice of husband. To Shy his misfortunes smelled like dice and debts, but since her own course through life had hardly been the straightest she thought she'd hold off on criticism and let misfortunes stand. Of child-stealing bandits, among many other things, he was entirely ignorant. As his parting shot he invited her and Lamb to a hand of cards that night. Stakes would be small, he promised, though in Shy's experience they always begin that way and don't have to rise far to land everyone in trouble. She politely declined that, too, and suggested a man who'd suffered so much misfortune might take pains not to court any more. He took the point with ruddy-faced good humour and called the same offer to Gentili and the boys. Lady Ingelstad looked like she'd be killing the lot of them with her teeth before she saw a hand dealt.

The next wagon might have been the biggest in the Fellowship, with glass windows and *The Famous Iosiv Lestek* written along the side in already peeling purple paint. Seemed to Shy that if a man was that famous he wouldn't have to paint his name on a wagon, but since her own brush with fame had been through bills widely posted for her arrest she hardly considered herself an expert.

A scratty-haired boy was driving and the great man sat swaying beside him, old and gaunt and leached of all colour, swaddled in a threadbare Ghost blanket. He perked up at the opportunity to boast as Shy and Lamb trotted over.

'I . . . am Iosiv Lestek.' It was a shock to hear the voice of a king boom from that withered head, rich and deep and fruity as plum sauce. 'I daresay the name is familiar.'

'Sorry to say we don't get often to the theatre,' said Lamb.

'What brings you to the Far Country?' asked Shy.

'I was forced to abandon a role at Adua's House of Drama due to illness. The ensemble was crushed to lose me, of course, quite *crushed*, but I am fully recovered.'

'Good news.' She dreaded to picture him before his recovery. He seemed a corpse raised by sorcery now.

'I am in transit to Crease to take a leading part in a cultural extravaganza!'

'Culture?' Shy eased up her hat brim to survey the empty country ahead, grey grass and ill scrub and parched slopes of baked brown boulder, no sign of life but for a couple of hopeful hawks circling on high. 'Out there?'

'Even the meanest hearts hunger for a glimpse of the sublime,' he informed them.

'I'll take your word on that,' said Lamb.

Lestek was busy smiling out at the reddening horizon, a hand so pale as almost to be see-through clutched against his chest. She got the feeling he was one of those men didn't really see the need for two sides to a conversation. 'My greatest performance is yet ahead of me, that much I know.'

'Something to look forward to,' muttered Shy, turning her horse.

A group of a dozen or so Suljuks watched the exchange, clustered to themselves around a rotten-looking wagon. They spoke no common, and Shy could barely recognise a word of Suljuk let alone understand one, so she just nodded to them as she rode by and they nodded back, pleasantly inscrutable to each other.

Ashjid was a Gurkish priest, fixed on being the first to spread the word of the Prophet west to Crease. Or actually the second, since a man called Oktaadi had given up after three months there and been skinned by the Ghosts on the return trip. Ashjid was having a good stab at spreading the word to the Fellowship in the meantime through daily blessings, though so far his only convert was a curious retard responsible for collecting drinking water. He had no information for them beyond the revelation of the scripture, but he asked God to smile upon their search and Shy thanked him for that. Seemed better to her to have blessings than curses, for all time's plough would more'n likely turn up what it turned regardless.

The priest pointed out a stern-looking type on a neatly kept wagon as Savian, a man not to be fiddled with. He'd a long sword at his side looked like it had seen plenty of action and a grey-stubbled face looked like it had seen plenty more, eyes narrowed to slits in the shadow of his low hat-brim.

'My name's Shy South, this is Lamb.' Savian just nodded, like he accepted that was a possibility but had no set opinion on it. 'I'm looking for my brother and sister. Six years and ten.' He didn't even nod to that. A tight-mouthed bastard, and no mistake. 'They were stole by a man named Grega Cantliss.'

'Can't help you.' A trace of an Imperial accent, and all the while Savian looked at her long and level, like he'd got just her measure and wasn't moved by it. Then his eyes shifted to Lamb, and took his measure, too, and wasn't moved by that either. He put a fist over his mouth and gave a long, gravelly cough.

'That cough sounds bad,' she said.

'When's a cough good?'

Shy noticed a flatbow hooked to the seat beside him. Not loaded, but full-drawn and with a wedge in the trigger. Exactly as ready as it needed to be. 'You along to fight?'

'Hoping I won't have to.' Though the whole set of him said his hopes hadn't always washed out in that regard.

'What kind of a fool hopes for a fight, eh?'

'Sad to say there's always one or two about.'

Lamb snorted. 'There's the sorry truth.'

'What's your business in the Far Country?' asked Shy, trying to chisel something more from that hardwood block of a face.

'My business.' And he coughed again. Even when he did that his mouth hardly moved. Made her wonder if he'd any muscles in his head.

'Thought we might try our hand at prospecting.' A woman had poked her face out from the wagon. Lean and strong, hair cut short and with these blue, blue eyes looked like they saw a long way. 'I'm Corlin.'

'My niece,' added Savian, though there was something odd about the way they looked at each other. Shy couldn't quite get it pegged.

'Prospecting?' she asked, pushing her hat back. 'Don't see a lot of women at that business.'

'Are you saying there's a limit on what a woman can do?' asked Corlin.

Shy raised her brows. 'Might be one on what she's dumb enough to try.'

'It seems neither sex has a monopoly on hubris.'

'Seems not,' said Shy, adding, under her breath, 'whatever the fuck that means.' She gave the two of them a nod and pulled her horse about. 'Be seeing you on the trail.'

Neither Corlin nor her uncle answered, just gave each other some deadly competition at who could stare after her the hardest.

'Something odd about them two,' she muttered to Lamb as they rode off. 'Didn't see no mining gear.'

'Maybe they mean to buy it in Crease.'

'And pay five times the going rate? You look in their eyes? Don't reckon they're a pair used to making fool deals.'

'You don't miss a trick, do you?'

'I try to be aware of 'em, at least, in case they end up being played on me. You think they're trouble?'

Lamb shrugged. 'I think you're best off treating folk the way you'd want to be treated and leaving their choices to them. We're all of us trouble o' one kind or another. Half this whole crowd probably got a sad story to tell. Why else would they be plodding across the long and level nowhere with the likes of us for company?'

All Raynault Buckhorm had to tell about was hopes, though he did it with something of a stutter. He owned half the cattle with the Fellowship, employed a good few of the men to drive 'em, and was making his fifth trip to Crease where he said there was always call for meat, this time bringing his wife and children and planning to stay. The exact number of children was hard to reckon but the impression was of many. Buckhorm asked Lamb if he'd seen the grass out there in the Far Country. Best damn grass in the Circle of the World, he thought. Best water, too. Worth facing the weather and the Ghosts and the murderous distance for that grass and that water. When Shy told him about Grega Cantliss and his band he shook his head and said he could still be surprised by how low men could sink. Buckhorm's wife Luline – possessed of a giant smile but a tiny body you could hardly believe had produced such a brood – shook her head too, and said it was the most awful thing she'd ever heard, and she wished there was something she could do, and probably would've hugged her if they hadn't had the height of a horse between them. Then she gave Shy a little pie and asked if she'd spoken to Hedges.

Hedges was a shifty sort with a wore-out mule, not enough gear and a charmless habit of talking to her from the neck down. He'd never heard of Grega Cantliss but he did point out his ruined leg, which he said he'd got leading a charge at the battle of Osrung. Shy had her doubts about that story. Still, her mother used to say, *you're best off looking for the best in people*, and it was good advice even if the woman never had taken it herself. So Shy offered Hedges Luline Buckhorm's pie and he looked her in the eye finally and said, 'You're all right.'

'Don't let a pie fool you.' But when she rode off he was still looking down at it in his dirty hand, like it meant so much he couldn't bring himself to eat it.

Shy went on around them 'til her voice was sore from sharing her troubles and her ears from lending them to others' dreams. A Fellowship was a good name for it, she reckoned, 'cause they were a good-humoured and a giving company, in the main. Raw and strange and foolish, some of them, but all fixed on finding a better tomorrow. Even Shy felt it, time and trouble-toughened, work and weather-worn, weighed down with worries about Pit and Ro's future and Lamb's past. The new wind on her face and the new hopes ringing in her ears and she found a dopey smile creeping under her nose as she threaded between the wagons, nodding to folks she didn't know, slapping the backs of those she'd only just met. Soon as she'd remember why she was there and wipe that smile away she'd find it was back, like pigeons shouted off a new-sown field.

Soon enough she stopped trying. Pigeons'll ruin your crop, but what harm will smiles do, really?

So she let it sit there. Felt good on her.

'Lots of sympathy,' she said, once they'd talked to almost everyone, and the sun had sunk to a gilt sliver ahead of them, the first torches lit so the Fellowship could slog another mile before making camp. 'Lots of sympathy but not much help.'

'I guess sympathy's something,' said Lamb. She waited for more but he just sat hunched, nodding along to the slow walk of his horse.

'They seem all right, though, mostly.' Gabbing just to fill the hole, and feeling annoyed that she had to. 'Don't know how they'll fare if the Ghosts come and things get ugly, but they're all right.'

'Guess you never know how folk'll fare if things get ugly.'

She looked across at him. 'You're damn right there.'

He caught her eye for a moment, then guiltily looked away. She opened her mouth but before she could say more, Sweet's deep voice echoed through the dusk, calling halt for the day.

The Rugged Outdoorsman

Temple wrenched himself around in his saddle, heart suddenly bursting—

And saw nothing but moonlight on shifting branches. It was so dark he could scarcely see that. He might have heard a twig torn loose by the wind, or a rabbit about its harmless nocturnal business in the brush, or a murderous Ghost savage daubed with the blood of slaughtered innocents, fixed on skinning him alive and wearing his face as a hat.

He hunched his shoulders as another chilly gust whipped up, shook the pines and chilled him to his marrow. The Company of the Gracious Hand had enveloped him in its foul embrace for so long he had come to take the physical safety it provided entirely for granted. Now he keenly felt its loss. There were many things in life one did not fully appreciate until one had cavalierly tossed them aside. Like a good coat. Or a very small knife. Or a few-score hardened killers and an affable geriatric villain.

The first day he had ridden hard and worried only that they would catch him. Then, when the second morning dawned chill and vastly empty, that they wouldn't. By the third morning he was feeling deeply aggrieved at the thought that they might not even have tried. Fleeing the Company, directionless and unequipped, into the unmapped wasteland, was looking less and less like the easy way to anything.

Temple had played many parts during his thirty ill-starred years alive. Beggar, thief, unwilling trainee priest, ineffective surgeon, disgusted butcher, sore-handed carpenter, briefly a loving husband and even more briefly a doting father followed closely by a wretched mourner and bitter drunk, overconfident confidence trickster, prisoner of the Inquisition then informant for them, translator, accountant and lawyer, collaborator with a whole range of different wrong sides, accomplice to mass murder, of course, and, most recently and disastrously, man of conscience. But rugged outdoorsman made no appearance on the list.

Temple did not even have the equipment to make a fire. Or, had he had it, known how to use it. He had nothing to cook anyway. And now he was lost in every sense of the word. The barbs of hunger, cold and fear had quickly come to bother him vastly more than the feeble prodding of his conscience ever had. He should probably have thought more carefully before fleeing, but flight and careful thought are like oil and water, ever reluctant to mix. He blamed Cosca. He blamed Lorsen. He blamed Jubair, and Sheel, and Sufeen. He blamed every fucker available excepting, of course, the one who was actually to blame, the one sitting in his saddle and getting colder, hungrier, and more lost with every unpleasant moment.

'Shit!' he roared at nothing.

His horse checked, ears swivelling, then plodded on. It was becoming resignedly immune to his outbursts. Temple peered up through the crooked branches, the moon casting a glow through the fast-moving streaks of cloud.

'God?' he muttered, too desperate to feel a fool. 'Can you hear me?' No answer, of course. God does not answer, especially not the likes of him. 'I know I haven't been the best man. Or even a particularly good one . . .' He winced. Once you accept He's up there, and all-knowing and all-seeing and so on, you probably have to accept that there's no point gilding the truth for Him. 'All right, I'm a pretty poor one, but . . . far from the worst about?' A proud boast, that. What a headstone it would make. Except, of course, there would be no one to carve it when he died out here alone and rotted in the open. 'I am sure I could improve, though, if you could just see your way to giving me . . . one more chance?' Wheedling, wheedling. 'Just . . . *one* more?'

No reply but another chill gust filling the trees with whispers. If there was a God, He was a tight-mouthed bastard, and no—

Temple caught the faintest glimmer of flickering orange through the trees.

A fire! Jubilation sprang to life in his breast!

Then caution smothered it.

Whose fire? Ear-collecting barbarians, but a step above wild animals?

He caught a whiff of cooking meat and his stomach gave a long, squelching growl, so loud he worried it might give him away. Temple had spent a great deal of his early life hungry and become quite adept at it, but, as with so many things, to do it well one has to stay in practice.

He gently reined in his horse, slid as quietly as he could from the saddle and looped the reins around a branch. Keeping low, he eased through the brush, tree-limbs casting clawing shadows towards him, breathing curses as he caught his clothes, his boots, his face on snatching twigs.

The fire had been built in the middle of a narrow clearing, a small animal neatly skinned and spitted on sticks above it. Temple suppressed a powerful impulse to dive at it teeth first. A single blanket was spread out between the fire and a worn saddle. A round shield leaned against a tree, metal rim and wooden front marked with the scars of hard use. Next to it was an axe with a heavy bearded head. It took no expert in the use of weapons to see this was a tool not for chopping wood but people.

The gear of one man, but clearly a man it would be a bad idea to be caught stealing the dinner of.

Temple's eyes crawled from meat to axe and back, and his mouth watered with an intensity almost painful. Possible death by axe loomed large at any time, but at that moment certain death from hunger loomed larger yet. He slowly straightened, preparing to—

'Nice night for it.' Northern words in a throaty whisper of a voice, just behind Temple's ear.

He froze, small hairs tingling up his neck. 'Bit windy,' he managed to croak.

'I've seen worse.' A cold and terrible point pricked at the small of Temple's back. 'Let's see your weapons, slow as snails in winter.'

'I am . . . unarmed.'

A pause. 'You're what?'

'I had a knife, but . . .' He had given it to a bony farmer who killed his best friend with it. 'I lost it.'

'Out in the big empty without a blade?' As though it was strange as to be without a nose. Temple gave a girlish squeak as a big hand slipped under his arm and started to pat him down. 'Nor have you, 'less you're hiding one up your arse.' An unpleasing notion. 'I ain't looking there.' That was some relief. 'You a madman?'

'I am a lawyer.'

'Can't a man be both?'

Self-evidently. 'I . . . suppose.'

Another pause. 'Cosca's lawyer?'

'I was.'

'Huh.' The point slipped away, its absence leaving a prickling spot in Temple's back. Even unpleasant things can be sorely missed, apparently, if you have lived with them long enough.

A man stepped past Temple. A great, black, shaggy shape, knife-blade glinting in one hand. He dragged a long sword from his belt and tossed it on the blanket, then lowered himself cross-legged, firelight twinkling red and yellow in the mirror of his metal eye.

'Life takes you down some strange paths, don't it?' he said.

'Caul Shivers,' muttered Temple, not at all sure whether to feel better or worse.

Shivers reached out and turned the spit between finger and thumb, fat dripping into the flames. 'Hungry?'

Temple licked his lips. 'Is that just a question . . . or an invitation?'

'I've got more'n I can eat. You'd best bring that horse up before it shakes loose. Watch your step, though.' The Northman jerked his head back into the trees. 'There's a gorge that way might be twenty strides deep, and with some angry water at the bottom.'

Temple brought the horse up and hobbled it, stripped its saddle and the damp blanket beneath, abandoned it to nuzzle at whatever grass it could find. A sad fact, but the hungrier a man is the less he tends to care about the hunger of others. Shivers had carved the carcass down to the bones and was eating from a tin plate with the point of his knife. More meat lay gleaming on some torn-off bark on the other side of the fire. Temple sank to his knees before it as though it were a most hallowed altar.

'My very great thanks.' He closed his eyes as he began to eat, sucking the juice from every morsel. 'I was starting to think I'd die out here.'

'Who says you won't?'

A shred of meat caught in Temple's throat and he gave an awkward cough. 'Are you alone?' he managed to gasp out – anything but more of the crushing silence.

'I've learned I make poor company.'

'You aren't worried about the Ghosts?'

The Northman shook his head.

'I hear they've killed a lot of people in the Far Country.'

'Once they've killed me I'll worry.' Shivers tossed down his plate and leaned back on one elbow, his ruined face shifting further into the darkness. 'A man can spend the time he's given crapping his arse out over what might be, but where does it get you?'

Where indeed? 'Still hunting for your nine-fingered man?'

'He killed my brother.'

Temple paused with another piece of meat halfway to his mouth. 'I'm sorry.'

'You're sorrier'n me, then. My brother was a shit. But family is family.'

'I wouldn't know.' Temple's relatives had rarely stayed long in his life. A dead mother, a dead wife, a dead daughter. 'Closest thing I have to family is . . .' He realised he had been about to say Sufeen, and now he was dead as well. 'Nicomo Cosca.'

Shivers grunted. Almost a chuckle. 'In my experience, he ain't the safest man to have at your back.'

'What is your experience?'

'We were both hired to kill some men. In Styria, ten years ago or so. Friendly, too. Some others. A poisoner. A torturer.'

'Sounds quite the merry company.'

'I ain't the wag I seem. Things got . . .' Shivers scratched ever so gently at the great scar under his metal eye. 'A bit unpleasant.'

'Things tend to get unpleasant when Cosca's involved.'

'They can get plenty unpleasant without him.'

'More so with,' muttered Temple, looking into the fire. 'He never cared much, but he used to care a little. He's got worse.'

'That's what men do.'

'Not all of them.'

'Ah.' Shivers showed his teeth. 'You're one of them optimists I've heard about.'

'No, no, not me,' said Temple. 'I always take the easy way.'

'Very wise. I find hoping for a thing tends to bring on the opposite.' The Northman slowly turned the ring on his little finger round and around, the stone glittering the colour of blood. 'I had my dreams of being a better man, once upon a time.'

'What happened?'

Shivers stretched out beside the fire, boots up on his saddle, and started to shake a blanket over himself. 'I woke up.'

Temple woke to that first washed out, grey-blue touch of dawn, and found himself smiling. The ground was cold and hard, the blanket was far too small and smelled powerfully of horse, the evening meal had been inadequate, and yet it was a long time since he had slept so soundly. Birds twittered, wind whispered and through the trees he could hear the faint rushing of water.

Fleeing the Company suddenly seemed a masterful plan, boldly executed. He wriggled over under his blanket. If there was a God, it turned out He was the forgiving fellow Kahdia had always—

Shivers' sword and shield had gone and another man squatted on his blanket.

He was stripped to the waist, his pale body a twisted mass of sinew. Over his bottom half he wore a filthy woman's dress, slit up the middle then stitched with twine to make loose trousers. One side of his head was shaved, the orange hair on the other scraped up into stiff spikes with some kind of fat. In one dangling hand he held a hatchet, in the other a bright knife.

A Ghost, then.

He stared unblinking across the dead fire at Temple with piercing blue eyes and Temple stared back, considerably less piercingly, and found he had gently pulled his horse-stinking blanket up under his chin in both fists.

Two more men slipped silently from the trees. One wore as a kind of helmet, though presumably not for protection against any earthly weapon, an open box of sticks joined at the corners with feathers and secured to a collar made from an old belt. The other's cheeks were striped with self-inflicted scars. In different circumstances – on stage, perhaps, at a Styrian carnival – they might have raised quite the laugh. Here, in the untracked depths of the Far Country and with Temple their only audience, merriment was notable by its absence.

'Noy.' A fourth Ghost had appeared as if from nowhere, between man and boy with yellow hair about his pale face and a line of dried-out brown paint under his eyes. Temple hoped it was paint. The bones of some small animal, stitched to the front of a shirt made from a sack, rattled as he danced from one foot to the other, smiling radiantly all the while. He beckoned Temple up.

'Noy.'

Temple very slowly got to his feet, smiling back at the boy, and then at the others. Keep smiling, keep smiling, everything on a friendly footing. 'Noy?' he ventured.

The boy hit him across the side of the head.

It was the shock more than the force that put Temple down. So he told himself. The shock, and some kind of primitive understanding that there was nothing to be gained by staying up. The world swayed as he lay there. His hair was tickly. He touched his scalp and there was blood on his fingers.

Then he saw the boy had a rock in his hand. A rock painted with blue rings. And now with just a few spots of Temple's red blood.

'Noy!' called the boy, beckoning again.

Temple was in no particular rush to rise. 'Look,' he said, trying common first. The boy slapped him with his empty hand. 'Look!' Giving Styrian a go. The boy slapped him a second time. He tried Kantic. 'I do not have any—' The boy hit him with the rock again, caught him across the cheek and put him on his side.

Temple shook his head. Groggy. Couldn't hear that well.

He grabbed at the nearest thing. The boy's leg, maybe.

He clambered up as far as his knees. His knees or the boy's knees. Someone's knees.

His mouth tasted of blood. His face was throbbing. Not hurting exactly. Numb.

The boy was saying something to the others, raising his arms as if asking for approval.

The one with the spikes of hair nodded gravely and opened his mouth to speak, and his head flew off.

The one beside him turned, slightly impeded by his stick helmet. Shivers' sword cut his arm off above the elbow and thudded deep into his chest, blood flooding from the wound. He stumbled wordlessly back, the blade lodged in his ribs.

The one with the scarred face flew at Shivers, stabbing at him, clawing at his shield, the two of them lurching about the clearing, feet kicking sparks from the embers of the fire.

All this in a disbelieving, wobbly breath or two, then the boy hit Temple over the head again. That seemed ridiculously unfair. As if Temple was the main threat. He dragged himself up the leg with a surge of outraged innocence. Shivers had forced the scarred Ghost onto his knees now and was smashing his head apart with the rim of his shield. The boy hit Temple again but he clung on, caught a fistful of bone-stitched shirt as his knees buckled.

They went down, scratching, punching, gouging. Temple was on the bottom, teeth bared, and he forced his thumb up the Ghost's nose and wrestled him over and all the while he could not help thinking how amazingly silly and wasteful this all was, and then that effective fighters probably leave the philosophising until after the fight.

The Ghost kneed at him, screaming in his own language, and they were rolling between the trees, sliding downhill, and Temple was punching at the Ghost's bloody face with his bloody knuckles, screeching as the Ghost caught his forearm and bit it, and then there were no trees, only loose earth under them, then the sound of the river grew very loud, and there was no earth at all, and they were falling.

He vaguely remembered Shivers saying something about a gorge.

Wind rushed, and turning weightlessness, and rock and leaf and white water. Temple let go of the Ghost, both of them falling without a sound. It all felt so unlikely. Dreamlike. Would he wake soon with a jolt, back with the Company of the—

The jolt came when he hit the water.

Feet-first, by blind luck, and then he was under, gripped by cold, crushed by the surging weight of it, ripped five ways at once in a current so strong it felt as though it would tear his arms from their sockets. Over and over, a leaf in the torrent, helpless.

His head left the flood and he heaved in a shuddering breath, spray in his face, roar of the furious water. Dragged under again and something thumped hard at his shoulder and twisted him over, showed him the sky for just a moment. Limbs so heavy now, a sore temptation to stop fighting. Temple had never been much of a fighter.

He caught a glimpse of driftwood, dried-out and bleached bone-white by sun and water. He snatched at it, lungs bursting, clawed at it as he came right-side-up. It was part of a tree. A whole tree-trunk with leafless branches still attached. He managed to heave his chest over it, coughing, spitting, face scraping against rotten wood.

He breathed. A few breaths. An hour. A hundred years.

Water lapped at him, tickled him. He raised his head so he could see the sky. A mighty effort. Clouds shifted across the deep and careless blue.

'Is this your idea of a fucking joke?' he croaked, before a wave slapped him in the face and made him swallow water. No joke, then. He lay still. Too tired and hurting for anything else. The water had calmed now, at least. The river wider, slower, the banks lower, long grass shelving down to the shingle.

He let it all slide by. He trusted to God, since there was no one else. He hoped for heaven.

But he fully expected the alternative.

Driftwood

'Whoa!' called Shy. 'Whoa!'

Maybe it was the noise of the river, or maybe they somehow sensed she'd done some low-down things in her life, but, as usual, the oxen didn't take a shred of notice and kept on veering for the deeper water. Dumb stubborn bloody animals. Once they'd an idea in mind they'd keep towards it regardless of all urgings to the contrary. Nature giving her a taste of her own cooking, maybe. Nature was prone to grudges that way.

'Whoa, I said, you bastards!' She gripped at her soaked saddle with her soaked legs, wound the rope a couple of times around her right forearm and gave a good haul. The other end was tight-knotted to the lead yoke and the line snapped taut and sprayed water. Same time Leef nudged his pony up from the downstream side and snapped out a neat little flick with his goad. He'd turned out to have quite a knack as a drover. One of the front pair gave an outraged snort but its blunt nose shifted left, back to the chosen course, towards the stretch of wheel-scarred shingle on the far bank where the half of the Fellowship already across was gathered.

Ashjid the priest was one of them, arms thrust up to heaven like his was the most important job around, chanting a prayer to calm the waters. Shy had observed no becalming. Not of the waters, and for damn sure not of her.

'Keep 'em straight!' growled Sweet, who'd reined his dripping horse up on a sandbar and was taking his ease – something he took an aggravating amount of.

'Keep them straight!' echoed Majud from behind, gripping so hard to the seat of his wagon it was a wonder he didn't rip it off. He wasn't comfortable with water, apparently, which was quite an inconvenience in a frontiersman.

'What d'you think I'm aiming to do, you idle old fucks?' hissed Shy, digging her horse out left and giving the rope another heave. 'See us all flushed out to sea?'

It didn't look unlikely. They'd doubled up the oxen, teams of six or eight or even a dozen hitched to the heaviest loads, but still it was far from easy going. If the wagons weren't hitting deep water and threatening to float away, they were doing the opposite and getting bogged in the shallows.

One of Buckhorm's wagons was stranded now and Lamb was in the river to his waist, straining at the back axle while Savian leaned from his horse to smack at the lead oxen's rump. He hit it that hard Shy was worried he'd break the beast's back, but in the end he got it floundering on and Lamb sloshed back wearily to his horse. Unless your name was Dab Sweet, it was hard work all round.

But then work had never scared Shy. She'd learned early that once you were stuck with a task you were best off giving it your all. The hours passed quicker then, and you were less likely to get a belting, too. So she'd worked hard at errands soon as she could run, at farming when a woman grown, and between the two at robbing folk and been damn good at it, though that was probably better not dwelt on. Her work now was finding her brother and sister, but since fate had allotted her oxen to drive through a river in the meantime, she reckoned she'd try her hardest at that in spite of the smell and the strain on her sore arms and the freezing water washing at her arse-crack.

They finally floundered out onto the sandbar, animals streaming and blowing, cartwheels crunching in the shingle, Shy's horse trembling under her and that the second one she'd blowed out that day.

'Call this a damn ford?' she shouted at Sweet over the noise of the water.

He grinned back at her, leathery face creased up with good humour. 'What'd you call it?'

'A stretch of river 'bout the same as any other, and just as apt to be drowned in.'

'You should've told me if you couldn't swim.'

'I can, but this wagon's no fucking salmon, I can tell you that.'

Sweet turned his horse about with the slightest twist of his heel. 'You disappoint me, girl. I had you marked for an adventurer!'

'Never by choice. You ready?' she called out to Leef. The lad nodded. 'How about you?'

Majud waved a weak hand. 'I fear I will never be ready. Go. Go.'

So Shy wound the rope tight again, heaved in a good breath, gave herself a thought of Ro's face and Pit's, and set off after Sweet. Cold gripped her calves, then her thighs, oxen peering nervous towards the far bank, her horse snorting and tossing its head, none of them any keener on another dip than she was, Leef working the goad and calling out, 'Easy, easy.'

The last stretch was the deepest, water surging around the oxen and making white bow-waves on their upstream flanks. Shy hauled at the rope, making them strain into the current at a diagonal just to end up with a straight course, while the wagon jolted over the broken stream-bed, wheels half-under, then squealing axles under, then the whole thing halfway to floating and a damn poor shape for a boat.

She saw one of the oxen was swimming, neck stretched as it struggled to keep its flaring nostrils above the water, then two, scared eyes rolling towards her, then three, and Shy felt the rope tugging hard, and she wound it tighter about her forearm and put all her weight into it, hemp gripping at her leather glove, biting at the skin above it.

'Leef!' she growled through her gritted teeth, 'Get it over to—'

One of the leaders slipped, craggy shoulder-blades poking up hard as it struggled for a footing, and then it veered off to the right and took its neighbour's legs away too and the pair of them were torn sideways by the river. The rope jerked Shy's right arm straight like it would rip her muscles joint from joint, dragging her half-out of the saddle before she knew a thing about it.

Now the front two oxen were thrashing, sending up spray, dragging the next yoke out of true while Leef screeched and lashed at them. Might as well have been lashing at the river, which he mostly was. Shy dragged with all her strength. Might as well have been dragging at a dozen dead oxen. Which she soon would be.

'Fuck!' she gasped, rope slipping suddenly through her right hand and zipping around her forearm, just managing to hold on, blood in the hemp and mixing with the beaded water, spray in her face and wet hair and the terrified lowing of the animals and the terrified wailing of Majud.

The wagon was skidding, grinding, near to floating, near to tipping. The first animal had found ground again somehow and Savian was smacking at it and snarling, Shy with neck stretched back and dragging, dragging, rope ripping at her arm and her horse shuddering under her.

Glimpse of the far bank, people waving, their shouts and her breath and the thrashing of the beasts making just one echoing throb in her skull.

'Shy.' Lamb's voice. And there was a strong arm around her and she knew she could let go.

Like when she fell off the barn roof and Lamb had lifted her up. 'All right, now. Quiet, now.' Sun flickering through her lids and her mouth tasting like blood, but not scared any more. Later, years later, him bandaging the burns on her back. 'It'll pass. It'll pass.' And her walking up to the farm after that black time gone, not knowing what she'd find there, or who, and seeing him sat by the door with that same smile as always. 'Good to have you back,' like she'd only left a moment before, hugging her tight and feeling that prickle of tears under her closed lids . . .

'Shy?'

'Uh.' Lamb was setting her down on the bank, blurred faces flickering into focus around her.

'You all right, Shy?' Leef was calling. 'She all right?'

'Give her some room.'

'Let her breathe, now.'

'I'm breathing,' she grunted, waving their pawing hands away, fighting up to sitting though she wasn't sure what'd happen when she got there.

'Hadn't you better stay still a while?' asked Lamb. 'You have to be—'

'I'm fine,' she snapped, swallowing the need to puke. 'Grazed my pride a little, but that'll scab over.' It had scars enough on it already, after all. 'Gave my arm a scrape.' She winced as she pulled her glove off with her teeth, every joint in her right arm throbbing, grunted as she worked the trembling fingers. The raw rope-burn coiled bloody around her forearm like a snake up a branch.

'Scraped it bad.' Leef slapped at his forehead. 'My fault! If I'd just—'

'No one's fault but my own. Should've let go the damn rope.'

'I for one am grateful you did not.' Majud must've finally prised his fingers free of his wagon-seat. Now he draped a blanket over Shy's shoulders. 'I am far from a strong swimmer.'

Shy squinted at him and that brought the burning to the back of her throat again, so she looked to the wet shingle between her knees instead. 'You ever think a journey over twenty unbridged rivers might've been a mistake?'

'Every time we cross one, but what can a merchant do when he smells opportunity at the other side? Much as I detest hardship, I love profit more.'

'Just what we need out here.' Sweet twisted his hat back firm onto his head as he stood. 'More greed. All right! Drama's done, everyone, she yet lives! Let's get these teams unhitched and back across, the rest of them wagons ain't going to fly over!'

Corlin shoved between Lamb and Leef with a bag in one hand and knelt next to Shy, taking her arm and frowning down at it. She'd such a manner of knowing exactly what she was about made you hardly even think to ask whether she did.

'You going to be all right?' asked Leef.

Shy waved him away. 'You can go on. You all can.' She'd known some folks couldn't get enough pity, but it'd always made her feel uncomfortable right into her arse.

'You're sure?' asked Lamb, looking down at her from what seemed a great height.

'I daresay you've got better places to be than in my way,' snapped Corlin, already cleaning the cuts.

They drifted off, back towards the ford, Lamb with one last worried look over his shoulder, leaving Corlin to bind Shy's arm with quick, deft hands, wasting no time and making no mistakes.

'Thought they'd never leave.' And she slipped a little bottle out of her bag and into Shy's free hand.

'Now that's good doctoring.' Shy took a sneaky swig and curled her lips back at the burning.

'Why do a thing badly?'

'I'm always amazed how some folk can't help themselves.'

'True enough.' Corlin glanced up from her work towards the ford, where they were manhandling Gentili's rickety wagon to the far bank, one of the ancient prospectors waving his spindly arms as a wheel caught in the shallows. 'There's a few like that along on this trip.'

'I guess most of 'em mean well.'

'Someday you can build a boat from meaning well and see how it floats.'

'Tried that. Sank with me on it.'

The corner of Corlin's mouth twitched up. 'I think I might have been on that voyage. Icy water, wasn't it?' Lamb had dropped in beside Savian, the two old men straining at the stuck wheel, the whole wagon rocking with their efforts. 'You see a lot of strong men out here in the wilderness. Trappers and hunters hardly spent a night of their lives under a roof. Men made of wood and leather. Not sure I ever saw one stronger than your father, though.'

'He ain't my father,' muttered Shy, taking another swig from the bottle. 'And your uncle's no weakling neither.'

Corlin cut a bandage from the roll with a flick of a bright little knife. 'Maybe we should give up on oxen and get those two old bastards to haul the wagons.'

'Expect we'd get there faster.'

'You reckon you could get Lamb into a yoke?'

'Easily, but I don't know how Savian might respond to a whipping.'

'You'd probably break your whip on him.'

The wagon finally ground free and lurched on, Gentili's old cousin flailing about in the seat. Behind in the water, Savian gave Lamb an approving thump on the shoulder.

'They've struck up quite the friendship,' said Shy. 'For two men never say a word.'

'Ah, the unspoken camaraderie of veterans.'

'What makes you think Lamb's a veteran?'

'Everything.' And Corlin slid a pin neatly through the bandage to hold it closed. 'You're done.' She glanced towards the river, the men calling out as they splashed around in the water, and suddenly she sprang up and shouted, 'Uncle, your shirt!'

Seemed like mad over-modesty to panic about a torn sleeve when half the men in the Fellowship were stripped to the waist and a couple all the way to their bare arses. Then, as Savian twisted to look, Shy caught a glimpse of his bare forearm. It was blue-black with tattooed letters.

No need to ask what he was a veteran of. He was a rebel. More than likely he'd been fighting in Starikland and was on the run, for all Shy knew hotly pursued by his Majesty's Inquisition.

She looked up, and Corlin looked down, and neither one of them quite managed to hide what they were thinking.

'Just a torn shirt. Nothing to worry about.' But Corlin's blue, blue eyes were narrowed and Shy realised she still had that bright little knife in her hand and of a sudden felt the need to pick her words with care.

'I daresay we've all got a rip or two behind us.' Shy handed the bottle back to Corlin and slowly stood. 'Ain't none of my affair to go picking at other folks' stitches. Their business is their business.'

Corlin took a swig of her own, looking at Shy all the while over the bottle. 'That's a fine policy.'

'And this a fine bandage.' Shy grinned as she worked her fingers. 'Can't say I've ever had a better.'

'You had a lot?'

'Been cut enough, but mostly I just had to let 'em bleed. No one interested in doing the bandaging, I guess.'

'Sad story.'

'Oh, I can tell 'em all day long . . .' She frowned towards the river. 'What's that?'

A dead tree was washing slowly towards them, snagging in the shallows then drifting on, tangles of foamy grass caught up in its branches. There was something draped over the trunk. Someone, limbs trailing. Shy threw her blanket off and hurried to the bank, slid into the water, cold gripping her legs again and making her shiver.

She waded out and caught hold of a branch, winced as pain shot through all the joints of her right arm and into her ribs, had to flounder around to use her left instead.

The passenger was a man, head turned so she couldn't see his face, only a mass of black hair, wet shirt rucked up to show a patch of brown midriff.

'That's a funny-looking fish,' said Corlin, looking down from the bank with hands on hips.

'You want to leave the jokes 'til you've helped me land him?'

'Who is he?'

'He's the Emperor of fucking Gurkhul! How should I know who he is?'

'That's exactly my point.'

'Maybe we can ask once we've dragged him out?'

'That might be too late.'

'Once he's washed out to sea it surely will be!'

Corlin sucked sourly at her teeth, then stomped down the bank and into the river without breaking stride. 'On your head be it if he turns out a murderer.'

'No doubt it will be.' Together they heaved the tree and its human cargo grinding onto the bank, broken branches leaving grooves through the gravel, and stood looking down, soaked through, Shy's stomach sticking unpleasantly to her wet shirt with each shivering in-breath.

'All right, then.' Corlin reached down to take the man under his arms. 'Keep your knife handy, though.'

'My knife's always handy,' said Shy.

With a grunt and a heave, Corlin twisted him over and onto his back, one leg flopping after. 'Any idea what the Emperor of Gurkhul looks like?'

'Better fed,' muttered Shy. He had a lean look to him, fibres in his stretched-out neck, sharp cheekbones, one with an ugly cut down it.

'Better dressed,' said Corlin. He had nothing but the torn clothes he was tangled with, and one boot. 'Older, too.' He couldn't have been much over thirty, short black beard on his cheeks, grey scattered in his hair.

'Less . . . earnest,' said Shy. It was the best word she could think of for that face. He looked almost peaceful in spite of the cut. Like he'd just closed his eyes to philosophise a moment.

'It's the earnest-looking bastards need the most watching.' Corlin tipped his face one way, then the other. 'But he is pretty. For flotsam.' She leaned further to put her ear over his mouth, then rocked back on her haunches, considering.

'He alive?' asked Shy.

'One way to find out.' Corlin slapped him across the face, and none too gently.

When Temple opened his eyes he saw only a blinding brightness.

Heaven!

But should heaven hurt so much?

Hell, then.

But surely hell would be hot?

And he felt very cold.

He tried to lift his head and decided it was far too much effort. Tried to move his tongue and decided that was no better. A wraith-like figure floated into view, surrounded by a nimbus of sparkling light, painful to look upon.

'God?' Temple croaked.

The slap made a hollow boom in his head, brought fire to the side of his face and snapped everything into focus.

Not God.

Or not the way He was usually portrayed.

This was a woman, and a pale-skinned one. Not old in years, but

Temple got the feeling those years had been testing. A long, pointed face, made to look longer by the red-brown hair hanging about it, stuck to pale cheeks with wet, wedged under a ragged hat salt-stained about the band. Her mouth was set in a suspicious frown, with faint lines at the corners that suggested it often was. She looked used to hard work and hard choices, but there was a soft dusting of freckles across the narrow bridge of her nose.

Another woman's face hovered behind. Older and squarer with short hair stirred by the wind and blue eyes that looked as if they were stirred by nothing.

Both women were wet. So was Temple. So was the shingle under him. He could hear the washing of a river and, fainter in the background, the calls of men and beasts. There was only one explanation, reached gradually and by a process of ponderous elimination.

He was still alive.

These two women could scarcely have seen as weak, watery and unconvincing a smile as he mustered at that moment. 'Hello,' he croaked.

'I'm Shy,' said the younger.

'You needn't be,' said Temple. 'I feel we know each other quite well already.'

Under the circumstances he thought it a solid effort, but she did not smile. People rarely find jokes based on their own name amusing. They, after all, have heard them a thousand times.

'My name is Temple.' He tried to rise again, and this time made it as far as his elbows before giving up.

'Not the Emperor of Gurkhul, then,' muttered the older woman, for some reason.

'I am . . .' Trying to make up his mind exactly what he was now. 'A lawyer.'

'So much for earnest.'

'Don't know that I ever been this close to a lawyer before,' said Shy.

'Is it all you hoped for?' asked the other woman.

'So far it's middling.'

'You're not catching me at my best.' With a little help from the two women he dragged himself to sitting, noting with a pang of nervousness that Shy kept one hand on the grip of a knife. Not a shy knife, judging by the sheath, and that hard set to her mouth made him think she would not be shy about using it.

He was careful to make no sudden moves. Not that it was difficult. Painstaking ones were enough of a challenge.

'How does a lawyer get into a river?' asked the older woman. 'Give bad advice?'

'It's good advice usually lands you in trouble.' He tried another smile, somewhat closer to his usual winning formula. 'You did not tell me your name.'

It won nothing from her. 'No. You weren't pushed, then?'

'Me and another man sort of . . . pushed each other.'

'What happened to him?'

Temple gave a helpless shrug. 'For all I know he'll float by presently.'

'You armed?'

'He ain't even shod,' said Shy.

Temple peered down at his bare foot, tendons standing stark from the skin as he wriggled the toes. 'I used to have a very small knife but . . . that didn't turn out too well. I think it's fair to say . . . I've had a bad week.'

'Some days work out.' Shy started to help him up. 'Some don't.'

'You sure about this?' asked her companion.

'What's the choice, throw him back in the water?'

'I've heard worse ideas.'

'You can stay here, then.' And Shy dragged Temple's arm around her neck and hauled him to his feet.

God, he was hurting. His head felt like a melon someone had taken a hammer to. God, he was cold. He could hardly have been colder if he had died in the river. God, he was weak. His knees trembled so badly he could hear them flapping at the insides of his wet trousers. Just as well he had Shy to lean on. She did not feel like she would collapse any time soon. Her shoulder was firm as wood under his hand.

'Thank you,' he said, and meant it, too. 'Thank you so much.' He had always been at his best with someone strong to lean on. Like a flowering creeper adorning a deep-rooted tree. Or a songbird perched on a bull's horn. Or a leech on a horse's arse.

They struggled up the bank, his booted foot and his bare foot scraping at the mud. Behind them, cattle were being driven across the river, riders leaning from saddles to wave their hats or their ropes, yipping and calling, the beasts swarming, swimming, clambering one over another, thrashing up clouds of spray.

'Welcome to our little Fellowship,' said Shy.

A mass of wagons, animals and people were gathered in the lee of a wind-bent copse just beyond the river. Some worked timber for repairs. Some struggled to get stubborn oxen into yokes. Some were busy changing clothes soaked in the crossing, sharp tan-lines on bare limbs. A pair of women were heating soup over a fire, Temple's stomach giving a painful grumble at the smell of it. Two children laughed as they chased a three-legged dog around and around.

He did his best to smile, and nod, and ingratiate himself as Shy helped him through their midst with her strong hand under his armpit, but a few curious frowns were his whole harvest. Mostly these people were fixed on their work, all of them aimed squarely at grinding a profit out of this unforgiving new land with one kind of hard labour or another. Temple winced, and not just from the pain and the cold. When he'd signed up with Nicomo Cosca, it had been on the understanding that he'd never come this close to hard work again.

'Where is the Fellowship heading?' he asked. It would be just his luck to hear Squaredeal or Averstock, settlements whose remaining citizens he rather hoped never to be reacquainted with.

'West,' said Shy. 'Right across the Far Country to Crease. That suit?'

Temple had never heard of Crease. Which was the highest recommendation for the place. 'Anywhere but where I came from suits well enough. West will be wonderful. If you'll have me.'

'Ain't me you got to convince. It's these old bastards.'

There were five of them, standing in a loose group at the head of the column. Temple was slightly unnerved to see the nearest was a Ghost woman, long and lean with a face worn tough as saddle-leather, bright eyes looking straight through Temple and off to the far horizon. Next to her, swaddled in a huge fur coat and with a pair of knives and a gilt-sheathed hunting sword at his belt, a smallish man with a shag of grey hair and beard and a curl to his mouth as if Temple was a joke he didn't find funny but was too polite to frown at.

'This here is the famous scout Dab Sweet and his associate Crying Rock. And this the leader of our merry Fellowship, Abram Majud.' A bald, sinewy Kantic, face composed of unforgiving angles with two careful, slanted eyes in the midst. 'This is Savian.' A tall man, with iron grey stubble and a stare like a hammer. 'And this is . . .' Shy paused, as though trying to think up the right word. 'Lamb.'

Lamb was a huge old Northman, slightly hunched as if he was trying to look smaller than he was, a piece missing from his ear and a face that, through a tangle of hair and beard, looked as if it had seen long use as a millstone. Temple wanted to wince just looking at that collection of breaks, nicks and scars, but he grinned through it like the professional he was, and smiled at each of these geriatric adventurers as though he never saw in one place such a collection of the beautiful and promising.

'Gentlemen, and . . .' He glanced at Crying Rock, realised the word hardly seemed to fit but had entirely backed himself into a corner. 'Lady . . . it is my honour to meet you. My name is Temple.'

'Speaks nice, don't he?' rumbled Sweet, as though that was a black mark against him already.

'Where did you find him?' growled Savian. Temple had not failed at as many professions as he had without learning to recognise a dangerous man, and he feared this one straight away.

'Fished him out of the river,' said Shy.

'You got a reason not to throw him back?'

'Didn't want to kill him, I guess.'

Savian looked straight at Temple, flint-eyed, and shrugged. 'Wouldn't be killing him. Just letting him drown.'

There was a moment of silence for Temple to consider that, while the wind blew chill through his soaked trousers and the five old worthies treated him each to their own style of appraisal, suspicion or scorn.

It was Majud who spoke first. 'And where did you float in from, Master Temple? You do not appear to be native to these parts.'

'No more than you, sir. I was born in Dagoska.'

'An excellent city for commerce in its day, rather less so since the demise of the Guild of Spicers. And how does a Dagoskan come to be out here?'

Here is the perennial trouble with burying your past. Others are forever trying to dig it up. 'I must confess . . . I had fallen in with some bad company.'

Majud indicated his companions with a graceful gesture. 'It happens to the best of us.'

'Bandits?' asked Savian.

All that and worse. 'Soldiers,' said Temple, putting it in the best light possible short of an outright lie. 'I left them and struck out on my own. I was set upon by Ghosts, and in the struggle rolled down a slope and . . . into a gorge.' He pressed gently at his battered face, remembering that sickening moment when he ran out of ground. 'Followed by a long fall into water.'

'I been there,' murmured Lamb, with a faraway look.

Sweet puffed up his chest and adjusted his sword-belt. 'Whereabouts did you run across these Ghosts?'

Temple could only shrug. 'Upriver?'

'How far and how many?'

'I saw four. It happened at dawn and I've been floating since.'

'Might be no more'n twenty miles south.' Sweet and Crying Rock exchanged a long glance, grizzled concern on his part, stony blankness on hers. 'We'd best ride out and take a look that way.'

'Hmm,' murmured the old Ghost.

'Do you expect trouble?' asked Majud.

'Always. That way you'll only be pleasantly surprised.' Sweet walked between Lamb and Savian, giving each of them a slap on the shoulder as he passed. 'Good work at the river. Hope I'm as useful when I reach your age.' He slapped Shy, too. 'And you, girl. Might want to let go the rope next time, though, eh?' It was only then that Temple noticed the bloody bandage around her limp arm. He had never been particularly sensitive to the hurts of others.

Majud showed off a gold front tooth as he smiled. 'I imagine you would be grateful to travel with our Fellowship?'

Temple sagged with relief. 'Beyond grateful.'

'Every member has either paid for their passage or contributes their skills.'

Temple unsagged. 'Ah.'

'Do you have a profession?'

'I have had several.' He thought quickly through the list for those that were least likely to land him immediately back in the river. 'Trainee priest, amateur surgeon—'

'We've got a surgeon,' said Savian.

'And a priest, more's the pity,' added Shy.

'Butcher—'

'We have hunters,' said Majud.

'—carpenter—'

'A wagon-man?'

Temple winced. 'House-builder.'

'We need no houses out here. Your most recent work?'

Mercenary usually won few friends. 'I was a lawyer,' he said, before realising that often won still fewer.

Savian was certainly not one of them. 'There's no law out here but what a man brings with him.'

'Have you ever driven oxen?' asked Majud.

'I am afraid not.'

'Herded cattle?'

'Sadly, no.'

'Handled horses?'

'One at a time?'

'Experience in combat?' grated Savian.

'Very little, and that far more than I'd like.' He feared this interview was not showing him in his best light, if there was such a thing. 'But . . . I am determined to start fresh, to earn my place, to work as hard as any man – or woman – here and . . . keen to learn,' he finished, wondering if so many exaggerations had ever been worked into one sentence.

'I wish you every success with your education,' said Majud, 'but passengers pay one hundred and fifty marks.'

A brief silence as they all, particularly Temple, considered the likelihood of his producing such a sum. Then he patted at his wet trouser-pockets. 'I find myself a little short.'

'How short?'

'One hundred and fifty marks-ish?'

'You let us join for nothing and I reckon you're getting your money's worth,' said Shy.

'Sweet made that deal.' Majud ran an appraising eye over Temple and he found himself trying to hide his bare foot behind the other. Without success. 'And you at least brought two boots apiece. This one will need clothes, and footwear, and a mount. We simply cannot afford to take in every stray that happens across our path.'

Temple blinked, not entirely sure where this left him.

'Where does that leave him?' asked Shy.

'Waiting at the ford for a Fellowship with different requirements.'

'Or another set of Ghosts, I guess?'

Majud spread his hands. 'If it were up to me I would not hesitate before helping you, but I have the feelings of my partner Curnsbick to consider, and he has a heart of iron where business is concerned. I am sorry.' He did look a little sorry. But he did not look like he would be changing his mind.

Shy glanced sideways at Temple. All he could do was stare back as earnestly as possible.

'Shit.' She planted her hands on her hips and shook her head at the sky for a moment, then curled back her top lip to show a noticeable gap between her front teeth and neatly spat through it. 'I'll buy him in, then.'

'Really?' asked Majud, brows going up.

'Really?' asked Temple, no less shocked.

'That's right,' she snapped. 'You want the money now?'

'Oh, don't trouble yourself.' Majud had the trace of a smile about his lips. 'I know your touch with figures.'

'I don't like this.' Savian propped the heel of his hand on the grip of one of his knives. 'This bastard could be anyone.'

'So could you,' said Shy. 'I've no notion what you were doing last month, or what you'll get to next, and for a fact it's none o' my business. I'm paying, he's staying. You don't like it, you can float off downriver, how's that?' She glared right into Savian's stony face all the while and Temple found he was liking her more and more.

Savian pursed his thin lips a fraction. 'Got anything to say about this, Lamb?'

The old Northman looked slowly from Temple to Shy and back. It appeared he did nothing quickly. 'I reckon everyone should get a chance,' he said.

'Even those don't deserve it?'

'Especially them, maybe.'

'You can trust me,' said Temple, treating the old men to his most earnest look. 'I won't let you down, I promise.' He had left a trail of broken promises across half the Circle of the World, after all. One extra would hardly keep him out of heaven.

'You saying so don't necessarily make it so, does it?' Savian leaned forward, narrowing his eyes even further, a feat that might have been considered impossible but a moment before. 'I'm watching you, boy.'

'That is . . . a tremendous comfort,' squeaked Temple as he backed slowly away. Shy had already turned on her heel and he hurried to catch her up.

'Thank you,' he said. 'Truly. I'm not sure what I can do to repay you.'

'Repay me.'

He cleared his throat. 'Yes. Of course.'

'With one-quarter interest. I ain't no charity.'

Now he was liking her less. 'I begin to see that. Principal plus a quarter. Far more than fair. I always pay my debts.' Except, perhaps, the financial ones.

'Is it true you're keen to learn?'

He was keener to forget. 'I am.'

'And to work as hard as any man here?'

Judging by the dustiness, sweatiness, sunburn and generally ruined appearance of most of the men, that claim seemed now rather rash. 'Yes?'

'Good, 'cause I'll work you, don't worry on that score.'

He was worrying on several scores, but the lack of hard labour had not been among them. 'I can . . . hardly wait to start.' He was getting the distinct sensation that he had whisked his neck from one noose only to have another whipped tight around it. Looked at with the benefit of hindsight, his life, which at the time had felt like a series of ingenious escapes, resembled rather more closely a succession of nooses, most of them self-tied. The self-tied ones will still hang you, though.

Shy was busy kneading at her injured arm and planning strategy. 'Might be Hedges has some clothes'll fit. Gentili's got an old saddle will serve and Buckhorm's got a mule I believe he'd sell.'

'A mule?'

'If that's too fucking lowly you can always walk to Crease.'

Temple thought it unlikely he would make it as far as the mule on foot, so he smiled through the pain and consoled himself with the thought that he would repay her. For the indignity, if not the money.

'I shall feel grateful for every moment spent astride the noble beast,' he forced out.

'You should feel grateful,' she snapped.

'I will,' he snapped back.

'Good,' she said.

'Good.'

A pause. 'Good.'

Reasons

'Some country, ain't it?'

'Looks like quite a bloody lot of country to me,' said Leef.

Sweet spread his arms and pulled in such a breath you'd have thought he could suck the whole world through his nose. 'It's the Far Country, true enough! Far 'cause it's so damn far from anywhere a civilised man would care to go. And Far 'cause it's so damn far from here to anywhere else he'd want to go.'

'Far 'cause it's so damn far to anything at all,' said Shy, staring out across that blank expanse of grass, gently shifting with the wind. A long, long way off, so pale they might've been no more'n wishes, the grey outline of hills.

'But damn civilised men, eh, Lamb?'

Lamb raised a mild eyebrow. 'We can't just let 'em be?'

'Maybe even borrow some hot water off 'em once in a while,' muttered Shy, scratching at her armpit. She'd a fair few passengers along for the ride now, not to mention dust crusted to every bit of her and her teeth tasting of salt dirt and dry death.

'Damn 'em, say I, and hot water, too! You can strike off south to the Empire and ask old Legate Sarmis for a bath if that's your style. Or trek back east to the Union and ask the Inquisition.'

'Their water might be too hot for comfort,' she muttered.

'Just tell me where a body can feel as free as this!'

'Can't think of nowhere,' she admitted, though to her mind there was something savage in all that endless empty. You could come to feel squashed by all that room.

But not Dab Sweet. He filled his lungs to bursting one more time. 'She's easy to fall in love with, the Far Country, but she's a cruel mistress. Always leading you on. That's how it's been with me, ever since I was younger'n Leef here. The best grass is always just past the horizon.

The sweetest water's in the next river. The bluest sky over some other mountain.' He gave a long sigh. 'Afore you know it, your joints snap of a morning and you can't sleep two hours together without needing to piss and of a sudden you realise your best country's all behind you, never even appreciated as you passed it by, eyes fixed ahead.'

'Summers past love company,' mused Lamb, scratching at the star-shaped scar on his stubbled cheek. 'Seems every time you turn around there's more o' the bastards at your back.'

'Comes to be everything reminds you of something past. Somewhere past. Someone. Yourself, maybe, how you were. The now gets fainter and the past more and more real. The future worn down to but a stub.'

Lamb had a little smile at his mouth's corner as he stared into the distance. 'The happy valleys o' the past,' he murmured.

'I love old-bastard talk, don't you?' Shy cocked a brow at Leef. 'Makes me feel healthy.'

'You young shrimps think tomorrow can be put off for ever,' grumbled Sweet. 'More time got like money from a bank. You'll learn.'

'If the Ghosts don't kill us all first,' said Leef.

'Thanks for raising that happy possibility,' said Sweet. 'If philosophy don't suit, I do have other occupation for you.'

'Which is?'

The old scout nodded down. Scattered across the grass, flat and white and dry, were a bumper harvest of cow-leavings, fond mementoes of some wild herd roving the grassland. 'Collecting bullshit.'

Shy snorted. 'Ain't he collected bullshit enough listening to you and Lamb sing the glories o' yesteryear?'

'You can't burn fond remembrances, more's the pity, or I'd be toasty warm every night.' Sweet stuck an arm out to the level sameness in every direction, the endless expanse of earth and sky and sky and earth away to nowhere. 'Ain't a stick of timber for a hundred miles. We'll be burning cow flats 'til after we cross the bridge at Sictus.'

'And cooking over 'em, too?'

'Might improve the flavour o' what we been eating,' said Lamb.

'All part o' the charm,' said Sweet. 'Either way, all the young 'uns are gathering fuel.'

Leef's eyes flickered to Shy. 'I ain't that young.' And as though to prove it he fingered his chin where he'd started to lovingly cultivate a meagre harvest of blond hairs.

Shy wasn't sure she couldn't have fielded more beard and Sweet was unmoved. 'You're young enough to get shitty-handed in service of the Fellowship, lad!' And he slapped Leef on the back, much to the lad's hunch-shouldered upset. 'Why, brown palms are a mark of high courage and distinction! The medal of the plains!'

'You want the lawyer to lend you a hand?' asked Shy. 'For three bits he's yours for the afternoon.'

Sweet narrowed his eyes. 'I'll give you two for him.'

'Done,' she said. It was hardly worth haggling when the prices were so small.

'Reckon he'll enjoy that, the lawyer,' said Lamb, as Leef and Sweet headed back towards the Fellowship, the scout holding forth again on how fine things used to be.

'He ain't along for his amusement.'

'I guess none of us are.'

They rode in silence for a moment, just the two of them and the sky, so big and deep it seemed any moment there might be nothing holding you to the ground any more and you'd just fall into it and never stop. Shy worked her right arm a little, shoulder and elbow still weak and sore, grumbles up into her neck and down into her ribs but getting looser each day. For sure she'd lived through worse.

'I'm sorry,' said Lamb, out of nowhere.

Shy looked over at him, hunched and sagging like he'd an anchor chained around his neck. 'I've always thought so.'

'I mean it, Shy. I'm sorry. For what happened back there in Averstock. For what I did. And what I didn't do.' He spoke slower and slower until Shy got the feeling each word was a battle to fight. 'Sorry that I never told you what I was . . . before I came to your mother's farm . . .' She watched him all the while, mouth dry, but he just frowned down at his left hand, thumb rubbing at that stump of a finger over and over. 'All I wanted was to leave the past buried. Be nothing and nobody. Can you understand that?'

Shy swallowed. She'd a few memories at her back she wouldn't have minded sinking in a bog. 'I reckon.'

'But the seeds of the past bear fruit in the present, my father used to say. I'm that much of a fool I got to teach myself the same lesson over and over, always pissing into the wind. The past never stays buried. Not one like mine, leastways. Blood'll always find you out.'

'What were you?' Her voice sounded a tiny croak in all that space. 'A soldier?'

That frown of his got harder still. 'A killer. Let's call it what it is.'

'You fought in the wars? Up in the North?'

'In wars, in skirmishes, in duels, in anything offered, and when I ran out of fights I made my own, and when I ran out of enemies I turned my friends into more.'

She'd thought any answers would be better than none. Now she wasn't so sure. 'I guess you had your reasons,' she muttered, so weak it turned into a wheedling question.

'Good ones, at first. Then poor ones. Then I found you could still shed blood without 'em and gave up on the bastards altogether.'

'You got a reason now, though.'

'Aye. I've a reason now.' He took a breath and drew himself up straighter. 'Those children . . . they're all the good I done in my life. Ro and Pit. And you.'

Shy snorted. 'If you're counting me in your good works you got to be desperate.'

'I am.' He looked across at her, so fixed and searching she'd trouble meeting his eye. 'But as it happens you're about the best person I know.'

She looked away, working that stiff shoulder again. She'd always found soft words a lot tougher to swallow than hard. A question of what you're used to, maybe. 'You got a damn limited circle of friends.'

'Enemies always came more natural to me. But even so. I don't know where you got it, but you've a good heart, Shy.'

She thought of him carrying her from that tree, singing to the children, putting the bandages on her back. 'So have you.'

'Oh, I can fool folk. The dead know I can fool myself.' He looked back to the flat horizon. 'But no, Shy, I don't have a good heart. Where we're going, there'll be trouble. If we're lucky, just a little, but luck ain't exactly stuck to me down the years. So listen. When I next tell you to stay out of my way, you stay out, you hear?'

'Why? Would you kill me?' She meant it half as a joke, but his cold voice struck her laughter dead.

'There's no telling what I'll do.'

The wind gusted into the silence and swept the long grass in waves and Shy thought she heard shouting sifting on it. An unmistakable note of panic.

'You hear that?'

Lamb turned his horse towards the Fellowship. 'What did I say about luck?'

They were in quite the spin, all bunched up and shouting over or riding into each other, wagons tangled and dogs darting under the wheels and children crying and a mood of terror like Glustrod had risen from the grave up ahead and was fixed on their destruction.

'Ghosts!' Shy heard someone wail. 'They'll have our ears!'

'Calm down!' Sweet was shouting. 'It ain't bloody Ghosts and they don't want your ears! Travellers like us, is all!'

Peering off to the north Shy saw a line of slow-moving riders, wriggling little specks between the vast black earth and the vast white sky.

'How can you be sure?' shrieked Lord Ingelstad, clutching a few prized possessions to his chest as if he was about to make a dash for it, though where he'd dash to was anyone's guess.

''Cause Ghosts fixed on blood don't just trot across the horizon! You lot sit tight here and try not to injure yourselves. Me and Crying Rock'll go parley.'

'Might be these travellers know something about the children,' said Lamb, and he spurred his horse after the two scouts, Shy following.

She'd thought their own Fellowship worn down and dirty, but they were a crowd of royalty beside the threadbare column of beggars they came upon, broken-down and feverish in the eyes, their horses lean round the rib and yellow at the tooth, a handful of wagons lurching after and a few flyblown cattle dragging at the rear. A Fellowship of the damned and no mistake.

'How do,' said Sweet.

'How do?' Their leader reined in, a big bastard in a tattered Union soldier's coat, gold braid around the sleeves all torn and dangling. 'How do?' He leaned from his horse and spat. 'A year older'n when we come the other way and not a fucking hour richer, that's how we do. Enough of the Far Country for these boys. We're heading back to Starikland. You want our advice, you'll do the same.'

'No gold up there?' asked Shy.

'Maybe there's some, girl, but I ain't dying for it.'

'No one's ever giving aught away,' said Sweet. 'There's always risks.'

The man snorted. 'I was laughing at the risks when I came out last year. You see me laughing now?' Shy didn't, much. 'Crease is at bloody war, killings every night and new folk piling in every day. They hardly even bother to bury the bodies any more.'

'They were always keener there on digging than filling in, as I recall,' said Sweet.

'Well, they got worse. We pushed on up to Beacon, into the hills, to find us a claim to work. Place was crawling with men hoping for the same.'

'Beacon was?' Sweet snorted. 'It weren't more'n three tents last time I was there.'

'Well, it's a whole town now. Or was, at least.'

'Was?'

'We stopped there a night or two then off into the wilds. Come back to town after we'd checked a few creeks and found naught but cold mud . . .' He ran out of words, just staring at nothing. One of his fellows took his hat off, the brim half-torn away, and looked into it. Strange to see in that hammered-out face, but there were tears in his eyes.

'And?' asked Sweet.

'Everyone gone. Two hundred people in that camp, or more. Just gone, you understand?'

'Gone where?'

'To fucking hell was our guess, and we ain't planning on joining 'em. The place empty, mark you. Meals still on the table and washing still hung out and all. And in the square we find the Dragon Circle painted ten strides across.' The man shivered. 'Fuck that, is what I'm saying.'

'Fuck it to hell,' agreed his neighbour, jamming his ruined hat back on.

'Ain't been no Dragon People seen in years,' said Sweet, but looking a little worried. He never looked worried.

'Dragon People?' asked Shy. 'What are they? A kind of Ghosts?'

'A kind,' grunted Crying Rock.

'They live way up north,' said Sweet. 'High in the mountains. They ain't to be dabbled with.'

'I'd sooner dabble with Glustrod his self,' said the man in the Union coat. 'I fought Northmen in the war and I fought Ghosts on the plains and I fought Papa Ring's men in Crease and I gave not a stride to any of 'em.' He shook his head. 'But I ain't fighting those Dragon bastards. Not if the mountains was made of gold. Sorcerers, that's what they are. Wizards and devils and I'll have none of it.'

'We appreciate the warning,' said Sweet, 'but we've come this far and I reckon we'll go on.'

'May you all get rich as Valint and Balk combined, but you'll be doing it without me.' He waved on his slumping companions. 'Let's go!'

Lamb caught him by the arm as he was turning back. 'You heard of Grega Cantliss?'

The man tugged his sleeve free. 'He works for Papa Ring, and you won't find a blacker bastard in the Far Country. A Fellowship of thirty got killed and robbed up in the hills near Crease last summer, ears cut off and skinned and interfered with, and Papa Ring said it must be Ghosts and no one proved it otherwise. But I heard a whisper it was Cantliss did it.'

'Him and us got business,' said Shy.

The man turned his sunken eyes on her. 'Then I'm sorry for you, but I ain't seen him in months and I don't plan to lay eyes on the bastard ever again. Not him, not Crease, not any part of this blasted country.' And he clicked his tongue and rode away, heading eastwards.

They sat there a moment and watched the defeated shamble back the long way to civilisation. Not a sight to make anyone too optimistic about the destination, even if they'd been prone to optimism, which Shy wasn't.

'Thought you knew everyone in the Far Country?' she said to Sweet.

The old scout shrugged. 'Those who been about a while.'

'Not this Grega Cantliss, though?'

His shrug rose higher. 'Crease is crawling with killers like a tree-stump with woodlice. I ain't out there often enough to tell one from another. We both get there alive, I can make you an introduction to the Mayor. Then you can get some answers.'

'The Mayor?'

'The Mayor runs things in Crease. Well, the Mayor and Papa Ring run things, and it's been that way ever since there was two planks nailed together in that place, and all that time neither one's been too friendly with the other. Sounds like they're getting no friendlier.'

'The Mayor can help us find Cantliss?' asked Lamb.

Sweet's shrug went higher yet. Any further and it'd knock his hat off. 'The Mayor can always help you. If you can help the Mayor.' And he gave his horse his heels and trotted back towards the Fellowship.

Oh God, the Dust

'Wake up.'

'No.' Temple strove to pull his miserable scrap of blanket over his face. 'Please, God, no.'

'You owe me one hundred and fifty-three marks,' said Shy, looking down. Every morning the same. If you could even call it morning. In the Company of the Gracious Hand, unless there was booty in the offing, few would stir until the sun was well up, and the notary stirred last of all. In the Fellowship they did things differently. Above Shy the brighter stars still twinkled, the sky about them only a shade lighter than pitch.

'Where did the debt begin?' he croaked, trying to clear yesterday's dust from his throat.

'One hundred and fifty-six.'

'What?' Nine days of back-breaking, lung-shredding, buttock-skinning labour and he had shaved a mere three marks from the bill. Say what you will about Nicomo Cosca, the old bastard had been a handsome payer.

'Buckhorm docked you three for that cow you lost yesterday.'

'I am no better than a slave,' Temple murmured bitterly.

'You're worse. A slave I could sell.' Shy poked him with her foot and he struggled grumbling up, pulled his oversized boots onto feet dewy from sticking out beyond the bottom of his undersized blanket, shrugged his fourth-hand coat over his one sweat-stiffened shirt and limped for the cook's wagon, clutching at his saddle-bludgeoned backside. He badly wanted to weep but refused to give Shy the satisfaction. Not that anything satisfied her.

He stood, sore and miserable, choking down cold water and half-raw meat that had been buried under the fire the previous night. Around him men readied themselves for the day's labours and spoke in hushed tones, words smoking on the dawn chill, of the gold that awaited them at trail's end, eyes wide with wonder as if, instead of yellow metal, it was the secret of existence they hoped to find written in the rocks of those unmapped places.

'You're riding drag again,' said Shy.

Many of Temple's previous professions had involved dirty, dangerous, desperate work but none had approached, for its excruciating mixture of tedium, discomfort, and minute wages, the task of riding drag behind a Fellowship.

'Again?' His shoulders slumped as if he had been told he would be spending the morning in hell. Which he more or less had been.

'No, I'm joking. Your legal skills are in high demand. Hedges wants you to petition the King of the Union on his behalf, Lestek's decided to form a new country and needs advice on the constitution and Crying Rock's asked for another codicil to her will.'

They stood there in the almost-darkness, the wind cutting across the emptiness and finding out the hole near his armpit.

'I'm riding drag.'

'Yes.'

Temple was tempted to beg, but this time his pride held out. Perhaps at lunch he would beg. Instead he took up the mass of decayed leather that served him for saddle and pillow both and limped for his mule. It watched him approach, eyes inflamed with hatred.

He had made every effort to cast the mule as a partner in this unfortunate business but the beast could not be persuaded to see it that way. He was its arch-enemy and it took every opportunity to bite or buck him, and had on one occasion most memorably pissed on his ill-fitting boots while he was trying to mount. By the time he had finally saddled and turned the stubborn animal towards the back of the column, the lead wagons were already rolling, their grinding wheels already sending up dust.

Oh God, the dust.

Concerned about Ghosts after Temple's encounter, Dab Sweet had led the Fellowship into a dry expanse of parched grass and sun-bleached bramble, where you only had to look at the desiccated ground to stir up dust. The further back in the column you were, the closer companions you and dust became, and Temple had spent six days at the very back. Much of the time it blotted out the sun and entombed him in a perpetual soupy gloom, landscape expunged, wagons vanished, often the cattle just ahead made insubstantial phantoms. Every part of him was dried out by wind and impregnated by dirt. And if the dust did not choke you the stink of the animals would finish the job.

He could have achieved the same effect by rubbing his arse with wire wool for fourteen hours while eating a mixture of sand and cow-shit.

No doubt he should have been revelling in his luck and thanking God that he was alive, yet he found it hard to be grateful for this purgatory of dust. Gratitude and resentment are brothers eternal, after all. Time and again he considered how he might escape, slip from beneath his smothering debt and be free, but there was no way out, let alone an easy one. Surrounded by hundreds of miles of open country and he was imprisoned as surely as if he had been in a cage. He complained bitterly to everyone who would listen, which was no one. Leef was the nearest rider, and the boy was self-evidently in the throes of an adolescent infatuation with Shy, had cast her somewhere between lover and mother, and exhibited almost comical extremes of jealousy whenever she talked or laughed with another man, which, alas for him, was often. Still, he need not have worried. Temple had no romantic designs on the ringleader of his tormentors.

Though he had to concede there was something oddly interesting about that swift, strong, certain way she had, always on the move, first to work and last to rest, standing when others sat, fiddling with her hat, or her belt, or her knife, or the buttons on her shirt. He did occasionally catch himself wondering whether she was as hard all over as her shoulder had been under his hand. As her side had been pressed up against his. Would she kiss as fiercely as she haggled . . . ?

When Sweet finally brought them to a miserable trickle of a stream, it was the best they could do to stop a stampede from cattle and people both. The animals wedged in and clambered over each other, churning the bitter water brown. Buckhorn's children frolicked and splashed. Ashjid thanked God for His bounty while his idiot nodded and chuckled and filled the drinking barrels. Iosiv Lestek dabbed his pale face and quoted pastoral poetry at length. Temple found a spot upstream and flopped down on his back in the mossy grass, smiling wide as the damp soaked gently through his clothes. His standard for a pleasurable sensation had decidedly lowered over the past few weeks. In fact he was greatly enjoying the sun's warmth on his face, until it was suddenly blotted out.

'My daughter getting her money's worth out of you?' Lamb stood over him. Luline Buckhorm had cut her childrens' hair that morning and the Northman had reluctantly allowed himself to be put at the back of the queue. He looked bigger, and harder, and even more scarred with his grey hair and beard clipped short.

'I daresay she'll turn a profit if she has to sell me for meat.'

'I wouldn't put it past her,' said Lamb, offering a canteen.

'She's a hard woman,' said Temple as he took it.

'Not all through. Saved you, didn't she?'

'She did,' he was forced to admit, though he wondered whether death would have been kinder.

'Reckon she's just soft enough, then, don't you?'

Temple swilled water around his mouth. 'She certainly seems angry about something.'

'She's been often disappointed.'

'Sad to say I doubt I'll be reversing that trend. I've always been a deeply disappointing man.'

'I know that feeling.' Lamb scratched slowly at his shortened beard. 'But there's always tomorrow. Doing better next time. That's what life is.'

'Is that why you two are out here?' asked Temple, handing back the canteen. 'For a fresh beginning?'

Lamb's eyes twitched towards him. 'Didn't Shy tell you?'

'When she talks to me it's mostly about our debt and how slowly I'm clearing it.'

'I hear that ain't moving too quick.'

'Every mark feels like a year off my life.'

Lamb squatted beside the stream. 'Shy has a brother and a sister. They were . . . taken.' He held the canteen under the water, bubbles popping. 'Bandits stole 'em, and burned our farm, and killed a friend of ours. They stole maybe twenty children all told and took them up the river towards Crease. We're following on.'

'What happens when you find them?'

He pushed the cork back into the canteen, hard enough that the scarred knuckles of his big right hand turned white. 'Whatever needs to. I made a promise to their mother to keep those children safe. I broken a lot of promises in my time. This one I mean to keep.' He took a long breath. 'And what brought you floating down the river? I've always been a poor judge of men, but you don't look the type to carve a new life from the wilderness.'

'I was running away. One way and another I've made quite a habit of it.'

'Done a fair bit myself. I find the trouble is, though, wherever you run to . . . there y'are.' He offered out his hand to pull Temple up, and Temple reached to take it, and stopped.

'You have nine fingers.'

Suddenly Lamb was frowning at him, and he didn't look like such a slow and friendly old fellow any more. 'You a missing-finger enthusiast?'

'No, but . . . I may have met one. He said he'd been sent to the Far Country to find a nine-fingered man.'

'I probably ain't the only man in the Far Country missing a finger.'

Temple felt the need to pick his words carefully. 'I have a feeling you're the sort of man that sort of man might be looking for. He had a metal eye.'

No flash of recognition. 'A man with a missing eye after a man with a missing finger. There's a song in there somewhere, I reckon. He give a name?'

'Caul Shivers.'

Lamb's scarred face twisted as though he'd bitten into something sour. 'By the dead. The past just won't stay where you put it.'

'You do know him, then?'

'I did. Long time back. But you know what they say – old milk turns sour but old scores just get sweeter.'

'Talking of scores.' A second shadow fell across him and Temple squinted around. Shy stood over him again, hands on her hips. 'One hundred and fifty-two marks. And eight bits.'

'Oh God! Why didn't you just leave me in the river?'

'It's a question I ask myself every morning.' That pointed boot of hers poked at his back. 'Now up you get. Majud wants a Bill of Ownership drawn up on a set of horses.'

'Really?' he asked, hope flickering in his breast.

'No.'

'I'm riding drag again.'

Shy only grinned, and turned, and walked away.

'Just soft enough, did you say?' Temple muttered.

Lamb stood, wiping his hands dry on the seat of his trousers. 'There's always tomorrow.'

Sweet's Crossing

'**D**id I exaggerate?' asked Sweet.

'For once,' said Corlin, 'no.'

'It surely is a big one,' muttered Lamb.

'No doubt,' added Shy. She wasn't a woman easily impressed, but the Imperial bridge at Sictus was some sight, specially for those who'd scarcely seen a thing you could call a building in weeks. It crossed the wide, slow river in five soaring spans, so high above the water you could hardly fathom the monstrous scale of it. The sculptures on its pitted pedestals were wind-worn to melted lumps, its stonework sprouted with pink-flowered weeds and ivy and even whole spreading trees, and all along its length and in clusters at both ends it was infested with itinerant humanity. Even so diminished by time it was a thing of majesty and awe, more like some wonder of the landscape than a structure man's ambition could ever have contemplated, let alone his hands assembled.

'Been standing more'n a thousand years,' said Sweet.

Shy snorted. 'Almost as long as you been sitting that saddle.'

'And in all that time I've changed my trousers but twice.'

Lamb shook his head. 'Ain't something I can endorse.'

'Changing 'em so rarely?' asked Shy.

'Changing 'em at all.'

'This'll be our last chance to trade before Crease,' said Sweet. ' 'Less we have the good luck to run into a friendly party.'

'Good luck's never a thing to count on,' said Lamb.

'Specially not in the Far Country. So make sure and buy what you need, and make sure you don't buy what you don't.' Sweet nodded at a polished chest of drawers left abandoned beside the way, fine joints all sprung open from the rain, in which a colony of huge ants appeared to have taken up residence. They'd been passing all kinds of weighty possessions over the past few miles, scattered like driftwood after a flood. Things folk had thought they couldn't live without when they and civilisation parted. Fine furniture looked a deal less appealing when you had to carry it. 'Never own a thing you couldn't swim a river with, old Corley Ball used to tell me.'

'What happened to him?' asked Shy.

'Drowned, as I understand.'

'Men rarely live by their own lessons,' murmured Lamb, hand resting on the hilt of his sword.

'No, they don't,' snapped Shy, giving him a look. 'Let's get on down there, hope to make a start on the other side before nightfall.' And she turned and waved the signal to the Fellowship to move on.

'Ain't long before she takes charge, is it?' she heard Sweet mutter.

'Not if you're lucky,' said Lamb.

Folk had swarmed to the bridge like flies to a midden, sucked in from across the wild and windy country to trade and drink, fight and fuck, laugh and cry and do whatever else folk did when they found themselves with company after weeks or months or even years without. There were trappers and hunters and adventurers, all with their own wild clothes and hair but the same wild smell and that quite ripe. There were peaceable Ghosts set on selling furs or begging up scraps or tottering about drunk as shit on their profits. There were hopeful folk on their way to the gold-fields seeking to strike it rich and bitter folk on the way back looking to forget their failures, and merchants and gamblers and whores aiming to build their fortunes on the backs of both sets and each other. All as boisterous as if the world was ending tomorrow, crowded at smoky fires among the furs staked out to dry and the furs being pressed for the long trip back where they'd make some rich fool in Adua a hat to burn their neighbours up with jealousy.

'Dab Sweet!' growled a fellow with a beard like a carpet.

'Dab Sweet!' called a tiny woman skinning a carcass five times her size.

'Dab Sweet!' shrieked a half-naked old man building a fire out of smashed picture-frames, and the old scout nodded back and gave a how-do to each, by all appearances known intimately to half the plains.

Enterprising traders had draped wagons with gaudy cloth for stalls, lining the buckled flags of the Imperial road leading up to the bridge and making a bazaar of it, ringing with shouted prices and the complaints of livestock and the rattle of goods and coinage of every stamp. A woman with eyeglasses sat behind a table made from an old door with a set of dried-out, stitched up heads arranged on it. Above a sign read *Ghost Skulls Bought and Sold.* Food, weapons, clothing, horses, spare wagon parts and anything else that might keep a man alive out in the Far Country was going for five times its value. Treasured possessions from cutlery to windowpanes, abandoned by naïve colonists, were hawked off by cannier opportunists for next to nothing.

'Reckon there'd be quite a profit in bringing swords out here and hauling furniture back,' muttered Shy.

'You've always got your eye open for a deal,' said Corlin, grinning sideways at her. You couldn't find a calmer head in a crisis but the woman had a sticky habit the rest of the time of always seeming to know better.

'They won't seek you out.' Shy dodged back in her saddle as a streak of bird shit spattered the road beside her horse. There were crowds of birds everywhere, from the huge to the tiny, squawking and twittering, circling high above, sitting in beady-eyed rows, pecking at each other over the flyblown rubbish heaps, waddling up to thieve every crumb not currently held on to and a few that were, leaving bridge, and tents, and even a fair few of the people all streaked and crusted with grey droppings.

'You'll be needing one o' these!' a merchant screamed at them, thrusting a disgruntled tomcat at Shy by the scruff of the neck while all around him from tottering towers of cages other mangy specimens stared out with the haunted look of the long-imprisoned. 'Crease is crawling with rats the size o' horses!'

'Then you'd best get some bigger cats!' Corlin shouted back, and then to Shy, 'Where's your slave got to?'

'Helping Buckhorm drive his cattle through this shambles, I daresay. And he ain't a slave,' she added, further niggled. She seemed to be forever calling upon herself to defend from others a man she'd sooner have been attacking herself.

'All right, your man-whore.'

'Ain't that either, far as I'm aware.' Shy frowned at one example of the type, peering from a greasy tent-flap with his shirt open to his belly. 'Though he does often say he's had a lot of professions . . .'

'He might want to think about going back to that one. It's about the only way I can see him clearing that debt of yours out here.'

'We'll see,' said Shy. Though she was starting to think Temple wasn't much of an investment. He'd be paying that debt 'til doomsday if he didn't die first – which looked likely – or find some other fool to stick to and slip away into the night – which looked even more likely. All those times she'd called Lamb a coward. He'd never been scared of work, at least. Never once complained, that she could recall. Temple could hardly open his mouth without bitching on the dust or the weather or the debt or his sore arse.

'I'll give him a sore arse,' she muttered, 'useless bastard . . .'

Maybe you're best off looking for the best in people but if Temple had one he was keeping it well hid. Still. What can you expect when you fish men out of the river? Heroes?

Two towers had once stood watch at each end of the bridge. At the near side they were broken off a few strides up and the fallen stone scattered and overgrown. A makeshift gate had been rigged between them – as shoddy a piece of joinery as Shy ever saw and she'd done some injuries to wood herself – bits of old wagon, crate and cask bristling with scavenged nails and even a wheel lashed to the front. A boy was perched on a sheared-off column to one side, menacing the crowds with about the most warlike expression Shy ever saw.

'Customers, Pa!' he called as Lamb and Sweet and Shy approached, the wagons of the Fellowship spread out in the crush and jolting after.

'I see 'em, son. Good work.' The one who spoke was a hulking man, bigger'n Lamb even and with a riot of ginger beard. For company he had a stringy type with the knobbliest cheeks you ever saw and a helmet looked like it had been made for a man with cheeks of only average knobbliness. It fit him like a teacup on a mace end. Another worthy made himself known on top of one of the towers, bow in hand. Red Beard stepped in front of the gate, his spear not quite pointed at them, but surely not pointed away.

'This here's our bridge,' he said.

'It's quite something.' Lamb pulled off his hat and wiped his forehead. 'Wouldn't have pegged you boys for masonry on this scale.'

Ginger Beard frowned, not sure whether he was being insulted. 'We didn't build it.'

'But it's ours!' shouted Knobbly, as though it was the shouting of it made it true.

'You big idiot!' added the boy from his pillar.

'Who says it's yours?' asked Sweet.

'Who says it isn't?' snapped Knobbly. 'Possession is most o' the law.'

Shy glanced over her shoulder but Temple was still back with the herd. 'Huh. When you actually want a bloody lawyer there's never one to hand . . .'

'You want to cross, there's a toll. A mark a body, two marks a beast, three marks a wagon.'

'Aye!' snarled the boy.

'Some doings.' Sweet shook his head as if at the decay of all things worthy. 'Charging a man just to roll where he pleases.'

'Some people will turn a profit from anything.' Temple had finally arrived astride his mule. He'd pulled the rag from his dark face and the dusty yellow stripe around his eyes lent him a clownish look. He offered up a watery smile, like it was a gift Shy should feel grateful for.

'One hundred and forty-four marks,' she said. His smile slipped and that made her feel a little better.

'Guess we'd better have a word with Majud,' said Sweet. 'See about a whip-around for the toll.'

'Hold up there,' said Shy, waving him down. 'That gate don't look up to much. Even I could kick that in.'

Red Beard planted the butt of his spear on the ground and frowned up at her. 'You want to try it, woman?'

'Try it, bitch!' shouted the boy, his voice starting somewhat to grate at Shy's nerves.

She held up her palms. 'We've no violent intentions at all, but the Ghosts ain't so peaceful lately, I hear . . .' She took a breath, and let the silence do her work for her. 'Sangeed's got his sword drawed again.'

Red Beard shifted nervously. 'Sangeed?'

'The very same.' Temple hopped aboard the plan with some nimble-ness of mind. 'The Terror of the Far Country! A Fellowship of fifty was massacred not a day's ride from here.' He opened his eyes very wide and drew his fingers down his ears. 'Not an ear left between them.'

'Saw it ourselves,' threw in Sweet. 'They done outrages upon those corpses it pains me to remember.'

'Outrages,' said Lamb. 'I was sick.'

'Him,' said Shy, 'sick. Things as they are I'd want a decent gate to hide behind. The one at the other end bad as this?'

'We don't got a gate at the other end,' said the boy, before Red Beard shut him up with a dirty look.

The damage was done, though. Shy took a sharper breath. 'Well, that's up to you, I reckon. It is your bridge. But . . .'

'What?' snapped Knobbly.

'It so happens we got a man along by the name of Abram Majud. A wonder of a smith, among other things.'

Red Beard snorted. 'And he brought his forge with him, did he?'

'Why, that he did,' said Shy. 'His Curnsbick patent portable forge.'

'His what?'

'As wondrous a creation of the modern age as your bridge is one of the ancient,' said Temple, earnest as you like.

'Half a day,' said Shy, 'and he'll have you a set of bands, bolts and hinges both ends of this bridge it'd take an army to get through.'

Red Beard licked his lips, and looked at Knobbly, and he licked his lips, too. 'All right, I tell you what, then. Half price if you fix up our gates—'

'We go free or not at all.'

'Half-price,' growled Red Beard.

'Bitch!' added his son.

Shy narrowed her eyes at him. 'What do you reckon, Sweet?'

'I reckon I've been robbed before and at least they didn't dress it up any, the—'

'Sweet?' Red Beard's tone switched from bullying to wheedling. 'You're Dab Sweet, the scout?'

'The one killed that there red bear?' asked Knobbly.

Sweet drew himself up in his saddle. 'Twisted that furry fucker's head off with these very fingers.'

'Him?' called the boy. 'He's a bloody midget!'

His father shut him up with a wave. 'No one cares how big he is. Tell you what, could we use your name on the bridge?' He swept one hand through the air, like he could see the sign already. 'We'll call it Sweet's Crossing.'

The celebrated frontiersman was all bafflement. 'It's been here a thousand years, friend. Ain't no one going to believe I built it.'

'They'll believe you use it, though. Every time you cross this river you come this way.'

'I come whatever way makes best sense on that occasion. Reckon I'd be a piss-poor pilot were it any other how, now, wouldn't I?'

'But we'll say you come this way!'

Sweet sighed. 'Sounds a damn fool notion to me but I guess it's just a name.'

'He usually charges five hundred marks for the usage of it,' put in Shy.

'What?' said Red Beard.

'What?' said Sweet.

'Why,' said Temple, nimble with this notion, too, 'there is a manu-facturer of biscuits in Adua who pays him a thousand marks a year just to put his face on the box.'

'What?' said Knobbly.

'What?' said Sweet.

'But,' went on Shy, 'seeing as we're using your bridge ourselves—'

'And it is a wonder of the ancient age,' put in Temple.

'—we can do you a cut-price deal. One hundred and fifty only, our Fellowship cross free and you can put his name to the bridge. How's that? You've made three hundred and fifty marks today and you didn't even move!'

Knobbly looked delighted with his profit. Red Beard yet doubted. 'We pay you that, what's to stop you selling his name to every other bridge, ford and ferry across the Far Country?'

'We'll draw up a contract, good and proper, and all make our marks to it.'

'A con . . . tract?' He could hardly speak the word, it was that unfamiliar. 'Where the hell you going to find a lawyer out here?'

Some days don't work out. Some days do. Shy slapped a hand down on Temple's shoulder, and he grinned at her, and she grinned back. 'We've got the good fortune to be travelling with the best damn lawyer west of Starikland!'

'He looks like a fucking beggar to me,' sneered the boy.

'Looks can lie,' said Lamb.

'So can lawyers,' said Sweet. 'It's halfway a habit with those bastards.'

'He can draw up the papers,' said Shy. 'Just twenty-five marks.' She spat in her free hand and offered it down.

'All right, then.' Red Beard smiled, or at least it looked like he might've in the midst of all that beard, and he spat, and they shook.

'In what language shall I draft the papers?' asked Temple.

Red Beard looked at Knobbly and shrugged. 'Don't matter. None of us can read.' And they turned away to see about getting the gate open.

'One hundred and nineteen marks,' muttered Temple in her ear, and while no one was looking nudged his mule forward, stood in his stirrups and shoved the boy off his perch, sending him sprawling in the mud next to the gate. 'My humble apologies,' he said. 'I did not see you there.'

He probably shouldn't have, just for that, but Shy found afterwards he'd moved up quite considerably in her estimation.

Dreams

Hedges hated this Fellowship. That stinking brown bastard Majud and that stuttering fuck Buckhorm and that old fake Sweet and their little-minded rules. Rules about when to eat and when to stop and what to drink and where to shit and what size of dog you could have along. It was worse'n being in the bloody army. Strange thing about the army – when he was in it he couldn't wait to get out, but soon as he was out he missed it.

He winced as he rubbed at his leg, trying to knead out the aches, but they was always there, laughing at him. Damn, but he was sick of being laughed at. If he'd known the wound would go bad he never would've stabbed himself. Thinking he was the clever one as he watched the rest of the battalion charge off after that arsehole Tunny. Little stab in the leg was a whole lot better than the big one through the heart, wasn't it? Except the enemy had left the wall the night before and they hadn't even had to fight. The battle over and him the only casualty, kicked out of the army with one good leg and no prospects. Misfortunes. He'd always been dogged by 'em.

The Fellowship weren't all bad, though. He turned in his battered saddle and picked out Shy South, riding back there near the cattle. She wasn't what you'd call a beauty but there was something to her, not caring about nothing, shirt dark with sweat so you could get a notion of her shape – and there was nothing wrong with it, far as he could tell. He'd always liked a strong woman. She weren't lazy either, always busy at something. No notion why she was laughing with that spice-eating arsehole Temple, worthless brown fuck if ever there was, she should've come over to him, he'd have given her something to smile at.

Hedges rubbed at his leg again, and shifted in his saddle, and spat. She was all right, but most of 'em were bastards. His eyes found Savian, swaying on his wagon-seat next to that sneering bitch of his, sharp chin up like she was better'n everyone else and Hedges in particular. He spat again. Spit was free so he might as well use plenty.

People spoke over him, looked through him, and when they passed a bottle round it never got to him, but he had eyes, and he had ears, and he'd seen that Savian in Rostod, after the massacre, dishing out orders like he was the big man, that hard-faced bitch of a niece loitering, too, maybe, and he'd heard the name *Conthus*. Heard it spoken soft and the rebels scraping the bloodstained ground with their noses like he was great Euz his self. He'd seen what he'd seen and he'd heard what he'd heard and that old bastard weren't just some other wanderer with dreams of gold. His dreams were bloodier. The worst of rebels, and no notion anyone knew it. Look at him sitting there like the last word in the argument, but Hedges would be the one had the last word. He'd had his misfortunes but he could smell an opportunity, all right. Just a case of finding out the moment to turn his secret into gold.

In the meantime, wait, and smile, and think about how much he hated that stuttering fuck Buckhorm.

He knew it was a waste of strength he didn't have, but sometimes Raynault Buckhorm hated his horse. He hated his horse, and he hated his saddle, and his canteen and his boots and his hat and his face-rag. But he knew his life depended on them sure as a climber's on his rope. There were plenty of spectacular ways to die out in the Far Country, skinned by a Ghost or struck by lightning or swept away in a flood. But most deaths out here would make a dull story. A mean horse in your string could kill you. A broken saddle-girth could kill you. A snake under your bare foot could kill you. He'd known this would be hard. Everyone had said so, shaking their heads and clucking like he was mad to go. But hearing it's one thing, and living it another. The work, the sheer graft of it, and the weather always wrong. You were burned by the sun or chafed by the rain and forever torn at by the wind, ripping across the plains to nowhere.

Sometimes he'd look out at the punishing emptiness ahead and wonder — has anyone else ever stood here? The thought would make him dizzy. How far had they come? How far still to go? What happened if Sweet didn't come back from one of his three-day scouts? Could they find their way through this ocean of grass without him?

He had to appear fixed, though, had to stay cheerful, had to be strong. Like Lamb. He took a look sideways at the big Northman, who'd got down to roll Lord Ingelstad's wagon out of a rut. Buckhorn didn't think him and all his sons could've managed it, but Lamb just shrugged it free without a word. Ten years Buckhorn's senior at the least, but might as well have been carved out of rock still, never tiring, never complaining. Folk were looking to Buckhorn for an example, and if he weakened everyone might, and then what? Turn back? He glanced over his shoulder, and though every direction looked about the same, saw failure that way.

He saw his wife, too, plodding away from the column with some of the other women to make water. He'd a sense she wasn't happy, which was a heavy burden and a sore confusion to him. Wasn't as if all this was for his benefit, was it? He'd been happy enough in Hormring, but a man should work to give his wife and children the things they haven't got, grab them a better future, and out there in the west was where he'd seen it. He didn't know what to do to make her happy. Did his husband's duties every night, didn't he, sore or not, tired or not?

Sometimes he felt like asking her – what do you want? The question sitting on his clumsy tongue but his bloody stutter would come on hard then and he never could spit it free. He'd have liked to get down and walk with her a spell, talk like they used to, but then who'd keep the cattle moving? Temple? He barked a joyless laugh at that, turned his eyes on the drifter. There was one of those fellows thought the world owed him an easy ride. One of those men floats from one disaster to another pretty as a butterfly leaving others to clean up his spillings. He wasn't even minding the task he was being paid for, just toddling along on his mule clowning with Shy South. Buckhorn shook his head at that odd couple. Out of the two of them, no doubt she was the better man.

Luline Buckhorn took her place in the circle, studiously looking outwards.

Her wagon was at a halt, as it always was unless she was on hand to shift it by force of will, three of her older children fighting over the reins, their mindless bickering floating out over the grass.

Sometimes she hated her children, with their whining and their sore spots and their endless, gripping, crushing needs. When do we stop? When do we eat? When do we get to Crease? Their impatience all the harder to bear because of her own. All desperate for anything to break up the endless plodding sameness of the trek. Must have been well into autumn now, but except for the wind having an even chillier slap to it, how could you even tell the time of year out here? So flat, so endlessly flat, and yet she still felt they were toiling always uphill, the incline greater with every day trudged by.

She heard Lady Ingelstad dropping her skirts and felt her push into place beside. It was a great equaliser, the Far Country. A woman who wouldn't have deigned to look at her back in civilisation, whose husband had sat on the Open Council of the Union, fool though he was, and here they were making piss together. Sisbet Peg took up her place in the middle of the circle, squatting over the bucket, safe from prying eyes, no more than sixteen and just married, still fresh in love and talking like her husband was the answer to every question, bless her. She'd learn.

'A good man, your husband,' said Lady Ingelstad approvingly. 'You can always rely on him to do the decent thing.'

'That you can,' said Luline, making sure she sounded proud as any wife could be.

Sometimes she hated her husband, with his grinding ignorance of her struggles, and his chafing assumptions of what was woman's work and what was man's. Like knocking in a fence-post then getting drunk was real labour, but minding a crowd of children all day and night was fun to feel grateful for. She looked up and saw white birds high in the sky, flying in a great arrow to who knew where, and wished she could join them. How many steps had she trudged beside that wagon, now?

She'd liked it in Hormring, good friends and a house she'd spent years getting just so. But no one ever asked what her dream was, oh no, she was just expected to sell her good chair and the good fire it had stood beside and chase off after his. She watched him trot up to the head of the column, pointing something out to Majud. The big men, with the big dreams to discuss.

Did it never occur to him that she might want to ride, and feel the fresh wind, and smile at the wide-open country, and rope cattle, and consider the route, and speak up in the meetings while he trudged beside the squealing wagon, and changed the shitty wrappings on their youngest, and shouted at the next three in line to stop shouting, and had his nipples chewed raw every hour or two while still being expected to have a good dinner ready and do the wifely duties every bloody night, sore or not, tired or not?

A fool question. It never did occur to him. And when it occurred to her, which was plenty, there was always something stopped her tongue sure as if she had the stutter, and made her just shrug and be sulky silent.

'Will you look at that?' murmured Lady Ingelstad. Shy South had swung down from her saddle not a dozen strides from the column and was squatting in the long grass in the shadow of her horse making a spatter, reins in her teeth and trousers around ankles, the side of her pale arse plain to see.

'Incredible,' someone muttered.

She pulled her trousers up, gave a friendly wave, then closed her belt, spat the reins into her hand and was straight back in the saddle. The whole business had taken no time at all, and been done exactly when and how she wanted. Luline Buckhorm frowned around at the outward-facing circle of women, changing over so that one of the whores could take her turn above the bucket. 'There a reason we can't do the same?' she muttered.

Lady Ingelstad turned an iron frown upon her. 'There most certainly is!' They watched Shy South ride off, shouting something to Sweet about closing the wagons up. 'Although, at present, I must confess it eludes me.'

A sharp cry from the column that sounded like her eldest daughter and Luline's heart near leaped from her chest. She took a lurching step, wild with panic, then saw the children were just fighting on the wagon's seat again, shrieking and laughing.

'Don't you worry,' said Lady Ingelstad, patting her hand as she stepped back into place in the circle. 'All's well.'

'Just so many dangers out here.' Luline took a breath and tried to calm her beating heart. 'So much could go wrong.' Sometimes she hated her family, and sometimes her love for them was like a pain in her. Probably it was a puzzle there was no solving.

'Your turn,' said Lady Ingelstad.

'Right.' Luline started hitching up her skirts as the circle closed around her. Damn, had there ever been so much trouble taken over making piss?

The famous Iosiv Lestek grunted, and squeezed, and finally spattered a few more drops into the can. 'Yes . . . yes . . .' But then the wagon jolted, pans and chests all rattling, he released his prick to grab the rail, and when he steadied himself the tap of joy was turned firmly off.

'Why is man cursed with such a thing as age?' he murmured, quoting the last line of *The Beggar's Demise*. Oh, the silence into which he had murmured those words at the peak of his powers! Oh, the applause that had flooded after! Tremendous acclaim. And now? He had supposed himself in the wilderness when his company had toured the provinces of Midderland, never guessing what real wilderness might look like. He peered out of the window at the endless grass. A great ruin hove into view, some forgotten fragment of the Empire, countless years abandoned. Toppled columns, grass-seeded walls. There were many of them scattered across this part of the Far Country, their glories faded, their stories unknown, their remains scarcely arousing interest. Relics of an age long past. Just as he was.

He remembered, with powerful nostalgia, a time in his life when he had pissed bucket-loads. Sprayed like a handpump without even considering it, then whisked onstage to bask in the glow of the sweet-smelling whale-oil lamps, to coax the sighs from the audience, to wallow in the fevered applause. That ugly pair of little trolls, playwright and manager, entreating him to stay on another season, and begging, and grovelling, and offering more while he refused to dignify them with a reply, busy with his powder. He had been invited to the Agriont to tread the stage of the palace itself before his August Majesty and the entire Closed Council! He had played the First of the Magi before the First of the Magi – how many actors could say the same? He had pranced upon a pavement of abject critics, of ruined competitors, of adoring enthusiasts and scarcely even noticed them beneath his feet. Failure was for other men to consider.

'Oh, treachery, thy noisome visage shown—'

The wagon lurched and the miserable dribblings he had laboured the last hour for slopped from the can and over his hand. He scarcely even noticed. He rubbed at his sweaty jaw. He needed to shave. Some standards had to be maintained. He was bringing culture to the wasteland, was he not? He picked up Camling's letter and scanned it once again, mouthing the words to himself. He was possessed of an excessively ornamented style, this Camling, but was pleasingly abject in his praise and appreciation, in his promises of fine treatment, in his plans for an epoch-making event to be staged within the ancient Imperial amphitheatre of Crease. A show for the ages, as he put it. A cultural extravaganza!

Iosiv Lestek was not finished yet. Not he! Redemption can come in the most unlooked-for places. And it was some while since his last hallucinatory episode. Definitely on the mend! Lestek set down the letter and boldly took up prick once again, gazing through the window at the slowly passing ruins.

'My best performance is ahead of me . . .' he grunted, gritting his teeth as he squeezed a few more drops into the can.

'Wonder what it's like,' said Sallit, staring wistfully at that bright-coloured wagon, *The Famous Iosiv Lestek* written along the side in purple letters. Not that she could read it. But that was what Luline Buckhorm had told her it said.

'What what's like?' asked Goldy, twitching the reins.

'Being an actor. Up on stage in front of an audience and all.' She'd seen some players once. Her mother and father took her. Before they died. Of course before that. Not big-city actors, but even so. She'd clapped until her hands hurt.

Goldy scraped a loose lock of hair back under her battered hat. 'Don't you play a role every time you get a customer?'

'Not quite the same, is it?'

'Never been that good at pretending,' Sallit muttered. Not pretending to like it, anyway. Got in the way of pretending not to be there at all.

'Ain't always about the fucking. Not always. Not just the fucking, anyway.' Goldy had been around. She was hellish practical. Sallit wished she could be practical. Maybe she'd get there. 'Just treat 'em like they're somebody. That's all anyone wants, ain't it?'

'I suppose.' Sallit would've liked to be treated like somebody, instead of a thing. Folk looked at her, they just saw a whore. She wondered if anyone in the Fellowship knew her name. Less feeling than for cattle, and less value placed on you, too. What would her parents have made of this, their girl a whore? But they lost their say when they died, and it seemed Sallit had lost her say as well. She guessed there was worse.

'Just a living. That's the way to look at it. You're young, love. You've got time to work.' A heated bitch was trotting along beside the column and a crowd of a dozen or more dogs of every shape and size were loping hopefully after. 'Way o' the world,' said Goldy, watching them pass. 'Put the work in, you can come out rich. Rich enough to retire comfortable, anyway. That's the dream.'

'Is it?' Sounded like a pretty poor kind of dream to Sallit. To not have the worst.

'Not much action now, that's true, but we get to Crease, you'll see the money come in. Lanklan knows what he's about, don't you worry on that score.'

Everyone wanted to get to Crease. They'd wake up talking of the route, begging Sweet to know how many miles they'd gone, how many still to go, counting them off like days of a hard sentence. But Sallit dreaded the place. Sometimes Lanklan would talk about how many lonely men were out there, eyes aglitter, and how they'd have fifty clients a day like that was something to look forward to. Sounded like hell to Sallit. Sometimes she didn't much like Lanklan, but Goldy said as pimps went he was a keeper.

Najis' squealing was building to a peak now, impossible to ignore.

'How far is it still to go?' asked Sallit, trying to cover over it with talk.

Goldy frowned out towards the horizon. 'Lot of ground and a lot of rivers.'

'That's what you said weeks back.'

'It was true then and it's true now. Don't worry, love. Dab Sweet'll get us there.'

Sallit hoped he didn't. She hoped the old scout led 'em round in a great circle and all the way back to New Keln and her mother and father smiling in the doorway of the old house. That was all she wanted. But they were dead of the shudders, and out here in the great empty was no place for dreams. She took a hard breath, rubbed the pain out of her nose, making sure not to cry. That wasn't fair on the rest. Didn't help her when they cried, did it?

'Good old Dab Sweet.' Goldy snapped the reins and clucked at the oxen. 'Never been lost in his life, I hear.'

'Not lost, then,' said Crying Rock.

Sweet took his eyes off the coming rider to squint up at her, perched on top of one of the broken walls with the sinking sun behind, swinging a loose leg, that old flag unwrapped from her head for once and her hair shook out long, silver with a few streaks of gold still in it. 'When have you ever known me to be lost?'

'When I'm not there to point the way?'

He gave a sorry grin at that. Only a couple of times on this trip he'd needed to slip off in the darkness on a clear night to fiddle at his astrolabe and take a proper bearing. He'd won it off a retired sea-captain in a card game and it had proved damned useful down the years. It was like being at sea, sometimes, the plains. Naught but the sky and the horizon and the moaning bloody cargo. A man needed a trick or two to keep pace with his legend.

That red bear? It was a spear he'd killed it with, not his bare hands, and it had been old, and slow, and not that big. But it had been a bear, and he'd killed it, all right. Why couldn't folk be satisfied with that? Dab Sweet killed a bear! But no, they had to paint a taller picture with every telling – bare hands, then saving a woman, then there were three bears – until he himself could only disappoint beside it. He leaned back against a broken pillar, arms folded, and watched that horseman coming at a gallop, no saddle, Ghost fashion, with a sour, sour feeling in his gut.

'Who made me fucking admirable?' he muttered. 'Not me, that's sure.'

'Huh,' said Crying Rock.

'I never had an elevated motive in my life.'

'Uh.'

There was a time he'd heard tales of Dab Sweet and he'd stuck thumbs in his belt and chin to the sky and tricked himself that was how his life had been. But the years scraped by hard as ever and he got less and the stories more 'til they were tales of a man he'd never met succeeding at what he'd never have dreamed of attempting. Sometimes they'd stir some splinter of remembrance of mad and desperate fights or tedious slogs to nowhere or withering passages of cold and hunger and he'd shake his head and wonder by what fucking alchemy these episodes of rank necessity were made noble adventures.

'What do they get?' he asked. 'A parcel o' stories to nod their heads to. What do I got? Naught to retire on, that's sure. Just a worn-out saddle and a sack full of other men's lies to carry.'

'Uh,' said Crying Rock, like that was just the way of things.

'Ain't fair. Just ain't fair.'

'Why would it be fair?'

He grunted his agreement to that. He wasn't getting old no more. He *was* old. His legs ached when he woke and his chest ached when he lay down and the cold got in him deep and he looked at the days behind and saw how heavily they outnumbered those ahead. He'd set to wondering how many more nights he could sleep under the pitiless sky, yet still men looked at him awestruck like he was great Juvens, and if they landed in a real fix he'd sing a storm to sleep or shoot down Ghosts with lightning from his arse. He had no lightning, not he, and sometimes after he'd talked to Majud and played that role of knows-it-all-and-never-shirks better than Iosiv Lestek himself could have managed, he'd mount his horse and his hands would be all atremble and his eye dim and he'd say to Crying Rock, 'I've lost my nerve,' and she'd just nod like that was the way of things.

'I was something once, wasn't I?' he muttered.

'You're still something,' said Crying Rock.

'What, though?'

The rider reined in a few strides distant, frowning at Sweet, and at Crying Rock, and at the ruins they were waiting in, suspicious as a spooked stag. After a moment he swung a leg over and slid down.

'Dab Sweet,' said the Ghost.

'You can speak to me.'

'I can, but why should I?'

Locway bristled up, all chafe and pout like the young ones always were. Most likely Sweet had been no different in his youth. Most likely he'd been worse, but damn if all the posturing didn't make him tired these days. He waved the Ghost down. 'All right, all right, we'll talk.' He took a breath, that sour feeling getting no sweeter. He'd been planning this a long time, argued every side of it and picked his path, but taking the last step was still proving an effort.

'Talk, then,' said Locway.

'I'm bringing a Fellowship, might be a day's quick ride south of us. They've got money.'

'Then we will take it,' said Locway.

'You'll do as you're fucking told is what you'll do,' snapped Sweet. 'Tell Sangeed to be at the place we agreed on. They're jumpy as all hell as it is. Just show yourselves in fighting style, do some riding round, shout a lot and shoot an arrow or two and they'll be keen to pay you off. Keep things easy, you understand?'

'I understand,' said Locway, but Sweet had his doubts that he knew what easy looked like.

He went close to the Ghost, their faces level since he was fortunately standing upslope, and put his thumbs in his sword-belt and jutted his jaw out. 'No killing, you hear? Nice and simple and everyone gets paid. Half for you, half for me. You tell Sangeed that.'

'I will,' said Locway, staring back, challenging him. Sweet had a sore temptation to stab him and damn the whole business. But better sense prevailed. 'What do you say to this?' Locway called to Crying Rock.

She looked down at him, hair shifting with the breeze, and kept swinging that loose leg. Just as if he hadn't spoke at all. Sweet had himself a bit of a chuckle.

'Are you laughing at me, little man?' snapped Locway.

'I'm laughing and you're here,' said Sweet. 'Draw your own fucking conclusions. Now off and tell Sangeed what I said.'

He frowned after Locway for a long time, watching him and his horse dwindle to a black spot in the sunset and thinking how this particular episode weren't likely to show up in the legend of Dab Sweet. That sour feeling was worse'n ever. But what could he do? Couldn't be guiding Fellowships for ever, could he?

'Got to have something to retire on,' he muttered. 'Ain't too greedy a dream, is it?'

He squinted up at Crying Rock, binding her hair back into that twisted flag again. Most men would've seen nothing, maybe. But he who'd known her so many years caught the disappointment in her face. Or maybe just his own, reflected back like in a still pool.

'I never been no fucking hero,' he snapped. 'Whatever they say.'

She just nodded, like that was the way of things.

The Folk were camped among the ruins, Sangeed's tall dwelling built in the angle of the fallen arm of a great statue. No one knew now who the statue had been. An old God, died and fallen away into the past, and it seemed to Locway that the Folk would soon join him.

The camp was quiet and the dwellings few, the young men ranging far to hunt. On the racks only lean shreds of meat drying. The shuttles of the blanket weavers clacked and rattled, chopping the time up into ugly moments. Brought to this, they who had ruled the plains. Weaving for a pittance, and stealing money so they could buy from their destroyers the things that should have been theirs already.

The black spots had come in the winter and carried away half the children, moaning and sweating. They had burned their dwellings and drawn the sacred circles in the earth and said the proper words but it made no difference. The world was changing, and the old rituals held no power. The children had still died, the women had still dug, the men had still wept, and Locway had wept most bitterly of all.

Sangeed had put his hand upon his shoulder and said, 'I fear not for myself. I had my time. I fear for you and the young ones, who must walk after me, and will see the end of things.' Locway feared, too. Sometimes he felt that all his life was fear. What way was that for a warrior?

He left his horse and picked his way through the camp. Sangeed was brought from his lodge, his arms across the shoulders of his two strong daughters. His spirit was being taken piece by piece. Each morning there was less of him, that mighty frame before which the world had trembled withered to a shell.

'What did Sweet say?' he whispered.

'That a Fellowship is coming, and will pay. I do not trust him.'

'He has been a friend to the Folk.' One of Sangeed's daughters wiped the spit from the corner of his slack mouth. 'We will meet him.' And already he was starting to sleep.

'We will meet him,' said Locway, but he feared what might happen.

He feared for his baby son, who only three nights before had given his first laugh and so become one of the Folk. It should have been a moment for rejoicing, but Locway had only fear in him. What world was this to be born into? In his youth the Folk's flocks and herds had been strong and numerous, and now they were stolen by the new-comers, and the good grazing cropped away by the passing Fellowships, and the beasts hunted to nothing, and the Folk scattered and taken to shameful ways. Before, the future had always looked like the past. Now he knew the past was a better place, and the future full of fear and death.

But the Folk would not fade without a fight. And so Locway sat beside his wife and son as the stars were opened, and dreamed of a better tomorrow he knew would never come.

The Wrath of God

'Don't much care for the look o' that cloud!' called Leef, pushing hair out of his face that the wind straight away snatched back into it.

'If hell has clouds,' muttered Temple, 'they look like that one.' It was a grey-black mountain on the horizon, a dark tower boiling into the very heavens, making of the sun a feeble smudge and staining the sky about it strange, warlike colours. Every time Temple checked it was closer. All the endless, shelterless Far Country to cast into shadow and where else would it go but directly over his head? Truly, he exerted an uncanny magnetism on anything dangerous.

'Let's get these fires lit and back to the wagons!' he called, as though some planks and canvas would be sure protection against the impending fury of the skies. The wind was not helping with the task. Nor did the drizzle, when it began to fall a moment later. Nor did the rain that came soon after that, whipping from everywhere at once, cutting through Temple's threadbare coat as if he was wearing nothing. He bent cursing over his little heap of cow-leavings, dissolving rapidly in his wet hands into their original, more fragrant state while he fumbled with a smouldering stick of wood.

'Ain't much fun trying to set fire to wet shit, is it?' shouted Leef.

'I've had better jobs!' Though the same sense of distasteful futility had applied to most of them, now Temple considered it.

He heard hooves and saw Shy swing from her saddle, hat clasped to her head. She had to come close and shout over the rising wind and Temple found himself momentarily distracted by her shirt, which had stuck tight to her with wet and come open a button, showing a small tanned triangle of skin below her throat and a paler one around it, sharp lines of her collarbones faintly glistening, perhaps just the suggestion of—

'I said, where's the herd?' she bellowed in his face.

'Er . . .' Temple jerked a thumb over his shoulder. 'Might be a mile behind us!'

'Storm was making 'em restless.' Leef's eyes were narrowed against the wind, or possibly at Temple, it was hard to say which.

'Buckhorm was worried they might scatter. He sent us to light some fires around the camp.' Temple pointed out the crescent of nine or ten they had managed to set a flame to before the rain came. 'Maybe steer the herd away if they panic!' Though their smouldering efforts did not look capable of diverting a herd of lambs. The wind was blowing up hard, ripping the smoke from the fires and off across the plain, making the long grass thrash, dragging the dancing seed heads out in waves and spirals. 'Where's Sweet?'

'No telling. We'll have to work this one out ourselves.' She dragged him up by his wet coat. 'You'll get no more fires lit in this! We need to get back to the wagons!'

The three of them struggled through what was now lashing rain, stung and buffeted by gusts, Shy tugging her nervous horse by the bridle. A strange gloom had settled over the plain and they scarcely saw the wagons until they stumbled upon them in a mass, folk tugging desperately at oxen, trying to hobble panicked horses and tether snapping livestock or wrestling with their own coats or oilskins, turned into thrashing adversaries by the wind.

Ashjid stood in the midst, eyes bulging with fervour, sinewy arms stretched up to the pouring heavens, the Fellowship's idiot kneeling at his feet, the whole like a sculpture of some martyred Prophet. 'There is no running from the sky!' he was shrieking, finger outstretched. 'There is no hiding from God! God is always watching!'

It seemed to Temple he was that most dangerous kind of priest – one who really believes. 'Have you ever noticed that God is wonderful at watching,' he called, 'but quite poor when it comes to helping out?'

'We got bigger worries than that fool and his idiot,' snapped Shy. 'Got to get the wagons closed up – if the herd charges through here there's no telling what'll happen!'

The rain was coming in sheets now, Temple was as wet as if he had been dunked in the bath. His first in several weeks, come to think of it. He saw Corlin, teeth gritted and her hair plastered to her skull, struggling with ropes as she tried to get some snapping canvas lashed. Lamb was near her, heavy shoulder set to a wagon and straining as if he might move it on his own. He even was, a little. Then a couple of bedraggled Suljuks jumped in beside him and between them got it rolling. Luline Buckhorn was lifting her children up into a wagon and Temple went to help them, scraping the hair from his eyes.

'Repent!' shrieked Ashjid. 'This is no storm, this is the wrath of God!'

Savian dragged him close by his torn robe. 'This is a storm. Keep talking and I'll show you the wrath of God!' And he flung the old man on the ground.

'We need to get . . .' Shy's mouth went on but the wind stole her words. She tugged at Temple and he staggered after, no more than a few steps but they might as well have been miles. It was black as night, water coursing down his face, and he was shivering with cold and fear, hands helplessly dangling. He turned, bearings suddenly fled and panic gripping him.

Which way were the wagons? Where was Shy?

One of his fires still smouldered nearby, sparks showering out into the dark, and he tottered towards it. The wind came up like a door slamming on him and he pushed and struggled, grappling at it like one drunkard with another. Then, suddenly, a sharper trickster than he, it came at him the other way and bowled him over, left him thrashing in the grass, Ashjid's mad shrieking echoing in his ears, calling on God to smite the unbeliever.

Seemed harsh. You can't just choose to believe, can you?

He crawled on hands and knees, hardly daring to stand in case he was whisked into the sky and dashed down in some distant place, bones left to bleach on earth that had never known men's footsteps. A flash split the darkness, raindrops frozen streaks and the wagons edged with white, figures caught straining as if in some mad tableau then all sunk again in rain-lashed darkness.

A moment later thunder ripped and rattled, turning Temple's knees to jelly and seeming to shake the very earth. But thunder should end and this only drummed louder and louder, the ground trembling now for certain, and Temple realised it was not thunder but hooves. Hundreds of hooves battering the earth, the cattle driven mad by the storm, so many dozen tons of meat hurtling at him where he knelt helpless. Another flash and he saw them, rendered devilish by the darkness, one heaving animal with hundreds of goring horns, a furious mass boiling across the plain towards him.

'Oh God,' he whispered, sure that, slippery as he was, death's icy grip was on him at last. 'Oh God.'

'Come on, you fucking idiot!'

Someone tugged at him and another flash showed Shy's face, hatless with hair flattened and her lips curled back, all dogged determination, and he had never been so glad to be insulted in his life. He stumbled with her, the pair of them jerked and buffeted by the wind like corks in a flood, the rain become a scriptural downpour, like to the fabled flood with which God punished the arrogance of old Sippot, the thunder of hooves merged with the thunder of the angry sky to make one terrifying din.

A double blink of lightning lit the back of a wagon, canvas awning madly jerking, and below it Leef's face, wide-eyed, shouting encouragements drowned in the wind, one arm stretched starkly out.

And suddenly that hand closed around Temple's and he was dragged inside. Another flash showed him Luline Buckhorn and some of her children, huddled together amongst the sacks and barrels along with two of the whores and one of Gentili's cousins, all wet as swimmers. Shy slithered into the wagon beside him, Leef dragging her under the arms, while outside he could hear a veritable river flowing around the wheels. Together they wrestled the flapping canvas down.

Temple fell back, in the pitch darkness, and someone sagged against him. He could hear their breath. It might have been Shy, or it might have been Leef, or it might have been Gentili's cousin, and he hardly cared which.

'God's teeth,' he muttered, 'but you get some weather out here.'

No one answered. Nothing to say, or too drained to say it, or perhaps they could not hear him for the hammering of the passing cattle and the hail battering the waxed canvas just above their heads.

The path the herd had taken wasn't hard to follow – a stretch of muddied, trampled earth veering around the camp and spreading out beyond as the cattle had scattered, here or there the corpse of a dead cow huddled, all gleaming and glistening in the bright wet morning.

'The good people of Crease may have to wait a little longer for the word of God,' said Corlin.

'Seems so.' Shy had taken it at first for a heap of wet rags. But crouching beside it she'd seen a corner of black cloth flapping with some white embroidery, and recognised Ashjid's robe. She took off her hat. Felt like the respectful thing to do. 'Ain't much left of him.'

'I suppose that's what happens when a few hundred cattle trample a man.'

'Remind me not to try it.' Shy stood and jammed her hat back on. 'Guess we'd best tell the others.'

It was all activity in the camp, folk putting right what the storm spoiled, gathering what the storm scattered. Some of the livestock might've wandered miles, Leef and a few others off rounding them up. Lamb, Savian, Majud and Temple were busy mending a wagon that the wind had dragged over and into a ditch. Well, Lamb and Savian were doing the lifting while Majud was tending to the axle with grip and hammer. Temple was holding the nails.

'Everything all right?' he asked as they walked up.

'Ashjid's dead,' said Shy.

'Dead?' grunted Lamb, setting the wagon down and slapping his hands together.

'Pretty sure,' said Corlin. 'The herd went over him.'

'Told him to stay put,' growled Savian. That man was all sentiment.

'Who's going to pray for us now?' Majud even looked worried about it.

'You need praying for?' asked Shy. 'Didn't pick you for piety.'

The merchant stroked at his pointed chin. 'Heaven is at the bottom of a full purse, but . . . I have become used to a morning prayer.'

'And me,' said Buckhorm, who'd drifted over to join the conversation with a couple of his several sons.

'What do you know,' muttered Temple. 'He made some converts after all.'

'Say, lawyer!' Shy called at him. 'Wasn't priest among your past professions?'

Temple winced and leaned in to speak quietly. 'Yes, but of all the many shameful episodes in my past, that is perhaps the one that shames me most.'

Shy shrugged. 'There's always a place for you behind the herd if that suits you better.'

Temple thought a moment, then turned to Majud. 'I was given personal instruction over the course of several years by Kahdia, High Haddish of the Great Temple in Dagoska and world-renowned orator and theologist.'

'So . . .' Buckhorm pushed his hat back with a long finger. 'Cuh . . . can you say a prayer or can't you?'

Temple sighed. 'Yes. Yes, I can.' He added in a mutter to Shy. 'A prayer from an unbelieving preacher to an unbelieving congregation from a score of nations where they all disbelieve in different things.'

Shy shrugged. 'We're in the Far Country now. Guess folk need something new to doubt.' Then, to the rest, 'He'll say the best damn prayer you ever heard! His name's Temple, ain't it? How religious can you get?'

Majud and Buckhorm traded sceptical glances. 'If a Prophet can fall from the sky, I suppose one can wash from a river, too.'

'Ain't exactly raining . . . other options.'

'It's rained everything else,' said Lamb, peering up at the heavens.

'And what shall be my fee?' asked Temple.

Majud frowned. 'We did not pay Ashjid.'

'Ashjid's only care was for God. I have myself to consider also.'

'Not to mention your debts,' added Shy.

'Not to mention those.' Temple gave Majud an admonishing glance. 'And, after all, your support for charity was clearly demonstrated when you refused to offer help to a drowning man.'

'I assure you I am as charitable as anyone, but I have the feelings of my partner Curnsbick to consider and Curnsbick has an eye on every bit.'

'So you often tell us.'

'And you were not drowning at the time, only wet.'

'One can still be charitable to the wet.'

'You weren't,' added Shy.

Majud shook his head. 'You two would sell eyeglasses to a blind man.'

'No less use than prayers to a villain,' put in Temple, with a pious fluttering of his lashes.

The merchant rubbed at his bald scalp. 'Very well. But I buy nothing without a sample. A prayer now, and if the words convince me I will pay a fair price this morning and every morning. I will hope to write it off to sundry expenses.'

'Sundry it is.' Shy leaned close to Temple. 'You wanted a break from riding drag, this could be a steady earner. Give it some belief, lawyer.'

'All right,' Temple muttered back. 'But if I'm the new priest, I want the old one's boots.' He clambered up onto one of the wagons, makeshift congregation shuffling into an awkward crescent. To Shy's surprise it was nearly half the Fellowship. Nothing moves people to prayer like death, she guessed, and last night's demonstration of God's wrath didn't hurt attendance either. All the Suljuks were there. Lady Ingelstad tall and curious. Gentili with his ancient family. Buckhorm with his young one. Most of the whores and their pimp, too, though Shy had a suspicion he was keeping an eye on his goods rather than moved by love of the Almighty.

There was a silence, punctuated only by the scraping of Hedges' knife as he salvaged the dead cattle for meat, and the scraping of Savian's shovel as he put the remains of the Fellowship's previous spiritual advisor to rest. Without his boots. Temple held one hand in the other and humbly turned his face towards the heavens. Deep and clear now, with no trace of last night's fury.

'God—'

'Close, but no!' And at that moment old Dab Sweet came riding up, reins dangling between two fingers. 'Morning, my brave companions!'

'Where the hell have you been?' called Majud.

'Scouting. It's what you pay me for, ain't it?'

'That and help in storms.'

'I can't hold your hand across every mile o' the Far Country. We been out north,' jerking his thumb over his shoulder.

'Out north,' echoed Crying Rock, who had somehow managed to ride into the encampment from the opposite direction in total silence.

'Following some Ghost signs, trying to guide you clear of any nasty surprises.'

'Ghost signs?' asked Temple, looking a little sick.

Sweet held up a calming hand. 'No need for anyone to shit their britches yet. This is the Far Country, there's always Ghosts around. Question is which ones and how many. We was worried those tracks might belong to some o' Sangeed's people.'

'And?' asked Corlin.

''Fore we could get a sight of 'em, that storm blew in. Best thing we could do was find a rock to shelter by and let it blow along.'

'Hah huh,' grunted Crying Rock, presumably in agreement.

'You should have been here,' grumbled Lord Ingelstad.

'Even I can't be everywhere, your Lordship. But keep complaining, by all means. Scorn is the scout's portion. Everyone's got a better way of doing things 'til they're called on to actually tell you what it might be. It was our surmise that among the whole Fellowship you'd enough stout hearts and level heads to see it through – not that I'd count your Lordship with either party – and what do you know?' Sweet stuck out his bottom lip and nodded around at the dripping camp and its bedraggled occupants. 'Few head of cattle lost but that was quite a storm last night. Could've been plenty worse.'

'Shall I get down?' asked Temple.

'Not on my account. What you doing up there, anyhow?'

'He was about to say the morning prayer,' said Shy.

'He was? What happened to the other God-tickler? What's his name?'

'Herd ran over him in the night,' said Corlin, without emotion wasted on the fact.

'I guess that'll do it.' Sweet reached into his saddlebag and eased out a half-full bottle. 'Well, then, have at it, lawyer.' And he treated himself to a long swig.

Temple sighed, and looked at Shy. She shrugged, and mouthed, 'Drag,' at him. He sighed again and turned his eyes skywards.

'God,' he began for a second time. 'For reasons best known to yourself, you have chosen to put a lot of bad people in the world. People who would rather steal a thing than make it. Who would rather break a thing than grow it. People who will set fire to a thing just to watch it burn. I know. I've run across a few of them. I've ridden with them.' Temple looked down for a moment. 'I suppose I've been one of them.'

'Oh, he's good,' muttered Sweet, handing the bottle to Shy. She took a taste, making sure it wasn't too deep.

'Perhaps they seem like monsters, these people.' Temple's voice rose high and fell low, hands stroking and plucking and pointing in a fashion Shy had to concede was quite arresting. 'But the truth is, it takes no sorcery to make a man do bad things. Bad company. Bad choices. Bad luck. A no more than average level of cowardice.' Shy offered the bottle to Lamb but he was fixed so tight to the sermon he didn't notice. Corlin took it instead.

'But gathered here today, humbly seeking your blessing, you see a different kind of people.' Quite a few of them, in fact, as the flock was steadily swelling. 'Not perfect, surely. Each with their faults. Some uncharitable.' And Temple gave Majud a stern look. 'Some prone to drink.' Corlin paused with the bottle halfway to her mouth. 'Some just a little on the grasping side.' His eye fell on Shy, and damn it if she didn't even feel a little shamed for a moment, and that took some heavy doing.

'But every one of these people came out here to make something!' A ripple of agreement went through the Fellowship, heads bobbing as they nodded along. 'Every one of them chose to take the hard way! The right way!' He really was good. Shy could hardly believe it was the same man who moaned ten times a day about dust, pouring out his heart like he'd God's words in him after all. 'To brave the perils of the wilderness so they could build new lives with their hands and their sweat and their righteous effort!' Temple spread his own hands wide to encompass the gathering. 'These are the good people, God! Your children, ranged before you, hopeful and persevering! Shield them from the storm! Guide them through the trials of this day, and every day!'

'Hurrah!' cried the idiot, leaping up and punching the air, faith switched smoothly to a new Prophet, whooping and capering and shouting, 'Good people! Good people!' until Corlin caught hold of him and managed to shut him up.

'Good words,' said Lamb as Temple hopped down from the wagon. 'By the dead, those were some good words.'

'Mostly another man's, if I'm honest.'

'Well, you surely say 'em like you believe 'em,' said Shy.

'A few days riding drag and you'll believe in anything,' he muttered. The congregation was drifting apart, heading to their morning tasks, a couple of them thanking Temple as they moved off to get under way. Majud was left, lips appraisingly pressed together.

'Convinced?' asked Shy.

The merchant reached into his purse – which wasn't far from a miracle in itself – and pulled out what looked like a two mark piece. 'You should have stuck to prayers,' he said to Temple. 'They're in greater demand than laws out here.' And he flicked the coin spinning into the air, flashing with the morning sun.

Temple grinned, reaching out to catch it.

Shy snatched it from the air first.

'One hundred and twelve,' she said.

The Practical Thinkers

'You owe me—'

'One hundred and two marks,' said Temple, turning over. He was already awake. He had started waking before dawn, lately, ready the moment his eyes came open.

'That's right. Get up. You're wanted.'

'I've always had that effect on women. It's a curse.'

'For them, no doubt.'

Temple sighed as he started to roll up his blanket. He was a little sore, but it would wear off. He was getting hard from the work. Tough in places that had been soft a long time. He had been obliged to tighten his belt by a couple of notches. Well, not notches exactly, but he had twice shifted the bent nail that served for a buckle in the old saddle-girth that served for a belt.

'Don't tell me,' he said. 'I'm riding drag.'

'No. Once you've led the Fellowship in prayer, Lamb's lending you his horse. You're coming hunting with me and Sweet today.'

'Do you have to taunt me like this every morning?' he asked as he pulled his boots on. 'What happened to make you this way?'

She stood looking at him, hands on hips. 'Sweet found a stretch of timber over yonder and reckons there might be game. If you'd rather ride drag, you can ride drag. Thought you might appreciate the break is all, but have it your way.' And she turned and started to walk off.

'Wait, you're serious?' Trying to hurry after her and pull on his other boot at the same time.

'Would I toy with your feelings?'

'I'm going hunting?' Sufeen had asked him to go hunting a hundred times and he had always said he could not imagine anything more boring. After a few weeks with the dust, had he been the quarry he would have dashed off laughing across the plains.

'Calm down,' said Shy. 'No one's fool enough to give you a bow. Me and Sweet'll do the shooting while Crying Rock scares up the game. You and Leef can follow on and skin, butcher and cart. Wouldn't be a bad idea to grab some wood for a shitless fire or two either.'

'Skinning, butchering and shitless fires! Yes, my Queen!' He remembered those few months butchering cattle in the sweltering meat district of Dagoska, the stink and the flies, the back-breaking effort and horrible clamour. He had thought it like hell. Now he dropped to his knees, and grabbed her hand, and kissed it in thanks for the chance.

She jerked it free. 'Stop embarrassing yourself.' It was still too dark to see her face, but he thought he could hear a smile in her voice. She slid her sheathed knife from her belt. 'You'll need this.'

'A knife of my own! And quite a large one!' He stayed on his knees and thrust his fists into the sky. 'I'm going hunting!'

One of Gentili's venerable cousins, on his way shambling past to empty his bladder, shook his head and grumbled, 'Who gives a fuck?'

As the first signs of dawn streaked the sky and the wheels of the Fellowship began to turn, the five of them rode off across the scrubby grass, Leef on an empty wagon for carrying the carcasses, Temple trying to persuade Lamb's horse that they were on the same side. They crested the edge of what passed for a valley out here but would barely have qualified as a ditch anywhere else, some ill-looking trees huddling in its base, browned and broken. Sweet sat slumped in his saddle, scanning those unpromising woods. God only knew what for.

'Look about right?' he grunted to Crying Rock.

'About.' The Ghost gave her old grey a tap with her heels and they were off down the long slope.

The lean deer that came bouncing from the trees and straight into Sweet's bolts and Shy's arrows were a different prospect from the big, soft oxen that had swung from the hooks in Dagoska's stinking warehouses, but the principles came back quickly enough. Soon Temple was making a few swift slits with the blade then peeling the skins off whole while Leef held the front hooves. He even took a sprinkling of pride in the way he got the guts sliding out in one mass, steaming in the chill morning. He showed Leef the trick of it and soon they were bloody to their elbows, and laughing, and flicking bits of gut at each other like a pair of boys.

Soon enough they had five tough little carcasses stretched out and glistening in the back of the wagon and the last skinned and headed, the offal in a flyblown heap and the hides in a red and brown tangle like clothes discarded by a set of eager swimmers.

Temple wiped Shy's knife on one of them and nodded off up the rise. 'I'd best see what's keeping those two.'

'I'll get this last one gutted.' Leef grinned up at him as he dragged himself onto Lamb's horse. 'Thanks for the pointers.'

'Teaching is the noblest of callings, Haddish Kahdia used to tell me.'

'Who's he?'

Temple thought about that. 'A good, dead man, who gave his life for mine.'

'Sounds like a shitty trade,' said Leef.

Temple snorted. 'Even I think so. I'll be back before you know it.' He pushed up the valley, following the treeline, enjoying the turn of speed he got from Lamb's horse and congratulating himself that he was finally making some progress with that boy. A hundred strides further on and he saw Sweet and Shy watching the trees from horseback.

'Can't you sluggards kill any faster?' he called at them.

'You finish that lot already?' asked Shy.

'Skinned, gutted and eager for the pot.'

'I'll be damned,' grunted Sweet, ivory-stocked flatbow propped on his thigh. 'Reckon someone who knows the difference better check up on the lawyer's handiwork. Make sure he hasn't skinned Leef by mistake.'

Shy brought her horse around and they rode back towards the wagon. 'Not bad,' she said, giving him an approving nod. It might well have been the first he had received from her, and he found he quite liked having one. 'Reckon we might make a plainsman o' you yet.'

'That or I'll make snivelling townsfolk of the lot of you.'

'Take stronger stuff than you're made of to get that done.'

'I'm made of pretty weak stuff, all in all.'

'I don't know.' She was looking sideways at him, one appraising brow up. 'I'm starting to think there might be some metal under all that paper.'

He tapped his chest with a fist. 'Tin, maybe.'

'Well, you wouldn't forge a sword from it, but tin'll make a decent bucket.'

'Or a bath.'

She closed her eyes. 'By the dead, a bath.'

'Or a roof.'

'By the dead, a roof,' as they crested the rise and looked down towards the trees, 'can you remember what a roof—'

The wagon came into view below, and the heap of skins, and next to them Leef lying on the ground. Temple knew it was him because of his boots. He couldn't see the rest, because two figures knelt over him. His first thought was that the lad must have had a fall and the other two were helping him up.

Then one turned towards them, and he was dressed in a dozen different skins all patchwork-stitched and carried a red knife. He gave a hellish shriek, tongue sticking stiff from his yawning mouth, high and heedless as a wolf at the moon, and started to bound up the slope towards them.

Temple could only sit and gawp as the Ghost rushed closer, until he could see the eyes bulging in his red-painted face. Then Shy's bowstring hummed just by his ear, and the arrow flickered across the few strides between them and into the Ghost's bare chest, stopped him cold like a slap in the face.

Temple's eyes darted to the other Ghost, standing now in a cloak of grass and bones, slipping his own bow off his back and reaching for an arrow from a skin quiver tied to his bare leg. Shy rode down the hill, giving a scream hardly more human than the Ghost's had been, tugging out that short-sword she wore.

The Ghost got his arrow free, then spun around and sat down. Temple looked over to see Sweet lowering his flatbow. 'There'll be more!' he shouted, hooking the stirrup on the end of his bow over one boot and hauling the string back with one hand, turning his horse with a twitch of the other and scanning the treeline.

The Ghost tried to lift his arrow and fumbled it, tried to reach for another, couldn't straighten his arm because of the bolt in it. He screamed something at Shy as she rode up, and she hit him across the face with her sword and sent him tumbling.

Temple spurred down the slope after her and slid from his saddle near Leef. One of the boy's legs kicked as if he was trying to get up. Shy leaned over him and he touched her hand and opened his mouth but only blood came. Blood from his mouth and from his nose and from the jagged leavings where his ear used to be and the knife-cuts in his arms and the arrow wound in his chest. Temple stared down, hands twitching in dumb helplessness.

'Get him on your horse!' snarled Shy, and Temple came alive of a sudden and seized Leef under his arms. Crying Rock had come from somewhere and was beating the Ghost Shy had shot with a club. Temple could hear the crunching of it as he started dragging Leef towards his horse, stumbled and fell, struggled up and on again.

'Leave him!' shouted Sweet. 'He's all done, a fool can see it!'

Temple ignored him, teeth gritted, trying to haul Leef up onto the horse by belt and bloody shirt. For a skinny lad he was quite the weight. 'Not leaving him,' hissed Temple. 'Not leaving him . . . not leaving him . . .'

The world was just him and Leef and the horse, just his aching muscles and the boy's dead weight and his mindless, bubbling groan. He heard the hooves of Sweet's horse thumping away. Heard shouting in no language he knew, voices hardly human. Leef lolled, and slipped, and the horse shifted, then Shy was there next to him, growling in her throat, effort and fear and anger, and together they hauled Leef up over the saddle horn, broken arrow-shaft sticking black into the air.

Temple's hands were covered in blood. He stood looking at them for a moment.

'Go!' shrieked Shy. 'Go you fucking idiot!'

He scrambled into the saddle, fumbling for the reins with sticky fingers, hammering with his heels, almost falling off as his horse – Lamb's horse – leaped into life, and he was riding, riding, wind whipping in his face, whipping the garbled shouting from his mouth, whipping the tears from his eyes. The flat horizon bounced and shuddered and Leef jolted over the saddle horn, Sweet and Crying Rock two wriggling specks against the sky. Shy up ahead, bent low over the saddle, tail of her horse streaming, and she snatched a look behind, and he saw the fear in her face, didn't want to look, had to look.

There they were at his heels like messengers from hell. Painted faces, painted horses, childishly daubed and stuck with skins, feathers, bones, teeth and one with a human hand dried and shrunken bouncing around his neck and one with a headdress made of bulls' horns and one wearing a great copper dish as a breastplate, shining and flashing with the afternoon sun, a mess of flying red and yellow hair and brandished weapons hooked and beaked and jagged-edged all screaming furiously and fixed on his most horrible murder and Temple went freezing cold right into his arse.

'Oh God oh God oh fuck oh God . . .'

His brainless swearing drumming away like the hooves of his horse

– Lamb's horse – and an arrow flickered past and into the grass. Shy screamed at him over her shoulder but the words were gone in the wind. He clung to the reins, clung to the back of Leef's shirt, his breath whooping and his shoulders itching and knowing for sure that he was a dead man and worse than dead and all he could think was that he should have ridden drag after all. Should have stayed on the hill above Averstock. Should have stepped forward when the Gurkish came for Kahdia instead of standing in that silent, helpless line of shame with all the others.

Then he saw movement up ahead and realised it was the Fellowship, shapes of wagons and cattle on the flat horizon, riders coming out to meet them. He glanced over his shoulder and saw the Ghosts were dropping back, peeling away, could hear their whooping calls, one of them sending an arrow looping towards him and falling well short and he sobbed with relief, had just the presence of mind left to rein in as he came close, his horse – Lamb's horse – quivering almost as much as he was.

Chaos among the wagons, panic spreading as if there had been six hundred Ghosts instead of six, Luline Buckhorm screaming for a missing child, Gentili all tangled up with a rust-stained breastplate even older than he was, a couple of cattle loose and charging through the midst and Majud standing on his wagon's seat and yelling demands for calm no one could hear.

'What happened?' growled Lamb, steady as ever, and Temple could only shake his head. No words in him. Had to force his aching hand open to let go of Leef's shirt as Lamb slid him from the horse and lowered him to the ground.

'Where's Corlin?' Shy was shouting, and Temple slithered from the saddle, legs numb as two dry sticks. Lamb was cutting Leef's shirt, fabric ripping under the blade, and Temple leaned down, wiping the blood away from the arrow shaft, wiping the blood but as soon as he wiped it there was more, Leef's body all slick with it.

'Give me the knife,' snapping his fingers, and Lamb pushed it into his hand and he stared at that arrow, what to do, what to do, pull it out, or cut it out, or push it through, and trying to remember what Kahdia had told him about arrow-wounds, something about what the best chance was, the best chance, but he couldn't fix on anything, and Leef's eyes were crossed, his mouth hanging open and his hair all matted with blood.

Shy scrambled down next to him and said, 'Leef? Leef?' And Lamb gently laid him flat, and Temple stuck the knife in the earth and rocked back on his heels. They came to him then in a strange rush, all the things he knew about the boy. That he'd been in love with Shy, and that Temple had been starting to win him round, that he'd lost his parents, that he'd been trying to find his brother stolen by bandits, that he'd been a good man with oxen and a hard worker . . . but all that now was hacked off in the midst and would never be resolved, all his dreams and hopes and fears ended here on the trampled grass and cut out from the world forever.

Hell of a thing.

Savian was roaring, and coughing, and pointing everywhere with his flatbow, trying to get the wagons dragged into some kind of fort with barrels and clothes-chests and rope coils stacked up to hide behind, the cattle corralled inside and the women and children to the safest place, though Shy had no notion where that might be. Folk were scrambling about like the idea of Ghosts had never been discussed before, running to do what they were told or exactly what they hadn't been, to tug at stubborn animals or find stowed weapons or save their gear or their children or just to stare and clutch at themselves like they were stabbed and their ears off already.

Iosiv Lestek's big wagon had run into a ditch and a couple of men were struggling to rock it free. 'Leave it!' shouted Savian. 'We ain't going to act our way out o' this!' And they left it colourfully advertising the world's finest theatrical entertainment to the empty plains.

Shy shouldered her way through the madness and up onto Majud's wagon. Away to the south, across the waving, shifting grass, three Ghosts rode around in circles, one shaking a horned lance at the sky, and Shy thought she could hear them singing, high and joyful. Sweet watched, his loaded flatbow propped on one knee, rubbing at his bearded jaw, and it felt like there was a small piece of calm around him she gratefully squatted in.

'How's the boy?'

'Dead,' said Shy, and it made her sick that was all she had to say.

'Ah, damn it.' Sweet gave a bitter grimace, and closed his eyes and pressed them with finger and thumb. 'Damn it.' Then he trained them on the mounted Ghosts on the horizon, shaking his head. 'Best fix ourselves on making sure the rest of us don't go the same way.'

Savian's cracked voice shouted on and all around folk were clambering onto the wagons with bows in unpractised hands, new ones never drawn with purpose and antiques long out of service.

'What are they singing of?' asked Shy, pulling an arrow from her quiver and slowly turning it round and round, feeling the roughness against her fingertips like wood was a new thing never felt before.

Sweet snorted. 'Our violent demise. They reckon it's near at hand.'

'Is it?' she couldn't help asking.

'Depends.' Sweet's jaw muscles worked under his beard, then he slowly, calmly spat. 'On whether those three are some of Sangeed's main warband or he's split it up into smaller parties.'

'And which is it?'

'Guess we can count 'em when they arrive, and if there's a few dozen we'll know we've a chance, and if there's a few hundred we'll have our profound fucking doubts.'

Buckhorm had clambered up on the wagon, a mail shirt flapping at his thighs that suited him even worse than it fitted him. 'Why are we just waiting?' he hissed, the Ghosts chased his stutter away for now. 'Why don't we move?'

Sweet turned his slow grey eyes on him. 'Move where? Ain't no castles nearby.' He looked back to the plains, empty in every direction, and the three Ghosts circling at the edge of that shallow valley, faint singing keening across the empty grass. 'One patch of nowhere's as good to die on as another.'

'Our time's better spent getting ready for what's coming than running from it.' Lamb stood tall on the next wagon. He'd built up quite the collection of knives the last few weeks and now he was checking them one by one, calm as if he was getting ready to plough a field back on the farm instead of fight for his life in wild and lawless country. More than calm, now Shy thought about it. Like it was a field he'd long dreamed of ploughing but was only now getting the chance at.

'Who are you?' she said.

He looked up from his blades for a moment. 'You know me.'

'I know a big, soft Northman scared to whip a mule. I know a beggar turned up to our farm in the night to work for crusts. I know a man used to hold my brother and sing when he had the fever. You ain't that man.'

'I am.' He stepped across the gap between the wagons, and he put his arms around her crushing tight, and she heard him whisper in her ear. 'But that's not all I am. Stay out of my way, Shy.' Then he hopped down from the wagon. 'You'd better keep her safe!' he called to Sweet.

'You joking?' The old scout was busy sighting down his bow. 'I'm counting on her to save me!'

Just then Crying Rock gave a high shout and pointed off to the south, and over the crest they boiled as if from some nightmare, relics of a savage age long past, toothed with a hundred jagged stolen blades and chipped-stone axes and sharp arrows glinting and a lifetime of laughed-at stories of massacre came boiling with them and stole Shy's breath.

'We're all going to lose our ears!' someone whimpered.

'Ain't like you use 'em now, is it?' Sweet levelled his flatbow with a grim smile. 'Looks like a few dozen to me.'

Shy knelt there trying to count them but some horses had other horses painted on their sides and some had no riders and some had two or carried scarecrow figures made to look like men and others flapping canvas stretched on sticks to make them giants bloated like bodies drowned, all swimming and blurring before her leaking eyes, mindless and deadly and unknowable as a plague.

Shy thought she could hear Temple praying. She wished she knew how.

'Easy!' Savian was shouting. 'Easy!' Shy hardly knew what he meant. One Ghost wore a hood crusted with fragments of broken glass that sparkled like jewels, mouth yawning in a spit-stringed scream. 'Stand and live! Run and die!' She'd always had a knack for running and no stomach for standing, and if there'd ever been a time to run, her whole body was telling her that time was now. 'Under that fucking paint they're just men!' A Ghost stood in his or her or its stirrups and shook a feathered lance, naked but for paint and a necklace of ears bouncing and swinging around its neck.

'Stand together or die alone!' roared Savian, and one of the whores whose name Shy had forgotten stood with a bow in her hand and her yellow hair stirred by the wind, and she nodded to Shy and Shy nodded back. Goldy, that was it. Stand together. That's why they call it a Fellowship, ain't it?

The first bowstring went, panicky and pointless, arrow falling well short, then more and Shy shot her own, barely picking out one target there were so many. Arrows flickered down and fell among the waving grass and the heaving flesh and here or there a shape tumbled from a saddle or a horse veered. The Ghost with the hood slumped back, Savian's bolt through its painted chest, but the rest swarmed up to the feeble ring of wagons and swallowed it whole, whirling and rearing and sending up a murk of dust until they and their painted horses were phantoms indeed, their screams and shrieks and animal howls disembodied and treacherous as the voices a madman hears.

Arrows dropped around Shy, zip and clatter as one tumbled from a crate, another lodged in a sack just beside her, a third left trembling in the wagon's seat. She nocked a shaft and shot again, and again, and again, shot at nothing, at anything, crying with fear and anger and her teeth crushed together and her ears full of joyous wailing and her own spat curses. Lestek's mired wagon was a red hump with shapes crawling over it, hacking it with axes, stabbing it with spears like hunters that had brought down some great beast.

A pony stuck with arrows tottered sideways past, biting at its neighbour and, while Shy stared at it, a ragged shape came hurtling over the side of the wagon. She saw just a bulging eye in a face red-painted like an eye and she grabbed at it, her finger in a mouth and ripping at a cheek and together they tumbled off the wagon, rolling in the dust. There were strong hands around her head, lifting it and twisting it while she snarled and tried to find her knife and suddenly her head burst with light and the world was quiet and strange all shuffling feet and choking dust and she felt a burning, ripping pain under her ear and she screamed and thrashed and bit at nothing but couldn't get free.

Then the weight was off and she saw Temple wrestling with the Ghost, both gripping a red knife and she clambered up, slow as corn growing, fumbled her sword free and took a step through the rocking world and stabbed the Ghost, realised it was Temple she'd stabbed they were so tangled. She caught the Ghost around the throat and clutched him close and pushed the sword into his back, dragged at it and shoved at it, scraping on bone until she had it all the way into him, hand slippery hot.

Arrows fluttered down, gentle as butterflies, and fell among the cattle and they snorted their upset, some feathered and bloodied. They jostled unhappily at each other and one of Gentili's old cousins knelt on the ground with two arrows in his side, one dangling broken.

'There! There!' And she saw something slithering in under a wagon, a clawing hand, and she stomped on it with her boot and nearly fell, and one of the miners was beside her hacking with a shovel and some of the whores stabbing at something with spears, screaming and stabbing like they were chasing a rat.

Shy caught sight of a gap between the wagons and beyond the Ghosts flooding up on foot in a gibbering crowd, and she heard Temple breathe something in some tongue of his own and a woman near her moan – or was it her voice? The heart went out of her and she took a cringing step back, as though an extra stride of mud would be a shield, all thoughts of standing far in a vanished past as the first Ghost loomed up, an antique greatsword brown with rust clutched in painted fists and a man's skull worn over its face as a mask.

Then with a roar that was half a laugh Lamb was in their midst, twisted face a grinning mockery of the man she knew, more horrible to her than any mask a Ghost might wear. His swung sword was a blur and the skull-face burst in a spray of black, body sagging like an empty sack. Savian was stabbing from a wagon with a spear, stabbing into the shrieking mass and Crying Rock beating with her club and others cutting at them and mouthing curses in every language in the Circle of the World, driving them back, driving them out. Lamb swung again and folded a ragged shape in half, kicked the corpse away, opened a great wound in a back, white splinters in red, hacking and chopping and he lifted a wriggling Ghost and dashed its head against the rim of a barrel. Shy knew she should help but instead she sat down on a wagon-wheel and was sick while Temple watched her, lying on his side, clutching at his rump where she'd stabbed him.

She saw Corlin stitching up a cut in Majud's leg, thread in her teeth, cool as ever though with sleeves red speckled to the elbow from the wounds she'd tended. Savian was already shouting out, voice gravelly hoarse, to close up the wagons, plug that gap, toss the bodies out, show 'em they were ready for more. Shy didn't reckon she was ready for more. She sat with hands braced against her knees to stop everything from shaking, blood tickling at the side of her face, sticky in her hair, staring at the corpse of the Ghost she'd killed.

They were just men, like Savian said. Now she got a proper look, she saw this one was a boy no older than Leef. No older than Leef had been. Five of the Fellowship were killed. Gentili's cousin shot with arrows, and two of Buckhorm's children found under a wagon with their ears cut off, and one of the whores had been dragged away and no one knew how or when.

There weren't many who didn't have some cuts or scrapes and none who wouldn't start when they heard a wolf howl for all their days. Shy couldn't make her hands stop trembling, ear burning where the Ghost had made a start at claiming it for a prize. She wasn't sure whether it was just a nick or if her ear was hanging by a flap and hardly dared find out.

But she had to get up. She thought of Pit and Ro out in the far wilderness, scared as she was, and that put the heat into her and got her teeth gritted and her legs moving and she growled as she dragged herself up onto Majud's wagon.

She'd half-expected the Ghosts would have vanished, drifted away like smoke on the wind, but they were there, still of this world and this time even if Shy could hardly believe it, milling in chaos or rage away across the grass, singing and wailing to each other, steel still winking.

'Kept your ears, then?' asked Sweet, and frowned as he pressed his thumb against the cut and made her wince. 'Just about.'

'They'll be coming again,' she muttered, forcing herself to look at those nightmare shapes.

'Maybe, maybe not. They're just testing us. Figuring whether they want to give us a proper try.'

Savian clambered up beside him, face set even harder and eyes even narrower than usual. 'If I was them I wouldn't stop until we were all dead.'

Sweet kept staring out across the plain. Seemed he was a man made for that purpose. 'Luckily for us, you ain't them. Might look a savage but he's a practical thinker, your average Ghost. They get angry quick but they hold no grudges. We prove hard to kill, more'n likely they'll try to talk. Get what they can by way of meat and money and move on to easier pickings.'

'We can buy our way out of this?' asked Shy.

'Ain't much God's made can't be bought out of if you've got the coin,' said Sweet, and added in a mutter, 'I hope.'

'And once we've paid,' growled Savian, 'what's to stop them following on and killing us when it suits?'

Sweet shrugged. 'You wanted predictable, you should've stayed in Starikland. This here is the Far Country.'

And at that moment the axe-scarred door of Lestek's wagon banged open and the noted actor himself struggled out, in his nightshirt, rheumy eyes wild and sparse white hair in disarray. 'Bloody critics!' he boomed, shaking an empty can at the distant Ghosts.

'It will be all right,' Temple said to Buckhorm's son. His second son, he thought. Not one of the dead ones. Of course not one of them, because it would not be all right for them, they already had lost everything. That thought was unlikely to comfort their brother, though, so Temple said, 'It will be all right,' again, and tried to make it earnest, though the painful pounding of his heart, not to mention of his wounded buttock, made his voice wobble. It sounds funny, a wounded buttock. It is not.

'It *will* be all right,' he said, as if the emphasis made it a cast-iron fact. He remembered Kahdia saying the same to him when the siege had begun, and the fires burned all across Dagoska, and it was painfully clear that nothing would be all right. It had helped, to know that someone had the strength to tell the lie. So Temple squeezed the shoulder of Buckhorm's second son and said, 'It . . . will be . . . all right,' his voice surer this time, and the boy nodded, and Temple felt stronger himself, that he could give strength to someone else. He wondered how long that strength would last when the Ghosts came again.

Buckhorm thrust his shovel into the dirt beside the graves. He still wore his old chain-mail shirt, still with the buckles done up wrong so it was twisted at the front, and he wiped his sweaty forehead with the back of his hand and left a smear of dirt across it.

'It'd mean a lot to us if you'd suh . . . say something.'

Temple blinked at him. 'Would it?' But perhaps worthwhile words could come from worthless mouths, after all.

The great majority of the Fellowship were busy strengthening the defences, such as they were, or staring at the horizon while they chewed their fingernails bloody, or too busy panicking about the great likelihood of their own deaths to concern themselves with anyone else's. In attendance about the five mounds of earth were Buckhorm, his stunned and blinking wife and their remaining brood of eight, who ranged from sorrow to terror to uncomprehending good humour; two of the whores and their pimp, who had been nowhere to be seen during the attack but had at least emerged in time to help with the digging; Gentili and two of his cousins; and Shy, frowning down at the heaped earth over Leef's grave, shovel gripped white-knuckle hard in her fists. She had small hands, Temple noticed suddenly, and felt a strange welling of sympathy for her. Or perhaps that was just self-pity. More than likely the latter.

'God,' he croaked, and had to clear his throat. 'It seems . . . sometimes . . . that you are not out here.' It had mostly seemed to

Temple, with all the blood and waste that he had seen, that He was not anywhere. 'But I know you are,' he lied. He was not paid for the truth. 'You are everywhere. Around us, and in us, and watching over us.' Not doing much about it, mind you, but that was God for you. 'I ask you . . . I beg you, watch over these boys, buried in strange earth, under strange skies. These men and women, too. You know they had their shortcomings. But they set out to make something in the wilderness.' Temple felt the sting of tears himself, had to bite his lip for a moment, look to the sky and blink them back. 'Take them to your arms, and give them peace. There are none more deserving.'

They stood in silence for a while, the wind tugging at the ragged hem of Temple's coat and snatching Shy's hair across her face, then Buckhorm held out his palm, coins glinting there. 'Thank you.'

Temple closed the drover's calloused hand with both of his. 'My honour to do it.' Words did nothing. The children were still dead. He would not take money for that, whatever his debts.

The light was starting to fade when Sweet swung down from Majud's wagon, the sky pinking in the west and streaks of black cloud spread across it like breakers on a calm sea. 'They want to talk!' he shouted. 'They've lit a fire halfway to their camp and they're waiting for word!' He looked pretty damn pleased about it. Probably Temple should have been pleased, but he was sitting near Leef's grave, weight uncomfortably shifted off his throbbing buttock, feeling as if nothing would ever please him again.

'*Now* they want to talk,' said Luline Buckhorm, bitterly. 'Now my two boys are dead.'

Sweet winced. 'Better'n when all your boys are. I'd best go out there.'

'I'll be coming,' said Lamb, dry blood still speckled on the side of his face.

'And me,' said Savian. 'Make sure those bastards don't try anything.'

Sweet combed at his beard with his fingers. 'Fair enough. Can't hurt to show 'em we've got iron in us.'

'I will be going, too.' Majud limped up, grimacing badly so that gold tooth glinted, trouser-leg flapping where Corlin had cut it free of his wound. 'I swore never to let you negotiate in my name again.'

'You bloody won't be going,' said Sweet. 'Things tend sour we might have to run, and you're running nowhere.'

Majud ventured some weight on his injured leg, grimaced again, then nodded over at Shy. 'She goes in my place, then.'

'Me?' she muttered, looking over. 'Talk to those fuckers?'

'There is no one else I trust to bargain. My partner Curnsbick would insist on the best price.'

'I could get to dislike Curnsbick without ever having met the man.'

Sweet was shaking his head. 'Sangeed won't take much to a woman being there.'

It looked to Temple as though that made up Shy's mind. 'If he's a practical thinker he'll get over it. Let's go.'

They sat in a crescent about their crackling fire, maybe a hundred strides from the Fellowship's makeshift fort, the flickering lights of their own camp dim in the distance. The Ghosts. The terrible scourge of the plains. The fabled savages of the Far Country.

Shy tried her best to stoke up a towering hatred for them, but when she thought of Leef cold under the dirt, all she felt was sick at the waste of it, and worried for his brother and hers who were still lost as ever, and worn through and chewed up and hollowed out. That and, now she saw them sitting tame with no death cries or shook weapons, she'd rarely seen so wretched-looking a set of men, and she'd spent a good stretch of her life in desperate straits and most of the rest bone-poor.

They wore half-cured hides, and ragged skins, and threadbare fragments of a dozen different scavenged costumes, the bare skin showing stretched pale and hungry-tight over the bone. One was smiling, maybe at the thought of the riches they were soon to win, and he'd but one rotten tooth in his head. Another frowned solemnly under a helmet made from a beaten-out copper kettle, spout sticking from his forehead. Shy took the old Ghost in the centre for the great Sangeed. He wore a cloak of feathers over a tarnished breastplate looked like it had made some general of the Empire proud a thousand years ago. He had three necklaces of human ears, proof she supposed of his great prowess, but he was long past his best. She could hear his breathing, wet and crackly, and one half of his leathery face sagged, the drooping corner of his mouth glistening with stray spit.

Could these ridiculous little men and the monsters that had come screaming for them on the plain be the same flesh? A lesson she should've remembered from her own time as a fearsome bandit – between the horrible and pitiful there's never much of a divide, and most of that is in how you look at it.

If anything, it was the old men on her side of the fire that scared her more now – deep-lined faces made devilish strangers by the shifting flames, eyes gleaming in chill-shadowed sockets, the head of the bolt in Savian's loaded flatbow coldly glistening, Lamb's face bent and twisted like a weather-worn tree, etched with old scars, no clue to his thoughts, not even to her who'd known him all these years. Especially not to her, maybe.

Sweet bowed his head and said a few words in the Ghosts' tongue, making big gestures with his arms. Sangeed said a few back, slow and grinding, coughed, and managed a few more.

'Just exchanging pleasantries,' Sweet explained.

'Ain't nothing pleasant about this,' snapped Shy. 'Let's get done and get back.'

'We can talk in your words,' said one of the Ghosts in a strange sort of common like he had a mouthful of gravel. He was a young one, sitting closest to Sangeed and frowning across the fire. His son, maybe. 'My name is Locway.'

'All right.' Sweet cleared his throat. 'Here's a right fucking fuck up, then, ain't it, Locway? There was no call for no one to die here. Now look. Corpses on both sides just to get to where we could've started if you'd just said how do.'

'Every man takes his life in his hands who trespasses upon our lands,' said Locway. Looked like he took himself mighty seriously, which was quite the achievement for someone wearing a ripped-up pair of old Union cavalry trousers with a beaver pelt over the crotch.

Sweet snorted. 'I was ranging these plains long before you was sucking tit, lad. And now you're going to tell me where I can ride?' He curled his tongue and spat into the fire.

'Who gives a shit who rides where?' snapped Shy. 'Ain't like it's land any sane man would want.'

The young Ghost frowned at her. 'She has a sour tongue.'

'Fuck yourself.'

'Enough,' growled Savian. 'If we're going to deal, let's deal and go.'

Locway gave Shy a hard look, then leaned to speak to Sangeed, and the so-called Emperor of the Plains mulled his words over for a moment, then croaked a few of his own.

'Five thousands of your silver marks,' said Locway, 'and twenty of cattle, and twenty of horses, and you leave with your ears. That is the word of dread Sangeed.' And the old Ghost lifted his chin and grunted.

'You can have two thousand,' said Shy.

'Three thousand, then, and the animals.' His haggling was almost as piss-weak as his clothes.

'My people agreed to two. That's what you're getting. Far as cattle go, you can have the dozen you were fool enough to make meat of with your arrows, that's all. The horses, no.'

'Then perhaps we will come and take them,' said Locway.

'You can come and fucking try.'

His face twisted and he opened his mouth to speak but Sangeed touched his shoulder and mumbled a few words, looking all the time at Sweet. The old scout nodded to him, and the young Ghost sourly worked his mouth. 'Great Sangeed accepts your offering.'

Sweet rubbed his hands on his crossed legs and smiled. 'All right, then. Good.'

'Uh.' Sangeed broke out in a lopsided grin.

'We are agreed,' said Locway, no smile of his own.

'All right,' said Shy, though she took no pleasure in it. She was worn down to a nub, just wanted to sleep. The Ghosts stirred, relaxing a little, the one with the rotten tooth grinning wider'n ever.

Lamb slowly stood, the sunset at his back, a towering piece of black with the sky all bloodstained about him.

'I've a better offer,' he said.

Sparks whirled about his flicking heels as he jumped the fire. There was a flash of orange steel and Sangeed clutched his neck, toppling backwards. Savian's bowstring went and the Ghost with the kettle fell, bolt through his mouth. Another leaped up but Lamb buried his knife in the top of his head with a crack like a log splitting.

Locway scrambled to his feet just as Shy was doing the same, but Savian dived and caught him around the neck, rolling over onto his back and bringing the Ghost with him, thrashing and twitching, a hatchet in his hand but pinned helpless, snarling at the sky.

'What you doing?' called Sweet, but there wasn't much doubt by then. Lamb was holding up the last of the Ghosts with one fist and punching him with the other, knocking out the last couple of teeth, punching him so fast Shy could hardly tell how many times, whipping sound of his arm inside his sleeve and his big fist crunching, crunching and the black outline of the Ghost's face losing all shape, and Lamb tossed his body fizzling in the fire.

Sweet took a step back from the shower of sparks. 'Fuck!' His hands tangled in his grey hair like he couldn't believe what he was seeing.

Shy could hardly believe it either, cold all over and sitting frozen, each breath whooping a little in her throat, Locway snarling and struggling still but caught tight in Savian's grip as a fly in honey.

Sangeed tottered up, one hand clutching at his chopped-open throat, clawing fingers shining with blood. He had a knife but Lamb stood waiting for it, and caught his wrist as though it was a thing ordained, and twisted it, and forced Sangeed down on his knees, drooling blood into the grass. Lamb planted one boot in the old Ghost's armpit and drew his sword with a faint ringing of steel, paused a moment to stretch his neck one way and the other, then lifted the blade and brought it down with a thud. Then another. Then another, and Lamb let go of Sangeed's limp arm, reached down and took his head by the hair, a misshapen thing now, split open down one cheek where one of Lamb's blows had gone wide of the mark.

'This is for you,' he said, and tossed it in the young Ghost's lap.

Locway stared at it, chest heaving against Savian's arm, a strip of tattoo showing below the old man's rucked-up sleeve. The Ghost's eyes moved from the head to Lamb's face, and he bared his teeth and hissed out, 'We will be coming for you! Before dawn, in the darkness, we will be coming for you!'

'No.' Lamb smiled, his teeth and his eyes and the blood streaked down his face all shining with the firelight. 'Before dawn . . .' He squatted in front of Locway, still held helpless. 'In the darkness . . .' He gently stroked the Ghost's face, the three fingers of his left hand leaving three black smears down pale cheek. 'I'll be coming for you.'

They heard sounds, out there in the night. Talking at first, muffled by the wind. People demanded to know what was being said and others hissed at them to be still. Then Temple heard a cry and clutched at Corlin's shoulder. She brushed him off.

'What's happening?' demanded Lestek.

'How can we know?' snapped Majud back.

They saw shadows shifting around the fire and a kind of gasp went through the Fellowship.

'It's a trap!' shouted Lady Ingelstad, and one of the Suljuks started yammering in words not even Temple could make sense of. A spark of panic, and there was a general shrinking back in which Temple was ashamed to say he took a willing part.

'They should never have gone out there!' croaked Hedges, as though he had been against it from the start.

'Everyone be calm.' Corlin's voice was hard and level and did no shrinking whatsoever.

'There's someone coming!' Majud pointed out into the darkness. Another spark of panic, another shrinking back in which, again, Temple was a leading participant.

'No one shoot!' Sweet's gravel bass echoed from the darkness. 'That's all I need to crown my fucking day!' And the old scout stepped into the torchlight, hands up, Shy behind him.

The Fellowship breathed a collective sigh of relief, in which Temple was among the loudest, and rolled away two barrels to let the negotiators into their makeshift fort.

'What happened?'

'Did they talk?'

'Are we safe?'

Sweet just stood there, hands on hips, slowly shaking his head. Shy frowned off at nothing. Savian came behind, narrowed eyes giving away as little as ever.

'Well?' asked Majud. 'Do we have a deal?'

'They're thinking it over,' said Lamb, bringing up the rear.

'What did you offer? What happened, damn it?'

'He killed them,' muttered Shy.

There was a moment of confused silence. 'Who killed who?' squeaked Lord Ingelstad.

'Lamb killed the Ghosts.'

'Don't overstate it,' said Sweet. 'He let one go.' And he pushed back his hat and sagged against a wagon tyre.

'Sangeed?' grunted Crying Rock. Sweet shook his head. 'Oh,' said the Ghost.

'You . . . killed them?' asked Temple.

Lamb shrugged. 'Out here when a man tries to murder you, maybe you pay him for the favour. Where I come from we got a different way of doing things.'

'He killed them?' asked Buckhorm, eyes wide with horror.

'Good!' shouted his wife, shaking one small fist. 'Good someone had the bones to do it! They got what they had coming! For my two dead boys!'

'We've got eight still living to think about!' said her husband.

'Not to mention every other person in this Fellowship!' added Lord Ingelstad.

'He was right to do it,' growled Savian. 'For those that died and those that live. You trust those fucking animals out there? Pay a man to hurt you, all you do is teach him to do it again. Better they learn to fear us.'

'So *you* say!' snapped Hedges.

'That I do,' said Savian, flat and cold. 'Look on the upside – we might've saved a great deal of money here.'

'Scant comfort if it cuh . . . if it costs us all our lives!' snapped Buckhorm.

The financial argument looked to have gone a long way towards bringing Majud around, though. 'We should have made the choice together,' he said.

'A choice between killing and dying ain't no choice at all.' And Lamb brushed through the gathering as though they were not there and to an empty patch of grass beside the nearest fire.

'Hell of a fucking gamble, ain't it?'

'A gamble with our lives!'

'A chance worth taking.'

'You are the expert,' said Majud to Sweet. 'What do you say to this?'

The old scout rubbed at the back of his neck. 'What's to be said? It's done. Ain't no undoing it. Less your niece is so good a healer she can stitch Sangeed's head back on?'

Savian did not answer.

'Didn't think so.' And Sweet climbed back up onto Majud's wagon and perched in his place behind his arrow-prickled crate, staring out across the black plain, distinguishable from the black sky now only by its lack of stars.

Temple had suffered some long and sleepless nights during his life. The night the Gurkish had finally broken through the walls and the Eaters had come for Kahdia. The night the Inquisition had swept the slums of Dagoska for treason. The night his daughter died, and the night not long after when his wife followed. But he had lived through none longer than this.

People strained their eyes into the inky nothing, occasionally raising breathless alarms at some imagined movement, the bubbling cries of one of the prospectors who had an arrow-wound in his stomach, and who Corlin did not expect to last until dawn, as the backdrop. On Savian's order, since he had stopped making suggestions and taken unquestioned command, the Fellowship lit torches and threw them out into the grass beyond the wagons. Their flickering light was almost worse than darkness because, at its edges, death always lurked.

Temple and Shy sat together in silence, with a palpable emptiness where Leef's place used to be, Lamb's contented snoring stretching out the endless time. In the end Shy nodded sideways, and leaned against him, and slept. He toyed with the idea of shouldering her off into the fire, but decided against. It could well have been his last chance to feel the touch of another person, after all. Unless he counted the Ghost who would kill him tomorrow.

As soon as there was grey light enough to see by, Sweet, Crying Rock and Savian mounted up and edged towards the trees, the rest of the Fellowship gathered breathless on the wagons to watch, hollow-eyed from fear and lack of sleep, clutching at their weapons or at each other. The three riders came back into view not long after, calling out that in the lee of the timber there were fires still smoking on which the Ghosts had burned their dead.

But they were gone. It turned out they were practical thinkers after all.

Now the enthusiasm for Lamb's courage and swift action was unanimous. Luline Buckhorm and her husband were both tearful with gratitude on behalf of their dead sons. Gentili would have done just the same in his youth, apparently. Hedges would have done it if it weren't for his leg, injured in the line of duty at the Battle of Osrung. Two of the whores offered a reward in kind, which Lamb looked minded to accept until Shy declined on his behalf. Then Lestek clambered on a wagon and suggested in quavering tones that Lamb be rewarded with four hundred marks from the money saved, which he looked minded to refuse until Shy accepted on his behalf.

Lord Ingelstad slapped Lamb on the back, and offered him a swig from his best bottle of brandy, aged for two hundred years in the family cellars in faraway Keln which were now, alas, the property of a creditor.

'My friend,' said the nobleman, 'you're a bloody hero!'

Lamb looked at him sideways as he raised the bottle. 'I'm bloody, all right.'

The Fair Price

It was cold as hell up in them hills. The children all cold, and scared, huddling together at night close to the fires with cheeks pinched and pinked and their breath smoking in each other's faces. Ro took Pit's hands and rubbed them between hers and breathed on them and tried to wrap the bald furs tighter against the dark.

Not long after they got off the boat, a man had come and said Papa Ring needed everyone and Cantliss had cursed, which never took much, and sent seven of his men off. That left just six with that bastard Blackpoint but no one spoke of running now. No one spoke much at all, as if with each mile poled or rode or trod the spirit went out of them, then the thought, and they became just meat on the hoof, trailing slack and wretched to whatever slaughterhouse Cantliss had in mind.

The woman called Bee had been sent off, too, and she'd cried and asked Cantliss, 'Where you taking the children?' And he'd sneered, 'Get back to Crease and mind your business, damn you.' So it was up to Ro and the boy Evin and a couple of the other older ones to see to the blisters and fears of the rest.

High they went into the hills, and higher, twisting by scarce-trodden ways cut by the water of long ago. They camped among great rocks that had the feel of buildings fallen, buildings ancient as the mountains. The trees grew taller and taller until they were pillars of wood that seemed to pierce the sky, their lowest branches high above, creaking in the silent forest bare of brush, without animals, without insects.

'Where you taking us?' Ro asked Cantliss for the hundredth time, and for the hundredth time he said, 'On,' jerking his unshaved face towards the grey outlines of the peaks beyond, his fancy clothes worn out to rags.

They passed through some town, all wood-built and not built well, and a lean dog barked at them but there were no people, not a one.

Blackpoint frowned up at the empty windows and licked at the gap in his teeth and said, 'Where did they all go to?' He spoke in Northern but Lamb had taught Ro enough to understand. 'I don't like it.'

Cantliss just snorted. 'You ain't meant to.'

Up, and on, and the trees withered to brown and stunted pine then twisted twig then there were no trees. It turned from icy cold to strangely warm, the soft breeze across the mountainside like breath, and then too hot, too hot, the children toiling on, pink faces sweat-beaded, up bare slopes of rock yellow with crusted sulphur, the ground warm to touch as flesh, the very land alive. Steam popped and hissed from cracks like mouths and in cupped stones lay salt-crusted pools, the water bubbling with stinking gas, frothing with multicoloured oils and Cantliss warned them not to drink for it was poison.

'This place is wrong,' said Pit.

'It's just a place.' But Ro saw the fear in the eyes of the other children, and in the eyes of Cantliss' men, and felt it, too. It was a dead place.

'Is Shy still following?'

'Course she is.' But Ro didn't think she could be, not so far as this, so far it seemed they weren't in the world any more. She could hardly remember what Shy looked like, or Lamb, or the farm as it had been. She was starting to think all that was gone, a dream, a whisper, and this was all there was.

The way grew too steep for horses, then for mules, so one man was left waiting with the animals. They climbed a deep, bare valley where the cliffs were riddled with holes too square for nature to have made, heaped mounds of broken rock beside the way that put Ro in mind of the spoil of mines. But what ancient miners had delved here and for what excavated in this blasted place she could not guess.

After a day breathing its ugly fume, noses and throats raw from the stink, they came upon a great needle of rock set on its end, pitted and stained by weather and time but bare of moss or lichen or plant of any kind. As they came close in a group all tattered reluctance, Ro saw it was covered with letters, and though she couldn't read them knew it for a warning. In the rocky walls above, the blue sky so far away, were more holes, many more, and towering, creaking scaffolds of old wood held platforms, ropes and buckets and evidence of fresh diggings.

Cantliss held up his open hand. 'Stop here.'

'What now?' asked Blackpoint, fingering the hilt of his sword.

'Now we wait.'

'How long?'

'Not long, brother.' A man leaned against a rock, quite at his ease. How Ro had missed him there she could not tell because he was by no means small. Very tall, and dark-skinned, head shaved to the faintest silver stubble, and he wore a simple robe of undyed cloth. In the crook of one heavy-muscled arm he had a staff as tall as he was, in the other hand a small and wrinkled apple. Now he bit into it and said, 'Greetings,' with his mouth half-full, and he smiled at Cantliss, and at Blackpoint and the other men, his face alive with friendly creases unfitting to these grim surroundings, and he smiled at the children, and at Ro in particular, she thought. 'Greetings, children.'

'I want my money,' said Cantliss.

The smile did not leave the old man's face. 'Of course. Because you have a hole in you and you believe gold will fill it.'

'Because I got a debt, and if I don't pay I'm a dead man.'

'We are all dead men, brother, in due course. It is how we get there that counts. But you will have your fair price.' His eyes moved over the children. 'I count but twenty.'

'Long journey,' said Blackpoint, one hand resting on his sword. 'Bound to be some wastage.'

'Nothing is bound to be, brother. What is so is so because of the choices we make.'

'I ain't the one buys children.'

'I buy them. I do not kill them. Is it the hurting of weak things that fills the hole in you?'

'I ain't got no hole in me,' said Blackpoint.

The old man took a last bite from his apple. 'No?' And he tossed the core to Blackpoint. The Northman reached for it on an instinct, then grunted. The old man had covered the ground between them in two lightning steps and struck him in the chest with the end of his staff.

Blackpoint shuddered, letting fall the core and fumbling for his sword but he had no strength left to draw it, and Ro saw it was not a staff but a spear, the long blade sticking bloody from Blackpoint's back. The old man lowered him to the ground, put a gentle hand on his face and closed his eyes.

'It is a hard thing to say, but I feel the world is better without him.'

Ro looked at the Northman's corpse, clothes already dark with blood, and found that she was glad, and did not know what that meant.

'By the dead,' breathed one of Cantliss' men, and looking up Ro saw many figures had come silent from the mines and out onto the scaffolds, looking down. Men and women of all races and ages, but all wearing the same brown cloth and all with heads shaved bald.

'A few friends,' said the old man, standing.

Cantliss' voice quavered, thin and wheedling. 'We did our best.'

'It saddens me, that this might be your best.'

'All I want is the money.'

'It saddens me, that money might be all a man wants.'

'We had a deal.'

'That also saddens me, but so we did. Your money is there.' And the old man pointed out a wooden box sitting on a rock they had passed on the way. 'I wish you joy of it.'

Cantliss snatched up the box and Ro saw the glitter of gold inside. He smiled, dirty face warm with the reflected glow. 'Let's go.' And he and his men backed off.

One of the little children started snivelling then, because little children will come to love even the hateful if that is all they have, and Ro put a hand on her shoulder and said, 'Shhh,' and tried to be brave as the old man walked up to stand towering over her.

Pit clenched his little fists and said, 'Don't hurt my sister!'

The man swiftly knelt so that his bald head was level with Ro's, huge-looking so close, and he put one great hand gently upon Ro's shoulder and one upon Pit's and he said, 'Children, my name is Waerdinur, the thirty-ninth Right Hand of the Maker, and I would never harm either one of you, nor allow anyone else so to do. I have sworn it. I have sworn to protect this sacred ground and the people upon it with my last blood and breath and only death will stop me.'

He brought out a fine chain and hung it around Ro's neck, and strung upon it, resting on her chest, was a piece of dull, grey metal in the shape of a teardrop.

'What's this?' she asked.

'It is a dragon's scale.'

'A real one?'

'Yes, a real one. We all have them.' He reached into his robe and pulled out his own to show to her.

'Why do I have one?'

He smiled, eyes glimmering with tears. 'Because you are my daughter now.' And he put his arms around her and held her very tight.

III
CREASE

'The town, with less than one thousand permanent
residents, was filled with so much vileness that
the very atmosphere appeared impregnated with
the odour of abomination; murder ran riot,
drunkenness was the rule, gambling a universal
pastime, fighting a recreation.'

J. W. Buel

Hell on the Cheap

Crease at night?

Picture hell on the cheap. Then add more whores.

The greatest settlement of the new frontier, that prospector's paradise, the Fellowship's long-anticipated destination, was wedged into a twisting valley, steep sides dotted with the wasted stumps of felled pines. It was a place of wild abandon, wild hope, wild despair, everything at extremes and nothing in moderation, dreams trodden into the muck and new ones sucked from bottles to be vomited up and trodden down in turn. A place where the strange was commonplace and the ordinary bizarre, and death might be along tomorrow so you'd best have all your fun today.

At its muddy margins, the city consisted mostly of wretched tents, scenes better left unwitnessed by mankind assaulting the eye through wind-stirred flaps. Buildings were botched together from split pine and high hopes, held up by the drunks slumped against both sides, women risking their lives to lean from wonky balconies and beckon in the business.

'It's got bigger,' said Corlin, peering through the jam of wet traffic that clogged the main street.

'Lot bigger,' grunted Savian.

'I'd have trouble saying better, though.'

Shy was trying to imagine worse. A parade of crazed expressions reeled at them through the litter-strewn mud. Faces fit for some nightmare stage show. A demented carnival permanently in town. Off-key giggling split the jagged night and moans of pleasure or horror, the calls of pawnbrokers and the snorts of livestock, the groaning of ruined bedsteads and the squeaking of ruined violins. All composing a desperate music together, no two bars alike, spilling into the night through ill-fitting doors and windows, roars of laughter at a joke or a good spin of the gaming wheel hardly to be told from roars of anger at an insult or the bad turn of a card.

'Merciful heaven,' muttered Majud, one sleeve across his face against the ever-shifting stench.

'Enough to make a man believe in God,' said Temple. 'And that He's somewhere else.'

Ruins loomed from the wet night. Columns on inhuman scale towered to either side of the main street, so thick three men couldn't have linked their arms around them. Some were toppled short, some sheared off ten strides up, some still standing so high the tops were lost to the dark above, the shifting torchlight picking out stained carvings, letters, runes in alphabets centuries forgotten, mementoes of ancient happenings, winners and losers a thousand years dust.

'What did this place used to be?' muttered Shy, neck aching from looking up.

'Cleaner, at a guess,' said Lamb.

Shacks had sprouted around those ancient columns like unruly fungi from the trunks of dead trees. Folk had built teetering scaffolds up them, and chiselled bent props into them, and hung ropes from the tops and even slung walkways between, until some were entirely obscured by incompetent carpentry, turned to nightmare ships run thousands of miles aground, decked out in torches and lanterns and garish advertising for every vice imaginable, the whole so precarious you could see the buildings shifting when the breeze got stiff.

The valley opened up as the remnants of the Fellowship threaded its way further and the general mood intensified to something between orgy, riot and an outbreak of fever. Wild-eyed revellers rushed at it all open-mouthed, fixed on ripping through a lifetime of fun before sunup, as if violence and debauch wouldn't be there on the morrow.

Shy had a feeling they would.

'It's like a battle,' grunted Savian.

'But without any sides,' said Corlin.

'Or any victory,' said Lamb.

'Just a million defeats,' muttered Temple.

Men tottered and lurched, limped and spun with gaits grotesque or comical, drunk beyond reason, or crippled in head or body, or half-mad from long months spent digging alone in high extremities where words were a memory. Shy directed her horse around a man making a spatter all down his own bare legs, trousers about ankles in the muck, cock in one wobbling hand while he slobbered at a bottle in the other.

'Where the hell do you start?' Shy heard Goldy asking her pimp. He had no answer.

The competition was humbling, all right. The women came in every shape, colour and age, lolling in the national undress of a score of different nations and displaying flesh by the acre. Gooseflesh, mostly, since the weather was tending chilly. Some cooed and simpered or blew kisses, others shrieked unconvincing promises about the quality of their services at the torchlit dark, still others abandoned even that much subtlety and thrust their hips at the passing Fellowship with the most warlike expressions. One let a pair of pendulous, blue-veined teats dangle over the rail of a balcony and called out, 'What d'you think o' these?'

Shy thought they looked about as appealing as a pair of rotten hams. You never can tell what'll light the fire in some folk, though. A man looked up eagerly with one hand down the front of his trousers noticeably yanking away, others stepping around him like a wank in the street was nothing to remark upon. Shy blew out her cheeks.

'I been to some low-down places and I done some low-down shit when I got there, but I never saw the like o' this.'

'Likewise,' muttered Lamb, frowning about with one hand resting on the hilt of his sword. Seemed to Shy it rested there a lot these days, and had got pretty comfortable too. He weren't the only one with steel to hand, mind you. The air of menace was thick enough to chew, gangs of ugly-faced and ugly-purposed men haunting the porches, armed past their armpits, aiming flinty frowns across at groups no better favoured on the other side of the way.

While they were stopped waiting for the traffic to clear, a thug with too much chin and nowhere near enough forehead stepped up to Majud's wagon and growled, 'Which side o' the street you on?'

Never a man to be rushed, Majud considered a moment before answering. 'I have purchased a plot on which I mean to site a business, but until I see it—'

'He ain't talking about plots, fool,' snorted another tough with hair so greasy he looked like he'd dipped his head in cold stew. 'He means are you on the Mayor's side or Papa Ring's side?'

'I am here to do business.' Majud snapped his reins and his wagon lurched on. 'Not to take sides.'

'Only thing on neither side o' the street is the sewer!' shouted Chinny after him. 'You want to go in the fucking sewer, do you?'

The way grew wider and busier still, a crawling sea of muck, the columns even higher above it, the ruin of an ancient theatre cut from the hillside where the valley split in two ahead of them. Sweet was waiting near a sprawling heap of building like a hundred shacks piled on top of each other. Looked as if some optimist had taken a stab at it with whitewash but given up halfway and left the rest to slowly peel, like a giant lizard in the midst of moulting.

'This here is Papa Ring's Emporium of Romance, Song and Dry Goods, known locally as the Whitehouse,' Sweet informed Shy as she hitched her horse. 'Over yonder,' and the old scout nodded across the stream that split the street in two, serving at once for drinking water and sewer and crossed by a muddle of stepping stones, wet planks and improvised bridges, 'is the Mayor's Church of Dice.'

The Mayor had occupied the ruins of some old temple – a set of pillars with half a moss-caked pediment on top – and filled in the gaps with a riot of planks to consecrate a place of worship for some very different idols.

'Though, being honest,' continued Sweet, 'they both offer fucking, drink and gambling so the distinction is largely in the signage. Come on, the Mayor's keen to meet you.' He stepped back to let a wagon clatter past, showering mud from its back wheels over all and sundry, then set off across the street.

'What shall I do?' called Temple, still on his mule with a faceful of panic.

'Take in the sights. Reckon there's a lifetime of material for a preacher. But if you're tempted by a sample, don't forget you got debts!' Shy forded the road after Lamb, trying to pick the firmest patches as the slop threatened to suck her boots right off, around a monstrous boulder she realised was the head of a fallen statue, half its face mud-sunk while the other still wore a pitted frown of majesty, then up the steps of the Mayor's Church of Dice, between two groups of frowning thugs and into the light.

The heat was a slap, such a reek of sweltering bodies that Shy – no stranger to the unwashed – felt for a moment like she might drown in it. Fires were stoked high and the air was hazy with their smoke, and chagga smoke, and the smoke from cheap lamps burning cheap oil with a fizz and sputter, and her eyes set right away to watering. Stained walls half green wood and half moss-crusted stone trickled with the wet of desperate breath. Mounted in alcoves above the swarming humanity were a dozen sets of dusty Imperial armour that must've belonged to some general of antiquity and his guards, the proud past staring down in faceless disapproval at the sorry now.

'It gets worse?' muttered Lamb.

'What gets better?' asked Sweet.

The air rang with the rattle of thrown dice and bellowed odds, thrown insults and bellowed warnings. There was a band banging away like their lives were at stake and some drunken prospectors were singing along but didn't know even a quarter of the words and were making up the balance with swears at random. A man reeled past clutching at a broken nose and blundered into the counter – gleaming wood and more'n likely the only thing in the place that came near clean – stretching what looked like half a mile and every inch crammed with clients clamouring for drink. Stepping back, Shy nearly tripped over a card-game. One of the players had a woman astride him, sucking at his face like he'd a gold nugget down his gullet and with just a bit more effort she'd get her tongue around it.

'Dab Sweet?' called a man with a beard seemed to go right up to his eyes, slapping the scout on the arm. 'Look, Sweet's back!'

'Aye, and brought a Fellowship with me.'

'No trouble with old Sangeed on the way?'

'There was,' said Sweet. 'As a result of which he's dead.'

'Dead?'

'No doubt o' that.' He jerked his thumb at Lamb. 'It was this lad did—'

But the man with all the beard was already clambering up on the nearest table sending glasses, cards and counters clattering. 'Listen up, all o' you! Dab Sweet killed that fucker Sangeed! That old Ghost bastard's dead!'

'A cheer for Dab Sweet!' someone roared, a surge of approval battered the mildewed rafters and the band struck up an even wilder tune than before.

'Hold on,' said Sweet, 'Wasn't me killed him—'

Lamb steered him on. 'Silence is the warrior's best armour, the saying goes. Just show us to the Mayor.'

They threaded through the heaving crowd, past a cage where a pair of clerks weighed out gold dust and coins in a hundred currencies and transformed it through the alchemy of the abacus to gambling chips and back. A few of the men Lamb brushed out of the way didn't much care for it, turned with a harsh word in mind, but soon reconsidered when they saw his face. Same face that, slack and sorry, boys used to laugh at back in Squaredeal. He was a man much changed since those days, all right. Or maybe just a man revealed.

A couple of nail-eyed thugs blocked the bottom of the stairs but Sweet called, 'These two are here to see the Mayor!' and bundled them up with a deal of back-slappery, along a balcony overlooking the swarming hall and to a heavy door flanked by two more hard faces.

'Here we go,' said Sweet, and knocked.

It was a woman who answered. 'Welcome to Crease,' she said.

She wore a black dress with a shine to the fabric, long-sleeved and buttoned all the way to her throat. Late in her forties was Shy's guess, hair streaked with grey. She must've been quite the beauty in her day, though, and her day weren't entirely past either. She took Shy's hand in one of hers and clasped it with the other one besides and said, 'You must be Shy. And Lamb.' She gave Lamb's weathered paw the same treatment, and he thanked her too late in a creaky voice and took his battered hat off as an afterthought, sparse hair overdue for a cut left flapping at all angles.

But the woman smiled like she'd never been treated to so gallant a gesture. She shut the door and with its solid click into the frame the madness outside was shut away and all was calm and reasonable. 'Do sit. Master Sweet has told me of your troubles. Your stolen children. A terrible thing.' And she had such pain in her face you'd have thought it was her babies had vanished.

'Aye,' muttered Shy, not sure what to do with that much sympathy.

'Would either of you care for a drink?' She poured four healthy measures of spirit without need for an answer. 'Please forgive this place, it's a struggle to get good furniture out here, as you can imagine.'

'Guess we'll manage,' said Shy, even though it was about the most comfortable chair she'd ever sat in and about the nicest room besides, Kantic hangings at the windows, candles in lamps of coloured glass, a great desk with a black leather top just a little stained with bottle rings.

She'd real fine manners, Shy thought, this woman, as she handed out the drinks. Not that haughty, down-the-nose kind that idiots thought lifted you above the crowd. The kind that made you feel you were worth something even if you were dog-tired and dog-filthy and had near worn the arse out of your trousers and not even you could tell how many hundred miles of dusty plain you'd covered since your last bath.

Shy took a sip, noted the drink was just as far out of her class as everything else, cleared her throat and said, 'We were hoping to see the Mayor.'

The woman perched herself against the edge of the desk – Shy had a feeling she'd have looked comfortable sitting on an open razor – and said, 'You are.'

'Hoping?'

'Seeing her.'

Lamb shifted awkwardly in his chair, like it was too comfortable for him to be comfortable in.

'You're a woman?' asked Shy, head somewhat scrambled from the hell outside and the clean calm in here.

The Mayor only smiled. She did that a lot but somehow you never tired of it. 'They have other words for what I am on the other side of the street, but, yes.' She tossed down her drink in a way that suggested it wasn't her first, wouldn't be her last and wouldn't make much difference either. 'Sweet tells me you're looking for someone.'

'Man by the name of Grega Cantliss,' said Shy.

'I know Cantliss. Preening scum. He robs and murders for Papa Ring.'

'Where can we find him?' asked Lamb.

'I believe he's been out of town. But I expect he'll be back before long.'

'How long are we talking about?' asked Shy.

'Forty-three days.'

That kicked the guts out of her. She'd built herself up to good news, or at least to news. Kept herself going with thoughts of Pit and Ro's smiling faces and happy hugs of reunion. Should've known better but hope's like damp – however much you try to keep it out there's always a little gets in. She knocked back the balance of her drink, not near so sweet now, and hissed, 'Shit.'

'We've come a long way.' Lamb carefully placed his own glass on the desk, and Shy noticed with a hint of worry his knuckles were white with pressure. 'I appreciate your hospitality, no doubt I do, but I ain't in any mood to fuck around. Where's Cantliss?'

'I'm rarely in the mood to fuck around either.' The rough word sounded double harsh in the Mayor's polished voice, and she held

Lamb's eye like manners or no she wasn't someone to be pushed. 'Cantliss will be back in forty-three days.'

Shy had never been one to mope. A moment to tongue at the gap between her teeth and dwell on all the unfairness the world had inflicted on her undeserving carcass and she was on to the what nexts. 'Where's the magic in forty-three days?'

'That's when things are coming to a head here in Crease.'

Shy nodded towards the window and the sounds of madness drifting through. 'Strikes me they always are.'

'Not like this one.' The Mayor stood and offered out the bottle.

'Why not?' said Shy, and Lamb and Sweet were turning nothing down either. Refusing to drink in Crease seemed wrong-headed as refusing to breathe. Especially when the drink was so fine and the air so shitty.

'Eight years we've been here, Papa Ring and I, staring across the street at each other.' The Mayor drifted to the window and looked out at the babbling carnage below. She had a trick of walking so smooth and graceful it seemed it must done with wheels rather'n legs. 'There was nothing on the map out here but a crease when we arrived. Twenty shacks among the ruins, places where trappers could see out the winter.'

Sweet chuckled. 'You were quite a sight among 'em.'

'They soon got used to me. Eight years, while the town grew up around us. We outlasted the plague, and four raids by the Ghosts, and two more by bandits, and the plague again, and after the big fire came through we rebuilt bigger and better and were ready when they found the gold and the people started coming. Eight years, staring across the street at each other, and snapping at each other, and in the end all but at war.'

'You going to come near a point?' asked Shy.

'Our feud was getting bad for business. We agreed to settle it according to mining law, which is the only kind out here for the moment, and I can assure you people take it very seriously. We treated the town as a plot with two rival claims, winner takes all.'

'Winner of what?' asked Lamb.

'A fight. Not my choice but Papa Ring manoeuvred me into it. A fight, man against man, bare-fisted, in a Circle marked out in the old amphitheatre.'

'A fight in the Circle,' muttered Lamb. 'To the death, I daresay?'

'I understand more often than not that's where these things end up. Master Sweet tells me you may have some experience in that area.'

Lamb looked over at Sweet, then glanced at Shy, then back to the Mayor and grunted, 'Some.'

There was a time, not all that long ago, Shy would've laughed her arse off at the notion of Lamb in a fight to the death. Nothing could've been less funny now.

Sweet was chuckling as he put down his empty glass, though. 'I reckon we can drop the pretence, eh?'

'What pretence?' asked Shy.

'Lamb,' said Sweet. 'That's what. You know what I call a wolf wearing a sheep mask?'

Lamb looked back at him. 'I've a feeling you can't keep it to yourself.'

'A wolf.' The old scout wagged a finger across the room, looking quite decidedly pleased with himself. 'I'd a crazy guess about you the moment I saw a big nine-fingered Northman kill the hell out o' two drifters back in Averstock. When I saw you crush Sangeed like a beetle I was sure. I must admit it did occur when I asked you along that you and the Mayor might be the answer to each other's problems—'

'Ain't you a clever little bastard?' snarled Lamb, eyes burning and the veins suddenly popping from his thick neck. 'Best be careful when you pull that mask off, fucker, you might not like what's under there!'

Sweet twitched, Shy flinched, the comfortable room of a sudden feeling balanced on the brink of a great pit and that an awful dangerous place for a chat. Then the Mayor smiled as if this was all a joke between friends, gently took Lamb's trembling hand and filled his glass, fingers lingering on his just a moment.

'Papa Ring's brought in a man to fight for him,' she carried on, smooth as ever. 'A Northman by the name of Golden.'

'Glama Golden?' Lamb shrank back into his chair like he'd been embarrassed by his own temper.

'I've heard the name,' said Shy. 'Heard it'd be a fool who'd bet against him in a fight.'

'That would depend who he was fighting. None of my men is a match for him, but you . . .' She leaned forwards and the sweet whiff of perfume, rare as gold among the reeks of Crease, even got Shy a little warm under the collar. 'Well, from what Sweet tells me, you're more than a match for anyone.'

There was a time Shy would have laughed her arse off at that, too. Now, she wasn't even near a chuckle.

'Might be my best years are behind me,' muttered Lamb.

'Come, now. I don't think either one of us is over the hill quite yet. I need your help. And I can help you.' The Mayor looked Lamb in the face and he looked back like no one else was even there. Shy got a worried feeling, then. Like she'd somehow been out-bartered by this woman without prices even being mentioned.

'What's to stop us finding the children some other how?' she snapped, her voice sounding harsh as a graveyard crow's.

'Nothing,' said the Mayor simply. 'But if you want Cantliss, Papa Ring will put himself in your way. And I'm the only one who can get him out of it. Would you say that's fair, Dab?'

'I'd say it's true,' said Sweet, still looking a little unnerved. 'Fair I'll leave to better judges.'

'But you needn't decide now. I'll arrange a room for you over at Camling's Hostelry. It's the closest thing to neutral ground we have here. If you can find your children without my help, go with my blessing. If not . . .' And the Mayor gave them one more smile. 'I'll be here.'

''Til Papa Ring kicks you out of town.'

Her eyes flickered to Shy's and there was anger there, hot and sharp. Just for a moment, then she shrugged. 'I'm still hoping to stay.' And she poured another round of drinks.

Plots

'It is a plot,' said Temple.

Majud slowly nodded. 'Undeniably.'

'Beyond that,' said Temple, 'I would not like to venture.'

Majud slowly shook his head. 'Nor I. Even as its owner.'

It appeared the amount of gold in Crease had been drastically overstated, but no one could deny there had been a mud strike here of epic proportions. There was the treacherous slop that constituted the main street and in which everyone was forced to take their wading, cursing, shuffling chances. There was the speckly filth that showered from every wagon-wheel to inconceivable heights when it was raining, sprinkling every house, column, beast and person. There was an insidious, watery muck that worked its way up from the ground, leaching into wood and canvas and blooming forth with moss and mould, leaving black tidemarks on the hems of every dress in town. There was an endless supply of dung, shit, crap and night soil, found in every colour and configuration and often in the most unlikely places. Finally, of course, there was the all-pervasive moral filth.

Majud's plot was rich in all of these and more.

An indescribably haggard individual stumbled from one of the wretched tents pitched higgledy-piggledy upon it, hawked up at great length and volume, and spat upon the rubbish-strewn mud. Then he turned the most bellicose of expressions towards Majud and Temple, scratched at his infested beard, dragged up his decaying full-body undershirt so it could instantly slump once more, and returned to the unspeakable darkness whence he came.

'The location is good,' said Majud.

'Excellent,' said Temple.

'Right on the main street.' Although Crease was so narrow that it was virtually the only street. Daylight revealed a different side to the thoroughfare: no cleaner, perhaps even less so, but at least the sense of a riot in a madhouse had faded. The flood of intoxicated criminals between the ruined columns had become a more respectable trickle. The whorehouses, gaming pits, husk-shacks and drinking dens were no doubt still taking customers but no longer advertising as if the world would end tomorrow. Premises with less spectacular strategies for fleecing passers-by came to the fore: eateries, money changers, pawnshops, blacksmiths, stables, butchers, combined stables and butchers, ratters and hatters, animal and fur traders, land agents and mineral consultancies, merchants in mining equipment of the most execrable quality, and a postal service whose representative Temple had seen dumping letters in a stream scarcely even out of town. Groups of bleary prospectors slogged miserably back to their claims, probably in hopes of scraping enough gold dust from the freezing stream-beds for another night of madness. Now and again a dishevelled Fellowship came chasing their diverse dreams into town, usually wearing the same expressions of horror and amazement that Majud and Temple had worn when they first arrived.

That was Crease for you. A place where everyone was passing through.

'I have a sign,' said Majud, patting it affectionately. It was painted clean white with gilt lettering and proclaimed: *Majud and Curnsbick Metalwork, Hinges, Nails, Tools, Wagon Fixings, High-Quality Smithing of All Varieties.* Then it said *Metalwork* in five other languages – a sensible precaution in Crease, where it sometimes seemed no two people spoke quite the same tongue, let alone read it. In Northern it had been spelled wrong, but it was still vastly superior to most of the gaudy shingles dangling over the main street. A building across the way sported a red one on which yellow letters had run into drips on the bottom edge. It read, simply, *Fuck Palace.*

'I brought it all the way from Adua,' said Majud.

'It is a noble sign, and embodies your high achievement in coming so far. All you need now is a building to hang it on.'

The merchant cleared his throat, its prominent knobble bobbing. 'I remember house-builder being among your impressive list of previous professions.'

'I remember you being unimpressed,' said Temple. ' "We need no houses out here," were your very words.'

'You have a sharp memory for conversations.'

'Those on which my life depends in particular.'

'Must I apologise at the start of our every exchange?'

'I see no pressing reason why not.'

'Then I apologise. I was wrong. You have proved yourself a staunch travelling companion, not to mention a valued leader of prayer.' A stray dog limped across the plot, sniffed at a turd, added one of its own and moved on. 'Speaking as a carpenter—'

'Ex-carpenter.'

'—how would you go about building on this plot?'

'If you held a knife to my throat?' Temple stepped forwards. His boot sank in well beyond the ankle, and it was only with considerable effort he was able to drag it squelching free.

'The ground is not the best,' Majud was forced to concede.

'The ground is always good enough if one goes deep enough. We would begin by driving piles of fresh hardwood.'

'That task would require a sturdy fellow. I will have to see if Master Lamb can spare us a day or two.'

'He is a sturdy fellow.'

'I would not care to be a pile under his hammer.'

'Nor I.' Temple had felt very much like a pile under a hammer ever since he had abandoned the Company of the Gracious Hand, and was hoping to stop. 'A hardwood frame upon the piles, then, jointed and pegged, beams to support a floor of pine plank to keep your customers well clear of the mud. Front of the ground floor for your shop, rear for office and workshop, contract a mason for a chimney-stack and a stone-built addition to house your forge. On the upper floor, quarters for you. A balcony overlooking the street appears to be the local fashion. You may festoon it with semi-naked women, should you so desire.'

'I will probably avoid the local fashion to that degree.'

'A steeply pitched roof would keep off the winter rains and accommodate an attic for storage or employees.' The building took shape in Temple's imagination, his hand sketching out the rough dimensions, the effect only slightly spoiled by a clutch of feral Ghost children frolicking naked in the shit-filled stream beyond.

Majud gave a curt nod of approval. 'You should have said architect rather than carpenter.'

'Would that have made any difference?'

'To me it would.'

'But, don't tell me, not to Curnsbick.'

'His heart is of iron—'

'I got one!' A filth-crusted individual rode squelching down the street into town, pushing his blown nag as fast as it would hobble, one arm raised high as though it held the word of the Almighty. 'I got one!' he roared again. Temple caught the telltale glint of gold in his hand. Men gave limp cheers, called out limp congratulations, gathered around to clap the prospector on the back as he slid from his horse, hoping perhaps his good fortune might rub off.

'One of the lucky ones,' said Majud as they watched him waddle, bow-legged, up the steps into the Mayor's Church of Dice, a dishevelled crowd trailing after, eager at the chance even of seeing a nugget.

'I fully expect he'll be destitute by lunchtime,' said Temple.

'You give him that long?'

One of the tent-flaps was thrust back. A grunt from within and an arc of piss emerged, spattered against the side of one of the other tents, sprinkled the mud, drooped to a dribble and stopped. The flap closed.

Majud gave vent to a heavy sigh. 'In return for your help in constructing the edifice discussed, I would be prepared to pay you the rate of one mark a day.'

Temple snorted. 'Cursbick has not chased all charity from the Circle of the World, then.'

'The Fellowship may be dissolved but still I feel a certain duty of care towards those I travelled with.'

'That, or you expected to find a carpenter here but now perceive the local workmanship to be . . . inferior.' Temple cocked a brow at the building beside the plot, every door and window-frame at its own wrong angle, leaning sideways even with the support of an ancient stone block half-sunk in the ground. 'Perhaps you would like a place of business that will not wash away in the next shower. Does the weather get harsh here, do you suppose, in winter?'

A brief pause while the wind blew up chill and made the canvas of the tents flap and the wood of the surrounding buildings creak alarmingly. 'What fee would you demand?' asked Majud.

Temple had been giving serious consideration to the idea of slipping away and leaving his debt to Shy South forever stalled at seventy-six marks. But the sad fact was he had nowhere to slip to and no one to slip with, and was even more useless alone than in company. That left him with money to find. 'Three marks a day.' A quarter of what Cosca used to pay him, but ten times his wages riding drag.

Majud clicked his tongue. 'Ridiculous. That is the lawyer in you speaking.'

'He is a close friend of the carpenter.'

'How do I know your work will be worth the price?'

'I challenge you to find anyone less than entirely satisfied with the quality of my joinery.'

'You have built no houses here!'

'Then yours shall be unique. Customers will flock to see it.'

'One and a half marks a day. Any more and Curnsbick will have my head!'

'I would hate to have your death upon my conscience. Two it is, with meals and lodging provided.' And Temple held out his hand.

Majud regarded it without enthusiasm. 'Shy South has set an ugly precedent for negotiation.'

'Her ruthlessness approaches Master Curnsbick's. Perhaps they should go into business together.'

'If two jackals can share a carcass.' They shook. Then they considered the plot again. The intervening time had in no way improved it.

'The first step would be to clear the ground,' said Majud.

'I agree. Its current state is a veritable offence against God. Not to mention public health.' Another occupant had emerged from a structure of mildewed cloth sagging so badly that it must have been virtually touching the mud inside. This one wore nothing but a long grey beard not quite long enough to protect his dignity, or at least everyone else's, and a belt with a large knife sheathed upon it. He sat down in the dirt and started chewing savagely at a bone. 'Master Lamb's help might come in useful there also.'

'Doubtless.' Majud clapped him on the shoulder. 'I shall seek out the Northman while you begin the clearance.'

'Me?'

'Who else?'

'I am a carpenter, not a bailiff!'

'A day ago you were a priest and cattleman and a moment before that a lawyer! A man of your varied talents will, I feel sure, find a way.' And Majud was already hopping briskly off down the street.

Temple rolled his eyes from the earthbound refuse to the clean, blue heavens. 'I'm not saying I don't deserve it, but you surely love to test a man.' Then he hitched up his trouser-legs and stepped gingerly towards the naked beggar with the bone, limping somewhat since the buttock Shy pricked on the plains was still troubling him in the mornings.

'Good day!' he called.

The man squinted up at him, sucking a strip of gristle from his bone. 'I don't fucking think so. You got a drink?'

'I thought it best to stop.'

'Then you need a good fucking reason to bother me, boy.'

'I have a reason. Whether you will consider it a good one I profoundly doubt.'

'You can but try.'

'The fact is,' ventured Temple, 'we will soon be building on this plot.'

'How you going to manage that with me here?'

'I was hoping you could be persuaded to move.'

The beggar checked every part of his bone for further sustenance and, finding none, tossed it at Temple. It bounced off his shirt. 'You ain't going to persuade me o' nothing without a drink.'

'The thing is, this plot belongs to my employer, Abram Majud, and—'

'Who says so?'

'Who . . . says?'

'Do I fucking stutter?' The man took out his knife as if he had some everyday task that required one, but the subtext was plain. It really was a very large blade and, given the prevailing filthiness of everything else within ten strides, impressively clean, edge glittering with the morning sun. 'I asked who says?'

Temple took a wobbly step back. Straight into something very solid. He spun about, expecting to find himself face to face with one of the other tent-dwellers, probably sporting an even bigger knife – God knew there were so many big knives in Crease the distinction between them and swords was a total blur – and was hugely relieved to find Lamb towering over him.

'*I* say,' said Lamb to the beggar. 'You could ignore me. You could wave that knife around a little more. But you might find you're wearing it up your arse.'

The man looked down at his blade, perhaps wishing he had opted for a smaller one after all. Then he put it sheepishly away. 'Reckon I'll just move along.'

Lamb gave that a nod. 'I reckon.'

'Can I get my trousers?'

'You'd fucking better.'

He ducked into his tent and came out buttoning up the most ragged article of clothing Temple ever saw. 'I'll leave the tent, if it's all the same. Ain't that good a one.'

'You don't say,' said Temple.

The man loitered a moment longer. 'Any chance of that drink do you—'

'Get gone,' growled Lamb, and the beggar scampered off like he'd a mean dog at his heels.

'There you are, Master Lamb!' Majud waded over, trouser-legs held up by both hands to display two lean lengths of muddy calf. 'I was hoping to persuade you to work on my behalf and here I find you already hard at it!'

'It's nothing,' said Lamb.

'Still, if you could help us clear the site I'd be happy to pay you—'

'Don't worry about it.'

'Truly?' The watery sun gleamed from Majud's golden tooth. 'If you were to do me this favour I would consider you a friend for life!'

'I should warn you, friend o' mine can be a dangerous position.'

'I feel it is worth the risk.'

'If it'll save a couple of bits,' threw in Temple.

'I got all the money I need,' said Lamb, 'but I always been sadly short on friends.' He frowned over at the vagrant with the underclothes, just poking his head out of his tent and into the light. 'You!' And the man darted back inside like a tortoise into its shell.

Majud raised his brows at Temple. 'If only everyone was so accommodating.'

'Not everyone has been obliged to sell themselves into slavery.'

'You could've said no.' Shy was on the rickety porch of the building next door, leaning on the rail with boots crossed and fingers dangling. For a moment Temple hardly recognised her. She had a new shirt, sleeves rolled up with her tanned forearms showing, one with the old rope burn coiled pink around it, a sheepskin vest on top which was no doubt yellow by any reasonable estimation but looked white as a heavenly visitation in the midst of all that dirt. The same stained hat but tipped back, hair less greasy and more red, stirring in the breeze.

Temple stood and looked at her, and found he quite enjoyed it. 'You look . . .'

'Clean?'

'Something like that.'

'You look . . . surprised.'

'Little bit.'

'Did you think I stunk out of choice?'

'No, I thought you couldn't help yourself.'

She spat daintily through the gap between her front teeth, narrowly missing his boots. 'Then you discover your error. The Mayor was kind enough to lend me her bath.'

'Bathing with the Mayor, eh?'

She winked. 'Moving up in the world.'

Temple plucked at his own shirt, only held together by the more stubborn stains. 'Do you think she'd give me a bath?'

'You could ask. But I reckon there's about a four in five chance she'd have you killed.'

'I like those odds. Lots of people are five in five on my untimely death.'

'Something to do with you being a lawyer?'

'As of today, I will have you know, I am a carpenter and architect.'

'Well, your professions slip on and off easy as a whore's drawers, don't they?'

'A man must follow the opportunities.' He turned to take in the plot with an airy wave. 'I am contracted to build upon this unrivalled site a residence and place of business for the firm of Majud and Curnsbick.'

'My congratulations on leaving the legal profession and becoming a respectable member of the community.'

'Do they have such a thing in Crease?'

'Not yet, but I reckon it's on the way. You stick a bunch of drunken murderers together, ain't long before some turn to thieving, then to lying, then to bad language, and pretty soon to sobriety, raising families and making an honest living.'

'It's a slippery slope, all right.' Temple watched Lamb shepherd a tangle-haired drunkard off the plot, few possessions dragging in the muck behind him. 'Is the Mayor going to help you find your brother and sister?'

Shy gave a long sigh. 'Maybe. But she's got a price.'

'Nothing comes for free.'

'Nothing. How's carpenter's pay?'

Temple winced. 'Barely enough to scrape by on, sadly—'

'Two marks a day, plus benefits!' called Majud as he dismantled the most recently vacated tent. 'I've known bandits kinder to their victims!'

'Two marks from that miser?' Shy gave an approving nod. 'Well done. I'll take a mark a day towards the debt.'

'A mark,' Temple managed to force out. 'Very reasonable.' If there was a God His bounty was only lent, never given.

'I thought the Fellowship dissolved!' Dab Sweet pulled his horse up beside the plot, Crying Rock haunting his shoulder. Neither of them appeared to have ventured within spitting range of a bath, or a change of clothes either. Temple found that strangely reassuring. 'Buckhorm's out of town with his grass and his water, Lestek's dressing the theatre for his grand debut and most of the rest split up to dig gold their own way, but here's the four of you still, inseparable. Warms my heart that I forged such camaraderie out in the wilderness.'

'Don't pretend you got a heart,' said Shy.

'Got to be something pumps the black poison through my veins, don't there?'

'Ah!' shouted Majud. 'If it is not the new Emperor of the Plains, the conqueror of great Sangeed, Dab Sweet!'

The scout gave Lamb a nervous sideways glance. 'I've made no effort to spread that rumour.'

'And yet it has taken to this town like fire to tinder! I have heard half a dozen versions, none particularly close to my own remembrance. Most recently, I was told you shot the Ghost from a mile's distance and with a stiff side wind.'

'I heard you impaled him on the horns of an enraged steer,' said Shy.

'And in the newest version to reach my ear,' said Temple, 'you killed him in a duel over the good name of a woman.'

Sweet snorted. 'Where the hell do they get this rubbish? Everyone knows there's no women o' my acquaintance with a good name. This your plot?'

'It is,' said Majud.

'It is a plot,' said Crying Rock solemnly.

'Majud has contracted me to build a shop upon it,' said Temple.

'More buildings?' Sweet wriggled his shoulders. 'Bloody roofs hanging over you. Walls bearing in on you. How can you take a breath in those things?'

Crying Rock shook her head. 'Buildings.'

'A man can't think of nothing when he's in one but how to get back out. I'm a wanderer and that's a fact. Born to be under the sky.' Sweet watched Lamb drag another wriggling drunk from a tent one-handed and toss him rolling into the street. 'Man has to be what he is, don't he?'

Shy frowned up. 'He can try to be otherwise.'

'But more often than not it don't stick. All that trying, day after day, it wears you right through.' The old scout gave her a wink. 'Lamb taking up the Mayor's offer?'

'We're thinking on it,' she snapped back.

Temple looked from one to the other. 'Am I missing something?'

'Usually,' said Shy, still giving Sweet the eyeball. 'If you're heading on out of town, don't let us hold you up.'

'Wouldn't dream of it.' The old scout pointed down the main street, busier with traffic as the day wore on, weak sun raising a little steam from the wet mud, the wet horses, the wet roofs. 'We're signed up to guide a Fellowship of prospectors into the hills. Always work for guides around Crease. Everyone here wants to be somewhere else.'

'Not I,' said Majud, grinning as Lamb kicked another tent over.

'Oh no.' Sweet gave the plot a final glance, smile lurking at the corner of his mouth. 'You lot are right where you belong.' And he trotted on out of town, Crying Rock at his side.

Words and Graces

Shy didn't much care for pretension, and despite having crawled through more than her share was no high enthusiast for dirt. The dining room of Camling's Hostelry was an unhappy marriage of the two uglier by far than either one alone. The tabletops were buffed to a prissy shine but the floor was caked with boot-mud. The cutlery had bone handles but the walls were spattered hip high with ancient food. There was a gilt-framed painting of a nude who'd found something to smirk about but the plaster behind was blistered with mould from a leak above.

'State o' this place,' muttered Lamb.

'That's Crease for you,' said Shy. 'Everything upside down.'

On the trail she'd heard the stream-beds in the hills were lined with nuggets, just itching for greedy fingers to pluck them free. Some lucky few who'd struck gold in Crease might've dug it from the earth but it looked to Shy like most had found a way to dig it out of other folks. It weren't prospectors crowding the dining room of Camling's and forming a grumpy queue besides, it was pimps and gamblers, racketeers and money lenders, and merchants pedalling the same stuff they might anywhere else at half the quality and four times the price.

'A damn superfluity of shysters,' muttered Shy as she stepped over a pair of dirty boots and dodged a careless elbow. 'This the future of the Far Country?'

'Of every country,' muttered Lamb.

'Please, please, my friends, do sit!' Camling, the proprietor, was a long, oily bastard with a suit wearing through at the elbows and a habit of laying soft hands where they weren't wanted which had already nearly earned him Shy's fist in his face. He was busy flicking crumbs from a table perched on an ancient column top some creative carpenter had laid the floorboards around. 'We try to stay neutral but any friend of the Mayor's is a friend of mine, indeed they are!'

'I'll face the door,' said Lamb, shifting his chair around.

Camling drew out the other for Shy. 'And may I say how positively radiant you are this morning?'

'You can say it, but I doubt anyone'll be taking your word over the evidence o' their senses.' She levered her way to sitting, not easy since the ancient carvings on the column were prone to interfere with her knees.

'On the contrary, you are a positive ornament to my humble dining room.'

Shy frowned up. A slap in the face she could take in good part but all this fawning she didn't trust in the least. 'How about you bring the food and hold on to the blather?'

Camling cleared his throat. 'Of course.' And slipped away into the crowd.

'That Corlin over there?'

She was wedged into a shadowy corner, eyeing the gathering with her mouth pressed into that tight line of hers, like it'd take a couple of big men with pick and crowbar to get a word out.

'If you say so,' said Lamb, squinting across the room. 'My eyes ain't all they were.'

'I say so. And Savian, too. Thought they were meant to be prospecting?'

'Thought you didn't believe they would be?'

'Looks like I was right.'

'You usually are.'

'I'd swear she saw me.'

'And?'

'And she ain't given so much as a nod.'

'Maybe she wishes she hadn't seen you.'

'Wishing don't make it so.' Shy slipped from the table, having to make room for a big bald bastard who insisted on waving his fork around when he talked.

'. . . there's still a few coming in but less than we hoped. Can't be sure how many more'll turn up. Sounds like Mulkova was bad . . .' Savian stopped short when he saw Shy coming. There was a stranger wedged even further into the shadows between him and Corlin, under a curtained window.

'Corlin,' said Shy.

'Shy,' said Corlin.

'Savian,' said Shy.

He just nodded.

'I thought you two were out digging?'

'We're putting it off a while.' Corlin held Shy's eye all the time. 'Might leave in a week. Might be later.'

'Lot of other folks coming through with the same idea. You want to claim aught but mud you'd best get into them hills.'

'The hills have been there since great Euz drove the devils from the world,' said the stranger. 'I predict that they will persist into next week.' He was an odd one, with bulging eyes, a long tangle of grey beard and hair and eyebrows hardly shorter. Odder yet, Shy saw now he had a pair of little birds, tame as puppies, pecking seed from his open palm.

'And you are?' asked Shy.

'My name is Zacharus.'

'Like the Magus?'

'Just like.'

Seemed a foolish sort of thing to take the name of a legendary wizard, but then you might have said the same for naming a woman after social awkwardness. 'Shy South.' She reached for his hand and an even smaller bird hopped from his sleeve and snapped at her finger, gave her the hell of a shock and made her jerk it back. 'And, er, that's Lamb over there. We rolled out from the Near Country in a Fellowship with these two. Faced down Ghosts and storms and rivers and an awful lot of boredom. High times, eh?'

'Towering,' said Corlin, eyes narrowed to blue slits. Shy was getting the distinct feeling they wanted her somewhere else and that was making her want to stay. 'And what's your business, Master Zacharus?'

'The turning of ages.' He had a trace of an Imperial accent, but it was strange somehow, crackly as old papers. 'The currents of destiny. The rise and fall of nations.'

'There a good living in that?'

He flashed a faintly crazy smile made of a lot of jagged yellow teeth. 'There is no bad living and no good death.'

'Right y'are. What's with the birds?'

'They bring me news, companionship, songs when I am melancholy and, on occasion, nesting materials.'

'You have a nest?'

'No, but they think I should.'

'Course they do.' The old man was mad as a mushroom, but she doubted folk hard-headed as Corlin and Savian would be wasting time on him if that was the end of the story. There was something off-putting to the way those birds stared, heads on one side, unblinking. Like they'd figured her for a real idiot.

She thought the old man might share their opinion. 'What brings you here, Shy South?'

'Come looking for two children stole from our farm.'

'Any luck?' asked Corlin.

'Six days I been up and down the Mayor's side of the street asking every pair of ears, but children ain't exactly a common sight around here and no one's seen a hair of them. Or if they have they ain't telling me. When I say the name Grega Cantliss they shut up like I cast a spell of silence.'

'Spells of silence are a challenging cloth to weave,' mused Zacharus, frowning up into an empty corner. 'So many variables.' There was a flapping outside and a pigeon stuck its head through the curtains and gave a burbling coo. 'She says they are in the mountains.'

'Who?'

'The children. But pigeons are liars. They only tell you what you want to hear.' And the old man stuck his tongue in the seeds in his palm and started crunching them between his yellow front teeth.

Shy was already minded to beat a retreat when Camling called from behind. 'Your breakfast!'

'What do you reckon those two are about?' asked Shy as she slipped back into her chair and flicked away a couple of crumbs their host had missed.

'Prospecting, I heard,' said Lamb.

'You ain't been listening to me at all, have you?'

'I try to avoid it. If they want our help I daresay they'll ask. 'Til then, it ain't our business.'

'Can you imagine either of them asking for help?'

'No,' said Lamb. 'So I reckon it'll never be our business, will it?'

'Definitely not. That's why I want to know.'

'I used to be curious. Long time ago.'

'What happened?'

Lamb waved his three-fingered hand at his scar-covered face.

Breakfast was cold porridge, runny egg and grey bacon, and the porridge weren't the freshest and the bacon may well not have derived from a pig. All whisked in front of Shy on imported crockery with trees and flowers painted into it in gilt, Camling with an air of smarmy pride like there was no finer meal to be had anywhere in the Circle of the World.

'This from a horse?' she muttered to Lamb, prodding at that meat and half-expecting it to tell her to stop.

'Just be thankful it ain't from the rider.'

'On the trail we ate shit, but at least it was honest shit. What the hell's this?'

'Dishonest shit?'

'That's Crease for you. You can get fine Suljuk plates but only slops to eat off 'em. Everything back to bloody front . . .' She realised the chatter had all faded, the scraping of her fork about the only noise. Hairs prickled on the back of her neck and she slowly turned.

Six men were adding their boot-prints to the mud-caked floor. Five were the kind of thugs you saw a lot of in Crease, spreading out among the tables to find watchful places, each wearing that ready slouch said they were better'n you 'cause there were more of them and they all had blades. The sixth was a different prospect. Short but hugely wide and with a big belly on him, too, a suit of fine clothes bulging at the buttons like the tailor had been awful optimistic with the measurements. He was black-skinned with a fuzz of grey hair, one earlobe stretched out around a thick golden ring, hole in the middle big enough almost for Shy to have got her fist through.

He looked pleased with himself to an untold degree, smiling on everything as though it was all exactly the way he liked it. Shy disliked him right off. Most likely jealousy. Nothing ever seemed to be the way she liked it, after all.

'Don't worry,' he boomed in a voice spilling over with good humour, 'you can all keep on eating! If you want to be shitting water all day!' And he burst out laughing, and slapped one of his men on the back and near knocked him into some fool's breakfast. He made his way between the tables, calling out hellos by name, shaking hands and patting shoulders, a long stick with a bone handle tapping at the boards.

Shy watched him come, easing a little sideways in her chair and slipping the bottom button of her vest open so the grip of her knife poked out nice and perky. Lamb just sat eating with eyes on his food. Not looking up even when the fat man stopped right next to their table and said, 'I'm Papa Ring.'

'I'd made a prediction to that effect,' said Shy.

'You're Shy South.'

'It ain't a secret.'

'And you must be Lamb.'

'If I must, I guess I must.'

'Look for the big fucking Northman with the face like a chopping block, they told me.' Papa Ring swung a free chair away from the next-door table. 'Mind if I sit?'

'What if I said yes?' asked Shy.

He paused halfway down, leaning heavy on his stick. 'Most likely I'd say sorry but sit anyway. Sorry.' And he lowered himself the rest of the way. 'I've got no fucking graces at all, they tell me. Ask anyone. No fucking graces.'

Shy took the quickest glance across the room. Savian hadn't even looked up, but she caught the faintest gleam of a blade ready under the table. That made her feel a little better. He didn't give much to your face, Savian, but he was a reassurance at your back.

Unlike Camling. Their proud host was hurrying over now, rubbing his hands together so hard Shy could hear them hiss. 'Welcome, Papa, you're very welcome.'

'Why wouldn't I be?'

'No reason, no reason at all.' If Camling had rubbed his hands any faster he might've made fire. 'As long as there's no . . . trouble.'

'Who'd want trouble? I'm here to talk.'

'Talk's how it always begins.'

'Talk's how everything begins.'

'My concern is how it will conclude.'

'How's a man to know that 'til he's talked?' asked Lamb, still not looking up.

'Exactly so,' said Papa Ring, smiling like it was the best day of his life.

'All right,' said Camling, reluctantly. 'Will you be taking food?'

Ring snorted. 'Your food is shit, as these two unfortunates are only now discovering. You can lose yourself.'

'Now look, Papa, this is my place—'

'Happy chance.' Of a sudden Ring's smile seemed to have an edge to it. 'You'll know just where to lose yourself.'

Camling swallowed, then scraped away with the sourest of expressions. The chatter gradually came up again, but honed to a nervous point now.

'One of the strongest arguments I ever saw for there being no God is the existence of Lennart Camling,' muttered Ring, as he watched their host depart. The joints of his chair creaked unhappily as he settled back, all good humour again. 'So how are you finding Crease?'

'Filthy in every sense.' Shy poked her bacon away, then tossed her fork down and pushed the plate away, too. There could never be too great a distance between her and that bacon, far as she was concerned. She let her hands flop into her lap where one just happened to rest right on her knife's handle. Imagine that.

'Dirty's how we like it. You meet the Mayor?'

'I don't know,' said Shy, 'did we?'

'I know you did.'

'Why ask, then?'

'Watching my manners, such as they are. Though I don't deceive myself they come close to hers. She's got graces, don't she, our Mayor?' And Ring gently rubbed the polished wood of the table with one palm. 'Smooth as mirror glass. When she talks you feel swaddled in a goose-down blanket, don't you? The worthier folks around here, they tend to move in her orbit. Those manners. That way. The worthy folks lap that stuff up. But let's not pretend you all are two of the worthy ones, eh?'

'Could be we're aspiring to be worthier,' said Shy.

'I'm all for aspiration,' said Ring. 'God knows I came here with nothing. But the Mayor won't help you better yourselves.'

'And you will?'

Ring gave a chuckle, deep and joyful, like you might get from a kindly uncle. 'No, no, no. But at least I'll be honest about it.'

'You'll be honest about your dishonesty?'

'I never claimed to do anything other than sell folk what they want and make no judgements on 'em for their desires. Daresay the Mayor gave you the impression I'm quite the evil bastard.'

'We can get that impression all by ourselves,' said Shy.

Ring grinned at her. 'Quick, aren't you?'

'I'll try not to leave you behind.'

'She do all the talking?'

'The vast majority,' said Lamb, out the side of his mouth.

'Reckon he's waiting for something worth replying to,' said Shy.

Ring kept grinning. 'Well that's a very reasonable policy. You seem like reasonable folks.'

Lamb shrugged. 'You ain't really got to know us yet.'

'That's the very reason I came along. To get to know you better. And maybe just to offer some friendly advice.'

'I'm getting old for advice,' said Lamb. 'Even the friendly kind.'

'You're getting old for brawling, too, but I do hear tell you might be involving yourself in some bare-fist business we got coming to Crease.'

Lamb shrugged again. 'I fought a bout or two in my youth.'

'I see that,' said Ring, with an eye on Lamb's battered face, 'but, keen devotee though I am of the brawling arts, I'd rather this fight didn't happen at all.'

'Worried your man might lose?' asked Shy.

She really couldn't drag Ring's grin loose at all. 'Not really. My man's famous for beating a lot of famous men, and beating 'em bad. But the fact is I'd rather the Mayor packed up nice and quiet. Don't get me wrong, I don't mind seeing a little blood spilled. Shows people you care. But too much is awful bad for business. And I got big plans for this place. Good plans . . . But you don't care about that, do you?'

'Everyone's got plans,' said Shy, 'and everyone thinks theirs are good. It's when one set of good plans gets tangled with another things tend to slide downhill.'

'Just tell me this, then, and if the answer's yes I'll leave you to enjoy your shitty breakfast in peace. Have you given the Mayor a certain yes or can I still make you a better offer?' Ring's eyes moved between them, and neither spoke, and he took that for encouragement, and maybe it was. 'I may not have the graces but I'm always willing to deal. Just tell me what she's promised you.'

Lamb looked up for the first time. 'Grega Cantliss.'

Shy was watching him hard and she saw Ring's smile slip at the name. 'You know him, then?' she asked.

'He works for me. Has worked for me, at times.'

'Was he working for you when he burned my farm, and killed my friend, and stole two children from me?' asked Lamb.

Ring sat back, rubbing at his jaw, a trace of frown showing. 'Quite an accusation. Stealing children. I can tell you now I'd have no part of that.'

'Seems you got one even so,' said Shy.

'Only your word for it. What kind of a man would I be if I gave my people up on your say-so?'

'I don't care one fucking shit what kind of man y'are,' snarled Lamb, knuckles white around his cutlery, and Ring's men stirred unhappily, and Shy saw Savian sitting up, watchful, but Lamb took no notice of any of it. 'Give me Cantliss and we're done. Get in my way, there'll be trouble.' And he frowned as he saw he'd bent his knife at a right angle against the tabletop.

Ring mildly raised his brows. 'You're very confident. Given nobody's heard of you.'

'I been through this before. I got a fair idea how it turns out.'

'My man ain't bent cutlery.'

'He will be.'

'Just tell us where Cantliss is,' said Shy, 'and we'll be on our way and out of yours.'

Papa Ring looked for the first time like he might be running short of patience. 'Girl, do you suppose you could sit back and let me and your father talk this out?'

'Not really. Maybe it's my Ghost blood but I'm cursed with a contrary temperament. Folk warn me off a thing, I just start thinking on how to go about it. Can't help myself.'

Ring took a long breath and forced himself back to reasonable. 'I understand. Someone stole my children, there'd be nowhere in the Circle of the World for those bastards to run to. But don't make me your enemy when I can every bit as easily be your friend. I can't just hand you Cantliss. Maybe that's what the Mayor would do but it ain't my way. I tell you what, though, next time he comes to town we can all sit down and talk this out, get to the truth of it, see if we can't find your young ones. I'll help you every way I can, you got my word.'

'Your word?' And Shy curled back her lip and spat onto her cold bacon. If it was bacon.

'I got no graces but I got my word.' And Ring stabbed at the table with his thick forefinger. 'That's what everything stands on, on my side of the street. Folk are loyal to me 'cause I'm loyal to them. Break that, I got nothing. Break that, I am nothing.' He leaned closer, beckoning like he had the killer offer to make. 'But forget my word and just look at it this way – you want the Mayor's help, you're going to have to fight for it and, believe me, that'll be one hell of a fight. You want my help?' He gave the biggest shrug his big shoulders could manage, like even considering an alternative was madness. 'All you got to do is *not* fight.'

Shy didn't like the feel of this bastard one bit, but she didn't like the feel of the Mayor much more and she had to admit there was something in what he was saying.

Lamb nodded as he straightened out his knife between finger and thumb and tossed it on his plate. Then he stood. 'What if I'd rather fight?' And he strode for the door, the queue for breakfast scurrying to part for him.

Ring blinked, brows drawn in with puzzlement. 'Who'd rather fight?' Shy got up without answering and hurried after, weaving between the tables. 'Just think about it, that's all I'm asking! Be reasonable!'

And they were out into the street. 'Hold up there, Lamb! Lamb!'

She dodged through a bleating mass of little grey sheep, had to lurch back to let a pair of wagons squelch past. She caught sight of Temple, sitting high up astride a big beam, hammer in hand, the strong square frame of Majud's shop already higher than the slumping buildings on either side. He raised one hand in greeting.

'Seventy!' she bellowed at him. She couldn't see his face but the shoulders of his silhouette slumped in a faintly heartening way.

'Will you hold up?' She caught Lamb by the arm just as he was getting close to the Mayor's Church of Dice, the thugs around the door, hardly to be told from the ones who'd come with Papa Ring, watching them hard-eyed. 'What do you think you're doing?'

'Taking the Mayor up on her offer.'

'Just 'cause that fat fool rubbed you the wrong way?'

Lamb came close and suddenly it seemed that he was looming over her from quite the height. 'That and 'cause his man stole your brother and sister.'

'You think I'm happy about that?' she hissed at him, getting angry now. 'But we don't know the ins and outs of it! He seemed reasonable enough, considering.'

Lamb frowned back towards Camling's. 'Some men only listen to violence.'

'Some men only talk it. Never took you for one of 'em. Did we come for Pit and Ro or for blood?'

She'd meant to make a point not ask a question but for a moment it looked like he had to consider the answer. 'I'm thinking I might get all three.'

She stared at him for a moment. 'Who the fuck *are* you? There was a time men could rub your face in the dung and you'd just thank 'em and ask for more.'

'And you know what?' He peeled her fingers from his arm with a grip that was almost painful. 'I've remembered I didn't like it much.' And he stomped muddy footprints up the steps of the Mayor's place, leaving Shy behind in the street.

That Simple

Temple tapped a few more shavings from the joint, then nodded to Lamb and together they lowered the beam, tenon sliding snugly into mortise.

'Hah!' Lamb slapped Temple on the back. 'Naught so nice as to see a job done well. You got clever hands, lad. Damn clever for a man washes up out of streams. Sort of hands you can turn to anything.' He looked down at his own big, battered, three-fingered hand and made a fist of it. 'Mine only ever really been good for one thing.' And he thumped at the beam until it came flush.

Temple had expected carpentry to be almost as much of a chore as riding drag, but he had to admit he was enjoying himself, and it was getting harder every day to pretend otherwise. There was something in the smell of fresh-sawn timber – when the mountain breeze slipped into the valley long enough for one to smell anything but shit – that wafted away his suffocating regrets and let him breathe free. His hands had found old skills with hammer and chisel and he had worked out the habits of the local wood, pale and straight and strong. Majud's hirelings silently conceded he knew his business and soon were taking his instructions without a second word, working at scaffold and pulleys with little skill but great enthusiasm, the frame sprouting up twice as fast and twice as fine as Temple had hoped.

'Where's Shy?' he asked, offhand, as though it was no part of a plan to dodge his latest payment. It was getting to be a game between them. One he never seemed to win.

'She's still touring town, asking questions about Pit and Ro. New folk coming in every day to ask. Probably she's trying Papa Ring's side of the street by now.'

'Is that safe?'

'I doubt it.'

'Shouldn't you stop her?'

Lamb snorted as he pushed a peg into Temple's fishing hand. 'Last time I tried to stop Shy she was ten years old and it didn't stick then.'

Temple worked the peg into its hole. 'Once she has a destination in mind, she isn't one to stop halfway.'

'Got to love that about her.' Lamb had a trace of pride in his voice as he passed the mallet. 'She's no coward, that girl.'

'So why are you helping me not her?'

''Cause I reckon I've found a way to Pit and Ro already. I'm just waiting for Shy to come round to the cost.'

'Which is?'

'The Mayor wants a favour.' There was a long pause, measured out by the tapping of Temple's mallet, accompanied by the distant sounds of other hammers on other more slovenly building sites scattered about the town. 'She and Papa Ring bet Crease on a fight.'

Temple looked around. 'They bet Crease?'

'They each own half the town, more or less.' Lamb looked out at it, crammed thoughtlessly into both sides of that winding valley like the place was an almighty gut, people and goods and animals squeezing in one end and shit and beggars and money squirting out the other. 'But the more you get the more you want. And all either one o' them wants is the half they haven't got.'

Temple puffed out his cheeks as he twisted at the next peg. 'I imagine one of them is sure to be disappointed.'

'At least one. The worst enemies are those that live next door, my father used to tell me. These two have been squabbling for years and neither one's come out on top, so they're putting on a fight. Winner takes all.' A group of half-tame Ghosts had spilled from one of the worse whorehouses – the better ones wouldn't let them in the door – and had knives out, taunting each other in common, knowing no words but swearing and the language of violence. That was more than enough to get by on in Crease. 'Two men in a Circle,' murmured Lamb, 'more'n likely with a considerable audience and a fair few side bets. One comes out alive, one comes out otherwise, and everyone else comes out thoroughly entertained.'

'Shit,' breathed Temple.

'Papa Ring's brought in a man called Glama Golden. A Northman. Big name in his day. I hear he's been fighting for money in pits and pens all across the Near Country and done a lot of winning, too. The

Mayor, well, she's been searching high and low for someone to stand up for her . . .' He gave Temple a long look and it was easy enough to guess the rest.

'Shit.' It was one thing to fight for your life out there on the plains when the Ghosts were coming at you and offering no alternatives. Another to wait weeks for the moment, choose to step out in front of a crowd and batter, twist and crush the life from a man with your hands. 'Have you had any practice at . . . that sort of thing?'

'As luck would have it – my luck being what it is – more'n a little.'

'Are you sure the Mayor's on the right side of this?' asked Temple, thinking of all the wrong sides he had taken.

Lamb frowned down at the Ghosts, who had evidently resolved their differences without bloodshed and were noisily embracing. 'In my experience there's rarely such a thing as a right side, and when there is I've an uncanny knack of picking out the other. All I know is Grega Cantliss killed my friend and burned my farm and stole two children I swore to protect.' Lamb's voice had a cold edge on it as he shifted his frown to the Whitehouse, cold enough to bring Temple out in gooseflesh all over. 'Papa Ring's standing by him, so he's made himself my enemy. The Mayor's standing against him, and that makes her my friend.'

'Are things ever really that simple?'

'When you step into a Circle with the intention of killing a man, it's best if they are.'

'Temple?' The sun was low and the shadow of one of the great columns had fallen across the street below, so it took a moment to work out who was calling from the swirling traffic. 'Temple?' Another moment before he placed the smiling face tipped towards him, bright-eyed and with a bushy yellow beard. 'That you up there?' Still a third before he connected the world in which he knew that man to the world he lived in now, and recognition washed over him like a bucket of ice-water over a peaceful sleeper.

'Bermi?' he breathed.

'Friend of yours?' asked Lamb.

'We know each other,' Temple managed to whisper.

He slipped down the ladder with shaky hands, all the time tingling with the rabbit's urge to run. But where to? He had been beyond lucky to survive the last time he fled the Company of the Gracious Hand and was far from sure his divine support would stretch to another effort.

He picked his way to Bermi with reluctant little steps, plucking at the hem of his shirt, like a child that knows he has a slap coming and more than likely deserves it.

'You all right?' asked the Styrian. 'You look ill.'

'Is Cosca with you?' Temple could hardly get the words out he felt that sick. God might have blessed him with clever hands but He'd cursed him with a weak stomach.

Bermi was all smiles, though. 'I'm happy to say he's not, nor any of those other bastards. I daresay he's still floundering about the Near Country bragging to that bloody biographer and searching for ancient gold he'll never find. If he hasn't given up and gone back to Starikland to get drunk.'

Temple closed his eyes and expelled a lungful of the most profound relief. 'Thank heaven.' He put his hand on the Styrian's shoulder and leaned over, bent nearly double, head spinning.

'You sure you're all right?'

'Yes, I am.' He grabbed Bermi around the back and hugged him tight. 'Better than all right!' He was ecstatic! He breathed free once again! He kissed Bermi's bearded cheek with a noisy smack. 'What the hell brings you to the arse of the world?'

'You showed me the way. After that town – what was the name of it?'

'Averstock,' muttered Temple.

Bermi's eyes took on a guilty squint. 'I've done things I'm not proud of, but that? Nothing else but murder. Cosca sent me to find you, afterwards.'

'He did?'

'Said you were the most important man in the whole damn Company. Other than him, of course. Two days out I ran into a Fellowship coming west to mine for gold. Half of them were from Puranti – from my home town, imagine that! It's as if God has a purpose!'

'Almost as if.'

'I left the Company of the Fucking Finger and off we went.'

'You put Cosca behind you.' Cheating death once again had given Temple a faintly drunken feeling. 'Far, far behind.'

'You a carpenter now?'

'One way to clear my debts.'

'Shit on your debts, brother. We're heading back into the hills. Got a claim up on the Brownwash. Men are just sieving nuggets out of the mud up there!' He slapped Temple on the shoulder. 'You should come with us! Always room for a carpenter with a sense of humour. We've a cabin but it could do with some work.'

Temple swallowed. How often on the trail, choking on the dust of Buckhorn's herd or chafing under the sting of Shy's jibes, had he dreamed of an offer just like this? An easy way, unrolling before his willing feet. 'When do you leave?'

'Five days, maybe six.'

'What would a man need to bring?'

'Just some good clothes and a shovel, we've got the rest.'

Temple looked for the trick in Bermi's face but there was no sign of one. Perhaps there was a God after all. 'Are things ever really that simple?'

Bermi laughed. 'You're the one always loved to make things complicated. This is the new frontier, my friend, the land of opportunities. You got anything keeping you here?'

'I suppose not.' Temple glanced up at Lamb, a big black shape on the frame of Majud's building. 'Nothing but debts.'

Yesterday's News

'I'm looking for a pair of children.'

Blank faces.

'Their names are Ro and Pit.'

Sad shakes of the head.

'They're ten and six. Seven. He'd be seven now.'

Sympathetic mumbles.

'They were stole by a man named Grega Cantliss.'

A glimpse of scared eyes as the door slammed in her face.

Shy had to admit she was getting tired. She'd near worn her boots through tramping up and down the crooked length of main street, which wormed longer and more crooked every day as folk poured in off the plains, throwing up tents or wedging new hovels into some sliver of mud or just leaving their wagons rotting alongside the trail. Her shoulders were bruised from pushing through the bustle, her legs sore from scaling the valley sides to talk to folk in shacks clinging to the incline. Her voice was a croak from asking the same old questions over and over in the gambling halls and husk-dens and drinking sheds until she could hardly tell them apart one from another. There were a good few places they wouldn't let her in, now. Said she put off the customers. Probably she did. Probably Lamb had the right of it just waiting for Cantliss to come to him, but Shy had never been much good at waiting. *That's your Ghost blood*, her mother would've said. But then her mother hadn't been much good at waiting either.

'Look here, it's Shy South.'

'You all right, Hedges?' Though she could tell the answer at a glance. He'd never looked flushed with success but he'd had a spark of hope about him on the trail. It had guttered since and left him greyed out and ragged. Crease was no place to make your hopes healthier. No place to make anything healthier, far as she could tell. 'Thought you were looking for work?'

'Couldn't find none. Not for a man with a leg like this. Wouldn't have thought I led the charge up there at Osrung, would you?' She wouldn't have, but he'd said so already so she kept her silence. 'Still looking for your kin?'

'Will be until I find 'em. You heard anything?'

'You're the first person said more'n five words together to me in a week. Wouldn't think I led a charge, would you? Wouldn't think that.' They stood there awkward, both knowing what was coming next. Didn't stop it coming, though. 'Can you spare a couple o' bits?'

'Aye, a few.' She delved in her pocket and handed him the coins Temple had handed her an hour before, then headed on quick. No one likes to stand that close to failure, do they? Worried it might rub off.

'Ain't you going to tell me not to drink it all?' he called after her.

'I'm no preacher. Reckon folk have the right to pick their own method of destruction.'

'So they do. You're not so bad, Shy South, you're all right!'

'We'll have to differ on that,' she muttered, leaving Hedges to shuffle for the nearest drinking hole, never too many steps away in Crease even for a man whose steps were miserly as his.

'I'm looking for a pair of children.'

'I cannot assist you there, but I have other tidings!' This woman was a strange-looking character, clothes that must've been fine in their time but their time was long past and the months since full of mud and stray food. She drew back her sagging coat with a flourish and produced a sheaf of crumpled papers.

'What are they, news-bills?' Shy was already regretting talking to this woman but the path here was a narrow stretch of mud between sewer-stream and rotten porches and her bulging belly wasn't giving space to pass.

'You have a keen eye for quality. You wish to make a purchase?'

'Not really.'

'The faraway happenings of politics and power are of no interest?'

'They never seem to bear much on my doings.'

'Perhaps it is your ignorance of current affairs keeps you down so?'

'I always took it to be the greed, laziness and ill-temper of others plus a fair share of bad luck, but I reckon you'll have it your way.'

'Everyone does.' But the woman didn't move.

Shy sighed. Given her knack for upsetting folk she thought she might give indulgence a try. 'All right, then, deliver me from ignorance.'

The woman displayed the upmost bill and spoke with mighty self-importance. 'Rebels defeated at Mulkova – routed by Union troops under General Brint! How about that?'

'Unless they been defeated there a second time, that happened before I even left the Near Country. Everyone knows it.'

'The lady requires something fresher,' muttered the old woman, rooting through her thumbed-over bundle. 'Styrian conflict ends! Sipani opens gates to the Snake of Talins!'

'That was at least two years before.' Shy was starting to think this woman was touched in the head, if that even meant anything in a place where most were happy-mad, dismal-mad, or some other kind of mad that defied further description.

'A challenge indeed.' The woman licked a dirty finger to leaf through her wares and came up with one that looked a veritable antique. 'Legate Sarmis menaces border of the Near Country? Fears of Imperial incursion?'

'Sarmis has been menacing for decades. He's the most menacing Legate you ever heard of.'

'Then it's true as it ever was!'

'News spoils quick, friend, like milk.'

'I say it gets better if carefully kept, like wine.'

'I'm glad you like the vintage, but I ain't buying yesterday's news.'

The woman cradled her papers like a mother hiding an infant from bird attack, and as she leaned forward Shy saw the top was tore off her tall hat and got a view of the scabbiest scalp imaginable and a smell of rot almost knocked her over. 'No worse than tomorrow's, is it?' And the woman swept her aside and strode on waving her old bills over her head. 'News! I have news!'

Shy took a long, hard breath before she set off. Damn, but she was tired. Crease was no place to get less tired, far as she could tell.

'I'm looking for a pair of children.'

The one in the middle treated her to something you'd have had to call a leer. 'I'll give you children, girl.'

The one on the left burst out laughing. The one on the right grinned, and a bit of chagga juice dribbled out of his mouth and ran down into his beard. From the look of his beard it wasn't his first dribble either. They were an unpromising trio all right, but if Shy had stuck to the promising she'd have been done in Crease her first day there.

'They were stolen from our farm.'

'Probably nothing else there worth stealing.'

'Being honest, I daresay you're right. Man called Grega Cantliss stole 'em.'

The mood shifted right off. The one on the right stood up, frowning. The one on the left spat juice over the railing. Leery leered more'n ever. 'You got some gall asking questions over here, girl. Some fucking gall.'

'You ain't the first to say so. Probably best I just take my gall away on down the street.'

She made to move on but he stepped down from the porch to block her way, pointed a waving finger towards her face. 'You know what, you've got kind of a Ghosty look to you.'

'Half-breed, maybe,' grunted one of his friends.

Shy set her jaw. 'Quarter, as it goes.'

Leery took his leer into realms of facial contortion. 'Well, we don't care for your kind over on this side o' the street.'

'Better quarter-Ghost than all arsehole, surely?'

There was that knack for upsetting folk. His brows drew in and he took a step at her. 'Why, you bloody—'

Without thinking she put her right hand on the grip of her knife and said, 'You'd best stop right there.'

His eyes narrowed. Annoyed. Like he hadn't expected straight-up defiance but couldn't back down with his friends watching. 'You'd best not put your hand on that knife unless you're going to use it, girl.'

'Whether I use it or not depends on whether you stop there or not. My hopes ain't high but maybe you're cleverer than you look.'

'Leave her be.' A big man stood in the doorway. Big hardly did him justice. His fist up on the frame beside him looked about the size of Shy's head.

'You can stay out o' this,' said Leery.

'I could, but I'm not. You say you're looking for Cantliss?' he asked, eyes moving over to Shy.

'That's right.'

'Don't tell her nothing!' snapped Squinty.

The big man's eyes drifted back. 'You can shut up . . .' He had to duck his head to get through the doorway. 'Or I can shut you up.' The other two men backed off to give him room – and he needed a lot. He looked bigger still as he stepped out of the shadows, taller'n Lamb, even, and maybe bigger in the chest and shoulder, too. A real monster, but he spoke soft, accent thick with the North. 'Don't pay these idiots no mind. They've got big bones for fights they're sure of winning but otherwise not enough for a toothpick.' He took the couple of steps down into the street, boards groaning under his great boots, and stood towering over Leery.

'Cantliss is from the same cloth,' he said. 'A puffed-up fool with a lot of vicious in him.' For all his size there was a sad sag to his face. A droop to his blond moustache, a sorry greying to the stubble about it. 'More or less what I used to be, if it comes to that. He owes Papa Ring a lot of money, as I heard it. Ain't been around for a while now, though. Not much more I can tell you.'

'Well, thanks for that much.'

'My pleasure.' The big man turned his washed-out blue eyes on Leery. 'Get out of her way.'

Leery gave Shy a particularly nasty leer, but Shy had been treated to a lot of harsh expressions in her time and after a while they lose their sting. He made to go back up the steps but the big man didn't let him. 'Get out of her way, that way.' And he nodded over at the stream.

'Stand in the sewer?' said Leery.

'Stand in the sewer. Or I'll lay you out in it.'

Leery cursed to himself as he clambered down the slimy rocks and stood up to his knees in shitty water. The big man put one hand on his chest and with the other offered Shy the open way.

'My thanks,' she said as she stepped past. 'Glad I found someone decent this side of the street.'

The man gave a sad snort. 'Don't let a small kindness fool you. Did you say you're looking for children?'

'My brother and sister. Why?'

'Might be I can help.'

Shy had learned to treat offers of help, and for that matter everything else, with a healthy suspicion. 'Why would you?'

'Because I know how it feels to lose your family. Like losing a part of you, ain't it?' She thought about that for a moment, and reckoned he had it right. 'Had to leave mine behind, in the North. I know it was the best thing for 'em. The only thing. But it still cuts at me now. Didn't ever think it would. Can't say I valued 'em much when I had 'em. But it cuts at me.'

He'd such a sorry sag to his great shoulders then that Shy had to take pity on him. 'Well, you're welcome to follow along, I guess. It's been my observation that folk take me more serious when I've a great big bastard looking over my shoulder.'

'That is a sadly universal truth,' he said as he fell into step, two of his near enough to every three of hers. 'You here alone?'

'Came with my father. Kind of my father.'

'How can someone be kind of your father?'

'He's managed it.'

'He father to these other two you're looking for?'

'Kind of to them, too,' said Shy.

'Shouldn't he be helping look?'

'He is, in his way. He's building a house, over on the other side of the street.'

'That new one I've seen going up?'

'Majud and Curnsbick's Metalwork.'

'That's a good building. And that's a rare thing around here. Hard to see how it'll find your young ones, though.'

'He's trusting someone else to help with that.'

'Who?'

Normally she'd have kept her cards close, so to speak, but something in his manner brought her out. 'The Mayor.'

He took a long suck of breath. 'I'd sooner trust a snake with my fruits than that woman with anything.'

'She sure is a bit too smooth.'

'Never trust someone who don't use their proper name, I was always told.'

'You haven't told me your name yet.'

The big man gave a weary sigh. 'I was hoping to avoid it. People tend to look at me different, once they know what it is.'

'One o' those funny ones, is it? Arsehowl, maybe?'

'That'd be a mercy. My name'll make no one laugh, sad to say. You'd never believe how I worked at blowing it up bigger. Years of it. Now there ain't no getting out from under its shadow. I've forged the links of my own chain and no mistake.'

'I reckon we're all prone to do that.'

'More'n likely.' He stopped and offered one huge hand, and she took it, her own seeming little as a child's in its great warm grip. 'My name's—'

'Glama Golden!'

Shy saw the big man flinch a moment, and his shoulders hunch, then he slowly turned. A young man stood in the street behind. A big lad, with a scar through his lips and a tattered coat. He had an unsteady look to him made Shy think he'd been drinking hard. To puff his courage up, maybe, though folk didn't always bother with a reason to drink in Crease. He raised an unsteady finger to point at them, and his other hand hovered around the handle of a big knife at his belt.

'You're the one killed Stockling Bear?' he sneered. 'You're the one won all them fights?' He spat in the mud just near their feet. 'You don't look much!'

'I ain't much,' said the big man, softly.

The lad blinked, not sure what to do with that. 'Well . . . I'm fucking calling you out, you bastard!'

'What if I ain't listening?'

The lad frowned at the people on the porches, all stopped their business to watch. He ran his tongue around the inside of his mouth, not sure of himself. Then he looked over at Shy, and took one more stab at it. 'Who's this bitch? Your fucking—'

'Don't make me kill you, boy.' Golden didn't say it like a threat. Pleading, almost, his eyes sadder'n ever.

The lad flinched a little, and his fingers twitched, and he came over pale. The bottle's a shifty banker – it might lend you courage but it's apt to call the debt in sudden. He took a step back and spat again. 'Ain't fucking worth it,' he snapped.

'No, it ain't.' Golden watched the lad as he backed slowly off, then turned and walked away fast. A few sighs of relief, a few shrugs, and the talk started building back up.

Shy swallowed, mouth suddenly dried out and sticky-feeling. 'You're Glama Golden?'

He slowly nodded. 'Though I know full well there ain't much golden about me these days.' He rubbed his great hands together as he watched that lad lose himself in the crowd, and Shy saw they were shaking. 'Hell of a thing, being famous. Hell of a thing.'

'You're the one standing for Papa Ring in this fight that's coming?'

'That I am. Though I have to say I'm hopeful it won't happen. I hear the Mayor's got no one to fight for her.' His pale eyes narrowed as he looked back to Shy. 'Why, what've you heard?'

'Nothing,' she said, trying her best to smile and failing at it. 'Nothing at all.'

Blood Coming

It was just before dawn, clear and cold, the mud crusted with frost. The lamps in the windows had mostly been snuffed, the torches lighting the signs had guttered out and the sky was bright with stars. Hundreds upon hundreds of them, sharp as jewels, laid out in swirls and drifts and twinkling constellations. Temple opened his mouth, cold nipping at his cheeks, turning, turning until he was dizzy, taking in the beauty of the heavens. Strange, that he had never noticed them before. Maybe his eyes had been always on the ground.

'You reckon there's an answer up there?' asked Bermi, his breath and his horse's breath smoking on the dawn chill.

'I don't know where the answer is,' said Temple.

'You ready?'

He turned to look at the house. The big beams were up, most of the rafters and the window and door-frames, too, the skeleton of the building standing bold and black against the star-scattered sky. Only that morning Majud had been telling him what a fine job he was doing, how even Curnsbick would have considered his money well spent. He felt a flush of pride, and wondered when he had last felt one. But Temple was a man who abandoned everything half-done. That was a long-established fact.

'You can ride on the packhorse. It's only a day or two into the hills.'

'Why not?' A few hundred miles on a mule and his arse was carved out of wood.

Over towards the amphitheatre the carpenters were already making a desultory start. They were throwing up a new bank of seating at the open side so they could cram in a few score more onlookers, supports and cross-braces just visible against the dark hillside, bent and badly bolted, some of the timbers without the branches even properly trimmed.

'Only a couple of weeks to the big fight.'

'Shame we'll miss it,' said Bermi. 'Better get on, the rest of the lads'll be well ahead by now.'

Temple pushed his new shovel through one of the packhorse's straps, moving slower, and slower, then stopping still. It had been a day or two since he'd seen Shy, but he kept reminding himself of the debt in her absence. He wondered if she was out there somewhere, still doggedly searching. You could only admire someone who stuck at a thing like that, no matter the cost, no matter the odds. Especially if you were a man who could never stick at anything. Not even when he wanted to.

Temple thought about that for a moment, standing motionless up to his ankles in half-frozen mud. Then he walked to Bermi and slapped his hand down on the Styrian's shoulder. 'I won't be going. My bottomless thanks for the offer, but I've a building to finish. That and a debt to pay.'

'Since when do you pay your debts?'

'Since now, I suppose.'

Bermi gave him a puzzled look, as if he was trying to work out where the joke might be. 'Can I change your mind?'

'No.'

'Your mind always shifted with the breeze.'

'Looks like a man can grow.'

'What about your shovel?'

'Consider it a gift.'

Bermi narrowed his eyes. 'There's a woman involved, isn't there?'

'There is, but not in the way you're thinking.'

'What's she thinking?'

Temple snorted. 'Not that.'

'We'll see.' Bermi hauled himself into his saddle. 'I reckon you'll regret it, when we come back through with nuggets big as turds.'

'I'll probably regret it a lot sooner than that. Such is life.'

'You're right there.' The Styrian swept off his hat and raised it high in salute. 'No reasoning with the bastard!' And he was off, mud flicking from the hooves of his horse as he headed out up the main street, scattering a group of reeling-drunk miners on the way.

'Iosiv Lestek?' Temple twitched up his trousers to squelch out into the street. 'What happened to you?'

'Disgrace!' croaked the actor, beating at his breast. 'The crowd . . . wretched. My performance . . . abject. The cultural extravaganza . . . a debacle!' He clawed at Temple's shirt. 'I was pelted from the stage. I!

234

Iosiv Lestek! He who ruled the theatres of Midderland as if they were a private fief!' He clawed at his own shirt, stained up the front. 'Pelted with *dung*! Replaced by a trio of girls with bared bubs. To rapturous applause, I might add. Is that all audiences care for these days? Bubs?'

'I suppose they've always been popular—'

'All finished!' howled Lestek at the sky.

'Shut the fuck up!' someone roared from an upstairs window.

'Camling!' Lestek tore free, waving his bottle. 'That cursed maggot! That treacherous cuckoo! He has ejected me from his Hostelry! I! Me! Lestek! I will be revenged upon him, though!'

'Doubtless.'

'He will see! They will all see! My best performance is yet ahead of me!'

'You will show them, but perhaps in the morning. There are other hostelries—'

'I am penniless! I sold my wagon, I let go my props, I pawned my costumes!' Lestek dropped to his knees in the filth. 'I have nothing but the rags I wear!'

Temple gave a smoking sigh and looked once more towards the star-prickled heavens. Apparently he was set on the hard way. The thought made him oddly pleased. He reached down and helped the old man to his feet. 'I have a tent big enough for two, if you can stand my snoring.'

Lestek stood swaying for a moment. 'I don't deserve such kindness.'

Temple shrugged. 'Neither did I.'

'My boy,' murmured the actor, opening wide his arms, tears gleaming again in his eyes.

Then he was sick down Temple's shirt.

Shy frowned. She'd been certain Temple was about to get on that packhorse and ride out of town, trampling her childish trust under hoof and no doubt the last she'd ever hear of him. But all he'd done was give a man a shovel and wave him off. Then haul some shit-covered old drunk into the shell of Majud's building. People are a mystery there's no solving, all right.

She was awake a lot in the nights, now. Watching the street. Maybe thinking she'd see Cantliss ride in – not that she even had the first clue what he looked like. Maybe thinking she'd catch a glimpse of Pit and Ro, if she even recognised them any more. But mostly just picking at her worries. About her brother and sister, about Lamb, about the fight that was coming. About things and places and faces she'd rather have forgotten.

Jeg with his hat jammed down saying, 'Smoke? Smoke?' and Dodd all surprised she'd shot him and that bank man saying so politely, 'I'm afraid I can't help you,' with that puzzled little smile like she was a lady come for a loan rather'n a thief who'd ended up murdering him for nothing. That girl they'd hanged in her place whose name Shy had never known. Swinging there with a sign around her twisted neck and her dead eyes asking, *why me and not you?* and Shy still no closer to an answer.

In those slow, dark hours her head filled with doubts like a rotten rowboat with bog water, going down, going down for all her frantic bailing, and she'd think of Lamb dead like it was already done and Pit and Ro rotting in the empty somewhere and she'd feel like some kind of traitor for thinking it, but how do you stop a thought once it's in there?

Death was the one sure thing out here. The one fact among the odds and chances and bets and prospects. Leef, and Buckhorn's sons, and how many Ghosts out there on the plain? Men in fights in Crease, and folk hung on tissue-paper evidence or dead of fever or of silly mishaps like that drover kicked in the head by his brother's horse yesterday, or the shoe-merchant they found drowned in the sewer. Death walked among them daily, and presently would come calling on them all.

Hooves in the street and Shy craned to see, a set of torches flickering, folk retreating to their porches from the flying mud of a dozen horsemen. She turned to look at Lamb, a big shape under his blanket, shadow pooled in its folds. At the head-end she could just see his ear, and the big notch out of it. Could just hear his soft, slow breathing.

'You awake?'

He took a longer breath. 'Now I am.'

The men had reined in before the Mayor's Church of Dice, torchlight shifting over their hard-used, hard-bitten faces, and Shy shrank back. Not Pit or Ro and not Cantliss either. 'More thugs arrived for the Mayor.'

'Lots of thugs about,' grunted Lamb. 'Don't take no reader of the runes to see blood coming.'

Hooves thumped on by in the street and a flash of laughter and a woman shouting then quiet, with just the quick tap-tap of a hammer from over near the amphitheatre to remind them that the big show was on its way.

'What happens if Cantliss don't come?' She spoke at the dark. 'How do we find Pit and Ro then?'

Lamb slowly sat up, scrubbing his fingers through his grey hair. 'We'll just have to keep looking.'

'What if . . .' For all the time she'd spent thinking it she hadn't crossed the bridge of actually making the words 'til now. 'What if they're dead?'

'We keep looking 'til we're sure.'

'What if they died out there on the plains and we'll never know for sure? Every month passes there's more chance we'll never know, ain't there? More chance they'll just be lost, no finding 'em.' Her voice was turning shrill but she couldn't stop it rising, wilder and wilder. 'They could be anywhere by now, couldn't they, alive or dead? How do we find two children in all the unmapped empty they got out here? When do we stop, is what I'm asking? When *can* we stop?'

He pushed his blanket back, padded over and winced as he squatted, looking up into her face. 'You can stop whenever you want, Shy. You come this far and that's a long, hard way, and more'n likely there's a long, hard way ahead yet. I made a promise to your mother and I'll keep on. Long as it takes. Ain't like I got better offers knocking my door down. But you're young, still. You got a life to lead. If you stopped, no one could blame you.'

'I could.' She laughed then, and wiped the beginnings of a tear on the back of her hand. 'And it ain't like I got much of a life either, is it?'

'You take after me there,' he said, pulling back the covers on her bed, 'daughter or not.'

'Guess I'm just tired.'

'Who wouldn't be?'

'I just want 'em back,' as she slid under the blankets.

'We'll get 'em back,' as he dropped them over her and laid a weighty hand on her shoulder. She could almost believe him, then. 'Get some sleep now, Shy.'

Apart from the first touch of dawn creeping between the curtains and across Lamb's bedspread in a grey line, the room was dark.

'You really going to fight that man Golden?' she asked, after a while. 'He seemed all right to me.'

Lamb was silent long enough she started to wonder whether he was asleep. Then he said, 'I've killed better men for worse reasons, I'm sorry to say.'

The Sleeping Partner

In general, Temple was forced to concede, he was a man who had failed to live up to his own high standards. Or even to his low ones. He had undertaken a galaxy of projects. Many of those any decent man would have been ashamed of. Of the remainder, due to a mixture of bad luck, impatience and a shiftless obsession with the next thing, he could hardly remember one that had not tailed off into disappointment, failure or outright disaster.

Majud's shop, as it approached completion, was therefore a very pleasant surprise.

One of the Suljuks who had accompanied the Fellowship across the plains turned out to be an artist of a roofer. Lamb had applied his nine digits to the masonry and proved himself more than capable. More recently the Buckhorms had shown up in full numbers to help saw and nail the plank siding. Even Lord Ingelstad took a rare break from losing money to the town's gamblers to give advice on the paint. Bad advice, but still.

Temple took a step back into the street, gazing up at the nearly completed façade, lacking only for balusters to the balcony and glass in the windows, and produced the broadest and most self-satisfied grin he had entertained in quite some time. Then he was nearly pitched on his face by a hearty thump on the shoulder.

He turned, fully expecting to hear Shy grate out the glacial progress of his debt to her, and received a second surprise.

A man stood at his back. Not tall, but broad and possessed of explosive orange sideburns. His thick eyeglasses made his eyes appear minute, his smile immense by comparison. He wore a tailored suit, but his heavy hands were scarred across the backs by hard work.

'I had despaired of finding decent carpentry in this place!' He raised an eyebrow at the new seating haphazardly sprouting skywards around the ancient amphitheatre. 'But what should I find, just at my lowest ebb?' And he seized Temple by the arms and pointed him back towards Majud's shop. 'But this invigorating example of the joiner's craft! Bold in design, diligent in execution and in a heady fusion of styles aptly reflecting the many-cultured character of the adventurers braving this virgin land. And all on my behalf! Sir, I am quite humbled!'

'Your . . . behalf?'

'Indeed!' He pointed towards the sign above the front door. 'I am Honrig Curnsbick, the better half of Majud and Curnsbick!' And he flung his arms around Temple and kissed him on both cheeks, then rooted in his waistcoat pocket and produced a coin. 'A little something extra for your trouble. Generosity repays itself, I have always said!'

Temple blinked down at the coin. It was a silver five-mark piece. 'You have?'

'I have! Not always financially, not always immediately, but in goodwill and friendship which ultimately are beyond price!'

'They are? I mean . . . you think they are?'

'I do! Where is my partner, Majud? Where is that stone-hearted old money-grubber?'

'I do not believe he is expecting your arrival—'

'Nor do I! But how could I stay in Adua while . . . *this*,' and he spread his arms wide to encompass swarming, babbling, fragrant Crease, 'all *this* was happening without me? Besides, I have a fascinating new idea I wish to discuss with him. Steam, now, is the thing.'

'Is it?'

'The engineering community is in an uproar following a demonstration of Scibgard's new coal-fired piston apparatus!'

'Whose what?'

Curnsbick perched eyeglasses on broad forehead to squint at the hills behind the town. 'The results of the first mineral investigations are quite fascinating. I suspect the gold in these mountains is black, my boy! Black as . . .' He trailed off, staring up the steps of the house. 'Not . . . can it be . . .' He fumbled down his eyeglasses and let fall his jaw. 'The famous Iosiv Lestek?'

The actor, swaddled in a blanket and with several days' grey growth upon his grey cheeks, blinked back from the doorway. 'Well, yes—'

'My dear sir!' Curnsbick trotted up the steps, caused one of Buckhorn's sons to fumble his hammer by flicking a mark at him, seized the actor by the hand and pumped it more vigorously than any piston apparatus could have conceived of. 'An honour to make your acquaintance, sir, a perfect honour! I was transported by your Bayaz on one occasion back in Adua. Veritably transported!'

'You do me too much kindness,' murmured Lestek as Majud's ruthlessly pleasant partner steered him into the shop. 'Though I feel sure my best work still lies ahead of me . . .'

Temple blinked after them. Curnsbick was not quite what he had been led to expect. But then what was in life? He stepped back once again, losing himself again in happy contemplation of his building, and was nearly knocked onto his face by another slap on the shoulder. He rounded on Shy, decidedly annoyed this time.

'You'll get your money, you bloodsucking—'

A monstrous fellow with a tiny face perched on an enormous bald head stood at his back. 'The Mayor . . . wants . . . to see you,' he intoned, as though they were lines for a walk-on part badly memorised.

Temple was already running through the many reasons why someone powerful might want him dead. 'You're sure it was me?' The man nodded. Temple swallowed. 'Did she say why?'

'Didn't say. Didn't ask.'

'And if I would rather remain here?'

That minuscule face crinkled smaller still with an almost painful effort of thought. 'Wasn't an option . . . she discussed.'

Temple took a quick glance about but there was no help in easy reach and, in any case, the Mayor was one of those inevitable people. If she wanted to see him, she would see him soon enough. He shrugged, once more whisked helpless as a leaf on the winds of fate, and trusted to God. For reasons best known to Himself, He'd been coming through for Temple lately.

The Mayor gazed across her desk in thoughtful silence for a very long time.

People with elevated opinions of themselves no doubt delight in being looked upon in such a manner, mentally listing the many wonderful characteristics the onlooker must be in dumbstruck admiration of. For Temple it was torture. Reflected in that estimating gaze he saw all his own disappointment in himself, and wriggled in his chair wishing the ordeal would end.

'I am hugely honoured by the kind invitation, your . . . Mayor . . . ness,' he ventured, able to bear it no longer, 'but—'

'Why are we here?'

The old man by the window, whose presence was so far a mystery, gave vent to a crackly chuckle. 'Juvens and his brother Bedesh debated that very question for seven years and the longer they argued, the further away was the answer. I am Zacharus.' He leaned forward, holding out one knobbly-knuckled hand, black crescents of dirt ingrained beneath the fingernails.

'Like the Magus?' asked Temple, tentatively offering his own.

'Exactly like.' The old man seized his hand, twisted it over and probed at the callus on his middle finger, still pronounced even though Temple had not held a pen in weeks. 'A man of letters,' said Zacharus, and a group of pigeons perched on the window sill all at once reared up and flapped their wings at each other.

'I have had . . . several professions.' Temple managed to worm his hand from the old man's surprisingly powerful grip. 'I was trained in history, theology and law in the Great Temple of Dagoska by Haddish Kahdia—' The Mayor looked up sharply at the name. 'You knew him?'

'A lifetime ago. A man I greatly admired. He always preached and practised the same. He did what he thought right, no matter how difficult.'

'My mirror image,' muttered Temple.

'Different tasks need different talents,' observed the Mayor. 'Do you have experience with treaties?'

'As it happens, I negotiated a peace agreement and trimmed a border or two last time I was in Styria.' He had served as a tool in a shameful and entirely illegal land-grab, but honesty was an advantage to carpenters and priests, not to lawyers.

'I want you to prepare a treaty for me,' said the Mayor. 'One that brings Crease, and a slab of the Far Country around it, into the Empire and under its protection.'

'Into the Old Empire? The great majority of the settlers come from the Union. Would that not be the natural—'

'Absolutely not the Union.'

'I see. Not wishing to talk myself into trouble – I do that rather too often – but . . . the only laws people seem to respect out here are the ones with a point on the end.'

'Now, perhaps.' The Mayor swept to the window and looked down into the swarming street. 'But the gold will run out and the prospectors will drift off, and the fur will run out and the trappers will drift off, then the gamblers, then the thugs, then the whores. Who will remain? The likes of your friend Buckhorn, building a house and raising cattle a day's ride out of town. Or your friend Majud, whose very fine shop and forge you have been chafing your hands on these past weeks. People who grow things, sell things, make things.' She gracefully acquired a glass and bottle on the way back. 'And those kinds of people like laws. They don't like lawyers much, but they consider them a necessary evil. And so do I.'

She poured out a measure but Temple declined. 'Drink and I have had some long and painful conversations and found we simply can't agree.'

'Drink and I can't agree either.' She shrugged and tossed it down herself. 'But we keep on having the argument.'

'I have a rough draft . . .' Zacharus rummaged in his coat, producing a faint smell of musty onions and a grubby sheaf of odd-sized papers, scrawled upon with the most illegible handwriting imaginable. 'The principal points covered, as you see. The ideal is the status of a semi-independent enclave under the protection of and paying nominal taxes to the Imperial government. There is precedent. The city of Calcis enjoys similar status. Then there is . . . was . . . what's it called? Thingy. You know.' He screwed up his eyes and slapped at the side of his head as if he could knock the answer free.

'You have some experience with the law,' said Temple as he leafed through the document.

The old man waved a dismissive and gravy-stained hand. 'Imperial law, a long time ago. This treaty must be binding under Union law and mining traditions also.'

'I will do the best I can. It will mean nothing until it is signed, of course, by a representative of the local population and, well, by the Emperor, I suppose.'

'An Imperial Legate speaks for the Emperor.'

'You have one handy?'

Zacharus and the Mayor exchanged a glance. 'The legions of Legate Sarmis are said to be within four weeks' march.'

'I understand Sarmis is . . . not a man anyone would choose to invite. His legions even less so.'

The Mayor gave a resigned shrug. 'Choice does not enter into it. Papa Ring is keen for Crease to be brought into the Union. I understand his negotiations in that direction are well advanced. That *cannot* be allowed to happen.'

'I understand,' said Temple. That their escalating squabble had acquired an international dimension and might well escalate further still. But escalating squabbles are meat and drink to a lawyer. He had to confess some trepidation at the idea of going back to that profession, but it certainly looked like the easy way.

'How long will it take you to prepare the document?' asked the Mayor.

'A few days. I have Majud's shop to finish—'

'Make this a priority. Your fee will be two hundred marks.'

'Two . . . hundred?'

'Is that sufficient?'

Most definitely the easy way. Temple cleared his throat and said in a voice slightly hoarse, 'That will be adequate but . . . I must complete the building first.' He surprised himself with that even more than the Mayor had surprised him with the fee.

Zacharus nodded approvingly. 'You are a man who likes to see things through.'

Temple could only smile. 'The absolute opposite but . . . I've always liked the idea of being one.'

Fun

They were all in attendance, more or less. The whole Fellowship reunited. Well, not Leef, of course, or the others left in the dirt out there on the flat and empty. But the rest. Laughing and backslapping and lying about how well things were going now. Some misting up at rose-tinted remembrances of the way things had been on the trail. Some observing what a fine building the firm of Majud and Curnsbick had to work with. Probably Shy should've been joshing away with the rest. How long since she had some fun, after all? But she'd always found fun was easier talked of and looked forward to than actually had.

Dab Sweet was complaining about the faithlessness of those prospectors he'd guided into the mountains and who'd stiffed him on the payment before he could stiff them. Crying Rock was nodding along and grumbling, 'Mmm,' at all the wrong moments. Iosiv Lestek was trying to impress one of the whores with tales of his heyday on the stage. She was asking whether that was before the amphitheatre got built, which by most estimates was well over a thousand years ago. Savian was swapping grunts with Lamb in one corner, tight as if they'd known each other since boys. Hedges was lurking in another, nursing a bottle. Buckhorm and his wife still had a fair old brood running about folks' legs despite the ones they'd lost in the wilderness.

Shy gave a sigh and drank another silent toast to Leef and the rest who couldn't be there. Probably the company of the dead suited her better right then.

'I used to ride drag behind an outfit like this!'

She turned towards the door and got quite the shock. Temple's more successful twin stood there in a new black suit, all tidy as a princess, his dusty tangle of hair and beard barbered close. He'd come upon a new hat and a new manner besides, swaggering in more like owner than builder.

Wasn't until she felt a sting of disappointment to see him so unfamiliar that she realised how much she'd been looking forward to seeing him the same.

'Temple!' came the merry calls and they crowded round to approve of him.

'Who'd have thought you could fish such a carpenter from a river?' Curnsbick was asking, an arm around Temple's shoulders like he'd known him all his life.

'A lucky find indeed!' said Majud, like he was the one did the fishing and lent the money and Shy hadn't been within a dozen miles at the time.

She worked her tongue around, reflecting that it surely was hard to get even the little credit you deserved, leaned to spit through the gap in her teeth, then saw Luline Buckhorm watching her with a warning eyebrow up and swallowed it instead.

Probably she should've been glad she'd saved a man from drowning and steered him to a better life, her faith justified against all contrary opinion. Let ring the bells! But instead she felt like a secret only she'd enjoyed was suddenly common knowledge, and found she was brooding on how she might go about spoiling it all for him, and then was even more annoyed that she was thinking like a mean child, and turned her back on the room and took another sour pull at her bottle. The bottle never changed unexpectedly, after all. It always left you equally disappointed.

'Shy?'

She made sure she looked properly surprised, like she'd no idea he'd be in the room. 'Well, if it ain't everyone's favourite chunk o' driftwood, the great architect himself.'

'The very same,' said Temple, tipping that new hat.

'Drink?' she asked him, offering the bottle.

'I shouldn't.'

'Too good to drink with me these days?'

'Not good enough. I can never stop halfway.'

'Halfway to where?'

'Face down in the shit was my usual destination.'

'You take a sip, I'll try and catch you if you fall, how's that?'

'I suppose it wouldn't be the first time.' He took the bottle, and a sip, and grimaced like she'd kicked him in the fruits. 'God! What the hell's it made of?'

'I've decided it's one of those questions you're happier without an answer to. Like how much that finery o' yours cost.'

'I haggled hard,' thumping at his chest as he tried to get his voice back. 'You would've been proud.'

Shy snorted. 'Pride ain't common with me. And it still must've cost a fair sum for a man with debts.'

'Debts, you say?'

Here was familiar ground, at least. 'Last we spoke it was—'

'Forty-three marks?' Eyes sparkling with triumph, he held out one finger. A purse dangled from the tip, gently swinging.

She blinked at it, then snatched it from his finger and jerked it open. It held the confusion of different coinage you usually found in Crease, but mostly silver, and at a quick assay there could easily have been sixty marks inside.

'You turned to thievery?'

'Lower yet. To law. I put ten extra in there for the favour. You did save my life, after all.'

She knew she should be smiling but somehow she was doing just the opposite. 'You sure your life's worth that much?'

'Only to me. Did you think I'd never pay?'

'I thought you'd grab your first chance to wriggle out of it and run off in the night. Or maybe die first.'

Temple raised his brows. 'That's about what I thought. Looks like I surprised us both. Pleasantly, though, I hope.'

'Of course,' she lied, pocketing the purse.

'Aren't you going to count it?'

'I trust you.'

'You do?' He looked right surprised about it and so was she, but she realised it was true. True of a lot of folk in that room.

'If it ain't all there I can always track you down and kill you.'

'It's nice to know that's an option.'

They stood side by side, in silence, backs to the wall, watching a room full of their friends' chatter. She glanced at him and he slowly looked sideways, like he was checking whether she was looking, and when he got there she pretended she'd been looking past him at Hedges all along. Tense having him next to her of a sudden. As if without that debt between them they were pressed up too close for comfort.

'You did a fine job on the building,' was the best she could manage after digging away for something to say.

'Fine jobs and paid debts. I can think of a few acquaintances who wouldn't recognise me.'

'I'm not sure I recognise you.'

'That good or bad?'

'I don't know.' A long pause, and the room was getting hot from all the folk blathering in it, and her face was hot in particular, and she passed Temple the bottle, and he shrugged and took a sip and passed it back. She took a bigger one. 'What do we talk about, now you don't owe me money?'

'The same things as everyone else, I suppose.'

'What do they talk about?'

He frowned at the crowded room. 'The high quality of my craftsman-ship appears to be a popular—'

'Your head swells any bigger you won't be able to stand.'

'A lot of people are talking about this fight that's coming—'

'I've heard more'n enough about that.'

'There's always the weather.'

'Muddy, lately, in main street, I've observed.'

'And I hear there's more mud on the way.' He grinned sideways at her and she grinned back, and the distance didn't feel so great after all.

'Will you say a few words before the fun starts?' It was when Curns-bick loomed suddenly out of nowhere Shy realised she was already more'n a bit drunk.

'Words about what?' she asked.

'I apologise, my dear, but I was speaking to this gentleman. You look surprised.'

'Not sure which shocks me more, that I'm a dear or he's a gentleman.'

'I stand by both appellations,' said the inventor, though Shy wasn't sure what the hell he meant by it. 'And as ex-spiritual advisor to this ex-Fellowship, and architect and chief carpenter of this outstanding edifice, what gentleman better to address our little gathering at its completion?'

Temple raised his palms helplessly as Curnsbick hustled him off and Shy took another swig. The bottle was getting lighter all the time. And she was getting less annoyed.

Probably there was a link between the two.

*

'My old teacher used to say you know a man by his friends!' Temple called at the room. 'Guess I can't be quite the shit I thought I was!'

A few laughs and some shouts of, 'Wrong! Wrong!'

'Not long ago I barely knew one person I could have called decent. Now I can fill a room I built with them. I used to wonder why anyone would come out to this God-forsaken arse of the world who didn't have to. Now I know. They come to be part of something new. To live in new country. To be new people. I nearly died out on the plains, and I can't say I would have been widely mourned. But a Fellowship took me in and gave me another chance I hardly deserved. Not many of them were keen to begin with, I'll admit, but . . . one was, and that was enough. My old teacher used to say you know the righteous by what they give to those who can't give back. I doubt anyone who's had the misfortune to bargain with her would agree, but I will always count Shy South among the righteous.'

A general murmur of agreement, and some raised glasses, and he saw Corlin slapping Shy on the back and her looking sour beyond belief.

'My old teacher used to say there is no better act than the raising of a good building. It gives something to those that live in it, and visit it, and even pass it by every day it stands. I haven't really tried at much in life, but I've tried to make a good building of this. Hopefully it will stand a little longer than some of the others hereabouts. May God smile on it as He has smiled on me since I fell in that river, and bring shelter and prosperity to its occupants.'

'And liquor is free to all!' bellowed Curnsbick. Majud's horrified complaints were drowned out in the stampede towards the table where the bottles stood. 'Especially the master carpenter himself.' And the inventor conjured a glass into Temple's hand and poured a generous measure, smiling so broadly Temple could hardly refuse. He and drink might have had their disagreements, but if the bottle was always willing to forgive, why shouldn't he? Was not forgiveness neighbour to the divine? How drunk could one get him?

Drunk enough for another, as it turned out.

'Good building, lad, I always knew you had hidden talents,' rambled Sweet as he sloshed a third into Temple's glass. 'Well hidden, but what's the point in an obvious hidden talent?'

'What indeed?' agreed Temple, swallowing a fourth. He could not have called it a pleasant taste now, but it was no longer like swallowing red-hot wire wool. How drunk could four get him, anyway?

Buckhorm had produced a fiddle now and was hacking out a tune while Crying Rock did injury to a drum in the background. There was dancing. Or at least well-meaning clomping in the presence of music if not directly related to it. A kind judge would have called it dancing and Temple was feeling like a kind judge then, and with each drink – and he'd lost track of the exact number – he got more kind and less judging, so that when Luline Buckhorm laid small but powerful hands upon him he did not demur and in fact tested the floorboards he had laid only a couple of days before with some enthusiasm.

The room grew hotter and louder and dimmer, sweat-shining faces swimming at him full of laughter and damn it but he was enjoying himself like he couldn't remember when. The night he joined the Company of the Gracious Hand, maybe, and the mercenary life was all a matter of good men facing fair risks together and laughing at the world and nothing to do with theft, rape and murder on an industrial scale. Lestek tried to add his pipe to the music, failed in a coughing fit and had to be escorted out for air. Temple thought he saw the Mayor, talking softly to Lamb under the watchful eyes of a few of her thugs. He was dancing with one of the whores and complimenting her on her clothes, which were repugnantly garish, and she couldn't hear him anyway and kept shouting, 'What?' Then he was dancing with one of Gentili's cousins, and complimenting him on his clothes, which were dirt-streaked from prospecting and smelled like a recently opened tomb, but the man still beamed at the compliment. Corlin came past in stately hold with Crying Rock, both of them looking grave as judges, both trying to lead, and Temple near choked on his tongue at the unlikeliness of the couple. Then suddenly he was dancing with Shy and to his mind they were making a pretty good effort at it, quite an achievement since he still had a half-full glass in one hand and she a half-empty bottle.

'Never thought you'd be a dancer,' he shouted in her ear. 'Too hard for it.'

'Never thought you'd be one,' her breath hot against his cheek. 'Too soft.'

'No doubt you're right. My wife taught me.'

She stiffened then, for a moment. 'You've got a wife?'

'I did have. And a daughter. They died. Long time ago, now. Sometimes it doesn't feel so long.'

She took a drink, looking at him sideways over the neck of the bottle, and there was something to that glance gave him a breathless tingle. He leaned to speak to her and she caught him around the head and kissed him quite fiercely. If he'd had time he would've reasoned she wasn't the type for gentle kisses but he didn't get time to reason, or kiss back, or push her off, or even work out which would be his preference before she twisted his head away and was dancing with Majud, leaving him to be manhandled about the floor by Corlin.

'You think you're getting one from me you've another think coming,' she growled.

He leaned against the wall, head spinning, face sweating, heart pounding as if he had a dose of the fever. Strange, what sharing a little spit can do. Well, along with a few measures of raw spirits on a man ten years sober. He looked at his glass, thought he'd be best off throwing the contents down the wall, then decided he put more value on the wall than himself and drank them instead.

'You all right?'

'She kissed me,' he muttered.

'Shy?'

Temple nodded, then realised it was Lamb he'd said it to, and shortly thereafter that it might not have been the cleverest thing to say.

But the big Northman only grinned. 'Well, that's about the least surprising thing I ever heard. Everyone in the Fellowship saw it coming. The snapping and arguing and niggling over the debt. Classic case.'

'Why did no one say anything?'

'Several talked of nothing else.'

'I mean to me.'

'In my case, 'cause I had a bet with Savian on when it would happen. We both thought a lot sooner'n this, but I won. He can be a funny bastard, that Savian.'

'He can . . . what?' Temple hardly knew what shocked him more, that Shy kissing him came as no surprise, or that Savian could be funny. 'Sorry to be so predictable.'

'Folk usually prefer the obvious outcome. Takes bones to defy expectation.'

'Meaning I don't have any.'

Lamb only shrugged as though that was a question that hardly needed answering. Then he picked up his battered hat.

'Where are you going?' asked Temple.

'Ain't I got a right to my own fun?' He put a hand on Temple's shoulder. A friendly, fatherly hand, but a frighteningly firm one, too. 'Be careful with her. She ain't as tough as she looks.'

'What about me? I don't even look tough.'

'That's true. But if Shy hurts you I won't break her legs.'

By the time Temple had worked that one out, Lamb was gone. Dab Sweet had commandeered the fiddle and was up on a table, stomping so the plates jumped, sawing away at the strings like they were around his sweetheart's neck and he had moments to save her.

'I thought we were dancing?'

Shy's cheek had colour in it and her eyes were shining deep and dark and for reasons he couldn't be bothered to examine but probably weren't all that complicated anyway she looked dangerously fine to him right then. So, fuck it all, he tossed down his drink with a manly flick of the wrist then realised the glass was empty, threw it away, snatched her bottle while she grabbed his other hand and they dragged each other in amongst the lumbering bodies.

It was a long time since Shy had got herself properly reeling drunk but she found the knack came back pretty quick. Putting one foot in front of the other had become a bit of a challenge but if she kept her eyes wide open on the ground and really thought about it she didn't fall over too much. The hostelry was way too bright and Camling said something about a policy on guests and she laughed in his face and told him there were more whores than guests in this fucking place and Temple laughed as well and snorted snot down his beard. Then he chased her up the stairs with his hand on her arse which was funny to begin with then a bit annoying and she slapped him and near knocked him down the steps he was that surprised, but she caught him by the shirt and dragged him after and said sorry for the slap and he said what slap and started kissing her on the top landing and tasted like spirits. Which wasn't a bad way to taste in her book.

'Isn't Lamb here?'

'Staying at the Mayor's place now.'

Bloody hell things were spinning by then. She was fumbling in her trousers for the key and laughing and then she was fumbling in his trousers and they were up against the wall and kissing again her mouth full of his breath and his tongue and her hair then the door banging open and the two of them tumbling through and across the dim-lit floorboards. She crawled on top of him and they were grunting away, room reeling, and she felt the burn of sick at the back of her throat but swallowed it and didn't much care as it tasted no worse than the first time and Temple seemed to be a long way from complaining or probably even noticing either, he was too busy struggling with the buttons on her shirt and couldn't have been making harder work of it if they'd been the size of pinheads.

She realised the door was open still and kicked out at it but judged the distance all wrong and kicked a hole in the plaster beside the frame instead, started laughing again. Got the door shuddering shut with the next kick and he had her shirt open now and was kissing at her chest which felt all right actually if a bit ticklish, her own body looking all pale and strange to her and she was wondering when was the last time she did anything like this and deciding it was way too long. Then he'd stopped and was staring down in the darkness, eyes just a pair of glimmers.

'Are we doing the right thing?' he asked, so comic serious for a moment she wanted to laugh again.

'How the fuck should I know? Get your trousers off.'

She was trying to wriggle free of her own but still had her boots on and was getting more and more tangled, knew she should've taken the boots off first but it was a bit late now and she grunted and kicked and her belt thrashed about like a snake cut in half, her knife flopping off the end of it and clattering against the wall, until she got one boot off and one trouser-leg and that seemed good enough for the purpose.

They'd made it to the bed somehow and were tangled up with each other more naked than not, warm and pleasantly wriggling, his hand between her legs and her shoving her hips against it, both laughing less and grunting more, slow and throaty, bright dots fizzing on the inside of her closed lids so she had to open her eyes so she didn't feel like she'd fall right off the bed and out the ceiling. Eyes open was worse, the room turning around her loud with her breath and her thudding heartbeat and the warm rubbing of skin on skin and the springs in the old mattress shrieking with complaint but no one giving too much of a shit for their objections.

Something about her brother and sister niggled at her, and Gully swinging, and Lamb and a fight, but she let it all drift past like smoke and spin away with the spinning ceiling.

How long since she had some fun, after all?

*

'Oh,' groaned Temple. 'Oh no.'

He moaned a piteous moan as of the cursed dead in hell, facing an eternity of suffering and regretting most bitterly their lives wasted in sin.

'God help me.'

But God had the righteous to assist and Temple could not pretend to be in that category. Not after last night's fun.

Everything hurt him. The blanket across his bare legs. A fly buzzing faintly up near the ceiling. The sun sneaking around the edges of the curtains. The sounds of Crease life and Crease death beyond them. He remembered now why he had stopped drinking. What he could not remember was why it had felt like a good idea to start again.

He winced at the hacking, gurgling noise that had woken him, managed to lift his head a few degrees and saw Shy kneeling over the night pot. She was naked except for one boot and her trousers tangled around that ankle, ribs standing stark as she retched. A strip of light from the window cut over one shoulder-blade bright, bright, and found a big scar, a burn like a letter upside down.

She rocked back, turned eyes sunken in dark rings on him and wiped a string of spit from the corner of her mouth. 'Another kiss?'

The sound he made was indescribable. Part laugh, part belch, part groan. He could not have made it again in a year of trying. But why would he have wanted to?

'Got to get some air.' Shy dragged up her trousers but left the belt dangling and they sagged off her arse as she tottered to the window.

'Don't do it,' moaned Temple, but there was no stopping her. Not without moving, and that was inconceivable. She hauled the curtains away and pushed the window wide, while he struggled feebly to shield his eyes from the merciless light.

Shy was cursing as she fished around under the other bed. He could hardly believe it when she came up with a quarter-full bottle, pulled the cork with her teeth and sat there gathering her courage, like a swimmer staring into an icy pool.

'You're not going to—'

She tipped the bottle up and swallowed, clapped the back of her hand to her mouth, stomach muscles fluttering, and burped, and grimaced, and shivered, and offered it to him.

'You?' she asked, voice wet with rush back.

He wanted to be sick just looking. 'God, no.'

'It's the only thing'll help.'

'Is the cure for a stab-wound really another one?'

'Once you set to stabbing yourself it can be hard to stop.'

She shrugged her shirt over that scar, and after doing a couple of buttons realised she had them in the wrong holes and the whole front twisted, gave up and slumped down on the other bed. Temple wasn't sure he'd ever seen anyone look so worn out and defeated, not even in the mirror.

He wondered whether he should put his clothes on. Some of the muddy rags scattered across the boards bore a faint resemblance to part of his new suit, but he could not be sure. Could not be sure of anything. He forced himself to sit, dragging his legs off the bed as if they were made of lead. When he was sure his stomach would not immediately rebel, he looked at Shy and said, 'You'll find them, you know.'

'How do I know?'

'Because no one deserves a good turn of the card more.'

'You don't know what I deserve.' She slumped back on her elbows, head sinking into her bony shoulders. 'You don't know what I've done.'

'Can't be worse than what you did to me last night.'

She didn't laugh. She was looking past him, eyes focused far away. 'When I was seventeen I killed a boy.'

Temple swallowed. 'Well, yes, that is worse.'

'I ran off from the farm. Hated it there. Hated my bitch mother. Hated my bastard stepfather.'

'Lamb?'

'No, the first one. My mother got through 'em. I had some fool notion I'd open a store. Things went wrong right off. Didn't mean to kill that boy, but I got scared and I cut him.' She rubbed absently under her jaw with a fingertip. 'He wouldn't stop bleeding.'

'Did he have it coming?'

'Guess he must've. Got it, didn't he? But he had a family, and they chased me, and I ran, and I got hungry so I started stealing.' She droned it all out in a dead monotone. 'After a while I got to thinking no one gives you a fair chance and taking things is easier than making 'em. I fell in with some low company and dragged 'em lower. More robbing, and more killings, and maybe some had it coming, and maybe some didn't. Who gets what they deserve?'

Temple thought of Kahdia. 'I'll admit God can be a bit of a shit that way.'

'In the end there were bills up over half the Near Country for my arrest. Smoke, they called me, like I was something to be scared of, and put a price on my head. About the only time in my life I was thought worth something.' She curled her lips back from her teeth. 'They caught some woman and hanged her in my place. Didn't even look like me, but she got killed and I got away with it and I don't know why.'

There was a heavy silence, then. She raised the bottle and took a couple of good, long swallows, neck working with the effort, and she came up gasping for air with eyes watering hard. That was an excellent moment for Temple to mumble his excuses and run. A few months ago, the door would have been swinging already. His debts were settled, after all, which was better than he usually managed on his way out. But he found this time he did not want to leave.

'If you want me to share your low opinion of yourself,' he said, 'I'm afraid I can't oblige. Sounds to me like you made some mistakes.'

'You'd call all that mistakes?'

'Some pretty stupid ones, but yes. You never chose to do evil.'

'Who chooses evil?'

'I did. Pass me that bottle.'

'What's this?' she asked as she tossed it across. 'A shitty-past competition?'

'Yes, and I win.' He closed his eyes and forced down a swallow, burning and choking all the way. 'After my wife died, I spent a year as the most miserable drunk you ever saw.'

'I've seen some pretty fucking miserable ones.'

'Then picture worse. I thought I couldn't get any lower, so I signed up as lawyer for a mercenary company, and found I could.' He raised the bottle in salute. 'The Company of the Gracious Hand, under Captain General Nicomo Cosca! Oh, noble brotherhood!' He drank again. It felt good in a hideous way, like picking at a scab.

'Sounds fancy.'

'That's what I thought.'

'Wasn't fancy?'

'A worse accumulation of human scum you never saw.'

'I've seen some pretty fucking bad ones.'

'Then picture worse. To begin with I believed there were good reasons for what they did. What *we* did. Then I convinced myself there were good reasons. Then I knew there weren't even good excuses, but did it anyway because I was too coward not too. We were sent to the Near

Country to root out rebels. A friend of mine tried to save some people. He was killed. And them. They killed each other. But I squirmed away, as always, and I ran like the coward I am, and I fell in a river and, for reasons best known only to Himself, God sent a good woman to fish my worthless carcass out.'

'As a point of fact, God sent a murdering outlaw.'

'Well, His ways are damned mysterious. I can't say I took to you right away, that's true, but I'm starting to think God sent exactly what I needed.' Temple stood. It wasn't easy, but he managed it. 'I feel like all my life I've been running. Maybe it's time for me to stick. To try it, at least.' He sank down beside her, the creaking of the bedsprings going right through him. 'I don't care what you've done. I owe you. Only my life, now, but still. Let me stick.' He tossed the empty bottle aside, took a deep breath, licked his finger and thumb-tip and smoothed down his beard. 'God help me, but I'll take that kiss now.'

She squinted at him, every colour in her face wrong – skin a little yellow, eyes a little pink, lips a little blue. 'You serious?'

'I may be a fool, but I'm not letting a woman who can fill a sick pot without spilling pass me by. Wipe your mouth and come here.'

He shifted towards her, someone clattering in the corridor outside, and her mouth twitched up in a smile. She leaned towards him, hair tickling his shoulder, and her breath smelled foul and he did not care. The doorknob turned and rattled, and Shy bellowed at the door, so close and broken-voiced it felt like a hatchet blow in Temple's forehead, 'You got the wrong fucking room, idiot!'

Against all expectation, the door lurched open anyway and a man stepped in. A tall man with close-cropped fair hair and sharp clothes. He had a sharp expression too as his eyes wandered unhurried about the place, as if this was his room and he was both annoyed and amused to find someone else had been fucking in it.

'I think I got it right,' he said, and two other men appeared in the doorway, and neither looked like men you'd be happy to see anywhere, let alone uninvited in your hotel room. 'I heard you been looking for me.'

'Who the fuck are you?' growled Shy, eyes flickering to the corner where her knife was lying sheathed on the floor.

The newcomer smiled like a conjuror about to pull off the trick you won't believe. 'Grega Cantliss.'

Then a few things happened at once. Shy flung the bottle at the doorway and dived for her knife. Cantliss dived for her, the other two tangled in the doorway behind him.

And Temple dived for the window.

Statements about sticking notwithstanding, before he knew it he was outside, air whooping in his throat in a terrified squeal as he dropped, then rolling in the cold mud, then floundering up and sprinting naked across the main street, which in most towns would have been considered poor form but in Crease was not especially remarkable. He heard someone bellow and forced himself on, slipping and sliding and his heart pounding so hard he thought he might have to hold his skull together, the Mayor's Church of Dice lurching closer.

When the guards at the door saw him they smiled, then they frowned, then they caught hold of him as he scrambled up the steps.

'The Mayor's got a rule about trousers—'

'Got to see Lamb. Lamb!'

One of them punched him in the mouth, snapped his head back and sent him stumbling against the door-frame. He knew he deserved it more than ever, but somehow a fist in the face always came as a surprise.

'Lamb!' he screeched again, covering his head as best he could. 'La— ooof.' The other's fist sank into his gut and doubled him up, drove his wind right out and dropped him to his knees, blowing bloody bubbles. While he was considering the stones under his face in breathless silence, one of the guards grabbed him by the hair and started dragging him up, raising his fist high.

'Leave him be.' To Temple's great relief, Savian caught that fist before it came down with one knobbly hand. 'He's with me.' He grabbed Temple under the armpit with the other and dragged him through the doorway, shrugging off his coat and throwing it around Temple's shoulders. 'What the hell happened?'

'Cantliss,' croaked Temple, limping into the gaming hall, waving a weak arm towards the hostelry, only able to get enough breath for one wheezing word at a time. 'Shy—'

'What happened?' Lamb was thumping down the steps from the Mayor's room, barefooted himself and with his shirt half-buttoned, and for a moment Temple was wondering why he came that way, and then he saw the drawn sword in Lamb's fist and felt very scared, and then he saw something in Lamb's face that made him feel more scared still.

'Cantliss . . . at Camling's . . .' he managed to splutter.

Lamb stood a moment, eyes wide, then he strode for the door, brushing the guards out of his way, and Savian strode after.

'Everything all right?' The Mayor stood on the balcony outside her rooms in a Gurkish dressing gown, a pale scar showing in the hollow between her collar bones. Temple blinked up, wondering if Lamb had been in there with her, then pulled his borrowed coat around him and hurried after the others without speaking. 'Put some trousers on!' she called after him.

When Temple struggled up the steps of the hostelry, Lamb had Camling by the collar and had dragged him most of the way over his own counter with one hand, sword in the other and the proprietor desperately squealing, 'They just dragged her out! The Whitehouse, maybe, I have no notion, it was none of my doing!'

Lamb shoved Camling tottering away and stood, breath growling in his throat. Then he put the sword carefully on the counter and his palms flat before it, fingers spreading out, the wood gleaming in the space where the middle one should have been. Savian walked around behind the counter, shouldering Camling out of the way, took a glass and bottle from a high shelf, blew out one then pulled the cork from the other.

'You need a hand, you got mine,' he grunted as he poured.

Lamb nodded. 'You should know lending me a hand can be bad for your health.'

Savian coughed as he nudged the glass across. 'My health's a mess.'

'What are you going to do?' asked Temple.

'Have a drink.' And Lamb picked up the glass and drained it, white stubble on his throat shifting. Savian tipped the bottle to fill it again.

'Lamb!' Lord Ingelstad walked in somewhat unsteadily, his face pale and his waistcoat covered in stains. 'He said you'd be here!'

'Who said?'

Ingelstad gave a helpless chuckle as he tossed his hat on the counter, a few wisps of stray hair left standing vertically from his head. 'Strangest thing. After that fun at Majud's place, I was playing cards over at Papa Ring's. Entirely lost track of time and I was somewhat behind financially, I'll admit, and a gentleman came in to tell Papa something, and he told me he'd forget my debt if I brought you a message.'

'What message?' Lamb drank again, and Savian filled his glass again.

Ingelstad squinted at the wall. 'He said he's playing host to a friend of yours . . . and he'd very much like to be a gracious host . . . but you'll have to kiss the mud tomorrow night. He said you'll be dropping anyway, so you might as well drop willingly and you can both walk out of Crease free people. He said you have his word on that. He was very particular about it. You have his word, apparently.'

'Well, ain't I the lucky one,' said Lamb.

Lord Ingelstad squinted over at Temple as though only just noticing his unusual attire. 'It appears some people have had an even heavier night than I.'

'Can you take a message back?' asked Lamb.

'I daresay a few more minutes won't make any difference to Lady Ingelstad's temper at this point. I am *doomed* whatever.'

'Then tell Papa Ring I'll keep his word safe and sound. And I hope he'll do the same for his guest.'

The nobleman yawned as he jammed his hat back on. 'Riddles, riddles. Then off to bed for me!' And he strutted back out into the street.

'What are you going to do?' whispered Temple.

'There was a time I'd have gone charging over there without a thought for the costs and got bloody.' Lamb lifted the glass and looked at it for a moment. 'But my father always said patience is the king of virtues. A man has to be realistic. Has to be.'

'So what are you going to do?'

'Wait. Think. Prepare.' Lamb swallowed the last measure and bared his teeth at the glass. 'Then get bloody.'

High Stakes

'Atrim?' asked Faukin, directing his blank, bland, professional smile towards the mirror. 'Or something more radical?'

'Shave it all off, hair and beard, close to the skull as you can get.'

Faukin nodded as though that would have been his choice. The client always knows best, after all. 'A wet shave of the pate, then.'

'Wouldn't want to give the other bastard anything to hold on to. And I reckon it's a little late to damage my looks, don't you?'

Faukin gave his blank, bland, professional chuckle and began, comb struggling with the tangles in Lamb's thick hair, the snipping of the scissors cutting the silence up into neat little fragments. Outside the window the noise of the swelling crowd grew louder, more excited, and the tension in the room swelled with it. The grey cuttings spilled down the sheet, scattered across the boards in those tantalising patterns that looked to hold some meaning one could never quite grasp.

Lamb stirred at them with his foot. 'Where does it all go, eh?'

'Our time or the hair?'

'Either one.'

'In the case of the time, I would ask a philosopher rather than a barber. In the case of the hair, it is swept up and thrown out. Unless on occasion one might have a lady friend who would care to be entrusted with a lock . . .'

Lamb glanced over at the Mayor. She stood at the window, keeping one eye on Lamb's preparations and the other on those in the street, a slender silhouette against the sunset. He dismissed the notion with an explosive snort. 'One moment it's a part of you, the next it's rubbish.'

'We treat whole men like rubbish, why not their hair?'

Lamb sighed. 'I guess you've got the right of it.'

Faukin gave the razor a good slapping on the strap. Clients usually appreciated a flourish, a mirror flash of lamplight on steel, an edge of drama to proceedings.

'Careful,' said the Mayor, evidently in need of no extra drama today. Faukin had to confess to being considerably more scared of her than he was of Lamb. The Northman he knew for a ruthless killer, but suspected him of harbouring principles of a kind. He had no such suspicions about the Mayor. So he gave his blank, bland, professional bow, ceased his sharpening, brushed up a lather and worked it into Lamb's hair and beard, then began to shave with patient, careful, hissing strokes.

'Don't it ever bother you that it always grows back?' asked Lamb. 'There's no beating it, is there?'

'Could not the same be said of every profession? The merchant sells one thing to buy another. The farmer harvests one set of crops to plant another. The blacksmith—'

'Kill a man and he stays dead,' said Lamb, simply.

'But . . . if I might observe without causing offence . . . killers rarely stop at one. Once you begin, there is always someone else that needs killing.'

Lamb's eyes moved to Faukin's in the mirror. 'You're a philosopher after all.'

'On a strictly amateur footing.' Faukin worked the warm towel with a flourish and presented Lamb shorn, as it were, a truly daunting array of scars laid bare. In all his years as a barber, including three in the service of a mercenary company, he had never attended upon a head so battered, dented and otherwise manhandled.

'Huh.' Lamb leaned closer to the mirror, working his lopsided jaw and wrinkling his bent nose as though to convince himself it was indeed his own visage gazing back. 'There's the face of an evil bastard, eh?'

'I would venture to say a face is no more evil than a coat. It is the man beneath, and his actions, that count.'

'No doubt.' Lamb looked up at Faukin for a moment, and then back to himself. 'And there's the face of an evil bastard. You done the best a man could with it, though. Ain't your fault what you're given to work with.'

'I simply try to do the job exactly as I'd want it done to me.'

'Treat folk the way you'd want to be treated and you can't go far wrong, my father used to tell me. Seems our jobs are different after all. Aim o' mine is to do to the other man exactly what I'd least enjoy.'

'Are you ready?' The Mayor had silently drifted closer and was looking at the pair of them in the mirror.

Lamb shrugged. 'Either a man's always ready for a thing like this or he'll never be.'

'Good enough.' She came closer and took hold of Faukin's hand. He felt a strong need to back away, but clung to his blank, bland professionalism a moment longer. 'Any other jobs today?'

Faukin swallowed. 'Just the one.'

'Across the street?'

He nodded.

The Mayor pressed a coin into his palm and leaned close. 'The time is fast approaching when every person in Crease will have to choose one side of the street. I hope you choose wisely.'

Sunset had lent the town a carnival atmosphere. There was a single current to the crowds of drunk and greedy and it flowed to the amphitheatre. As he passed, Faukin could see the Circle marked out on the ancient cobbles at its centre, six strides across, torches on close-set poles to mark the edge and light the action. The ancient banks of stone seating and the new teetering stands of bodged-together carpentry were already boiling with an audience such as that place had not seen in centuries. Gamblers screeched for business and chalked odds on high boards. Hawkers sold bottles and hot gristle for prices outrageous even in this home of outrageous prices.

Faukin gazed at all those people swarming over each other, most of whom could hardly have known what a barber was let alone thought of employing one, reflected for the hundredth time that day, the thousandth time that week, the millionth time since he arrived that he should never have come here, clung tight to his bag and hurried on.

Papa Ring was one of those men who liked to spend money less the more of it he had. His quarters were humble indeed by comparison with the Mayor's, the furniture an improvised and splinter-filled collection, the low ceiling lumpy as an old bedspread. Glama Golden sat before a cracked mirror lit by smoking candles, something faintly absurd in that huge body crammed onto a stool and draped in a threadbare sheet, his head giving the impression of teetering on top like a cherry on a cream cake.

Ring stood at the window just as the Mayor had, his big fists clamped behind his back, and said, 'Shave it all off.'

'Except the moustache.' Golden gathered up the sheet so he could stroke at his top lip with huge thumb and forefinger. 'Had that all my life and it's going nowhere.'

'A most resplendent article of facial hair,' said Faukin, though in truth he could see more than a few grey hairs despite the poor light. 'To remove it would be a deep regret.'

In spite of being the undoubted favourite in the coming contest, Golden's eyes had a strange, haunted dampness as they found Faukin's in the mirror. 'You got regrets?'

Faukin lost his blank, bland, professional smile for a moment. 'Don't we all, sir?' He began to cut. 'But I suppose regrets at least prevent one from repeating the same mistakes.'

Golden frowned at himself in that cracked mirror. 'I find however high I stack the regrets, I still make the same mistakes again and again.'

Faukin had no answer for that, but the barber holds the advantage in such circumstances: he can let the scissors fill the silence. Snip, snip, and the yellow cuttings scattered across the boards in those tantalising patterns that looked to hold some meaning one could never quite grasp.

'Been over there with the Mayor?' called Papa Ring from the window.

'Yes, sir, I have.'

'How'd she seem?'

Faukin thought about the Mayor's demeanour and, more importantly, about what Papa Ring wanted to hear. A good barber never puts truth before the hopes of his clients. 'She seemed very tense.'

Ring stared back out of the window, thick thumb and fingers fussing nervously behind his back. 'I guess she would be.'

'What about the other man?' asked Golden. 'The one I'm fighting?'

Faukin stopped snipping for a moment. 'He seemed thoughtful. Regretful. But fixed on his purpose. In all honesty . . . he seemed very much like you.' Faukin did not mention what had only just occurred.

That he had, in all likelihood, given one of them their last haircut.

Bee was mopping up when he passed by the door. She hardly even had to see him, she knew him by his footsteps. 'Grega?' She dashed out into the hall, heart going so hard it hurt. 'Grega!'

He turned, wincing, like hearing her say his name made him sick. He looked tired, more'n a little drunk, and sore. She could always tell his moods. 'What?'

She'd made up all kinds of little stories about their reunion. One where he swept her into his arms and told her they could get married now. One where he was wounded and she'd to nurse him back to health. One where they argued, one where they laughed, one where he cried and said sorry for how he'd treated her.

But she hadn't spun no stories where she was just ignored.

'That all you got to say to me?'

'What else would there be?' He didn't even look her in the eye. 'I got to go talk to Papa Ring.' And he made off up the hall.

She caught his arm. 'Where are the children?' Her voice all shrill and bled out from her own disappointment.

'Mind your own business.'

'I am. You made me help, didn't you? You made me bring 'em!'

'You could've said no.' She knew it was true. She'd been so keen to please him she'd have jumped in a fire on his say-so. Then he gave a little smile, like he'd thought of something funny. 'But if you must know, I sold 'em.'

She felt cold to her stomach. 'To who?'

'Those Ghosts up in the hills. Those Dragon fuckers.'

Her throat was all closed up, she could hardly talk. 'What'll they do with 'em?'

'I don't know. Fuck 'em? Eat 'em? What do I care? What did you think I was going to do, start up an orphanage?' Her face was burning now, like he'd slapped her. 'You're such a stupid sow. Don't know that I ever met anyone stupider than you. You're stupider than—'

And she was on him and tearing at his face with her nails and she'd probably have bitten him if he hadn't hit her first, just above the eye, and she tumbled into the corner and caught a faceful of floor.

'You mad bitch!' She started to push herself up, all groggy, that familiar pulsing in her face, and he was touching his scratched cheek like he couldn't believe it. 'What did you do that for?' Then he was shaking out his fingers. 'You hurt my fucking hand!' And he took a step towards her as she tried to stand and kicked her in the ribs, folded her gasping around his boot.

'I hate you,' she managed to whisper, once she was done coughing.

'So?' And he looked at her like she was a maggot.

She remembered the day he'd chosen her out of all the room to dance with and nothing had ever felt so fine, and of a sudden it was like she saw the whole thing fresh, and he seemed so ugly, so petty and vain and selfish beyond enduring. He just used people and threw them away and left a trail of ruin behind him. How could she ever have loved him?

Just because for a few moments he'd made her feel one step above shit. The rest of the time ten steps below.

'You're so small,' she whispered at him. 'How did I not see it?'

He was pricked in his vanity then and he took another step at her, but she found her knife and whipped it out. He saw the blade, and for a moment he looked surprised, then he looked angry, then he started laughing like she was a hell of a joke.

'As if you've got the bones to use it!' And he sauntered past, giving her plenty of time to stab him if she'd wanted to. But she just knelt there, blood leaking out her nose and tapping down the front of her dress. Her best dress, which she'd worn three days straight 'cause she knew he'd be coming.

Once the dizziness had passed she got up and went to the kitchen. Everything was trembling but she'd taken worse beatings and worse disappointments, too. No one there so much as raised a brow at her bloody nose. The Whitehouse was that kind of place.

'Papa Ring said I need to feed that woman.'

'Soup in the pot,' grunted the cook's boy, perched on a box to look out of a high little window where all he got was a view of boots outside.

So she put a bowl on a tray with a cup of water and carried it down the damp-smelling stair to the cellar, past the big barrels in the darkness and the bottles on the racks gleaming with the torchlight.

The woman in the cage uncrossed her legs and stood, sliding her tight-bound hands up the rail behind her, one eye glinting through the hair tangled across her face as she watched Bee come closer. Warp sat in front at his table, ring of keys on it, pretending to read a book. He loved to pretend, thought it made him look right special, but even Bee, who weren't no wonder with her letters, could tell he had it upside down.

'What d'you want?' And he turned a sneer on her like she was a slug in his breakfast.

'Papa Ring said to feed her.'

She could almost see his brain rattling around in his big fat head. 'Why? Ain't like she'll be here much longer.'

'You think he tells me why?' she snapped. 'But I'll go back and tell Papa you wouldn't let me in if you—'

'All right, get it done, then. But I've got my eye on you.' He leaned close and blasted her with his rotting breath. 'Both eyes.'

He unlocked the gate and swung it squealing open and Bee ducked inside with her tray. The woman watched her. She couldn't move far from the rail, but even so she was backed up tight against it. The cage smelled of sweat and piss and fear, the woman's and all the others' who'd been kept in here before and no bright futures among 'em, that was a fact. No bright futures anywhere in this place.

Bee set the tray down and took the cup of water. The woman sucked at it thirstily, no pride left in her if she'd had any to begin with. Pride don't last long in the Whitehouse, and especially not down here. Bee leaned close and whispered.

'You asked me about Cantliss before. About Cantliss and the children.'

The woman stopped swallowing and her eyes flickered over to Bee's, bright and wild.

'He sold the children to the Dragon People. That's what he said.' Bee looked over her shoulder but Warp was already sitting back at his table and pulling at his jug, not looking in the least. He wouldn't think Bee would do anything worth attending to in her whole life. Right now that worked for her. She stepped closer, slipped out the knife and sawed through the ropes around one of the woman's rubbed-raw wrists.

'Why?' she whispered.

'Because Cantliss needs hurting.' Even then she couldn't bring herself to say killing, but they both knew what she meant. 'I can't do it.' Bee pressed the knife, handle first, into the woman's free hand where it was hidden behind her back. 'Reckon you can, though.'

Papa Ring fidgeted at the ring through his ear, an old habit went right back to his days as a bandit in the Badlands, his nerves rising with the rising noise in a painful lump under his jaw. He'd played a lot of hands, rolled a lot of dice, spun a lot of wheels, and maybe the odds were all stacked on his side, but the stakes had never been higher. He wondered whether she was nervous, the Mayor. No sign of it, standing alone on her balcony bolt upright with the light behind her, that stiff pride of hers showing even at this distance. But she had to be scared. Had to be.

How often had they stood here, after all, glaring across the great divide, planning each other's downfall by every means fair or foul, the number of men they paid to fight for them doubling and doubling again, the stakes swelling ever higher. A hundred murders and stratagems and manoeuvrings and webs of petty alliances broken and re-formed, and it all came down to this.

He slipped into one of his favourite furrows of thought, what to do with the Mayor when he won. Hang her as a warning? Have her stripped naked and beaten through town like a hog? Keep her as his whore? As anyone's? But he knew it was all fancy. He'd given his word she'd be let go and he'd keep it. Maybe folk on the Mayor's side of the street took him for a low bastard and maybe they were right, but all his life he'd kept his word.

It could give you some tough moments, your word. Could force you into places you didn't want to be, could serve you up puzzles where the right path weren't easy to pick. But it wasn't meant to be easy, it was meant to be right. There were too many men always did the easy thing, regardless.

Grega Cantliss, for instance.

Papa Ring looked sourly sideways. Here he was, three days late as always, slumped on Ring's balcony as if he had no bones in him and picking his teeth with a splinter. In spite of a new suit he looked sick and old and had fresh scratches on his face and a stale smell about him. Some men use up fast. But he'd brought what he owed plus a healthy extra for the favour. That was why he was still breathing. Ring had given his word, after all.

The fighters were coming out now with an accompanying rise in the mood of the mob. Golden's big shaved head bobbed above the crowd, a knot of Ring's men around him clearing folks away as they headed for the theatre, old stones lit up orange in the fading light. Ring hadn't mentioned the woman to Golden. He might be a magician with his fists but that man had a bad habit of getting distracted. So Ring had just told him to let the old man live if he got the chance, and considered that a promise kept. A man's got to keep his word but there has to be some give in it or you'll get nothing done.

He saw Lamb now, coming down the steps of the Mayor's place between the ancient columns, his own entourage of thugs about him. Ring fussed with his ear again. He'd a worry the old Northman was one of those bastards you couldn't trust to do the sensible thing. A right wild card, and Papa Ring liked to know what was in the deck. Specially when the stakes were high as this.

'I don't like the looks of that old bastard,' Cantliss said.

Papa Ring frowned at him. 'Do you know what? Neither do I.'

'You sure Golden'll take him?'

'Golden's taken everyone else, hasn't he?'

'I guess. Got a sad sort o' look to him though, for a winner.'

Ring could've done without this fool picking at his worries. 'That's why I had you steal the woman, isn't it? Just in case.'

Cantliss rubbed at his stubbly jaw. 'Still seems a hell of a risk.'

'One I wouldn't have had to take if you hadn't stole that old bastard's children and sold 'em to the savage.'

Cantliss' head jerked around with surprise.

'I can add two and two,' growled Ring, and felt a shiver like he was dirty and couldn't clean it off. 'How much lower can a man stoop? Selling children?'

Cantliss looked deeply wounded. 'That's so *fucking* unfair! You just said get the money by winter or I'd be a dead man. You didn't concern yourself with the source. You want to give me the money back, free yourself of its base origins?'

Ring looked at the old box on the table, and thought about that bright old gold inside, and frowned back out into the street. He hadn't got where he'd got by giving money back.

'Didn't think so.' Cantliss shook his head like stealing children was a fine business scheme for which he deserved the warmest congratulation. 'How was I to know this old bastard would wriggle out the long grass?'

'Because,' said Ring, speaking very slow and cold, 'you should have learned by now there's consequences when you *fucking* do a thing, and a man can't wander through life thinking no further ahead than the end of his cock!'

Cantliss worked his jaw and muttered, 'So fucking unfair,' and Ring was forced to wonder when was the last time he'd punched a man in the face. He was sorely, sorely tempted. But he knew it would solve nothing. That's why he'd stopped doing it and started paying other people to do it for him.

'Are you a child yourself, to whine about what's fair?' he asked. 'You think it's fair I have to stand up for a man can't tell a good hand of cards from a bad but still has to bet an almighty pile of money he don't have on the outcome? You think it's fair I have to threaten some girl's life to make sure of a fight? How does that reflect on me, eh? How's that for the start of my new era? You think it's fair I got to keep my word to men don't care a damn about theirs? Eh? What's God-fucked fair about all that? Go and get the woman.'

'Me?'

'Your bloody mess I'm aiming to clean up, isn't it? Bring her up here so our friend Lamb can see Papa Ring's a man of his word.'

'I might miss the start,' said Cantliss, like he couldn't believe he'd be inconvenienced to such an extent by a pair of very likely deaths.

'You keep talking you'll be missing the rest of your fucking life, boy. Get the woman.'

Cantliss stomped for the door and Ring thought he heard him mutter, 'Ain't fair.'

He gritted his teeth as he turned back towards the theatre. That bastard made trouble everywhere he went and had a bad end coming, and Ring was starting to hope it'd come sooner rather than later. He straightened his cuffs, and consoled himself with the thought that once the Mayor was beaten the bottom would fall right out of the henchman market and he could afford to hire himself a better class of thug. The crowd was falling silent now, and Ring reached for his ear then stopped himself, stifling another swell of nerves. He'd made sure the odds were all stacked on his side, but the stakes had never been higher.

'Welcome all!' bellowed Camling, greatly relishing the way his voice echoed to the very heavens, 'To this, the historic theatre of Crease! In the many centuries since its construction it can rarely have seen so momentous an event as that which will shortly be played out before your fortunate eyes!'

Could eyes be fortunate independently of their owners? This question gave Camling an instant's pause before he dismissed it. He could not allow himself to be distracted. This was his moment, the torchlit bowl crammed with onlookers, the street beyond heaving with those on tiptoe for a look, the trees on the valley side above even carrying cargoes of intrepid observers in their upper branches, all hanging upon his every word. Noted hotelier he might have been, but he was without doubt a sad loss to the performing arts.

'A fight, my friends and neighbours, and what a fight! A contest of strength and guile between two worthy champions, to be humbly refereed by myself, Lennart Camling, as a respected neutral party and long-established leading citizen of this community!'

He thought he heard someone call, 'Cockling!' but ignored it.

'A contest to settle a dispute between two parties over a claim, according to mining law—'

'Get the fuck on with it!' someone shouted.

There was a scattering of laughs, boos and jeers. Camling gave a long pause, chin raised, and treated the savages to a lesson in cultured gravity.

The type of lesson he had been hoping Iosiv Lestek might administer, what a farce *that* had turned out to be. 'Standing for Papa Ring, a man who needs no introduction—'

'Why give him one, then?' More laughter.

'—who has forged a dread name for himself across the fighting pits, cages and Circles of the Near and Far Countries ever since he left his native North. A man undefeated in twenty-two encounters. Glama . . . Golden!'

Golden shouldered his way into the Circle, stripped to the waist, his huge body smeared with grease to frustrate an opponent's grasp, great slabs of muscle glistening white by torchlight and reminding Camling of the giant albino slugs he sometimes saw in his cellar and was irrationally afraid of. With his skull shaved, the Northman's luxuriant moustache looked even more of an absurd affectation, but the volume of the crowd's bellows only increased. A breathless frenzy had descended upon them and they no doubt would have cheered an albino slug if they thought it might bleed for their entertainment.

Camling leaned close to whisper, 'Just that for a name?'

'Good as another,' said the old Northman, without removing his steady gaze from his opponent. No doubt everyone considered him the underdog. Certainly Camling had almost discounted him until that very moment: the older, smaller, leaner man, the gambler's odds considerably against him, but Camling noticed something in his eye that gave him pause. An eager look, as though he had an awful hunger and Golden was the meal.

The bigger man's face, by contrast, held a trace of doubt as Camling ushered the two together in the centre of the Circle. 'Do I know you?' he called over the baying of the audience. 'What's your real name?'

Lamb stretched his neck out to one side and then the other. 'Maybe it'll come to you.'

Camling held one hand high. 'May the best man win!' he shrieked.

Over the sudden roar he heard Lamb say, 'It's the worst man wins these.'

This would be Golden's last fight. That much he knew.

They circled each other, footwork, footwork, step and shuffle, each feeling out the other, the wild noise of the crowd and their shaken fists and twisted faces pushed off to one side. No doubt they were eager for the fight to start. They didn't realise that oftentimes the fight was won and lost here, in the slow moments before the fighters even touched.

By the dead, though, Golden was tired. Failures and regrets dragging after him like chains on a swimmer, heavier with each day, with each breath. This had to be his last fight. He'd heard the Far Country was a place where men could find their dreams, and come searching for a way to claim back all he'd lost, but this was all he'd found. Glama Golden, mighty War Chief, hero of Ollensand, who'd stood tall in the songs and on the battlefield, admired and feared in equal measure, rolling in the mud for the amusement of morons.

A tilt of the waist and a dip of the shoulder, a couple of lazy ranging swings, getting the other man's measure. He moved well, this Lamb, whatever his age. He was no stranger to this business – there was a snap and steadiness to his movements and he wasted no effort. Golden wondered what his failures had been, what his regrets. What dream had he come chasing after into this Circle?

'Leave him alive if you can,' Ring had said, which only showed how little he understood in spite of his endless bragging about his word. There were no choices in a fight like this, life and death on the Leveller's scales. There was no place for mercy, no place for doubts. He could see in Lamb's eyes that he knew it, too. Once two men step into the Circle, nothing beyond its edge can matter, past or future. Things fall the way they fall.

Golden had seen enough.

He squeezed his teeth together and rushed across the Circle. The old man dodged well but Golden still caught him by the ear and followed with a heavy left in the ribs, felt the thud right up his arm, warming every joint. Lamb struck back but Golden brushed it off and as quickly as they'd come together they were apart, circling again, watching, a gust swirling around the theatre and dragging out the torch flames.

He could take a punch, this old man, still moving calm and steady, showing no pain. Golden might have to break him down piece by piece, use his reach, but that was well enough. He was warming to the task. His breath came faster and he growled along with it, his face finding a fighting snarl, sucking in strength and pushing out doubt, all his shame and disappointment made tinder for his anger.

Golden slapped his palms together hard, feinted right then hissed as he darted in, faster and sharper than before, catching the old man with two more long punches, bloodying his bent nose, staggering him and dancing away before he could think of throwing back, the stone bowl ringing with encouragements and insults and fresh odds in a dozen languages.

Golden settled to the work. He had the reach and the weight and the youth but he took nothing for granted. He would be cautious. He would make sure.

This would be his last fight, after all.

'I'm coming, you bastard, I'm coming!' shouted Pane, hobbling down the hall on his iffy leg.

Bottom of the pile, that's what he was. But he guessed every pile needs someone on the bottom, and probably he didn't deserve to be no higher. The door was jolting in its frame from the blows outside. They should've had a slot to look through. He'd said that before but no one took no notice. Probably they couldn't hear him through that heap of folks on top. So he had to wrestle the bolt back and haul the door open a bit to see who was calling.

There was an old drunk outside. Tall and bony with grey hair plastered to one side of his head and big hands flapping and a tattered coat with what looked like old vomit down one side and fresh down the other. 'I wanna get fucked,' he said in a voice like rotten wood splitting.

'Don't let me stop you.' And Pane swung the door shut.

The old man wedged a boot in it and the door bounced back open. 'I wanna get fucked, I says!'

'We're closed.'

'You're what?' The old man craned close, most likely deaf as well as drunk.

Pane heaved the door open wider so he could shout it. 'There's a fight on, case you didn't notice. We're closed!'

'I did notice and I don't care a shit. I want fucking and I want it now. I got dust and I heard tell the Whitehouse is never closed to business. Not never.'

'Shit,' hissed Pane. That was true. 'Never closed,' Papa Ring was always telling 'em. But then they'd been told to be careful, and triple careful today. 'Be triple careful today,' Papa had told them all. 'I can't stand a man ain't careful.' Which had sounded strange, since no one round here was ever the least bit careful.

'I want a fuck,' grunted the old man, hardly able to stand up straight, he was that drunk. Pane pitied the girl got that job, he stank like all the shit in Crease. Usually there'd be three guards at the door but the others had all snuck off to watch the fight and left him on his own, bottom of the bloody heap that he was.

He gave a strangled groan of upset, turned to shriek for someone just a little higher up the heap, and to his great and far from pleasant surprise an arm slipped tight around his neck and a cold point pressed into his throat and he heard the door swing shut behind.

'Where's the woman you took?' The old man's breath stank like a still but his hands were tight as vices. 'Shy South, skinny thing with a big mouth. Where is she?'

'I don't know nothing about no woman,' Pane managed to splutter, trying to say it loud enough to get someone's attention but half-swallowing his words from the pressure.

'Guess I might as well open you up, then.' And Pane felt the point of the knife dig into his jaw.

'Fuck! All right! She's in the cellar!'

'Lead on.' And the old man started moving him. One step, two, and suddenly it just got to Pane what a damn indignity this was on top of everything else, and without thinking he started twisting and thrashing and elbowing away, struggling like this was his moment to get out from under the bottom of that heap and finally be somebody worthy of at least his own respect.

But the old man was made of iron. That knotty hand clamped Pane's windpipe shut so he couldn't make more'n a gurgle and he felt the knife's point burning across his face, right up under his eye.

'Struggle any more and that eye's coming out,' and there was a terrible coldness in the old man's voice froze all the fight right out. 'You're just the fool who opens the door, so I reckon you don't owe Papa Ring too much. He's finished anyway. Take me to the woman and do nothing stupid, you'll live to be the fool who opens someone else's door. Make sense?'

The hand released enough for him to choke, 'Makes sense.' It did make sense, too. That was about as much fight as Pane had showed in his whole life and where'd it got him? He was just the fool who opened the door.

Bottom of the pile.

Golden had bloodied the old man's face up something fierce. Drizzle was streaking through the light about the torches, cool on his forehead but he was hot inside now, doubts banished. He had Lamb's measure and even the blood in his mouth tasted like victory.

This would be his last fight. Back to the North with Ring's money and win back his lost honour and his lost children, cut his revenge out of Cairm Ironhead and Black Calder, the thought of those hated names and faces bringing up the fury in a sudden blaze.

Golden roared and the crowd roared with him, carried him across the Circle as if on the crest of a wave. The old man pushed away one punch and slipped under another, found a hold on Golden's arm and they slapped and twisted, fingers wriggling for a grip, hands slippery with grease and drizzle, feet shuffling for advantage. Golden strained, and heaved, and finally with a bellow got Lamb off his feet, but the old man hooked his leg as he went down and they crashed together onto the stones, the crowd leaping up in joy as they fell.

Golden was on top. He tried to get a hand around the old man's throat, fumbled with a notch out of his ear, tried to rip at it but it was too slippery, tried to inch his hand up onto Lamb's face so he could get his thumbnail in his eye, the way he had with that big miner back in the spring, and of a sudden his head was dragged down and there was a burning, tugging pain in his mouth. He bellowed and twisted and growled, clawed at Lamb's wrist with his nails and, with a stinging and ripping right through his lip and into his gums he tore himself free and thrashed away.

As Lamb rolled up he saw the old man had yellow hairs caught in one fist and Golden realised he'd torn half his moustache out. There was laughter in the crowd, but all he heard was the laughter years behind him as he trudged from Skarling's Hall and into exile.

The rage came up white-hot and Golden charged in shrieking, no thoughts except the need to smash Lamb apart with his fists. He caught the old man square in the face and sent him staggering right out of the Circle, folk on the front row of stone benches scattering like starlings. Golden came after him, spewing curses, raining blows, fists knocking Lamb left and right like he was made of rags. The old man's hands dropped, face slack, eyes glassy, and Golden knew the moment was come. He stepped in, swinging with all his strength, and landed the father of all punches right on the point of Lamb's jaw.

He watched the old man stumble, fists dangling, waiting for Lamb's knees to buckle so he could spring on top of him and put an end to it.

But Lamb didn't fall. He tottered back a pace or two into the Circle and stood, swaying, blood drooling from his open mouth and his face tipped into shadow. Then Golden caught something over the thunder of the crowd, soft and low but there was no mistaking it.

The old man was laughing.

Golden stood, chest heaving, legs weak, arms heavy from his efforts, and he felt a chill doubt wash over him because he wasn't sure he could hit a man any harder than that.

'Who are you?' he roared, fists aching like he'd been beating a tree.

Lamb gave a smile like an open grave, and stuck out his red tongue, and smeared blood from it across his cheek in long streaks. He held up his left fist and gently uncurled it so he looked at Golden, eyes wide and weeping wet like two black tar-pits, through the gap where his middle finger used to be.

The crowd had fallen eerily quiet, and Golden's doubt turned to a sucking dread because he finally knew the old man's name.

'By the dead,' he whispered, 'it can't be.'

But he knew it was. However fast, however strong, however fearsome you make yourself, there's always someone faster, stronger, more fearsome, and the more you fight the sooner you'll meet him. No one cheats the Great Leveller for ever and now Glama Golden felt the sweat turn cold on him, and the fire inside guttered out and left only ashes.

And he knew this would be his last fight indeed.

'So fucking unfair,' Cantliss muttered to himself.

All that effort spent dragging those mewling brats across the Far Country, all that risk taken bringing 'em to the Dragon People, every bit repaid and interest too and what thanks? Just Papa Ring's endless moaning and another shitty task to get through besides. However hard he worked things never went his way.

'A man just can't get a fair go,' he snapped at nothing, and saying it made his face hurt and he gingerly pressed the scratches and that made his hand hurt and he reflected bitterly on the wrong-headed stupidity of womankind.

'After everything I done for that whore . . .'

That idiot Warp was pretending to read as Cantliss stalked around the corner.

'Get up, idiot!' The woman was still in the cage, still tied and helpless, but she was watching him in a style made him angrier than ever, level and steady like she'd something on her mind other than fear. Like she'd a plan and he was a piece of it. 'What d'you think you're looking at, bitch?' he snapped.

Clear and cold she said, 'A fucking coward.'

He stopped short, blinking, hardly able to believe it at first. Even this skinny thing disrespecting him? Even this, who should have been snivelling for mercy? If you can't get a woman's respect tying her up and beating her, when can you fucking get it? 'What?' he whispered, going cold all over.

She leaned forwards, mocking eyes on him all the way, curled her lips back, pressed her tongue into the gap between her teeth, and with a jerk of her head spat across the cage and through the bars and it spattered against Cantliss' new shirt.

'Coward cunt,' she said.

Taking a telling from Papa Ring was one thing. This was another. 'Get that cage open!' he snarled, near choking on fury.

'Right y'are.' Warp was fumbling with his ring of keys, trying to find the right one. There were only three on there. Cantliss tore it out of his hand, jammed the key in the lock and ripped back the gate, edge clanging against the wall and taking a chunk out of it.

'I'll learn you a fucking lesson!' he screamed, but the woman watched him still, teeth bared and breathing so hard he could see the specks of spit off her lips. He caught a twisted handful of her shirt, half-lifting her, stitches ripping, and he clamped his other hand around her jaw, crushing her mouth between his fingers like he'd crush her face to pulp and—

Agony lanced up his thigh and he gave a whooping shriek. Another jolt and his leg gave so he tottered against the wall.

'What you—' said Warp, and Cantliss heard scuffling and grunting and he twisted around, only just staying on his feet for the pain right up into his groin.

Warp was against the cage, face a picture of stupid surprise, the woman holding him up with one hand and punching him in the gut with the other. With each punch she gave a spitty snort and he gave a cross-eyed gurgle and Cantliss saw she had a knife, strings of blood slopping off it and spattering the floor as she stabbed him. Cantliss realised she'd stabbed him, too, and he gave a whimper of outrage at the hurt and injustice of it, took one hopping step and flung himself at her, caught her around the back and they tumbled through the cage door and crashed together onto the packed-dirt floor outside, the knife bouncing away.

She was slippery as a trout, though, slithered out on top and gave him a couple of hard punches in the mouth, snapping his head against the ground before he knew where he was. She lunged for the knife but he caught her shirt before she got there and dragged her back, ragged thing ripped half-off, the pair of them wriggling across the dirt floor towards the table, grunting and spitting. She punched him again but it only caught the top of his skull and he tangled his hand in her hair and dragged her head sideways. She squealed and thrashed but he had her now and smacked her skull into the leg of the table, and again, and she went limp long enough for him to drag his weight on top of her, groaning as he tried to use his stabbed leg, all wet and warm now from his leaking blood.

He could hear her breath whooping in her throat as they twisted and strained and she kneed at him but his weight was on her and he finally got his forearm across her neck and started pressing on it, shifted his body and reached out, stretching with his fingers, and gathered in the knife, and he chuckled as his hand closed around it because he knew he'd won.

'Now we'll thucking thee,' he hissed, a bit messed-up with his lips split and swollen, and he lifted the blade so she got a good look at it, her face all pinked from lack of air with bloody hair stuck across it, and her bulging eyes followed the point as she strained at his arm, weaker and weaker, and he brought the knife high, did a couple of fake little stabs to taunt her, enjoying the way her face twitched each time. 'Now we'll thee!' He brought it higher still to do the job for real.

And Cantliss' wrist was suddenly twisted right around and he gasped as he was dragged off her, and as he was opening his mouth something smashed into it and sent everything spinning. He shook his head, could hear the woman coughing what sounded like a long way away. He saw the knife on the ground, reached for it.

A big boot came down and smashed his hand into the dirt floor. Another swung past and its toe flicked the blade away. Cantliss groaned and tried to move his hand but couldn't.

'You want me to kill him?' asked an old man, looking down.

'No,' croaked the girl, stooping for the knife. 'I want to kill him.' And she took a step at Cantliss, spitting blood in his face through the gap between her teeth.

'No!' he whimpered, trying to scramble back with his useless leg but still with his useless hand pinned under the old man's boot. 'You need me! You want your children back, right? Right?' He saw her face and knew he had a chink to pick at. 'Ain't easy getting up there! I can show you the ways! You need me! I'll help! I'll put it right! Wasn't my fault, it was Ring. He said he'd kill me! I didn't have no choice! You need me!' And he blathered and wept and begged but felt no shame because when he's got no other choice a sensible man begs like a bastard.

'What a thing is this,' muttered the old-timer, lip curled with contempt.

The girl came back from the cage with the rope she'd been bound with. 'Best keep our options open, though.'

'Take him with us?'

She squatted down and gave Cantliss a red smile. 'We can always kill him later.'

Abram Majud was deeply concerned. Not about the result, for that no longer looked in doubt. About what would come after.

With each exchange Golden grew weaker. His face, as far as could be told through the blood and swelling, was a mask of fear. Lamb's smile, by terrible contrast, split wider with every blow given or received. It had become the demented leer of a drunkard, of a lunatic, of a demon, no trace remaining of the man Majud had laughed with on the plains, an expression so monstrous that observers in the front row scrambled back onto the benches behind whenever Lamb lurched close.

The audience was turning almost as ugly as the show. Majud dreaded to imagine the total value of wagers in the balance, and he had already seen fights break out among the spectators. The sense of collective insanity was starting to remind him strongly of a battle – a place he had very much hoped never to visit again – and in a battle he knew there are always casualties.

Lamb sent Golden reeling with a heavy right hand, caught him before he fell, hooked a finger in his mouth and ripped his cheek wide open, blood spotting the nearest onlookers.

'Oh my,' said Curnsbick, watching the fight through his spread fingers.

'We should go.' But Majud saw no easy way to manage it. Lamb had hold of Golden's arm, was wrapping his own around it, forcing him onto his knees, the pinned hand flopping uselessly. Majud heard

Golden's bubbling scream, then the sharp pop as his elbow snapped back the wrong way, skin horribly distended around the joint.

Lamb was on him like a wolf on the kill, giggling as he seized Golden around the throat, arching back and smashing his forehead into his face, and again, and again, the crowd whooping their joy or dismay at the outcome.

Majud heard a wail, saw bodies heaving in the stands, what looked like two men stabbing another. The sky was suddenly lit by a bloom of orange flame, bright enough almost to feel the warmth of. A moment later a thunderous boom shook the arena and terrified onlookers flung themselves down, hands clasped over their heads, screams of bloodlust turned to howls of dismay.

A man staggered into the Circle, clutching at his guts, and fell not far from where Lamb was still intent on smashing Golden's head apart with his hands. Fire leaped and twisted in the drizzle on Papa Ring's side of the street. A fellow not two strides away was hit in the head by a piece of debris as he stood and knocked flying.

'Explosive powder,' muttered Curnsbick, his eyeglasses alive with the reflections of fire.

Majud seized him by the arm and dragged him along the bench. Between the heaving bodies he could see Lamb's hacked-out smile lit by one guttering torch, beating someone's head against one of the pillars with a regular crunch, crunch, the stone smeared black. Majud had a suspicion the victim was Camling. The time for referees was plainly long past.

'Oh my,' muttered Curnsbick. 'Oh my.'

Majud drew his sword. The one General Malzagurt had given him as thanks for saving his life. He hated the damn thing but was glad of it now. Man's ingenuity has still developed no better tool for getting people out of the way than a length of sharpened steel.

Excitement had devolved into panic with the speed of a mudslide. On the other side of the Circle, the new-built stand was starting to rock alarmingly as people boiled down it, trampling each other in their haste to get away. With a tortured creak the whole structure lurched sideways, buckling, spars splintering like matchsticks, twisting, falling, people pitching over the poorly made railings and tumbling through the darkness.

Majud dragged Curnsbick through it all, ignoring the fighting, the injured, a woman propped on her elbows staring at the bone sticking out of her leg. It was every man for himself and perhaps, if they were lucky, those closest to him, no choice but to leave the rest to God.

'Oh my,' burbled Curnsbick.

In the street it was no longer like a battle, it was one. People dashed gibbering through the madness, lit by the spreading flames on Ring's side of the street. Blades glinted, men clashed and fell and rolled, floundered in the stream, the sides impossible to guess. He saw someone toss a burning bottle whirling onto a roof where it shattered, curling lines of fire shooting across the thatch and catching hungrily in spite of the wet.

He glimpsed the Mayor, still staring across the maddened street from her balcony. She pointed at something, spoke to a man beside her, calmly directing. Majud acquired the strong impression that she had never intended to sit back and meekly abide by the result.

Arrows flickered in the darkness. One stuck in the mud near them, burning. Majud's ears rang with words screeched in languages he did not know. There was another thunderous detonation and he cowered as timbers spun high, smoke roiling up into the wet sky.

Someone had a woman by the hair, was dragging her kicking through the muck.

'Oh my,' said Curnsbick, over and over.

A hand clutched at Majud's ankle and he struck out with the flat of his sword, tore free and struggled on, not looking back, sticking to the porches of the buildings on the Mayor's side of the street. High above, at the top of the nearest column, three men were silhouetted, two with bows, a third lighting their pitch-soaked arrows so they could calmly shoot them at the houses across the way.

The building with the sign that said *Fuck Palace* was thoroughly ablaze. A woman leaped from the balcony and crumpled in the mud, wailing. Two corpses lay nearby. Four men stood with naked swords, watching. One was smoking a pipe. Majud thought he was a dealer from the Mayor's Church of Dice.

Curnsbick tried to pull his arm free. 'We should—'

'No!' snapped Majud, dragging him on. 'We shouldn't.'

Mercy, along with all the trappings of civilised behaviour, was a luxury they could ill afford. Majud tore out the key to their shop and thrust it into Curnsbick's trembling hand while he faced the street, sword up.

'Oh my,' the inventor was saying as he struggled with the lock, 'oh my.'

They spilled inside, into the still safety, the darkness of the shop flickering with slashes of orange and yellow and red. Majud shouldered the door shut, gasped with relief as he felt the latch drop, spun about when he felt a hand on his shoulder and nearly took Temple's head off with his flailing sword.

'What the hell's going on?' A strip of light wandered across one half of Temple's stricken face. 'Who won the fight?'

Majud put the point of his sword on the floor and leaned on the pommel, breathing hard. 'Lamb tore Golden apart. Literally.'

'Oh my,' whimpered Curnsbick, sliding down the wall until his arse thumped against the floor.

'What about Shy?' asked Temple.

'I've no idea. I've no idea about anything.' Majud eased the door open a crack to peer out. 'But I suspect the Mayor is cleaning house.'

The flames on Papa Ring's side of the street were lighting the whole town in garish colours. The Whitehouse was ablaze to its top floor, fire shooting into the sky, ravenous, murderous, trees burning on the slopes above, ash and embers fluttering in the rain.

'Shouldn't we help?' whispered Temple.

'A good man of business remains neutral.'

'Surely there's a moment to cease being a good man of business, and try to be merely a good man.'

'Perhaps.' Majud heaved the door shut again. 'But this is not that moment.'

Old Friends

'Well, then!' shouted Papa Ring, and he swallowed, and he blinked into the sun. 'Here we are, I guess!' There was a sheen of sweat across his forehead, but Temple could hardly blame him for that. 'I haven't always done right!' Someone had ripped the ring from his ear and the distorted lobe flopped loose as he turned his head. 'Daresay most of you won't miss me none! But I've always done my best to keep my word, at least! You'd have to say I always kept my—'

Temple heard the Mayor snap her fingers and her man booted Ring in the back and sent him lurching off the scaffold. The noose jerked tight and he kicked and twisted, rope creaking as he did the hanged man's dance, piss running from one of his dirty trouser-legs. Little men and big, brave men and cowards, powerful men and meagre, they all hang very much the same. That made eleven of them dangling. Ring, and nine of his henchmen, and the woman who had been in charge of his whores. A half-hearted cheer went up from the crowd, more habit than enthusiasm. Last night's events had more than satisfied even Crease's appetite for death.

'And that's the end of that,' said the Mayor under her breath.

'It's the end of a lot,' said Temple. One of the ancient pillars the Whitehouse had stood between had toppled in the heat. The other loomed strangely naked, cracked and soot-blackened, the ruins of the present tangled charred about the ruins of the past. A good half of the buildings on Ring's side of the street had met the same fate, yawning gaps burned from the jumble of wooden shack and shanty, scavengers busy among the wreckage.

'We'll rebuild,' said the Mayor. 'That's what we do. Is that treaty ready yet?'

'Very nearly done,' Temple managed to say.

'Good. That piece of paper could save a lot of lives.'

'I see that saving lives is our only concern.' He trudged back up the steps without waiting for a reply. He shed no tears for Papa Ring, but he had no wish to watch him kick any longer.

With a fair proportion of the town's residents dead by violence, fire or hanging, a larger number run off, a still larger number even now preparing to leave, and most of the rest in the street observing the conclusion of the great feud, the Mayor's Church of Dice was eerily empty, Temple's footsteps echoing around the smoke-stained rafters. Dab Sweet, Crying Rock and Corlin sat about one table, playing cards under the vacant gaze of the ancient armour ranged about the walls.

'Not watching the hanging?' asked Temple.

Corlin glanced at him out of the corner of her eye and treated him to a hiss of contempt. More than likely she had heard the story of his naked dash across the street.

'Nearly got hanged myself one time, up near Hope,' said Sweet. 'Turned out a misunderstanding, but even so.' The old scout hooked a finger in his collar and dragged it loose. 'Strangled my enthusiasm for the business.'

'Bad luck,' intoned Crying Rock, seeming to stare straight through her cards, half of which faced in and the other half out. Whether it was the end of Sweet's enthusiasm, or his near-hanging, or hanging in general that was bad luck she didn't clarify. She was not a woman prone to clarification.

'And when there's death outside is the one time a man can get some room in here.' Sweet rocked his chair back on two legs and deposited his dirty boot on the table. 'I reckon this place has turned sour. Soon there'll be more money in taking folk away than bringing 'em in. Just need to round up a few miserable failures desperate to see civilisation again and we're on our way back to the Near Country.'

'Maybe I'll join you,' said Temple. A crowd of failures sounded like ideal company for him.

'Always welcome.' Crying Rock let fall a card and started to rake in the pot, her face just as slack as if she'd lost. Sweet tossed his hand away in disgust. 'Twenty years I been losing to this cheating bloody Ghost and she still pretends she don't know how to play the game!'

Savian and Lamb stood at the counter, warming themselves at a bottle. Shorn of hair and beard the Northman looked younger, even bigger, and a great deal meaner. He also looked as if he had made every effort to fell a tree with his face. It was a misshapen mass of scab and bruise, a ragged cut across one cheekbone roughly stitched and his hands both wrapped in stained bandages.

'All the same,' he was grunting through bloated lips, 'I owe you big.'

'Daresay I'll find a way for you to pay,' answered Savian. 'Where d'you stand on politics?'

'These days, as far away from it as I can . . .'

They shut up tight when they saw Temple. 'Where's Shy?' he asked.

Lamb looked at him, one eye swollen nearly shut and the other infinitely tired. 'Upstairs in the Mayor's rooms.'

'Will she see me?'

'That's up to her.'

Temple nodded. 'You've got my thanks as well,' he said to Savian. 'For what that's worth.'

'We all give what we can.'

Temple wasn't sure whether that was meant to sting. It was one of those moments when everything stung. He left the two old men and made for the stairs. Behind him he heard Savian mutter, 'I'm talking about the rebellion in Starikland.'

'The one just finished?'

'That and the next one . . .'

He lifted his fist outside the door, and paused. There was nothing to stop him letting it drop and riding straight out of town, to Bermi's claim, maybe, or even on to somewhere no one knew what a disappointing cock he was. If there was any such place left in the Circle of the World. Before the impulse to take the easy way could overwhelm him, he made himself knock.

Shy's face looked little better than Lamb's, scratched and swollen, nose cut across the bridge, neck a mass of bruises. It hurt him to see it. Not as much as if he'd taken the beating, of course. But it hurt still. She didn't look upset to see him. She didn't look that interested. She left the door open, limping slightly, and showed her teeth as she sank down on a bench under the window, bare feet looking very white against the floorboards.

'How was the hanging?' she asked.

He stepped inside and gently pushed the door to. 'Very much like they always are.'

'Can't say I've ever understood their appeal.'

'Perhaps it makes people feel like winners, seeing someone else lose so hard.'

'Losing hard I know all about.'

'Are you all right?'

She looked up and he could hardly meet her eye. 'Bit sore.'

'You're angry with me.' He sounded like a sulking child.

'I'm not. I'm just sore.'

'What good would I have done if I'd stayed?'

She licked at her split lip. 'I daresay you'd just have got yourself killed.'

'Exactly. But instead I ran for help.'

'You ran all right, that I can corroborate.'

'I got Savian.'

'And Savian got me. Just in time.'

'That's right.'

They looked at each other in silence, while outside in the street the hanging crowd started to drift away. Then he sank into a chair facing her. 'I'm fucking ashamed of myself.'

'I've got no excuse.'

'And yet I feel one's coming.'

His turn to grimace. 'I'm a coward, simple as that. I've been running away so long it's come to be a habit. Not easy, changing old habits. However much we might—'

'Don't bother.' She gave a long, pained sigh. 'I got low expectations. To be fair, you already exceeded 'em once when you paid your debt. So you tend to the cowardly. Who doesn't? You ain't the brave knight and I ain't the swooning maiden and this ain't no storybook, that's for sure. You're forgiven. You can go your way.' And she waved him out the door with the scabbed back of her hand.

That was closer to forgiveness than he could have hoped for, but he found he was not moving. 'I don't want to go.'

'I'm not asking you to jump again, you can use the stairs.'

'Let me make it right.'

She looked up at him from under her brows. 'We're heading into the mountains, Temple. That bastard Cantliss'll show us where these Dragon People are, and we're going to try and get my brother and sister back, and I can't promise there'll be anything made right at all. A few promises I can make – it'll be hard and cold and dangerous and there won't even be any windows to jump out of. You'll be about as useful there as a spent match, and let's neither one of us offend honesty by pretending otherwise.'

'Please.' He took a wheedling step towards her, 'Please give me one more—'

'Leave me be,' she said, narrowing her eyes at him. 'I just want to sit and hurt in peace.'

So that was all. Maybe he should have fought harder, but Temple had never been much of a fighter. So he nodded at the floor, and quietly shut the door behind him, and went back down the steps, and over to the counter.

'Get what you wanted?' asked Lamb.

'No,' said Temple, spilling a pocketful of coins across the wood. 'What I deserved.' And he started drinking.

He was vaguely aware of the dull thud of hooves out in the street, shouting and the jingle of harness. Some new Fellowship pulling into town. Some new set of forthcoming disappointments. But he was too busy with his own even to bother to look up. He told the man behind the counter to leave the bottle.

This time there was no one else to blame. Not God, not Cosca, certainly not Shy. Lamb had been right. The trouble with running is wherever you run to, there you are. Temple's problem was Temple, and it always had been. He heard heavy footsteps, spurs jingling, calls for drink and women, but he ignored them, inflicted another burning glassful on his gullet, banged it down, eyes watering, reached for the bottle.

Someone else got there first.

'You'd best leave that be,' growled Temple.

'How would I drink it then?'

At the sound of that voice a terrible chill prickled his spine. His eyes crawled to the hand on the bottle – aged, liver-spotted, dirt beneath the cracked nails, a gaudy ring upon the first finger. His eyes crawled past the grubby lacework on the sleeve, up the mud-spotted material, over the breastplate, gilt peeling, up a scrawny neck speckled with rash, and to the face. That awfully familiar, hollowed visage: the nose sharp, the eyes bright, the greyed moustaches waxed to curling points.

'Oh God,' breathed Temple.

'Close enough,' said Nicomo Cosca, and delivered that luminous smile of which only he was capable, good humour and good intentions radiating from his deep-lined face. 'Look who it is, boys!'

At least two dozen well-known and deeply detested figures had made their way in after the Old Man. 'Whatever are the odds?' asked Brachio, showing his yellow teeth. He had a couple fewer knives in his bandolier than when Temple had left the Company, but was otherwise unchanged.

'Rejoice, ye faithful,' rumbled Jubair, quoting scripture in Kantic, 'for the wanderer returns.'

'Scouting, were you?' sneered Dimbik, smoothing his hair down with a licked finger and straightening his sash, which had devolved into a greasy tatter of indeterminate colour. 'Finding us a path to glory?'

'Ah, a drink, a drink, a drink . . .' Cosca took a long and flamboyant swig from Temple's bottle. 'Did I not tell you all? Wait long enough and things have a habit of returning to their proper place. Having lost my Company, I was for some years a penniless wanderer, buffeted by the winds of fate, most *roughly* buffeted, Sworbreck, make a note of that.' The writer, whose hair had grown considerably wilder, clothes shabbier, nostril rims pinker and hands more tremulous since last they met, fumbled for his pencil. 'But here I am, once more in command of a band of noble fighting men! You will scarcely believe it, but Sergeant Friendly was at one time forced into the criminal fraternity.' The neckless sergeant hoisted one brow a fraction. 'But he now stands beside me as the staunch companion he was born to be. And you, Temple? What role could fit your high talents and low character so well as that of my legal advisor?'

Temple hopelessly shrugged. 'None that I can think of.'

'Then let us celebrate our inevitable reunion! One for me.' The Old Man took another hefty swig, then grinned as he poured the smallest dribble of spirit into Temple's glass. 'And one for you. I thought you stopped drinking?'

'It felt like a perfect moment to start again,' croaked Temple. He had been expecting Cosca to order his death but, almost worse, it appeared the Company of the Gracious Hand would simply reabsorb him without breaking stride. If there was a God, He had clearly taken a set dislike to Temple over the past few years. But Temple supposed he could hardly blame Him. He was coming to feel much the same.

'Gentlemen, welcome to Crease!' The Mayor came sweeping through the doorway. 'I must apologise for the mess, but we have—' She saw the Old Man and her face drained of all colour. The first time Temple had seen her even slightly surprised. 'Nicomo Cosca,' she breathed.

'None other. You must be the Mayor.' He stiffly bowed, then looking slyly up added, 'These days. It is a morning of reunions, apparently.'

'You know each other?' asked Temple.

'Well,' muttered the Mayor. 'What . . . astonishing luck.'

'They do say luck is a woman.' The Old Man made Temple grunt by poking him in the ribs with the neck of his own bottle. 'She's drawn to those who least deserve her!'

Out of the corner of his eye, Temple saw Shy limping down the stairs and over towards Lamb who, along with Savian, was watching the new arrivals in careful silence. Cosca, meanwhile, was strutting to the windows, spurs jingling. He took a deep breath, apparently savouring the odour of charred wood, and started to swing his head gently in time to the creaking of the bodies on their scaffold. 'I love what you've done with the place,' he called to the Mayor. 'Very . . . apocalyptic. You make something of a habit of leaving settlements you preside over in smoking ruins.'

Something they had in common, as far as Temple could tell. He realised he was picking at the stitches holding his buttons on and forced himself to stop.

'Are these gentlemen your whole contingent?' asked the Mayor, eyeing the filthy, squinting, scratching, spitting mercenaries slouching about her gaming hall.

'Dear me, no! We lost a few on the way across the Far Country – the inevitable desertions, a round of fever, a little trouble with the Ghosts – but these stalwarts are but a representative sample. I have left the rest beyond the city limits because if I were to bring some three hundred—'

'Two hundred and sixty,' said Friendly. The Mayor looked paler yet at the number.

'Counting Inquisitor Lorsen and his Practicals?'

'Two hundred and sixty-eight.' At the mention of the Inquisition, the Mayor's face had turned positively deathly.

'If I were to bring two hundred and sixty eight travel-sore fighting men into a place like this, there would, frankly, be carnage.'

'And not the good sort,' threw in Brachio, dabbing at his weepy eye.

'There is a good sort?' murmured the Mayor.

Cosca thoughtfully worked one moustache-tip between thumb and forefinger. 'There are . . . *degrees*, anyway. And here he is!'

His black coat was weather-worn, a patchy yellow-grey beard had sprouted from cheeks more gaunt than ever, but Inquisitor Lorsen's eyes

288

were just as bright with purpose as they had been when the Company left Mulkova. More so, if anything.

'This is Inquisitor Lorsen.' Cosca scratched thoughtfully at his rashy neck. 'My current employer.'

'An honour.' Though Temple detected the slightest strain in the Mayor's voice. 'If I may ask, what business might his Majesty's Inquisition have in Crease?'

'We are hunting escaped rebels!' called Lorsen to the room at large. 'Traitors to the Union!'

'We are far from the Union here.'

The Inquisitor's smile seemed to chill the whole room. 'The reach of his Eminence lengthens yearly. Large rewards are being offered for the capture of certain persons. A list will be posted throughout town, at its head the traitor, murderer and chief fomenter of rebellion, Conthus!'

Savian gave vent to a muffled round of coughing and Lamb slapped him on the back, but Lorsen was too busy frowning down his nose at Temple to notice. 'I see you have been reunited with this slippery liar.'

'Come now.' Cosca gave Temple's shoulder a fatherly squeeze. 'A degree of slipperiness, and indeed of lying, is a positive boon in a notary. Beneath it all there has never been a man of such conscience and moral courage. I'd trust him with my life. Or at least my hat.' And he swept it off and hung it over Temple's glass.

'As long as you trust him with none of my business.' Lorsen waved to his Practicals. 'Come. We have questions to ask.'

'He seems charming,' said the Mayor as she watched him leave.

Cosca scratched at his rash again and held up his fingernails to assess the results. 'The Inquisition makes a point of recruiting only the most well-mannered fanatical torturers.'

'And the most foul-mannered old mercenaries too, it would appear.'

'A job is a job. But I have my own reasons for being here also. I came looking for a man called Grega Cantliss.'

There was a long pause as that name settled upon the room like a chilly snowfall.

'Fuck,' he heard Shy breathe.

Cosca looked about expectantly. 'The name is not unknown, then?'

'He has at times passed through.' The Mayor had the air of choosing her words very carefully. 'If you were to find him, what then?'

'Then I and my notary – not to mention my employer the noble Inquisitor Lorsen – could be very much out of your way. Mercenaries have, I am aware, a poor reputation, but believe me when I say we are not here to cause trouble.' He swilled some spirit lazily around in the bottom of the bottle. 'Why, do you have some notion of Cantliss' whereabouts?'

A pregnant silence ensued while a set of long glances were exchanged. Then Lamb slowly lifted his chin. Shy's face hardened. The Mayor graced them with the tiniest apologetic shrug. 'He is chained up in my cellar.'

'Bitch,' breathed Shy.

'Cantliss is ours.' Lamb pushed himself up from the counter and stood tall, bandaged left hand sitting loose on the hilt of his sword.

Several of the mercenaries variously puffed themselves up and found challenging stances of one kind or another, like tomcats opening hostilities in a moonlit alley. Friendly only watched, dead-eyed, dice clicking in his fist as he worked them gently around each other.

'Yours?' asked Cosca.

'He burned my farm and stole my son and daughter and sold 'em to some savages. We've tracked him all the way from the Near Country. He's going to take us up into the mountains and show us where these Dragon People are.'

The Old Man's body might have stiffened down the years but his eyebrows were still some of the most limber in the world, and they reached new heights now. 'Dragon People, you say? Perhaps we can help each other?'

Lamb glanced about the dirty, scarred and bearded faces. 'Guess you can never have too many allies.'

'Quite so! A man lost in the desert must take such water as he is offered, eh, Temple?'

'Not sure I wouldn't rather go thirsty,' muttered Shy.

'I'm Lamb. That's Shy.' The Northman raised his glass, the stump of his middle finger plainly visible in spite of the bandages.

'A nine-fingered Northman,' mused the captain general. 'I do believe a fellow called Shivers was looking for you in the Near Country.'

'Haven't seen him.'

'Ah.' Cosca waved his bottle at Lamb's injuries. 'I thought perhaps this might be his handiwork.'

'No.'

'You appear to have many enemies, Master Lamb.'

'Sometimes it seems I can't shit without making a couple more.'

'It all depends who you shit on, I suppose? A fearsome fellow, Caul Shivers, and I would not judge the years to have mellowed him. We knew each other back in Styria, he and I. Sometimes I feel I have met everyone in the world and that every new place is peopled with old faces.' His considering gaze came to rest on Savian. 'Although I do not recognise this gentleman.'

'I'm Savian.' And he coughed into his fist.

'And what brings you to the Far Country? Your health?'

Savian paused, mouth a little open, while an awkward silence stretched out, several of the mercenaries still with hands close to weapons, and suddenly Shy said, 'Cantliss took one of his children, too, he's been tracking 'em along with us. Lad called Collem.'

The silence lasted a little longer then Savian added, almost reluctantly, 'My lad, Collem.' He coughed again, and raspingly cleared his throat. 'Hoping Cantliss can lead us to him.'

It was almost a relief to see two of the Mayor's men dragging the bandit across the gaming hall. His wrists were in manacles, his once fine clothes were stained rags and his face as bruised as Lamb's, one hand hanging useless and one leg dragging on the boards behind him.

'The elusive Grega Cantliss!' shouted Cosca as the Mayor's men flung him cringing down. 'Fear not. I am Nicomo Cosca, infamous soldier of fortune, et cetera, et cetera, and I have some questions for you. I advise you to consider your answers carefully as your life may depend upon them, and so forth.'

Cantliss registered Shy, Savian, Lamb and the score or more of mercenaries, and with a coward's instinct Temple well recognised quickly perceived the shift in the balance of power. He eagerly nodded.

'Some months ago you bought some horses in a town called Greyer. You used coins like these.' Cosca produced a tiny gold piece with a magician's flourish. 'Antique Imperial coins, as it happens.'

Cantliss' eyes flickered over Cosca's face as though trying to read a script. 'I did. That's a fact.'

'You bought those horses from rebels, fighting to free Starikland from the Union.'

'I did?'

'You did.'

'I did!'

Cosca leaned close. 'Where did the coins come from?'

'Dragon People paid me with 'em,' said Cantliss. 'Savages in the mountains up beyond Beacon.'

'Paid you for what?'

He licked his scabbed lips. 'For children.'

'An ugly business,' muttered Sworbreck.

'Most business is,' said Cosca, leaning closer and closer towards Cantliss. 'They have more of these coins?'

'All I could ever want, that's what he said.'

'Who said?'

'Waerdinur. He's their leader.'

'All I could ever want.' Cosca's eyes glimmered as brightly as his imagined gold. 'So you are telling me these Dragon People are in league with the rebels?'

'What?'

'That these savages are funding, and perhaps harbouring, the rebel leader Conthus himself?'

There was a silence while Cantliss blinked up. 'Er . . . yes?'

Cosca smiled very wide. 'Yes. And when my employer Inquisitor Lorsen asks you the same question, what will your answer be?'

Now Cantliss smiled, too, sensing that his chances might have drastically improved. 'Yes! They got them that Conthus up there, no doubt in my mind! Hell, he's more'n likely going to use their money to start a new war!'

'I knew it!' Cosca poured a measure of spirit into Lamb's empty glass. 'We must accompany you into the mountains and pull up this very root of insurrection! This wretched man will be our guide and thereby win his freedom.'

'Yes, indeed!' shouted Cantliss, grinning at Shy and Lamb and Savian, then squawking as Brachio hauled him to his feet and manhandled him towards the door, wounded leg dragging.

'Fuckers,' whispered Shy.

'Realistic,' Lamb hissed at her, one hand on her elbow.

'What luck for all of us,' Cosca was expounding, 'that I should arrive as you prepare to leave!'

'Oh, I've always had the luck,' muttered Temple.

'And me,' murmured Shy.

'Realistic,' hissed Lamb.

'A party of four is easily dismissed,' Cosca was telling the room. 'A party of three hundred, so much less easily!'

'Two hundred and seventy-two,' said Friendly.

'If I could have a word?' Dab Sweet was approaching the counter. 'You're planning on heading into the mountains, you'll need a better scout than that half-dead killer. I stand ready and willing to offer my services.'

'So generous,' said Cosca. 'And you are?'

'Dab Sweet.' And the famous scout removed his hat to display his own thinning locks. Evidently he had caught the scent of a more profitable opportunity than shepherding the desperate back to Starikland.

'The noted frontiersman?' asked Sworbreck, looking up from his papers. 'I thought you'd be younger.'

Sweet sighed. 'I used to be.'

'You're aware of him?' asked Cosca.

The biographer pointed his nose towards the ceiling. 'A man by the name of Marin Glanhorm – I refuse to use the term writer in relation to him – has penned some most inferior and far-fetched works based upon his supposed exploits.'

'Those was unauthorised,' said Sweet. 'But I've exploited a thing or two, that's true. I've trodden on every patch of this Far Country big enough to support a boot, and that includes them mountains.' He beckoned Cosca closer, spoke softer. 'Almost as far as Ashranc, where those Dragon People live. Their sacred ground. My partner, Crying Rock, she's been even further, see . . .' He gave a showman's pause. 'She used to be one of 'em.'

'True,' grunted Crying Rock, still occupying her place at the table, though Corlin had vanished leaving only her cards.

'Raised up there,' said Sweet. 'Lived up there.'

'Born up there, eh?' asked Cosca.

Crying Rock solemnly shook her head. 'No one is born in Ashranc.' And she stuck her dead chagga pipe between her teeth as though that was her last word on the business.

'She knows the secret ways up there, though, and you'll need 'em, too, 'cause those Dragon bastards won't be extending no warm welcomes once you're on their ground. It's some strange, sulphurous ground they've got but they're jealous about it as mean bears, that's the truth.'

'Then the two of you would be an invaluable addition to our expedition,' said Cosca. 'What would be your terms?'

'We'd settle for a twentieth share of any valuables recovered.'

'Our aim is to root out rebellion, not valuables.'

Sweet smiled. 'There's a risk of disappointment in any venture.'

'Then welcome aboard! My notary will prepare an agreement!'

'Two hundred and seventy-four,' mused Friendly. His dead eyes drifted to Temple. 'And you.'

Cosca began to slosh out drinks. 'Why are all the really interesting people always advanced in years?' He nudged Temple in the ribs. 'Your generation really isn't producing the goods.'

'We cower in giants' shadows and feel our shortcomings most keenly.'

'Oh, you've been missed, Temple! If I've learned one thing in forty years of warfare, it's that you have to look on the funny side. The tongue on this man! Conversationally, I mean, not sexually, I can't vouch for that. Don't include that, Sworbreck!' The biographer sullenly crossed something out. 'We shall leave as soon as the men are rested and supplies gathered!'

'Might be best to wait 'til winter's past,' said Sweet.

Cosca leaned close. 'Do you have any notion what will happen if I leave my Company quartered here for four months? The state of the place now barely serves as a taster.'

'You got any notion what'll happen if three hundred men get caught in a real winter storm up there?' grunted Sweet, pulling his fingers through his beard.

'None whatsoever,' said Cosca, 'but I can't wait to find out. We must seize the moment! That has always been my motto. Note that down, Sworbreck.'

Sweet raised his brows. 'Might not be long 'til your motto is, "I can't feel my fucking feet." '

But the captain general was, as usual, not listening. 'I have a premonition we will all find what we seek in those mountains!' He threw one arm about Savian's shoulders and the other about Lamb's. 'Lorsen his rebels, I my gold, these worthy folk their missing children. Let us toast our alliance!' And he raised Temple's nearly empty bottle high.

'Shit on this,' breathed Shy through gritted teeth.

Temple could only agree. But that appeared to be all his say in the matter.

Nowhere to Go

Ro pulled off the chain with the dragon's scale and laid it gently on the furs. Shy once told her you can waste your life waiting for the right moment. Now was good as any.

She touched Pit's cheek in the dark and he stirred, the faintest smile on his face. He was happy here. Young enough to forget, maybe. He'd be safe, or safe as he could be. In this world there are no certainties. Ro wished she could say goodbye but she was worried he'd cry. So she gathered her bundle and slipped out into the night.

The air was sharp, snow gently falling but melting as soon as it touched the hot ground and dry a moment later. Light spilled from some of the houses, windows needing neither glass nor shutter cut from the mountain or from walls so old and weathered Ro couldn't tell them from the mountain. She kept to the shadows, rag-wrapped feet silent on the ancient paving, past the great black cooking slab, surface polished to a shine by the years, steam whispering from it as the snow fell.

The Long House door creaked as she passed and she pressed herself against the pitted wall, waiting. Through the window she could hear the voices of the elders at their Gathering. Three months here and she already knew their tongue.

'The Shanka are breeding in the deeper tunnels.' Uto's voice. She always counselled caution.

'Then we must drive them out.' Akosh. She was always bold.

'If we send enough for that there will be few left behind. One day men will come from outside.'

'We put them off in the place they call Beacon.'

'Or we made them curious.'

'Once we wake the Dragon it will not matter.'

'It was given to me to make the choice.' Waerdinur's deep voice. 'The Maker did not leave our ancestors here to let his works fall into decay.

We must be bold. Akosh, you will take three hundred of us north into the deep places and drive out the Shanka, and keep the diggings going over winter. After the thaw you will return.'

'I worry,' said Uto. 'There have been visions.'

'You always worry . . .'

Their words faded into the night as Ro padded past, over the great sheets of dulled bronze where the names were chiselled in tiny characters, thousands upon thousands stretching back into the fog of ages. She knew Icaray was on guard tonight and guessed he would be drunk, as always. He sat in the archway, head nodding, spear against the wall, empty bottle between his feet. The Dragon People were just people, after all, and each had their failings like any other.

Ro looked back once and thought how beautiful it was, the yellow-lit windows in the black cliff-face, the dark carvings on the steep roofs against a sky blazing with stars. But it wasn't her home. She wouldn't let it be. She scurried past Icaray and down the steps, hand brushing the warm rock on her right because on her left, she knew, was a hundred strides of empty drop.

She came to the needle and found the hidden stair, striking steeply down the mountainside. It scarcely looked hidden at all but Waerdinur had told her that it had a magic, and no one could see it until they were shown it. Shy had always told her there were no such things as Magi or demons and it was all stories, but out here in this far, high corner of the world all things had their magic. To deny it felt as foolish as denying the sky.

Down the winding stair, switching back and forth, away from Ashranc, the stones growing colder underfoot. Into the forest, great trees on the bare slopes, roots catching at her toes and tangling at her ankles. She ran beside a sulphurous stream, bubbling through rocks crusted with salt. She stopped when her breath began to smoke, the cold biting in her chest, and she bound her feet more warmly, unrolled the fur and wrapped it around her shoulders, ate and drank, tied her bundle and hurried on. She thought of Lamb plodding endlessly behind his plough and Shy swinging the scythe sweat dripping from her brows and saying through her gritted teeth, *You just keep on. Don't think of stopping. Just keep on*, and Ro kept on.

The snow had settled in slow melting patches here, the branches dripping tap, tap and how she wished she had proper boots. She heard wolves sorrowful in the high distance and ran faster, her feet wet and her legs sore, downhill, downhill, clambering over jagged rock and sliding in scree, checking with the stars the way Gully taught her once, sitting out beside the barn in the dark of night when she couldn't sleep.

The snow had stopped falling but it was drifted deep now, sparkling as dawn came fumbling through the forest, her feet crunching, her face prickling with the cold. Ahead the trees began to thin and she hurried on, hoping perhaps to look out upon fields or flower-filled valleys or a merry township nestled in the hills.

She burst out at the edge of a dizzy cliff and stared far over high and barren country, sharp black forest and bare black rock slashed and stabbed with white snow fading into long grey rumour without a touch of people or colour. No hint of the world she had known, no hope of deliverance, no heat now from the earth beneath and all was cold inside and out and Ro breathed into her trembling hands and wondered if this was the end of the world.

'Well met, daughter.' Waerdinur sat cross-legged behind her, his back against a tree-stump, his staff, or his spear – Ro still was not sure which it was – in the crook of one arm. 'Do you have meat there in your bundle? I was not prepared for a journey and you have led me quite a chase.'

In silence she gave him a strip of meat and sat down beside him and they ate and she found she was very glad he had come.

After a time he said, 'It can be difficult to let go. But you must see the past is done.' And he pulled out the dragon scale that she had left behind and put the chain around her neck and she did not try to stop him.

'Shy'll be coming . . .' But her voice sounded tiny, thinned by the cold, muffled in the snow, lost in the great emptiness.

'It may be so. But do you know how many children have come here in my lifetime?'

Ro said nothing.

'Hundreds. And do you know how many families have come to claim them?'

Ro swallowed, and said nothing.

'None.' Waerdinur put his great arm around her and held her tight and warm. 'You are one of us now. Sometimes people choose to leave us. Sometimes they are made to. My sister was. If you really wish to go, no one will stop you. But it is a long, hard way, and to what? The world out there is a red country, without justice, without meaning.'

Ro nodded. That much she'd seen.

'Here life has purpose. Here we need you.' He stood and held out his hand. 'Can I show you a wondrous thing?'

'What thing?'

'The reason why the Maker left us here. The reason we remain.'

She took his hand and he hoisted her up easily onto his shoulders. She put her palm on the smooth stubble of his scalp and said, 'Can we shave my head tomorrow?'

'Whenever you are ready.' And he set off up the hillside the way she had come, retracing her footprints through the snow.

IV
DRAGONS

'There are many humorous things in the world,
among them the white man's notion that he
is less savage than the other savages.'
Mark Twain

In Threes

'**F**uck, it's cold,' whispered Shy.

They'd found a shred of shelter wedged in a hollow among frozen tree-roots, but when the wind whipped up it was still like a slap in the face, and even with a piece of blanket double-wrapped around her head so just her eyes showed, it left Shy's face red and stinging as a good slapping might've. She lay on her side, needing a piss but hardly daring to drop her trousers in case she ended up with a yellow icicle stuck to her arse to add to her discomforts. She dragged her coat tight around her shoulders, then the frost-crusted wolfskin Sweet had given her tight around that, wriggled her numb toes in her icy boots and pressed her dead fingertips to her mouth so she could make the most of her breath while she still had some.

'Fuck, it's cold.'

'This is nothing,' grunted Sweet. 'Got caught in drifts one time in the mountains near Hightower for two months. So cold the spirits froze in the bottles. We had to crack the glass off and pass the booze around in lumps.'

'Shhh,' murmured Crying Rock, faintest puff of smoke spilling from her blued lips. 'Til that moment Shy had been wondering whether she'd frozen to death hours before with her pipe still clamped in her mouth. She'd scarcely even blinked all morning, staring through the brush they'd arranged the previous night as cover and down towards Beacon.

Not that there was much to see. The camp looked dead. Snow in the one street was drifted up against doors, thick on roofs toothed with glinting icicles, pristine but for the wandering tracks of one curious wolf. No smoke from the chimneys, no light from the frozen flaps of the half-buried tents. The old barrows were just white humps. The broken tower which in some forgotten past must've held the beacon the place was named for held nothing but snow now. Aside from wind sad in the mangy pines and making a shutter somewhere tap, tap, tap, the place was silent as Juvens' grave.

Shy had never been much for waiting, that wasn't news, but lying up here in the brush and watching reminded her too much of her outlaw days. On her belly in the dust with Jeg chewing and chewing and spitting and chewing in her ear and Neary sweating an inhuman quantity of salt water, waiting for travellers way out of luck to pass on the road below. Pretending to be the outlaw, Smoke, half-crazy with meanness, when what she really felt like was a painfully unlucky little girl, half-crazy with constant fear. Fear of those chasing her and fear of those with her and fear of herself most of all. No clue what she'd do next. Like some hateful lunatic might seize her hands and her mouth and use them like a puppet any moment. The thought of it made her want to wriggle out of her own sore skin.

'Be still,' whispered Lamb, motionless as a felled tree.

'Why? There's no one bloody here, place is dead as a—'

Crying Rock raised one gnarled finger, held it in front of Shy's face, then gently tilted it to point towards the treeline on the far side of the camp.

'You see them two big pines?' whispered Sweet. 'And them three rocks like fingers just between? That's where the hide is.'

Shy stared at that colourless tangle of stone and snow and timber until her eyes ached. Then she caught the faintest twitch of movement.

'That's one of them?' she breathed.

Crying Rock held up two fingers.

'They go in pairs,' said Sweet.

'Oh, she's good,' whispered Shy, feeling a proper amateur in this company.

'The best.'

'How do we flush 'em out?'

'They'll flush 'emselves out. Long as that drunk madman Cosca comes through on his end of it.'

'Far from a certainty,' muttered Shy. In spite of Cosca's talk about haste his Company had loitered around Crease like flies around a turd for a whole two weeks to resupply, which meant to cause every kind of unsavoury chaos and steadily desert. They'd taken even longer slogging across the few dozen miles of high plateau between Crease and Beacon as the weather turned steadily colder, a good number of Crease's most ambitious whores, gamblers and merchants straggling after in hopes of wrenching free any money the mercenaries had somehow left unspent. All the while the Old Man smiled upon this tardy shambles like it was exactly the plan discussed, spinning far-fetched yarns about his glorious past for the benefit of his idiot biographer. 'Seems to me talk and action have come properly uncoupled for that bastard—'

'Shhh,' hissed Lamb.

Shy pressed herself against the dirt as a gang of outraged crows took off clattering into the frozen sky below. Shouting drifted deadened on the wind, then the rattle of gear, then horsemen came into view. Twenty or more, floundering up through the snow drifted in the valley and making damned hard work of it, dipping and bobbing, riders slapping at their mounts' steaming flanks to keep them on.

'The drunk madman comes through,' muttered Lamb.

'This time.' Shy had a strong feeling Cosca didn't make a habit of it.

The mercenaries dismounted and spread out through the camp, digging away at doorways and windows, ripping open tents with canvas frozen stiff as wood, raising a whoop and a clamour which in that winter deadness sounded noisy as the battle at the end of time. That these scum were on her side made Shy wonder whether she was on the right side, but she was where she was. Making the best from different kinds of shit was the story of her life.

Lamb touched her arm and she followed his finger to the hide, caught a dark shape flitting through the trees behind it, keeping low, quickly vanished among the tangle of branch and shadow.

'There goes one,' grunted Sweet, not keeping his voice so soft now the mercenaries were raising hell. 'Any luck, that one'll run right up to their hidden places. Right up to Ashranc and tell the Dragon People there's twenty horsemen in Beacon.'

'When strong seem weak,' muttered Lamb, 'when weak seem strong.'

'What about the other one?' asked Shy.

Crying Rock tucked away her pipe and produced her beaked club, as eloquent an answer as was called for, then slipped limber as a snake around the tree she had her back to and into cover.

'To work,' said Sweet, and started to wriggle after her, a long stretch faster than Shy had ever seen him move standing. She watched the two old scouts crawl between the black tree-trunks, through the snow and the fallen pine needles, working their way towards the hide and out of sight.

She was left shivering on the frozen dirt next to Lamb, and waiting some more.

Since Crease he'd stuck to shaving his head and it was like he'd shaved all sentiment off, too, hard lines and hard bones and hard past laid bare. The stitches had been pulled with the point of Savian's knife and the marks of the fight with Glama Golden were fast fading, soon to be lost among all the rest. A lifetime of violence written so plain into that beaten anvil of a face she'd no notion how she never read it there before.

Hard to believe how easy it had been to talk to him once. Or talk at him, at least. Good old cowardly Lamb, he'll never surprise you. Safe and comfortable as talking to herself. Now there was a wider and more dangerous gulf between them each day. So many questions swimming round her head but now she finally got her mouth open, the one that dropped out she hardly cared about the answer to.

'Did you fuck the Mayor, then?'

Lamb left it long enough to speak, she thought he might not bother. 'Every which way and I don't regret a moment.'

'I guess a fuck can still be a wonderful thing between folk who've reached a certain age.'

'No doubt. Specially if they didn't get many beforehand.'

'Didn't stop her knifing you in the back soon as it suited her.'

'Get many promises from Temple 'fore he jumped out your window?'

Shy felt the need for a pause of her own. 'Can't say I did.'

'Huh. I guess fucking someone don't stop them fucking you.'

She gave a long, cold, smoking sigh. 'For some of us it only seems to increase the chances . . .'

Sweet came trudging from the pines near the hide, ungainly in his swollen fur coat, and waved up. Crying Rock followed and bent down, cleaning her club in the snow, leaving the faintest pink smear on the blank white.

'I guess that's it done,' said Lamb, wincing as he clambered up to a squat.

'I guess.' Shy hugged herself tight, too cold to feel much about it but cold. She turned, first time she'd looked at him since they started speaking. 'Can I ask you a question?'

The jaw muscles worked on the side of his head. 'Sometimes ignorance is the sweetest medicine.' He turned this strange, sick, guilty look on her, like a man who's been caught doing murder and knows the game's all up. 'But I don't know how I'd stop you.' And she felt worried to the pit of her stomach and could hardly bring herself to speak, but couldn't stand to stay silent either.

'Who are you?' she whispered. 'I mean . . . who were you? I mean—shit.'

She caught movement – a figure flitting through the trees towards Sweet and Crying Rock.

'Shit!' And she was running, stumbling, blundering, snagged a numb foot at the edge of the hollow and went tumbling through the brush, floundered up and was off across the bare slope, legs so caught in the virgin snow it felt like she was dragging two giant stone boots after her.

'Sweet!' she wheezed. The figure broke from the trees and over the unspoiled white towards the old scout, hint of a snarling face, glint of a blade. No way Shy could get there in time. Nothing she could do.

'Sweet!' she wailed one more time, and he looked up, smiling, then sideways, eyes suddenly wide, shrinking away as the dark shape sprang for him. It twisted in the air, fell short and went tumbling through the snow. Crying Rock rushed up and hit it over the head with her club. Shy heard the sharp crack a moment after.

Savian pushed some branches out of his way and trudged through the snow towards them, frowning at the trees and calmly cranking his flatbow.

'Nice shot,' called Crying Rock, sliding her club into her belt and jamming that pipe between her teeth.

Sweet pushed back his hat. 'Nice shot, she says! I've damn near shat myself.'

Shy stood with her hands on her hips and tried to catch her smoking breath, chest on fire from the icy coldness of it.

Lamb walked up beside her, sheathing his sword. 'Looks like they sometimes go in threes.'

Among the Barbarians

'They hardly look like demons.' Cosca nudged the Dragon Woman's cheek with his foot and watched her bare-shaved head flop back. 'No scales. No forked tongues. No flaming breath. I feel a touch let down.'

'Simple barbarians,' grunted Jubair.

'Like the ones out on the plains.' Brachio took a gulp of wine and peered discerningly at the glass. 'A step above animals and not a high step.'

Temple cleared his sore throat. 'No barbarian's sword.' He squatted down and turned the blade over in his hands: straight, and perfectly balanced, and meticulously sharpened.

'These ain't no common Ghosts,' said Sweet. 'They ain't really Ghosts at all. They aim to kill and know how. They don't scare at nothing and know each rock o' this country, too. They did for every miner in Beacon without so much as a struggle.'

'But clearly they bleed.' Cosca poked his finger into the hole made by Savian's flatbow bolt and pulled it out, fingertip glistening red. 'And clearly they die.'

Brachio shrugged. 'Everyone bleeds. Everyone dies.'

'Life's one certainty,' rumbled Jubair, rolling his eyes towards the heavens. Or at least the mildewed ceiling.

'What is this metal?' Sworbreck pulled an amulet from the Dragon Woman's collar, a grey leaf dully gleaming in the lamplight. 'It is very thin but . . .' He bared his teeth as he strained at it. 'I cannot bend it. Not at all. The workmanship is remarkable.'

Cosca turned away. 'Steel and gold are the only metals that interest me. Bury the bodies away from the camp. If I've learned one thing in forty years of warfare, Sworbreck, it's that you have to bury the bodies far from camp.' He drew his cloak tight at the icy blast as the door was opened. 'Damn this cold.' Hunched jealously over the fire, he looked like nothing so much as an old witch over her cauldron, thin hair hanging lank, grasping hands like black claws against the flames. 'Reminds me of the North, and that can't be a good thing, eh, Temple?'

'No, General.' Being reminded of any moment in the past ten years was no particularly good thing in Temple's mind – the whole a desert of violence, waste and guilt. Except, perhaps, gazing out over the free plains from his saddle. Or down on Crease from the frame of Majud's shop. Or arguing with Shy over their debt. Dancing, pressed tight against her. Leaning to kiss her, and her smile as she leaned to kiss him back . . . He shook himself. All thoroughly, irredeemably fucked. Truly, you never value what you have until you jump out of its window.

'That cursed retreat.' Cosca was busy wrestling with his own failures. There were enough of them. 'That damned snow. That treacherous bastard Black Calder. So many good men lost, eh, Temple? Like . . . well . . . I forget the names, but my point holds.' He turned to call angrily over his shoulder. 'When you said "fort" I was expecting something more . . . substantial.'

Beacon's chief building was, in fact, a large log cabin on one and a half floors, separated into rooms by hanging animal skins and with a heavy door, narrow windows, access to the broken tower in one corner and a horrifying array of draughts.

Sweet shrugged. 'Standards ain't high in the Far Country, General. Out here you put three sticks together, it's a fort.'

'I suppose we must be glad of the shelter we have. Another night in the open you'd have to wait for spring to thaw me out. How I long for the towers of beautiful Visserine! A balmy summer night beside the river! The city was mine, once, you know, Sworbreck?'

The writer winced. 'I believe you have mentioned it.'

'Nicomo Cosca, Grand Duke of Visserine!' The Old Man paused to take yet another swig from his flask. 'And it shall be mine again. My towers, my palace, and my respect. I have been often disappointed, that's true. My back is a tissue of metaphorical scars. But there is still time, isn't there?'

'Of course.' Sworbreck gave a false chuckle. 'You have many successful years ahead of you, I'm sure!'

'Still a little time to make things right . . .' Cosca was busy staring at the wrinkled back of his hand, wincing as he worked the knobbly fingers. 'I used to be a wonder with a throwing knife, you know,

Sworbreck. I could bring down a fly at twenty paces. Now?' He gave vent to an explosive snort. 'I can scarcely see twenty paces on a clear day. That's the most wounding betrayal of all. The one by your own flesh. Live long enough, you see everything ruined . . .'

The next whirlwind heralded Sergeant Friendly's arrival, blunt nose and flattened ears slightly pinked but otherwise showing no sign of discomfort at the cold. Sun, rain or tempest all seemed one to him.

'The last stragglers are into camp along with the Company's baggage,' he intoned.

Brachio poured himself another drink. 'Hangers-on swarm to us like maggots to a corpse.'

'I am not sure I appreciate the image of our noble brotherhood as a suppurating carcass,' said Cosca.

'However accurate it may be,' murmured Temple.

'Who made it all the way here?'

Friendly began the count. 'Nineteen whores and four pimps—'

'They'll be busy,' said Cosca.

'—twenty-two wagon-drivers and porters including the cripple Hedges, who keeps demanding to speak to you—'

'Everyone wants a slice of me! You'd think I was a feast-day currant cake!'

'—thirteen assorted merchants, pedlars and tinkers, six of whom complain of having been robbed by members of the Company—'

'I consort with criminals! I was a Grand Duke, you know. So many disappointments.'

'—two blacksmiths, a horse trader, a fur trader, an undertaker, a barber boasting of surgical qualifications, a pair of laundry women, a vintner with no stock, and seventeen persons of no stated profession.'

'Vagrants and layabouts hoping to grow fat on my crumbs! Is there no honour left, Temple?'

'Precious little,' said Temple. Certainly his own stock was disgracefully meagre.

'And is Superior Pike's . . .' Cosca leaned close to Friendly and after taking another swallow from his flask whispered, entirely audibly, '*secret wagon* in the camp?'

'It is,' said Friendly.

'Place it under guard.'

'What's in it, anyway?' asked Brachio, wiping some damp from his weepy eye with a fingernail.

'Were I to share that information, it would no longer be a secret wagon, merely . . . a wagon. I think we can agree that lacks mystique.'

'Where will all this flotsam find shelter?' Jubair wished to know. 'There is hardly room for the fighting men.'

'What of the barrows?' asked the Old Man.

'Empty,' said Sweet. 'Robbed centuries ago.'

'I daresay they'll warm up something snug. The irony, eh, Temple? Yesterday's heroes kicked from their graves by today's whores!'

'I thrill to the profundity,' muttered Temple, shivering at the thought of sleeping in the dank innards of those ancient tombs, let alone fucking in them.

'Not wanting to spoil your preparations, General,' said Sweet, 'but I'd best be on my way.'

'Of course! Glory is like bread, it stales with time! Was it Farans who said so, or Stolicus? What is your plan?'

'I'm hoping that scout'll run straight back and tell his Dragon friends there's no more'n twenty of us down here.'

'The best opponent is one befuddled and mystified! Was that Farans? Or Bialoveld?' Cosca treated Sworbreck, busy with his notebooks, to a contemptuous glare. 'One *writer* is very much like another. You were saying?'

'Reckon they'll set to wondering whether to stay tucked up at Ashranc and ignore us, or come down and wipe us out.'

'They'll trip over a shock if they try it,' said Brachio, jowls wobbling as he chuckled.

'That's just what we want 'em to do,' said Sweet. 'But they ain't prone to come down without good reason. A little trespass on their ground should hook 'em. Prickly as all hell about their ground. Crying Rock knows the way. She knows secret ways right into Ashranc, but that's a hell of a risk. So all we do is creep up there and leave some sign they won't miss. A burned-out fire, some nice clear tracks across their road—'

'A turd,' said Jubair, pronouncing the word as solemnly as a prophet's name.

Cosca raised his flask. 'Marvellous! Lure them with a turd! I'm reasonably sure Stolicus never recommended *that*, eh, Temple?'

Brachio squeezed his big lower lip thoughtfully between finger and thumb. 'You're sure they'll fall for this turd trap?'

'They've been the big dogs around here for ever,' said Sweet. 'They're used to slaughtering Ghosts and scaring off prospectors. All that winning's made 'em arrogant. Set in old ways. But they're dangerous, still. You'd best be good and ready. Don't reel 'em in 'til they've swallowed the hook.'

Cosca nodded. 'Believe me when I say I have stood at both ends of an ambush and fully understand the principles. What would be your opinion of this scheme, Master Cantliss?'

The wretched bandit, his clothes splitting at the seams and stuffed with straw against the cold, had until then been sitting in the corner of the room nursing his broken hand and quietly sniffling. He perked up at the sound of his name and nodded vigorously, as though his support might be help to any cause. 'Sounds all right. They think they own these hills, that I can chime with. And that Waerdinur killed my friend Blackpoint. Snuffed him out casual as you please. Can I . . .' licking his scabbed lips and reaching towards Cosca's flask.

'Of course,' said Cosca, draining it, upending it to show it was empty, then shrugging. 'Captain Jubair has picked out eight of his most competent men to accompany you.'

Sweet looked less than reassured as he gave the hulking Kantic a sidelong glance. 'I'd rather stick with folks I know I can count on.'

'So would we all, but are there truly any such in life, eh, Temple?'

'Precious few.' Temple certainly would not have counted himself among their number, nor anyone else currently in the room.

Sweet affected an air of injured innocence. 'You don't trust us?'

'I have been often disappointed by human nature,' said Cosca. 'Ever since Grand Duchess Sefeline turned on me and poisoned my favourite mistress I have tried never to encumber working relationships with the burden of trust.'

Brachio gave vent to a long burp. 'Better to watch each other carefully, stay well armed and mutually suspicious, and keep our various self-interests as the prime motives.'

'Nobly said!' And Cosca slapped his thigh. 'Then, like a knife in the sock, we make trust our secret weapon in the event of emergencies.'

'I tried a knife in the sock,' muttered Brachio, patting the several he had stowed in his bandolier. 'Chafed terribly.'

'Shall we depart?' rumbled Jubair. 'Time is wasting, and there is God's work to be done.'

'There's work, anyway,' said Sweet, pulling the collar of his big fur coat up to his ears as he ducked out into the night.

Cosca tipped up his flask, realised it was empty and held it aloft for a refill. 'Bring me more spirit! And Temple, come, talk to me as you used to! Offer me comfort, Temple, offer me advice.'

Temple took a long breath. 'I'm not sure what advice I can offer. We're far beyond the reach of the law out here.'

'I don't speak of the law, man, but of the righteous path! Thank you.' This as Sergeant Friendly began to decant a freshly opened bottle into Cosca's waving flask with masterful precision. 'I feel I am adrift upon strange seas and my moral compass spins entirely haywire! Find me an ethical star to steer by, Temple! What of God, man, what of God?'

'I fear we may be far beyond the reach of God as well,' muttered Temple as he made for the door. Hedges limped in as he opened it, clutching tight to his ruin of a hat and looking sicker than ever, if that was possible.

'Who's this now?' demanded Cosca, peering into the shadows.

'The name's Hedges, Captain General, sir, one of the drovers from Crease. Injured at Osrung, sir, leading a charge.'

'The very reason charges are best left led by others.'

Hedges sidled past into the room, eyes nervously darting. 'Can't say I disagree, sir. Might I have a moment?' Grateful for the distraction, Temple slipped out into the bitter darkness.

In the camp's one street, secrecy did not seem a prime concern. Men swathed in coats and furs, swaddled in torn-up blankets and mismatched armour stomped cursing about, churning the snow to black slush, holding rustling torches high, dragging reluctant horses, unloading boxes and barrels from listing wagons, breath steaming from wrappings around their faces.

'Might I accompany you?' asked Sworbreck, threading after Temple through the chaos.

'If you're not scared my luck will rub off.'

'It could be no worse than mine,' lamented the biographer.

They passed a group huddled in a hut with one missing wall, playing dice for bedding, a man sharpening blades at a shrieking grindstone, sparks showering into the night, three women arguing over how best to get a cook-fire started. None had the answer.

'Do you ever feel . . .' Sworbreck mused, face squashed down for warmth into the threadbare collar of his coat, 'as though you have somehow blundered into a situation you never intended to be in, but now cannot see your way clear of?'

Temple looked sidelong at the writer. 'Lately, every moment of every day.'

'As if you were being punished, but you were not sure what for.'

'I know what for,' muttered Temple.

'I don't belong here,' said Sworbreck.

'I wish I could say the same. But I fear that I do.'

Snow had been dug away from one of the barrows and torchlight flickered in its moss-caked archway. One of the pimps was busy hanging a worn hide at the entrance of another, a disorderly queue already forming outside. A shivering pedlar had set up shop between the two, offering belts and boot-polish to the heedless night. Commerce never sleeps.

Temple caught Inquisitor Lorsen's grating tones emerging from a cabin's half-open door, '. . . Do you really believe there are rebels in these mountains, Dimbik?'

'Belief is a luxury I have not been able to afford for some time, Inquisitor. I simply do as I'm told.'

'But by whom, Captain, by whom is the question. I, after all, have the ear of Superior Pike, and the Superior has the ear of the Arch Lector himself, and a recommendation from the Arch Lector . . .' His scheming was lost in the babble.

In the darkness at the edge of the camp, Temple's erstwhile fellows were already mounting up. It had begun to snow again, white specks gently settling on the manes of the horses, on Crying Rock's grey hair and the old flag it was bound up with, across Shy's shoulders, hunched as she steadfastly refused to look over, on the packages Lamb was busy stowing on his horse.

'Coming with us?' asked Savian as he watched Temple approach.

'My heart is willing but the rest of me has the good sense to politely decline.'

'Crying Rock!' Sworbreck produced his notebook with a flourish. 'It is a most intriguing name!'

She stared down at him. 'Yes.'

'I daresay an intriguing story lies behind it.'

'Yes.'

'Would you care to share it?'

Crying Rock slowly rode off into the gathering darkness.

'I'd call that a no,' said Shy.

Sworbreck sighed. 'A writer must learn to flourish on scorn. No passage, sentence or even word can be to the taste of *every* reader. Master Lamb, have you ever been interviewed by an author?'

'We've run across just about every other kind of liar,' said Shy.

The biographer persisted. 'I've heard it said that you have more experience of single combat than any man alive.'

Lamb pulled the last of the straps tight. 'You believe everything you hear?'

'Do you deny it, then?'

Lamb did not speak.

'Have you any insights into the deadly business, for my readers?'

'Don't do it.'

Sworbreck stepped closer. 'But is it true what General Cosca tells me?'

'From what I've seen, I wouldn't rate him the yardstick of honesty.'

'He told me you were once a king.'

Temple raised his brows. Sweet cleared his throat. Shy burst out laughing, but then she saw Lamb wasn't, and trailed off.

'He told me you were champion to the King of the Northmen,' continued Sworbreck, 'and that you won ten duels in the Circle in his name, were betrayed by him but survived, and finally killed him and took his place.'

Lamb dragged himself slowly up into his saddle and frowned off into the night. 'Men put a golden chain on me for a while, and knelt, because it suited 'em. In violent times folk like to kneel to violent men. In peaceful times they remember they're happier standing.'

'Do you blame them?'

'I'm long past blaming. That's just the way men are.' Lamb looked over at Temple. 'Can we count on your man Cosca, do you reckon?'

'Absolutely not,' said Temple.

'Had a feeling you'd say that.' And Lamb nudged his horse uphill into the darkness.

'And they say I've got stories,' grumbled Sweet as he followed.

Sworbreck stared after them for a moment, then fumbled out his pencil and began to scratch feverishly away.

Temple met Shy's eye as she turned her mount. 'I hope you find them!' he blurted. 'The children.'

'We will. Hope you find . . . whatever you're looking for.'

'I think I did,' he said softly. 'And I threw it away.'

She sat there a moment as though considering what to say, then clicked her tongue and her horse walked on.

'Good luck!' he called after her. 'Take care of yourself, among the barbarians!'

She glanced over towards the fort, from which the sounds of off-key singing were already beginning to float, and raised one eyebrow. 'Likewise.'

Bait

The first day they rode through towering forest, trees far bigger'n Shy ever saw, branch upon branch upon branch blocking out the sun so she felt they stole through some giant's crypt, sombre and sacred. The snow had found its way in still, drifted a stride deep between the crusted trunks, frozen to a sparkling crust that skinned the horse's legs, so they had to take turns breaking new ground. Here and there a freezing fog had gathered, curling round men and mounts as they passed like spirits jealous of their warmth. Not that there was much of that to be had. Crying Rock gave a warning hiss whenever anyone started in to talk so they just nodded in dumb misery to the crunching of snow and the laboured breaths of the struggling horses, Savian's coughing and a soft mumbling from Jubair which Shy took for prayers. He was a pious bastard, the big Kantic, that you couldn't deny. Whether piety made him a safe man to have at your back she profoundly doubted. Folk she'd known to be big on religion had tended to use it as an excuse for doing wrong rather'n a reason not to.

Only when the light had faded to a twilight glimmer did Sweet lead them to a shallow cave under an overhang and let them stop. By then the mounts and the spare mounts were all blown and shuddering and Shy wasn't in a state much better, her whole body one stiff and aching, numbed and prickling, chafed and stinging competition of complaints.

No fire allowed, they ate cold meat and hard biscuit and passed about a bottle. Savian put a hard face over his coughing like he did over everything else, but Shy could tell he was troubled with it, bent and hacking and his pale hands clawing his coat shut at his neck.

One of the mercenaries, a Styrian with a jutting jaw by the name of Sacri, who struck Shy as the sort whose only comfort in life is others' discomfort, grinned and said, 'You got a cough, old man. You want to go back?'

Shy said, 'Shut your mouth,' with as much fire as she could muster which right then wasn't much.

'What'll you do?' he sneered at her. 'Slap me?'

That struck a hotter spark from her. 'That's right. With a fucking axe. Now shut your mouth.'

This time he did shut it, too, but by the moon's glimmering she gathered he was working out how to even the score, and reckoned she'd better mind her back even closer than before.

They kept watch in pairs, one from the mercenaries, one from the Fellowship that had been, and they watched each other every bit as hard as they watched the night for Dragon People. Shy marked time by Sweet's snoring, and when the moment came she shook Lamb and whispered in his ear.

'Wake up, your Majesty.'

He gave a grunting sigh. 'Wondered how long it'd be 'fore that floated up again.'

'Pardon the foolishness of a witless peasant. I'm just overcome at having the King of the Northmen snoring in my blankets.'

'I spent ten times as long poorer'n a beggar and without a friend to my name. Why does no one want to talk about that?'

'In my case 'cause I know well enough what that feels like. I haven't had occasion to wear a crown that often.'

'Neither have I,' he said, crawling stiffly clear of the bedding. 'I had a chain.'

'A golden one?'

'With a diamond like that.' And he made a shape the size of a hen's egg with his thumb and forefinger and eyed her through it.

She still wasn't sure whether this was all some kind of a joke. 'You.'

'Me.'

'That got through a whole winter in one pair of trousers.'

He shrugged. 'I'd lost the chain by then.'

'Any particular way I should act around royalty?'

'The odd curtsy wouldn't go amiss.'

She snorted. 'Fuck yourself.'

'Fuck yourself, *your Majesty*.'

'King Lamb,' she muttered, crawling into the blankets to make the most of his already fading warmth. 'King Lamb.'

'I had a different name.'

Shy looked sideways at him. 'What name?'

He sat there in the wide mouth of the cave, hunched black against the star-speckled night, and she couldn't guess at what was on his face. 'Don't matter,' he said. 'No good ever came of it.'

Next morning the snow whirled down on a wind that came from every way at once, bitter as a bankrupt. They mounted up with all the joy of folk riding to their own hangings and pressed on, uphill, uphill. The forest thinned out, trees shrinking, withering, twisting like folk in pain. They threaded through bare rocks and the way grew narrow – an old stream bed, maybe, though sometimes it looked more like a man-made stair worn almost smooth by years and weather. Jubair sent one of his men back with the horses and Shy half-wished she was going with him. The rest of them toiled on by foot.

'What the hell are these Dragon bastards doing up here anyhow?' Shy grunted at Sweet. Didn't seem like a place anyone in their right mind would want to visit, let alone live in.

'Can't say I know exactly . . . why they're up here.' The old scout had to talk in rushes between his heaving breaths. 'But they been here a long time.'

'She hasn't told you?' asked Shy, nodding at Crying Rock, striding on hard up ahead.

'I reckon it's on account . . . o' my reluctance to ask those kind o' questions . . . she's stuck with me down the years.'

'Ain't for your good looks, I can tell you that.'

'There's more to life than looks.' He glanced sideways at her. 'Luckily for us both.'

'What would they want with children?'

He stopped to take a swallow of water and offered one to her while the mercenaries laboured past under the considerable burden of their many weapons. 'The way I hear it, no children are born here. Some-thing in the land. They turn barren. All the Dragon People were taken from someone else, one time or another. Used to be that meant Ghosts mostly, maybe Imperials, the odd Northman strayed down from the Sea of Teeth. Looks like since the prospectors drove the Ghosts out they're casting their net wider. Buying children off the likes of Cantliss.'

'Less talk!' hissed Crying Rock from above. 'More walk!'

The snow came down weightier than ever but didn't drift as deep, and when Shy peeled the wrappings off her face she found the wind wasn't half so keen. An hour later the snow was slippery slush on the wet rock, and she pulled her soaked gloves off and could still feel her fingertips. An hour after that the snow still fell but the ground was bare, and Shy was sweating fast enough she had to strip her coat off and wedge it in her pack. The others were doing the same. She bent and pressed her palm to the earth and there was a strange warmth, like it was the wall of a baker's and the oven was stoked on the other side.

'There is fire below,' said Crying Rock.

'There is?' Shy snatched her hand back like flames might pop from the dirt then and there. 'Can't say that notion floods a woman with optimism.'

'Better'n freezing the crap up my arse, ain't it?' said Sweet, pulling his shirt off to reveal another underneath. Shy wondered how many he had on. Or if he'd keep taking them off until he disappeared altogether.

'Is that why the Dragon People live up here?' Savian pressed his own palm to the warm dirt. 'Because of the fire?'

'Or because they live here there is a fire.' Crying Rock stared up the slope, bare rock and scree now, crusted in places with stains of yellow sulphur, overlooked by a towering bastard of a rock face. 'This way may be watched.'

'Certainly it will be,' said Jubair. 'God sees all.'

'Ain't God as'll put an arrow in your arse if we keep on this path,' said Sweet.

Jubair shrugged. 'God puts all things where they must be.'

'What now, then?' asked Savian.

Crying Rock was already uncoiling a rope from her pack. 'Now we climb.'

Shy rubbed at her temples. 'Had a nasty feeling she'd say that.'

Damn it if the climbing wasn't even harder than the walking and a long drop scarier. Crying Rock swarmed up like a spider and Lamb wasn't much slower, seeming well at home among the mountains, the two of them getting ropes ready for the rest. Shy brought up the rear with Savian, cursing and fumbling at the slick rock, arms aching from the effort and her hands burning from the hemp.

'Haven't had the chance to thank you,' she said as she waited on a ledge.

He didn't make a sound but the hissing of the rope through his gnarled hands as he pulled it up behind them.

'For what you did back in Crease.' Silence. 'Ain't had my life saved so often that I overlook it.' Silence. 'Remember?'

She thought he gave the tiniest shrug.

'Get the feeling you've been avoiding mention of it.'

Silence. He avoided mentioning anything wherever possible.

'Probably you ain't much of a one for taking thanks.'

More silence.

'Probably I ain't much of a one for giving 'em.'

'You're taking your time about it, all right.'

'Thanks, then. Reckon I'd be good and dead if it weren't for you.'

Savian pressed his thin lips together even tighter and gave a throaty grunt. 'Reckon you or your father would've done the same for me.'

'He ain't my father.'

'That's between you two. But if you were to ask, I'd say you could do worse.'

Shy snorted. 'I used to think so.'

'This isn't what he wanted, you know. Or the way he wanted it.'

'I used to think that, too. Not so sure any more. Family, eh?'

'Family.'

'Where's Corlin got to?'

'She can look after herself.'

'Oh, no doubt.' Shy dropped her voice. 'Look, Savian, I know what you are.'

He looked up at her hard. 'That so?'

'I know what you got under there,' and she moved her eyes down to his forearms, blue with tattoos, she knew, under his coat.

'Can't fathom your meaning,' but tweaking one of his sleeves down even so.

She leaned closer and whispered, 'Just pretend you can, then. When Cosca got to talking about rebels, well, my big fucking mouth ran away with me, like always. I meant well, like always, trying to help out . . . but I haven't, have I?'

'Not a lot.'

'My fault you're in this fix. If that bastard Lorsen finds out what you got there . . . what I'm saying is, you should go. This ain't your fight. Naught to stop you slipping away, and no shortage of empty to slip into.'

'And you'd say what? Forgot all about my lost boy, did I? It'd just make 'em curious. Might make trouble for you. Might make trouble for me, in the end. Reckon I'll keep my head down and my sleeves down too and stick with you. Best all round.'

'My big fucking mouth,' she hissed to herself.

Savian grinned. It might have been the first time she'd ever seen him do it and it was like a lantern uncovered, the lines shifting in his weathered face and his eyes suddenly gleaming. 'You know what? Your big fucking mouth ain't to everyone's taste but I've almost got to like it.' And he put his hand down on her shoulder and gave it a squeeze. 'You'd best watch out for that prick Sacri, though. Don't think he sees it that way.'

Nor did she. Not long after that, a rock came clattering down that missed her head by a whisker. She saw Sacri grinning above and was sure he'd kicked it loose on purpose. Soon as she got the chance she told him so and where she'd stick her knife if another rock came along. The other mercenaries were quite tickled by her language.

'I should teach you some manners, girl,' snapped Sacri, sticking his jutting jaw out even further, trying to save what face he could.

'You'd have to fucking know some to teach some.'

He put his hand on his sword, more bluster than meaning to use it, but before he even got the chance Jubair loomed between them.

'There will be weapons drawn, Sacri,' he said, 'but when and against whom I say. These are our allies. We need them to show us the way. Leave the woman be or we will quarrel and a quarrel with me is a heavy weight to carry.'

'Sorry, Captain,' said Sacri, scowling.

Jubair offered him the way with one open hand. 'Regret is the gateway to salvation.'

Lamb scarcely even looked over while they were arguing, and trudged off when they were done like none of it was his concern.

'Thanks for your help back there,' she snapped as she caught him up.

'You'd have had it if you'd needed it. You know that.'

'A word or two wouldn't have hurt.'

He leaned close. 'Way I see it, we've got two choices. Try and use these bastards, or kill 'em all. Hard words have never won a battle yet, but they've lost a few. You mean to kill a man, telling him so don't help.'

Lamb walked on, and left her to think about that.

They camped near a steaming stream that Sweet said not to drink from. Not that anyone was keen to try since it smelled like feast-day farts. All night the water hissing in Shy's ears and she dreamed of falling. Woke sweating with her throat raw from the warm stink to see Sacri on guard and watching her and thought she caught the gleam of metal in his hand. She lay awake after that, her own knife drawn in her fist. The way she had long ago when she was on the run. The way she'd hoped she never would again. She found herself wishing that Temple was there. Surely the man was no hero, but somehow he made her feel braver.

In the morning, grey shadows of crags loomed over them that through the shifting veil of snow looked like the ruins of walls, towers, fortresses. Holes were cut in the rock, too square to be natural, and near them mounds of spoil.

'Prospectors get this far?' one of the mercenaries asked.

Sweet shook his head. 'Nowhere near. These is older diggings.'

'How much older?'

'Much older,' said Crying Rock.

'Seems like the closer we get the more I worry,' Shy muttered at Lamb as they set off, bent and sore.

He nodded. 'Starting to think about all the thousand things could go wrong.'

'Scared we won't find 'em.'

'Or scared we will.'

'Or just plain scared,' she muttered.

'Scared is good,' he said. 'The dead are fearless and I don't want either of us joining 'em.'

They stopped beside a deep gorge, the sound of water moving far below, steam rising and everywhere the reek of brimstone. An arch spanned the canyon, black rock slick with wet and bearded with dripping icicles of lime. From its middle a great chain hung, links a stride high, rust-eaten metal squealing faintly as the wind stirred them. Savian sat with his head back, breathing hard. The mercenaries slouched in a group nearby, passing round a flask.

'And here she is!' Sacri chuckled. 'The child hunter!' Shy looked at him, and at the drop beside him, and thought how dearly she'd like to introduce one to the other. 'What kind of fool would hope to find children alive in a place like this?'

'Why do big mouths and little brains so often go together?' she muttered, but she thought about Lamb's words, realised her question might apply to herself just as easily, and stopped her tongue for once.

'Nothing to say?' Sacri grinned down his nose as he tipped his flask up. 'At least you've learned some—'

Jubair put out a great arm and brushed him off the cliff. The Styrian made a choking whoop, flask tumbling from his hand, and he was gone.

A thump and a clatter of stones, then another, and another, fading out of hearing in the gorge below.

The mercenaries stared, one with a piece of dried meat halfway to his open mouth. Shy watched, skin prickling, as Jubair stepped to the brink, lips thoughtfully pursed, and looked down. 'The world is filled with folly and waste,' he said. 'It is enough to shake a man's faith.'

'You killed him,' said one of the mercenaries, with that talent for stating the obvious some men have.

'God killed him. I was but the instrument.'

'God sure can be a thorny bastard, can't He?' croaked Savian.

Jubair solemnly nodded. 'He is a terrible and a merciless God and all things must bend to His design.'

'His design's left us a man short,' said Sweet.

Jubair shrugged his pack over his shoulder. 'Better that than discord. We must be together in this. If we disagree, how can God be for all of us?' He waved Crying Rock forward, and let his surviving men step, more than a little nervously, past him, one swallowing as he peered down into the gorge.

Jubair took Sacri's fallen flask from the brink. 'In the city of Ul-Nahb in Gurkhul, where I was born, thanks be to the Almighty, death is a great thing. All efforts are taken with the body and a family wails and a procession of mourners follows the flower-strewn way to the place of burial. Out here, death is a little thing. A man who expects more than one chance is a fool.' He frowned out at the vast arch and its broken chain, and took a thoughtful swig. 'The further I go into the unmapped extremes of this country, the more I become convinced these are the end times.'

Lamb plucked the flask from Jubair's hand, drained it, then tossed it after its owner. 'All times are end times for someone.'

They squatted among ruined walls, between stones salt-streaked and crystal-crusted, and watched the valley. They'd been watching it for what felt like for ever, squinting into the sticky mist while Crying Rock hissed at them to keep low, stay out of sight, shut their mouths. Shy was getting just a little tired of being hissed at. She was getting a little tired altogether. Tired, and sore, and her nerves worn down to aching stubs with fear, and worry, and hope. Hope worst of all.

Now and again Savian broke out in muffled coughs and Shy could hardly blame him. The very valley seemed to breathe, acrid steam rising from hidden cracks and turning the broken boulders to phantoms, drifting down to make a fog over the pool in the valley's bottom, slowly fading only to gather again.

Jubair sat cross-legged, eyes closed and arms folded, huge and patient, lips silently moving, a sheen of sweat across his forehead. They all were sweating. Shy's shirt was plastered to her back, hair stuck clammy to her face. She could hardly believe she'd felt close to death from cold a day or two before. She'd have given her teeth to strip and drop into a snowdrift now. She crawled over to Crying Rock, the stones wet and sticky-warm under her palms.

'They're close?'

The Ghost shifted her frown up and down a fraction.

'Where?'

'If I knew that, I would not have to watch.'

'We leave this bait soon?'

'Soon.'

'I hope it ain't really a turd you got in mind,' grunted Sweet, surely down to his last shirt now, ''cause I don't fancy dropping my trousers here.'

'Shut up,' hissed Crying Rock, sticking her hand out hard behind her.

A shadow was shifting in the murk on the valley's side, a figure hopping from one boulder to another. Hard to tell for the distance and the mist but it looked like a man, tall and heavy-built, dark-skinned, bald-headed, a staff carried loose in one hand.

'Is he whistling?' Shy muttered.

'Shh,' hissed Crying Rock.

The old man left his staff beside a flat rock at the water's edge, shrugged off his robe and left it folded carefully on top, then did a little dance, spinning naked in and out of some broken pillars at the shoreline.

'He don't look all that fearsome,' whispered Shy.

'Oh, he is fearsome,' said Crying Rock. 'He is Waerdinur. My brother.'

Shy looked at her, pale as new milk, then back to the dark-skinned man, still whistling as he waded out into the pool. 'Ain't much resemblance.'

'We came of different wombs.'

'Good to know.'

'What is?'

'Had a feeling you might've hatched from an egg, you're that pain-less.'

'I have my pains,' said Crying Rock. 'But they must serve me, not the other way about.' And she stuck the stained stem of her pipe between her jaws and chomped down hard on it.

'What is Lamb doing?' came Jubair's voice.

Shy turned and stared. Lamb was scurrying through the boulders and down towards the water, already twenty strides away.

'Oh, hell,' muttered Sweet.

'Shit!' Shy forced her stiff knees into life and vaulted over the crumbling wall. Sweet made a grab at her but she slapped his hand off and threaded after Lamb, one eye on the old man still splashing happily below them, his whistling floating through the mist. She winced and skidded over the slick rocks, almost on all fours, ankles aching as her feet were jarred this way and that, burning to shout to Lamb but knowing she couldn't make a peep.

He was too far ahead to catch, had made it all the way down to the water's edge. She could only watch as he perched on that flat rock with the folded robe as a cushion, laid his drawn sword across one knee, took out his whetstone and licked it. She flinched as he set it to the blade and gave it a single grating stroke.

Shy caught the surprise in the tightening of Waerdinur's shoulders, but he didn't move right off. Only as the second stroke cut the silence did he slowly turn. A kind face, Shy would've said, but she'd seen kind-looking men do some damned mean things before.

'Here is a surprise.' Though he seemed more puzzled than shocked as his dark eyes shifted from Lamb to Shy and back again. 'Where did you two come from?'

'All the way from the Near Country,' said Lamb.

'The name means nothing to me.' Waerdinur spoke common without much of an accent. More'n likely he spoke it better'n Shy did. 'There is only here and not here. How did you get here?'

'Rode some, walked the rest,' grunted Lamb. 'Or do you mean, how did we get here without you knowing?' He gave his sword another shrieking stroke. 'Maybe you ain't as clever as you think you are.'

Waerdinur shrugged his broad shoulders. 'Only a fool supposes he knows everything.'

Lamb held up the sword, checked one side and the other, blade flashing. 'I've got some friends waiting, down in Beacon.'

'I had heard.'

'They're killers and thieves and men of no character. They've come for your gold.'

'Who says we have any?'

'A man named Cantliss.'

'Ah.' Waerdinur splashed water on his arms and carried on washing. 'That is a man of no substance. A breeze would blow him away. You are not one such, though, I think.' His eyes moved across to Shy, weighing her, no sign of fear at all. 'Neither of you. I do not think you came for gold.'

'We came for my brother and sister,' grated Shy, voice harsh as the stone on the blade.

'Ah.' Waerdinur's smile slowly faded as he considered her, then he hung his head, water trickling down his shaved scalp. 'You are Shy. She said you would come and I did not believe her.'

'Ro said?' Her throat almost closing up around the words. 'She's alive?'

'Healthy and flourishing, safe and valued. Her brother, too.'

Shy's knees went for a moment and she had to lean on the rock beside Lamb.

'You have come a long, hard way,' said Waerdinur. 'I congratulate you on your courage.'

'We didn't come for your fucking congratulations!' she spat at him. 'We came for the children!'

'I know. But they are better off with us.'

'You think I care a fuck?' There was a look on Lamb's face then, vicious as an old fighting dog, made Shy go cold all over. 'This ain't about them. You've stolen from me, fucker. From *me*!' Spit flicked from his bared teeth as he stabbed at his chest with a finger. 'And I'll have back what's mine or I'll have blood.'

Waerdinur narrowed his eyes. 'You, she did not mention.'

'I got one o' those forgettable faces. Bring the children down to Beacon, you can forget it, too.'

'I am sorry but I cannot. They are my children now. They are Dragon People, and I have sworn to protect this sacred ground and those upon it with my last blood and breath. Only death will stop me.'

'He won't stop me.' Lamb gave his sword another grinding lick. 'He's had a thousand chances and never took a one.'

'Do you think death fears you?'

'Death loves me.' Lamb smiled, black-eyed, wet-eyed, and the smile was worse even than the snarl had been. 'All the work I done for him? The crowds I've sent his way? He knows he ain't got no better friends.'

The leader of the Dragon People looked back sad and level. 'If we must fight it would be . . . a shame.'

'Lot o' things are,' said Lamb. 'I gave up trying to change 'em a long time ago.' He stood and slid his sword back into its sheath with a scraping whisper. 'Three days to bring the children down to Beacon. Then I come back to your sacred ground.' He curled his tongue and blew spit into the water. 'And I'll bring death with me.' And he started picking his way back towards the ruins on the valley side.

Shy and Waerdinur looked at each other a moment longer. 'I am sorry,' he said. 'For what has happened, and for what must happen now.'

She turned and hurried to catch up to Lamb. What else could she do?

'You didn't mean that, did you?' she hissed at his back, slipping and sliding on the broken rocks. 'About the children? That this ain't about them? That it's about blood?' She tripped and skinned her shin, cursed and stumbled on. 'Tell me you didn't mean that!'

'He got my meaning,' snapped Lamb over his shoulder. 'Trust me.'

But there was the problem – Shy was finding that harder every day. 'Weren't you just saying that when you mean to kill a man, telling him so don't help?'

Lamb shrugged. 'There's a time for breaking every rule.'

'What the hell did you do?' hissed Sweet when they clambered back into the ruin, scrubbing at his wet hair with his fingernails and no one else looking too happy about their unplanned expedition either.

'I left him some bait he'll have to take,' said Lamb.

Shy glanced back through one of the cracks towards the water. Waerdinur was only now wading to the shore, scraping the wet from his body, putting on his robe, no rush. He picked up his staff, looked towards the ruins for a while, then turned and strode away through the rocks.

'You have made things difficult.' Crying Rock had already stowed her pipe and was tightening her straps for the trip back. 'They will be coming now, and quickly. We must return to Beacon.'

'I ain't going back,' said Lamb.

'What?' asked Shy.

'That was the agreement,' said Jubair. 'That we would draw them out.'

'You draw 'em out. Delay's the parent o' disaster, and I ain't waiting for Cosca to blunder up here drunk and get my children killed.'

'What the hell?' Shy was tiring of not knowing what Lamb would do one moment to the next. 'What's the plan now, then?'

'Plans have a habit o' falling apart when you lean on 'em,' said Lamb. 'We'll just have to think up another.'

The Kantic cracked a bastard of a frown. 'I do not like a man who breaks an agreement.'

'Try and push me off a cliff.' Lamb gave Jubair a flat stare. 'We can find out who God likes best.'

Jubair pressed one fingertip against his lips and considered that for a long, silent moment. Then he shrugged. 'I prefer not to trouble God with every little thing.'

Savages

'I've finished the spear!' called Pit, doing his best to say the new words just the way Ro had taught him, and he offered it up for his father to see. It was a good spear. Shebat had helped him with the binding and declared it excellent, and everyone said that the only man who knew more about weapons than Shebat was the Maker himself, who knew more about everything than anyone, of course. So Shebat knew a lot about weapons, was the point, and he said it was good, so it must be good.

'Good,' said Pit's father, but he didn't really look. He was walking fast, bare feet slapping against the ancient bronze, and frowning. Pit wasn't sure he'd ever seen him frown before. Pit wondered if he'd done wrong. If his father could tell his new name still sounded strange to him. He felt ungrateful, and guilty, and worried that he'd done something very bad even though he hadn't meant to.

'What have I done?' he asked, having to hurry to keep up, and realised he'd slipped back to his old talk without thinking.

His father frowned down, and it seemed then he did it from a very long way up.

'Who is Lamb?'

'Lamb's my father,' he said without thinking, then put it right, '*was* my father, maybe . . . but Shy always said he wasn't.' Maybe neither of them were his father or maybe both, and thinking about Shy made him think about the farm and the bad things, and Gully saying run, run, and the journey across the plains and into the mountains and Cantliss laughing and he didn't know what he'd done wrong and he started to cry and he felt ashamed and so he cried more, and he said, 'Don't send me back.'

'No!' said Pit's father. 'Never!' Because he was Pit's father, you could see it in the pain in his face. 'Only death will part us, do you understand?'

Pit didn't understand the least bit but he nodded anyway, crying now with relief that everything would be all right, and his father smiled, and knelt beside him, and put his hand on Pit's head.

'I am sorry.' And Waerdinur was sorry, truly and completely, and he spoke in the Outsiders' tongue because he knew it was easier on the boy. 'It is a fine spear, and you a fine son.' And he patted his son's shaved scalp. 'We will go hunting, and soon, but there is business I must see to first, for all the Dragon People are my family. Can you play with your sister until I call for you?'

He nodded, blinking back tears. He cried easily, the boy, and that was a fine thing, for the Maker taught that closeness to one's feelings was closeness to the divine.

'Good. And . . . do not speak to her of this.'

Waerdinur strode to the Long House, his frown returning. Six of the Gathering were naked in the hot dimness, hazy in the steam, sitting on the polished stones around the fire-pit, listening to Uto sing the lessons, words of the Maker's father, all-mighty Euz, who split the worlds and spoke the First Law. Her voice faltered as he strode in.

'There were outsiders at the Seeking Pool,' he growled as he stripped off his robe, ignoring the proper forms and not caring.

The others stared upon him, shocked, as well they might be. 'Are you sure?' Ulstal's croaking voice croakier still from breathing the Seeing Steam.

'I spoke to them! Scarlaer?'

The young hunter stood, tall and strong and the eagerness to act hot in his eye. Sometimes he reminded Waerdinur so much of his younger self it was like gazing in Juvens' glass, through which it was said one could look into the past.

'Take your best trackers and follow them. They were in the ruins on the north side of the valley.'

'I will hunt them down,' said Scarlaer.

'They were an old man and a young woman, but they might not be alone. Go armed and take care. They are dangerous.' He thought of the man's dead smile, and his black eye, like gazing into a great depth, and was sore troubled. 'Very dangerous.'

'I will catch them,' said the hunter. 'You can depend on me.'

'I do. Go.'

He bounded from the hall and Waerdinur took his place at the fire-pit, the heat of it close to painful before him, perching on the rounded stone where no position was comfortable, for the Maker said they should never be comfortable who weigh great matters. He took the ladle and poured a little water on the coals, and the hall grew gloomier yet with steam, rich with the scents of mint and pine and all the blessed spices. He was already sweating, and silently asked the Maker that he sweat out his folly and his pride and make pure choices.

'Outsiders at the Seeking Pool?' Hirfac's withered face was slack with disbelief. 'How did they come to the sacred ground?'

'They came to the barrows with the twenty Outsiders,' said Waerdinur. 'How they came further I cannot say.'

'Why have they come?' Uto leaned forward into the light, shadow patching in the hollows of her skull. 'What do they want?'

Waerdinur glanced around the old sweat-beaded faces and licked his lips. If they knew the man and woman had come for his children they might ask him to give them up. A faint chance, but a chance, and he would give them up to no one but death. It was forbidden to lie to the Gathering, but the Maker set down no prohibition on offering half the truth.

'What all outsiders want,' said Waerdinur. 'Gold.'

Hirfac spread her gnarled hands. 'Perhaps we should give it to them? We have enough.'

'They would always want more.' Shebat's voice was low and sad. 'Theirs is a hunger never satisfied.'

A silence while all considered, and the coals shifted and hissed in the pit and sparks whirled and glowed in the dark and the sweet smell of the Seeing Steam washed out among them.

The colours of fire shifted across Akarin's face as he nodded. 'We must send everyone who can hold a blade. Eighty of us are there, fit to go, who did not travel north to fight the Shanka?'

'Eighty swords upon my racks.' Shebat shook his head as if that was a matter for regret.

'It worries me to leave Ashranc guarded only by the old and young,' said Hirfac. 'So few of us now—'

'Soon we will wake the Dragon.' Ulstal smiled at the thought. 'Soon.'

'Soon.'

'Next summer,' said Waerdinur, 'or perhaps the summer after. But for now we must protect ourselves.'

'We must drive them out!' Akarin slapped knobbly fist into palm. 'We must journey to the barrows and drive out the savages.'

'Drive them out?' Uto snorted. 'Call it what it is, since you will not be the one to wield the blade.'

'I wielded blades enough in my time. Kill them, then, if you prefer to call it that. Kill them all.'

'We killed them all, and here are more.'

'What should we do, then?' he asked, mocking her. 'Welcome them to our sacred places with arms wide?'

'Perhaps the time has come to consider it.' Akarin snorted with disgust, Ulstal winced as though at blasphemy, Hirfac shook her head, but Uto went on. 'Were we not all born savage? Did not the Maker teach us to first speak peace?'

'So he did,' said Shebat.

'I will not hear this!' Ulstal struggled to his feet, wheezing with the effort.

'You will.' Waerdinur waved him down. 'You will sit and sweat and listen as all sit and listen here. Uto has earned her right to speak.' And Waerdinur held her eye. 'But she is wrong. Savages at the Seeking Pool? Outsiders' boots upon the sacred ground? Upon the stones where trod the Maker's feet?' The others groaned at each new outrage, and Waerdinur knew he had them. 'What should we do, Uto?'

'I do not like that there are only six to make the choice—'

'Six is enough,' said Akarin.

Uto saw they were all fixed on the steel road and she sighed, and reluctantly nodded. 'We kill them all.'

'Then the Gathering has spoken.' Waerdinur stood, and took the blessed pouch from the altar, knelt and scooped up a handful of dirt from the floor, the sacred dirt of Ashranc, warm and damp with life, and he put it in the pouch and offered it to Uto. 'You spoke against this, you must lead.'

She slipped from her stone and took the pouch. 'I do not rejoice in this,' she said.

'It is not necessary that we rejoice. Only that we do. Prepare the weapons.' And Waerdinur put his hand on Shebat's shoulder.

*

Shebat slowly nodded, slowly rose, slowly put on his robe. He was no young man any more and it took time, especially since, even if he saw the need, there was no eagerness in his heart. Death sat close beside him, he knew, too close for him to revel in bringing it to others.

He shuffled from the steam and to the archway as the horn was sounded, shrill and grating, to arms, to arms, the younger people putting aside their tasks and stepping out into the evening, preparing themselves for the journey, kissing their closest farewell. There would be no more than sixty left behind, and those children and old ones. Old and useless and sitting close to death, as he was.

He passed the Heartwoods, and patted his fondly, and felt the need to work upon it, and so he took out his knife, and considered, and finally stripped the slightest shaving. That would be today's change. Tomorrow might bring another. He wondered how many of the People had worked upon it before his birth. How many would work upon it after his death.

Into the stone darkness he went, the weight of mountains heavy above him, the flickering oil wicks making gleam the Maker's designs, set into the stone of the floor in thrice-blessed metal. Shebat's footsteps echoed in the silence, through the first hall to the place of weapons, his sore leg dragging behind him. Old wound, old wound that never heals. The glory of victory lasts a moment, the wounds are always. Though he loved the weapons, for the Maker taught the love of metal and of the thing well made and fitted for its purpose, he gave them out only with regret.

'For the Maker taught also that each blow struck is its own failure,' he sang softly as one blade at a time he emptied the racks, wood polished smooth by the fingertips of his forebears. 'Victory is only in the hand taken, in the soft word spoken, in the gift freely given.' But he watched the faces of the young ones as they took from him the tools of death, hot and eager, and feared they heard his words but let their meaning slip away. Too often of late the Gathering spoke in steel.

Uto came last, as fitted the leader. Shebat still thought she should have been the Right Hand, but in these hard days soft words rarely found willing ears. Shebat handed her the final blade.

'This one I kept for you. Forged with my own hands, when I was young and strong and had no doubts. My best work. Sometimes the metal . . .' and he rubbed dry fingertips against thumb as he sought the words, 'comes out *right*.'

She sadly smiled as she took the sword. 'Will this come out right, do you think?'

'We can hope.'

'I worry we have lost our way. There was a time I felt so sure of the path I had only to walk forward and I would be upon it. Now I am hemmed in by doubts and know not which way to turn.'

'Waerdinur wants what is best for us.' But Shebat wondered if it was himself he struggled to convince.

'So do we all. But we disagree on what is best and how to get it. Waerdinur is a good man, and strong, and loving, and can be admired for many reasons.'

'You say that as if it is a bad thing.'

'It makes us likely to agree when we had better consider. The soft voices are all lost in the babble. Because Waerdinur is full of fire. He burns to wake the Dragon. To make the world as it was.'

'Would that be such a bad thing?'

'No. But the world does not go back.' She lifted the blade he had given her and looked at it, the flickering reflection of the lights on her face. 'I am afraid.'

'You?' he said. 'Never!'

'Always. Not of our enemies. Of ourselves.'

'The Maker taught us it is not fear, but how we face it that counts. Be well, my old friend.' And he folded Uto in his arms, and wished that he was young again.

They marched through the High Gate swift and sure, for once the Gathering has debated the arguments and spoken its judgement there is no purpose in delay. They marched with swords sharpened and shields slung that had been ancient in the days of Uto's great-grandfather's great-grandfather. They marched over the names of their ancestors, etched in bronze, and Uto asked herself whether those Dragon People of the past would have stood shoulder to shoulder with this cause of theirs. Would the Gatherings of the past have sent them out to kill? Perhaps. Times rarely change as much as we suppose.

They left Ashranc behind, but they carried Ashranc with them, the sacred dirt of their home kept in her pouch. Swift and sure they marched and it was not long before they reached the valley of the Seeking Pool, the mirror of the surface still holding a patch of sky. Scarlaer was waiting in the ruin.

'Have you caught them?' asked Uto.

'No.' The young hunter frowned as if the Outsiders' escape was an insult to him alone. Some men, especially young ones, are fixed on taking offence at everything, from a rain shower to a fallen tree. From that offence they can fashion an excuse for any folly and any outrage. He would need watching. 'But we have their tracks.'

'How many are they?'

Maslingal squatted over the ground, lips pressed tight together. 'The marks are strange. Sometimes it has the feel of two trying to seem a dozen, sometimes of a dozen trying to seem like two. Sometimes it has the feel of carelessness, sometimes the feel of wanting to be followed.'

'They will receive their wish and far more than they wished for, then,' growled Scarlaer.

'It is best never to give your enemy what they most desire.' But Uto knew she was without choice. Who has choice, in the end? 'Let us follow. But let us be watchful.'

Only when snow came and hid the moon did Uto give the sign to stop, lying awake under the burden of leadership as the time slipped by, feeling the warmth of the earth and fearing for what would come.

In the morning they felt the first chill and she waved to the others to put on their furs. They left the sacred ground and passed into the forest, jogging in a rustling crowd. Scarlaer led them fast and merciless after the tracks, always ahead, always beckoning them on, and Uto ached and trembled and breathed hard, wondering how many more years she could run like this.

Uto squatted, and looked across that clean whiteness. Once the Gathering has debated the arguments and spoken its judgement there is no place for regrets, and yet she had kept hers, as often checked and polished and as jealously guarded as any miser's hoard. Something of her own, perhaps.

The Dragon People had fought, always. Won, always. They fought to protect the sacred ground. To protect the places where they mined for the Dragon's food. To take children so that the Maker's teaching and the Maker's work might be passed on and not be lost like smoke on the wind of time. The bronze sheets reminded them of those who had fought and those fallen, of what was won and what lost in those battles of the past, and the far past, back into the Old Time and beyond. Uto did not think the Dragon People had ever killed so many to so little purpose as they had here.

Evening was settling when they looked down upon Beacon. The snow had stopped but the sky was gloomy with more. A flame twinkled in the top of the broken tower and she counted four more lights at the windows, but otherwise the place was dark. She saw the shapes of wagons, one very large, almost like a house on wheels. A few horses huddled at a rail. What she might have expected for twenty men, all unwary, except . . .

Tracks sparkled faintly with the twilight, filled with fresh snow so they were no more than dimples, but once she saw one set, like seeing one insect then realising the ground crawled with them, she saw more, and more. Criss-crossing the valley from treeline to treeline and back. Around the barrows and in at their fronts, snow dug away from their entrances. Now she saw the street between the huts, rutted and trampled, the ancient road up to the camp no better. The snow on the roofs was dripping from warmth inside. All the roofs.

Too many tracks for twenty men. Far too many, even careless as the Outsiders were. Something was wrong. She held her hand up for a halt, watching, studying.

Then she felt Scarlaer move beside her, looked around to see him already slipping through the brush, without orders.

'Wait!' she hissed at him.

He sneered at her. 'The Gathering made their decision.'

'And they decided I lead! I say wait!'

He snorted his contempt, turned for the camp, and she lunged for his heels.

Uto snatched at him but she was weak and slow and Scarlaer brushed off her fumbling hand. Perhaps she had been something in her day, but her day was long past and today was his. He bounded down the slope, swift and silent, scarcely leaving marks in the snow, up to the corner of the nearest hut.

He felt the strength of his body, the strength of his beating heart, the strength of the steel in his hand. He should have been sent north to fight the Shanka. He was ready. He would prove it whatever Uto might say, the withered-up old hag. He would write it in the blood of the Outsiders and make them regret their trespass on the sacred ground. Regret it in the instant before they died.

No sound from within the shack, built so poorly of split pine and cracking clay it almost hurt him to look upon its craftsmanship. He slipped low beside the wall, under the dripping eaves and to the corner, looking into the street. A faint crust of new snow, a few new trails of boot-prints and many, many older tracks. Maker's breath but they were careless and filthy, these Outsiders, leaving dung scattered everywhere. So much dung for so few beasts. He wondered if the men shat in the street as well.

'Savages,' he whispered, wrinkling his nose at the smell of their fires, of their burned food, of their unwashed bodies. No sign of the men, though, no doubt all deep in drunken sleep, unready in their arrogance, shutters and doors all fastened tight, light spilling from cracks and out into the blue dawn.

'You damned fool!' Uto slipped up, breathing hard from the run, breath puffing before her face. But Scarlaer's blood was up too hot to worry at her carping. 'Wait!' This time he dodged her hand and was across the street and into the shadow of another shack. He glanced over his shoulder, saw Uto beckoning and the others following, spreading out through the camp, silent shadows.

Scarlaer smiled, hot all over with excitement. How they would make these Outsiders pay.

'This is no game!' snarled Uto, and he only smiled again, rushed on towards the iron-bound door of the largest building, feeling the folk behind him in a rustling group, strong in numbers and strong in resolve—

The door opened and Scarlaer was left frozen for a moment in the lamplight that spilled forth.

'Morning!' A wispy-haired old man leaned against the frame in a bedraggled fur with a gilded breastplate spotted with rust showing beneath. He had a sword at his side, but in his hand only a bottle. He raised it now to them, spirit sloshing inside. 'Welcome to Beacon!'

Scarlaer lifted his blade and opened his mouth to make a fighting scream, and there was a flash at the top of the tower, a pop in his ears and he was shoved hard in the chest and found himself on his back.

He groaned but could not hear it. He sat up, head buzzing, and stared into oily smoke.

Isarult helped with the cooking at the slab and smiled at him when he brought the kill home blooded, and sometimes, if he was in a generous mood, he smiled back. She had been ripped apart. He could tell it was her corpse by the shield on her arm but her head was gone, and the other arm, and one leg so that it hardly looked like it could ever have been a person but just lumps of stuff, the snow all around specked, spattered, scattered with blood and hair and splinters of wood and metal, other friends and lovers and rivals flung about and torn and smouldering.

Tofric, who was known to be the best skinner anywhere, staggered two stiff-legged steps and dropped to his knees. A dozen wounds in him turned dark the furs he wore and one under his eye dripped a black line. He stared, not looking pained, but sad and puzzled at the way the world had changed so suddenly, all quiet, all in silence, and Scarlaer wondered, *What sorcery is this?*

Uto lay next to him. He put a hand under her head and lifted it. She shuddered, twitched, teeth rattling, red foam on her lips. She tried to pass the blessed pouch to him but it was ripped open and the sacred dust of Ashranc spilled across the bloodied snow.

'Uto? Uto?' He could not hear his own voice.

He saw friends running down the street to their aid, Canto in the lead, a brave man and the best to have beside you in a fix. He thought how foolish he had been. How lucky he was to have such friends. Then as they passed one of the barrows smoke burst from its mouth and Canto was flung away and over the roof of the shack beside. Others tumbled sideways, spun about, reeled blinking in the fog or strained as if into a wind, hands over their faces.

Scarlaer saw shutters open, the glint of metal. Arrows flitted silently across the street, lodged in wooden walls, dropped harmlessly in snow, found tottering targets, brought them to their knees, on their faces, clutching, calling, silently screaming.

He struggled to his feet, the camp tipping wildly. The old man still stood in the doorway, pointing with the bottle, saying something. Scarlaer raised his sword but it felt light, and when he looked at his hand his bloody palm was empty. He tried to search for it and saw there was a short arrow in his leg. It did not hurt, but it came upon him like a shock of cold water that he might fail. And then that he might die. And suddenly there was a fear upon him like a weight.

He tottered for the nearest wall, saw an arrow flicker past and into the snow. He laboured on, chest shuddering, floundering up the slope. He snatched a look over his shoulder. The camp was shrouded in smoke as the Gathering was in the Seeing Steam, giant shadows moving inside. Some of his people were running for the trees, stumbling, falling, desperate. Then shapes came from the whirling fog like great devils – men and horses fused into one awful whole. Scarlaer had heard tales of this obscene union and laughed at its foolishness but now he saw them and was struck with horror. Spears and swords flashed, armour glittered, towering over the runners, cutting them down.

Scarlaer struggled on but his arrow-stuck leg would hardly move, a trail of blood following him up the slope and a horse-man following that, his hooves mashing the snow, a blade in his hand.

Scarlaer should have turned and shown his defiance, at least, proud hunter of the Dragon People that he was. Where had his courage gone? Once there had seemed no end to it. Now there was only the need to run, as desperate as a drowning man's need to breathe. He did not hear the rider behind him but he felt the jarring blow across his back and the snow cold, cold on his face as he fell.

Hooves thumped about him, circling him, showering him with white dust. He fought to get up but he could get no further than his hands and knees, trembling with that much effort. His back would not straighten, agony, all burning, and he whimpered and raged and was helpless, his tears melting tiny holes in the snow beneath his face, and someone seized him by the hair.

Brachio put his knee in the lad's back and forced him down into the snow, pulled a knife out and, taking care not to make a mess of it, which was something of a challenge with the lad still struggling and gurgling, cut his ears off. Then he wiped the knife in the snow and slipped it back into his bandolier, reflecting that a bandolier of knives was a damn useful thing to have in his business and wondering afresh why it hadn't caught on more widely. Might be the lad was alive when Brachio winced and grunted his bulk back up into his saddle, but he wasn't going anywhere. Not with that sword-cut in him.

Brachio chuckled over his trophies and, riding down to the camp, thought they'd be the perfect things to scare his daughters with when Cosca had made him rich and he finally came home to Puranti. Genuine Ghost ears, how about that? He imagined the laughter as he chased them around the parlour, though in his imaginings they were little girls still, and it made him sad to think they would be nearly women grown when he saw them again.

'Where does the time go?' he muttered to himself.

Sworbreck was standing at the edge of the camp, staring, mouth open as the horsemen chased the last few savages up into the woods. He was a funny little fellow but Brachio had warmed to him.

'You're a man of learning,' he called as he rode up, holding high the ears. 'What do you think I should do? Dry them? Pickle them?' Sworbreck did not answer, only stood there looking decidedly bilious. Brachio swung down from his saddle. There was riding to do but damn it if he'd be hurrying anywhere, he was out of breath already. No one was as young as they used to be, he supposed. 'Cheer up,' he said. 'We won, didn't we?' And he clapped the writer on his scrawny back.

Sworbreck stumbled, put out a hand to steady himself, felt a warmth, and realised he had sunk his fingers into a savage's steaming guts, separated by some distance from the ruined body.

Cosca took another deep swallow from his bottle – if Sworbreck had read in print the quantity of spirits the Old Man was currently drinking each day he would have cursed it for an outrageous lie – and rolled the corpse over with his boot, then, wrinkling his pinked nose, wiped the boot on the side of the nearest shed.

'I have fought Northmen, Imperials, Union men, Gurkish, every variety of Styrian and plenty more whose origin I never got to the bottom of.' Cosca gave a sigh. 'And I am forced to consider the Dragon Person vastly overrated as an opponent. You may quote me on that.' Sworbreck only just managed to swallow another rush of nausea while the Old Man burbled on. 'But then courage can often be made to work against a man in a carefully laid ambuscade. Bravery, as Verturio had it, is the dead man's virtue— Ah. You are . . . discomfited. Sometimes I forget that not everyone is familiar with such scenes as this. But you came to witness battle, did you not? Battle is . . . not always glorious. A general must be a realist. Victory first, you understand?'

'Of course,' Sworbreck found he had mumbled. He had reached the point of agreeing with Cosca on instinct, however foul, ridiculous or outrageous his utterances. He wondered if he had ever come close to hating anyone as much as he did the old mercenary. Or relying on anyone so totally for everything. No doubt the two were not unrelated. 'Victory first.'

'The losers are always the villains, Sworbreck. Only winners can be heroes.'

'You are absolutely right, of course. Only winners.'

'The one good way to fight is that which kills your enemy and leaves you with the breath to laugh . . .'

Sworbreck had come to see the face of heroism and instead he had seen evil. Seen it, spoken with it, been pressed up against it. Evil turned out not to be a grand thing. Not sneering Emperors with world-conquering designs. Not cackling demons plotting in the darkness beyond the world. It was small men with their small acts and their small reasons. It was selfishness and carelessness and waste. It was bad luck, incompetence and stupidity. It was violence divorced from conscience or consequence. It was high ideals, even, and low methods.

He watched Inquisitor Lorsen move eagerly among the bodies, turning them to see their faces, waving away the thinning, stinking smoke, tugging up sleeves in search of tattoos. 'I see no sign of rebels!' he rasped at Cosca. 'Only these savages!'

The Old Man managed to disengage lips from bottle for long enough to shout back, 'In the mountains, our friend Cantliss told us! In their so-called sacred places! In this town they call Ashranc! We will begin the pursuit right away!'

Sweet looked up from the bodies to nod. 'Crying Rock and the rest'll be waiting for us.'

'Then it would be rude to delay! Particularly with the enemy so denuded. How many did we kill, Friendly?'

The sergeant wagged his thick index finger as he attempted to number the dead. 'Hard to say which pieces go with which.'

'Impossible. We can at least tell Superior Pike that his new weapon is a great success. The results scarcely compare to when I blew up that mine beneath the fortress of Fontezarmo but then neither does the effort involved, eh? It employs explosive powders, Sworbreck, to propel a hollow ball which shatters upon detonation sending splinters—boom!' And Cosca demonstrated with an outward thrusting of both hands. An entirely unnecessary demonstration, since the proof of its effectiveness was distributed across the street in all directions, bloody and raw and in several cases barely recognisable as human.

'So this is what success looks like,' Sworbreck heard Temple murmur. 'I have often wondered.'

The lawyer saw it. The way he took in the charnel-house scene with his black eyes wide and his jaw set tight and his mouth slightly twisted. It was some small comfort to know there was one man in this gang who, in better company, might have approached decency, but he was just as helpless as Sworbreck. All they could do was watch and, by doing nothing more, participate. But how could it be stopped? Sworbreck cowered as a horse thundered past, showering him with gory snow. He was one man, and that one no fighter. His pen was his only weapon and, however highly the scribes might rate its power, it was no match for axe and armour in a duel. If he had learned nothing else the past few months, he had learned that.

He let them drop, too tired to ride let alone write. People do not realise the crushing effort of creation. The pain of dragging the words from a tortured mind. Who read books out here, anyway? Perhaps he would lie down. He began to shamble for the fort.

'Take care of yourself, author,' said Temple, looking grimly down from horseback.

'You too, lawyer,' said Sworbreck, and patted him on the leg as he passed.

The Dragon's Den

'**W**hen do we go?' whispered Shy.

'When Savian says go,' came Lamb's voice. He was close enough she could almost feel his breath, but all she could see in the darkness of the tunnel was the faintest outline of his stubbled skull. 'Soon as he sees Sweet bring Cosca's men up the valley.'

'Won't these Dragon bastards see 'em, too?'

'I expect so.'

She wiped her forehead for the hundredth time, rubbing the wet out of her eyebrows. Damn, but it was hot, like squatting in an oven, the sweat tickling at her, hand slippery-slick on the wood of her bow, mouth sticky-dry with heat and worry.

'Patience, Shy. You won't cross the mountains in a day.'

'Easily said,' she hissed back. How long had they been there? Might've been an hour, might've been a week. Twice already they'd had to slink back into the deeper blackness of the tunnel when Dragon People had strayed close, all pressed together in a baking panic, her heart beating so hard it made her teeth rattle. So many hundreds of thousands of things that could go wrong she could hardly breathe for their weight.

'What do we do when Savian says go?' she asked.

'Open the gate. Hold the gate.'

'And after?' Providing they were still alive after, which she wouldn't have wanted to bet good money on.

'We find the children,' said Lamb.

A long pause. 'Starting to look like less and less of a plan, ain't it?'

'Do the best you can with what there is, then.'

She puffed her cheeks out at that. 'Story of my life.'

She waited for an answer but none was forthcoming. She guessed danger makes some folk blather and some clamp tight. Sadly, she was in the former camp, and surrounded by the latter. She crept forwards on all fours, stone hot under her hands, up next to Crying Rock, wondering afresh what the Ghost woman's interest in all this was. Didn't seem the type to be interested in gold, or rebels, or children neither. No way of knowing what went on behind that lined mask of a face, though, and she wasn't shining any lights inward.

'What's this Ashranc place like?' asked Shy.

'A city carved from the mountain.'

'How many are in there?'

'Thousands once. Few now. Judging from those who left, very few, and mostly the young and old. Not good fighters.'

'A bad fighter sticks a spear in you, you're just as dead as with a good one.'

'Don't get stuck, then.'

'You're just a mine of good advice, ain't you?'

'Fear not,' came Jubair's voice. Across the passageway she could only see the gleam of his eyes, the gleam of his ready sword, but she could tell he was smiling. 'If God is with us, He will be our shield.'

'If He's against?' asked Shy.

'Then no shield can protect us.'

Before Shy could tell him what a great comfort that was there was scuffling behind, and a moment later Savian's crackling voice. 'It's time. Cosca's boys are in the valley.'

'All of them?' asked Jubair.

'Enough of them.'

'You're sure?' The shudder of nerves up Shy's throat almost choked her. For months now she'd been betting everything she had on finding Pit and Ro. Now the moment might've come she would've given anything to put it off.

'Course I'm bloody sure! Go!'

A hand shoved at her back and she knocked into someone and almost fell, staggered on a few steps, fingers brushing the stone to keep her bearings. The tunnel made a turn and suddenly she felt cooler air on her face and was out blinking into the light.

Ashranc was a vast mouth in the mountainside, a cavern cut in half, its floor scattered with stone buildings, a huge overhang of rock shadowing everything above. Ahead of them, beyond a daunting drop, a grand expanse of sky and mountain opened out. Behind the cliff was riddled with openings – doorways, windows, stairways, bridges, a confusion of wall and walkway on a dozen levels, houses half-built into the rock face, a city sunk in stone.

An old man stared at them, shaved bald, a horn frozen on the way to his mouth. He muttered something, took a shocked step back, then Jubair's sword split his head and he went over in a shower of blood, horn bouncing from his hand.

Crying Rock darted right and Shy followed, someone whispering, 'Shit, shit, shit,' in her ear and she realised it was her. She rushed along low beside a crumbling wall, breath punching hard, every part of her singing with an unbearable fear and panic and rage, so wild and strong she thought she might burst open with it, sick it up, piss it out. Shouting from high above. Shouting from all around. Her boots clanked over metal plates polished smooth and scrawled with writing, grit pinging and rattling from her heels. A tall archway in a cleft in the rocks, bouncing and shuddering as she ran. A heavy double-door, one leaf already closed, two figures straining to haul the other fast, a third on the wall above, pointing at them, bow in hand. Shy went down on one knee and nocked her own arrow. A shaft looped down, missed one of the running mercenaries and clattered away across the bronze. Snap of the bowstring as Shy let fly and she watched her own arrow cover the distance, hanging in the still air. It caught the archer in the side and she gave a yelp – a woman's voice, or maybe a child's – staggered sideways and off the parapet, bounced from the rock and fell crumpled beside the gate.

The two Dragon People who'd been shutting the doors had found weapons. Old men, she saw now, very old. Jubair hacked at one and sent him reeling into the rock face. Two of the mercenaries caught up with the other and cut him down, swearing, chopping, stamping.

Shy stared at the girl she'd shot, lying there. Not much older'n Ro, she reckoned. Part Ghost, maybe, from the whiteness of her skin and the shape of her eyes. Just like Shy. Blame it on your Ghost blood. She stared down and the girl stared up, breathing fast and shallow, saying nothing, eyes so dark and wet and blood across her cheek. Shy's free hand opened and closed, useless.

'Here!' roared Jubair, raising one hand. Shy heard a faint answering call, through the gate saw men struggling up the mountainside. Cosca's men, weapons drawn. Caught a glimpse of Sweet, maybe, struggling along on foot. The other mercenaries started dragging the doors wide to let them through. Doors of metal four fingers thick but swinging as smooth as a box lid.

'God is with us,' said Jubair, his grin spotted with blood.

God might've been, but Lamb was nowhere to be seen. 'Where's Lamb?' she asked, staring about.

'Don't know.' Savian only just managed to force the words out. He was breathing hard, bent over. 'Went the other way.'

She took off again.

'Wait!' Savian wheezed after her, but he weren't running anywhere. Shy dashed to the nearest house, about enough thought in her pounding head to sling her bow over her shoulder and pull her short-sword. Wasn't sure she'd ever swung a sword in anger. When she killed that Ghost that killed Leef, maybe. Wasn't sure why she was thinking about that now. Heaved in a great breath and tore aside the hide that hung in the doorway, leaped in, blade-first.

Maybe she'd been expecting Pit and Ro to look up, weeping grateful tears. Instead a bare room, naught there but strips of light across a dusty floor.

She barrelled into another house, empty as the first.

She dashed up a set of steps and through an archway in the rock face. This room had furniture, polished by time, bowls neatly stacked, no sign of life.

An old man blundered from the next doorway and right into Shy, slipped and fell, a big pot dropping from his hands and shattering across the ground. He scrambled away, holding up a trembling arm, muttering something, cursing Shy, or pleading for his life, or calling on some forgotten god, and Shy lifted the sword, standing over him. Took an effort to stop herself killing him. Her body burned to do it. But she had to find the children. Before Cosca's men boiled into this place and caught the killing fever. Had to find the children. If they were here. She let the old man crawl away through a doorway.

'Pit!' she screamed, voice cracking. Back down the steps and into another dim, hot, empty room, an archway at the back leading to another yet. The place was a maze. A city built for thousands, like Crying Rock had said. How the hell to find two children in this? A roar came from somewhere, strange, echoing.

'Lamb?' She clawed sweaty hair out of her face.

Someone gave a panicked screech. There were people spilling from the doorways now, from the low houses below, some with weapons, others with tools, one grey-haired woman with a baby in her arms. Some stared about, sensing something was wrong but not sure what.

Others were hurrying off, away from the gate, away from Shy, towards a tall archway in the rock at the far end of the open cavern.

A black-skinned man stood beside it, staff in hand, beckoning people through into the darkness. Waerdinur. And close beside him a much smaller figure, thin and pale, shaven-headed. But Shy knew her even so.

'Ro!' she screamed, but her voice was lost. The clatter of fighting echoed from the rocky ceiling, bounced from the buildings, coming from everywhere and nowhere. She vaulted over a parapet, hopped a channel where water flowed, startled as a huge figure loomed over her, realised it was a tree-trunk carved into a twisted man-shape, ran on into an open space beside a long, low building and slid to a stop.

A group of Dragon People had gathered ahead of her. Three old men, two old women and a boy, all shaven-headed, all armed, and none of them looking like they planned to move.

Shy hefted her sword and screamed, 'Get out o' my fucking way!'

She knew she wasn't that imposing a figure, so it was something of a shock when they began to back off. Then a flatbow bolt flitted into the stomach of one of the old men and he clutched at it, dropping his spear. The others turned and ran. Shy heard feet slapping behind her and mercenaries rushed past, whooping, shouting. One of them hacked an old woman across the back as she tried to limp away.

Shy looked towards that archway, flanked by black pillars and full of shadow. Waerdinur had vanished inside now. Ro too, if it had been her. It must have been.

She set off running.

In so far as Cosca had a best, danger brought it out in him. Temple hurried cringing along, sticking so close to the walls that he would occasionally scrape his face upon them, his fingernails so busy with the hem of his shirt he was halfway to unravelling the whole thing. Brachio scuttled bent almost double. Even Friendly prowled with shoulders suspiciously hunched. But the Old Man had no fear. Not of death, at least. He strode through the ancient settlement utterly heedless of the arrows that occasionally looped down, chin high, eyes aglitter, steps only slightly wayward from drink, snapping out orders that actually made sense.

'Bring down that archer!' Pointing with his sword at an old woman on top of a building.

'Clear those tunnels!' Waving towards some shadowy openings beside them.

'Kill no children if possible, a deal is a deal!' Wagging a lecturing finger at a group of Kantics already daubed with blood.

Whether anyone took any notice of him, it was hard to say. The Company of the Gracious Hand were not the most obedient at the best of times, and these times in no way qualified.

Danger brought no best from Temple. He felt very much as he had in Dagoska, during the siege. Sweating in that stinking hospital, and cursing, and fumbling with the bandages, and tearing up the clothes of the dead for more. Passing the buckets, all night long, lit by fires, water slopping, and for nothing. It all burned anyway. Weeping at each death. Weeping with sorrow. Weeping with gratitude that it was not him. Weeping with fear that it would be him next. Months in fear, always in fear. He had been in fear ever since.

A group of mercenaries had gathered around an ancient man, growling unintelligible insults through clenched teeth in a language something like Old Imperial, swinging a spear wildly in both hands. It did not take long for Temple to realise he was blind. The mercenaries darted in and out. When he turned, one would poke him in the back with a weapon, when he turned again, another would do the honours. The old man's robe was already dark with blood.

'Should we stop them?' muttered Temple.

'Of course,' said Cosca. 'Friendly?'

The sergeant caught the blind man's spear just below the blade in one big fist, whipped a cleaver from his coat with the other and split his head almost in half in one efficient motion, letting his body slump to the ground and tossing the spear clattering away.

'Oh God,' muttered Temple.

'We have work to do!' snapped the Old Man at the disappointed mercenaries. 'Find the gold!'

Temple tore his hands away from his shirt and scratched at his hair instead, scrubbed at it, clawed at it. He had promised himself, after Averstock, that he would never stand by and watch such things again. The same promise he had made in Kadir. And before that in Styria. And here he was, standing uncomplaining by. And watching. But then he had never been much for keeping promises.

Temple's nose kept running, tickling, running. He rubbed it with the heel of his hand until it bled, and it ran again. He tried to look only at the ground, but sounds kept jerking his wet eyes sideways. To crashes and screams and laughs and bellows, to whimpers and gurgles and sobs and screeches. Through the windows and the doorways he caught glimpses, glimpses he knew would be with him as long as he lived and he rooted his running eyes on the ground again and whispered to himself, 'Oh God.'

How often had he whispered it during the siege? Over and over as he hurried through the scorched ruins of the Lower City, the bass rumble of the blasting powder making the earth shake as he rolled over the bodies, seeking for survivors, and when he found them burned and scarred and dying, what could he do? He had learned he was no worker of miracles. Oh God, oh God. No help had come then. No help came now.

'Shall we burn 'em?' asked a bow-legged Styrian, hopping like a child eager to go out and play. He was pointing up at some carvings chiselled from ancient tree-trunks, wood polished to a glow by the years, strange and beautiful.

Cosca shrugged. 'If you must. What's wood for, after all, if not to take a flame?' He watched the mercenary shower oil on the nearest one and pull out his tinderbox. 'The sad fact is I just don't care much any more, either way. It bores me.'

Temple startled as a naked body crashed into the ground next to them. Whether it had been alive or dead on the way down, he could not say. 'Oh God,' he whispered.

'Careful!' bellowed Friendly, frowning up at the buildings on their left.

Cosca watched the blood spread from the corpse's broken skull, scarcely interrupted in his train of thought. 'I look at things such as this and feel only . . . a mild ennui. My mind wanders on to what's for dinner, or the recurrent itch on the sole of my foot, or when and where I might next be able to get my cock sucked.' He started to scratch absently at his codpiece, then gave up. 'What horror, eh, to be bored by such as this?' Flames flickered merrily up the side of the nearest carving, and the Styrian pyromaniac skipped happily over to the next. 'The violence, treachery and waste that I have seen. It's quite squeezed the enthusiasm out of me. I am numbed. That's why I need you, Temple. You must be my conscience. I want to believe in something!'

He slapped a hand down on Temple's shoulder and Temple twitched, heard a squeal and turned just in time to see an old woman kicked from the precipice.

'Oh God.'

'Exactly what I mean!' Cosca slapped him on the shoulder again. 'But if there is a God, why in all these years has He not raised a hand to stop me?'

'Perhaps we are His hand,' rumbled Jubair, who had stepped from a doorway wiping blood from his sword with a cloth. 'His ways are mysterious.'

Cosca snorted. 'A whore with a veil is mysterious. God's ways appear to be . . . insane.'

Temple's nose tickled with perfumed smoke as the wood burned. It had smelled that way in Dagoska when the Gurkish finally broke into the city. The flames spraying the slum buildings, spraying the slum-dwellers, people on fire, flinging themselves from the ruined docks into the sea. The noise of fighting coming closer. Kahdia's face, lit in flickering orange, the low murmur of the others praying and Temple tugging at his sleeve and saying, 'You must go, they will be coming,' and the old priest shaking his head, and smiling as he squeezed at Temple's shoulder, and saying, 'That is why I must stay.'

What could he have done then? What could he do now?

He caught movement at the corner of his eye, saw a small shape flit between two of the low stone buildings. 'Was that a child?' he muttered, already leaving the others behind.

'Why does everyone pout so over children?' Cosca called after him. 'They'll turn out just as old and disappointing as the rest of us!'

Temple was hardly listening. He had failed Sufeen, he had failed Kahdia, he had failed his wife and daughter, he had sworn always to take the easy way, but perhaps this time . . . he rounded the corner of the building.

A boy stood there, shaven-headed. Pale-skinned. Red-brown eyebrows, like Shy's. The right age, perhaps, could it—

Temple saw he had a spear in his hands. A short spear, but held with surprising purpose. In his worry for others, Temple had for once neglected to feel worried for himself. Perhaps that showed some level of personal growth. The self-congratulations would have to wait, however.

'I'm scared,' he said, without needing to dissemble. 'Are you scared?'

No response. Temple gently held out his hands, palms up. 'Are you Pit?'

A twitch of shock across the boy's face. Temple slowly knelt and tried to dig out that old earnestness, not easy with the noises of destruction filtering from all around them. 'My name is Temple. I am a friend of Shy's.' That brought out another twitch. 'A good friend.' A profound exaggeration at that moment, but a forgivable one. The point of the spear wavered. 'And of Lamb's too.' It started to drop. 'They came to find you. And I came with them.'

'They're here?' It was strange to hear the boy speak the common tongue with the accent of the Near Country.

'They're here,' he said. 'They came for you.'

'Your nose is bleeding.'

'I know.' Temple wiped it on his wrist again. 'No need to worry.'

Pit set down his spear, and walked to Temple and hugged him tight. Temple blinked for a moment, then hesitantly put his arms around the boy and held him.

'You are safe now,' he said. 'You are safe.'

It was hardly the first lie he had ever told.

Shy padded down the hallway, desperate to run on and scared to the point of shitting herself at once, clinging to the slippery grip of her sword. The place was lit only by flickering little lamps that struck a gleam from the metal designs on the floor – circles within circles, letters and lines – and from the blood smeared across them. Her eyes flicked between the tricking shadows, jumped from body to body – Dragon People and mercenaries, too, hacked and punctured and still leaking.

'Lamb?' she whispered, but so quietly even she could hardly hear it.

Sounds echoed from the warm rock, spilled from the openings to either side – screams and crashes, whispering steam, weeping and laughter leaching through the walls. The laughter worst of all.

'Lamb?'

She edged to the archway at the end of the hall and pressed herself to the wall beside it, a hot draught sweeping past. She clawed the wet hair from her stinging eyes again, flicked sweat from her fingertips and gathered her tattered courage. For Pit and Ro. No turning back now.

She slipped through and her jaw fell. A vast emptiness opened before her, a great rift, an abyss inside the mountain. A ledge ahead was scattered with benches, anvils, smith's tools. Beyond a black gulf yawned, crossed by a bridge no more than two strides wide, no handrail, arching through darkness to another ledge and another archway, maybe fifty strides distant. The heat was crushing, the bridge lit underneath by fires that growled far out of sight below, streaks of crystal in the rocky walls sparkling, everything metal from the hammers and anvils and ingots to her own sword catching a smelter's glow. Shy swallowed as she edged out towards that empty plunge and the far wall dropped down, down, down. As if this were some upper reach of hell the living never should've broached.

'You'd think they'd give it a fucking rail,' she muttered.

Waerdinur stood on the bridge behind a great square shield, a dragon worked into the face, bright point of a spear-blade showing beside it, blocking the way. One mercenary lay dead in front of him, another was trying to ease back to safety, poking away wildly with a halberd. A third knelt not far from Shy, cranking a flatbow. Waerdinur lunged and smoothly skewered the halberdier with his spear, then stepped forward and brushed him off the bridge. He fell without a sound. Not of his falling. Not of his reaching the bottom.

The Dragon Man set himself again, bottom edge of that big shield clanging against the bridge as he brought it down, and he shouted over his shoulder in words Shy didn't understand. People shuffled through the shadows behind him – old ones, and children, too, and a girl running last of all.

'Ro!' Shy's scream was dead in the throbbing heat and the girl ran on, swallowed in the shadows at the far end of the bridge.

Waerdinur stayed, squatting low behind his shield and watching her over the rim, and she gritted her teeth and gave a hiss of frustrated fury. To come so close, and find no way around.

'Have this, arsehole!' The last mercenary levelled his flatbow and the bolt rattled from Waerdinur's dragon shield and away into the dark, spinning end-over-end, a tiny orange splinter in all that inky emptiness. 'Well, he's going nowhere.' The archer fished a bolt from his quiver and set to cranking back the string again. 'Couple more bows up here and we'll get him. Sooner or later. Don't you fucking worry about—'

Shy saw a flicker at the corner of her eye and the mercenary lurched against the wall, Waerdinur's spear right through him. He said, 'Oh,' and slid to sitting, setting his bow carefully on the ground. Shy was just taking a step towards him when she felt a gentle touch on her shoulder.

Lamb was at her back, but no kind of reassurance. He'd lost his coat and stood in his leather vest all scar and twisted sinew and his sword broken off halfway, splintered blade slathered in blood to his elbow.

'Lamb?' she whispered. He didn't even look at her, just brushed her away with the back of his arm, black eyes picking up a fiery glimmer and fixed across that bridge, muscles starting from his neck, head hanging on one side, pale skin all sweat-beaded, blood-dotted, his bared teeth shining in a skull-grin. Shy shrank out of his way like death itself had come tapping at her shoulder. Maybe it had.

As if it was a meeting long arranged, Waerdinur drew a sword, straight and dull, a silver mark glinting near the hilt.

'I used to have one o' those.' Lamb tossed his own broken blade skittering across the floor and over the edge into nothingness.

'The work of the Maker himself,' said Waerdinur. 'You should have kept it.'

'Friend o' mine stole it.' Lamb stepped towards one of the anvils, fingers whitening as he wrapped them around a great iron bar that lay against it, tall as Shy was. 'And everything else.' Metal grated as he dragged it after him towards the bridge. 'And it was better'n I deserved.'

Shy thought about telling him not to go but the words didn't come. Like she couldn't get the air to speak. Wasn't another way through that she could see, and it wasn't as if she was about to turn back. So she sheathed her sword and shrugged her bow into her hand. Waerdinur saw it and took a few cautious steps away, light on the balls of his bare feet, calm as if he trod a dance floor rather'n a strip of stone too narrow for the slimmest of wagons to roll down.

'Told you I'd be back,' said Lamb as he stepped out onto the bridge, the tip of the metal bar clattering after him.

'And so you are,' said Waerdinur.

Lamb nudged the corpse of the dead mercenary out of his way with a boot and it dropped soundless into the abyss. 'Told you I'd bring death with me.'

'And so you have. You must be pleased.'

'I'll be pleased when you're out o' my way.' Lamb stopped a couple of paces short of Waerdinur, a trail of glistening footprints left behind him, the two old men facing each other in the midst of that great void.

'Do you truly think the right is with you?' asked the Dragon Man.

'Who cares about right?' And Lamb sprang, lifting that big length of metal high and bringing it down on Waerdinur's shield with a boom made Shy wince, leaving a great dent in the dragon design and one corner bent right back. The Dragon Man was driven sprawling, legs kicking as he scrambled from the brink. Before the echoes had faded Lamb was roaring as he swung again.

This time Waerdinur was ready, though, angled his shield so the bar glanced clear and swung back. Lamb jerked away snake-quick and the sword missed him by a feather, jerked forward snake-quick and caught Waerdinur under the jaw, sent him tottering, spitting blood. He found his balance fast, though, lashed left and right, sent sparks and splinters flying from the metal bar as Lamb brought it up to block.

Shy drew a bead but even close as she was the two old men were moving too fast – deadly, murderous fast so any step or twitch could be their last – no telling who she'd hit if she let loose the arrow. Her hand jerked about as she eased onto the bridge, trying to find the shot, always a few moments behind, sweat tickling at her flickering eyelids as she looked from the fight ahead to the void under her feet.

Waerdinur saw the next blow coming and slipped clear, nimble for all his size. The bar caught the bridge with a shrieking crash, struck sparks, left Lamb off balance long enough for the Dragon Man to swing. Lamb jerked his head away and rather'n splitting his skull the bright point left a red line down his face, drops of blood flicking into nothingness. He staggered three steps, heel slapping at the very brink on the last, space opening between the two men for just a breath as Waerdinur brought his sword back to thrust.

Shy might not have been much at waiting but when the moment came she'd always had a talent for just diving in. She didn't even think about shooting. Her arrow flitted through the darkness, glanced the edge of the shield and into Waerdinur's sword-arm. He grunted, point of his blade dropping and scraping harmlessly against the bridge as Shy lowered her bow, hardly believing she'd taken the shot, still less hit the target.

Lamb bellowed like a mad bull, swinging that length of metal as if it was no heavier than a willow switch, knocking Waerdinur this way and that, sending him reeling along the bridge, no chance to hit back even if he'd been able with Shy's arrow through his arm, no chance to do anything but fight to keep his footing. Lamb kept after, tireless, merciless, driving him off the bridge and onto the ledge at the far end. One last blow tore the shield from Waerdinur's arm and sent it tumbling away into the darkness. He stumbled against the wall, sword clattering from his limp hand, bloody now from the leaking arrow-wound.

A shape came flying from the shadows in the archway, the flash of a knife as it sprang on Lamb and he staggered back towards the brink, wrestled with it, flung it off and into the wall. A shaven-headed girl crumpled against the floor. Changed, so changed, but Shy knew her.

She threw her bow away and ran, no thought for the drop to either side, no thought for anything but the space between them.

Lamb plucked the knife out of his shoulder along with a string of blood and flicked it away like a spent toothpick, face still locked in that red smile, bloody as a new wound, seeing nothing, caring for nothing. Not the man who'd sat beside her on that wagon so many swaying miles, or patiently ploughed the field or sang to the children or warned her to be realistic. Another man, if he was a man at all. The one who'd murdered those two bandits in Averstock, who'd hacked Sangeed's head off on the plains, who'd killed Glama Golden with his hands in the Circle. Death's best friend indeed.

He arched back with that length of metal in his fists, cuts and notches from the Maker's sword all angrily glinting, and Shy screamed out but it was wasted breath. He'd no more mercy in him now than the winter. All those miles she'd come, all that ground struggled over, and just those few paces left were too many as he brought the bar hissing down.

Waerdinur flung himself on top of Ro and the metal caught his big forearm and snapped it like a twig, crashed on into his shoulder, opened a great gash down his head, knocked him senseless. Lamb raised the bar again, screaming froth on his twisted lips, and Shy caught hold of the other end of it as she hurtled off the bridge, whooped as she was jerked into the air. Wind rushed, the glowing cavern flipped over, and she crashed upside down into stone.

Then all quiet.

Just a faint ringing.

Shuffling boots.

Get up, Shy.

Can't just lie around all day.

Things need doing on a farm.

But breathing was quite the challenge.

She pushed against the wall, or the floor, or the ceiling, and the world spun right over, everything whirling like a leaf on a flood.

Was she standing? No. On her back. One arm dangling. Dangling over the edge of the drop, blackness and fire, tiny in the distant depth. That didn't seem a good idea. She rolled the other way. Managed to find her knees, everything swaying, trying to shake the fog from her skull.

People were shouting, voices vague, muffled. Something knocked against her and she nearly fell again.

A tangle of men, shuffling, wrestling. Lamb was in the midst, face wild as an animal's, red wet from a long cut right across it, squealing and gurgling sounds that weren't even halfway to swearing.

Cosca's big sergeant, Friendly, was behind him with one arm around his neck, sweat standing from his forehead with the effort but his face just faintly frowning like he was teasing out a troubling sum.

Sweet was trying to keep a grip on Lamb's left arm, getting dragged about like a man who'd roped a crazy horse. Savian had Lamb's right and he was croaking, 'Stop! Stop, you mad fucker!' Shy saw he had a knife drawn and didn't think she could stop him using it. Didn't even know if she wanted to.

Lamb had tried to kill Ro. All they'd gone through to find her and he'd tried to kill her. He would've killed Shy, too, whatever he'd promised her mother. He would've killed all of them. She couldn't make sense of it. Didn't want to.

Then Lamb went rigid, near dragging Sweet off the edge of the cliff, whites of his eyes showing under flickering lids. Then he sagged, gasping, whimpering, and he put his bloody three-fingered hand over his face, all the fight suddenly put out.

And Savian patted Lamb on the chest, drawn knife still held behind his back and said, 'Easy, easy.'

Shy tottered up, the world more or less settled but her head throbbing, blood tickling at the back of her skull.

'Easy, easy.'

Right arm hard to move and her ribs aching so it hurt to breathe but she started shuffling for the archway. Behind her she could hear Lamb sobbing.

'Easy . . . easy . . .'

A narrow passageway, hot as a forge, black but for a flaring glow up ahead and glimmering spots across the floor. Waerdinur's blood. Shy limped after, remembered her sword, managed to get it drawn but could hardly grip the thing in her numb right hand, fumbled it across to her left and went on, getting steadier, halfway to jogging now, the tunnel getting brighter, hotter still, and an opening ahead, a golden light spilling across the stones. She burst through and slid to a sudden stop, went over on her arse and lay still, propped on her elbows, gaping.

'Fuck,' she breathed.

They were called Dragon People, that much she knew. But she'd never guessed they actually had a dragon.

It lay there in the centre of a vast domed chamber like the big scene from a storybook – beautiful, terrible, strange, its thousand thousand metal scales dull-glistered with the light of fires.

It was hard to judge its size, coiled about and about as it was, but its tapered head might've been long as a man was tall. Its teeth were dagger-blades. No claws. Each of its many legs ended in a hand, golden rings upon the graceful metal fingers. Beneath its folded paper wings gears gently clicked and clattered, wheels slowly, slowly turned, and the faintest breath of steam issued from its vented nostrils, the tip of a tongue like a forked chain softly rattling, a tiny slit of emerald eye showing under each of its four metal eyelids.

'Fuck,' she whispered again, eyes drifting down to the dragon's bed, no less of a child's daydream than the monster itself. A hill of money. Of ancient gold and silver plate. Of chains and chalices, coins and coronets. Of gilded arms and armour. Of gem-encrusted everythings. The silver standard of some long-lost legion thrust up at a jaunty angle. A throne of rare woods adorned with gold leaf stuck upside down from the mass. There was so much it became absurd. Priceless treasures rendered to gaudy trash by sheer quantity.

'Fuck,' she muttered one last time, waiting for the metal beast to wake and fall in blazing rage upon this tiny trespasser. But it didn't stir, and Shy's eyes crept down to the ground. The dotted tracks of blood became a smear, then a trickle, and now she saw Waerdinur, lying back against the dragon's foreleg, and Ro beside him, staring, face streaked with blood from a cut on her scalp.

Shy struggled up, and crept down the bowl-shaped floor of the chamber, the stone underfoot all etched with writing, gripping tight to her sword, as though that feeble splinter of steel was anything more than a petty reassurance.

She saw other things among the hoard as she came closer. Papers with heavy seals. Miners' claims. Bankers' drafts. Deeds to buildings long ago fallen. Wills to estates long ago divided. Shares in Fellowships, and companies, and enterprises long deceased. Keys to who knew what forgotten locks. Skulls, too. Dozens of them. Hundreds. Coins and gemstones cut and raw spilling from their empty eye sockets. What things more valued than the dead?

Waerdinur's breath came shallow, robe blood-soaked, shattered arm limp beside him and Ro clutching at the other, Shy's broken arrow still lodged near the shoulder.

'It's me,' Shy whispered, scared to raise her voice, edging forward, stretching out her hand. 'Ro. It's me.'

She wouldn't let go of the old man's arm. It took him reaching up and gently peeling her hand away. He nudged her towards Shy, spoke some soft words in his language and pushed again, more firmly. More words and Ro hung her shaved head, tears in her eyes, and started to shuffle away.

Waerdinur looked at Shy with pain-bright eyes. 'We only wanted what was best for them.'

Shy knelt and gathered the girl up in her arms. She felt thin, and stiff, and reluctant, nothing left of the sister she'd had so long ago. Scarcely the reunion Shy had dreamed of. But it was a reunion.

'Fuck!' Nicomo Cosca stood in the entrance of the chamber, staring at the dragon and its bed.

Sergeant Friendly walked towards it, sliding a heavy cleaver from inside his coat, took one crunching step onto the bed of gold and bones and papers, coins sliding in a little landslip behind his boot-heel and, reaching forward, tapped the dragon on the snout.

His cleaver made a solid clank, as if he'd tapped an anvil.

'It is a machine,' he said, frowning down.

'Most sacred of the Maker's works,' croaked Waerdinur. 'A thing of wonder, of power, of—'

'Doubtless.' Cosca smiled wide as he walked into the chamber, fanning himself with his hat. But it wasn't the dragon that held his eye. It was its bed. 'How great a sum, do you think, Friendly?'

The sergeant raised his brows and took a long breath through his nose. 'Very great. Shall I count it?'

'Perhaps later.'

Friendly looked faintly disappointed.

'Listen to me . . .' Waerdinur tried to prop himself up, blood oozing from around the shaft in his shoulder, smearing the bright gold behind him. 'We are close to waking the dragon. So close! The work of centuries. This year . . . perhaps next. You cannot imagine its power. We could . . . we could share it between us!'

Cosca grimaced. 'Experience has taught me I'm no good at sharing.'

'We will drive the Outsiders from the mountains and the world will

357

be right again, as it was in the Old Time. And you . . . whatever you want is yours!'

Cosca smiled up at the dragon, hands on hips. 'It certainly is a remarkable curiosity. A magnificent relic. But against what is already boiling across the plains? The legion of the dumb? The merchants and farmers and makers of trifles and filers of papers? The infinite tide of greedy little people?' He waved his hat towards the dragon. 'Such things as this are worthless as a cow against a swarm of ants. There will be no place in the world to come for the magical, the mysterious, the strange. They will come to your sacred places and build . . . tailors' shops. And dry-goods emporia. And lawyers' offices. They will make of them bland copies of everywhere else.' The old mercenary scratched thoughtfully at his rashy neck. 'You can wish it were not so. I wish it were not so. But it is so. I tire of lost causes. The time of men like me is passing. The time of men like you?' He wiped a little blood from under his fingernails. 'So long passed it might as well have never been.'

Waerdinur tried to reach out, his hand dangling from the broken forearm, skin stretched around the splintered bones. 'You do not understand what I am offering you!'

'But I do.' And Cosca set one boot upon a gilded helmet wedged into the hoard and smiled down upon the Maker's Right Hand. 'You may be surprised to learn this, but I have been made many outlandish offers. Hidden fortunes, places of honour, lucrative trading rights along the Kadiri coast, an entire city once, would you believe, though admittedly in poor condition. I have come to realise . . .' and he peered discerningly up at the dragon's steaming snout, 'a painful realisation, because I enjoy a fantastic dream just as much as the next man . . .' and he fished up a single golden coin and held it to the light. 'That one mark is worth a great deal more than a thousand promises.'

Waerdinur slowly let his broken arm drop. 'I tried to do . . . what was best.'

'Of course.' Cosca gave him a reassuring nod, and flicked the coin back onto the heap. 'Believe it or not, so do we all. Friendly?'

The sergeant leaned down and neatly split Waerdinur's head with his cleaver.

'No!' shrieked Ro, and Shy could hardly hold on to her, she started thrashing so much.

Cosca looked mildly annoyed at the interruption. 'It might be best if you removed her. This really is no place for a child.'

Greed

They set off in a happy crowd, smiling, laughing, congratulating one another on their work, comparing the trophies of gold and flesh they had stolen from the dead. Ro had not thought ever in her life to look upon a man worse than Grega Cantliss. Now they were everywhere she turned. One had Akarin's pipe and he tooted a mindless three-noted jig and some danced and capered down the valley, their clothes made motley by the blood of Ro's family.

They left Ashranc in ruins, the carvings smashed and the Heartwoods smoking charcoal and the bronze panels gouged up and the Long House burned with the blessed coals from its fire-pit, all forever stained with death. They despoiled even the most sacred caves and tipped the Dragon over so they could steal the coins that made its bed, then they sealed it in its cavern and brought down the bridge with a burning powder that made the very earth shake in horror at the heresy.

'Better to be safe,' the murderer Cosca had said, then leaned towards the old man called Savian and asked, 'Did you find your boy? My notary salvaged several children. He's discovered quite the talent for it.'

Savian shook his head.

'A shame. Will you keep searching?'

'Told myself I'd go this far. No further.'

'Well. Every man has his limit, eh?' And Cosca gave him a friendly slap on the arm then chucked Ro under the chin and said, 'Cheer up, your hair will grow back in no time!'

And Ro watched him go, wishing she had the courage, or the presence of mind, or the anger in her to find a knife and stab him, or rip him with her nails, or bite his face.

They set off briskly but soon slowed, tired and sore and gorged on destruction. Bent and sweating under the weight of their plunder, packs and pockets bulging with coins. Soon they were jostling and cursing each other and arguing over fallen trinkets. One man tore the pipe away and smashed it on a rock and the one who had been playing it struck him and the great black man had to drag the two of them apart and spoke about God, as if He was watching, and Ro thought, if God can see anything, why would He watch this?

Shy talked, talked, different than she had been. Pared down and pale and tired as a candle burned to the stub, bruised as a beaten dog so Ro hardly recognised her. Like a woman she saw in a dream once. A nightmare. She blathered, nervous and foolish with a mask of a smile. She asked the nine children to tell their names and some gave their old names and some their new, hardly knowing who they were any more.

Shy squatted in front of Evin when he told his name, and said, 'Your brother Leef was with us, for a bit.' She put the back of her hand to her mouth and Ro saw it was trembling. 'He died out on the plains. We buried him in a good spot, I reckon. Good as you get out there.' And she put her hand on Ro's shoulder then and said, 'I wanted to bring you a book or something, but . . . didn't work out.' And the world in which there were books was a half-remembered thing, and the faces of the dead so real and new about her, Ro could not understand it. 'I'm sorry . . . we took so long.' Shy looked at her with wet in the corners of her pink rimmed eyes and said, 'Say something, can't you?'

'I hate you,' said Ro, in the language of the Dragon People so she would not understand.

The dark-skinned man called Temple looked sadly at her and said, in the same tongue, 'Your sister came a long way to find you. For months you have been all she has wanted.'

Ro said, 'I have no sister. Tell her that.'

Temple shook his head. 'You tell her.'

All the while the old Northman watched them, eyes wide but looking through her, as if he had seen an awful thing far-off, and Ro thought of him standing over her with that devil smile and her father giving his life for hers and wondered who this silent killer was who looked so much like Lamb. When his cut face started bleeding, Savian knelt near him to stitch it and said, 'Hardly seemed like demons, in the end, these Dragon Folk.'

The man who looked like Lamb didn't flinch as the needle pierced his skin. 'The real demons you bring with you.'

When Ro lay in the darkness, even with fingers stuck in her ears all she could hear was Hirfac screaming and screaming as they burned her on the cooking-slab, the air sweet with the smell of meat. Even with her hands over her eyes, all she could see was Ulstal's face, sad and dignified, as they pushed him off the cliff with their spears and he fell without a cry, the bodies left broken at the foot, good people she had laughed with, each with their own wisdom, made useless meat and she could not understand the waste of it. She felt she should have hated all these Outsiders beyond hating but somehow she was only numb and withered inside, as dead a thing as her family herded off the cliff, as her father with his head split, as Gully swinging from his tree.

The next morning, men were missing and gold and food missing with them. Some said they had deserted and some that they had been lured by spirits in the night and some that the Dragon People were following, vengeful. While they argued, Ro looked back towards Ashranc, a pall of smoke still hanging over the mountainside in the pale blue, and felt she was stolen from her home once again, and she reached inside her robe and clutched the dragon scale her father had given her, cool against her skin. Beside her on a rock, the old Ghost Woman stood frowning.

'Bad luck to look back too long, girl,' said the white-bearded one called Sweet, though Ro reckoned the Ghost fifty years old at the least, only a few yellow hairs left among the grey she had bound up with a rag.

'It does not feel so fine as I thought it would.'

'When you spend half your life dreaming of a thing, its coming to pass rarely measures up.'

Ro saw Shy look at her, then down at the ground, and she curled her lip back and spat through the gap in her teeth. A memory came up then all unbidden of Shy and Gully having a contest at spitting in a pot and Ro laughing, and Pit laughing, and Lamb watching and smiling, and Ro felt a pain in her chest and looked away, not knowing why.

'Maybe the money'll make it feel finer,' Sweet was saying.

The old Ghost woman shook her head. 'A rich fool is still a fool. You will see.'

Sick of waiting for their missing friends, the men went on. Bottles were opened and they got drunk and slowed under the weight of their booty, toiling in the heat over broken rocks, straining and cursing with mighty burdens as though gold was worth more than their own flesh, more than their own breath. Even so they left discarded baubles scattered in their wake, sparkling like a slug's trail, some picked up by those behind only to be dropped a mile further on. More food had gone in the night and more water and they squabbled over what was left, a haunch of bread worth its weight in gold, then ten times its weight, jewels given over for half a flask of spirits. A man killed another for an apple and Cosca ordered him hanged. They left him swinging behind them, still with the silver chains rattling around his neck.

'Discipline must be maintained!' Cosca told everyone, wobbling with drunkenness in the saddle of his unfortunate horse, and up on Lamb's shoulders Pit smiled, and Ro realised she had not seen him smile in a long time.

They left the sacred places behind and passed into the forest, and the snow began to fall, and then to settle, and the Dragon's warmth faded from the earth and it grew bitter chill. Temple and Shy handed out furs to the children as the trees reared taller and taller around. Some of the mercenaries had thrown their coats away so as to carry more gold, and now shivered where they had sweated before, curses smoking on the chill, cold mist catching at their heels.

Two men were found dead in the trees, shot in the back with arrows while they were shitting. Arrows that the mercenaries had themselves abandoned in Ashranc so they could stuff their quivers with loot.

They sent out other men to find and kill whoever had done the shooting but they did not come back and after a while the rest pressed on, but with a panic on them now, weapons drawn, staring into the trees, starting at shadows. Men kept vanishing, one by one, and one man took another who had strayed for an enemy and shot him down, and Cosca spread his hands and said, 'In war, there are no straight lines.' They argued over how they might carry the wounded man or whether they should leave him, but before they decided he died anyway and they picked things from his body and kicked it into a crevasse.

Some of the children gave each other grins because they knew their own family must be following, the bodies left as a message to them, and Evin walked close beside her and said in the Dragon People's tongue, 'Tonight we run,' and Ro nodded.

The darkness settled without stars or moon and the snow falling thick and soft and Ro waited, trembling with the need to run and the fear of being caught, marking the endless time by the sleeping breath of the Outsiders, Shy's quick and even and Savian's crackling loud in his chest and the Ghost Woman prone to mutter as she turned, more to say when she was sleeping than waking. Until the old man Sweet, who she took for the slowest runner among them, was roused for his watch and grumbled to a place on the other side of their camp. Then she tapped Evin's shoulder, and he nodded to her, and prodded the others, and in a silent row they stole away into the darkness.

She shook Pit awake and he sat. 'Time to go.' But he only blinked. 'Time to go!' she hissed, squeezing his arm.

He shook his head. 'No.'

She dragged him up and he struggled and shouted, 'I won't go! Shy!' And someone flung back their blankets, a can clattering, all commotion, and Ro let go Pit's hand and ran, floundering in the snow, away into the trees, caught her boot on a root and tumbled over and over and up and on. Struggling, striving, this time she would get free. Then a terrible weight took her around the knees and she fell.

She screeched and kicked and punched but she might as well have struggled with a stone, with a tree, with the mighty earth itself. The weight was around her hips, then her chest, trapping her helpless. She thought she saw Evin as the snow swirled, looking back, and she strained towards him with one hand and shouted, 'Help me!'

Then he was lost in the darkness. Or she was.

'Damn you!' Ro snarled and wept and twisted but all in vain.

She heard Lamb's voice in her ear. 'I'm already damned. But I ain't letting you go again,' and he held her so tight she could scarcely move, could scarcely breathe.

So that was all.

V
TROUBLE

'Each land in the world produces its own men
individually bad – and, in time, other bad men
who kill them for the general good.'
Emerson Hough

The Tally

They smelled Beacon long before they saw it. A waft of cooking meat set the famished column shambling downhill through the trees, men slipping and barging and knocking each other over in their haste, sending snow showering. An enterprising hawker had set sticks of meat to cook high up on the slope above the camp. Alas for her, the mercenaries were in no mood to pay and, brushing her protests aside, plundered every shred of gristle as efficiently as a horde of locusts. Even meat as yet uncooked was fought over and wolfed down. One man had his hand pressed into the glowing brazier in the commotion and knelt moaning in the snow, clutching his black-striped palm as Temple laboured past, hugging himself against the cold.

'What a set o' men,' muttered Shy. 'Richer than Hermon and they'd still rather steal.'

'Doing wrong gets to be a habit,' answered Temple, teeth chattering.

The smell of profit must have drifted all the way to Crease because the camp itself was positively booming. Several more barrows had been dug out and several new shacks thrown up and their chimneys busily smoking. More pedlars had set up shop and more whores set down mattress, all crowding happily out to offer succour to the brave conquerors, price lists surreptitiously amended as salesmen noticed, all avaricious amaze, the weight of gold and silver with which the men were burdened.

Cosca was the only one mounted, leading the procession on an exhausted mule. 'Greetings!' He delved into his saddlebag and with a carefree flick of the wrist sent a shower of ancient coins into the air. 'And a happy birthday to you all!'

A stall was toppled, pots and pans clattering as people dived after the pinging coins, huddling about the hooves of the Old Man's mount and jostling each other like pigeons around a handful of seed. An emaciated fiddler, undeterred by his lack of a full complement of strings, struck up a merry jig and capered among the mercenaries, toothlessly grinning.

Beneath that familiar sign proclaiming *Majud and Curnsbick Metalwork*, to which had been carefully added *Weapons and Armour Manufactured and Repaired*, stood Abram Majud, a couple of hirelings keeping the patent portable forge aglow on a narrow strip of ground behind him.

'You've found a new plot,' said Temple.

'A small one. Would you build me a house upon it?'

'Perhaps later.' Temple clasped the merchant's hand, and thought with some nostalgia of an honest day's work done for a half-honest master. Nostalgia was becoming a favoured hobby of his. Strange, how the best moments of our lives we scarcely notice except in looking back.

'And are these the children?' asked Majud, squatting down before Pit and Ro.

'We found 'em,' said Shy, without displaying much triumph.

'I am glad.' Majud offered the boy his hand. 'You must be Pit.'

'I am,' he said, solemnly shaking.

'And you, Ro.'

The girl frowned away, and did not answer.

'She is,' said Shy. 'Or . . . was.'

Majud slapped his knees. 'And I am sure will be again. People change.'

'You sure?' asked Temple.

The merchant put a hand on his shoulder. 'Does not the proof stand before me?'

He was wondering whether that was a joke or a compliment when Cosca's familiar shriek grated at his ear. 'Temple!'

'Your master's voice,' said Shy.

Where was the purpose in disputing it? Temple nodded his apologies and slunk off towards the fort like the beaten dog he was. He passed a man ripping a cooked chicken apart with his hands, face slick with grease. Two others fought over a flask of ale, accidentally pulled the stopper, and a third dived between them, mouth open, in a vain effort to catch the spillings. A cheer rang out as a whore was hoisted up on three men's shoulders, festooned with ancient gold, a coronet clasped lopsided to her head and screeching, 'I'm the Queen of the fucking Union! I'm the fucking Queen of the fucking Union!'

'I am glad to see you well.' Sworbreck clapped him on the arm with what felt like genuine warmth.

'Alive, at least.' It had been some time since Temple last felt well.

'How was it?'

Temple considered that. 'No stories of heroism for you to record, I fear.'

'I have given up hope of finding any.'

'I find hope is best abandoned early,' muttered Temple.

The Old Man was beckoning his three captains into a conspiratorial and faintly unpleasant-smelling huddle in the shadow of Superior Pike's great fortified wagon.

'My trusted friends,' he said, starting, as he would continue, with a lie. 'We stand upon the heady pinnacle of attainment. But, speaking as one who has often done so, there is no more precarious perch and those that lose their footing have far to fall. Success tests a friendship far more keenly than failure. We must be doubly watchful of the men and triply cautious in our dealings with all outsiders.'

'Agreed,' nodded Brachio, jowls trembling.

'Indeed,' sneered Dimbik, sharp nose pinked by the cold.

'God knows it,' rumbled Jubair, eyes rolling to the sky.

'How can I fail with three such pillars to support me? The first order of business must be to collect the booty. If we leave it with the men they will have frittered the majority away to these vultures by first light.'

Men cheered as a great butt of wine was tapped, red spots spattering the snow beneath, and began happily handing over ten times the price of the entire barrel for each mug poured.

'By that time they will probably find themselves in considerable debt,' observed Dimbik, slicking back a loose strand of hair with a dampened fingertip.

'I suggest we gather the valuables without delay, then, observed by us all, counted by Sergeant Friendly, notarised by Master Temple, and stored in this wagon under triple-lock.' And Cosca thumped the solid wood of which the wagon was made as though to advertise the good sense and dependability of his suggestion. 'Dimbik, set your most loyal men to guard it.'

Brachio watched a fellow swing a golden chain around his head, jewels sparkling. 'The men won't hand their prizes over happily.'

'They never do, but if we stand together and provide enough distractions they will succumb. How many do we number now, Friendly?'

'One hundred and forty-three,' said the sergeant.

Jubair shook his heavy head at the faithlessness of mankind. 'The Company dwindles alarmingly.'

'We can afford no further desertions,' said Cosca. 'I suggest all mounts be gathered, corralled and closely watched by trusted guards.'

'Risky.' Brachio scratched worriedly at the crease between his chins. 'There are some skittish ones among 'em—'

'That's horses for you. See it done. Jubair, I want a dozen of your best in position to make sure our little surprise goes to plan.'

'Already awaiting your word.'

'What surprise?' asked Temple. God knew, he was not sure he could endure any further excitement.

The captain general grinned. 'A surprise shared is no surprise at all. Don't worry! I feel sure you'll approve.' Temple was in no way reassured. His idea of a good thing and Cosca's intersected less with every passing day. 'Each to our work, then, while I address the men.'

As he watched his three captains move off, Cosca's smile slowly faded, leaving him with eyes narrowed to slits of suspicion. 'I don't trust those bastards further than I could shit.'

'No,' said Friendly.

'No,' said Temple. Indeed, the only man he trusted less stood beside him now.

'I want the two of you to account for the treasure. Every brass bit properly tallied, noted and stored away.'

'Counted?' said Friendly.

'Absolutely, my old friend. And see to it also that there is food and water in the wagon, and a team of horses hitched and at the ready. If things turn . . . ugly here, we may require a swift exit.'

'Eight horses,' said Friendly. 'Four pairs.'

'Now help me up. I have a speech to make.'

With a great deal of grimacing and grumbling, the Old Man managed to clamber onto the seat and then the roof of the wagon, fists bunched upon its wooden parapet, facing out into the camp. By that stage, those not already thoroughly occupied had begun a chant in his honour, weapons, bottles and half-devoured morsels shaken at the evening sky. Tiring of their burden, they unceremoniously deposed the newly crowned Queen of the Union screeching in the mud and plundered her of her borrowed valuables.

'Cosca! Cosca! Cosca!' they roared as the captain general removed his hat, smoothed the white wisps across his pate and spread his arms wide to receive their adulation. Someone seized the beggar's fiddle and smashed it to pieces, then further ensured his silence with a punch in the mouth.

'My honoured companions!' bellowed the Old Man. Time might have dulled some of his faculties but the volume of his voice was unimpaired. 'We have done well!' A rousing cheer. Someone threw money in the air, provoking an ugly scuffle. 'Tonight we celebrate! Tonight we drink, and sing, and revel, as befits a triumph worthy of the heroes of old!' Further cheers, and brotherly embraces, and slapping of backs. Temple wondered whether the heroes of old would have celebrated the herding of a few dozen ancients from a cliff. More than likely. That's heroes for you.

Cosca held up a gnarled hand for quiet, eventually achieved aside from the soft sucking sounds of a couple who were beginning the celebrations early. 'Before the revelry, however, I regret that there must be an accounting.' An immediate change in mood. 'Each man will surrender his booty—' Angry mutterings now broke out. '*All* his booty!' Angrier yet. 'No swallowed jewels, no coins up arses! No one wants to have to look for them there.' A few distinct boos. 'That our majestic haul may be properly valued, recorded, safely kept under triple-lock in this very wagon, to be dispersed as appropriate when we have reached civilisation!'

The mood now verged on the ugly. Temple noted some of Jubair's men, threading watchfully through the crowd. 'We start out tomorrow morning!' roared Cosca. 'But for tonight each man will receive one hundred marks as a bonus to spend as he sees fit!' Some amelioration of the upset at that. 'Let us not spoil our triumph with sour dissent! Remain united, and we can leave this benighted country rich beyond the dreams of greed. Turn against each other, and failure, shame and death will be our just deserts.' Cosca thumped one fist against his breastplate. 'I think, as ever, only of the safety of our noble brotherhood! The sooner your booty is tallied, the sooner the fun begins!'

'What of the rebels?' rang out a piercing voice. Inquisitor Lorsen was shoving his way through the press towards the wagon, and from the look on his gaunt face the fun would not be starting any time soon. 'Where are the rebels, Cosca?'

'The rebels? Ah, yes. The strangest thing. We scoured Ashranc from top to bottom. Would you use the word "scoured", Temple?'

'I would,' said Temple. They had smashed anything that might hold a coin, let alone a rebel.

'But no sign of them?' growled Lorsen.

'We were deceived!' Cosca thumped the parapet in frustration. 'Damn, but these rebels are a slippery crowd! The alliance between them and the Dragon People was a ruse.'

'Their ruse or yours?'

'Inquisitor, you wrong me! I am as disappointed as you are—'

'I hardly think so!' snapped Lorsen. 'You have lined your own pockets, after all.'

Cosca spread his hands in helpless apology. 'That's mercenaries for you.'

A scattering of laughter from the Company but their employer was in no mood to participate. 'You have made me an accomplice to robbery! To murder! To massacre!'

'I held no dagger to your neck. Superior Pike did ask for chaos, as I recall—'

'To a purpose! You have perpetrated mindless slaughter!'

'Mind*ful* slaughter would surely be even worse?' Cosca burst out in a chuckle but Lorsen's black-masked Practicals, scattered about the shadows, lacked all sense of humour.

The Inquisitor waited for silence. 'Do you believe in anything?'

'Not if I can help it. Belief alone is nothing to be proud of, Inquisitor. Belief without evidence is the very hallmark of the savage.'

Lorsen shook his head in amazement. 'You truly are disgusting.'

'I would be the last to disagree, but you fail to see that you are worse. No man capable of greater evil than the one who thinks himself in the right. No purpose more evil than the higher purpose. I freely admit I am a villain. That's why you hired me. But I am no hypocrite.' Cosca gestured at the ragged remnants of his Company, fallen silent to observe the confrontation. 'I have mouths to feed. You could just go home. If you are set on doing good, make something to be proud of. Open a bakery. Fresh bread every morning, there's a noble cause!'

Inquisitor Lorsen's thin lip curled. 'There truly is nothing in you of what separates man from animal, is there? You are bereft of conscience. An utter absence of morality. You have no principle beyond the selfish.'

Cosca's face hardened as he leaned forwards. 'Perhaps when you have faced as many disappointments and suffered as many betrayals as I, you will see it – there is no principle beyond the selfish, Inquisitor, and men *are* animals. Conscience is a burden we choose to bear. Morality is the lie we tell ourselves to make its bearing easier. There have been many times in my life when I have wished it was not so. But it is so.'

Lorsen slowly nodded, bright eyes fixed on Cosca. 'There will be a price for this.'

'I am counting on it. Though it seems an almost ludicrous irrelevance now, Superior Pike promised me fifty thousand marks.'

'For the capture of the rebel leader Conthus!'

'Indeed. And there he is.'

There was a scraping of steel, a clicking of triggers, a rattling of armour as a dozen of Jubair's men stepped forward. A circle of drawn swords, loaded flatbows, levelled polearms all suddenly pointed in towards Lamb, Sweet, Shy and Savian. Gently, Majud drew the wide-eyed children close to him.

'Master Savian!' called Cosca. 'I deeply regret that I must ask you to lay down your weapons. Any and all, if you please!'

Betraying no emotion, Savian slowly reached up to undo the buckle on the strap across his chest, flatbow and bolts clattering to the mud. Lamb watched him do it, and calmly bit into a leg of chicken. No doubt that was the easy way, to stand and watch. God knew, Temple had taken that way often enough. Too often, perhaps . . .

He dragged himself up onto the wagon to hiss in Cosca's ear. 'You don't have to do this!'

'Have to? No.'

'Please! How does it help you?'

'Help *me*?' The Old Man raised one brow at Temple as Savian unbuttoned his coat and one by one shed his other weapons. 'It helps me not at all. That is the very essence of selflessness and charity.'

Temple could only stand blinking.

'Are you not always telling me to do the right thing?' asked Cosca. 'Did we not sign a contract? Did we not accept Inquisitor Lorsen's noble cause as our own? Did we not lead him a merry chase up and down this forsaken gulf of distance? Pray be silent, Temple. I never thought to say this, but you are impeding my moral growth.' He turned away to shout, 'Would you be kind enough to roll up your sleeves, Master Savian?'

Savian cleared his throat, metal rattling as the mercenaries nervously shifted, took the button at his collar and undid it, then the next, then the next, the fighters and pedlars and whores all watching the drama unfold in silence. Hedges too, Temple noticed, for some reason with a smile of feverish delight on his face. Savian shrugged his shirt off and stood stripped to the waist, and his whole body from his pale neck to his pale hands was covered in writing, in letters large and tiny, in slogans in a dozen languages: *Death to the Union, Death to the King. The only good Midderlander is a dead one. Never kneel. Never surrender. No Mercy. No Peace. Freedom. Justice. Blood.* He was blue with them.

'I only asked for the sleeves,' said Cosca, 'but I feel the point is made.'

Savian gave the faintest smile. 'What if I said I'm not Conthus?'

'I doubt we'd believe you.' The Old Man looked over at Lorsen, who was staring at Savian with a hungry intensity. 'In fact, I very much doubt we would. Do you have any objections, Master Sweet?'

Sweet blinked around at all that sharpened metal and opted for the easy way. 'Not me. I'm shocked as anyone at this surprising turn of events.'

'You must be quite discomfited to learn you've been travelling with a mass-murderer all this time.' Cosca grinned. 'Well, two, in fact, eh, Master Lamb?' The Northman still picked at his drumstick as though there was no steel pointed in his direction. 'Anything to say on behalf of your friend?'

'Most o' my friends I've killed,' said Lamb around a mouthful. 'I came for the children. The rest is mud.'

Cosca pressed one sorry hand to his breastplate. 'I have stood where you stand, Master Savian, and entirely sympathise. We all are alone in the end.'

'It's a hard fucking world,' said Savian, looking neither right nor left.

'Seize him,' growled Lorsen, and his Practicals swarmed forwards like dogs off the leash. For a moment it looked as if Shy's hand was creeping towards her knife but Lamb held her arm with his free hand, eyes on the ground as the Practicals marched Savian towards the fort. Inquisitor Lorsen followed them inside, smiled grimly out into the camp and slammed the door with a heavy bang.

Cosca shook his head. 'Not even so much as a thank you. Doing right is a dead end, Temple, as I have often said. Queue up, my boys, it's time for an accounting!'

Brachio and Dimbik began to circulate, ushering the men into a grumbling queue, the excitement of Savian's arrest already fading. Temple stared across at Shy, and she stared back at him, but what could either of them do?

'We will need sacks and boxes!' Cosca was shouting. 'Open the wagon and find a table for the count. A door on trestles, then, good enough! Sworbreck? Fetch pen and ink and ledger. Not the writing you came to do, but no less honourable a task!'

'Deeply honoured,' croaked the writer, looking slightly sick.

'We'd best be heading out.' Dab Sweet had made his way over to the wagon and was looking up. 'Get the children back to Crease, I reckon.'

'Of course, my friend,' said Cosca, grinning down. 'You will be sorely missed. Without your skills – let alone the fearsome talents of Master Lamb – the task would have been nigh impossible. The tall tales don't exaggerate in your cases, eh, Sworbreck?'

'They are legends made flesh, captain general,' mumbled the writer.

'We will have to give them a chapter to themselves. Perhaps two! The very best of luck to you and your companions. I will recommend you wherever I go!' Cosca turned away as though that concluded their business.

Sweet looked to Temple, and Temple could only shrug. There was nothing he could do about this either.

The old scout cleared his throat. 'There's just the matter of our share o' the proceeds. As I recall, we discussed a twentieth—'

'What about my share?' Cantliss elbowed his way past Sweet to stare up. 'It was me told you there'd be rebels up there! Me who found those bastards out!'

'Why, so you did!' said Cosca. 'You are a veritable child-stealing Prophet and we owe you all our success!'

Cantliss' bloodshot eyes lit with a fire of greed. 'So . . . what am I due?'

Friendly stepped up from behind, innocuously slipped a noose over his head, and as Cantliss glanced around, Jubair hauled with all his considerable weight on the rope, which had been looped over a beam projecting from the side of the broken tower. Hemp grated as the bandit was hoisted off his feet. One kicking foot knocked a black spray of ink across Sworbreck's ledger and the writer stumbled up, ashen-faced, as Cantliss pawed feebly at the noose with his broken hand, eyes bulging.

'Paid in full!' shouted Cosca. Some of the mercenaries half-heartedly cheered. A couple laughed. One threw an apple core and missed. Most barely raised an eyebrow.

'Oh God,' whispered Temple, picking at the stitching on his buttons and staring at the tarred planks under his feet. But he could still see Cantliss' squirming shadow there. 'Oh God.'

Friendly wound the rope about a tree-stump and tied it off. Hedges, who'd been shoving his way towards the wagon, cleared his throat and carefully retreated, smiling no longer. Shy spat through the gap in her front teeth, and turned away. Lamb stood watching until Cantliss stopped twisting about, one hand resting slack on the hilt of the sword he had taken from the Dragon People. Then he frowned towards the door through which Savian had been taken, and flicked his stripped chicken bone into the mud.

'Seventeen times,' said Friendly, frowning up.

'Seventeen times what?' asked Cosca.

'He kicked. Not counting that last one.'

'That last one was more of a twitch,' said Jubair.

'Is seventeen a lot?' asked the Old Man.

Friendly shrugged. 'About average.'

Cosca looked down at Sweet, grey brows high. 'You were saying something about a share, I think?'

The old scout watched Cantliss creaking back and forth, with a hooked finger gently loosened his collar and opted for the easy way again. 'Must've misremembered. Reckon I'll just be heading on back to Crease, if that's all the same with you.'

'As you wish.' Below them, the first man in line upended his pack and sent gold and silver sliding across the table in a glittering heap. The captain general plumped his hat back on and flicked the feather. 'Happy journey!'

Going Back

'That fucking old shit-fucker!' snarled Sweet, slashing with a stick at a branch that hung across the road and showering snow all over himself. 'Prickomo fucking Cocksca! That bastard old arsehole-fucker!'

'You said that one already, as I recall,' muttered Shy.

'He said old arsehole bastard-fucker,' said Crying Rock.

'My mistake,' said Shy. 'That's a whole different thing.'

'Ain't fucking disagreeing, are you?' snapped Sweet.

'No I'm not,' said Shy. 'He's a hell of a fucker, all right.'

'Shit . . . fuck . . . shit . . . fuck . . .' And Sweet kicked at his horse and whipped at the tree-trunks in a rage as he passed. 'I'll get even with that maggot-eaten bastard, I can tell you that!'

'Let it be,' grunted Lamb. 'Some things you can't change. You got to be realistic.'

'That was my damn retirement got stole there!'

'Still breathing, ain't you?'

'Easy for you to say! You didn't lose no fortune!'

Lamb gave him a look. 'I lost plenty.'

Sweet worked his mouth for a moment, then shouted, 'Fuck!' one last time and flung his stick away into the trees.

A cold and heavy quiet, then. The iron tyres of Majud's wagon scrape-scraping and some loose part in Curnsbick's apparatus in the back clank-clanking under its canvas cover and the horse's hooves crunch-crunching in the snow on the road, rutted from the business flowing up from Crease. Pit and Ro lay in the back under a blanket, faces pressed up against each other, peaceful now in sleep. Shy watched them rocking gently as the axles shifted.

'I guess we did it,' she said.

'Aye,' said Lamb, but looking a long stretch short of a celebration. 'Guess so.'

They rounded another long bend, road switching back one last time as it dropped down steep off the hills, the stream beside half-frozen, white ice creeping out jagged from each bank to almost meet in the middle.

Shy didn't want to say anything. But once a thought was in her head she'd never been much good at keeping it there, and this thought had been pricking at her ever since they left Beacon. 'They're going to be cutting into him, ain't they? Asking questions.'

'Savian?'

'Who else?'

The scarred side of Lamb's face twitched a little. 'That's a fact.'

'Ain't a pretty one.'

'Facts don't tend to be.'

'He saved me.'

'Aye.'

'He saved you.'

'True.'

'We really going to fucking leave him, then?'

Lamb's face twitched again, jaw-muscles working as he frowned out hard across the country ahead. The trees were thinning as they dropped out of the mountains, the moon fat and full in a clear sky star-dusted, spilling light over the high plateau. A great flat expanse of dry dirt and thorny scrub looked like it could never have held life, all half carpeted now with sparkling snow. Through the midst, straight as a sword-cut, the white strip of the old Imperial Road, a scar through the country angling off towards Crease, wedged somewhere in the black rumour of hills on the horizon.

Lamb's horse slowed to a walk, then stopped.

'Shall we halt?' asked Majud.

'You told me you'd be my friend for life,' said Lamb.

The merchant blinked. 'And I meant it.'

'Then keep on.' Lamb turned in his saddle to look back. Behind them, somewhere high up in the folded, forested ridges there was a glow. The great bonfire the mercenaries had stacked high in the middle of Beacon to light their celebrations. 'Got a good road here and a good moon to steer by. Keep on all night, quick and steady, you might make Crease by dark tomorrow.'

'Why the rush?'

Lamb took a long breath, looked to the starry sky and breathed out smoke in a grumbling sigh. 'There's going to be trouble.'

'We going back?' asked Shy.

'You're not.' The shadow of his hat fell across his face as he looked at her so his eyes were just two gleams. 'I am.'

'What?'

'You're taking the children. I'm going back.'

'You always were, weren't you?'

He nodded.

'Just wanted to get us far away.'

'I've only had a few friends, Shy. I've done right by even fewer. Could count 'em on one hand.' He turned his left hand over and looked at the stump of his missing finger. 'Even this one. This is how it has to be.'

'Ain't nothing has to be. I ain't letting you go alone.'

'Yes y'are.' He eased his horse closer, looking her in the eye. 'Do you know what I felt, when we came over that hill and saw the farm all burned out? The first thing I felt, before the sorrow and the fear and the anger caught up?'

She swallowed, her mouth all sticky-dry, not wanting to answer, not wanting to know the answer.

'Joy,' whispered Lamb. 'Joy and relief. 'Cause I knew right off what I'd have to do. What I'd have to be. Knew right off I could put an end on ten years of lying. A man's got to be what he is, Shy.' He looked back at his hand and made a three-fingered fist of it. 'I don't . . . *feel* evil. But the things I done. What else can you call 'em?'

'You ain't evil,' she whispered. 'You're just . . .'

'If it hadn't been for Savian I'd have killed you in them caves. You and Ro.'

Shy swallowed. She knew it well enough. 'If it hadn't been for you, we'd never have got the children back.'

Lamb looked at the pair of 'em, Ro with her arm over Pit. Stubble of hair showing dark now, almost grown over the scratch down her scalp. Both so changed. 'Did we get 'em back?' he asked, and his voice was rough. 'Sometimes I think we just lost us, too.'

'I'm who I was.'

Lamb nodded, and it seemed he had the glimmer of tears in his eyes. 'You are, maybe. But I don't reckon there's any going back for me.' He leaned from his saddle then and hugged her tight. 'I love you. And them. But my love ain't a weight anyone should have to carry. Best of luck, Shy. The very best.' And he let her go, and turned his horse, and he rode away, following their tracks back towards the trees, and the hills, and the reckoning beyond.

'What the hell happened to being realistic?' she called after him.

He stopped just a moment, a lonely figure in all that moonlit white. 'Always sounded like a good idea but, being honest? It never worked for me.'

Slow, and numb, Shy turned her back on him. Turned her back and rode on across the plateau, after the wagon and Majud's hired men, after Sweet and Crying Rock, staring at the white road ahead but seeing nothing, tongue working at the gap between her teeth and the night air cold, cold in her chest with each breath. Cold and empty. Thinking about what Lamb had said to her. What she'd said to Savian. Thinking about all the long miles she'd covered the last few months and the dangers she'd faced to get this far, and not knowing what she could do. This was how it had to be.

Except when folk told Shy how things had to be, she started thinking on how to make 'em otherwise.

The wagon hit a lump and with a clatter Pit got jolted awake. He sat up, and he stared blinking about him, and said, 'Where's Lamb?' And Shy's hands went slack on the reins, and she let her horse slow, then stop, and she sat there solemn.

Majud looked over his shoulder. 'Lamb said keep on!'

'You got to do what he tells you? He ain't your father, is he?'

'I suppose not,' said the merchant, pulling up the horses.

'He's mine,' muttered Shy. And there it was. Maybe he wasn't the father she'd want. But he was still the only one she'd got. The only one all three of 'em had got. She'd enough regrets to live with.

'I've got to go back,' she said.

'Madness!' snapped Sweet, sitting his horse not far off. 'Bloody madness!'

'No doubt. And you're coming with me.'

A silence. 'You know there's more'n a hundred mercenaries up there, don't you? Killers, every man?'

'The Dab Sweet I heard stories of wouldn't take fright at a few mercenaries.'

'Don't know if you noticed, but the Dab Sweet you heard stories of ain't much like the one wearing my coat.'

'I hear you used to be.' She rode up to him and reined in close. 'I hear you used to be quite a man.'

Crying Rock slowly nodded. 'That is true.'

Sweet frowned at the old Ghost woman, and frowned at Shy, and finally frowned at the ground, scratching at his beard and bit by bit slumping down in his saddle. 'Used to be. You're young and got dreams ahead of you still. You don't know how it is. One day you're something, so promising and full o' dares, so big the world's too small a place to hold you. Then, 'fore you know it, you're old, and you realise all them things you had in mind you'll never get to. All them doors you felt too big to fit through have already shut. Only one left open and it leads to nothing but nothing.' He pulled his hat off and scrubbed at his white hair with his dirty nails. 'You lose your nerve. And once it's gone where do you find it? I got scared, Shy South. And once you get scared there ain't no going back, there just ain't no—'

Shy caught a fist of his fur coat and dragged him close. 'I ain't giving up this way, you hear me? I just ain't *fucking* having it! Now I need that bastard who killed a red bear with his hands up at the source of the Sokwaya, whether it bloody well happened or not. You hear me, you old shit?'

He blinked at her for a moment. 'I hear you.'

'Well? You want to get even with Cosca or you just want to swear about it?'

Crying Rock had brought her horse close. 'Maybe do it for Leef,' she said. 'And those others buried on the plains.'

Sweet stared at her weather-beaten face for a long moment, for some reason with the strangest, haunted look in his eye. Then his mouth twitched into a smile. 'How come after all this time you're still so damn beautiful?' he asked.

Crying Rock just shrugged, like facts were facts, and stuck her pipe between her teeth.

Sweet reached up and brushed Shy's hand away. He straightened his fur coat. He leaned from his saddle and spat. He looked with narrowed eyes up towards Beacon and set his jaw. 'If I get killed I'm going to haunt your skinny arse for life.'

'If you get killed I doubt my life'll be too long a stretch.' Shy slipped down from her saddle and crunched stiff-legged to the wagon, stood looking down at her brother and sister. 'Got something to take care of,' she said, putting a gentle hand on each of them. 'You go on with Majud. He's a little on the stingy side but he's one of the good ones.'

'Where you going?' asked Pit.

'Left something behind.'

'Will you be long?'

She managed to smile. 'Not long. I'm sorry, Ro. I'm sorry for everything.'

'So am I,' said Ro. Maybe that was something. For sure it was all she'd get.

She touched Pit's cheek. Just a brush with her fingertips. 'I'll see you two in Crease. You'll hardly notice I'm gone.'

Ro sniffed, sleepy and sullen, and wouldn't meet her eye, and Pit stared at her, face all tracked with tears. She wondered if she really would see them in Crease. Madness, like Sweet said, to come all this way just to let them go. But there was no point to long goodbyes. Sometimes it's better to do a thing than live with the fear of it. That's what Lamb used to say.

'Go!' she shouted at Majud, before she had the chance to change her mind. He nodded to her, and snapped the reins, and the wagon rolled on.

'Better to do it,' she whispered at the night sky, and she clambered back into her saddle, turned her horse about, and gave it her heels.

Answered Prayers

Temple drank. He drank like he had after his wife died. As if there was something at the bottom of the bottle he desperately needed. As if it was a race he had bet his life on. As if drinking was a profession he planned on rising right to the top of. Tried most of the others, hadn't he?

'You should stop,' said Sworbreck, looking worried.

'You should start,' said Temple, and laughed, even if he'd never felt like laughing less. Then he burped and there was some sick in it, and he washed the taste away with another swallow.

'You have to pace yourself,' said Cosca, who was not pacing himself in the least. 'Drinking is an art, not a science. You caress the bottle. You tease it. You romance it. A drink . . . a drink . . . a drink . . .' kissing at the air with each repetition, eyelids flickering. 'Drinking is like . . . *love*.'

'What the fuck do you know about love?'

'More than I'd like,' answered the Old Man, a faraway look in his yellowed eye, and he gave a bitter laugh. 'Despicable men still love, Temple. Still feel pain. Still nurse wounds. Despicable men most of all, maybe.' He slapped Temple on the back, sent a searing swig the wrong way and induced a painful coughing fit. 'But let's not be maudlin! We're rich, boy! All rich. And rich men need make no apologies. To Visserine for me. Take back what I lost. What was stolen.'

'What you threw away,' muttered Temple, quietly enough not to be heard over the racket.

'Yes,' mused Cosca. 'Soon there'll be space for a new captain general.' He took in the noisy, crowded, sweltering room with a sweep of his arm. 'All this will be yours.'

It was quite a scene of debauch to cram into a one-roomed hovel, lit by a single guttering lamp and hazy with chagga smoke, noisy with laughter and conversations in several languages. Two big Northmen were wrestling, possibly in fun, possibly with the intention of killing each other, people occasionally lurching out of their way. Two natives of the Union and an Imperial bitterly complained as their table was jogged in the midst of a card-game, bottles tottering on top. Three Styrians had shared a husk-pipe and were blissfully lounging on a burst mattress in one corner, somewhere between sleep and waking. Friendly was sitting with legs crossed and rolling his dice between them, over and over and over, frowning down with furious concentration as though the answers to everything would soon appear on their dozen faces.

'Hold on,' muttered Temple, his pickled mind only now catching up. 'Mine?'

'Who better qualified? You've learned from the best, my boy! You're a lot like me, Temple, I've always said so. Great men march often in the same direction, did Stolicus say?'

'Like you?' whispered Temple.

Cosca tapped his greasy grey hair. 'Brains, boy, you've got the brains. Your morals can be stiff at times but they'll soon soften up once you have to make the tough choices. You can talk well, know how to spot people's weaknesses, and above all you understand the *law*. The strong-arm stuff's all going out of fashion. I mean, there'll always be a place for it, but the law, Temple, that's where the money's going to be.'

'What about Brachio?'

'Family in Puranti.'

'Really?' Temple blinked across the room at Brachio, who was in a vigorous embrace with a large Kantic woman. 'He never mentioned them.'

'A wife and two daughters. Who talks about their family with scum like us?'

'What about Dimbik?'

'Pah! No sense of humour.'

'Jubair?'

'Mad as a plum jelly.'

'But I'm no soldier. I'm a fucking coward!'

'Admirable thing in a mercenary.' Cosca stretched forward his chin and scratched at his rashy neck with the backs of his yellowed nails. 'I'd have done far better with a healthy respect for danger. It's not as if you'll be swinging the steel yourself. The job's all talk. Blah, blah, blah and big hats. That and knowing when not to keep your word.'

He wagged a knobbly finger. 'I was always too bloody emotional. Too bloody loyal. But you? You're a treacherous bastard, Temple.'

'I am?'

'You abandoned me when it suited and found new friends, then when it suited you abandoned them and sauntered straight back without so much as a by-your-leave!'

Temple blinked at that. 'I rather had the feeling you'd have killed me otherwise.'

Cosca waved it away. 'Details! I've had you marked as my successor for some time.'

'But . . . no one respects me.'

'Because you don't respect yourself. Doubt, Temple. Indecision. You simply worry too much. Sooner or later you have to do something, or you'll never do anything. Overcome that, you could be a wonderful captain general. One of the greats. Better than me. Better than Sazine. Better than Murcatto, even. You might want to cut down on the drinking, though.' Cosca tossed his empty bottle away, pulled the cork from another with his teeth and spat it across the room. 'Filthy habit.'

'I don't want to do this any more,' Temple whispered.

Cosca waved that away, too. 'You say that all the time. Yet here you are.'

Temple lurched up. 'Got to piss.'

The cold air slapped him so hard he nearly fell against one of the guards, sour-faced from having to stay sober. He stumbled along the wooden side of Superior Pike's monstrous wagon, thinking how close his palm was to a fortune, past the stirring horses, breath steaming out of their nosebags, took a few crunching steps into the trees, sounds of revelry muffled behind him, shoved his bottle down in the frozen snow and unlaced with drunken fingers. Bloody hell, it was cold still. He leaned back, blinking at the sky, bright stars spinning and dancing beyond the black branches.

Captain General Temple. He wondered what Haddish Kahdia would have thought of that. He wondered what God thought of it. How had it come to this? He'd always had good intentions, hadn't he? He'd always tried to do his best.

It's just that his best had always been shit.

'God?' he brayed at the sky. 'You up there, you bastard?' Perhaps He was the mean bully Jubair made Him out to be, after all. 'Just . . .

give me a sign, will you? Just a little one. Just steer me the right way. Just . . . just give me a nudge.'

'I'll give you a nudge.'

He froze for a moment, still dripping. 'God? Is that you?'

'No, fool.' There was a crunch as someone pulled his bottle out of the snow.

He turned. 'I thought you left.'

'Came back.' Shy tipped the bottle up and took a swig, one side of her face all dark, the other lit by the flickering bonfire in the camp. 'Thought you'd never come out o' there,' she said, wiping her mouth.

'Been waiting?'

'Little while. Are you drunk?'

'Little bit.'

'That works for us.'

'It works for me.'

'I see that,' she said, glancing down.

He realised he hadn't laced-up yet and started fumbling away. 'If you wanted to see my cock that badly, you could just have asked.'

'No doubt a thing o' haunting beauty but I came for something else.'

'Got a window needs jumping through?'

'No. I might need your help.'

'Might?'

'Things run smooth you can just creep back to drowning your sorrows.'

'How often do things run smooth for you?'

'Not often.'

'Is it likely to be dangerous?'

'Little bit.'

'Really a little bit?'

She drank again. 'No. A lot.'

'This about Savian?'

'Little bit.'

'Oh God,' he muttered, rubbing at the bridge of his nose and willing the dark world to be still. Doubt, that was his problem. Indecision. Worrying too much. He wished he was less drunk. Then he wished he was more. He'd asked for a sign, hadn't he? Why had he asked for a sign? He'd never expected to get one.

'What do you need?' he muttered, his voice very small.

Sharp Ends

Practical Wile slid a finger under his mask to rub at the little chafe marks. Not the worst part of the job, but close.

'There it is, though,' he said, rearranging his cards, as if that made his hand any less rotten, 'I daresay she's found someone else by now.'

'If she's got any sense,' grunted Pauth.

Wile nearly thumped the table, then worried that he might hurt his hand and stopped short. 'This is what I mean by undermining! We're supposed to look out for each other but you're always talking me down!'

'Weren't nothing in the oaths I swore about not talking you down,' said Pauth, tossing a couple of cards and sliding a couple more off the deck.

'Loyalty to his Majesty,' threw out Bolder, 'and obedience to his Eminence and the ruthless rooting out of treasons, but nothing about looking out for no one.'

'Doesn't mean it's a bad idea,' grumbled Wile, rearranging his rotten hand.

'You're confusing how you'd like the world to be with how it is,' said Bolder. 'Again.'

'A little solidarity is all I'm asking. We're all stuck in the same leaky boat.'

'Start baling and stop bloody moaning, then.' Pauth had a good scratch under his own mask. 'All the way out here you've done nothing but moan. The food. The cold. Your mask sores. Your sweetheart. My snoring. Bolder's habits. Lorsen's temper. It's enough to make a man quite aggravated.'

'Even if life weren't aggravating enough to begin with,' said Ferring, who was out of the game and had been sitting with his boots up on the table for the best part of an hour. Ferring had the most unnatural patience with doing nothing.

Pauth eyed him. 'Your boots are pretty damn aggravating.'

Ferring eyed him back. Those sharp blue eyes of his. 'Boots is boots.'

'Boots is boots? What does that even mean? Boots is boots?'

'If you've nothing worth saying, you two might consider not saying it.' Bolder nodded his lump of a head towards the prisoner. 'Take a page out of his book.' The old man hadn't said a word to Lorsen's questions. Hadn't done much more than grunt even when they burned him. He just watched, eyes narrowed, raw flesh glistening in the midst of his tattoos.

Ferring's eyes shifted over to Wile's. 'You think you'd take a burning that well?'

Wile didn't reply. He didn't like thinking about taking a burning. He didn't like giving one to someone else, whatever oaths he'd sworn, whatever treasons, murders or massacres the man was meant to have masterminded. One thing holding forth about justice at a thousand miles removed. Another having to press metal into flesh. He just didn't like thinking about it at all.

It's a steady living, the Inquisition, his father had told him. *Better asking the questions than giving the answers anyway, eh?* And they'd laughed together at that, though Wile hadn't found it funny. He used to laugh a lot at unfunny things his father said. He wouldn't have laughed now. Or maybe that was giving himself too much credit. He'd a bad habit of doing that.

Sometimes Wile wondered whether a cause could be right that needed folk burned, cut and otherwise mutilated. Hardly the tactics of the just, was it, when you took a step back? Rarely seemed to produce any truly useful results either. Unless pain, fear, hate and mutilation were what you were after. Maybe it *was* what they were after.

Sometimes Wile wondered whether the torture might cause the very disloyalty the Inquisition was there to stop, but he kept that notion very much to himself. Takes courage to lead a charge, but you've got people behind you there. Takes a different and rarer kind to stand up all alone and say, 'I don't like the way we do things.' Especially to a set of torturers. Wile didn't have either kind of courage. So he just did as he was told and tried not to think about it, and wondered what it would be like to have a job you believed in.

Ferring didn't have that same problem. He liked the work. You could see it in those blue, blue eyes of his. He grinned over at the tattooed old man now and said, 'Doubt he'll be taking a burning that well by the time he gets back to Starikland.' The prisoner just sat and watched, blue-painted ribs shifting with his crackly breathing. 'Lot of nights between here and there. Lot of burnings, maybe. Yes, indeedy. Reckon he'll be good and talkative by—'

'I already suggested you shut up,' said Bolder. 'Now I'm thinking o' making it an instruction. What do you—'

There was a knock at the door. Three quick knocks, in fact. The Practicals looked at each other, eyebrows up. Lorsen back with more questions. Once Lorsen had a question in mind, he wasn't a man to wait for an answer.

'You going to get that?' Pauth asked Ferring.

'Why would I?'

'You're closest.'

'You're shortest.'

'What's that got to fucking do with anything?'

'It amuses me.'

'Maybe my knife up your arse will amuse me!' And Pauth slipped his knife out of his sleeve, blade appearing as if by magic. He loved to do that. Bloody show-off.

'Will you two infants *please* shut up?' Bolder chucked down his cards, levered his bulk from his chair and slapped Pauth's knife aside. 'I came out here to get a break from my bloody children, not to mind three more.'

Wile rearranged his cards again, wondering if there was some way he could win. One win, was that too much to ask? But such a rotten hand. His father had always said *there are no rotten hands, only rotten players*, but Wile believed otherwise.

Another insistent knocking. 'All right, I'm coming!' snapped Bolder, dragging back the bolts. 'It's not as if—'

There was a clatter, and Wile looked up to see Bolder lurching against the wall looking quite put out and someone barging past. Seemed a bit strong even if they'd taken a while to answer the door. Bolder obviously agreed, because he opened his mouth to complain, then looked surprised when he gurgled blood everywhere instead. That was when Wile noticed there was a knife-handle sticking from his fat throat.

He dropped his cards.

'Eh?' said Ferring, trying to get up, but his boots were tangled with the table. It wasn't Lorsen who'd been knocking, it was the big Northman, the one with all the scars. He took a stride into the room, teeth bared, and crunch! Left a knife buried in Ferring's face to the cross-piece, his nose flattened under it and blood welling and Ferring wheezed and arched back and kicked the table over, cards and coins flying.

Wile stumbled up, the Northman turning to look at him, blood dotting his face and pulling another knife from inside his coat, and—

'Stop!' hissed Pauth. 'Or I kill him!' Somehow he'd got to the prisoner, kneeling behind the chair he was roped to, knife blade pressed against his neck. Always been a quick thinker, Pauth. Good thing someone was.

Bolder had slid to the floor, was making a honking sound and drooling blood into a widening pool.

Wile realised he was holding his breath and took a great gasp.

The scarred Northman looked from Wile, to Pauth, and back, lifted his chin slightly, then gently lowered his blade.

'Get help!' snapped Pauth, and he tangled his fingers in the prisoner's grey hair and pulled his head back, tickling his stubbled neck with the point of his knife. 'I'll see to this.'

Wile circled the Northman, his knees all shaky, pushing aside one of the leather curtains that divided up the fort's downstairs, trying to keep as safe a distance as possible. He slithered in Bolder's blood and nearly went right over, then dived out of the open door and was running.

'Help!' he screeched. 'Help!'

One of the mercenaries lowered a bottle and stared at him, cross-eyed. 'Wha?' The celebrations were still half-heartedly dragging on, women laughing and men singing and shouting and rolling in a stupor, none of them enjoying it but going through the motions anyway like a corpse that can't stop twitching, all garishly lit by the sizzling bonfire. Wile slid over in the mud, staggered up, dragging down his mask so he could shout louder.

'Help! The Northman! The prisoner!'

Someone was pointing at him and laughing, and someone shouted at him to shut up, and someone was sick all over the side of a tent, and Wile stared about for anyone who might exert some control over this shambles and suddenly felt somebody clutch at his arm.

'What are you jabbering about?' None other than General Cosca, dewy eyes gleaming with the firelight, lady's white powder smeared across one hollow, rash-speckled cheek.

'That Northman!' squealed Wile, grabbing the captain general by his stained shirt. 'Lamb! He killed Bolder! And Ferring!' He pointed a trembling finger towards the fort. 'In there!'

To give him his due, Cosca needed no convincing. 'Enemies in the camp!' he roared, flinging his empty bottle away. 'Surround the fort! You, cover the door, make sure no one leaves! Dimbik, get men around the back! You, put that woman down! Arm yourselves, you wretches!'

Some snapped to obey. Two found bows and pointed them uncertainly towards the door. One accidentally shot an arrow into the fire. Others stared baffled, or continued with their revelry, or stood grinning, imagining that this was some elaborate joke.

'What the hell happened?' Lorsen, black coat flapping open over his nightshirt, hair wild about his head.

'It would appear our friend Lamb attempted a rescue of your prisoner,' said Cosca. 'Get away from that door, you idiots – do you think this is a joke?'

'Rescue?' muttered Sworbreck, eyebrows raised and eyeglasses skewed, evidently having recently crawled from his bed.

'Rescue?' snapped Lorsen, grabbing Wile by the collar.

'Pauth took the prisoner . . . prisoner. He's seeing to it—'

A figure lurched from the fort's open door, took a few lazy steps, eyes wide above his mask, hands clasped to his chest. Pauth. He pitched on his face, blood turning the snow around him pink.

'You were saying?' snapped Cosca. A woman shrieked, stumbled back with a hand over her mouth. Men started to drag themselves from tents and shacks, bleary-eyed, pulling on clothes and bits of armour, fumbling with weapons, breath smoking in the cold.

'Get more bows up here!' roared Cosca, clawing at his blistered neck with his fingernails. 'I want a pincushion of anything that shows itself! Clear the bloody civilians away!'

Lorsen was hissing in Wile's face. 'Is Conthus still alive?'

'I think so . . . he was when I . . . when I—'

'Cravenly fled? Pull your mask up, damn it, you're a disgrace!'

Probably the Inquisitor was right, and Wile was a disgraceful Practical. He felt strangely proud of that possibility.

'Can you hear me, Master Lamb?' called Cosca, as Sergeant Friendly helped him into his gilded, rusted breastplate, a combination of pomp and decay that rather summed up the man.

'Aye,' came the Northman's voice from the black doorway of the fort. The closest thing to silence had settled over the camp since the mercenaries returned in triumph the previous day.

'I am so pleased you have graced us with your presence again!' The captain general waved half-dressed bowmen into the shadows around the shacks. 'I wish you'd sent word of your coming, though, we could have prepared a more suitable reception!'

'Thought I'd surprise you.'

'We appreciate the gesture! But I should say I have some hundred and fifty fighting men out here!' Cosca took in the wobbling bows, dewy eyes and bilious faces of his Company. 'Several of them are very drunk, but still. Long established admirer though I am of lost causes, I really don't see the happy ending for you!'

'I've never been much for happy endings,' came Lamb's growl. Wile didn't know how a man could sound so steady under these circumstances.

'Nor me, but perhaps we can engineer one between us!' With a couple of gestures Cosca sent more men scurrying down either side of the fort and ordered a fresh bottle. 'Now why don't you two put your weapons down and come out, and we can all discuss this like civilised men!'

'Never been much for civilisation either,' called Lamb. 'Reckon you'll have to come to me.'

'Bloody Northmen,' muttered Cosca, ripping the cork from his latest bottle and flinging it away. 'Dimbik, are any of your men not drunk?'

'You wanted them as drunk as possible,' said the captain, who had got himself tangled with his bedraggled sash as he tried to pull it on.

'Now I need them sober.'

'A few who were on guard, perhaps—'

'Send them in.'

'And we want Conthus alive!' barked Lorsen.

Dimbik bowed. 'We will do our best, Inquisitor.'

'But there can be no promises.' Cosca took a long swallow from his bottle without taking his eyes from the house. 'We'll make that Northern bastard regret coming back.'

*

'You shouldn't have come back,' grunted Savian as he loaded the flatbow.

Lamb edged the door open to peer through. 'Regretting it already.' A thud, splinters, and the bright point of a bolt showed between the planks. Lamb jerked his head back and kicked the door wobbling shut. 'Hasn't quite gone the way I'd hoped.'

'You could say that about most things in life.'

'In my life, no doubt.' Lamb took hold of the knife in the Practical's neck and ripped it free, wiped it on the front of the dead man's black jacket and tossed it to Savian. He snatched it out of the air and slid it into his belt.

'You can never have too many knives,' said Lamb.

'It's a rule to live by.'

'Or die by,' said Lamb as he tossed over another. 'You need a shirt?'

Savian stretched out his arms and watched the tattoos move. The words he'd tried to live his life by. 'What's the point in getting 'em if you don't show 'em off? I've been covering up too long.'

'Man's got to be what he is, I reckon.'

Savian nodded. 'Wish we'd met thirty years ago.'

'No you don't. I was a mad fucker then.'

'And now?'

Lamb stuck a dagger into the tabletop. 'Thought I'd learned something.' He thumped another into the doorframe. 'But here I am, handing out knives.'

'You pick a path, don't you?' Savian started drawing the string on the other flatbow. 'And you think it's just for tomorrow. Then thirty years on you look back and see you picked your path for life. If you'd known it then, you'd maybe have thought more carefully.'

'Maybe. Being honest, I've never been much for thinking carefully.'

Savian finally fumbled the string back, glancing at the word *freedom* tattooed around his wrist like a bracelet. 'Always thought I'd die fighting for the cause.'

'You will,' said Lamb, still busy scattering weapons around the room. 'The cause of saving my fat old arse.'

'It's a noble calling.' Savian slipped a bolt into place. 'Reckon I'll get upstairs.'

'Reckon you'd better.' Lamb drew the sword he'd taken from Waerdinur, long and dull with that silver letter glinting. 'We ain't got all night.'

'You'll be all right down here?'

'Might be best if you just stay up there. That mad fucker from thirty years ago – sometimes he comes visiting.'

'Then I'll leave the two of you to it. You shouldn't have come back.' Savian held out his hand. 'But I'm glad you did.'

'Wouldn't have missed it.' Lamb took a grip on Savian's hand and gave it a squeeze, and they looked each other in the eye. Seemed in that moment they had as good an understanding between them as if they had met thirty years ago. But the time for friendship was over. Savian had always put more effort into his enemies, and there was no shortage outside. He turned and took the stairs three at a time, up into the garret, a flatbow in each hand and the bolts over his shoulder.

Four windows, two to the front, two to the back. Straw pallets around the walls and a low table with a lit lamp, and in its flickering pool of light a hunting bow and a quiver of arrows, and a spiked mace, too, metal gleaming. One handy thing about mercenaries, they leave weapons lying about wherever they go. He slipped in a crouch to the front, propped one of the flatbows carefully under the left-hand window and then scurried over to the right with the other, hooking the shutters open and peering out.

There was a fair bit of chaos under way outside, lit by the great bonfire, sparks whirling, folk hurrying this way and that on the far side. Seemed some of those who'd come to get rich on the Company's scraps hadn't reckoned on getting stuck in the middle of a fight. The corpse of one of the Practicals was stretched out near the door but Savian shed no tears for him. He'd cried easily as a child, but his eyes had good and dried up down the years. They'd had to. With what he'd seen, and what he'd done, too, there wouldn't have been enough salt water in the world.

He saw archers, squatting near the shacks, bows trained towards the fort, made a quick note of the positions, of the angles, of the distances. Then he saw men hurrying forward, axes at the ready. He snatched the lamp off the table and tossed it spinning through the dark, saw it shatter on the thatch roof of one of the shacks, streaks of fire shooting hungrily out.

'They're coming for the door!' he shouted.

'How many?' came Lamb's voice from downstairs.

'Five, maybe!' His eyes flickered across the shadows down there around the bonfire. 'Six!' He worked the stock of the flatbow into his shoulder, settling down still and steady around it, warm and familiar as curling around a lover's back. He wished he'd spent more of his time curled around a lover and less around a flatbow, but he'd picked his path and here was the next step along it. He twitched the trigger and felt the bow jolt and one of the axemen took a tottering step sideways and sat down.

'Five!' shouted Savian as he slipped away from the window and over to another, setting down the first bow and hefting the second. Heard arrows clatter against the frame behind, one spinning into the darkness of the room. He levelled the bow, caught a black shape against the fire and felt the shot, a mercenary staggered back and tripped into the flames and even over the racket Savian could hear him screaming as he burned.

He slid down, back against the wall under the window. Saw an arrow flit through above him and shudder into a rafter. He was caught for a moment with a coughing fit, managed to settle it, breath rasping, the burns around his ribs all stinging fresh. Axes at the door, now, he could hear them thudding. Had to leave that to Lamb. Only man alive he'd have trusted alone with that task. He heard voices at the back, quiet, but he heard them. Up onto his feet and he scuttled to the back wall, taking up the hunting bow, no time to buckle the quiver, just wedging it through his belt.

He dragged in a long, crackling breath, stifled a cough and held it, nocked an arrow, drew the string, in one movement poked the limb of the bow behind the shutters and flicked them open, stood, leaned out and pushed the air slow through his pursed lips.

Men crouched in the shadows against the foot of the back wall. One looked up, eyes wide in his round face, and Savian shot him in his open mouth no more than a stride or two away. He nocked another shaft. An arrow whipped past him, flicking his hair. He drew the bow, calm and steady. He could see light gleam on the archer's arrowhead as he did the same. Shot him in the chest. Drew another arrow. Saw a man running past. Shot him too and saw him crumple in the snow. Crunching of footsteps as the last of them ran away. Savian took a bead and shot him in the back, and he crawled and whimpered and coughed, and Savian nocked an arrow and shot him a second time, elbowed the shutters closed and breathed in again.

He was caught with a coughing fit and stood shuddering against the wall. He heard a roar downstairs, clash of steel, swearing, crashing, ripping, fighting.

He stumbled to the front window again, nocking an arrow, saw two men rushing for the door, shot one in the face and his legs went from under him. The other skidded to a stop, scuttled off sideways. Arrows were frozen in the firelight, clattering against the front of the building as Savian twisted away.

A crack and the shutters in the back window swung open showing a square of night sky. Savian saw a hand on the sill, let fall the bow and snatched up the mace as he went, swinging it low and fast to miss the rafters and smashing it into a helmeted head as it showed itself, knocking someone tumbling out into the night.

He spun, black shape in the window as a man slipped into the attic, knife in his teeth. Savian lunged at him but the haft of the mace glanced off his shoulder and they grappled and struggled, growling at each other. Savian felt a burning in his gut, fell back against the wall with the man on top of him, reached for the knife at his belt. He saw one half of the mercenary's snarling face lit by firelight and Savian stabbed at it, ripped it open, black pulp hanging from his head as he stumbled, thrashing blindly around the attic. Savian clawed his way up and fell on him, dragged him down and stabbed and coughed and stabbed until he stopped moving, knelt on top of him, each cough ripping at the wound in his guts.

A bubbling scream had started downstairs, and Savian heard someone squealing, 'No! No! No!' slobbering, desperate, and he heard Lamb growl, 'Yes, you fucker!' Two heavy thuds, then a long silence.

Lamb gave a kind of groan downstairs, another crash like he was kicking something over.

'You all right?' he called, his own voice sounding tight and strange.

'Still breathing!' came Lamb's, even stranger. 'You?'

'Picked up a scratch.' Savian peeled his palm away from his tattooed stomach, blood there gleaming black. Lot of blood.

He wished he could talk to Corlin one last time. Tell her all those things you think but never say because they're hard to say and there'll be time later. How proud he was of what she'd become. How proud her mother would've been. To carry on the fight. He winced. Or maybe to give up the fight, because you only get one life and do you want to look back on it and see just blood on your hands?

But it was too late to tell her anything. He'd picked his path and here was where it ended. Hadn't been too poor a showing, all told. Some good and some bad, some pride and some shame, like most men. He crawled coughing to the front, took up one of the flatbows and started wrestling at the string with sticky hands. Damn hands. Didn't have the strength they used to.

He stood up beside the window, men still moving down there, and the shack he threw the lamp on sending up a roaring blaze now, and he bellowed out into the night. 'That the best you can do?'

'Sadly for you,' came Cosca's voice. 'No!'

Something sparked and fizzled in the darkness, and there was a flash like daylight.

It was a noise like to the voice of God, as the scriptures say, which levelled the city of the presumptuous Nemai with but a whisper. Jubair peeled his hands from his ears, all things still ringing even so, and squinted towards the fort as the choking smoke began to clear.

Much violence had been done to the building. There were holes finger-sized, and fist-sized, and head-sized rent through the walls of the bottom floor. Half of the top floor had departed the world, splintered planks smouldering in places, three split beams still clinging together at one corner as a reminder of the shape of what had been. There was a creaking and half the roof fell in, broken shingles clattering to the ground below.

'Impressive,' said Brachio.

'The lightning harnessed,' murmured Jubair, frowning at the pipe of brass. It had nearly leaped from its carriage with the force of the blast and now sat skewed upon it, smoke still issuing gently from its blackened mouth. 'Such a power should belong only to God.'

He felt Cosca's hand upon his shoulder. 'And yet He lends it to us to do His work. Take some men in there and find those two old bastards.'

'I want Conthus alive!' snapped Lorsen.

'If possible.' The Old Man leaned close to whisper. 'But dead is just as good.'

Jubair nodded. He had come to a conclusion long years before that God sometimes spoke through the person of Nicomo Cosca. An unlikely prophet, some might say – a treacherous, lawless pink drunkard who had never uttered a word of prayer in all his long life – but from the first moment Jubair had seen him in battle, and known he had no fear, he had sensed in him some splinter of the divine. Surely he walked in God's shadow, as the Prophet Khalul had walked naked through a rain of arrows with only his faith to protect him and emerged untouched, and so forced the Emperor of the Gurkish to honour his promise and abase himself before the Almighty.

'You three,' he said, picking out some of his men with a finger, 'on my signal go in by the door. You three, come with me.'

One of them, a Northman, shook his head with starting eyes round as full moons. 'It's . . . *him*,' he whispered.

'Him?'

'The . . . the . . .' And in dumbstruck silence he folded the middle finger on his left hand back to leave a gap.

Jubair snorted. 'Stay then, fool.' He trotted around the side of the fort, through shadow and deeper shadow, all the same to him for he carried the light of God within. His men peered up at the building, breathing hard, afraid. They supposed the world was a complicated place, full of dangers. Jubair pitied them. The world was simple. The only danger was in resisting God's purpose.

Fragments of timber, rubbish and dust were scattered across the snow behind the building. That and several arrow-shot men, one sitting against the wall and softly gurgling, hand around a shaft through his mouth. Jubair ignored them and quietly scaled the back wall of the fort. He peered into the ruined loft, furniture ripped apart, a mattress spilling straw, no signs of life. He brushed some embers away and pulled himself up, slid out his sword, metal glinting in the night, fearless, righteous, godly. He eased forward, watching the stairwell, black with shadows. He heard a sound from down there, a regular thump, thump, thump.

He leaned out at the front of the building and saw his three men clustered below. He hissed at them, and the foremost kicked the door wide and plunged inside. Jubair pointed the other two to the stairwell. He felt something give beneath the sole of his boot as he turned. A hand. He bent and dragged a timber aside.

'Conthus is here!' he shouted.

'Alive?' came Lorsen's shrill bleat.

'Dead.'

'Damn it!'

Jubair gathered up what was left of the rebel and rolled it over the ragged remnant of the wall, tumbling down the snow drifted against the side of the building to lie broken and bloody, tattoos ripped with a score of wounds. Jubair thought of the parable of the proud man. God's judgement comes to great and small alike, all equally powerless before the Almighty, inevitable and irreversible, and so it was, so it was. Now there was only the Northman, and however fearsome he might be, God had a sentence already in mind—

A scream split the night, a crashing below, roars and groans and a metal scraping, then a strange hacking laugh, another scream. Jubair strode to the stairs. A wailing below, now, as horrible as the sinful dead consigned to hell, blubbering off into silence. The point of Jubair's sword showed the way. Fearless, righteous . . . He hesitated, licking at his lips. To feel fear was to be without faith. It is not given to man to understand God's design. Only to accept his place in it.

And so he clenched his jaw tight, and padded down the steps.

Black as hell below, light shining in rays of flickering red, orange, yellow, through the holes in the front wall, casting strange shadows. Black as hell and like hell it reeked of death, so strong the stench it seemed a solid thing. Jubair half-held his breath as he descended, step by creaking step, eyes adjusting to the darkness by degrees.

What revelation?

The leather curtains that had divided up the space hung torn, showered and spotted with black, stirred a little as if by wind though the space was still. His boot caught something on the bottom step and he looked down. A severed arm. Frowning, he followed its glistening trail to a black slick, flesh humped and mounded and inhumanly abused, hacked apart and tangled together in unholy configurations, innards dragged out and rearranged and unwound in glistening coils.

In the midst stood a table and upon the table a pile of heads, and as the light shifted from the flames outside they looked upon Jubair with expressions awfully vacant, madly leering, oddly questioning, angrily accusatory.

'God . . .' he said. Jubair had done butchery in the name of the Almighty and yet he had seen nothing like this. This was written in no scripture, except perhaps in the forbidden seventh of the seven books, sealed within the tabernacle of the Great Temple in Shaffa, in which were recorded those things that Glustrod brought from hell.

'God . . .' he muttered. And jagged laughter bubbled from the shadows, and the skins flapped, and rattled the rings they hung upon. Jubair darted forward, stabbed, cut, slashed at darkness, caught nothing but dangling skin, blade tangled with leather and he slipped in gore, and fell, and rose, turning, turning, the laughter all around him.

'God?' mumbled Jubair, and he could hardly speak the holy word for a strange feeling, beginning in his guts and creeping up and down his spine to set his scalp to tingle and his knees to shake. All the more terrible for being only dimly remembered. A childish recollection, lost in darkness. For as the Prophet said, the man who knows fear every day becomes easy in its company. The man who knows not fear, how shall he face this awful stranger?

'God . . .' whimpered Jubair, stumbling back towards the steps, and suddenly there were arms around him.

'Gone,' came a whisper. 'But I am here.'

'Damn it!' snarled Lorsen again. His long-cherished dream of presenting the infamous Conthus to the Open Council, chained and humbled and plastered with tattoos that might as well have read *give Inquisitor Lorsen the promotion he has so long deserved*, had gone up in smoke. Or down in blood. Thirteen years minding a penal colony in Angland, for this. All the riding, all the sacrifice, all the indignity. In spite of his best efforts the entire expedition had devolved into a farce, and he had no doubt upon which undeserving head would be heaped the blame. He slapped at his leg in a fury. 'I wanted him alive!'

'So did he, I daresay.' Cosca stared narrow-eyed through the haze of smoke towards the ruined fort. 'Fate is not always kind to us.'

'Easy for you to say,' snapped Lorsen. To make matters worse – if that were possible – he had lost half his Practicals in one night, and that the better half. He frowned over at Wile, still fussing with his mask. How was it possible for a Practical to look so pitiably unthreatening? The man positively radiated doubt. Enough to plant the seeds of doubt in everyone around him. Lorsen had entertained doubts enough over the years but he did what one was supposed to, and kept them crushed into a tight little packet deep inside where they could not leak out and poison his purpose.

The door slowly creaked open and Dimbik's archers shifted nervously, flatbows all levelled towards that square of darkness.

'Jubair?' barked Cosca. 'Jubair, did you get him? Answer me, damn it!'

Something flew out, bounced once with a hollow clonk and rolled across the snow to rest near the fire.

'What is that?' asked Lorsen.

Cosca worked his mouth. 'Jubair's head.'

'Fate is not always kind,' murmured Brachio.

Another head arced from the doorway and bounced into the fire. A third landed on the roof of one of the shacks, rolled down it and lodged in the gutter. A fourth fell among the archers and one of them let his bow off as he stumbled away from it, the bolt thudding into a barrel nearby. More heads, and more, hair flapping, tongues lolling, spinning, and dancing, and scattering spots of blood.

The last head bounced high and rolled an elliptical course around the fire to stop just next to Cosca. Lorsen was not a man to be put off by a little gore, but even he had to admit to being a little unnerved by this display of mute brutality.

Less squeamish, the captain general stepped forward and angrily kicked the head into the flames. 'How many men have those two old bastards killed between them?' Though the Old Man was no doubt a good deal older than either.

'About twenty, now,' said Brachio.

'We'll fucking run out at this rate!' Cosca turned angrily upon Sworbreck, who was frantically scratching away in his notebook. 'What the hell are you writing for?'

The author looked up, reflected flames dancing in his eyeglasses. 'Well, this is . . . rather dramatic.'

'Do you find?'

Sworbreck gestured weakly towards the ruined fort. 'He came to the rescue of his friend against impossible odds—'

'And got him killed. Is not a man who takes on impossible odds generally considered an incorrigible idiot rather than a hero?'

'The line between the two has always been blurry . . .' murmured Brachio.

Sworbreck raised his palms. 'I came for a tale to stir the blood—'

'And I've been unable to oblige you,' snapped Cosca, 'is that it? Even my bloody biographer is deserting me! No doubt I'll end up the villain in the book I commissioned while yonder decapitating madman is celebrated to the rafters! What do you make of this, Temple? Temple? Where's that bloody lawyer got to? What about you, Brachio?'

The Styrian wiped fresh tears from his weepy eye. 'I think the time has come to put an end to the ballad of the nine-fingered Northman.'

'Finally some sense! Bring up the other tube. I want that excuse for a fort levelled to a stump. I want that meddling fool made mush, do you hear? Someone bring me another bottle. I am sick of being taken fucking lightly!' Cosca slapped Sworbreck's notebook from his hands.

'A little respect, is that too much to ask?' He slapped the biographer to boot and the man sat down sharply in the snow, one hand to his cheek in surprise.

'What's that noise?' said Lorsen, holding up a palm for silence. A thumping and rumbling spilled from the darkness, rapidly growing louder, and he took a nervous step towards the nearest shack.

'Bloody hell,' said Dimbik.

A horse came thundering from the night, eyes wild, and a moment later dozens more, surging down the slope towards the camp, snow flying, a boiling mass of animals, a flood of horseflesh coming at the gallop.

Men flung their weapons down and ran, dived, rolled for any cover. Lorsen tripped over his flapping coat-tail and sprawled in the mud. He heard a whooping and caught a glimpse of Dab Sweet, mounted at the rear of the herd, grinning wildly, lifting his hat in salute as he skirted the camp. Then the horses were among the buildings and all was a hell of milling, kicking, battering hooves, of screaming, thrashing, rearing beasts, and Lorsen flattened himself helplessly against the nearest hovel, clinging with his fingernails to the rough-sawn wood.

Then suddenly there was silence. A throbbing, ringing silence. Lorsen unpeeled himself from the side of the shack and took a wobbling step or two through the hoof-hammered mud, blinking into the haze of smoke and settling dirt.

'They stampeded the horses,' he muttered.

'Do you fucking think so?' shrieked Cosca, tottering from the nearest doorway.

The camp was devastated. Several of the tents had ceased to be, the canvas and their contents – both human and material – trampled into the snow. The ruined fort continued to smoulder. Two of the shacks were thoroughly aflame, burning straw fluttering down and leaving small fires everywhere. Bodies were humped between the buildings, trampled men and women in various states of dress. The injured howled or wandered dazed and bloodied. Here and there a wounded horse lay, kicking weakly.

Lorsen touched one hand to his head. His hair was sticky with blood. A trickle tickling his eyebrow.

'Dab fucking Sweet!' snarled Cosca.

'I did say he had quite a reputation,' muttered Sworbreck, fishing his tattered notebook from the dirt.

'Perhaps we should have paid him his share,' mused Friendly.

'You can take it to him now if you please!' Cosca pointed with a clawing finger. 'It's in . . . *the wagon*.' He trailed off into a disbelieving croak.

The fortified wagon that had been Superior Pike's gift, the wagon in which the fire tubes had been carried, the wagon in which the Dragon People's vast treasure had been safely stowed . . .

The wagon was gone. Beside the fort there was only a conspicuously empty patch of darkness.

'Where is it?' Cosca shoved Sworbreck out of the way and ran to where the wagon had stood. Clearly visible in the snowy mud among the trampled hoof-prints were two deep wheel-ruts, angling down the slope towards the Imperial Road.

'Brachio,' Cosca's voice rose higher and higher until it was a demented shriek, 'find some fucking horses and *get after them*!'

The Styrian stared. 'You wanted all the horses corralled together. They're stampeded!'

'Some must have broken from the herd! Find half a dozen and get after those bastards! Now! Now! Now!' And he kicked snow at Brachio in a fury and nearly fell over. 'Where the hell is Temple?'

Friendly looked up from the wagon-tracks and raised an eyebrow.

Cosca closed his hands to trembling fists. 'Everyone who can, get ready to *move*!'

Dimbik exchanged a worried look with Lorsen. 'On foot? All the way to Crease?'

'We'll gather mounts on the way!'

'What about the injured?'

'Those who can walk are welcome. Any who cannot mean greater shares for the rest of us. Now get them moving, you damned idiot!'

'Yes, sir,' muttered Dimbik, pulling off and sourly flinging away his sash which, already a ruin, had become thoroughly besmirched with dung when he dived for cover.

Friendly nodded towards the fort. 'And the Northman?'

'Fuck the Northman,' hissed Cosca. 'Soak the building with oil and burn it. They've stolen our gold! They've stolen my dreams, do you understand?' He frowned off down the Imperial Road, the wagon-tracks vanishing into the darkness. 'I will *not* be disappointed again.'

Lorsen resisted the temptation to echo Cosca's sentiments that fate is not always kind. Instead, as the mercenaries scrambled over each other in their preparations to leave, he stood looking down at Conthus' forgotten body, lying broken beside the fort.

'What a waste,' he muttered. In every conceivable sense. But Inquisitor Lorsen had always been a practical man. A man who did not balk at hardship and hard work. He took his disappointment and crushed it down into that little packet along with his doubts, and turned his thoughts to what could be salvaged.

'There will be a price for this, Cosca,' he muttered at the captain general's back. 'There will be a price.'

Nowhere Fast

Every bolt, bearing, plank and fixing in that monster of a wagon banged, clattered or screeched in an insane cacophony so deafening that Temple could scarcely hear his own squeals of horror. The seat hammered at his arse, bounced him around like a heap of cheap rags, threatening to rattle the teeth right out of his head. Tree-limbs came slicing from the darkness, clawing at the wagon's sides, slashing at his face. One had snatched Shy's hat off and now her hair whipped around her staring eyes, fixed on the rushing road, lips peeled back from her teeth as she yelled the most blood-curdling abuse at the horses.

Temple dreaded to imagine the weight of wood, metal and above all gold they were currently hurtling down a mountainside on top of. Any moment now, the whole, surely tested beyond the limits of human engineering, would rip itself apart and the pair of them into the bargain. But dread was a fixture of Temple's life, and what else could he do now but cling to this bouncing engine of death, muscles burning from fingertips to armpits, stomach churning with drink and terror. He hardly knew whether eyes closed or eyes open was the more horrifying.

'Hold on!' Shy screamed at him.

'What the fuck do you think I'm—'

She dragged back on the brake lever, boots braced against the footboard and her shoulders against the back of the seat, fibres starting from her neck with effort. The tyres shrieked like the dead in hell, sparks showering up on both sides like fireworks at the Emperor's birthday. Shy hauled on the reins with her other hand and the whole world began to turn, then to tip, two of the great wheels parting company with the flying ground.

Time slowed. Temple screamed. Shy screamed. The wagon screamed. Trees off the side of the bend hurtled madly towards them, death in their midst. Then the wheels jolted down again and Temple was almost flung over the footboard and among the horses' milling hooves, biting his tongue and choking on his own screech as he was tossed back into the seat.

Shy let the brake off and snapped the reins. 'Might've taken that one a little too fast!' she shouted in his ear.

The line between terror and exultation was ever a fine one and Temple found, all of a sudden, he had broken through. He punched at the air and howled, 'Fuck you, Coscaaaaaaaa!' into the night until his breath ran out and left him gasping.

'Feel better?' asked Shy.

'I'm alive! I'm free! I'm rich!' Surely there was a God. A benevolent, understanding, kindly grandfather of a God and smiling down indulgently upon him even now. 'Sooner or later you have to do something, or you'll never do anything,' Cosca had said. Temple wondered if this was what the Old Man had in mind. It did not seem likely. He grabbed hold of Shy and half-hugged her and shouted in her ear, 'We did it!'

'You sure?' she grunted, snapping the reins again.

'Didn't we do it?'

'The easy part.'

'Eh?'

'They won't just be letting this go, will they?' she called over the rushing wind as they picked up pace. 'Not the money! Not the insult!'

'They'll be coming after us,' he muttered.

'That was the whole point o' the exercise!'

Temple cautiously stood to look behind them, wishing he was less drunk. Nothing but snow and dirt spraying up from the clattering back wheels and the trees to either side vanishing into the darkness.

'They've got no horses, though?' His voice turning into a hopeful little whine at the end.

'Sweet slowed 'em down, but they'll still be coming! And this contraption ain't the fastest!'

Temple took another look back, wishing he was more drunk. The line between exultation and terror was ever a fine one and he was rapidly crossing back over. 'Maybe we should stop the wagon! Take two of the horses! Leave the money! Most of the money, anyway—'

'We need to give Lamb and Savian time, remember?'

'Oh, yes. That.' The problem with courageous self-sacrifice was the self-sacrifice part. It had just never come naturally to him. The next jolt brought a wash of scalding vomit to the back of Temple's mouth and he tried to swallow it, choked, spluttered and felt it burning all the way up his nose with a shiver. He looked up at the sky, stars vanished now and shifting from black to iron-grey as the dawn came on.

'Woah!' Another bend came blundering from the gloom and Shy dragged the shrieking brakes on again. Temple could hear the cargo sliding and jingling behind them as the wagon bounded around the corner, the earnest desire of all that weight to plunge on straight and send them tumbling down the mountainside in ruin.

As they clattered back onto the straight there was an almighty cracking and Shy reeled in her seat, one leg kicking, yelling out as she started to tumble off the wagon. Temple's hand snapped closed around her belt and hauled her back, the limb of the bow over her shoulder nearly taking his eye out as she fell against him, reins flapping.

She held something up. The brake lever. And decidedly no longer attached. 'That's the end of that, then!'

'What do we do?'

She tossed the length of wood over her shoulder and it bounced away up the road behind them. 'Not stop?'

The wagon shot from the trees and onto the plateau. The first glimmer of dawn was spilling from the east, a bright shaving of sun showing over the hills, starting to turn the muddy sky a washed-out blue, the streaked clouds a washed-up pink, setting the frozen snow that blanketed the flat country to glitter.

Shy worked the reins hard and insulted the horses again, which felt a little unfair to Temple until he remembered how much better insults had worked on him than encouragement. Their heads dipped and manes flew and the wagon picked up still more speed, wheels spinning faster on the flat, and faster yet, the snowy scrub whipping past and the wind blasting at Temple's face and plucking at his cheeks and rushing in his cold nose.

Far ahead he could see horses scattering across the plateau, Sweet and Crying Rock no doubt further off with most of the herd. No dragon's hoard to retire on, but they'd cash in a decent profit on a couple of hundred mounts. When it came to stock, people out here were more concerned with price than origin.

'Anyone following?' called Shy, without taking her eyes off the road.

Temple managed to pry his hand from the seat long enough to stand and look behind them. Just the jagged blackness of the trees, and a rapidly growing stretch of flat whiteness between them and the wagon.

'No!' he shouted, confidence starting to leak back. 'No one . . . wait!' He saw movement. A rider. 'Oh God,' he muttered, confidence instantly draining. More of them. 'Oh God!'

'How many?'

'Three! No! Five! No! Seven!' They were still a few hundred strides behind, but they were gaining. 'Oh God,' he said again as he dropped back down into the shuddering seat. 'Now what's the plan?'

'We're already off the end of the plan!'

'I had a nasty feeling you'd say that.'

'Take the reins!' she shouted, thrusting them at him.

He jerked his hands away. 'And do what?'

'Can't you drive?'

'Badly!'

'I thought you'd done everything?'

'Badly!'

'Shall I stop and give you a fucking lesson? Drive!' She pulled her knife from her belt and offered that to him as well. 'Or you could fight.'

Temple swallowed. Then he took the reins. 'I'll drive.' Surely there was a God. A mean little trickster laughing His divine arse off at Temple's expense. And hardly for the first time.

Shy wondered how much of her life she'd spent regretting her last decision. Too much, that was sure. Looked like today was going to plough the same old furrow.

She dragged herself over the wooden parapet and onto the wagon's tar-painted roof, bucking under her feet like a mean bull trying to toss a rider. She lurched to the back, shrugged her bow off into her hand, clawed away her whipping hair and squinted across the plateau.

'Oh, shit,' she muttered.

Seven riders, just like Temple said, and gaining ground. All they had to do was get ahead of the wagon, bring down a horse or two in the team and that'd be that. They were out of range still, specially shooting from what might as well have been a raft in rapids. She wasn't bad with a bow but she was no miracle-worker either. Her eyes went to the hatch on the roof, and she tossed the bow down and slithered over to it on her hands and knees, drew her sword and jammed it into the hasp the padlock was on. Way too strong and heavy. The tar around the hinges was carelessly painted, though, the wood more'n halfway rotten. She jammed the point of the sword into it, twisted, gouged, working out the fixings, digging at the other hinge.

'Are they still following?' she heard Temple shriek.

'No!' she forced through her gritted teeth as she wedged her sword under the hatch and hauled back on it. 'I've killed them all!'

'Really?'

'No, not fucking really!' And she went skittering over on her arse as the hatch ripped from its hinges and flopped free. She flung the sword away, thoroughly bent, dragged the hatch open with her fingertips, started clambering down into the darkness. The wagon hit something and gave a crashing jolt, snatched the ladder from her hands and flung her on her face.

Light spilled in from above, through cracks around the shutters of the narrow windows. Heavy gratings down both sides, padlocked and stacked with chests and boxes and saddlebags bouncing and thumping and jingling, treasure spilling free, gold gleaming, gems twinkling, coins sliding across the plank floor, five king's ransoms and change left over for a palace or two. There were a couple of sacks under her, too, crunchy with money. She stood, bouncing from the gratings to either side as the wagon twitched left and right on its groaning springs, started dragging the nearest sack towards the bright line between the back doors. Heavy as all hell but she'd hauled a lot of sacks in her time and she wasn't about to let this one beat her. Shy had taken beatings enough but she'd never enjoyed them.

She fumbled the bolts free, cursing, sweat prickling her forehead, then, holding tight to the grate beside her, booted the doors wide. The wind whipped in, the bright, white emptiness of the plateau opening up, the clattering blur of the wheels and the snow showering from them, the black shapes of the riders following, closer now. Much closer.

She whipped her knife out and hacked the sack gaping open, dug her fist in and threw a handful of coins out the back, and another, and the other hand, and then both, flinging gold like she was sowing seed on the farm. It came to her then how hard she'd fought as a bandit and slaved as a farmer and haggled as a trader for a fraction of what she was flinging away with every movement. She jammed the next fistful down into her pocket 'cause – well, why not die rich? Then she scooped more out with both hands, threw the empty bag away and went back for seconds.

The wagon hit a rut and tossed her in the air, smashed her head into the low ceiling and sent her sprawling. Everything reeled for a moment, then she staggered up and clawed the next sack towards the swinging, banging doors, growling curses at the wagon, and the ceiling, and her bleeding head. She braced herself against the grate and shoved the sack out with her boot, bursting open in the snow and showering gold across the empty plain.

A couple of the riders had stopped, one already off his horse and on his hands and knees after the coins, dwindling quickly into the distance. But the others came on regardless, more determined than she'd hoped. That's hopes for you. She could almost see the face of the nearest mercenary, bent low over his horse's dipping head. She left the doors banging and scrambled back up the ladder, dragged herself out onto the roof.

'They still following?' shrieked Temple.

'Yes!'

'What are you doing?'

'Having a fucking lie down before they get here!'

The wagon was hurtling into broken land, the plateau folded with little streams, scattered with boulders and pillars of twisted rock. The road dropped down into a shallow valley, steep sides blurring past, wheels rattling harder than ever. Shy wiped blood from her forehead with the back of her hand, slithered across the shuddering roof to the rear, scooping up the bow and drawing an arrow. She squatted there for a moment, breathing hard.

Better to do it than live with the fear of it. Better to do it.

She came up. The nearest rider wasn't five strides back from the swinging doors. He saw her, eyes going wide, yellow hair and a broad chin and cheeks pinked from the wind. She thought she'd seen him writing a letter back in Beacon. He'd cried while he did it. She shot his horse in the chest. Its head went back, it caught one hoof with the other and horse and rider went down together, tumbling over and over, straps and tackle flapping in a tangle, the others swerving around the wreckage as she ducked back down to get another arrow, thought she could hear Temple muttering something.

'You praying?'

'No!'

'Better start!' She came up again and an arrow shuddered into the wood just beside her. A rider, black against the sky on the valley's edge, drawing level with them, horse's hooves a blur, standing in his stirrups with masterful skill and already pulling back his string again.

'Shit!' She dropped down and the shaft flitted over her head and clicked into the parapet on the other side. A moment later another joined it. She could hear the rest of the riders now, shouting to each other just at the back of the wagon. She put her head up to peer over and a shaft twitched into the wood, point showing between two planks not a hand's width from her face, made her duck again. She'd seen some Ghosts damn good at shooting from horseback, but never as good as this. It was bloody unfair, that's what it was. But fair has never been an enforceable principle in a fight to the death.

She nocked her shaft, took a breath and stuck her bow up above the parapet. Right away an arrow flitted between the limb and the string, and up she came. She knew she was nowhere near as good with a bow as he was, but she didn't have to be. A horse is a pretty big target.

Her shaft stuck to the flights in its ribs and it lost its footing right off, fell sideways, rider flying from his saddle with a howl, his bow spinning up in the air and the pair of them tumbling down the side of the valley behind.

Shy shouted, 'Ha!' and turned just in time to see a man jump over the parapet behind her.

She got a glimpse of him. Kantic, with eyes narrowed and his teeth showing in a black beard, a hooked blade in each hand he must've used for climbing the side of the speeding wagon, an endeavour she'd have greatly admired if he hadn't been fixed on killing her. The threat of murder surely can cramp your admiration for a body.

She threw her bow at him and he knocked it away with one arm while he swung at her overhand with the other. She twisted to the side and the blade thudded into the parapet. She caught his other arm as it came at her and punched him in the ribs as she slipped around him. The wagon jolted and ditched her on her side. He twisted his curved blade but couldn't get it free of the wood, jerked his hand out of the thong around his wrist. By then she was up in a crouch and had her knife out, drawing little circles in the air with the point, circles, circles, and they watched each other, both with boots planted wide and knees bent low and the juddering wagon threatening to shake them off their feet and the wind threatening to buffet them right over.

'Hell of a spot for a knife-fight,' she muttered.

The wagon bumped and he stumbled a little, took his eye off her just long enough. She sprang at him, raising the knife like she'd stab him overhand, then whipped down low and past, slashing at his leg as she went, turning to stab him in the back, but the wagon jumped and spun her all the way round and grunting into the parapet.

When she turned he was coming at her roaring, cutting at the wind and her jerking back from the first slash and weaving away from the second, roof of the wagon treacherous as quicksand under her boot-heels and her eyes crossed on that blur of metal. She caught the third cut on her own blade, steel scraping on steel and off and slitting her left forearm, ripped sleeve flapping.

They faced each other again, both breathing hard, both a little bit knifed but nothing too much changed. Her arm sang as she squeezed her bloody fingers but they still worked. She feinted, and a second, trying to draw him into a mistake, but he kept watching, swishing that hooked knife in front of him as if he was trying to snag a fish, the broken valley still thundering past on both sides.

The wagon bounced hard and Shy was off her feet a moment, yelping as she toppled sideways. He slashed at her and missed, she stabbed at him and the blade just grazed his cheek. Another jolt flung them together and he caught her wrist with his free hand, tried to stab at her but got his knife tangled in her coat and she grabbed his wrist, twisted it up, not that she wanted the fucking thing but there was no letting go of it now, their knives both waggling hopelessly at the sky, streaked with each other's blood as they staggered around the bucking roof.

She kicked at his knee and made it buckle but he had the strength, and step by wobbling step he wrestled her to the parapet and started to bend her over it, his weight on top of her. He twisted his knife, twisting her grip loose, getting it free, both of them snarling spit at each other, wood grinding into her back and the wagon's wheels battering the ground not so far behind her head, specks of dirt stinging her cheek, his snarling face coming closer and closer and closer—

She darted forwards and sank her teeth into his nose, biting, biting, her mouth salty with blood and him roaring and twisting and pulling away and suddenly she was right over backwards, breath whooping in as she tumbled over the parapet, plummeted down and smashed against the side of the wagon, breath groaning out, her fallen knife pinging from the road and somehow holding on by one clutching hand, all the fibres in her shoulder strained right to the point of tearing.

She swung wriggling around, road rushing underneath her, honking mad sounds through gritted teeth, legs milling at the air as she tried to get her other hand onto the parapet. Made a grab and missed and swung away and the whirling wheel clipped her boot and near snatched her off. Made another grab and got her fingertips over, worked her hand, groaning and whimpering and almost out of effort, everything numb, but she wouldn't be beaten and she growled as she dragged herself back over.

The mercenary was staggering about with an arm around his neck, Temple's face next to his, both of them grunting through bared teeth. She lunged at him, half-falling, grabbed hold of his knife-arm in both hands and twisted it, twisted it down, both arms straining, and his jowls were trembling, torn nose oozing blood, eyes rolling towards the point of his knife as she forced it down towards him. He said something in Kantic, shaking his head, the same word over and over, but she wasn't in a mood to listen even if she'd understood. He wheezed as the point cut through his shirt and into his chest, mouth going wide open as the blade slid further, right to the cross-piece, and she fell on top of him, blood slicking the roof of the wagon.

There was something in her mouth. The tip of his nose. She spat it out and mumbled at Temple, 'Who'th driving?'

The wagon tipped, there was a grinding jolt, and Shy was flying.

Temple groaned as he rolled over to lie staring at the sky, arms out wide, the snow pleasantly cool against his bare neck—

'Uh!' He sat up, wincing at a range of stabbing pains, and stared wildly about.

A shallow canyon with walls of streaked stone and earth and patched snow, the road down the centre, the rest strewn with boulders and choked with thorny scrub. The wagon lay on its side a dozen strides away, one door ripped off and the other hanging wide, one of the uppermost wheels gone and the other still gently turning. The tongue had sheared through and the horses were still going, no doubt delighted by their sudden liberation, already a good way down the road and dwindling into the distance.

The sun was just finding its way into the bottom of the canyon, making gold glitter, a trail of treasure spilled from the back of the stricken wagon and for thirty strides or so behind. Shy sat in the midst of it.

He started running, immediately fell and took a mouthful of snow, spat out a tiny golden coin and floundered over. She was trying to stand, torn coat tangled in a thorn bush, and sank back down as he got there.

'My leg's fucked,' she forced through gritted teeth, hair matted and face streaked with blood.

'Can you use it?'

'No. Hence *fucked*.'

He hooked an arm around her, managed with an effort to get them both to standing, her on one good leg, him on two shaky ones. 'Got a plan yet?'

'Kill you and hide in your body?'

'Better than anything I've got.' He looked about the canyon sides for some means of escape, started tottering over to the most promising place with Shy hopping beside him, both of them wheezing with pain and effort. It might almost have been comical had he not known his erstwhile colleagues must be near. But he did know. So it wasn't.

'Sorry I got you into this,' she said.

'I got myself into this. A long time ago.' He grabbed at a trailing bush but it came free and tumbled hopelessly down in a shower of earth, most of which went straight into his mouth.

'Leave me and run,' said Shy.

'Tempting . . .' He cast about for another way up. 'But I already tried that and it didn't work out too well.' He picked at some roots, brought down some gravel, the slope as unreliable as he'd been down the years. 'I'm trying not to make the same mistakes over and over these days . . .'

'How's that going for you?' she grunted.

'Right now it could be better.' The lip was only a couple of strides above his hand but it might as well have been a mile distant, there was no—

'Hey, hey, Temple!'

A single horseman came up the road at an easy walk, between the two ruts the wagon-wheels had left. Everyone else was thinner than when they left Starikland, but somehow not Brachio. He stopped not far away, leaning his bulk over his saddle horn and speaking in Styrian. 'That was quite a chase. Didn't think you had it in you.'

'Captain Brachio! What a pleasure!' Temple twisted around to put himself between Shy and the mercenary. A pathetic effort at gallantry, he was almost embarrassed to have made it. He felt her take his hand,

414

though, fingers sticky with blood, and was grateful, even if it was just to keep her balance.

Some more earth slid down behind and, looking around, he saw another rider above them, loaded flatbow loose in his hands. Temple realised his knees were shaking. God, he wished he was a brave man. If only for these last few moments.

Brachio nudged his horse lazily forward. 'I told the Old Man you couldn't be trusted, but he always had a blind spot for you.'

'Well, good lawyers are hard to find.' Temple stared around as though the means of their salvation might suddenly present themselves. They did not. He struggled to put some confidence in his creaking voice. 'Take us back to Cosca and maybe I can tidy this up—'

'Not this time.' Brachio drew his heavy sword, steel scraping, and Shy's fingers tightened around Temple's. She might not have understood the words but a naked blade never needs translating. 'Cosca's on his way, and I think he'll want everything tidy when he gets here. That means you dead, in case you were wondering.'

'Yes, I'd gathered,' croaked Temple. 'When you drew the sword. But thanks for the explanation.'

'Least I could do. I like you, Temple. I always have. You're easy to like.'

'But you're going to kill me anyway.'

'You say it like there's a choice.'

'I blame myself. As always. Just . . .' Temple licked his lips, and twisted his hand free of Shy's, and looked Brachio in his tired eyes, and tried to conjure up that earnestness. 'Maybe you could let the girl go? You could do that.'

Brachio frowned at Shy for a moment, who'd sunk back against the bank and was sitting silent. 'I'd like to. Believe it or not, I get no pleasure from killing women.'

'Of course not. You wouldn't want to take a thing like that back to your daughters.' Brachio worked his shoulders uncomfortably, knives shifting across his belly, and Temple felt a crack there that he could work at. He dropped on his knees in the snow, and he clasped his hands, and he sent up a silent prayer. Not for him, but for Shy. She actually deserved saving. 'It was all my idea. All me. I talked her into it. You know I'm awful that way, and she's gullible as a child, poor thing. Let her go. You'll feel better about it in the long run. Let her go. I'm begging you.'

Brachio raised his brows. 'That is quite moving, in fact. I was expecting you to blame her for the whole thing.'

'I'm somewhat moved,' agreed the man with the flatbow.

'We're none of us monsters.' And Brachio reached up and dabbed some tears from his leaky eye. The other one stayed dry, however. 'But she tried to rob us, whoever's idea it was, and the trouble her father caused . . . No. Cosca wouldn't understand. And it isn't as if you'll be repaying the favour, is it?'

'No,' muttered Temple. 'No, I wouldn't have thought so.' He floundered for something to say that might at least delay the inevitable. That might borrow him a few more moments. Just an extra breath. Strange. It was hardly as though he was enjoying himself all that much. 'Would it help if I said I was very drunk?'

Brachio shook his head. 'We all were.'

'Shitty childhood?'

'Mummy used to leave me in a cupboard.'

'Shitty adulthood?'

'Whose isn't?' Brachio nudged his horse forward again, its great shadow falling over Temple. 'Stand up, then, eh? I'd rather get it done quick.' He worked the shoulder of his sword-arm. 'Neither one of us wants me hacking away at you.'

Temple looked back at Shy, sitting there bloody and exhausted. 'What did he say?' she asked.

He gave a tired shrug. She gave a tired nod. It looked like even she had run out of fight. He blinked up at the sky as he got to his feet. An unremarkable, greyish sky. If there was a God, He was a humourless banker. A bloodless pedant, crossing off His debts in some cosmic ledger. All take their loan and, in the end, all must repay.

'Nothing personal,' said Brachio.

Temple closed his eyes, the sun shining pink through the lids. 'Hard not to take it personally.'

'I guess so.'

There was a rattling sound. Temple winced. He'd always dreamed of facing death with some dignity, the way Kahdia had. But dignity requires practice and Temple had none. He couldn't stop himself cringing. He wondered how much it would hurt, having your head cut off. Did you feel it? He heard a couple of clicks, and a grunt, and he cringed even more. How could you not feel it? Brachio's horse snuffled, pawing the ground, then the metallic clatter of a sword falling.

Temple prised one eye open. Brachio was looking down, surprised. There was an arrow through his neck and two others in his chest. He opened his mouth and blathered blood down his shirt, then slowly tipped from the saddle and crumpled face down on the ground next to Temple's boots, one foot still tangled in its stirrup.

Temple looked around. The man with the flatbow had vanished. His mount stood peacefully riderless at the top of the canyon wall.

'Here's a surprise,' croaked Shy.

A horse was approaching. In the saddle, hands crossed over the horn and the breeze stirring her short hair about her sharp-boned frown, sat Corlin. 'A pleasant one, I hope.'

'Little late.' Shy took hold of Temple's limp hand and used it to drag herself wincing up. 'But I guess we'll live with the timing.'

Horses appeared at the valley sides, and riders on the horses, perhaps three dozen of them, all well armed and some armoured. There were men and women, old and young, some faces Temple recognised from Crease, others strange to him. Three or four held half-drawn bows. They weren't pointed right at Temple. But they weren't pointed far away either. Some had forearms showing, and on the forearms were tattoos. *Doom to the Union. Death to the King. Rise up!*

'Rebels,' whispered Temple.

'You always did have a talent for stating the obvious.' Corlin slid from the saddle, kicked Brachio's boot from his stirrup and rolled his corpse over with her foot, leaving him goggling at the sky, fat face caked with dirt. 'That arm all right?'

Shy pulled her ripped sleeve back with her teeth to show a long cut, still seeping, blood streaked down to her fingertips. The sight of it made Temple's knees weak. Or even weaker. It was a surprise he was still standing, all in all. 'Bit sore,' she said.

Corlin pulled a roll of bandage from her pocket. 'Feels as if we've been here before, doesn't it?' She turned her blue, blue eyes on Temple as she started to unroll it around Shy's arm. She never seemed to blink. Temple would have found that unnerving if he'd had any nerves left. 'Where's my uncle?'

'In Beacon,' he croaked, as the rebels dismounted and began to lead their horses down the steep sides of the canyon, scattering dirt.

'Alive?'

'We don't know,' said Shy. 'They found out he was Conthus.'

'That so?' Corlin took Temple's limp hand and clamped it around Shy's wrist. 'Hold that.' She started to unbutton her coat.

'Lamb went back for him but they ran into some trouble. That's when we took the wagon. Sweet stampeded the horses, to give them some . . . time . . .'

Corlin shrugged off her coat and tossed it over her horse's neck, her sinewy arms blue with letters, words, slogans from shoulder to wrist.

'I'm Conthus,' she said, pulling a knife from her belt.

There was a pause.

'Oh,' said Temple.

'Ah,' said Shy.

Corlin, or Conthus, cut the bandage with one quick movement then pushed a pin through it. Her narrowed eyes moved towards the wreckage of the wagon, calmly taking in the gold twinkling in the snow. 'Looks like you came into some money.'

Temple cleared his throat. 'Little bit. Lawyers' fees have been shooting up lately—'

'We could use a couple of horses.' Shy twisted her bandaged forearm free of Temple's grip and worked the fingers. 'Nicomo Cosca won't be far behind us.'

'You just can't stay clear of trouble, can you?' Corlin patted Brachio's mount on the neck. 'We have two spare, as it goes. But it'll cost.'

'Don't suppose you feel like haggling?'

'With you? I don't think so. Let's just call it a generous contribution to the liberation of Starikland.' She jerked her head at her fellows and they hurried forward, sacks and saddlebags at the ready. One big lad nearly knocked Temple over with a shoulder in his hurry. Some started rooting on hands and knees, scooping up the gold scattered about the wreck. Others wriggled inside and soon could be heard smashing the gratings and breaking open the boxes to steal the dragon's hoard for a third time that week.

A few moments ago, Temple had been rich beyond the hopes of avarice, but since a few moments later he had been on the point of losing his head, it felt rude to complain about this outcome.

'A noble cause,' he whispered. 'Do help yourselves.'

Times Change

The Mayor stood in her accustomed position at her balcony, hands at their familiar, polished places on the rail, and watched Curnsbick's men hard at work on his new manufactory. The huge frame already towered over the amphitheatre, the new over the ancient, cobwebbed with scaffolding on the site Papa Ring's Whitehouse had once occupied. That had been a repugnant building in every sense. A building towards which for years she had directed all her hatred, cunning and fury. And how she missed it.

Never mind Mayor, she had been Queen of the Far Country when Ring stopped swinging, but no sooner had she clutched the garland of triumph than it had withered to wretched stalks. The violence and the fires drove off half the population. Whispers mounted that the gold was running dry. Then word came of a strike to the south near Hope and suddenly people were pouring out of Crease by the hundred. With no one left to fight she had dismissed most of her men. Disgruntled, they had dabbled in arson on their way out of town and burned down a good part of what remained. Even so there were buildings empty, and no rents coming in. Lots in town and claims in the hills that men had killed for lost all value overnight. The gaming halls and the bawdy houses were mostly boarded up, only a trickle of passing custom below her in the Church of Dice, where once she had coined money as though she ran a mint.

Crease was her sole dominion. And it was next to worthless.

Sometimes the Mayor felt she had spent her life building things, with painstaking sweat and blood and effort, only to watch them destroyed. Through her own hubris, and others' vindictiveness, and the fickle thrashings of that blind thug fate. Fleeing one debacle after another. Abandoning even her name, in the end. Even now, she always kept a bag packed. She drained her glass and poured herself another.

That's what courage is. Taking your disappointments and your failures, your guilt and your shame, all the wounds received and inflicted, and sinking them in the past. Starting again. Damning yesterday and facing tomorrow with your head held high. Times change. It's those that see it coming, and plan for it, and change themselves to suit that prosper. And so she had struck her deal with Curnsbick, and split her hard-won little empire again without so much as a harsh word spoken.

By that time his small manufactory, which had looked pretty damn big when he converted it from an empty brothel, was already belching black smoke from its two tin chimneys, then from three brick ones, which smogged the whole valley on a still day and chased the few whores still plying a threadbare trade off their balconies and back indoors.

By the looks of it, his new manufactory would have chimneys twice the size. The biggest building within a hundred miles. She hardly even knew what the place was for, except that it had something to do with coal. The hills had hidden little gold in the end but they were surrendering the black stuff in prodigious quantities. As the shadows of the manufactory lengthened, the Mayor had started to wonder whether she might have been better off with Ring across the street. Him, at least, she had understood. But Ring was gone, and the world they had fought over was gone with him, drifted away like smoke on the breeze. Curnsbick was bringing men in to build, and dig, and stoke his furnaces. Cleaner, calmer, more sober men than Crease was used to, but they still needed to be entertained.

'Times change, eh?' She held her drink up in salute to no one. To Papa Ring, maybe. Or to herself, when she still had a name. She caught something through the distorting window of her glass, and lowered it. Two riders were coming down the main street, looking as if they'd been going hard, one cradling an injured arm. It was that girl Shy South. Her and Temple, the lawyer.

The Mayor frowned. After twenty years dodging catastrophes she could smell danger at a thousand paces, and her nose was tickling something fierce as those two riders reined in at her front door. Temple slithered from his horse, fell in the mud, stumbled up and helped down Shy, who was limping badly.

The Mayor drained her glass and sucked the liquor from her teeth. As she crossed her rooms, buttoning her collar tight, she glanced at the cupboard where she kept that packed bag, wondering if today would be its day.

Some people are trouble. Nicomo Cosca was one. Lamb was another. Then there are people who, without being troublesome in themselves, always manage to let trouble in when they open your door. Temple, she had always suspected, was one of those. Looking at him now as she swept down the stairs, leaning against the counter in her sadly deserted gaming hall, she was sure of it. His clothes were torn and bloodied and caked in dust, his expression wild, his chest heaving.

'You look as if you've come in a hurry,' she said.

He glanced up, the slightest trace of guilt in his eye. 'You might say that.'

'And ran into some trouble on the way.'

'You might say that, too. Might I ask you for a drink?'

'Can you pay for it?'

'No.'

'I'm no charity. What are you doing here?'

He took a moment to prepare and then produced, like a magician's trick, an expression of intense earnestness. It put her instantly on her guard. 'I have nowhere else to go.'

'Are you sure you've tried hard enough?' She narrowed her eyes. 'Where's Cosca?'

He swallowed. 'Funny you should ask.'

'I'm not laughing.'

'No.'

'So it's not funny?'

'No.' He visibly abandoned earnestness and settled for simple fear. 'I would guess he's no more than a few hours behind us.'

'He's coming here?'

'I expect so.'

'With all his men?'

'Those that remain.'

'Which is how many?'

'Some died in the mountains, a lot deserted—'

'How many?'

'I would guess at least a hundred still.'

The Mayor's nails dug at her palms as she clenched her fists. 'And the Inquisitor?'

'Very much present, as far as I am aware.'

421

'What do they want?'

'The Inquisitor wants to torture his way to a brighter tomorrow.'

'And Cosca?'

'Cosca wants a fortune in ancient gold that he stole from the Dragon People, and that . . .' Temple picked nervously at his frayed collar. 'I stole from him.'

'And where is this twice-stolen fortune now?'

Temple grimaced. 'Stolen. The woman Corlin took it. She turns out to be the rebel leader Conthus. It's been a day of surprises,' he finished, lamely.

'So . . . it . . . appears,' whispered the Mayor. 'Where is Corlin?'

Temple gave that helpless shrug of which he was so fond. 'In the wind.'

The Mayor was less fond of that shrug. 'I have not the men to fight them,' she said. 'I have not the money to pay them off. I have no ancient hoard for Nicomo *bloody* Cosca and for damn sure no brighter tomorrow for Inquisitor *fucking* Lorsen! Is there any chance your *head* will pacify them?'

Temple swallowed. 'I fear not.'

'So do I. But in the absence of a better suggestion I may have to make the offer.'

'As it happens . . .' Temple licked his lips. 'I have a suggestion.'

The Mayor took a fistful of Temple's shirt and dragged him close. 'Is it a good one? Is it the best suggestion I ever heard?'

'I profoundly doubt it, but, circumstances being what they are . . . do you have that treaty?'

'I'm tired,' said Corporal Bright, glancing unimpressed at the piled-up hovels of Crease.

'Aye,' grunted Old Cog in reply. He kept having to force his eyelids up, they were that heavy from last night's revelry, then the terror o' the stampede, then a healthy trek on foot and a hard ride to follow.

'And dirty,' said Bright.

'Aye.' The smoke of last night's fires, and the rolling through the brush running from stomping horses, then the steady showering of dirt from the hooves of the galloping mounts in front.

'And sore,' said Bright.

'No doubt.' Last night's revelry again, and the riding again, and Cog's arm still sore from the fall in the mountains and the old wound in his arse always aching. You wouldn't think an arrow in the arse would curse you all your days but there it is. Arse armour. That was the key to the mercenary life.

'It's been a testing campaign,' said Cog.

'If you can apply the word to half a year's hard riding, hard drinking, killing and theft.'

'What else would y'apply it to?'

Bright considered that a moment. 'True. Have you seen a worse, though? You been with Cosca for years.'

'The North was colder. Kadir was dustier. That last Styrian mess was bloodier. Full-on revolt in the Company at one point.' He shifted the manacles at his belt. 'Gave up on using chains and had to go with hangings for every infraction. But all considered, no. I ain't seen a worse.' Cog sniffed up some snot, worked it thoughtfully about his mouth, gathering a good sense of its consistency, then leaned back and spat it arcing through a hovel's open window.

'Never saw a man could spit like you,' said Bright.

'It's all about putting the practice in,' said Cog. 'Like anything else.'

'Keep moving!' roared Cosca over his shoulder, up at the head of the column. If you could call eighteen men a column. Still, they were the lucky ones. The rest of the Company were most likely still slogging across the plateau on foot. The ones that were still alive, anyway.

Bright's thoughts were evidently marching in the same direction. 'Lost a lot o' good men these last few weeks.'

'Good might be stretching it.'

'You know what I mean. Can't believe Brachio's gone.'

'He's a loss.'

'And Jubair.'

'Can't say I'm sorry that black bastard's head ain't attached no more.'

'He was a strange one, right enough, but a good ally in a tough corner.'

'I'd rather stay out o' the tough corners.'

Bright looked sideways at him, then dropped his horse back a stretch so the others up front wouldn't mark him. 'Couldn't agree more. I want to go home, is what I'm saying.'

'Where's home to men like us?'

'I want to go anywhere but here, then.'

Cog glanced about at the tangled mass of wood and ruins that was Crease, never a place to delight a cultured fellow and less so than ever now by the looks of things, parts of it burned out and a lot of the rest near deserted. Those left looked like the ones who couldn't find a way to leave, or were too far gone to try. A beggar of truly surpassing wretchedness hobbled after them for a few strides with his hand out before falling in the gutter. On the other side of the street a toothless old woman laughed, and laughed, and laughed. Mad. Or heard something real funny. Mad seemed likelier.

'I take your point,' said Cog. 'But we've got that money to find.' Even though he weren't entirely sure he wanted to find it. All his life he'd been clutching at every copper he could get his warty fingers around. Then suddenly he had so much gold none of it seemed worth anything any more. So much the world seemed to make no sense in the light of it.

'Didn't you keep a little back?'

'O' course. A little.' More than a little, in fact, the pouch under his armpit was heavy with coins. Not so much it made him sweat, but a tidy haul.

'We all did,' muttered Bright. 'So it's Cosca's money we're after really, ain't it?'

Cog frowned. 'There's the principle 'n all.'

'Principle? Really?'

'Can't let folks just up and rob you.'

'We robbed it ourselves, didn't we?' said Bright, an assertion Cog could by no means deny. 'I'm telling you, it's cursed. From the moment we laid our hands on it things have gone from shit to shitter.'

'No such thing as curses.'

'Tell it to Brachio and Jubair. How many of us set off from Starikland?'

'More'n four hundred, according to Friendly, and Friendly don't get a count wrong.'

'How many now?'

Cog opened his mouth, then closed it. The point was obvious to all.

'Exactly,' said Bright. 'Hang around out here much longer we'll be down to none.'

Cog sniffed, and grunted, and spat again, right into a first-floor window this time around. An artist has to challenge himself, after all. 'Been with Cosca a long time.'

'Times change. Look at this place.' Bright nodded towards the vacant hovels that a month or two before had boiled over with humanity. 'What's that stink, anyway?'

Cog wrinkled his nose. The place had always stunk, o' course, but that healthy, heartening stench of shit and low living that had always smelled like home to him. There was an acrid sort of a flavour on the air now, a pall of brownish smoke hanging over everything. 'Don't know. Can't say I care for it one bit.'

'I want to go home,' said Bright, miserably.

The column was coming to the centre of town now, in so far as the place had one. They were building something on one side of the muddy street, teetering scaffold and lumber stacked high. On the other side the Church of Dice still stood, where Cog had spent several very pleasant evenings a month or two before. Cosca held up his fist for a halt in front of it and with the help of Sergeant Friendly disentangled himself from the saddle and clambered stiffly down.

The Mayor stood waiting on the steps in a black dress buttoned to the neck. What a woman that was. A lady, Cog would almost have said, dusting the word off in the deepest recesses of his memory.

'General Cosca,' she said, smiling warmly. 'I did not think—'

'Don't pretend you're surprised!' he snapped.

'But I am. You come at a rather inopportune time, we are expecting—'

'Where is my gold?'

'I'm sorry?'

'By all means play the wide-eyed innocent. But we both know better. Where is my damned notary, then?'

'Inside, but—'

The Old Man shouldered past her and limped grumbling up the steps, Friendly, Sworbreck, and Captain Dimbik following.

The Mayor caught Lorsen's arm with a gentle hand. 'Inquisitor Lorsen, I must protest.'

He frowned back. 'My dear Lady Mayor, I've been protesting for months. Much good it has done me.'

Cosca had seemed heedless of the half dozen frowning thugs lounging on either side of the door. But Cog noted them well enough as he climbed the steps after the others, and from the worried look on Bright's face he did too. Might be that the Company had the numbers, and more coming across the plateau as fast as they could walk, but Cog didn't fancy fighting right then and there.

He didn't fancy fighting one bit.

*

Captain Dimbik straightened his uniform. Even if the front was crusted with dirt. Even if it was coming apart at the seams. Even if he no longer even belonged to any army, had no nation, fought for no cause or principle a sane man could believe in. Even if he was utterly lost and desperately concealing a bottomless hatred and pity for himself, even then.

Better straight than crooked.

The place had changed since last he visited. The gaming hall had been largely cleared to leave an expanse of creaking boards, the dice- and card-tables shifted against the walls, the women ushered away, the clients vanished. Only ten or so of the Mayor's thugs remained, notice-ably armed and scattered watchfully about under the empty alcoves in the walls, a man wiping glasses behind the long counter, and in the centre of the floor a single table, recently polished but still showing the stains of hard use. Temple sat there before a sheaf of papers, peculiarly unconcerned as he watched Dimbik's men tramp in to surround him.

Could you even call them men? Ragged and haggard beyond belief and their morale, never the highest, ebbed to a sucking nadir. Not that they had ever been such very promising examples of humanity. Dimbik had tried, once upon a time, to impose some discipline upon them. After his discharge from the army. After his disgrace. He remembered, dimly, as if seen through a room full of steam, that first day in uniform, so handsome in the mirror, puffed up on stories of derring-do, a bright career at his fingertips. He miserably straightened the greasy remnants again. How could he have sunk so low? Not even scum. Lackey to scum.

He watched the infamous Nicomo Cosca pace across the empty floor, bent spurs jingling, his eyes fixed upon Temple and his rat-like face locked in an expression of vengeful hatred. To the counter, he went, of course, where else? He took up a bottle, spat out its cork and swallowed a good quarter of the contents in one draught.

'So here he is!' grated the Old Man. 'The cuckoo in the nest! The serpent in the bosom! The . . . the . . .'

'Maggot in the shit?' suggested Temple.

'Why not, since you mention it? What did Verturio say? Never fear your enemies, but your friends, *always*. A wiser man than I, no doubt! I forgave you! *Forgave* you and how am I repaid? I hope you're taking notes, Sworbreck! You can prepare a little parable, perhaps, on the myth of redemption and the price of betrayal.' The author scrambled to produce his pencil as Cosca's grim smile faded to leave him simply grim. 'Where is my gold, Temple?'

'I don't have it.' The notary held up his sheaf of papers. 'But I do have this.'

'It better be valuable,' snapped Cosca, taking another swallow. Sergeant Friendly had wandered to one of the dice-tables and was sorting dice into piles, apparently oblivious to the escalating tension. Inquisitor Lorsen gave Dimbik a curt nod as he entered. Dimbik respectfully returned it, licked a finger and slicked his front hairs into position, wondering if the Inquisitor had been serious about securing him a new commission in the King's Own when they returned to Adua. Most likely not, but we all need pretty dreams to cling to. The hope of a second chance, if not the chance itself . . .

'It is a treaty.' Temple spoke loudly enough for the whole room to hear. 'Bringing Crease and the surrounding country into the Empire. I suspect his Radiance the Emperor will be less than delighted to find an armed party sponsored by the Union has encroached upon his territory.'

'I'll give you an encroachment you won't soon forget.' Cosca let his left hand rest on the hilt of his sword. 'Where the hell is my *gold*?'

With a draining inevitability, the atmosphere ratcheted towards bloodshed. Coats were flicked open, itchy fingers crept to ready grips, blades were loosened in sheaths, eyes were narrowed. Two of Dimbik's men eased the wedges from the triggers of their loaded flatbows. The glass-wiper had put a surreptitious hand on something beneath the counter, and Dimbik did not doubt it would have a point on the end. He watched all this with a helpless sense of mounting horror. He hated violence. It was the uniforms he'd become a soldier for. The epaulettes, and the marching, and the bands—

'Wait!' snapped Lorsen, striding across the room. Dimbik was relieved to see that someone in authority still had a grip on their reason. 'Superior Pike said most clearly there were to be no Imperial entanglements!' He snatched the treaty from Temple's hand. 'This expedition has been enough of a disaster without our starting a war!'

'You cannot mean to dignify this charade,' sneered Cosca. 'He lies for a living!'

'Not this time.' The Mayor glided into the room with another pair of her men, one of whom had lost an eye but in so doing gained considerably in menace. 'That document is endorsed by elected representatives of the townspeople of Crease and is fully binding.'

'I consider it my best work.' If he was lying, Temple was even more smug about it than usual. 'It makes use of the principle of inviolate ownership enshrined at the formation of the Union, refers back to the earliest Imperial claim on the territory, and is even fully binding under mining law. I feel confident you will find it incontestable in any court.'

'Alas, my lawyer departed my service under something of a cloud,' forced Cosca through gritted teeth. 'If we contest your treaty it will have to be in the court of sharp edges.'

Lorsen snorted. 'It's not even signed.' And he tossed the document flapping onto the table.

Cosca narrowed his bloodshot eyes. 'What if it were? You of all people should know, Temple, that the only laws that matter are those backed by force. The nearest Imperial troops are weeks away.'

Temple's smile only widened. 'Oh, they're a little closer than that.'

The doors were suddenly flung wide and, under the disbelieving eyes of the heavily armed assembly, soldiers tramped into the Church of Dice. Imperial troops, in gilded greaves and breastplates, with broad-bladed spears in their fists and short-bladed swords at their hips, with round shields marked with the hand of Juvens, and the five thunderbolts, and the sheaf of wheat, and all looking as if they had marched straight from antiquity itself.

'What the *shit* . . .' muttered Cosca.

In the centre of this bizarre honour guard strode an old man, his short beard white as snow, his gilded helm adorned with a tall plume. He walked slowly, deliberately, as though it caused him pain, yet perfectly erect. He looked neither to the left nor to the right, as if Cosca and his men, the Mayor and her men, Temple and Lorsen and everyone else were all insects utterly beneath his notice. As if he were a god obliged for this moment to walk among the filth of humanity. The mercenaries edged nervously away, repelled not so much by fear of the Emperor's legions as by this old man's aura of untouchable command.

The Mayor prostrated herself at his feet in a rustling of skirts. 'Legate Sarmis,' she breathed. 'Your Excellency, we are inexpressibly honoured by your presence . . .'

Dimbik's jaw dropped. Legate Sarmis, who had crushed the Emperor's enemies at the Third Battle of Darmium and ordered every prisoner put to death. Who across the Circle of the World was famous for his military brilliance and infamous for his ruthlessness. Who they had all supposed was many hundreds of miles away to the south. Standing before them now, in the flesh. Dimbik somehow felt he had seen that magnificent face before, somewhere. On a coin, perhaps.

'You *are* honoured,' pronounced the old man, 'for my presence is the presence of his Radiance, the Emperor, Goltus the First.' The Legate's body might have been withered by age but his voice, seasoned with the slightest Imperial accent, was that of a colossus, booming from the lofty rafters, as awe-inspiring as deep thunder close at hand. Dimbik's knees, always weakened by authority, positively itched to bend.

'Where is the instrument?' intoned the Legate.

The Mayor rose and abjectly indicated the table, on which Temple had arranged pen and document. Sarmis grunted as he stiffly leaned over it.

'I sign with the name Goltus, for this hand is the hand of the Emperor.' With a flourish that would have been outrageous under any other circumstances, he signed. 'And so it is done. You stand now upon Imperial soil, and are Imperial subjects under the protection of his Radiance! Warmed by his bounty. Humbled beneath his law.' The ringing echoes faded and he frowned, as though he had only just become aware of the mercenaries. His merciless gaze swept over them and Dimbik felt a chill to his very core.

Sarmis formed his words with fearsome precision. 'Who are these . . . people?'

Even Cosca had been silenced by the theatre of the moment, but now, much to everyone's dismay, he found his voice again. It sounded cracked, weak, almost ridiculous after the Legate's, but he found it nonetheless, waving his half-emptied bottle for added emphasis. 'I am Nicomo Cosca, Captain General of the Company of the Gracious Hand, and—'

'And we were just leaving!' snapped Lorsen, seizing Cosca's elbow.

The Old Man refused to be moved. 'Without my gold? I hardly think so!'

Dimbik did not care in the least for the way things were going. Probably no one did. There was a gentle rattle as Friendly threw his dice. The Mayor's one-eyed thug suddenly had a knife in his hand. That did not strike him as a positive development.

'Enough!' hissed Lorsen, halfway now to wrestling the Old Man by his armpit. 'When we reach Starikland every man will get a bonus! Every man!'

Sworbreck was crouching against the counter, apparently trying to vanish into the floor while madly scribbling in his notebook. Sergeant

Cog was edging towards the doorway, and he had good instincts. The odds had changed, and not for the better. Dimbik had begged Cosca to wait for more men, the old fool, but he might as well have argued with the tide. And now all it would take was a loose trigger and there would be a bloodbath.

Dimbik held one hand up to the flatbowmen as to a skittish horse. 'Easy . . .'

'I shit on your bonus!' snarled Cosca, struggling with scant dignity to shake Lorsen off. 'Where's my fucking gold?'

The Mayor was backing away, one pale hand against her chest, but Sarmis only appeared to grow in stature, his white brows drawing inwards. 'What is this impertinence?'

'I can only apologise,' blathered Temple, 'we—'

Sarmis struck him across the face with the back of his hand and knocked him to the floor. 'Kneel when you address me!'

Dimbik's mouth was dry, the pulse pounding in his head. That he would have to die for Cosca's absurd ambitions seemed horribly unfair. His sash had already given its life for the dubious cause and that seemed more than sacrifice enough. Dimbik had once been told that the best soldiers are rarely courageous. That was when he had been sure it was the career for him. He started to slide one hand towards his sword, far from sure what he would do with it once it reached the hilt.

'I will not be disappointed again!' shrieked the Old Man, struggling to reach his own hilt with Lorsen restraining him and a half-full bottle still clutched in his other fist. 'Men of the Gracious Hand! Draw your—'

'No!' Lorsen's voice barked out like a slamming door. 'Captain General Dimbik, take the traitor Nicomo Cosca under arrest!'

There was the very slightest pause.

Probably no more than a breath, for all it felt far longer. While everyone assessed the odds and the outcomes. While everyone judged just where the shifting power sat. While everything dropped into place in Dimbik's mind and, no doubt, the minds of every other person present. Just a breath, and everything was rearranged.

'Of course, Inquisitor,' said Dimbik. The two flatbowmen raised their weapons to point them at Cosca. They looked slightly surprised that they were doing it, but they did it nonetheless.

Friendly looked up from his dice and frowned slightly. 'Two,' he said.

Cosca gazed slack-jawed at Dimbik. 'So that's how it is?' The bottle dropped from his nerveless fingers, clattered to the floor and rolled away, dribbling liquor. 'That's how it is, is it?'

'How else would it be?' said Dimbik. 'Sergeant Cog?'

That venerable soldier stepped forward, for once, with an impressive degree of military snap. 'Sir?'

'Please disarm Master Cosca, Master Friendly, and Master Sworbreck.'

'Place them in irons for the trip,' said Lorsen. 'They will face trial on our return.'

'Why me?' squeaked Sworbreck, eyes wide as saucers.

'Why not you?' Corporal Bright looked the author over and, finding no weapon, he jerked the pencil from his hand, tossed it on the floor and made great show of grinding it under his heel.

'Prisoner?' muttered Friendly. For some reason he had the faintest smile on his face as the manacles were snapped around his wrists.

'I'll be back!' snarled the Old Man, spraying spit over his shoulder as Cog dragged him wriggling away, empty scabbard flapping. 'Laugh while you can, because Nicomo Cosca always laughs last! I'll be revenged on the whole pack of you! I will not be disappointed again! I will—' The door swung shut upon him.

'Who was that drunkard?' asked Sarmis.

'Nicomo Cosca, your Excellency,' muttered Temple, still on his knees and with one hand pressed to his bloody mouth. 'Infamous soldier of fortune.'

The Legate grunted. 'Never heard of him.'

Lorsen placed one hand upon his breast and bowed low. 'Your Excellency, I pray that you accept my apologies for any and all inconveniences, trespasses and—'

'You have eight weeks to leave Imperial territory,' said Sarmis. 'Any of you found within our borders after that time will be buried alive.' He slapped dust from his breastplate. 'Have you such a thing as a bath?'

'Of course, your Excellency,' murmured the Mayor, virtually grovelling. 'We will do the very best we can.' She turned her eyes to Dimbik as she ushered the Legate towards the stairs. 'Get out,' she hissed.

The brand-new captain general was by no means reluctant to oblige. With the greatest of relief, he and his men spilled into the street and prepared their tired mounts for the trip out of town. Cosca had been manhandled into his saddle, sparse hair in disarray, gazing down at Dimbik with a look of stunned upset.

'I remember when I took you on,' he muttered. 'Drunk, and spurned,

431

and worthless. I graciously offering my hand.' He attempted to mime the offering of his hand but was prevented by his manacles.

Dimbik smoothed down his hair. 'Times change.'

'Here is justice, eh, Sworbreck? Here is loyalty! Take a good look, all of you, this is where charity gets you! The fruits of polite behaviour and thought for your fellow man!'

'For pity's sake, someone shut him up,' snapped Lorsen, and Cog leaned from his saddle and stuffed a pair of socks in Cosca's mouth.

Dimbik leaned closer to the Inquisitor. 'It might be best if we were to kill them. Cosca still has friends among the rest of the Company, and—'

'A point well made and well taken, but no. Look at him.' The infamous mercenary did indeed present a most miserable picture, sitting hunched on horseback with hands manacled behind him, his torn and muddied cloak all askew, the gilt on his breastplate all peeling and rust showing beneath, his wrinkled skin blotchy with rash, one of Cog's socks dangling from his mouth. 'Yesterday's man if ever there was one. And in any case, my dear Captain General . . .' Dimbik stood tall and straightened his uniform at the title. He very much enjoyed the ring of it. 'We need someone to blame.'

In spite of the profound pain in his stomach, the ache in his legs, the sweat spreading steadily under his armour, he remained resplendently erect upon the balcony, rigid as a mighty oak, until long after the mercenaries had filed away into the haze. Would the great Legate Sarmis, ruthless commander, undefeated general, right hand of the Emperor, feared throughout the Circle of the World, have allowed himself to display the least trace of weakness, after all?

It felt an age of agony before the Mayor stepped out onto the balcony with Temple behind her, and spoke the longed for words, 'They're gone.'

Every part of him sagged and he gave a groan from the very bottom of his being. He removed that ridiculous helmet, wiping the sweat from his forehead with a trembling hand. He could scarcely recall having donned a more absurd costume in all his many years in the theatre. No garlands of flowers flung by an adoring audience, perhaps, as had littered the broad stage of Adua's House of Drama after his every appearance as the First of the Magi, but his satisfaction was no less complete.

'I told you I had one more great performance in me!' said Lestek.

'And so you did,' said the Mayor.

'You both provided able support, though, for amateurs. I daresay you have a future in the theatre.'

'Did you have to hit me?' asked Temple, probing at his split lip.

'Someone had to,' muttered the Mayor.

'Ask yourself rather, would the terrible Legate Sarmis have struck you, and blame him for your pains,' said Lestek. 'A performance is all in the details, my boy, all in the details! One must inhabit the role entirely. Which occurs to me, do thank my little legion before they disperse, it was an ensemble effort.'

'For five carpenters, three bankrupt prospectors, a barber and a drunk, they made quite an honour guard,' said Temple.

'That drunk scrubbed up surprisingly well,' said Lestek.

'A good find,' added the Mayor.

'It really worked?' Shy South had limped up to lean against the door frame.

'I told you it would,' said Temple.

'But you obviously didn't believe it.'

'No,' he admitted, peering up at the skies. 'There really must be a God.'

'Are you sure they'll believe it?' asked the Mayor. 'Once they've joined up with the rest of their Company and had time to think it over?'

'Men believe what they want to,' said Temple. 'Cosca's done. And those bastards want to go home.'

'A victory for culture over barbarity!' said Lestek, flicking the plume on the helmet.

'A victory for law over chaos,' said Temple, fanning himself with his worthless treaty.

'A victory for lying,' said the Mayor, 'and only by the narrowest of margins.'

Shy South shrugged and said, with her talent for simplicity, 'A win's a win.'

'All too true!' Lestek took a long breath through his nose and, even with the pain, even though he knew he did not have long left, perhaps because he knew it, he breathed out with the deepest fulfilment. 'As a young man I found happy endings cloying but, call me soppy, with age, I have come to appreciate them more and more.'

The Cost

Shy scooped up water and splashed it on her face, and groaned at the cold of it, just this side of ice. She worked her fingertips into her sore eyelids, and her aching cheeks, and her battered mouth. Stayed there, bent over the basin, her faint reflection sent scattering by the drops from her face. The water was pink with blood. Hard to say where from exactly. The last few months had left her beaten as a prizefighter. Just without the prize.

There was the long rope-burn coiling around one forearm and the new cut down the other, blood spotted through the bandage. Her hands were ripped up front and back, crack-nailed and scab-knuckled. She picked at the scar under her ear, a keepsake from that Ghost out on the plains. He'd almost got the whole ear to remember her by. She felt the lumps and scabs on her scalp, the nicks on her face, some of them she couldn't even remember getting. She hunched her shoulders and wriggled her spine and all the countless sores and grazes and bruises niggled at her like a choir of ugly little voices.

She looked down into the street and watched the children for a moment. Majud had found them some new clothes – dark suit and shirt for Pit, green dress with lace at the sleeves for Ro. Better than Shy had ever been able to buy them. They might've passed for some rich man's children if it hadn't been for their shaved heads, the dark fuzz just starting to grow back. Curnsbick was pointing to his vast new building, talking with big, enthusiastic gestures, Ro watching and listening solemnly, taking it all in, Pit kicking a stone about the mud.

Shy sniffed, and swallowed, and splashed more water on her face. Couldn't be crying if her eyes were wet already, could she? She should've been leaping with joy. In spite of the odds, the hardships, the dangers, she'd got them back.

But all she could think of was the cost.

The people killed. A few she'd miss and a lot she wouldn't. Some she'd even have called evil, but no one's evil to themselves, are they? They were still people dead, could do no good now, could make no amends and right no wrongs, people who'd taken a lifetime to make, plucked out from the world and turned to mud. Sangeed and his Ghosts. Papa Ring and his crooks. Waerdinur and his Dragon People. Leef left under the dirt out on the plains, and Grega Cantliss doing the hanged man's dance, and Brachio with the arrows in him, and—

She stuck her face in the cloth and rubbed, hard, like she could rub them all away, but they were stuck tight to her. Tattooed into her sure as the rebel slogans into Corlin's arms.

Was it her fault? Had she set it all rolling when she came out here like the kicked pebble that starts the landslide? Or was it Cantliss' fault, or Waerdinur's, or Lamb's? Was it everyone's? Her head hurt from trying to pull apart the tapestry of everything happened and follow her own nasty little thread through it, sifting for blame like a fevered miner dredging at a stream-bed. No point picking at it any more than at a scab. But still, now it was behind her, she couldn't stop looking back.

She limped to the bed and sat with a groaning of old springs, arms around herself, wincing and twitching at flashes of things happened like they were happening now.

Cantliss smashing her head against a table leg. Her knife sliding into flesh. Grunting in her face. Things she'd had to do. Wrestling with a crazy Ghost. Leef without his ears. Sangeed's head coming off, thud. It had been them or her. Looking down at that girl she'd shot, not much older'n Ro. Arrow in a horse and the rider tumbling. No choice, she'd had no choice. Lamb flinging her against the wall, Waerdinur's skull split, click, and she was flying from the wagon, and over, and over, and over—

She jerked her head up at a knock, wiped her eyes on her bandage. 'Who's there?' Doing her best to sound like it was any other morning.

'Your lawyer.' Temple swung the door open, that earnest look on his face which she could never quite be sure was genuine. 'Are you all right?'

'I've had easier years.'

'Anything I can do?'

'Guess it's a little late to ask you to keep that wagon on the road.'

'A little.' He came and sat down on the bed next to her. Didn't feel uncomfortable. You go through what they'd been through together, maybe uncomfortable goes off the menu. 'The Mayor wants us gone. She says we're bad luck.'

'Hard to argue with her. I'm surprised she hasn't killed you.'

'I suppose she still might.'

'Just need to wait a little longer.' Shy grunted as she wormed her foot into her boot, trying to work out how bad the ankle hurt. Bad enough she stopped trying. 'Just 'til Lamb comes back.'

There was a silence then. A silence in which Temple didn't say, 'Do you really think he's coming back?' Instead he just nodded, as if Lamb coming was as sure as tomorrow, and she was grateful for that much. 'Then where are you heading?'

'That's a question.' New lives out west didn't look much different to the old ones. No short cuts to riches, leastways, or none a sane woman might want to take. And it was no place for children neither. She'd never thought farming would look like the comfortable option, but now she shrugged. 'The Near Country for me, I reckon. It's no easy life but I've spotted nothing easier.'

'I hear Dab Sweet and Crying Rock are putting together a Fellowship for the trip back. Majud's going along, aiming to make some deals in Adua. Lord Ingelstad too.'

'Any Ghosts turn up his wife can frown 'em to death.'

'She's staying. I hear she bought Camling's Hostelry for a song.'

'Good for her.'

'The rest will be heading east within the week.'

'Now? 'Fore the weather breaks?'

'Sweet says now's the time, before the meltwater swells the rivers and the Ghosts get tetchy again.'

She took a long breath. Could've done with a year or two in bed but life hadn't often served her what she ordered. 'Might be I'll sign up.'

Temple looked across from under his brows. Nervous, almost. 'Maybe . . . I'll tag on?'

'Can't stop you, can I?'

'Would you want to?'

She thought about that. 'No. Might need someone to ride drag. Or jump out of a window. Or drive a wagon full of gold off a road.'

He puffed himself up. 'As it happens, I am expert in all three. I'll talk to Sweet and let him know we'll be joining up. I suppose it's possible he won't value my skills as highly as you do, though . . . I might have to buy my way in.'

They looked at each other for a moment. 'You coming up a little short?'

'You didn't exactly give me time to pack. I've nothing but the clothes I'm wearing.'

'Lucky for you I'm always willing to help out.' She reached into her pocket and drew out a few of the ancient coins she'd taken while the wagon sped across the plateau. 'Will that cover it?'

'I'd say so.' He took them between finger and thumb but she didn't let go.

'Reckon that's about two hundred marks you owe.'

He stared at her. 'Are you trying to upset me?'

'I can do that without trying.' And she let go the coins.

'I suppose a person should stick to what they're good at.' He smiled, and flicked one of the coins spinning up and snatched it from the air. 'Seems I'm at my best in debt.'

'Tell you what.' She grabbed a bottle from the table by her bed and wedged it in her shirt pocket. 'I'll pay you a mark to help me downstairs.'

Outside a sleety drizzle had set in, falling brown around Curnsbick's belching chimneys, his workmen struggling in the mush on the far side of the street. Temple helped her to the rail and she leaned against it, watching. Funny thing. She didn't want to let go of him.

'I'm bored,' said Pit.

'One day, young man, you will learn what a luxury it is to be bored.' Temple offered him his hand. 'Why not help me seek out that noted scout and frontiersman, Dab Sweet? There may even be gingerbread in it for you. I have recently come into some money.'

'All right.' Temple lifted the boy onto his shoulders and they set off down the rattling porches at half a jog, Pit laughing as he bounced.

He had a touch with the children, had Temple. More than she had, now, it seemed. Shy hopped to the bench against the front of the house and dropped onto it, stretched her hurt leg out in front of her and eased back. She grunted as she let her muscles go soft by slow degrees, and finally pulled the cork from her bottle with that echoing *thwop* that sets your mouth watering. Oh, the simple joy of doing nothing. Thinking nothing. She reckoned she could allow herself a rest.

It had been hard work, the last few months.

She lowered that bottle, looking up the street, liquor burning at the cuts in her mouth in a way that wasn't entirely unpleasant. There was a rider coming through the murk of smoke and drizzle. A particularly slouching rider coming at a slow walk, taking shape as he came closer – big, and old, and battered. His coat was torn, and dirtied, and ash-smeared. He'd lost his hat, short scrub of grey hair matted with blood and rain, face streaked with dirt, mottled with bruise, scabbed and grazed and swollen.

She took another sip from her bottle. 'I was wondering when you'd turn up.'

'You can stop,' grunted Lamb, stopping himself, his old horse looking like it didn't have another stride in it. 'The children all right?'

'They're as well as they were.'

'How about you?'

'Don't know when I was last all right, but I'm still just about alive. You?'

'Just about.' He clambered down from his horse, teeth gritted, not even bothering to tie it up. 'Say one thing for me . . . say I'm a survivor.' He held his ribs as he limped up the steps and onto the porch. He looked at the bench, then his sword, realised he wouldn't be able to sit with it on, started struggling with the buckle on the belt, his knuckles scabbed raw and two of the fingers he still had bandaged together and held stiff.

'By . . . the . . . fucking—'

'Here.' She leaned and flicked the buckle open and he pulled the sword off, belt dangling, cast about for somewhere to put it, then gave up and dropped it on the boards, sank down beside her and slowly, slowly stretched his legs out next to hers.

'Savian?' she asked.

Lamb shook his head a little. Like shaking it a lot would hurt him. 'Where's Cosca?'

'Gone.' She passed him the bottle. 'Temple lawyered him off.'

'Lawyered him?'

'With a little help from the Mayor and a final performance of remarkable quality.'

'Well, I never did.' Lamb took a long swig and wiped his scabbed lips, looking across the street at Curnsbick's manufactory. A couple of doors down, above an old card-hall, they were hauling up a sign reading *Valint and Balk, Bankers*. Lamb took another swallow. 'Times sure are changing.'

'Feel left out?'

He rolled one eye to her, half-swollen shut and all blown and blood-shot, and offered the bottle back. 'For a while now.'

They sat there, looking at each other, like two survivors of an avalanche. 'What happened, Lamb?'

He opened his mouth, as if he was thinking about where to start, then just shrugged, looking even more tired and hurt than she did. 'Does it matter?'

If there's nothing needs saying, why bother? She lifted the bottle. 'No. I guess not.'

Last Words

'Just like old times, eh?' said Sweet, grinning at the snow-patched landscape.

'Colder,' said Shy, wriggling into her new coat.

'Few more scars,' said Lamb, wincing as he rubbed gently at the pinked flesh around one of his face's recent additions.

'Even bigger debts,' said Temple, patting his empty pockets.

Sweet chuckled. 'Bunch o' bloody gripers. Still alive, ain't you, and found your children, and got the Far Country spread out ahead? I'd call that a fair result.'

Lamb frowned off towards the horizon. Shy grumbled her grudging agreement. Temple smiled to himself, and closed his eyes, and tipped his face back to let the sun shine pink through his lids. He was alive. He was free. His debts were deeper than ever, but still, a fair result. If there was a God, He was an indulgent father, who always forgave no matter how far His children strayed.

'Reckon our old friend Buckhorm's prospered,' said Lamb, as they crested a rise and looked down on his farmstead.

It had been carefully sited beside a stream, a set of solid-looking cabins arranged in a square, narrow windows facing outwards, a fence of sharpened logs closing up the gaps and a wooden tower twice a man's height beside the gate. A safe, and civilised, and comfortable-looking place, smoke slipping gently up from a chimney and smudging the sky. The valley around it, as far as Temple could see, was carpeted with tall green grass, patched white with snow in the hollows, dotted brown with cattle.

'Looks like he's got stock to trade,' said Shy.

Sweet stood in his stirrups to study the nearest cow. 'Good stock, too. I look forward to eating 'em.' The cow peered suspiciously back, apparently less enamoured of that idea.

'Maybe we should pick up some extra,' said Shy, 'get a herd together and drive 'em back to the Near Country.'

'Always got your eyes open for a profit, don't you?' asked Sweet.

'Why close your eyes to one? Specially when we've got one of the world's foremost drag riders sitting idle.'

'Oh God,' muttered Temple.

'Buckhorm?' bellowed Sweet as the four of them rode up. 'You about?' But there was no reply. The gate stood ajar, a stiff hinge faintly creaking as the breeze moved it. Otherwise, except for the cattle lowing in the distance, all was quiet.

Then the soft scrape as Lamb drew his sword. 'Something ain't right.'

'Aye,' said Sweet, laying his flatbow calmly across his knees and slipping a bolt into place.

'No doubt.' Shy shrugged her own bow off her shoulder and jerked an arrow from the quiver by her knee.

'Oh God,' said Temple, making sure he came last as they eased through the gateway, hooves of their horses squelching and crunching in the half-frozen mud. Was there no end to it? He peered at the doors and into the windows, grimacing with anticipation, expecting any and every horror from a welter of bandits, to a horde of Ghosts, to Waerdinur's vengeful dragon erupting from the earth to demand its money back.

'Where's my gold, Temple?'

The dragon would have been preferable to the awful phantom that now stooped beneath the low lintel of Buckhorm's house and into the light. Who else but that infamous soldier of fortune, Nicomo Cosca?

His once-fine clothes were reduced to muddy rags, corroded breast-plate lost and his filthy shirt hanging by two buttons, one trouser-leg torn gaping and a length of scrawny, trembling white calf exposed. His magnificent hat was a memory, the few strands of grey hair he had so carefully cultivated to cross his liver-spotted pate now floating about his skull in a grease-stiffened nimbus. His rash had turned crimson, scabbed with nail marks and, like mould up a cellar wall, spread flaking up the side of his head to speckle his waxy face. His hand quivered on the door, his gait was uncertain, he looked like nothing so much as a corpse exhumed, brought to a mockery of life by sorcerous intervention.

He turned his mad, bright, feverish eyes on Temple and slapped the hilt of his sword. One trapping of glory he had managed to retain. 'Like the ending of a cheap storybook, eh, Sworbreck?' The writer crept from the darkness behind Cosca, equally filthy and with bare feet to add to his wretchedness, one lens of his eyeglasses cracked, his empty hands fussing with each other. 'One final appearance for the villains!'

Sworbreck licked his lips, and remained silently loitering. Perhaps he could not tell who were the villains in this particular metaphor.

'Where's Buckhorm?' snapped Shy, training her drawn bow on Cosca and prompting his biographer to cower behind him for cover.

The Old Man was less easily rattled. 'Driving some cattle down to Hope with his three eldest sons, I understand. The lady of the house is within but, alas, cannot see visitors just at present. Ever so slightly tied up.' He licked at his chapped lips. 'I don't suppose any of you have a drink to hand?'

'Left mine over the rise with the rest of the Fellowship.' Shy jerked her head towards the west. 'I find if I have it, I drink it.'

'I've always had the very same problem,' said Cosca. 'I would ask one of my men to pour me a glass, but thanks to Master Lamb's fearsome talents and Master Temple's underhanded machinations, my Company is somewhat reduced.'

'You played your own hand in that,' said Temple.

'Doubtless. Live long enough, you see everything ruined. But I still hold a few cards.' Cosca gave a high whistle.

The doorway of the barn banged open and several of Buckhorm's younger children shuffled through into the courtyard, wide-eyed and fearful, some of their faces streaked with tears. Sergeant Friendly was their shepherd, an empty manacle swinging by the chain, the other still locked around his thick wrist. The blade of his cleaver glimmered briefly in the sun.

'Hello, Temple,' he said, showing as little emotion as if they'd been reunited at a tavern counter.

'Hello,' croaked Temple.

'And Master Hedges was good enough to join us.' Cosca pointed past them, finger shaking so badly it was hard at first to tell at what. Looking around, Temple saw a black outline appear at the top of the little turret by the gate. The self-professed hero of the Battle of Osrung, and pointing a flatbow down into the yard.

'Real sorry about this!' he shouted.

'You're that sorry, you can drop the bow,' growled Shy.

'I just want what I'm owed!' he called back.

'I'll give you what you're fucking owed, you treacherous—'

'Perhaps we can establish exactly what everyone is owed once the money is returned?' suggested Cosca. 'As a first step, I believe throwing down your weapons would be traditional?'

Shy spat through the gap in her front teeth. 'Fuck yourself.' The point of her arrow did not deviate by a hair.

Lamb stretched his neck out one way, then the other. 'We don't hold much with tradition.'

Cosca frowned. 'Sergeant Friendly? If they do not lay down their arms within the count of five, kill one of the children.'

Friendly shifted his fingers around the grip of his cleaver. 'Which one?'

'What do I care? You pick.'

'I'd rather not.'

Cosca rolled his eyes. 'The biggest one, then, and work your way down. Must I manage every detail?'

'I mean I'd rather not—'

'One!' snapped the Old Man.

Nobody gave the slightest impression of lowering their weapons. Quite the reverse. Shy stood slightly in her stirrups, scowling down her arrow. 'One o' those children dies, you're next.'

'Two!'

'Then you!' For that of a war hero, Hedges' voice had risen to a decidedly unheroic register.

'Then the fucking lot of you,' growled Lamb, hefting his heavy sword.

Sworbreck stared at Temple around Cosca's shoulder, palms open, as though to say, *What can reasonable men do under such circumstances?*

'Three!'

'Wait!' shouted Temple. 'Just . . . wait, damn it!' And he scrambled down from his horse.

'What the hell are you doing?' Shy snarled around the flights of her arrow.

'Taking the hard way.'

Temple began to walk slowly across the courtyard, mud and straw squelching under his boots, the breeze stirring his hair, the breath cold in his chest. He did not go with a smile, as Kahdia had gone to the Eaters when they padded into the Great Temple, black figures in the darkness, giving his life for the lives of his students. It took a mighty effort, wincing as if he was walking into a gale. But he went.

The sun found a chink in the clouds and glinted on the drawn steel, each edge and point picked out with painful brightness. He was scared.

He wondered if he might piss himself with each step. This was not the easy way. Not the easy way at all. But it was the right way. If there is a God, He is a solemn judge, and sees to it that each man receives his rightful deservings. So Temple knelt in the dung before Nicomo Cosca, and looked up into his bloodshot eyes, wondering how many men he had killed during that long career of his.

'What do you want?' he asked.

The ex-captain general frowned. 'My gold, of course.'

'I'm sorry,' said Temple. He even was a little. 'But it's gone. Conthus has it.'

'Conthus is dead.'

'No. You got the wrong man. Conthus took the money and it isn't coming back.' He did not try to be earnest. He simply gazed into Cosca's worn-out face and told the truth. In spite of the fear, and the high odds on his imminent death, and the freezing water leaking through the knees of his trousers, it felt good.

There was a pause pregnant with doom. Cosca stared at Temple, and Shy at Cosca, and Hedges at Shy, and Sweet at Hedges, and Friendly at Sweet, and Lamb at Friendly, and Sworbreck at everyone. All poised, all ready, all holding their breath.

'You betrayed me,' said Cosca.

'Yes.'

'After all I did for you.'

'Yes.'

The Old Man's wriggling fingers drifted towards his sword hilt. 'I should kill you.'

'Probably,' Temple was forced to admit.

'I want my money,' said Cosca, but the slightest plaintive note had crept into his voice.

'It isn't your money. It never was. Why do you even want it?'

Cosca blinked, hand hovering uncertainly. 'Well . . . I can use it to take back my dukedom—'

'You didn't want the dukedom when you had it.'

'It's . . . money.'

'You don't even like money. When you get it you throw it away.'

Cosca opened his mouth to refute that statement, then had to accept its obvious truth. He stood there, rashy, quivering, hunched, aged even beyond his considerable years, and looked down at Temple as though

444

he was seeing him for the first time. 'Sometimes,' he muttered, 'I think you're hardly like me at all.'

'I'm trying not to be. What do you want?'

'I want . . .' Cosca blinked over at the children, Friendly with one hand on the shoulder of the eldest and his cleaver in the other. Then at Lamb, grim as a gravedigger with his sword drawn. Then at Shy, bow trained on him, and at Hedges, bow trained on her. His bony shoulders sagged.

'I want a chance to do it all again. To do it . . . *right*.' Tears showed in the Old Man's eyes. 'How ever did it go so wrong, Temple? I had so many advantages. So many opportunities. All squandered. All slipped away like sand through a glass. So many disappointments . . .'

'Most of them you brought on yourself.'

'Of course.' Cosca gave a ragged sigh. 'But they're the ones that hurt the worst.' And he reached for his sword.

It was not there. He frowned down, puzzled. 'Where's my— uh?'

The blade slid out of his chest. He and Temple both stared at it, equally shocked, sun glinting on the point, blood spreading quickly out into his filthy shirt. Sworbreck let go of the hilt and stepped back, mouth hanging open.

'Oh,' said Cosca, dropping to his knees. 'There it is.'

Behind him Temple heard a flatbow go off and, almost simultaneously, another. He spun clumsily about, falling in the muck on one elbow.

Hedges gave a cry, bow tumbling from his hand. There was a bolt through the palm of the other. Sweet lowered his own bow, at first looking shocked, then rather pleased with himself.

'I stabbed him,' muttered Sworbreck.

'Am I shot?' asked Shy.

'You'll live,' said Lamb, flicking at the flights of Hedges' bolt. It was stuck through her saddle horn.

'My last words . . .' With a faint groan, Cosca toppled onto his side in the mud next to Temple. 'I had some wonderful ones . . . worked out. What were they now?' And he broke out into that luminous smile of which only he was capable, good humour and good intentions radiating from his deep-lined face. 'Ah! I remember . . .'

Nothing more. He was still.

'He's dead,' said Temple, voice flat. 'No more disappointments.'

'You were the last,' said Friendly. 'I told him we'd be better off in prison.' He tossed his cleaver in the muck and patted Buckhorm's eldest son on the shoulder. 'You four can go inside to your mother.'

'You shot me!' shrieked Hedges, clutching at his skewered hand.

Sworbreck adjusted his broken eyeglasses as though he could scarcely credit the evidence of his senses. 'Astonishing skill!'

'I was aiming for his chest,' said the scout, under his breath.

The author stepped gingerly around Cosca's corpse. 'Master Sweet, I wonder whether I might speak to you about a book I have in mind.'

'Now? I really don't see—'

'A generous share of the profits would be forthcoming.'

'—any way I could turn you down.'

Cold water was leaking through the seat of Temple's trousers, gripping his arse in its icy embrace, but he found he could not move. Facing death certainly can take it out of you. Especially if you've spent most of your life doing your best to avoid facing anything.

He realised Friendly was standing next to him, frowning down at Cosca's body. 'What do I do now?' he asked.

'I don't know,' said Temple. 'What does anyone do?'

'I plan an authentic portrait of the taming and settlement of the Far Country,' Sworbreck was blathering. 'A tale for the ages! One in which you have played a pivotal role.'

'I'm pivotal, all right,' said Sweet. 'What's pivotal?'

'My hand!' shrieked Hedges.

'You're lucky it's not through your face,' said Lamb.

Somewhere inside, Temple could hear the tearful sounds of the Buckhorm children being reunited with their mother. Good news, he supposed. A fair result.

'My readers will thrill to your heroic exploits!'

'I've certainly thrilled to 'em,' snorted Shy. 'The heroic scale of your digestive gases would never be believed back east.'

Temple looked up, and watched the clouds moving. If there was a God, the world seemed exactly the way it would be if there wasn't one.

'I must insist on absolute honesty. I will entertain no more exaggeration! Truth, Master Sweet, is at the heart of all great works of art.'

'No doubt at all. Which makes me wonder – have you heard of the time I killed a great red bear with naught but these two hands . . .'

Some Kind of Coward

Nothing was quite the way she remembered it. All small. All drab. All changed.

Some new folks had happened by and built a house where theirs had stood, and a new barn, too. Couple of fields tilled and coming up nice, by all appearances. Flowers blooming around the tree they'd hanged Gully from. The tree Ro's mother was buried under.

They sat there, on horseback, frowning down, and Shy said, 'Somehow I thought it'd be the way we left it.'

'Times move on,' said Lamb.

'It's a nice spot,' said Temple.

'No it's not,' said Shy.

'Shall we go down?'

Shy turned her horse away. 'Why?'

Ro's hair was grown back to a shapeless mop. She'd taken Lamb's razor one morning meaning to shave it off again, and sat there by still water, holding her dragon scale and thinking of Waerdinur. Couldn't picture his face no more. Couldn't remember his voice or the Maker's lessons he'd so carefully taught her. How could it all have washed away so fast? In the end she just put the razor back and let her hair grow.

Times move on, don't they?

They'd moved on in Squaredeal, all right, lots of land about cleared and drained and put under the plough, and new buildings sprung up all over and new faces everywhere passing through or stopping off or settling down to all sorts of business.

Not everything had prospered. Clay was gone and there was a drunk idiot running his store and it had no stock and half the roof had fallen in. Shy argued him down to one Imperial gold piece and a dozen bottles of cheap spirit and bought the place as a going concern. Nearly going, at least. They all set to work next morning like it was the last day of creation, Shy haggling merciless as a hangman for stock, Pit and Ro laughing as they swept dust over each other, Temple and Lamb hammering away at the carpentry, and it weren't long before things got to feel a bit like they used to. More than Ro had ever thought they would.

Except sometimes she'd think of the mountains and cry. And Lamb still wore a sword. The one he'd taken from her father.

Temple took a room over the road and put a sign above the door saying *Temple and Kahdia: Contracts, Clerking and Carpentry*.

Ro said to him, 'This Kahdia ain't around much, is he?'

'Nor will he be,' said Temple. 'But a man should have someone to blame.'

He started doing law work, which might as well have been magic far as most folk around there were concerned, children peering in at his window to watch him write by candlelight. Sometimes Ro went over there and listened to him talk about the stars, and God, and wood, and the law, and all kinds of faraway places he'd been on his travels, and in languages she'd never even heard before.

'Who needs a teacher?' Shy asked. 'I was taught with a belt.'

'Look how that turned out,' said Ro. 'He knows a lot.'

Shy snorted. 'For a wise man he's a hell of a fool.'

But once Ro woke in the night and came down, restless, and saw them out the back together, kissing. There was something in the way Shy touched him made it seem she didn't think he was quite the fool she said he was.

Sometimes they went out around the farmsteads, more buildings springing up each week that passed, buying and selling. Pit and Ro swaying on the seat of the wagon next to Shy, Lamb riding along beside, always frowning hard at the horizon, hand on that sword.

Shy said to him, 'There's naught to worry about.'

And without looking at her he said, 'That's when you'd better worry.'

They got in one day at closing time, the long clouds pinking overhead as the sun sank in the west and the lonely wind sighing up and sweeping dust down the street and setting that rusty weathervane to squeak. No Fellowships coming through and the town quiet and still, some children laughing somewhere and a grandmother creaking in her rocker on her porch and just one horse Ro didn't know tied up at the warped rail.

'Some days work out,' said Shy, looking at the back of the wagon, just about empty.

'Some don't,' Ro finished for her.

Calm inside the store, just Wist soft snoring in his chair with his boots up on the counter. Shy slapped 'em off and woke him with a jolt. 'Everything good?'

'Slow day,' said the old man, rubbing his eyes.

'All your days are slow,' said Lamb.

'Like you're so bloody quick. Oh, and there's someone been waiting for you. Says you and him got business.'

'Waiting for me?' asked Shy, and Ro heard footsteps in the back of the store.

'No, for Lamb. What did you say your name was?'

A man pushed a hanging coil of rope aside and came into the light. A great, tall man, his head brushing the low rafters, a sword at his hip with a grip of scored grey metal, just like Lamb's. Just like her father's. He had a great scar angled across his face and the guttering candle-flame twinkled in his eye. A silver eye, like a mirror.

'My name's Caul Shivers,' he said, voice quiet and all croaky soft and every hair Ro had stretched up.

'What's your business?' muttered Shy.

Shivers looked down at Lamb's hand, and the stump of the missing finger there, and he said, 'You know my business, don't you?'

Lamb just nodded, grim and level.

'You're after trouble, you can fucking ride on!' Shy's voice, harsh as a crow's. 'You hear me, bastard? We've had all the trouble we—'

Lamb put his hand on her forearm. The one with the scar coiling around it. 'It's all right.'

'It's all right if he wants my knife up his—'

'Stay out of it, Shy. It's an old debt we got. Past time it was paid.' Then he spoke to Shivers in Northern. 'Whatever's between me and you, it don't concern these.'

Shivers looked at Shy, and at Ro, and it seemed to her there was no more feeling in his living eye than in his dead. 'It don't concern these. Shall we head outside?'

They walked down the steps in front of the store, not slow and not fast, keeping a space between them, eyes on each other all the way. Ro, and Shy, and Pit, and Wist edged after them onto the porch, watching in a silent group.

'Lamb, eh?' said Shivers.

'One name's good as another.'

'Oh, not so, not so. Threetrees, and Bethod, and Whirrun of Bligh, and all them others forgotten. But men still sing your songs. Why's that, d'you reckon?'

''Cause men are fools,' said Lamb.

The wind caught a loose board somewhere and made it rattle. The two Northmen faced each other, Lamb's hand dangling loose at his side, stump of the missing finger brushing the grip of his sword, and Shivers gently swept his coat clear of his own hilt and held it back out of the way.

'That my old sword you got there?' asked Lamb.

Shivers shrugged. 'Took it off Black Dow. Guess it all comes around, eh?'

'Always.' Lamb stretched his neck out one way, then the other. 'It always comes around.'

Time dragged, dragged. Those children were still laughing somewhere, and maybe the echoing shout of their mother calling them in. That old woman's rocker softly creak, creaking on the porch. That weathervane squeak, squeaking. A breeze blew up then and stirred the dust in the street and flapped the coats of the two men, no more than four or five strides of dirt between them.

'What's happening?' whispered Pit, and no one answered.

Shivers bared his teeth. Lamb narrowed his eyes. Shy's hand gripped almost painful hard at Ro's shoulder, the blood pounding now in her head, the breath crawling in her throat, slow, slow, the rocker creaking and that loose board rattling and a dog barking somewhere.

'So?' growled Lamb.

Shivers tipped his head back, and his good eye flickered over to Ro. Stayed on her for a long moment. And she bunched her fists, and clenched her teeth, and she found herself wishing he'd kill Lamb. Wishing it with all her being. The wind came again and stirred his hair, flicked it around his face.

Squeak. Creak. Rattle.

Shivers shrugged. 'So I'd best be going.'

'Eh?'

'Long way home for me. Got to tell 'em that nine-fingered bastard is back to the mud. Don't you think, Master Lamb?'

Lamb curled his left hand into a fist so the stump didn't show, and swallowed. 'Long dead and gone.'

'All for the best, I reckon. Who wants to run into him again?' And just like that Shivers walked to his horse and mounted up. 'I'd say I'll be seeing you but . . . I think I'd best not.'

Lamb still stood there, watching. 'No.'

'Some men just ain't stamped out for doing good.' Shivers took a deep breath, and smiled. A strange thing to see on that ruined face. 'But it feels all right, even so. To let go o' something.' And he turned his horse and headed east out of town.

They all stood stock still a while longer, with the wind, and the creaking rocker, and the sinking sun, then Wist gave a great rattling sigh and said, 'Bloody hell I near shit myself!'

It was like they could all breathe again, and Shy and Pit hugged each other, but Ro didn't smile. She was watching Lamb. He didn't smile either. Just frowned at the dust Shivers left behind him. Then he strode back to the store, and up the steps, and inside without a word. Shy headed after. He was pulling things down from the shelves like he was in a hurry. Dried meat, and feed, and water, and a bedroll. All the things you'd need for a trip.

'What're you doing, Lamb?' asked Shy.

He looked up for a moment, guilty, and back to his packing. 'I always tried to do the best I could for you,' he said. 'That was the promise I made your mother. The best I can do now is go.'

'Go where?'

'I don't know.' He stopped for a moment, staring at the stump of his middle finger. 'Someone'll come, Shy. Sooner or later. Got to be realistic. You can't do the things I've done and walk away smiling. There'll always be trouble at my back. All I can do is take it with me.'

'Don't pretend this is for us,' said Shy.

Lamb winced. 'A man's got to be what he is. Got to be. Say my goodbyes to Temple. Reckon you'll do all right with him.'

He scooped up those few things and back out into the street, wedged them into his saddlebags and like that he was ready.

'I don't understand,' said Pit, tears on his face.

'I know.' Lamb knelt in front of him, and it seemed his eye was wet too. 'And I'm sorry. Sorry for everything.' He leaned forward and gathered the three of them in an awkward embrace.

'The dead know I've made mistakes,' said Lamb. 'Reckon a man could steer a perfect course through life by taking all the choices I didn't. But I never regretted helping raise you three. And I don't regret that I brought you back. Whatever it cost.'

'We need you,' said Shy.

Lamb shook his head. 'No you don't. I ain't proud o' much but I'm proud o' you. For what that's worth.' And he turned away, and wiped his face, and hauled himself up onto his horse.

'I always said you were some kind of coward,' said Shy.

He sat looking at them for a moment, and nodded. 'I never denied it.'

Then he took a breath, and headed off at a trot towards the sunset. Ro stood there on the porch, Pit's hand in her hand, and Shy's on her shoulder, and they watched him.

Until he was gone.

Acknowledgments

As always, four people without whom:

Bren Abercrombie, whose eyes are sore from reading it.
Nick Abercrombie, whose ears are sore from hearing about it.
Rob Abercrombie, whose fingers are sore from turning the pages.
Lou Abercrombie, whose arms are sore from holding me up.

Then, my heartfelt thanks:

To all the lovely and talented folks at my UK Publisher, Gollancz, and their parent Orion, particularly Simon Spanton, Jon Weir, Jen McMenemy, Mark Stay and Jon Wood. Then, of course, all those who've helped make, publish, publicise, translate and above all *sell* my books wherever they may be around the world.

To the artists responsible for somehow continuing to make me look classy: Didier Graffet, Dave Senior and Laura Brett.

To editors across the Pond: Devi Pillai and Lou Anders.

For keeping the wolf on the right side of the door: Robert Kirby.

To all the writers whose paths have crossed mine on the internet, at the bar, or in some cases on the D&D table and the shooting range, and who've provided help, support, laughs and plenty of ideas worth the stealing. You know who you are.

And lastly, yet firstly:

My partner in crimes against fantasy fiction, Gillian Redfearn. I mean, Butch Cassidy wasn't gloriously slaughtered on his own, now, was he?